RIVER GOD

Also by Wilbur Smith

THE COURTNEYS

When the Lion Feeds
The Sound of Thunder
A Sparrow Falls
Birds of Prey
Monsoon

THE COURTNEYS OF AFRICA

The Burning Shore
Power of the Sword
Rage
A Time to Die
Golden Fox

THE BALLANTYNE NOVELS

A Falcon Flies
Men of Men
The Angels Weep
The Leopard Hunts in Darkness

Also

The Dark of the Sun
Shout at the Devil
Gold Mine
The Diamond Hunters
The Sunbird
The Eagle of the Tiger
Cry Wolf
Hungry as the Sea
Wild Justice
Elephant Song
River God
The Seventh Scroll
Warlock
Triumph of the Sun

WILBUR SMITH

RIVER GOD

River God first published 1993 by MacMillan
an imprint of Pan Macmillan Ltd
Pan Macmillan, 20 New Wharf Road, London N1 9RR
Basingstoke and Oxford
www.panmacmillan.com

Warlock first published 2001 by Macmillan
an imprint of Pan Macmillan Ltd
25 Eccleston Place, London SW1W9NF
Basingstoke and Oxford
www.panmacmillan.com
Associated companies throughout the world
www.macmillan.com

This omnibus edition published 2006 by Pan Macmillan Ltd

ISBN 0 230 01505 0
ISBN 978 0230 01515 0

River God. Copyright © Wilbur Smith 1993
Warlock. Copyright © Wilbur Smith 2001

The right of Wilbur Smith to be identified as the author of this work has been asserted by him in accordance with the Copyright, Designs and Patents Act 1988.

All rights reserved. No part of this publication may be reproduced, stored in or introduced into retrieval system, or transmitted, in any form, or by any means (electronic, mechanical, photocopying, recording or otherwise) without the prior written permission of the publisher. Any person who does any unauthorized act in relation to this publication may be liable to criminal prosecution and civil claims for damages.

2 4 6 8 10 9 7 5 3 1

A CIP catalogue record for this book is available from the British Library.

River God – Typeset by Cambridge Composing (UK) Ltd, Cambridge
Warlock – Typeset by SetSystems Ltd, Saffron Walden, Essex
Printed and bound in Australia by McPherson's Printing Group

The hieroglyphs write the name of the god of the Nile inundation, Hapi, from the papyrus of Ani (P BM 10470).

This book, like so many others before it, is for my wife, Danielle Antoinette.

The Nile that flows through this story has both of us in her thrall. We have spent days of delight voyaging together upon her waters and idling upon her banks. As we are, so is she a creature of this very Africa of ours.

Yet this great river runs neither so strongly nor so deeply as my love for you, my darling.

THE RIVER lay heavily upon the desert, bright as a spill of molten metal from a furnace. The sky smoked with heat-haze and the sun beat down upon it all with the strokes of a coppersmith's hammer. In the mirage the gaunt hills flanking the Nile seemed to tremble to the blows.

Our boat sped close in beside the papyrus beds; near enough for the creaking of the water buckets of the shadoof, on their long, counter-balanced arms, to carry from the fields across the water. The sound harmonized with the singing of the girl in the bows.

Lostris was fourteen years of age. The Nile had begun its latest flood on the very day that her red woman's moon had flowered for the first time, a coincidence that the priests of Hapi had viewed as highly propitious. Lostris, the woman's name that they had then chosen to replace her discarded baby-name, meant 'Daughter of the Waters'.

I remember her so vividly on that day. She would grow more beautiful as the years passed, become more poised and regal, but never again would that glow of virgin womanhood radiate from her so overpoweringly. Every man aboard, even the warriors at the rowing-benches, were aware of it. Neither I nor any one of them could keep our gaze off her. She filled me with a sense of my own inadequacy and a deep and poignant longing; for although I am a eunuch I was gelded only after I had known the joy of a woman's body.

'Taita,' she called to me, 'sing with me!' And when I obeyed she smiled with pleasure. My voice was one of the many reasons that, whenever she was able, she kept me near her; my tenor complemented her lovely soprano to perfection. We sang one of the old peasant love songs that I had taught her, and which was still one of her favourites:

> My heart flutters up like a wounded quail
> when I see my beloved's face
> and my cheeks bloom like the dawn sky
> to the sunshine of his smile—

From the stern another voice joined with ours. It was a man's voice, deep and powerful, but it lacked the clarity and purity of my own. If my voice was that of a dawn-greeting thrush, then this was the voice of a young lion.

Lostris turned her head and now her smile shimmered like the sunbeams on the surface of the Nile. Although the man upon whom she played that smile was my friend, perhaps my only true friend, still I felt the bitter gall of envy burn the back of my throat. Yet I forced myself to smile at Tanus, as she did, with love.

Tanus' father, Pianki, Lord Harrab, had been one of the grandees of the Egyptian nobility, but his mother had been the daughter of a freed Tehenu slave. Like so many of her people, she had been fair-headed and blue-eyed. She had died of the swamp fever while Tanus was still a child, so my memory of her was imperfect. However, the old women said that seldom before had such beauty as hers been seen in either of the two kingdoms.

On the other hand, I had known and admired Tanus' father, before he lost all his vast fortune and the great estates that had once almost rivalled those of Pharaoh himself. He had been of dark complexion, with Egyptian eyes the colour of polished obsidian, a man with more physical strength than beauty, but with a generous and noble heart – some might say too generous and too trusting, for he had died destitute, with his heart broken by those he had thought his friends, alone in the darkness, cut off from the sunshine of Pharaoh's favour.

Thus it seemed that Tanus had inherited the best from both his parents, except only worldly wealth. In nature and in power he was as his father; in beauty as his mother. So why should I resent my mistress loving him? I loved him also, and, poor neutered thing that I am, I knew that I could never have her for myself, not even if the gods had raised my status above that of slave. Yet such is the perversity of human nature that I hungered for what I could never have and dreamed of the impossible.

Lostris sat on her cushion on the prow with her slave girls sprawled at her feet, two little black girls from Cush, lithe as panthers, entirely naked except for the golden collars around their necks. Lostris herself wore only a skirt of bleached linen, crisp and white as an egret's wing. The skin of her upper body, caressed by the sun, was the colour of oiled cedar wood from the mountains beyond Byblos. Her breasts were the size and shape of ripe figs just ready for plucking, and tipped with rose garnets.

She had set aside her formal wig, and wore her natural hair in a side-lock that fell in a thick dark rope over one breast. The slant of her eyes was enhanced by the silver-green of powdered malachite cunningly touched to the upper lids. The colour of her eyes was green also, but the darker, clearer green of the Nile when its waters have shrunk and deposited their burden of precious silts. Between her breasts, suspended on a gold chain, she wore a figurine of Hapi, the goddess of the Nile, fashioned in gold and precious lapis lazuli. Of course it was a superb piece, for I had made it with my own hands for her.

Suddenly Tanus lifted his right hand with the fist clenched. As a single man the rowers checked their stroke and held the blades of their paddles aloft, glinting in the sunlight and dripping water. Then Tanus thrust the steering-oar hard over, and the men on the port bank stabbed their backstroke deeply, creating a series of tiny whirlpools in the surface of the green water. The starboard side pulled strongly ahead. The boat spun so sharply that the deck canted over at an alarming angle. Then both banks pulled together and she shot forward. The sharp prow, with the blue eyes of Horus emblazoned upon it, brushed aside the dense stands of papyrus, and she lanced her way out of the flow of the river and into the still waters of the lagoon beyond.

Lostris broke off the song and shaded her eyes to gaze ahead. 'There they are!' she cried, and pointed with a graceful little hand. The other boats of Tanus' squadron were cast like a net across the southern reaches of the lagoon, blocking the main entrance to the great river, cutting off any escape in that direction.

Naturally, Tanus had chosen for himself the northern station, for he knew that this was where the sport would be most furious. I wished it was not so. Not that I am a coward, but I have always the safety of my mistress to consider. She had inveigled herself aboard the *Breath of Horus* only after much intrigue in which, as always, she had deeply involved me. When her father learned, as he surely would, of her presence in the thick of the hunt, it would go badly enough for me, but if he learned also that I was responsible for allowing her to be in the company of Tanus for a full day, not even my privileged position would protect me from his wrath. His instructions to me regarding this young man were unequivocal.

However, I seemed to be the only soul aboard the *Breath of Horus* who was perturbed. The others were simmering with excitement. Tanus checked the rowers with a peremptory hand-signal, and the boat glided to a halt and lay rocking gently upon the green waters that were so still that when I glanced overboard and saw my own reflection look back at me, I was struck, as always, by how well my beauty had carried over the years. To me it seemed that my face was more lovely than the cerulean blue lotus blooms that framed it. I had little time to admire it, however, for the crew were all abustle.

One of Tanus' staff officers ran up his personal standard to the masthead. It was the image of a blue crocodile, with its great coxcombed tail held erect and its jaws open. Only an officer of the rank of Best of Ten Thousand was entitled to his own standard. Tanus had achieved such rank, together with the command of the Blue Crocodile division of Pharaoh's own elite guard, before his twentieth birthday.

Now the standard at the masthead was the signal for the hunt to begin. On the horizon of the lagoon the rest of the squadron were tiny with distance, but their paddles began to beat rhythmically, rising and falling like the wings of wild geese in flight, glistening in the sunlight. From their sterns the multiple wavelets of their wakes were drawn out across the placid waters and lay for a long while on the surface, as though moulded from solid clay.

Tanus lowered the gong over the stern. It was a long bronze tube. He allowed the end of it to sink below the surface. When struck with a hammer of the same metal the shrill, reverberating tones would be transmitted through the water, filling our quarry with consternation. Unhappily for my equanimity, I knew that this could readily turn to a murderous rage.

Tanus laughed at me. Even in his own excitement he had sensed my qualms. For a rude soldier he had unusual perception. 'Come up here in the stern-tower, Taita!' he ordered. 'You can beat the gong for us. It will take your mind off the safety of your own beautiful hide for a while.'

I was hurt by his levity, but relieved by the invitation, for the stern-tower is high above the water. I moved to do his bidding without undignified haste, and, as I passed him, I paused to exhort him sternly, 'Have a care for the safety of my mistress. Do you hear me, boy? Do not encourage her to recklessness, for she is every bit as wild as you are.' I could speak thus to an illustrious commander of ten thousand, for he was once my pupil and I had wielded the cane on more than one occasion across those martial buttocks. He grinned at me now as he had in those days, as cocky and impudent as ever.

'Leave that lady in my hands, I implore you, old friend. There is nothing I would relish more, believe me!' I did not admonish him for such a disrespectful tone, for I was in some small haste to take my place in the tower. From there I watched him take up his bow.

Already that bow was famous throughout the army, indeed throughout the length of the great river from the cataracts to the sea. I had designed it for him when he had grown dissatisfied with the puny weapons that, up until that time, were all that were available to him. I had suggested that we should try to fashion a bow with some new material other than those feeble woods that grow in our narrow riverine valley; perhaps with exotic timbers such as the heartwood of the olive from the land of the

Hittites or of the ebony from Cush; or with even stranger materials such as the horn of the rhinoceros or the ivory tusk of the elephant.

No sooner had we made the attempt than we came upon a myriad of problems, the first of which was the brittleness of these exotic materials. In their natural state none of them would bend without cracking, and only the largest and therefore the most expensive elephant tusk would allow us to carve a complete bowstock from it. I solved both these problems by splitting the ivory of a smaller tusk into slivers and gluing these together in sufficient girth and bulk to form a full bow. Unfortunately it was too rigid for any man to draw.

However, from there it was an easy and natural step to laminate together all four of our chosen materials – olive wood, ebony, horn and ivory. Of course, there were many months of experimentation with combinations of these materials, and with various types of glue to hold them together. We never did succeed in making a glue strong enough. In the end I solved this last problem by binding the entire bowstock with electrum wire to prevent it from flying apart. I had two big men assist Tanus in twisting the wire on to it with all their combined strength, while the glue was still hot. When it cooled, it set to an almost perfect combination of strength and pliability.

Then I cut strands from the gut of a great black-maned lion that Tanus hunted and killed with his bronze-bladed war spear out in the desert. These I tanned and twisted together to form a bowstring. The result was this gleaming arc of such extraordinary power that only one man out of all the hundreds who had made the attempt could draw it to full stretch.

The regulation style of archery as taught by the army instructors was to face the target and draw the nocked arrow to the sternum of the chest, hold that aim for a deliberate pause, then loose on command. However, not even Tanus had the strength to draw this bow and hold his aim steadily. He was forced to develop a completely new style. Standing sideways to the target, addressing it over his left shoulder, he would throw up the bow with his left arm outstretched and, with a convulsive heave, draw back the arrow until the feathered flights touched his lips and the muscles of his arms and chest stood proud with the effort. In that same instant of full extension, seemingly without aiming, he would loose.

At first, his arrows flew at random as wild bees leave the hive, but he practised day after day and month after month. The fingers of his right hand became raw and bleeding from the chafing of the bowstring, but they healed and toughened. The inside of his left forearm was bruised and excoriated where the bowstring slashed past it on the release of the arrow, but I fashioned a leather guard to protect it. And Tanus stood at the butts and practised and practised.

Even I lost confidence in his ability to master the weapon but Tanus never gave up. Slowly, agonizingly slowly, he gained control of it to the point where, finally, he could launch three arrows with such rapidity that they were all in the air at the same instant. At least two of the three would strike the target, a copper disc the size of a man's head set up at a distance of fifty paces from where Tanus stood. Such was the force of those arrows that they would fly cleanly through the metal which was the thickness of my little finger.

Tanus named this mighty weapon Lanata which was, quite coincidentally, the discarded baby-name of my mistress. Now he stood in the bows with the woman at his side, and her namesake in his left hand. They made a marvellous couple, but too obviously so for my peace of mind.

I called sharply, 'Mistress! Come back here immediately! It is unsafe where you are.' She did not even deign to glance over her shoulder, but made a sign at me behind her back. Every one of the crew of the galley saw it, and the boldest of them guffawed. One of those little black vixens that were her handmaidens must have taught Lostris that gesture, which was more appropriate to the ladies of the riverside taverns than to a highborn daughter of the House of Intef. I considered remonstrating with her, but at once abandoned such an imprudent course, for my mistress is amenable to restraint only in certain of her moods. Instead, I applied myself to beating the bronze gong with sufficient vigour to disguise my chagrin.

The shrill, reverberating tone carried across the glassy waters of the lagoon, and instantly the air was filled with the susurration of wings and a shade was cast over the sun as, from the papyrus beds and the hidden pools and open water, a vast cloud of water-fowl rose into the sky. They were of a hundred varieties: black and white ibis with vulturine heads, sacred to the goddess of the river; flights of honking geese in russet plumage, each with a ruby droplet in the centre of its chest; herons of greenish-blue or midnight black, with bills like swords and ponderous wing-beats; and ducks in such profusion that their numbers challenged the eye and the credibility of the beholder.

Wild-fowling is one of the most ardent pursuits of the Egyptian nobility, but that day we were after different game. At that moment, I saw far ahead a disturbance upon the glassy surface. It was weighty and massive, and my spirits quailed, for I knew what terrible beast had moved there. Tanus also had seen it, but his reaction was altogether different from mine. He gave tongue like a hunting hound, and his men shouted with him and bent to their paddles. The *Breath of Horus* shot forward as though she were one of the birds that darkened the sky above us, and my mistress shrieked with excitement and beat with one small fist upon Tanus' muscled shoulder.

The waters roiled once more and Tanus signalled to his steersman to follow the movement, while I hammered upon the gong to bolster and sustain my courage. We reached the spot where last we had seen movement, and the vessel glided to a standstill while every man upon her decks gazed around eagerly.

I alone glanced directly over the stern. The water beneath our hull was shallow and almost as clear as the air above us. I shrieked as loudly and as shrilly as my mistress had and leapt back from the stern-rail, for the monster was directly under us.

The hippopotamus is the familiar of Hapi, the goddess of the Nile. It was only with her special dispensation that we could hunt it. To that end Tanus had prayed and sacrificed at the goddess's temple that morning, with my mistress close by his side. Of course, Hapi is her patron goddess, but I doubted that alone was the reason for her avid participation in the ceremony.

The beast that I saw beneath us now was an enormous old bull. To my eye, he seemed as large as our galley, a gigantic shape that lumbered along the bottom of the lagoon, his movements slowed down by the drag of the water so that he moved like a creature from a nightmare. He raised puffs of mud from beneath his hooves the same way that a wild oryx stirs the dust as it races across the desert sands.

With the steering-oar Tanus spun the boat about and we sped after the bull. But even at that slow and mannered gallop he rapidly drew away from us. His dark shape faded into the green depths of the lagoon ahead of us.

'Pull! By Seth's foul breath, pull!' Tanus howled at his men, but when one of his officers shook out the knotted lash of the whip, Tanus frowned and shook his head. I have never seen him ply the lash where it was not warranted.

Suddenly the bull broke through the surface ahead of us and blew a great cloud of fetid steam from his lungs. The stink of it washed over us, even though he was well out of bowshot. For a moment his back formed a gleaming granite island in the lagoon, then he drew a whistling breath and with a swirl was gone again.

'After him!' Tanus bellowed.

'There he is,' I cried, as I pointed over the side, 'he's doubling back.'

'Well done, old friend,' Tanus laughed at me, 'we'll make a warrior of you yet.' That notion was ridiculous, for I am a scribe, a sage and an artist. My heroics are of the mind. None the less, I felt a thrill of pleasure, as I always do at Tanus' praise, and my trepidation was, for the moment, lost in the excitement of the chase.

To the south of us the other galleys of the squadron had joined the hunt. The priests of Hapi had kept a strict count of the number of these great beasts in the lagoon, and had given sanction for fifty of them to be slaughtered for the coming festival of Osiris. This would leave almost three hundred of the goddess's flock remaining in the temple lagoon, a number that the priests considered ideal to keep the waterways free of choking weed, to prevent the papyrus beds from encroaching upon the arable lands and to provide a regular supply of meat for the temple. Only the priests themselves were allowed to eat the flesh of the hippopotamus outside the ten days of the festival of Osiris.

So the hunt spun out across the waters like some intricate dance, with the ships of the squadron weaving and pirouetting while the frenzied beasts fled before them, diving and blowing and grunting as they surfaced to dive again. Yet each dive was shorter than the last, and the swirling breaches at the surface became more frequent as their lungs were emptied and could not be fully recharged before the pursuing ships bore down upon them and forced them to dive again. All the while the bronze gongs in the stern-tower of each galley rang out to blend with the excited cries of the rowers and the exhortations of the helmsmen. All was wild uproar and confusion and I found myself shouting and cheering along with the most bloodthirsty of them.

Tanus had concentrated all his attention on the first and largest bull. He ignored the females and younger animals that breached within bowshot, and followed the great beast through all his convolutions, drawing inexorably closer to him each time he surfaced. Even in my excitement I could not but admire the skill with which Tanus handled the *Breath of Horus* and the manner in which his crew responded to his signals. But then, he always had the knack of getting the very best out of those he commanded. How otherwise, with neither fortune nor great patron to sustain him, could he have risen so swiftly to exalted rank? What he had achieved he had done on his own merit, and that despite the malignant influence of hidden enemies who had placed every obstacle in his way.

Suddenly the bull burst through the surface not thirty paces from the bows. He came out gleaming in the sunshine, monstrous black and awful, clouds of steamy vapour spurting from his nostrils like that creature from the underworld that devours the hearts of those who are found wanting by the gods.

Tanus had an arrow nocked and now he threw up the great bow and loosed it in the same fleeting instant. Lanata played her dreadful shimmering music, and the arrow leaped out in a blur that deceived the eye. While it still hissed in flight, another followed it and then another. The bowstring hummed like a lute, and the arrows struck one after the other. The bull bellowed as they buried themselves full-length in his broad back, and he dived again.

These were missiles that I had devised especially for this occasion. The feathered flights had been removed from the arrows and replaced by tiny floats of baobab wood such as the fishermen use to buoy their nets. They slipped over the butt of the shaft in such a way that they were secure in flight but would become dislodged once the beast dived and dragged them through the water. They were attached to the bronze arrow-head by a fine linen thread that was wound around the shaft, but which unravelled once the float was detached. So now, as the bull sped away beneath the water, the three tiny floats popped to the surface and bobbed along behind him. I had painted them bright yellow so that the eye was drawn to them and the bull's position was instantly revealed, even though he was deep in the lagoon.

Thus Tanus was able to anticipate each of the bull's wild rushes and to send the *Breath of Horus* speeding to head him off and to place another set of arrows deep in the glistening black back as it bulged out of the water. By now the bull was towing a garland of pretty yellow corks behind him, and the waters were streaking and swirling red with his blood. Despite the wild emotions of the moment I could not help but feel pity for the stricken creature each time it came bellowing to the surface to be met by another hail of the deadly hissing arrows. My sympathy was not shared by my young mistress, who was in the very thick of the fray and shrieking with the delicious terror and excitement of it all.

Once again the bull came up dead ahead, but this time facing the *Breath of Horus* as she bore down upon him. His jaws gaped so wide that I could see far down his throat. It was a tunnel of bright red flesh that could easily have engulfed a man entirely. The jaws were lined with such an array of fangs that my breath stopped and my flesh chilled. In his bottom jaw they were huge ivory sickles designed to harvest the tough and sinewy stalks of standing papyrus. In his upper jaw they were gleaming white shafts as thick as my wrist that could shear through the hull timbers of the *Breath of Horus* as easily as I would bite through a cake of cornflour. I had recently had the opportunity of examining the corpse of a peasant woman who, while cutting papyrus on the river-bank, had disturbed a cow hippo that had just given birth to a calf. The woman had been severed in half so neatly that it seemed she had been struck with the keenest of bronze blades.

Now this enraged monster with his maw filled with these gleaming teeth was bearing down upon us, and even though I was high in the stern-tower and as far from him as I could possibly be, yet I found myself as incapable of sound or movement as a temple statue, frozen with terror.

Tanus loosed yet another arrow which flew squarely down the gaping throat, yet the creature's agony was already so terrible that he seemed not to notice this further injury, although it must eventually prove fatal. He charged without check or hesitation straight at the bows of the *Breath of Horus*. Such a fearsome roar of fury and of mortal anguish issued from the tortured throat that an artery ruptured deep within it and gouts of blood were sent spraying from his open jaws. The spewing blood turned to clouds of red mist in the sunlight, both beautiful and horrible at the same time. Then the bull crashed headlong into the bows of our galley.

The *Breath of Horus* was cutting through the water at the speed of a running gazelle, but the bull was even swifter in his rage and his bulk was so solid that it seemed as though we had run aground on a rocky shore. The rowers were sent sprawling from their benches, while I was hurled forwards with such force against the rail of the stern-tower that the air was driven from my lungs and replaced by a solid rock of pain in my chest.

Yet even in my own distress my concern was all for my mistress. Through tears of agony I saw her flung forward by the impact. Tanus threw out his arm to try to save her, but he was also off-balance from the shock, and the bow in his left hand hindered him. He was only able to check her impetus for a moment, but then she teetered at the rail with her arms windmilling desperately, and her back arched out over the drop.

'Tanus!' she screamed, and reached out one hand to him. He recovered his balance with the nimbleness of an acrobat and tried to catch her hand. For an instant their fingers touched, then it seemed that she was plucked away and dashed over the side.

From my elevated position in the stern I was able to follow her fall. She flipped over in the air like a cat, and the white skirts streamed upwards to expose the exquisite length of her thighs. To me it seemed that she fell for ever, and my own anguished cry blended with her despairing wail.

'My baby!' I cried. 'My little one!' For I was certain that she was lost. It seemed that all her life, as I had known it, replayed itself before my eyes. I saw her again as a toddling infant and heard the baby endearments that she bestowed on me, her adoring nursemaid. I saw her grow to womanhood, and I remembered every joy and every heartache that she had caused me. I loved her then in the moment of losing her even more than I had done in all those fourteen long years.

She fell upon the vast, blood-splattered back of the infuriated bull, and for an instant lay spread-eagled there like a human sacrifice upon the altar of some obscene religion. The bull whirled about, mounting high out of the water, and he twisted his huge deformed head backwards, trying to reach her. His bloodshot piggy eyes glared with the insanity of his rage, and his great jaws clashed as he snapped at her.

Somehow Lostris managed to gather herself and cling to a pair of the arrow-shafts that protruded from the bull's broad back as though they were handles. She lay with her arms and legs spread wide. She was not screaming now, all her art and strength employed in staying alive. Those curved ivory fangs rang upon each other like the blades of duelling warriors as they gnashed in air. At each bite they seemed to miss her by only a finger's-breadth, and any instant I expected one of her lovely limbs to be pruned away like a delicate shoot from the vine, and to see her sweet young blood mingle with those brutish effusions that streamed from the bull's wounds.

In the prow Tanus recovered swiftly. For an instant I saw his face and it was terrible. He tossed aside the bow, for it was useless to him now, and he seized instead the hilt of his sword and jerked the blade free of its crocodile-skin scabbard. It was a gleaming length of bronze as long as his arm, and the edges were honed until they could shave the hair from the back of his hand.

He leaped up on to the gunwale and balanced there for an instant, watching the wild gyrations of the mortally wounded bull in the water below him. Then he launched himself outwards and dropped like a stooping falcon with the sword held in both hands and pointing downwards.

He dropped across the bull's thick neck, landing astride it as though he were about to ride it into the underworld. The full weight of his body and the impetus of that wild leap were behind the sword as he struck. Half the length of the blade was driven into the hippopotamus's neck at the base of the skull, and, seated upon it like a rider, Tanus worried and worked the keen bronze deeper, using both arms and the strength of those broad shoulders. At the goad of the blade the bull went berserk. His strivings up to that point seemed feeble in comparison to this fresh outburst. The bull reared most of his enormous bulk out of the lagoon, swinging his head from side to side, throwing solid sheets of water so high in the air that they crashed down on the deck of the galley and, like a curtain, almost obscured the scene from my horrified gaze.

Through it all I watched the couple on the monster's back tossed about mercilessly. The shaft of one of the arrows that Lostris was holding snapped, and she was almost thrown clear. If this had happened she would surely have been savaged by the bull and chopped into bloody tatters by those ivory fangs. Tanus reached backwards and with one arm seized and steadied her, while with his right hand he never ceased working the bronze blade deeper into the nape of the bull's neck.

Unable to reach them, the hippopotamus slashed at his own flanks, inflicting terrible gaping wounds in his sides so that for fifty paces around the galley the waters were incarnadined, and both Lostris and Tanus were painted entirely crimson from the tops of their heads to the soles of their feet by the spurting blood. Their faces were turned to grotesque masks from which their eyes whitely glared.

The violent death-throes of the bull had carried them far from the galley's side, and I was the first aboard to recover my wits. I yelled to the rowers, 'Follow them! Don't let them get away,' and they sprang to their stations and sent the *Breath of Horus* in pursuit.

At that instant it seemed that the point of Tanus' blade must have found the joint of the vertebrae in the beast's neck and slipped through. The immense carcass stiffened and froze. The bull rolled on to his back with all four legs extended rigidly, and he plunged below the waters of the lagoon, bearing Lostris and Tanus with him into the depths.

I choked back the wail of despair that rose in my throat, and bellowed an order to the deck below. 'Back-water! Do not overrun them! Swimmers to the bows!' Even I was startled by the power and authority of my own voice.

The galley's forward way was checked, and before I could reflect on the prudence of what I was doing, I found myself heading a rush of hulking warriors across the deck. They would probably have cheered while they watched any other officer drown, but not their Tanus.

As for myself, I had already stripped off my skirt and was naked. Not the threat of a hundred lashes would have made me do this in any other circumstances, for I have let only one other person ever see those injuries that the state executioner inflicted upon me so long ago, and he was the one who had ordered the castrating knife used upon me in the first place. But now, for once, I was totally oblivious of the gross mutilation of my manhood.

I am a strong swimmer, and although in retrospect such foolhardiness makes me shudder, I truly believe that I might have dived over the side and swum down through those blood-dyed waters in an attempt to rescue my mistress. However, as I poised myself at the ship's rail, the waters directly below me opened and two heads bobbed out, both of them streaming water and as close as a pair of mating otters. One was dark and the other fair, but from both of them issued the most unlikely sound I had ever heard. They were laughing. They were howling and shrieking and spluttering with laughter as they floundered towards the ship's side, locked so firmly in each other's arms that I was certain that they were in real danger of drowning one another.

All my concern turned instantly to outrage at this levity, and at the thought of the dreadful folly which I had been on the point of committing. Like a mother whose first instinct on finding her lost child is to thrash it, I heard my own voice lose all its previous deep authority and turn shrill and querulous. I was still berating my mistress with all my famous eloquence as she and Tanus were dragged by a dozen willing hands from the water on to the deck.

'You reckless, unbridled little savage!' I railed at her. 'You thoughtless, selfish, undisciplined little hoyden! You promised me! You swore an oath on the maidenhead of the goddess—'

She ran to me and threw both arms around my neck. 'Oh, Taita!' she cried, still bubbling with laughter. 'Did you see him? Did you see Tanus spring to my rescue? Was it not the noblest deed that ever you heard of? Just like the hero of one of your very best stories.'

The fact that I had been on the point of making a similar heroic gesture was quite ignored, and this only increased my irritation. Added to which I suddenly realized that Lostris had lost her skirt, and that the cold, wet body she pressed to mine was entirely naked. She was displaying to the rude gaze of officers and men the neatest, tightest pair of buttocks in all Egypt.

I snatched up the nearest shield and used it to cover both our bodies while I shouted at her slave girls to find another skirt for her. Their giggles only increased my fury, and as soon as both Lostris and I were once again decently covered, I rounded on Tanus.

'As for you, you careless ruffian, I shall report you to my Lord Intef! He will have the skin flogged from your back.'

'You will do no such thing,' Tanus laughed at me, and threw one wet muscled arm around my shoulders to hug me so soundly that I was lifted off my feet, 'for he would have you flogged just as merrily. Nevertheless, thank you for your concern, old friend.'

He looked around quickly, with one arm still encircling my shoulder, and frowned. The *Breath of Horus* was separated from the other ships of the squadron, but by now the hunt was over. Every galley but ours had taken its full share of the bag that the priests had sanctioned us.

Tanus shook his head. 'We did not make the most of our chances, did we?' he grunted, and ordered one of his officers to hoist the recall signal to the squadron.

Then he forced a smile. 'Let us broach a jug of beer together, for now we have a while to wait and this has been thirsty work.' He went to the bows where the slave girls were fussing over Lostris. At first I was still so angry that I would not join their impromptu picnic on the deck. Instead I maintained an aloof dignity in the stern.

'Oh, let him sulk a while,' I heard Lostris' stage-whisper to Tanus as she recharged his cup with foaming beer. 'The old darling gave himself an awful scare, but he will get over it as soon as he is hungry. He does so love his food.'

She is the epitome of injustice, is my mistress. I never sulk, I am no glutton, and at that time I was barely thirty years of age, although to a fourteen-year-old anyone above twenty is an ancient, and I admit that, when it comes to food, I do have the refined tastes of a connoisseur. The roast wild goose with figs that she was ostentatiously displaying was one of my favourite dishes, as she very well knew.

I made them suffer for a while longer, and it was only when Tanus brought me a jug of beer with his own hand and cajoled me with all his charm that I deigned to relent a little and let him lead me to the prow. Still, I was a little stiff with them until Lostris kissed my cheek and said, loud enough for all to hear, 'My girls tell me that you took command of the ship like a veteran, and that you would have dived overboard to rescue me. Oh, Taita, what would I ever do without you?' Only then would I smile at her and accept the slice of goose she pressed upon me. It was delicious, and the beer was of three-palm quality. Even so, I ate sparingly, for I have my figure to consider and her earlier jibe about my appetite still rankled a little.

Tanus' squadron was scattered widely across the lagoon, but now it began to regroup. I saw that some of the other galleys had suffered damage, as we had. Two ships had collided in the heat of the chase, while four others had been attacked by the quarry. However, they reassembled swiftly and took up their battle stations. Then, in line astern and with strings of gay pennants fluttering at the mastheads to proclaim the size of each galley's bag, they dashed past us. The crews raised a cheer as they came level with the *Breath of Horus*. Tanus saluted them with a clenched fist and the Blue Crocodile standard was dipped at the masthead, for all the world as though we had just achieved a famous victory against daunting odds. Boyish display, perhaps, but then I am still enough of a boy to enjoy military ceremonial.

As soon as it was over, the squadron resumed its battle stations and was holding its position against the light breeze that had sprung up, with skilful use of paddles and steering-oars. Of course, there was no sign of the slaughtered hippopotami as yet. Although every galley had killed at least one, while some had killed two and even three, the carcasses had all sunk away into the green depths of the lagoon. I knew that Tanus was secretly lamenting the fact that the *Breath of Horus* had not been the most successful boat, and that our protracted encounter with the bull had limited our score to only that single animal. He was accustomed to excelling. Anyway, he was not his usual ebullient self and he soon left us on the prow and went to supervise the repairs to the hull of the *Breath of Horus*.

The bull's charge had sprung the underwater planking and we were taking enough water to necessitate constant bailing of the bilges with leather buckets. This was a most inefficient procedure which diverted men from their duties as rowers and warriors. Surely it could be improved upon, I thought to myself.

So while we waited for the carcasses of the dead beasts to rise, I sent one of the slave girls to fetch the basket that contained my writing instruments. Then, after a little further thought, I began to sketch out an idea for mechanically removing the water from the bilges of a fighting galley in action, a method which did not demand the efforts of half the crew. It was based on the same principle as the shadoof water buckets. I thought that two men might operate it instead of a dozen at the buckets, as was now the case.

When I had completed the sketch, I pondered on the collision that had caused the original damage. Historically, the tactics used in battles between squadrons of river galleys had always been the same as those of land engagements. The ships would lie alongside each other and exchange volleys of arrows. They would then close and grapple and board, and finish the business with the sword. The galley captains were always careful to avoid collision, as this was considered sloppy seamanship.

'But what if—' I thought suddenly, and I began a sketch of a galley with a reinforced bow. As the idea took firm root I added a horn like that of the rhinoceros at the water line. It could be carved from hardwood and clad with bronze. Angled forwards and slightly downwards, it could be driven through the hull of an opposing vessel to rip out her belly. I was so engrossed that I did not hear Tanus come up behind me. He snatched the papyrus scroll from me and studied it avidly.

Of course, he understood instantly what I was about. When his father had lost his fortune, I had tried everything in my power to find a rich patron to sponsor him to enter one of the temples as a novice scribe, there to continue his studies and his learning. For I truly believed that, with my tutelage, he had every prospect of developing into one of the great minds of Egypt, perhaps in time a name to rank with that of Imhotep who, one thousand years before, had designed those first marvellous pyramids at Saqqarah.

I had been unsuccessful, naturally enough, for the same enemy whose spite and guile had destroyed Tanus' father had set out to bar the way to Tanus himself. No man in the land could prevail against such a baleful influence. So instead I had helped Tanus to enter the army. Despite my disappointment and misgivings, this had been his own choice of career ever since he had first stood upright and wielded a wooden sword on the other infants in the playground.

'By the carbuncles on Seth's buttocks!' he exclaimed now, as he studied my drawings. 'You and that designing-brush of yours are worth ten full squadrons to me!'

Tanus' casual blasphemy on the name of the great god Seth always alarms me. For although both he and I are Horus men, still I do not believe in flagrantly offering offence to any member of the pantheon of Egyptian gods. I personally never pass a shrine without offering a prayer or making a small sacrifice, no matter how humble or unimportant the god it houses. It is, to my mind, simple common sense and good insurance. One has sufficient enemies amongst men without deliberately seeking out others amongst the gods. I am particularly obsequious to Seth, for his formidable reputation terrifies me. I suspect that Tanus knows all this and deliberately does it to tease me. However, my discomfort was soon forgotten in the warm glow of his praise.

'How do you do it?' he demanded. 'I am the soldier, and today I saw everything that you did. Why did not the same ideas occur to me?'

We were instantly immersed in a lively discussion of my designs. Of course, Lostris could not be excluded for long, and she came to join us. Her handmaidens had dried and rebraided her hair and retouched her make-up. Her loveliness was a distraction, especially since she stood beside me and nonchalantly draped one slim arm over my shoulder. She would never have touched a man like that in public, for it would have offended against custom and modesty. But then I am not a man, and though she leaned against me, her eyes never left Tanus' face.

Her preoccupation with him went back to when she had first learned to walk. She had stumbled along adoringly behind the lordly ten-year-old Tanus, faithfully trying to copy his every gesture and word. When he spat, she spat. When he swore, she lisped the same oath, until Tanus had complained bitterly to me, 'Can you not make her leave me alone, Taita? She's just a baby!' He was not doing much complaining now, I noticed.

At last we were interrupted by a hail from the lookout in the bows, and we all hurried forward and peered eagerly across the lagoon. The first hippopotamus carcass was rising to the surface. It came up belly first as the gases in its intestines expanded and the guts distended like a child's balloon made from a goat's bladder. It bobbed on the surface with all its legs extended stiffly. One of the galleys sped across to recover it. A sailor scrambled out on to the carcass and secured a line to one of the legs. As soon as this was done, the galley towed it away towards the distant shore.

By now the huge corpses were surfacing all around us. The galleys gathered them up and dragged them away. Tanus secured two of them to our stern-hawser and the rowers strained at their paddles to move them through the water.

As we approached the shore I shaded my eyes against the slanting sun's rays and peered ahead. It seemed that every man, woman and child in Upper Egypt was waiting upon the bank. They were a vast multitude, dancing and singing and waving palm-fronds to welcome the incoming fleet. The restless movement of their white robes seemed like a storm surf breaking upon the edge of the placid lagoon.

As each galley drew up against the bank, teams of men clad only in the briefest loin-cloths waded out as deep as their armpits to fasten ropes to the bloated carcasses. In their excitement they were oblivious to the ever-present threat of crocodiles lurking in the opaque green waters. Every season these ferocious dragons devour hundreds of our people. Sometimes they are so bold that they rush out on to dry land to seize a child playing near the water's edge or a peasant woman washing clothes or drawing water for her family.

Now, in the vast meat-hunger that gripped them, the people were interested in only one thing. They seized the ropes and hauled the carcasses ashore. As they slithered up the muddy bank, scores of tiny silver fish that had been feasting on the open wounds were slow to relinquish their hold and were drawn out with the carcasses. Stranded upon the mud-banks, they flopped and quivered like stars that had fallen to earth.

Men and women, all wielding knives or axes, swarmed like ants over the bodies. In a delirium of greed they howled and snarled at each other like vultures and hyenas on a lion's kill, disputing each titbit as they hacked at the gigantic carcasses. Blood and bone chips flew in sheets as the blades hacked and hewed. There would be long lines of wounded at the temple that evening, awaiting treatment from the priests for their missing fingers and gashes down to the bone where the careless blades had slipped.

I too would be busy half the night, for in some quarters I have a reputation as a medical doctor that surpasses even that of the priests of Osiris. In all modesty I must admit that this reputation is not entirely unwarranted, and Horus knows my fees are much more reasonable than those of the holy men. My Lord Intef allows me to keep for myself a third part of all that I earn. Thus I am a man of some substance, despite my slave status.

From the stern-tower of the *Breath of Horus* I watched the pantomime of human frailty that was being played out below me. Traditionally the populace is allowed to eat its fill of the meats of the hunt upon the foreshore, just as long as none of the spoils are carried away. Living as we do in a verdant land which is fertilized and watered by the great river, our people are well fed. However, the staple diet of the poorer classes is grain, and months may pass between their last mouthful of meat and the next. Added to which, the festival was a time when all the normal restraints of everyday life were thrust aside. There was licence to excess in all things of the body, in food and drink and carnal passion. There would be sore bellies and aching heads and matrimonial recriminations on the morrow, but this was the first day of the festival and there was no check on any appetite.

I smiled as I watched a mother, naked to the waist and plastered from head to toe with blood and fat, emerge from the belly cavity of a hippopotamus, clutching a running lump of liver which she threw to one of her brood in the jostling, shrieking pack of children that surrounded the carcass. The woman ducked back into the interior of the beast, while, clutching his prize, the child darted away to one of the hundreds of cooking-fires that burned along the shore. There an elder brother snatched the hunk of liver from him and threw it on the coals, while a pack of younger urchins crowded forward impatiently, slavering like puppies.

The eldest child hooked the barely scorched liver off the fire with a green twig, and his brothers and sisters fell upon it and devoured it. Immediately it was consumed they bayed for more, with fat and juice running down their faces and dripping from their chins. Many of the younger ones had probably never tasted the delicious flesh of the river-cow before. It is sweet and tender and fine-grained, but most of all it is fat, fatter than beef or striped wild ass, and the marrow-bones are truly a delicacy fit for the great god Osiris himself. Our people are starved of animal fat and the taste of it drove them wild. They gorged themselves, as was their right on this day.

I was content to keep aloof from this riotous mob, happy in the knowledge that my Lord Intef's bailiffs would secure the finest cuts and marrow-bones for the palace kitchens where the cooks would prepare my personal platter to perfection. My precedence in the vizier's household exceeds all other, even that of his major-domo or the commander of his bodyguard, both of whom are free-born. Of course, it is never openly spoken of, but all tacitly acknowledge my privileged and superior position and few would dare challenge it.

I watched the bailiffs at work now, claiming the share of my lord, the governor and grand vizier of all the twenty-two nomes of Upper Egypt. They swung their long staves with the expertise born of long practice, whacking any bare back or set of naked buttocks that presented themselves as targets, and shouting their demands.

The ivory teeth of the animals belonged to the vizier, and the bailiffs collected every one of them. They were as valuable as the elephant tusks that are brought down in trade from the land of Cush, beyond the cataracts. The last elephant had been killed in our Egypt almost one thousand years ago, in the reign of one of the pharaohs of the Fourth Dynasty, or so the hieroglyphics on the stele in his temple boast. Naturally, from the fruits of the hunt my lord was expected to tithe the priests of Hapi who were the titular shepherds of the goddess's flock of river-cows. However, the amount of the tithe was in my lord's discretion, and I who was in overall charge of the palace accounts knew where the lion's share of the treasure would end up. My Lord Intef does not indulge in unnecessary generosity, even towards a goddess.

As for the hides of the hippopotamus, these belonged to the army and would be turned into war shields for the officers of the guards regiments. The army quartermasters were supervising the skinning-out and the handling of the hides, each of which was almost the size of a Bedouin tent.

The meat that could not be consumed on the bank would be pickled in brine, or smoked or dried. Ostensibly it would be used to feed the army, the members of the law courts, the temples and other civil servants of the state. However, in practice a large part of it would be discreetly sold, and the proceeds would filter down quite naturally into my lord's coffers. As I have said before, my lord was the wealthiest man in the Upper Kingdom after Pharaoh himself, and growing richer every year.

A fresh commotion broke out behind me, and I turned quickly. Tanus' squadron was still in action. The galleys were drawn up in line of battle, stem to stern, parallel to the shore-line, but fifty paces off it on the edge of the deeper water. On each ship harpooneers stood at the rails with their weapons poised and pointed down at the surface of the lagoon.

The taint of blood and offal in the water had attracted the crocodiles. Not only from all over the lagoon, but from as far off as the main course of the Nile, they had come swarming to the feast. The harpooneers were waiting for them. Each long harpoon pole was tipped with a relatively small bronze head, viciously barbed. Spliced to an eye in the metal head was a tough flax rope.

The skill of the harpooneers was truly impressive. As one of these scaly saurians came slipping through the green water, with its great crested tail flailing, moving like a long dark shadow, silent and deadly beneath the surface, they would be waiting for it. They would allow the crocodile to pass beneath the galley, and then, as it emerged on the far side with the harpooneer's movements screened from it by the ship's hull, he would lean out over it and stab downwards.

It was not a violent blow, but an almost delicate dab with the long pole. The bronze head was as sharp as a surgeon's needle, and its full length was buried deep beneath the reptile's thick, scaly hide. The harpooneer aimed for the back of the neck, and so skilful were these thrusts that many of them pierced the spinal cord and killed the creature instantly.

However, when a blow missed its mark, the water exploded as the wounded crocodile burst into wild convulsions. With a twist of the harpoon pole the metal head was detached and remained buried in the reptile's armoured neck. Then four men took the creature on the flax line to control its contortions. If the crocodile was a large one – and some of them were four times the length of a man stretched out on the ground – then the coils of line were whipped away smoking over the gunwale, scorching the palms of the men who were trying to hold it.

When this happened, even the hungry crowds on the beach paused for a while to cheer and shout encouragement, and to watch the struggle as the crocodile was eventually subdued or the rope parted like a whiplash and the sailors were sent tumbling backwards across the deck. More often, the stout flax line held. As soon as the crew were able to turn the reptile's head towards them, it could no longer swim out into the deep water. They could then drag it in a turmoil of froth and white water to the ship's side where another gang was waiting with clubs to crush the rock-hard skull.

When the carcasses of the crocodiles were dragged to the bank, I went ashore to examine them. The skinners of Tanus' regiment were already at work.

It was the grandfather of our present king who had granted the regiment the honorific 'the Blue Crocodile Guards' and bestowed upon them the standard of the Blue Crocodile. Their battle armour is made from the horny skins of these dragons. Properly treated and cured, it becomes hard enough to stop an arrow or turn the edge of an enemy sword-cut. It is far lighter in weight than metal, and much cooler to wear in the desert sun. Tanus, in his crocodile-skin helmet all decorated with ostrich plumes, and his breastplate of the same hide, polished and starred with bronze rosettes, is a sight to strike terror into the heart of an enemy, or turmoil into the belly of any maiden who looks upon him.

As I measured and noted the length and girth of each carcass, and watched the skinners at work, I felt not even the most fleeting sympathy for these hideous monsters as I had for the slaughtered river-cows. To my mind there is no more loathsome beast in nature than the crocodile, with the possible exception of the venomous asp.

My revulsion was increased a hundredfold when a skinner slit open the belly of one of the largest of these grotesque animals, and out on to the mud slithered the partly digested remains of a young girl. The crocodile had swallowed the entire top half of her body, from the waist upwards. Although the flesh was bleached soft and pasty-white by the digestive juices and was sloughing from the skull, the girl's top-knot was still intact and neatly plaited and coiled above the ghastly, ruined face. As a further macabre touch, there was a necklace around her throat and pretty bracelets of red and blue ceramic beads on the skeletal wrists.

No sooner was this gruesome relic revealed than there came a shriek so high and heart-rending that it cut through the hubbub of the throng, and a woman elbowed aside the soldiers and ran forward to drop on her knees beside the pitiful remains. She tore her clothing and keened the dreadful ululation of mourning.

'My daughter! My little girl!' She was the same woman who had come to the palace the previous day to report her daughter missing. The officials had told her that the child had probably been abducted and sold into slavery by one of the gangs of bandits who were terrorizing the countryside. These gangs had become a force in the land, blatantly conducting their lawless depredations in broad daylight right up to the gates of the cities. The palace officials had warned the woman that there was nothing they could do about recovering her daughter, for the gangs were beyond any control that the state could exert upon them.

For once this dire prediction had proved unfounded. The mother had recognized the ornaments which still decorated the pathetic little corpse. My heart went out to the stricken woman, as I sent a slave to fetch an empty wine jar. Although the woman and her child were both strangers to me, I could not prevent my own tears from welling up as I helped her to gather the remains and place them in the jar for decent burial.

As she staggered away into the uncaring multitude of revellers, carrying the jar clutched to her breast, I reflected that despite all the rites and prayers that the mother would lavish upon her daughter, and even in the unlikely event that she could afford the staggering cost of the most rudimentary mummification, the child's shade could never find immortality in the life beyond the grave. For that to happen, the corpse must be intact and whole before embalming. My feelings were all for the unfortunate mother. It is a weakness of mine that I so often lament, that I take upon myself the cares and sorrows of every unfortunate that crosses my path. It would be easier to have a harder heart, and a more cynical turn of mind.

As always when I am saddened or distressed, I reached for my brush and scroll and began to record all that was taking place around me, everything from the harpooneers, the bereaved mother, the skinning and the butchery of the dead river-cows and crocodiles on the beach, to the unfettered behaviour of the feasting, revelling populace.

Already those who were stuffed with meat and gorged with beer were snoring where they had fallen, oblivious of being kicked and trampled by the others still capable of remaining upright. The younger and more shameless were dancing and embracing and using the gathering darkness and the inadequate cover of the scanty bushes and the trampled papyrus beds to screen their blatant copulations. This wanton behaviour was merely a symptom of the malaise that afflicted the entire land. It would not have been thus if only there had been a strong pharaoh, and a moral and upright administration in the nome of Greater Thebes. The common people take their example from those above them.

Although I disapproved most strongly of it all, still I recorded it faithfully. Thus an hour sped away while I sat cross-legged and totally absorbed upon the poop-deck of the *Breath of Horus*, scribbling and sketching. The sun sank and seemed to quench itself in the great river, leaving a coppery sheen on the water and a smoky glow in the western sky as though it had set fire to the papyrus beds.

The crowds on the beach were becoming ever more raucous and unrestrained. The harlots were doing a brisk trade. I watched a plump and matronly love-priestess, wearing the distinctive blue amulet of her calling upon her forehead, lead a skinny sailor who was half her size from one of the galleys into the shadows beyond the firelight. There she dropped her skirts and fell to her knees in the dust, presenting him with a quivering pair of monumental buttocks. With a happy cry the little fellow was upon her like a dog on a bitch, and within seconds she was yapping as loudly as he was. I began to sketch their antics, but the light faded swiftly, and I was forced to quit for the day.

As I set my scroll aside, I realized with a start that I had not seen my mistress since before the incident with the dead child. I leaped to my feet in a panic. How could I have been so remiss? My mistress had been strictly raised, I had seen to that. She was a good and moral child, fully aware of the duties and obligations which law and custom placed upon her. She was aware also of the honour of the high family to which she belonged, and of her place in society. What was more, she stood in as much awe as I did of her father's authority and temper. Of course I trusted her.

I trusted her as much as I would have trusted any other strong-willed young creature in the first flush of passionate womanhood on a night such as this, alone somewhere in the darkness with the handsome and equally passionate young soldier with whom she was totally infatuated.

My panic was not so much for the fragile maidenhead of my mistress, that ethereal talisman which once lost is seldom mourned, as for the much more substantial risk of damage to my own skin. On the morrow we would return to Karnak and the palace of my Lord Intef, where there would be wagging tongues aplenty to carry the tale of any lapse or indiscretion on any of our parts to him.

My lord's spies permeated every layer of society and every corner of our land, from the docks and the fields to the palace of Pharaoh itself. They were even more numerous than my own, for he had more money to pay his agents, although many of them served both of us impartially and our networks interlocked at many levels. If Lostris had disgraced us all, father, family, and me her tutor and guardian, then my Lord Intef would know of it by morning, and so would I.

I ran from one end of the ship to the other, searching for her. I climbed into the stern-tower and scanned the beach in desperation. I could see nothing of her or of Tanus, and my worst fears were encouraged.

Where to search for them in this mad night I could not begin to think. I caught myself wringing my hands in an agony of frustration, and stopped myself immediately. I am always at pains to avoid any appearance of effeminacy. I do so abhor those obese, mincing, posturing creatures who have suffered the same mutilation as I have. I always try to conduct myself like a man rather than a eunuch.

I controlled myself with an effort and assumed the same coldly determined mien that I had seen on Tanus' features in the heat of battle, whereupon my wits were restored to me and I became rational once again. I considered how my mistress was likely to behave. Of course, I knew her intimately. After all, I had studied her for fourteen years. I realized that she was much too fastidious and conscious of her noble rank brazenly to mingle with the drunken, uncouth throng upon the beach, or to creep away into the bushes to play the beast with two backs, as I had watched the sailor and the fat old harlot do. I knew that I could call upon no one else to assist me in my search, for that would have guaranteed that my Lord Intef would hear all about it. I had to do it all myself.

To what secret place had Lostris allowed herself to be carried away? Like most young girls of her age she was enchanted with the idea of romantic love. I doubted that she had ever seriously considered the more earthy aspects of the physical act, despite the best efforts of those two little black sluts of hers to enlighten her. She had not even displayed any great deal of interest in the mechanics of the business when I had attempted, as was my duty, to warn her, at least sufficiently to protect her from herself.

I realized then that I must look for her in some place that would live up to her sentimental expectations of love. If there had been a cabin on the *Breath of Horus* I would have hurried to it, but our river galleys are small, utilitarian fighting ships, stripped down for speed and manoeuvrability. The crew sleep on the bare deck, while even the captain and his officers have only a reed awning for a night shelter. This was not rigged at the moment, and so there was no place aboard where they could be hiding.

Karnak and the palace were half a day's travel away. The slaves were only now erecting our tents on one of the small inshore islands that had been set aside to give our party privacy from the common herd of humanity. It was remiss of the slaves to be so tardy, but they had been caught up in the festivities. In the torchlight I could see that a few of them were more than a little unsteady on their feet as they struggled with the guy-ropes. They had not yet erected Lostris' personal tent, so the luxurious comforts of carpets and embroidered hangings and down-filled mattresses and linen sheets were not available to the lovers. So where then might they be?

At that moment a soft yellow glow of torchlight farther out on the lagoon caught my attention. Immediately my intuition was aroused. I realized that, given my mistress's connections with the goddess Hapi, her temple on its picturesque little granite island in the middle of the lagoon would be exactly the place that would draw Lostris irresistibly. I searched the beach for some means of reaching the island. Although there were shoals of small craft drawn up on the shore, the ferrymen were mostly falling-down drunk.

Then I spotted Kratas on the beach. The ostrich feathers on his helmet stood high above the heads of the crowd, and his proud bearing marked him out.

'Kratas!' I yelled at him, and he looked across at me and waved. Kratas was Tanus' chief lieutenant and, apart from myself, the firmest of his multitude of friends. I could trust Kratas as I dared trust no other.

'Get me a boat!' I screamed at him. 'Any boat!' I was so distraught and my tone so shrill that it carried clearly to him. It was typical of the man that he wasted not a moment in question or indecision. He strode to the nearest felucca on the shore. The ferryman was lying like a log in his own bilges. Kratas took him by the scruff of the neck and lifted him out bodily. He dropped him on the beach, and the ferryman never moved, but lay in a stupor of cheap wine, twisted in the attitude that Kratas had dumped him in. Kratas launched the craft himself and, with a few thrusts of the punt pole, laid alongside the *Breath of Horus*. In my haste I tumbled from the tower and landed in a heap in the bows of the tiny craft.

'To the temple, Kratas,' I pleaded with him as I scrambled up, 'and may the sweet goddess Hapi grant we are not already too late!'

With the evening breeze in the lateen sail we were whisked across the dark waters to the stone jetty below the temple. Kratas secured the painter to one of the mooring-rings, and made as if to follow me ashore, but I stopped him.

'For Tanus' sake, not mine,' I told him, 'do not follow me, please.'

He hesitated a moment, then nodded. 'I will be listening for your call.' He drew his sword and offered it to me, hilt first. 'Will you need this?'

I shook my head. 'It is not that kind of danger. Besides, I have my dagger. But thank you for your trust.' I left him in the boat and hurried up the granite steps to the entrance of the temple of Hapi.

The rush torches in their brackets on the tall entrance pillars threw a ruddy, wavering light that seemed to bring to life the bas-relief carvings on the walls and make them dance. The goddess Hapi is one of my favourites. Strictly speaking, she is neither god nor goddess, but a strange, bearded, hermaphroditic creature possessed of both a massive penis and an equally cavernous vagina, and bounteous breasts that give milk to all. She is the deification of the Nile, and the goddess of the harvest. The two kingdoms of Egypt and all the peoples in them depend utterly upon her and the periodic flooding of the great river which is her alter ego. She is able to change her gender or, like many of the other gods of this very Egypt, take on the shape of any animal at will. Her favourite guise is that of the hippopotamus. Despite the god's ambiguous sexuality, my mistress Lostris always considered her to be female, and so do I. The priests of Hapi may differ from us on this view.

Her images upon the stone walls were vast and motherly. Painted in hectic primary colours of red and yellow and blue, she beamed down with the head of a kindly river-cow, and seemed to invite all of nature to be fruitful and to multiply. The implied invitation was most inappropriate to my present anxiety. It was my fear that my precious charge might even at this moment be availing herself of the goddess's indulgence.

A priestess was kneeling at the side-altar, and I ran to her, seized her by the hem of her cape and tugged at it urgently. 'Holy sister, tell me, have you seen the Lady Lostris, daughter of the grand vizier?' There were very few citizens of Upper Egypt who did not know my mistress by sight. They all loved her for her beauty, her gay spirit and her sweet disposition, and they clustered around her and cheered her in the streets and market-places when she walked abroad.

The priestess grinned at me, all wrinkled and toothless, and she laid one bony finger on the side of her nose with such a sly and knowing expression that all my worst fears were confirmed.

I shook her again, but less gently. 'Where is she, revered old mother? I beseech you, speak!' But instead she wagged her head and rolled her eyes towards the portals of the inner sanctum.

I sped across the granite flags, my heart outrunning my frantic feet, but even in my distress I wondered at the boldness of my mistress. Although as a member of the high nobility she had right of access to the holy of holies, was there another in all of Egypt who would have the nerve to choose such a place for her love tryst?

At the entrance to the sanctum I paused. My instinct had been right.

There they were, the two of them, just as I had dreaded. I was so obsessed by my own certainty of what was taking place that I almost yelled aloud to them to stop it. Then I checked myself.

My mistress was fully clad, more so than was usual, for her breasts were covered and she had spread a blue woollen shawl over her head. She was kneeling before the gigantic statue of Hapi. The goddess beamed down upon her, bedecked in wreaths of blue water-lilies.

Tanus knelt beside her. He had laid aside his weapons and his armour. They were piled at the door of the sanctuary. He was dressed only in a linen shift and short tunic, with sandals on his feet. The young couple were holding hands, and their faces were almost touching as they whispered solemnly together.

My base suspicions were refuted, and I was struck with remorse and shame. How could I ever have doubted my mistress? Quietly I began to withdraw, although I would go only as far as the side-altar, where I would give thanks to the goddess for her protection, and from where I could keep a discreet eye on further proceedings.

However, at that moment Lostris rose to her feet and diffidently approached the statue of the goddess. I was so enthralled by her girlish grace that I lingered a moment longer to watch her.

From around her neck she unclasped the lapis lazuli figurine of the goddess which I had made for her. I realized with a pang that she was about to offer it as a sacrifice. That jewel had been crafted with all my love for her, and I hated to see it leave her throat. Lostris stood on tiptoe to hang it on the idol's neck. Then she knelt and kissed the stone foot while Tanus watched, still kneeling where she had left him.

She rose and turned to go back to him, but then she saw me in the doorway. I tried to melt away into the shadows, for I was embarrassed at having spied upon so intimate a moment. However, her face lit with joy and before I could escape, she ran to me and seized my hands.

'Oh, Taita, I am so glad that you are here – you of all people! It is so fitting. It makes it all so perfect.' She led me forward into the sanctum and Tanus rose to his feet and came smiling to take my other hand.

'Thank you for coming. I know we can always count upon you.' I wished that my motives had been as pure as they believed them to be, so I hid my guilty heart from them with a loving smile.

'Kneel here!' Lostris ordered me. 'Here, where you can hear every word we say to each other. You will bear witness for us before Hapi and all the gods of Egypt.' She pressed me to my knees, and then she and Tanus resumed their places in front of the goddess and took each other's hands, looking full into each other's eyes.

Lostris spoke first. 'You are my sun,' she whispered. 'My day is dark without you.'

'You are the Nile of my heart,' Tanus told her quietly, 'The waters of your love feed my soul.'

'You are my man, through this world and all the worlds to come.'

'You are my woman, and I pledge you my love. I swear it to you on the breath and the blood of Horus,' Tanus said clearly and openly, so that his voice echoed through the stone halls.

'I take up your pledge and return it to you one hundredfold,' Lostris cried. 'No one can ever come between us. Nothing can ever part us. We are one, for ever.'

She offered her face to his and he kissed her, deeply and lingeringly. As far as I was aware, it was the first kiss that the couple had ever exchanged. I felt that I was privileged to have witnessed such an intimate moment.

As they embraced, a sudden chill wind off the lagoon swirled through the dimly lit halls of the temple and fluttered the torch flames, so that for an instant the faces of the two lovers blurred before my eyes and the image of the goddess seemed to stir and quiver. The wind passed as swiftly as it had come, but the whisper of it around the great stone pillars was like the distant sardonic laughter of the gods, and I shuddered with superstitious awe.

It is always dangerous to pique the gods with extravagant demands, and Lostris had just asked for the impossible. This was the moment that for years I had known was coming, and which I had dreaded more bitterly than the day of my own death. The pledge that Tanus and Lostris had made to each other could never endure. No matter how deeply they meant it, it could never be. I felt my own heart tearing within me as, at last, they broke the kiss and both turned back to me.

'Why so sad, Taita?' Lostris demanded, her own face flooded with joy. 'Rejoice with me, for this is the happiest day of my life.'

I forced my lips to smile, but I could find no word of comfort or of felicitation for these two, the ones I loved best in all the world. I remained upon my knees, with that fixed, idiotic smile on my lips and desolation in my soul.

Now Tanus lifted me to my feet and embraced me. 'You will speak to Lord Intef on my behalf, won't you?' he demanded as he hugged me.

'Oh yes, Taita,' Lostris joined her plea to his. 'My father will listen to you. You are the only one who can do it for us. You won't fail us, will you, Taita? You have never let me down, never once in all my life. You'll do it for me, won't you?'

What could I say to them? I could not be so cruel as to tell them the blunt truth. I could not find the words to blight this fresh and tender love. They were waiting for me to speak, to express my joy for them, and to promise them my help and support. But I was struck dumb, my mouth was as dry as if I had bitten into an unripe pomegranate.

'Taita, what is it?' I watched the joy wither upon my mistress's beloved countenance. 'Why do you not rejoice for us?'

'You know that I love you both, but—' I could not continue.

'But? But what, Taita?' Lostris demanded. 'Why do you give me "buts" and a long face on this happiest of all possible days?' She was becoming angry, her jaw was setting, but at the same time there were tears gathering deep in her eyes. 'Don't you want to help us? Is this the real value of all the promises you have made to me over the years?' She came to me and thrust her face close to mine in challenge.

'Mistress, please don't talk like that. I do not deserve that treatment. No, listen to me!' I placed my fingers on her lips to forestall another outburst. 'It is not me. It is your father, my Lord Intef—'

'Exactly.' Impatiently Lostris plucked my hand away from her mouth. 'My father! You will go to him and speak to him the way you always do, and it will be all right.'

'Lostris,' I began, and it was a sign of my distress that I used her name in this familiar fashion, 'you are no longer a child. You must not delude yourself with childish fantasies. You know that your father will never agree—'

She would not listen to me, she did not want to hear the truth that I would speak, so she rushed in with words to drown out mine. 'I know that Tanus has no fortune, yes. But he has a marvellous future ahead of him. One day he will command all the armies of Egypt. One day he will fight the battles which will reunite the two kingdoms, and I will be at his side.'

'Mistress, please hear me out. It is not only the lack of Tanus' fortune. It is more, much more.'

'His blood-line and his breeding, then? Is that what troubles you? You know full well that his family is as noble as ours. Pianki, Lord Harrab was my own father's equal and his dearest friend.' She had closed her ears to me. She did not realize the depth of the tragedy on which we were embarking. Neither she nor Tanus did, but then I was probably the only person in the kingdom who understood it fully.

I had protected her from the truth all these years and, of course, I had never been able to tell Tanus either. How could I explain it to her now? How could I reveal to her the depths of the hatred that her father bore towards the young man she loved? It was a hatred born out of guilt and envy, and yet all the more implacable for these reasons.

However, my Lord Intef was a crafty and devious man. He was able to conceal his feelings from those around him. He was able to dissemble his hatred and his spite, and to kiss the one he would destroy and heap rich gifts and lulling flattery upon him. He had the patience of the crocodile buried in the mud at the drinking-place on the river, waiting for the unsuspecting gazelle. He would wait years, even a decade, but when the opportunity arose, he was as swift as that reptile to strike and drag his prey under.

Lostris was blithely unaware of the depths of her father's rancour. She even believed that he had loved Pianki, Lord Harrab, as Tanus' father had loved him. But then how could she know the truth of it, for I had always shielded her from it? In her sweet innocence Lostris believed that the only objections that her father would have to her lover were those of fortune and family.

'You know it is true, Taita. Tanus is my equal in the lists of the nobility. It is written in the temple records for all to see. How can my father deny it? How can you deny it?'

'It is not for me to deny or to accede, mistress—'

'Then you will go to my father for us, won't you, dear Taita? Say you will, please say you will!'

I could only bow my head in acquiescence, and to hide the hopeless expression in my eyes.

THE FLEET was heavily laden on the return to Karnak. The galleys were low in the water under their cargoes of rawhides and salted meat. Thus our progress against the Nile's current was slower than on our outward journey, but still too swift for my heavy heart and mounting dread.

The lovers were gay and euphoric with their newly declared love and their trust in me to remove the obstacles from their path. I could not bring myself to deny them this day of happiness, for I knew that it would be one of the very last they would share. I think that if I could have found the words or summoned the courage, I would have urged them, there and then, to seek the consummation of their love that I had so opposed the night before. There would never be another chance for them, not after I had alerted my Lord Intef with my foredoomed attempt at matchmaking. Once he knew what they were about, he would come between them and thrust them apart for ever.

So instead I laughed and smiled as gaily as they did, and tried to hide my fears from them. They were so blinded by love that I succeeded, whereas at any other time my mistress would have seen through me immediately. She knows me almost as well as I know her.

We sat together in the prow, the three of us, and we discussed the re-enactment of the passion of Osiris that would be the highlight of the festival. My Lord Intef had made me the impresario of the pageant, and I had cast both Lostris and Tanus in leading roles.

The festival is held every second year, at the rising of the full moon of Osiris. There was a time when it was an annual event. However, the expense and disruption of royal life caused by having to remove the court from Elephantine to Thebes was so great that Pharaoh decreed a greater interval between the festivals. He was always a prudent man with his gold, was our Pharaoh.

The plans for the pageant provided me with a fine distraction from the looming confrontation with my Lord Intef, and so now I rehearsed the two lovers in their lines. Lostris was to play Isis, the wife of Osiris, while Tanus would take on the major role of Horus. They were both vastly amused at the idea of Tanus playing Lostris' son, and I had to explain that the gods were ageless, and it was quite possible that a goddess could appear younger than her offspring.

I had written a new script for the pageant to replace the one that had remained unchanged for almost a thousand years. The language of the ancient one was archaic and unsuitable for a modern audience. Pharaoh would be the guest of honour when the pageant was performed in the temple of Osiris on the final night of the festival, so I was particularly anxious that it should be a success. I had already encountered opposition to my new version of the passion from the more conservative nobles and priests. Only my Lord Intef's intervention had prevailed against their objections.

My lord is not a deeply religious man and would not normally have interested himself in theological arguments. However, I had included a few lines that were designed to amuse and flatter him. I read them to him out of context, and then tactfully pointed out to him that the chief opposition to my version came from the high priest of Osiris, a prissy old man who had once frustrated my Lord Intef's interest in a comely young acolyte. This was a trespass for which my lord had never forgiven the high priest.

Thus it was that my version would be performed for the first time. It was essential that the actors bring out the full glory of my poetry, or it might well be the last time it would be heard.

Both Tanus and Lostris possessed marvellous speaking voices, and they were determined to reward me for my promise to help them. They gave me of their best, and thus the rehearsal was so absorbing, their recitations so startling, that for a while I could forget myself.

Then I was brought back from the passion of the gods to my own mundane preoccupations by a cry from the lookout. The fleet was sweeping around the last bend in the river, and there lay the twin cities of Luxor and Karnak, that between them made up Greater Thebes, strung out along the bank before us and sparkling like a necklace of pearls in the stark Egyptian sunlight. Our fantastic interlude had ended, and we must face reality once again. My spirits tumbled as I scrambled to my feet.

'Tanus, you must transfer Lostris and myself to the galley of Kratas before we come any closer to the city. My lord's minions will be watching us from the land. They must not see us in your company.'

'A little late, is it not?' Tanus smiled at me. 'You should have thought of that some days ago.'

'My father will learn about us soon enough,' Lostris endorsed his objection. 'It might make your task easier if we forewarn him of our intentions.'

'If you know better than I, then you must do it your way and I will take no further part in this crazy business of yours.' I put on my most stiff and offended air, and they relented immediately.

Tanus signalled Kratas' galley alongside, and the lovers had only a few moments for their farewells. They dared not embrace before the eyes of half the fleet, but the glances and the loving words they exchanged were almost as fulfilling.

From the stern-tower of Kratas' ship we waved to the *Breath of Horus* as she turned from us, and with her paddles flashing like the wings of a dragonfly, she bore away to her moorings in front of the city of Luxor, while we continued on up-river towards the palace of the grand vizier.

IMMEDIATELY we docked at the palace wharf, I made enquiry as to the whereabouts of my master and was relieved to learn that he had crossed the river to undertake a last-minute inspection of Pharaoh's tomb and funerary temple on the west bank. The king's temple and tomb had been under construction for the past twelve years, ever since the first day that he had donned the double white and red crown of the two kingdoms. It was nearing completion at last, and the king would be anxious to visit it as soon as the festival was over and he was free to do so. My Lord Intef was anxious that the king should not be disappointed. One of my lord's many titles and honours was Guardian of the Royal Tombs, and it was a serious responsibility.

His absence afforded me a further day in which to prepare my case and plan my strategy. However, the solemn promise that the two lovers had extracted from me was to speak out for them at the first opportunity, and I knew that would be on the morrow when my lord held his weekly assize.

As soon as I had seen my mistress safely ensconced in the harem, I hurried to my own quarters in that wing of the palace which is reserved for the special companions of the grand vizier.

My Lord Intef's domestic arrangements were as devious as the rest of his existence. He had eight wives, all of whom brought to his marriage-bed either substantial dowry or influential political connections. However, only three of these women had ever borne him children. Apart from my Lady Lostris, there were two sons.

As far as I was aware, and I was aware of everything that happened in the palace and most of what happened outside it, my lord had not visited the harem in the last fifteen years. The getting of Lostris had been the last occasion that he had performed his matrimonial duties. His sexual tastes lay in other directions. The special companions of the grand vizier who lived in our wing of the palace were as pretty a collection of slave boys as you could find in the Upper Kingdom, where over the previous hundred years pederasty had replaced wild-fowling and hunting as the favourite preoccupation of most of the nobility. This was merely another symptom of the ills that beset our lovely land.

I was the eldest of this select company of slave boys. Unlike so many others over the years whom, once their physical beauty had begun to fade or pall, my lord had sent to the auction block in the slave-market, I had endured. He had come to value me for virtues other than my physical beauty alone. Not that this had faded – on the contrary, it had grown more striking as I had matured. You must not think me vain if I mention this, but I have determined to set down nothing but the truth in these accounts. They are remarkable enough without my having to resort to false modesty.

No, my lord seldom pleasured himself with me in those days, a neglect for which I was truly thankful. When he did so, it was usually only to punish me. He knew full well the physical pain and the humiliation his attentions always caused me. Although I had still been a child when I first learned to hide my revulsion, and to simulate pleasure in the perverse acts that he forced upon me, I never succeeded in deceiving him.

Strangely, my feelings of disgust and my loathing for this unnatural congress never detracted from his own enjoyment, rather they seemed to enhance it. He was neither a gentle nor a compassionate man, my Lord Intef. I have counted in the hundreds the slave boys who, over the years, were brought to me weeping and torn after their first night of love with my master. I doctored them and tried my best to comfort them. That is perhaps why they called me *Akh-Ker* in the slave boys' quarters, a name which means Elder Brother.

I might no longer be my master's favourite plaything, but he valued me much more highly than that. I was many other things to him –

physician and artist, musician and scribe, architect and bookkeeper, adviser and confidant, engineer and nursemaid to his daughter. I am not so naïve as to believe that he loved me or that he trusted me, but I think that at times he came as close to it as he was capable. That was why Lostris had prevailed upon me to plead on her behalf.

My Lord Intef had no concern for his only daughter, other than to maintain her marriage value at its optimum, and this was another duty that he delegated entirely to me. Sometimes he did not speak a single word to her from one flooding of the Nile to the next. He showed no discernible interest in the regular reports which I made to him of her training and schooling.

Of course, I was always at pains to conceal from him my true feelings for Lostris, knowing that he would certainly use them against me at the first opportunity. I always tried to give him the impression that I found her tuition and her care a tedious duty that I mildly resented having thrust upon me, and that I shared his own disdain and distaste for all of womankind. I don't think he ever realized that, despite my emasculation, I had the feelings and desires of a natural man towards the opposite sex.

My lord's disinterest in his daughter was the reason why I was occasionally tempted, on the urging of my mistress, to run such insane risks as this latest escapade of ours on board the *Breath of Horus*. There was usually at least a chance that we would get away with it.

That evening I retired early to my private quarters, where my first concern was to feed and pamper my darlings. I have a love for birds and animals, and a way with them that amazes even myself. I had an intimate friendship with a dozen cats, for no one can ever claim to own a cat. I owned, on the other hand, a pack of fine dogs. Tanus and I used them to hunt the oryx and the lion out in the desert.

The wild birds flocked to my terrace to enjoy the hospitality I provided for them. They competed raucously amongst themselves for a perch on my shoulder or on my hand. The boldest of them would take food from between my lips. My tame gazelle would brush against my legs like one of the cats, and my two falcons squawk at me from their perches on the terrace. They were the rare desert Sakers, beautiful and fierce. Whenever we were able, Tanus and I would take them out into the desert to fly them against the giant bustards. I took great pleasure from their speed and aerial grace as they stooped down on their prey. Anyone else who attempted to fondle them would feel the cutting edge of those hooked yellow bills, but with me they were as gentle as sparrows.

Only once I had taken care of my menagerie did I call one of the slave boys to bring my evening meal. On the terrace overlooking the wide green expanse of the Nile I savoured the exquisite little dish of wild quail cooked in honey and goat's milk that the head chef had prepared especially to welcome me home. From there I was able to watch for the return of my lord's barge from the far bank. It came with the sunset glowing on the single square sail, and I felt my spirits sink. He might send for me this evening, and I was not ready to face him.

Then with relief I heard Rasfer, the commander of the palace guard, shouting for my lord's favourite of the moment, a sloe-eyed Bedouin lad, barely ten years old. A short while later I heard the child protesting in a terrified treble as Rasfer dragged him past my door towards the curtained entrance of the grand vizier's chambers. Although I had heard it so many times before, I never could harden myself to the sounds of the children, and I felt the familiar pang of pity. Still, I was relieved that it was not I who would be called that evening. I would need a good night's sleep so as to look my best in the morning.

I woke before dawn with the feeling of dread still strong upon me. Even my ritual swim in the cool waters of the Nile did nothing to relieve it. I hurried back to my chamber where two of the slave boys were waiting to oil my body and comb out my hair. I detested the new fashion amongst the nobility of wearing make-up. My own skin and complexion were fine enough not to require it, but my lord liked his boys to use it, and I wanted to please him especially that day.

Even though my image in the bronze mirror reassured me, I could find no appetite for my breakfast. I was the first member of my lord's entourage awaiting his arrival in the water-garden where he held his assize every morning.

While I waited for the rest of the court to assemble I watched the kingfishers at work. I had designed and supervised the building of the water-garden. It was a marvellous complex of channels and ponds which overflowed from one into the other. The flowering plants had been collected from every part of the kingdom and beyond, and they were a dazzle of colour. The ponds were stocked with all the hundreds of varieties of fish that the Nile yields up to the nets of the fishermen, but they had to be replenished daily as a result of the depredations of the kingfishers.

My Lord Intef enjoyed watching the birds hovering in the air like jewels of lapis lazuli, then darting down to hit the water in a flash of spray, and rising again with a silver sliver quivering in their long bills. I think he saw himself as a fellow predator, a fisher of men, and that he looked upon the birds as his kin. He never allowed the gardeners to discourage the birds.

Gradually I was joined by the rest of the court. Many of them were dishevelled and yawning from sleep. My Lord Intef keeps early hours and likes to complete the bulk of the business of state before the main heat of the day. We waited respectfully in the first rays of the sun for my lord's arrival.

'He's in a good mood this morning,' the chamberlain whispered, as he took his place beside me, and I felt a tiny prickle of hope. I might yet be able to escape the serious consequences of my foolhardy promise to Lostris.

There was a stirring and a murmuring amongst us as when the river breeze moves through the papyrus beds, and my Lord Intef came out to us.

His walk was stately and his manner was sumptuous, for he was mighty with the weight of his honours and his power. Around his neck he wore the Gold of Praise, that necklace of red gold from the mines of Lot which Pharaoh had laid upon him with his own hands. His praise-singer preceded him, a stump-legged dwarf chosen for his misshapen body and stentorian tones. It amused my lord to surround himself with curiosities, either beautiful or grotesque. Cavorting and prancing on his bowed legs, the dwarf chanted the lists of my lord's titles and honours.

'Behold the Support of Egypt! Greet the Guardian of the Waters of the Nile! Bow down before Pharaoh's Companion!' These were all titles granted by the king, and many of them imposed specific duties and obligations on him. As Guardian of the Waters, for instance, he was responsible for monitoring the levels and flows of the seasonal floods of the Nile, a duty which was naturally delegated to that faithful, indefatigable slave, Taita.

I had spent half a year with a team of engineers and mathematicians working under me, measuring and carving the rock cliffs at Assoun so that the height of the waters rising up them could be accurately gauged and the volume of the flood calculated. From these figures I was able to estimate the size of the harvest months in advance. This enabled both famine and plenty to be anticipated and planned for by the administration. Pharaoh had been delighted with my work and bestowed further honours and reward upon my Lord Intef.

'Bend the knee for the Nomarch of Karnak and the Governor of all the twenty-two nomes of Upper Egypt! Greet the Lord of the Necropolis and the Keeper of the Royal Tombs!' My lord was by these titles responsible for designing, building and maintaining the monuments to pharaohs long dead and the one still living. Once again, these duties were unloaded upon a long-suffering slave's shoulders. My lord's visit to Pharaoh's tomb the day before had been the first that he had undertaken since the previous festival of Osiris. It was I who was sent out in the dust and the heat to cajole and curse the lying builders and the conniving masons. I often regretted having let my master realize the extent of my talents.

He singled me out now without seeming to have done so. The yellow eyes, as implacable as those of a wild leopard, touched mine, and he inclined his head slightly. I stepped in behind him as he passed, and I was struck as always by his height and the width of his shoulders. He was an outrageously handsome man with long, clean limbs and a flat, hard belly. His head was leonine and his hair dense and lustrous. At this time he was forty years of age, and I had been his slave for almost twenty of those.

My Lord Intef led us to the barrazza in the centre of the garden, a thatched building without enclosing walls, open to the cool breeze off the river. He seated himself cross-legged on the paved floor at the low table on which lay the state scrolls, and I took my usual place behind him. The day's business began.

Twice during the morning my lord leaned back slightly towards me. He did not turn his head nor did he say a word, but he was asking my advice. I barely moved my lips and I kept my voice pitched so low that no one else could hear me and very few were even aware of the exchanges between us.

Once I murmured, 'He is lying,' and a second time, 'Retik is a better man for the post, and he has offered a gift of five gold rings to my lord's private treasury.' And though I did not mention it then, another ring of gold to me if the post were secured.

At noon my lord dismissed the congregation of officials and petitioners and called for his midday meal. For the first time that day we were alone together, except for Rasfer, who was both the commander of the palace guard and the official state executioner. Now he took his post at the gate to the garden, within sight of the barrazza but out of earshot.

With a gesture my lord invited me to move up to his elbow, and to taste the delicious meats and fruits that had been laid out before him. While we waited for the effects of any possible poisoning to manifest themselves upon me, we discussed the morning's business in detail.

Then he questioned me about the expedition to the lagoon of Hapi and the great hippopotamus hunt. I described it all to him and gave him the figures of the profits that he might expect from the meat and hides and teeth of the river-cows. I inflated the estimate of profits a little, and he smiled. His smile is frank and charming. Once you have seen it, it is easier to understand my Lord Intef's ability to manipulate and control men. Even I, who should have known better, was once again lulled by it.

As he bit into a succulent cold cut of river-cow fillet, I drew a breath, screwed up my courage and began my plea. 'My lord should know that I allowed your daughter to accompany me on the expedition.' I could see by his eyes that he already knew this and that he had been waiting for me to attempt to conceal it from him.

'You did not think to obtain my permission beforehand?' he asked mildly, and I avoided his eyes and concentrated on peeling a grape for him as I answered, 'She only asked as we were on the point of departure. As you know, the goddess Hapi is her patron, and she wished to worship and make sacrifice at the lagoon temple.'

'Still you did not ask me?' he repeated, and I offered him the grape. He parted his lips and allowed me to slip it into his mouth. That could only mean that he was well disposed towards me, so obviously he had not yet found out the full truth about Tanus and Lostris.

'My lord was in council with the nomarch of Assoun at the time. I would not have dared disturb you. Besides, there was no harm in it that I could fathom. It was a simple domestic decision which I thought beneath your concern.'

'You are so glib, aren't you, my darling?' he chuckled. 'And so beautiful today. I like the way you have painted your eyelids, and what is that perfume you are wearing?'

'It is distilled from the petals of the wild violet,' I replied. 'I am happy that you like it, for I have a flask of it as a small gift for you, my lord.' I produced the flask from my purse and went on my knees to offer it to him. He placed his finger under my chin and lifted my face to kiss me on the lips. Dutifully I responded to the kiss until he drew back and patted my cheek.

'Whatever it is you are up to, you are still very attractive, Taita. Even after all these years you can still make me smile. But tell me, you took good care of the Lady Lostris, did you not? You never let her out of your sight or care for a moment, did you?'

'As always, my lord,' I agreed vehemently.

'So there is nothing unusual concerning her that you wish to report to me, is there?'

I was still on my knees in front of him, and my next attempt to speak failed. My voice dried up.

'Do not squeak at me, my old darling,' he laughed, 'Speak out like a man, even though you are not.' It was a cruel little jibe, but it steeled me.

'There is indeed something I wish humbly to bring to my lord's attention,' I said. 'And it does indeed concern the Lady Lostris. As I have already reported, your daughter's red moon rose for the first time at the flooding of the great river. Since then the courses of her moon have flowed strongly each month.'

My lord made a small grimace of distaste, the functions of the feminine body repelled him. I found this ironic, considering his own preoccupation with those far less savoury reaches of the masculine anatomy.

I hurried on, 'The Lady Lostris is now of marriageable age. She is a woman of an ardent and loving nature. I believe it would be wise to find a husband for her, as soon as we can.'

'No doubt you have one to suggest?' he asked drily, and I nodded. 'There is indeed a suitor, my lord.'

'Not one, Taita. You mean another one, don't you? I know of at least six, including the nomarch of Assoun and the governor of Lot, who have already made offers.'

'I did mean another one, but this time one that the Lady Lostris approves of. As you recall, she referred to the nomarch as that fat toad, and to the governor as a randy old goat.'

'The child's approval or disapproval is of no interest to me whatsoever.' He shook his head, and smiled and stroked my cheek to encourage me. 'But go on, Taita, tell me the name of this lovelorn swain who will do me the honour of becoming my son-in-law in return for the richest dowry in Egypt.' I steeled myself to reply, but he stopped me. 'No, wait! Let me guess.'

His smile turned into that sly and foxy grin that I knew so well, and I realized that he had been toying with me.

'For Lostris to welcome him, he must be young and handsome.' He pretended to muse on it. 'And for you to speak out for him, he must be a friend or a protégé of yours. There must have been an opportunity for this paragon to declare his suit and to solicit your support. What would be the time and the place for that to have happened, I wonder? Could it have been at midnight in the temple of Hapi, perhaps? Am I on the right trail, Taita?'

I felt myself pale. How did he know so much? He slid his hand around behind my head and caressed the nape of my neck. This was often his prelude to love-making, and he kissed me again.

'I can see by your face that my guesses are close to the target.' He took a handful of my hair and twisted it lightly. 'Now it remains only to divine the name of this bold lover. Could it be Dakka? No, no, Dakka is not so stupid as to incur my wrath.' He twisted my hair just hard enough to bring tears to my eyes. 'Kratas, then? He is handsome and foolhardy enough to take the risk.' He twisted harder and I felt a clump of my hair come away in his hand with a tearing sound. I choked back the whimper in my throat.

'Answer me, my darling, was it Kratas?' He forced my face down into his lap.

'No, my lord,' I whispered painfully. I was not surprised to find that he was fully aroused. He pushed my face down upon himself and held me there.

'Not Kratas, are you sure?' He pretended to be puzzled. 'If it was not Kratas, then I am at a loss to guess who else might be so insolent, so insulting and so mortally stupid as to approach the virgin daughter of the grand vizier of Upper Egypt.'

Abruptly, he raised his voice. 'Rasfer!' he cried. My head was twisted in his lap so that through streaming eyes I could watch Rasfer approach.

In Pharaoh's menagerie on Elephantine Island at Assoun there was a huge black bear brought in many years ago by one of the trade caravans from the East. That vicious, scarred brute always reminded me strongly of the commander of my lord's bodyguard. They both had the same vast, shapeless body and the raw, savage power to crush a man to death. However, in loveliness of face and sweetness of disposition, the bear had been favoured far beyond Rasfer.

I watched Rasfer approach now at a trot that was surprisingly swift and agile for those heavy, tree-like legs and the swell of his hairy gut, and I was transported back over the years to the day that my manhood had been plucked from me.

It all seemed so familiar, as though I was being forced to live once more through that terrible day. Every detail of it was still so clear in my mind that I wanted to shriek aloud. The actors in that long-ago tragedy were the same. My Lord Intef, Rasfer the brute, and me. Only the girl was missing.

Her name had been Alyda. She had been the same age as me, sixteen sweet innocent years. Like me, she had been a slave. I remember her now as having been beautiful, but it is likely that my memory cheats me, for had she been so she would have gone into a harem of one of the great houses and not been relegated to the kitchen. I do know for certain that she had skin the colour and lustre of polished amber that was warm and soft to the touch. I will never forget the feel of Alyda's body, for I will never experience anything like it again. In our misery we had found comfort and deep solace in each other. I never discovered who it was that betrayed us. I am not usually a vengeful man, but I still dream that one day I will find the person who delivered us up.

At that time I had been my Lord Intef's favourite, his special darling. When he discovered that I had been faithless to him, the affront to his self-esteem was such as to drive him to the very frontier of madness.

Rasfer had come to fetch us. He dragged us to my lord's chamber, one of us in each hand, as easily as if we had been a pair of kittens. There he had stripped us naked while my Lord Intef sat cross-legged on the floor, just as he was doing now. Rasfer bound Alyda's wrists and ankles with rawhide thongs. She was pale and shivering but she did not weep. My love for her and my admiration for her courage had never been stronger than at that moment.

My Lord Intef beckoned me to kneel in front of him and he took a lock of my hair and whispered endearments to me. 'Do you love me, Taita?' he asked, and because I was afraid, and because in some dim way I thought that it might spare Alyda's suffering, I answered, 'Yes, my lord, I love you.'

'Do you love anyone else, Taita?' he asked in a voice of silk and, coward and traitor that I was, I answered him, 'No, my lord, I love only you.' It was only then that I heard Alyda begin to weep. It was one of the most harrowing sounds of my life.

He called to Rasfer, 'Bring the slut here. Place her so that they can see each other clearly. Taita must be able to see everything that is done to her.'

As Rasfer pushed the girl into my line of vision I could see that he was grinning. Then my master raised his voice slightly: 'Very well, Rasfer, you may proceed.'

Rasfer slipped a loop of braided rawhide rope over Alyda's forehead. At close intervals the rope was knotted, so that it looked like a headband such as the Bedouin women wear. Standing behind the girl, Rasfer thrust a short, stout baton of olive wood through the rawhide loop and twisted it until it came up tight against her smooth, unblemished skin. The knots of harsh leather bit into her flesh and Alyda grimaced with the pain.

'Slowly, Rasfer,' my lord warned him. 'We still have a long way to go.'

The olive-wood baton seemed like a child's toy in Rasfer's huge, hairy paws. He twisted it with careful deliberation, a quarter of a turn at a time. The knots bit in deeper, and Alyda's mouth dropped open and her lungs emptied in a gasping rush of air. All the colour drained from her skin so that it turned to the colour of dead ashes. She struggled to fill her empty lungs with air and then released it in one long, penetrating scream.

Still grinning, Rasfer twisted the baton and the line of leather knots buried themselves in Alyda's forehead. Her skull changed shape. At first I thought it was a trick of my overwrought mind, then I realized that her head was, in truth, constricting and elongating as the loop tightened. Her scream was now a single unbroken peal that plunged into my heart like a sword-blade. It went on and on for what seemed like for ever.

Then her skull burst. I heard the bone collapse with a sound like a palm-nut crushed in the jaws of a feeding elephant. That terrible, piercing scream was cut off abruptly, as Alyda's corpse sagged in Rasfer's hands, and my soul was filled to overflowing with my sorrow and despair.

After what seemed like an eternity my lord lifted my head and looked into my eyes. His expression was sad and regretful as he told me, 'She has gone, Taita. She was evil and she led you astray. We must make certain that it never happens again. We must protect you from any further temptations.'

Once again he signalled to Rasfer and he took Alyda's naked body by the heels and dragged it out on to the terrace. The back of her crushed head bumped down the steps and her hair streamed out behind her. With a heave of his massive shoulders, Rasfer threw her far out into the river. Her slack limbs flashed and tumbled as she fell and struck the water. She sank swiftly with her hair spreading out around her like trailing fronds of the river-weed.

Rasfer turned away and went to the end of the terrace where two of his men were tending a brazier of burning charcoal. Beside the brazier a full set of surgeon's instruments were laid out on a wooden tray. He glanced over them and then nodded with satisfaction. He returned and bowed before my Lord Intef. 'All is in readiness.'

My master wiped my tear-streaked face with one finger, then lifted the finger to his lips as though he were tasting my sorrow. 'Come, my pretty darling,' he whispered, and lifting me to my feet he led me out on to the terrace. I was so distraught and blinded by my tears that I did not realize my own peril until the soldiers seized me. They threw me down and held me spread-eagled on the terracotta tiles, pinning me at wrists and ankles so that I could move only my head.

My master knelt at my head, while Rasfer knelt between my spread thighs.

'You will never do this evil thing again, Taita.' Only then did I become aware of the bronze scalpel that Rasfer had concealed in his right hand. My master nodded at him and he reached down with his free hand and seized me and stretched me out, until it felt as though he were plucking my entrails out through my groin.

'What a fine pair of eggs we have here!' Rasfer grinned and showed me the scalpel, holding it up before my eyes. 'But I am going to feed them to the crocodiles, just as I did with your little girl-friend.' He kissed the blade.

'Please, my lord,' I begged, 'have mercy—' but my entreaties ended in a shrill cry as Rasfer slashed down with the blade. It felt as though a red-hot skewer had been thrust up into my belly.

'Say goodbye to them, pretty boy.' Rasfer held up the sac of pale wrinkled skin and its pathetic contents. Then he began to rise, but my lord stopped him. 'You have not finished,' he told Rasfer quietly. 'I want all of it.'

Rasfer stared at him for a moment, not understanding the order. Then he began to chuckle until his belly bounced. 'By the blood of Horus,' he roared, 'from now on pretty boy will have to squat like a girl when he wants to piss!' He struck again, then bellowed with laughter as he held up the finger of flesh that had once been the most intimate part of my body.

'Never mind, boy. You'll walk a lot lighter without that weight to carry around with you.' Staggering with laughter, he started towards the edge of the terrace as if to hurl them into the river, but once again my lord called to him sharply.

'Give them to me!' he ordered, and obediently Rasfer placed the bloody fragments of my manhood in his hands. For a few seconds my lord examined them curiously, and then he spoke to me again. 'I am not so cruel as to deprive you for ever of such fine trophies, my darling. I will send these to the embalmers, and when they are ready I will have them placed on a necklace surrounded with pearls and lapis lazuli. They will be my present to you at the next festival of Osiris. Thus at the day of your burial they can be placed in your tomb with you, and if the gods are kind, you may have the use of them in the afterlife.'

Those terrible memories should have ended at the moment when Rasfer staunched the bleeding with a ladle of boiling embalming lacquer from the brazier, and I was plunged into blessed oblivion by the unbearable intensity of the pain, but now I was trapped in the nightmare. It was all happening again. Only this time little Alyda was missing, and instead of the gelding-knife Rasfer held the whip of hippo-hide in his great hairy fist.

The whip was as long as the full stretch of Rasfer's arms and it tapered to the thickness of his little finger at the point. I had watched him whittling it himself, shaving off the coarse outer layer from the long strip of cured hide until the inner skin was exposed, periodically pausing to test the balance and the heft of it, cutting it through the air until it keened and whined like the desert wind through the canyons of the hills of Lot. It was the colour of amber and Rasfer had polished it lovingly until it was smooth and translucent as glass, but so supple that he could bend it into a perfect arc between those bear-like paws. He had allowed the blood of a hundred victims to dry upon it and to dye the thin end of it to a lustrous patina that was aesthetically quite beautiful.

Rasfer was an artist with this awful tool. He could flick out and leave on the tender thigh of a young girl only a crimson weal that never broke the skin, but stung as viciously as a scorpion and left his victim writhing and weeping with the agony of it; or with a dozen hissing strokes he could strip the skin and flesh from a man's back and leave his ribs and the crest of his spine exposed.

He stood over me now and grinned as he flexed the long lash in his hands. Rasfer loved his work, and he hated me with all the force of his envy and the feelings of inferiority that my intelligence and looks and favour engendered in him.

My Lord Intef stroked my naked back and sighed. 'You are so wicked sometimes, my old darling. You try to deceive me to whom you owe the deepest loyalty. Nay, more than simple loyalty – to whom you owe your very existence.' He sighed again. 'Why do you force this unpleasantness upon me? You should know much better than to press the suit of that young jackanapes upon me. It was a ludicrous attempt, but I suppose that I understand why you made it. That childlike sense of compassion is one of your many weaknesses, and one day will probably be the cause of your complete downfall. However, at times I find it rather quaint and endearing and I might readily have forgiven you for it, but I cannot overlook the fact that you have endangered the market value of the goods that I placed in your care.' He twisted my head up so that my mouth was free to answer him. 'For that, you must be punished. Do you understand me?'

'Yes, my lord,' I whispered, but I rolled my eyes to watch the whip in Rasfer's hands. Once again my Lord Intef buried my face in his lap, and then he spoke to Rasfer above my head.

'With all your cunning, Rasfer. Do not break the skin, please. I do not want this delightfully smooth back marred permanently. Ten will do as a start. Count them aloud for us.'

I had watched a hundred or more unfortunates undergo this punishment, some of them warriors and vaunted heroes. Not one of them was able to remain silent under the lash of Rasfer. In any event it was best not to do so, for he took silence as a personal challenge to his skill. I knew this well, having travelled this bitter road before. I was quite prepared to swallow any stupid pride and pay tribute to Rasfer's art in a loud voice. I filled my lungs in readiness.

'One!' grunted Rasfer, and the lash fluted. The way a woman later forgets the full pain of childbirth, I had forgotten the exquisite sting of it, and I screamed even louder than I had intended.

'You are fortunate, my dear Taita,' my Lord Intef murmured in my ear. 'I had the priests of Osiris examine the goods last night. They are still intact.' I squirmed in his lap. Not only from the pain, but also at the thought of those lascivious old goats from the temple probing and prying into my little girl.

Rasfer had his own little ritual to draw out the punishment and to ensure that both he and his victim were able to savour the moment to the full. Between each stroke he jogged in a small circle around the barrazza, grunting exhortations and encouragement to himself, holding the whip at high port like a ceremonial sword. As he completed the circle he was in position for the next stroke, and he raised the lash high.

'Two!' he cried, and I shrieked again.

ONE OF Lostris' slave girls was waiting for me on the broad terrace of my quarters when I limped painfully up the steps from the garden.

'My mistress bids you attend her immediately,' she greeted me.

'Tell her that I am indisposed.' I tried to avoid the summons and, shouting for one of the slave boys to dress my injuries, I hurried through into my chamber in an attempt to rid myself of the girl. I could not face Lostris yet, for I dreaded having to report my failure, and having at last to make her face the reality and the impossibility of her love for Tanus. The black girl followed me, ogling the livid weals across my back with delicious horror.

'Go tell your mistress that I am injured, and that I cannot come to her,' I snapped over my shoulder.

'She told me that you would try to wriggle out of it, but she told me also that I was to stay with you and see to it that you did not.'

'You are insolent for a slave,' I reprimanded her sternly as the boy anointed my back with a healing salve of my own concoction.

'Yes,' agreed the imp with a grin. 'But then so are you.' And she dodged the half-hearted slap I aimed at her with ease. Lostris is much too soft with her handmaidens.

'Go tell your mistress that I will come to her,' I capitulated.

'She said I must wait and make sure you did.'

So I had an escort as I passed the guards at the gate of the harem. The guards were eunuchs like myself, but, unlike me, they were portly and androgynous. Despite their corpulence, or perhaps because of it, they were powerful men and fierce. However, I had used my influence to secure both of them this cosy sinecure, so they passed me through into the women's quarters with a respectful salute.

The harem was not nearly as grand nor as comfortable as the quarters of the slave boys, and it was clear where my Lord Intef's real interest lay. It was a compound of mud-brick hutments surrounded by a high mud wall. The only gardens or decorations were those that Lostris and her maids had undertaken, with my assistance. The vizier's wives were too fat and lazy and caught up in the scandals and intrigues of the harem to exert themselves.

Lostris' quarters were those closest to the main gate, surrounded by a pretty garden with a lily pond and song-birds twittering in cages woven of split bamboo. The mud walls were decorated with bright murals of Nile scenes, of fish and birds and goddesses, that I had helped her paint.

Her slave girls were huddled in a subdued group at the doorway, and more than one of them had been weeping. Their faces were streaked with tears. I pushed my way past them into the cool, dark interior, and at once heard my mistress's sobs from the inner chamber. I hurried to her, ashamed that I had been so craven as to try to avoid my duty to her.

She was lying face down on the low bed, her entire body shaking with the force of her grief, but she heard me enter and whirled off the bed and rushed to me.

'Oh, Taita! They are sending Tanus away. Pharaoh arrives in Karnak tomorrow, and my father will prevail upon him to order Tanus to take his squadron up-river to Elephantine and the cataracts. Oh, Taita! It is twenty days' travel to the first cataract. I shall never see him again. I wish I were dead. I shall throw myself into the Nile and let the crocodiles devour me. I don't want to live without Tanus—' All this in one rising wail of despair.

'Softly, my child.' I rocked her in my arms. 'How do you know all these terrible things? They may never happen.'

'Oh, they will. Tanus has sent me a message. Kratas has a brother in my father's personal bodyguard. He heard my father discussing it with Rasfer. Somehow my father has found out about Tanus and me. He knows that we were in the temple of Hapi alone. Oh, Taita, my father sent the priests to examine me. Those filthy old men did horrid things to me. It hurt so, Taita.'

I hugged her gently. It is not too often that I have the opportunity to do so, but now she hugged me back with all her strength. Her thoughts turned from her own injuries to her lover.

'I shall never see Tanus again,' she cried, and I was reminded of how young she truly was, not much more than a child, vulnerable and lost in her grief. 'My father will destroy him.'

'Even your father cannot touch Tanus,' I tried to reassure her. 'Tanus is a commander of a regiment of Pharaoh's own elite guard. He is the king's man. Tanus takes his orders only from Pharaoh, and he enjoys the full protection of the double crown of Egypt.' I did not add that this was probably the only reason that her father had not already destroyed him, but went on gently, 'While as for never seeing Tanus again, you will be playing opposite him in the pageant. I will make certain that there is a chance for the two of you to speak to each other between the acts.'

'My father will never let the pageant go on now.'

'He has no alternative, unless he is prepared to ruin my production and risk Pharaoh's displeasure, and you can be certain that he will never do that.'

'He will send Tanus away, and have another actor play Horus,' she sobbed.

'There is no time to rehearse another actor. Tanus will play the god Horus. I will make that clear to my Lord Intef. You and Tanus will have a chance to talk. We will find a way out for the two of you.'

She gulped back her tears and looked up at me with complete trust. 'Oh, Taita. I know that you will find a way. You always do—' She broke off suddenly and her expression changed. Her hands moved over my back, exploring the ridged welts that Rasfer's whip had raised across it.

'I am sorry, mistress. I tried to put forward Tanus' suit, as I promised you I would, and all this is the consequence of my stupidity.'

She stepped behind me and lifted the light linen tunic I had donned to hide my injuries, and she gasped. 'This is Rasfer's work. Oh, my poor dear Taita, why did you not warn me that this would happen, that my father was so violently opposed to Tanus and to me?'

I was hard put not to gasp at this artless piece of effrontery, I who had pleaded and warned them and in return been accused of disloyalty. I managed to hold my peace, however, although my back still throbbed abominably.

At least my mistress's own misery was forgotten for the moment in her concern for my superficial injuries. She ordered me to sit on her bed and remove my tunic while she ministered to me, her genuine love and compassion making up for the lack of her medicinal skills. This distraction lifted her from the utter depths of her despair. Soon she was chattering away in her usual ebullient fashion, making plans to thwart her father's wrath and to reunite herself with Tanus.

Some of these plans demonstrated her good common sense, while others, more far-fetched, merely pointed to her trusting youth and lack of knowledge and experience in the wicked ways of the world. 'I shall play such a fine role of Isis in the pageant,' she declared at one stage, 'and I shall make myself so agreeable to Pharaoh that he will grant me any boon that I ask of him. Then I shall beg him for Tanus as my husband, and he will say—' here she mimicked the king's pompous ceremonial tones so cleverly that I was forced to grin, 'and he will say, "I declare the betrothal of Tanus, Lord Harrab, son of Pianki, and of the Lady Lostris, daughter of Intef, and I raise my good servant Tanus to the rank of Great Lion of Egypt and commander of all my armies. I further order that all the former estates of his father, the noble Pianki, Lord Harrab be returned to him—"' Here she broke off in the middle of her ministrations to my wounds and flung her arms around my neck.

'It could happen like that, could it not, dear Taita? Please say that it could!'

'No natural man could resist you, mistress,' I smiled at her nonsense. 'Not even great Pharaoh himself.' If I had known then how close my words would turn out to being the truth, I think I should have placed a live coal on my tongue before I spoke them.

Her face was shining with hope once again. That was enough reward for me, and I donned my tunic again to bring to an end her too enthusiastic ministrations to my back.

'But now, mistress, if you are to make a beautiful and irresistible Isis, you must get some rest.' I had brought with me a potion of the powder of the sleeping-flower which is called the Red Shepenn. The seeds of this precious flower had first been brought into this very Egypt by the trade caravans from a mountainous land somewhere far to the east. I now cultivated the red blooms in my garden, and when the petals were fallen I scratched the seed carapace with a gold fork of three tines. Thick white milk flowed from these wounds, which I gathered and dried and treated in accordance with the formula I had evolved. The powder could induce sleep, conjure up strange dreams or smooth out pain.

'Stay with me awhile, Taita,' she murmured as she settled down on the bed, curled like a sleepy kitten. 'Cuddle me to sleep like you did when I was a baby.' She was a baby still, I thought, as I took her in my arms.

'It will all turn out all right, won't it?' she whispered. 'We will live happily ever after, just like they do in your stories, won't we, Taita?'

When she was asleep, I kissed her forehead softly and covered her with a fur rug before I stole from her chamber.

ON THE fifth day of the festival of Osiris, Pharaoh came down-river to Karnak from his palace on Elephantine Island which was ten days' travel away by swift river galley. He came in full state with all his retinue to officiate at the festival of the god.

Tanus' squadron had left Karnak three days previously, speeding away upstream to meet the great flotilla and escort it on the last stage of the voyage, so neither Lostris nor I had seen him since we had all three returned from the great river-cow hunt. It was a special joy for both of us then to see his galley come flying around the bend in the river, full on the current and with a strong desert wind abeam. The *Breath of Horus* was in the van of the fleet, leading it up from the south.

Lostris was in the grand vizier's train, standing behind her two brothers, Menset and Sobek. The two boys were comely and well-favoured, but there was too much of their father in them for my taste. Menset, the elder of the two, I particularly mistrusted, and the younger followed where his brother led.

I was standing further back in the ruck of courtiers and lesser functionaries from where I could keep an eye both on Lostris and on my Lord Intef. I saw the back of her neck flush with pleasure and excitement at the glimpse she had of Tanus' tall figure on the stern-tower of the *Breath of Horus*. The scales on his crocodile-skin breastplate gleamed in the sunlight, and the spray of ostrich feathers on his helmet floated in the draught of the galley's passage.

Lostris was hopping with excitement and waving both slim arms above her head, but her squeals and her antics were lost in the roar of the vast crowd that lined both banks of the Nile to welcome their pharaoh. Thebes is the most populous city in the world, and I guessed that almost a quarter of a million souls had turned out to welcome the king.

Meanwhile Tanus looked neither left nor right, but stared sternly ahead with his unsheathed sword held before his face in salute. The rest of his squadron followed the *Breath of Horus* in the wide vee of the egret formation, named for the pattern that those birds fly in as they return in the sunset to their roosts. All their standards and battle honours were streaming out in a fluttering blaze of rainbow colours, a noble show that set the crowds cheering and waving their palm-fronds wildly.

It was some time before the first vessel of the main convoy came wallowing round the bend behind them. It was laden with ladies and nobles of the king's entourage. It was followed by another, and then by a great untidy horde of vessels great and small. They came swarming downstream, transports filled with palace servants and slaves and all their accoutrements and paraphernalia, barges laden with oxen and goats and chickens for the kitchens, gilded and gaily painted vessels bearing cargoes of palace furniture and treasure, of nobles and lesser creatures, all uncomfortably jumbled together in a most unseamanlike fashion. In what contrast was the display put up by Tanus' squadron as it rounded-to downstream and held its geometrically spaced formation against the swift Nile current!

At last Pharaoh's state barge lumbered around the bend, and the cheering of the crowd rose to a crescendo. This huge vessel, the largest ever built by man, made its ponderous way towards where we were waiting to welcome it at the stone wharf below the grand vizier's palace.

I had plenty of time in which to study it and to muse how aptly its size and design, and the handling of it, reflected the present state and government of this very Egypt of ours – Egypt as she stood in the twelfth year of the rule of Pharaoh Mamose, the eighth of that name and line, and the weakest yet of a weak and vacillating dynasty. The state barge was as long as five of the fighting galleys laid end to end, but its height and breadth were so ill-proportioned that they gravely offended my artistic instincts. Its massive hull was painted in the riotous colours that were the fashion of the age, and the figurehead of Osiris on the bows was gilded with real gold leaf. However, as she drew closer to the landing where we waited, I could see that the brilliant colours were faded in patches and her sides were zebra-striped in dun where her crew had defecated over the rail.

Amidships stood a tall deck-house, Pharaoh's private quarters, that was so solidly constructed of thick planks of precious cedar, and so stuffed with heavy furniture that the sailing characteristics of the barge were sadly affected. Atop this grotesque edifice, behind an ornate railing that was woven of fresh lilies, beneath a canopy of finely tanned gazelle skins skilfully sewn together and painted with images of all the major gods and goddesses, sat Pharaoh in majestic isolation. On his feet were sandals of gold filigree and his robe was of linen so pure that it shone like the high cumulus clouds of full summer. On his head he wore the tall double crown; the white crown of Upper Egypt with the head of the vulture goddess Nekhbet, combined with the red crown and the cobra head of Buto, the goddess of the Delta.

Despite the crown, the ironic truth was that this beloved sovereign of ours had lost the Delta almost ten years previously. In our turbulent days another pharaoh ruled in Lower Egypt, one who also wore the double crown, or at least his own version of it, a pretender who was our sovereign's deadly adversary, and whose constant wars against us drained both kingdoms of gold and the blood of the young men. Egypt was divided and torn by internal strife. Over the thousand or so years of our history, it had always been thus when weak men took on the mantle of pharaoh. It needed a strong, bold and clever man to hold the two kingdoms in his fists.

In order to turn the unwieldy vessel into the current and bring her to her moorings at the palace wharf, the captain should have steered close in to the far bank. If he had done so, he would have had the full breadth of the Nile in which to complete his turn. However, he had obviously misjudged the strength of wind and current and he began his turn from midstream. At first the barge swung ponderously across the current, listing heavily as the height of the deck-house caught the hot desert wind like a sail. Half a dozen boatswains raged about the lower deck with their whips rising and falling, the snapping of the lash on bare shoulders carrying clearly across the water.

Under the goading of the lash the rowers plied their paddles in a frenzy that churned the waters alongside the hull to foam, one hundred paddles a side pulling against each other and none of them making any effort to synchronize the stroke. Their curses and cries blended with the shouted orders of the four helmsmen who were struggling with the long steering-oar in the stern. Meanwhile, on the poop-deck, Nembet, the geriatric admiral and captain of the barge, alternately combed his fingers through his long scraggy grey beard and flapped his hands in impotent agitation.

High above this pandemonium sat Pharaoh, motionless as a statue and aloof from it all. Oh, verily this was our Egypt.

Then the rate of the barge's turn bled away until she was no longer swinging but heading straight for where we stood on the bank, locked in chains by the pull of the current and the contrary push of the wind. Captain and crew, despite all their wild and erratic exertions, seemed powerless either to complete the manoeuvre and head her into the current, or to heave-to and prevent her from ploughing headlong into the granite blocks of the wharf and staving in her great gilded bows.

As everyone realized what was about to happen, the cheers of the crowd watching from the shore slowly died away and an awful hush fell upon both banks of the Nile into which the shouting and the turmoil on the decks of the huge vessel carried all the more clearly.

Then suddenly all the eyes of the crowd were drawn downstream, as the *Breath of Horus* broke from her station at the head of the squadron and came tearing up-river, driven by the flying paddles. In perfect unison those paddles dipped and pulled and swung and dipped again. She cut in so sharply under the bows of the barge that the crowd gasped with a sound higher than the wind in the papyrus beds. Collision seemed inevitable, but at the last possible moment Tanus signalled with a clenched fist lifted above his head. Simultaneously both banks of rowers backed water and the helmsman put the steering-oar hard over.

The *Breath of Horus* checked and paid away before the ponderous advance of the great barge. The two vessels touched as lightly as a virgin's kiss, and for an instant the stern-tower of the *Breath of Horus* was almost level with the barge's main deck.

In that instant Tanus poised himself on the bulwark of the tower. He had kicked off his sandals, divested himself of his armour, and thrown aside his weapons. Around his waist he had tied the end of a light flax line. With the line trailing behind him he leaped out across the gap between the two vessels.

As though awakening from a stupor, the crowd stirred and shook itself. If there was still one amongst them who did not know who Tanus was, he would know before this day was out. Of course, Tanus' fame had already been won in the river wars against the legions of the usurper in the Lower Kingdom. However, only his own troops had ever seen him in action. The reported deed never carries the same weight as the one that the eye sees for itself.

Now, before the gaze of Pharaoh, the royal flotilla and the entire populace of Karnak, Tanus leaped from one deck to the other and landed as lightly as a leopard.

'Tanus!' I am sure that it was my mistress, Lostris, who first called out his name, but I was next.

'Tanus!' I yelled, and then all those around me took up the cry. 'Tanus! Tanus! Tanus!' They chanted it like an ode to some newly discovered god.

The moment he landed on the deck of the barge, Tanus whirled and raced into the bows, hauling in the thin line hand over hand as he ran. The crew of his galley had spliced a heavy hawser, as thick as a man's arm, to the end of the carrying-line. Now they sent it across as Tanus lay back against the weight of it. With the muscles of his arms and back shining with sweat, he dragged it in.

By this time a handful of the barge's crew had realized what he was about, and rushed forward to help him. Under Tanus' direction they took three turns with the end of the hawser about the barge's bowsprit, and the instant it was secured Tanus signalled his galley away.

The *Breath of Horus* leaped into the current, gathering speed swiftly. Then abruptly she came up short against the hawser, and the weight of the heavy vessel on the other end threw her back on her haunches. For a dreadful moment I thought she might capsize and be dragged under, but Tanus had anticipated the shock and signalled his crew to cushion it by skilfully backing the long paddles.

Although she was dragged down so low that she took in green water over her stern, the galley weathered it, bobbed up and came back taut on the hawser. For a long moment nothing happened. The galley's puny weight made no impression on the great ship's ponderous way. The two vessels were locked together as though a crocodile had an old bull buffalo by the snout but could not drag him from the bank. Then Tanus in the bows of the barge turned to face the disorganized crew. He made one authoritative gesture that caught all their attention, and a remarkable change came over them. They were waiting for his command.

Nembet was the commander of all Pharaoh's fleet with the rank of Great Lion of Egypt. Years ago he had been one of the mighty men, but now he was old and feeble. Tanus took over from him effortlessly, as though it were as natural as the force of the current and the wind, and the crew of the barge responded immediately.

'Pull!' He gestured to the port bank of oarsmen and they bent their backs and pulled with a will.

'Back-water!' He stabbed his clenched fist at the starboard side and they dug in hard with the pointed blades of their paddles. Tanus stepped to the rail and signalled to the helmsman of the *Breath of Horus*, masterfully coordinating the efforts of both crews. Still the barge was bearing down upon the wharf and now only a narrow strip of open water separated the vessel from the granite blocks.

Then at last, slowly, too slowly, she began to respond. The gaudily painted bows began to swing up into the current as the galley dragged them round. Once again the cheering died away and that fateful hush fell upon us all as we waited for the enormous ship to crash into the wharf and tear out her own guts on the rock. When that happened there was no doubt what the consequences must be for Tanus. He had snatched command from the senile admiral and so must bear the full responsibility for all the old man's mistakes. When Pharaoh was dashed from his throne by the collision, when the double crown and all his dignity were sent rolling across the deck, and when the state barge sank beneath him and he was dragged from the river like a drowning puppy before the gaze of all his subjects, then there would be both the insulted Admiral Nembet and my Lord Intef to encourage Pharaoh to bring the full weight of his displeasure to bear upon the presumptuous young upstart.

I stood helplessly and trembled for my dear friend, and then a miracle occurred. The barge was already so close to running aground and Tanus so near to where I stood that his voice carried clearly to me. 'Great Horus, help me now!' he cried.

There is no doubt at all in my mind that the gods often take a hand in the affairs of men. Tanus is a Horus man, and Horus is the god of the wind.

The desert wind had blown for three days and nights out of the western desolation of the Sahara. It had blown at the strength of half a gale without a check for all that time, but now it dropped. It did not taper off, it simply ceased to blow at all. The wavelets that had flecked the surface of the river flattened out, and the palms along the waterfront that had been vigorously shaking their fronds fell still, as though frozen by a sudden frost.

Released from the claws of the wind, the barge rolled back on to an even keel and yielded to the pull of the *Breath of Horus*. Her elephantine bows turned up into the current, and she came parallel with the wharf at the exact moment that her side touched the dressed stone and the rush of the Nile killed her forward-way and stalled her motionless in the water.

One last command from Tanus and, before the ship could gather stern-way, the mooring ropes were cast on to the wharf and swiftly gathered up by eager hands and made fast to the stone bollards. Lightly as a goose-down feather floating on the water, the great barge of state lay safe and serene at her berth, and neither the throne upon which Pharaoh sat, nor the high crown upon his head, had been disturbed by her moorage.

We, the onlookers, burst out in a roar of praise for the feat, and the name of Tanus rather than that of Pharaoh was on all our tongues. Modestly, and very prudently, Tanus made no attempt to acknowledge our applause. To draw any further attention to himself that might detract from the welcome that awaited the king would have been folly indeed, and would certainly have negated any royal favour that his exploit had earned him. Pharaoh was always jealous of his royal dignity. Instead, Tanus surreptitiously signalled the *Breath of Horus* alongside. When she was hidden from our view by the bulk of the barge, he dropped overside on to the galley's deck, quitting the stage on which he had just earned such distinction, and leaving it now to his king.

However, I saw the expression of fury and chagrin on the face of Nembet, the ancient admiral, the Great Lion of Egypt, as he came ashore behind Pharaoh, and I knew that Tanus had made himself another powerful enemy.

I WAS able to make good my promise to Lostris that very evening when I put the cast of the pageant through their dress rehearsal. Before the performance began I was able to give the two lovers almost an hour alone together.

In the precincts of the temple of Osiris, which was to be our theatre for the pageant, I had set up tents to act as dressing-rooms for each of the principal players. I had purposely placed Lostris' tent a little apart from the others, screened from them by one of the huge stone columns that support the roof of the temple. While I stood on sentry duty at the entrance to the tent, Tanus lifted the opposite panel and slipped in under it.

I tried not to eavesdrop on their cries of delight as they first embraced, nor to the whispering and cooing, to the muffled laughter and to the small moans and gasps of their decorous love-making which followed. Although at this stage I would not have made any attempt to prevent it, I was convinced that they would not carry this love-making to its ultimate conclusion. Long afterwards both Lostris and Tanus separately confirmed this for me. My mistress had been a virgin on her wedding day. If only any of us had known how close upon us that wedding day was, I wonder how differently we might have acted then.

Although I was acutely aware that every minute that they were alone together in the tent increased the danger for all of us, still I could not bring myself to call enough and separate them. Although the welts on my back that Rasfer's whip had raised still burned, and although deep in that morass of my soul where I attempt to hide all my unworthy thoughts and instincts my envy for the lovers burned as painfully, still I let them stay together much longer than I should have done.

I did not hear my Lord Intef coming. He used to have his sandals shod in the softest kid-skin to muffle his footfalls. He moved silently as a ghost, and many a courtier and slave felt either Rasfer's whip or his noose on account of a careless word that my lord overheard on his noiseless peregrinations through the halls and corridors of the palace. However, over the years I developed an instinct that enabled me most times to sense his presence before he materialized out of the shadows. This instinct was not infallible, but that evening it stood me in good stead. When I looked round suddenly he was almost upon me, gliding between the pillars of the hypostyle hall towards me, slim and tall and deadly as an erect cobra.

'My Lord Intef!' I cried loudly enough to startle myself, 'I am honoured that you have come to witness our rehearsals. I would be deeply grateful for any advice or suggestions—' I was gabbling wildly in an attempt to cover my confusion and to alert the lovers in the tent behind me.

In both objects I succeeded better than I had any right to expect. I heard the sudden scuffle of consternation within the dressing-tent behind me as the lovers broke apart, and then the flutter of the rear panel of the tent as Tanus ducked out the way he had entered.

At any other time I would never have succeeded so easily in deceiving my Lord Intef. He would have read the guilt upon my face as clearly as I read the hieroglyphics on the temple walls or my own characters on this scroll; but that evening he was blinded by his own wrath, and intent only on taking me to task for my latest misdemeanour. He did not rage or roar with anger. My Lord is at his most dangerous when his tone is mild and his smile silky.

'Dear Taita.' It was almost a whisper. 'I hear that you have altered some of the arrangements for the opening act of the pageant, despite the fact that I personally ordered them. I could not believe that you have been so presumptuous. I had to come all this way in the heat to find out for myself.'

I knew it was of no avail to feign innocence or ignorance, so I bowed my head and tried to look aggrieved. 'My lord. It was not I who ordered the changes. It was His Holiness, the abbot of the temple of Osiris—'

But my lord broke in impatiently, 'Yes, of course he did, but only after you put him up to it. Do you think I do not know both you and that mumbling old priest? He never had an original thought in his head, while you have nothing but.'

'My lord!' I protested.

'What devious little trick was it this time? Was it one of those convenient dreams sent to you by the gods?' my lord asked, his voice as soft as the rustle of one of the sacred cobras that infested the temple, sliding across the stone flags of the floor.

'My lord!' I did my best to look shocked by the accusation, although I had indeed given the good abbot a rather fanciful account of how Osiris in the guise of a black crow had visited me in my sleep to complain of the spilling of blood in his temple.

Up until that time the priest had voiced no objection to the realistic piece of theatre that my Lord Intef had planned for the amusement of Pharaoh. I had only resorted to dreams when all my efforts to dissuade my lord had failed. It was deeply abhorrent to me to be party to such an abomination as my lord had ordered to be performed in the first act of the pageant. Of course I am aware that certain savage peoples in the eastern lands make human sacrifice to their gods. I have heard that the Kassites, who live beyond the twin rivers Tigris and Euphrates, cast newborn babes into a fiery furnace. The caravan masters who have travelled in those distant lands speak of other atrocities performed in the name of religion, of young virgins slaughtered to promote the harvest or captives of war beheaded before the statues of a triple-headed god.

However, we Egyptians are a civilized people and we worship wise and just gods, not blood-crazed monsters. I had tried to convince my master of this. I had pointed out to him that only once before had a pharaoh made human sacrifice; when Menotep had slit the throats of the seven rebel princes in the temple of Seth and quartered their corpses and sent the embalmed fragments to the governors of each of the nomes as a warning. History still remembered the deed with distaste. Menotep is known to this day as the Bloody King.

'It is not human sacrifice,' my master had contradicted me. 'Merely a well-merited execution, to be carried out in a rather novel fashion. You will not deny, dear Taita, that the death penalty has always been an important part of our system of justice, will you? Tod is a thief. He has stolen from the royal coffers and he must die, if only as an example to others.'

It sounded reasonable, except that I knew he was not at all interested in justice, but rather in protecting his own treasure and in impressing Pharaoh, who so loved pageant and theatre. This had left me with no alternative but to dream for the benefit of the good abbot. Now my Lord Intef's lip lifted in a smile which exposed his perfect teeth but which chilled my blood and raised the hairs on the nape of my neck.

'Here is a little piece of advice,' he whispered close to my face. 'I suggest that you have another dream tonight, so that whichever god it was that visited you last time has an opportunity to countermand his previous instructions to the abbot and to endorse my arrangements. If this does not happen, I will find some more work for Rasfer – that is my solemn promise to you.' He turned and strode away, leaving me both relieved that he had not discovered the lovers and miserable that I was forced to go ahead with the vile display which he had ordered.

Nevertheless, after my master had left, the rehearsal was a heartening success that revived my spirits. Lostris was in such a glow of happiness after her tryst with Tanus that her beauty was indeed divine, and Tanus in his youth and power was the young Horus incarnate.

Naturally I was perturbed by the entrance of my Osiris to the stage, aware as I now was of the fate that my Lord Intef had ordered for him. My Osiris was played by a handsome, middle-aged man named Tod who had been one of the bailiffs until he had been caught dipping into my Lord Intef's coffers to support a young and expensive courtesan of whom he was enamoured. I was not proud that it was my examination of the accounts that had brought to light the discrepancies.

My lord had released him from custody, where he was awaiting formal trial and sentencing, to play the part of the god of the underworld in the pageant. My lord had promised not to take the matter further if he fulfilled the role of Osiris satisfactorily. The unfortunate Tod was unaware of the hidden menace in this offer and threw himself into the act with pathetic enthusiasm, believing that he was about to earn his pardon. He could not know that, in the meantime, my lord had secretly signed his death warrant and handed the scroll to Rasfer, who was not only the state executioner but my choice to play Seth in our little production. It was my lord's intention that he should combine both roles on the following evening when the pageant was performed before Pharaoh. Although Rasfer was a natural choice for the role of Seth, I regretted having cast him in it as I watched him rehearse the opening scene with Tod, and I shuddered as I imagined how the main performance would differ from the rehearsal.

After the rehearsal it was my most pleasant duty to escort my mistress back to the harem compound. She would not let me leave but kept me late listening to her excited résumé of the day's extraordinary events and the role that Tanus had played in them.

'Did you see how he called upon the great god Horus and how the god came at once to his aid? Surely he has the full favour and protection of Horus, don't you agree? Horus will not let any evil befall us, of that I am now certain.'

There was much more of this happy fantasy, and no more talk of parting and suicide. How swiftly the winds of young love shift!

'After what Tanus did today, the way he saved the state barge from wrecking, surely he must also have earned Pharaoh's high favour, don't you think so, Taita? With favour of both the god and Pharaoh, my father can never succeed in having Tanus sent away now, can he, Taita?'

I was called upon to endorse every happy thought that occurred to her, and I was not allowed to leave the harem until I had memorized at least a dozen messages of undying love which I was sworn to carry to Tanus personally.

When, exhausted, I finally reached my own quarters, there was still no rest for me. Nearly all the slave boys were waiting for me, as excited and as garrulous as my mistress had been. They also wanted to have my opinion of the day's events, and particularly of Tanus' rescue of Pharaoh's ship and the significance of that deed. They crowded around me on the terrace above the river as I fed my pets, and vied with each other for my attention.

'Elder brother, is it true that Tanus called upon the god for his help, and Horus intervened immediately? Did you see it happen? Some even say that the god appeared in his falcon shape and hovered over Tanus' head, spreading protective wings over him. Is it true?'

'Is it true, *Akh*, that Pharaoh has promoted Tanus to Companion of Pharaoh, and given him an estate of five hundred feddan of fertile land on the riverside as reward?'

'Elder brother, they say that the oracle at the desert shrine of Thoth, the god of wisdom, has cast a horoscope for Tanus. The oracle divines that he will be the greatest warrior in the history of our Egypt and that, one day, Pharaoh will favour him above all others.' It is amusing now to look back on these childish prattles, and to realize the strange truths that were adumbrated in them, but at the time I dismissed them as I did the children, with mock severity.

As I composed myself to sleep, my last thought was that the populace of the twin towns of Luxor and Karnak had taken Tanus to their hearts completely, but that this was an onerous and dubious distinction. Fame and popularity breed envy in high places, and the adulation of the mob is fickle. They often take as much pleasure in tearing down the idols that they have grown tired of, as they did in elevating them in the first place.

It is safer by far to live unseen and unremarked, as I always attempt to do.

ON THE afternoon of the sixth day of the festival, Pharaoh moved in solemn procession from his villa in the midst of the royal estates in the open country between Karnak and Luxor, down the ceremonial avenue lined with statues of granite lions, to the temple of Osiris on the bank of the Nile.

The great sledge on which he rode was so tall that the dense crowds lining the avenue were forced to strain their necks backwards to look up at him on his great gilded throne as he trundled by, drawn by twenty pure white bullocks with massive humped shoulders and wreaths of flowers on their horned heads. The skids of the sledge ground harshly over the paving and scarred the stone slabs.

One hundred musicians led the procession, strumming the lyre and the harp, beating the cymbal and the drum, shaking the rattle and the sistrum, and blowing on the long straight horn of the oryx and on the curling horn of the wild ram. A choir of a hundred of the finest voices in Egypt followed them, singing hymns of praise to Pharaoh and that other god Osiris. Naturally I led the choir. Behind us followed an honour guard from the Blue Crocodile regiment led by Tanus himself. The crowds raised a special cheer for him as, all plumed and armoured, he strode past. The unmarried maidens shrieked and more than one of them sank swooning in the dust, overcome by the hysteria that his new-won fame engendered.

Behind the guard of honour came the vizier and his high-office bearers, then the nobles and their wives and children, then a detachment of the Falcon regiment, and finally Pharaoh's great sledge. In all, this was an assembly of several thousand of the most wealthy and influential persons in the Upper Kingdom.

As we approached the temple of Osiris, the abbot and all his priests were drawn up on the staircase between the tall entrance pylons to welcome Pharaoh Mamose. The temple had been freshly painted and the bas-relief on the outer walls was dazzling with colour in the warm yellow glow of the sunset. A gay cloud of banners and flags fluttered from their poles set in the recesses of the outer wall.

At the base of the staircase Pharaoh descended from his carriage and in solemn majesty began the climb up the one hundred steps. The choir lined both sides of the staircase. I was on the fiftieth step and so I was able to study the king minutely during the few seconds that it took for him to pass close to me.

I already knew him well, for he had been a patient of mine, but I had forgotten how small he was – that is, small for a god. He stood not as tall as my shoulder, although the high double crown made him seem much more impressive. His arms were folded across his chest in the ritual posture and he carried the crook and the flail of his royal office and his godhead. I remarked as I had before that his hands were hairless, smooth and almost feminine, and that his feet also were small and neat. He wore rings on all his fingers and on his toes, amulets on his upper arms and bracelets on his wrists. The massive pectoral plate of red gold on his chest was inlaid with many colours of faience depicting the god Thoth bearing the feather of truth. That piece of jewellery was a splendid treasure almost five hundred years old and had been worn by seventy kings before him.

Under the double crown, his face was powdered dead white like that of a corpse. His eyes were dramatically outlined with startling jet black and his lips were rouged crimson. Under the heavy make-up his expression was petulant, and his lips were thin and straight and humourless. His eyes were shifty and nervous, as well they might be, I reflected.

The foundations of this great House of Egypt were cracked, and the kingdom riven and shaken. Even a god has his worries. Once his domain had stretched from the sea, across the seven mouths of the Delta, southwards to Assoun and the first cataract – the greatest empire on earth. He and his ancestors had let it all slip away, and now his enemies swarmed at his shrunken borders, clamouring like hyena and jackal and vulture to feast on the carcass of our Egypt.

In the south were the black hordes of Africa, in the north along the coast of the great sea were the piratical sea-people, and along the lower reaches of the Nile the legions of the false Pharaoh. In the west were the treacherous Bedouin and the sly Libyan, while in the east new hordes seemed to rise up daily, their names striking terror into a nation grown timid and hesitant with defeat. Assyrians and Medes, Kassites and Hurrians and Hittites – there seemed no end to their multitudes.

What advantage remained in our ancient civilization if it were grown feeble and effete with its great age? How were we to resist the barbarian in his savage vigour, his cruel arrogance and his lust for rapine and plunder? I was certain that this pharaoh, like those who had immediately preceded him, was not capable of leading the nation back to its former glories. He was incapable even of breeding a male heir.

This lack of an heir to the empire of Egypt seemed to obsess him even more than the loss of the empire itself. He had taken twenty wives so far. They had given him daughters, a virtual tribe of daughters, but no son. He would not accept that the fault lay with him as sire. He had consulted every doctor of renown in the Upper Kingdom and visited every oracle and every important shrine.

I knew all this because I was one of the learned doctors he had sent for. I admit that at the time I had felt some trepidation in prescribing to a god, and that I had wondered why he should need to consult a mere mortal on such a delicate subject. Nevertheless, I had recommended a diet of bull's testicles fried in honey and counselled him to find the most beautiful virgin in Egypt and take her to his marriage-bed within a year of the first flowering of her woman's moon.

I had no great faith in my own remedy, but bull's testicles, when cooked to my recipe, are a tasty dish, while I reckoned that the search for the most beautiful virgin in the land might distract Pharaoh and prove not only amusing but pleasurable as well. From a practical point of view, if the king bedded a sufficient number of young ladies, then surely one of them must eventually drop a male pup into his harem.

Anyhow, I consoled myself that my treatment was not as drastic as some of the others proposed by my peers, particularly those disgusting remedies dreamed up by the quacks in the temple of Osiris who call themselves doctors. If not actually efficacious, my recommendations would at least do no harm. That was what I believed. How wrong the fates would prove me, and if only I had known the consequences of my folly, I would have taken Tod's place in the pageant rather than have given Pharaoh such frivolous counsel.

I was amused and flattered when I heard that Pharaoh must have taken my advice seriously, and that he had ordered his nomarchs and his governors to scour the length of the land from El Amarna to the cataracts to find bulls with succulent balls and any virgin who might fit my specifications for the mother of his first son. My sources at the king's court informed me that he had already rejected hundreds of aspiring applicants for the title of the most beautiful virgin in the land.

Then the king was swiftly past me and gone into the temple to the keening of the priests and the obsequious bobbing of the abbot. The grand vizier and all his train followed closely, and then there was an undignified rush of lesser citizens to find places from which to watch the passion play. Space in the temple was limited. Only the mighty and the noble and those rich enough to bribe the thieving priests were allowed into the inner courtyard. The others were forced to watch through the gates from the outer court. Many thousands of the citizenry would be disappointed and would have to be content with a secondhand account of the pageant. Even I, the impresario, had great difficulty in fighting my way through the press of humanity, and I only succeeded when Tanus saw my predicament and sent two of his men to rescue me and force a path for me into the precincts reserved for the actors.

Before the pageant could begin, we were obliged to endure a succession of flowery speeches, firstly from the local functionaries and government ministers, and then from the grand vizier in person. This interlude of speechifying gave me the opportunity to make certain that all the arrangements for the pageant were perfect. I went from tent to tent, checking the costumes and the make-up of each of my actors, and soothing last-minute attacks of temperament and stage-fright.

The unfortunate Tod was nervously dreading the possibility that his performance might not please my Lord Intef. I was able to assure him that it most certainly would, and then I administered to him a draught of the Red Shepenn, which would deaden the pain that he was about to have inflicted upon him.

When I came to Rasfer's tent he was drinking wine with two of his cronies from the palace guard and, with a whetstone, laying an edge on his short bronze sword. I had created his make-up to render him even more repulsive, which was not an easy feat given the high plateau of ugliness from which we started. I realized how well I had succeeded as he leered at me with blackened teeth and offered me a cup of the wine.

'How does your back feel now, pretty boy? Have a taste of a man's drink! Perhaps it will give you balls again.' I am accustomed to his taunts and I kept my dignity as I told him that my Lord Intef had countermanded the abbot's orders and that the first act was to be played out in the original form.

'I have spoken to Lord Intef already.' He held up the sword. 'Feel the edge, eunuch. I want to make certain that it meets with your approval.' I left him feeling a little queasy.

Although Tanus would not be on stage until the second act, he was already in costume. Relaxed and smiling, he clasped my shoulder. 'Well, old friend, this is your opportunity. After this evening your fame as a playwright will spread throughout Egypt.'

'As yours has already. Your name is on every lip,' I told him, but he laughed it away with careless modesty as I went on, 'Do you have your closing declamation prepared, Tanus? Would you like to recite it to me now?'

Traditionally, the actor who played Horus would close the pageant with a message to Pharaoh, ostensibly from the gods but in reality from his own subjects. In olden times this had been the one occasion during the year when the populace, through the agency of the actor, could bring to the king's notice matters of concern which they were not able to address to him at any other time. However, during the rule of this last dynasty of kings the tradition had fallen away, and the closing speech had become merely another eulogy to the divine pharaoh.

For days past I had been asking Tanus to rehearse his speech for me, but every time he had put me off with excuses so lame that I was by now thoroughly suspicious of his intentions. 'This is the last opportunity,' I insisted, but he laughed at me.

'I have decided to let my speech be as much a surprise to you as I hope it will be to Pharaoh. That way you should both enjoy it more.' And there was nothing I could do to persuade him. At times he can be far and away the most headstrong and obstinate young ruffian I have ever encountered. I left him in not a little dudgeon, and went to find more convivial company.

As I stooped in through the entrance of Lostris' dressing-tent, I froze with shock. Even though I had designed her costume myself and instructed her handmaidens as to exactly how I wanted her powder and rouge and eye-paint applied, still I was not prepared for the ethereal vision that stood before me now. For a moment I was convinced that another miracle had taken place and that the goddess had indeed risen up from the underworld to take my mistress's place. I gasped aloud and had actually begun to sink to my knees in superstitious awe when my mistress giggled and roused me from my delusion.

'Isn't this fun? I cannot wait to see Tanus in full costume. I am sure he must look like the god himself.' She turned slowly to allow me to appraise her own costume, smiling at me over her shoulder.

'No more godlike than you, my lady,' I whispered.

'When will the play begin?' she demanded impatiently. 'I am so excited that I can wait no longer.'

I cocked my ear to the panel of the tent and listened for a moment to the drone of the speeches in the great hall. I realized that this was the final oration and that at any moment my Lord Intef would call upon my players to perform.

I took Lostris' hand and squeezed it. 'Remember the long pause and the haughty look before you begin your opening speech,' I cautioned her, and she slapped my shoulder playfully.

'Away with you, you old fuss-pot, it will all go perfectly, you'll see.' And at that moment I heard my Lord Intef's voice raised.

'The divine god Pharaoh Mamose, the Great House of Egypt, the Support of the Realm, the Just, the Great, the All-Seeing, the All-Merciful—' The titles and honorifics continued while I hurried out of Lostris' tent and made my way to my opening position behind the central pillar. I peered around the column and saw that the inner courtyard of the temple was packed and that Pharaoh and his senior wives sat in the front rank on low benches of cedar wood, sipping cool sherbet or nibbling dates and sweetmeats.

My Lord Intef was addressing them from the front of the raised platform below the altar that was our stage. The main body of the stage was still hidden from the audience by the linen curtains. I surveyed it for one last time, although it was too late to do anything further about it now.

Behind the curtains the set was decorated with palms and acacia trees that the palace gardeners had transplanted under my instruction. My masons had been taken from the work on the king's tomb to build a stone cistern at the back of the temple from which a stream could be diverted across the stage to represent the river Nile.

At the rear of the stage, hanging from floor to ceiling, were tightly stretched sheets of linen on which the artists from the necropolis had painted marvellous landscapes. In the half-light of the dusk and the flicker of the torches in their brackets the effect was so realistic as to transport the beholder into a different world in a distant time.

There were other delights that I had prepared for Pharaoh's amusement, from cages of animals, birds and butterflies that would be released to simulate the creation of the world by the great god Ammon-Ra, to flares and torches that I had doctored with chemicals to burn with brilliant flames of crimson and green, and flood the stage with eerie light and smoke-clouds, like those of the underworld where the gods live.

'Mamose, son of Ra, may you be granted eternal life! We your loyal subjects, the citizens of Thebes, beg you to draw nigh and give your divine attention to this poor play that we dedicate to Your Majesty.'

My Lord Intef concluded his address of welcome and resumed his seat. To a fanfare of hidden rams' horns, I stepped out from behind the pillar and faced the audience. They had endured discomfort and boredom on the hard flagstones, and by now were ripe for the entertainment to begin. A raucous cheer greeted my entrance and even Pharaoh smiled in anticipation.

I held up both hands for silence, and only when it was total did I begin to speak my overture.

'While I walked in the sunlight, young and filled with the vigour of youth, I heard the fatal music in the reeds by the bank of the Nile. I did not recognize the sound of this harp, and I had no fear, for I was in the full bloom of my manhood and secure in the affection of my beloved.

'The music was of surpassing beauty. Joyously I went to find the musician, and could not know that he was Death and that he played his harp to summon me alone.' We Egyptians are fascinated by death, and I had at once touched a deep chord within my audience. They sighed and shuddered.

'Death seized me and bore me up in his skeletal arms towards Ammon-Ra, the sun god, and I was become one with the white light of his being. At a great distance I heard my beloved weep, but I could not see her and all the days of my life were as though they had never been.' This was the first public recitation of my prose, and I knew almost at once that I had them, their faces were fascinated and intent. There was not a sound in the temple.

'Then Death set me down in a high place from which I could see the world like a shining round shield in the blue sea of the heavens. I saw all men and all creatures who have ever lived. Like a mighty river, time ran backwards before mine eyes. For a hundred thousand years I watched their strivings and their deaths. I watched all men go from death and old age to infancy and birth. Time became more and more remote, going back until the birth of the first man and the first woman. I watched them at the moment of their birth and then before. At last there were no men upon the earth and only the gods existed.

'Yet still the river of time flowed back beyond the time of the gods into Nun, into the time of darkness and primordial chaos. The river of time could flow no further back and so reversed itself. Time began to run forward in the manner that was familiar to me from my days of life upon the earth, and I watched the passion of the gods played out before me.' My audience were all of them well versed in the theology of our pantheon, but none of them had ever heard the mysteries presented in such a novel fashion. They sat silent and enthralled as I went on.

'Out of the chaos and darkness of Nun rose Ammon-Ra, He-Who-Creates-Himself. I watched Ammon-Ra stroke his generative member, masturbating and spurting out his seminal seed in mighty waves that left the silver smear that we know as the Milky Way across the dark void. From this seed were generated Geb and Nut, the earth and the heaven.'

'*Bak-her!*' a single voice broke the tremulous silence of the temple. '*Bak-her!* Amen!' The old abbot had not been able to contain himself, and now he endorsed my vision of the creation. I was so astonished by his change of heart that I almost forgot my next line. After all, he had been my sternest critic up to that time. I had won him over completely, and my voice soared in triumph.

'Geb and Nut coupled and copulated, as man and women do, and from their dreadful union were born the gods Osiris and Seth, and the goddesses Isis and Nephthys.'

I made a wide gesture and the linen curtains were drawn slowly aside to reveal the fantasy world that I had created. Nothing like this had ever been seen in Egypt before and the audience gasped with amazement. With measured tread I withdrew, and my place upon the stage was taken by the god Osiris. The audience recognized him instantly by the tall, bottle-shaped head-dress, by his arms crossed over his chest and by the crook and the flail he held before him. Every household kept his statuette in the family shrine.

A droning cry of reverence went up from every throat, and indeed the sedative that I had administered to Tod glittered weirdly in his eyes and gave him a strange, unearthly presence that was convincingly godlike. With the crook and the flail Osiris made mystical gestures and declaimed in sonorous tones, 'Behold Atur, the river!'

Once more the audience rustled and murmured as they recognized the Nile. The Nile was Egypt and the centre of the world.

'*Bak-her!*' another voice called out, and, watching from my hidden place amongst the pillars, I was astonished and delighted as I realized who had spoken. It was Pharaoh. My play had both secular and divine endorsement. I was certain that from now on mine would become the authorized version, replacing the thousand-year-old original. I had found my place in immortality. My name would live on down the millennium.

Joyfully I signalled for the cistern to be opened and the waters began to flow across our stage. At first the audience did not comprehend, and then they realized that they were actually witnessing the revelation of the great river, and a shout went up from a thousand throats, '*Bak-her! Bak-her!*'

'Behold the waters rise!' cried Osiris, and obediently the Nile was swollen by the inundation.

'Behold the waters fall!' cried the god, and they shrank at his command. 'Now they will rise again!'

I had arranged for buckets of dye to be added to the water as it poured out of the cistern at the rear of the temple. First a green dye to simulate the low-water period, and then, as it rose again, a darker dye that faithfully emulated the colour of the silt-laden waters of the high inundation.

'Now behold the insects and birds upon the earth!' ordered Osiris, and the cages at the rear of the stage were opened and a shrieking, chattering, swirling cloud of wild birds and gorgeously coloured butterflies filled the temple.

The watchers were like children, enchanted and enthralled, reaching up to snatch the butterflies from the air and then release them again to fly out between the high pillars of the temple. One of the wild birds, a long-billed hoopoe marvellously patterned in colours of white and cinnamon and black, flew down unafraid and settled on Pharaoh's crown.

The crowd was delighted. 'An omen!' they cried. 'A blessing on the king. May he live for ever!' and Pharaoh smiled.

It was naughty of me, but afterwards I hinted to my Lord Intef that I had trained the bird to single out Pharaoh, and although it was of course quite impossible, he believed me. Such is my reputation with animals and birds.

On the stage Osiris wandered through the paradise that he had created, and the mood was set for the dramatic moment when, with a blood-chilling shriek, Seth bounded on to the stage. Although they had been expecting it, still the powerful and hideous presence shocked the audience, and the women screamed and covered their faces, only to peer out again from between trembling fingers.

'What is this you have done, brother?' Seth bellowed in jealous rage. 'Do you set yourself above me? Am I not also a god? Do you hold all creation to yourself alone, that I, your brother, may not share it with you?'

Osiris answered him calmly, his dignity remote and cool as the drug held him in its thrall. 'Our father, Ammon-Ra, has given it to us both. However, he has also given us the right to choose how we dispose of it, for good or for evil—' The words that I had put into the mouth of the god reverberated through the temple. They were the finest that I had written, and the audience hung upon them. However, I alone of all of them knew what was coming, and the beauty and the power of my own composition were soured as I steeled myself for it.

Osiris drew to the close of his speech. 'This is the world as I have revealed it. If you wish to share it in peace and brotherly love, then you are welcome. However, if you come in warlike rage, if evil and hatred fill your heart, then I order you gone.' He lifted his right arm all draped in the gleaming diaphanous linen of his robe and pointed the way for Seth to leave the paradise of Earth.

Seth hunched those huge, hairy shoulders like a buffalo bull, and he bellowed so that the spittle flew from his lips in a cloud that was flavoured by the rotting teeth in his jaws. I could smell it from where I stood. He lifted high the bronze broad-sword and rushed at his brother. This had never been rehearsed, and it took Osiris completely by surprise. He stood with his right arm still outstretched, and the blade hissed with the power of the stroke as it swung down. The hand was lopped off at the wrist as cleanly as I would prune a shoot from the vine that grows over my terrace. It fell at Osiris' feet and lay there with the fingers fluttering feebly.

The surprise was so complete and the sword so sharp that for a long moment Osiris did not move, except to sway slightly on his feet. The audience must have believed that this was another theatrical trick, and that the fallen hand was a dummy. The blood did not come at once, which lulled them further. They were intensely interested but not alarmed, until suddenly Osiris reeled back and with a dreadful cry clutched at the stump of his lower arm. Only then did the blood burst out between his fingers and sprayed down his white robe, staining it like spilt wine. Still clutching his stump, Osiris staggered across the stage and began to scream. That scream, high and clear with mortal agony, broke the mood of the spectators' complacency. They knew then for the first time that what they were witnessing was not make-believe, but they were trapped in horrified silence.

Before Osiris could reach the edge of the stage, Seth came bounding after him on those thick bow-legs. He seized the stump of Osiris' arm and used it as a handle to drag him back into the centre of the stage, where he threw him sprawling full-length on the stone flags. The tinsel crown tumbled from Osiris' head and the plaits of dark hair fell to his shoulders as he lay in a spreading puddle of his own blood.

'Please spare me,' Osiris shrieked, as Seth stood over him, and Seth laughed. It was a full-throated roar of genuine amusement. Rasfer had become Seth, and Seth was hugely enjoying himself.

That savage laughter woke the audience from its trance. However, the illusion was complete. They no longer believed that they were watching a play, and for all of them this terrible spectacle had become reality. Women screamed and men roared with fury as they witnessed the murder of their god.

'Spare him! Spare the great god Osiris!' they howled, but not one of them rose from his seat or rushed on to the stage to attempt to prevent the tragedy from being played out. They knew that the struggles and passions of the gods were beyond the influence of mortal men.

Osiris reached up and pawed at Seth's legs with his one remaining hand. Still laughing, Seth grabbed his wrist and pulled his arm out to its full length, inspecting it as a butcher might inspect the shoulder of a goat before he sections it.

'Cut it off!' screamed a voice in the crowd, thick with the lust for blood. The mood had swung again.

'Kill him!' screamed another. It has always troubled me how the sight of blood and violent death affects even the mildest of men. Even I was stirred by this terrible scene, sickened and horrified, it is true, but beneath it stirred by a revolting excitement.

With a casual sweep of the blade, Seth struck off the arm, and Osiris fell back, leaving the twitching limb in Seth's red fist. He was trying to rise to his feet, but he had no hands to support himself. His legs kicked spasmodically, and his head whipped from side to side, and still he screamed. I tried to force myself to turn away, but though my gorge rose and scalded the back of my throat, still I had to watch.

Seth hacked the arm into three pieces through the joint of the wrist and the elbow. One at a time he hurled the fragments into the packed ranks of the audience. As they spun through the air they sprinkled those below with drops of ruby. They roared like the lions in Pharaoh's zoo at feeding-time, and held up their hands to catch these holy relics of their god.

Seth worked on with dedicated gusto. Osiris' feet he chopped off at the ankles. Then the calves at the knees, and the thighs at the hip joints. As he threw each of these to them, the mob clamoured for more.

'The talisman of Seth!' howled a voice amongst them. 'Give us the talisman of Seth!' and the cry was taken up. According to the myth, the talisman is the most powerful of all the magical charms. The person who has it in his possession controls all the dark forces of the underworld. It is the only one of the fourteen segments of Osiris' body that was never recovered by Isis and her sister Nephthys from the far corners of the earth to which Seth scattered them. The talisman of Seth is that same part of the body that Rasfer deprived me of, and which forms the centrepiece of that beautiful necklace that was the cynical gift of my Lord Intef.

'Give us the talisman of Seth!' the mob howled, and Seth reached down and lifted the red sodden tunic of the limbless trunk at his feet. He was still laughing. I shuddered as I recognized that merciless sound that I had heard so often at my own punishment sessions. In sympathy I experienced once again the sudden fire in my groin as the short sword flashed in Seth's hairy paw, already wet and running with his victim's blood, and he lifted on high the piteous relic.

The crowd pleaded for it. 'Give it to us,' they begged him. 'Give us the power of the talisman.' The spectacle had transformed them into ravening beasts.

Seth ignored their pleas. 'A gift,' he cried. 'A gift from one god to another. I Seth, god of darkness, dedicate this talisman to the god-Pharaoh, Mamose the divine.' And he hopped down the stone stairs on those powerful bow-legs and placed the relic at Pharaoh's feet.

To my amazement the king leaned forward and gathered it up to himself. His expression beneath the powder and paint was spellbound, as though this was the true relic of the god. I am sure that at that moment he truly believed it was. He held it in his right hand through all that ensued.

His gift accepted, Seth rushed back on to the stage to complete his butchery. The thing that haunts me still is that the poor dismembered creature was alive and sensate to the very end. I realized that the drug I had given Tod had done little to dull his senses. I saw the terrible agony in his eyes as he lay in the lake of his own blood and rolled his head from side to side, the only part that remained to him to move.

For me, then, it came as an intense relief when at last Seth struck off the head and held it up by its thick plaited locks for the crowd to admire. Even then, the poor creature's eyes swivelled wildly in their sockets as he looked for the very last time on this world. At last they dulled and glazed over, and Seth tossed the head to them.

Thus the first act of our pageant ended in swelling and rapturous applause that threatened to shake the granite pillars of the temple from their bases.

DURING THE intermission my slave helpers cleaned away the gruesome evidence of the slaughter from the set. I was particularly concerned that my Lady Lostris should not realize what had truly taken place in the first act. I wished her to believe that all had gone as we had rehearsed it. So I had arranged that she stay in her tent, and that one of Tanus' men remain at the entrance to keep her there, and also to ensure that none of her Cushite maidens were allowed to peep out at the first act and rush back to Lostris with a report. I knew that if she realized the truth, she would be too distraught to play her part. While my helpers used buckets of water from our stage Nile to wash away the ghastly evidence, I hurried to my mistress's tent to reassure her and to satisfy myself that my precautions to shield her had been effective.

'Oh, Taita, I heard the applause,' she greeted me happily. 'They love your play. I am so happy for you. You so richly deserve this success.' She chuckled in a conspiratorial fashion. 'It sounded as though they believed the murder of Osiris was real, and the buckets of ox-blood with which you drenched Tod were truly the blood of the god.'

'Indeed, my lady, they seemed totally deceived by our little tricks,' I agreed, although I still felt faint and ill from what I had just lived through.

My Lady Lostris suspected nothing, and when I led her out on to the stage, she barely glanced at the grisly stains that remained upon the stones. I posed her in her opening position, and adjusted the torchlight to flatter her. Even though I was accustomed to it, still her beauty choked my throat and made my eyes sting with tears.

I left her concealed by the linen curtains, and stepped out to face my audience. There was no sarcastic applause to greet me this time. Every one of them, from Pharaoh to the meanest vassal, was captive to my voice, as in my lambent prose I described the mourning of Isis and her sister Nephthys at the death of their brother.

When I stepped down and the curtain was drawn aside to reveal the grieving figure of Isis, the audience gasped aloud at her loveliness. After the horror and blood of the first act, her presence was all the more moving.

Isis began to sing the lament for the dead, and her voice thrilled through the gloomy halls of the temple. As her head moved to the cadence of her voice, the torchlight was reflected in a darting and flickering shaft from the bronze moon that surmounted her horned head-dress.

I watched Pharaoh attentively as she sang. His eyes never left her face, and his lips moved silently in sympathy with the words that swelled from her throat.

> My heart is a wounded gazelle,
> torn by the lion claws of my grief—

She lamented and the king and all his train grieved with her.

> There is no sweetness in the honeycomb,
> no perfume remains in the desert blossom.
> My soul is an empty temple,
> deserted by the god of love.

In the front rank one or two of the king's wives were snuffling and blubbering, but nobody even glanced at them.

> I look on death's grim face with a smile.
> Gladly would I follow him,
> if he could lead me to the arms of my dear lord.

By now not only the royal wives but every one of the women were weeping, and most of the men also. Her words and her beauty were too much for them to resist. It seemed impossible that a god should show the same emotions as mortal men, but the slow tears were cutting runnels through the white powder on Pharaoh's cheeks, and he blinked his heavy, kohl-darkened eyelids like an owl as he stared at my Lady Lostris.

Nephthys entered and sang a duet with her sister, then hand-in-hand the two women went in search of the scattered fragments of Osiris' corpse.

Of course I had not placed the actual dismembered portions of Tod's corpse for them to find. During the intermission my helpers had retrieved these and carried them away to the embalmers on my instructions. I would pay for Tod's funeral out of my own purse. It seemed the very least that I could do to compensate the unfortunate creature for my own part in his murder. Despite the missing portion of his anatomy that Pharaoh still held in his hand, I hoped the gods might make an exception in his case and allow Tod's shade to pass into the underworld, and that there he might not think too badly of me. It is wise to have friends wherever you can, in this world and the next.

To represent the body of the god I had the funeral artists from the necropolis build for me a magnificent mummy cartonnage, depicting Osiris in his full regalia and in the death pose with his arms folded across his chest. This container I had cut into thirteen sections that fitted together like a child's building-blocks.

As the sisters retrieved each of these sections they sang a hymn of praise to the god's parts, to his hands and feet, to his limbs and trunk, and finally to his divine head.

> Such eyes, like stars set in the heavens,
> must shine for ever.
> Death should never dim such beauty,
> nor the funeral wrappings contain such majesty.

When at last the two sisters had reassembled the complete body of Osiris, except for the missing talisman, they pondered aloud how they could return it to life once more.

This was my opportunity to add to the pageant that essential element that makes any theatrical production appeal to the popular taste. There is a broad lascivious streak in most of us, and the playwright and the poet does well to bear this in mind if he hopes to have his work appreciated by the main body of his audience.

'There is but one certain way to bring our dear lord and brother back to life.' I placed the words in the mouth of the goddess Nephthys. 'One of us must perform the act of generation with his shattered body to make it whole again and to fan the spark of life within it.'

The audience stirred and leaned forward with anticipation at this suggestion. It had elements to appeal to even the most prurient of those present, including incest and necrophilia.

I had agonized over how I would represent upon the stage this episode in the myth of the resurrection of Osiris. My mistress had shocked me when she had declared herself willing to carry her role through to the end. She had even had the effrontery to point out, with that impudent grin of hers, that she might gain some valuable knowledge and experience from doing so. I was not certain if she was jesting or if she would really have gone through with it; however, I would not give her the opportunity to demonstrate her good faith or lack of it. Her reputation and the honour of her family were too valuable to trifle with.

So it was that at my signal, the linen curtains were drawn once more and my Lady Lostris quickly left the stage. Her place was taken by one of the upper-class courtesans who usually plied her trade in a palace of love near the port. I had hired this wench, from amongst several that I had interviewed, because of her fine young body that so much resembled that of my mistress. Of course, in facial beauty she could not come close to my Lady Lostris, but then I know of none who could.

As soon as the substitute goddess was in position, the torches at the rear of the stage were lit so as to cast her shadow upon the curtain. She began to disrobe in the most provocative manner. The males in the audience cheered on her shadowy gyrations, convinced that they were watching my Lady Lostris. The harlot responded to this encouragement with an increasingly lewd display that was almost as well received as the slaughter of Osiris in the first act.

Now came that action of the play that had given me, the author, considerable pause, for how could I contrive fecundity without a stout peg to hang it on? We had just seen Osiris forcefully deprived of his. In the end I was forced to stoop to that tired old theatrical device that I so scorned in the work of other playwrights, namely the intervention of the gods and their supernatural powers.

While my Lady Lostris spoke from the wings, her shadowy alter ego on stage stood over the mummiform figure of Osiris and made a series of mystical gestures. 'My dear brother, by the rare and marvellous powers granted to me by our forefather, Ammon-Ra, I restore to you those manly parts that cruel Seth so brutally tore from you,' intoned my mistress.

I had equipped the mummy case with a device that I could raise by hauling on a length of fine linen twine that ran over a pulley in the temple roof directly above where Osiris lay. At Isis' words the wooden phallus, hinged to the god's pudenda, rose in majestic splendour, as long as my arm, into full erection. The audience gasped with admiration.

When Isis caressed it, I jerked the string to make it leap and twitch. The audience loved it, but loved it even better when the goddess mounted the supine mummy of the god. Judging by the convincing acrobatics of her simulated ecstasy, the harlot I had chosen to play the part must have been one of the truly great exponents of her art. The audience gave full recognition to her superior performance, egging her on with whistling and hooting and shouting ribald advice.

At the climax of this exhibition the torches were extinguished and the temple plunged into darkness. In the darkness the substitution was made once more and when the torches were re-lit my Lady Lostris stood in mid-stage with a new-born infant in her arms. One of the kitchen slaves had been considerate enough to give birth a few days previously, and I had borrowed her whelp for the occasion.

'I give you the new-born son of Osiris, god of the underworld, and of Isis, goddess of the moon and of the stars.' My Lady Lostris lifted the infant high and he, astonished by the sea of strangers before him, screwed up his tiny face and turned bright red as he howled.

Isis raised her voice above his and cried, 'Greet the young Lord Horus, god of the wind and the sky, falcon of the heavens!' Half the audience were Horus men and their enthusiasm for their patron was unbounded. They came to their feet in a roaring tumult, and the second act ended in another triumph for me and in mortification for the infant god, who on later examination was found to have prodigiously soiled his swaddling-cloth.

I OPENED the final act with another of my recitations describing the childhood and the coming to manhood of Horus. I spoke of the sacred charge laid upon him by Isis, and as I did so, the curtains were drawn aside to reveal the goddess in the centre of the stage.

Isis was bathing in the Nile, attended by her handmaidens. Her wet robe clung to her body so that the pale glory of her skin shone through. The indistinct outlines of her breasts were tipped with tiny rose-buds of virgin pink.

Tanus as Horus entered from the wings, and immediately dominated the stage. In his polished armour and his warrior's pride he was a perfect counterpoint for the beauty of the goddess. The long list of his battle honours in the river wars, together with his most recent exploit in saving the royal barge, had focused the attention of the populace full upon him. For this moment Tanus was the darling of the crowd. Before he could speak, they began to cheer him, and the applause continued so long that the actors were forced to freeze in their opening positions.

While the cheering swirled around Tanus, I picked out certain faces in the audience and watched their reactions. Nembet, the Great Lion of Egypt, scowled and muttered fiercely into his beard, making no attempt to hide his animosity. Pharaoh smiled graciously and nodded slightly, so that those seated behind him were made aware of his approbation, and their own enthusiasm was encouraged. My Lord Intef, never one to fly against the prevailing winds, smiled his most silky smile and nodded his head in concert with his king. His eyes, however, when seen from my vantage-point, were deadly.

At last the applause abated and Tanus could speak his lines, not without difficulty, however, for every time he paused to draw breath another outburst of cheering broke out. It was only when Isis began to sing that complete silence fell upon them once more.

> The suffering of your father,
> the terrible fate that hangs over our house,
> all these must be expunged.

In verse Isis warned her noble son, and held out her arms to him in supplication and in command.

> The curse of Seth is upon us all,
> and only you can break it.
> Seek out your monstrous uncle.
> By his arrogance and his ferocity,
> you will know him.
> When you find him,
> strike him down.
> Chain him,
> bind him to your will,
> that the gods and all men
> will be freed for ever from his ghastly sway.

Still singing, the goddess withdrew and left her son to his quest. Like children following a well-loved nursery rhyme, the audience knew full well what to expect and leaned forward eagerly and hummed with anticipation.

When at last Seth came leaping back on stage for the cataclysmic battle, the age-old struggle between good and evil, beauty and ugliness, duty and dishonour, the audience was ready for him. They greeted Seth with a chorus of hatred that was spontaneous and unfeigned. In defiance Rasfer leered and gibbered at them, strutting about the stage, cupping his genitalia in his hands and thrusting his hips out at them in a mocking and obscene gesture that drove them wild with fury.

'Kill him, Horus!' they howled. 'Smash in his ugly face!' And Seth pranced before them, stoking their fury.

'Kill the murderer of the great god Osiris!' they roared in a paroxysm of loathing.

'Smash in his face!'

'Rip out his guts!'

The congregation's reaction to him was in no way moderated by the fact that it knew, deep down, that this was Rasfer and not Seth.

'Hack off his head!' they screamed.

'Kill him! Kill him!'

At last Seth pretended to see his nephew for the first time, and swaggered up to him, lolling his tongue out between his blackened teeth, drooling like an idiot so that silver strands of saliva slimed down on to his chest. I would never have believed that Rasfer could make himself more repulsive than nature had already accomplished, but now he proved me wrong.

'Who is this child?' he demanded, and belched full in the face of Horus. Tanus was unprepared for this and stepped back involuntarily, his expression of disgust unfeigned as he smelled Rasfer's breath and the contents of his stomach, the sour wine still fermenting in it.

Tanus recovered swiftly and spoke his next line. 'I am Horus, son of Osiris.'

Seth let out a mocking peal of laughter. 'And what is it you seek, boy child of a dead god?'

'I seek vengeance for the murder of my noble father. I seek the assassin of Osiris.'

'Then search no further,' Seth shouted, 'for I am Seth the vanquisher of lesser gods. I am Seth the eater of stars, and the destroyer of worlds.'

The two gods drew their swords and rushed at each other, to meet in mid-stage with a ringing clash of bronze as blade struck blade. In an attempt to reduce the chances of accidental injury, I had attempted to substitute wooden swords for bronze, but neither of my actors would have any of it. My Lord Intef had intervened when Rasfer had appealed to him. He had ordered that they be allowed to wield their real battle weapons, and I had been forced to yield to this higher authority. At least it added to the realism of the scene as they stood now chest to chest, with blades locked, and glared into each other's face.

They made an extraordinary pair, so totally dissimilar, pointing up the moral of the play, the eternal conflict of good against evil. Tanus was tall and fair and comely. Seth was swarthy and thick-set, bow-legged and hideous. The contrast was direct and visceral. The mood of the audience was as fiery and as fiercely partisan as that of the two protagonists.

Simultaneously they pushed each other backwards and then rushed in again, thrusting and cutting, feinting and parrying. They were both highly trained and skilled swordsmen, amongst the finest in all Pharaoh's armies. Their blades whirled and glinted in the torchlight so that they seemed as insubstantial as the sunlight reflected from the wind-ruffled surface of the great river. The sound of their flight was that of the wings of the birds startled from their roosts in the gloomy heights of the temple, but when they clashed together it was with the heavy ring of hammers at the coppersmith's forge.

What seemed to the observer to be the chaos of real battle was in fact a meticulously choreographed ballet which had been carefully rehearsed. Each man knew exactly how each blow must be launched and each parry timed. These were two superb athletes engaged in the activity for which they had trained their entire warrior's lifetime, and they made it seem effortless.

When Seth thrust, Horus left his parry so late that the point actually touched his breastplate and left a tiny bright scratch on the metal. Then when Horus launched himself forward in riposte, his edge flew so close to Seth's head that a coil of his coarse matted hair was shorn from his skull, as if by a barber's razor. Their footwork was as graceful and intricate as that of the temple dancers, and they were swift as falcons and lithe as hunting cheetahs.

The crowd was mesmerized and so was I. Therefore it must have been some deep instinct that warned me, perhaps even a nudge from the gods, who knows? At any rate, something outside myself made me tear my eyes away from the spectacle and glance at my Lord Intef where he sat in the front row.

Again, was it instinct or my own deep knowledge of him, or the intervention of the god who protects Tanus that placed the thought in my mind? A little of all three of these, perhaps, but I knew with instant and utter certainty the reason for that wolfish smile on my Lord Intef's handsome features.

I knew why he had chosen Rasfer to play Seth. I knew why he had made no effort to exclude Tanus from the role of Horus, even after he had found out about the relationship between him and my Lady Lostris. I knew why he had ordered the use of real swords, and I knew why he was smiling now. The massacre was not over for the evening. He was looking forward to more. Before this act was played out, Rasfer would ply his special talents once again.

'Tanus!' I screamed, as I started forward. 'Beware! It's a trap. He intends—' My cries were drowned out by the thunder of the crowd, and I had not taken a second step when I was seized by each arm from behind. I tried to struggle free, but two of Rasfer's ruffians held me fast and started to drag me away. They had been placed there for just such a moment as this, to prevent me from warning my friend.

'Horus, give me strength!' I rendered up a swift and silent entreaty, and instead of resisting them I hurled myself back in the same direction as they were pulling me. For an instant they were thrown off-balance, and I broke half-free of their grasp. I managed to reach the edge of the stage before they could control me again.

'Horus, give me voice!' I prayed, and then screamed with all my breath, 'Tanus, beware! He means to kill you.'

This time my voice carried above that of the mob, and Tanus heard me. I saw his head flick and his eyes narrow slightly. However, Rasfer heard me as well. He responded instantly, breaking the rehearsed routine. Instead of dropping back before the whirlwind of cuts and thrusts that Tanus was aiming close to his brutish head, he stepped in and, with an upward sweep of his own blade, he forced Tanus' sword-arm high.

Without the benefit of surprise he would never have made the opening into which he now launched a thrust behind which was the full weight of those massive shoulders and mighty trunk. The point of his blade was aimed an inch below the rim of Tanus' helmet and directly at his right eye. It should have skewered his eye and cleaved his skull through and through.

However, my shouted warning had given Tanus that fleeting moment of grace in which to react. He recovered his guard just in time. With the pommel of his sword he managed to touch a glancing blow to Rasfer's wrist. It had just sufficient force to deflect the sword-point a finger's-width, and at the same moment Tanus tucked in his chin and rolled his head. It was too late to avoid the blow entirely. However, the stroke that might have skewered his eye and split his skull like a rotten melon, merely laid open his eyebrow to the bone, and then flew on over his shoulder.

Instantly a sheet of blood gushed from the shallow wound and flowed over Tanus' face, blinding his right eye. He was forced to fall back before the savage onslaught that Rasfer now launched at him. Desperately he gave ground, blinking at the blood and trying to wipe it away with his free hand. It seemed impossible that he would be able to defend himself, and if only I had not been held so securely by the palace guards, I would have drawn the little jewelled dagger at my belt and rushed to his aid.

Even without my assistance Tanus was able to survive that first murderous attack. Though he was wounded twice more, a gouge across the left thigh and a nick on the biceps of his sword-arm, he kept weaving and parrying and ducking. Rasfer kept coming at him, never letting him recover his balance or his full vision. Within minutes Rasfer was blowing and grunting like a giant forest hog, and running with sweat, his misshapen torso gleaming in the torchlight, but the speed and fury of his assault never faltered.

Though no great swordsman myself, I am a student of the art. So often had I watched Rasfer at practice in the weapons-yard that I knew his style intimately. I knew he was an exponent of the attack *khamsin*, the attack 'like the desert wind'. It was a manoeuvre that perfectly suited his brute strength and physique. I had seen him practise it on a hundred occasions and now I divined by his footwork that he was gathering himself for it, for that one last effort that would end it all.

Struggling in the grip of my captors, I screamed at Tanus again, '*Khamsin*! Be ready!' I thought that my warning had been drowned and washed away by the uproar that filled the temple, for Tanus showed no reaction. Later he told me he had indeed heard me, and that with his impaired vision that second warning of mine had certainly saved him once again.

Rasfer dropped back a half-pace, the classic prelude to the *khamsin*, relaxing the pressure for an instant to position his opponent for the coup. Then his weight shifted and his left foot swung forward into the lead. He used his momentum and all the strength of his right leg to launch his entire body into the attack, like some grotesque carrion-bird taking to flight. As both his feet left the ground, the point of his blade was aimed at Tanus' throat. It was inexorable. Nothing could prevent that deadly blade from flying true to its mark except the one classic defence, the stop-hit.

At the precise instant that Rasfer was fully committed to the stroke, Tanus launched himself with equal power and superior grace. Like an arrow leaving the bowstring, he flew straight at his opponent. As they met in mid-air Tanus gathered up Rasfer's blade with his own and let it run down on to the pommel, where it came up hard and short, stopping it dead. It was the perfectly executed stop-hit.

The mass and speed of the two big men were thrown on to the bronze blade in Rasfer's fist, and it could not withstand the shock. It snapped cleanly, and left him clutching only the sheared-off hilt. Then they were locked chest-to-chest once more. Although Tanus' sword was still undamaged, Rasfer had got in under his guard and he could not wield it. Both Tanus' hands, the sword still held in his right fist, were locked behind Rasfer's back as the two men heaved and strained at each other.

Wrestling is one of the military disciplines in which every warrior in the Egyptian army is trained. Bound to each other by the crushing embrace of arms, they spun about the stage, each attempting to throw the other off-balance, snarling into each other's eyes, hooking a heel to trip, butting at each other with the visors of their helmets, equally matched thus far in strength and determination.

The audience had long since sensed that this was no longer a mock engagement, but a fight to the death. I wondered that their appetites had not been jaded by all they had witnessed that evening, but it was not so. They were insatiable, howling for blood and yet more blood.

At last Rasfer tore his arm free of Tanus' encircling grip. He still clutched the hilt of the broken sword in his fist, and with the jagged edge he struck at Tanus' face, deliberately aiming at his eyes and the wound in his brow, trying to enlarge and aggravate it. Tanus twisted his head to avoid the blows, catching them on the peak of his bronze helmet. Like a python shifting its coils around its prey, he used the moment to adjust his crushing hold around Rasfer's chest. The strain that he was exerting was such that Rasfer's features began to swell and engorge with blood. The air was being forced out of him, and he struggled against suffocation. He began visibly to weaken. Tanus kept up the pressure until a carbuncle on Rasfer's back was stretched to bursting-point and the yellow pus erupted in a stinking stream and trickled down into the waistband of his kilt.

Already suffocating, Rasfer grimaced at the pain of the bursting abscess and checked. Tanus felt him falter, and he summoned some deep reserve of strength. He changed the angle of his next effort, dropping his shoulders slightly and forcing his opponent backwards and upwards on to his heels. Rasfer was off-balance, and Tanus heaved again and forced him back a pace. Once he had him moving backwards, he kept the momentum going. Still locked to his opponent, he ran Rasfer backwards across the stage, steering him towards one of the gigantic stone pillars. For a moment none of us realized Tanus' intention, and then we saw him drop the point of his sword to the horizontal and press the hilt hard against Rasfer's spine.

At a full run the point of Tanus' sword hit the unyielding column. The metal screeched against the granite, and the shock was transmitted up the blade. It stopped those two big men in their tracks, and the force of it drove the hilt into Rasfer's spine. It would have killed a lesser man, and even Rasfer was paralyzed by it. With the last gust of his foul breath he let out a cry of agony, and his arms flew open. The broken haft of his own sword spun from his grip and skidded away across the stone pavement.

Rasfer's knees buckled, and he sagged in Tanus' arms. Tanus thrust his hip into him, and, with a heave of his upper body, hurled Rasfer over backwards. He landed so heavily that I heard more than one of his ribs crackle like dry twigs in the flames of the camp-fire. The back of his skull bounced upon the stone flags with a sound like a desert melon dropped from on high, and the breath from his lungs whistled out of his throat.

He groaned in agony. He had barely the strength to lift his arms to Tanus in capitulation. Tanus was so carried away by battle-rage, and inflamed by the roar of the crowd, that he was a man berserk. He stood over Rasfer and lifted his sword on high, gripping the hilt with both hands. He was a dreadful sight. Blood from the wound in his forehead had painted his visage into a glistening devil mask. Sweat and blood had soaked the hair of his chest and stained his clothing.

'Kill him!' roared the congregation. 'Kill the evil one!'

The point of Tanus' sword was aimed at the centre of Rasfer's chest, and I steeled myself for the down-stroke that would impale that gross body. I willed Tanus to do it, for I hated Rasfer more than any of them. The gods know that I had reason, for here was the monster who had gelded me, and I longed for my revenge.

It was in vain. I should have known my Tanus better than expect him to skewer a surrendered enemy. I saw the fires of madness begin to fade from his eyes. He shook his head slightly, as if to regain control of himself. Then, instead of stabbing down, he lowered his sword-point slowly until it just pricked Rasfer's chest. The keen point raised a drop of blood, bright as a garnet amongst the coarse hair of Rasfer's chest. Then Tanus picked up the lines of his script.

'Thus I bind you to my will, and I expel you from the light. May you wander through all eternity in the dark places. May you never more have power over the noble and the good amongst men. I give you to rule over the thief and the coward, over the bully and the cheat, over the liar and the murderer, over the grave-robber and the violater of virtuous women, over the blasphemer and the breaker of faith. From henceforth you are the god of all evil. Get you gone, and carry away with you the curse of Horus and of his resurrected father, Osiris.'

Tanus lifted the point of his sword from Rasfer's chest and tossed the weapon aside, deliberately disarming himself in the presence of his enemy to demonstrate his disdain and scorn. The blade clattered on the flagstones and Tanus strode to the running waters of our stage Nile and went down on one knee to scoop a handful and dash it into his own face, washing away the blood. Then he tore a strip of linen from the hem of his kilt and swiftly bound up the wound on his forehead to stem the bleeding.

Rasfer's two apes released me and rushed on stage to succour their fallen commander. They lifted him to his feet, and he staggered between them, heaving and blowing like a great obscene bullfrog. I saw that he was grievously injured. They dragged him from the stage, and the crowd howled its derision and hatred at him.

I watched my Lord Intef, and his expression was for the moment unguarded. I saw every one of my suspicions confirmed there. This was how he had planned to wreak his vengeance on Tanus – to have him slain before the eyes of the entire populace – and on his own daughter: to have her lover killed before her eyes – that was to have been Lostris' punishment for flouting her father's will.

My Lord Intef's frustration and disappointment now were enough to make me feel a smug satisfaction as I considered what retribution must be in store for Rasfer. He might have preferred more of the rough treatment that Tanus had dealt out to him, to the punishment that my Lord Intef would inflict upon him. My master was ever harsh with those who failed him.

Tanus was still gasping from the exertions of the duel, but now, as he moved to the front of the stage, he drew a dozen deep breaths to steady himself for the declamation that would bring the pageant to an end. As he faced the congregation it fell silent, for in blood and anger he was an awe-inspiring sight.

Tanus lifted up both his hands to the temple roof and cried out in a loud voice, 'Ammon-Ra, give me voice! Osiris, give me eloquence!' The traditional entreaty of the orator.

'Give him voice! Give him eloquence!' the crowd responded, and their faces were still rapt with all they had witnessed, but hungry for more entertainment.

Tanus was that unusual creature, a man of action who was also a man of words and ideas. I am sure that he would have been generous enough to admit that many of those ideas were planted in his mind by that lowly slave, Taita. However, once planted, they were in fertile ground.

When it came to oratory, Tanus' exhortations to his squadrons on the eve of battle were famous. Of course, I had not been present at all of these, but they had been relayed to me verbatim by Kratas, his faithful friend and lieutenant. I had copied many of these speeches down on a set of papyrus scrolls, for they were worthy of preservation.

Tanus had the common touch, and the ability to appeal directly to the ordinary man. I often thought that much of this special power of his sprang from his transparent honesty and his forthright manner. Men trusted him and followed willingly wherever he led them, even unto death itself.

I was still overwrought by the conflict we had all just witnessed and the closeness of Tanus' escape from the trap that my Lord Intef had laid for him. Nevertheless, I was eager to listen to the declamation that Tanus had prepared without my help or advice. To be truthful, I was still a little resentful that he had declined my assistance, and more than a little nervous as to what he might come out with. Tact and subtlety have never been Tanus' most notable virtues.

Now Pharaoh made a gesture of invitation to him to speak, crossing and uncrossing the ceremonial crook and flail, and inclining his head gracefully. The congregation was silent and intent, leaning forward eagerly so as not to miss a single word.

'It is I, Horus the falcon-headed, that speaks,' Tanus began, and they encouraged him.

'It is verily the falcon-headed! Hear him!'

'*Ha-Ka-Ptah!*' Tanus used the archaic form from which the present name of Egypt was derived. Very few realized that the original meaning was the temple of Ptah. 'I speak to you of this ancient land given to us ten thousand years since, in the time when all the gods were young. I speak to you of the two kingdoms that in nature are one and indivisible.'

Pharaoh nodded. This was the standard dogma, approved by both temporal and religious authority that neither recognized the impostor in the Lower Kingdom, nor even acknowledged his existence.

'Oh, *Kemit!*' Tanus used another ancient name for Egypt: the Black

Land, after the colour of the Nile mud brought down by the annual inundation. 'I speak to you of this land riven and divided, torn by civil war, bleeding and drained of treasure.' My own shock was mirrored on the faces of all those who listened to him. Tanus had just given voice to the unspeakable. I wanted to rush on to the stage and clap my hand over his mouth to prevent him from going on, but I was transfixed.

'Oh, *Ta-Meri!*' Another old name: the Beloved Earth. Tanus had learned well the history I had taught him. 'I speak to you of old and feeble generals, and admirals too weak and indecisive to wrest back the stolen kingdom from the usurper. I speak to you of ancient men in their dotage who waste your treasure and spill the blood of your finest young men as though it were the lees of bitter wine.'

In the second row of the audience I saw Nembet, the Great Lion of Egypt, flush with anger and scratch furiously with chagrin at his beard. The other elderly military men around him frowned and moved restlessly on their benches, rattling their swords in their scabbards as a sign of their disapproval. Amongst them all, only my Lord Intef smiled as he watched Tanus escape from one trap only to blunder into the next.

'Our *Ta-Meri* is beset by a host of enemies, and yet the sons of the nobles prefer to cut off their own thumbs rather than to carry the sword to protect her.' As he said this, Tanus looked keenly at Menset and Sobek, Lostris' older brothers, where they sat beside their father in the second row. The king's decree exempted from military service only those with such physical disability as to render them unfit. The surgeon priests at the temple of Osiris had perfected the art of removing the top joint of the thumb with little pain or danger of infection, thus rendering it impossible for that hand to wield a sword or pluck a bowstring. The young bucks proudly flaunted their mutilations as they sat gambling and carousing in the riverside taverns. They considered the missing digit a mark not of cowardice, but of sophistication and independent spirit.

'War is the game played by old men with the lives of the young,' I had heard Lostris' brothers argue. 'Patriotism is a myth conceived by those old rogues to draw us into the infernal game. Let them fight as they will, but we want no part of it.' In vain I had remonstrated with them that the privilege of Egyptian citizenship carried with it duties and responsibilities. They dismissed me with the arrogance of the young and ignorant.

Now, however, beneath Tanus' level stare they fidgeted and concealed their left hands in the folds of their clothing. They were both of them right-handed, but had convinced the recruiting officer to the contrary, with their eloquence and a dash of gold.

The common people at the rear of the great hall hummed and stamped their feet in agreement with what Tanus had said. It was their sons who filled the rowing-benches of the war galleys, or marched under arms through the desert sands.

However, in the wings of the stage I wrung my hands in despair. With that little speech Tanus had made an enemy of fifty of the young nobles in the audience. They were men who would one day inherit power and influence in the Upper Kingdom. Their enmity outweighed a hundred times the adoration of the common herd and I prayed for Tanus to cease. In a few minutes he had done enough damage to last us all a hundred years, but he went on blithely.

'Oh, *Ta-Nutri!*' This was yet another ancient name: the Land of the Gods. 'I speak to you of the wrong-doer and the robber who waits in ambush on every hilltop and in every thicket. The farmer is forced to plough with his shield at his side, and the traveller must go with his sword bared.'

Again the commoners applauded. The depredations of the robber bands were a terrible scourge upon them all. No man was safe beyond the mud walls of the towns, and the robber chieftains who called themselves the Shrikes were arrogant and fearless. They respected no law but their own, and no man was safe from them.

Tanus had struck exactly the right note with the people, and suddenly I was moved by the notion that this was all much deeper than it seemed. Revolutions have been forged and dynasties of pharaohs overturned by just such appeals to the masses. With Tanus' next words my suspicion was strengthened.

'While the poor cry out under the lash of the tax-collector, the nobles anoint the buttocks of their fancy boys with the most precious oils of the orient—' A roar went up from the rear of the hall, and my fears were replaced by a tremulous excitement. Had this been carefully planned? Was Tanus more subtle and devious than I had ever given him credit for?

'By Horus!' I cried in my heart. 'The land is ripe for revolution, and who better to lead it than Tanus?' I felt only disappointment that he had not taken me into his confidence and made me party to his design. I could have planned a revolution as skilfully and as cunningly as I could design a water-garden or write a play.

I craned to look over the heads of the congregation, expecting at the very next moment to see Kratas and his brother officers burst into the temple at the head of a company of warriors from the squadron. I felt the hair on my forearms and at the nape of my neck lift with excitement as I pictured them snatching the double crown from Pharaoh's head and placing it upon the blood-smeared brow of Tanus. With what joy I would have joined the cry of 'Long live Pharaoh! Long live King Tanus!'

Heady images swirled before my eyes as Tanus went on speaking. I saw the prophecy of the desert oracle fulfilled. I dreamed of Tanus, with my Lady Lostris beside him, seated on the white throne of this very Egypt, with myself standing behind them resplendent in the apparel of the grand vizier of the Upper Kingdom. But why, oh why, had he not consulted me before embarking on this perilous venture?

With his next breath he made the reason plain. I had misjudged my Tanus, my honest, plain and good Tanus, my noble, straight and trustworthy Tanus, lacking only in guile and stealth and deceit.

This was no plot. This was simply Tanus speaking his mind without fear or favour. The commoners, who only moments before had been clinging enraptured to every word that fell from his tongue, were now quite unexpectedly given the sharp edge of that organ as he rounded upon them.

'Hear me, oh Egypt! What is to become of a land where the mean-spirited try to suppress the mighty amongst them; where the patriot is reviled; where there is no man of yesterday revered for his wisdom; where the petty and the envious seek to tear down the men of worth to their own base level?'

There was no cheering now as those at the back of the hall recognized themselves in this description. Effortlessly my Tanus had succeeded in alienating every man amongst them, great and small, rich and poor. Oh, why had he not consulted me, I mourned, and the answer was plain. He had not consulted me because he knew I would have counselled him against it.

'What order is there in society where the slave is free with his tongue, and counts himself as equal to those of noble birth?' he blazed at them. 'Should the son revile his father and scorn the wisdom paid for in grey hairs and wrinkled brow? Should the waterfront harlot wear rings of lapis lazuli and set herself above the virtuous wife?'

By Horus, he would not spare one of them from the lash of his tongue, I thought bitterly. As always, he was completely oblivious to his own safety in the pursuit of what he saw as the right and open way.

Only one person in the temple was enchanted with what he had to tell them. Lostris appeared at my side and gripped my arm.

'Isn't he wonderful, Taita?' she breathed. 'Every word he utters is the truth. Tonight he is truly a young god.'

I could find neither the words nor the heart to agree with her, and I hung my head in sorrow as Tanus went on relentlessly.

'Pharaoh, you are the father of the people. We cry out to you for protection and for succour. Give the affairs of state and war into the hands of honest and clever men. Send the rogues and the fools to rot on their estates. Call off the faithless priests and the usurious servants of the state, those parasites upon the body of this *Ta-Meri* of ours.'

Horus knows that I am as good a priest-hater as the best of them, but only a fool or very brave man would call down the wrath of every god-botherer in Egypt upon his own head, for their power is infinite and their hatred implacable. While as for the civil servants, their lines of influence and corruption have been set up over the centuries and my Lord Intef was the chief of them all. I shuddered in pity for my dear blunt friend as he went on handing out instructions to Pharaoh on how to restructure the whole of Egyptian society.

'Heed the words of the sage! Oh, king, honour the artist and the scribe. Reward the brave warrior and the faithful servant. Root out the bandits and the robbers from their desert fastnesses. Give the people example and direction in their lives, so that this very Egypt may once again flourish and be great.'

Tanus fell to his knees in the centre of the stage and spread his arms wide. 'Oh, Pharaoh, you are our father. We protest our love to you. In return, show us now a father's love. Hear our entreaties, we beg of you.'

Up to that moment I had been stupefied by the depths of my friend's folly, but now, much too late, I regained my wits and signalled frantically for my stage-hands to drop the curtain before Tanus could do any further damage. As the gleaming folds of cloth floated down and hid him from their view, the audience sat in stunned silence, as though they did not believe all that they had heard and seen that night.

It was Pharaoh himself who broke the spell. He rose to his feet, and his face behind the stiff white make-up was inscrutable. As he swept from the temple, the congregation prostrated itself before him. Before he too went down in obeisance, I saw my Lord Intef's expression. It was triumphant.

I ESCORTED Tanus back from the temple to his own sparsely furnished quarters close to the dock at which his squadron was moored. Although I walked beside him with my hand on the hilt of my dagger, prepared for the consequences of his foolhardy honesty to be visited on us immediately, Tanus was quite unrepentant. Indeed, he seemed oblivious to the depths of his folly and inordinately pleased with himself. I have often remarked how a man freshly released from terrible strain and mortal danger becomes garrulous and elated. Even Tanus, the hardened warrior, was no exception.

'It was time somebody stood up and said what needed to be said, don't you agree, old friend?' His voice rang clear and loud down the darkened alley, as though he were determined to summon any awaiting assassin to us. I kept my agreement muted.

'You did not expect it of me, did you now? Be honest with me, Taita. It took you quite by surprise, did it not?'

'It surprised us all.' This time I could agree with a little more enthusiasm. 'Even Pharaoh was taken aback, as well he might be.'

'He listened, Taita. He took it all in, I could tell. I did good work this evening, don't you think so?'

When I attempted to raise the subject of Rasfer's treacherous attack upon him and broach the possibility that it might have been inspired by my Lord Intef, Tanus would have none of it. 'That is impossible, Taita. You dreamed it. Lord Intef was my father's dearest friend. How could he wish me ill? Besides, I am to be his son-in-law, am I not?' And despite his injuries he let out such a happy shout of laughter that it roused the sleepers in the darkened huts that we were passing and they shouted grumpily back at us to be quiet. Tanus ignored their protests.

'No, no, I am sure that you are wrong,' he cried. 'It was simply Rasfer working out his spite in his own charming way. Well, he'll know better next time.' He threw his arm around my shoulders and hugged me so hard that it hurt. 'You saved me twice tonight. Without your warnings Rasfer would have had me both times. How do you do these things, Taita? I swear you are a secret warlock, and have the gift of the inner eye.' He laughed again.

How could I stifle his joy? He was like a boy, a big rumbustious boy. I could not help but love him all the more. This was not the time to point out the danger in which he had placed himself and all of us who were his friends.

Let him have his hour, and tomorrow I would sound the voice of reason and of caution. So I took him home and stitched the gash in his forehead, and washed his other wounds and anointed them with my special mixture of honey and herbs to prevent mortification. Then I gave him a stiff draught of the Red Shepenn and left the good Kratas to guard his slumbers.

When I reached my own quarters well after midnight, there were two summonses awaiting me: one from my Lady Lostris and the other from the vanquished Rasfer. There was no doubt as to which of them I would have responded to if I had been given the choice, but I was not. Rasfer's two thugs almost dragged me away to where he lay on a sweat-soaked mattress, cursing and moaning by turns, and calling on Seth and all the gods to witness his pain and his fortitude.

'Good Taita!' he greeted me, raising himself painfully on one elbow, 'you will not believe the pain. My chest is afire. I swear every bone in it is crushed, and my head aches as though it is bound by thongs of rawhide.'

With very little effort I was able to force back my tears of pity, but it is a strange thing about those of us who are doctors and healers that we cannot find it in our hearts to deny our skills to even the most abominable creatures that require them. I sighed with resignation, unpacked the leather bag that contained my medical equipment and set out my instruments and unguents.

I was delighted to find that Rasfer's self-diagnosis was perfectly valid, and that apart from numerous contusions and shallow wounds, at least three of his ribs were broken and there was a lump on the back of his head almost the size of my fist. I had, therefore, a perfectly legitimate reason for adding considerably to his discomfort. One of the broken ribs was seriously out of alignment and there was genuine danger that it might pierce the lung. While his two thugs held him down and Rasfer squealed and howled most gratifyingly, I manipulated the rib back into place and strapped up his chest with linen bandages well soaked in vinegar to shrink as they dried.

Then I addressed myself to the lump on the back of his skull where it had struck the stone paving. The gods are often generous. When I held a lamp to Rasfer's eyes the pupils did not dilate. There was not the least doubt in my mind as to what treatment was required. Bloody fluid was gathering inside that unlovely skull. Without my help Rasfer would be dead by the following sunset. I thrust aside the obvious temptation and reminded myself of the surgeon's duty to his patient.

There are probably only three surgeons in all of Egypt who are capable of trepanning a skull with a good chance of success, and personally I would not put much faith in the other two. Once again I ordered Rasfer's two oafs to take hold of him to control his struggles, and to hold him face down on his mattress. By the roughness of their handling and their obvious disregard for their master's injured ribs, I surmised that they were not exactly overflowing with loving feeling towards their master.

Once again a chorus of howls and squeals turned the night hideous and gladdened my labours, as I made a semi-circular incision around the lump on his scalp, and then peeled a large flap of skin away from the bone. Now not even those two strapping ruffians could hold him down. His struggles were splashing blood as high as the ceiling of the room and sprinkling us all, so that we seemed to be inflicted with a red pox. At last, in exasperation, I ordered them to bind his ankles and wrists to the bedposts with leather straps.

'Oh, gentle and sweet Taita, the pain is beyond belief. Give me but a drop of that flower juice, I beg you, dear friend,' he blubbered.

Now that he was safely bound to the bed, I could afford to be frank with him. 'I understand, my good Rasfer, just how you feel. I also would have been grateful for a little of the flower when last you took the knife to me. Alas, old comrade, my store of the drug is finished, and there will not be another eastern caravan for at least a month,' I lied cheerfully, for very few knew that I cultivated the Red Shepenn myself. Knowing that the best was yet to come, I reached for my bone-drill.

The human head is the only part of the body that puzzles me as a doctor. At the orders of my Lord Intef the corpses of all executed criminals are handed over to me. In addition Tanus has been able to bring me many fine specimens from the battlefield, suitably pickled in vats of brine. All these I have dissected and studied so that I know every bone and how it fits into its exact place in the skeleton. I have traced the route by which food enters the mouth and passes through the body. I have found that great and wondrous organ, the heart, nestling between the pale air-bladders of the lungs. I have studied the rivers of the body through which the blood flows, and I have observed the two types of blood which determine the moods and emotions of man.

There is, of course, that bright joyous blood that, when released by the cut of a scalpel or the headsman's axe, spurts out in regular impulses. This is the blood of happy thoughts and fine emotions, it is the blood of love and kindness. Then there is that darker sullen blood that flows without the vigour and the bounding joy of the other. This is the blood of anger and of sorrow, of melancholic thoughts and evil deeds.

All these matters I have studied, and have filled one hundred papyrus rolls with my observations. There is no man in the world that I know of who has gone to such lengths, certainly none of those quacks in the temple with their amulets and their incantations have done so. I doubt any one of them could tell the liver from the sphincter of the anus without an invocation to Osiris, a casting of the divining dice and a fat fee paid in advance.

In all modesty I can say that I have never met a man who understands the human body better than I, and yet the head is still a puzzle to me. Naturally I understand that the eyes see, the nose smells, the mouth tastes and the ears hear – but what is the purpose of that pale porridge that fills the gourd of the skull?

I have never been able to fathom it myself, and no man has ever been able to offer me a satisfactory explanation, except that Tanus came closest to it. After he and I had spent an evening together sampling the latest vintage of red wine, he had woken in the dawn and suggested with a groan, 'Seth has placed this thing in our heads as his revenge on mankind.'

I once met a man who was travelling with a caravan from beyond those legendary twin rivers, the Tigris and the Euphrates, who professed to have studied the same problem. He was a wise man and together we debated many mysteries over the course of half a year. At one point he suggested that all human emotion and thought sprang not from the heart, but from those soft amorphous curds that make up the brain. I mention this naïve assertion only to demonstrate how gravely even an intelligent and learned man can err.

Nobody who has ever considered that mighty organ, the heart, leaping with its own life in the centre of our body, fed by great rivers of blood, protected by the palisades of bone, can doubt that this is the fountain from which all thought and emotion springs. The heart uses the blood to disseminate these emotions throughout the body. Have you ever felt your heart stir within you and quicken to beautiful music, or a lovely face, or the fine words of a moving speech? Have you ever felt anything leaping around inside your head? Even the wise man from the East had to capitulate before my ruthless logic.

No rational man can believe that a bloodless puddle of curdled milk lying inert in its bony jar could conjure up the lines of a poem or the design of a pyramid, could cause a man to love or to wage war. Even the embalmers scoop it out and discard it when they prepare a corpse for the long journey.

There is, however, a paradox here in that if this glutinous mass is interfered with, even by the pressure of trapped fluid upon it, the patient is certainly doomed. It requires an intimate knowledge of the structure of the head and a quite marvellous dexterity to be able to drill through the skull without disturbing the sac that contains this porridge. I have both these attributes.

As I ground down slowly through the bone, encouraged by Rasfer's bellows, I paused regularly to wash away the bone chips and filings by splashing vinegar into the wound. The sting of the liquid added little to the patient's well-being, but revived the flagging volume of his voice.

Suddenly the sharp bronze drill bit cleanly through the skull, and a tiny but perfect circle of bone was blown out of the wound by the pressure within. It was followed immediately by a spurt of dark, clotted blood that hit me in the face. Immediately Rasfer relaxed under me. I knew, not without a sneaking pang of regret, that he would survive. As I stitched the flap of scalp back into place, covering the aperture in the depths of which the dura mater pulsed ominously, I wondered if I had truly done mankind a great service by preserving this specimen of it.

When I left Rasfer with his head swathed in bandages, snoring and whimpering in porcine self-pity, I found that I was completely exhausted. The excitements and alarums of the day had expended even my vast store of energy. However, there was to be no rest for me yet, for my Lady Lostris' messenger still hovered on the terrace of my quarters and pounced on me as I set foot on the first step. I was allowed only sufficient grace to wash away Rasfer's blood and change my soiled raiment.

As I tottered into her chamber, barely able to place one foot before the other, my Lady Lostris met me with blazing eyes and ominously tapping foot. 'Just where do you think you have been hiding yourself, Master Taita?' she lashed out at me immediately. 'I sent for you before the second watch, and it's now not much short of dawn. How dare you keep me waiting so? Sometimes you forget your station. You know full well the punishment for impertinent slaves—' She was in full flight, having let her impatience brew for all these hours. In anger her beauty is stunning, and when she stamped her foot in that adorable gesture that was so typically her own, I thought that my heart must burst with my love for her.

'Don't you stand there grinning at me!' she flared at me. 'I am so truly angry that I could order you flogged.' She stamped her foot again, and I felt the tiredness fall from my shoulders like a heavy load. Her mere presence had the power to revitalize me.

'My lady, what a wondrous role you played this night. It seemed to me and all who watched you that it was indeed the divine goddess that walked amongst us—'

'Don't you dare try your tricks with me.' She stamped for the third time, but without conviction. 'You'll not wriggle out of this so easily—'

'Truly, my lady, as I walked back from the temple through the crowded streets, your name was on every tongue. They said your singing was the finest they had ever heard, and had quite stolen every heart.'

'I believe not a word,' she declared, but she was clearly having difficulty sustaining her fury. 'In fact I thought my voice was awful this evening. I was flat at least once, and off-key on numerous—'

'I must contradict you, mistress. You were never better. And what beauty! It lit the whole temple.' She is not truly vain, my Lady Lostris, but she is a woman.

'You awful man!' she cried in exasperation. 'I was ready to have you flogged this time, I truly was. But come and sit beside me on the bed and tell me all about it. I am still so excited that I am sure I will not sleep for a week.' She took my hand and led me to the bed, babbling on happily about Tanus, and how he must have won every heart as well as Pharaoh's with his wonderful performance and fearless speech, and how the infant Horus had beshat her dress, and did I truly think that she had sung even passing well, and wasn't I just saying so?

At last I had to stop her. 'My lady, it is almost dawn and we must be ready to leave with all the court to accompany the king when he crosses the river to inspect his funerary temple and his tomb. You must get some sleep if you are to look your best on such an important state occasion.'

'I'm not sleepy, Taita,' she protested, and went chattering on, only to slump against my shoulder a few minutes later, fallen asleep in mid-sentence.

Gently, I slipped her head down on to the carved wooden headrest and covered her with a rug of colobus monkey furs. I could not bring myself to leave immediately but hovered beside her bed. At last I placed a gentle kiss upon her cheek. She did not open her eyes, but whispered sleepily, 'Do you think there will be an opportunity for me to speak to the king tomorrow? Only he will be able to prevent my father sending Tanus away.'

I could think of no ready answer for her, and while I still dithered, she fell fully asleep.

I COULD scarcely drag myself from my couch at dawn, for I seemed barely to have closed my eyes to sleep before it was time to open them again. My reflection in the bronze mirror was haggard and my eyes were underscored in purple. Swiftly I touched on make-up to cover the worst of my sorry condition, enhancing the hollows of my eyes with kohl and my pale features with a brushing of antimony. Two of the slave boys combed out my hair and I was so pleased with the result that I felt almost cheerful as I hurried down to the grand vizier's private dock where the great state barge lay moored.

I was amongst the last to join the throng upon the quay, but no one seemed to notice my late arrival, not even my Lady Lostris who was already on the deck of the barge. I watched her for a while.

She had been invited to join the royal women. These comprised not only the king's wives, but his numerous concubines and all his daughters. Of course these last were the cause of much of Pharaoh's unhappiness, a flock of them ranging in age from crawlers and toddlers to others of marriageable age, and not a son amongst them. How was Pharaoh's immortality to be maintained without a male line to carry it forward?

It was difficult to believe that, like me, Lostris had not slept more than an hour or two, for she seemed as sweet and fresh as one of the desert roses in my garden. Even in that glittering array of feminine beauty that had been hand-picked by Pharaoh's factors or sent to him in tribute by his satraps at the ends of the empire, Lostris stood out like a swallow in a flock of drab little desert larks.

I looked for Tanus, but his squadron was already lying well upstream, ready to escort Pharaoh's crossing, and the reflection of the rising sun turned the surface of the river into a dazzling silver sheet that blinded the eye. I could not look into it.

At that moment there was the steady boom of a drum, and the populace craned to watch Pharaoh's stately progress down from the palace to the royal barge.

This morning he wore the light *nemes* crown of starched and folded linen, secured around his forehead with the gold band of the *uraeus*. The erect golden cobra, with its hood flared and its garnet eyes glittering, rose up from his brow. The cobra was the symbol of the powers of life and death that Pharaoh held over his subjects. The king was not carrying the crook and flail, only the golden sceptre. After the double crown itself, this was the most holy treasure of all the crown jewels and was reputed to be over a thousand years old.

Despite all the regalia and the ceremonial, Pharaoh wore no make-up. Under the direct rays of the early sun, and without make-up to disguise the fact, Mamose himself was unremarkable. Just a soft little godling of late middle age, with a small round paunch bulging over the waistband of his kilt and features intricately carved with lines of worry.

As he passed where I stood, it seemed he recognized me, for he nodded slightly. I immediately prostrated myself on the paving, and he paused and made a sign for me to approach. I crawled forward on hands and knees, and knocked my forehead three times on the ground at his feet.

'Are you not Taita, the poet?' he asked in that thin and petulant voice of his.

'I am Taita the slave, your Majesty,' I replied. There are times when a little humility is called for. 'But I am also a poor scribbler.'

'Well, Taita the slave, you scribbled to good effect last night. I have never been so well entertained by a pageant. I shall issue a royal edict declaring your poor scribblings to be the official version.'

He announced this loud enough for all the court to hear, and even my Lord Intef, who followed him closely, beamed with pleasure. As I was his slave, the honour belonged to him more than to me. However, Pharaoh was not finished with me yet.

'Tell me, Taita the slave, are you not also the same surgeon who recently prescribed to me?'

'Majesty, I am that same humble slave who has the temerity to practise a little medicine.'

'Then when shall your cure take effect?' He dropped his voice so that only I could hear the question.

'Majesty, the event will take place nine months after you have fulfilled all those conditions that I listed for you.' As we were now in a surgeon-

and-patient relationship, I felt emboldened to add, 'Have you followed the diet I set you?'

'By Isis' bountiful breasts!' he exclaimed with an unexpected twinkle in his eye. 'I am so full of bull's balls, it is a wonder that I do not bellow when a herd of cows passes the palace.'

He was in such pleasant mood that I tried a little joke of my own. 'Has Pharaoh found the heifer I suggested?'

'Alas, doctor, it is not as simple as it would seem. The prettiest flowers are soonest visited by the bee. You did stipulate that she must be completely untouched, did you not?'

'Virgin and untouched, and within a season of her first red moon,' I added quickly, making it as difficult as possible to put my recipe to the test. 'Have you found one who meets that description, Majesty?'

His expression changed again, and he smiled thoughtfully. The smile looked out of place on those melancholy features. 'We shall see,' he murmured. 'We shall see.' And he turned and mounted the boarding-ladder of the barge. As my Lord Intef drew level with me, he made a small gesture, ordering me to fall in behind him, and so I followed him up on to the deck of the royal barge.

The wind had dropped during the night and the dark waters of the river seemed heavy and quiet as oil in the jar, disturbed only by those streaks and whirlpools upon the surface where the eternal current ran deep and swift. Even Nembet should be able to make the crossing in these conditions, although Tanus' squadron stood by in most unflattering fashion, as if Tanus was preparing to rescue him from error once again.

My Lord Intef drew me aside as soon as we reached the deck. 'You still have the power to surprise me sometimes, my old darling,' he whispered, and squeezed my arm. 'Just when I was seriously beginning to doubt your loyalty.'

I was taken aback by this sudden flush of goodwill, since the welts from Rasfer's lash across my back still ached. However, I bowed my head to shield my expression and waited for him to give me direction before committing myself, which he did immediately.

'I could not have written a more appropriate declamation for Tanus to recite before Pharaoh if I had tried myself. Where that imbecile Rasfer failed so dismally, you retrieved the day for me in your usual style.' It was only then that it all fell into place. He believed that I was the author of Tanus' monumental folly, and that I had composed it for his benefit. In the uproar of the temple he could not have heard my shouted warnings to Tanus, or he would have known better.

'I am pleased that you are pleased,' I whispered back to him. I felt an enormous sense of relief. My position of influence had not been compromised. It was not my own skin I was thinking of at that moment – well, not entirely. I was thinking of Tanus and Lostris. They would need every bit of help and protection that I could give them during the stormy days that lay ahead for both of them. I was grateful that I was still in a position to be of some use to them.

'It was no less than my duty.' Thus I made the most of this windfall.

'You will find me grateful,' my Lord Intef replied. 'Do you remember the piece of ground on the canal behind the temple of Thoth that we discussed some time ago?'

'Indeed, my lord.' We both knew that I had hankered after that plot for ten years. It would make a perfect writer's retreat and a place to which I could retire in my old age.

'It is yours. At my next assize, bring the deed to me for my signature.' I was stunned and appalled by the vile manner in which it had come into my possession, as payment for an imagined piece of treachery on my part. For a moment I thought of rejecting the gift, but only for a moment. By the time I had recovered from my shock we were across the river and pulling into the mouth of the canal that led across the plain to Pharaoh Mamose's great funerary temple.

I had surveyed this canal with only minimal help from the royal architects, as I had planned virtually single-handed the whole complicated business of the transport of Pharaoh's body from the place of his death to the funerary temple where the mummification process would take place.

I had assumed that he would die at his palace on lovely little Elephantine Island. Therefore his corpse would be brought down-river in the state barge. I had designed the canal to accommodate the huge ship snugly. So now she slipped into it as neatly as the sword into its scabbard.

Straight as the blade of my dagger, the canal cut through the black loam soil of the riparian plain two thousand paces to the foot of the gaunt Saharan foothills. Tens of thousands of slaves had laboured over the years to build it, and to line it with stone blocks. As the barge nosed into the canal, two hundred sturdy slaves seized the tow-ropes from the bows and began to draw her smoothly across the plain. They sang one of the sad melodious work chants as they marched in ranks along the towpath. The peasants working in the fields beside the canal ran to welcome us. They crowded to the bank, calling blessing on the king and waving palm-fronds, as the great barge moved majestically by.

When at last we slid into the stone dock below the outer walls of the half-finished temple, the slaves made the tow-ropes fast to the mooring-rings. So precise was my design that the entry port in the bulwark of the state barge lined up exactly with the portals of the main gate to the temple.

As the huge vessel came to rest, the trumpeter in the bows blew a fanfare on his gazelle horn, and the portcullis was raised slowly, to reveal the royal hearse waiting in the gateway attended by the company of embalmers in their crimson robes and fifty priests of Osiris in rank behind them.

The priests began to chant as they trundled the hearse forward on its wooden rollers, on to the deck of the barge. Pharaoh clapped his hands with delight and hurried forward to examine this grotesque vehicle.

I had taken no part in the conception of this celebration of bad taste. It was entirely the work of the priests. Suffice it only to say that in the naked sunlight, the superabundant gold-work shone so brightly as to offend the eye almost as painfully as did the actual design. Such weight of gold forced the priests to pant and sweat as they manhandled the clumsy ark on to the deck, and it listed even the great ship alarmingly. That weight of gold could have filled all the grain stores of the Upper Kingdom, or built and fitted out fifty squadrons of fighting ships and paid their crews for ten years. Thus the inept craftsman attempts to hide the paucity of his inspiration behind a dazzle of treasure. If only they had given me such material to work with, they might have seen something different.

This monstrosity was destined to be sealed in the tomb with Pharaoh's dead body. No matter that its construction had contributed largely to the financial ruin of the kingdom, Pharaoh was delighted with it.

At my Lord Intef's suggestion, the king mounted the vehicle and took his seat on the platform designed to carry his sarcophagus. From there he beamed about him, all his dignity and royal reserve forgotten. He was probably enjoying himself as much as he ever had in all his gloomy life, I reflected with a pang of pity. His death was to be the pinnacle to which most of his living energy and anticipation were directed.

On what was clearly an impulse, he beckoned my Lord Intef to join him on the ark and then looked around the crowded deck as if seeking someone else in the throng. He seemed to find who he wanted, for he stooped slightly and said something to the grand vizier.

My Lord Intef smiled and, following his direction, singled out my Lady Lostris. With a gesture he ordered her to come to him on the ark. She was clearly flustered, and blushed under her make-up, a rare phenomenon for one who was so seldom caught out of countenance. However, she recovered swiftly, and mounted the carriage with girlish, long-legged grace that as usual carried every eye with her.

She knelt before the king and touched her forehead three times to the floor of the platform. Then, in front of all the priests and the entire court, Pharaoh did an extraordinary thing. He reached down and took Lostris' hand, and lifted her to her feet, and seated her beside him on the platform. It was beyond all protocol, there was no precedent for it, and I saw his ministers exchange looks of amazement.

Then something else happened of which even they were not aware. When I was very young there had lived in the boys' quarters an old deaf slave who had befriended me. It was he who had taught me to read men's speech not only by the sound of it, but also by the shape of their lips as they formed the words. It was a very useful accomplishment. With it I could follow a conversation at the far end of a crowded hall, with musicians playing and a hundred men around me laughing and shouting at each other.

Now, before my eyes I saw Pharaoh say softly to my Lady Lostris, 'Even in daylight you are as divine as was the goddess Isis in the torchlight of the temple.'

The shock of it was like the blow of a fist in my stomach. Had I been blind, I berated myself desperately, or had I merely been stupid? Surely any imbecile must have anticipated the direction in which my capricious meddling must incline the order in which the dice of destiny might fall.

My facetious advice to the king must inevitably have had the effect of directing his attention towards my Lady Lostris. It was as though some malignant impulse below the surface of my mind had set out to describe her precisely to him as the mother of his first-born son. The most beautiful virgin in the land, to be taken within the first season after her moon had flowered – it was her exactly. And then, of course, by casting her as the leading female in the pageant, I had managed to display her to the king in the kindest possible light.

What I suddenly realized was about to happen was all of it my fault, as much as though I had deliberately engineered it. What is more, there was nothing I could do about it now. I stood in the sunlight so appalled and stricken with remorse that for a while I was deprived of the powers of speech and of reason.

When the sweating priests shoved the hearse off the deck and through the gateway, the crowd around me started after it and I was borne along with them willy-nilly, as though I were a leaf upon a stream without direction of my own. Before I was able to recover my wits I found myself within the forecourt of the funerary temple. I began to push my way forward, jostling those ahead of me to get past them and to reach the side of the hearse before it came to the main entrance of the royal mortuary.

As one team of priests pushed the vehicle forward, a second team picked up the wooden rollers that were left behind it and ran forward to place them ahead of the ponderous golden vehicle. There was a short delay as the carriage reached that area of the courtyard that had not yet been paved. While the priests spread straw ahead of the rollers to smooth the passage over this rough ground, I slipped quickly around the back of the row of huge carved stone lions that lined the carriageway, and hurried down this clear space until I was level with the ark. When one of the priests tried to bar my way and prevent me reaching the side of the vehicle, I gave him such a look as would have made one of the stone lions quail, and spat a single word at him that was seldom heard in the temple confines and caused him to step hurriedly aside and let me pass.

When I reached the near side of the ark I found myself directly below Lostris, close enough to stretch up and touch her arm, and to hear every word she addressed to the king. I could tell at once that she had completely recovered her poise which Pharaoh's unexpected interest in her had disturbed, and was now setting out to be as agreeable as possible to him. Miserably, I recalled how she had planned to do exactly this, and to use his favour to secure his agreement to her marriage to Tanus. As recently as last evening I had dismissed it as girlish prattle, but now it was happening, and it was beyond my power to prevent it or to warn her of the dangerous waters into which she was steering.

If, earlier in this chronicle, I have given the impression that my Lady Lostris was a flighty child with not a thought in her pretty head other than romantic nonsense and her own frivolous enjoyment of life, then I have fallen short in my efforts as historian of these extraordinary events. Although still so young, she was at times mature far beyond her years. Our Egyptian girls bloom early in the Nile sunlight. She was also a diligent scholar, with a bright mind and a thoughtful and enquiring side to her nature, all of which I had done my very best over the years to foster and develop.

Under my tutelage she had reached the stage where she could debate with the priests the most obscure religious dogma, could hold her own with the palace lawyers on such matters as the Land Tenure Acts and the extremely complicated Irrigation Act that regulated the usage of the waters from the Nile. Of course, she had read and absorbed every single one of the scrolls in the palace library. These included several hundred of which I was the author, from my medical treatises to my definitive essays on the tactics of naval warfare, together with my astrological scrolls on the names and natures of all the heavenly bodies, and my manuals on archery and swordsmanship, horticulture and falconry. She could even argue with me my own principles of architecture, and compare them to those of the great Imhotep.

Thus she was perfectly equipped to discuss any subject from astrology to the practice of war, from politics or the building of temples to the measurement and regulation of the Nile waters, all of which were subjects that fascinated Pharaoh. In addition she could rhyme and riddle and coin an amusing pun, and her vocabulary was almost as extensive as my own.

In short, she was an accomplished conversationalist, with a ready sense of humour. She was articulate and had an enchanting voice and a merry little laugh. Truly, no man or god could resist her, especially if she could offer to someone without a son the promise of an heir.

I had to warn her, and yet how could a slave intrude upon the congress of persons so infinitely high above his own station? I skipped nervously beside the carriage, listening to my Lady Lostris' voice at its most enthralling as she set herself out to engage the king's fancy.

She was describing to him the manner in which his funerary temple had been laid out to conform to the most propitious astronomical aspects, those of the moon and the zodiac at the time of Pharaoh's birth. Of course she was merely repeating knowledge that she had gleaned from me, for I was the one who had surveyed and orientated the temple to the heavenly bodies. However, she was so convincing that I found myself following her explanations as though I was hearing them for the first time.

The funeral ark passed between the pylons of the inner court of the temple and rolled down the long colonnaded atrium, past the barred and guarded doors to the six treasuries in which were manufactured and stored the funerary offerings which would go with the king to his tomb. At the end of the atrium the acacia-wood doors, on which were carved the images of all the gods of the pantheon, were swung open, and we entered the mortuary where Pharaoh's corpse would one day be embalmed.

Here in this solemn chapel the king dismounted from the carriage, and went forward to inspect the massive table on which he would lie for the ritual of mummification. Unlike the embalming of a commoner, royal embalming took seventy days to accomplish. The table had been sculpted from a single block of diorite, three paces long and two wide. Into the dark, mottled surface of the stone had been chiselled the indentation that fitted the back of the king's head, and the grooves which would drain the blood and other bodily fluids released by the scalpels and the instruments of the embalmers.

The grand master of the guild of embalmers was standing beside the table, ready to explain the entire process to the king, and he had an attentive audience, for Pharaoh seemed fascinated by every gruesome detail. At one stage it seemed that he might so far forget his dignity as to climb up upon the diorite block and try its fit, very much as though it were a new costume of linen presented by his tailor.

However, he restrained himself with an obvious effort, and instead devoted himself to the mortician's description of how the first incision would be made from his gullet to his groin, and how his viscera would be lifted out cleanly and then divided into their separate parts – liver, lungs, stomach and entrails. The heart, as the hearth of the divine spark, would be left in place, as would the kidneys with their associations with water and thus with the Nile, the source of life.

After this edifying instruction, Pharaoh minutely examined the four Canopic jars that would receive his viscera. They stood on another smaller granite table close at hand. The jars were carved from gleaming translucent alabaster the colour of milk. Their stoppers were fashioned in the shapes of the animal-headed gods: Anubis the jackal, Sobeth the crocodile, Thoth the ibis-headed, Sekhmet with the head of a lioness. They would be the guardians of Pharaoh's divine parts until his awakening in the eternal life.

On the same granite table that held the Canopic jars, the embalmers had laid out their instruments and the full array of pots and amphorae that contained the natron salts, lacquers and other chemicals that they would use in the process. Pharaoh was fascinated by the glistening bronze scalpels which would disembowel him, and when the embalmer showed him the long pointed spoon that would be pushed up his nostrils to scoop out the contents of his skull, those cheesy curds over which I had pondered so long and fruitlessly, the king was fascinated and handled the grisly instrument with reverential awe.

Once the king had satisfied his curiosity at the mortuary table, my Lady Lostris directed his attention to the painted bas-relief engravings that covered the walls of the temple from floor to ceiling. The decorations were not yet completed, but were none the less quite striking in their design and execution. I had drawn most of the original cartoons with my own hand, and had closely supervised the others drawn by the palace artists. These had been traced on to the walls with charcoal sticks. Once the tracings were in place, I had corrected and perfected them in freehand. Now a company of master sculptors was engraving them into the sandstone blocks, while behind them a second company of artists was painting in the completed bas-relief.

The dominant colour I had chosen for these designs was blue in all its variation: the blue of the starling's wing, the blues of the sky and the Nile in the sunlight, the blues of the petals of the desert orchid and the shimmering blue of the river perch quivering in the fisherman's net. However, there were other colours as well, all those vibrant reds and yellows that we Egyptians love so well.

Pharaoh, accompanied closely by my Lord Intef, in his capacity of Keeper of the Royal Tombs, made a slow circuit of the high walls, examining every detail, and commenting on most of them. Naturally the theme I had chosen for the mortuary was the *Book of the Dead*, that detailed map and description of the route to the underworld that Pharaoh's shade must follow, and the depictions of all the trials and dangers he would confront along the way.

He paused for a long while before my drawing of the god Thoth, with his bird head and long curved ibis beak, weighing Pharaoh's disembodied heart on the scales against the feather of truth. Should the heart be impure, it would tip the scales against the feather, and the god would immediately toss it to the crocodile-headed monster that waited close at hand to devour it. Softly, the king quoted the protective mantra laid down in the book to shield himself from such a calamity, and then passed on to my next engraving.

It was almost noon before Pharaoh had completed his inspection of the mortuary temple and led the way out into the forecourt where the palace chefs had laid out a sumptuous open-air banquet.

'Come and sit here, where I can speak to you further on the matter of the stars!' Once again the king ignored precedent to place my Lady Lostris close to him at the banquet table, even moving one of his senior wives to make a place for her. During the meal he directed most of his conversation towards my mistress. She was now completely at her ease and kept the king and all those around her enthralled and merry with her wit and charm.

Of course, as a slave I did not have a seat at the table, nor could I even inveigle myself within range of my mistress to warn her to moderate her demeanour in the king's presence. Instead, I found myself a place on the pedestal of one of the granite lions, from where I could look down the length of the banquet table and watch everything that took place there. I was not the only observer, for my Lord Intef sat close to the king and yet withdrawn, watching it all with glittering, implacable eyes, like a handsome but deadly spider at the centre of his web.

At one stage of the meal a yellow-billed kite wheeled high over head, and uttered a screech, a sardonic and mocking cry. Hurriedly I made the sign against the evil eye, for who knows what god it was that had taken the form of the bird to muddle and confuse our petty endeavours?

After the midday meal it was customary for the court to rest for an hour or so, especially at this the hottest season of the year. However, Pharaoh was so wrought up that today he would have none of it.

'Now we will inspect the treasuries,' he announced. The guards at the doors of the first treasury stood aside and presented arms as the royal party approached, and the doors were swung open from within.

I had planned these six treasuries not only as store-rooms to hold the vast funerary treasure that Pharaoh had been collecting for the past twelve years, ever since his accession to the double throne, but also as workshops in which a small army of craftsmen and artisans was permanently employed in adding to that treasure.

The hall that we entered was the armoury that housed the collection of weapons and accoutrements of the battlefield and the wild chase, both practical and ceremonial, which the king would take with him into the afterworld. With my Lord Intef's concurrence, I had arranged for the craftsmen to be at their benches so that the king would have the opportunity of watching them at work.

As Pharaoh passed slowly down the row of benches, his questions were so astute and technical that those nobles and priests to whom he addressed himself could provide no answers, and they looked around frantically for someone who could. I was summoned hastily from the back of the crowd and pushed forward to face the king's interrogation.

'Ah, yes,' Pharaoh grimaced bleakly as he recognized me. 'It is none other than the humble slave who writes pageants and cures the sick. No one here seems to know the composition of this electrum wire that binds the stock of the war-bow that this man is making for me.'

'Gracious Pharaoh, the metal is a mixture of one part of copper to five parts of silver and four of gold. The gold is of the red variety found only in the mines of Lot in the western desert. No other gives the wire the same pliability or elasticity, of course.'

'Of course,' the king agreed wryly. 'And how do you make the strands so thin? These are no thicker than the hairs of my head.'

'Majesty, we extrude the hot metal by swinging it in a special pendulum that I designed for the purpose. Later we can watch the process in the gold foundry, if Your Majesty so wishes.'

Thus during the rest of the tour I was able to remain at the king's side and to deflect some of his attention away from Lostris, but I still could not find the opportunity to speak to her alone.

Pharaoh passed down the armoury to inspect the huge array of weapons and armour already in store. Some of these had belonged to his forefathers and had been employed in famous battles; others were newly manufactured and would never be used in war. All of them were magnificent, each a pinnacle of the armourer's art. There were helmets and breastplates of bronze and silver and gold, battle swords with ivory hilts set with precious stones, full-dress ceremonial uniforms of the commander-in-chief of each of the king's elite regiments, shields and bucklers in hippo-hide and crocodile-skin, all starred with rosettes of gold. It made a splendid array.

From the armoury we crossed the atrium to the furniture store, where a hundred cabinet-makers laboured with cedar and acacia and precious ebony wood to build the funeral furnishings for the king's long journey.

Very few substantial trees grow in our riparian valley, and wood is a scarce and costly commodity, worth very nearly its weight in silver. Almost every stick of it must be carried hundreds of leagues across the desert, or shipped downstream from those mysterious lands to the south. Here it was piled in extravagant stacks, as though it were commonplace, and the fragrance of fresh sawdust perfumed the hot air.

We watched while craftsmen inlaid the head-board of Pharaoh's bed with patterns of mother-of-pearl and woods of contrasting colour. Others decorated the arm-rests of the chairs with golden falcons and the back-rests of the padded sofas with the heads of silver lions. Not even the halls of the royal palace at Elephantine Island contained such delicate workmanship as would grace the rock cell of the king's tomb.

From the furniture treasury we passed on to the hall of the sculptors. In marble and sandstone and granite of a hundred differing hues, the sculptors whittled and chipped away with chisel and file so that a fine, pale dust hung in the air. The masons covered their noses and mouths with strips of linen on which the dust settled and their features were powdered white with the insidious stuff. Some of the men coughed behind their masks as they worked, a persistent, dry cough that was peculiar to their profession. I had dissected the corpses of many old sculptors who had worked thirty years and died at their trade. I found their lungs petrified and turned to stone in their bodies, thus I spent as little time as possible in the masons' shop lest I contract the same malady.

None the less, their products were wondrous to contemplate, statues of the gods and of Pharaoh himself that seemed to vibrate with life. There were life-sized images of Pharaoh seated on his throne or walking abroad, alive and dead, in his god form or in the shape of a mortal man. These statues would line the long causeway that led from the funerary temple on the valley floor up into the wall of black hills from which his final tomb was even at this moment being excavated. At his death the golden hearse, drawn by a train of one hundred white bullocks, was to bear his massive sarcophagus along that causeway to its final resting-place.

This granite sarcophagus, only partially completed, lay in the centre of the masons' hall. Originally it had been a single block of pink granite quarried from the mines at Assoun, and ferried down-river in a barge especially constructed for that purpose. It had taken five hundred slaves to haul it ashore and drag it over wooden rollers to where it now lay, an oblong of solid stone five paces long, three wide and three tall.

The masons had begun by sawing a thick slab from the top of it. Upon this granite lid a master mason was fashioning the likeness of the mummiform Pharaoh, with his arms crossed and the crook and flail gripped in his dead hands. Another team of masons was now engaged in hollowing out the interior of the main granite block to provide a nest into which the cluster of inner coffins would fit perfectly. Including the huge outer sarcophagus, there would be seven coffins in all, fitting one within the other like a child's puzzle-toy. Seven was, of course, one of the magical numbers. The innermost coffin would be of pure gold, and later we watched it being beaten out of the formless mass of metal in the hall of the goldsmiths.

It was this multiple sarcophagus, this mountain of stone and gold housing the king's wrapped corpse, that the great golden hearse would carry along the causeway to the hills, a slow journey that would take seven whole days to complete. The hearse would stop each night in one of the small shrines that were spaced at intervals along the causeway.

A fascinating adjunct to the hall of statues was the *ushabti* shop at the rear where the servants and retainers who would escort the dead king were being carved. These were perfect little manikins of wood representing all the grades and orders of Egyptian society who would work for the king in the hereafter, so as to enable him to maintain his estate and the style of his existence in the underworld.

Each *ushabti* was a delightfully carved wooden doll dressed in the authentic uniform of his calling and bearing the appropriate tools. There were farmers and gardeners, fishermen and bakers, beer-brewers and handmaidens, soldiers and tax-collectors, scribes and barbers, and hundreds upon hundreds of common labourers to perform every menial task and to go forward in the king's place if ever he were called upon by the other gods to work in the underworld.

At the head of this congregation of little figures there was even a grand vizier whose miniature features closely resembled those of my Lord Intef. Pharaoh picked out this manikin and examined him closely, turning him over to read the description on his back.

> My name is Lord Intef, grand vizier of the Upper Kingdom, Pharaoh's sole companion, three times the recipient of the Gold of Praise. I am ready to answer for the king.

Pharaoh passed the doll to my Lord Intef. 'Is your physique truly so muscular, my Lord Intef?' he asked with a smile just below the surface of his dour expression, and the grand vizier bowed slightly.

'The sculptor has failed to do me justice, Your Majesty.'

The last treasury that the king visited that day was the hall of the goldsmiths. The infernal glow of the furnaces cast a strange glow on the features of the jewellers as they worked with total concentration at their benches. I had coached them well. At the entrance of the royal entourage, the goldsmiths knelt in unison to make the triple obeisance to Pharaoh, and then rose and resumed their work.

Even in that large hall the heat of the furnace flames was so sulphurous as almost to stop the breath, and we were soon bathed in our own sweat. However, the king was so fascinated by the treasure displayed for him that he seemed not to notice the oppressive atmosphere. He went directly to the raised dais in the centre of the hall where the most experienced and skilful smiths were at work upon the golden inner coffin. They had perfectly captured Pharaoh's living face in the shimmering metal. The mask would fit exactly over his bandaged head. It was a divine image with eyes of obsidian and rock-crystal, and with the cobra-headed *uraeus* encircling the brow. I truly believe that no finer masterpiece of the goldsmith's art has ever been fashioned in all the thousand years of our civilization. This was the peak and the zenith. All the unborn ages might one day marvel at its splendour.

Even after Pharaoh had admired the golden mask from every angle, he seemed unable to tear himself too far from it. He spent the remainder of the day on the dais beside it, seated on a low stool while box after cedar-wood box of exquisite jewels were laid at his feet and the contents catalogued for him.

I cannot believe that such a treasure was ever before accumulated in one place at one time. To make a bald list of the items does not in the least way suggest the richness and the diversity of it all. None the less, let me tell you at the outset that there were six thousand four hundred and fifty-five pieces already in the cedar-wood boxes, and that each day more were added to the collection as the jewellers worked on tirelessly.

There were rings for Pharaoh's toes as well as his fingers; there were amulets and charms, and gold figurines of the gods and goddesses; there were necklaces and bracelets and pectoral medallions and belts on which were inlaid falcons and vultures and all the other creatures of the earth and the sky and the river; there were crowns and diadems studded with lapis lazuli and garnets and agate and carnelians and jasper and every gemstone that civilized man holds dear.

The artistry with which all this had been designed and manufactured eclipsed all that had been created over the preceding one thousand years. It is often in decline that a nation creates its most beautiful works of art. In the formative years of empire the obsession is with conquest and the building-up of wealth. It is only once this has been achieved that there is leisure and a desire to develop the arts, and – more importantly – rich and powerful men to sponsor them.

The weight of gold and silver already used in the manufacture of the hearse and the funeral mask and all the rest of this breathtaking collection of treasure was in excess of five hundred takhs; thus it would have taken five hundred strong men to lift it all. I had calculated that this was almost one-tenth of the total weight of these precious metals that had been mined in the entire one thousand years of our recorded history. All of this the king intended taking with him to the tomb.

Who am I, a humble slave, to question the price that a king was willing to pay for eternal life? Suffice it only to state that in assembling this treasure, while at the same time conducting the war against the Lower Kingdom, Pharaoh had, almost alone and unaided, plunged this very Egypt of ours into beggary.

No wonder, then, that Tanus in his declamation had singled out the depredation of the tax-collectors as one of the most terrible afflictions visited upon the populace. Between them and the robber bands that ravaged unchecked and unhindered through the countryside, we were all ruined and crushed under the financial yoke that was too heavy for any of us to bear. To survive at all, we had to evade the tax-collector's net. So as he set out to beggar us for his own aggrandizement, the king made criminals of us at the same moment. Very few of us, great or small, rich or poor, slept well at night. We lay awake dreading at any moment the heavy knock of the tax-collector upon the door.

Oh, sad and abused land, how it groaned beneath the yoke!

LAVISH quarters had been prepared in the necropolis in which the king would spend that night upon the west bank of the Nile, close to his own final resting-place in the gaunt black hills.

The necropolis, the city of the dead, was almost as extensive as Karnak itself. It was home to all those associated with the building and the care of the funerary temple and the royal tomb. There was a full regiment of the elite guard to protect the holy places, for the usurper in the north was as avaricious for treasure as was our own dear king, while the robber barons in the desert became each day bolder and more daring. The treasuries of the funerary temple were a sore temptation to every predator in the two kingdoms, and beyond.

In addition to the guards there were the companies of the craftsmen and the artisans and all their apprentices to house. I was responsible for the records of wages and rations, so I knew exactly how many there were. On the last pay-day their number had been four thousand eight hundred and eleven. Added to this, there were over ten thousand slaves employed upon the work.

I will not weary myself by listing the numbers of oxen and sheep that had to be slaughtered each day to feed them all, nor the cartloads of fish that were brought up from the Nile, nor the thousands of jars of beer that were brewed daily to slake the summer thirst of this multitude as they laboured under the watchful eye and the ready lash of the overseers.

The necropolis was a city, and in that city was a palace for the king. It was with relief that we moved into it to spend the night, for it had been a wearying day. But once again there was little rest for me.

I tried to reach my Lady Lostris, but it was almost as if there existed a conspiracy to keep me away from her. According to her little black maids, first she was at toilet, and after that she was in her bath, and then she was resting and could not be disturbed. Finally, as I still waited in the ante-chamber of her quarters, a summons reached me from her father, and I could linger no longer, but must hurry to my master.

As soon as I entered my Lord Intef's bedchamber he dismissed all the others in the room. When we were alone, he kissed me. I was once more surprised by his benevolence and disturbed by his excited manner. Seldom had I seen him in such mood, and always before it had adumbrated calamitous events.

'How often the gateway to power and fortune is found in the most unexpected place!' he laughed at me, and caressed my face. 'This time it lies between the thighs of a woman. No, my old darling, don't play the innocent. I know just what a cunning hand you have taken in all of this. Pharaoh has told me how you cajoled him into it by promising him a male heir to his line. By Seth, but you are the cunning one, are you not? Not a word to me of your design, but you schemed it all on your own account.'

He laughed again, and twisted a lock of my hair between his fingers. 'You must have divined my ultimate ambition all along, even though we have never discussed it openly. So you set out to achieve it for me. Of course, I should have you punished for your presumption,' he twisted the lock of hair until tears started into my eyes, 'but how can I be angry with you when you have placed the double crown within my grasp?' He released the tress of my hair and kissed me again. 'I have just come from the king's presence. In two days, at the culmination of the festival, he will announce his betrothal to my daughter, Lostris.' I felt a sudden darkness behind my eyes, and a chilly dew formed on my skin.

'The wedding will take place the same day, immediately after the closing ceremony of the festival, I saw to that. We don't want any delay in which something might happen to prevent it, do we?'

Such a swift royal wedding was unusual but not unheard of. When brides were chosen to seal a political union, or to consolidate the conquest of a new territory, the wedding often took place the very same day it was decided. Pharaoh Mamose the First, forefather of our present pharaoh, had married the daughter of a conquered Hurrian chieftain on the actual battlefield. However, such historical precedents were of little comfort to me now as I faced the bleak maturation of my worst fears.

My Lord Intef seemed not to notice my distress. He was too concerned with his own immediate interests, and he went on speaking. 'Before I gave my formal consent to the union, I prevailed on the king to concede that if she bore him a son then he would elevate my daughter to the rank of principal wife and queen consort.' He clapped his hands in unrestrained triumph.

'Of course, you realize what that means. If Pharaoh should die before my grandson is of age to rule, then I as his grandfather and closest male line would become regent—' He broke off suddenly and stared at me, and I knew him so well that I understood exactly what was running through his mind. He was bitterly regretting that indiscretion, nobody should ever have heard that thought expressed. It was purest treason. If Lostris bore a son to Pharaoh, then the father would not live long thereafter. We both understood that. My Lord Intef had given voice to regicide, and he was considering removing the only one who had heard it spoken, the humble slave, Taita. We both understood that clearly.

'My lord, I am only grateful that it has turned out the way I planned it. I admit now that I have worked deviously to place your daughter in the king's way, and that I described her to him as the mother of his future son. I used the pageant as a show-piece to focus his attention upon her. However, I could not bring myself to speak to you of such momentous affairs until they had been successfully engineered. But there still remains a great deal for us to do, before we can count ourselves secure—' and I began swiftly to extemporize a list of all that might go awry before he could gain control of the crown and the golden sceptre of Egypt. Tactfully I made it clear how much he still needed me if he were to achieve his design. I saw him relax as he followed my arguments, and I knew that at least for the immediate future I was safe.

It was some time before I could reasonably escape from his presence and hurry to warn my Lady Lostris of the terrible predicament in which I had placed her. However, before I reached her door I realized that my warning to her would serve no purpose other than to distress her to the point of dementia or even suicide. I could waste no further time if I were to prevent events from rushing to their tragic conclusion.

There was only one person to whom I could turn now.

I LEFT the necropolis and set off alone along the tow-path of the canal, back towards the river-bank where I knew that Tanus' squadrons were encamped. The moon was only three days from full and it lit the jagged hills of the western horizon with a cold yellow radiance and threw black shadows on the plain below.

As I hurried along, I recited to myself a full list of all the possible calamities and misfortunes that might befall Tanus, my Lady Lostris and myself in the days ahead. I was goading myself the same way that a black-maned desert lion lashes up his temper with the bony spike in the end of his tail before he charges at the huntsman. Thus I was in fulminating mood long before I reached the bank of the Nile.

I found Tanus' encampment without difficulty, hard by the bank of the Nile and the mouth of the canal. The ships of the squadron were anchored below the camp. The sentries challenged me and then, when they recognized me, led me to Tanus' tent.

Tanus was at late supper with Kratas and four other of his subordinate officers. He rose to greet me with a smile and offered me the beer tankard in his hand. 'This is such an unexpected pleasure, old friend. Sit down beside me and have a pull of my beer while my slave brings you a cup and platter. You look hot and out of sorts—'

I cut short these pleasantries by rounding on him furiously. 'To Seth with you, you great senseless oaf! Do you not understand what jeopardy you have placed us in? You and that flapping jawbone of yours! Do you have no thought for the safety and the well-being of my mistress?' In truth I had not meant to be so harsh on him, but once I had started, it seemed that I was unable to control my emotions, and all my fear and anxiety came tumbling out in a flood of invective. Not all that I accused him of was true or fair, but it made me feel better to have it out.

Tanus' expression changed and he held up one hand as though to shield himself. 'Whoa! You take me unawares. I am unarmed and unable to defend myself from such a murderous assault.' In front of his officers his tone was jocular, but his smile was thin as he seized my arm and steered me out of the tent into the darkness, and half-dragged me beyond the regimental lines into the open moonlit fields beyond. I was like a child in the grip of that right hand that was trained to wield the sword and draw the great bow Lanata.

'Now puke it up!' he ordered me grimly. 'What has happened to put you in such vile humour?'

I was still angry, but more afraid than angry, and my tongue took flight again. 'I have spent half my life trying to protect you from your own stupidity, and I am sick of it. Don't you understand anything of life?

Did you truly believe that you would be allowed to escape unscathed from the incredible folly into which you threw all of us last night?'

'Are you talking about my declamation at the pageant?' He looked puzzled, and released the crushing grip on my arm. 'How can you say it was folly? All my officers, and every other person I have spoken to since then, are all delighted with what I had to say—'

'You fool, don't you see that the opinions of all your officers and all your friends count for the price of a rotten fish in the scheme of things? Under any other ruler you would already be dead, and even this weak and vacillating old man of ours cannot afford to let you escape the consequences of your insolence. It is more than his throne is worth. There will be a bill for you to pay, Tanus, Lord Harrab. Horus knows, it will be a heavy bill.'

'You are speaking in riddles,' he snapped at me. 'I did the king a great service. He is surrounded by fawning toadies who feed him the lies they think he wants to hear. It was past time that he learned the truth, and I know in my heart that once he considers it, he will be grateful to me.'

My anger began to evaporate before his simple and steadfast belief in the triumph of good. 'Tanus, my dearest friend, what an innocent you are! No man is ever grateful for having the unpalatable truth rammed down his throat. But apart from that, you have played directly into the hands of my Lord Intef.'

'My Lord Intef?' he stared at me hard. 'What of my Lord Intef? You speak of him as though he were my enemy. The grand vizier was my father's dearest friend. I know that I can trust him to protect me. He swore an oath to my father as he lay on his death-bed—'

I could see that despite his sunny disposition and our friendship, he was becoming truly angry with me, probably for the first time in his life. I knew also that, although it was slow to rouse, Tanus' anger was something to fear.

'Oh, Tanus!' I curbed my own anger at last. 'I have been unfair to you. There is so much that I should have told you, and never did. Nothing was as you thought it. I was a coward, but I could not tell you that Intef was your own father's deadliest enemy.'

'How can this be true?' Tanus shook his head. 'They were friends, the dearest friends. My earliest memories are of them laughing together. My father told me that I could trust my very life to my Lord Intef.'

'The noble Pianki, Lord Harrab believed that, it is true. His faith cost him his entire fortune, and in the end his life which he placed in Intef's hands.'

'No, no, you must be mistaken. My father was the victim of a series of misfortunes—'

'And every one of those misfortunes was engineered by my Lord Intef. He envied your father for his virtues and his popularity, for his wealth and his influence with Pharaoh. He realized that Lord Harrab would be appointed grand vizier before him and he hated him for all these things.'

'I cannot believe you. I cannot bring myself to believe you.' Tanus shook his head in denial, and the last of my anger was snuffed out.

'I will explain it all to you, as I should have done long ago. I will give you all the proof you need. But there is no time for it now. You must trust me. My Lord Intef hates you even as he hated your father. Both you and my Lady Lostris are in danger. In danger of more than simply life itself, in danger of losing each other for ever.'

'But how is that possible, Taita?' He was confused and shaken by my words. 'I thought that my Lord Intef had agreed to our union. Have you not spoken to him, then?'

'Yes, I have spoken to him,' I cried, and I seized Tanus' hand and thrust it up under the back of my tunic. 'That was his reply. Feel the welts left by the lash! He had me flogged for even suggesting the marriage between you and my Lady Lostris. That is how much he hates you and your family.'

Tanus stared at me speechlessly, but I saw that he believed me at last, and so I was able to come to the subject that was dominating my thoughts more even than his intemperate speech, or the vendetta that the grand vizier had conducted so successfully against him over so many years.

'Hear me now, my dear friend, and brace yourself for the very worst tidings yet.' There was no other way to tell him, except as directly as Tanus would have told me. 'Far from agreeing to your marriage, my Lord Intef has this very night pledged his daughter's hand to another. She is to be married immediately to Pharaoh Mamose, and after she bears his first son she will become his principal wife and consort. The king will make the announcement himself at the end of the festival of Osiris. The marriage will take place that very same evening.'

Tanus swayed on his feet and in the moonlight his face turned ghostly pale. Neither of us could speak for a long while and then Tanus turned away from me and walked out alone into the field of standing corn. I trailed behind him, keeping him in sight, until at last he found an outcrop of black rock and seated himself upon it with the weary air of a very old man. I came up softly and seated myself below him. Deliberately I remained silent until he sighed and asked quietly, 'Has Lostris consented to this marriage?'

'Of course not. As yet she probably knows nothing about it. But do you think for one moment that her objections would count against the will of her father and the king? She will have no say in the matter.'

'What are we to do, old friend?'

Even in my distress I was grateful to him that he used the plural, including me, reassuring me of our friendship. 'There is one other probability that we must face,' I warned him. 'And that is that in the same speech that Pharaoh announces his betrothal to Lostris, he will order your imprisonment, or worse still, issue your death warrant. My Lord Intef has the king's ear and he will certainly put him up to it. In truth he would have good reason. You are certainly guilty of sedition.'

'I do not care to live without Lostris as my wife. If the king takes her from me, then he is welcome to my head as a marriage gift.' He said it simply, without histrionics, so that I had difficulty in feigning anger and putting the edge of contempt into my voice.

'You sound like a weak and pitiful old woman, giving herself up to the fates without a struggle. What a fine and undying love is yours, if you will not even fight for her!'

'How do you fight a king and a god?' Tanus asked quietly. 'A king to whom you have sworn allegiance, and a god who is as remote and as unassailable as the sun?'

'As a king he does not deserve your allegiance. You set that out clearly in your declamation. He is a weak and dithering old man who has divided the two kingdoms and brought our *Ta-Meri* bleeding to her knees.'

'And as a god?' Tanus again asked quietly, as though he were not really interested in the answer, although I knew him to be a devout and religious man, as so many great warriors are.

'A god?' I made my tone derisive. 'You have more of the godhead in your sword-arm than he has in all his soft little body.'

'Then what do you suggest?' he asked with deceptive mildness. 'What would you have me do?'

I drew a deep breath and then blurted it out. 'Your officers and your men would follow you to the gates of the underworld. The populace loves you for your courage and your honour—' I faltered, for his expression in the moonlight gave me no encouragement to continue.

He was silent for twenty beats of my racing heart and then he ordered me softly, 'Go on! Say what you have to say.'

'Tanus, you would make the noblest pharaoh that this *Ta-Meri*, this mother-land, has known for a thousand years. You with my Lady Lostris on the throne beside you could lead this land and this people back to greatness. Call out your squadrons, and lead your men down the causeway to where that unworthy pharaoh lies unprotected and vulnerable. By dawn tomorrow you could be ruler of the Upper Kingdom. By this time next year you could have defeated the usurper and have reunited the two kingdoms.' I leaped to my feet and faced him. 'Tanus, Lord Harrab, your destiny and that of the woman you love await you. Seize them in both your strong warrior's hands!'

'Warrior's hands, yes.' He held them up before my face. 'Hands that have fought for my mother-land and have protected her rightful king. You do me a disservice, old friend. They are not the hands of a traitor. Nor is this the heart of a blasphemer, that would seek to cast down and destroy a god, and take his place in the pantheon.'

I groaned aloud in my frustration. 'You would be the greatest pharaoh of the last five hundred years, and you need not proclaim your godhead, not if the idea offends you. Do it, I beseech you, for the sake of this very Egypt of ours, and of the woman that we both love!'

'Would Lostris still love a traitor as she loved a soldier and a patriot? I think not.' He shook his head.

'She would love you no matter what—' I began, but he cut me short.

'You cannot convince me. She is a woman of virtue and of honour. As a traitor and a thief, I would forfeit all right to her respect. What is of equal importance, I would never respect myself again, or consider myself worthy of her sweet love, if I did what you urge. Speak of it no more, as you value our friendship. I have no claim to the double crown, nor will I ever make such claim. Horus, hear me, and turn your face away from me if ever I should break this pledge.'

The matter was closed, I knew him so well, that great infuriating oaf, whom I loved with all my heart. He meant exactly what he said, and would cleave to it at any cost.

'Then what will you do, damn your stubborn heart?' I flared at him. 'Nothing that I say has any weight with you. Do you want to face this on your own? Are you suddenly too wise to heed my counsel?'

'I'm willing to take your counsel, just as long as it has sense to it.' He reached out and drew me down beside him. 'Come, Taita, help us. Lostris and I need you now as never before. Don't desert us. Help us find the honourable way.'

'I fear there is no such thing,' I sighed, my emotions bobbing and spinning like a piece of flotsam caught in the Nile flood. 'But if you will not seize the crown, then you dare not stay here. You must sweep Lostris up in your arms and bear her away.'

He stared at me in the moonlight. 'Leave Egypt? You cannot be serious. This is my world. This is Lostris' world.'

'No!' I reassured him. 'That is not what I had in mind. There is another pharaoh in Egypt. One who has need of warriors and honest men. You have much to offer such a king. Your fame in the Lower Kingdom is as great as it is here at Karnak. Place Lostris on the deck of the *Breath of Horus* and send your galley flying northwards. No other ship can catch you. In ten days, with this wind and current, you can present yourself at the court of the red pharaoh in Memphis, and swear allegiance to—'

'By Horus, you are determined to make a traitor of me yet,' he cut across me. 'Swear allegiance to the usurper, you say? Then what of the allegiance I swore to the true Pharaoh Mamose? Does that count for nothing with you? What kind of man am I, that can make the same oath to every king or renegade that crosses my path? An oath is not something to be bartered or reclaimed, Taita, it is for life. I gave my oath to the true Pharaoh Mamose.'

'That true Pharaoh is the same one who will marry your love, and will order the strangling-rope to be twisted around your neck,' I pointed out grimly, and this time even he wavered.

'You are right, of course. We should not stay in Karnak. But I will not make myself a traitor or break my solemn oath by taking up the sword against my king.'

'Your sense of honour is too complicated for me.' I could not keep the tone of sarcasm from my voice. 'All I know is that it bodes fair to make corpses of us all. You have told me what you will not do. Now tell me what you will do to save yourself, and rescue my Lady Lostris from a hateful fate.'

'Yes, old friend, you have every right to be angry with me. I asked for your help and advice. When you gave it freely, I scorned it. I beg your patience. Bear with me a while longer.' Tanus sprang to his feet and began to prowl about like the leopard in Pharaoh's menagerie, back and forth, muttering to himself, shaking his head and bunching his fists, as if to face an adversary.

At last he stopped in front of me. 'I am not prepared to play the traitor, but with a heavy heart I will force myself to play the coward. If Lostris agrees to accompany me, and only if she agrees, then I am prepared to take flight. I will take her away from this land we both love so well.'

'Where will you go?' I asked.

'I know that Lostris can never leave the river. It is not only her life and mine, but her god also. We must stay with Hapi, the river. That leaves only one direction open to us.' He raised his right arm, gleaming with muscle in the moonlight, and pointed south. 'We will follow the Nile southwards into the depths of Africa, into the land of Cush and beyond. We will go up beyond the cataracts into the unfathomed wilderness where no civilized man has ever gone before. There, perhaps, if the gods are kind, we will carve out another *Ta-Meri* for ourselves.'

'Who will be your companions?'

'Kratas, of course, and those of my officers and men who are game for the adventure. I'll address them tonight and give them the choice. Five ships, perhaps, and the men to work them. We must be ready to leave by dawn. Will you go back to the necropolis and fetch Lostris to me?'

'And me?' I asked quietly. 'You'll take me with you?'

'You?' He laughed at me. Now that the decision was made, his mood took flight, high as the bating falcon launched from the gloved fist. 'Would you truly give up your garden and your books, your pageants and your building of temples? The road will be dangerous, and the life hard. Do you truly want that, Taita?'

'I could not let you go alone, without my restraining hand upon your shoulder. What folly and danger would you lead my mistress into, if I were not there to guide you?'

'Come!' he ordered, and clapped me on the back. 'I never doubted that you would come with us. I know that Lostris would not leave without you, anyway. Enough chatter! We have work to do. First, we will tell Kratas and the others what we intend, and let them make their choice. Then you must go back to the necropolis and fetch Lostris, while I make the preparations for our departure. I'll send a dozen of my best men with you, but we must hurry. It is past midnight, and well into the third watch.'

Silly romantic fool that I am, but I was as excited as he was as we hurried back to the regiment's encampment below the temple and the causeway. I was so elated that my sense of danger was dulled. It was Tanus who picked out the sinister movement in the moonlight ahead of us and seized my arm and drew me beneath the shelter of a stunted carob tree.

'An armed party,' he whispered, and I saw the glint of bronze spearheads. There was a large band of men, thirty or forty, I estimated.

'Bandits, perhaps, or a raiding party from the Lower Kingdom,' Tanus growled, and even I was alarmed by the stealthy behaviour of the armed men ahead of us. They were not using the tow-path of the canal, but creeping through the open fields, spreading out to surround Tanus' encampment on the river-bank.

'This way!' With a soldier's eye for ground he picked out a shallow wadi that ran down to join the river, and he steered me to it. We jumped down and ran doubled over until we reached the perimeter of the camp. Then Tanus sprang out of the wadi and roused the camp with a bellow.

'Stand to arms! On me, the Blues! Form on me!' It was the rallying cry of the Blue Crocodile Guards, and it was taken up at once by the sergeants of each company. Instantly the camp boiled to life. The men sleeping round the fires leaped to their feet and snatched up their stacked weapons, while the officers' tents burst open as though the men within had never slept but had been waiting, tensed and ready for Tanus' command. Sword in hand, they raced to their stations, and I saw Kratas in the forefront.

I was amazed by the swiftness of their response, even though I knew that these were all battle-tested veterans. Before I could draw a dozen excited breaths they had formed in their phalanxes, with overlapping shields and long spears thrust outwards facing the darkness. The strange band out there in the night must have been as startled as I was by this militant display, for although I could still make out the vague shapes of many men and the gleam of their weapons in the gloom, the murderous charge we were all expecting from them never materialized.

The instant that Tanus had his formations in line, he ordered the advance. We had often debated the advantages of offensive action over defence, and now the massed squadrons moved forward, poised to break into a full charge at Tanus' command. It must have been a daunting spectacle to the men out there in the darkness, for a voice hailed us with an edge of panic in its tone. 'We are Pharaoh's men on the king's business. Hold your attack!'

'Hold hard, the Blues!' Tanus stopped the menacing advance, and then called back, 'Which pharaoh do you serve, the red usurper or the true pharaoh?'

'We serve the true king, the divine Mamose, ruler of the Upper and the Lower Kingdoms. I am the king's messenger.'

'Come forward, king's messenger, who creeps around in the night like a thief. Come forward and state your business!' Tanus invited him, but under his breath he told Kratas, 'Be ready for treachery. The smell of it is thick in the air. Have the fires built up. Give us light to see.'

Kratas gave the order and bundles of dry rushes were flung on to the watch-fires. The flames leaped up, and the darkness was thrown back. Into this ruddy glow the leader of the strange band stepped forward and shouted, 'My name is Neter, Best of Ten Thousand. I am the commander of Pharaoh's bodyguard. I bear the hawk seal for the arrest and detention of Tanus, Lord Harrab.'

'By Horus, he lies in his teeth,' Kratas growled. 'You are no felon with a warrant on your head. He insults you and the regiment. Let us at them and I'll thrust that hawk seal up between his buttocks.'

'Hold!' Tanus restrained him. 'Let us hear the fellow out.' He raised his voice again; 'Show us the seal, Captain Neter.'

Neter held it aloft. A small statuette in glistening blue faience, in the shape of the royal hawk. The hawk seal was the king's personal empowerment. The bearer acted with all the force and validity of Pharaoh himself. On pain of death, no man could question or hinder him in the course and commission of the royal business. The bearer answered only to the king.

'I am Tanus, Lord Harrab,' Tanus conceded. 'And I acknowledge the hawk seal.'

'My lord, my lord!' Kratas whispered urgently. 'Do not go to the king. It will mean your certain death. I have spoken to the other officers. The regiment is behind you, nay, the entire army is behind you. Give us the word. We'll make you king before the new day breaks.'

'My ear is deaf to those words,' Tanus told him softly, but with a weight of menace in his tone more telling than any growl or bellow. 'But only this once, Kratas, son of Maydum. Next time that you speak treason, I will deliver you to the king's wrath with my own hands.'

He turned from Kratas to me, and drew me a little to one side. 'It is too late, old friend. The gods frown on our enterprise. I must trust myself to the king's good sense. If he is truly a god, then he will be able to look into my heart and see for himself that it contains no evil.' He touched my arm, and that light gesture was to me more significant than the warmest embrace. 'Go to Lostris, tell her what has happened, tell her why it has happened. Tell her I love her and, whatever happens, I will do so through this life and the next. Tell her I will wait for her, to the ends of eternity, if need be.'

Then Tanus ran his sword back into the scabbard at his side and with empty hands stepped forward to meet the bearer of the hawk seal. 'I stand ready to do the king's bidding,' he said simply.

Behind him his own men hissed and growled, and rattled their swords against their bucklers, but Tanus turned and quieted them with a gesture and a frown, then strode out to confront Neter. The king's guard closed in around him, and then at a trot they moved away along the tow-path of the canal, back towards the necropolis.

The camp was filled with angry, bitter young men when I left it and followed Tanus and his escort at a discreet interval. When I reached the necropolis, I went directly to my Lady Lostris' quarters. I was distressed to find them deserted except for three of her little black maids, who in their usual lazy and lackadaisical manner were packing the last of their mistress's clothing into a cedar-wood chest.

'Where is your mistress?' I demanded, and the eldest and most insolent of them picked her nose as she gave me an airy reply, 'Where you can't reach her, eunuch.' The others tittered at her powers of repartee. They are all of them jealous of my favour with my Lady Lostris.

'Answer me straight, or I'll whip your insolent backside, you little baggage.' I had done so before, so she relented and muttered sulkily, 'They have taken her to Pharaoh's own harem. You have no influence there. Despite your missing balls, the guards will never let you pass amongst the royal women.'

She was right, of course, but still I had to make the attempt. My mistress would need me now, as much as she ever had in all her life.

As I feared, the guards at the gate to the king's harem were intractable. They knew who I was, but they had orders that no one, not even the closest members of Lostris' retinue, was to be allowed to go to her.

It cost me a gold ring, but the best I could achieve, even with that extravagance, was the promise that one of the guards would take my message to her. I wrote it out on a scrap of papyrus parchment, a bland little attempt at encouragement. I dared not relate all that had befallen us, nor the peril in which Tanus now stood. I could not even mention him by name, and yet I had to reassure her of his love and protection. As an investment, it was not worth the price I was forced to pay. Hardest of all to bear, I learned later that my gold had been entirely wasted and that she never received the message. Is there no man we can trust in this perfidious world?

I was not to see either Tanus or my Lady Lostris again until the evening of the last day of the festival of Osiris.

THE FESTIVAL ended in the temple of the god. It seemed once more that all the populace of Greater Thebes was packed into the courtyards. We were jammed so tightly that I could scarcely breathe in the press and the heat.

I was feeling wretched, for I had slept little for two nights in succession on account of the worry and the strain. Apart from the uncertainty of the fate of Tanus, I had been further burdened by my Lord Intef with the onerous duty of arranging the wedding ceremony of the king to his daughter, a duty that ran so contrary to my own desires. Added to which, I was parted from my mistress, and I could scarcely bear it. I do not know how I came through it. Even the slave boys were concerned about me. They declared that they had never seen my beauty so impaired, or my spirits so low.

Twice during Pharaoh's interminable speech from the throne, I found myself swaying on my feet, on the very point of fainting. However, I forced myself to hold on, while the king droned out the platitudes and half-truths with which he sought to disguise the true state of the kingdom and to placate the populace.

As was only to be expected, he never referred directly to the red pharaoh in the north or the civil war in which we were embroiled, except in such broad terms as 'these troubled times' or 'the defection and insurrection'. However, after he had spoken for a while it suddenly became plain to me that he was referring to every one of the issues that

Tanus had raised in his declamation, and attempting to find remedies for each of them.

It was true that he was doing so in his usual inept and vacillating fashion, but the simple fact that he had taken notice of what Tanus had said braced me and focused my wandering attention. I edged forward in the press of humanity until I had a better view of the throne, by which time the king was speaking about the impudence of the slaves and the disrespectful behaviour of the lower classes of our society. This was another issue that Tanus had mentioned, and I was amused to hear Pharaoh's solution. 'From henceforth the slave-owner may order fifty lashes to the insolent slave, without recourse to the magistrate to sanction such punishment,' he announced.

I smiled when I remembered how this same king had almost wrecked the state twelve years previously with another proclamation that ran in the exact opposite direction to this latest pronouncement. Still idealistic at his coronation, he had set out actually to abolish the ancient and honourable institution of slavery. He had wanted to turn every slave in Egypt loose and make him a free man.

Even at this remove in time, such folly is still incomprehensible to me. Though I am myself a slave, I believe that slavery and serfdom are the institutions on which the greatness of nations is founded. The rabble cannot govern itself. Government should be entrusted only to those born and trained to it. Freedom is a privilege, not a right. The masses need a strong master, for without control and direction anarchy would reign. The absolute monarch and slavery and serfdom are the pillars of a system that has allowed us to develop into civilized men.

It had been instructive to see how the slaves themselves had rebelled at the prospect of having freedom thrust upon them. I had been very young at the time, but I too had been alarmed at the prospect of being turned out from my warm and secure niche in the boys' quarters to scavenge on the rubbish-heaps for my next crust of bread with a horde of other freed slaves. A bad master is better than no master at all.

Of course, the kingdom had been thrown into chaos by this folly. The army had been upon the brink of revolt. Had the red pharaoh in the north seized the opportunity, then history might have been written differently. In the end our own pharaoh had hastily withdrawn his misguided decree of manumission, and managed to cling to his throne. Now here he was little more than a decade later proclaiming increased punishments for the impudence of a slave. It was so typical of this hesitant and muddling pharaoh that I pretended to mop my brow in order to cover the first smile that had creased my face in the last two days.

'The practice of self-mutilation for the purpose of avoiding military service will in future be strongly discouraged,' the king droned on. 'Any eligible young man claiming exemption under this dispensation is to appear before a tribunal of three army officers, at least one of whom is to be a centurion or officer of superior rank.' This time my smile was one of reluctant approval. For once Pharaoh was on the right tack. I would dearly love to see Menset and Sobek displaying their missing thumbs to some hardened old veteran of the river wars. What tender sympathy they could expect! 'The fine for such an offence will be one thousand rings of gold.' By Seth's bulging belly, that would make those two young dandies pause, and my Lord Intef would have to meet the fine on their behalf.

Despite my other concerns, I was beginning to feel a little more cheerful, as Pharaoh continued, 'From this day forward it will be an offence punishable by a fine of ten gold rings for a harlot to ply for trade in any public place, other than one set aside by the magistrates for that purpose.' This time I could barely prevent myself from laughing aloud. Vicariously Tanus would make puritans and honest men of all of Thebes. I wondered how the sailors and the off-duty soldiers would welcome this interference in their sporting lives. Pharaoh's period of lucidity had been short-lived. Any fool knows the folly of trying to legislate to man's sexual foibles.

Despite my doubts as to the wisdom of the king's remedies, still I found myself overtaken by a tremulous excitement. It was clear that the king had taken serious notice of every issue that Tanus had brought forward in his declamation. Could he now go on to condemn Tanus for sedition, I wondered?

However, Pharaoh had not finished yet. 'It has been brought to my notice that certain officials of the state have abused the trust and faith that I have placed in them. These officials, concerned with the collection of taxes and the handling of public funds, will be called upon to account for the monies placed in their care. Those found guilty of embezzlement and corruption will be summarily sentenced to death by strangulation.' The populace stirred and sighed with disbelief. Would the king truly seek to restrain his tax-collectors?

Then a single voice at the back of the hall cried out, 'Pharaoh is great! Long live Pharaoh!' The cry was taken up until the temple rang with the cheering. It must have been an unusual sound for the king to hear, that spontaneous applause. Even at the distance that I was from the throne I could tell that he enjoyed it. His lugubrious expression lightened and the double crown seemed to weigh less heavily on his head. I was certain that all of this must improve Tanus' chances of escaping the executioner's noose.

When the cheering eventually subsided, the king went on in his particular style to diminish everything that he had just achieved. 'My trusted grand vizier, the noble Lord Intef, will be placed in sole and absolute charge of this investigation of the civil service, with the full powers of search and arrest, of life and of death vested in him.' There was just the softest echo of applause to greet this appointment, and I used it to disguise a sardonic chuckle. Pharaoh was sending a hungry leopard to count the birds in his chicken-coop. What sport my Lord Intef would have amongst the royal treasuries, and what a redistribution of the nation's wealth would now take place with my master doing the counting, and milking the tax-collectors of their secret hoards of savings!

Pharaoh had a rare talent for capsizing or running the noblest sentiments and intentions on to the rocks with his blundering helmsmanship. I wondered what other folly he would manage to perpetrate before he finished speaking that day, and I did not have too long to wait.

'For some time it has been a cause for great concern to me that a state of lawlessness exists in the Upper Kingdom, placing the lives and the estates of honest citizens in the gravest jeopardy. I had made dispositions to deal with this state of affairs at an appropriate time. However, the matter was recently presented to me in such an untimely and ill-advised manner as to reek of sedition. It was done under the dispensation of the festival of Osiris. However, that dispensation does not cover treason or the crime of blasphemy, an attack on the person and divinity of the king.' Pharaoh paused significantly. It was clear that he was speaking of Tanus, and I was once again critical of his judgement. A strong pharaoh would not explain his motives to the people, or seek to win their approval for his actions. He would simply have pronounced sentence and have had done with the matter.

'I speak, of course, of Tanus, Lord Harrab who played the role of the great god Horus at the pageant of Osiris. He has been arrested for the crime of sedition. My councillors are divided on the subject of this person's guilt. There are those amongst them who wish him to pay the supreme penalty—' I saw my Lord Intef, standing below the throne, avert his gaze for a moment, and it confirmed what I already knew, that he was the chief amongst those who wished to see Tanus executed '—and there are those who feel that his declamation at the festival was indeed inspired by divine forces and that it was not the voice of Tanus, Lord Harrab, that spoke out on these matters, but the veritable voice of the god Horus. If this latter be the case, then clearly there can be no culpability to the mortal through whom the god chose to speak.'

The reasoning was fair, but what pharaoh worth the double crown would deign to explain it to this horde of common soldiers and sailors and farmers, of tradesmen and labourers and slaves, most of whom were still suffering from the ill-effects of too much wine and revelry? While I still pondered this, the king gave a command to the captain of his bodyguard who stood below the throne. I recognized him as Neter, the officer who had been sent to arrest Tanus. Neter marched away smartly and returned a moment later, leading Tanus from the sanctuary at the rear of the hall.

My heart leaped at the sight of my friend, and then with joy and hope I realized that he was unbound, there were no chains on his ankles. Although he carried no weapons and wore no badge of rank, and was dressed in a simple white kilt, he walked with his accustomed elastic step and jaunty grace. Apart from the healing scab on his forehead where Rasfer had struck him, he was unmarked. He had not been beaten or tortured, and I felt my optimism revived. They were not treating him as a condemned man.

A moment later all my hopes were dashed to pieces. Tanus made his obeisance before the throne, but when he rose to his feet again, Pharaoh looked down upon him severely and spoke in a voice without pity. 'Tanus, Lord Harrab, you stand accused of treason and sedition. I find you guilty of both these crimes. I sentence you to death by strangulation, the traditional punishment of the traitor.'

As Neter placed the noose of linen rope around Tanus' neck to mark him as one condemned to die, a groan went up from the people who watched. A woman wailed, and soon the temple was filled with cries of lamentation and the ululation of mourning. Never before had such a display accompanied the passing of the death sentence. Nothing could demonstrate more clearly the love which the populace bore Tanus. I wailed with them and the tears broke from my lids and streamed down my face to pour like a waterfall on to my chest.

The bodyguards fell upon the crowd, using the butts of their long spears in an attempt to beat the mourners into silence. It was in vain, and I screamed out over their heads, 'Mercy, bountiful Pharaoh! Mercy for the noble Tanus!'

One of the guards struck me on the side of the head, and I fell to the ground half-stunned, but my cry was taken up. 'Mercy, we beseech you, oh divine Mamose!' It took all the efforts of the guards to restore some order, but still a few of the women were sobbing.

Only when Pharaoh raised his voice again were we at last silent, so that every one of us heard his next pronouncement. 'The condemned man has complained of the lawless state of the kingdom. He has called upon the throne to stamp out the bands of robbers who ravage the land. The condemned man has been called a hero, and there are those who say that he is a mighty warrior. If this be true, then he himself would be better suited than any other to carry out those measures he demands.'

Now the people were confused and silent, and I struck the tears from my face with my forearm as I strained to catch the next word. 'Therefore, the sentence of death is deferred for two years. If the condemned man was truly inspired by the god Horus when he made his seditious speech, then the god will assist him in the task I now place upon him.'

The silence was profound. None of us seemed able to understand what we were hearing, although hope and despair filled my soul in equal measure.

At a signal from the king one of the ministers of the crown stepped forward and offered Pharaoh a tray on which lay a tiny blue statuette. Pharaoh held it aloft and announced, 'I issue to Lord Harrab the hawk seal of the pharaohs. Under the auspice of the seal he may recruit all the men and materials of war that he deems necessary to his task. He may employ whatever means he chooses, and no man may prevent him. For two full years he is the king's man, and he answers only to the king. At the end of that time, on the last day of the next festival of Osiris, he will come before the throne once again, wearing the noose of death around his neck. If he has failed in his task, the noose will be tightened and he will be strangled to death on the spot where he now stands. If he has completed his task, then I, Pharaoh Mamose, will lift the noose from around his neck with my own hands and replace it with a chain of gold.'

Still none of us could speak or move, and we stared in fascination as Pharaoh made a gesture with the crook and the flail. 'Tanus, Lord Harrab, I charge you with the task of eradicating from the Upper Kingdom of Egypt the outlaws and robber bands that are terrorizing this land. Within two years you will restore order and peace to the Upper Kingdom. Fail me at your peril.'

A roar went up from the congregation, wild as the sound of storm surf beating on a rocky shore. Though they cheered unthinkingly, I lamented. The task that Pharaoh had set was too great for any mortal man to achieve. The cloud of death had not been lifted from over Tanus. I knew that in two years from today he would die on the very same spot where he now stood so young and proud and tall.

FORLORN AS a lost waif, she stood alone in the midst of the multitude, with the river that was her patron god at her back and before her a sea of faces.

The long linen shift that fell to her ankles was dyed with the juice of shellfish to the colour of the finest wine, a colour that proclaimed her as a virgin bride. Her hair was loose. It flowed down on to her shoulders in a soft dark tide that shone in the sunlight as though with an inner fire. On those shining locks she wore the bridal wreath woven from the long stems of the water-lily. The blossoms were an unearthly cerulean blue, with throats of the clearest gold.

Her face was as white as freshly ground cornflour. Her eyes were so large and dark that they reminded me heartbreakingly of the little girl whom, in years gone by, I had so often woken from the grip of nightmare, and lit the lamp and sat beside her cot until she slept again. This time I could not help her, for the nightmare was reality.

I could not go to her, for the priests and Pharaoh's guard surrounded her, as they had all these days past, and they would not let me near unto her. She was lost to me for ever, my little girl, and I could not support the thought of it.

The priests had built the wedding canopy of river rushes on the bank above the Nile, and my Lady Lostris waited beneath it for her bridegroom to come to claim her. At her side stood her father, with the Gold of Praise glittering around his neck and the smile of the cobra on his lips.

The royal bridegroom came at last, to the solemn beat of the drum and the bleat of gazelle-horn trumpets, and to me this wedding march was the saddest sound in all the earth.

Pharaoh wore the *nemes* crown and carried the sceptre, but behind the pomp and the regalia, he was still a little old man with a pot-belly and a sad face. I could not help but think of the other bridegroom who might have stood under the canopy beside my mistress, if only the gods had been kinder.

Pharaoh's ministers and high officials attended him so closely that my view of my mistress was obscured. Despite the fact that it was I who had been forced to arrange every detail of it, I was excluded from the wedding, and I had only glimpses of my Lady Lostris during the ceremony.

The high priest of Osiris washed the hands and the feet of both the bride and the groom with water freshly drawn from the Nile to symbolize the purity of their union. Then the king broke a morsel from the ritual corn-loaf and offered it to his young bride as a pledge. I glimpsed my mistress's face as he placed the crust between her lips. She could neither chew nor swallow but stood with it in her mouth as though it were a stone.

Once again she was hidden from my view, and it was only when I heard the crunch of the empty jug that had contained the marriage wine as the bridegroom shattered it with a blow of his sword, that I knew that it was done and that Lostris was for ever more beyond the reach of Tanus' arms.

The crowd beneath the canopy opened and Pharaoh led his newest bride forward to the front of the platform to present her to the people. They showed their love for Lostris in a chorus of adulation that went on and on until my ears rang and my head swam.

I wanted to escape from the press and go to find Tanus. Although I knew that he had been released from detention and was once again at liberty, he had not attended the ceremony. He was perhaps the only man in Thebes who had not come to the riverside today. I knew that wherever he might be, he stood in as dire need of me as I was of him. The only small comfort that either of us might find on this tragic day was with each other. However, I could not tear myself away. I had to see it out to the final harrowing moment.

At last my Lord Intef came forward to take his farewell of his daughter. As the crowd subsided into silence he embraced her.

Lostris was like a corpse in his embrace. Her arms hung limply at her side, and her face was pale as death. Her father released her, but kept a grip on her hand as he turned and faced the congregation to offer the ritual gift to his daughter. Traditionally, this gift was made over and above the dowry that went directly to the bridegroom. However, only the nobility observed this custom, which was designed to give the bride an independent income.

'Now that you go from my house and from my protection to the house of your husband, I bestow upon you the gift of parting, that you will remember me always as the father that loved you.' The words were inappropriate to the circumstances, I thought bitterly. My Lord Intef had never loved another living soul. However, he continued the ancient formula, as though the sentiments were his own. 'Ask any boon of me, my beloved child. I will refuse you nothing on this joyous day.'

It was the usual practice for the extent of the gift to be agreed in private between father and daughter before the ceremony. In this case, however, my Lord Intef had told his daughter unequivocally what she was entitled to ask for. He had done me the honour of discussing the matter with me the previous day, before informing Lostris of his decision. 'I don't want to be extravagant, but on the other hand I do not wish to appear parsimonious in Pharaoh's eyes,' he had mused. 'Let us say, five thousand gold rings and fifty feddan of land – not on the riverfront, mind you.'

He had, with my prompting, finally decided on five thousand gold rings and one hundred feddan of prime irrigable land as being a suitable gift for a royal wedding. On his instruction I had already drawn up the deed of grant for the land, and set aside the gold from a secret store that my master kept out of the way of the tax-collectors.

The matter was settled. It remained only for Lostris to give voice to the request before her groom and all the wedding guests. But she stood pale and silent and withdrawn, seeming neither to see nor hear what was going on around her.

'Speak up, my child. What is it that you desire from me?' My Lord

Intef's tones of paternal love were becoming strained, and he shook his daughter's hand to rouse her. 'Come, tell your father what he can do to make this happy day complete.'

My Lady Lostris stirred as though coming awake from a dreadful dream. She looked about her and her tears welled up and threatened to break over her quivering eyelids. She opened her mouth to speak, but what came from her throat was the weak little cry of a wounded bird. She closed her lips again and shook her head speechlessly.

'Come, child. Speak out.' My Lord Intef was having difficulty sustaining an expression of paternal affection. 'Name your marriage gift, and I will give it to you, whatever it is that you desire.'

The effort that Lostris had to make was apparent to me, even though I stood so far from her, but this time when she opened her mouth her request rang out over our heads, clear as the music of the lyre. There could not have been a soul in the crowd who did not hear every word of it.

'For my gift give me the slave, Taita!'

My Lord Intef reeled back a pace as though she had thrust a dagger into his belly. He stared at her aghast, his mouth opening and closing without a sound escaping. Only he and I knew the value of the gift that Lostris had demanded. Not even he, with the store of wealth and treasure that he had garnered over a lifetime, could afford such a payment.

He recovered swiftly. His expression was once more calm and benign, though his lips stretched tight. 'You are too restrained, my darling daughter. A single slave is no fitting gift for Pharaoh's bride. Such stinginess is not in my nature. I would rather you accepted a gift of real value, five thousand rings of gold and—'

'Father, you have always been too generous with me, but I want only Taita.'

My Lord Intef smiled a white smile, white teeth, white lips and white rage. While he still stared at Lostris I could see that his mind was racing.

I was the most valuable of all his possessions. It was not simply my wide range of extraordinary talents that made up the full measure of my worth to him. Even more, it was that I knew intimately every convoluted thread of the intricate tapestry of his affairs. I knew every informer and spy in his network, every person whom he had ever bribed and who had bribed him. I knew which favours were outstanding on each account, which favours remained to be settled, and which grudges were still to be paid off.

I knew all his enemies, a long list; and I knew those he counted his friends and allies, a much shorter list. I knew where every nugget of his vast treasure was hidden, who were his bankers and his agents and his nominees, and how he had concealed the ownership of great tracts of land and stores of precious metals and gemstones in the legal labyrinth of deeds and titles and servitudes. All of this was information that would delight the tax-collectors and cause Pharaoh to revise his opinion of his grand vizier.

I doubted that my Lord Intef himself could remember and trace all his wealth without my assistance. He could not properly order and control his sprawling, shadowy empire without me, for he had kept himself aloof and separated from the most unsavoury aspects of it. He had preferred to send me to take care of those details which, if discovered, might incriminate him.

So it was that I knew a thousand dark secrets, and I knew of a thousand fearful deeds, of embezzlement and extortion, of robbery and bloodiest murder, all of which taken together could destroy even a man as powerful as the grand vizier.

I was indispensable. He could not let me go. And yet, before Pharaoh and the entire population of Thebes, he could not deny Lostris her request.

My Lord Intef is a man full of ire and hatred. I have seen such rage in him that must have made Seth, the god of anger, start up and take notice. But I had never seen such fury as now that his own daughter had him cornered.

'Let the slave Taita stand forward,' he called, and I saw that it was a ruse for him to gain a respite. I pushed my way as swiftly as I was able to the foot of the wedding platform, to give him as little time as possible to plan his next mischief.

'I am here, my lord,' I cried, and he stared down at me with those deadly eyes. We have been together so long that he can speak to me with a look almost as clearly as with the spoken word. He stared at me in silence until my heart was racing and my fingers fluttered with fear, then at last he said in soft, almost affectionate tones, 'Taita, you have been with me since you were a child. I have come to regard you as a brother more than as a slave. Still, you have heard my daughter's request. I am by nature a fair and kind man. After all the years it would be inhuman of me to discard you against your wishes. I know that it is unusual for a slave to be given a say in his own disposal, but then your circumstances are indeed unusual. Choose, Taita. If you wish to stay in your home, the only home you have ever known, then I cannot find the heart to send you away. Not even at the request of my own daughter.' He never took his eyes off me, those terrible yellow eyes. I am not a coward but I am careful of my safety. I realized that I was staring into the eyes of death, and I could not find my voice.

I tore my gaze from his, and looked towards my Lady Lostris. There was such appeal there, such loneliness and terror, that my own safety counted for nothing. I could not desert her now, not at any price or under any threat.

'How can a poor slave deny the wish of Pharaoh's wife? I am ready to do the bidding of my new mistress,' I cried out at the top of my lungs, and I hoped that my voice had a manly ring to it and was not as shrill as it sounded in my own ears.

'Come, slave!' my new mistress ordered. 'Take your place behind me.'

As I mounted the platform, I was forced to pass close to my Lord Intef. His white, stiff lips barely moved as he spoke for my ears alone. 'Farewell, my old darling. You are a dead man.'

I shuddered as though a poisonous cobra had slid across my path and I hurried to take my place in the retinue of my mistress, as though I truly believed that I could find safety in her protection.

I STAYED close to Lostris during the rest of the ceremony and I waited on her personally at the wedding feast, hovering at her elbow and trying to make her eat a little of the meats and fine fare that was spread before her. She was so wan and sickly that I was certain that she had eaten nothing in the last two days, not since her betrothal and the condemnation of Tanus.

In the end I succeeded in getting her to take a little watered wine, but that was all. Pharaoh saw her drink and thought that she was toasting him. He lifted his own gold chalice, and smiled at her over the rim as he returned the toast, and the wedding guests cheered the couple delightedly.

'Taita,' she whispered to me as soon as the king's attention was diverted by the grand vizier who sat at his other hand, 'I fear that I am going to vomit. I cannot stay here another moment. Please take me back to my chamber.'

It was an impudence and a scandal, and had I not been able to adopt the role of surgeon, I could never have achieved it, but I was able to creep on my knees to the king's side, and to whisper to him without causing an undue comment amongst the wedding guests, most of whom were well along in wine at this stage.

As I grew to know him better, I found that Pharaoh was a kindly man, and this was the first proof he gave me of it. He listened to my explanations and then clapped his hands and addressed the guests. 'My bride will go to her chamber now to prepare for the night ahead,' he told them, and they leered and greeted the announcement with lewd comment and lascivious applause.

I helped my mistress to her feet, but she was able to make her obeisance to the king and leave the banquet hall without my support. In her bedchamber she threw up the wine she had drunk into the bowl that I held for her, and then she collapsed upon the bed. The wine was all her stomach contained and my suspicion that she had been starving herself was confirmed.

'I don't want to live without Tanus.' Her voice was weak, but I knew her well enough to recognize that her will was as strong as ever.

'Tanus is alive,' I tried to console her. 'He is strong and young and will live for another fifty years. He loves you and he promises to wait for you to the end of time. The king is an old man, he cannot live for ever—'

She sat up on the fur bedcover and her voice became stern and determined. 'I am Tanus' woman and no other man shall have me. I would rather die.'

'We all die in the end, mistress.' If only I could distract her for the first few days of this marriage, I knew I could see her through. But she understood me too well.

'I know what you are up to, but all your pretty words will do you no good. I am going to kill myself. I order you to prepare a draught of poison for me to drink.'

'Mistress, I am not versed in the science of poison.' It was a forlorn attempt, and she crushed it effortlessly.

'Many is the time that I have seen you give poison to a suffering animal. Do you not remember your old dog, the one with abscesses in its ears, and your pet gazelle that was mauled by a leopard? You told me that the poison was painless, that it was the same as going to sleep. Well, I want to go to sleep and be embalmed and go on to the other world to wait for Tanus there.'

I had to try other persuasion. 'But what about me, mistress? You have only this day taken possession of me. How can you abandon me? What will become of me without you? Have pity on me.' I saw her waver, and I thought I had her, but she lifted her chin stubbornly.

'You will be all right, Taita. You will always be all right. My father will take you back gladly after I am dead.'

'Please, my little one,' I used the childhood endearment in a last attempt to cajole her, 'let us talk of this in the morning. Everything will be different in the sunlight.'

'It will be the same,' she contradicted me. 'I will be parted from Tanus, and that wrinkled old man will want me in his bed to do horrid things to me.' Her voice was raised so that the other members of the king's harem might hear every word. Fortunately most of them were still at the wedding feast, but I trembled at the thought of her description of him being relayed to Pharaoh.

Her voice became shriller with the edge of hysteria in it. 'Mix me the poison draught now, this instant, while I watch you do it. I order you to do it. You dare not disobey me!' This command was so loud that even the guards at the outer gates must be able to hear her, and I dared not argue longer.

'Very well, my lady. I will do it. I must fetch my chest of medicine from my rooms.'

When I returned with the chest under my arm, she was up from the bed and pacing around her chamber with glittering eyes in that pale, tragic face.

'I am watching you. Don't try any of your tricks on me now,' she warned me, as I prepared the draught from the scarlet glass bottle. She knew that colour warned of the lethal contents.

When I handed the bowl to her, she showed no fear, and paused only to kiss my cheek. 'You have been both father and loving brother to me. I thank you for this last kindness. I love you, Taita, and I shall miss you.'

She lifted the bowl in both hands as though it were a wassail cup rather than a fatal potion.

'Tanus, my darling,' she toasted him with it, 'they shall never take me from you. We shall meet again on the far side!' And she drained the bowl at a swallow, then dropped it to shatter on the floor. At last, with a sigh, she fell back upon the bed.

'Come, sit beside me. I am afraid to be alone when I die.'

Taken on her empty stomach, the effect of the draught was very rapid. She had only time to turn her face to me and whisper, 'Tell Tanus again how much I loved him. Unto the portals of death, and beyond.' Then her eyes closed and she was gone.

She lay so still and pale that for a moment I was truly alarmed, afraid that I had misjudged the strength of the powder of the Red Shepenn which I had substituted for the essence of the deadly Datura Pod. It was only when I held a bronze hand-mirror to her mouth that the clouded surface reassured me she still breathed. I covered her gently, and tried to convince myself that in the morning she would be resigned to the fact that she was still alive, and that she would forgive me.

At that moment there was a peremptory knock upon the door of the outer chamber and I recognized the voice of Aton, the royal chamberlain, demanding entrance. He was another eunuch, one of the special brotherhood of the emasculated, so I could count him as a friend. I hurried through to greet him.

'I have come to fetch your little mistress to the king's pleasure, Taita,' he told me, in high girlish tones so incongruous with such a large frame. He had been gelded before puberty. 'Is she ready?'

'There has been a small mishap,' I explained, and led him through to see Lostris for himself.

He puffed out his rouged cheeks with consternation when he saw her condition. 'What can I tell Pharaoh?' he cried. 'He will have me beaten. I will not do it. The woman is your responsibility. You must answer to the king, and stand before his wrath.'

It was not a duty that I relished, but Aton's distress was real, and at least I had my medical status to afford me some protection from the king's frustrated expectations. Reluctantly, I agreed to accompany him to the royal bedchamber. However, I made sure that there was one of the older and more reliable slave maids in attendance in my mistress's outer chamber before I left her alone.

Pharaoh had removed his crown and his wig. His head was shaved as bare and white as an ostrich egg. The effect startled even me, and I wondered how my mistress would have responded to the sight. I doubt that it would have raised either her ardour or her opinion of him.

The king seemed as startled to see me as I was to see him. We stared at each other for a moment before I fell to my knees and made my obeisance.

'What is this, Taita the slave? I sent for another—'

'Merciful Pharaoh, on behalf of the Lady Lostris I come to beg your understanding and indulgence.' I launched into a harrowing description of my Lady Lostris' condition, larding it with obscure medical terms and explanations that were intended to divert the royal appetite. Aton stood beside me, nodding in emphatic corroboration of all I had to say.

I am sure that it would not have worked with a younger and more vigorous bridegroom, ready and rearing to get to the business, but Mamose was an old bull. It would have been impossible to tally all the lovely women who over the past thirty years or so had enjoyed his services. In single file they would probably have encircled the city of Thebes of a hundred gates, possibly more than once.

'Your Majesty,' Aton interrupted my explanations at last, 'with your permission, I will fetch you another female companion for the night. Perhaps the little Hurrian with the unusual control of her—'

'No, no,' the king dismissed him. 'There will be plenty of time for it when the child is recovered from her indisposition. Leave us now, chamberlain. There is some other matter that I wish to discuss with the doctor – I mean, with this slave.'

As soon as we were alone the king lifted his shift to display his belly. 'What do you think is the cause of this, doctor?' I examined the rash that adorned his protuberant paunch, and found it to be an infestation of the common ringworm. Some of the royal women washed less frequently than is desirable in our hot climate. I have noted that filth and the contagious itch go together. The king had probably contracted the infection from one of them.

'Is it dangerous? Can you cure it, doctor?' Fear makes commoners of us all. He was deferring to me now as would any other patient.

With his permission, I went to my quarters to fetch my medicine chest, and when I returned, I ordered him to lie on the ornate gold and ivory marquetry bed while I massaged an ointment into the inflamed red circle of skin on his belly. The ointment was of my own concoction and would heal the rash within three days, I assured him.

'In a great measure you are responsible for the fact that I have married this child who is your new mistress,' he told me as I worked. 'Your ointment may cure my rash, but will your other treatment provide me with a son?' he demanded. 'These are troubled times. I must have an heir before I am another year older. The dynasty is in jeopardy.'

We physicians are always reluctant to guarantee our cures, but then so is the lawyer and the astrologer. While I procrastinated he gave me the escape I was searching for.

'I am no longer a young man, Taita. You are a doctor and I can tell you this. My weapon has been in many a fierce battle. Its blade is no longer as keen as once it was. Of late it has failed me when I most had need of it. Do you have something in that box of yours that would stiffen the wilting stem of the lily?'

'Pharaoh, I am pleased that you have discussed this with me. Sometimes the gods work in mysterious ways—' we both made the sign to avert evil before I went on, 'your first congress with my virgin mistress must be perfectly executed. Any faltering, any bending from our purpose, any failure to raise on high the royal sceptre of your manhood, will frustrate our efforts. There will be only one opportunity, the first union must be successful. If we have to try again there will be the danger of your fathering yet another female.' My medical grounds for this prognosis were rather insubstantial. Nevertheless, we both looked grave, he graver than I did.

I held up my forefinger. 'Had we made the attempt tonight, and—' I said no more, but let my forefinger droop suggestively, and shook my head. 'No, we are fortunate to have been given another chance by the gods.'

'What must we do?' he demanded anxiously, and I was silent for a long while, kneeling in deep thought beside his bed.

It was difficult not to let my relief and satisfaction become apparent. Within the first day of my mistress's marriage, I was already working my way into a position of influence with the king, and I had been offered a perfect excuse for keeping her maidenhead intact for at least a little longer, long enough perhaps for me to be able to prepare her for the brutal shock of her first act of procreation with a man whom she did not love and who was, indeed, physically distasteful to her. I told myself that with clever management of the situation, I might be able to draw out this period of grace indefinitely.

'Yes indeed, Your Majesty, I can help you, but it will take some time. It will not be as easy as curing this rash.' My mind was racing. I had to wring every drop out of this sponge. 'We will have to go on to a very strict diet.'

'No more bull's balls, I beseech you, doctor.'

'I think you have had enough of those now. However, we will need to warm your blood and sweeten your generative fluids for the fateful attempt. Goat's milk, warm goat's milk and honey three times a day, and of course the special potions I will prepare for you from the horn of the rhinoceros and the root of the mandrake.'

He looked relieved. 'You are certain this will work?'

'It has never failed before, but there is one other measure that is essential.'

'What is that?' His relief evaporated, and he sat up and peered at me anxiously.

'Complete abstinence. We must allow the royal member to rest and regain its full strength and force once again. You must forsake your harem and all its pleasures for a while.' I said this with the dogmatic air of the physician that cannot be gainsaid, for it was the one sure way to ensure that my Lady Lostris would remain untouched. However, I was worried by what his reaction would be. He could conceivably have flown into a rage at the thought of being denied his conjugal pleasures. He might have rejected me, and I could have lost all the advantage that I had so newly won. But I had to take the risk for the benefit of my mistress. I had to protect her just as long as I was able.

The king's reaction surprised me. He simply lay back on his headrest and smiled complacently to himself. 'For how long?' he asked quite cheerfully, and I was struck by the realization that my strictures had come as a relief to him. For me, to whom the act of love with a beautiful woman would always be an unattainable and elusive dream, it took an immense effort to understand that Pharaoh was content to be relieved of a once pleasurable duty that, by reason of being so often performed, had become onerous.

There must have been at least three hundred wives and concubines in his harem at that time, and some of those Asian women were notorious for their insatiable appetites. I tried to sympathize with the effort that it must require to act like a god night after night, and year after year. The prospect did not daunt me as the actuality seemed to have wearied the king.

'Ninety days,' I said.

'Ninety days?' he repeated thoughtfully. 'Nine Egyptian weeks of ten days each?'

'At least,' I said firmly.

'Very well.' He nodded without rancour and changed the subject easily.

'My chamberlain tells me, doctor, that apart from your medical skills, you are also one of the three most eminent astrologers in this very Egypt of ours?'

I wondered why my friend the chamberlain had qualified his assertion. For the life of me I could not think who the other two might be, but I inclined my head modestly. 'He flatters me, Your Majesty, but perhaps I do have some little knowledge of the heavenly bodies.'

'Cast a horoscope for me!' he ordered, sitting up eagerly.

'Now?' I asked with surprise.

'Now!' he agreed. 'Why not? For on your orders there is nothing that I should rather be doing at this moment.' That unexpected smile of his was really quite endearing, and despite what he meant to Tanus and my mistress, I found myself liking him.

'I shall have to fetch some of my scrolls from the palace library.'

'We have all night,' he pointed out. 'Fetch whatever you need.'

The exact time and date of the king's birth were well documented and I had in the scrolls all the observations of the movements of the heavenly bodies made by fifty generations of astrologers before me. While the king watched avidly, I made the first cast of the royal horoscope, and before I had half finished it I saw the character of the man, as I had observed it, perfectly endorsed by his stars. The great red wandering star, that we know as the eye of Seth, dominated his destiny. It was the star of conflict and uncertainty, of confusion and war, of sadness and misfortune, and in the end of violent death.

But how could I tell him all these things?

I extemporized and put together a scantily veiled résumé of the well-documented facts of his life, and laced these with a few less well-known details that I had gathered from my spies, one of whom was the royal chamberlain. Then I followed with the usual assurances of good health and long life that every client wants to hear.

The king was impressed. 'You have all the skills that your reputation made me expect.'

'Thank you, Your Majesty. I am pleased that I have been able to be of service.' I began to gather up my scrolls and my writing instruments preparatory to taking my leave. It was very late by now. From the darkness beyond the palace walls I had already heard the first cockerel crow.

'Wait, Taita. I have not given you permission to leave. You have not told me what I really want to know. Will I have a son and will my dynasty survive?'

'Alas, Pharaoh, those matters cannot be predicted by the stars. They can give only the general inclination of your fate, and the overall direction that your life will take, without making clear such details—'

'Ah, yes,' he interrupted me, 'but there are other means of seeing into the future, are there not?' I was alarmed by the direction in which his questions were leading, and I attempted to head him off, but he was determined.

'You interest me, Taita, and I have made enquiry about you. You are an adept of the Mazes of Ammon-Ra.' I was distressed. How had he found this out? Very few knew of this esoteric gift of mine, and I wanted it to remain thus. However, I could not blatantly deny it, so I remained silent.

'I saw the Mazes hidden at the bottom of your medicine chest,' he said, and I was relieved that I had not attempted to deny my gift and been caught out in the lie. I shrugged with resignation, for I knew what was coming.

'Work the Mazes for me, and tell me if I am to have an heir and whether or not my dynasty will survive,' he ordered.

A horoscope is one thing; it requires only a knowledge of the configuration of the stars and their properties. Some little patience, and the correct procedure will result in a fairly accurate prediction. A divination by the Mazes of Ammon-Ra is another matter entirely. It requires an expenditure of the life-forces, a burning up of something deep inside the seer that leaves him worn out and exhausted.

These days I will go to lengths to avoid having to exercise this gift. It is true that on rare occasions I can still be persuaded to work the Mazes, but then for days thereafter I am spiritually and physically depleted. My Lady Lostris, who knows of this strange power of mine, also knows of the effect that it has upon me, and she has forbidden me, for my own sake, to practise it, except occasionally on her behalf.

However, a slave cannot deny a king, and with a sigh I reached for the leather bag in the bottom of my chest that contained the Mazes. I set the bag aside and prepared a mixture of the herbs that are necessary to open the eyes of the soul, to enable them to look into the future. I drank the potion, and then waited until the familiar but dreaded sensation of rising out of my own body assailed me. I felt dreamy and far from reality as I brought out the leather bag which contained the Mazes.

The Mazes of Ammon-Ra consist of ten ivory discs. Ten is the mystical number of the greatest potency. Each disc represents a single facet of human existence, from birth to death and the hereafter. With my own hands I had carved the symbols on the face of each of the Mazes. Each one was a tiny masterpiece. By constantly handling and breathing upon them over the years I had endowed them with part of my own life-force.

I poured them from the bag and began to fondle them, concentrating all my powers upon them. Soon they began to feel warm as living flesh to my touch, and I experienced the familiar sensation of depletion as my own strength flowed from me into the ivory discs. I arranged the Mazes face-down in two random stacks and invited Pharaoh to take up each pile in turn, to rub them between his fingers and to concentrate all his attention upon them at the same time as he repeated his questions aloud: 'Will I have a son? Will my dynasty survive?'

I relaxed completely and opened my soul to allow the spirits of prophecy to enter. The sound of his voice began to penetrate into my soul, deeper and deeper with each repetition, like missiles from a slingshot striking upon the same spot.

I began to sway slightly where I sat, the same way that the cobra dances to the flute of the snake-charmer. The drug took its full effect. I felt as though my body had no weight to it and that I was floating in air. I spoke as if from a great distance and my voice echoed strangely in my own head, as though I sat in a cavern below the surface of the earth.

I ordered the king to breathe upon each stack and then to divide it into halves, setting aside one half and retaining the other. Again and again I made him split each pile and then combine the remainder, until he was left with only two of the coin-shaped Mazes.

For the last time he breathed upon them and then at my instruction placed one in each of my hands. I held them tightly and pressed them to my breast. I could feel my heart pounding against my clenched fists as it absorbed the influence of the Mazes.

I closed my eyes and from the darkness saw shapes begin to emerge, and strange sounds filled my ears. There was no form or coherence to them, it was all confusion. I felt dizzy, and my senses blurred. I felt myself grow lighter still, until I seemed to float in space. I allowed myself to be carried upwards as though I were a blade of dry grass caught in a whirlwind, one of those dust devils of the Saharan summer.

The sounds in my head became clearer, and the dark images firmed.

'I hear a new-born infant cry.' My voice was distorted, as though my palate had been riven at birth.

'Is it a boy?' Pharaoh's question throbbed in my head, so that I felt rather than heard it.

Then slowly my vision began to harden, and I looked down a long tunnel through the darkness to a light at the far end. The ivory Mazes in my hands were hot as embers from the hearth and seared the flesh of my palms.

In the nimbus of light at the end of the tunnel I saw a child, lying in the bloody puddle of its own birth-waters, with the fat python of the placenta still coiled upon its belly.

'I see a child,' I croaked.

'Is it a boy?' Pharaoh demanded from out of the surrounding darkness.

The infant wailed and kicked both legs in the air, and I saw rising from between the chubby thighs a pale finger of flesh surmounted by a cap of wrinkled skin.

'A boy,' I confirmed, and I felt an unexpected tenderness towards this phantom of my mind, as though it were truly flesh and blood. I reached out to it with my heart, but the image faded, and the birth cry receded and was lost in the blackness.

'The dynasty? What will become of my line? Will it endure?' The king's voice reached me, and then was lost in a cacophony of other sounds that filled my head — the sound of battle trumpets, the shouts of men in mortal conflict, and the ring of bronze on bronze. I saw the sky above me, and the air was dark with flights of arrows arcing overhead.

'War! I see a mighty battle that will change the shape of the world,' I cried to make myself heard above the sounds of conflict that filled my head.

'Will my line survive?' The king's voice was frantic, but I paid it no heed, for there was a mighty roaring in my ears, like the sound of the *khamsin* wind, or the waters of the Nile boiling through the great cataracts. I saw a strange yellow cloud that obscured the horizon of my vision, and the cloud was shot through with flashes of light, which I knew were the reflection of the sun from weapons of war.

'What of my dynasty?' Pharaoh's voice tugged at my mind, and the vision faded. There was a silence in my head and I saw a tree standing upon the bank of the river. It was a great acacia in full leaf, and its branches were heavy with fruit pods. On the topmost branch was perched a hawk, the royal hawk, but even as I watched, the hawk changed shape and colour. It was transformed into the double crown of Egypt, red and white, the papyrus and the lotus of the two kingdoms entwined. Then, before my eyes, the waters of the Nile rose and fell, and rose and fell again. Five times in all I saw the waters flood.

While still I stared with burning eyes, abruptly the sky above the tree darkened with flying insects, and a dense cloud of locusts descended upon the tree. They covered it completely. When they rose again the tree was devastated and bare of the last trace of green. Not a leaf remained on the dry brown twigs. Then the dead tree toppled and fell ponderously to earth. The fall shattered the trunk and the crown was smashed into pieces. The fragments turned to dust and were blown away on the wind. Nothing remained but the wind and the driven sands of the desert.

'What is it that you see?' Pharaoh demanded, but it all faded and I found myself once more seated on the floor of the king's bedchamber. I was gasping for breath, as though I had run a great distance, and salt sweat scalded my eyes and poured down my body in rivulets to soak the linen of my kilt and to form a pool on the tiles beneath me. I was shaking with a burning fever and there was that familiar sick and heavy feeling in the pit of my stomach that I knew would be with me for days to come.

Pharaoh was staring at me and I realized what a haggard and dreadful sight I presented to him. 'What did you see?' he whispered. 'Will my line survive?'

I could not tell him the truth of my vision, so I invented another to satisfy him. 'I saw a forest of great trees that reached to the horizon of my dream. There was no end to their number and on top of each tree there was a crown, the red and the white crown of the two kingdoms.'

Pharaoh sighed and covered his eyes with his hands for a while. We sat in silence, he in the release that my lie had given him, and I in sympathy for him.

At last I lied softly. 'The forest that I saw was the line of your descendants,' I whispered, to spare him. 'They reach to the boundaries of time, and each of them wears the crown of Egypt.'

He uncovered his eyes, and his gratitude and his joy were pathetic to watch. 'Thank you, Taita. I can see how the divination has taxed your strength. You may go now and rest. Tomorrow the court will sail for my palace on Elephantine Island. I will have a galley set aside for the safe passage of you and your mistress. Guard her with your life, for she is the vessel that contains the seeds of my immortality.'

I was so weak that I had to use the frame of the bed to lift myself to my feet. I tottered to the door and steadied myself against the jamb. However, I was not so weakened that I could not think of my duty to my mistress.

'There is the matter of the marriage sheet. The populace will expect to have it displayed,' I reminded him. 'Both your reputation and that of my mistress is at stake.'

'What do you suggest, Taita?' This soon he was relying on me. I told him what must be done, and he nodded. 'See to it!'

Carefully I folded the sheet that covered the royal bed. It was of the finest linen, white as the high cirrus clouds of summer, embroidered with the rare silk thread that the trade caravans occasionally bring in from the East. I carried the folded sheet with me when I left the king's bed-chamber and made my way back through the still dark and silent palace to the harem.

My mistress was sleeping like a dead woman, and I knew that with the amount of the Red Shepenn I had given her, she would sleep the day away and would probably only wake that evening. I sat beside her bed for a while. I felt exhausted and depressed for the Mazes had drained my soul. The images they had evoked still troubled me. I felt certain that the infant I had seen was that of my mistress, but then how could the rest of my vision be explained? There seemed to be no answer to the riddle, and I set the thought aside for I still had work to do.

Squatting beside Lostris' bed, I spread the embroidered sheet upon the floor. The blade of my dagger was sharp enough to shave the hair from my forearm. I picked out one of the blue rivers of blood beneath the smooth skin on the inside of my wrist, and I pricked it with the point of the dagger and let the dark slow blood trickle on to the sheet. When I was satisfied with the extent of the stain, I bound up my wrist with a strip of linen to staunch the bleeding, and bundled the soiled sheet.

The slave girl was still in attendance in the outer chamber. I ordered that Lostris was to be allowed to sleep undisturbed. Knowing that she would be well cared for, I was content to leave her, and climb the ladder to the top of the outer wall of the harem.

The dawn was only just breaking, but already an inquisitive crowd of old women and loiterers had gathered below the walls. They looked up expectantly when I appeared.

I made a show of shaking out the sheet before I draped it over the ramparts of the outer wall. The bloodstain in the centre of the cloud-white ground was the shape of a flower, and the crowd buzzed with gossip at this badge of my mistress's virginity and her bridegroom's virility.

At the rear of the crowd stood a figure taller than those around him. His head was covered by a striped woollen shawl. It was only when he threw this back and exposed his face and his head of red-gold hair that I recognized him.

'Tanus!' I shouted. 'I must speak to you.'

He looked up at me upon the wall, and his eyes were filled with such pain as I wished never to see again. That stain upon the sheet had destroyed his life. I also had known the agony of lost love and remembered every detail of it even after all the long years. Tanus' heart wound was fresh and bleeding still, more agonizing than any hurt that he had received on the battlefield.

He needed my help now, if he were to survive it. 'Tanus! Wait for me.'

He threw the shawl over his head, covering his face, and he turned from me. Unsteady as a drunkard, he stumbled away.

'Tanus!' I shouted after him. 'Come back! I must talk to you.' He did not look round, but quickened his pace.

By the time that I had climbed down from the wall and run out of the main gates, he had disappeared into the maze of alleys and mud huts of the inner city.

I SEARCHED for Tanus half the morning, but his quarters were deserted and nobody had seen him in any of his customary haunts.

At last I had to abandon the search, and to make my way back to my own rooms in the quarters of the slave boys. The royal flotilla was preparing to sail for the south. I had still to assemble and pack my possessions if my mistress and I were to be ready for the departure. I forced aside the sense of gloom that the Mazes and my glimpse of Tanus had left me, and I set about bundling up my possessions and breaking up the only home that I had ever known.

My animals seemed to sense that something untoward was happening. They fretted and chirped and whined, each trying in his own way to attract my attention. The wild birds hopped and fluttered on the paved terrace outside, while in the corner nearest my bed, my beloved Saker falcons stretched their wings and raised the feathers along their backs, and screeched at me from their perches. The dogs and the cats and the tame gazelle crowded around my legs, trying to brush against me, and hindered my efforts to pack my possessions.

In exasperation I noticed the jug of soured goat's milk beside my bed. It is one of my favourite drinks, and the slave boys make certain that the jug is always refilled. My animals also enjoy the thickened milk, so to distract them I carried the jug out on to the terrace and filled their clay drinking-bowls. They crowded around the bowls, pushing and shoving each other, and I left them and went back to my task, closing the awnings of rush matting to keep them out.

It is curious how many possessions even a slave can gather about him over a lifetime. The boxes and bundles were piled high against one wall before I was at last finished. By this time my mood of depression and weariness was almost prostrating, but I was still sufficiently alert to be aware of the silence. I stood for a while in the centre of my room, listening uneasily. The only sound was the jingle of the tiny bronze bells on the jesses of my female falcon where she sat in the far corner and watched me with that intent, implacable gaze of the raptor. The tiercel, smaller but more handsome than she, was asleep on his own perch in the other corner, with the soft leather hood of the rufter covering his eyes. None of my other pets made a sound. Not one of the cats mewed or hissed at the dogs, nor did the wild birds chirrup or sing, none of my puppies growled or tumbled over each other in boisterous play.

I went to the rush awning and drew it aside. The sunlight burst into the room and blinded me for a moment. Then my vision returned and I cried out with horror. They were scattered upon the terrace and down into the garden every bird and animal.

They lay in the abandoned attitudes of death, every one of them where he had fallen. I rushed out to them, calling my favourites by name, kneeling to pick one of them up in my arms and hugging the slack warm body as I searched for signs of life. There was no flicker of it in any of them, though I went to each of them. The birds were small and light in my hand, their marvellous plumage undimmed by death.

I thought that my already heavy heart must now burst with the sheer weight of my grief. I knelt on the terrace with my family scattered around me and I wept.

It was some time before I could bring myself to think about the cause of this tragedy. Then I stood up and went to one of the empty bowls that lay on the tiles. They had licked it clean, but I sniffed at it to try and fathom the nature of the poison that had been intended for me. The odour of soured milk disguised any other smell; all I knew was that it had been swift and deadly.

I wondered who had placed the jug beside my bed, but it did not matter whose hand had carried the vessel to me. I knew with utter certainty who had given the order for it. 'Farewell, my old darling. You are a dead man,' Lord Intef had told me, and he had not waited long to transform the words into the deed.

The anger that seized me was a form of madness. It was aggravated by my unsteady state and sombre mood. I found that I was shaking with a rage that I had never known before. I drew the little dagger from my belt and before I realized what I was doing, I was rushing down the steps of the terrace with the naked blade in my hand. I knew that at this time of the morning Intef would be in his water-garden. I could no longer bear to think of him as my Lord Intef. The memory of every outrage he had ever visited upon me, every agony and every humiliation, was bright and clear in my mind. I was going to kill him now, stab him a hundred times through that cruel and evil heart.

I was in sight of the gate to the water-garden before I regained my sanity. There were half a dozen guards at the gate, and there would be as many more beyond. I would never get within dagger-thrust of the grand vizier before they cut me down. I forced my flying feet to check and turn back. I slipped the dagger into the jewelled leather sheath, and brought my breathing under control. I walked slowly back to the terrace and gathered up the pathetic bodies of my pets.

I had planned to plant a row of sycamore trees along the border of my garden. The holes to take them had already been dug. The trees would never be planted now that I was leaving Karnak, and the pits would serve as graves for my beloved creatures. It was the middle of the afternoon before I had filled the last grave, but my rage was unabated. If I could not yet have my full vengeance, at least I could give myself a foretaste of it.

There was still a little of the sour milk left in the jug beside my bed. I held the jug in my hands and tried to think of some way in which I could get it to the grand vizier's kitchens. It would be so fitting to pay him his own vile coin, although I knew in my heart that the idea was futile. Lord Intef was far too cunning to be taken so easily. I myself had helped him devise the system he used to keep himself secure from poison and assassination. He could not be reached without much careful planning. What was more, he would be especially on his guard now. I would have to be patient, but that was impossible. Even if I could not kill him yet, I could exact some lesser payment as a deposit against what I was determined must follow.

Still carrying the fatal jug, I slipped out of one of the side-doors of the boys' quarters into the street. I did not have to go far to find a milkman surrounded by his flock of nanny-goats. While I waited he stripped the rich milk from the swollen udders of one of them, topping the jug to the brim. Whoever had prepared the poison had used enough to murder half the citizens of Karnak. I knew that more than sufficient remained in the jug for my purpose.

One of the grand vizier's bodyguards loafed at the door to Rasfer's chamber. The fact that he had him under guard proved to me that Rasfer was still valuable to Lord Intef, and the loss of his personal lieutenant would annoy if not seriously discommode him.

The guard recognized me and waved me into the sick-room that smelled like a sty. Rasfer lay on his filthy bed, basting in his own sweat. However, I could tell at once that my surgery had been successful, for he opened his eyes and cursed me weakly. He must also be so certain of his own eventual recovery that he need no longer toady to me.

'Where have you been, you ball-less freak?' he growled at me, hardening my resolve and ridding me of the last traces of any pity that I might have felt for him. 'I have been in agony ever since you drilled into my skull. What kind of physician are you—'

There was much more in this style, which I pretended to ignore as I unwound the soiled bandage from around his head. My interest was purely academic as I examined the small wound that the trepan had left in his scalp. It was another perfectly executed operation, and I felt a certain professional regret that it would be wasted.

'Give me something for the pain, eunuch!' Rasfer tried to seize the front of my tunic, but I was too quick for him and stepped back out of his reach.

I made a fuss of shaking a few crystals of harmless salt from a glass vial into his drinking-bowl, and then topped it up with milk from my jug.

'If the pain becomes too bad, this will relieve it,' I told him as I set the bowl near to his hand. Even at this stage, I could not bring myself to hand it to him directly.

He heaved himself up on one elbow and reached for the bowl to guzzle it down. Before his fingers touched it, I pushed it out of his reach with my foot. At the moment I thought that this was merely a desire to prolong the anticipation, and I felt satisfaction at his distress as he whined at me, 'Good Taita, give me the potion. Let me drink. This pain in my head will drive me mad.'

'First let's talk a while, good Rasfer. Did you hear that the Lady Lostris asked for me as her parting gift from Lord Intef?'

Even in his pain, he grinned at me. 'You are a fool if you think he will let you go. You are a dead man.'

'The very words Lord Intef used. Will you mourn for me, Rasfer? Will you weep for me when I am gone?' I asked softly, and he began to chuckle, then broke it off and glanced at the bowl.

'In my own way, I have always been rather fond of you,' he grunted. 'Now let me have the bowl.'

'How fond of me were you when you castrated me?' I asked, and he stared up at me.

'Surely you do not still bear a grudge for that? It was long ago, and besides, I could not disobey the orders of Lord Intef. Be reasonable, Taita, let me have the bowl.'

'You laughed as you cut me. Why did you laugh? Did you enjoy it so much?'

He shrugged and then winced at the pain that the movement caused him. 'I am a jovial man. I always laugh. Come now, old friend, say you forgive me and let me have the bowl.'

I nudged it towards him with my foot. He reached out and seized it, his movements still uncoordinated. A few drops slopped over the rim as he raised it greedily to his mouth.

I didn't realize what I was about to do, until I had leapt forward and struck the bowl out of his hands. It hit the floor without shattering and rolled into the corner, splashing milk up on to the wall.

Rasfer and I stared at each other. I was appalled by my own stupidity and my weakness. If ever a man deserved a death by the agony of poison, it was this one. But then I saw again the contorted bodies of my pets strewn across the terrace, and I knew why I had not been able to allow Rasfer to drink. Only a fiend could commit such an act. I have too high a regard for myself ever to descend to the ignominy of the poisoner.

I saw understanding dawn in Rasfer's bloodshot eyes. 'Poison,' he whispered. 'The bowl was poisoned.'

'It was sent to me by Lord Intef.' I don't know why I told him this. Perhaps I was trying to excuse myself for the atrocity that I had almost committed. I don't know why I was behaving so strangely. Maybe it was still the after-effects of working the Mazes. I staggered slightly as I turned for the door.

Behind me Rasfer began to laugh, softly at first and then louder, until great gusty bellows of laughter seemed to shake the walls.

'You are a fool, eunuch,' he roared after me as I ran. 'You should have done it. You should have killed me, for now as surely as I have a hole between my buttocks, I will kill you.'

As I had expected, when at last I returned to her chamber my Lady Lostris was still asleep. I settled at the foot of her bed, intending to wait for her to wake on her own. However, the rigours and the exertions of the past day and night had been too much for me. I slumped down and fell asleep, curled like a puppy on the tiles.

I WOKE under attack. Something struck the side of my head such a painful blow that I was on my feet before I was properly awake. The next blow took me across the shoulder and stung like the bite of a hornet.

'You cheated me!' my Lady Lostris screamed at me. 'You did not let me die.' She swung the fan again. It was a formidable weapon, the bamboo handle was as long as twice the span of my arms, and the comb at its head that held the fan of ostrich feathers was of solid silver. Fortunately she was still groggy from the drug and from oversleeping, and her aim was erratic. I ducked under the blow, and the momentum of it swung her around so that she collapsed on the bed again.

She dropped the fan and burst into tears. 'I wanted to die. Why did you not let me die?'

It was some time before I could approach her, and put one arm around her to comfort her. 'Did I hurt you, Taita?' she asked. 'I have never beaten you before.'

'Your first attempt was a very good one,' I congratulated her ruefully. 'In fact you are so good at it that I do not think you need practise it further.' Theatrically I rubbed the side of my head, and she smiled through her tears.

'Poor Taita. I do treat you so badly. But you did deserve it. You cheated me. I wanted to die and you disobeyed me.'

I saw it was time to change the subject. 'Mistress, I have the most remarkable news for you. But you must promise to tell no one of it, not even your maids.' Not since she had first learned to talk had she been able to resist a secret, but then what woman can? The promise of one had always been enough to distract her, and it worked yet again.

Even with her heart broken and the threat of suicide hanging over her, she sniffed back the last of her tears and ordered, 'Tell me!'

Recently, I had accumulated a good store of secrets to choose from, and I paused for a moment to make my selection. I would not tell her of the poisoning of my pets, of course, nor of my glimpse of Tanus. I needed something to cheer her rather than to depress her further.

'Last night I went to Pharaoh's bedchamber and I spoke to him for half the night.'

The tears rose to the surface of her eyes once more, 'Oh, Taita, I hate him. He's an ugly old man. I don't want to have to—'

I wanted no more in that vein, in moments she would be weeping again, so I hurried on, 'I worked the Mazes for him.' Instantly I had her complete attention. My Lady Lostris is totally fascinated by my powers of divination. If it were not for the deleterious effect that the Mazes have upon my health, she would make me work them every single day.

'Tell me! What did you see?' She was riveted. No thought of suicide now, all sadness forgotten. She was still so young and artless that I felt ashamed of my trickery, even though it was for her own good.

'I had the most extraordinary visions, mistress. I have never had such clear images, such depths of sight—'

'Tell me! I declare I will die of impatience if you don't tell me immediately.'

'First you must swear secrecy. Not another soul must ever know what I saw. These are affairs of state and dire consequence.'

'I swear. I swear.'

'We cannot take these matters lightly—'

'Get on with it, Taita. You are teasing me now. I order you to tell me this very moment or, or,' she groped for a threat to coerce me, 'or I shall beat you again.'

'Very well. Listen to my vision. I saw a great tree upon the bank of the Nile. Upon the summit of the tree was the crown of Egypt.'

'Pharaoh! The tree was the king.' She saw it at once, and I nodded. 'Go on, Taita. Tell me the rest of it.'

'I saw the Nile rise and fall five times.'

'Five years, the passing of five years!' She clapped her hands with excitement. She loves to unravel the riddles of my dreams.

'Then the tree was devoured by locusts, and thrown down and turned to dust.'

She stared at me, unable to utter the words, so I spoke for her. 'In five years Pharaoh will be dead, and you will be a free woman. Free from your father's thrall. Free to go to Tanus, with no man to stop you.'

'If you are lying to me, it will be too cruel to bear. Please say it is true.'

'It is true, my lady, but there is more. In the vision, I saw a new-born babe, a boy child, a son. I felt my love go out to the infant, and I knew that you were the mother of the child.'

'The father, who was the father of my baby? Oh, Taita, tell me please.'

'In the dream I knew with absolute certainty that the father was Tanus.' This was the first deviation from the truth that I had allowed myself, but once again I had the consolation of believing that it was for her benefit.

She was silent for a long time, but her face shone with an inner glow that was all the reward I could ever ask for. Then at last she whispered, 'I can wait for five years. I was prepared to wait all eternity for him. It will be hard, but I can wait five years for Tanus. You were right not to let me die, Taita. It would have been an offence in the face of the gods.'

My relief buoyed me up, and I now felt more confident that I would be able to steer her safely through all that lay ahead.

AT DAWN the following day the royal flotilla sailed south from Karnak. As the king had promised, my Lady Lostris and all her entourage were on board one of the small, fast galleys of the southern squadron.

I sat with my mistress on the cushions under the awning on the poop that the captain had arranged especially for her. We looked back at the lime-washed buildings of the city shining in the first tangerine tints of the rising sun.

'I cannot think where he has gone.' She was fretting over Tanus as she had a score of times since we had set sail. 'Did you look everywhere for him?'

'Everywhere,' I confirmed. 'I spent half the morning scouring the inner city and the docks. He has disappeared. But I left your message with Kratas. You can be sure Kratas will deliver it to him.'

'Five years without him, will they ever pass?'

THE VOYAGE up-river passed pleasantly enough in long, leisurely days spent sitting on the poop-deck in conversation with my mistress. We discussed every detail of our changed circumstances in great depth, and examined all that we might expect and hope for in the future.

I explained to her all the complexities of life at the court, the precedent and the protocol. I traced for her the hidden lines of power and influence, and I listed all those whom it would be in our interest to cultivate and those whom we could safely ignore. I explained to her the issues of the day, and how Pharaoh stood on each of them. Then I went on to discuss with her the feeling and the mood of the citizenry.

In a large measure I was indebted to my friend Aton, the royal chamberlain, for all this intelligence. It seemed that over the last dozen years every ship that had come down-river from Elephantine Island to Karnak had carried a letter from him to me full of these fascinating details, and on its return to Elephantine Island had carried a golden token of my gratitude back to my friend, Aton.

I was determined that we would soon be at the centre of the court and in the mainstream of power. I had not trained my mistress all these years to see the weapons that I had placed in her armoury rust with disuse. The sum of her many accomplishments and her talents was already formidable, but I was patiently adding to it each day. She had a keen and restless mind. Once I had helped her to throw off the black mood that had threatened to destroy her, she was, as always, open to my instruction. Every chance I had, I fired up her ambition and her eagerness to take up the role I had planned for her.

I soon found that one of the most effective means of enlisting her attention and cooperation was to suggest that all this would be to the eventual benefit and advantage of Tanus. 'If you have influence at court, you will be better able to protect him,' I pointed out to her. 'The king has set him an almost impossible task to fulfil. Tanus will need us if he is to succeed, and if he fails only you will be able to save him from the sentence that the king has placed upon him.'

'What can we do to help him carry out his task?' At the mention of Tanus I immediately had all her attention. 'Tell me truly, will any man be able to stamp out the Shrikes? Is it not too difficult a mission, even for a man like Tanus?'

The bandits that terrorized the Upper Kingdom called themselves the Shrikes, after those fierce birds. Our Nile shrike is smaller than a dove; a handsome little creature with a white chest and throat and a black back and cap, it plunders the nests of other birds and makes a grisly display of the pathetic carcasses of its victims by hanging them on the thorns of the acacia tree. Its vernacular name is the Butcher Bird.

In the beginning the bandits had used it as a cryptic name to conceal their identity and to hide their existence, but since they had grown so strong and fearless, they had adopted it openly and often used the black and white feather of the Butcher Bird as their emblem.

In the beginning they would leave the feather on the doorway of a home they had robbed or on the corpse of one of their victims. But in those days, so bold and so organized had they become that at times they might send a feather to an intended victim as a warning. In most cases that was all that was necessary to make the victim pay over a half of all he owned in the world. That was preferable to having all of it pillaged, and having his wives and daughters carried off and raped, and he and his sons thrown into the burning ruins of their home to boot.

'Do you think it possible that even with the power of the hawk seal Tanus will be able to carry out the king's mission?' my mistress repeated. 'I have heard that all the bands of the Shrikes in the whole of the Upper Kingdom are controlled by one man, someone that they call the Akh-Seth, the brother of Seth. Is that true, Taita?'

I thought for a moment before I answered. I could not yet tell her all I knew of the Shrikes, for if I did so, then I would be forced to reveal how such knowledge had come into my possession. At this stage that would not be much to her advantage, nor to my credit. There might be a time for these disclosures later.

'I have also heard that rumour,' I agreed cautiously. 'It seems to me that if Tanus were to find and crush this one man, Akh-Seth, then the Shrikes would crumble away. But Tanus will need help that only I can give him.'

She looked at me shrewdly. 'How can you help him?' she demanded. 'And what do you know about this business?'

She is quick, and hard to deceive. She sensed at once that I was hiding something from her. I had to retreat swiftly and to play on her love of Tanus and her trust in me.

'For Tanus' sake, ask me no more now. Only give me your permission to do what I can to help him complete the task that Pharaoh has set him.'

'Yes, of course we must do all in our power. Tell me how I can help.'

'I will stay with you at the court on Elephantine Island for ninety days, but then you must give me leave to go to him—'

'No, no,' she interrupted me, 'if you can be of help to Tanus, you must go immediately.'

'Ninety days,' I repeated stubbornly. That was the period of grace that

I had won for her. Although I was torn between these two dear children of mine, my first duty was to my mistress.

I knew that I could not leave her alone at the court without a friend or a mentor. I also knew that I had to be with her when the king finally sent for her in the night.

'I cannot leave you yet, but don't worry. I have left a message for Tanus with Kratas. They will be expecting me, and I have explained to Kratas all that has to be done before I arrive back at Karnak.' I would not tell her more, and there can be few as obtuse or as evasive as I can be when I set myself to it.

The flotilla sailed only during the day. Neither the navigational skills of Admiral Nembet nor the comfort of the king and his court would stand up to a night passage, so every evening we moored and a forest of hundreds of tents sprang up on the river-bank. Always the royal stewards chose the most congenial spot to pitch camp, usually in a grove of palm trees or in the lee of a sheltering hillock, with a temple or a village nearby from which we were able to draw supplies.

The entire court was still in festive mood. Every camp was treated as a picnic. There was dancing and feasting in the light of the bonfires, while in the shadows the courtiers intrigued and flirted. Many an alliance both political and carnal was struck during those balmy nights, perfumed with the fruity aromas of the irrigated lands along the river and the spicier desert airs blown in from further afield.

I used every moment to the best advantage of both my mistress and myself. Of course she was now one of the royal ladies, but there were already several hundred of those, and she was still a very junior wife. Lord Intef's foresight might change her future status, but only if she bore Pharaoh a son. In the meantime it was up to me.

Almost every evening after we had gone ashore, Pharaoh sent for me, ostensibly to see to the cure of his ringworm, but in reality to review the preparations for begetting a male heir to the double crown. While he watched with interest, I prepared my tonic for potency and virility from grated rhinoceros horn and mandrake root, which I mixed with warm goat's milk and honey. When he had taken this, I examined the royal member and was delighted for the sake of my mistress to find that it possessed neither the length nor the girth that one would have expected from a god. I was of the opinion that my mistress, even in her virgin state, would be able to cope with its modest dimensions without too much discomfort. Naturally I would do all in my power to avoid the dread moment, but if I was unable to stave it off, then I was determined to ease the passage to womanhood for her.

Having found the king to be healthy if unremarkable in these regions, I recommended a poultice of cornflour mixed with olive oil and honey to be applied to the royal member at night before retiring, and then I went on to deal with the ringworm. To the king's intense gratification my ointment cured the condition within the three days that I had promised, and my already considerable reputation as a physician was enhanced. The king boasted of my accomplishment to his council of ministers, and within days I was in huge demand throughout the court. Then, when it was known that I was not only a healer but also an astrologer whom even the king consulted, my popularity became boundless.

Every evening there came to our tents a succession of messengers bearing expensive gifts for my mistress from this lady or that lord and begging that she allow me to visit them for a consultation. We acceded to only those with whom we wished to make better acquaintance. Once I was in the tent of a powerful and noble lord, he with his kilt up around his waist while I examined his haemorrhoids, it was a simple matter to extol my mistress and bring her many virtues to the attention of my patient.

The other ladies of the harem soon discovered that my Lady Lostris and I sang a beautiful duet together, and that we could compose the most intriguing riddles and tell even more amusing stories. We were in demand throughout the court, and especially amongst the children of the harem. This gave me special pleasure, for if there is anything I love more than animals, it is small children.

Pharaoh, who was responsible for our popularity in the first place, soon had the increase of it reported to him. This further spurred his interest in my mistress, if it were not already sufficiently intense. At sailing time on many mornings she was summoned on board the royal barge to spend the day in the king's company, while most evenings, at the royal invitation, my mistress dined at the king's board, and regaled him and the assembled company with her natural wit and childlike grace. Of course I was always in discreet attendance. When the king made no move to send for her in the night in order to force her to submit to those horrible but rather hazy terrors she had conjured up, her feelings towards him began to moderate.

Beneath his glum exterior Pharaoh Mamose was a kind and decent man. My Lady Lostris soon realized this, and like me, she began to grow quite fond of him. Before we reached Elephantine Island she was treating him like a favourite uncle, and quite unaffectedly would sit on his knee to tell him a story, or would play throwing-sticks with him on the deck of the royal barge, both of them flushed with the exertion and laughing like children. Aton confided to me that he had never seen the king so gay.

All this was watched and noted by the court, who very soon recognized her as the king's favourite. Soon there were other visitors to our tents in the evening, those who had a petition which they wished my mistress to bring to Pharaoh's notice. The gifts they proffered were even more valuable than those offered for my services.

My mistress had rejected her father's gift in favour of a single slave, so she had begun the journey southwards as a pauper, dependent on my own modest savings. However, before the voyage was done she had accumulated not only a comfortable fortune, but also a long list of favours owed by her new rich and powerful friends. I kept a careful accounting of all these assets.

I am not so conceited that I should pretend that my Lady Lostris would not have achieved this recognition without my help. Her beauty and her cleverness and her sweet, warm nature must have made her a favourite in any circumstances. I only suggest that I was able to make it happen a little sooner and a little more certainly.

Our success brought with it some drawbacks. As always, there was jealousy from those who felt themselves displaced in Pharaoh's favour, and there was also the matter of Pharaoh's mounting carnal interest in my mistress. This was aggravated by the period of abstinence that I had enforced upon him.

One evening in his tent after I had administered his rhinoceros horn, he confided in me, 'Taita, this cure of yours is really most efficacious. I have not felt so virile since I was a young man, way back before my coronation and my divinity. This morning when I awoke I had a stiffening of the member which was so gratifying that I sent for Aton to view it. He was mightily impressed and he wished forthwith to fetch your mistress.'

I was thoroughly alarmed by this news, and I put on my sternest expression and shook my head and sucked air through my teeth and tut-tutted to show my disapproval. 'I am grateful for your good sense in not agreeing to Aton's suggestion, Your Majesty. It could so easily have undone all our efforts. If you want a son, then you must follow my regime meticulously.'

This brought home to me the swift passage of time, and how soon the ninety days of grace would be up. I began to condition my mistress for that night which Pharaoh would soon insist upon.

First I must prepare her mind, and I set about this by pointing out to her that it was inevitable, and that if she wished to outlive the king and eventually to go to Tanus, then she would have to submit to the king's will. She was always a sensible girl.

'Then you will have to explain exactly what it is he expects of me, Taita,' she sighed. I was not the best guide in this area. My personal experience had been ephemeral, but I was able to outline the fundamentals and to make it seem so commonplace as not to alarm her unduly.

'Will it hurt?' she wanted to know, and I hastened to reassure her.

'The king is a kind man. He has much experience of young girls. I am sure he will be gentle with you. I will prepare an ointment for you that will make things much easier. I will apply it every night before you retire. It will open the gateway. Think to yourself that one day Tanus will pass through those same portals, and that you are doing this to welcome him and no other.'

I tried to remain the aloof physician and take no sensual pleasure in what I had to do to help her. The gods forgive me, but I failed in my resolution. She was so perfect in her womanly parts as to overshadow the most lovely blossom that I had ever raised in my garden. No desert rose ever bore petals so exquisite. When I smoothed the ointment upon them they raised their own sweet dew, more oleaginous and silky to the touch than any unguent that I could concoct.

Her cheeks turned rosy and her voice was husky as she murmured, 'Up until now, I thought that part of me was meant for only one purpose. Why is it that when you do that, I long so unbearably for Tanus?'

She trusted me so implicitly, and had so little understanding of these unfamiliar sensations, that it required the exercise of all my ethics as a physician to proceed with the treatment only as long as was necessary. However, I slept only fitfully that night, haunted by dreams of the impossible.

AS WE sailed deeper into the south, so the belts of green land on each side of the river narrowed. Now the desert began to squeeze in upon us. In places brooding cliffs of black granite trod the verdant fields under foot and pressed so close as to overhang the turgid waters of the Nile.

The most forbidding of these narrows was known as the Gates of Hapi, and the waters were whipped into a wild and wilful temper as they boiled through the gap in the high cliffs.

We made the passage of the Gates of Hapi, and came at last to Elephantine, the largest of a great assembly of islands that were strung through the throat of the Nile, where the harsh hills constricted its flow and forced it through the narrows.

Elephantine was shaped like a monstrous shark pursuing the shoal of lesser islands up the narrows. On either side of the river the encroaching deserts were distinct in colour and character. On the west bank, the Saharan dunes were hot orange and savage as the Bedouin who were the only mortals able to survive amongst them. To the east, the Arabian desert was dun and dirty grey, studded with black hills that danced dreamlike in the heat mirage. These deserts had one thing in common – both of them were killers of men.

What a delightful contrast was Elephantine Island, set like a glistening green jewel in the silver crown of the river. It took its name from the smooth grey granite boulders that clustered along its bank like a herd of the huge pachyderms and also from the fact that the trade in ivory brought down from the savage land of Cush beyond the cataract had for a thousand years centred upon this place.

Pharaoh's palace sprawled over most of the island, and the wags suggested that he had chosen to build it here at the southernmost point in his kingdom to be as far from the red pretender in the north as possible.

The wide stretch of water that surrounded the island secured it from the attack of an enemy, but the remainder of the city had overflowed on to both main banks. After great Thebes, west and east Elephantine together made up the largest and most populous city in the Upper Kingdom, a worthy rival to Memphis, the seat of the red pretender in the Lower Kingdom.

As at no other place in the whole of Egypt, Elephantine Island was clad with trees. Their seeds had been brought down by the river on a thousand annual floods, and they had taken root in the fertile loams that had themselves been transported by the restless waters.

On my last visit to Elephantine, when I had come up-river to do a survey of the river gauges for my Lord Intef in his capacity as Guardian of the Waters, I had spent many months on the island. With the assistance of the head gardener, I had catalogued the names and natural histories of all the plants in the palace gardens, so I was able to point them out to my mistress. There were *ficus* trees the like of which had never been seen elsewhere in Egypt. Their fruits grew not upon the branch but on the main trunk, and their roots twisted and writhed together like mating pythons. There were dragon's blood trees whose bark, when cut, poured out a bright red sap. There were Cushite sycamores and a hundred other varieties that spread a shady green umbrella over the lovely little island.

The royal palace was built upon the solid granite that lay below the fertile soil and formed the skeleton of the island. I have often wondered that our kings, the long line of pharaohs of fifty dynasties that stretches back over a thousand years, have each of them devoted so much of his life and treasure to the building of vast and eternal tombs of granite and marble, while in their lifetimes they have been content to live in palaces with mud walls and thatched roofs. In comparison to the magnificent funerary temple that I was building for Pharaoh Mamose at Karnak, this palace was a very modest affair, and the dearth of straight lines and symmetry offended the instincts of both the mathematician and the architect in me. I suppose the sprawling jumble of red clay walls and roofs canted at odd angles did have a sort of bucolic charm, yet I itched to get out my ruler and plumb-line.

Once we had gone ashore and found the quarters that had been set aside for us, the true appeal of Elephantine was even more apparent. Naturally we were lodged in the walled harem on the northern tip of the island, but the size and the furnishings of our lodgings confirmed our favoured position, not only with the king but with his chamberlain as well. Aton had made the allocation, and he, like most others, had proved completely defenceless against my mistress's natural charm, and was now one of her most shameless admirers.

He placed at our disposal a dozen spacious and airy rooms with our own courtyard and kitchens. A side-gate in the main wall led directly down to the riverside and a stone jetty. That very first day I purchased a flat-bottomed skiff which we could use for fishing and water-fowling. I kept it moored at the jetty.

As to the rest of our new home, however comfortable it might have been, neither my mistress nor I was satisfied, and we immediately set about improving and beautifying it. With the cooperation of my old friend the head gardener, I laid out and planted our own private garden in the courtyard, with a thatched barrazza under which we could sit in the heat of the day, and where I kept my Saker falcons tethered on their perches.

At the jetty I set up a shadoof to lift from the river a constant flow of water that I led through ceramic pipes to our own water-garden with lily-ponds and fish-pools. The overflow from the pools drained away in a narrow gutter. This gutter I directed through the wall of my mistress's chamber, across a screened corner of the room and out the far side, from whence it returned to the main flow of the Nile. I carved a stool of fragrant cedar wood, with a hole through the seat, and placed this over the gutter so that anything dropped through the bottom of the seat would be borne away by the never-ending flow of water. My mistress was delighted with this innovation and spent far more time perched upon the stool than was really necessary to accomplish the business for which it was originally intended.

The walls of our quarters were bare red clay. We designed a set of frescoes for each room. I drew the cartoons and transposed them on to the walls and then my mistress and her maids painted in the designs. The frescoes were scenes from the mythology of the gods, with fanciful landscapes peopled by wonderful animals and birds. Of course, I used my Lady Lostris as my model for the figure of Isis, but was it any wonder that the figure of Horus was central to every painting, or that on the insistence of my mistress, he was depicted as having red-gold hair and that he looked amazingly familiar?

The frescoes caused a stir throughout the harem and every one of the royal wives took turns to visit us, to drink sherbet and to view the paintings. We had set a fashion, and I was prevailed upon to advise on the redecoration of most of the private apartments in the harem, at a suitable fee, of course. In this process we made many new friends amongst the royal ladies and added considerably to our financial estate.

Very soon the king heard about the decorations and came in person to examine them. Lostris gave him the grand tour of her chambers. Pharaoh noticed her new water-stool of which my mistress was so proud that when the king asked her to demonstrate it for him she did so without hesitation, perching upon it and giggling as she sent a tinkling stream into the gutter.

She was still so innocent as not to realize the effect that this display had upon her husband. I could tell by his expression that any attempt that I might make to delay him beyond the promised ninety days was likely to be difficult.

After the tour, Pharaoh sat under the barrazza and drank a cup of wine while he actually laughed aloud at some of my mistress's sallies. At last he turned to me. 'Taita, you must build me a water-garden and a barrazza just like this – only much bigger, and whilst you are about it, you can make a water-stool for me as well.'

When at last he was ready to leave, he commanded me to walk a little way alone with him, ostensibly to discuss the new water-garden, but I knew better. No sooner had we left the harem than he was at me.

'Last night I dreamed of your mistress,' he told me, 'and when I awoke, I found that my seed had spilled out upon the sheets. That has not happened to me since I was a boy. This little vixen of yours has begun to fill my thoughts both sleeping and waking. I have no doubt that I can make a son with her, and that we should delay no longer. What do you think, doctor, am I not yet ready for the attempt?'

'I counsel you most strongly to observe the ninety days, Majesty. To make the attempt before that would be folly.' It was dangerous to label the king's desire as folly, but I was desperate to contain it. 'It would be most unwise to spoil all our chances of success for so short a period of time.' In the end I prevailed, and left him looking glummer than ever.

When I returned to the harem, I warned my mistress of the king's intentions, and so thoroughly had I conditioned her to accept the inevitable that she showed no undue distress. She was by this time completely resigned to her role as the king's favourite, while my promise that there would be a term to her captivity here on Elephantine Island made it easier for her to bear. In all fairness, our sojourn on the island could not truly be described as captivity. We Egyptians are the most civilized men on earth. We treat our women well. I have heard of others, the Hurrians and the Cushites and the Libyans, for example, who are most cruel and unnatural towards their wives and daughters.

The Libyans make of the harem a true prison in which the women live their entire lives without sight of a living male apart from the eunuchs and the children. They say that even male dogs and cats are forbidden to pass through the gates, so great is their possessive frenzy.

The Hurrians are even worse. Not only do they confine their women and make them cover their bodies from ankle to wrist, but they force them to go masked as well, even within the confines of the harem. Thus only a woman's husband ever lays eyes upon her face.

The primitive tribes of Cush are the worst of all of them. When their women reach the age of puberty they circumcize them in the most savage manner. They cut away the clitoris and the inner lips of the vagina to remove the seat of sexual pleasure so that they may never be tempted to stray from their husbands.

This may seem so bizarre as to defy belief, but I have seen the results of this brutal surgery with my own eyes. Three of my mistress's slave girls were captured by the slavers only after they were matured and had been subjected to the knife by their own fathers. When I examined the gaping, scar-puckered pits they had been left with, I was sickened, and my instincts as a healer were deeply offended by this mutilation of that masterpiece of the gods, the human body. It has been my observation that this circumcision does not achieve its object, for it seems to deprive the victim of the most desirable female traits, and leaves her cold and calculating and cruel. She becomes a sexless monster.

On the other hand, we Egyptians honour our women and treat them, if not as equals, at least with consideration. No husband may beat his wife without recourse to the magistrate, and he has a legal duty to dress and feed and maintain her in accordance with his own station in society. A wife of the king, or of one of the nobles, is not confined to the harem, but, if suitably escorted by her entourage, may walk abroad in city street or countryside. She is not forced to hide her charms, but, according to the fashion of the moment and her own whim, she may sit at her husband's dinner-table with her face uncovered and her breasts bared, and entertain his male companions with conversation and song.

She may hold, in her own right, slaves and land and fortune separately from the estate of her husband, although the children she bears belong to him alone. She may fish, and fly hawks, and even practise archery, although such masculine endeavours as wrestling and swordsmanship are forbidden to her. There are, quite rightly, certain activities from which she is barred, such as the practice of law and architecture, but a highborn wife is a person of consequence, possessed of legal rights and dignity. Naturally it is not the same for the concubine or for the wife of a common man. They have the same rights as the bullock or the donkey.

Thus my mistress and I were free to wander abroad to explore the twin cities on each bank of the Nile and the surrounding countryside. In the streets of Elephantine my Lady Lostris was very soon a favourite, and the common people gathered round her to solicit her blessing and her generosity. They applauded her grace and beauty, just as they had done in her native Thebes. I was instructed by her always to carry a large bag of cakes and sweetmeats from which she stuffed the cheeks of every ragamuffin we encountered who seemed to her to require nourishing. Wherever we went, we seemed always to be surrounded by a shrieking, dancing flock of children.

My mistress always seemed happy to sit in the doorway of a poor shanty with the housewife, or under a tree in the field of a peasant farmer and listen to their woes and grievances. At the first opportunity she would take these up with Pharaoh. Often he would smile indulgently and agree to the redress that she suggested. So her reputation as a champion of the common man was born. When she passed through even the saddest, poorest quarters of the city, she left smiles and laughter behind her.

On other days we fished together from our little skiff in the backwaters of the lagoons that the inundation of the Nile had created, or we laid out decoys for the wild duck. I had made a special bow for my mistress which was suited to her strength. Of course, it was nothing like the great bow, Lanata, that I had designed for Tanus, but it was adequate for the water-fowl we were after. My Lady Lostris was a better marksman than most men I have watched at the archery butts, and when she loosed an arrow it was very seldom that I was not required to plunge overside and swim out to retrieve the carcass of a duck or a goose.

Whenever the king went out hawking, my mistress was invited to attend. I would walk behind her with my Saker falcons on my arm, as we skirted the edge of the papyrus beds. As soon as a heron rose with heavy wing-beats from a hidden pool in the reeds, she would take one of the falcons from me and kiss its hooded head. 'Fly fast and true, my beauty!' she would whisper to it, and slip the rufter to unmask the fierce yellow eyes, and launch the splendid little killer aloft.

We would watch entranced as the falcon towered high above the quarry, and then folded those sickle wings and stooped with a speed that made the wind sing over his dappled plumage. The shock of impact carried clearly to us over a distance of two hundred paces. A puff of pale blue feathers was smeared across the darker blue of the sky, and then was carried away like smoke on the river breeze. The falcon bound to its prey with hooked talons to bring it smashing to earth. My mistress shrieked in triumph and ran as fast as a boy to retrieve the bird, to lavish praise upon it and pamper it, and then to feed it the severed head of the heron.

I love all creatures of the water and the land and the air. My mistress has the same feelings. Why is it then, I often wonder, that both of us are so moved by these sports of the chase? I have puzzled over it without finding an answer. Perhaps it is simply that man, and woman also, are the earth's fiercest predator. We feel a kinship with the falcon, with his beauty and his speed. The heron and the goose were given to the falcon by the gods as his rightful prey. In the same way, man has been given dominance over all other creatures on earth. We cannot deny these instincts with which the gods have endowed us.

From the earliest age, when she had first developed the strength and the stamina to stay with us, I had allowed my Lady Lostris to accompany Tanus and myself on our hunting and fishing forays. For, perhaps to mask his hatred of his rival, Lord Harrab, my Lord Intef consented to my hunting sorties with young Tanus.

Years before, Tanus and I had taken possession of a deserted fisherman's shack which we had discovered on the fringe of the swamp below Karnak. We had made this our secret hunting-lodge. It was only a short distance from the shack to the edge of the true desert. So from this comfortable base we had the options of fishing the lagoon or of wildfowling or of hawking that noble bird, the giant bustard, in the open desert.

In the beginning Tanus had resented the intrusion of this gawky nine-year-old girl, skinny and flat-chested as a boy, into our private world. Soon, however, he had grown accustomed to her presence and even found it convenient to have someone to run errands for him and perform the irksome little chores around camp.

Thus, little by little, Lostris had picked up the lore and the wisdom of the outdoors, until she knew every fish and bird by its proper name, and could wield a harpoon or a hunting-bow with equal skill. In the end Tanus had become as proud of her as if it had been he who had invited her to join us in the first place.

She had been with us in the black rock hills above the river valley on the day that Tanus had hunted the cattle-killer. The lion was a scarred old male with a black mane that waved like a field of corn in the wind as he walked, and a voice like the thunder of the heavens. We set my pack of hounds upon him and followed them as they bayed the lion up from the paddock beside the Nile where he had killed his last bullock. The dogs cornered him at the head of a rocky defile. The lion fixed on us as soon as we came up and brushed the dogs aside as he charged through them.

As he came grunting and roaring towards us, my mistress had stood unwavering, only a pace behind Tanus' left shoulder, with her own puny little bow at full draw. Of course, it had been Tanus who had killed the beast, sending an arrow from the great bow Lanata hissing down his gaping throat, but we had both seen Lady Lostris' courage displayed in full measure.

I think it was probably on that day that Tanus first became aware of his true feelings for her, while for my mistress, the hunt and the chase were for ever bound up with the images and memories of her lover. She had remained ever since an avid huntress. She had learned from Tanus and myself to respect and to love the quarry, but not to burden herself with guilt when she exercised her god-given rights over the other creatures of the earth, to use them as beasts of burden, to consume them as food, or to pursue them as game.

We may have dominance over the beasts, but in the same way, all men and women are Pharaoh's cattle, and none may gainsay him. Promptly on the ninetieth night the king sent Aton to fetch my mistress.

BECAUSE OF our friendship and his own feelings for my mistress, Aton had given me ample warning before he came. I was able to make my final preparations well in advance of his arrival.

For the last time I rehearsed my mistress in exactly what to say to the king and how to behave towards him. Then I applied the ointment that I had reserved for this occasion. It was not only a lubricant, but contained also the essence of a herb that I use on other patients to deaden the pain of tooth-ache and other minor afflictions. It had the property of numbing the sensitive mucous membranes of the body.

She was brave right up to the moment that Aton appeared in the doorway of her chamber, and then her courage deserted her and she turned to me with tears brimming against her lids. 'I cannot go alone. I am afraid. Please come with me, Taita.' She was pale beneath the make-up that I had applied so carefully, and a fit of shivering took hold of her so that her small white teeth chattered together softly.

'Mistress, you know that is not possible. Pharaoh has sent for you. This once I cannot help you.'

It was then that Aton came to her aid. 'Perhaps Taita could wait in the ante-chamber of the king's bedroom, with me. After all, he is the royal physician, and his services may be needed,' he suggested in his reedy voice, and my mistress stood on tiptoe to kiss his fat cheek.

'You are so kind, Aton,' she whispered, and he blushed.

My Lady Lostris held my hand tightly as we followed Aton through the labyrinth of passages to the king's apartments. In the ante-chamber she squeezed it hard, and then dropped my hand and went to the doorway to the king's chamber. She paused and looked back at me. She had never looked so lovely or so young and vulnerable. My heart was breaking, but I smiled at her to give her courage. She turned from me and stepped through the curtains. I heard the murmur of the king's voice as he greeted her and her soft reply.

Aton seated me on a stool at the low table, then without a word set up the bao board between us. I played without attention, moving the polished round stones in the cups carved into the wooden board, and Aton won three quick games in succession. He had very seldom beaten me before, but I was distracted by the voices from the room beyond, although they were too low for me to catch the actual words.

Then quite clearly I heard my mistress say, exactly as I had coached her, 'Please, Your Majesty, be gentle with me. I beseech you, do not hurt me,' and the appeal was so moving that even Aton coughed softly and blew his nose upon his sleeve, while it was all I could do to restrain myself from leaping to my feet and rushing through the curtain to drag her away.

For a while there was silence and then a single high, sobbing cry that rent my soul, and once again silence.

Aton and I sat hunched over the bao board, no longer making any pretence at playing. I do not know how long we waited, but it must have been in the last watch of the night when I heard at last the sound of an old man's snores from beyond the curtain. Aton looked up at me and nodded, then he rose ponderously to his feet.

Before he reached the curtains, they parted, and my mistress stepped through them and came directly to where I sat. 'Take me home, Taita,' she whispered.

Without thinking about it I picked her up in my arms, and she hugged me around the neck and laid her head on my shoulder, just like she used to as a little girl. Aton took up the oil lamp and lit the way for us back to the harem. He left us at the door to my mistress's bedchamber. I laid her on the bed, and while she drowsed I examined her gently. There was a little blood, just a smear of it on those silken thighs, but it had staunched itself.

'Is there any pain, my little one?' I asked softly, and she opened her eyes and shook her head.

Then quite unexpectedly she smiled at me. 'I don't know what all the fuss was about,' she murmured. 'In the end, it was not much worse than using your water-stool, and it didn't take much longer either.' And she curled herself in a ball and fell asleep without another sound.

I almost wept with relief. All my preparations and the numbing herbs I had employed had seen her through without damage to either her body or her sweet spirit.

IN THE morning we went out hawking as though nothing untoward had happened, and my mistress mentioned the subject only once during the day. As we picnicked on the bank of the river, she asked thoughtfully, 'Will it be the same with Tanus, do you think, Taita?'

'No, mistress. You and Tanus love each other. It will be different. It will be the most wonderful moment in your entire life,' I assured her.

'Yes, I know deep in my heart that is how it should be,' she whispered, and involuntarily both of us looked northwards along the sweep of the Nile, towards Karnak far below the horizon.

Although I knew well where my duty towards Tanus lay, life on the island was so idyllic, and I so much enjoyed the exclusive company of my mistress, that I delayed my departure with the excuse that she still needed me. In truth, although Pharaoh sent for her night after night, my mistress had a tough and resilient streak in her and was blessed with the instinct of survival in full measure. Very swiftly she learned how to please the king, but at the same time to remain untouched and emotionally unmoved by it. She did not need me as much as Tanus did. Indeed, it was she who began to nag me to leave her at Elephantine and to journey down-river once again.

I procrastinated until one evening, after a full day out in the field with the king, we returned late to the palace. I saw to it that my mistress was bathed and her evening meal was laid out for her before I went to my own rooms.

As I entered my chamber the delicious odour of ripe mangoes and pomegranates filled the air. In the centre of the floor stood a large closed basket which I could tell was filled with these two favourite fruits of mine. I was not surprised to find it there, for never a day passed without gifts being sent to my mistress and me by someone seeking our favours.

I wondered who it was this time, and my mouth filled with saliva as another whiff of the fragrance filled my nostrils. I had not eaten since noon. As I lifted the woven lid and reached for the reddest and ripest of the pomegranates, the fruit spilled and rolled across the floor. There was a sharp hissing sound and a great black ball of writhing coils and gleaming scales flopped out of the basket and lashed out at my legs.

I leaped backwards, but not fast enough. The open jaws of the serpent struck the leather heel of my sandal with such force that I very nearly lost my balance. A cloud of venom was released from the curved fangs. The clear but deadly fluid drenched the skin of my ankle, but with another leap, I managed to evade the second strike that followed immediately upon the first. I threw myself back against the wall in the far corner of the room.

The cobra and I confronted each other across the width of the floor. Half its body was coiled upon itself, but the front portion of it was raised as high as my shoulder. Its hood was extended to display the broad black and white bands which patterned it. Like some dreadful black lily of death swaying upon its stem, it watched me with those glittering, beady eyes, and I realized that it stood between me and the only door to the chamber.

It is true that some cobras are kept as pets. They are given the run of the household, and they keep down the numbers of rats and mice that infest the building. They will drink milk from a jug and become as tame as kittens. There are others of these serpents that are trained by methods of torment and provocation to become deadly tools of the assassin. I was in no doubt as to which kind of cobra this was standing before me now.

I sidled along the wall, trying to outflank it and to reach safety. It launched itself at me, and the gape of its jaw was a pale sickly yellow and tendrils of venom drooled from the tips of its fangs. Involuntarily I yelled with terror as I sprang away from it and cowered in my corner again. The serpent recovered swiftly from the strike, and reared upright. It was still between me and the doorway. I knew that its poison sacs were charged with sufficient venom to kill a hundred strong men. As I watched, its lower body uncoiled slowly and it began to glide across the floor towards me, its flaring head held high and those terrible, bright little eyes fastened upon me.

I have seen one of these snakes mesmerize a fowl so that it made no move to escape at this sinuous approach, but lay before it with a patent air of resignation. I was paralyzed in the same way, and found that I could neither move nor cry out again as death glided towards me.

Then suddenly I saw a movement beyond the swaying cobra. My Lady Lostris appeared in the doorway, summoned by my first terrified cry. I found my voice again, and I screamed at her, 'Be careful! Come no closer!'

She paid no heed to my warning as she took in the scene at a glance. A moment's delay or hesitation on her part, and the serpent would have struck at me for the third and last time. My mistress had been at her dinner when she heard my cry for help. She stood now with a half-eaten melon in one hand and a silver knife in the other, and she reacted with the swift instinct of a true huntress.

Tanus had taught her to forsake the awkward double-jointed manner of throwing that is natural to the female, and she hurled the melon she held with the force and aim of a trained javelineer. It struck the cobra upon the back of its extended hood, and for a fleeting instant the blow knocked it flat upon the tiled floor. Like the release of a war bow, the serpent whipped erect and turned its dreadful head towards my mistress and then sped at her across the room in full attack.

I was released from my trance at last and started forward to help her, but I was too slow. Using its tail as a fulcrum, the cobra swung forward and aimed at her with its jaws so widely distended that venom sprayed from its erect fangs in a fine, pale mist. My mistress leaped back, agile and swift as a gazelle before the rush of the hunting cheetah. The cobra missed its strike, and for an instant the impetus threw it flat at her feet, extended to its full glistening, scaly length.

I do not know what possessed her, but she had never lacked in courage. Before the cobra could recover, she hopped forward again and landed with both those neat little sandalled feet upon the back of its head, pinning it to the tiles with her full weight.

Perhaps she had expected to crush its spine, but the snake was as thick as her wrist and resilient as the lash of Rasfer's whip. Although its head was pinned, the rest of its long body whipped up and over and coiled around her legs. A woman of lesser sense and nerve might have tried to escape that loathsome embrace. If she had done so my mistress would have died, for the instant the cobra's head was freed the death-strike would have followed.

Instead, she kept both feet planted firmly upon the writhing serpent, spreading her arms to balance herself, and she screamed out, 'Help me, Taita!'

I was already halfway across the room, and now I dived full length and thrust my hands into the coils of the serpent's body that boiled around her legs. I groped along its sinuous length, down to where it narrowed into the neck, and I seized it and locked both my hands around the cobra's throat, with my fingers entwined.

'I have him!' I yelled, almost incoherent with my own horror and loathing for this cold, scaly creature that struggled in my grip. 'I have him! Get away from us! Stand clear!'

My mistress leaped back obediently, and I came to my feet clutching the creature with a frantic strength, trying to keep its gaping jaws away from my face. The tail whipped back and wound around my shoulders and my neck, threatening to strangle me as I clung to the head. With this grip upon me the snake now had purchase, and its strength was terrifying. I found that I could not hold it, even with both my fists locked around its throat. It was gradually forcing its head free, drawing it inexorably back through my fingers. I realized that the instant it broke out of my grip, it would lash out at my unprotected face.

'I can't hold it!' I screamed, more to myself than to Lady Lostris. I was holding it at arm's-length, but it was pulling itself towards my face, drawing closer to my eyes every moment as waves of power pulsed through it, contracting and tightening the coils around my throat, forcing the head back through my fingers.

Although my knuckles were white with the strength of my grip, the cobra was so close to my face that I could see the fangs flicking back and forth in the roof of its wide gaping jaws. The cobra was able to erect or to flatten them at will. They were bony white needles, and pale, smoky jets of venom spurted from their tips. I knew that if even a droplet of that poison entered my eyes, it would blind me, and the burning pain of it might drive me half-mad.

I twisted the snake's head away from my face so that the spray of poison was discharged into the air, and I screamed again in despair, 'Call one of the slaves to help me!'

'On the table!' my mistress spoke close beside me. 'Hold its head on the table!' I was startled. I had thought that she had obeyed my order and run to find help, but she was at my side, and I saw that she still brandished the silver table-knife.

Carrying the cobra with me, I staggered across the floor and fell to my knees beside the low table. With a supreme effort I managed to force the snake's head down across one edge of the table, and to hold it there. It gave my mistress a chopping-block against which to wield the knife. She hacked at the base of the cobra's neck, behind the hideous head.

The snake felt the first cut and redoubled its struggles. Coil after coil of rubbery flesh lashed and contorted around my head. Hissing bursts of air flew from its gape, almost deafening us, the awful din mingling with the spurts of venom from its fangs.

The little blade was sharp, and the scaly flesh parted under it. Slippery, cool, ophidian blood welled up over my fingers, but the blade bit down to the bone of the spine. With all her strength and with her face contorted by the effort, my mistress sawed at the bone, but now my fingers were lubricated by the cobra's blood. I felt the head slither out between them and the serpent was free, but at the same moment the knife found the joint between the vertebrae and slipped through, cleaving the spine.

Dangling by a thread of skin, the head was thrown about loosely by the cobra's death-throes. Although almost severed from the body, the fangs still flickered and oozed poison. The lightest touch would be enough to drive them into my flesh. I tore at the body with frenzied, bloody fingers and at last managed to unwind it from around my throat, and to hurl it to the floor.

As the two of us backed away to the door, the snake continued its grotesque contortions, knotting itself and coiling into a ball, scaly turns sliding over each other.

'Are you harmed, my lady?' I asked, without being able to tear my eyes away from the death-throes of the carcass. 'Is there any of the venom in your eyes or on your skin?'

'I am all right,' she whispered. 'And you, Taita?' The tone of her voice alarmed me enough to make me forget my own distress, and I looked at her face. The reaction from danger had already seized her, and she was beginning to shake. Her dark green eyes were too large to fit that glassy white face. I had to find some way to release her from the icy grip of shock.

'Well,' I said briskly, 'that takes care of tomorrow evening's dinner. I do so love a nice piece of roast cobra.'

For a moment she stared at me blankly and then she let out a peal of hysterical laughter. My own laughter was no less wild and unrestrained. We clung helplessly to each other and laughed until tears poured down our cheeks.

I WOULD not trust our cook with it, so I prepared the cobra myself. I skinned and gutted it and stuffed it with wild garlic and other herbs, together with a dollop of mutton fat from the tail of a prime ram. Then I coiled it in a ball and wrapped it in banana leaves and covered the whole bundle with a thick coating of wet clay. I built over the lump of clay a hot fire which I kept burning all day.

That evening when I cracked open the hard-baked ball of clay, the aroma released by the succulent white flesh flooded our mouths with saliva. There are those who have dined at my table who say they have never eaten tastier food than that which I prepare, and who am I to contradict my friends?

I served the flaky fillets to my mistress with a wine of five-palm quality that Aton had chanced upon in Pharaoh's store-rooms. My Lady Lostris insisted that I sit with her under the barrazza in the courtyard and share the meal. We agreed that it was better than the tail of crocodile, or even than the flesh of the finest perch from the Nile.

It was only when we had eaten our fill and sent the rest of it to her slave maidens that we broached the matter of who it was that had sent me the gift of the basket of fruit.

I tried not to alarm my mistress, and made a joke of it: 'It must have been somebody who does not like my singing!' However, she was not to be put off so easily.

'Don't play the clown with me, Taita. It is one direction in which you have little talent. I think you know who it was, and I think I do as well.'

I stared at her, not sure how to deal with what I suspected was coming. I had always protected her, even from the truth. I wondered how far she had seen through me.

'It was my father,' she said with such finality that there was no reply or denial I could give her. 'Tell me about him, Taita. Tell me all the things I should know about him, but which you never dared tell me.'

It came hard at first. A lifetime of reticence cannot be overcome in a moment. It was still difficult to realize that I was no longer completely under the thrall of Lord Intef. Deeply as I had always hated him, he had dominated me body and soul since my childhood, and there persisted a kind of perverse loyalty that made it difficult for me to speak out freely against him. Weakly I attempted to fob her off with only the barest outlines of her father's clandestine activities, but she cut across me impatiently.

'Come now! Don't take me for a fool. I know more about my father than you ever dreamed. It is time for me to learn the rest of it. I charge you straight, tell me everything.'

So I obeyed her, and there was so much to tell that the full moon was halfway up the sky before I was done. We sat in silence for a long time afterwards. I had left out nothing, nor had I tried to deny or to excuse my own part in any of it.

'No wonder he wants you dead,' she whispered at last. 'You know enough to destroy him.' She was silent a little longer, and then she went on, 'My father is a monster. How is it possible that I am any different from him? Why, as his daughter, am I not also possessed by such unnatural instincts?'

'We must thank all the gods that you are not. But mistress, do you not despise me also for what I have done?'

She reached across and touched my hand. 'You forget that I have known you all my life, since the day that my mother died giving birth to me. I know what you really are. Anything you did, you were forced to do, and freely I forgive you for it.'

She sprang to her feet and paced restlessly around the lily pond before she returned to where I sat.

'Tanus is in terrible danger from my father. I never realized just how much until this evening. He must be warned so that he will be able to protect himself. You must go to him now, Taita, without delaying another day.'

'Mistress—' I began, but she cut me off brusquely.

'No, Taita, I will not listen to any more of your sly excuses. You will leave for Karnak tomorrow.'

SO BEFORE sunrise the next morning I set out fishing, alone in the skiff. However, I made certain that at least a dozen slaves and sentries saw me leave the island.

In a backwater of the lagoon I opened the leather bag in which I had concealed a tom-cat that had befriended me. He was a sad old animal riddled with mange and with agonizing canker in both ears. For some time I had been steeling myself to give him release from his misery. Now I fed him a lump of raw meat laced with Datura essence. I held him on my lap and stroked him as he ate, and he purred contentedly. As soon as he slipped painlessly into oblivion, I cut his throat.

I sprinkled the blood over the skiff, and dropped the carcass of the cat overboard where I knew that the crocodiles would soon dispose of it. Then, leaving my harpoons and lines and other gear on board, I pushed the skiff out into the slow current and waded through the papyrus beds to hard ground.

We had agreed that my mistress would wait until nightfall before she raised the alarm. It would be noon tomorrow before they found the blood-smeared skiff and concluded that I had been taken by a crocodile or been murdered by a band of the Shrikes.

Once I was ashore, I changed swiftly into the costume I had brought with me. I had chosen to impersonate one of the priests of Osiris. I would often ape their stilted gait and pompous manners for the amusement of my mistress. It needed only a wig, a touch of make-up and the correct costume to make the transformation. The priests are always on the move, up and down along the river, travelling between one temple and another, begging or rather demanding alms along the way. I would excite little interest, and my disguise might help to discourage an attack by the Shrikes. On superstitious grounds they were often reluctant to interfere with the holy men.

I skirted the lagoon and entered the town of West Elephantine through the poor quarter. At the docks I approached one of the barge captains who was loading a cargo of corn in leather bags and clay jugs of oil. With the right degree of arrogance I demanded free passage to Karnak in the name of the god, and he shrugged and spat on the deck, but allowed me to come aboard. All men are resigned to the extortions of the brotherhood. They may despise the priests, but they also fear their power, both spiritual and secular. Some say that the priesthood wields almost as much power as does Pharaoh himself.

The moon was full and the barge captain a more intrepid mariner than Admiral Nembet. We did not anchor at night. With the breeze and the full flood of the Nile behind us, we made a fair passage and on the fifth day rounded the bend of the river and saw the city of Karnak lying before us.

My stomach was queasy as I went ashore, for this was my town and every beggar and idler knew me well. If I were recognized, Lord Intef would hear about it before I could reach the city gates. However, my disguise held up, and I kept to the back alleys as I hurried in a purposeful and priestly manner to Tanus' house near the squadron base.

His front door was unbarred. I entered as though I had the right, and closed the door securely behind me. The starkly furnished rooms were deserted and when I searched them, I found nothing to give me any indication of his whereabouts. Tanus had obviously been gone for a long time, possibly since my mistress and I had left Karnak. The milk in a jug by the window had thickened and dried like hard cheese, and a crust of sorghum bread on the plate beside it was covered with a blue mould.

As far as I could see, nothing was missing; even the bow Lanata still hung on its rack above his bed. For Tanus to have left that was extraordinary. Usually it was like an extension of his body. I hid it away carefully in a secret compartment below his sleeping-place, which I had built for him when first he had moved into these lodgings. I wished to avoid moving around the city in daylight, so I remained in Tanus' rooms for the rest of that afternoon, occupying myself with cleaning up the dust and filth that had accumulated.

At nightfall I slipped out and went down to the riverside. I saw immediately that the *Breath of Horus* was at her moorings. She had obviously been in action since last I had seen her, and had suffered battle damage. Her bows were shattered and her timbers amidships had been scorched and charred.

I noted with a stir of proprietary pride that Tanus had made the modifications to her hull that I had designed. The gilded metal horn protruded from her bows, just above the water-line. From its battered condition I surmised that it had done fierce execution amongst the fleets of the red pretender.

However, I could see that neither Tanus nor Kratas was on deck. A junior officer whom I recognized had the watch, but I discarded the idea of hailing him, and instead set out to tour the sailors' haunts around the area of the docks.

It says a great deal for the morals and the sanctity of the priests of Osiris that I was welcomed in the dives and whorehouses like an habitué. In one of the more respectable taverns I recognized the impressive figure of Kratas. He was drinking and playing at dice with a group of his brother officers. I made no move to approach him, but I watched him across the crowded room. Meanwhile I fended off the advances of a succession of pleasure-birds of both sexes who were progressively lowering their tariffs in their efforts to tempt me out into the dark alleyway to sample their well-displayed charms. None of them were in the least deterred by my priestly collar of blue glass beads.

When Kratas at last gave his companions a hearty goodnight and made his way out into the alley, I followed his tall figure with relief.

'What is it you want from me now, beloved of the gods?' he growled at me with scorn when I hurried up beside him. 'Is it my gold or my bum-splitter you crave?' Many of the priests had taken enthusiastically to this modern vogue for pederasty.

'I'll take the gold,' I told him. 'You have more of that than the other, Kratas.' He stopped dead in his tracks and stared at me suspiciously. His bluff and handsome features were only a little flushed and befuddled by liquor.

'How do you know my name?' He seized me by the shoulder and dragged me into a lighted doorway, and studied my face. At last he snatched the wig from off my head. 'By the piles between Seth's buttocks, it's you, Taita!' he roared.

'I'd be obliged if you would refrain from shouting out my name to all the world,' I told him, and he turned serious at once.

'Come! We'll go to my rooms.'

Once we were alone, he poured two mugs of beer. 'Haven't you had enough of that?' I asked, and he grinned at me.

'We'll only know the answer to that in the morning. How now, Taita! Don't be too strict with me. We have been down-river raiding the red usurper's fleet for the past three weeks. Sweet Hapi, but that bow-horn of yours works wonders. We cut up nearly twenty of his galleys and we chopped the heads off a couple of hundred of his rascals. Although it was thirsty work, not a drop of anything stronger than water has passed my lips in all that time. Don't begrudge me a mouthful of beer now. Drink with me!' He raised his mug, and I was also thirsty. I saluted him in return, but as I put the mug down again, I asked, 'Where is Tanus?'

He sobered instantly. 'Tanus has disappeared,' he said, and I stared at him.

'Disappeared? What do you mean, disappeared? Did he not lead the raid down-river?'

Kratas shook his head. 'No. He's gone. Vanished. I have had my men scour every street and every house in all of Thebes. There is no sign of him. I tell you, Taita, I am worried, really worried.'

'When did you last see him?'

'Two days after the royal wedding, after the Lady Lostris married the king, on the evening of the day that you sailed with the royal flotilla for

Elephantine. I tried to talk some sense into his thick head, but he would not listen.'

'What did he say?'

'He handed over the command of the Breath of Horus and the entire squadron to me.'

'He could not do that, surely?'

'Yes, he could. He used the authority of Pharaoh's hawk seal.'

I nodded. 'And then? What did he do?'

'I have just told you. He disappeared.'

I sipped at the mug of beer as I tried to think it out. Meanwhile Kratas went to the window and urinated through it. It splashed noisily into the street below and I heard a startled passer-by shout up at him, 'Careful where you spray, you filthy pig!'

Kratas leaned out and quite cheerfully offered to crack his skull for him, and the man's grumblings receded rapidly. Chortling with this small victory, Kratas came back to me and I asked, 'What mood was Tanus in when he left you?'

Kratas turned serious again. 'The blackest and most ugly temper I have ever witnessed. He cursed the gods and Pharaoh. He even cursed the Lady Lostris and called her a royal whore.'

I winced to hear it. Yet I knew that this was not my Tanus speaking. It was the voice of despairing and hopeless love.

'He said that Pharaoh could carry out his threat to have him strangled for sedition and he would welcome the release. No, he was in terrible straits and there was nothing that I could do or say to comfort him.'

'That was all? He gave you no hint as to what he intended?' Kratas shook his head and refilled his beer mug.

'What happened to the hawk seal?' I asked.

'He left it with me. He said he had no further use for it. I have it safe aboard the Breath of Horus.'

'What of the other arrangements that I discussed with you? Have you done what I asked?'

He looked into his mug guiltily and muttered, 'I began to make the arrangements, but after Tanus was gone, there seemed no point to it. Besides, I have been busy down-river since then.'

'It is not like you, Kratas, to be so unreliable.' I had found that with Kratas hurt disappointment was more effective than anger. 'My Lady Lostris was relying on you. She told me that she trusted you completely. Kratas is a great rock of strength – those were her exact words.'

I could see that it was working yet again, for Kratas is also one of my mistress's ardent admirers. Even a hint of her displeasure would move him.

'Damn you, Taita, you make me sound like a weak-kneed idiot—' I kept silent, but silence can be more irksome than words. 'What in the name of Horus does the Lady Lostris want me to do?'

'Nothing more than I asked you to do before I left for Elephantine,' I told him, and he slammed down his mug.

'I am a soldier. I cannot leave my duties and take half the squadron to go off on some mad adventure. It was one thing when Tanus had the hawk seal—'

'You have the hawk seal now,' I told him softly.

He stared at me. 'I cannot use it without Tanus—'

'You are his lieutenant. Tanus gave you the hawk seal to use. You know what to do with it. Do it! I will find Tanus and bring him back, but you must be ready by then. There is desperate and bloody work ahead, and Tanus needs you. Don't let him down, not again.'

He flushed with anger at the jibe. 'I'll make you swallow those words,' he promised.

'And that will be the finest meal you could set for me,' I told him. I love brave and honest men, they are so easily manipulated.

I WAS uncertain as to how I would make good my promise to find Tanus, but I left Kratas to sleep off his debauch, and I went out into the town again to try. Once more I made the rounds of every one of his old haunts and questioned anyone who could possibly have seen him. I had no illusions as to the risk I was taking in pursuing my enquiries about Tanus, or as to just how flimsy was my disguise if I should run into anybody who knew me well, but I had to find him. I kept going through the night, until even the shebeens and whorehouses along the waterfront had thrown out the last drunken customers and doused their lamps.

As the dawn broke over the river, I stood tired and disconsolate on the bank of the Nile, and tried to think if there was some possibility I had overlooked. A wild honking cry made me look up. High above me a straggling skein of Egyptian geese was outlined against the pale gold and coppery tones of the eastern sky. Immediately they brought to my mind those happy days that the three of us, Tanus and the Lady Lostris and myself, had spent wild-fowling in the swamps.

'Fool!' I reviled myself. 'Of course that's it.'

By this time the alleyways of the souk were filled with a noisy, jostling crowd. Thebes is the busiest city in the world, no man is idle here. They blow glass and work gold and silver, they weave flax and throw pots. The merchant deals and haggles, the lawyer cants, the priest chants and the whore swives. It is an exciting, flamboyant city and I love it.

I forced my way through the throng and the hubbub of banter and bargaining as the merchants and the farmers displayed their wares for the housewives and the bailiffs of the rich households. The souk stank fulsomely of spices and fruits, of vegetables and fish and meats, some of which were far from fresh. Cattle bellowed and goats bleated and added their dung to the human contribution of excrement that trickled down the open gutters towards old Mother Nile.

I thought of buying an ass, for it would be a long walk in this hottest season of the year, and there were some sturdy beasts on offer. In the end I decided against such extravagance, not only on the grounds of economy, for I knew that once I was out in the open countryside, an expensive animal would certainly attract the attention of the Shrikes. For such a prize they might overcome their religious scruples. Instead, I purchased only a few handfuls of dates and a loaf of bread, a leather bag to carry these provisions and a gourd water-bottle. Then I set out through the narrow streets for the main gate of the city.

I had not reached the gates when there was a commotion in the street ahead of me and a detachment of the palace guards came towards me, using their staves to force a passage through the market crowds. Close behind them a half-dozen slaves carried an ornate and curtained litter at a jog-trot. I was trapped against the clay-daub walls of one of the buildings and though I recognized both the litter and the commander of the bodyguards, I could not avoid a confrontation.

Panic seized me. I might survive a casual scrutiny from Rasfer, but I was certain that even under my disguise, my Lord Intef would know me instantly. Standing beside me was an old slave woman with breasts like two great amphorae of olive oil and a backside like a hippopotamus's. I wriggled sideways until her bulk hid me. Then I settled my wig over my eyes and peeped out from behind her.

Despite my fears I felt a tingle of professional pride that Rasfer was on his feet again so soon after my surgery. He led his troop of bodyguards towards where I hid, but it was only when he drew almost level that I noticed that one side of his face had collapsed. It was as though his unlovely features had been modelled in wax and then held close to a naked flame. This condition is often the consequence of even the most skilful trepanning. The other half of his face was set in its customary scowl. If Rasfer had been hideous before, now he should cause the children to cry and their elders to make the sign against the evil eye when they looked upon him.

He passed close by where I stood, and the litter followed him. Through a chink in the embroidered curtains I caught a glimpse of Lord Intef as he sprawled elegantly on pillows of pure silk imported from the East that must have cost at least five gold rings each.

His cheeks were freshly shaved and his hair was dressed in formal ringlets. On top of his coiffure was set a cone of perfumed beeswax that would melt in the heat and trickle over his scalp and down his neck to cool and soothe his skin. One hand, the fingers stiff with jewelled rings, lay languidly on the smooth brown thigh of a pretty little slave boy who must have been a recent addition to his collection, for I did not recognize him.

I was taken off-guard by the strength of my own hatred as I looked at my old master. All the countless injuries and humiliations that I had suffered at his hands rushed back to torment me, and these were aggravated by his most recent outrage. By sending the cobra to me he had endangered the life of my mistress. If I had been able to forgive all else, I would never be able to forgive him that.

He began to turn his head in my direction, but before our eyes could meet, I sank down behind the mountainous woman in front of me. The litter was borne away down the narrow alley, and as I stared after it, I found that I was trembling just as I had after my struggle with the cobra.

'Divine Horus, hear this plea. Grant me no rest until he is dead and gone to his master, Seth,' I whispered, and I pushed my way on towards the city gate.

THE INUNDATION was at its height, and the lands along the river were in the fecund embrace of the Nile. As she had done every season from the beginning of time, she was laying down on our fields another rich layer of black silt. When she receded again, those glistening expanses would once more bloom with that shade of green that is peculiar to this very Egypt. The rich silt and the sunshine would raise three crops to harvest before the Nile poured over its banks once more to deliver its bounty.

The borders of the flooded fields were hemmed with the raised dykes that controlled the flood and also served as roadways. I followed one of these footpaths eastward until I reached the rocky ground along the foothills, then I turned southward. As I went, I paused occasionally to turn over a rock beside the path, until I found what I was looking for. Then I struck out with more determination.

I kept a wary eye on the rough and broken ground on my right-hand side, for that was just the type of terrain that would afford a fine ambush for a band of Shrikes. I was crossing one of the rocky ravines that lay across the pathway when I was hailed from close at hand.

'Pray for me, beloved of the gods!' My nerves were so tightly strung that I had let out a startled cry and leapt in the air before I could prevent it.

A shepherd boy sat on the edge of the ravine just above me. He was not more than ten years old, but he seemed as old as man's first sin. I knew that the Shrikes often used these children as their scouts and their sentinels. This grubby little imp looked perfect for that role. His hair was matted with filth, and he wore a badly tanned goat's skin that I could smell from where I stood. His eyes were as bright and as avaricious as those of a crow as he ran them over me, assessing my costume and my baggage.

'Where are you headed, and what is your business, good father?' he asked, and blew a long warbling note on his reed flute that could have been a signal to somebody hidden further up the hillside.

It took another few moments for my heart to steady its wild pace, and my voice was a little breathless as I told him, 'You are impertinent, child. What business is it of yours who I am or where I go?'

Immediately he changed his demeanour towards me. 'I am starved, gentle priest, an orphan forced to fend for myself. Don't you have a crust for me in that big bag of yours?'

'You look well-nourished to me.' I turned away, but he scrambled down the bank and danced beside me.

'Let me see in your bag, kind father,' he insisted. 'Alms, I beg of you, gentle sir.'

'Very well, you little ruffian.' Out of the bag I brought a ripe date. He reached out for it, but before his fingers touched it, I closed my hand and when I opened it again the date had been transformed into a purple scorpion. The poisonous insect lifted its tail menacingly over its head, and the boy screamed and fled back up the bank.

At the top he paused only long enough to howl at me, 'You are not a priest. You are one of the desert djinn. You are a devil, not a man.' Frantically he made the sign against the evil eye and spat three times on the ground, and then he raced away up the hill.

I had captured the scorpion from under a flat rock farther back along the path. Naturally, I had nipped the sting from the end of its tail before slipping it into my bag in readiness for just such an eventuality. The old slave who had taught me to read lips, had showed me a few other tricks while he was about it. One of them was sleight-of-hand.

At the shoulder of the next hill I paused to look back. The shepherd boy was on the crest far above me, but he was not alone. There were two men with him. They stood in a group looking down at me, and the child was gesticulating vehemently. As soon as they saw I had spotted them, all three of them disappeared over the skyline. I doubted they would want further truck with a demon priest.

I had not gone much farther when I saw movement on the track ahead of me, and I stopped short and shaded my eyes against the dazzle of the noonday sun. I was relieved to make out a small and innocent-seeming party coming in my direction. I moved forward cautiously to meet it, and as we drew together, my heart leaped as I thought I recognized Tanus. He was leading a donkey. The doughty little animal was heavily burdened. Atop the large bundle on its back sat a woman and a child, but it trotted on gamely. I saw that the woman was herself heavily burdened, her belly swelling out with her pregnancy. The child balanced behind her was a girl on the verge of puberty.

I was about to hail Tanus and hurry forward to meet him, when I realized that I was mistaken and the man was a stranger. It was his tall, broad-shouldered figure, the limber way he moved and the shining shock of gold-blond hair that had deceived me. He was watching me suspiciously and had drawn his sword. Now he pulled the donkey off the path and interposed himself between me and the precious burden it carried.

'The blessings of the gods upon you, good fellow.' I played out my role as priest, and he grunted and kept the point of the sword aimed at my belly. No man trusted a stranger in this very Egypt of ours.

'You risk the life of your family on this road, my friend. You should have sought out the protection of a caravan. There are brigands in the hills.' I was truly worried for them. The woman seemed gentle and decent, while the child was on the verge of tears at my warning.

'Pass on, priest!' the man ordered. 'Keep your advice for those who value it.'

'You are kind, gentle sir,' the woman whispered. 'We waited a week at Qena for the caravan, and could not wait longer. My mother lives at Luxor, and she will help with the birth of my baby.'

'Silence, woman!' her husband growled at her. 'We want no truck with strangers, even though they wear the robes of the priesthood.'

I hesitated, trying to fathom if there was anything that I could do for them. The girl was a pretty little thing with dark obsidian eyes, and she had quite touched my heart. However, at that moment the husband urged the donkey past where I stood, and with a helpless shrug, I watched them go.

'You cannot bleed for all of mankind,' I told myself. 'Nor can you force your advice on those who reject it.' Without looking back again, I went on northwards.

It was late afternoon before I looked down on the spur of rock that thrust out into the green swampland. Even from this vantage-point it was impossible to pick out the shanty. It was hidden deep in the papyrus beds, and the roof was of papyrus stems, so the concealment was perfect. I ran down the path, leaping from rock to rock, until I reached the edge of the water. This far from the main course of the Nile, the flood was not so significant.

I found our old dilapidated boat tied up at the landing. It was half-flooded and I had to bale it out before committing it to the water. I poled out cautiously along the tunnel through the papyrus. At low ebb of the Nile the shanty stood on dry land, but now there was sufficient water under the stilts that supported it to drown a standing man.

There was an empty boat in better shape than mine tied to one of the hut stilts. I moored mine beside it, climbed the rickety ladder and peered into our old hunting-lodge. It consisted of a single room, and the sunshine streamed in through the holes in the thatched roof, but no matter, for it never rains in Upper Egypt.

The hut had not been in such disorder since the day Tanus and I had first discovered it. Clothing and weapons and cooking-pots were scattered around like the debris of a battlefield. The stink of liquor was even more powerful than that of old food and unwashed bodies.

Those unwashed bodies were lying on an equally unwashed mattress in the far corner. I crossed the littered floor gingerly to inspect them for signs of life, and at that moment the woman grunted and rolled over. She was young and her naked body was full and enticing, with big round breasts and a thatch of crisp curls at the base of her belly. However, even in repose, her face was hard and common. I had no doubt that Tanus had found her on the waterfront.

I had always known him to be fastidious, and he was never a drinking man. This creature and the empty wine jars that were stacked against every wall were merely an indication of how far he had been brought down. I looked at him now as he slept, and hardly recognized him. His face was mottled and bloated with drink and covered with untrimmed beard. It was clear that he had not shaved since last I had seen him outside the harem walls.

At that moment the woman woke. Her eyes focused on me and in a single catlike movement she was off the mattress and reaching for the sheathed dagger hanging on the wall beside me. I snatched the weapon away before she could reach it and offered her the naked point.

'Go!' I ordered softly. 'Before I give you something in your belly that even you have never felt before.'

She gathered up her clothes and pulled them on hurriedly, all the while staring at me venomously.

'He has not paid me,' she said, once she was dressed.

'I am sure you have already helped yourself generously.' I gestured towards the door with the dagger.

'He promised me five rings of gold.' She changed her tone and began to whine. 'I have worked hard for him these last twenty days or more. I have done everything for him, cooked and kept his house, serviced him and cleaned up his puke when he was drunk. I must be paid. I will not leave until you pay me—'

I seized her by a lock of her long black hair and ushered her to the doorway. I helped her, still by means of her hair, into the more dilapidated of the two boats. Once she had poled out of my reach, she turned upon me such a stream of abuse that the egrets and other waterfowl were frightened from the reed-beds around us.

When I returned to where Tanus lay, he had not moved. I checked the wine jars. Most of them were empty, but there were still two or three that were full. I wondered how he had accumulated such a store of liquor, and guessed that he had probably sent the woman back to Karnak to find a ferryman to ship it out to him. There had been enough to keep the entire corps of the Blue Crocodile Guards drunk for a season. Little wonder that he was in such a condition.

I sat beside his mattress for a while, letting my sympathy for him run its full course. He had tried to destroy himself. I understood that, and did not despise him for it. His love for my mistress was such that without it he did not wish to continue living.

Of course I was also angry with him for abusing himself in such a fashion, and for succumbing to such self-indulgent folly. However, even in this pitiful drink-sodden state, I could still find much that was noble and admirable about him. After all, he was not alone in guilt. My mistress had tried to take poison for the very same reason as he had tried to destroy himself. I had understood and forgiven her. Could I do less for Tanus? I sighed for these two young people who were all that I had in life of any real value. Then I stood up and got to work.

Firstly, I stood over Tanus for a while, bolstering my anger to the extent that I could be really harsh with him. Then I took him by the heels and dragged him across the floor of the hut. He came half out of his stupor and cursed weakly, but I took no notice of his protests and tumbled him through the doorway. He plunged into the swamp head-first and raised a mighty splash as he went under. I waited for him to come up and flounder about groggily on the surface, still only half-conscious.

I dropped in beside him, grabbed a double handful of his hair and thrust his head back under-water. For a moment he struggled only weakly and I was able to hold him under with ease. Then his natural instincts of survival took over and he heaved up with all his old strength. I was lifted clear of the surface and thrown aside like a twig in a storm.

Tanus came out bellowing in the effort to draw breath, and striking out blindly at his unseen adversary. One of those blows would have stunned a hippopotamus, and I backed away hurriedly and watched him from a distance.

Coughing and choking, he floundered to the ladder and hung upon it with his hair streaming into his eyes. He had obviously swallowed so much water and sucked so much of it into his lungs that I felt a tingle of alarm. My cure might have been a little too vigorous. I was just about to go to his aid, when he opened his mouth wide and a foul mixture of swamp water and rotten wine erupted out of him. I was astonished by the quantity of it.

He hung on to the ladder, gasping and gurgling for breath. I swam to one of the stilts of the hut and waited until he had vomited again before I told him, putting all the contempt I could muster into my voice, 'My Lady Lostris would be so proud to see you now.'

He peered about with streaming eyes and focused on me at last. 'Taita, damn you! Was it you that tried to drown me? You idiot, I could have killed you.'

'In your present condition the only damage you could do would be to a jar of wine. What a sorry, disgusting sight you are!' I climbed the ladder into the hut and left him in the water, shaking his head and mumbling to himself. I set about tidying up the mess and the filth.

It was some time before Tanus followed me up the ladder and sat shamefacedly in the doorway. I ignored him and went on with my work, until at last he was forced to break the silence.

'How are you, old friend? I have missed you.'

'Others have missed you also. Kratas, for one. The squadron has been fighting down-river. They could have found use for another sword. My Lady Lostris, for another. She speaks of you every day, and holds her love pure and true. I wonder what she would think of that trollop I chased out of your bed?'

He groaned and held his head. 'Oh, Taita, don't speak your mistress's name. To be reminded of her is unbearable—'

'So broach another jug of wine and wallow in your own filth and your self-pity,' I suggested angrily.

'I have lost her for ever. What would you have me do then?'

'I would want you to have faith and fortitude, as she has.'

He looked up at me pitifully. 'Tell me about her, Taita. How is she? Does she still think of me?'

'More is the pity,' I grunted digustedly. 'She thinks of little else. She holds herself ready for the day that you two are brought together again.'

'That will never be. I have lost her for ever and I don't want to go on living.'

'Good!' I agreed briskly. 'Then I'll not waste further time here. I'll tell my mistress that you did not want to hear her message.' I pushed past him, swarmed down the ladder and dropped into the skiff.

'Wait, Taita!' he called after me. 'Come back!'

'To what purpose? You want to die. Then get on with it. I'll send the embalmers out to pick up the corpse later.'

He grinned with embarrassment. 'All right, I am being a fool. The drink has fuddled my mind. Come back, I beg of you. Give me the message from Lostris.'

With a show of reluctance I climbed back up the ladder, and he followed me into the hut, staggering only a little.

'My mistress bids me tell you that her love for you is untouched by any of the things that have been thrust upon her. She is still and will always be your woman.'

'By Horus, she puts me to shame,' he muttered.

'No,' I disagreed. 'Your shame is of your own making.'

He snatched his sword from the scabbard that hung above the filthy bed and slashed out at the row of wine amphorae that stood against the far wall. As each one burst, the wine poured out and trickled through the slats of the floor.

He was panting as he came back to me, and I scoffed at him. 'Look at you! You have let yourself go until you are as soft and as short of wind as an old priest—'

'Enough of that, Taita! You have had your say. Mock me no more, or you will regret it.'

I could see he was becoming as angry as I had intended. My insults were stiffening him up nicely. 'My mistress would have you take up the challenge thrown to you by Pharaoh so that you will still be alive and a man of honour and worth in five years' time, when she is free to come to you.'

I had his full attention now. 'Five years? What is this about, Taita? Will there truly be a term to our suffering?'

'I worked the Mazes for Pharaoh. He will be dead in five years from now,' I told him simply. He stared at me in awe and I saw a hundred different emotions pursue each other across his features. He is as easy to read as this scroll on which I write.

'The Mazes!' he whispered at last. Once long ago he had been a doubter, and had disparaged my way with the Mazes. That had changed and he was now an even firmer believer in my powers than my mistress. He had seen my visions become reality too often to be otherwise.

'Can you wait that long for your love?' I asked. 'My mistress swears that she can wait for you through all eternity. Can you wait a few short years for her?'

'She has promised to wait for me?' he demanded.

'Through all eternity,' I repeated, and I thought he might begin to weep. I could not have faced that, not watched a man like Tanus in tears, so I went on hastily, 'Don't you want to hear the vision that the Mazes gave me?'

He thrust back the tears. 'Yes! Yes!' he agreed eagerly, and so we began to talk. We talked until the night fell, and then we sat in the darkness and talked some more.

I told him the things that I had told my Lady Lostris, all the details that I had kept from them both over the years. When I came to the details of how his father, Pianki, Lord Harrab, had been ruined and destroyed by his secret enemy, Tanus' anger was so fierce that it burned away the last effects of the debauchery from his mind, and by the time the dawn broke over the swamps, his resolve was once more clear and strong.

'Let us get on with this enterprise of yours, for it seems the right and proper way.' He sprang to his feet and girded on his sword scabbard. Although I thought it wise to rest a while and let him recover fully from the effects of the wine, he would have no part of it.

'Back to Karnak at once!' he insisted. 'Kratas is waiting, and the lust to avenge my father's memory and to lay eyes on my own sweet love again burns like a fire in my blood.'

ONCE WE had left the swamp, Tanus took the lead along the rocky path, and I followed him at a run. As soon as the sun came up above the horizon, the sweat burst out across his back and streamed down to soak the waistband of his kilt. It was as though the rancid old wine was being purged from his body. Although I could hear him panting wildly, he never paused to rest or even moderated his pace, but ran on into the rising heat from the desert without a check.

It was I who pulled him up with a shout, and we stood shoulder to shoulder and stared ahead. The birds had caught my attention. I had picked out the commotion of their wings from afar.

'Vultures,' Tanus grunted with ragged breath. 'They have something dead amongst the rocks.' He drew his sword and we went forward cautiously.

We found the man first, and chased the vultures off him in a flurrying storm of wings. I recognized him by the shock of blond hair as the husband I had met on the road the previous day. There was nothing left of his face, for he had lain upon his back and the birds had eaten the flesh away to the bones of the skull. They had picked out his eyes, and the empty sockets stared at the cloudless sky. His lips were gone and he grinned with bloody teeth, as though at the futile joke of our brief existence upon this earth. Tanus rolled him on to his stomach, and we saw at once the stab-wounds in his back that had killed him. There were a dozen of these thrust through his ribs.

'Whoever did this was making sure of the job,' Tanus remarked, hardened to death as only a seasoned soldier can be.

I walked on into the rocks and a buzzing black cloud of flies rose from the dead body of the wife. I have never understood where the flies come from, how they materialize so swiftly out of the searing dry heat of the desert. I guessed that the wife had aborted while they were busy with her. They must have left her alive after they had taken their pleasure with her. With the last of her strength she had taken the infant protectively in her arms. She had died like that, huddled against a boulder, shielding her still-born infant from the vultures.

I went on deeper into the broken ground, and once again the flies led me to where the bandits had dragged the little girl. At least one of them had summoned up the compassion to cut her throat after they had finished with her, rather than let her bleed slowly to death.

One of the flies settled on my lips. I brushed it away and began to weep. Tanus found me still weeping.

'Did you know them?' he asked, and I nodded and cleared my throat to answer.

'I met them on the road yesterday. I tried to warn—' I broke off, for it was not easy to continue. I took a deep breath. 'They had a donkey. The Shrikes will have taken it.'

Tanus nodded. His expression was bleak as he turned away and made a rapid cast amongst the rocks.

'This way!' he called, and broke into a run, heading out into the rocky desert.

'Tanus!' I yelled after him. 'Kratas is waiting—' But he took not the least notice and I was left with no option but to follow him. I caught up with him again when he lost the tracks of the donkey on a bad piece of ground and was forced to cast ahead.

'I feel for that family even more than you do,' I insisted. 'But this is folly. Kratas waits for us. We do not have time to waste—'

He cut me off without even glancing in my direction, 'How old was that child? Not more than nine years? I always have time to see justice done.' His face was cold and vengeful. It was clear to see that he had recovered all his former mettle. I knew better than to argue further.

The image of the little girl was still strong and clear in my mind. I joined him and we picked up the trail again. Now, with the two of us cooperating, we went forward even more swiftly.

Tanus and I had tracked gazelle and oryx, and even lion, in this fashion and we had both become adept at this esoteric art. We worked as a team, running on each side of the spurs that our quarry had left, and signalling every twist or change in it to each other. Very soon our quarry reached a rough track that led eastward from the river and still deeper into the desert. They had joined it, and made our task of catching up with them that much simpler.

It was almost noon, and our water-bottles were empty when at last we spotted them far ahead. There were five of them, and the donkey. It was clear that they had not expected to be followed deep into the desert which was their fastness, and they were moving carelessly. They had not even taken the trouble to cover their back-trail.

Tanus pulled me down behind the shelter of a rock while we caught our breath, and he growled at me, 'We'll circle out ahead of them. I want to see their faces.'

He jumped up and led me in a wide detour out to one side of the track. We overtook the band of Shrikes, but well beyond their line of sight. Then we cut in again to meet the track ahead of them. Tanus had a soldier's eye for ground, and set up the ambuscade unerringly.

We heard them coming from afar, the clatter of the donkey's hooves and the sing-song of their voices. While we waited for them, I had the first opportunity to contemplate the prudence of my decision to follow along so unquestioningly. When the party of Shrikes at last came into view I was convinced that I had been over-hasty. They were as murderous-looking a bunch of ruffians as I had ever laid eyes upon, and I was armed only with my little jewelled dagger.

Just short of where we lay, the tall, bearded Bedouin who was obviously their leader stopped suddenly, and ordered one of the men who followed him to unload the water-skin from the donkey. He drank first and then passed it on to the others. My throat closed in sympathy as I watched them swallow down the precious stuff.

'By Horus, look at the stains of the women's blood on their robes. I wish I had Lanata with me now,' Tanus whispered, as we crouched amongst the rocks. 'I could put an arrow through that one's belly and drain the water from him like beer from the vat.' Then he laid a hand on my arm. 'Don't move until I do, do you hear me? I want no heroics from you now, mind.' I nodded vigorously, and felt not the slightest inclination to protest against these very reasonable instructions.

The Shrikes came on again directly to where we waited. They were all heavily armed. The Bedouin walked ahead. His sword was strapped between his shoulder-blades, but with the handle protruding up over his left shoulder, ready to hand. He had the cowl of his woollen cloak drawn over his head to protect him from the fierce sunlight. It impaired his side-vision and he did not notice us as he passed close in front of us.

Two others followed him closely, one of them leading the donkey. The last two sauntered along behind the animal, engrossed in a listless squabble over a piece of gold jewellery that they had taken from the murdered woman. All their weapons were sheathed, except for the short, bronze-headed stabbing spears carried by the last pair.

Tanus let them all pass, and then he stood up quietly and moved in behind the last two men in the column. He appeared to move casually, as the leopard does, but it was in reality only a breath before he swung his sword at the neck of the man on the right.

Although I had intended backing Tanus up to the full, somehow my good intentions had not been translated into action, and I still crouched behind my comforting rock. I justified myself with the thought that I would probably only have hindered him if I had followed him too closely.

I had never watched Tanus kill a man before. Although I knew that it was his vocation and that he had, over the years, had every opportunity to hone these gruesome skills, still I was astonished by his virtuosity. As he struck, his victim's head leapt from its shoulders like a desert spring-hare from its burrow, and the decapitated trunk actually took another step before the legs buckled under it. As the blow reached the limit of its arc, Tanus smoothly reversed the stroke. With the same movement he struck back-handed at the next brigand. The second neck severed just as cleanly. The head toppled off and fell free, while the carcass slumped forward with the blood fountaining high in the air.

The splash of blood and the weighty thump-thump of the two disembodied heads striking the rocky earth alerted the other three Shrikes. They spun about in alarm, and for a moment stared in bewildered disbelief at the sudden carnage in their ranks. Then with a wild shout they drew their swords and rushed at Tanus in a body. Rather than retreating before them, Tanus charged them ferociously, splitting them apart. He swung to face the man he had isolated from his mates, and his thrust ripped a bloody flesh-wound down the side of his chest. The man squealed and reeled backwards. But before Tanus was able to finish him off, the other two fell upon him from behind. Tanus was forced to spin round to face them, and bronze clashed on bronze as he stopped their charge. He held them off at sword's-length, engaging first one and then the other, until the lightly wounded man recovered and came at him from his rear.

'Behind you!' I yelled at him, and he whipped round only just in time to catch the thrust on his own blade. Instantly the other two were upon him again, and he was forced to give ground in order to defend himself from all sides. His swordsmanship was breathtaking to watch. So swift was his blade that it seemed that he had erected a glittering wall of bronze around himself against which the blows of his enemies clattered ineffectually.

Then I realized that Tanus was tiring. The sweat streamed from his body in the heat, and his features were contorted with the effort. The long weeks of wine and debauchery had taken their toll of what had once been his limitless strength and stamina.

He fell back before the next rush with which the bearded Bedouin drove at him, until he pressed his back to one of the boulders on the opposite side of the track from where I still crouched helplessly. With the rock to cover his back, all three of his attackers were forced to come at him from the front. But this was no real respite. Their attack was relentless. Led by the Bedouin, they howled like a pack of wild dogs as they bayed him, and Tanus' right arm tired and moved slower.

The spear carried by the first man whom Tanus had beheaded had fallen in the middle of the track. I realized that I must do something immediately if I were not to watch Tanus hacked down before my eyes. With a huge effort I gathered up my slippery courage, and crept from my hiding-place. The Shrikes had forgotten all about me in their eagerness for the kill. I reached the spot where the spear lay without any one of them noticing me, and I snatched it up. With the solid weight of the weapon in my hands, all my lost courage came flooding back.

The Bedouin was the most dangerous of the three of Tanus' adversaries, and he was also the closest to me. His back was towards me, and his whole attention was on the unequal duel. I levelled the spear and rushed at him.

The kidneys are the most vulnerable target in the human back. With my knowledge of anatomy, I could aim my thrust exactly. The spear-point went in a finger's-width to one side of the spinal column, all the way in. The broad spear-head opened a gaping wound, and skewered his right kidney with a surgeon's precision. The Bedouin stiffened and froze like a temple statue, instantly paralysed by my thrust. Then, as I viciously twisted the blade in his flesh the way Tanus had taught me, mincing his kidney to pulp, the sword fell from his fist and he collapsed with such a dreadful cry that his comrades were distracted enough to give Tanus his chance.

Tanus' next thrust took one of them in the centre of his chest, and despite his exhaustion it still had sufficient power in it to fly cleanly through the man's torso and for the blood-smeared point to protrude a hand-span from between his shoulder-blades. Before Tanus was able to clear his blade from the clinging embrace of live flesh and to kill the last Shrike, the survivor spun round and ran.

Tanus took a few paces after him, then gasped, 'I'm all done in. After him, Taita, don't let that murderous jackal get away.'

There are very few men that can outrun me. Tanus is the only one I know of, but he has to be on top form to do it. I put my foot in the centre of the Bedouin's back and held him down as I jerked the spearhead out of his flesh, and then I went after the last Shrike.

I caught him before he had gone two hundred paces, and I was running so lightly that he did not hear me coming up behind him. With the edge of the spear-head I slashed the tendon in the back of his heel, and he went down sprawling. The sword flew out of his hand. As he lay on his back kicking and screaming at me, I danced around him, pricking him with the point of the spear, goading him into position for a good clean killing thrust.

'Which of the women did you enjoy the best?' I asked him, as I stabbed him in the thigh. 'Was it the mother, with her big belly, or was it the little girl? Was she tight enough for you?'

'Please spare me!' he screamed. 'I did nothing. It was the others. Don't kill me!'

'There is dried blood on the front of your kilt,' I said, and I stabbed him in the stomach, but not too deeply. 'Did the child scream as loudly as you do now?' I asked.

As he rolled over into a ball to protect his stomach, I stabbed him in the spine, by a lucky chance finding the gap between the vertebrae. Instantly he was paralysed from the waist down, and I stepped back from him.

'Very well,' I said. 'You ask me not to kill you, and I won't. It would be too good for you.'

I turned away and walked back to join Tanus. The maimed Shrike dragged himself a little way after me, his paralysed legs slithering after him like a fisherman dragging a pair of dead carp. Then the effort was too much and he collapsed in a whimpering heap. Although it was past noon, the sun still had enough heat in it to kill him before it set.

Tanus looked at me curiously as I came back to join him. 'There is a savage streak in you that I never suspected before.' He shook his head in wonder. 'You never fail to amaze me.'

He pulled the water-skin from the back of the donkey and offered it to me, but I shook my head. 'You first. You need it more than I do.'

He drank, his eyes tightly closed with the pleasure of it, and then gasped, 'By the sweet breath of Isis, you are right. I am soft as an old woman. Even that little piece of sword-play nearly finished me.' Then he looked around at the scattered corpses, and grinned with satisfaction. 'But all in all, not a bad start on Pharaoh's business.'

'It was the poorest of beginnings,' I contradicted him, and when he crooked an eyebrow at me I went on, 'We should have kept at least one of them alive to lead us to the Shrikes' nest. Even that one', I gestured towards the dying man lying out there amongst the rocks, 'is too far-gone to be of any use to us. It was my fault. I allowed my anger to get the better of me. We won't make the same mistake again.'

We were halfway back to where we had left the bodies of the murdered family before my true nature reasserted itself, and I began bitterly to regret my callous and brutal treatment of the maimed brigand.

'After all, he was a human being, as we are,' I told Tanus, and he snorted.

'He was an animal, a rabid jackal, and you did a fine job. You have mourned him far too long. Forget him. Tell me, instead, why we must make this detour back to look at dead men, instead of heading straight for Kratas' camp.'

'I need the husband's body.' I would say no more until we stood over the mutilated corpse. The pathetic relic was already stinking in the heat. The vultures had left very little flesh on the bones.

'Look at that hair,' I told Tanus. 'Who else do you know with a bush like that?' For a moment he looked puzzled, and then he grinned and ran his fingers through his own dense ringlets.

'Help me load him on the donkey,' I ordered. 'Kratas can take him into Karnak to the morticians for embalming. We'll buy him a good funeral and a fine tomb with your name on the walls. Then, by sunset tomorrow, all of Thebes will know that Tanus, Lord Harrab perished in the desert, and was half-eaten by the birds.'

'If Lostris hears of it—' Tanus looked worried.

'I'll send a warning letter to her. The advantage we will win by letting the world believe you dead will far outweigh any risk of alarming my mistress.'

KRATAS WAS camped at the first oasis on the caravan road to the Red Sea, less than a day's march from Karnak. He had with him a hundred men of the Blue Crocodile Guards, all of them carefully selected, as I had commanded. Tanus and I reached the encampment in the middle of the night. We had travelled hard and were close to exhaustion. We fell on our sleeping-mats beside the camp-fire and slept until dawn.

At first light, Tanus was up and mingling with his men. Their delight at having him back was transparent. The officers embraced him and the men cheered him, and grinned with pride as he greeted each of them by name.

At breakfast Tanus gave Kratas instructions to take the putrefying corpse back to Karnak for burial and to make certain that the news of his death was the gossip of all Thebes. I gave Kratas a letter for my Lady Lostris. He would find a trustworthy messenger to carry it up-river to Elephantine.

Kratas selected an escort of ten men, and they prepared to set off with the donkey and its odorous burden, back towards the Nile and Thebes.

'Try to catch up with us on the road to the sea. If you cannot, then you'll find us camped at the oasis of Gebel Nagara. We will wait for you there,' Tanus shouted after him, as the detachment trotted out of the encampment. 'And remember to bring Lanata, my bow, when you return!'

NO SOONER was Kratas out of sight beyond the first rise on the westerly road than Tanus formed up the rest of the regiment and led us away in the opposite direction along the caravan road towards the sea.

The caravan road from the banks of the river Nile to the shores of the Red Sea was long and hard. A large, unwieldy caravan usually took twenty days to make the journey. We covered the distance in four days, for Tanus pushed us in a series of forced marches. At the outset, he and I were probably the only ones of all the company who were not in superb physical condition. However, by the time we reached Gebel Nagara, Tanus had burned the excess fat off his frame and sweated out the last poisons from the wine jar. He was once again lean and hard.

As for myself, it was the first time that I had ever made a forced march with a company of the guards. For the first few days I suffered all the torments of thirst and aching muscles, of blistered feet and exhaustion that the *Ka* of a dead man must be forced to endure on the road to the underworld. However, my pride would not allow me to fall behind, apart from the fact that to do so in this wild and savage landscape would have meant certain death. To my surprise and pleasure, I found that after the first few days, it became easier and easier to keep my place in the ranks of trotting warriors.

Along the way, we passed two large caravans moving towards the Nile, with the donkeys bow-legged under their heavy loads of trade goods, and escorts of heavily armed men far surpassing in number the merchants and their retainers who made up the rest of the company. No caravan was safe from the depredations of the Shrikes unless it was protected by a force of mercenaries such as these, or unless the merchants were prepared to pay the crippling toll money that the Shrikes demanded to allow them free passage.

When we met these strangers, Tanus pulled his shawl over his head to mask his face and hide that golden bush of hair. He was too distinctive a figure to risk being recognized and his continued existence being reported in Karnak. We did not respond to the greetings and questions that were flung at us by these other travellers, but ran past them in aloof silence without even glancing in their direction.

When we were still a day's march from the coast, we left the main caravan route and swung away southwards, following an ancient disused track that had been shown to me some years previously by one of the wild Bedouin whom I had befriended. The wells at Gebel Nagara lay on this old route to the sea, and were seldom visited by humans these days, only by the Bedouin and the desert bandits, if you can call these human.

By the time we reached the wells, I was as slim and physically fit as I had ever been in my life, but I lamented the lack of a mirror, for I was convinced that this new energy and force that I felt within myself must be reflected in my features, and that my beauty must be enhanced by it. I would have welcomed the opportunity to admire it myself. However, there seemed to be no dearth of others to admire it in my place. At the camp-fire in the evenings, many a prurient glance was flashed in my direction, and I received more than a few sly offers from my companions, for even such an elite fighting corps as the guards was contaminated by the new sexual licence that permeated our society.

I kept my dagger beside me in the night and when I pricked the first uninvited visitor to my sleeping-mat with the needle-point, his yells caused much hilarity amongst the others. After that, I was spared any further unwelcome attentions.

Even once we had reached the wells, Tanus would allow us little rest. While we waited for Kratas to catch up, he kept his men exercising at arms, and at competitions of archery and wrestling and running. I was pleased to see that Kratas had chosen these men strictly in accordance with my instructions to him. There was not a single hulking brute amongst them. Apart from Tanus himself, they were all small, agile men aptly suited to the role that I planned for them.

Kratas arrived only two days behind us. Taking into account his return to Karnak and the time taken up by the tasks that Tanus had set for him there, this meant that he must have travelled even more swiftly than we had done.

'What held you up?' Tanus greeted him. 'Did you find a willing maid on the way?'

'I had two heavy burdens to carry,' Kratas replied, as they embraced. 'Your bow, and the hawk seal. I am glad to be rid of both of them.' He handed over both the weapon and the statuette with a grin, delighted as ever to be back with Tanus.

Tanus immediately took Lanata out into the desert. I went with him and helped him stalk close to a herd of gazelle. With these fleet little creatures racing and leaping across the plain, it was an extraordinary sight to watch Tanus bowl over a dozen of them at full run with as many arrows. That night, as we feasted on grilled livers and fillets of gazelle, we discussed the next stage of my plan.

In the morning we left Kratas in command of the guards, and Tanus and I set out alone for the coast. It was only half a day's travel to the small fishing village which was our goal, and at noon we topped the last rise and looked down from the hills on to the glittering expanse of the sea spread below us. From this height we could see clearly the dark outline of the coral reefs beneath the turquoise waters.

As soon as we entered the village, Tanus called for the headman, and so apparent from his bearing was Tanus' importance and authority, that the old man came at a run. When Tanus showed him the hawk seal, he fell to the earth in obeisance, as though it were Pharaoh himself who stood before him, and beat his head upon the ground with such force that I feared he might do himself serious injury. When I lifted him to his feet once more, he led us to the finest lodgings in the village, his own filthy hovel, and turned his numerous family out to make room for us.

Once we had eaten a bowl of the fish stew that our host provided and drunk a cup of the delicious palm wine, Tanus and I went down to the beach of dazzling white sand and bathed away the sweat and the dust of the desert in the warm waters of the lagoon that was enclosed by the jagged barricade of coral that lay parallel to the shore. Behind us the harsh mountains, devoid of the faintest green tinge of growing things, thrust up into the aching blue desert sky.

Sea, mountains and sky combined in a symphony of grandeur that stunned the senses. However, I had little time to appreciate it all, for the fishing fleet was returning. Five small dilapidated vessels with sails of woven palm-fronds were coming in through the pass in the reef. So great was the load of fish that each of them carried, that they seemed in danger of foundering before they could reach the beach.

I am fascinated by all the natural bounty that the gods provide for us, and I examined the catch avidly as it was thrown out upon the beach, and questioned the fishermen as to each of the hundred different species. The pile of fish formed a glittering treasure of rainbow colours, and I wished that I had my scrolls and paint-pots to record it all.

This interlude was too brief. As soon as the catch was unloaded, I embarked on one of the tiny vessels that stank so abundantly of its vocation, and waved back at Tanus on the beach as we put out through the pass in the reef. He was to remain here until I returned with the equipment that we needed for the next part of my plan. Once again, I did not want him to be recognized where I was going. His job now was to prevent any of the fishermen or their families from sneaking away into the desert to a secret meeting with the Shrikes, to report the presence in their village of a golden-headed lord who bore the hawk seal.

The tiny vessel threw up her bows at the first strong scend of the sea, and the helmsman tacked across the wind and headed her up into the north, running parallel to that dun and awful coast. We had but a short way to go, and before nightfall the helmsman pointed over the bows at the clustered stone buildings of the port of Safaga on the distant shoreline.

FOR A thousand years Safaga had been the entrepôt for all trade coming into the Upper Kingdom from the East. Even as I stood in the bows of our tiny craft, I could make out the shapes of other much larger vessels on the northern horizon as they came and went between Safaga and the Arabian ports on the eastern shore of the narrow sea.

It was dark by the time that I stepped ashore on the beach at Safaga, and nobody seemed to remark my arrival. I knew exactly where I was going, for I had visited the port regularly on Lord Intef's nefarious business. At this hour the streets were almost deserted, but the taverns were packed. I made my way swiftly to the home of Tiamat the merchant. Tiamat was a rich man and his home the largest in the old town. An armed slave barred the door to me.

'Tell your master that the surgeon from Karnak who saved his leg for him is here,' I ordered, and Tiamat himself limped out to greet me. He was taken aback when he saw my clerical disguise, but had the good sense not to remark on it, nor to mention my name in front of the slave. He drew me into his walled garden, and as soon as we were alone he exclaimed, 'Is it really you, Taita? I heard that you had been murdered by the Shrikes at Elephantine.'

He was a portly, middle-aged man, with an open, intelligent face and a shrewd mind. Some years previously he had been carried in to me on a litter. A party of travellers had found him beside the road, where he had been left for dead after his caravan had been pillaged by the Shrikes. I had stitched him together, and even managed to save the leg that had already mortified by the time I first saw it. However, he would always walk with a limp.

'I am delighted to see that the reports of your death are premature,' he chuckled, and clapped his hands to have his slaves bring me a cup of cool sherbet and a plate of figs and honeyed dates.

After a decent interval of polite conversation, he asked quietly, 'Is there anything I can do for you? I owe you my life. You have only to ask. My home is your home. All I have is yours.'

'I am on the king's business,' I told him, and drew out the hawk seal from under my tunic.

His expression became grave. 'I acknowledge the seal of Pharaoh. But it was not necessary to show it to me. Ask what you will of me. I cannot refuse you.'

He listened to all I had to say without another word, and when I had finished, he sent for his bailiff and gave him his orders in front of me. Before he sent the man away, he turned to me and said, 'Is there anything that I have forgotten? Anything else you need at all?'

'Your generosity is without limits,' I told him, 'However, there is one other thing. I long for my writing materials.'

He turned back to the bailiff. 'See to it that there are scrolls and brushes and ink-pot in one of the packs.'

After the bailiff had left, we sat on talking for half the night. Tiamat stood at the centre of the busiest trading route in the Upper Kingdom, and heard every rumour and whisper from the farthest reaches of the empire, and from beyond the sea. I learned as much in those few hours in his garden as I would in a month in the palace at Elephantine.

'Do you still pay your ransom to the Shrikes to allow your caravans through?' I asked, and he shrugged with resignation.

'After what they did to my leg, what option do I have? Each season their demands become more exorbitant. I must pay over one-quarter of the value of my goods to them as soon as the caravan leaves Safaga, and half my profits once the goods are sold in Thebes. Soon they will beggar us all, and grass will grow on the caravan roads, and the trade of the kingdom will wither and die.'

'How do you make these payments?' I asked. 'Who determines the amount, and who collects them?'

'They have their spies here in the port. They watch every cargo that is unloaded, and they know what each caravan carries when it leaves Safaga. Before it even reaches the mountain pass, it will be met by one of the robber chieftains who will demand the ransom they have set.'

It was long past midnight before Tiamat called a slave to light me to the chamber he had set aside for me.

'You will be gone before I rise tomorrow.' Tiamat embraced me. 'Farewell, my good friend. My debt to you is not yet paid in full. Call upon me again, whenever you have need.'

The same slave woke me before dawn, and led me down to the seafront in the darkness. A fine trading vessel of Tiamat's fleet was moored inside the reef. The captain weighed anchor as soon as I came aboard.

In the middle of the morning we crept in through the pass in the coral and dropped anchor in front of the little fishing village where Tanus stood on the beach to welcome me.

DURING MY absence Tanus had managed to gather together six decrepit donkeys, and the sailors from Tiamat's ship waded ashore carrying the bales that we had brought with us from Safaga, and loaded them on to these miserable creatures. Tanus and I left the captain of the trading vessel with strict orders to await our return, then, leading the string of donkeys, we headed back inland towards the wells at Gebel Nagara.

Kratas' men had obviously suffered the heat and the sand-flies and the boredom with poor grace, for they accorded us a welcome that was out of keeping with the period that we had been absent. Tanus ordered Kratas to parade them. The ranks of warriors watched as I unpacked the first bale that we had brought in on the donkey train. Almost immediately their interest gave way to mild amusement as I laid out the costume of a slave girl. In its turn, this was replaced by a buzz of speculation and argument as the bales yielded up a further seventy-nine complete female costumes.

Kratas and two of his officers helped me place one of these on the sand in front of each guardsman, and then Tanus gave the order: 'Disrobe! Put on the dress in front of you!' There was a roar of protest and incredulous hilarity, and it was only when Kratas and his officers passed down the ranks with assumed expressions of sternness to reinforce the order, that they began to obey it.

Unlike our women who dress but lightly and often leave their bosom bared and their legs free and naked, the women of Assyria wear skirts that sweep the ground and sleeves that cover their arms to the wrist. For reasons of misplaced modesty they even veil their faces when they walk abroad, although perhaps these restrictions are placed upon them by the possessive jealousy of their menfolk. Then again there is a wide difference between the sunny land of Egypt and those more sombre climes where water falls from the sky and turns solid white upon the mountaintops, and the winds chill the flesh and the bones of men like death.

Once they had weathered the first shock of seeing each other in this outlandish apparel, the men entered into the spirit of the moment. Soon there were eighty veiled slave girls prancing and mincing about in the long skirts that reached to their ankles, tweaking each other's buttocks and casting exaggerated sheep's eyes at Tanus and his officers.

The officers could no longer maintain their gravity. Perhaps it is because of my peculiar circumstances that I have always found the spectacle of men dressed as women to be vaguely repulsive, but it is strange how few other men share my feelings of distaste, and it needs only some hairy ruffian to don a skirt to reduce his audience to a state of incontinence.

In the midst of this uproar, I congratulated myself that I had insisted that Kratas choose only the smallest and slimmest men from the squadron. Looking them over now, I was certain that they would be able to carry through the deception. They would need only a little schooling in feminine deportment.

THE FOLLOWING morning our strange caravan passed through the little fishing village and wound its way down on to the beach, where the trading vessel waited. Kratas and eight of his officers made up the escort. Complete lack of any armed escort for such a valuable consignment would surely have aroused suspicion. Nine armed men dressed in the motley garb of mercenaries would be sufficient to allay this, but would not deter a large raiding party of Shrikes.

At the head of the caravan marched Tanus, dressed in the rich robes and beaded head-dress of a wealthy merchant from beyond the Euphrates river. His beard had grown out densely, and I had curled it for him into those tight ringlets that the Assyrians favoured. Many of these Asians, particularly those from the high mountainous regions further north, have the same complexion and skin coloration as Tanus, so he looked the part I had chosen for him.

I followed close behind him. I had overcome my aversion to wearing female garb, and donned the long skirts and veil, together with the gaudy jewellery of an Assyrian wife. I was determined not to be recognized when I returned to Safaga.

The voyage was enlivened by the sea-sickness of most of the slave girls and not a few of the officers, for they were accustomed to sail on the placid waters of the great river. At one stage so many of them were lining the rail to make their offerings to the gods of the sea, that the ship took on a distinct list.

We were all relieved to step on to the beach at Safaga, where we caused much excitement. The Assyrian girls were famous for their skills on the love couch. It was said that some of them were capable of tricks that could bring a thousand-year-old mummy back to life. It was obvious to those who watched us come ashore that behind the veils our slave girls must be images of feminine loveliness. A shrewd Asian merchant would not transport his wares so far and at such expense, unless he was certain of a good price in the slave-markets on the Nile.

One of the Safaga merchants approached Tanus immediately and offered to buy the entire bevy of girls on the spot, and spare him the onerous journey across the desert with them. Tanus waved him away with a scornful chuckle.

'Have you been warned of the perils of the journey that you intend making?' the merchant insisted. 'Before you reach the Nile, you will be forced to pay a ransom for your safe passage that will eat up most of your profits.'

'Who will force me to pay?' Tanus demanded. 'I pay only what I owe.'

'There are those who guard the road,' the merchant warned him. 'And even though you pay what they demand, there is no certainty that they will let you pass unharmed, especially with such tempting goods as you have with you. The vultures on the road to the Nile are so fat from feeding on the carcasses of stubborn merchants that they can hardly fly. Sell to me now at a good profit—'

'I have armed guards', Tanus indicated Kratas and his small squad, 'who will be a match for any robbers we may meet.' And the onlookers who had listened to the exchange tittered and nudged each other at the boast.

The merchant shrugged. 'Very well, my brave friend. On my next journey through the desert, I will look for your skeleton beside the road. I will recognize you by that blustering red beard of yours.'

As he had promised me he would, Tiamat had forty donkeys waiting for us. Twenty of them were laden with filled water-skins, and the remainder with pack-saddles to carry the bales and bundles that we brought ashore from the trading ship.

I was anxious that we should spend as little time as possible in the port, under all those prying eyes. It would take only a single lapse by one of the slave girls to reveal his true gender, and we would be undone. Kratas and his escort hurried them through the narrow streets, keeping the bystanders at a distance, and making certain that the slave girls kept their veils in place and their eyes downcast, and that none of them responded in gruff masculine tones to the ribald comment that followed us, until we were out into the open country beyond the town.

We camped that first night still within sight of Safaga. Although I did not anticipate an attack until we were beyond the first mountain pass, I was certain that we were already being watched by the spies of the Shrikes.

While it was still light, I made sure that our slave girls conducted themselves as women, that they kept their faces and bodies covered, and that when they went into the nearby wadi to attend to nature's demands, they squatted in decorous fashion and did not uncouthly spray their water while standing.

It was only after darkness fell that Tanus ordered the bundles carried by the donkeys to be opened and the weapons they contained to be issued to the slave girls. Each of them slept with his bow and his sword concealed under his sleeping-mat.

Tanus posted double sentries around the camp. After we had inspected them and made sure that they were all well placed and fully alert, Tanus and I slipped away, and in the darkness returned to the port of Safaga. I led him through the dark streets to the house of Tiamat. The merchant was expecting our arrival, and had a meal laid ready to welcome us. I could see that he was excited to meet Tanus.

'Your fame proceeds you, Lord Harrab. I knew your father. He was a man indeed,' he greeted Tanus. 'Although I have heard persistent rumours that you died in the desert not a week since, and that even at this moment your body lies with the morticians on the west bank of the Nile, undergoing the ritual forty days of the embalming process, you are welcome in my humble house.'

While we enjoyed the feast he provided, Tanus questioned him at length on all he knew of the Shrikes, and Tiamat answered him freely and openly.

At last Tanus glanced at me and I nodded. Tanus turned back to Tiamat and said, 'You have been a generous friend to us, and yet we have been less than honest with you. This was from necessity, for it was of vital importance that no one should guess at our real purpose in this endeavour. Now I will tell you that it is my purpose to smash the Shrikes and deliver their leaders up to Pharaoh's justice and wrath.'

Tiamat smiled and stroked his beard. 'This comes as no great surprise to me,' he said, 'for I have heard of the charge that Pharaoh placed upon you at the festival of Osiris. That and your patent interest in those murderous bandits left little doubt in my mind. I can say only that I will sacrifice to the gods for your success.'

'To succeed, I will need your help again,' Tanus told him.

'You have only to ask.'

'Do you think that the Shrikes are as yet aware of our caravan?'

'All of Safaga is talking about you,' Tiamat replied. 'Yours is the richest cargo that has arrived this season. Eighty beautiful slave girls will be worth at least a thousand gold rings each in Karnak.' He chuckled and shook his head at the joke. 'You can be certain that the Shrikes already know all about you. I saw at least three of their spies in the crowd at the waterfront watching you. You can expect them to meet you and make their demands even before you reach the first pass.'

When we rose to take our leave, he walked with us as far as his own door. 'May all the gods attend your endeavours. Not only Pharaoh, but every living soul in the entire kingdom will be in your debt if you can stamp out this terrible scourge that threatens to destroy our very civilization, and drive us all back into the age of barbarism.'

IT WAS still cool and dark the following morning when the column started out. Tanus, with Lanata slung over his shoulder, was at the head of the caravan, with myself, in all my womanly grace and beauty, following him closely.

Behind us the donkeys were harnessed in single file, moving nose to tail down the middle of the well-beaten track. The slave girls were in double columns on the outer flanks of the file of donkeys. Their weapons were concealed in the packs upon the backs of the animals. Any of the men needed only to reach out to lay a hand upon the hilt of his sword.

Kratas had split his escort into three squads of six men each, commanded by Astes, Remrem and himself. Astes and Remrem were warriors of renown and more than deserving of their own commands. However, both of them had, on numerous occasions, refused promotion in order to remain with Tanus. That was the quality of loyalty that Tanus inspired in all who served under him. I could not help thinking yet again what a pharaoh he would have made.

The escorts now slouched along beside the column, making every attempt to forsake their military bearing. It would seem to the spies who were certainly watching us from the hills that they were there solely to prevent any of the slaves from escaping. In truth they were fully occupied with preventing their charges from breaking into marching step and sounding off a chorus of one of the rowdy regimental songs.

'You there, Kernit!' I heard Remrem challenge one of them. 'Don't take such long steps, man, and swing that fat arse of yours a little! Try to make yourself alluring.'

'Give me a kiss, captain,' Kernit called back, 'and I'll do anything you say.'

The heat was rising, and the mirage was beginning to make the rocks dance. Tanus turned back to me. 'Soon I will call our first rest-stop. One cup of water for each—'

'Good husband,' I interrupted him, 'your friends have arrived. Look ahead!'

Tanus turned back, and instinctively gripped the stock of the great bow that hung at his side. 'And what fine fellows they are, too!'

At that moment our column was winding through the first foothills below the desert plateau. On either hand we were walled in by the steep sides of the rocky hills. Now three men stood in the track ahead of us. The one who led them was a tall, menacing figure swathed in the woollen robe of the desert traveller, but his head was bared. His skin was very dark, and deeply pitted with the scars of the smallpox. He had a nose that was hooked like the beak of a vulture, and his right eye was an opaque jelly from the blind-worm that burrows deep into the eyeball of its victims.

'I know the one-eyed villain,' I said softly, so that Tanus alone could hear. 'His name is Shufti. He is the most notorious of the barons of the Shrikes. Be wary of him. The lion is a gentle beast compared to this one.'

Tanus gave no sign of having heard me, but lifted his right hand to show that it held no weapon, and called out cheerfully, 'May all your days be scented with jasmine, gentle traveller, and may a loving wife welcome you at your own front door when at last your journey is done.'

'May your water-skins stay filled and cool breezes fan your brow when you cross the Thirsty Sands,' Shufti called back, and he smiled. That smile was fiercer than a leopard's snarl, and his single eye glared horribly.

'You are kind, my noble lord,' Tanus thanked him. 'I would like to offer you a meal and the hospitality of my camp, but I pray your indulgence. We have a long road before us, and we must pass on.'

'Just a little more of your time, my fine Assyrian.' Shufti moved forward to block the path. 'I have something which you need, if you and your caravan are ever to reach the Nile in safety.' He held up a small object.

'Ah, a charm!' Tanus exclaimed. 'You are a magician, perhaps? What manner of charm is this you are offering me?'

'A feather.' Shufti was still smiling. 'The feather of a shrike.'

Tanus smiled, as though to humour a child. 'Very well then, give me this feather and I'll delay you no longer.'

'A gift for a gift. You must give me something in return,' Shufti told him. 'Give me twenty of your slaves. Then, when you return from Egypt, I will meet you on the road again and you will give me half the profits from the sale of the other sixty.'

'For a single feather?' Tanus scoffed. 'That sounds like a sorry bargain to me.'

'This is no ordinary feather. It is a shrike's feather,' Shufti pointed out. 'Are you so ill-informed that you have never heard of that bird?'

'Let me see this magical feather.' Tanus walked towards him with his right hand outstretched, and Shufti came forward to meet him. At the same time Kratas, Remrem and Astes wandered up inquisitively, as though to examine the feather.

Instead of taking the gift from his hand, suddenly Tanus seized Shufti's wrist and twisted it up between his shoulder-blades. With a startled cry,

Shufti fell to his knees and Tanus held him easily. At the same time Kratas and his men darted forward, taking the other two bandits by as much surprise as their chief. They knocked the weapons out of their hands, and dragged them to where Tanus stood.

'So, you little birds think to frighten Kaarik, the Assyrian, with your threats, do you? Yes, my fine vendor of feathers, I have heard of the Shrikes. I have heard that they are a flock of chattering, cowardly little fledglings, that make more noise than a flock of sparrows.' He twisted Shufti's arm more viciously, until the bandit yelled with pain and fell flat on his face. 'Yes, I have heard of the Shrikes, but have you heard of Kaarik, the terrible?' He nodded at Kratas, and quickly and efficiently they stripped the three Shrikes stark naked and pinned them spread-eagled upon the rocky earth.

'I want you to remember my name, and fly away like a good little shrike when next you hear it,' Tanus told him, and nodded to Kratas again. Kratas flexed the lash of his slave-whip between his fingers. It was of the same type as Rasfer's famous tool, whittled from the cured hide of a bull hippopotamus. Tanus held out his hand for it, and reluctantly Kratas handed it over to him.

'Don't look so sad, slave-master,' Tanus told him. 'I'll let you have your turn later. But Kaarik, the Assyrian, always takes the first spoonful from the pot.'

Tanus slashed the whip back and forth through the air, and it whistled like the wing of a goose in flight. Shufti squirmed where he lay, and twisted his head around to hiss at Tanus, 'You are mad, you Assyrian ox! Do you not realize that I am a baron of the Shrike clan? You dare not do this to me—' His naked back and buttocks were stippled with pox scars.

Tanus lifted the whip on high, and then brought it down in a full-armed stroke with all his weight behind it. He laid a purple welt as fat as my forefinger across Shufti's back. So intense was the pain of it that the bandit's entire body convulsed and the air hissed out of his lungs, so that he could not scream. Tanus lifted the lash and then meticulously laid another ridged welt exactly parallel to the first, almost, but not quite, touching it. This time Shufti filled his lungs and let out a hoarse bellow, like a buffalo bull caught in a pitfall. Tanus ignored his struggles and his outraged roars, and worked on assiduously, laying on the strokes as though he were weaving a carpet.

When at last he was done, his victim's legs, buttocks and back were latticed with the fiery weals. Not one of the blows had overlaid another. The skin was intact and not a drop of blood had spilled out, but Shufti was no longer wriggling or screaming. He lay with his face in the dirt, his breath snoring in his throat, so that each exhalation raised a puff of dust. When Remrem and Kratas released him, he made no effort to sit up. He did not even stir.

Tanus tossed the whip to Kratas. 'The next one is yours, slave-master. Let us see what a pretty pattern you can tattoo on his back.'

Kratas' strokes hummed with power, but lacked the finesse that Tanus had demonstrated. Soon the bandit's back was leaking like a flawed jar of red wine. The droplets of blood fell into the dust and rolled into tiny balls of mud.

Sweating lightly, Kratas was satisfied at last, and he passed the whip to Astes as he indicated the last victim. 'Give that one something to remind him of his manners, as well.'

Astes had an even more rustic touch than Kratas. By the time he had finished, the last bandit's back looked like a side of fresh beef that had been cut up by a demented butcher.

Tanus signalled the caravan to move forward, towards the pass through the red rock mountains. We lingered a while beside the three naked men.

At last Shufti stirred and lifted his head, and Tanus addressed him civilly. 'And so, my friend, I beg leave of you. Remember my face, and step warily when you see it again.' Tanus picked up the fallen shrike's feather and tucked it into his headband. 'I thank you for your gift. May all your nights be cradled in the arms of lovely ladies.' He touched his heart and lips in the Assyrian gesture of farewell, and I followed him up the road after the departing caravan.

I looked back before we dropped over the next rise. All three Shrikes were on their feet, supporting each other to remain upright. Even at this distance I could make out the expression on Shufti's face. It was hatred distilled to its essence.

'Well, you have made certain that we will have every Shrike this side of the Nile upon us, the moment we take our first step beyond the pass,' I told Kratas and his ruffians, and I could not have pleased them more, had I promised them a shipload of beer and pretty girls.

FROM THE crest of the pass we looked back at the cool blue of the sea for the last time and then dropped down into that sweltering wilderness of rock and sand that stood between us and the Nile.

As we moved forward, the heat came at us like a mortal enemy. It seemed to enter through our mouths and nostrils as we gasped for breath. It sucked the moisture from our bodies like a thief. It dried out our skin and cracked it until our lips burst open like over-ripe figs. The rocks beneath our feet were hot, as though fresh from the pot-maker's kiln, and they scalded and blistered our feet, even through the leather soles of our sandals. It was impossible to continue the march during the hottest hours of the day. We lay in the flimsy shade of the linen tents that Tiamat had provided, and panted like hunting dogs after the chase.

When the sun sank towards the jagged rock horizon, we went on. The desert around us was charged with such a brooding nameless menace that even the high spirits of the Blue Crocodile Guards were subdued. The long slow column wound like a maimed adder through the black rock outcrops and tawny lion-coloured dunes, following the ancient road along which countless other travellers had passed before us.

When night fell at last, the sky came alive with such a dazzle of stars and the desert was lit so brightly that, from my place at the head of the caravan, I could recognize the shape of Kratas at the tail, although two hundred paces separated us. We marched on for half the night before Tanus gave the order to fall out. Then he had us up before dawn and we marched on until the heat-mirage dissolved the rocky outcrops around us and made the horizon swim so that it seemed to be moulded from melting pitch.

We saw no other sign of life, except that once a troop of dog-headed baboons barked at us from the cliffs of a stark rock tableland as we passed below them, and the vultures soared so high in the hot blue sky that they appeared to be but dust motes swirling in slow and deliberate circles high above us.

When we rested in the middle of the day the whirlwinds pirouetted and swayed with the peculiar grace of dancing houris across the plains, and the cupful of water that was our ration seemed to turn to steam in my mouth.

'Where are they?' Kratas growled angrily. 'By Seth's sweaty scrotum, I hope these little birds will soon puff up their courage and come in to roost.'

Although they were all tough veterans and inured to hardship and discomfort, nerves and tempers were wearing thin. Good comrades and old friends began to snarl at each other for no reason, and bicker over the water ration.

'Shufti is a cunning old dog,' I told Tanus. 'He will gather his forces and wait for us to come to him, rather than hurry to meet us. He will let us tire ourselves with the journey, and grow careless with our fatigue, before he strikes.'

On the fifth day I knew that we were approaching the oasis of Gallala when I saw that the dark cliffs ahead of us were riddled with the caves of ancient tombs. Centuries ago, the oasis had supported a thriving city, but then an earthquake had shaken the hills and damaged the wells. The water had dwindled to a few seeping drops. Even though the wells had been dug deeper to reach the receding water, and the earthen steps reached down to where the surface of the water was always in shade, the city had died. The roofless walls stood forlorn in the silence, and lizards sunned themselves in the courtyards where rich merchants had once dallied with their harems.

Our very first concern was to refill the water-skins. The voices of the men drawing water at the bottom of the well were distorted by the echoes in the deep shaft. While they were busy, Tanus and I made a swift tour of the ruined city. It was a lonely and melancholy place. In its centre was the dilapidated temple to the patron god of Gallala. The roof had fallen in and the walls were collapsing in places. It had but a single entrance through the crumbling gateway at the western end.

'This will do admirably,' Tanus muttered as he strode across it, measuring it with his soldier's eye for fortification and ambuscade. When I questioned him on his intentions, he smiled and shook his head. 'Leave that part of it to me, old friend. The fighting is my business.'

As we stood at the centre of the temple I noticed the tracks of a troop of baboons in the dust at our feet, and I pointed them out to Tanus, 'They must come to drink at the wells,' I told him.

That evening when we sat around the small, smoky fires of dried donkey dung in the ancient temple, we heard the baboons again, the old bull apes barking a challenge in the hills that surrounded the ruined city. Their voices boomed back and forth along the cliffs, and I nodded at Tanus across the fire. 'Your friend, Shufti, has arrived at last. His scouts are in the hills up there watching us now. It is they who have alarmed the baboons.'

'I hope you are right. My blackguards are close to mutiny. They know this is all your idea, and if you are wrong, I might have to give them your head or your backside to appease them,' Tanus growled, and went to speak to Astes at the neighbouring cooking-fire.

Swiftly a new mood infected the camp as they realized that the enemy was near. The scowls evaporated and the men grinned at each other in the firelight, as they surreptitiously tested the edges of the swords concealed beneath the sleeping-mats on which they sat. However, they were canny veterans and they went through the motions of normal caravan life, so as not to alert the watchers in the dark hills above us. At last we were all bundled on our mats, and the fires died down, but none of us slept. I could hear them coughing and fidgeting restlessly all around me in the dark. The long hours drew out, and through the open roof I watched the great constellations of the stars wheel in stately splendour overhead, but still the attack never came.

Just before dawn, Tanus made his round of the sentries for the last time, and then, on his way back to his place beside the cooling ashes of last night's fire, he stopped by my mat for a moment and whispered, 'You and your friends the baboons, you deserve each other. All of you bark at shadows.'

'The Shrikes are here. I can smell them. The hills are full of them,' I protested.

'All you can smell is the promise of breakfast,' he grunted. He knows how I detest the suggestion that I am a glutton. Rather than reply to such callow humour, I went out into the darkness to relieve myself behind the nearest pile of ruins.

As I squatted there, a baboon barked again, the wild, booming cry shattering the preternatural silences of that last and darkest of the night-watches. I turned my head in that direction and heard, faint and faraway, the sound of metal strike rock, as though a nervous hand had dropped a dagger up there on the ridge, or a careless shield had brushed against a granite outcrop as an armed man hurried to take up his station before the dawn found him out.

I smiled complacently to myself; there are few pleasures in my life compared to that of making Tanus eat his words. As I returned to my mat, I whispered to the men that I passed, 'Be ready. They are here,' and I heard my warning passed on from mouth to sleepless mouth.

Above me the stars began to fade away, and the dawn crept up on us as stealthily as a lioness stalking a herd of oryx. Then abruptly I heard a sentry on the west wall of the temple whistle, a liquid warble that might have been the cry of a nightjar except that we all knew better, and instantly a stir ran through the camp. It was checked by the low but urgent whispers of Kratas and his officers, 'Steady, the Blues! Remember your orders. Hold your positions!' and not a man stirred from his sleeping-mat.

Without rising, and with my shawl masking my face, I turned my head slowly and looked up at the crests of the cliffs that stood higher than the temple walls. The shark's-tooth silhouette of the granite hills began to alter most subtly. I had to blink my eyes to be certain of what I was seeing. Then slowly I turned my head in a full circle, and it was the same in whichever direction I looked. The skyline all about us was picketed with the dark and menacing shapes of armed men. They formed an unbroken palisade around us through which no fugitive could hope to escape.

I knew then why Shufti had delayed his retaliation so long. It would have taken him all this time to gather together such an army of thieves. There must be a thousand or more of them, although in the poor light it was not possible to count their multitudes. We were outnumbered at least ten to one, and I felt my spirits quail. It was poor odds, even for a company of the Blues.

The Shrikes stood as still as the rocks around them, and I was alarmed at this evidence of their discipline. I had expected them to come streaming down upon us in an untidy rabble, but they were behaving like trained warriors. Their stillness was more menacing and intimidating than any wild shouting and brandishing of weapons would have been.

As the light strengthened swiftly, we could make them out more clearly. The first rays of the sun glanced off the bronze of their shields and their bared sword-blades, and struck darts of light into our eyes. Every one of them was muffled up, a scarf of black wool wound around each head so that only their eyes showed in the slits, eyes as malevolent as those of the ferocious blue sharks that terrorize the waters of the sea we had left behind us.

The silence drew out until I thought that my nerves might tear and my heart burst with the pressure of blood within it. Then suddenly a voice rang out, shattering the dawn silence and echoing along the cliffs. 'Kaarik! Are you awake?'

I recognized Shufti then, despite the scarf that masked him. He stood in the centre of the west wall of the cliff, where the road cut through it. 'Kaarik!' he called again. 'It is time for you to pay what you owe me, but the price has risen. I want everything now. Everything!' he repeated, and flung aside the scarf so that his pock-marked features were revealed. 'I want everything you have, including your stupid and arrogant head.'

Tanus rose from his mat and threw aside his sheepskin rug. 'Then you will have to come down and take it from me,' he shouted back, and drew his sword.

Shufti raised his right arm, and his blind eye caught the light and gleamed like a silver coin. Then he brought his arm down abruptly.

At his signal, a shout went up from the ranks of men that lined the high ground, and they lifted their weapons and shook them to the pale yellow dawn sky. Shufti waved them forward and they streamed down the cliffs in a torrent into the narrow valley of Gallala.

Tanus raced to the centre of the temple court where the ancient inhabitants had raised a tall stone altar to their patron Bes, the dwarf god of music and drunkenness. Kratas and his officers ran to join him, while the slave girls and I crouched on our mats and covered our heads, wailing with terror.

Tanus leaped up on to the altar, and went down on one knee as he flexed the great bow Lanata. It took all of his strength to string it, but when he stood erect again it shimmered in its coils of silver electrum wire, as though it were a living thing. He reached over his shoulder and drew an arrow from the quiver on his back and faced the main gateway through which the horde of Shrikes must enter.

Below the altar, Kratas had drawn up his men into a single rank, and they also had strung their bows and faced the entrance to the square. They made a pitifully small cluster around the altar, and I felt a lump rise in my throat as I watched them. They were so heroic and undaunted. I would compose a sonnet in their honour, I decided on a sudden impulse, but before I could find the first line, the head of the mob of bandits burst howling through the ruined gateway.

Only five men abreast could climb the steep stairway into the opening, and the distance to where Tanus stood on the altar was less than forty paces. Tanus drew and let his first arrow fly. That single arrow killed three men. The first of them was a tall rogue dressed in a short kilt, with long greasy tresses of hair streaming down his back. The arrow took him in the centre of his naked chest and passed through his torso as cleanly as though he were merely a target cut from a sheet of papyrus.

Slick with the blood of the first man, the arrow struck the man behind him in the throat. Although the force of it was dissipating now, it still went through his neck and came out behind him, but it could not drive completely through. The fletchings at the back of the shaft snagged in his flesh, while the barbed bronze arrow-head buried itself in the eye of the third man who had crowded up close behind him. The two Shrikes were pinned together by the arrow, and they staggered and thrashed about in the middle of the gateway, blocking the opening to those who were trying to push their way past them into the courtyard. At last the arrow-head tore out of the third man's skull, with the eye impaled upon the point. The two stricken men fell apart, and a throng of screaming bandits poured over them into the square. The small band around the altar met them with volley after volley of arrows, shooting them down so that their corpses almost blocked the opening, and those coming in from behind were forced to scramble over the mounds of dead and wounded.

It could not last much longer, the pressure of warriors from behind was too great and their numbers too overwhelming. Like the bursting of an earthen dyke unable to stem the rising flood of the Nile, they forced the opening, and a solid mass of fighting men poured into the square and surrounded the tiny band around the altar of the god Bes.

It was too close quarters for the bows now, and Tanus and his men cast them aside and drew their swords. 'Horus, arm me!' Tanus shouted his battle-cry, and the men around him took it up, as they went to work. Bronze rang on bronze as the Shrikes tried to come at them, but they had formed a ring around the altar, facing outwards. No matter from which side they came, the Shrikes were met by the point and the deadly sword-play of the guards. The Shrikes were not short of courage, and they pressed in serried ranks around the altar. As one of them was cut down, another leaped into his place.

I saw Shufti in the gateway. He was holding back from the fray, but cursing his men and ordering them into the thick of it with horrid howls of rage. His blind eye rolled in its socket as he exhorted them, 'Get me the Assyrian alive. I want to kill him slowly and hear him squeal.'

The bandits completely ignored the women who still cowered on their sleeping-mats, their heads covered, wailing and screeching with terror. I wailed with the best of them, but the struggle in the centre of the yard was too uncomfortable for my liking. By this time, there were over a thousand men crowded into the confined space. Choking in the dust, I was kicked and pummelled by the sandalled feet of the battling horde, until I managed to crawl away into a corner of the wall.

One of the bandits turned aside from the fighting and stooped over me. He tore the shawl away from my face and for a moment stared into my eyes. 'Mother of Isis,' he breathed, 'you are beautiful!'

He was an ugly devil with gaps in his teeth and a scar down one cheek. His breath stank like a sewerage gutter as he lusted into my face. 'Wait until this business is over. Then I'll give you something to make you squeal with joy,' he promised, and twisted my face up to his. He kissed me.

My natural instinct was to pull away from him, but I resisted it and returned his kiss. I am an artist of the love arts, for I learned my skills in the boys' quarters of Lord Intef. My kisses can turn a man to water.

I kissed him with all my skill, and he was transfixed by it. While he was still paralysed, I slipped my dagger from its sheath beneath my blouse and slid the point through the gap between his fifth and sixth ribs. When he screamed, I muffled the sound with my own lips and clasped him lovingly to my breast, twisting the blade in his heart until, with a shudder, he relaxed completely against me, and I let him roll over on his side.

I looked around me quickly. In the few moments that it had taken me to dispose of my admirer, the plight of the small group of guards around the altar had worsened. There were gaps in their single rank. Two men were down and Amseth was wounded. He had switched his sword into his left hand, while the other arm hung bleeding at his side.

With a rush of relief I saw that Tanus was still untouched, still laughing with the savage joy of it all as he plied the sword. But he had left it too late to spring the trap, I thought. The entire band of Shrikes were crowded into the square and baying around him like hounds around a treed leopard. Within moments he and his gallant little band must be cut down.

Even as I watched, Tanus killed another of them with a straight thrust through the throat, and then he jerked his blade free of the clinging flesh and stepped back. He threw back his head and let loose a bellow that rang from the crumbling walls around us. 'On me, the Blues!'

On the instant every one of the cringing slave girls leapt up and flung aside their trailing robes. Their swords were already bared and they fell upon the rear of the robber horde. The surprise was complete and overwhelming. I saw them kill a hundred or more before their victims even realized what they were about, and could rally to meet them. But when they did turn to face this fresh attack, they exposed their backs to Tanus and his little band.

They fought well, I'll give them that, though I am sure it was terror, rather than courage, that drove them on. However, their ranks were too close-packed to allow them free play with the sword, and the men they faced were some of the finest troops in Egypt, which is to say the entire world.

For a while yet they held on. Then Tanus bellowed again from the midst of the turmoil. For a moment I thought it was another command, then I realized that it was the opening bar of the battle hymn of the guards. Though I had often heard it spoken in awe that the Blues always sang when the battle was at its height, I had never truly believed it possible. Now all around me the song was taken up by a hundred straining voices:

> We are the breath of Horus,
> hot as the desert wind,
> we are the reapers of men—

Their swords beat an accompaniment to the words, like the clangour of hammers on the anvils of the underworld. In the face of such arrogant ferocity the remaining Shrikes wavered, and then suddenly it was no longer a battle, but a massacre.

I have seen a pack of wild dogs surround and tear into a flock of sheep. This was worse. Some of the Shrikes threw down their swords and fell to their knees begging quarter. There was no mercy shown them. Others tried to reach the gateway, but guardsmen waited for them there, sword in hand.

I danced on the fringes of the fighting, screaming across at Tanus, trying to make myself heard in the uproar, 'Stop them. We need prisoners.'

Tanus could not hear me, or more likely he simply ignored my entreaties. Singing and laughing, with Kratas at his left hand and Remrem on the other, he tore into them. His beard was soaked with the spurted blood of those he had killed, and his eyes glittered in the running red mask of his face with a madness I had never seen in them before. Joyous Hapi, how he thrived on the heady draught of battle!

'Stop it, Tanus! Don't kill them all!' This time he heard me. I saw the madness fade, and he was once more in control of himself.

'Give quarter to those who plead for it!' he roared, and the guards obeyed him. But in the end, out of the original thousand, fewer than two hundred Shrikes grovelled unarmed on the bloody stone flags and pleaded for their lives.

For a while I stood dazed and uncertain on the fringe of this carnage, and then from the corner of my eye I caught a furtive movement.

Shufti had realized that he could not escape through the gateway. He threw down his sword and darted to the east wall of the court, close to where I stood. This was the most ruined section, where the wall was reduced to half its original height. The tumbled mud-bricks formed a steep ramp, and Shufti scrambled up it, slipping and falling, but rapidly nearing the top of the wall. It seemed that I was the only one who had noticed his flight. The guards were busy with their other prisoners, and Tanus had his back turned to me as he directed the mopping-up of the shattered enemy.

Almost without thinking, I stooped and picked up half a mud-brick. As Shufti topped the wall, I hurled the brick up at him with all my strength. It thumped against the back of his skull with such force that he dropped to his knees, and then the treacherous pile of loose rubble gave way beneath him and he came sliding back down in a cloud of dust to land at my feet, only half-conscious.

I pounced upon him where he lay, straddling his chest, and I pressed the point of my dagger to his throat. He stared up at me, his single eye still glazed with the crack I had dealt him.

'Lie still,' I cautioned him, 'or I will gut you like a fish.'

I had lost my shawl and head-dress, and my hair had come down on to my shoulders. He recognized me then, which was no surprise. We had met often, but in different circumstances.

'Taita, the eunuch!' he mumbled. 'Does Lord Intef know what you are about?'

'He will find out soon enough,' I assured him, and pricked him until he grunted, 'but you will not be the one to enlighten him.'

Without removing the point from his throat, I shouted to two of the nearest guards to take him. They flipped him on to his face and bound his wrists together with linen twine before they dragged him away.

Tanus had seen me capture Shufti, and he strode across to me now, stepping over the dead and wounded. 'Good throw, Taita! You have forgotten nothing that I taught you.' He clapped me on the back so hard that I staggered. 'There is plenty of work for you still. We've lost four men killed, and there are at least a dozen wounded.'

'What about their camp?' I asked, and he stared at me.

'What camp?'

'A thousand Shrikes did not spring up from the sands like desert flowers. They must have pack-animals and slaves with them. Not far from here, either. You must not let them escape. Nobody must escape to tell the tale of today's battle. None of them must be allowed to carry the news to Karnak that you are still alive.'

'Sweet Isis, you are right! But how will we find them?' It was obvious that Tanus was still bemused with battle lust. Sometimes I wondered what he would do without me.

'Back-track them,' I told him impatiently. 'A thousand pairs of feet will have trodden a road for us to follow back to where they came from.'

His expression cleared, and he hailed Kratas across the length of the temple. 'Take fifty men. Go with Taita. He will lead you to their base-camp.'

'The wounded—' I began to protest. I had enjoyed enough fighting for one day, but he brushed my objections aside. 'You are the best tracker I have. The wounded can wait for your care, my ruffians are all as tough as fresh buffalo steaks, very few of them will die before you return.'

FINDING THEIR camp was as simple as I had made it sound. With Kratas and fifty men following me closely, I made a wide cast around the city, and behind the first line of hills I picked up the broad track that they had made as they came in and deployed to surround us. We followed it back at a trot, and had covered less than a mile before we topped a rise and found the camp of the Shrikes in the shallow valley below us.

Their surprise was complete. They had left fewer than twenty men to guard the donkeys and women. Kratas' men overran them at the first rush, and this time I was too late to save any prisoners. They spared only the women, and once the camp was secure, Kratas let his men have them as part of the traditional reward of the victors.

The women seemed to me to be a more comely selection than I would have expected in such company. I saw quite a few pretty faces amongst them. They submitted to the rituals of conquest with a remarkably good grace. I even heard some of them laughing and joking as the guardsmen threw dice for them. The vocation of camp-follower to a band of Shrikes could not be considered the most delicate calling, and I doubted that any of these ladies were blushing virgins. One by one, they were led by their new owners behind the cover of the nearest clump of rocks, where their skirts were lifted without further ceremony.

New moon follows the death of the old, spring follows winter, none of the ladies showed any signs of mourning for their erstwhile spouses. Indeed, it seemed probable that new and perhaps lasting relationships were being struck up here on the desert sand.

For myself, I was more interested in the pack-donkeys and what they carried. There were over a hundred and fifty of these, and most of them were sturdy animals in prime condition which would fetch good prices in the market at Karnak or Safaga. I reckoned that I should be entitled to at least a centurion's share when the prize money was divided up. After all, I had already dispensed large amounts of my own savings in the furtherance of this enterprise, and should be entitled to some compensation. I would speak seriously to Tanus about it, and could expect his sympathy. His is a generous spirit.

By the time we returned to the city of Gallala, leading the captured pack-animals laden with booty and followed by a straggle of women who had attached themselves quite naturally to their new menfolk, the sun had set.

One of the smaller ruined buildings near the wells had been turned into a field hospital. There I worked through the night, by the light of torch and oil lamp, sewing together the wounded guardsmen. As always, I was impressed by their stoicism, for many of their wounds were grave and painful. None the less, I lost only one of my patients before dawn broke. Amseth succumbed to loss of blood from the severed arteries in his arm. If I had attended to him immediately after the battle, instead of going off into the desert, I might have been able to save him. Even though the responsibility rested with Tanus, I felt the familiar guilt and sorrow in the face of a death that I might have prevented. However, I was confident that my other patients would heal swiftly and cleanly. They were all strong young men in superb condition.

There were no wounded Shrikes to attend. Their heads had been lopped off where they lay on the battlefield. As a physician, I was perturbed by this age-old custom of dealing with the wounded enemy, yet I suppose there was logic in it. Why should the victors waste their resources on the maimed vanquished, when it was unlikely they would have any value as slaves, and, if left alive, might recover to fight against them another day?

I worked all night with only a swallow of wine and a few mouthfuls of food taken with bloody hands to sustain me, and I was almost exhausted, but there was to be no rest for me yet. Tanus sent for me as soon as it was light.

THE UNWOUNDED prisoners were being held in the temple of Bes. Their wrists were bound behind their backs, and they were squatting in long lines along the north wall, with the guards standing over them.

As soon as I entered the temple, Tanus called me to where he stood with a group of his officers. I was still in the dress of an Assyrian wife, so I lifted my blood-splattered skirts and picked my way across the floor littered with the debris of the battle.

'There are thirteen clans of Shrikes – isn't that what you told me, Taita?' Tanus asked, and I nodded. 'Each clan with its own baron. We have Shufti. Let's see if you recognize any of the other barons amongst this gathering of the fair and gentle people.' He indicated the prisoners with a chuckle, and took my arm to lead me down the ranks of squatting men.

I kept my face veiled so that none of the prisoners could recognize me. I glanced at each face as I passed, and recognized two of them. Akheku was head of the southern clan that preyed on the lands around Assoun, Elephantine and the first cataract, while Setek was from further north, the baron of Kom-Ombo.

It was clear that Shufti had gathered together whatever men he could find at such short notice. There were members of all the clans amongst those that we had captured. As I identified their leaders with a tap on the shoulder, they were dragged away.

When we reached the end of the line Tanus asked, 'Are you sure that you missed none of them?'

'How can I be sure? I told you that I never met all of the barons.'

Tanus shrugged. 'We could not hope to catch every little bird with one throw of the net. We must count ourselves fortunate that we have taken as many as three so soon. But let us look at the heads. We might be lucky enough to find a few more amongst them.'

This was a gruesome business that might have affected a more delicate stomach than mine, but human flesh, both dead and living, is my stock-in-trade. While we sat at our ease on the steps of the temple enjoying our breakfast, the severed heads were displayed to us, held up one at a time by the blood-caked hair, tongues lolling from between slack lips, and dull eyes powdered with dust staring into the other world whither they were bound.

My appetite was as healthy as ever, for I had eaten very little during the last two days. I devoured the delicious cakes and fruits that Tiamat had provided, while I pointed out those heads I recognized. There was a score or so of common thieves that I had encountered during the course of my work for Lord Intef, but only one more of the barons. He was Nefer-Temu of Qena, a lesser member of the ghastly brotherhood.

'That makes four of them,' Tanus grunted with satisfaction, and ordered Nefer-Temu's head to be placed on the pinnacle of the pyramid of skulls that he was erecting in front of the well of Gallala.

'So now we have accounted for four of them. We must find the other nine barons. Let us begin by putting the question to our prisoners.' He stood up briskly, and I hastily gulped down the remains of my breakfast and followed him reluctantly back into the temple of Bes.

Although I was the one who had made clear to Tanus the necessity of having informers from within the clans, and indeed it was I who had suggested how we should recruit them, still now that the time to act upon my suggestion had arrived, I was stricken with remorse and guilt. It was one thing to suggest ruthless action, but another thing entirely to stand by and watch it practised.

I made a feeble excuse that the wounded men in the makeshift hospital might need me, but Tanus brushed it away cheerfully. 'None of your fine scruples now, Taita. You will stay with me during the questioning to make certain that you overlooked none of your old friends on your first inspection.'

The questioning was swift and merciless, which I suppose was only appropriate to the character of the men we were dealing with.

To begin with, Tanus sprang up on to the stone altar of Bes, and, with the hawk seal in one hand, he looked down on the ranks of squatting prisoners with a smile that must have chilled them, even though they sat in the full rays of the desert sun.

'I am the bearer of the hawk seal of Pharaoh Mamose, and I speak with his voice,' he told them grimly, as he held the statuette high. 'I am your judge and your executioner.' He paused and let his gaze pass slowly over their upturned faces. As each of them met his eyes, they dropped their own. Not one of them could hold firm before his penetrating scrutiny.

'You have been taken in the act of pillage and murder. If there is one of you who would deny it, let him stand before me and declare his innocence.'

He waited while the impatient shadows of the vultures, circling in the sky above us, criss-crossed the dusty courtyard. 'Come now! Speak up, you innocents.' He glanced upwards at the circling birds with their grotesque pink bald heads. 'Your brethren grow impatient for the feast. Let us not keep them waiting.'

Still none of them spoke or moved, and Tanus lowered the hawk seal. 'Your actions, which all here have witnessed, condemn you. Your silence confirms the verdict. You are guilty. In the name of the divine Pharaoh, I pass sentence upon you. I sentence you to death by beheading. Your severed heads will be displayed along the caravan routes. All law-abiding men who pass this way will see your skulls grinning at them from the roadside, and they will know that the Shrike has met the eagle. They will know that the age of lawlessness has passed from the land, and that peace has returned to this very Egypt of ours. I have spoken. Pharaoh Mamose has spoken.'

Tanus nodded, and the first prisoner was dragged forward and forced to his knees before the altar.

'If you answer three questions truthfully, your life will be spared. You will be enlisted as a trooper in my regiment of the guards, with all the pay and privileges. If you refuse to answer the questions, your sentence will be carried out immediately,' Tanus told him.

He looked down on the kneeling prisoner sternly. 'This is the first question. What clan do you belong to?'

The condemned man made no reply. The blood oath of the Shrikes was too strong for him to break.

'This is the second question. Who is the baron that commands you?' Tanus asked, and still the man was silent.

'This is the third and the last question. Will you lead me to the secret places where your clan hides?' Tanus asked, and the man looked up at him, hawked in his throat and spat. His phlegm spattered yellow upon the stones. Tanus nodded to the guardsman who stood over him with the sword.

The stroke was clean and the head toppled on to the steps at the foot of the altar. 'One more head for the pyramid,' Tanus said quietly, and nodded for the next prisoner to be brought forward.

He asked the same three questions, and when the Shrike answered him with a defiant obscenity, Tanus nodded. This time the headsman mistimed the blow and the corpse flopped about with the neck only half-severed. It took three more strokes before the head bounced down the steps.

Tanus lopped twenty-three heads, I was counting them to distract myself from the waves of debilitating compassion that assailed me, until the first of the condemned men broke down. He was young, not much more than a boy. In a shrill voice he gabbled out the replies before Tanus could actually pose the three questions to him.

'My name is Hui. I am a blood-brother of the clan of Basti the Cruel. I know his secret places, and I will lead you to them.' Tanus smiled with grim satisfaction and gestured for the lad to be led away. 'Care for him well,' he warned his gaolers. 'He is now a trooper of the Blues, and your companion-in-arms.'

After the defection of one of them, it went more readily, although there were still many who defied Tanus. Some of them cursed him, while others laughed their defiance at him until the blade swept down, and their bravado ended with their very last breath that burst from the severed windpipe in a crimson gust.

I was filled with admiration for those who, after a base and despicable life, at the end chose to die with some semblance of honour. They laughed at death. I knew that I was not capable of that quality of courage. Offered that choice, I am certain that I would have responded as some of the weaker prisoners did.

'I am a member of the clan of Ur,' one confessed.

'I am of the clan of Maa-En-Tef, who is baron of the west bank as far as El Kharga,' said another, until we had informers to lead us to the strongholds of every one of the remaining robber barons, and a shoulder-high pile of recalcitrant heads to add to the pyramid beside the well.

ONE OF the matters to which Tanus and I had given much thought was the disposal of the three robber barons we had already captured, and the score of informers we had gleaned from the ranks of the condemned Shrikes.

We knew that the influence of the Shrikes was so pervasive that we dared not keep our captives in Egypt. There was not a prison secure enough to prevent Akh-Seth and his barons from reaching them, either to set them free by bribery or force, or to have them silenced by poison or some other unpleasant means. We knew that Akh-Seth was like an octopus whose head was hidden, but whose tentacles reached into every facet of our government and into the very fabric of our existence.

This was where my friend Tiamat, the merchant of Safaga, came into my reckoning.

Marching now as a unit of the Blue Crocodile Guards, and not as a slave caravan, we returned to the port on the Red Sea in half the time that it had taken us to reach Gallala. Our captives were hustled aboard one of Tiamat's trading vessels that was waiting for us in the harbour, and the captain set sail immediately for the Arabian coast, where Tiamat maintained a secure slave-compound on the small off-shore island of Jez Baquan, run by his own warders. The waters around the island were patrolled by packs of ferocious blue sharks. Tiamat assured us that no one who had attempted escape from the island had ever avoided both the vigilance of the warders and the appetites of the sharks.

Only one of our captives was not sent to the island. He was Hui from the clan of Basti the Cruel, the same youngster who had been the first to capitulate to the threat of execution. During the march to the sea, Tanus had kept the lad close to him and had turned all the irresistible force of his personality upon him. By this time Hui was his willing slave. This special gift of Tanus' to win loyalty and devotion from the most unlikely quarters never failed to amaze me. I was sure that Hui, who had buckled so swiftly under the threat of execution, would now willingly lay down his worthless life for Tanus.

Under Tanus' spell, Hui poured out every detail that he could remember of the clan to which he had once sworn a blood-oath. I listened quietly, with my writing-brush poised, as Tanus questioned him and I recorded all he had to tell us.

We learned that the stronghold of Basti the Cruel was in the fastness of that awful desert of Gebel-Umm-Bahari, on the summit of one of the flat-topped mountains that was protected by sheer cliffs on every side. Hidden and impregnable, but less than two days' march from the east bank of the Nile and the busy caravan routes that ran along its banks, it was the perfect nest for the raptor.

'There is one path to the top, cut like a stairway from the rock. It is wide enough for only one man to climb at a time,' Hui told us.

'There is no other way to the summit?' Tanus asked, and Hui grinned and laid his finger along his nose in a conspiratory gesture.

'There is another route. I have used it often, to return to the mountain after I had deserted my post to visit a lady friend. Basti would have had me killed if he had known I was missing. It is a dangerous climb, but a dozen good men could make it and hold the top of the cliff while the main force came up the pathway to them. I will lead you up it, Akh-Horus.'

It was the first time that I heard the name. Akh-Horus, the brother of the great god Horus. It was a good name for Tanus. Naturally, Hui and our other captives could not know Tanus' real identity. They knew only in their simple way that Tanus must be some kind of god. He looked like a god and he fought like a god, and he invoked the name of Horus in the midst of battle. So, they had reasoned, he must be the brother of Horus.

Akh-Horus! It was a name that all Egypt would come to know well in the months ahead. It would be shouted from hilltop to hilltop. It would be carried along the caravan routes. It would travel the length of the river on the lips of the boatmen, from city to city, and from kingdom to kingdom. The legend would grow up around the name, as the accounts of his deeds were repeated and exaggerated at each telling.

Akh-Horus was the mighty warrior who appeared from nowhere, sent by his brother Horus to continue the eternal struggle against evil, against Akh-Seth, the lord of the Shrikes.

Akh-Horus! Each time the people of Egypt repeated the name, it would fill their hearts with fresh hope.

All that was in the future as we sat in the garden of Tiamat the merchant. Only I knew how hot Tanus was for Basti, and how eager to lead his men into the Gebel-Umm-Bahari to hunt him down. It was not only that Basti was the most rapacious and pitiless of all the barons. There was much more to it than that. Tanus had a very personal score to settle with that bandit.

From me, Tanus had learned that Basti had been the particular instrument that Akh-Seth had used to destroy the fortune of Pianki, Lord Harrab, Tanus' father.

'I can lead you up the cliffs of Gebel-Umm-Bahari,' Hui promised. 'I can deliver Basti into your hands.'

Tanus was silent awhile in the darkness as he savoured that promise. We sat and listened to the nightingale singing at the bottom of Tiamat's garden. It was a sound totally alien from the evil and desperate affairs that we were discussing. After a while Tanus sighed and dismissed Hui.

'You have done well, lad,' he told him. 'Fulfil your promise, and you will find me grateful.'

Hui prostrated himself, as though before a god, and Tanus nudged him irritably with his foot. 'Enough of that nonsense. Away with you now.'

This recent, unlooked-for elevation to the godhead embarrassed Tanus. No one could ever accuse him of being either modest or humble, but he was at least a pragmatist, with no false illusions of his own station; he never aspired to become either a pharaoh or a divine, and he was always short with any servility or obsequious behaviour from those around him.

As soon as the lad was gone, Tanus turned back to me. 'So often I lie awake in the night and consider all that you have told me about my father. I ache in every fibre of my body and soul for revenge against the one who drove him into penury and disgrace and hounded him to his death. I can barely restrain myself. I am filled by the desire to abandon this devious way that you have devised of trapping Akh-Seth. Instead, I long to seek him out directly, and tear out his foul heart with my bare hands.'

'If you do that, you will lose everything,' I said. 'You know that well. Do it my way and you will restore not only your own reputation, but that of your noble father into the bargain. My way, you will retrieve the estate and the fortune that was stolen from you. My way will not only give you your full measure of revenge, but will also lead you back to Lostris and the fulfilment of the vision that I divined for the pair of you in the Mazes of Ammon-Ra. Trust me, Tanus. For your sake and the sake of my mistress, trust me.'

'If I don't trust you, then who can I trust?' he asked, and touched my arm. 'I know you are right, but I have always lacked patience. For me the swift and direct road has always been easiest.'

'For the time being, put Akh-Seth out of your mind. Think only of the next step along the devious way that we must travel together. Think of Basti the Cruel. It was Basti who destroyed your father's trade caravans as they returned from the East. For five seasons, not one of the caravans of Lord Harrab ever returned to Karnak. They were all attacked and looted along the road. It was Basti who destroyed your father's copper-mines at Sestra and murdered the engineers, and their slave workers. Since then those rich veins of ore have lain untapped. It was Basti who systematically pillaged your father's estates along the Nile, who slaughtered his slaves in the fields and burned the crops, until in the end, only weeds grew in Lord Harrab's fields, and he was forced to sell them at a fraction of their real worth.'

'All that may be true, but it was Akh-Seth who gave Basti his orders.'

'No one will believe that. Pharaoh will not believe that, unless he hears Basti confess it,' I told him impatiently. 'Why are you always so stubborn? We have gone over this a hundred times. The barons first, and then at last the head of the snake, Akh-Seth.'

'Yours is the voice of wisdom, I know it. But it is hard to bear the waiting. I long for my revenge. I long to cleanse the stain of sedition and treason from my honour, and I long – oh, how I long – for Lostris!'

He leaned across and clasped my shoulder with a grip that made me wince. 'You have done enough here, old friend. I could never have accomplished so much without you. If you had not come to find me, I might still be sodden with drink and lying in the embrace of some stinking whore. I owe you more than I can ever repay, but I must send you away now. You are needed elsewhere. Basti is my meat, and I don't need you to share the feast with me. You will not be coming with me to Gebel-Umm-Bahari. I am sending you back where you belong – where I also belong, but where I cannot be – at the side of the Lady Lostris. I envy you, old friend, I would give up my hope of immortality to be going to her in your place.'

I protested most prettily, of course. I swore that all I wanted was another chance at those villains, and that I was his companion and that I would be seriously aggrieved if he would not give me a place at his side in the next campaign. All the time I was secure in the knowledge that when Tanus set his mind on a course of action he was adamant and could not easily be dissuaded, except very occasionally by his friend and adviser, Taita the slave.

The truth was that I had enjoyed my fill of wild heroics and people trying to kill me. I was not by nature a soldier, not some insensitive clod of a trooper. I hated the rigours of campaigning in the desert. I could not bear another week of heat and sweat and flies without even a glimpse of the sweet green waters of Mother Nile. I longed for the feel of clean linen against my freshly bathed and anointed skin. I missed my mistress more than I could express in mere words. Our quiet, civilized life in the painted rooms on the Island of Elephantine, our music and long, leisurely conversations together, my pets and my scrolls, all these exerted an irresistible draw upon me.

Tanus was right, he no longer needed me, and my place was with my mistress. However, to acquiesce too readily to his orders might lower his opinion of me, and I did not want that either.

At last I allowed him to convince me, and, concealing my eagerness, I began my preparations for my return to Elephantine.

TANUS HAD ordered Kratas back to Karnak, to assemble and bring up reinforcements for the expedition into the desert of Gebel-Umm-Bahari. I was to travel under his protection as far as Karnak, but taking leave of Tanus was not a simple matter. Twice when I had already left the house of Tiamat to join Kratas where he waited for me on the outskirts of the town, Tanus called me back to give me another message to take to my mistress.

'Tell her that I think of her every hour of every day!'

'You have already given me that message,' I protested.

'Tell her that my dreams are filled with images of her lovely face.'

'And that one also. I can recite them by heart. Give me something new,' I pleaded.

'Tell her that I believe the vision of the Mazes, that in a few short years we will be together—'

'Kratas is waiting for me. If you keep me here, how can I deliver your message?'

'Tell her that everything I do is for her. Every breath I draw is for her—' he broke off, and embraced me. 'The truth is, Taita, I doubt I can live another day without her.'

'Five years will pass like that single day. When next you meet her, your honour will be restored and you will once more stand high in the land. She can only love you the more for that.'

He released me. 'Take good care of her until I am able to assume that joyous duty from you. Now, away with you. Speed to her side.'

'That has been my intention this hour past,' I told him wryly, and made good my escape.

With Kratas at the head of our small detachment, we made the journey to Karnak in under a week. Fearful of discovery by Rasfer or Lord Intef, I spent as little time in my beloved city as it took me to find passage on one of the barges heading southwards. I left Kratas busily recruiting from amongst the elite regiments of Pharaoh's guards the thousand good men that Tanus had demanded, and I went aboard the barge.

We had the north wind in our sails all the way, and we tied up at the wharf of East Elephantine twelve days after leaving Thebes. I was still dressed in the wig and garb of the priesthood, and nobody recognized me as I came ashore.

For the price of a small copper ring I hired a felucca to take me across the river to the royal island, and it put me down at the steps that led up to the water-gate to our garden in the harem. My heart pounded against my ribs as I bounded up the stairs. I had been away from my mistress far too long. It was at times such as these that I realized the full strength of my feelings for her. I was certain that Tanus' love was but a light river breeze in comparison to the *khamsin* of my own emotions.

One of Lostris' Cushite maidens met me at the gate, and tried to prevent me from entering. 'My mistress is unwell, priest. There is another doctor with her at this moment. She will not see you.'

'She will see me,' I told her, and stripped off my wig.

'Taita!' she squealed, and fell to her knees, frantically making the sign to ward off evil. 'You are dead. This is not you, but some evil apparition from beyond the grave.'

I brushed her aside and hurried to my mistress's private quarters, to be met at the doors by one of those priests of Osiris who consider themselves physicians.

'What are you doing here?' I demanded of him, appalled that one of these quacks had been anywhere near my mistress. Before he could answer, I bellowed at him, 'Out! Get out of here! Take your spells and charms and filthy potions, and don't come back.'

He looked as though he were prepared to argue, but I placed my hand between his shoulder-blades and gave him a running start towards the gate. Then I rushed to my mistress's bedside.

The odour of sickness filled the chamber, sour and strong, and a wild grief seized me as I looked down at the Lady Lostris. She seemed to have shrunk in size, and her skin was pale as the ashes of an old camp-fire. She was asleep or in a coma, I could not be certain which, but there were dark, bruised shadows beneath her closed eyelids. Her lips had that dry and crusty look that filled me with dread.

I drew back the linen sheet that covered her and beneath it she was naked. I stared in horror at her body. The flesh had melted off her. Her limbs were thin as sticks and her ribs and the bones of her pelvis stuck out through the unhealthy skin, like those of drought-stricken kine. Tenderly, I placed my hand in her armpit to feel for the heat of fever, but her skin was cool. What kind of disease was this, I fretted. I had not encountered any like it before.

Without leaving her side, I yelled for her slave girls, but none of them had the courage to face the ghost of Taita. In the end I had to storm into their quarters and drag one of them whimpering from under her bed.

'What have you done to your mistress to bring her to this pass?' I kicked her fat backside to focus her attention on my question, and she whined and covered her face, so as not to have to look upon me.

'She will not eat. Barely a mouthful in all these weeks. Not since the mummy of Tanus, Lord Harrab was laid in his tomb in the Valley of the Nobles. She has even lost the child of Pharaoh that she was carrying in her womb. Spare me, kind ghost, I have done you no harm.'

I stared down at her in bewilderment for a moment, until I realized what had happened. My message of comfort to the Lady Lostris had never been delivered. Intuitively I guessed that the messenger whom Kratas had dispatched from Luxor to carry my letter to my mistress, had never reached Elephantine. He had probably become one more victim of the Shrikes, just another corpse floating down the river with an empty purse and a gaping wound in his throat. I hoped that my letter had fallen into the hands of some illiterate thief, and not been taken to Akh-Seth. There was no time to worry about that now.

I rushed back to my mistress's side and fell on my knees beside her bed. 'My darling,' I whispered, and stroked her haggard brow. 'It is me, Taita, your slave.'

She stirred slightly and mumbled something I could not catch. I realized that there was little time to spare; she was far-gone. It was over a month since Tanus' purported death. If the slave girl had spoken the truth, and she had indeed taken no food in all that time, then it was a wonder that she was still alive.

I leaped up again and ran to my own rooms. Despite my 'demise' nothing had been changed, and my medicine chest was in the alcove where I had left it. With it in my arms, I hurried back to my mistress. My hands were shaking as I lit a twig of the scorpion bush from the flame of the oil lamp beside her bed, and held the glowing end under her nose. Almost immediately she gasped and sneezed and struggled to avoid the pungent smoke.

'Mistress, it is I, Taita. Speak to me.'

She opened her eyes and I saw the dawn of pleasure in them swiftly extinguished by the fresh realization of her bereavement. She held out her thin, pale arms to me, and I took her to my breast.

'Taita,' she sobbed softly. 'He is dead. Tanus is dead. I cannot live without him.'

'No! No! He is alive. I come directly from him with messages of love and devotion from him to you.'

'You are cruel to mock me so. I know he is dead. His tomb is sealed—'

'It was a subterfuge to mislead his enemies,' I cried. 'Tanus lives. I swear it to you. He loves you. He waits for you.'

'Oh, that I could believe you! But I know you so well. You will lie to protect me. How can you torment me with false promises? I hate you so—' She tried to break from my arms.

'I swear it. Tanus is alive.'

'Swear on the honour of the mother you never knew. Swear on the wrath of all the gods.' She hardly had the strength to challenge me.

'On all these I swear, and on my love and duty to you, my mistress.'

'Can it be?' I saw the strength of hope flow back into her, and a faint flush of colour bloom in her cheeks. 'Oh, Taita, can it truly be?'

'Would I look so joyful, if it were not? You know I love him almost as much as you do. Could I smile thus, if Tanus were truly dead?'

While she stared into my eyes, I launched into a recitation of all that had occurred since I had left her side so many weeks ago. I excluded only the details of the condition in which I had discovered Tanus in the old shack in the swamps, and the female company I had found him keeping.

She said not a word, but her eyes never left my face as she devoured my words. Her pale face, almost translucent with starvation, glowed like a pearl as she listened to my account of our adventures at Gallala, of how Tanus led the fighting like a god, and of how he sang with the wild joy of battle.

'And so you see, it is true. Tanus is alive,' I ended, and she spoke for the first time since I had begun.

'If he is alive, then bring him to me. I will not eat a mouthful until I set my eyes upon his face once more.'

'I will bring him to your side as swiftly as I can send a messenger to him, if that is what you wish,' I promised, and reached for the polished bronze mirror from my chest.

I held the mirror before her eyes, and asked softly, 'Do you want him to see you as you are now?'

She stared at her own gaunt, hollow-eyed image.

'I will send for him today, if you order it. He could be here within a week, if you really want that.'

I watched her struggle with her emotions. 'I am ugly,' she whispered. 'I look like an old woman.'

'Your beauty is still there, just below the surface.'

'I cannot let Tanus see me like this.' Feminine vanity had triumphed over all her other emotions.

'Then you must eat.'

'You promise,' she wavered, 'you promise that he is still alive, and that you will bring him to me as soon as I am well again? Place your hand on my heart and swear it to me.'

I could feel her every rib and her heart fluttering like a trapped bird beneath my fingers. 'I promise,' I said.

'I will trust you this time, but if you are lying I will never trust you again. Bring me food!'

As I hurried to the kitchen, I could not help but feel smug. Taita, the crafty, had got his own way yet again.

I mixed a bowl of warm milk and honey. We would have to begin slowly, for she had driven herself to the very edge of starvation. She vomited up the contents of the first bowl, but was able to keep down the second. If I had delayed my return by another day, it might have been too late.

SPREAD BY the chattering slave girls, the news of my miraculous return from the grave swept through the island like the smallpox.

Before nightfall Pharaoh sent Aton to fetch me to an audience. Even my old friend Aton was strained and reserved in my presence. He leaped away nimbly when I tried to touch him, as though my hand might pass through his flesh like a puff of smoke. As he led me through the palace, slaves and nobles alike scurried out of my path, and inquisitive faces watched me from every window and dark corner as we passed.

Pharaoh greeted me with a curious mixture of respect and nervousness, most alien to a king and a god.

'Where have you been, Taita?' he asked, as though he did not really want to hear the answer.

I prostrated myself at his feet. 'Divine Pharaoh, as you yourself are part of the godhead, I understand that you ask that question to test me. You know that my lips are sealed. It would be sacrilege for me to speak of these mysteries, even to you. Please convey to the other deities who are your peers, and particularly to Anubis, the god of the cemeteries, that I have been true to the charge laid upon me. That I have kept the oath of silence imposed upon me. Tell them that I have passed the test that you set me.'

His expression glazed as he considered this, and he fidgeted nervously. I could see him forming question after question, and then discarding each of them in turn. I had left him no opening to exploit.

In the end he blurted out lamely, 'Indeed, Taita, you have passed the test I set you. Welcome back. You have been missed.' But I could see that all his suspicions were confirmed, and he treated me with that respect due to one who had solved the ultimate mystery.

I crawled closer to him and dropped my voice to a whisper. 'Great Egypt, you know the reason I have been sent back?'

He looked mystified, but nodded uncertainly. I came to my feet and glanced around suspiciously, as though I expected to be overlooked by supernatural forces. I made the sign against evil before I went on, 'The Lady Lostris. Her illness was caused by the direct influence of—' I could not say the name, but made the horn sign with two fingers, the sign of the dark god, Seth.

His expression changed from confusion to dread, and he shivered involuntarily and drew closer to me, as if for protection, as I went on, 'Before I was taken away, my mistress was already carrying in her womb the treasure of the House of Mamose when the Dark One intervened. Due to her illness, the son she was bearing you has been aborted from her womb.'

Pharaoh looked distraught. 'So that is the reason that she miscarried,' he began, and then broke off.

I picked up my cue smoothly. 'Never fear, Great Egypt, I have been sent back by forces greater than those of the Dark One to save her, so that the destiny that I foresaw in the Mazes of Ammon-Ra may run its allotted course. There will be another son to replace the one that was lost. Your dynasty will still be secured.'

'You must not leave the side of the Lady Lostris until she is well again.' His voice shook with emotion. 'If you save her and she bears me another son, you may ask from me whatever you wish, but if she dies—' he stopped as he considered what threat might impress one who had already returned from beyond, and in the end let it trail away.

'With your permission, Your Majesty, I shall go to her this instant.'

'This instant!' he agreed. 'Go! Go!'

MY MISTRESS'S recovery was so swift that I began to suspect that I had unwittingly invoked some force beyond my own comprehension, and I felt a superstitious awe at my own powers.

Her flesh filled out and firmed almost as I watched. Those pitiful empty sacs of skin swelled into plump, round breasts once again, sweet enough to make the stone image of the god Hapi which stood at the doorway to her chamber burn with envy. Fresh young blood suffused the chalk of her skin until it glowed once more, and her laughter tinkled like the fountains of our water-garden.

Very soon it was impossible to keep her to her bed. Within three weeks of my return to Elephantine, she was playing games of toss with her handmaidens, dancing about the garden and leaping high to reach the inflated bladder above the heads of the others, until, fearful that she might overtax her returning strength, I confiscated the ball and ordered her back to her chamber. She would obey me only after we had struck another bargain, and I had agreed to sing with her, or teach her the most arcane formulas of the bao board which would allow her to enjoy her first victory over Aton, who was an addict of the game.

Aton came almost every evening to enquire about my mistress's health on behalf of the king, and afterwards to play the board-game with us. Aton seemed to have decided at last that I was not a dangerous ghost, and although he treated me with a new respect, our old friendship survived my demise.

Each morning my Lady Lostris made me repeat my promise to her. Then she would reach for her mirror and study her reflection without the faintest trace of vanity, assessing every facet of her beauty to determine if it was ready yet to be looked upon by Lord Tanus.

'My hair looks like straw, and there is another pimple coming up on my chin,' she lamented. 'Make me beautiful again, Taita. For Tanus' sake make me beautiful.'

'You have done the damage to yourself, and then you call for Taita to make it better,' I grumbled, and she laughed and threw her arms around my neck.

'That's what you are here for, you old scallywag. To look after me.'

Each evening when I mixed a tonic for her and brought the steaming bowl to her as she prepared for sleep, she would make me repeat my promise to her. 'Swear you will bring Tanus to me, just as soon as I am ready to receive him.'

I tried to ignore the difficulties and the dangers that this promise would bring upon us all. 'I swear it to you,' I repeated dutifully, and she lay back against the ivory headrest and went to sleep with a smile upon her face. I would worry about fulfilling my promise when the time came.

FROM ATON, Pharaoh had a full report of Lostris' recovery and came in person to visit her. He brought her a new necklace of gold and lapis lazuli in the form of an eagle and sat until evening, playing word-games and setting riddles with her. When he was ready to leave, he called me to walk with him as far as his chambers.

'The change in her is extraordinary. It is a miracle, Taita. When can I take her to bed again? Already she seems well enough to bear my son and heir.'

'Not yet, Great Egypt,' I assured him vehemently. 'The slightest exertion on the part of my mistress might trigger a relapse.'

He no longer questioned my word, for now I spoke with all the authority of the once dead, although his previous awe of me had worn a little thin with familiarity.

The slave girls also were becoming accustomed to my resurrection, and were able to look at my face without having to make the sign. Indeed, my return from the underworld was no longer the most popular fare of the palace gossips. They had something else to keep them busy. This was the advent of Akh-Horus into the lives and consciousness of every person living in the land along the great river.

The first time I heard the name Akh-Horus whispered in the palace corridors, I did not immediately place it. The garden of Tiamat beside the Red Sea seemed so remote from the little world of Elephantine, and I had forgotten the name that Hui had bestowed on Tanus. When, however, I heard the accounts of the extraordinary deeds ascribed to this demi-god, I realized who they were speaking about.

In a fever of excitement, I ran all the way back to the harem and found my mistress in the garden, besieged by a dozen visitors, noble ladies and royal wives, for she had so far recovered from her illness as to resume once more her role as court favourite.

I was so wrought up that I forgot my place as a mere slave, and to be rid of them I was quite rude to the royal ladies. They flounced out of the garden squawking like a gaggle of offended geese, and my mistress rounded on me. 'That was unlike you. What on earth has come over you, Taita?'

'Tanus!' I said the name like an incantation, and she forgot all her indignation and seized both my hands.

'You have news of Tanus! Tell me! Quickly, before I die of impatience.'

'News? Yes, I have news of him. What news! What extraordinary news. What unbelievable news!'

She dropped my hands and picked up her formidable silver fan. 'Stop your nonsense this instant,' she threatened me with it. 'I'll not put up with your teasing. Tell me, or I swear you'll have more lumps on your head than a Nubian has fleas.'

'Come! Let's go where nobody can hear us.' I led her down to the jetty and handed her into our little skiff. Out in the middle of the river we were safe from the flapping ears that lurked behind each corner of the palace walls.

'There is a fresh, clean wind blowing through the land,' I told her. 'They call this wind Akh-Horus.'

'The brother of Horus,' she breathed it with reverence. 'Is this what they call Tanus now?'

'None of them know it is Tanus. They think he is a god.'

'He is a god,' she insisted. 'To me, he is a god.'

'That is how they see it also. If he were not a god, how then would he know where the Shrikes are skulking, how else would he march unerringly to their strongholds, how would he know instinctively where they are waiting to waylay the incoming caravans, and to surprise them in their own ambuscades?'

'Has he accomplished all these things?' she demanded in wonder.

'These deeds and a hundred others, if you can believe the wild rumours that are flying about the palace. They say that every thief and bandit in the land runs in terror of his life, that the clans of the Shrikes are being shattered one by one. They say that Akh-Horus sprouted wings, like those of an eagle, and flew up the inaccessible cliffs of Gebel-Umm-Bahari to appear miraculously in the midst of the clan of Basti the Cruel. With his own hands, he hurled five hundred of the bandits from the top of the cliffs—'

'Tell me more!' She clapped her hands, almost capsizing the skiff in her enthusiasm.

'They say that at every crossroads and beside every caravan route he has built tall monuments to his passing.'

'Monuments? What monuments are these?'

'Piles of human skulls, high pyramids of skulls. The heads of the bandits he has slain, as a warning to others.'

My mistress shuddered with delicious horror, but her face still shone. 'Has he killed so many?' she demanded.

'Some say he has slain five thousand, and some say fifty thousand. There are even some who say one hundred thousand, but I think those must be exaggerating a little.'

'Tell me more! More!'

'They say he has already captured at least six of the robber barons—'

'And chopped off their heads!' she anticipated me with ghoulish relish.

'No, they say that he has not killed them, but transformed them into baboons. They say he keeps them in a cage for his amusement.'

'Is all of this possible?' she giggled.

'For a god, anything is possible.'

'He is my god. Oh, Taita, when will you let me see him?'

'Soon,' I promised. 'Your beauty burns up brighter every day. Soon it will be fully restored.'

'In the meantime you must gather every story and every rumour of Akh-Horus and bring them to me.'

She sent me to the shipping wharf every day to question the crews of the barges coming down from the north for news of Akh-Horus.

'They are saying now that nobody has ever seen the face of Akh-Horus, for he wears a helmet with a visor that covers all but his eyes. They say also that in the heat of battle the head of Akh-Horus bursts into flame, a flame that blinds his enemies,' I reported to her after one such visit.

'In the sunlight I have seen Tanus' hair seem to burn with a heavenly light,' my mistress confirmed.

On another morning I could tell her, 'They say that he can multiply his earthly body like the images in a mirror, that he can be in many different places at one time, for on the same day he can be seen in Qena and Kom-Ombo, a hundred miles apart.'

'Is that possible?' she asked, with awe.

'Some say this is not true. They say that he can cover these great distances only because he never sleeps. They say that in the night hours he gallops through the darkness on the back of a lion, and in the day he soars through the sky on the back of an enormous white eagle to fall upon his enemies when they least expect it.'

'That could be true.' She nodded seriously. 'I do not believe about the mirror images, but the lion and the eagle might be true. Tanus could do something like that. I believe it.'

'I think it more likely that everybody in Egypt is eager to set eyes upon Akh-Horus, and that the desire is father to the act. They see him behind every bush. As to the speed of his travels, well, I have marched with the guards and I can vouch for—' She would not allow me to finish, but interrupted primly.

'There is no romance in your soul, Taita. You would doubt that the clouds are the fleece of Osiris' flocks, and that the sun is the face of Ra, simply because you cannot reach up and touch them. I, for my part, believe Tanus is capable of all these things.' Which assertion put an end to the argument, and I hung my head in submission.

IN THE afternoons the two of us resumed our old practice of strolling through the streets and the market-places. As before her illness, my mistress was welcomed by an adoring populace, and she stopped to speak with all of them, no matter their station or their calling. From priests to prostitutes, none was immune to her loveliness and her unfeigned charm.

Always she was able to turn the conversation to Akh-Horus, and the people were as eager as she was to discuss the new god. By this time he had been promoted in the popular imagination from demi-god to a full member of the pantheon. The citizens of Elephantine had already begun a subscription for the building of a temple to Akh-Horus, to which my mistress had made a most generous donation.

A site for the temple had been chosen on the bank of the river opposite the temple of Horus, his brother, and Pharaoh had made the formal declaration of his intention to dedicate the building in person. Pharaoh had every reason to be grateful. There was a new spirit of confidence abroad. As the caravan routes were made secure, so the volume of trade between the Upper Kingdom and the rest of the world blossomed.

Where before one caravan had arrived from the East, now four made a safe crossing of the desert, and as many set out on the return journey. To supply the caravan masters, pack-donkeys were needed in their thousands, and the farmers and breeders drove them into the cities, grinning at the expectation of the high prices they would receive.

Because it was now safe to work the fields furthest from the protection of the city walls, crops were planted where for decades only weeds had grown, and the farmers, who had been reduced to beggars, began to prosper again. The oxen drew the sledges piled high with produce along the roads that were now protected by the legions of Akh-Horus, and the markets were filled with fresh produce.

Some of the profits of the merchants and the land-owners from these ventures were spent in the building of new villas in the countryside, where it was once more deemed safe to take their families to live. Artisans and craftsmen, who had walked the streets of Thebes and Elephantine seeking employment for their skills, were suddenly in demand, and used their wages to buy not only the necessities of life but luxuries for themselves and their families. The markets were thronged.

The volume of traffic up and down the Nile swelled dramatically, so that more craft were needed, and the new keels were laid down in every shipyard. The captains and crews of the river boats and the shipyard workers spent their new wealth in the taverns and pleasure-houses, so that the prostitutes and the courtesans clamoured for fine clothes and baubles, and the tailors and the jewellers thrived and built new homes, while their wives prowled the markets with gold and silver in their purses, looking for everything from new slaves to cooking-pots.

Egypt was coming to life again, after being strangled for all these years by the depredations of Akh-Seth and the Shrikes.

As a result of all this, the state revenues burgeoned, and Pharaoh's tax-collectors circled above it all with as much relish as the vultures above the corpses of the bandits that Akh-Horus and his legions were strewing across the countryside. Of course, Pharaoh was grateful.

So were my mistress and I. At my suggestion, the two of us invested in a share of a trading expedition that was setting out eastwards into Syria. When the expedition returned six months later, we found that we had made a profit of fifty times our original investment. My mistress bought herself a string of pearls and five new female slaves to make my life miserable. Prudent as always, I used my share to acquire five plots of prime land on the east bank of the river, and one of the law scribes drew up the deeds and had them registered in the temple books.

THEN CAME the day that I had been dreading. One morning my mistress studied her reflection in the mirror with even more attention than usual, and declared that she was ready at last. In all fairness, I had grudgingly to agree that she had never looked more lovely. It was as though all she had suffered recently had tempered her to a new resilience. The last traces of girlishness, uncertainty, and puppy fat had evaporated from her features, and she had become a woman, mature and composed.

'I trusted you, Taita. Now prove to me that I was not silly to do so. Bring Tanus to me.'

When Tanus and I had parted at Safaga, we had been unable to agree on any sure method of exchanging messages.

'I will be on the march every day, and who can tell where this campaign will lead me. Do not let the Lady Lostris worry if she does not hear from me. Tell her I will send a message when my task is completed. But tell her that I will be there when the fruits of our love are ripe upon the tree, and are ready for plucking.'

Thus it was that we had heard nothing of him other than the wild rumours of the wharves and bazaars.

Once again it seemed that the gods had intervened to save me, this time from the wrath of my Lady Lostris. There was a fresh rumour in the market-place that day. A caravan coming down the northern road had encountered a recently erected pyramid of human heads at the roadside not two miles beyond the city walls. The heads were so fresh that they were stinking only a little and had not yet been cleaned of flesh by the crows and vultures.

'This means only one thing,' the gossips told each other. 'This means that Akh-Horus is in the nome of Assoun, probably within sight of the walls of Elephantine. He has fallen upon the remnants of the clan of Akheku, who have been skulking in the desert since their baron had his head hacked off at Gallala. Akh-Horus has slaughtered the last of the bandits, and piled their heads at the roadside. Thanks be to the new god, the south has been cleared of the dreaded Shrikes!'

This was news indeed, the best I had heard in weeks, and I was in a fever to take it to my mistress. I pushed my way through the throng of sailors and merchants and fishermen on the wharf to find a boatman to take me back to the island.

Somebody tugged at my arm, and I shrugged the hand away irritably. Despite the new prosperity sweeping the land, or perhaps because of it, the beggars were more demanding than ever. This one was not so easily put off, and I turned back to him, angrily raising my staff to drive him off.

'Do not strike an old friend! I have a message for you from one of the gods,' the beggar whined, and I stayed the blow and gaped at him.

'Hui!' My heart soared as I recognized the sly grin of the erstwhile robber. 'What are you doing here?' I did not wait for a reply to my fatuous question, but went on swiftly, 'Follow me at a distance.'

I led him to one of the pleasure-houses in a narrow alley beyond the harbour that provided rooms to couples, of the same or of mixed gender. They rented the rooms for a short period measured by a water-clock set at the door, and charged a large copper ring for this service. I paid this exorbitant fee and the moment we were alone, I seized Hui by his ragged cloak.

'What news of your master?' I demanded, and he chuckled with infuriating insolence.

'My throat is so dry I can hardly speak.' Already he had adopted all the swagger and insolent panache of a trooper of the Blues. How quickly a monkey learns new tricks! I shouted for the porter to bring up a pot of beer. Hui drank like a thirsty donkey, then lowered the pot and belched happily.

'The god Akh-Horus sends greetings, to you and to another whose name cannot be mentioned. He bids me tell you that the task is completed and that all the birds are in the cage. He reminds you that it lacks only a few months to the next festival of Osiris and it is time to write a new script for the passion play for the amusement of the king.'

'Where is he? How long will it take for you to return to him?' I demanded eagerly.

'I can be with him before Ammon-Ra, the sun god, plunges beyond the western hills,' Hui declared, and I glanced through the window at the sun which was halfway down the sky. Tanus was lying up very close to the city, and I rejoiced anew. How I longed to feel his rough embrace, and hear that great booming laugh of his!

Grinning to myself in anticipation, I paced up and down the filthy floor of the room while I decided on the message that I would give Hui to take back to him.

IT WAS almost dark when I stepped ashore on our little jetty and hurried up the steps. One of the slave girls was weeping at the gate, and rubbing her swollen ear.

'She struck me,' the girl whimpered, and I saw that her dignity had suffered more than her ear.

'Do not refer to the Lady Lostris as "she",' I scolded her. 'Anyway, what have you to complain of? Slaves are there to be struck.'

None the less, it was unusual for my mistress to lift a hand to anyone in her household. She must indeed be in a fine mood, I thought, and slowed my pace. Proceeding warily now, I arrived just as another of the girls fled weeping from the chamber. My mistress appeared in the doorway behind her, flushed with anger. 'You have turned my hair into a haystack—'

She saw me then and broke off her tirade. She rounded on me with such gusto that I knew that I was the true object of her ire.

'Where have you been?' she demanded. 'I sent you to the harbour before noon. How dare you leave me waiting so long?' She advanced upon me with such an expression that I backed off nervously.

'He is here,' I told her hastily, and then dropped my voice so that none of the slave girls could hear me. 'Tanus is here,' I whispered, 'the day after tomorrow I will make good my promise to you.'

Her mood swung in a full circle and she leaped up to throw her arms around my neck, then she went off to find her offended girls and to comfort them.

AS PART of his annual tribute the vassal king of the Amorites had sent Pharaoh a pair of trained hunting cheetahs from his kingdom across the Red Sea. The king was eager to run these magnificent creatures against the herds of gazelle that abounded in the desert dunes of the west bank. The entire court, including my mistress, had been commanded to attend the course.

We sailed across to the west bank in a fleet of small river craft, white sails and bright-coloured pennants fluttering. There was laughter and the music of lute and sistrum to accompany us. The annual flooding of the great river would begin within days, and this expectation, together with the prosperous new climate of the land, enhanced the carnival mood of the court.

My mistress was in a gayer mood than any of them, and she called merry greetings to her friends in the other boats as our felucca cut through the green summer waters at such a rate as to deck our bows with a lacy white garland of foam and leave a shining wake behind us.

It seemed that I was the only one who was not happy and carefree. The wind had a harsh, abrasive edge to it, and was blowing from the wrong quarter. I kept glancing anxiously at the western sky. It was cloudless and bright, but there was a brassy sheen to the heavens that was unnatural. It was almost as though another sun was dawning from the opposite direction to the one we knew so well.

I put aside my misgivings and tried to enter into the spirit of the outing. I failed in this, for I had more than the weather to worry about. If one part of my plan went awry, my life would be in danger, and perhaps other lives more valuable than mine would be at risk.

I must have shown all this on my face, for my mistress nudged me with her pretty painted toe and told me, 'So glum, Taita? Everyone who looks at you will know that you are up to something. Smile! I command you to smile.'

When we landed on the west bank, there was an army of slaves waiting for us there. Grooms holding splendid white riding donkeys from the royal stables, all caparisoned with silk. Pack-donkeys laden with tents and rugs and baskets of food and wine, and all the other provisions for a royal picnic. There was a regiment of slaves in attendance, some to hold sun-shades above the ladies, others to wait upon the noble guests. There were clowns and acrobats and musicians to entertain them, and a hundred huntsmen to provide the sport.

The cheetah cage was loaded on a sledge drawn by a team of white oxen, and the court gathered around the vehicle to admire these rare beasts. They did not occur naturally in our land, for they were creatures of the open grassy savannah, and there was none of this type of terrain along the river. They were the first that I had ever seen, and my curiosity was so aroused that for a while I forgot my other worries and went up as close to the cage as I could push through the crowd without jostling or treading on the toes of some irascible nobleman.

They were the most beautiful cats that I could imagine, taller and leaner than our leopards, with long, clean limbs and concave bellies. Their sinuous tails seemed to give expression to their mood. Their golden hides were starred with rosettes of deepest black, while from the inner corner of each of their eyes, a line of black was painted down the cheek like a runnel of tears. This, with their regal bearing, gave them a tragic and romantic air that I found enchanting. I longed to own one of these creatures, and I decided on the moment to put the thought into the mind of my mistress. Pharaoh had never refused one of her whims.

Too soon for my liking, the barque carrying the king across the river arrived on the west bank, and with the rest of the court we hurried to the landing to greet him.

Pharaoh was dressed in light hunting garb and for once seemed relaxed and happy. He stopped beside my mistress and while she made a ritual obeisance, he enquired graciously about her health. I was filled with dread that he might decide to keep her by his side throughout the day, which would have upset all my arrangements. However, the hunting cheetah caught his attention and he passed by without giving my mistress any order to follow.

We lost ourselves in the throng and made our way to where a donkey was being held for my Lady Lostris. While I helped her to mount, I spoke quietly to the groom. When he told me what I wanted to hear, I slipped a ring of silver into his hand, and it disappeared, as though by magic.

With one slave leading her and another holding a sun-shade over her, my mistress and I followed the king and the sledge out into the desert. With frequent stops for refreshment, it took us half the morning to reach the Valley of the Gazelles. On the way we passed at a distance the ancient cemetery of Tras which dated from the time of the very first pharaohs. Some of the wise men said that the tombs had been carved from the cliff of black rock three thousand years ago, although how they reached this conclusion I could not tell. Without making it obvious, I studied the entrances of the tombs keenly as we passed. However, from so far off I could make out no trace of recent human presence around them, and I was unreasonably disappointed. I kept glancing back, as we went on.

The Valley of the Gazelles was one of the royal hunting preserves, protected by the decrees of a long line of pharaohs. A company of royal gamekeepers was permanently stationed in the hills above the valley to enforce the king's proclamation reserving all the creatures in it to himself. The penalty for hunting here without the royal authority was death by strangulation.

The nobles dismounted on the crest of one of these hills overlooking the broad brown valley. With despatch the tents were set up to give them shade, and jars of sherbet and beer were broached to slake the thirst of their journey.

I made certain that my mistress and I secured a good vantage-point from which to watch the hunt, but one from which we could also withdraw discreetly without attracting undue attention to ourselves. In the distance I could make out the herds of gazelle through the wavering watery mirage on the floor of the valley. I pointed them out to my mistress.

'What do they find to eat down there?' My Lady Lostris asked. 'There is not a trace of green. They must eat stones, for there are enough of those.'

'Many of those are not stones at all, but living plants,' I told her. When she laughed in disbelief, I searched the rocky ground and plucked a handful of those miraculous plants.

'They are stones,' she insisted, until she held one in her hand and crushed it. The thick juice trickled over her fingers, and she marvelled at the cunning of whatever god had devised this deception. 'This is what they live on? It does not seem possible.'

We could not continue this conversation, because the hunt was beginning. Two of the royal huntsmen opened the cage and the hunting cheetahs leaped down to earth. I expected them to attempt to escape, but they were tame as temple cats and rubbed themselves affectionately against the legs of their handlers. The cats uttered a strange twittering sound, more like a bird than a savage predator.

Along the far side of the brown, scorched valley bottom I could make out the line of beaters, their forms tiny and distorted by distance and mirage. They were moving slowly in our direction, and the herds of antelope were beginning to drift ahead of them.

While the king and his huntsmen, with the cheetahs on leash, moved down the slope towards the valley bottom, we and the rest of the court remained on the crest. The courtiers were already placing wagers with one another, and I was as eager as any of them to watch the outcome of the hunt, but my mistress had her mind on other matters.

'When can we go?' she whispered. 'When can we escape into the desert?'

'Once the hunt begins, all their eyes will be upon it. That will be our opportunity.' Even as I spoke, the wind that had blown us across the river and cooled us on the march suddenly dropped. It was as though a coppersmith had opened the door of his forge. The air became almost too hot to breathe.

Once again I looked to the western horizon. The sky above it had turned a sulphurous yellow. Even as I watched, the stain seemed to spread across the heavens. It made me uneasy. However, I was the only one in the crowd who seemed to notice this strange phenomenon.

Although the hunting party was now at the bottom of the hill, it was still close enough for me to observe the great cats. They had seen the herds of gazelle which were being driven slowly towards them. This had transformed them from affectionate pets into the savage hunters they truly were. Their heads were up, intent and alert, ears pricked forward, leaning against the leash. Their concave bellies were sucked in, and every muscle was taut as a bowstring drawn to full stretch.

My mistress tugged at my skirt, and whispered imperatively, 'Let us be gone, Taita,' and reluctantly I began to edge away towards a clump of rocks that would cover our retreat and screen us from the rest of the company. The bribe of silver to the groom had procured for us a donkey that was now tethered out of sight amongst the rocks. As soon as we reached it, I checked that it carried what I had ordered, the water-skin and the leather bag of provisions. I found that they were all in order.

I could not restrain myself, and I pleaded with my mistress, 'Just one moment more.' Before she could forbid it, I scrambled to the top of the rocky outcrop and peeped down into the valley below.

The nearest antelope were crossing a few hundred paces in front of where Pharaoh held the pair of cheetahs on the leash. I was just in time to watch him slip them and send them away. They started out at an easy lope, heads up, as if they were studying the herds of daintily trotting antelope to select their prey. Suddenly the herds became aware of their rapid approach, and they burst into full flight. Like a flock of swallows they skimmed away across the dusty plain.

The cats stretched out their long bodies, reaching far ahead with their forepaws and then whipping their hindquarters through, doubling their lean torsos before stretching out again. Swiftly they built up to the top of their speed, and I had never seen an animal so swift. Compared to them, the herds of gazelle seemed suddenly to have run into swampy ground and to have had their flight impeded. With effortless elegance, the two cats overhauled the herd, and ran past one or two stragglers before they caught up with the victims of their choice.

The panic-stricken antelopes tried to dodge the deadly rush. They leaped high and changed direction in mid-air, twisting and doubling back the moment their dainty hooves touched the scorched earth. The cats followed each of the convolutions with graceful ease, and the end was inevitable. Each of them bore one of the gazelle to earth in a sliding, tumbling cloud of dust, and then crouched over it, jaws clamped across the windpipe to strangle it while the gazelle's back legs kicked out convulsively, and then at last stiffened into the rigor of death.

I found myself shaken and breathless with the excitement of it all. Then my mistress's voice roused me. 'Taita! Come down immediately. They will see you perched up there.' And I slid down to rejoin her.

Although I was still wrought up, I boosted her into the saddle and led the donkey down into the dead ground where we were out of sight of the company on the hilltop behind us. My mistress could not sustain her irritation with me for very long, and when I slyly mentioned Tanus' name again she forgot it entirely, and urged her mount on towards the rendez-vous.

Only after I had placed another ridge behind us and was certain that we were well clear of the Valley of the Gazelles, did I head back directly towards the cemetery of Tras. In the still, hot air, the sound of our donkey's hooves clinked and crackled on the stones as though it were passing over a bed of broken glass. Soon I felt the sweat break out upon my skin, for the air was close and heavy with a feeling of thunder. Long before we reached the tombs, I told my mistress, 'The air is dry as old bones. You should drink a little water—'

'Keep on! There will be plenty of time to drink your fill later.'

'I was thinking only of you, mistress,' I protested.

'We must not be late. Every moment you waste will give me that much less with Tanus.' She was right, of course, for we would have little enough time before we were missed by the others. My mistress was so popular that many would be looking to enjoy her company once the hunt was over and they were returning to the river.

As we drew closer to the cliffs, so her eagerness increased until she could no longer abide the pace of her mount. She leaped off its back and ran ahead to the next rise. 'There it is! That is where he will be waiting for me,' she cried, and pointed ahead.

As she danced on the skyline, the wind came at us like a ravening wolf, howling amongst the hills and canyons. It caught my mistress's hair and spread it like a flag, snapping and tangling it around her head. It lifted her skirts high above her slim brown thighs, and she laughed and pirouetted, flirting with the wind as though it were her lover. I did not share her delight.

I turned and looked back and saw the storm coming out of the Sahara. It towered into the sullen yellow heavens, dun and awful, billowing upon itself like surf breaking on a coral reef. The wind-blown sand scoured my legs and I broke into a run, dragging the donkey behind me on its lead. The wind thrusting into my back almost knocked me off my feet, but I caught my mistress.

'We must be quick,' I shouted above the wind. 'We must reach the shelter of the tombs before it hits us.'

High clouds of sand blew across the sun, dimming it until I could look directly at it with my naked eye. All the world was washed with that sombre shade of ochre, and the sun was a dull ball of orange. Flying sand raked the exposed skin of our limbs and the backs of our necks, until I wound my shawl around my mistress's head to protect her, and led her forward by the hand.

Sheets of driven sand engulfed us, blotting out our surroundings, so that I feared I had lost direction, until abruptly a hole opened in the curtains of sand, and I saw the dark mouth of one of the tombs appear ahead of us. Dragging my mistress with one hand and our donkey with the other, I staggered into the shelter of the cave. The entrance-shaft was carved from the solid rock. It led us deep into the hillside, and then made a sharp turn before entering the burial chamber where once the ancient mummy had been laid to rest. Centuries before, the grave-robbers had disposed of the embalmed body and all its treasures. Now all that remained were the faded frescoes upon the stone walls, images of gods and monsters that were ghostly in the gloom.

My mistress sank down against the rock wall, but her first thoughts were for her love. 'Tanus will never find us now,' she cried in despair, and I who had led her to safety was hurt by her ingratitude. I unsaddled our donkey and heaped the load in a corner of the tomb. Then I drew a cup of water from the skin and made her drink.

'What will happen to the others, the king and all our friends?' she asked, between gulps from the cup. It was her nature to think of the welfare of others, even in her own predicament.

'They have the huntsmen to care for them,' I told her. 'They are good men and know the desert.' But not well enough to have anticipated the storm, I thought grimly. Although I sought to reassure her, I knew it would go hard with the women and children out there.

'And Tanus?' she asked. 'What will become of him?'

'Tanus especially will know what to do. He is like one of the Bedouin. You can be sure he will have seen the storm coming.'

'Will we ever get back to the river? Will they ever find us here?' At last she thought of her own safety.

'We will be safe here. We have water enough for many days. When the storm blows itself out, we will find our way back to the river.' Thinking of the precious water, I carried the bulging skin further into the tomb, where the donkey would not trample it. By now it was almost completely dark, and I fumbled with the lamp that the slave had provided from the pack, and blew upon the smouldering wick. It flared and lit the tomb with a cheery yellow light.

While I was still busy with the lamp and my back was turned to the entrance, my mistress screamed. It was a sound so high and filled with such mortal terror that I was struck with equal dread, and the courses of my blood ran thick and slow as honey, although my heart raced like the hooves of the flying gazelle. I spun about and reached for my dagger, but when I saw the monster whose bulk filled the doorway, I froze without touching the weapon on my belt. I knew instinctively that my puny blade would avail us not at all against whatever this creature might be.

In the feeble light of the lamp the form was indistinct and distorted. I saw that it had a human shape, but it was too large to be a man, and the grotesque head convinced me that this was indeed that dreadful crocodile-headed monster from the underworld that devours the hearts of those who are found wanting on the scales of Thoth, the monster depicted on the walls of the tomb. The head gleamed with reptilian scales, and the beak was that of an eagle or a gigantic turtle. The eyes were deep and fathomless pits that stared at us implacably. Great wings sprouted from its shoulders. Half-furled, they flapped about the towering body like those of a falcon at bate. I expected the creature to launch itself on those wings and to rend my mistress with brazen talons. She must have dreaded this as much as I, for she screamed again as she crouched at the monster's feet.

Then suddenly I realized that the creature was not winged, but that the folds of a long woollen cape, such as the Bedouin wear, were flogging on the wind. While we were still frozen by this horrible presence, it raised both hands and lifted off the gilded war helmet with the visor fashioned like the head of an eagle. Then it shook its head and a mass of red-gold curls tumbled down on to the broad shoulders.

'From the top of the cliff I saw you coming through the storm,' it said in those dear familiar tones.

My mistress screamed again, this time with wildly ringing joy. 'Tanus!'

She flew to him, and he gathered her up as though she were a child and lifted her so high that her head brushed the rock roof. Then he brought her down and folded her to his chest. From the cradle of his arms, she reached up with her mouth for his, and it seemed that they might devour each other with the strength of their need.

I stood forgotten in the shadows of the tomb. Although I had conspired and risked so much to bring them together, I cannot bring myself to write down here the feelings that assailed me as I was made reluctant witness to their rapture. I believe that jealousy is the most ignoble of all our emotions, and yet I loved the Lady Lostris as well as Tanus did, and not with the love of a father or of a brother, either. I was a eunuch, but what I felt for her was the love of a natural man, hopeless of course, but all the more bitter because of that. I could not stay and watch them and I began to slink from the tomb like a whipped puppy, but Tanus saw me leaving and broke that kiss which was threatening to destroy my soul.

'Taita, don't leave me alone with the wife of the king. Stay with us to protect me from this terrible temptation. Our honour is in jeopardy. I cannot trust myself, you must stay and see that I bring no shame to the wife of Pharaoh.'

'Go,' cried my Lady Lostris from his arms. 'Leave us alone. I'll listen to no talk of shame or honour now. Our love has been too long denied. I cannot wait for the prophecy of the Mazes to run its course. Leave us alone now, gentle Taita.'

I fled from the chamber as though my life was in danger. I might have run out into the storm and perished there. That way I would have found surcease, but I was too much of a coward, and I let the wind drive me back. I stumbled to a corner of the shaft where the wind could no longer harry me, and I sank to the stone floor. I pulled my shawl over my head to stop my eyes and my ears, but although the storm roared along the cliff, it could not drown the sounds from the burial chamber.

For two days the storm blew with unabated ferocity. I slept for part of that time, forcing myself to seek oblivion, but whenever I awoke, I could hear them, and the sounds of their love tortured me. Strange that I had never known such distress when my mistress was with the king – but then on the other hand not so strange, for the old man had meant nothing to her.

This was another world of torment for me. The cries, the groans, the whispers tore at my heart. The rhythmic sobs of a young woman that were not those of pain threatened to destroy me. Her wild scream of final rapture was more agonizing to me than the cut of the gelding-knife.

At last the wind abated and died away, moaning at the foot of the cliffs. The light strengthened and I realized that it was the third day of my incarceration in the tomb. I roused myself and called to them, not daring to enter the inner chamber for fear of what I might discover. For a while there was no reply, and then my mistress spoke in a husky, bemused voice that echoed eerily down the shaft. 'Taita, is that you? I thought that I had died in the storm and been carried to the western fields of paradise.'

ONCE THE storm had dropped, we had little time remaining. The royal huntsmen would already be searching for us. The storm had given us the best possible excuse for our absence. I was sure that the survivors of the hunting party would be scattered across these terrible hills. But the search-party must not discover us in the company of Tanus.

On the other hand, Tanus and I had barely spoken during these last days, and there was much to discuss. Hastily we made our plans, standing in the entrance to the shaft.

My mistress was quiet and composed as I had seldom seen her before. No longer the irrepressible chatterbox, she stood beside Tanus, watching his face with a new serenity. She reminded me of a priestess serving before the image of her god. Her eyes never left his face, and occasionally she reached out to touch him, as if to reassure herself that it was truly he.

When she did this, Tanus broke off whatever he was saying and gave all his attention to those dark green eyes. I had to call him back to the business we still had not completed. In the presence of such manifest adoration, my own feelings were base and mean. I forced myself to rejoice for them.

It took longer to finish our business than I deemed wise, but at last I embraced Tanus in farewell and urged the donkey out into the sunlight that was filtered by the fine yellow dust that still filled the air. My mistress lingered, and I waited for her in the valley below.

Looking back, I saw them emerge from the cave at last. They stood gazing at each other for a long moment without touching, and then Tanus turned and strode away. My mistress watched until he was gone from her sight, then she came down to where I waited. She walked like a woman in a dream.

I helped her to mount, and while I adjusted the saddle girth, she reached down and took my hand. 'Thank you,' she said simply.

'I do not deserve your gratitude,' I demurred.

'I am the happiest creature in all the world. Everything that you told me of love is true. Please rejoice for me, even though—' she did not finish, and suddenly I realized that she had read my innermost feelings. Even in her own great joy, she grieved that she had caused me pain. I think I loved her more in that moment than I had ever done before.

I turned away and took up the reins, and led her back towards the Nile.

ONE OF the royal huntsmen spied us from a far hilltop, and hailed us heartily.

'We have been searching for you at the king's command,' he told us, as he hurried down to join us.

'Was the king saved?' I asked.

'He is safe in the palace on Elephantine Island, and he has commanded that the Lady Lostris be brought to him directly she is found.'

As we set foot on the palace jetty, Aton was there, puffing out his painted cheeks with relief and fussing over my mistress. 'They have found the bodies of twenty-three unfortunates who perished in the storm,' he told us with ghoulish relish. 'All were certain that you would be found dead also. However, I prayed at the temple of Hapi for your safe return.' He looked pleased with himself, and I was annoyed that he tried to claim the credit for her survival for himself. He allowed us only time enough to wash hastily and anoint our dry skin with perfumed oil, before he whisked us away to the audience with the king.

Pharaoh was truly moved to have my mistress returned to him. I am sure he had come to love her as much as any of the others, and not merely for the promise of immortality that he saw in her. A tear tangled in his eyelash and smeared the paint on his cheek as she knelt before him.

'I thought you were lost,' he told her, and would have embraced her, had etiquette permitted it. 'Instead I find you prettier and livelier than ever.' Which was true, for love had gilded her with its special magic.

'Taita saved me,' she told Pharaoh. 'He guided me to a shelter and protected me through all those terrible days. Without him I would have perished, like those other poor souls.'

'Is this true, Taita?' Pharaoh demanded of me directly, and I assumed my modest expression, and murmured, 'I am but a humble instrument of the gods.'

He smiled at me, for I knew he had become fond of me also. 'You have rendered us many services, oh humble instrument. But this is the most valuable of them all. Approach!' he commanded, and I knelt before him.

Aton stood beside him, holding a small cedar-wood box. He lifted the lid and proffered it to the king. From the case Pharaoh lifted out a gold chain. It was of the purest unalloyed gold, and bore the marks of the royal jewellers to attest its weight of twenty deben.

The king held the chain over my head and intoned, 'I bestow upon you the Gold of Praise.' He lowered it on to my shoulders, and the oppressive weight was a delight to me. This decoration was the highest mark of royal favour, usually reserved for generals and ambassadors, or for high officials such as Lord Intef. I doubted that ever in the history of this very Egypt had the gold chain been placed around the neck of a lowly slave.

That was not the end of the gifts and awards that were to be bestowed upon me, for my mistress was not to be outdone. That evening while I was attending her bath, she suddenly dismissed her slaves and, standing naked before me, she told me, 'You may help me to dress, Taita.' She allowed me this privilege when she was especially well pleased with me. She knew just how much I enjoyed having her to myself in these intimate circumstances.

Her loveliness was covered only by the glossy tresses of her sable hair. It seemed that those days she had spent with Tanus had filled her with a new quality of beauty. It emanated from deep within her. A lamp placed inside an alabaster jar will shine through the translucent sides; in the same way, the Lady Lostris seemed to glow.

'I never dreamed that such a poor vessel as this body of mine could contain such joy.' She stroked her own flanks as she said it and looked down at herself, inviting me to do the same. 'All that you promised me came to pass while I was with Tanus. Pharaoh has bestowed the Gold of Praise upon you, it is fitting that I also show my appreciation to you. I want you to share my happiness in some way.'

'Serving you is all the reward I could wish for.'

'Help me to dress,' she ordered, and lifted her hands above her head. Her breasts changed shape as she moved. Over the year I had watched them grow from tiny immature figs into these round, creamy pomegranates, more beautiful than jewels or marble sculptures. I held the diaphanous nightdress over her, and then let it float down over her body. It covered her, but did not obscure her loveliness, in the same way that the morning mist decks the waters of the Nile in the dawn.

'I have commanded a banquet, and sent invitations to the royal ladies.'

'Very well, my lady. I shall see to it.'

'No, no, Taita. The banquet is in your honour. You will sit beside me as my guest.'

This was as shocking as any of the wild schemes she had thought up recently. 'It is not fitting, mistress. You will offend against custom.'

'I am the wife of Pharaoh. I set the customs. During the banquet I will have a gift for you, and I will present it to you in the sight of all.'

'Will you tell me what this gift is?' I asked, with some trepidation. I was never sure of what mischief she would dream up next.

'Certainly I will tell you what it is.' She smiled mysteriously. 'It is a secret, that's what it is.'

EVEN THOUGH I was the guest of honour, I could not leave the arrangements for the banquet to cooks and giggling slave girls. After all, the reputation of my mistress as a hostess was at stake. I was at the market before dawn to procure the finest, freshest produce from the fields and the river.

I promised Aton that he would be invited, and he opened the king's wine cellar and let me make my selection. I hired and rehearsed the best musicians and acrobats in the city. I sent out the slaves to gather hyacinth and lily and lotus from the banks of the river to augment the masses of blooms that already decorated our garden. I had the weavers plait tiny arks of reeds on which I floated coloured glass lamps and set them adrift on the ponds of our water-garden. I set out leather cushions and garlands of flowers for each guest, and jars of perfumed oil to cool them in the sultry night and drive away the mosquitoes.

At nightfall the royal ladies began to arrive in all their frippery and high fashion. Some of them had even shaved their heads and replaced their natural hair with elaborate wigs woven from the hair which the wives of the poor were forced to sell, in order to feed their brats. This was a fashion I abhorred and I vowed to do all in my power to prevent my mistress from succumbing to such folly. Her lustrous tresses were amongst my chief delights, but when it comes to fashion, even the most sensible woman is not to be trusted.

When, at the insistence of my mistress, I seated myself on the cushion beside her, rather than taking my usual position behind her, I could see that many of our guests were scandalized by such indecorous behaviour, and they whispered to each other behind their fans. I was just as uncomfortable as they were, and to cover my embarrassment, I signalled the slaves to keep the wine cups filled, the musicians to play, and the dancers to dance.

The wine was robust, the music rousing, and the dancers were all male. They gave ample proof of their gender, for I had ordered them to perform in a state of nature. The ladies were so enchanted by this display that they soon forgot their decent outrage, and did justice to the wine. I had no doubt that many of the male dancers would not leave the harem before dawn. Some of the royal ladies had voracious appetites, and many had not been visited by the king in years.

In this convivial atmosphere my mistress rose to her feet and called for the attention of her guests. Then she commended me to them in terms so extravagant that even I blushed. She went on to relate amusing and touching episodes from the lifetime we had spent together. The wine seemed to have softened the attitude of the women towards me, and they laughed and applauded. A few of them even wept a little with wine and sentiment.

At last my mistress commanded me to kneel before her, and as I did so, there was a murmur of comment. I had chosen to wear a simple kilt of the finest linen, and the slave girls had dressed my hair in the fashion that best suited me. Apart from the Gold of Praise around my throat, I wore no other ornament. In the midst of such ostentation, my simple style was striking. With regular swimming and exercise I had kept the athletic body which had first attracted Lord Intef to me. In those years I was in my prime.

I heard one of the senior wives murmur to her neighbour, 'What a pity he has lost his jewels. He would make such a diverting toy.' This evening I could ignore the words that in other circumstances would have caused me intense pain.

My mistress was looking very pleased with herself. She had succeeded in keeping me ignorant of the nature of her gift. Usually she was not so adroit as to be able to outwit me. She looked down on my bowed head and spoke slowly and clearly, wringing the utmost enjoyment from the moment.

'Taita the slave. For all the years of my life you have been a shield over me. You have been my mentor and my tutor. You have taught me to read and to write. You have made clear to me the mysteries of the stars and the arcane arts. You have taught me to sing and to dance. You have shown me how to find happiness and contentment in many things. I am grateful.'

The royal ladies were once more beginning to become restive. They had never before heard a slave praised in such effusive terms.

'On the day of the *khamsin* you did me a service that I must reward. Pharaoh has bestowed the Gold of Praise upon you. I have my own gift for you.'

From under her robe she took a roll of papyrus secured with a coloured thread. 'You knelt before me as a slave. Now rise to your feet as a free man.' She held up the papyrus. 'This is your deed of manumission, prepared by the scribes of the court. From this day forward, you are a free man.'

I lifted my head for the first time and stared at her in disbelief. She pressed the roll of papyrus into my numbed fingers, and smiled down at me fondly.

'You did not expect this, did you? You are so surprised that you have no words for me. Say something to me, Taita. Tell me how grateful you are for this boon.'

Every word she spoke wounded me like a poisoned dart. My tongue was a rock in my mouth as I contemplated a life without her. As a freed man, I would be excluded from her presence for ever. I would never again prepare her food, nor attend her bath. I would never spread the covers over her as she prepared for sleep, nor would I rouse her in the dawn and be at her side when first she opened those lovely dark green eyes to each new day. I would never again sing with her, or hold her cup, or help her to dress and have the pleasure of gazing upon all her loveliness.

I was stricken, and I stared at her hopelessly, as one whose life had reached its end.

'Be happy, Taita,' she ordered me. 'Be happy in this new freedom I give you.'

'I will never be happy again,' I blurted. 'You have cast me off. How can I ever be happy again?'

Her smile faded away, and she stared at me in perturbation. 'I offer you the most precious gift that it is in my power to give you. I offer you your freedom.'

I shook my head. 'You inflict the most dire punishment upon me. You are driving me away from you. I will never know happiness again.'

'It is not a punishment, Taita. It was meant as a reward. Please, don't you understand?'

'The only reward I desire is to remain at your side for the rest of my life.' I felt the tears welling up from deep inside me, and I tried to hold them back. 'Please, mistress, I beg of you, don't send me away from you. If you have any feeling towards me, allow me to stay with you.'

'Do not weep,' she commanded. 'For if you do, then I will weep with you, in front of all my guests.' I truly believe that she had not, until that moment, contemplated the consequences of this misplaced piece of generosity that she had dreamed up. The tears broke over my lids and streamed down my cheeks.

'Stop it! This is not what I wanted.' Her own tears kept mine good company. 'I only thought to honour you, as the king has honoured you.'

I held up the roll of papyrus. 'Please let me tear this piece of foolery to shreds. Take me back into your service. Give me leave to stand behind you, where I belong.'

'Stop it, Taita! You are breaking my heart.' Loudly she snuffled up her tears, but I was merciless.

'The only gift I want from you is the right to serve you for all the days of my life. Please, mistress, rescind this deed. Give me your permission to tear it.'

She nodded vigorously, blubbering as she used to do when she was a little girl who had fallen and grazed her knees. I ripped the sheet of papyrus once and then again. Not satisfied with this destruction, I held the fragments to the lamp flame and let them burn to crispy black curls.

'Promise me that you will never try to drive me away again. Swear that you will never again try to thrust my freedom upon me.'

She nodded through her tears, but I would not accept that. 'Say it,' I insisted. 'Say it aloud for all to hear.'

'I promise to keep you as my slave, never to sell you, nor to set you free,' she whispered huskily through the tears, and then a beam of mischief shone out of those tragic dark green eyes. 'Unless, of course, you annoy me inordinately, then I will summon the law scribes immediately.' She put out a hand to lift me to my feet. 'Get up, you silly man, and attend to your duties. I swear my cup is empty.'

I resumed my proper position behind her, and refilled the cup. The tipsy company thought it all a bit of fun that we had arranged for their amusement, and they clapped and whistled and threw flower petals at us to show their appreciation. I could see that most of them were relieved that we had not truly flouted decorum, and that a slave was still a slave.

My mistress lifted the wine cup to her lips, but before she drank, she smiled at me over the rim. Though her eyes were still wet with tears, that smile lifted my spirits and restored my happiness. I felt as close to her then as ever I had in all the years.

THE MORNING after the banquet and my hour of freedom, we woke to find that during the night the river had swollen with the commencement of the annual flood. We had no warning of it until the joyous cries of the watchmen down at the port aroused us. Still heavy with wine, I left my bed and ran down to the riverside. Both banks were already lined with the populace of the city. They greeted the waters with prayers and songs and waving palm-fronds.

The low waters had been the bright green of the verdigris that grows on bars of copper. The waters of the inundation had flushed it all away, and now the river had swollen to an ominous grey. During the night it had crept halfway up the stone pylons of the harbour, and soon it would press against the earthworks of the embankment. Then it would force its way into the mouths of the irrigation canals that had been cracked and dry for so many months. From there it would swirl out and flood the fields, drowning the huts of the peasants, and washing away the boundary markers between the fields.

The surveying and replacement of the boundaries after each flood was the responsibility of the Guardian of the Waters. Lord Intef had multiplied his fortune by favouring the claims of the rich and the generous when the time came round each year to reset the marker stones.

From upstream echoed the distant rumble of the cataract. The rising flood overwhelmed the natural barrages of granite that were placed in its path, and, as it roared through the gorges, the spray rose into the hard blue sky, a silver column that could be seen from every quarter of the nome of Assoun. When the fine mist drifted across the island, it was cool and refreshing on our upturned faces. We delighted in this blessing, for it was the only rain we ever knew in our valley.

Even as we watched, the beaches around our island were eaten up by the flood. Soon our jetty would be submerged, and the river would lap at the gates of our garden. Where it would stop was a question that could only be calculated by a study of the levels of the Nilometer. On those levels hung prosperity or famine for the whole land and every person in it.

I hurried back to find my mistress and to prepare for the ceremony of the waters, in which I would play a prominent role. We dressed in our finest and I placed my new gold chain around my neck. Then, with the rest of our household and the ladies of the harem, we joined the spontaneous procession to the temple of Hapi.

Pharaoh and all the great lords of Egypt led us. The priests, plump with rich living, were waiting for us on the temple steps. Their heads were shaven, their pates shining with oil, and their eyes glittering with avarice, for the king would sacrifice lavishly today.

Before the king the statue of the god was carried from the sanctuary, and decked with flowers and fine crimson linen. Then the statue was drenched in oils and perfume while we sang psalms of praise and thanks to the god for sending down the flood.

Far to the south, in a land that no civilized man had ever visited, the god Hapi sat on top of his mountain and from two pitchers of infinite capacity he poured the holy waters into his Nile. The water from each pitcher was of a different colour and taste; one was bright green and sweet, the other grey and heavy with the silt which flooded our fields each season and charged them with new life and fertility.

While we sang, the king made sacrifice of corn and meats and wine and silver and gold. Then he called out his wise men, his engineers and his mathematicians, and bade them enter the Nilometer to begin their observations and their calculations.

In the time that I had belonged to Lord Intef, I had been nominated as one of the keepers of the water. I was the only slave in that illustrious company, but I consoled myself by the fact that very few others wore the Gold of Praise, and that they treated me with respect. They had worked with me before, and they knew my worth. I had helped to design the Nilometers that measured the flow of the river, and I had supervised the building of them. It was I who had worked out the complex formula to determine the projected height and the volume of each flood from the observations.

Our way lit by flickering torches of pitch-dipped rushes, I followed the high priest into the mouth of the Nilometer, a dark opening in the rear wall of the sanctuary. We descended the incline shaft, the stone steps slippery with slime and the effusions of the river. From under our feet, one of the deadly black water cobras slithered away, and with a furious hiss plunged into the dark water that had already risen halfway up the shaft.

We gathered on the last exposed step and by the light of the torches studied the marks that my masons had chiselled in the walls of the shaft. Each of the symbols had values, both magical and empirical, allotted to it.

We made the first and most crucial reading together with extreme care. Over the following five days we would take it in turns to watch and record the rising waters, and time the readings with the flow of a water-clock. From samples of the water, we would estimate the amount of silt it bore, and all these factors would influence our final conclusions.

When the five days of observation were completed, we embarked on a further three days of calculations. These covered many scrolls of papyrus. Finally, we were ready to present our findings to the king. On that day Pharaoh returned to the temple in royal state, accompanied by his nobles and half the population of Elephantine to receive the estimates.

As the high priest read them aloud, the king began to smile. We had forecast an inundation of almost perfect proportions. It would not be too low, to leave the fields exposed and baking in the sun, depriving them of the rich black layer of silt so vital to their fertility. Nor would it be so high as to wash away the canals and earthworks, and to drown the villages and cities along the banks. This season would bring forth bountiful harvests and fat herds.

Pharaoh smiled, not so much for the good fortune of his subjects, but for the bounty that his tax-collectors would gather in. The annual taxes were computed on the value of the flood, and this year there would be vast new treasures added to the store-rooms of his funerary temple. To close the ceremony of the blessing of the water in the temple of Hapi, Pharaoh announced the date of the biennial pilgrimage to Thebes to participate in the festival of Osiris. It did not seem possible that two years had passed since my mistress had played the part of the goddess in the last passion of Osiris.

I had as little sleep that night as when I had kept vigil in the shaft of the Nilometer, for my mistress was too excited to seek her own couch. She made me sit up with me until dawn, singing and laughing and repeating those stories of Tanus to which she never tired of listening.

In eight days the royal flotilla would sail northwards on the rising flood of the Nile. When we arrived, Tanus, Lord Harrab would be waiting for us in Thebes. My mistress was delirious with happiness.

THE FLOTILLA that assembled in the harbour roads of Elephantine was so numerous that it seemed to cover the water from bank to bank. My mistress remarked jokingly that a man might cross the Nile without wetting his feet by strolling over the bridge of hulls. With pennants and flags flying from every masthead, the fleet made a gallant show.

We and the rest of the court had already embarked on the vessels that had been allotted to us, and from the deck we cheered the king as he descended the marble steps from the palace and went aboard the great state barge. The moment he was safely embarked, a hundred horns sounded the signal to set sail. As one, the fleet squared away and pointed their bows into the north. With the rush of the river and the banks of oars driving us, we bore away.

There had been a different spirit abroad in the land since Akh-Horus had destroyed the Shrikes. The inhabitants of every village we passed came down to the water's edge to greet their king. Pharaoh sat high on the poop, wearing the cumbersome double crown, so that all might have a clear view of him. They waved palm-fronds and shouted, 'May all the gods smile on Pharaoh!' The river brought down to them not only their king, but also the promise of its own benevolence, and they were happy.

Twice during the days that followed, Pharaoh and all his train went ashore to inspect the monuments that Akh-Horus had raised to his passing at the crossroads of the caravan routes. The local peasants had preserved these gruesome piles of skulls as sacred relics of the new god. They had polished each skull until it shone like ivory, and bound the pyramids with building clay so that they would stand through the years. Then they had built shrines over them and appointed priests to serve these holy places.

At both these shrines my mistress left a gold ring as an offering, joyously accepted by the self-appointed guardians. It was to no avail that I protested this extravagance. My mistress often lacked the proper respect for the wealth that I was so painstakingly amassing on her behalf. Without my restraining hand, she would probably have given it all away to the grasping priesthood and the insatiable poor, smiling as she did so.

On the tenth night after leaving Elephantine, the royal entourage camped on a pleasant promontory above a bend in the river. The entertainment that evening was to include one of the most famous story-tellers in the land, and usually my mistress loved a good story above most other pleasures. Both she and I had been looking forward to this occasion and discussing it avidly since leaving the palace. It was therefore to my surprise and bitter disappointment that the Lady Lostris declared herself too fatigued and out of sorts to attend the story-teller. Although she urged me to go, and take the rest of our household with me, I could not leave her alone when she was unwell. I gave her a hot draught and I slept on the floor at the end of her bed, so that I could be near if she needed me during the night.

I was truly worried in the morning when I tried to wake her. Usually she would spring from her bed with a smile of anticipation, ready to seize and devour the new day, a glutton for the joy of living. However, this morning she pulled the covers back over her head and mumbled, 'Leave me to sleep a little longer. I feel as heavy and dull as an old woman.'

'The king has decreed an early start. We must be aboard before the sun rises. I will bring you a hot infusion that will cheer you.' I poured boiling water over a bowl of herbs that I had picked with my own hands during the most propitious phase of the last moon.

'Do stop fussing,' she grumped at me, but I would not let her sleep again. I prodded her awake and made her drink the tonic. She pulled a face. 'I swear you are trying to poison me,' she complained, and then, without warning and before I could do anything to prevent it, she vomited copiously.

Afterwards she seemed as shocked as I was. We both stared at the steaming puddle beside her bed in consternation.

'What is wrong with me, Taita?' she whispered. 'Nothing like this has ever happened to me before.'

Only then did the meaning of it all dawn on me.

'The *khamsin*!' I cried. 'The cemetery of Tras! Tanus!'

She stared at me blankly for a moment, and then her smile lit the gloom of the tent like a lamp. 'I am making a baby!' she cried.

'Not so loud, mistress,' I pleaded.

'Tanus' baby! I am carrying Tanus' son.' It could not be the king's infant, for I had successfully kept him from her bed since her starvation sickness and her miscarriage.

'Oh, Taita,' she purred, as she lifted her nightdress and inspected her flat, firm belly with awe. 'Just think of it! A little imp just like Tanus growing inside of me.' She palpated her stomach hopefully. 'I knew that such delights as I discovered in the tomb of Tras could not pass unremarked by the gods. They have given me a memory that will last all my lifetime.'

'You race ahead,' I warned her. 'It may be only a colic. I must make the tests before we can be sure.'

'I need no test. I know it in my heart and in the secret depths of my body.'

'We will still do the tests,' I told her wryly, and went to fetch the pot. She perched upon it to provide me with the first water of her day, and I divided this into two equal parts.

The first portion of her urine I mixed with an equal part of Nile water. Then I filled two jars with black earth and in each of them planted five seeds of dhurra corn. I watered one jar with pure Nile water, and the other with the mixture that my mistress had provided. This was the first test.

Then I hunted amongst the reeds in the lagoon near the camp and captured ten frogs. These were not the lively green and yellow variety with leaping back legs, but slimy, black creatures. Their heads are not separated from their sluggish, fat bodies by a neck, and their eyes sit on top of the flat skull, so that the children call them sky-gazers.

I placed five of each of the sky-gazers in two separate jars of river water. To the one I added my mistress's intimate emission and I left the other unadulterated. The following morning, in the privacy of my mistress's cabin on board the galley, we removed the cloth with which I had covered the jars and inspected the contents.

The corn watered by the Lady Lostris had thrown tiny green shoots, while the other seeds were still inert. The five sky-gazers who had not received my mistress's blessing were barren, but the other more fortunate five had each laid long silvery strings which were speckled with black eggs.

'I told you so!' my mistress chirruped smugly, before I could give my official diagnosis. 'Oh, thanks to all the gods! No more beautiful thing has happened to me in all my life.'

'I will speak to Aton immediately. You will share the king's couch this very night,' I told her grimly, and she stared at me in bewilderment.

'Even Pharaoh who believes most things I tell him, will not believe that you were impregnated by the seeds blown in on the *khamsin* wind. We must have a foster-father for this little bastard of ours.' Already I considered the infant ours, and not hers alone. Though I tried to conceal it behind my levity, I was every bit as delighted with her fecundity as she was.

'Don't you ever call him a bastard again,' she flared at me. 'He will be a prince.'

'He will be a prince only if I can find a royal sire for him. Prepare yourself. I am going to see the king.'

'LAST NIGHT I had a dream, Great Egypt,' I told Pharaoh. 'It was so amazing that to confirm it I worked the Mazes of Ammon-Ra.'

Pharaoh leaned forward eagerly, for he had come to believe in my dreams and the Mazes as much as any of my other patients.

'This time it is unequivocal, Majesty. In my dream the goddess Isis appeared and promised to counter the baleful influence of her brother Seth, who so cruelly deprived you of your first son when he struck down the Lady Lostris with the wasting disease. Take my mistress to your bed on the first day of the festival of Osiris, and you will be blessed with another son. That is the promise of the goddess.'

'Tonight is the eve of the festival.' The king looked delighted. 'In truth, Taita, I have been ready to perform this pleasant duty all these past months, had you only allowed me to do so. But you have not told me what you saw in the Mazes of Ammon-Ra.' Again he leaned forward eagerly, and I was ready for him.

'It was the vision as before, only this time it was stronger and more vivid. The same endless forest of trees growing along the banks of the river, each tree crowned and imperial. Your dynasty reaching into the ages, strong and unbroken.'

Pharaoh sighed with satisfaction. 'Send the child to me.'

When I returned to the tent, my mistress was waiting for me. She had prepared herself with good grace and humour.

'I shall close my eyes and imagine that I am back in the tomb of Tras with Tanus,' she confided, and then giggled saucily. 'Although to imagine the king as Tanus is to imagine that the tail of the mouse has become the trunk of the elephant.'

Aton came to fetch her to the king's tent soon after the king had eaten his dinner. She went with a calm expression and a firm step, dreaming perhaps of her little prince, and of his true father who waited for us in Thebes.

BELOVED THEBES, beautiful Thebes of the hundred gates – how we rejoiced as we saw it appear ahead of us, decorating the broad sweep of the river-bank with its temples and gleaming walls.

My mistress sang out with excitement as each of the familiar landmarks revealed itself to us. Then, as the royal barge put in to the wharf below the palace of the grand vizier, the joy of home-coming went out of both of us, and we fell silent. The Lady Lostris groped for my hand like a little girl frightened by tales of hob-goblins, for we had seen her father.

Lord Intef with his sons, Menset and Sobek, those two thumbless heroes, stood at the head of the great concourse of the nobles and the city fathers of Thebes that waited upon the quay to greet the king. Lord Intef was as handsome and suave as I had imagined him in my nightmares, and I felt my spirits quail.

'You must be vigilant now,' the Lady Lostris whispered to me. 'They will seek to have you out of their way. Remember the cobra.'

Not far behind the grand vizier stood Rasfer. During our absence he had obviously received high promotion. He now wore the head-dress of a Commander of Ten Thousand and carried the golden whip of rank. There had been no improvement in his facial muscles. One side of his face still sagged hideously and saliva dribbled from the corner of his mouth. At that moment he recognized me, and grinned at me with half his face across the narrow strip of water. He lifted his golden whip in ironic greeting.

'I promise you, my lady, that my hand will be upon my dagger and I will eat nothing but fruit that I have peeled with my own hands while Rasfer and I are in Thebes together,' I murmured, as I smiled at him and returned his salute with a cheery wave.

'You are to accept no strange gifts,' my mistress insisted, 'and you will sleep at the foot of my bed, where I can protect you at night. During the day you will stay at my side, and not go wandering off on your own.'

'I will not find that irksome,' I assured her, and over the following days I kept my promise to her and remained under her immediate protection, for I was certain that Lord Intef would not jeopardize his connection to the throne by putting his daughter in danger.

Naturally, we were often in the company of the grand vizier, for it was his duty to escort the king through all the ceremonies of the festival. During this time, Lord Intef played the role of loving and considerate father to the Lady Lostris, and he treated her with all the deference and consideration due to a royal wife. Each morning he sent her gifts, gold and jewels and exquisite little carvings of scarabs and godlets in ivory and precious woods. Despite my mistress's orders, I did not return these. I did not wish to warn the enemy, and besides, the gifts were valuable. I sold them discreetly and invested the proceeds in stores of corn held for us in the granaries of trustworthy merchants in the city, men who were my friends.

In view of the expected harvest, the price of corn was the lowest it had been for ten years. There was only one direction it could go, and that was up, although we might have to wait a while for our profits. The merchants gave me receipts in the name of my mistress which I deposited in the archives of the law courts. I kept only a fifth part to myself, which I felt was a very moderate commission.

This gave me some secret pleasure whenever I caught Lord Intef watching me with those pale leopard's eyes. That look left me in no doubt that his feelings towards me had not moderated. I remembered his patience and his persistence when dealing with an enemy. He waited at the centre of his web like a beautiful spider, and his eyes glittered as he watched me. I remembered the bowl of poisoned milk and the cobra, and despite all my precautions, I was uneasy.

Meanwhile the festival rolled on with all the ceremony and tradition, as it had for centuries past. However, this season it was not Tanus' Blues but another squadron that hunted the river-cows in the lagoon of Hapi, while another company of actors played out the passion in the temple of Osiris. Because Pharaoh's decree was observed and the version of the play was mine, the words were as powerful and moving. However, this new Isis was not as lovely as my mistress had portrayed her, nor was Horus as noble or striking as Lord Tanus. On the other hand, Seth was winsome and lovable in comparison to the way that Rasfer had played him.

The day after the passion, Pharaoh crossed the river to inspect his temple, and on this occasion he kept me close at hand throughout the day. On numerous occasions he openly consulted me on aspects of the works. Of course I wore my golden chain whenever it was proper to do so. None of this was missed by Lord Intef, and I could see him musing on the favour the king showed to me. I hoped that this might further serve to protect me from the grand vizier's vengeance.

Since I had left Thebes, another architect had been placed in charge of the temple project. It was perhaps unfair that Pharaoh should expect this unfortunate to be able to maintain the high standards that I had set, or to push the work forward at the same pace.

'By the blessed mother of Horus, I wish you were still in charge here, Taita,' Pharaoh muttered. 'If she would part with you, I would buy you from your mistress, and keep you here in the City of the Dead permanently to supervise the work. The cost seems to have doubled since this other idiot took over from you.'

'He is a naïve young man,' I agreed. 'The masons and the contractors will steal his testicles from him and he will not notice that they are missing.'

'It is my balls that they are stealing,' the king scowled. 'I want you to go over the bill of quantities with him and show him where we are being robbed.'

I was of course flattered by his regard, and there was nothing spiteful in my pointing out to Pharaoh the lapses of taste that the new architect had perpetrated when he redesigned the pediment to my temple façade, or the shoddy craftsmanship that those rogues in the guild of masons had been able to slip past him. The pediment was permeated with the decadent Syrian style that was all the rage in the Lower Kingdom, where the common tastes of the low-born red pretender were corrupting the classical traditions of Egyptian art.

As for the workmanship, I demonstrated to the king how it was possible to slip a fragment of papyrus between the joints of the stone blocks that made up the side-wall of the mortuary temple. Pharaoh ordered both the pediment and the temple wall to be torn down, and he fined the guild of masons five hundred deben of gold to be paid into the royal store-rooms.

Pharaoh spent the rest of that day and the whole of the next reviewing the treasures in the store-rooms of the funerary temple. Here at least he could find very little to complain of. In the history of the world never had such wealth been assembled in one place at one time. Even I, who love fine things, was soon jaded by the abundance of it, and my eyes were pained by the dazzle of gold.

The king insisted that the Lady Lostris remain at his side all this time. I think that his infatuation with her was slowly turning into real love, or as close a facsimile of it as he was capable of. The consequence of his affection for her was that when we returned across the river to Thebes, my mistress was exhausted, and I feared for the child she was carrying. It was too soon to tell the king of her condition and to suggest that he showed her more consideration. It was less than a week since she had returned to his couch, and such an early diagnosis of pregnancy even from me must arouse his suspicion. To him she was still a healthy and robust young woman, and he treated her that way.

THE FESTIVAL ended, as it had for centuries past, with the assembly of the people in the temple of Osiris to hear the proclamation from the throne.

On the raised stone dais in front of the sanctuary of Osiris, Pharaoh was seated on his tall throne so that all the congregation could have a clear view of him. He wore the double crown and carried the crook and the flail.

This time there was an alteration to the usual layout of the temple, for I had made a suggestion to the king which he had been gracious enough to adopt. Against three walls of the inner temple he had ordered the erection of timber scaffolding. These rose in tiers halfway up the massive stone walls, and provided seating for thousands of the notables of Thebes from which they had a privileged and uninterrupted view of the proceedings. I had suggested that these stands be decorated with coloured bunting and palm-fronds, to disguise their ugliness. It was the first time that these structures were built in our land. Thereafter, they were to become commonplace, and they were built at most public functions, along the routes of royal processions and around the fields of athletic games. To this day they are known as Taita stands.

There had been much bitter competition for seats upon these stands, but as their designer, I had been able to procure the very best for my mistress and myself. We were directly opposite the throne and a little above the height of the king's head, so we had a fine view of the whole of the inner courtyard. I had provided a leather cushion stuffed with lamb's-wool for the Lady Lostris and a basket of fruits and cakes, together with jars of sherbet and beer, to sustain us during the interminable ceremony.

All around us were assembled the noblest in the land, lords and ladies decked out in high fashion. The generals and admirals carrying their golden whips and proudly flaunting the honours and standards of their regiments, the guild masters and the rich merchants, the priests and the ambassadors from the vassal states of the empire, they were all here.

In front of the king extended the courts of the temple, one opening into another like the boxes in a children's puzzle-game, but such was the layout of the massive stone walls that the gates were all perfectly aligned. A worshipper standing in the Avenue of Sacred Rams outside the pylons of the main gate could look through the inner gates and clearly see the king on his high throne almost four hundred paces away.

All the courts of the temple were packed with the multitudes of the common people, and the overflow spilled out into the sacred avenue and the gardens beyond the temple walls. Though I had lived almost my entire life in Thebes, I had never seen such a gathering. It was not possible to count their numbers, but I estimated that there must have been two hundred thousand assembled that day. From them rose such a hubbub of sound that I felt myself but a single bee in the vast humming hive.

Around the throne was gathered a small group of the highest dignitaries, their heads at the level of Pharaoh's feet. Of course one of these was the high priest of Osiris. During the past year the old abbot had left this transitory world of ours and set off on his journey through the underworld to the western fields of the eternal paradise. This new abbot was a younger, firmer man. I knew that he would not be so easily manipulated by Lord Intef. In fact, he had collaborated with me in certain unusual arrangements for today's ceremony that I had put in hand while supervising the erection of the Taita stands.

However, the most impressive figure in the group, rivalling Pharaoh himself, was the grand vizier. Lord Intef drew all eyes. He was tall and stately in bearing, handsome as a legend. With the heavy chains of the Gold of Praise lying weightily upon his chest and shoulders, he was like a figure from the myth of the pantheon. Close behind him loomed the hideous shape of Rasfer.

Lord Intef opened the ceremony in the traditional manner by stepping into the clear space before the throne and beginning the address of welcome to the king from the twin cities of Thebes. As he spoke, I glanced sideways at my mistress, and even though I shared her loathing, I was shocked by the expression of anger and hatred that she made no attempt to conceal, and that she directed openly at her own father. I wanted to warn her to make it less obvious to all about her, but I knew that in doing so, I might merely draw further attention to her burning antagonism.

The grand vizier spoke at length, listing his own accomplishments and the loyal service he had rendered Pharaoh in the year past. The crowd murmured and rustled with boredom and discomfort. The heat was rising from so many bodies, and the rays of the sun beating down into the crowded courts were trapped within the temple walls. I saw more than one woman in the press swoon and collapse.

When at last Lord Intef finished speaking, the high priest stepped into his place. While the sun made its noon overhead, he reported to the king on the ecclesiastical affairs of Thebes. As he spoke, the heat and the stench increased; perfume and fragrant oils could no longer disguise the odour of hot, unwashed bodies and running sweat. There was no escape from the crowd to attend urgent bodily functions. Men and women simply squatted where they stood. The temple began to stink like a sty or a public latrine. I handed my mistress a silk kerchief drenched in perfume which she dabbed to her nose.

There was a sigh of relief when at last the high priest ended his address with a blessing on the king in the name of the god Osiris, and, with a deep bow, retreated to his place behind the grand vizier. For the first time since it had begun to assemble before dawn that morning, the crowd fell completely silent. The boredom and discomfort was forgotten, and they craned forward eagerly to hear Pharaoh speak.

The king rose to his feet. I wondered at the old man's fortitude, for he had sat all this time like a statue. He spread his arms in benediction, and at that moment the hallowed chalice of custom and tradition was shattered by an event that plunged the entire congregation – priests, nobles and commoners – into consternation. I was one of the few in the crowd who was not surprised by what followed, for I had done more than my share to arrange it all.

The great burnished copper doors to the sanctuary swung open. There seemed to be no human agency to the movement, it was as though the doors opened of their own accord.

A gasp, a sigh of expelled breath passed like a wind through temple courts, and rustled the densely packed ranks as though they were the leaves of a tamarind tree. Then suddenly a woman screamed, and immediately a groan of superstitious horror shook them all. Some fell to their knees, some lifted their hands above their heads in terror, others covered their faces with their shawls so that they should not be struck blind by looking on sights that were not for mortal eyes.

A god strode out through the sanctuary doors, a tall and terrifying god, whose cloak swirled about his shoulders as he moved. His helmet was crowned with a plume of egret's feathers, and his features were grotesque and metallic, half-eagle and half-man, with a hooked beak and dark slits for eyes.

'Akh-Horus!' screamed a woman, and she collapsed in a dead faint upon the stone flags.

'Akh-Horus!' the cry was taken up. 'It is the god!' Row after row, they fell upon their knees in the attitude of reverence. Those on the high tiers of stands knelt and many of them made the sign to avert misfortune. Even the group of nobles around the throne went down. In all the temple only two persons remained on their feet. Pharaoh posed on the steps of his throne like a painted statue; and the grand vizier of Thebes stood tall and arrogant.

Akh-Horus stopped in front of the king and looked up at him through those slitted eyes in the bronze mask, and even then Pharaoh never flinched. The king's cheeks were painted dead white, so I could not tell whether he blanched, but there was a glitter in his eyes that may have been either religious ecstasy, or terror.

'Who are you?' Pharaoh challenged. 'Are you ghost or man? Why do you disturb our solemn proceedings?' His voice was strong and clear. I could detect no tremor in it, and my admiration for him was enhanced. Weak and aging and gullible perhaps, but still the old man had his full share of courage. He could face up to man or god and stand his ground like a warrior.

Akh-Horus answered him in a voice that had commanded regiments in the desperate din of battle, a voice that echoed amongst the stone pillars. 'Great Pharaoh, I am a man, not a ghost. I am your man. I come before you in response to your command. I come before you to account to you for the duty that you laid upon me in this place on this very day of Osiris two years ago.'

He lifted the helmet from his head, and the fiery curls tumbled down. The congregation recognized him instantly. A shout went up that seemed to rock the foundations of the temple.

'Lord Tanus! Tanus! Tanus!'

It seemed to me that my mistress screamed the loudest of them all, fairly deafening me, who sat so close beside her.

'Tanus! Akh-Horus! Akh-Horus!' The two names mingled and crashed against the temple walls like storm-driven surf.

'He has risen from his tomb! He has become a god amongst us!'

It did not abate until suddenly Tanus drew the sword from his scabbard and held it aloft in an unmistakable command for silence. This was obeyed, and in the silence he spoke again.

'Great Egypt, do I have your permission to speak?'

I think by now the king could no longer rely on his powers of speech, for he made a gesture with crook and flail, and then his legs seemed to give way beneath him and he dropped back on his throne.

Tanus addressed him in ringing tones that carried to the outer court. 'Two years ago you charged me with the destruction of those viperous nests of murderers and robbers who were threatening the life of the state. You placed in my trust the royal hawk seal.'

From under his cloak, Tanus drew out the blue statuette and placed it on the steps of the throne. Then he stepped back and spoke again.

'In order better to carry out the king's orders, I pretended my own death and caused the mummy of a stranger to be sealed in my tomb.'

'*Bak-Her!*' shouted a single voice, and they took up the cry until Tanus once more commanded silence.

'I led a thousand brave men of the Blues into the deserts and the wild places and sought out the Shrikes in their secret fortresses. There we slew them in their hundreds and piled their severed heads at the roadside.'

'*Bak-Her!*' they screamed. 'It is true. Akh-Horus has done all these things.' Once again Tanus silenced them.

'I broke the power of the barons. I slaughtered their followers without mercy. In all this very Egypt of ours there remains only one who still calls himself a Shrike.'

Now at last they were silent, gobbling up every word he said, fascinated and intent. Even Pharaoh could not hold his impatience in check. 'Speak, Lord Tanus, whom men now know as Akh-Horus. Name this man. Give me his name so that he may come to know the wrath of Pharaoh.'

'He hides behind the name of Akh-Seth,' Tanus roared, 'His deeds of infamy rank with those of his brother, the dark god.'

'Give me his true name,' Pharaoh commanded, rising once more to his feet in his agitation. 'Name this last of all the Shrikes!'

Tanus drew out the moment. He looked around the temple slowly and deliberately. When our eyes met, I nodded so slightly that only he saw the movement, but his gaze passed on without a pause and he looked towards the open doors of the sanctuary.

The attention of all the congregation was so fixed upon Lord Tanus that they did not at first see the file of armed men that issued swiftly and silently from the sanctuary. Although they wore full armour and carried their war shields, I recognized most of them under the helmets. There were Remrem and Astes and fifty other warriors of the Blues. Swiftly, they formed up around the throne like a royal bodyguard, but, without making it obvious, Remrem and Astes moved up behind Lord Intef. As soon as they were in position, Tanus spoke again.

'I will name this Akh-Seth for you, Divine Pharaoh. He stands unashamedly in the shadow of your throne.' Tanus pointed with his sword. 'There he is, wearing the Gold of Praise about his traitor's throat. There he stands, Pharaoh's sole companion who has turned your kingdom into a playground for murderers and bandits. That is Akh-Seth, governor of the nome of Thebes, grand vizier of the Upper Kingdom.'

An awful hush fell upon the temple. There must have been ten thousand or more in the congregation who had suffered grievously at Lord Intef's hands and who had every reason to hate him, but not a voice spoke out in jubilation or in triumph against him. All knew just how terrible was his wrath, and just how certain his retribution. I could smell the stink of their fear in the air, thick as the incense smoke. Every one of them understood that even Tanus' reputation and his mighty deeds were not sufficient for his unproven accusation to prevail against such a person as Lord Intef. To show joy or open agreement at this stage would be mortal folly.

In that hush Lord Intef laughed. It was a sound full of disdain, and with a dismissive gesture he turned his back upon Tanus and spoke directly to the king. 'The desert sun has burned his brain. The poor lad has gone mad. There is not a single word of truth in all his ravings. I should be angry, but instead I am saddened that a warrior of reputation has fallen so low.' He held out both hands to Pharaoh, a dignified and loyal gesture. 'All my life I have served Pharaoh and my people. My honour is so invulnerable that I see no need to defend myself against these wild rantings. Without fear I place my trust in the wisdom and justice of the divine king. I let my deeds and my love of Pharaoh speak, in place of my tongue.'

I saw the confusion and indecision on the king's painted face. His lips trembled and his brow was furrowed, for he was not blessed with a swift and incisive mind. After a moment he opened his mouth to speak, but before he could utter any fateful or irredeemable judgement, Tanus lifted his sword again and pointed beyond the throne to the open doors of the sanctuary.

Through the doors came another procession of men so unusual that Pharaoh gaped at them with his mouth still open. Kratas led, with his visor raised and a sword in his right hand. Those who followed him wore only loin-cloths, and their heads and feet were bare. Their arms were bound behind their backs, and they shuffled like slaves on their way to the auction block.

I was watching Lord Intef's face, and I saw the shock assail him and force him to flinch, as though he had received a blow in the face. He had recognized the captives, but he had obviously believed that they were long dead, and their skulls grinning at the roadside. He darted a sideways glance at the small sacristy door in the wall that was almost hidden by the hanging linen bunting. It was his only escape from the crowded inner court, but Remrem moved one pace to his right and blocked his path to the doorway. Lord Intef looked back at the throne and lifted his chin in a confident and defiant gesture.

The six bound captives lined up before the throne and then, at a quiet order from Kratas, dropped to their knees and bowed their heads.

'Who are these creatures?' Pharaoh demanded, and Tanus stood over the first of them, seized his bound wrists and hauled him to his feet. The captive's skin was studded with the old healed scars of the smallpox and his blind eye reflected the light like a silver coin.

'The divine Pharaoh asks who you are,' Tanus said softly. 'Reply to the question.'

'Great Egypt, I am Shufti,' he said. 'I was once a baron of the Shrikes before Akh-Horus scattered and slew my clan at the city of Gallala.'

'Tell the king who was your overlord,' Tanus insisted.

'Akh-Seth was my overlord,' Shufti replied. 'I swore a blood-oath of allegiance to Akh-Seth, and I paid a bounty of one-quarter of all my plunder to him. In return Akh-Seth gave me immunity from the forces of law, and provided me with information on my intended victims.'

'Point out to the king the man you know as Akh-Seth,' Tanus ordered, and Shufti shuffled forward until he faced Lord Intef. He filled his mouth with spittle and spat it on to the grand vizier's gorgeous uniform. 'This is Akh-Seth,' he cried. 'And may the worms feast on his guts!'

Kratas dragged Shufti to one side and Tanus lifted the next captive to his feet. 'Tell the king who you are,' he ordered.

'I am Akheku, and I was a baron of the Shrikes, but all my men are killed.'

'Who was your overlord? To whom did you pay your bounty?' Tanus demanded.

'Lord Intef was my overlord. I paid my bounty into the coffers of the grand vizier.'

Lord Intef stood proud and aloof, showing no emotion as these accusations were hurled at him. He offered no defence as, one after the other, the barons were dragged before him and each made the same declaration.

'Lord Intef was my overlord. Lord Intef is Akh-Seth.'

The silence of the multitudes in the temple was as oppressive as the heat. They watched in horror, or in silent hatred, or in confusion and disbelief. However, not one of them dared yet to speak out against Lord Intef, or to show emotion until Pharaoh had first spoken.

The last of the barons was brought forward to confront the grand vizier. He was a tall, lean man with stringy muscles and sun-blasted skin. There was Bedouin blood in his veins, for his eyes were black and his nose beaked. His beard was thick and curling, and his expression arrogant.

'My name is Basti.' He spoke more clearly than any of the others. 'Men call me Basti the Cruel, though I know not the reason why.' He grinned with a raffish hangman's humour. 'I was a baron of the Shrikes until Akh-Horus destroyed my clan. Lord Intef was my overlord.'

This time he was not dragged away as the others had been. Tanus spoke to him again. 'Tell the king. Did you know Pianki, Lord Harrab, who in former times was a nobleman of Thebes?'

'I knew him well. I had dealings with him.'

'What were these dealings?' Tanus asked, with death in his voice.

'I plundered his caravans. I burned his crops in the fields. I raided his mines at Sestra, and I slew the miners in such amusing fashion that no others ever came to work the copper there. I burned his villas. I sent my men into the cities to speak evil of him, so that his honesty and his loyalty to the state were tarnished. I helped others to destroy him so that in the end he drank the poisonous Datura seed from his own cup.'

I saw the hand of Pharaoh that held the royal flail shake as he listened, and one of his eyelids twitched in a manner that I had noticed before when he was sore distressed.

'Who was it that ordered these things?'

'Lord Intef commanded these things and rewarded me with a takh of pure gold.'

'What did Lord Intef hope to gain from this persecution of Lord Harrab?'

Basti grinned and shrugged. 'Lord Intef is grand vizier, while Pianki, Lord Harrab is dead. It seems to me Lord Intef achieved his purpose.'

'You acknowledge that I have offered you no clemency in return for this confession? Do you understand that death awaits you?'

'Death?' Basti laughed. 'I have never been afraid of that. It is the flour of the loaf I bake. I have fed it to countless others, so now why should I be afraid to feast on it myself?' Was he fool or brave man, I wondered, as I listened to the boast. Either way, I could find neither pity nor admiration for him in my heart. I remembered that Pianki, Lord Harrab had been a man like his son, and that is where my pity and my admiration lay.

I saw the merciless expression in the eyes of Tanus. I knew that he shared my feelings, and his grip upon the hilt of his sword tightened until his fingers turned as white as those of a drowned man.

'Take him away!' he grated. 'Let him await the king's pleasure.' I saw him compose himself with an effort, then he turned back to face the king. He went down on one knee before him.

'I have done all that you asked of me, Divine Mamose, god and ruler of *Kemit*. I wait for you to command me further.' His dignity and his grace closed up my throat so that I could not swallow. It took an effort to compose myself.

The silence in the temple persisted. I could hear my mistress's laboured breathing beside me and then I felt her take my hand and squeeze it with a strength that threatened to crack my finger-bones.

At last Pharaoh spoke, but with dismay I heard the doubt in his voice, and I sensed intuitively that he did not want any of this to be true. He had trusted Lord Intef so deeply for so long that it shook the foundations of his faith.

'Lord Intef, you have heard the accusations against you. How say you to them?'

'Divine Pharaoh, are these indeed accusations? I thought them merely the fantasies of a young man driven insane with envy and jealousy. He is the son of a convicted criminal and a traitor. Lord Tanus' motives are plain to see. He has convinced himself that the traitor Pianki might have become grand vizier in my place. In some perverse fashion, he holds me responsible for his father's downfall.'

With a wave of his hand he dismissed Tanus. It was so skilfully done that I saw the king waver. His doubts were growing stronger. For a lifetime he had implicitly trusted Lord Intef, and it was difficult for him to adjust his thinking. He wanted to believe in his innocence.

'What of the accusations of the barons?' Pharaoh asked at last. 'What reply do you make to them?'

'Barons?' Lord Intef asked. 'Must we flatter them with such a title? By their own testimony they are criminals of the basest kind – murderers, thieves, violators of women and children. Should we look for truth in them any more than we should look for honour and conscience in the beasts of the field?' Lord Intef pointed to them, and they were indeed half-naked and bound like animals. 'Let us gaze upon them, Divine Majesty. Are these not the kind of men that can be bribed or beaten into saying anything for the sake of their own skins? Would you take the word of one of these against a man who has served you faithfully all his life?'

I saw the small, involuntary nod of the king's head as he accepted the reasoning of the man he had looked upon as a friend, the man upon whom he had heaped trust and rewards.

'All you say is true. You have always served me without vice. These rogues are strangers to truth and honour. It is possible that they may have been coerced.' He vacillated, and Lord Intef sensed his advantage.

'So far I have had only words thrown at me. Surely there must be some other evidence to support such mortal charges against me? Is there one person in this very Egypt who will bring evidence against me, real evidence and not mere words? If there is, let him come forward. Then I will answer this charge. If there is no one who has this evidence, then I have nothing to answer to.'

His words troubled Pharaoh deeply, I could see that. He gazed about the hall as if seeking the evidence that Lord Intef demanded, and then he obviously reached a decision.

'Lord Tanus, what proof do you have of these things, apart from the words of murderers and criminals?'

'The beast has covered his tracks well,' Tanus admitted, 'and he has taken cover in the densest thicket where it is difficult to come at him. I have no further evidence against Lord Intef, but there may be some other who does, somebody who will be inspired by what he has heard here today. I beg you, Royal Egypt, ask your people if there is not one of them who can bring forth anything to help us here.'

'Pharaoh, this is provocation. My enemies will be emboldened to come out of the shadows where they lurk to attack me,' cried Lord Intef in vehement protest, but Pharaoh silenced him with a brusque gesture. 'They will bear false witness against you at their peril,' he promised, and then addressed the congregation.

'My people! Citizens of Thebes! You have heard the accusations made against my trusted and well-beloved grand vizier. Is there one of you who can provide the proof that Lord Tanus lacks? Can any of you bring forward evidence against the Lord Intef? If so, I charge you to speak.'

I was standing before I realized what I had done, and my voice was so loud in my own ears that it startled me.

'I am Taita, who was once the slave of Lord Intef,' I shouted, and Pharaoh looked across at me and frowned. 'I have aught that I wish to show Your Majesty.'

'You are known to us, Taita the physician. You may approach.'

As I left my seat on the stand and went down to stand before the king, I looked across at Lord Intef and I missed my step. It was as though I had walked into a stone wall, so tangible was his hatred.

'Divine Egypt, this thing is a slave.' Lord Intef's voice was cold and tight. 'The word of a slave against a lord of the Theban circle, and a high officer of the state – what mockery is this?'

I was still so conditioned to respond to his voice and to succumb to his word, that my resolve wavered. Then I felt Tanus' hand on my arm. It was only a brief touch, but it manned and sustained me. However, Lord Intef had noticed the gesture, and he pointed it out to the king.

'See how this slave is in the thrall of my accuser. Here is another one of Lord Tanus' trained monkeys.' Lord Intef's voice was once more smooth as warm honey. 'His insolence is unbounded. There are penalties laid down in the law codes—'

Pharaoh silenced him with a gesture of his flail. 'You presume on our good opinion of you, Lord Intef. The codes of law are mine to interpret or amend. In them there are penalties laid down for the high-born as well as the common man. You would be well advised to remember that.'

Lord Intef bowed in submission and remained silent, but suddenly his face was haggard and drawn as he realized his predicament.

Now the king looked down at me. 'These are unusual cirumstances, such as allow of unprecedented remedy. However, Taita the slave, let me warn you that if your words should prove frivolous, should they lack proof or substance, the strangling-rope awaits you.'

That threat and the poisonous bane of Lord Intef's gaze upon me made me stutter. 'While I was the slave of the grand vizier, I was his messenger and his emissary to the barons. I know all these men.' I pointed to the captives that Kratas held near to the throne. 'It was I who carried Lord Intef's commands to them.'

'Lies! More words, lacking proof,' Lord Intef called out, but now the edge of desperation was in his voice. 'Where is the proof?'

'Silence!' the king thundered with sudden ferocity. 'We will hear the testimony of Taita the slave.' He was looking directly at me, and I drew breath to continue.

'It was I who carried the command of Lord Intef to Basti the Cruel. The command was to destroy the estate and the fortune of Pianki, Lord Harrab. At that time I was the confidant of Intef, I knew that he desired the position of grand vizier to himself. All these things that Lord Intef commanded were accomplished. Lord Harrab was destroyed, and he was deprived of Pharaoh's favour and love, so that he drank the Datura cup. I, Taita, attest all these things.'

'It is so.' Basti the Cruel lifted his bound arms to the throne. 'All that Taita says is the truth.'

'*Bah-Her!*' shouted the barons. 'It is the truth. Taita speaks the truth.'

'Still these are only words,' the king mused. 'Lord Intef has demanded proof. I, your Pharaoh, demand proof.'

'For half my lifetime I was the scribe and the treasurer of the grand vizier. I kept the record of his fortune. I noted his profits and his expenses on my scrolls. I gathered in the bounty that the barons of the Shrikes paid to Lord Intef, and I disposed of all this wealth.'

'Can you show me these scrolls, Taita?' Pharaoh's expression shone like the full moon at the mention of treasure. Now I had his avid attention.

'No, Majesty, I cannot do so. The scrolls remained always in the possession of Lord Intef.'

Pharaoh made no effort to conceal his chagrin, his face hardened towards me, but I went on doggedly, 'I cannot show you the scrolls, but perhaps I can lead you to the treasure that the grand vizier has stolen from you, and from the people of your realm. It was I who built his secret treasuries for him, and hid within them the bounty that I gathered from the barons. It was in these store-rooms that I placed the wealth that Pharaoh's tax-collectors never saw.'

The king's excitement rekindled, hot as the coals on the coppersmith's forge. He leaned forward intently. Although every eye in the temple was fastened upon me, and the nobles were crowding forward the better to hear each word, I was watching Lord Intef without seeming to look in his direction. The burnished copper doors of the sanctuary were tall mirrors in which his reflection was magnified. Every nuance of his expression and every movement he made, however slight, was clear to me.

I had taken a fatal risk in assuming that his treasure still remained in the secret places where I had stored it for him. He might have moved it at any time during the past two years. Yet moving such quantities of treasure would have been a major work and the risk of doing so as great as letting it rest where it lay. He would have been forced to take others into his trust, and that was not easy for Lord Intef to do. He was by nature a suspicious man. Added to which was the fact that, until recently, he had believed me dead, and my secret with me.

I calculated that my chances were evenly balanced, and I risked my life on it. Now I held my breath as I watched Lord Intef's reflection in the copper doors. Then my heart raced and my spirits soared on the wings of eagles. I saw from the pain and panic in his expression that the arrow I had fired at him had struck the mark. I had won. The treasure was where I had left it. I knew that I could lead Pharaoh to the plunder and the loot that Lord Intef had gathered up over his lifetime.

But he was not yet defeated. I was rash to believe it would be so easily accomplished. I saw him make a gesture with his right hand that puzzled me, and while I dallied, it was almost too late.

In my triumph, I had forgotten Rasfer. The signal that Lord Intef gave him was a flick of the right hand, but Rasfer responded like a trained boar-hound to the huntsman's command to attack. He launched himself at me with such sudden ferocity that he took all of us by complete surprise. He had only ten paces to cover to reach me, and his sword rasped from its scabbard as he came.

There were two of Kratas' men standing between us, but their backs were turned to him, and Rasfer barged into them and knocked them off their feet, so that one of them sprawled across the stone flags in front of Tanus and blocked his path when he tried to spring to my aid. I was on my own, defenceless, and Rasfer threw up his sword with both hands to cleave through my skull to my breast-bone. I lifted my hands to ward off the blow, but my legs were frozen with shock and terror, and I could not move or duck away from the hissing blade.

I never saw Tanus throw his sword. I had eyes for nothing but the face of Rasfer, but suddenly the sword was in the air. Terror had so enhanced my senses that time seemed to pass as slowly as spilled oil dribbling from the jar. I watched Tanus' sword turning end over end, spinning slowly on its axis, flashing at each revolution like a sheet of summer lightning, but it had not completed a full turn when it struck, and it was the hilt and not the point that crashed into Rasfer's head. It did not kill him, but it snapped his head over, whipping his neck like the branch of a willow in the wind, so that his eyes rolled back blindly in their sockets.

Rasfer never completed the blow he aimed at me. His legs collapsed under him and he fell in a pile at my feet. His sword flew from his nerveless fingers, spinning high in the air, and then fell back. It pegged into the side of Pharaoh's throne, and quivered there. The king stared at it in shocked disbelief. The razor edge had touched his arm, and split the skin. As we all watched, a line of ruby droplets oozed from the shallow wound, and dripped on to Pharaoh's cloud-white linen kilt.

Tanus broke the horrified silence. 'Great Egypt, you saw who gave the signal for this beast to attack. You know who was to blame for endangering your royal person.' He leaped over the downed guardsman and seized Lord Intef by the arm, twisting it until he fell to his knees and cried out with pain.

'I did not want to believe this of you.' Pharaoh's expression was sorrowful as he looked down on his grand vizier. 'I have trusted you all my life, and you have spat upon me.'

'Great Egypt, hear me!' Lord Intef begged on his knees, but Pharaoh turned his face away from him.

'I have listened to you long enough.' Then he nodded to Tanus. 'Have your men guard him well, but show him courtesy, for his guilt is not yet fully proven.'

Finally Pharaoh addressed the congregation. 'These are strange and unprecedented events. I adjourn these proceedings to consider fully the evidence that Taita the slave will present to me. The population of Thebes will assemble once again to hear my judgement in this same place at noon tomorrow. I have spoken.'

WE ENTERED through the main doorway to the audience hall of the grand vizier's palace. Pharaoh paused at the threshold. Although the wound from Rasfer's sword was slight, I had bandaged it with linen and placed his arm in a sling.

Pharaoh surveyed the hall slowly. At the far end of the long room stood the grand vizier's throne. Carved from a solid block of alabaster, it was hardly less imposing than Pharaoh's own in the throne room at Elephantine. The high walls were plastered with smooth clay and on this background were painted some of the most impressive frescoes that I had ever designed. They transformed the huge room into a blazing garden of delights. I had painted them while I was Lord Intef's slave, and even though they were my own creations, they still gave me a deep thrill of pleasure when I looked upon them.

I have no doubt that these works alone, without consideration of any other of my achievements, would support my claim to the title of the most significant artist in the history of our land. It was sad that I who had created them was now to demolish them. It detracted from the triumph of this tumultuous day.

I led Pharaoh down the hall. For once we had dispensed with all protocol, and Pharaoh was as eager as a child. He followed me so closely that he almost trod upon my heels, and his royal train fell in as eagerly behind him.

I led them to the throne wall and we stopped below the huge mural depicting the sun god, Ammon-Ra, on his daily journey across the heavens. Even in his excitement, I could see the reverent expression in the king's eyes as he looked up at the painting.

Behind us, the great hall was half-filled with the king's train, the courtiers and the warriors and the noble lords, to say nothing of the royal wives and concubines who would rather have given up all their rouges and paint-boxes of cosmetics than miss such an exciting moment as I had promised them. Naturally, my mistress was in the forefront. Tanus marched only a pace behind the king. He and his Blues had taken over the duties of the royal bodyguard.

The king turned back to Tanus now. 'Have your men bring forward the Lord Intef!'

Treating him with elaborate and icy courtesy, Kratas led Intef to face the wall, but he interposed himself between the prisoner and the king and stood with his naked blade at the ready.

'Taita, you may proceed,' the king told me, and I measured the wall, stepping out exactly thirty paces from the furthest corner and marking the distance with the lump of chalk that I had brought with me for the purpose.

'Behind this wall lie the private quarters of the grand vizier,' I explained to the king. 'Certain alterations were made when last the palace was renovated. Lord Intef likes to have his wealth close at hand.'

'Sometimes you are garrulous, Taita.' Pharaoh was less than captivated by my lecture on the palace architecture. 'Get on with it, fellow. I am aflame to see what is hidden here.'

'Let the masons approach!' I called out, and a small band of these sturdy rogues in their leather aprons came down the aisle and dropped their leather tool-bags at the foot of the throne wall. I had summoned them across the river from their work on Pharaoh's tomb. The white stone-dust in their hair gave them an air of age and wisdom that few of them deserved.

I borrowed a wooden set-square from their foreman, and with it marked out an oblong shape on the clay-plastered wall. Then I stepped back and addressed the master mason. 'Gently now! Damage the frescoes as little as you can. They are great works of art.'

With their wooden mallets and their chisels of flint, they fell upon the wall, and they paid little heed to my strictures. Paint and plaster flew in clouds as slabs of the outer wall were stripped away and thumped to the marble floor. The dust offended the ladies and they covered their mouths and noses with their shawls.

Gradually from under the layer of plaster emerged the outline of the stone blocks. Then Pharaoh exclaimed aloud and, ignoring the flying dust, he drew closer, and peered at the design that appeared from beneath the plaster skin. The regular courses of stone blocks were marred by an oblong of alien-coloured stone that followed almost exactly the outline I had chalked upon the outer layer of plaster.

'There is a hidden door in there,' he cried. 'Open it immediately!'

Under the king's urging, the masons attacked the sealed doorway with a will, and once they had removed the keystone, the other blocks came out readily. A dark opening was revealed, and Pharaoh, who had by now taken charge of the work, called excitedly for torches to be lit.

'The entire space behind this wall is a secret compartment,' I told Pharaoh, while we waited for the torches to be brought to us. 'I had it constructed on Lord Intef's orders.'

When the torches were brought, Tanus took one of them and lit the king's way into the gaping secret door. The king stepped through, and I was the next to enter after him and Tanus.

It was so long since I had last been in there that I looked around me with as much interest as the others. Nothing had changed in all that time. The chests and casks of cedar and acacia wood were stacked exactly as I had left them. I pointed out to the king those cases to which he should first devote his attention, and he ordered, 'Have them carried out into the audience hall.'

'You will need strong men to carry them,' I remarked drily. 'They are rather heavy.'

It took three of the biggest men of the Blues to lift each case and they staggered out through the jagged opening in the wall with them.

'I have never seen these boxes before,' Lord Intef protested, as the first of them was carried out and laid on the dais of the grand vizier's throne. 'I had no knowledge of a secret chamber behind the wall. It must have been built by my predecessor, and the cases placed there at his command.'

'Your Majesty, observe the seal on this lid.' I pointed it out to him and the king peered at the clay tablet.

'Whose seal is this?' he demanded.

'Observe the ring on the left forefinger of the grand vizier, Majesty,' I murmured. 'May I respectfully suggest that Pharaoh match it to the seal on this chest?'

'Lord Intef, hand me your ring if you please,' the king asked with exaggerated courtesy, and the grand vizier hid his left hand behind his back.

'Great Egypt, the ring has been on my finger for twenty years. My flesh has grown around it and it cannot now be removed.'

'Lord Tanus.' The king turned to him. 'Take your sword. Remove Lord Intef's finger and bring it to me with the ring upon it.' Tanus smiled cruelly as he stepped forward to obey, half-drawing his blade.

'Perhaps I am mistaken,' Lord Intef admitted with alacrity. 'Let me see if I cannot free it.' The ring slipped readily enough from his finger, and Tanus went down on one knee to hand it to the king.

Pharaoh bent studiously over the chest and made the comparison of ring to seal. When he straightened up again his face was dark with anger.

'It is a perfect match. This seal was struck from your ring, Lord Intef.' But the grand vizier made no reply to the accusation. He stood with his arms folded and his expression stony.

'Break the seal. Open the chest!' Pharaoh ordered, and Tanus cut away the clay tablet and prised up the lid with his sword.

The king cried out involuntarily as the lid fell away and the contents were revealed, 'By all the gods!' And his courtiers crowded forward without ceremony to gaze into the chest, exclaiming and jostling each other for a better view.

'Gold!' The king scooped both hands full with the glittering yellow rings, and then let them cascade back between his fingers. He kept a single ring in his hand and held it close to his face to study the mint marks upon it. 'Two deben weight of fine gold. How much will this case contain, and how many cases are there in the secret store-room?' His question was rhetorical, and he was not expecting an answer, but I gave him a reply nevertheless.

'This case contains—' I read the manifest that I had inscribed on the lid so many years before. 'It contains one takh and three hundred deben of pure gold. As to how many cases of gold, if my memory serves me well, there should be fifty-three of gold and twenty-three of silver in this store. However, I have forgotten exactly how many chests of jewellery we hid here.'

'Is there no one I can trust? You, Lord Intef, I treated as my brother. There was no kindness that you did not receive from my hands, and this is how you have repaid me.'

AT MIDNIGHT the chancellor and the chief inspector of the royal taxes came to the king's chamber where I was changing the dressing on his injured arm. They presented their final tally of the amount of the treasure and Pharaoh read it with awe. Once again, his emotions warred with each other, outrage vying with euphoria at this staggering windfall.

'The rogue was richer than his own king. There is no punishment harsh enough for such evil. He has cheated and robbed me and my tax-collectors.'

'As well as murdering and plundering Lord Harrab and tens of thousands of your subjects,' I reminded him, as I secured the bandage on his arm. It was perhaps impudent of me. However, he was by now so deep in my debt that I could risk it.

'That too,' he agreed readily enough, my sarcasm wasted upon him. 'His guilt is deep as the sea and high as the heaven. I will have to devise a suitable punishment. The strangler's rope is too kind for Lord Intef.'

'Majesty, as your physician, I must insist that you rest now. It has been a day that has taxed even your great strength and endurance.'

'Where is Intef? I cannot rest until I am assured that he is well taken care of.'

'He is under guard in his own quarters, Majesty. A senior captain and a detachment of the Blues have that duty.' I hesitated delicately. 'Rasfer is also under guard.'

'Rasfer, that ugly drooling animal of his? The one who tried to kill you in the temple of Osiris? Did he survive the crack that Lord Tanus gave him?'

'He is well if not happy, Pharaoh,' I assured him. 'Did Your Majesty know that Rasfer is the one who, so long ago, used the gelding-knife upon me?' I saw the beam of pity in the king's eye, as I blurted it out.

'I will deal with him as I deal with his master,' Pharaoh promised. 'He will suffer the same punishment as Lord Intef. Will that satisfy you, Taita?'

'Your Majesty is just and omniscient.' I backed out of his presence and went to find my mistress.

She was waiting for me and, although it was after midnight and I was exhausted, she would not let me sleep. She was far too overwrought, and she insisted that for the rest of the night I sit beside her bed and listen to her chatter about Tanus and other topics of lesser importance.

DESPITE THE dearth of sleep, I was bright and clear-headed when I took my place in the temple of Osiris the following morning.

If anything, the congregation was even larger than it had been the day before. There was not a soul in Thebes who had not heard of the downfall of the grand vizier, and who was not eager to witness his ultimate humiliation. Even those of his underlings, who had most prospered under his corrupt administration, now turned upon him, like a pack of hyena who devour their leader when he is sick and wounded.

The barons of the Shrikes were led before the throne in their rags and bonds, but when Lord Intef entered the temple, he wore fine linen and silver sandals. His hair was freshly curled, his face painted, and the chains of the Gold of Praise hung around his neck.

The barons knelt before the king, but even when one of the guards pricked him with the sword, Lord Intef refused to bend the knee, and the king made a gesture for the guard to desist.

'Let him stand!' the king ordered. 'He will lie in his tomb long enough.' Then Pharaoh rose and stood before us in all his grandeur and his rage. This once he seemed a true king, as the first of his dynasty had been, a man of might and force. I, who had come to know him and his weaknesses so well, found that I was overcome with a sense of awe.

'Lord Intef, you are accused of treason and murder, of brigandage and piracy, and of a hundred other crimes no less deserving of punishment. I have heard the supported testimony of fifty of my subjects from all walks and stations of life, from lords and freemen and slaves. I have seen the contents of your secret treasury wherein you hid your stolen wealth from the royal tax-collectors. I have seen your personal seal upon the treasure chests. By all these matters your guilt is proven a thousand times over. I, Mamose the eighth of that name, Pharaoh and ruler of this very Egypt, hereby find you guilty of all the crimes of which you are accused, and deserving of neither royal clemency nor mercy.'

'Long live Pharaoh!' shouted Tanus, and the salute was taken up and repeated ten times by the people of Thebes. 'May he live for ever!'

When silence fell, Pharaoh spoke again. 'Lord Intef, you wear the Gold of Praise. The sight of that decoration on the breast of a traitor offends me.' He looked across at Tanus. 'Centurion, remove the gold from the prisoner.'

Tanus lifted the chains from Lord Intef's neck and carried them to the king. Pharaoh took the gold in his two hands, but when Tanus started to withdraw, he stayed him with a word.

'The name Lord Harrab was tarnished with the slur of treason. Your father was hounded to a traitor's death. You have proven your father's innocence. I rescind all sentences passed against Pianki, Lord Harrab, and posthumously restore to him all his honours and titles that were stripped from him. Those honours and titles descend to you, his son.'

'*Bak-Her!*' shouted the congregation. 'May Pharaoh live for ever! Hail, Tanus, Lord Harrab!'

'In addition to those titles which now come down to you as your inheritance, I bestow upon you new distinction. You have carried out my charge to you. You have destroyed the Shrikes and delivered their overlord to justice. In recognition of this service to the crown, I bestow upon you the Gold of Valour. Kneel, Lord Harrab, and receive the king's favour.'

'*Bak-Her!*' they cried, as Pharaoh placed the jangling gold chains, that had so recently belonged to Lord Intef, but to which he had now added the star pendant of the warrior's decoration, about Tanus' neck. 'Hail, Lord Harrab!'

As Tanus withdrew, Pharaoh turned his attention back to the prisoners. 'Lord Intef, you are deprived of your title as a lord of the Theban circle. Your name and rank will be erased from all the public monuments, and from your tomb that you have prepared in the Valley of the Nobles. Your estates and all your possessions, including your illicit treasure, are forfeited to the crown, except only those estates that once belonged to Pianki, Lord Harrab, and which by fell means have come into your possession. These are now returned in their entirety to his heir, my goodly Tanus, Lord Harrab.'

'*Bak-Her!* Pharaoh is wise! May he live for ever!' the people cheered wildly, and beside me my mistress was weeping unashamedly, but then so were half the royal women. Very few of them could resist that heroic figure whose golden hair seemed to dim the chains upon his breast.

Now the king took me by surprise. He looked directly at where I sat beside my mistress. 'There is one other who has done the crown loyal service, the one who revealed the whereabouts of the stolen treasure. Let the slave, Taita, stand forth.'

I went down to stand before the throne, and the king's voice was gentle. 'You have suffered unspeakable harm at the hands of the traitor Intef and his henchman Rasfer. You have been forced by them to commit nefarious deeds and capital crimes against the state, by conniving with bandits and robbers and by concealing your master's treasure from the royal tax-collectors. However, these were not crimes of your own inspiration. As a slave, you were forced to the will of your master. Therefore I absolve you from all guilt and liability. I find you innocent of any crime, and I reward you for your service to us with a bounty of two takhs of fine gold to be paid out of the treasure confiscated from the traitor, Intef.'

A murmur of astonishment greeted this announcement, and I gasped aloud. It was a staggering amount. A fortune to match those of all but the wealthiest lords in the land, enough to buy great tracts of the most fertile land along the river, and to furnish magnificent villas upon that land, to buy three hundred strong slaves to work the land, enough to fit out a fleet of trading vessels and send them to the ends of the earth to bring back more treasure. It was a sum large enough to boggle even my imagination, but the king had not finished.

'As a slave, this bounty will be paid not to you, but to your mistress, the Lady Lostris, who is a junior wife of Pharaoh.' I should have guessed that Pharaoh would keep it in the family.

I, who for a fleeting moment had been one of the richest men in Egypt, bowed to the king and returned to my place beside my mistress. She squeezed my hand to console me, but in truth I was not unhappy. Our destinies were so entwined that I was a part of her, and I knew that we would never again want for any material thing. I was already planning how I would invest my mistress's fortune for her.

At last the king was ready to pass sentence on the line of prisoners, though he looked only at Intef as he spoke.

'Your crimes are unparalleled. No punishment before meted out is harsh enough to fit your case. This then is the sentence I pass upon you. At dawn on the day after the end of the festival of Osiris, you will be marched through the streets of Thebes, bound and naked. While you still live you will be nailed by your feet to the main gate of the city, with your heads hanging downwards. You will be left there until your bones are picked clean by the crows. Then your bones will be taken down and ground to powder and cast into Mother Nile.'

Even Intef paled and swayed on his feet as he listened to the sentence. By dispersing their earthly bodies so that they could never be embalmed and preserved, Pharaoh was condemning the prisoners to oblivion. For an Egyptian there could be no harsher punishment. They were being denied for all eternity the fields of paradise.

WHEN MY mistress expressed her determination to attend the executions and to watch her father being nailed upside-down to the main gate, I do not think that she truly realized the horror of what she would witness. I was equally determined that she should not be there to see it. There had never been a sadistic streak in her. I believe that her decision was influenced by the fact that most of the other royal women were going to enjoy the diverting spectacle, and that Tanus would be in command of the execution. She would never pass up an opportunity to gaze at him, even from a distance.

In the end I persuaded her only by employing the most poignant argument in my arsenal. 'My lady, such cruel sights as these will certainly affect your unborn son. Surely you do not wish to blight his young unformed mind.'

'That is not possible,' she faltered for the first time in our argument. 'My son could know nothing of it.'

'He will see through your eyes, and the screams of his dying grandfather will pass through the walls of your stomach and enter his tiny ears.' It was an evocative choice of words, and they had the effect I was striving for.

She thought about it at length, and then sighed. 'Very well then, but I shall expect you to bring me back a full description of it all. You are not to miss a single detail. Especially I will want to know what the other royal wives were wearing.' Then she grinned at me wickedly to prove that she had not been totally gulled by my arguments. 'You can whisper it all to me, so the child sleeping in my belly cannot overhear us.'

At dawn on the day of the execution the gardens of the palace were still shrouded in darkness when I left the harem. I hurried through the water-gardens, and the stars were reflected in the black surfaces of the ponds. As I approached the wing of the palace where Lord Intef was being held in his own quarters, I saw the blaze of torches and lamps lighting the windows, and heard the frantic yelling of orders and invective from within.

I knew instantly that something was seriously amiss, and I broke into a run. I was almost speared by the guard at the door to Lord Intef's private quarters, but he recognized me at the last moment before he skewered me, and lifted his weapon and let me pass.

Tanus was in the centre of the ante-chamber. He was roaring like a black-maned lion in a trap, and aiming blows with his clenched fists at whoever came within range. Even though he had always had a stormy temper, I had never before seen him so incapacitated by rage. He seemed to have lost the power of reason or of articulate speech. His men, those mighty heroes of the Blues, cowered away from him, and the rest of the palace wing was in an uproar.

I went straight up to him, ducked under another wild punch, and shouted in his face, 'Tanus! It is I! Control yourself! In the name of all the gods, are you mad?'

He almost struck me, and I saw him wrestle with his emotions and at last take control of them.

'See what you can do for them.' He pointed at the bodies that were scattered about the ante-chamber as though a battle had raged through it.

With horror I recognized that one of them was Khetkhet, a senior captain of the regiment and a man I respected. He was curled in the corner clutching his stomach, with such agony etched on his rigid features that I hoped never to see again. I touched his cheek and the skin was cold and dead.

I shook my head, 'He is past all help that I can give him.' I lifted his eyelid with my thumb and gazed into his dead eye, then I leaned forward and smelled his mouth. The faint musty odour of mushrooms on it was dreadfully familiar.

'Poison.' I stood up. 'The others will be the same.' There were five of them curled on the tiles.

'How?' asked Tanus, in a tone of forced calm, and I picked up one of the bowls piled on the low table from which they had obviously eaten their dinner, and I sniffed it. The smell of mushrooms was stronger.

'Ask the cooks,' I suggested. Then, in a sudden access of anger, I hurled the bowl against the wall. The crumpled bodies reminded me of my pets who had died the same death, and Khetkhet had been my friend.

I took a deep breath to calm myself before I asked, 'No doubt your prisoner has escaped?' Tanus did not reply, but led me through into the grand vizier's bedchamber. Immediately I saw the painted panel that had been removed from the far wall of the empty room, and the opening behind it.

'Did you know that there was a secret passage?' Tanus demanded coldly, and I shook my head.

'I thought I knew all his secrets, but I was wrong.' My voice was resigned. I think that in my heart I had known all along that we would never bring Intef to justice. He was a favourite of the dark gods and enjoyed their protection.

'Has Rasfer escaped with him?' I asked, and Tanus shook his head.

'I have him locked in the arsenal with the barons. But Intef's two sons, Menset and Sobek, have disappeared. Almost certainly they were the ones who arranged this murder of my men, and their father's escape.' Tanus had full control of that wild temper of his once more, but his anger was still there beneath it. 'You know Intef so well, Taita. What will he do? Where will he go? How can I catch him?'

'One thing I know, he will have made plans against such a day as this. I know he has treasure stored for him in the Lower Kingdom, with merchants and lawyers there. He has even had commerce with the false pharaoh. I think that he sold military information to him and his generals. He would receive a friendly welcome in the north.'

'I have already sent five fast galleys to the north, with orders to search all vessels that they overtake,' Tanus told me.

'He has friends across the Red Sea,' I said. 'And he has sent treasure to merchants in Gaza on the shores of the northern sea, to be held for him. He has had dealings with the Bedouin. Many of them are in his pay. They would help him to cross the desert.'

'By Horus, he is like a rat with a dozen escape-routes to his hole,' swore Tanus. 'How can I cover all of them?'

'You cannot,' I said. 'And now Pharaoh is waiting to witness the executions. You will have to report this to him.'

'The king will be angry, and with good reason. By allowing Intef to escape, I have failed in my duty.'

But Tanus was wrong. Pharaoh accepted the news of Intef's escape with remarkable equanimity. I cannot fathom the reason for this, except perhaps that the vast quantity of treasure he had acquired so unexpectedly had mellowed him. Deep in his heart he may still have cherished some sneaking affection for his grand vizier. On the other hand, Pharaoh was a kindly man, and may not have truly relished the prospect of watching Lord Intef being nailed to the city gates.

It is true he showed some passing annoyance, and spoke of justice being cheated, but all the time we were in his presence, he was surreptitiously studying the manifest of the treasure. Even when Tanus admitted his responsibility for the prisoner's escape, Pharaoh brushed it aside.

'The fault lies with the captain of the guard, and he has already been sufficiently punished from the poison bowl that Intef provided for him. You have sent galleys and troops in pursuit of the fugitive. You have done all that can be expected of you, Lord Harrab. It remains only for you to carry out my sentence on these other criminals.'

'Is Pharaoh ready to witness the execution?' Tanus asked, and Pharaoh looked about him for an excuse to remain with his manifests and tax-collectors' reports.

'I have much to do here, Lord Tanus. Proceed without me. Report to me when the sentences have been carried out.'

SO GREAT was the public interest in the executions that the city fathers had erected a Taita stand in front of the main gates. They charged a silver ring for a seat upon it. There was no lack of customers, and the stand was packed to capacity. The crowds who could not find a seat upon it overflowed out into the fields beyond the walls. Many of them had brought beer and wine to make a celebration of it, and to toast the barons on their way. Very few of them had not suffered from the ravages of the Shrikes, and many of them had lost husbands or brothers or sons to them.

Stark naked and bound together, as Pharaoh had ordered, the condemned men were led through the streets of Karnak. The crowd lined their way and hurled dung and filth at them as they passed, screaming insults and shaking their fists. The children danced ahead of the procession singing bits of doggerel made up on the spur of the moment;

> Nails in my tooties, bare bum to the sky,
> I am a baron, and that's how I die.

Obedient to my mistress's wishes, I had taken up a place on the stand to watch the sentence carried out. In truth I had no eyes for the clothing and jewellery of the women of fashion around me when the prisoners were at last led through the open gates. I looked instead at Rasfer and I tried to revive and inflate my hatred for him. I forced myself to recite every cruel and wicked act that he had ever committed against me, to relive the agony of the lash and the knife that he had inflicted upon me. Yet there he stood with his white belly sagging almost to his knees, with excrement in his hair and filth streaking his face and running down his grotesque body. It was difficult to hate him as much as he deserved.

He saw me on the stand and he grinned up at me. The paralysed muscles on one side of his face made it only half a grin, a sardonic grimace, and he called, 'Thank you for coming to wish me godspeed, eunuch. Perhaps we will meet again in the fields of paradise, where I hope to have the pleasure of cutting off your balls once again.'

That taunt should have made it easier for me to hate him, but somehow it failed, although I called back to him, 'You are going no further than the mud in the river bottom, old friend. The next catfish that I roast on the spit I will call Rasfer.'

He was the first prisoner to be lifted on to the wooden gate. It took three men on the parapet of the wall, straining on the rope, while at the same time, four more shoved from below. They held him there as one of the regimental armourers climbed the ladder beside him with a stone-headed mallet in his fist.

There were no more jokes from Rasfer when the first of the thick copper nails was driven through the flesh and bones of his huge, calloused feet. He roared and swore and twisted in the grip of the men who held him, and the crowd cheered and laughed and urged on the sweating armourer.

It was only when the nails had been driven home and the hammerman had climbed down to admire his handiwork that the flaws in this novel form of punishment became evident. Rasfer howled and roared, swinging upside-down, with the blood trickling slowly down his legs. The hang of his pendulous paunch was reversed, and the huge hairy bunch of his genitalia flapped against his belly-button. As he twisted and struggled, the nails slowly ripped through the web of flesh between his toes, until finally they tore entirely free. Rasfer fell back to earth and flopped around like a beached fish. The spectators loved the show, and howled with mirth at his antics.

Encouraged by the spectators, his executioners lifted him back on to the gate, and the armourer with his hammer climbed back up the ladder to drive in more nails. In order to pin Rasfer more securely and to prevent him struggling, Tanus ordered his hands as well as his feet to be nailed to the gate.

This time it was more successful. Rasfer hung head down, his limbs spread like some monstrous star-fish. He was no longer bellowing, for the mass of intestines in his belly were sagging down and pressing on his lungs. He struggled for every breath he drew, and had none over for shouting.

One at a time, the other condemned men were lifted on to the gate and nailed there, and the crowd hooted and applauded. Only Basti the Cruel made no sound and gave them poor sport.

As the day wore on, the sun beat down upon the crucified victims, and the heat grew steadily stronger. By noon the prisoners were so weak with pain and thirst and loss of blood that they hung as quietly as the carcasses on butchers' hooks. The spectators began to lose interest and drifted away. Some of the barons lasted longer than the others. Basti went on breathing all that day. Only as the sun was setting did he take one deep shuddering breath and finally hang inert.

Rasfer was the toughest of them all. Long after Basti was gone, he hung on. His face was filled with dark blood so it swelled to twice its normal size. His tongue protruded from between his lips, like a thick slice of purple liver. Once in a while he would utter a deep groan and his eyes would flutter open. Every time this happened, I shared his agony. The last of my hatred for him had long ago shrivelled and died, and I was racked with pity, as I would have been for any other tortured animal.

The crowd had long ago dispersed, and I sat alone on the empty stand.

Not attempting to hide his disgust at such a brutal duty thrust upon him by the royal command, Tanus had stood to his post until sunset. Then finally he had handed over the death watch to one of his captains, and strode back into the city, leaving us to our vigil.

There were only the ten guards below the gate, myself on the stand and a few beggars lying like bundles of rags at the foot of the wall. The torches on either side of the gate guttered and flickered in the night breeze off the river, casting an eerie light over the macabre scene.

Rasfer groaned again, and I could stand it no longer. I took a jar of beer from my basket and climbed down to speak to the captain. We knew each other from the desert, and he laughed and shook his head at my request. 'You are a soft-hearted fool, Taita. The bastard is so far-gone, he is not worth worrying about,' he told me. 'But I will look the other way for a while. Be quick about it.'

I went to the gate, and Rasfer's head was on a level with my own. I called his name softly, and his eyes fluttered open. I had no way of telling how much he understood, but I whispered, 'I have a little beer to wet your tongue.'

He made a soft gulping sound in his throat. His eyes were looking at me. If he still had feeling, I knew his thirst must be a torment of hell. I dribbled a few drops from the jar over his tongue, careful not to let any of it run back into his nose. He made a weak and futile effort to swallow. It would have been impossible, even if he had been stronger; the liquid ran out of the corners of his mouth and down his cheeks into the dung-caked hair.

He closed his eyes, and that was the moment I was waiting for. I slipped my dagger out of the folds of my shawl. Carefully I placed the point behind his ear, and then with a sharp movement drove it in to the hilt. His back arched in the final spasm, and then he relaxed into death. I drew out the blade. There was very little blood, and I hid the dagger in my shawl and turned away.

'May dreams of paradise waft you through the night, Taita,' the captain of the guard called after me, but I had lost my voice and could not reply. I never thought that I would weep for Rasfer, and maybe I never did so. Perhaps I wept only for myself.

AT PHARAOH'S command the return of the court to Elephantine was initially delayed for a month. The king had his new treasure to dispose of and was in buoyant mood. In all the time I had known him, I had never seen him so happy and contented. I was pleased for him. By this time I held the old man in real and warm affection. Some nights I sat up late with him and his scribes, going over the accounts of the royal treasury, which now emitted a decidedly rosy glow.

At other times, I was summoned by Pharaoh to consultations on the alterations to the mortuary temple and the royal tomb that he was now better able to afford. I calculated that at least half of the recently revealed treasure would go into the tomb with Pharaoh. He selected all the finest jewellery from Intef's hoard and sent almost fifteen takhs of bullion to the goldsmiths in his temple, to be turned into funerary objects.

Nevertheless, he found time to send for Tanus to advise him on military matters. He had now recognized Tanus as one of the foremost generals in his army.

I was present at some of these meetings. The threat from the false pharaoh in the Lower Kingdom was ever-present and preyed on all our minds. Such was Tanus' favour with the king that he was able to make the most of these fears and to persuade Pharaoh to divert a small part of Intef's treasure to the building of five new squadrons of war galleys, and to re-equipping all the guards regiments with new weapons and sandals – although he was unable to persuade the king to make up the arrears in pay for the army. Many of the regiments had not been paid for the last half-year. Morale in the army was much boosted by these reinforcements, and every soldier knew whom to thank for them. They roared like lions and raised their clenched right fists in salute, when Tanus inspected their massed formations.

Most times when Tanus was summoned to the royal audience, my mistress found some excuse to be present. Although she had the good sense to keep in the background on these occasions, she and Tanus directed such looks at each other that I feared they might scorch the false beard of the Pharaoh. Fortunately nobody but myself seemed to notice these flashing messages of passion.

Whenever my mistress knew that I was to see Tanus in private, she burdened me with long and ardent messages for him. On my return I carried his replies which matched hers in length and fire. Fortunately these outpourings were highly repetitive, and memorizing them was not a great hardship.

My Lady Lostris never tired of urging me to find some subterfuge by which she and Tanus might be alone together once more. I admit that I feared enough for my own skin and for the safety of my mistress and our unborn child, not to devote all my energies and ingenuity to satisfying this request of hers. Once when I did tentatively approach Tanus with my mistress's invitation to a meeting, he sighed and refused it with many protestations of love for her.

'That interlude in the tombs of Tras was sheer madness, Taita. I never intended to compromise the Lady Lostris' honour, but for the *khamsin*, it would never have happened. We cannot take that risk again. Tell her that I love her more than life itself. Tell her our time will come, for the Mazes of Ammon-Ra have promised it to us. Tell her I will wait for her through all the days of my life.'

On receiving this loving message, my mistress stamped her foot, called her true love a stubborn fool who cared nothing for her, broke a cup and two bowls of coloured glass, hurled a jewelled mirror which had been a gift from the king into the river, and finally threw herself on the bed where she wept until suppertime.

APART FROM his military duties, which included supervising the building of the new fleet of galleys, Tanus, these days, was much occupied with the reorganization of his father's estates that he had at last inherited.

On these matters he consulted me almost daily. Not surprisingly, the estates had never been preyed upon by the Shrikes while they belonged to Lord Intef, and accordingly they were all prosperous and in good repair. Thus Tanus had become overnight one of the most wealthy men in the Upper Kingdom. Although I tried my best to dissuade him, he spent much of this private fortune in making up the arrears in pay to his men and in re-equipping his beloved Blues. Of course his men loved him all the more for this generosity.

Not content with these profligate expenditures, Tanus sent out his captains, Kratas and Remrem and Astes, to gather up all the crippled and blinded veterans of the river wars who now existed by begging in the streets of Thebes. Tanus installed this riff-raff in one of the large country villas that formed part of his inheritance, and although slops and kitchen refuse would have been too good for them, he fed them on meat and corn-cakes and beer. The common soldiers cheered Tanus in the streets and drank his health in the taverns.

When I told my mistress of Tanus' mad extravagances, she was so encouraged by them that she immediately spent hundreds of deben of the gold that I had earned for her, in buying and equipping a dozen buildings which she turned into hospitals and hostels for the poor people of Thebes. I had already earmarked this gold for investment in the corn market, and though I wrung my hands and pleaded with her, she could not be moved.

Needless to say, it was the long-suffering slave Taita who was responsible for the day-to-day management of this latest folly of his mistress, although she visited her charity homes every day. Thus it was possible for any loafer and drunkard in the twin cities to scrounge a free meal and a comfortable bed from us. If that was not enough, they could have their bowl of soup served to them by my mistress's own fair hand, and their running sores and purging bowels treated by one of the most eminent physicians in this very Egypt.

I was able to find a few young unemployed scribes and disenchanted priests who loved people more than gods or money. My mistress took them into her employ. I led this little band on nocturnal hunts through the back alleys and slum quarters of the city. Nightly we gathered up the street orphans. They were a filthy, verminous bunch of little savages, and very few of them came with us willingly. We had to pursue and catch them like wild cats. I received many lusty bites and scratches in the process of bathing their filth-encrusted little bodies and shaving their hair that was so thick with lice and nits that it was impossible to drag a comb through it.

We housed them in one of my mistress's new hostels. Here the priests began the tedious process of taming them, while the scribes started on the long road of their education. Most of our captives escaped within the first few days, and returned to the gutters where they belonged. However, some of them stayed on in the hostel. Their slow transformation from animals to human beings delighted my mistress and gave me more pleasure than I had suspected could ever come from such an unlikely source.

All my protests against the manner in which my mistress was wasting our substance were in vain, and I vowed that if I were to be embalmed and laid in my tomb before my allotted time, the blame would surely rest entirely with these two young idiots whom I had taken under my wing, and who rewarded me by consistently ignoring my best advice.

Needless to say, it was my mistress and not me whom the widows and the cripples blessed and presented with their pitiful little gifts of wilting wild flowers, cheap beads and tattered scraps of papyrus containing poorly written texts from the *Book of the Dead*. As she walked abroad, the common people held up their brats for her blessing and tried to touch the hem of her skirt as though it were some religious talisman. She kissed the grubby babies, a practice which I warned her would endanger her health, and she scattered copper pieces to the loafers with as much care as a tree drops its autumn leaves.

'This is my city,' she told me. 'I love it and I love every person in it. Oh, Taita, I dread the return to Elephantine. I hate to leave my beautiful Thebes.'

'Is it the city you hate to leave?' I asked. 'Or is it a certain uncouth soldier who lives here?' She slapped me, but lightly.

'Is there nothing you hold sacred, not even love that is pure and true? For all your scrolls and grand language, you are at heart a barbarian.'

THUS THE days passed swiftly for all of us, until one morning I consulted my calendar and discovered that over two months had passed since my Lady Lostris had resumed her marital duties on Pharaoh's couch. Although she still showed no evidence of her condition, it was time to apprise the king of his great good fortune, his approaching paternity.

When I told my mistress what I intended, only one matter engaged her consideration. She made me promise that before I discussed it with the king, I must first tell Tanus that he was the true father of the child she was carrying. I set out to fulfil my promise that very afternoon. I found Tanus at the shipyards on the west bank of the river, where he was swearing at the shipwrights and threatening to throw them into the river to feed the crocodiles. He forgot his anger when he saw me, and took me on board the galley that they had launched that morning. Proudly, he showed me the new pump to remove water from the bilges, if the ship should ever be damaged in battle. He seemed to have forgotten that I had designed the equipment for him, and I had to remind him tactfully.

'Next you will want me to pay you for your ideas, you old rogue. I swear you are as stingy as any Syrian trader.' He clapped me on the back, and led me to the far end of the deck where none of the sailors could overhear us. He dropped his voice.

'How goes it with your mistress? I dreamed about her again last night. Tell me, is she well? How are those little orphans of hers? What a loving heart she has, what beauty! All of Thebes adores her. I hear her name spoken wherever I go, and the sound of it is as sharp as a spear thrust in my chest.'

'There will soon be two of her for you to love,' I told him, and he stared at me with his mouth agape like a man suddenly bereft of his senses. 'It was much more than just the *khamsin* that struck that night in the tombs of Tras.'

He seized me in a hug so powerful that I could not breathe. 'What is this riddle? Speak plainly, or I shall throw you into the river. What are you saying, you old scallywag? Don't juggle words with me!'

'The Lady Lostris is carrying your child. She sent me to tell you so that you should be the first to know it, even before the king,' I gasped. 'Now set me free before I am permanently damaged.' He released me so suddenly, that I almost fell overboard.

'My child! My son!' he cried. It was amazing how both of them had made that immediate assumption of the poor little mite's gender. 'This is a miracle. This is a direct gift from Horus.' It was clear to Tanus in that moment that no other man in the history of the world had ever fathered an infant.

'My son!' he shook his head in wonder. He was grinning like an idiot. 'My woman and my son! I must go to them this very moment.' He set off down the deck, and I had to run to catch him. It took all my powers of persuasion to prevent him from storming the palace and bursting into the royal harem. In the end, I led him to the nearest riverside tavern to wet the baby's head. Fortunately a gang of off-duty Blues was already drinking there. I ordered and paid for a butt of the tavern's best wine and left them to it. There were men from some of the other regiments in the tavern, so there would probably be a riot later, for Tanus was in a rumbustious mood and the Blues never needed much encouragement to fight.

I went directly from the tavern to the palace, and Pharaoh was delighted to see me. 'I was about to send for you, Taita. I have decided that we have been too niggardly with the entrance-gates to my temple. I want something grander—'

'Pharaoh!' I cried. 'Great and Divine Egypt! I have wonderful tidings. The goddess Isis has kept her promise to you. Your dynasty will be eternal. The prophecy of the Mazes of Ammon-Ra will be fulfilled. The moon of my mistress has been trodden under the hooves of the mighty bull of Egypt! The Lady Lostris is bearing your son!'

For once all thought of funerals and temple-building was driven from Pharaoh's mind, and, like Tanus, his very first instinct was to go to her. Led by the king, we rushed through the palace corridors, a solid stream of nobles and courtiers turbulent as the Nile in spate, and my mistress was waiting for us in the garden of the harem. With the natural wiles of the female, she had composed the setting perfectly to show off her loveliness to full effect. She was seated on a low bench with flower-beds around her and the broad river behind her. For a moment I thought the king might throw himself to his knees in front of her, but even the prospect of immortality could not cause him to forget his dignity to that extent.

Instead, he showered her with congratulations and compliments and earnest enquiries after her health. All the while his fascinated gaze was fastened on her belly from which the miracle would in the fullness of time emerge. Finally he asked her, 'My dear child, is there anything that you lack for your happiness? Is there anything I can do to make you more comfortable during this trying time in your life?'

I was filled once more with admiration for my mistress. She would have made a great general or corn trader, for her sense of timing was impeccable. 'Your Majesty, Thebes is the city of my birth. I cannot be truly happy anywhere else in Egypt. I beg you in your generosity and understanding to allow your son to be born here in Thebes. Please do not make me return to Elephantine.'

I held my breath, the siting of the court was an affair of state. To remove from one city to another was a decision which affected the lives of thousands of citizens. It was not one to be made on the light whim of a child not yet sixteen years of age.

Pharaoh looked amazed at the request, and scratched his false beard. 'You want to live in Thebes? Very well, then, the court will move to Thebes!' He turned to me. 'Taita, design me a new palace.' He looked back at my mistress. 'Shall we site it there, on the west bank, my dear?' He pointed across the river.

'It is cool and pretty on the west bank,' my mistress agreed. 'I shall be very happy there.'

'On the west bank, Taita. Do not stint yourself in the design. It must be a fitting home for the son of Pharaoh. His name will be Memnon, the ruler of the dawn. We will call it the Palace of Memnon.'

With such simple ease my mistress saddled me with a mountain of labour, and accustomed the king to the first of many such demands in the name of the child in her womb. From this moment on, Pharaoh was not disposed to deny her aught that she asked for, whether it was titles of honour for those she loved or liked, alms for those she had taken under her protection, or rare and exotic dishes that were fetched for her from the ends of the empire. Like a naughty child, I think that she enjoyed testing the limits of this new power she wielded over the king.

She had never seen snow, though she had heard me speak of it from my fragmentary childhood memories of the mountainous land where I had been born. My mistress asked for some to be brought to her to cool her brow in the heat of the Nile valley. Pharaoh immediately commanded a special athletics games to be held, during which the hundred fastest runners in the Upper Kingdom were selected. They were despatched to Syria to bring back snow to my mistress in a special box of my design, which was intended to prevent it melting. This was probably the only one of all her whims that remained unsatisfied. All we received back from those far-off mountain peaks was a damp patch in the bottom of the box.

In all other things she was fully accommodated. On one occasion she was present when Tanus presented a report to the king on the order of battle of the Egyptian fleet. My mistress sat quietly in the background until Tanus had finished and taken his leave, then she remarked quietly, 'I have heard it said that Lord Tanus is the finest general we have. Don't you think it may be wise, divine husband, to promote him to Great Lion of Egypt and place him in command of the northern corps?' Once again I gasped at her effrontery, but Pharaoh nodded thoughtfully.

'That same thought had already occurred to me, my dear, even though he is still so young for high command.'

The following day, Tanus was summoned to a royal audience, from which he emerged as Great Lion of Egypt and the commander of the northern wing of the army. The ancient general who had preceded him was palmed off with a substantial pension and relegated to a sinecure in the royal household. Tanus now had three hundred galleys and almost thirty thousand men under his command. The promotion meant that he stood fourth in the army lists, with only Nembet and a couple of old dodderers above him.

'Lord Tanus is a proud man,' the Lady Lostris informed me, as if I were completely ignorant of this fact. 'If you should ever tell him that I had any hand in his promotion, I shall sell you to the first Syrian trader I come upon,' she threatened me ominously.

All this time her belly, once so smooth and shapely, was distending gradually. With all my other work I was obliged to relay daily bulletins on this progression, not only to the palace, but also to army headquarters, northern command.

I BEGAN work on the construction of the Palace of Memnon five weeks after Pharaoh had given me the original instructions, for it had taken me that long to draw up the final plans. Both my mistress and the king agreed that my designs exceeded their expectations, and that it would be by far the most beautiful building in the land.

On the same day that the work began, a blockade runner who had succeeded in bribing his way past the fleets of the red pretender in the north docked in Thebes with a cargo of cedar wood from Byblos. The captain was an old friend of mine and he had interesting news for me.

Firstly, he told me that Lord Intef had been seen in the city of Gaza. It was said that he was travelling in state with a large bodyguard towards the East. He must therefore have succeeded in crossing the Sinai desert, or he had found a vessel to carry him through the mouth of the Nile and thence east along the coast of the great sea.

The captain had other news that at the time seemed insignificant, but which was to change the destiny of this very Egypt and of all of us who lived along the river. It seemed that a new and warlike tribe had come out of an unknown land to the east of Syria, carrying all before them. Nobody knew much about these warrior people, except that they seemed to have developed a form of warfare that had never been seen before. They could cross vast distances very swiftly, and no army could stand against them.

There were always wild rumours of new enemies about to assail this very Egypt. I had heard fifty like this one before, and thought as little of this one as I had of all the others. However, the captain was usually a reliable source, and so I mentioned his story to Tanus when next we met.

'No one can stand against this mysterious foe?' Tanus smiled. 'I would like to see them come against my lads, I'll show them what the word invincible truly means. What did you say they are called, these mighty warriors who come like the wind?'

'It seems that they call themselves the Shepherd Kings,' I replied, 'the Hyksos.' The name would not have slid over my tongue so smoothly if I understood then what it would mean to our world.

'The shepherds, hey? Well, they will not find my rascals an easy flock to herd.' He dismissed them lightly, and was much more interested in my news of Lord Intef. 'If only we could be certain of his true whereabouts, I could send a detachment of men to arrest him, and bring him back to face up to justice. Wherever I walk on the estates that once belonged to my family, I feel the spirit of my father beside me. I know he will never rest until I avenge him.'

'Would that it were so easy.' I shook my head. 'Intef is as cunning as a desert fox. I don't think we will ever see him in Egypt again.' As I said this, the dark gods must have chuckled to themselves.

AS MY mistress's pregnancy advanced, I was able to insist that she limited her many activities. I forbade her to visit the hospitals or the orphanage, for fear of infecting herself and her unborn infant with the vermin and the diseases of the poor. During the heat of the day I made her rest under the barrazza that I had built in the water-garden for the grand vizier. When she protested at the boredom of this enforced inactivity, Pharaoh sent his musicians to the garden to entertain her, and I was persuaded to leave my work on the Palace of Memnon to keep her company, to tell her stories and to discuss Tanus' latest exploits with her.

I was very strict with her diet, and allowed her no wine or beer. I had the palace gardeners provide fresh fruits and vegetables each day, and I carved all the fat off her meat, for I knew that it would make the child in her belly sluggish. I prepared each of her meals myself and every night when I saw her to her bedchamber, I mixed a special potion with herbs and juices that would strengthen her infant.

Of course, when she suddenly declared that she must have a stew made from the liver and kidneys of a gazelle, or a salad of larks' tongues or the roasted breast of the wild bustard, the king immediately sent a hundred of his huntsmen into the desert to procure these delicacies for her. I refrained from telling Lord Tanus of these strange cravings of my mistress, for I dreaded to learn that rather than prosecuting the war against the false pharaoh, the northern army had been sent into the desert to hunt gazelle or larks or bustard.

As the day of her confinement approached, I lay awake at night worrying. I had promised the king a prince, but he was not expecting his heir to arrive so expeditiously. Even a god can count the days from the first of the festival of Osiris. There was nothing that I could do if the child turned out to be a princess, but at least I could prepare Pharaoh for her early arrival.

Pharaoh had now conceived an interest in the subject of pregnancy and parturition, which temporarily rivalled his obsession with temples and tombs. I had to reassure him almost daily that the Lady Lostris' rather narrow hips were no obstacle to a normal birth, and that her tender age, far from being prejudicial, was highly favourable to a successful conclusion to our enterprise.

I took the opportunity to inform him of the interesting but little-known fact that many of the great athletes, warriors and sages of history had been prematurely exposed to the light of day.

'I believe, Your Majesty, that it's rather like the case of the sluggard who lies too long abed, and thus wastes his energy, while the great men are invariably early risers. I have noticed that you, Divine Pharaoh, are always about before sunrise. It would not surprise me to learn that you were also a premature birth.' I knew that he was not, but naturally he could not now contradict me. 'It would be a most propitious circumstance if this prince of yours should imitate his sire, and start early from his mother's womb.' I hoped that I had not belaboured my point, but the king seemed convinced by my eloquence.

In the end, the child cooperated most handsomely by overstaying its allotted term by almost two weeks, and I did nothing to hurry it along. The time span was so close to the normal that no tongues could wag, but Pharaoh was blessed with the premature birth that he had come to believe was so desirable.

It was no surprise to me that my mistress began her labour at a most inconvenient hour. Her waters broke in the third watch of the night. She was not in the habit of making matters too easy for me. At least this gave me the excuse of dispensing with the services of a midwife, for I had little faith in those hags with the black, dried blood crusted under their long, ragged fingernails.

Once she had begun, my Lady Lostris carried it off with her usual despatch and aplomb. I had barely time to shake myself fully awake, scrub my hands in hot wine and bless my instruments in the flame of the lamp, before she grunted and said quite cheerfully, 'You had better take another look, Taita. I think something is happening.' Although I knew it was much too soon, I humoured her. One glance was enough, and I shouted for her slave girls.

'Hurry, you lazy strumpets! Fetch the royal wives!'

'Which ones?' The first girl to answer my call tottered into the room half-naked and half-asleep.

'All of them, any of them.' No prince could inherit the double crown unless his birth had been witnessed, and it was formally attested that no exchange had taken place.

The royal women began to arrive just as the child revealed itself for the first time. My lady was seized by an overpowering convulsion, and then the crown of the head appeared. I had dreaded that it might be surmounted by a shock of red-gold curls, but what I saw was a thick dark pelt like that of one of the river otters. It was much later that the colour would change and the red would begin to sparkle in the black locks, like points of polished garnets, and then only when the sun shone upon it.

'Push!' I called to my mistress. 'Push hard!' And she responded lustily. The young bones of her pelvis, not yet tempered to rigidity by the years, spread to give the infant fair passage, and the way was well oiled. The child took me unawares. It came out like a stone from a sling-shot, and the tiny, slippery body almost flew from my hands.

Before I had a good hold on it, my mistress struggled up on her elbows. Her hair was plastered to her scalp with sweat and her expression was desperate with anxiety. 'Is it a boy? Tell me! Tell me!'

The roomful of royal ladies crowding around the bed were witness to the very first act the child performed, as it entered this world of ours. From a penis as long as my little finger, the Prince Memnon, the first of that name, shot a fountain almost as high as the ceiling. I was full in the path of this warm stream, and it drenched me to the skin.

'Is it a boy?' my mistress cried again, and a dozen voices answered her together.

'A boy! Hail, Memnon, the royal prince of Egypt!'

I could not speak yet, for my eyes burned not only with royal urine, but with tears of joy and relief as his birth cry rang out, angry and hot with temper.

He waved his arms at me and kicked out so strongly that I almost lost my grip again. As my vision cleared I was able to make out the strong, lean body and the small, proud head with the thick pelt of dark hair.

I LOST count long ago of how many infants I have birthed, but there had been nothing in my experience to prepare me for this. I felt all the love and devotion of which I was capable crystallized into that moment. I knew that something which would last a lifetime, and which would grow stronger with each passing day, had begun. I knew that my life had taken another random turn, and that nothing would ever be the same again.

As I cut the cord and bathed the child, I was filled with a sense of religious awe such as I had never known in the sanctuary of any one of Egypt's manifold gods. I feasted my eyes and my soul upon that perfect little body and upon the red and wrinkled face in which the signs of strength and stubborn courage were stamped as clearly as upon the features of his true father.

I laid him in his mother's arms, and as he found and latched on to her swollen nipple like a leopard on to the throat of a gazelle, my mistress looked up at me. I could not speak, but then there were no words that could frame what passed silently between us. We both knew. It had begun, something so wonderful that as yet neither of us could fully comprehend it.

I left her to the joy of her son and went to report to the king. I was in no hurry. I knew that the news would have been carried to him long since. The royal ladies are not renowned for their reticence. He was probably on his way to the harem at this very moment.

I dawdled in the water-garden, possessed by a dreaming sense of unreality. The dawn was breaking, and the sun god, Ammon-Ra, showed the tip of his fiery disc above the eastern hills. I whispered a prayer of thanks to him. As I stood with my eyes uplifted, a flock of the palace pigeons circled above the gardens. As they turned, the rays of the sun caught their wings and they flashed like bright jewels in the sky.

Then I saw the dark speck high above the circling flock, and even at that distance I recognized it immediately. It was a wild falcon, come out of the desert. It folded back its sharp wings and began its stoop. It had chosen the leading bird in the flock, and the dive was deadly accurate and inexorable. It struck the pigeon in a burst of feathers, like a puff of pale smoke, and the bird was dead in the air. Always a falcon will bind to its prey and drop to earth with it gripped in its talons.

This time that did not happen. The falcon killed the pigeon and then opened his talons and released it. The shattered carcass of the bird fell free, and, with a harsh scream, the falcon circled over my head. Three times it circled and three times it uttered that thrilling, warlike call. Three is one of the most potent magical numbers. From all these things I realized that this was no natural occurrence. The falcon was a messenger, or even the god Horus in his other form.

The carcass of the pigeon fell at my feet, droplets of its warm blood splattered my sandals. I knew that it was a token from the god. A sign of his protection, and patronage for the infant prince. I understood also that it was a charge to me. The god was commending him to my care.

I took the dead pigeon in my hands, and lifted it to the sky. 'Joyfully I accept this trust that you have placed upon me, oh Horus. Through all the days of my life I will be true to it.'

The falcon called again, one last wild shriek, and then it banked away and on quick, stabbing wing-beats, flew out across the wide Nile waters and disappeared into the wilderness, back towards the western fields of paradise where the gods live.

I plucked a single wing-feather from the pigeon. Later I placed it under the mattress of the prince's cot, for good luck.

PHARAOH'S JOY and pride in his heir were unbounded. He declared a nativity feast in his honour. For one entire night the citizens of Upper Egypt sang and danced in the streets, and gorged on the meat and wine that Pharaoh provided, and they blessed the Prince Memnon with every bowlful that went down their gullets. The fact that he was the son of my Lady Lostris, whom they loved, made the occasion of his birth all the more joyous.

So young and resilient was my mistress that within days, she was well enough to appear before the full court of Egypt, bearing her infant at her breast. Seated on the lesser throne below that of the king, she made a picture of lovely young motherhood. When she opened her robe and lifted out one of her milk-swollen breasts and before the assembled court gave the infant suck, they cheered her so loudly as to startle the infant. He spat out the nipple and roared at them in scarlet-faced outrage, and the nation took him to its heart.

'He is a lion,' they declared. 'His heart is pumped up with the blood of kings and warriors.'

Once the prince had been quieted again, and his mouth stopped up with the nipple, Pharaoh rose to address us, his subjects.

'I acknowledge this child to be my issue and the direct line of my blood and succession. He is my first-born son, and shall be Pharaoh after me. To you noble lords and ladies, to all my subjects, I commend the Prince Memnon.'

The cheers went on and on, for no one amongst them wanted to be the first to fall silent and bring his loyalty into question.

During all of this I stood with other servants and slaves of the royal household in one of the upper galleries which overlooked the hall. By craning my head, I was able to pick out the tall figure of Lord Tanus. He was standing in the third rank below the throne with Nembet and the other military commanders. Although he cheered with the rest of them, I could read the expression on his broad, open face that he strove to disguise. His son was claimed by another and it was beyond his power to prevent it. Even I, who knew and understood him so well, could only guess at what agony he was suffering.

When at last the king ordered silence and he had their attention once more, he continued, 'I commend to you also the mother of the prince, the Lady Lostris. Know all men that she sits now closest to my throne. From this day forward she is elevated to the rank of chief consort and the senior wife of Pharaoh. From henceforth, in name she will become Queen Lostris, while in precedence and preferment she ranks after the king and his prince alone. Furthermore, until the prince has reached the age of his majority, Queen Lostris shall act as my regent and, when I am unable to do so, she will stand at the head of the nation in my stead.'

I do not think there was a soul in all the Upper Kingdom who did not love my mistress, except perhaps some of the royal wives who had been unable to provide the king with a male heir, and who now found themselves outranked by her and superseded in the order of precedence. All the rest showed their love in the acclaim with which they greeted this pronouncement.

To end the ceremony of the naming of Pharaoh's heir, the royal family left the hall. In the main courtyard of the palace, Pharaoh mounted the sledge of state, and with Queen Lostris seated at his side and the prince in her arms, they were drawn by the span of white bullocks down the Avenue of Rams to the temple of Osiris to make sacrifice to the god. Both sides of the sacred avenue were lined a hundred deep by the citizens of Thebes. With a mighty voice they demonstrated their devotion to the king and their love for the queen and her new-born prince.

That night, as I waited on her and the child, she whispered to me, 'Oh, Taita, did you see Tanus in the crowd? What a day of mixed joy and sorrow this has been. I could have wept for my love. He was so tall and brave, and he had to watch and listen when his son was taken from him. I wanted to jump to my feet in all that throng and cry out, "This is the son of Tanus, Lord Harrab, and I love them both."'

'I am pleased for the sake of all of us, Your Majesty, that for once you were able to restrain that wayward tongue of yours.'

She giggled. 'It is so strange to have you call me that – Your Majesty – it makes me feel like an impostor.' She transferred the prince from one breast to the other, and at the movement he released from both ends of his tiny body a double blast of air which in volume and resonance was truly imperial.

'It is apparent that he was conceived in a wind-storm,' I remarked drily, and she giggled again and then immediately afterwards sighed dolefully.

'My darling Tanus will never share these intimate moments with us. Do you realize that he has not yet held Memnon in his arms, and it is possible he never will? I think I am about to cry again.'

'Restrain yourself, mistress. If you weep, it might sour your milk.' A warning which was untrue but effective in bending her to my will. She sniffed back her tears.

'Is there no way that we can let Tanus enjoy our baby as we do?'

I thought about it for a while and then made a suggestion which caused her to cry out with pleasure. As if to endorse what I had said, the prince broke resounding wind once more.

The very next day when Pharaoh came to visit his son, the queen put my suggestion into effect. 'Dear and divine husband, have you given thought to selecting official tutors for Prince Memnon?'

Pharaoh laughed indulgently. 'He is still only an infant. Should he not first learn to walk and talk, before he is instructed in other skills?'

'I think his tutors should be appointed now, so they can grow to know him, and he them.'

'Very well.' The king smiled, and took the child on to his knee. 'Who do you suggest?'

'For his schooling we need one of our great scholars. Some person who understands all the sciences and mysteries.'

The king's eyes twinkled. 'I cannot think of one who answers that description,' and he grinned at me. The child had altered Pharaoh's disposition; since Memnon's birth, he had become almost jovial, and for a moment I expected him to wink at me. However, his new, congenial attitude to life did not extend quite that far.

The queen continued, unruffled by this exchange, 'Then we need a soldier well versed in the warlike arts, and the exercise of arms to train him as a warrior. He should, I think, be young and of good breeding. Trustworthy, of course, and loyal to the crown.'

'Who do you suggest for that position, my dear? Very few of my soldiers answer to all those virtues.' I do not think there was any guile or malice in Pharaoh's question, but nevertheless my mistress was no fool.

She inclined her head gracefully and said, 'The king is wise, and knows who, from all his generals, best suits that role.'

At the very next assize the king announced the prince's tutors. The slave and physician, Taita, was to be responsible for Memnon's schooling and deportment. This surprised very few, but there was a buzz of comment when the king went on, 'For his training in arms and in military tactics and strategy, the Great Lion of Egypt, Lord Harrab, shall henceforth be responsible.' Accordingly it became the duty of Lord Harrab, when he was not on campaign, to wait upon the prince at the beginning of each week.

While my mistress waited for her quarters in the new palace that I was building across the river to be completed, she had moved from the harem into a wing of the grand vizier's palace that overlooked the water-garden I had built for her father. This was in accordance with her new status as the senior wife and consort. The weekly audience that Prince Memnon held for his official tutors took place under the barrazza, with Queen Lostris in attendance. Very often there was a score of other officials or courtiers present, and occasionally Pharaoh himself arrived with all his train, so we were under considerable constraint.

However, once in a while there were just the four of us present. On the very first occasion that we had such privacy, Queen Lostris placed the prince in his father's arms for the first time and I was witness to the incoherent joy with which Tanus looked down into the face of his son. Memnon rose to the occasion by puking down the front of his father's uniform, but even then Tanus would not relinquish him.

From then onwards we reserved any special event in the child's life for when Tanus was with us. Tanus fed him his first spoonful of gruel, and the prince was so startled by this unaccustomed fare that he screwed up his face and spat the offending mess down his chin. Then he howled loudly for his mother's milk to wash the taste from his mouth. Queen Lostris took him on her lap and while Tanus watched fascinated, she gave him the breast. Suddenly Tanus reached across and tweaked the nipple from the tiny mouth. This amused everybody but the prince and me. Memnon was outraged at this cavalier treatment and made that fact known, while I was shocked. I imagined the king arriving unexpectedly to find the Great Lion of Egypt with a right royal handful which he seemed in no hurry to relinquish.

When I quite rightly protested, my mistress told me, 'Don't be such a prim old woman, Taita. We are only having a little innocent fun.'

'Fun, yes. However, there is some doubt as to the innocence of it,' I muttered, for I had seen both their faces light up at the intimate touch, and sensed their mutual passion like thunder in the air. I knew that they could not restrain themselves for much longer, and that even Tanus' sense of duty and honour must in the end succumb to so great a love as theirs.

That very evening I visited the temple of Horus and made a generous sacrifice. Then I prayed and asked the god, 'May the prophecy of the Mazes be not too long delayed, for they cannot help themselves. It will mean death and disgrace to all of us.'

Sometimes it is best for men not to attempt to interfere with destiny. Our prayers can be answered in ways which we do not expect and do not welcome.

I WAS physician to the prince, but in truth he had little need of my medical skills. He was blessed with his father's rude and abundant health, and precocious strength. His appetite and digestion were exemplary. Anything placed in his mouth was devoured with leonine voracity, and promptly re-emerged from his nether end in the desired shape and consistency.

He slept without interruption and woke bellowing for food. If I showed him a finger, he would watch it move from side to side with those huge dark eyes, and the moment it came within range, he would seize it and attempt to haul himself into a sitting position. In this he succeeded sooner than any other child that I had attended. He raised himself and crawled at the age when others had only begun to sit up. He took his first tottering step when others would only begin to crawl.

Tanus was present on that remarkable day. He had been on campaign for the past two months, for the forces of the red usurper had captured Asyut. That city was the pivot on which our northern defences turned, and Pharaoh had ordered Tanus down-river with all his fleet to retake the city.

Much later I heard from Kratas just how terrible had been the fighting, but in the end Tanus breached the walls and was at the head of his beloved Blues when they broke in. They drove the pretender from the city and back beyond his own borders with bloody losses.

Tanus sailed back to Thebes and the gratitude of the kingdom. Pharaoh laid another chain upon his shoulders, the Gold of Valour, and made up the back-pay of all the troops who had helped him achieve this victory.

Tanus came almost directly from the king to the barrazza in the water-garden where we were waiting for him. While I stood guard at the gateway, Tanus and my mistress embraced with all the fire that had burned up so brightly while they had been apart. At last I had to separate them, for that embrace could lead in only one direction.

'Lord Tanus,' I called sharply, 'Prince Memnon grows impatient.'

Reluctantly they drew apart, and Tanus went to where the infant sprawled naked on a robe of jackal skins that I had spread for him in the shade. Tanus went down on one knee before him.

'Greetings, Your Royal Highness. I bring you tidings of the triumph of our arms—' Tanus mocked him lovingly, and Memnon gave a happy shout as he recognized his father, and then the sparkling gold chain caught his eye. With a mighty heave he hoisted himself to his feet. He took four lurching steps, seized the chain and clung to it with both hands.

All of us applauded this feat, and, supporting himself by the chain, Memnon beamed about him, accepting this praise as his due.

'By the wings of Horus, he has as sharp an eye as you do for the yellow metal, Taita,' Tanus laughed.

'It is not the gold that draws him, but the winning of it,' my mistress declared. 'One day he too will wear the Gold of Valour upon his chest.'

'Never doubt it!' Tanus swung the boy high, and Memnon shrieked with pleasure and kicked his legs to urge Tanus to further rough play.

Thus, for Tanus and me, the child's advances seemed to mark the change of seasons, just as surely as did the rise and fall of the river. On the other hand my mistress's life revolved around those hours spent alone with the child and the man. Each interval between Tanus' visits seemed too long for my mistress to support, each visit too short for her to bear.

THE INUNDATION of that summer was as benevolent as any that we had forecast at the ceremony of the waters in Elephantine. When the flood receded, the fields glistened under their new coat of black mud. In their turn, they were soon obliterated by the dense green stands of corn and fruit. By the time the prince took his first upright step the granaries of Egypt were brimming, and the larders of even the poorest of her subjects were filled. On the west bank the Palace of Memnon was taking shape, and the war in the north was running in our favour. The gods smiled on Pharaoh and all his realm.

The only discontent in all this was that the two lovers, though close enough to touch, were cleaved apart by a gulf wider than the valley in which we lived. Each of them on separate but numerous occasions taxed me with the prophecy of the Mazes of Ammon-Ra, as though I were personally responsible for the fulfilment of the dream visions. It was in vain to protest that I was merely the mirror in which the future was reflected, and not the one who moved the stones on the bao board of destiny.

The old year died, and the river began to rise once more, completing the endless cycle. This was the fourth flood that the Mazes had foretold. I, as much as any of them, expected my vision of the Mazes to be fulfilled before the end of the season. When this did not happen, both my mistress and Tanus taxed me severely.

'When will I be free to go to Tanus?' Queen Lostris sighed. 'You must do something, Taita.'

'It is not me, but the gods, whom you must question. I can pray to them, but that is all I can do.'

Then another year passed without any change in our circumstances, and even Tanus was bitter. 'So much faith I have placed in you that I have based my future happiness on your word. I swear to you, Taita, that if you do not do something soon—' He broke off and stared at me. The threat was all the more forceful for not being spoken.

Yet another year drifted past, and even I began to lose faith in my own prophecy. I came to believe that the gods had changed their minds, or that what I had seen was my own wishful fantasy.

In the end Prince Memnon was almost five years old and his mother twenty-one, when the messenger came flying wild-eyed from the north, in one of our scouting galleys.

'The Delta has fallen. The red pretender is dead. The Lower Kingdom is in flames. The cities of Memphis and Avaris are destroyed. The temples are burned to the ground and the images of the gods thrown down,' he shouted to the king, and Pharaoh replied 'It is not possible. I long to believe this despatch, but I cannot. How could this thing come to pass without our knowledge? The usurper was possessed of great force, for more than fifteen years we have been unable to overthrow him. How has this been accomplished in a day, and by whom?'

The messenger was shaking with fear and exhaustion, for his journey had been onerous, and he knew how the bearers of disastrous tidings were treated in Thebes.

'The red pretender was destroyed with his sword still in the scabbard. His forces were scattered before the war trumpets could sound the alarm.'

'How was this accomplished?'

'Divine Egypt, I know not. They say that a new and terrible enemy has come out of the East, swift as the wind, and no nation can stand before his wrath. Though they have never seen him, our army is in full retreat from the northern borders. Even the bravest will not stay to face him.'

'Who is this enemy?' Pharaoh demanded, and for the first time we heard the fear in his voice.

'They call him the Shepherd King. The Hyksos.'

Tanus and I had jested with that name. We would never do so again.

PHARAOH CALLED his war council into secret conclave. It was only long afterwards that I learned from Kratas all that transpired in those deliberations. Tanus, of course, would never break his oath of secrecy, not even to me or my mistress. But I was able to worm it out of Kratas, for that lovable, brawling oaf was not proof against my wiles.

Tanus had promoted Kratas to the rank of Best of Ten Thousand, and had given him the command of the Blue Crocodile Guards. The bond between them was still as solid as a granite stele. Thus, as a regimental commander, Kratas was entitled to a seat on the war council, and although at his lowly rank he was not called upon to speak, he faithfully relayed all that was said, to me and my mistress.

The council was divided between the ancients, headed by Nembet, and the new blood of which Tanus was the leader. Unfortunately the final authority lay with the old men, and they forced their archaic views upon the others.

Tanus wanted to draw our main forces back from the frontier and to set up a series of deep defences along the river. At the same time, he intended sending forward scouting and reconnaissance parties to assess and study the nature of the mysterious enemy. We had spies in all of the northern cities, but for some unknown reason no reports from them had as yet been received. Tanus wanted to gather these in and study them, before he deployed his main force to battle.

'Until we know what we are facing, we cannot devise the correct strategy to meet it,' he told the council.

Nembet and his faction countered any of Tanus' suggestions. The old admiral had never forgiven Tanus for his humiliation on the day he saved the royal barge from destruction. His opposition to Tanus was based on principle rather than on reason or logic.

'We will not yield a cubit of our sacred soil. To suggest it is cowardice. We will meet the enemy and destroy him wherever we find him. We will not dance and flirt with him like a gaggle of village maidens.'

'My lord!' roared Tanus, incensed by the suggestion of cowardice. 'Only a fool, and an old fool at that, will make a decision before he knows the facts. We have no scrap of intelligence to act upon—'

It was in vain. The seniority of the three generals above Tanus on the army lists prevailed in the end.

Tanus was ordered north immediately, to steady and rally the retreating army. He was to hold the frontier, and make his stand on the boundary stones. He was forbidden to make a strategic withdrawal to the line of hills before Asyut, which was the natural defensive line, and from which the city walls provided a second line of defence. He would have the fleet and the northern army corps under his direct command, with three hundred warships to provide the transport, and to command the river.

In the meantime, Nembet would bring in the rest of the army, even those regiments on the southern border with Cush. The black threat from the African interior must be ignored now in the face of this more pressing danger. As soon as they were assembled, Nembet would rush these reinforcements northwards to join up with Tanus. Within a month, there would be an invincible army of sixty thousand men and four hundred galleys lying before Asyut. In the meantime, Tanus must hold the frontier at all costs.

Nembet ended with a strict injunction. 'Lord Harrab is further ordered to hold all his forces on the border. He is not to indulge in raids or scouting forays to the north.'

'My Lord Nembet, these orders blindfold me, and bind my sword-arm. You are denying me the means of conducting this campaign in a prudent and efficient manner,' Tanus protested in vain. Nembet sneered with the satisfaction of having forced his authority upon his young rival, and in having gained a measure of retribution. On such petty human emotions pivots the destiny of nations.

Pharaoh himself announced his intention of taking his rightful place at the head of his army. For a thousand years the pharaoh had been present on the field whenever the decisive battles of history had been fought out. Although I had to admire the king's courage, I wished he had not chosen this moment to demonstrate it. Pharaoh Mamose was no warrior, and his presence would do little to enhance our chances of victory. There might be some bolstering of morale when the troops saw him in the van, but on balance he and his train would be a greater hindrance than assistance to Lord Tanus.

The king would not travel northwards to the battle-front alone. His entire court would attend him, including his senior wife and his son. The queen must have her retinue and Prince Memnon his tutors, and so I would be going north to Asyut and the battle-front.

Nobody knew nor understood this enemy. I felt that my mistress and the prince were being placed in unnecessary danger. On the other hand, the safety of a slave was of no account, except to the slave himself. I slept little the night before we sailed northwards on the flood of the river for Asyut and the battle-front.

THE FARTHER north we sailed, the more numerous and troublesome were the rumours and reports coming down from the front to feed upon our contentment and confidence, like locusts upon the standing crops. Often during the voyage, Tanus came aboard our vessel, ostensibly to discuss these with me. However, on each visit he spent some time with the prince and his mother.

I have never held with the custom of women following the army into battle. In times of peace or war, they are a marvellous distraction – even a warrior of Tanus' calibre could be diverted from his main purpose. All his mind should have been on the task ahead, but when I told him so, he laughed and clapped my shoulder.

'They give me a reason to fight. Don't worry, old friend, I shall be a lion defending his cub.'

Soon we encountered the first elements of the retreating army, straggling groups of deserters who were looting the villages as they fled southwards along the banks of the river. With very little ceremony and no hesitation at all, Tanus beheaded several hundred of them and had their heads spiked on spears and planted along the bank as an example and a warning. Then he gathered up the others and regrouped them under reliable officers. There were no further desertions and the troops stood to the colours with a new spirit.

Our flotilla came to the walled city of Asyut, overlooking the river. In defiance of his orders from Nembet, Tanus left a small strategic reserve of five thousand men here under the command of Remrem. Then we sailed on northwards to take up our positions on the border, there to await the approach of the mysterious Shepherd King.

The fleet lay at anchor across the river in its battle formations, but the vessels were under skeleton crews. The fighting men were disembarked with the main body of infantry and deployed upon the east bank of the river.

I prevailed upon Pharaoh to allow my mistress and the prince to remain on board the large and comfortable barge that had brought them here. It was cooler and healthier out on the water, and their escape would be swifter if our army met with any reverse of arms.

The king went ashore with the army, and set up his camp on the higher ground above the inundated fields. There was a deserted village here; years ago the peasants had fled from this disputed border with the false pharaoh. There were always foraging troops and bloody little skirmishes hereabouts, and the farmers had given up any attempts to work these fertile but dangerous fields. The name of the derelict village was Abnub.

The flood of the Nile had begun to subside some weeks prior to our arrival at Abnub, and although the irrigation canals were still running strongly, and the fields were morasses of black mud, the main waters had retreated back between the permanent banks of the Nile.

Within the restrictions placed upon him by Nembet, Tanus set about preparing to meet the threat. The regiments encamped in their order of battle. Astes commanded the fleet on the river, Tanus himself had the centre with his left flank anchored on the Nile, while Kratas had the right wing.

The desert stretched to the eastern horizon, dun and forbidding. No army could survive out in that burning, waterless waste. It was our right flank, secure and impregnable.

All that we knew of the Hyksos was that he had come overland, and that he possessed no fleet of his own. Tanus expected to meet him on land, and to fight an infantry engagement. Tanus knew that he could prevent the Hyksos from crossing the river, and so he should be able to bring him to battle on the field of his own choice. Ideally, this would not have been at Abnub, but Nembet had made that decision for him.

The village of Abnub stood on a low ridge with open untended fields around it. At least it commanded a good view, and the enemy would be under our observation long before it could engage and drive in our pickets.

Tanus had thirty thousand of the finest troops in Egypt under his command. I had never seen such a large force. Indeed, I doubt that an army of this size had ever before been assembled in the valley of the Nile. Soon Nembet would arrive with another thirty thousand. Then it would be the greatest army in history.

I went with Tanus to inspect them, and the troops' morale had soared since he had taken command in person. Perhaps the presence of Pharaoh in the camp had also helped to steady them. They cheered Tanus as he strode along their massed ranks, and I felt much encouraged and relieved at the multitudes of their host, and the spirit in them.

I could not imagine an enemy powerful enough to overwhelm us. There were twelve thousand archers with polished leather helmets and padded leather breastplates that would stop an arrow, except if it were fired at very short range. There were eight thousand heavy spearmen, with long shields of hippo-skin as tough and hard as bronze. The ten thousand swordsmen in leopard-skin caps were also armed with slingshots, the stones from which could split a skull at fifty paces.

I felt more confident with each day that passed, as I watched Tanus exercising these huge masses of armed men. Yet it worried me that we still knew so little about the Hyksos and the forces that he commanded. I pointed out to Tanus that the war council had forbidden him to send land forces forward to reconnoitre, but had said nothing of vessels being used for this purpose.

'You should have been a law scribe,' Tanus laughed, 'you can make words dance to any tune you play.' But he ordered Hui to take a single squadron of fast galleys northwards as far as Minieh, or until he encountered the enemy. This was the same Hui whom we had captured at Gallala, and who had been one of Basti's Shrikes. Under Tanus' favour, that young rogue had advanced swiftly, and now commanded a squadron of galleys.

Hui had strict orders to avoid action and to report back within four days. Dutifully, he returned on the fourth day. He had reached Minieh without seeing another ship or encountering any resistance. The villages along the river were all deserted, and the town of Minieh itself had been sacked and was in flames.

Hui had, however, captured a handful of deserters from the false pharaoh's shattered army. These were the first persons we had questioned who were actual eye-witnesses of the Hyksos invasion. However, none of them had ever stood to engage and actually fight the Shepherd King. They had all fled at his first approach. Their reports were therefore so far-fetched and garbled as to be completely incredible.

How could we believe in the existence of an army that sailed across the open desert on ships that were as swift as the wind? According to our informants, the dust-clouds that hung over this strange fleet were so tall as to obscure their numbers and to strike terror into any army that watched their advance.

'These are not men,' the prisoners reported, 'they are fiends from the underworld, and they ride on the devil winds out of the desert.'

Having questioned the prisoners carefully, and finding that even hot coals on their heads could not make them alter their stories, Tanus ordered their summary execution. He did not want these wild tales circulating and spreading despondency amongst our forces who had only recently regained their courage.

ON THE tenth day of waiting at Abnub, we received word that Nembet was at last on his way with reinforcements, and that he expected to reach Asyut within the next two weeks. The effect on the men was marvellous to behold. They were transformed at a stroke from sparrows to eagles. Tanus issued an extra ration of beer and meat to celebrate the news, and the cooking-fires were a field of stars upon the plain before Abnub. The luscious odour of burning mutton fat filled the night, and the sound of laughter and singing only died away in the final watches.

I had left my mistress on board the barge with her son, and had come ashore in response to a summons from Tanus. He wanted me to attend the final war council with his regimental commanders. 'You are always a well of ideas and wisdom, you old rascal. Perhaps you can tell us how to sink a fleet of ships that comes sailing over dry land?'

Our deliberations went on until after midnight, and for once I was able to contribute very little of value. It was too late to return to the ship that night, so Tanus gave me a straw mattress in the corner of his tent. I awoke before dawn, as was my habit, but Tanus was gone from his bed, and beyond the coarse linen wall of the tent, the camp was already astir. I felt guilty of indolence, and hastened out to watch the dawn breaking over the desert.

I climbed the hill behind the camp. From there I looked first towards the river. The blue smoke from the cooking-fires was smeared out across the surface, mingling with the streamers of river mist. The riding lamps on board the ships were reflected in the dark waters. It was still too dark and far to pick out the vessel upon which my mistress lay.

I turned then towards the east and saw the light bloom over the desert with the nacreous glow of pearly oyster-shells. The light hardened and the desert was soft and lovely, the hillocks and dunes shaded with mauve and soft purple. In the limpid air the horizons seemed close enough to touch with an outstretched hand.

Then I saw the cloud suspended on the horizon beneath the unblemished aquamarine sheen of the sky. It was no larger than the end of my thumb, and my gaze wandered past it and then drifted back to it. I felt no initial alarm, for I had to stare at it for a while before I realized that it was moving.

'How strange,' I murmured aloud. 'The beginning of the *khamsin*, perhaps.' But it was out of season, and there had been no charging of the air with those malevolent forces which herald the desert storms. The morning was cool and balmy.

Even as I pondered it, the distant cloud spread and grew taller. The base of the cloud was upon the earth, not suspended above it, and yet it was too swift and wide to be of any earthly origin. A flock of birds might move that fast, locusts may rise that thickly to the skies, but this was neither of these things.

The cloud was ochre-yellow, but at first I could not believe it was dust. I have watched herds of scimitar-horned oryx galloping through the dunes in their hundreds upon their annual migrations, but they had never raised a dust-cloud such as this. It might have been the smoke from a fire, but there was nothing out there in the desert to burn. It had to be dust, and yet I still could not wholly believe it. Swiftly it grew, and drew ever closer, while I stared in wonder and in awe.

Suddenly I saw reflected light twinkle at the base of the towering cloud. Instantly I was transported back to the vision of the Mazes of Ammon-Ra. This was the same scene. The first had been fantasy, but this was reality. I knew that those beams of light were shot from war armour and from blades of polished bronze. I started to my feet, and alone upon the hilltop I shouted to the wind a warning that nobody heard.

Then I heard the war trumpets sounding in the camp below me. The pickets on the heights had at last seen the approaching dust-cloud and sounded the alarm. The sound of the trumpets was a part of my vision. Their urgent warning shrilled in my ears and threatened to split my skull, it thrilled my blood and chilled my heart. I knew from my vision that on this fateful day a dynasty would fall and the locusts from the East would devour the substance of this very Egypt. I was filled with dread, and with terror for my mistress and the child that was part of the dynasty.

The camp below me was a tumult of men running to arms. Their armour glinted and their spear-heads sparkled as they brandished them on high. They were bees from the overturned hive, massing and swarming in disarray. The shouts of the sergeants and the rallying cries of the captains were almost drowned by the braying horns.

I saw Pharaoh carried from his tent in the centre of a knot of armed men. They hustled him up the slope of the hill to where his throne was set amongst the rocks, overlooking the plain and the wide sweep of the river. They lifted him to the throne and placed the crook and the flail in his hands and the tall double crown upon his head. Pharaoh sat like a marble statue with an ash-white face, while below him his regiments fell into their battle formations. Tanus had trained and exercised them well, and out of the confusion of the first alarm, order swiftly emerged.

I ran down the hill to be near the king, and so rapid was the response of Lord Tanus' divisions that by the time I reached the foot of his throne, his army lay upon the plain like a coiled serpent to meet the menace of that boiling yellow dust-cloud that swept down upon it.

Kratas stood with his division on the right flank. I could recognize his tall figure on the first slope of the hill. His regimental officers were grouped around him, their plumes nodding and waving in the light morning breeze from the river. Tanus and his staff were directly below me, close enough for me to overhear their conversation. They discussed the advance of the enemy in cool, academic tones, as though this were a sandbox problem at an officers' training course.

Tanus had disposed his force in the classical formations. His heavy spearmen formed the front ranks. Their shields were interlocked and the spears' butts grounded. The bronze spear-heads sparkled in the early sunlight, and the men's demeanour was calm and grave. Drawn up behind them were the archers. Their bows were strung and ready. Behind each man stood his quiver boy with bundles of spare arrows. During the battle they would gather up the expended arrows of the enemy to replenish their own bundles. The swordsmen were in reserve, light and quick troops that could rush in to stop a breach or to exploit a weak point in the enemy formations.

The moves of any battle were like those of the bao board. There were classic openings with set defences that had been developed over the centuries. I had studied these and written three of the definitive scrolls on military tactics that were the prescribed reading of officers training in Thebes.

Now, reviewing Tanus' dispositions, I could find no fault in them, and my confidence soared. How could an enemy prevail against this mighty host of trained and battle-hardened veterans, and their brilliant young general, who had never lost a battle?

Then I looked once more beyond our ranks at that ominous, rolling yellow cloud, and my confidence wavered. This was something beyond military tradition, beyond the experience of any general in all our long, proud history. Were these mortal men that we were facing, or, as rumour suggested, were they fiends?

When I stared into the swirling clouds, they were now so close that I could make out dark shapes in the dun and gloomy veils of dust. My skin crawled with a kind of religious horror as I recognized the shiplike shapes that our prisoners had warned us of. But these were smaller and swifter than any vessel that had ever been launched on water, swifter even than any creature that had ever moved upon the surface of the earth.

It was difficult to follow one of these shapes with the eye, for they were ethereal and quick as moths in the light of a lantern. They wheeled and wove and disappeared in the moving clouds, so that when they reappeared, it was impossible to tell whether it was the same or another like it. There was no way to count their numbers, or even to guess at what followed the first ranks of their advance. Behind them, the dust-cloud extended back to the horizon from which they had come.

Although our own ranks stood firm and steady in the sunlight, I could sense the wonder and trepidation that gripped them all. The studied conversation of Tanus' officers had dried up, and they stood in silent awe and watched the enemy deploy before us.

Then I realized that the dust-cloud was no longer advancing upon us. It hung in the sky, and gradually began to settle and clear, so that I was able dimly to make out the stationary vehicles in the vanguard. But I was now so confused and alarmed that I could not tell whether there were a thousand of them or more.

We would learn later that this hiatus was always part of the Shepherd

King's attack plan. I did not know it then, but during this lull they were regrouping and watering and gathering themselves for the final advance.

A terrible stillness had fallen on our ranks. It was so profound that the whisper of the breeze was loud through the rocks and the wadis of the hill on which we stood. The only movement was the flutter and swirl of our battle standards at the head of each division. I saw the Blue Crocodile banner waving in the centre of our line, and I took comfort from it.

Slowly, the dust-clouds subsided and row after row of the Hyksos' craft were revealed to us. They were still too distant to make out details, but I saw that those in the rear were much larger than those leading their army. It seemed to me that they were roofed over with sails of cloth or leather. From these I saw that men were unloading what looked like large water jars and carrying them forward. I wondered what men could consume such large quantities of water. Everything these foreigners did was a puzzle and made no sense to me.

The silence and the waiting drew out until every muscle and nerve in my body screamed out with the strain. Then suddenly there was movement again.

From the front ranks of the Hyksos formations some of these strange vehicles started towards us. A murmur went up from our ranks as we saw how fast they were moving. After that short period of rest, they seemed to have doubled their speed. The range closed and another cry went up from our host as we realized that these vehicles were each being drawn by a pair of extraordinary beasts.

They stood as tall as the wild oryx, with the same stiff, upstanding mane along the crest of their arched necks. They were not horned like the oryx, but their heads were more gracefully formed. Their eyes were large and their nostrils flared. Their legs were long and hoofed. Striding out with a peculiar daintiness, they seemed merely to brush the surface of the desert.

Even now, after all these years, I can recapture the thrill of gazing at a horse for the first time. In my mind the beauty of the hunting cheetah paled beside these marvellous beasts. At the same time we were all filled with fear of them, and I heard one of the officers near me cry out, 'Surely these monsters are killers, and eaters of human flesh! What abomination is this that is visited upon us?'

A stirring of horror ran through our formations, as we expected these beasts to fall upon us and devour us, like ravening lions. But the leading vehicle swung away and sped parallel to our front rank. It moved on spinning discs, and I stared at it in wonder. For the first few moments I was so stunned by what I was looking at that my mind refused to absorb it all. If anything, my first sight of a chariot was almost as moving as the horses that drew it. There was a long yoke-pole between the galloping pair, connected to what I later came to know as the axle. The high dashboard was gilded with gold leaf and the side-panels were cut low to allow the archer to shoot his arrows to either side.

All this I took in at a glance, and then my whole attention focused on the spinning discs on which the chariot sailed so smoothly and swiftly over the rough ground. For a thousand years we Egyptians had been the most cultured and civilized men on earth; in the sciences and the religions we had far outstripped all other nations. However, in all our learning and wisdom we had conceived nothing like this. Our sledges churned the earth on wooden runners that dissipated the strength of the oxen that dragged them, or we hauled great blocks of stone over wooden rollers without taking the next logical step.

I stared at the first wheel I had ever seen, and the simplicity and the beauty of it burst in upon me like lightning flaring in my head. I understood it instantly, and scorned myself for not having discovered it of my own accord. It was genius of the highest order, and now I realized that we stood to be destroyed by this wonderful invention in the same way as it must have annihilated the red usurper in the Lower Kingdom.

The golden chariot sped across our front, just out of bowshot. As it drew opposite us, I dragged my gaze from those miraculously spinning wheels and the fierce and terrifying creatures that drew them, and I looked at the two men in the cockpit of the chariot. One was clearly the driver. He leaned out over the dashboard and he seemed to control the galloping team by means of long plaited cords of leather attached to their heads. The taller man who stood behind him was a king. There was no doubting his imperial bearing.

I saw instantly that he was an Asian, with amber skin and a hooked, aquiline nose. His beard was black and thick, cut square across his breastplates, curled and intricately plaited with coloured ribbons. His body armour was a glittering skin of bronze fish-scales, while his crown was tall and square; the gold was embossed with images of some strange god and set with precious stones. His weapons hung on the side-panel of the chariot, close to his hands. His broad-bladed sword in its leather and gold scabbard had a handle of ivory and silver. Beside it, two leather quivers bulged with arrows, and each shaft was fletched with bright feathers. Later I would come to know how the Hyksos loved gaudy colours. The king's bow on its rack beside him was of an unusual shape that I had never seen before. It was not the simple, clean arc of our Egyptian bows; on the Hyksos bow, the upper and lower limbs recurved at the tips.

As the chariot flew down our line, the king leaned out and planted a lance in the earth. It was tipped with a crimson pennant, and the men around me growled in perturbation. 'What is he doing? What purpose does the lance serve? Is it a religious symbol, or is it a challenge?'

I gaped at the fluttering pennant, but my wits were dulled by all that I had seen, it meant nothing to me. The chariot sped on, still just out of bowshot, and the crowned Asian planted another lance, then wheeled and came back. He had seen Pharaoh on his throne and he halted below him. The horses were lathered with sweat, it foamed on their flanks like lace. Their eyes rolled ferociously and their nostrils flared so that the pink mucous lining was exposed. They nodded their heads on long, arched necks and their manes flew like the tresses of a beautiful woman in the sunlight.

The Hyksos greeted Pharaoh Mamose, Son of Ra, Divine Ruler of the Two Kingdoms, May He Live For Ever, with contempt. It was a laconic and ironic wave of a mailed hand, and he laughed. The challenge was as clear as if it had been spoken in perfect Egyptian. His mocking laughter floated across to us, and the ranks of our army growled with anger, a sound like far-off thunder in the summer air.

A small movement below me caught my attention, and I looked down just as Tanus took one step forward and flung up the great bow Lanata. He loosed an arrow and it rose in a high arcing trajectory against the milky-blue sky. The Hyksos was out of range to any other bow, but not to Lanata. The arrow reached its zenith and then dropped like a stooping falcon, full at the centre of the Asian king's chest. The watching multitude gasped with the length and power and aim of that shot. Three hundred paces it flew, and at the very last moment the Hyksos threw up his bronze shield and the arrow buried its head in the centre of the target. It was done with such contemptuous ease that we were all amazed and confounded.

Then the Hyksos seized his own strangely shaped bow from the rack beside him. With one movement he nocked an arrow, and drew and let it fly. It rose higher than Tanus had reached, and it sailed over his head. Fluting like the wing of a goose, it dropped towards me. I could not move and it might have impaled me without my attempting to avoid it, but it passed my head by an arm's-length and struck the base of Pharaoh's throne behind me. It quivered in the cedar strut like an insult, and the Hyksos king laughed again and wheeled his chariot and sped away, back across the plain, to rejoin his own host.

I knew then that we were doomed. How could we stand against these speeding chariots, and the recurved bows that so easily outranged the finest archer in our ranks? I was not alone in my dreadful expectations. As the squadrons of chariots began their final fateful evolutions out on the plain and sped towards us in waves, a moan of despair went up from the army of Egypt. I understood then how the forces of the red pretender had been scattered without a struggle, and the usurper had died with his sword still in its scabbard.

On the run, the flying chariots merged into columns four abreast and came directly at us. Only then did my mind clear, and I started down the slope at full pelt. Panting, I reached Tanus' side and shouted at him, 'The pennant lances mark the weak points in our line! Their main strike will come through us there and there!'

Somehow the Hyksos had known our battle order, and had recognized the laps in our formation. Their king had planted his pennants exactly between our divisions. The idea of a spy or a traitor occurred to me even then, but in the urgency of the moment I thrust it aside, and it was for the moment forgotten.

Tanus responded to my warning instantly, and shouted an order for our pickets to race forward and seize the pennants. I wanted him to move them, so that we could receive the enemy thrust on our strongest front, but there was no time for that. Before our pickets could reach and throw down the markers, the spear-head of flying chariots bore down upon them. Some of our men were shot down with arrows from the bouncing, swerving chariots. The aim of the enemy charioteers was uncanny.

The survivors turned and raced back, trying to regain the illusory safety of our lines. The chariots overhauled them effortlessly. The drivers controlled the galloping, plunging teams of horses with a lover's touch. They did not run their victims down directly, but swerved to pass them at the length of less than a cubit. It was only then that I noticed the knives. They were curved outwards from the spinning hub of the wheels like the fangs of some monstrous crocodile.

I saw one of our men struck squarely by the whirling blades. He seemed to dissolve in a bright cloud of blood. One of his severed arms was thrown high in the air and the bleeding chunks of his mutilated torso were dashed into the rocky earth as the chariot flew on without the least check. The phalanx of chariots was still aimed directly at the lap in our front line, and though I heard Kratas yelling orders to reinforce it, it was far too late.

The column of chariots crashed into our defensive wall of shields and spears, and tore through it as though it were as insubstantial as a drift of river mist. In one instant our formation, that had stood the assault of the finest Syrian and Hurrian warriors, was cleaved and shattered.

The horses spurned our strongest and heaviest men under their hooves. The whirling wheel-knives hacked through their armour and lopped off heads and limbs, as though they were the tenderest shoots of the vine. From the high carriages the charioteers showered arrows and javelins into our tightly packed ranks, then they tore on through the breach they had forced, passing entirely through our formations, fanning out behind us and driving at full tilt along our rear files, still hurling their missiles into our unprotected rear.

When our troops turned to face this assault on their rear, another phalanx of racing chariots crashed into them from the open plain. The first assault split our army in twain, dividing Tanus from Kratas on the right wing. Then those that followed so swiftly cut up the two halves into smaller, isolated groups. We were no longer a cohesive whole. Little bands of fifty and a hundred men stood back-to-back and fought with the courage of the doomed.

Across the plain on wings of swirling dust, the Hyksos came on endlessly. Behind the light two-wheeled chariots followed the heavy four-wheeled war carts, each carrying ten men. The sides of the carts were screened with sheep fleeces. Our arrows slapped ineffectually into the thick, soft wool, our swords could not reach the men in the high body of the carts. They shot their points down into us and broke up the confused masses of our fighting men into scattered knots of terrified survivors. When one of our captains rallied a few men to counter-attack them, the war carts wheeled away and stopped out of range. With their awful recurved bows, they broke up our gallant charges, and the moment we wavered, they came rolling back upon us.

I was intensely aware of the moment when the conflict ceased to be a battle and became nothing more than a massacre. The remains of Kratas' division out on our right flank had fired the last of their arrows. The Hyksos had picked out their captains by their plumed helmets and shot nearly every one of them down. The men were disarmed and leaderless. They broke into rout. They threw down their weapons and ran for the river. But it was not possible to outrun a Hyksos chariot.

The broken troops ran into Tanus' divison below the hillock, and tangled with it. With their panicking, struggling masses they clogged and smothered what little resistance Tanus was still capable of offering. The terror was infectious and the centre of our line broke and tried to fly, but the deadly chariots circled them, like wolves around the flock.

In all that chaos, in the bloody shambles and the tumult of defeat, only the Blues stood firm around Tanus and the Crocodile standard. They were a little island in the torrent of defeated men, even the chariots could not break them up, for, with the instinct of a great general, Tanus had gathered them and pulled them back into the one patch of rocks and gulleys where the Hyksos could not come at them. The Blues were a wall, a bulwark around the throne of Pharaoh.

Because I had been at the king's side, I was in the centre of this ring of heroes. It was difficult to keep my feet, for all around me men struggled and surged, washed back and forth by the waves of battle, like seaweed clinging to a rock in the full stream of tide and surf.

I saw Kratas fight his way through from the shattered right wing to join us. His plumed helmet attracted the Hyksos arrows and they flew around his head thickly as locusts, but he came through unscathed, and our ring opened for him. He saw me, and he laughed with huge delight. 'By Seth's steaming turds, Taita, this is more fun than building palaces for little princes, is it not?' He was never famous for his repartee, was Kratas, and I was too busy staying on my feet to bother with a reply.

He and Tanus met close to the throne. Kratas grinned at him like an idiot. 'I'd not have missed this for all Pharaoh's treasure. I want one of those Hyksos sledges for myself.' Neither was Kratas one of Egypt's greatest engineers. Even now he still believed that the chariots were some type of sledge. That was as far as his imagination reached.

Tanus tapped the side of his helmet with the flat of his sword in greeting, and although his tone was light, his expression was grim. He was a general who had just lost a battle and an army, and an empire.

'Our work here is finished for today,' he told Kratas. 'Let us see if these Hyksos monsters can swim as well as they run. Back to the river!' Then, shoulder-to-shoulder, the two of them shoved their way through the ranks towards the throne where I still stood.

I could see over their heads, over the periphery of our little defensive ring, out over the plain where our broken army was streaming away towards the river, still harried by the squadrons of chariots.

I saw the golden chariot of the Hyksos king wheel out of formation and cleave its way towards us, trampling our men under the flying hooves and chopping them up with the glittering wheel-knives. The driver brought the horses to a rearing, plunging halt before he reached the barrier of rocks which protected us. Balancing easily on the footplates, the Hyksos drew his recurved bow and aimed at me, or so it seemed. Even as I ducked, I realized that the arrow was not meant for me. It shrieked over my head and I turned to watch its flight. It struck Pharaoh high in the chest, and buried half its length in his flesh.

Pharaoh gave a hoarse cry and tottered on his high throne. There was no blood, for the shaft had plugged the wound, but the feathers were a pretty scarlet and green. Pharaoh slid sideways and collapsed forward towards me, and I opened my arms to receive him. His weight bore me to my knees, so I did not see the Hyksos king's chariot wheel away, but I heard his mocking laughter receding as he dashed back across the plain to lead the slaughter.

Tanus stooped over me as I held the king. 'How badly is he struck?' he demanded.

'He is killed,' the reply rose to my lips unthinkingly. The angle of entry and the depth of the wound could mean that only one outcome was possible, but I choked off the words before they were spoken. I knew that our men would lose heart if Great Egypt was slain. Instead I said, 'He is hard hit. But if we carry him back aboard the state barge, he may recover.'

'Bring me a shield here!' Tanus roared, and when it came we gently lifted Pharaoh on to it. There was still no blood, but I knew his chest was filling like a wine jar. Quickly, I felt for the head of the arrow, but it had not emerged from his back. The point was still buried deep within the cage of his ribs. I snapped off the protruding shaft, and covered him with his linen shawl.

'Taita,' he whispered. 'Will I see my son again?'

'Yes, Mighty Egypt, I swear it to you.'

'And my dynasty will survive?'

'Even as the Mazes of Ammon-Ra have foretold.'

'Ten strong men here!' Tanus bellowed. They crowded around the makeshift litter, and lifted the king between them.

'Form the tortoise! Close up on me, the Blues!' With interlocking shields, the Blues formed a wall around the king.

Tanus raced to the Blue Crocodile which still waved in our midst and tore it from its pole. He wound it around his waist and knotted the ends across his belly.

'If the Hyksos want this rag, they had better come and take it from me,' he shouted, and his men cheered this piece of foolish bravado.

'All together now! Back to the ships! At the double!'

The moment we left the shelter of our little rocky redoubt, the chariots came at us.

'Leave the men!' Tanus had found the key. 'Kill their beasts!' As the first chariot bore down upon us, Tanus flexed Lanata. His bowmen drew with him, and they all fired on his example.

Half our arrows flew wide, for we were running over uneven ground and the archers were winded. Others struck the bodywork of the leading chariot, and the shafts snapped or pegged into the wood. Still other arrows rattled off the bronzed plates that covered the chests of the horses.

Only one arrow flew hard and true. From the great bow Lanata it sang with the wind in its feathers, and struck the offside horse in the forehead. The creature went down like a rockslide, tangling the traces and dragging its team-mate down in a cloud of dust and kicking hooves. The charioteers were hurled from the cockpit as the carriage somersaulted, and the other chariots veered away to avoid the wreckage. A jubilant shout went up from our ranks, and our pace picked up. This was our first success in all that dreadful day, and it manned and encouraged our little band of Blues.

'On me, the Blues!' Tanus roared, and then, incredibly, he began to sing. Immediately the men around him shouted the opening chorus of the regimental battle hymn. Their voices were strained and rough with thirst and effort, and there was little tune or beauty to it, but it was a sound to lift the heart and thrill the blood. I threw back my head and sang with them, and my voice soared clear and sweet.

'Horus bless you, my little canary,' Tanus laughed at me, and we raced for the river. The chariots circled us with the first wariness to their manoeuvres that they had demonstrated all that day. They had seen the fate of their comrade. Then three of them swung across the front of our tortoise, and in vee-formation charged at us head-on.

'Shoot at the heads of the beasts!' Tanus shouted, and led them with an arrow that brought another horse crashing to its knees. The chariot overturned and was smashed to pieces on the stony ground, and the other vehicles in the formation veered away.

As our formation passed the shattered chariot, some of our men ran out to stab the squealing horses that were trapped in the wreckage. Already they hated and feared these animals with an almost superstitious dread, which was reflected in this vindictive piece of cruelty. They killed the fallen charioteers also, but without the same rancour.

With two of their chariots destroyed, the Hyksos seemed reluctant to attack our little formation again, and we were rapidly approaching the morass of muddy fields and flooded irrigation ditches that marked the river-bank. I think that at that stage I was the only one of us who realized that the wheeled enemy could not follow us into the swamp.

Although I ran beside the king's litter, I could see, through the gaps in our ranks, the dying acts of the battle that were being played out around us.

Ours was the only surviving detachment that still showed any cohesion. The rest of the Egyptian army was a formless and terrified rabble streaming across the plain. Most of them had thrown aside their weapons. When one of the chariots drove at them, they dropped to their knees and held up their hands in supplication. The Hyksos showed them no quarter. They did not even waste arrows upon them but swung in close to chop them to tatters with the spinning wheel-knives, or to lean out of the cockpit with the lance and cut them down, or to smash in their skulls with the stone-headed maces. They dragged the victim behind them, still spiked on the lance, until the barbed spear-head disengaged, and only then did they leave the crumpled corpse lying in their dust.

I had never seen such butchery. I had never read of anything like it in all the accounts of ancient battles. The Hyksos slaughtered our people in their thousands and their tens of thousands. The plain of Abnub was like a field of dhurra corn after the reapers had been through it with their scythes. Our dead were piled in drifts and windrows.

For one thousand years our armies had been invincible and our swords had triumphed across the world. Here on the field of Abnub an age had come to an end. In the midst of this carnage the Blues sang, and I with them though my eyes burned with tears of shame.

The first irrigation ditch was just ahead when another chariot formation swung out on our flank and came driving hard at us, three abreast. Our arrows fell all about them, but they came on with the horses blowing hard through gaping red mouths and with the drivers screaming encouragement at them. I saw Tanus shoot twice, but each time his arrows were deflected or were cheated by the erratic swerve and bounce of the chariots. The formation thundered into us and broke the tortoise of interlocking shields.

Two of the men carrying Pharaoh's litter were cut to shreds by the wheel-knives, and the wounded king was tumbled to the earth. I dropped to my knees beside him and covered him with my own body to protect him from the Hyksos lances, but the chariots did not linger. It was their concern never to allow themselves to become entangled or surrounded. They raced on and clear before our men could reach them with the sword. Only then did they wheel and regroup, and come back.

Tanus reached down and hauled me to my feet. 'If you get yourself killed, who will be left to compose a hero's ode to us?' he scolded me, then he shouted for men. Between them they picked up the king's litter and ran with it for the nearest ditch.

I could hear the squeal of the chariot wheels bearing down on us, but I never looked back. In ordinary circumstances I am a strong runner, but now I outdistanced the litter-bearers as though their feet were chained to the earth. I attempted to hurdle the ditch, but it was too wide for me to cross in a single leap, and I landed knee-deep in the black mud. The chariot that was following me struck the bank of the ditch and one of its wheels shattered. The body of the vehicle toppled into the ditch and almost crushed me, but I managed to throw myself aside.

Swiftly the Blues stabbed and hacked the horses and men as they lay helplessly in the mud, but I took the moment to wade back to the chariot.

The up-ended wheel was still spinning in the air. I placed my hand upon it as I studied it, and let it rotate beneath my fingers. I stood there only as long as it took me to draw three deep breaths, but at the end of that time I had learned as much about wheel construction as any Hyksos, and had the first inkling of the improvements I could make to it.

'By Seth's melodious farts, Taita, you'll have us all killed, if you start daydreaming now!' Kratas yelled at me.

I shook myself and seized one of the recurved bows from the rack on the side of the chariot body and an arrow from the quiver. I wanted to examine these at my leisure. Then I waded across the ditch with them in my hand, just as the squadron of chariots came thundering back, running parallel to the ditch and firing their arrows down amongst us.

The men carrying the king were a hundred paces ahead of me, and I was the last of our little band. Behind me the charioteers roared with frustration that they were unable to follow us, and they shot their arrows around me as I ran. One of them struck my shoulder, but the point failed to penetrate and the shaft glanced away. It left a purple bruise which I only discovered much later.

Although I had started from so far behind them, I caught up with the litter-bearers by the time we reached the main bank of the Nile. The river-bank was crowded with the survivors of the battle. Nearly all of these were weaponless and very few were unwounded. They were all driven by a single desire, to return as swiftly as possible to the ships that had brought them down-river from Thebes.

Tanus singled me out and called me to him as the litter-bearers came up. 'I place Pharaoh in your hands now, Taita. Take him on board the royal barge and do all you can to save his life.'

'When will you come aboard?' I asked him.

'My duty is here, with my men. I must save all of them that I can, and get them embarked.' He turned from me and strode away, picking out the captains and commanders from amongst his beaten rabble, and shouting his orders.

I went to the king and knelt beside the litter. He was still alive. I examined him briefly and found that he hovered on the edge of consciousness. His skin was as clammy-cold as that of a reptile, and his breathing was shallow. There was only a thin rime of blood around that arrow-shaft which had seeped up from the wound, but when I laid my ear to his chest I heard the blood bubbling in his lungs with each breath he drew, and a thin red snake of it crawled from his mouth down his chin. I knew that whatever I could do to save him, I must do quickly. I shouted for a boat to take him out to the barge.

The litter-bearers lifted him into the skiff, and I sat in the bilges beside him as we sculled out to where the great state barge lay anchored in the main flow of the current.

THE KING'S suite crowded the ship's side to watch us approach. There was a gaggle of the royal women and all those courtiers and priests who had taken no part in the fighting. I recognized my mistress standing amongst them as we drew closer. Her face was very anxious and pale, and she held her young son by his hand.

As soon as those on board the barge looked down into our skiff and saw the king on his litter, with the blood on his face that I had been unable to wipe away, a terrible cry of alarm and mourning went up from them. The women keened and wailed, and the men howled with despair, like dogs.

Of all the women, my mistress stood closest at hand as the king was lifted up the ship's side and his litter laid on the deck. As the senior wife, hers was the duty to attend him first. The others gave her space as she stooped over him and wiped the mud and the blood from his haggard face. He recognized her, for I heard him breathe her name and ask for his son. My mistress called the prince to him, and he smiled softly and tried to raise his hand to touch the boy, but he did not have the strength, and the hand dropped back to his side.

I ordered the crew to carry Pharaoh to his quarters, and my mistress came to me quickly and asked low and urgently, 'What of Tanus? Is he safe? Oh, Taita, tell me that he is not slain by this dreadful enemy!'

'He is safe. Nothing can harm him. I have given you the vision of the Mazes. All this was foreseen. But now I must go to the king, and I will need your help. Leave Memnon with his nursemaids, and come with me.'

I was still black and crusted with river mud, and so was Pharaoh, for he had fallen in the same ditch as I had. I asked Queen Lostris and two of the other royal women to strip and bathe him and lay him on fresh white linen sheets, while I returned to the deck to bathe in buckets of river water that the sailors hauled up over the side. I never operate in filth, for I have found by experience that for some reason it affects the patient adversely and favours the accumulation of the morbid humours.

While I was thus occupied, I was watching the east bank where our broken army was huddled behind the protection of ditch and swamp. This sorry rabble had once been a proud and mighty force, and I was filled with shame and fear. Then I saw the tall figure of Tanus striding amongst them, and wherever he moved, the men stood up out of the mud, and reassembled into the semblance of military discipline. Once I even caught the sound of ragged and unconvincing cheers on the wind.

If the enemy should send their infantry through the swamps now, the slaughter and the rout would be complete. Not a man of all our mighty army would survive, for even Tanus would be able to offer little resistance. However, although I peered anxiously into the east, I could make out no sign of infantry shields in phalanx or the sparkle of advancing spear-heads at the shoulder-slope.

There was still that terrible dust-cloud hanging over the plain of Abnub, so the chariots were at work out there, but without enemy infantry falling upon him, Tanus could still salvage some little comfort out of this dreadful day. It was a lesson I was to remember, and which stood us in good stead in the years ahead. Chariots might win the battle, but only the foot-soldiers could consolidate it.

The battle out there on the river-bank was now entirely Tanus' affair, while I had another battle to fight with death in the cabin of the state barge.

'WE ARE not entirely without hope,' I whispered to my mistress, when I returned to the king's side. 'Tanus is rallying his troops, and if any man alive is capable of saving this very Egypt from the Hyksos, he is the one.' Then I turned to the king, and for the moment all else was forgotten but my patient.

As is often my way, I murmured my thoughts aloud as I examined the wound. It was less than an hour, measured by a water-clock, since the fateful arrow had struck, and yet the flesh around the broken-off stub of the shaft was swollen and empurpled.

'The arrow must come out. If I leave the barb in there, he will be dead by tomorrow's dawn.' I had thought the king could no longer hear me, but as I spoke, he opened his eyes and looked directly into mine.

'Is there a chance that I will live?' he asked.

'There is always a chance.' I was glib and insincere. I heard it in my own voice, and the king heard it also.

'Thank you, Taita. I know you will strive for me, and I absolve you now from all blame, if you should fail.' This was generous of him, for many physicians before me have felt the strangling-rope as punishment for letting the life of a king slip through their fingers.

'The head of the arrow is deeply lodged. There will be a great deal of pain, but I will give you the powder of the Red Shepenn, the sleeping-flower, to still it.'

'Where is my senior wife, Queen Lostris?' he asked, and my mistress replied immediately, 'I am here, my lord.'

'There is aught that I would say. Summon all my ministers and my scribes, that my proclamation may be witnessed and recorded.' They crowded into the hot little cabin and stood in silence.

Then Pharaoh reached out to my mistress. 'Take my hand, and listen to my words,' he ordered, and she sank down beside him and did as she was ordered, while the king went on speaking in a soft and breathless whisper.

'If I should die, Queen Lostris will stand as regent for my son. I have learned in the time that I have known her that she is a person of strength and good sense. If she were not, I would not have laid this charge upon her.'

'Thank you, Great Egypt, for your trust,' Queen Lostris murmured low, and now Pharaoh spoke directly to her, although every person in the cabin could hear him.

'Surround yourself with wise and honest men. Instruct my son in all the virtues of kingship that you and I have discussed. You know my mind on all these matters.'

'I will, Majesty.'

'When he is old enough to take up the flail and the crook, do not attempt to withhold it from him. He is my lineage and my dynasty.'

'Willingly I shall do what you order, for he is not only the son of his father, but my son also.'

'While you rule, rule wisely and care for my people. There will be many who seek to wrest the emblems of kingship from your grasp – not only this new and cruel enemy, this Hyksos, but others who stand even closer to your throne. But you must oppose them all. Keep the double crown intact for my son.'

'Even as you say, divine Pharaoh.'

The king fell silent for a while and I thought that he had slipped over the edge into unconsciousness, but suddenly he groped for the hand of my mistress again.

'There is one last charge I have for you. My tomb and my temple are incomplete. Now they are threatened, as is all my realm, by this terrible defeat that we have suffered. Unless my generals can stop them, these Hyksos will sweep on to Thebes.'

'Let us petition the gods that it does not come to pass,' my mistress murmured.

'I charge you most strictly that you will see me embalmed and interred with all my treasure in accordance with the strictest protocols of the *Book of the Dead*.'

My mistress was silent. I think that she realized even then just what an onerous charge this was that Pharaoh had laid upon her.

His grip upon her hand tightened until his knuckles turned white, and she winced. 'Swear this to me on your own life and hope for immortality. Swear it before my ministers of state and all my royal suite. Swear it to me in the name of Hapi, your patron god, and on the names of the blessed trinity, Osiris and Isis and Horus.'

Queen Lostris looked across at me with a piteous appeal in her eyes. I knew that once she had given it, she would honour her word at all and any cost to herself. In this, she was like her lover. She and Tanus were bound by the same code of chivalry. I knew also that those close to her must expect to pay the same price. An oath to the king now might one day return to burden us all, Prince Memnon and the slave Taita included. And yet there was no manner in which she could gainsay the king as he lay upon his death-bed. I nodded to her almost imperceptibly. Later I would examine the finer points of this oath, and like a law scribe I would mould it a little closer to reasonable interpretation.

'I swear on Hapi, and on all the gods,' Queen Lostris said, softly but clearly, and there would be a hundred times in the years ahead when I would wish she had not done so.

The king sighed with satisfaction and let her hand slip from his. 'Then I am ready for you, Taita. And for whatever fate the gods have decreed. Only let me kiss my son once more.'

While they brought our fine young prince to him, I drove the crowd of nobles from the cabin with little ceremony. Then I prepared a draught of the Red Shepenn for him and made it as strong as I dared, for I knew that pain could undo all my best efforts and destroy my patient as swiftly as a slip of my scalpel.

When he had drunk it all, I waited for the pupils of his eyes to contract to pinpoints, and for the lids to droop over them. Then I sent the prince away with his nursemaids.

ON LEAVING Thebes I had expected to have to deal with arrow wounds, so I had brought my spoons with me. I had designed this instrument myself, although there was a quack in Gaza and another in Memphis who both claimed it was their invention. I blessed the spoons and my scalpels in the lamp flame, and then washed my hands in hot wine.

'I do not think it is wise to use one of your spoons when the head of the arrow is so deep and so near the heart,' my mistress told me as she watched my preparations. There are occasions when she speaks as though the student had outpaced the master.

'If I leave the arrow, it will certainly mortify. I will have killed him just as surely as if I had chopped his head off his shoulders. This is the only way that I will have a chance of saving him.'

For a moment we looked into each other's eyes, and we spoke without words. This was the vision of the Mazes of Ammon-Ra. Did we wish to avoid the benevolent consequences to ourselves?

'He is my husband. He is Pharaoh.' My mistress took my hand to emphasize her words. 'Save him, Taita. Save him, if you can.'

'You know that I will,' I answered.

'Do you need me to help you?' She had assisted me so very often before. I nodded my assent, and stooped over the king.

There were three ways that I might have attempted to withdraw the arrow. The first would be to pluck it out. I have heard of a surgeon in Damascus who bends down the supple branch of a tree and attaches this to the shaft. When he releases the branch, the arrow is whipped out of the living flesh by the strength of the sapling. I have never tried such brutal treatment for I am convinced that very few men would survive it.

The second method would be to push the arrow through the limb or the torso until the barbed head emerges on the far side. To achieve this, it can be driven along its original path with a mallet, like a nail through a plank. Then the barb is sawn off and the shaft drawn free. This treatment is almost as brutal as the first.

My method is the Taita spoon. I have named the spoon after myself in all modesty, for the claims of those others are spurious, and posterity needs to be informed of my genius.

Firstly, I examined the Hyksos arrow that I had salvaged along with the bow from the overturned chariot. I was surprised to find that the arrow-head was of worked flint rather than of bronze. Of course, flint is cheaper and easier to procure in quantity, but I have seldom known a general who tries to economize when setting out to seize a kingdom. This flint arrow-head spoke eloquently of the Hyksos' limited resources, and suggested a reason for his savage attack upon this very Egypt. Wars are fought for land or wealth, and it seemed that the Hyksos was short of both these commodities.

I had to hope that the arrow-head buried in Pharaoh's breast was of the same shape and design. I matched a pair of my spoons to the razor-edged piece of stone. My spoons are of various sizes, and I selected a pair that enclosed the head snugly, masking the wicked barbs with smoothly polished metal.

By this time, the drug had worked its full magic, and Pharaoh lay unconscious upon his cloud-white linen sheets, with the snapped-off arrow standing out as far as my forefinger from the skin, which was wrinkled with age and covered with the frosted curls of his body hair. I laid my ear on his chest once more and heard his breath sigh and gurgle in his lungs. Satisfied that he still lived, I greased the spoons that I had selected with mutton fat, to lubricate their entry into the wound. I laid the spoons close at hand and took up one of my keenest scalpels.

I nodded to the four strong guards that Queen Lostris had selected for me while I was busy with my preparations, and they took hold of Pharaoh's wrists and ankles and held him down firmly. Queen Lostris sat at the king's head and placed the wooden tube from my medical chest between his lips and deep back into his throat. This would keep his windpipe clear and open. It would also prevent him from biting or swallowing his own tongue, or grinding his teeth together and snapping them off, when the pain assaulted him too fiercely.

'First I have to enlarge the wound around the shaft to enable me to reach the head of the arrow,' I muttered to myself, and I pressed the point of the scalpel down along the line of the shaft. Pharaoh's whole body stiffened, but the men held him down remorselessly.

I worked swiftly, for I have learned that speed is crucial in an operation of this nature, if the patient is to survive. I opened a slit on each side of the shaft. The human skin is tough and elastic and would inhibit the entry of the spoons, so I had to get through it.

I dropped the knife and took up the pair of lubricated spoons. Using the arrow-shaft as a guide, I eased them deeper and deeper into the wound, until only the long handles still protruded.

By this time Pharaoh was writhing and twisting in the grip of his restrainers. Sweat was pouring from every pore of his skin, and running back over his shaven skull with its stubble of thin grey hair. His screams rang through the tube in his mouth, and reverberated through the hull of the barge.

I had taught myself to ignore the agonized distress of my patients, and I slid the spoons deeper into the widely distended mouth of the wound until I felt them touch the flint of the arrow-head. This was the delicate part of the operation. Using the handles like a pair of tweezers, I levered the spoons apart and worked them over the arrow-head. When I felt them close of their own accord, I hoped that I had entirely enclosed the coarse flint and masked the barbs.

I took a careful grasp of the handles of the spoons and of the reed shaft of the arrow, and pulled back on them all together. If the barbs were still free, they would have immediately snagged in Pharaoh's flesh and resisted my pull. I could have shouted aloud with relief as I felt it all begin to yield. Still, the suction of the wet and clinging flesh was considerable, and I had to use all my strength to draw the shaft.

Pharaoh's agony was dreadful to hear and behold, as the mass of reed and stone and metal was dragged through his chest. The Red Shepenn drug had long ago ceased to be of any effect, and the pain was raw and savage. I knew I was doing fearful damage, and I could feel tissue and sinew tearing.

My own sweat ran down into my eyes and burned and half-blinded me, but I never released my pull until suddenly the blood-smeared arrow came free in my hands and I staggered backwards across the cabin and crashed into the bulkhead. I leaned against it for a moment, exhausted with the effort. I watched the dark, half-congealed blood trickle and spurt from the wound for a long moment, before I could rally myself and stagger back to stem it.

I smeared the wound with precious myrrh and crystallized honey, and then bound it up tightly with clean linen bandages. As I worked, I recited the incantation for the binding up of wounds:

> I bind thee up, oh creature of Seth.
> I stop up thy mouth.
> Retreat before me, red tide.
> Retire before me, red flower of death.
> I banish you, oh red dog of Seth.

This was the recitation for a bleeding wound caused by blade or arrow. There are specific verses for all types of wound, from burns to those inflicted by the fangs or claws of a lion. Learning these is a large part of the training of a physician. I am never certain in my own mind as to just how efficacious these incantations are; however, I believe that I owe it to my patients to employ any possible means at my disposal for their cure.

In the event, Pharaoh seemed much easier after the binding-up, and I could leave him sleeping in the care of his women and go back on deck. I needed the cool river airs to revive me, for the operation had drained me almost as much as it had Pharaoh.

By this time it was evening, and the sun was settling wearily upon the stark western hills and throwing its last ruddy glow over the battlefield. There had been no assault by the Hyksos infantry, and Tanus was still bringing off the remains of his vanquished army from the river-bank to the galleys anchored in the stream.

I watched the boatloads of wounded and exhausted men passing our anchored barge, and I felt a deep compassion for them, as I did for all our people. This would be for ever the most dire day in our history. Then I saw that the dust-cloud of the Hyksos chariots was already beginning to move southwards towards Thebes. The clouds were incarnadined by the sunset to the colour of blood. It was for me a sign, and my compassion turned to dread.

IT WAS dark by the time that Tanus himself came aboard the state barge. In the light of the torches he looked like one of the corpses from the battlefield. He was pale with fatigue and dust. His cloak was stiff with dried blood and mud, and there were dark, bruised shadows under his eyes. When he saw me, his first concern was to ask after Pharaoh.

'I have removed the arrow,' I told him. 'But the wound is deep and near the heart. He is very weak, but if he survives three days, then I will be able to save him.'

'What of your mistress and her son?' he always asked this, whenever we met.

'Queen Lostris is tired, for she helped me with the operation. But she is with the king now. The prince is as bonny as ever and sleeps now with his nurses.'

I saw Tanus reel on his feet, and knew that he was close to the end of even his great strength. 'You must rest now—' I began, but he shook off my hand.

'Bring lamps here,' he ordered. 'Taita, fetch your writing-brushes and ink-pots and scrolls. I must send a warning to Nembet, lest he walk into the Hyksos trap even as I did.'

So Tanus and I sat half that night on the open deck, and this was the despatch for Nembet that he dictated to me:

> I greet you Lord Nembet, Great Lion of Egypt, Commander of the Ra division of the army of Pharaoh. May you live for ever!
>
> Know you that we have encountered the enemy Hyksos at the plain of Abnub. The Hyksos in his strength and ferocity is a terrible foe, and possessed of strange, swift craft that we cannot resist.
>
> Know you further that we have suffered a defeat and that our army is destroyed. We can no longer oppose the Hyksos.
>
> Know you further that Pharaoh is gravely wounded and in danger of his life.
>
> We urge you not to meet the Hyksos in an open field, for his craft are like the wind. Therefore take refuge behind walls of stone, or wait aboard your ships, to turn the enemy aside.
>
> The Hyksos has no ships of his own, and it is by means of our ships alone that we may prevail against him.
>
> We urge you to await our coming before committing your forces to battle.
>
> I call the protection of Horus and all the gods down upon you.
>
> It is Tanus, Lord Harrab, Commander of the Ptah division of the army of Pharaoh, who speaks thus.

I wrote out four copies of this message, and as I completed each, Tanus called for messengers to carry them to the Lord Nembet, Great Lion of Egypt, who was advancing from the south to reinforce us. Tanus sent two fast galleys speeding up-river, each with a fair copy of the despatches. Then he put his best runners ashore on the west bank, the opposite side of the river from the Hyksos army, and sent them off to find Nembet.

'Surely one of your scrolls will win through to Nembet. You can do no more until morning,' I reassured him. 'You must sleep now, for if you destroy yourself, then all of Egypt is destroyed with you.'

Even then he would not go to a cabin, but curled on the deck like a dog, so that he could be instantly ready for any new emergency. But I went to the cabin to be near my king and to give comfort to my mistress.

I was on deck again before the first glimmer of dawn. I arrived to hear Tanus giving orders to burn our fleet. It was not for me to question this decision, but he saw me gape incredulously at him, and when the messengers had been sent away he told me brusquely, 'I have just received the roll-call from my regimental commanders. Of the thirty thousand of my men who stood yesterday on the plain of Abnub to meet the chariots of the Hyksos, only seven thousand remain. Five thousand of those are wounded, and many will still die. Of those who are unwounded, very few are sailors. I am left with only sufficient men to work half our fleet. I must abandon the rest of our ships, but I cannot let them fall into the hands of the Hyksos.'

They used bundles of reeds to start the fires, and once they were set, they burned fiercely. It was a sad and terrible sight to watch, even for me and my mistress, who were not sailors. For Tanus it was far worse. He stood alone in the bows of the state barge, with despair and grief in every line of his face and in the set of those wide shoulders, as he watched his ships burn. For him they were living things, and beautiful.

Before all the court my mistress could not go to his side where she belonged, but she took my hand surreptitiously, and the two of us mourned for Tanus and for all Egypt as we watched those gallant craft burn like torches. The roaring pillars of flame from each vessel were sullied with black smoke, but still their ruddy light rivalled the approach of the sunrise.

At last Tanus gave the order to his hundred remaining galleys to weigh anchor, and our little fleet, laden with wounded and dying men, turned back into the south.

Behind us, the smoke from the funeral pyre of our fleet stood high into the early morning sky, while ahead of us the yellow dust-cloud stretched taller and wider along the east bank of the Nile as the chariot squadrons of the Hyksos drove deeper into the Upper Kingdom, towards helpless Thebes and all her treasures.

It seemed that the gods had turned their backs on Egypt and deserted us completely, for the wind, which usually blew so strongly from the north at this season of the year, died away completely, and then sprang up again with renewed vigour from the south. Thus we were forced to contend with both current and wind, and our ships were deeply laden with their cargoes of wounded. We were slow and heavy in the water, with the depleted crews slaving at the oars. We could not keep pace with the Hyksos army, and it drew away from us inexorably.

I was absorbed with my duties as physician to the king. However, on every other vessel in the fleet, men whom I could have saved were dying in their scores. Every time that I went on deck for a little fresh air and a short break from my vigil at the bedside of Pharaoh, I saw corpses being thrown over the side of the other galleys near us. At each splash there was a swirl of crocodiles beneath the surface. Those awful reptiles followed the fleet like vultures.

Pharaoh rallied strongly, and on the second day I was able to feed him a small bowl of broth. That evening he asked to see the prince again, and Memnon was brought to him.

Memnon was already at the age when he was as restless as a grasshopper and as noisy as a flock of starlings. Pharaoh had always been good with the boy, if inclined to over-indulgence, and Memnon delighted in his company. Already he was a beautiful boy, with clean, strong limbs and his mother's skin and great dark green eyes. His hair was curled like the pelt of a new-born black lamb, but in the sunlight, it was sparked with the flames of Tanus' ruddy mop.

Pharaoh's delight in Memnon was even more poignant than usual. The child and the promise that he had wrung from my mistress were his hope of immortality. Against my wishes he kept the child with him until after sunset. I knew that Memnon's boundless energy and his demands for attention were tiring the king, but I could not intervene until it was time for the prince's supper and he was led away by his nurses.

My mistress and I stayed on at the king's bedside, but he fell almost instantly into a death-like sleep. Even without his white make-up, he was as pale as the linen sheets on which he lay.

The next day was the third since the wounding, and therefore the most dangerous. If he could survive this day, then I knew I could save him. But when I woke in the dawn the cabin was thick with the musky stench of corruption. When I touched Pharaoh's skin, it burned my fingers like a kettle from the hearth. I called for my mistress, and she came stumbling through from her alcove behind the curtain where she slept.

'What is it, Taita?' She got no further, for the answer was plain upon my face. She stood beside me as I unbound the wound. The binding-up is a high art of the surgeon's skills, and I had sewn the linen bandages in place. Now I snipped the threads that held them and peeled them away.

'Merciful Hapi, pray for him!' Queen Lostris gagged at the stench. The crusted black scab that corked the mouth of the wound burst open, and thick green pus poured out in a slow and viscous stream.

'Mortification!' I whispered. This was the surgeon's nightmare, this evil humour that struck upon the third day and spread through the body like winter fire in the dry papyrus beds.

'What can we do?' she asked, and I shook my head.

'He will be dead before nightfall,' I told her, but we waited beside his bed for the inevitable. As the word spread through the ship that Pharaoh was dying, so the cabin filled with priests and women and courtiers. We waited in silence.

Tanus was the last to arrive, and he stood at the back of the throng with his helmet under his arm, in the position of respect and mourning. His gaze rested not on the death-bed, but upon Queen Lostris. She kept her face averted from his, but I knew that she was aware of him in every fibre of her body.

She covered her head with an embroidered linen shawl, but above the waistband of her skirt, she was naked. Since the prince had been weaned, her breasts had lost their heavy burden of milk. She was as slim as a virgin, and childbirth had not scarred her bosom or her supple belly with silver lines of striae. Her skin was as smooth and unblemished as though it had been freshly anointed with perfumed oil.

I laid wet cloths upon Pharaoh's burning body in an attempt to cool the fever, but the heat evaporated the moisture and I was forced to change them at short intervals. Pharaoh tossed about restlessly and cried out in delirium, haunted by all the terrors and monsters of the other world, who waited to receive him.

At times he recited snatches from the *Book of the Dead*. From childhood the priests had taught him to memorize the book that was the key and the map through the shades to the far fields of paradise:

> The crystal path has twenty-one turnings.
> The narrow way is thin as the blade of bronze.
> The goddess who guards the second pylon
> is treacherous and her ways are devious.
> Lady of flame, whore of the universe,
> with the mouth of a lioness,

> your vagina swallows men up,
> they are lost in your milky dugs.

Gradually his voice and his movements became weaker, and a little after the sun had made its noon, he gave one last shuddering sigh and was still. I stooped over him and felt for the life-throb in his throat, but there was none, and the skin was cooling under my touch.

'Pharaoh is dead,' I said softly, and closed the lids over his staring eyes. 'May he live for ever!'

The mourning cry went up from all who were assembled there, and my mistress led the royal women in the wild ululation of grief. It was a sound that chilled me and made invisible insects crawl upon my skin, so I left the cabin as soon as I was able. Tanus followed me out on to the deck and seized my arm.

'You did all in your power to save him?' he demanded roughly. 'This was not another of your devices?'

I knew that this unkind treatment of me was an expression of his own guilt and fear, so I was gentle in my reply. 'He was slain by the Hyksos arrow. I did all that was in my power to save him. It was the destiny of the Mazes of Ammon-Ra, and there is no guilt or fault in any of us.'

He sighed and placed one strong arm around my shoulders. 'I had not foreseen any of this. I thought only of my love for the queen and for our son. I should rejoice that she is free, but I cannot. Too much is lost and destroyed. All of us are merely grains of dhurra corn in the grinding-mill of the Mazes.'

'There will be a time of happiness for all of us hereafter,' I reassured him, although I had no basis for this claim. 'But there is still a sacred duty on my mistress, and through her, on you and me also.' And I reminded him of the oath that Queen Lostris had sworn to the king, that she would preserve his earthly body and give it proper burial to allow his *Ka* to move on to the fields of paradise.

'Tell me how I can help in this,' Tanus replied simply, 'but remember that the Hyksos is sweeping through the Upper Kingdom ahead of us, and I cannot guarantee that Pharaoh's tomb will not be violated.'

'Then, if needs be, we must find another tomb for him. Our first concern must be to preserve his body. In this heat it will be decaying and crawling with maggots before the sun sets. I am not skilled in the embalmer's art, but I know of only one way in which we can keep our trust.'

Tanus sent his sailors down into the barge's hold, and they swung up one of the huge clay jars of pickled olives from our stores. Then, under my instructions, he emptied the jar and refilled it with boiling water. While the water was still hot, he mixed into it three sacks of the finest-quality sea salt. Then he filled four smaller wine jars with the same brine and set them all out on the deck to cool.

In the meantime I was working alone in the cabin. My mistress had wanted to help me. She felt that it was part of her duty to her dead husband, but I sent her away to care for the prince.

I slit open Pharaoh's corpse down his left flank from ribs to hip-bone. Through this opening I removed the contents of chest and belly, freeing them along the diaphragm with the knife. Naturally, I left his heart in place, for this is the organ of life and intelligence. I left the kidneys also, for these are the vessels of water and represent the sacred Nile. I packed the cavity with salt and then sutured it closed with cat-gut. I did not have an embalming-spoon to push up through the nostrils and remove that soft yellow mush from the gourd of the skull, so I left it in place. In any event, it was of no importance. The viscera I divided into its separate parts: liver, lungs, stomach and entrails. I washed out the stomach and intestines with brine, which was a loathsome task.

When this was done, I took the opportunity to examine the king's lungs minutely. The right lung was healthy and pink, but the left lung had been pierced by the arrow, and had collapsed like a punctured bladder. It was filled with rotten black blood and pus. I was amazed that the old man had lived so long with such an injury. I felt that I was absolved. No physician could have saved him, and there was no fault or failure in my treatment.

At last I ordered the sailors to bring in the cooled jars of brine. Tanus helped me to fold Pharaoh's body into the foetal position and we placed him in the olive vat. I made certain that he was completely immersed in the strong brine. We packed his viscera into the smaller Canopic wine jars. We sealed all the jars with pitch and wax, and lashed them securely into the reinforced compartment below decks in which the king stored his treasure. I think Pharaoh must have been content to rest thus, surrounded by gold and bars of silver.

I had done my best to help my mistress make good her vow. In Thebes I would hand the king's body over to the embalmers, if the Hyksos had not arrived there first, and if the city and its inhabitants still existed by the time we reached it.

WHEN WE reached the walled city of Asyut, it was apparent that the Hyksos had left only a small force to invest it, and had continued southwards with their main army. Even though it was merely a detachment with less than a hundred chariots, the Hyksos besiegers were far too strong for us to attack them with our decimated army.

Tanus' main aim was to rescue Remrem and his five thousand, who were within the city walls, and then to push on up-river to join forces with Lord Nembet and his thirty thousand reinforcements. Anchored out in the main stream of the river, secure from attack by those deadly chariots, Tanus was able to signal his intentions to Remrem on the city walls.

Years before, I had helped Tanus draw up a system of signals, using two coloured flags by means of which he could spell out a message to any other within sight, across a valley, from peak to peak, or from city wall to plain and river. With the flags Tanus was able to warn Remrem to be ready for us that night. Then, under cover of darkness, twenty of our galleys raced into the beach below the city walls. At the same moment, Remrem threw open the side-gates, and, at the head of his regiment, fought his way through the Hyksos pickets. Before the enemy were able to harness their horses, Remrem and all his men were safely embarked.

Immediately, Tanus signalled the rest of the flotilla to weigh anchor. He abandoned the city of Asyut to sack and plunder, and we bore on upstream under oars. For the rest of that night, whenever we looked back over the stern, we saw the flames of the burning city lighting the northern horizon.

'Let those poor bastards forgive me,' Tanus muttered to me. 'I had no choice but to sacrifice them. My duty lies south of here in Thebes.'

He was soldier enough to make the hard choice without flinching, but man enough to grieve bitterly over it. I admired him then as much as I loved him.

REMREM TOLD us that our signal frigates had sailed past Asyut the previous day, and that by now the despatches that I had drawn up on Tanus' behalf must be in Lord Nembet's hands.

Remrem was also able to give us some intelligence and news of the Hyksos, and his sweep to the south. Remrem had captured two Egyptian deserters and traitors who had gone over to the enemy and who had entered Asyut to spy on the defenders. Under torture they had howled like the jackals they were, and before they died, had told Remrem much about the Hyksos that was of value and interest to us.

The Hyksos king, whom we had so disastrously encountered on the plain of Abnub, was named Salitis. His tribe was of Semitic blood and originally a nomadic and pastoral people who had lived in the Zagros mountains near Lake Van. In this my first impression of these terrible Asians was confirmed. I had guessed at their Semitic origins from their features, but I wondered how a pastoral people had evolved such an extraordinary vehicle as a wheeled chariot, and where they had found that marvellous animal that we Egyptians now spoke of as a horse, and feared as though it were a creature from the underworld.

In other areas it seemed that the Hyksos were a backward people. They were unable to read or write, and their government was a harsh tyranny by their single king and ruler, this bearded Salitis. We Egyptians hated him and feared him even more than we did those wild creatures that drew his chariot.

The chief god of the Hyksos was named Sutekh, the god of storms. It needed no deep religious instruction to recognize in him our own dreaded Seth. Their choice of god was fitting, and their behaviour did the god honour. No civilized people would burn and plunder and murder as they did. The fact that we torture traitors cannot be weighed in the same scale as the atrocities committed by these barbarians.

It is a truth that I have often observed, that a nation chooses its gods to suit its own nature. The Philistines worship Baal, and cast live infants into the fiery furnace that is his mouth. The black Cushite tribes worship monsters and creatures from the underworld with the most bizarre rituals. We Egyptians worship just and decent gods who are benevolent towards mankind and make no demands for human sacrifice. Then the Hyksos have Sutekh.

It seemed that Remrem's captives were not the only Egyptian traitors travelling with the enemy host. With a hot coal in his anus, one of Remrem's captives had told of some great Egyptian lord from the Upper Kingdom who sat upon King Salitis' war council. When I heard this, I remembered how I had wondered at the knowledge that the Hyksos had displayed of our order of battle upon the plain of Abnub. I had guessed then at the presence of a spy among them who knew our secrets.

If any of this was true, then we must expect that the enemy knew all our strengths and weaknesses. They must know the plans and defences of all our cities. Especially they would know of that rich treasure that Pharaoh had accumulated in his funerary temple.

'Perhaps this explains the haste with which King Salitis is driving on towards Thebes,' I suggested to Tanus. 'We can expect them to attempt a crossing of the Nile at the first opportunity that presents itself to them.' And Tanus cursed bitterly.

'If Horus is kind, he will deliver this traitorous Egyptian lord into my hands.' He punched his fist into the palm of his other hand. 'We must prevent Salitis from crossing the river, our ships are the only advantage that we hold over him. I must exploit them to full advantage.'

He stamped about the deck, and looked up at the sky. 'When will this foul wind swing back into the north? Every hour the enemy's chariots draw farther ahead of us. Where is Nembet's fleet? We must join our forces and hold the river-line.'

THAT AFTERNOON on the poop-deck of the royal barge the state council of Upper Egypt convened before the throne. The high priest of Osiris represented the spiritual body, Lord Merseket the chancellor stood for the temporal body of the state, and Tanus, Lord Harrab stood for the military authority.

Between them the three lords lifted Queen Lostris to the throne of this very Egypt, and placed her son upon her lap. While every man and woman on board the barge raised their voices in a loyal salute, the other ships of the fleet sailed past, and even the wounded soldiers dragged themselves to the rail to cheer the new regent and the young heir to the great throne of Egypt.

The high priest of Osiris strapped the false beard of the kingship upon my mistress's chin, and it did nothing to detract from her beauty and manifest womanhood. Lord Merseket bound the lion's tail around her waist and settled the tall red and white crown upon her brow. Finally, Tanus mounted the throne to place the crook and golden flail in her hands. Now Memnon saw the shining toys that Tanus carried towards him, and reached out to snatch them from him.

'A king indeed! He knows the crook is his by right,' Tanus applauded proudly, and the court roared their approval of this precocious behaviour.

I think this was the first time that any of us had laughed since that dreadful day on the field of Abnub. It seemed to me that the laughter was a catharsis, and that it marked a new beginning for all of us. Up until that moment we had been overwhelmed by the shock of defeat and the loss of Pharaoh. But now, as the great lords of Egypt went forward one at a time to kneel before the throne on which sat this lovely young woman and her royal child, a fresh spirit sprang up in all of us. We were rescued from the apathy of despair, and our will to fight and to endure was resuscitated.

Tanus was last of all of them to kneel before the throne and swear his allegiance. As she looked down upon him, Queen Lostris' adoration for him was so evident that it suffused her lovely face and shone like the sunrise from those dark green eyes. I was amazed that no other in all that throng seemed aware of it.

That evening after the sun had set, my mistress sent me to the bridge of the state barge with a message for the commander of her armies. She summoned him to a council of war in the main cabin. This time Tanus dared not refuse her, for he had very recently sworn an oath of obedience.

This extraordinary war council of which I was the only witness had barely begun, before the new regent of Egypt imperiously banished me from the cabin, and sent me to guard the door and turn away all other visitors. The last glimpse that I had of them as I drew the heavy curtain was as they fell into each other's arms. So great was their need, and so long had they been denied, that they rushed at each other like deadly enemies joining in mortal combat, rather than lovers.

The happy sounds of this engagement persisted for most of the night, and I was relieved that we were not at anchor but driving on up-river in haste to join with Lord Nembet. The clunk and swish of the oars, the boom of the drum setting the stroke and the chants of the rowers on their benches almost drowned out the tumult in the royal cabin.

When he came to the poop-deck at the change of the night-watch, Tanus had the smile and the satisfied air of a general who had just won a famous victory. My mistress followed him on deck shortly afterwards, and she glowed with a new and ethereal beauty that startled even me, who was accustomed to her loveliness. For the rest of that day she was loving and kind to all around her, and found numerous occasions to consult the commander of her army. Thus Prince Memnon and I were able to spend most of the day together, a circumstance that suited both of us very well.

With the prince's dubious assistance I had already started carving a series of wooden models. One of these was a chariot and wooden horses. Another was a wheel on an axle that I was experimenting with.

Memnon stood on tiptoe to watch the wheel spin smoothly on its miniature hub.

'A solid disc is too heavy, don't you agree, Mem? See how swiftly it loses momentum and slows down.'

'Give it to me!' he demanded, and snatched at the spinning disc. It flew from his chubby fingers, dashed to the deck and shattered into four almost equal segments.

'You are a Hyksos ruffian,' I told him sternly, which he seemed to take as a great compliment, and I went down on my knees to gather up my poor model.

The broken segments still lay in a circular pattern, and, before my hand touched them, I had a strange aberration of vision. In the eye of my mind, the solid segments of wood became spaces, while the cracks between them appeared solid.

'Sweet breath of Horus! You've done it, Mem.' I hugged him. 'A rim supported by struts from the hub! When you are Pharaoh, what other miracles will you perform for us?'

Thus did the Prince Royal, Memnon the first of that name, Ruler of the Dawn – with just a little help from his friend – conceive of the spoked wheel. Little did I dream then that one day the two of us together would ride to glory upon it.

WE CAME upon the first of the Egyptian dead before noon. He came floating down the river with his bloated belly buoying him up, and his face gazing blankly at the sky. There was a black crow perched upon his chest. It picked out his eyes and threw back its head to swallow them one at a time.

In silence we stood at the ship's rail and watched the dead man float serenely by.

'He wears the kilt of the Lion Guards,' Tanus said quietly. 'The Lions are the spear-head of Nembet's army. I pray to Horus that there will be no others following this one down the river.'

But there were. Ten more, then a hundred. More and still more, until the surface of the river from bank to bank was carpeted by floating corpses. They were thick as the leaves of the water-hyacinth which clog the irrigation canals in summer.

At last we found one who still lived. He was a captain of the Lion Guards who had been seconded to Nembet's staff. He clung to a mat of floating papyrus stems in the current. We fished him from the water and I attended to his wounds. The head of a stone mace had shattered the bones of his shoulder and he would never use that arm again.

When he had recovered sufficiently to speak, Tanus squatted beside his mattress.

'What of Lord Nembet?'

'Lord Nembet is slain, and all his staff with him,' the captain told him hoarsely.

'Did Nembet not receive my despatch warning him of the Hyksos?'

'He received it on the eve of the battle, and he laughed as he read it.'

'Laughed?' demanded Tanus. 'How could he laugh?'

'He said that the puppy was destroyed – forgive me, Lord Tanus, but that was what he called you – and now sought to cover his stupidity and cowardice with spurious messages. He said that he would fight the battle in the classic manner.'

'The arrogant old fool,' Tanus lamented. 'But tell me the rest of it.'

'Lord Nembet deployed upon the east bank, with the river at his back. The enemy fell upon us like the wind, and drove us into the water.'

'How many of our men escaped?' Tanus asked softly.

'I believe that I am the only one of those who went ashore with Lord Nembet who survived. I saw no other left alive. The slaughter upon the river-bank was beyond my power to describe to you.'

'All our most famous regiments decimated,' Tanus mourned. 'We are left defenceless, except for our ships. What happened to Nembet's fleet? Was it anchored in midstream?'

'Lord Nembet anchored the greater part of the fleet, but he beached fifty galleys in our rear.'

'Why would he do that?' Tanus stormed. 'The safety of the ships is the first principle of our standard battle plan.'

'I do not know Lord Nembet's mind, except he may have kept them at hand to re-embark our troops expeditiously, should your warning have proved justified.'

'What then is the fate of our fleet? Nembet lost our army, but did he save the ships?' Tanus' tone was rough with anger and distress.

'Of the ships that were anchored in midstream, most are scuttled and burned by the skeleton crews. I saw the flames and the smoke even from where I lay on my papyrus float. A few of the others cut the anchor-lines and fled south towards Thebes. I shouted to the crews as they sailed past me, but so great was their terror that they would not heave-to and pick me from the water.'

'The fifty ships that lay upon the beach—' Tanus broke off and drew a deep breath before he finished the question. 'What has become of the squadron that was beached?'

'It has fallen into the hands of the Hyksos.' The captain trembled as he answered, for he dreaded Tanus' anger. 'I looked back as I drifted with the current, and I saw the enemy swarming aboard the galleys on the beach.'

Tanus stood up and strode to the bows. He stared upstream from where the corpses and the scorched and blackened planks of Nembet's fleet still drifted down upon the steady green flow of the river. I went to stand at his side, to be ready to halter his rage when it came.

'So the proud old fool has sacrificed his life, and the lives of all his men, simply to spite me. They should build a pyramid to his folly, for Egypt has never seen the like of it.'

'That is not all his folly,' I murmured, and Tanus nodded grimly.

'No, not all his folly. He has given the Hyksos the means to cross the river. Sweet milk of Isis' breast, but once they are across the Nile we are truly finished.'

Perhaps the goddess heard him call her name, for at that moment I felt the wind that had blown so long into our faces veer. Tanus felt it also. He spun on his heel and roared an order to his officers on the poop-deck.

'The wind turns fair. Make a general signal to the fleet. Set all sail. Relieve the men at the oars every hour by the water-clock. Drummers, increase the beat to flank speed. Make all haste southwards.'

The wind settled strongly into the north. Our sails filled and stiffened like the bellies of pregnant women. The drums gave the rowers the stroke, and we breasted the flow of the river as the whole battle-fleet raced southwards.

'All thanks to the goddess for this wind,' Tanus shouted. 'Divine Isis, let us be in time to catch them on the water.'

THE STATE barge was slow and ungainly. She began falling astern of the fleet. It seemed that the fates had intervened once more, for Tanus' old galley that he had loved so well, the *Breath of Horus*, was sailing close to us in the formation.

She was under a new captain now, but she was still a formidable little vessel, built for speed and attack. The sharp bronze ramming-horn protruded from her bows, just above the water line. Tanus hailed her alongside the barge and transferred his Blue Crocodile standard into her, taking over the command from her new captain.

My place was with my mistress and the prince. I am not certain how I found myself on board the *Breath of Horus*, standing on the poop beside Tanus, as we tore along upstream. Sometimes I am guilty of folly almost as monumental as that recently demonstrated by Lord Nembet. I remember only that as soon as the state barge began to fall away astern, I began bitterly to regret my impetuosity. I thought of telling Tanus that I had changed my mind, and asking him to put about and drop me once more on the deck of the barge. But after one glance at his face, I decided that I would rather face the Hyksos again.

From the deck of the *Breath of Horus*, Tanus issued his orders. By flag and voice-hail, they were passed from vessel to vessel. Without slackening the pace of our advance, Tanus redeployed the fleet. He gathered up the galleys around him, as he forged his way to the head of the flotilla.

The wounded and those no longer fit to fight were transferred to the slower vessels which fell back to keep pace with the state barge. The faster galleys in the van were cleared for action. They were manned mostly by Remrem's fresh troops whom we had relieved from the siege of Asyut. They were spoiling for a chance to avenge the disgrace of Abnub. Tanus hoisted the Blue Crocodile standard at his masthead of the *Breath of Horus*, and they roared with the lust of battle. How swiftly he had been able to stiffen their spirit since that bloody defeat!

The signs of Nembet's recent catastrophe became ever more obvious with each league that we covered. The corpses and wreckage and all the flotsam of war were stranded in the papyrus beds on each side of the river. Then, at last, in the sky ahead of us we saw once again the dust of the chariots mingling with the smoke from the cooking-fires of the Hyksos camp.

'It is as I had hoped,' Tanus exulted. 'They have halted their headlong advance on Thebes, now that Nembet has presented them with the means of crossing the river. But they are not sailors, and they will have difficulty embarking their men and chariots. If Horus is kind, we will arrive in time to help them on their way.'

In extended battle order we swept around the last wide bend of the river, and we found the Hyksos before us. By one of those happy freaks of war, we had arrived precisely at the moment that they were fully committed to the crossing of the Nile.

There were the fifty captured galleys straggling across the river in the most lubberly fashion. The sails and sheets were in a tangle and every oarsman was keeping his own stroke. The paddles were splashing and crab-catching. The steering of each vessel was shaky and erratic, completely out of phase with the ships around it.

We could see that most of the Hyksos manning the decks were in full bronze armour. Clearly they had not realized just how difficult it is to swim in that state of dress. They stared at us in consternation as we bore down upon them. Now at last the roles were reversed. We were in our element, and they were flying in the wind like a torn sail.

I had a few moments to study the enemy, as we closed. The vast bulk of the Hyksos army was still upon the east bank. They had gone into bivouac, and they were so numerous that their encampment stretched away to the foothills of the desert, as far as I could see from the deck of the *Breath of Horus*.

King Salitis was sending only a small force across the river. Almost certainly they were under orders to race down the west bank and to capture the funerary temple of Pharaoh Mamose, before we were able to remove the treasure.

We bore down rapidly on the convoy of Hyksos ships, and I shouted to Tanus above the beat of the drums and the bloodthirsty cheers of our rascals, 'They have taken their horses across already. Look over there!'

Almost unprotected, except for a few armed guards, there was a huge herd of these terrible animals gathered on the west bank. I guessed there were several hundred of them; even at this distance, we could make out their long, flowing manes and tails streaming in the strong north wind.

They were a disturbing sight to us. Some of the men around me shuddered and swore with loathing of them. I heard one of them mutter darkly, 'The Hyksos feed those monsters of theirs on human flesh, like tame lions or jackals. That is the reason for this slaughter. They must have food for them. We can only guess how many of our comrades are already in their bellies.'

I could not contradict him, and I even had a queasy feeling in my guts that he might be speaking the truth. I turned my attention from those beautiful but gory monsters to the galleys in the stream ahead of us.

'We have caught them taking the chariots and the men over,' I pointed out to Tanus. The decks of Nembet's captured vessels were piled high with chariots and equipment, and crowded with the Hyksos charioteers who were being ferried across. As they realized their predicament, some of the Hyksos tried to turn and run back for the east bank. They collided with the ships that followed them, and locked together, they drifted helplessly on the current.

Tanus laughed savagely to see their confusion, and shouted into the wind, 'General signal. Increase the beat to attack speed. Light the fire-arrows.'

The Hyksos had never experienced an attack with fire-arrows, and at the thought of what was coming, I laughed with Tanus, but nervously. Then suddenly I stiffened and my laughter choked off.

'Tanus!' I seized his arm. 'Look! Look at the galley dead ahead! On the poop. There is our traitor.'

For a moment Tanus did not recognize the tall, stately figure at the rail of the galley, for he wore fish-scale armour and a tall Hyksos war helmet. Then abruptly he roared with anger and outrage, 'Intef! Why did we not guess it was him?'

'I see it so clearly now. He has guided Salitis to this very Egypt. He went east and deliberately tempted the Hyksos with accounts of the treasures of Egypt.' My outrage and hatred matched those of Tanus.

Tanus threw up the bow Lanata and loosed an arrow, but the range was long and the point glanced off Lord Intef's armour. I saw his head jerk round at the shock, and he looked across the water directly at us. He singled us out, Tanus and myself, and for a moment I thought I saw fear in his eyes. Then he ducked out of sight below the gunwale of the galley.

Our leading squadron flew into the pack of confused and milling shipping. With a tearing crunch, our bronze ramming-horn struck Intef's galley amidships, and I was thrown off my feet by the impact. When I struggled up again, the oarsmen had already backed water, and with another rending screech of timbers we disengaged from the stricken ship.

At the same time, our archers were pouring a heavy rain of fire-arrows into her. The heads were bound with pitch-soaked papyrus stems that burned like comets, each leaving a trail of sparks and smoke as they flew into the sails and top hamper. The north wind fanned the flames and they leaped up the rigging with a fiendish exuberance.

The waters flooded in through the gaping hole we had ripped in her belly, and she listed over sharply. The sails caught fire and burned with startling rapidity. The heat singed my eyelashes even at that distance. The heavy mainsail, burning fiercely, fluttered down over the deck, trapping the crew and crowded charioteers beneath it. Their screams shrilled in our ears as their hair and clothing burst into flames. I remembered the plain at Abnub and felt no pity as they leaped in flames from the ship's side and were drawn under by the weight of their armour. Only a swirl of ripples and a lingering puff of steam marked where each of them had disappeared.

All down the line, the Hyksos galleys were burning and sinking. They had neither the experience nor the skill to counter our attack, and they were as helpless as we had been before the assault of their chariots. Our ships backed off and charged again, crushing in their hulls and sending torrents of flaming arrows into them.

I was watching the first galley that we had attacked, seeking another glimpse of Lord Intef. She was almost gone when suddenly he reappeared. He had thrown off his helmet and his armour, and wore only a linen breech clout. He balanced easily on the gunwale of the sinking ship, and then, as the flames reached out to embrace him, he joined his hands above his head and dived overboard.

He was a son of the Nile, at home in her waters. He knifed through the surface, and came up a minute later and fifty paces from where he had struck, with his long wet hair sleeked back, so that he looked like a swimming otter.

'There he goes!' I screamed at Tanus. 'Run the swine under.'

Instantly Tanus gave the order to turn the *Breath of Horus*, but quick as the helmsman was on the steering-oar, she was slow to come around. Meanwhile, Lord Intef slipped through the water like a fish, reaching out overarm for the east bank and the protection of his Hyksos allies.

'Swing hard!' Tanus signalled his starboard bank of oars, and they thrust the bows around. As soon as we were on line with the swimmer, Tanus gave the order to pull together, and we shot in pursuit. By now Lord Intef was far ahead and close in to the bank, where five thousand Hyksos archers waited with their long recurved bows strung and ready to give him covering fire.

'Seth piss on them!' Tanus yelled in defiance. 'We will take Intef out from under their noses.' And he drove the *Breath of Horus* directly at them, bearing down upon the lone swimming figure.

As we came within range of the shore, the Hyksos loosed a volley at us that darkened the sky, and their arrows fell in a whistling cloud around us. They dropped so thickly that the deck soon bristled with them like the quills in a goose's wing, and some of our sailors were struck and fell writhing and bleeding from their benches.

But we were already close on Intef, and he looked back over his shoulder and I saw the terror in his face as he realized he could not escape our sharp prow. I ignored the arrows and ran to the bows to scream down at him, 'I hated you from the first day we met. I hated every loathsome touch. I want to watch you die. You are evil! Evil!'

He heard me. I saw it in his eyes, and then his dark gods intervened yet again. One of the sinking Hyksos galleys drifted down upon us, spouting fire and smoke. If she had touched us we would have gone up with her in a tower of flame. Tanus was forced to put the steering-oar over, and to signal urgently for his oarsmen to back-water. The burning galley drifted between the shore and where we lay heaved-to. Lord Intef was hidden from my view, but when the burning galley was past, I saw him again. Three brawny Hyksos charioteers were dragging him from the water and up the steep bank.

He paused at the top of the bank and looked back at us, and then disappeared from sight, leaving me trembling with rage and frustration. Our men were still being struck down by the falling arrows, so Tanus gave the order, and we wheeled away and sped back to join in the destruction of those few vessels of the convoy that were still afloat.

As the last of these listed over and then rolled on to her back, the green Nile waters poured into her and quenched the flames in a hissing cloud of steam. Our archers leaned over the side and shot the few surviving Hyksos who splashed weakly on the surface.

Immediately they were all drowned, Tanus turned his attention to the west bank and to the small party of the enemy and the herd of horses that were stranded there. As our galley sped in to the shore, the Hyksos herders scattered and ran, but our men leaped ashore, sword in hand, and raced after them. The Hyksos were charioteers, and accustomed to riding into battle. Our lads were foot-soldiers and trained to run. Like a pack of hounds after a jackal, our men isolated and surrounded them. They hacked them down and left a hundred bleeding corpses scattered across the green fields of standing dhurra corn.

I had jumped ashore behind the first wave of our troops. I had serious business in mind. There was no point in making models and designing chariots without a means of driving the spoked wheels that I had seen in my imagination.

It required an enormous act of courage on my part to start towards that herd of terrible creatures that the Hyksos herders had abandoned close to the water's edge. Each step was an effort of will, for there were many hundreds of them, and they were obviously restless and alarmed by the shouting and the running of men and the clash of arms. I was certain that at any moment they would rush at me like wounded lions. I imagined them gobbling my still warm and twitching flesh, and my courage evaporated and I could go no closer. From a distance of a hundred paces, I stood staring in dreadful fascination at these savage predators, but I was poised to turn and rush back to the safety of the galley at the first sign of an attack.

This was the first opportunity that I had been given to study these animals. They were mostly of a dun colour, but with subtle shadings of bay and chestnut and roan. One or two of them were as black as Seth. They stood as tall as a man, with a full barrel-chest, and long necks that arched gracefully. Their manes were like the tresses of a beautiful woman, and their hides glowed in the sunlight, as though they had been burnished.

One of those nearest to me threw back its head and rolled its upper lip, and I recoiled as I saw the great square white teeth that lined its jaw. It kicked its hind-legs and emitted such a terrifying neighing sound that I turned and started back towards the ship with some alacrity.

Then a hoarse yell from one of our soldiers near me arrested my cowardly retreat. 'Kill the Hyksos monsters!'

'Kill the monsters!' The cry was taken up by the others.

'No!' I screamed, and my concern for my own safety was forgotten. 'No! Save the horses. We need them.'

My voice was lost in the angry war-cry of our troops, as they rushed at the herd of horses, with their shields raised and their swords still dripping with the blood of the herders. Some of the men paused to nock arrows to the bow and fire them into the herd.

'No!' I cried, as a glossy black stallion reared and screamed, with an arrow standing out of his withers.

'No! Please, no!' I cried again, as one of the sailors ran in with a light war-axe and hacked through the fetlock joint of a young mare. She was crippled by the blow and could not escape the next stroke of the axe that caught her between the ears and dropped her kicking in the dust.

'Leave them! Leave them!' I pleaded, but the arrows brought down a dozen of the animals, and the swords and axes maimed and killed a dozen more before the herd broke under the assault, and three hundred horses bolted and went galloping out in a mass across the dusty western plain towards the desert.

I shaded my eyes to watch them go, and it seemed to me that part of my heart went with them. When they had disappeared, I ran to protect and tend to those animals that were left maimed and arrowed amongst the papyrus beds. But the soldiers were ahead of me. So great was their fury that they gathered around the fallen carcasses. In a frenzy of hatred, they plunged their blades into the unresisting flesh and hacked at the broken heads.

A little to one side stood an isolated clump of papyrus reeds. Behind this, and screened from the rampaging soldiers, stood the black stallion that I had first seen hit by an arrow. He was sorely struck and staggering as he limped forward, the arrow deep in his chest. Without thought for my own safety, I ran towards him, and then stopped as he turned to face me.

Only then did I realize my danger. Here was a wounded beast that, like a lion in the same straits, must surely charge at me. The stallion and I stared at each other, and I felt fear fall away like a discarded cloak from my shoulders.

His eyes were huge and swimming with pain. Gentle eyes, beautiful eyes that made my heart swell with pity. He made a soft, fluttering sound, and limped towards me. I held out my hand and touched his muzzle and it felt like warm Arabian silk. He came directly to me, and pressed his forehead to my chest in a gesture of trust and appeal that was almost human. I knew that he was asking for my help.

Instinctively I flung my arms around his neck and embraced him. I wanted more than anything in my life at that moment to save him, but from his nostrils warm blood trickled down my chest. I knew he was hit through the lungs and that he was dying. He was far beyond any help that I could give him.

'My poor darling. What have those stupid, ignorant bastards done to you?' I whispered. Dimly in my distress and spiritual agony, I realized that my life had changed again, and that this dying creature had made that change. Somehow I seemed to sense that, in the years ahead, wherever I left my footsteps in the African earth, the hoof-prints of a horse would lie beside them. I had found another great love to fill my days.

The stallion made that fluttering sound once more and his breath was warm on my skin. Then his legs collapsed under him and he fell heavily on his side and lay gasping air into his punctured lungs. Bright red bubbles frothed from the wound in his chest. I went down beside him, and lifted that noble head into my lap and waited with him until he died. Then I stood up and went back to where the *Breath of Horus* was beached.

It was difficult to see my way, for my own hot tears blinded me. Once again I cursed myself for a soft and sentimental fool, but that never did much to help me brace myself. I was always so vulnerable to suffering in another creature, human or otherwise, especially in one that was noble and beautiful.

'Damn you, Taita! Where have you been?' Tanus railed at me as I scrambled aboard. 'There is a battle raging. The whole army cannot wait around while you have another of your famous daydreams.' Yet for all his bluster, he had not deserted me.

TANUS WOULD not even hear me out, but cut brusquely across my request for leave to follow the herd of runaway horses out into the desert, and for men to go with me.

'I want no truck with those foul and unholy creatures!' he shouted at me. 'I only regret that my men let them escape and that they did not slaughter the lot of them. Let us hope that the lions and the jackals make good that default.' I realized then that he hated them as much as did the most ignorant lout in his regiments.

'Were you there on the plain of Abnub?' I do not usually indulge in loud argument, but his intransigence infuriated me. 'Or was that some other dull-witted oaf standing beside me? Did you not see the future charge at you on hooves and wheels and chop your men to jackal-food? Do you not understand that without chariot and horse, you and this Egypt we know are finished?'

This amicable discussion was taking place on the poop-deck of the *Breath of Horus*. Tanus' officers were silent and stiff with shock to hear a slave address a Great Lion of Egypt and the commander of all her armies as a dull-witted oaf. However, I was past all restraint and I rushed on.

'The gods have given you this wonderful gift. Three hundred horses placed in your hands! I will build you the chariots to go with them. Are you so blind that you cannot see it?'

'I have my ships!' Tanus roared back at me. 'I don't need these foul man-eating beasts. They are an abomination in the face of decent men and all benevolent gods. They are creatures of Seth and Sutekh, and I want no part of them.'

Too late I realized that I had pushed Tanus into a position from which he could not retreat. He was a clever and intelligent man, until his pride hamstrung his reason. I moderated my tone and made my voice mellifluous.

'Tanus, please listen to me. I have held the head of one of these animals in my hands. They are strong, but strangely gentle. Their eyes shine with the intelligence of a faithful dog. They do not eat meat—'

'How could you tell that from one brief touch?' he sneered at me, still proud and affronted.

'The teeth,' I answered. 'They do not possess the fangs or claws of a carnivore. Pigs are the only hoofed creatures that eat flesh, and these are no pigs.'

I saw him waver at last, and I pressed my advantage. 'If that is not enough, look then at the stores that the Hyksos have brought across the river. Do they need that mountain of fodder to feed a pride of meat-eating lions?'

'Meat or fodder, I will not argue further. You have heard my decision. We will let those cursed horses perish in the wilderness. That is my decision, and it is final.' He stamped away, but I muttered under my breath, 'Final, is it? We will see about that.'

There have been very few occasions when I have not been able to have my own way with my mistress, and hers was now the highest authority in this very Egypt. I went to her that very evening, as soon as the royal barge came once more under the protection of the war galleys.

Without the knowledge of her commander and lover, I showed her the tiny working model of a chariot with the miniature carved horses in the traces, which I had crafted for her. Queen Lostris was enchanted by it. Naturally she had never seen the squadrons of war chariots in full flight, and had not conceived for them the same hatred as had the bulk of her army. Having captured her full attention with the model chariot, I then described the death of the stallion in such harrowing detail that both of us were reduced to tears. She can resist my tears as little as I am able to resist hers.

'You must go immediately and rescue these marvellous animals from the desert. When you have them, I order you to build a squadron of chariots for my armies,' she cried.

If Tanus had spoken to her before I had the chance to persuade her, I doubt that she would have given that order, and the history of our world would have been very different. As it was, Tanus was furious with my deception, and we came as close to a permanent rift in our relationship as we ever had in all the years.

It was fortunate that I had been summarily ordered ashore by Queen Lostris, and was able to escape the full force of his wrath. I had only a few hours in which to gather around me a few helpers, and the chief of these was the most unlikely of them all.

I had never taken to Hui, the Shrike whom we had captured at Gallala and who had commanded one of the galleys which Tanus had scuttled at Abnub. He was now a captain without a ship, and a man looking for a reason to go on. He sought me out as soon as rumour of my mission spread through the fleet.

'What do you know about horses?' he challenged me, which was a question I was not prepared to answer at that moment.

'Obviously not as much as you do?' I made it a cautious question.

'I was once a syce,' he boasted, in his usual endearing fashion.

'And what creature is that?'

'A groom, one who cares for horses,' he replied, and I stared at him in amazement.

'Where did you ever see a horse before that bloody day at Abnub?' I demanded.

'As an infant my parents were killed, and I was captured by a tribe of barbarians who roamed the plains far to the east, a year's travel beyond the Euphrates river. My captors were people of the horse and, as a child, I lived each day with those animals. Mare's milk was my food and I slept beneath the horses' bellies for shelter in the night, for a slave was not allowed into the tents of the tribe. When I escaped from slavery, it was upon the back of my favourite stallion. He carried me fast and far. But he died long before we reached the Euphrates.'

Thus Hui was with me when a galley set down my small party of reluctant horse-catchers upon the west bank. Sixteen men were all that I could recruit, and most of them were the dregs and riff-raff of the army. Tanus had seen to it that none of his best men would join me. He could not countermand the word of the regent of all Egypt, but he made it as difficult as he could for me to carry out her orders.

At Hui's suggestion, I had equipped my men with light linen ropes and bags of crushed dhurra corn. All of them, except Hui and myself, were terrified to the point of incontinence by the mere thought of the creatures that we had set out to follow. When I woke in the morning after our first night's camp, I found that every single one of these stalwarts had disappeared, and I never saw them again.

'We will have to turn back,' I despaired. 'There is nothing we can do alone. Lord Tanus will be pleased. This was exactly what he knew would happen.'

'You are not alone,' Hui pointed out cheerfully. 'You have me.' This was the first time that my feelings began to warm towards the young swaggerer. We divided the load of ropes and the leather bags of crushed corn, and we went on.

By this time the tracks of the horses were three days old, but they had stayed together in a single herd and so had beaten a road that was easy to follow. Hui assured me that the herd instinct was strong amongst them, and that with such lush grazing along the river-bank, they would not have wandered far. He was certain they would not have gone out into the desert, as I had feared that they might.

'Why would they do that? There is no food or water for them out there.' And in the end Hui proved right.

With the coming of the Hyksos, the peasants had deserted their farms and gone into the shelter of the walled towns. The fields were untended and the corn half-grown. We found the herd before noon the second day. It was spread out and grazing peacefully in one of the fields. Even after my experience with the wounded stallion, I was still rather nervous of these mysterious creatures.

'It will surely be a difficult and dangerous matter to capture a few of them,' I confided in Hui, seeking his reassurance and advice. At this stage, the notion of capturing all three hundred horses had not even occurred to me. I would have been satisfied with twenty, and delighted with fifty of them. I imagined that we would be forced to run each of them down and bind it with the ropes we had brought with us for that purpose.

'I have heard that you have the reputation of being a very clever slave,' Hui grinned at me, cocky and delighted by his superior understanding of the subject. 'Clearly, it is a reputation that is ill-founded.'

He showed me how to twist and braid a halter from the ropes. We made a dozen of these before he was satisfied. Then each of us armed himself with one of these and a leather sack of crushed corn, and we started towards the grazing herd. Following Hui's example, we never walked directly towards them, but strolled obliquely at a leisurely pace past the animals in the fringe of the herd.

'Slowly now,' Hui cautioned me, when they flung up their heads and studied us with that peculiarly frank and almost childlike gaze that I would come to know so well.

'Sit down.' We sank into the standing corn and remained motionless, until the horses started feeding again. Then we moved forward until they became restless once more.

'Down,' Hui ordered, and when we were crouched in the corn, he went on, 'They love the sound of a gentle voice. When I was a child, I sang to my horses to quieten them. Watch this!' He started to sing a refrain in a strange language, which I presumed was the barbaric tongue of his childhood captors.

Hui's voice was as melodious as the squawking of crows squabbling over the rotting carcass of a dead dog. The nearest horses stared at us curiously. I laid my hand on Hui's arm to quieten him. I was certain that the herd must find his efforts at song as distressing as I did.

'Let me try,' I whispered. I sang the lullaby that I had composed for my prince.

> Sleep, little Mem, who rules the dawn,
> sleep, little prince, who will rule the world,
> rest that curly head, filled with wondrous dreams,
> rest those arms, make them strong for sword and bow.

One of the mares closest to us took a few steps towards me, and when she stopped, she made that same soft fluttery sound with her lips. She was inquisitive, and I sang on softly and seductively. She had a foal at her heels, a lovely little bay-coloured creature with an appealing head and pricked-up ears.

With my special feeling for and understanding of birds and animals, I was already beginning to recognize the desirable points of breed in these new animals. I was learning swiftly and instinctively how to deal with them. I was no longer completely reliant on Hui to instruct me.

Still singing gently, I scooped up a handful of the crushed cornmeal and held it out to the mare. I could see at once that she had been handfed before, and that she understood my offer. She blew noisily through wide nostrils, and took another few paces towards me. Even now I can remember the thrill that almost stopped the beating of my heart when she took the last pace up to me, and delicately lowered her muzzle into my hand to taste the white meal. It powdered her whiskers as she ate, and I laughed with the joy and excitement of it. She made no effort to pull away from me as I slipped my other arm around her neck and laid my cheek softly against hers to inhale the strange, warm smell of her hide.

'The halter,' Hui reminded me softly, and I slipped it over her head, as he had shown me.

'She is yours,' Hui said.

'And I am hers,' I replied without thinking, but it was true. We had captured each other.

The rest of the herd had watched all this. As soon as the halter was on the mare, they settled down and trustingly allowed Hui and me to walk freely amongst them. They came to eat from the hand and allowed us to lift their hooves and stroke their necks and massive shoulders.

All this seemed to me at the time to be miraculous, but after only a little consideration I realized that it was quite natural. They were accustomed from birth to being handled and petted, to being fed and harnessed. They had lived always with the close and constant presence of man. The true miracle came later, when I realized that they recognized affection, and that they were able to return it in full measure.

Hui had selected and haltered one of the other mares, all the time lecturing me and displaying his learning and experience in matters equine. I was in such a euphoric mood that for once his bumptiousness did not annoy me.

'Very well,' he said at last, 'we will mount up now.' And to my utter astonishment he placed both hands on his mare's back, drew himself up and flung one leg over her, to sit astride her back. I gawked at him in disbelief, expecting the mare to react violently, to rear up and dash Hui to earth, or, at the very least, to seize his naked leg in those powerful white teeth and drag him from his perch. She did none of these things, but stood quietly and subserviently.

'Hi up, my darling!' he called to her, and dug his heels into her ribs. The mare started forward obediently, and when he urged her on again she broke into a trot and then a gallop. Hui guided her effortlessly in a manner that was not then apparent to me. Horse and rider traced out elegant patterns of movement across the field, and then circled back to where I stood.

'Come up, Taita. Try a gallop!' I could see that he was expecting me to refuse, and it was that which made me overcome my reluctance. I would not allow the little whippersnapper to have the better of me.

My first attempt at mounting up was unsuccessful, but the mare stood stoically, and Hui laughed. 'She has a great deal to teach you. You should call the poor animal Patience.' I did not see the humour of it then, but the name stuck and the mare was Patience from then onwards.

'Pull yourself higher before you swing your leg over, and be careful not to trap your balls under you when you come down,' Hui counselled, and then howled with laughter. 'And that's a piece of advice that you need not worry about. My guess is that you would love still to have a pair of those to sit on!'

All the warm feelings I was beginning to have towards Hui cooled again at that sally, and I threw myself on to the mare's back and clung with both hands around her neck, in fear of broken limbs and cracked skull.

'Sit up straight!' Hui began my instruction, and Patience assisted me with her sweet and forgiving nature.

I surprised myself by thinking of these creatures in human terms, but over the following days as we rode south towards Thebes, I discovered that they could be stupid or clever, suspicious or trusting, dour or mischievous, friendly or aloof, brave or timid, nervous or phlegmatic, long-suffering or impatient, surprising or predictable – in short, as close to man in temperament as any creature that walks on four legs. The more I learned about them, the more I wanted to learn. The longer I spent working with them, the more I grew to love them.

I rode ahead on Patience, her foal at heel. The herd trailed after us compliantly, all three hundred and sixteen of them. Hui brought up the rear to sweep up any stragglers. With each league we covered, I became more confident and proficient upon Patience's back, and the rapport between us became firmer. The mare became an extension of my own body, but so much swifter and stronger than my own feeble limbs. It felt so natural and right to be astride that broad and sturdy back that I was amazed that so few others were willing to share the experience with me.

Perhaps it was not only the terror that had struck them so devastatingly on the plain of Abnub, but also the words and attitude of Tanus, Lord Harrab that affected the regiments of our army. Whatever the reason, I could find no Egyptian who would mount upon the back of a horse, except Hui and, very much later, Prince Memnon. Of course, they learned to husband and breed the horse and care for him. Under my tutelage they became dexterous and dashing charioteers, but I never saw a man of them mounted on horseback, save only myself and Hui and the prince. When the chariots that I would design with their light, spoked wheels swept all before them, and made Egypt the master of this creation, Tanus never followed our example, and I never heard him express a kind sentiment towards those willing and brave animals who dragged him into battle.

Even in later years, when the horse was commonplace through all our realm, it was considered somehow indecent and obscene to mount them. When the three of us rode past astride, many of the common people spat on the ground three times and made the sign against the evil eye.

ALL THAT was in the future as I led my herd up the west bank of the river towards Thebes, and we arrived to the gratitude of my mistress, and to a gruff and unenthusiastic welcome from the commander-in-chief of the Egyptian armies.

'Just keep those evil brutes out of my sight,' Tanus told me. He still had not forgiven me for going above him to my mistress.

In fairness to him, he had more than enough excuse for his evil temper. The safety of the state and our nation were in the direst jeopardy. There had never been a time in our history when our civilization was so threatened by the barbarian.

Already Asyut was lost, and the whole east bank of the river as far as Dendera. Completely undaunted and undeterred by the naval reverse that Tanus had inflicted upon him, King Salitis with his chariots had swept on and surrounded the walled city of Thebes.

Those walls should have withstood siege for a decade, but that reckoned without the baleful presence of Lord Intef in the camp of the enemy. It transpired that while still grand vizier of the Upper Kingdom, he had secretly ordered the construction of a concealed passage beneath the city walls. Even I who knew most of his other secrets had never suspected this, and Lord Intef had murdered the workmen who had carried out this construction, so that he alone was aware of its existence. I have no idea why he should have constructed the tunnel in the first place, except that his devious mind was much given towards such devices. The palace was riddled with trap-doors and concealed corridors, like the warren of a rabbit or the lair of a desert fox.

When Lord Intef disclosed its existence to him, King Salitis sent a small party of his best men through the secret passage, and once within the walls, they stormed the unsuspecting Egyptian guards on the main gate, slaughtered them and threw the gates wide. The main Hyksos horde poured into the city, and within days of the siege commencing, the city was lost and half her inhabitants massacred.

From the west bank where Tanus now had his headquarters in the half-built Palace of Memnon, we could see the burnt and blackened roofs of those buildings in the city across the river that the Hyksos had put to the torch. Each day we watched the dust-clouds of their chariots, as they raced up and down the far bank, and the glint of their spear-heads at the shoulder-slope, as they prepared for the battle that all of us knew was coming.

With his sadly depleted fleet, Tanus had thus far managed to hold the river-line, and during my absence had beaten back another attempt by the Hyksos to get across the Nile in strength. However, our defences were thinly spread, for we had to guard a great sweep of the river, while the Hyksos could make a crossing at any point they chose. We learned from our spies on the east bank that they had commandeered every single craft they could lay hands on, from barge to skiff. They had captured many of our boatmakers, and had them at work in the boatyards of Thebes. Of course, we could be sure that Lord Intef would give them pertinent advice in all these matters, for he must have been every bit as eager as the barbarian Salitis to seize Pharaoh's treasure.

The crews of our galleys stood to arms every watch of the day and night, and Tanus only slept when he could, which was not often. Neither my mistress nor I saw much of him, and when we did, he was haggard and short-tempered.

Every night saw the arrival on the west bank of many hundreds of refugees. Of both sexes and all ages, they crossed the Nile in an odd assortment of rafts and small craft. Many of the stronger ones even swam the wide stretch of water. All of them were desperate to escape the Hyksos terror. They brought us horror-stories of rapine and plunder, but also detailed and up-to-date news of Hyksos movements.

Of course we welcomed these people, they were countrymen and relatives, but their numbers strained our resources. Our main granaries had all been in Thebes, and most of the herds of cattle and sheep had fallen into the hands of the enemy. Queen Lostris gave me the responsibility of gathering up all the supplies of grain and the herds on the west bank. I drew up lists and rosters for rationing our supplies of meat and grain. Fortunately, the date palms were in full bearing, and the supply of fish from the river was inexhaustible. The Hyksos could never starve us out.

My mistress had also appointed me Master of the Royal Horse. There was no intense competition for this appointment, particularly as no pay or privileges were attached to it. I made Hui my deputy, and he managed, by means of bribes, threats and blackmail, to recruit a hundred grooms to help him care for our little herd. Later we would train them as our first chariot-drivers.

It was no hardship for me to make time every day to visit our makeshift stables in the necropolis. The mare Patience always came running to greet me, and I carried corn-cakes for her and her foal. Often I was able to sneak Prince Memnon away from his mother and his nurses and carry him into the stables on my shoulders. He squealed with excitement as soon as he saw the horses.

I held the prince on my lap as Patience and I galloped along the river-bank, and he made clucking noises and rocked his little backside, imitating the way in which I urged Patience to a harder gallop. I made certain that the route we followed on these rides would never cross Tanus' path. He had still not forgiven me, and if he had seen his son on the back of a cursed horse, I knew that I would have been in physical danger.

I also spent a great deal of my time in the armoury workshop of Pharaoh's funerary temple, where I had the assistance of some of the finest craftsmen in the world to help me build my first chariot. It was here, while working on the design of these vehicles, that I conceived devices that were to become our first line of defence against the Hyksos chariots. These were simply long wooden staves sharpened at both ends, and with the points fire-hardened. Each of our infantrymen would carry ten of these in a bundle upon his back. At the approach of a squadron of cavalry, the staves were planted in the earth at an angle, with the points at the level of the horses' chests. Our men took up their positions behind this barrier of wicked spears, and fired their arrows over them.

When I demonstrated these to Tanus, he threw his arm around my shoulders for the first time since our quarrel over the horses, and said, 'Well, at least you have not turned senile on me yet,' and I knew that I had been at least partially forgiven.

The ground that I had gained with him here was almost completely lost over the affair of the Taita chariot.

My workmen and I at last completed the first chariot. The dashboard and sides were of split bamboo, woven into basketwork. The axle was of acacia wood. The hubs were of hand-forged bronze, greased with mutton fat, and the spoked wheels were bound with bronze rims. It was so light that two charioteers could lift it between them, and carry it over broken ground where the horses could not pull it. Even I realized that it was a masterpiece, and the workmen called it the Taita chariot. I did not object to the name.

Hui and I harnessed up two of our best horses, Patience and Blade, and took the Taita chariot for its first gallop. It took us some time to learn how to control the rig, but we learned swiftly, and the horses were bred to this and showed us the way. In the end, we were flying across the ground, and hurtling through tight turns at full gallop.

When we drove back into the stables, flushed with excitement and jubilant with our achievement, both of us were convinced that our chariot was swifter and handier than any that the Hyksos could send against us. We tested and modified this creation of mine for ten full days, working by lamplight in the armoury until the late watches of every night, before I was satisfied that I could show it to Tanus.

Tanus came to the stables with surly reluctance, and balked at climbing up into the cockpit of the chariot behind me.

'I trust this contraption of yours as much as I trust those cursed brutes who tow it,' he grumbled, but I was persuasive, and at last he stepped up gingerly on to the footplate and we were off.

At first I kept the horses to an easy trot, until I felt him relaxing and, despite himself, beginning to enjoy the exhilarating ride. Then I pushed them into a canter. 'See the speed of it. You can be upon the enemy before he knows you are there,' I exulted.

Tanus laughed for the first time, and I was encouraged. 'With your ships you rule the river. With this chariot you rule the land. Between the two, you rule the world. Nothing can stand against you.' I was careful not to disparage his beloved ships, or to make unfavourable comparisons.

'Is this your best speed?' he shouted in the wind and the pounding of hooves. 'With a fair wind, *Breath of Horus* is faster than this.' Which was a lie and a challenge.

'Hold on to the sides and take a deep breath,' I warned him. 'I am going to take you up where the eagles fly,' and I let Patience and Blade go.

No man has ever travelled faster. The wind seared our eyes, and the tears pouring from them were blown back into our hair.

'Sweet breath of Isis!' Tanus shouted with excitement. 'This is—' I never knew what he thought this was. Tanus never finished his sentence, for at that instant our off-wheel hit a rock and the rim exploded.

The chariot capsized and somersaulted, and both Tanus and I were thrown high and clear. I struck the hard earth with a force that should have crippled me, but I was so concerned with how Tanus would be affected by this little mishap, and how my dreams and plans would be dashed, that I felt no pain.

I bounded to my feet and saw Tanus crawl to his bleeding knees twenty paces beyond me. He was coated heavily with dust and seemed to have lost the skin from one half of his face. He tried to maintain his dignity as he pushed himself upright and staggered back to the wrecked chariot, but he was limping heavily.

He stood for a long minute gazing down at the shattered ruins of my creation, and then abruptly he let out a roar like a wounded bull, and launched such a mighty kick at it that it flipped over again, as though it were a child's toy. He turned on his heel without even a glance in my direction and limped away. I did not see him again for a week, and when we did meet, neither of us mentioned the chariot.

I think that might have been the end of the matter, and we would never have assembled our first chariot squadron, if it had not been for the fact that the stubbornness of my mistress's pride surpassed even that of her lover. She had given me the original order, and would not now retract it. When Tanus tried to inveigle her into doing so, he merely made my position stronger. Hui and I rebuilt the chariot within three days, and another identical to it.

By the time the embalmers in the funerary chapel had completed the ritual seventy days of royal mummification, we had our first squadron of fifty chariots, and had trained drivers for them.

SINCE WE had returned to the Palace of Memnon from our defeat at the battle of Abnub, my mistress had been occupied with the business of state thrust upon her by the regency. Long hours were spent with her ministers and advisers.

It was now that the initial training which I had given her in the Palace of Elephantine was to bear fruit. I had taught her to pick her way unerringly through the labyrinth of power and influence. She was just twenty-one years of age, but she was a queen, and ruled like one.

Very occasionally she encountered a problem which particularly vexed or perplexed her. Then she sent for me. I would drop my work in the armoury or the stables or in the small scribery that she had set aside for me just down the corridor from her audience chamber, and I would rush to her side.

On occasion I spent days sitting below her throne and steering her through some troublesome decisions. Once again, my ability to read the lips of men without hearing their words stood us in good stead. Some nobleman at the back of the audience never realized, as he plotted or schemed with his neighbour, that I was relaying his exact words to my mistress. She swiftly acquired a reputation of sagacity and prescience. Neither of us enjoyed much rest during these dark and worrisome days.

Even though our days were full, our nights were long. Those interminable councils of war and of state lasted well past midnight. No sooner was one crisis averted, than another loomed before us. Each day the Hyksos threatened us more directly, and Tanus' hold on the river-line weakened.

Slowly, a sense of doom and despair permeated all of us. Men smiled little and never laughed out loud. Even the play of the children was muted and subdued. We had only to look across the river, and the enemy was there, gathering himself, growing stronger each day.

After seventy days, the mummification of Pharaoh was completed. My early efforts in preserving the king's body had been highly successful, and the grand master of the guild of embalmers had commended me in the presence of my mistress. He had found no evidence of decay when he removed the king's corpse from the olive jar, and even his liver, which is the part most subject to mortification, was well preserved.

Once the king had been laid out on the diorite slab in his mortuary chapel, the grand master had inserted the spoon up his nostril and scooped out the curdled contents of his skull which the pickle had hardened to the consistency of cheese. Then, still in the foetal position, the king was placed in the bath of natron salt with only his head left uncovered by the harsh fluid. When he was removed from the bath thirty days later, all the fatty tissue had dissolved, and the outer layers of the skin had peeled off, except for that of the head.

They laid him upon the mottled stone slab once again and straightened him into an extended position. He was wiped and dried, and his empty stomach was filled with linen pads soaked in resins and wax and then sutured closed. Meanwhile, his internal organs were desiccated and placed in their milk-coloured alabaster Canopic jars, which were then sealed.

For the remaining forty days, the body of the king was allowed to dry out thoroughly. The doors of the chapel had been aligned with the direction of the warm, dry prevailing winds, so that they blew over the funeral slab. By the end of the ritual period of seventy days, Pharaoh's body was as dry as a stick of firewood.

His nails, which had been removed before he was soaked in the natron bath, were replaced and fixed in position on his fingers and toes with fine threads of gold wire. The first layer of pure white linen bandages was wound into place around his body, leaving his head and neck exposed. The binding was meticulous and intricate, with the bandages crossing and criss-crossing each other in elaborate patterns. Under the bindings were laid charms and amulets of gold and precious stones. The bandages were then soaked with lacquer and resins that dried to a stony hardness.

Now it was time for the ceremony of Opening-the-Mouth, which traditionally was performed by the dead pharaoh's next of kin. Memnon was too young to take this part, so his regent was called in his stead.

My mistress and I went to the chapel together in the gloom of dawn, and we were witnesses as the linen sheet that covered the king was drawn aside. Pharaoh's head was miraculously preserved. His eyes were closed and his expression was serene. The embalmers had rouged and painted his face, and he looked better in death than he had in life.

While the high priest of Ammon-Ra and the grand master of the guild of embalmers prepared the instruments for the ceremony, we sang the Incantation against Dying for the Second Time.

> He is the reflection and not the mirror.
> He is the music and not the lyre.
> He is the stone and not the chisel that forms it.
> He will live for ever.
> He will not die a second time.

Then the high priest handed my mistress the golden spoon and led her by the hand to the funeral slab.

Queen Lostris stooped over the body of Pharaoh and laid the spoon of life upon his painted lips.

> I open thy lips that thou mayest speak once more,
> I open thy nostrils that thou mayest breathe.

She intoned the words and then touched his eyelids with the spoon.

> I open thy eyes that thou mayest behold once more the glory
> of this world, and the nether-world of the gods where you
> shall dwell from this day forward.

She touched the spoon to his bandaged chest.

> I quicken your heart, so that you may live for ever.
> You shall not die a second time.
> You shall live for ever!

Then we waited while the embalmers bound up Pharaoh's head in the neat swathes of bandages and painted them with resin. They moulded the resin-wet bandages to the shape of his face beneath them. Finally, they placed over his blind bandaged face the first of the four funeral masks.

This was the same funeral mask that we had watched being fashioned from pure gold. While he was still alive, Pharaoh had posed for the sculptor, so the mask was amazingly lifelike. The eyes of shining rock-crystal and obsidian seemed to gaze upon me with all the humanity that the man beneath the mask had once possessed. The cobra head of the *uraeus* rose from the noble brow, regal and mystical.

Then the wrapped mummy was placed in the golden inner coffin, which was sealed, and this went into the second golden coffin with another death-mask embossed upon the lid. Half the treasure recovered from Lord Intef's hoard had gone to make up that enormous weight of precious metal and jewels.

There were seven coffins in all, including the massive stone sarcophagus standing upon the golden sledge, which waited ready to carry Pharaoh along the causeway to his tomb in the gaunt hills. But my mistress refused to give her sanction for this to happen.

'I have given my sacred vow. I cannot place my husband in a tomb that may be plundered by the Hyksos barbarians. Pharaoh will lie here until I am able to make good my promise to him. I will find a secure tomb in which he may lie through eternity. I have given my word that no one will disturb his rest.'

THE WISDOM of Queen Lostris' decision to delay the entombment was proved three nights later. The Hyksos made a determined effort to cross the river, and Tanus barely succeeded in turning them back. They made the attempt on an unguarded stretch of the river two miles north of Esna. They swam their horses across in a mass, and then followed with an armada of small boats which they had carried overland from Thebes in order to conceal their intentions from us.

They actually succeeded in making a beachhead on the west bank before Tanus could rush his galleys to the spot, but he arrived before they could unload their chariots and harness the horses to them. Tanus destroyed their boats with the chariots still on board, and he then had almost three thousand Hyksos stranded on our side of the river. Their horses scattered and bolted away into the night when Tanus' troops made their first charge.

Without their chariots the Hyksos were on even terms with our troops, but they had no means of escape and they fought with grim determination. In numbers they were almost evenly matched, for Tanus had managed to bring up only one full regiment. The rest of his army was thinly spread along the west bank. The fighting was bloody and ferocious, confused by the darkness which was lit only by the burning vessels that Tanus had fired on the beach.

It was only by the wildest coincidence, or by another nudge from the gods, that Hui and I had brought our little squadron of fifty chariots and fledgling charioteers to Esna on training manoeuvres. In truth, we had driven these twenty miles from Thebes principally to escape from Tanus' disapproval and interference.

We were encamped in the sacred grove of tamarind trees beside the temple of Horus at Esna. I was exhausted after a long day of galloping and manoeuvring at high speed. On return to our encampment, Hui had produced a jar of remarkably palatable wine, and I had been somewhat intemperate in my sampling of it. I was dead asleep when Hui staggered into my tent and shook me awake.

'There are fires burning on the bank of the river downstream,' he told me, 'and when the wind shifts, you can hear the sound of cheering, and a little while ago I thought I heard many voices singing the battle hymn of the Blues. I think there is a fight going on down there.'

I was as unsteady on my feet as he was, and reckless with wine, as I shouted for him to rouse the camp and harness the horses. We were all still novices, and it was almost dawn by the time we had caught the horses and put them in the traces. In the chilly drift of the river mist and the gloomy shiver of dawn, we trotted along the north road in column of route, two chariots abreast. I was driving the lead chariot, while Hui had command of the rear-guard. Our fifty chariots had been reduced to thirty by the previous day's exercises, for I had not yet succeeded in perfecting my spoked wheels. They had an alarming tendency to fly to pieces when driven at speed, and almost half my force was out of action.

The passage of the wind over my bare chest made me shiver again, and counteracted the bravado of the wine. I was beginning to hope that Hui had been mistaken, when suddenly from far ahead there came that unmistakable chorus of shouting and cheering, and the clank and clash of bronze on bronze that could mean only one thing. Once you have heard them, the sounds of battle are not readily forgotten or mistaken. The rough farmer's track we were following along the river-bank took a turn to the left. As we came through it, the field lay open before us.

The sun was just above the horizon, and it had turned the surface of the river into a shimmering sheet of beaten copper that was painful to the eye. The ships of Tanus' squadron lay just off-shore, crowding in close to, in an attempt to bring the archers on the decks in range of the Hyksos, and to cut off any retreat across the river.

The stranded Hyksos regiment was making a stand in the centre of a field of knee-high green corn. They had formed a circle, facing outwards, shoulder to shoulder, with their shields locked together and their spears thrust forward. As we came into view, they had just repulsed another attempt by Tanus' troops to break their circle. The Egyptian regiment was pulling back to regroup, leaving their dead and wounded scattered around the periphery of the enemy circle.

I am no soldier, although I have written scrolls on the conduct of war. I had accepted the rank of Commander of the Royal Horse, thrust upon me by my mistress, with the deepest reluctance. I had intended simply to perfect my chariot, train the first squadron, and then hand it over to Hui or some other person more suited to the warlike professions.

I was cold and still half-drunk as I heard my voice giving the order to deploy in arrow-head formation. It was the evolution that we had practised the previous day, and the chariots that followed mine flared out on either side with reasonable proficiency. I was acutely aware of the sound of hooves in the soft earth and the creak of the chariot harness, the squeal of the wheels turning on their metal-lined hubs, and the rattle of javelins as my charioteers drew their darts from the quivers. I looked left and right, reviewing our little squadron drawn up in the shape of an arrow-head with my chariot at the apex. It was a formation I had copied from the Hyksos. I drew a deep breath.

'Squadron will advance!' I screamed, and my voice shrilled with fear. 'At the gallop, forward!'

I had only to lift my left hand that held the traces, and Patience and Blade bounded forward. I was almost thrown over backwards, but I grabbed at the dashboard with my free hand, and we went straight at the Hyksos circle.

Beneath me the chariot leaped and jolted over the lumpy ploughed earth, and I looked over the plunging hindquarters of my horses and saw the wall of Hyksos shields, glittering and impenetrable in the early sunlight, drawing closer with every stride we took.

On either side of me, men were howling and cheering to hide their terror, and I howled with them, like a pariah dog at full moon. The horses were snorting and neighing, and suddenly Patience lifted the long plume of her tail and began to fart in rhythm and in time to her own stride. This struck me as immoderately funny. My howls of terror turned to screams of laughter. The helmet that I had borrowed from Hui was too large for me. It bounced off my head and the wind flung my hair out behind me.

Patience and Blade were the fastest pair in the squadron, and our chariot pulled ahead of the rest of the formation. I tried to slow our charge by hauling back on the traces, but Patience would have none of it. Her glee was evident, she was as excited as any of us, and she straightened her neck and ran away with me.

We tore through the retiring lines of Egyptian infantry coming back from the failed assault on the Hyksos circle, and they scattered out of our path and gawked at us in astonishment.

'Come on!' I howled with laughter. 'We will show you the way!' They turned and followed us back towards the enemy at the run. Behind me, I heard the trumpeters sounding the charge, and the braying horns seemed to spur our horses. Out on my right I saw Tanus' battle standard waving, and recognized his crested helmet standing taller than the other men around him.

'What do you think of my cursed brutes now?' I yelled at him, as we tore past, and Patience farted again, bringing on fresh gales of my nervous laughter.

The chariot on my left was running almost level with me, and then its near-side wheel burst under the strain and it went flying end over end, throwing the charioteers, and bringing the horses down screaming. The rest of us tore on without a check.

The first rank of the enemy was now so close that I could see their eyes staring at me over the top edge of their shields. Their arrows hissed around my ears. I could make out clearly the figures of beasts and demons embossed on their tall metal helmets, see the beads of sweat glittering in their plaited and beribboned beards, hear their chanted war-cry – and then we were into them.

My horses leaped together into the barrier of shields and it shattered before the weight and fury of our charge. I saw a man tossed head-high, and heard his bones crackle like kindling in the fire. On the footplate behind me, my javelineer was making deadly practice. I had chosen him as the best from amongst all my recruits, and he proved my choice now, as he stood firm and hurled his darts down into the enemy.

In succession the following chariots tore into the gap we had opened, and we hardly checked as we raced through, breaking out through the far side of the Hyksos circle, then wheeling in pods of three and coming back at them.

Tanus seized the moment and threw his infantry into the breach that we had torn open. The Hyksos formation broke up into knots of struggling men. These in turn disintegrated, and the Hyksos panicked and ran for the river. The moment they came within range, the archers on the decks of our galleys sent clouds of arrows over them.

Ahead of me there was an isolated pocket of Hyksos warriors still fighting back-to-back, and holding off our men. I swerved the chariot and drove at them in full gallop. Before I reached them, my right wheel burst asunder, the light carapace of the chariot flipped over, and I soared free and then, with a gut-tearing lurch, fell back to earth. My head struck first, and my eyes filled with stars and meteors of bright light. Then there was only darkness.

I woke again under the awning on the deck of Tanus' flagship. I found myself lying on a sheepskin mattress, with Tanus leaning over me. As soon as he saw that I was conscious, he masked the expression of concern and worry that had twisted his features.

'You crazy old fool.' He forced a grin at me. 'What, in the name of Horus, were you laughing about?'

I tried to sit up, but my head ached abominably and I groaned, then clutched his arm as it all came back to me.

'Tanus, the enemy horses that swam across last night – I must have them.'

'Don't worry that battered head of yours. I have already sent Hui to gather them up,' he assured me. 'If I am to have five hundred of those contraptions of yours for my new chariot division, I will need a thousand of those cursed brutes to pull them. However, those new-fangled wheels of yours are more dangerous than a regiment of Hyksos. I will not ride with you again until you do something about them.'

For a moment it did not penetrate my aching skull, then I realized that it had happened. Tanus had quashed his pride, and given in to me. My orphan chariot squadron was at last to be part of the standing army, and he would give me the men and gold to build five hundred more. He would even ride with me again, if only I could fix my wheels.

But what truly filled me with joy was that he had forgiven me at last, and we were friends once more.

THE SUCCESS of my chariots at Esna, and the feeling of confidence that it instilled in us all, were short-lived. Secretly, I had expected and dreaded what would happen next. It was the enemy's logical move, and both Salitis and Lord Intef should have made it much earlier.

We knew that when he swept through the Lower Kingdom, Salitis had captured most of the fleet of the red pretender intact. Those ships were lying abandoned in the docks of Memphis and Tanis in the Delta. However, there must be droves of renegade Egyptians from the usurper's navy available to Salitis, and even if that were not the case, it would certainly be possible to recruit enough mercenary Syrian sailors in Gaza and Joppa, and the other ports along the eastern coast of the great sea, to man several hundred of these galleys and transports.

I had realized that this must happen, but I had refrained from warning either Tanus or my mistress of the likelihood, for I did not wish to add to the feeling of gloom, and heighten the despondency of our people. I had searched my heart for a counter to this move when Salitis and Intef made it, but there was none that I could think of. Therefore, since I could do nothing to allay these fears, I thought it best to keep them to myself.

When it finally happened, and our spies on the east side of the river opposite Asyut warned us of the approach of this fleet from the Delta, Tanus rushed his own ships northwards to meet them. His fleet was superior in every way to the one which Salitis and Intef had assembled, but the battle they fought lasted for almost a week before Tanus destroyed or drove them back into the Delta.

However, Salitis had brought his transports up behind the screen of fighting galleys, and while the river battle still raged, he was able to embark almost two full regiments of horse and chariot, and ferry them intact to our side of the river, without our galleys being able to reach them.

These regiments comprised nearly three hundred of Salitis' fast war chariots, his elite divisions which he led himself. At last he had turned our flank. There was nothing to stop him now, as his chariots came bowling southwards along our side of the river. All our galleys could do was to try to keep pace with the dust-cloud he threw up, as he raced for the funerary temple of Mamose and all its treasures.

QUEEN LOSTRIS called her war council when the news of the Hyksos crossing reached us in the Palace of Memnon. She addressed her first question to Tanus.

'Now that he is across the river, can you check the barbarian?'

'I can slow him down, perhaps,' he replied frankly. 'We have learned a great deal about him. We can wait for him behind walls of stone, or behind barriers of the sharp staves that Taita has equipped us with. But Salitis need not give battle. His chariots are so fast that he can swing around our positions as he did at Asyut. No, I cannot stop him.'

Queen Lostris looked at me. 'Taita, what about your chariots? Can they not give battle to the Hyksos?'

'Your Majesty, I have forty chariots that I can send in to meet him. He has three hundred. My chariots are swifter than those of Salitis, but my men cannot match his in skill and training. There is also the matter of the wheels. I have not perfected them. Salitis will overwhelm and destroy us very easily. If I am given the time and the material, I can build new and better chariots with wheels that do not burst, but I cannot replace the horses. We dare not risk the horses. They are our only hope for eventual victory.'

While we thus debated, another messenger arrived, this time from the south. He had fled to us on the current and the wind, so his news was only a day old. Tanus ordered him into the council chamber, and the messenger fell to his knees before Queen Lostris.

'Speak, fellow,' Tanus invited him. 'What do you have to tell us?'

The messenger stuttered in fear of his life, 'Divine Majesty, while our fleet was busy at Asyut, the barbarian made another crossing at Esna. They swam the horses over as they did before, but this time there were none of our galleys ready to turn back their boats. Two Hyksos regiments are across. Their horses are in the traces and they are coming on a cloud of dust, swiftly as the flight of the swallow. They will be here in three days.'

None of us spoke until Tanus had sent the man away with orders that he be fed and cared for. The messenger, who had expected to be killed, kissed Queen Lostris' sandals.

When we were alone, Tanus said softly, 'Salitis has four regiments across the river. Six hundred chariots. It is over.'

'No!' my mistress's voice shook with the force of her denial. 'The gods cannot desert this very Egypt now. Our civilization cannot perish. We have too much to give to the world.'

'I can fight on, of course,' Tanus agreed. 'But in the end it will all be the same. We cannot prevail against their chariots.'

My mistress turned back to me. 'Taita, I have not asked you before, because I know how dearly it costs you. But I must ask you now before I make the final decision. I ask you to work the Mazes of Ammon-Ra for me. I must know what the gods require of us.'

I bowed my head in acquiescence, and whispered, 'I will fetch my chest.'

THE SITE that I chose for the divination was the inner sanctuary of the shrine to Horus in the half-completed Palace of Memnon. The shrine had not yet been dedicated to the god, and his image had not yet been set up, but I was certain that Horus had already cast his benevolent influence over the building.

My mistress sat before me with Tanus at her side, and watched in fascination as I drank the witches' potion to open the eyes of my soul, my *Ka*, the little bird-like creature that lives in the heart of every one of us, and which is our alter ego.

I laid the ivory Mazes before them and asked both Queen Lostris and Tanus to stroke and handle them, to endow them with their spirit and the spirit of the nation that they represented, this very Egypt. As I watched them divide the stacks of ivory counters, I felt the drug in my blood grow stronger, and the beat of my heart slowed as the little death crept over me.

I took up the two remaining Mazes from the last stack, and I held them to my breast. They began to grow hot against my skin, and my instinct was to draw back from the darkness that I felt coming over me. Instead, I surrendered to it and let it carry me away.

I heard my mistress's voice, as though from a great distance. 'What will become of the double crown? How can we resist the barbarian?'

The visions began to form before my eyes, and I was carried up into the days that were still to come, and I saw events that had not yet come to pass.

The morning sunlight was streaming through the aperture in the roof and striking the altar of Horus, when at last I returned from the far journey of the Mazes. I was shaken and nauseated with the effect of the hallucinatory drug, giddy and trembling with the memories of the strange sights that I had seen.

My mistress and Tanus had stayed with me during the long night. Their anxious faces were the first things that I saw on my return, but they were still so distorted and wavering that I thought they were part of the vision.

'Taita, are you all right? Speak to us. Tell us what you saw.' My mistress was concerned. She could not hide the guilt she felt at having forced me to enter the Mazes of Ammon-Ra once more.

'There was a serpent.' My voice still echoed strangely in my own ears, as though I stood apart. 'A great green serpent that crawled through the desert.'

I saw the puzzled expression on their faces, but I had not yet considered the meaning of it all myself, so I could give them no guidance.

'I am thirsty,' I whispered. 'My throat is dry and my tongue like a stone covered with moss.'

Tanus fetched a jar of wine and poured it into the bowl for me, and I drank greedily.

'Tell us of the serpent,' my mistress demanded, as soon as I lowered the bowl.

'There was no end to its sinuous body, and it shimmered green in the sunlight. It crawled through a strange land, in which lived tall naked men and strange and wonderful beasts.'

'Could you see the head or the tail of the serpent?' my mistress asked, and I shook my head.

'Where were you? Where did you stand?' she insisted. I had forgotten how keenly she enjoyed my visions, and what pleasure she took in interpreting them.

'I was riding upon the back of the serpent,' I answered. 'But I was not alone.'

'Who was with you?'

'You were at my side, mistress, and Memnon with you. Tanus was on my other hand, and the serpent carried us all.'

'The Nile! The serpent was the river,' she cried triumphantly. 'You foresaw a voyage that we were making upon the river.'

'Which way?' Tanus demanded. He was as rapt as she was. 'Which way did the river run?'

I made an effort to recall every detail. 'I saw the sun rise on my left hand.'

'South!' he cried.

'Into Africa,' said my mistress.

'At last I saw the heads of the serpent ahead of us. The body of the serpent was bifurcated, and on each branch was a head.'

'Does the Nile have two branches?' my mistress wondered aloud. 'Or is there some deeper meaning to the vision?'

'Let us hear the rest of what Taita has to tell us,' Tanus stopped her speculation. 'Continue, old friend.'

'Then I saw the goddess,' I went on. 'She sat upon a high mountain. Both the heads of the serpent worshipped her.'

My mistress could not restrain herself. 'Which of the goddesses did you see? Oh, tell me quickly who it was.'

'She had the bearded head of a man but the breasts and the pudenda of a woman. From her vagina she spurted out two great streams of water into the open mouths of the double-headed serpent.'

'It is the goddess Hapi, the river god,' Queen Lostris whispered. 'She generates the river within herself, and pours it out to flow through the world.'

'What else did the vision show you?' Tanus demanded.

'The goddess smiled at us, and her face shone with love and benevolence. She spoke in a voice that was the sound of the wind and the sea. The sound of thunder on the peaks of far-away mountains.'

'What did she say to us?' Queen Lostris asked in awe.

'She said, "Let my child come to me. I will make her strong so that she will prevail and my people will not perish in the face of the barbarian."' I repeated the words that still beat like a drum in my head.

'I am the child of the river goddess,' said my mistress simply. 'At birth I was dedicated to her. Now she summons me, and I must go to the place where she dwells at the end of the Nile.'

'This is the same voyage that Taita and I contemplated once before,' Tanus mused. 'And now the goddess commands it. We cannot refuse her.'

'Yes, we must go, but we will come back,' my mistress vowed. 'This is my land, this very Egypt. This is my city, this beautiful Thebes of the hundred gates. I cannot leave them for ever. I will return to Thebes. This I swear and I call upon the goddess Hapi to witness my oath. We shall return!'

THE DECISION to fly to the south, up above the cataracts into the wild and unexplored land beyond, was one that Tanus and I had made once before. The first time had been to escape the wrath and vengeance of Pharaoh. Now we were flying from an even more merciless foe. It was almost as though the gods were determined that we should undertake this voyage, and that they would not be denied.

There was little time for us to make our preparations for such a fateful departure. The Hyksos were coming down on us from two directions, and our pickets reported that their cohorts would be in view from the roof of the Palace of Memnon within three days at the very latest.

Tanus placed Kratas in charge of half his available force and sent him to meet King Salitis who was driving hard from Asyut in the north and was likely to be the first column to reach the necropolis and the palace. Kratas had orders to fight a running battle. Using the staves and defending every fortified position, he was to delay Salitis as long as was possible, without risking being cut off or overwhelmed. When he could hold them no longer, he was to evacuate his men on to the galleys.

Tanus himself took the other half of our army and moved south to fight another delaying battle against the Hyksos division coming at us from Esna.

While they were thus engaged, my mistress was to embark our people and all their possessions aboard the remaining ships of our fleet. My mistress delegated this duty to Lord Merkeset, but of course she made me his assistant. Lord Merkeset was not only well into his dotage, but had recently taken to himself a sixteen-year-old wife. He was not, therefore, of much use either to himself or to me. The entire planning and execution of the evacuation fell squarely on my shoulders.

However, before I could turn my mind to this, I had to take care of my horses. Even at this early stage I realized with stark clarity that they were the key to our survival as a nation and a civilized people. With those animals that we had captured at Esna, we now had several thousand in our herd. I split this herd into four parts so that they could more readily find grazing on the march. Further, the smaller herds would throw up less dust, and it would be easier for them to avoid the Hyksos scouts.

I sent Hui and my charioteers and grooms south with these herds towards Elephantine, with orders to avoid the river-bank down which the Hyksos chariots were advancing and to keep inland, closer to the edge of the desert.

Once the horses were despatched, I could turn my attention to the humans. I realized that we were limited by the number of ships available as to how many of our people were able to accompany us on the long voyage. I was certain that almost every Egyptian wanted to be part of the exodus. The cruelty and ferocity of the Hyksos were evident in every city they burned and in every atrocity that they inflicted on our people. All the unknown dangers of the African wilderness were preferable to these bloodthirsty monsters who were racing down upon us in their chariots.

In the end I calculated that we could accommodate only twelve thousand souls aboard the escaping fleet, and I reported this to my mistress.

'We will have to be ruthless in those we select and those we leave behind,' I told her, but she would not listen to my advice.

'These are my people. I would give up my own place rather than leave one of them to the Hyksos.'

'But, Majesty, what about the old and the decrepit? The sick and the very young?'

'Every citizen will be given the choice of coming with us. I will not leave a greybeard or a beggar, a day-old infant or a leper. They are my people, and if they cannot go, then Prince Memnon and I will stay with them.' Of course, she mentioned the prince to make doubly certain of her victory over me.

The ships would be gunwale-deep under this great weight of humanity, but I had no choice. Still, I had some satisfaction in first embarking all the most useful and creative citizens. I chose men from every trade and profession, masons and weavers, coppersmiths and potters, tanners and sailmakers, scribes and artists, shipbuilders and carpenters, all of them leaders in their particular discipline. These I saw safely on board the waiting transports. It gave me a particular pleasure to allocate the most uncomfortable berths in the most squalid vessels to the priesthood and the law scribes, those blood-sucking fleas on the healthy body of the state.

When all of these were boarded, I allowed the rabble to come swarming on to the wharf below the temple.

As a result of my mistress's intransigence, I had to be careful in choosing what cargo we would load. There would be no room for idle fripperies. I gathered up the weapons and tools and the raw materials that we would need to build up another civilization in the unknown lands. For the rest of the cargo I tried in every way to reduce weight and bulk. For instance, rather than grain and fruits, I loaded the seeds of every desirable plant in clay jars sealed with pitch and wax.

Every deben-weight of cargo that we loaded in our holds meant that something else must be left behind. Our voyage might last ten years or a lifetime. The road would be hard. We knew that the great cataracts lay ahead of us. We dared not burden ourselves with anything but the most essential, but then there remained my mistress's promise to Pharaoh. There was barely room for the living – how much space could we afford to give over to the dead?

'I gave my vow to the king as he lay dying,' my mistress insisted. 'I cannot leave him here.'

'Your Majesty, I will find a secure hiding-place for the king's body, an unmarked grave in the hills where no man will find him. When we return to Thebes, we will exhume him, and give him the royal burial that you promised him.'

'If I break my vow, the gods will desert us and our voyage will be doomed. The body of the king must go with us.'

One glance at her expression warned me that there would be no profit in further argument. We opened the massive granite sarcophagus and lifted out the six inner coffins. Even these were so bulky that it would have needed a galley to carry them alone.

I made a decision without consulting Queen Lostris. I had the workmen remove only the two innermost golden coffins. These we covered with a thick linen canvas shroud which we stitched over them as protection. The size and weight were thus reduced to acceptable proportions, and we stowed these two canvas-covered coffins in the hold of the *Breath of Horus*.

The bulk of Pharaoh's treasure, all the gold and silver and the precious stones, was packed into cedar-wood boxes. I ordered the goldsmiths to strip the bullion from the discarded coffins and from the wooden frame of the great funeral sledge, and melt it down into bars. I was secretly delighted to be the instrument of destruction of that tasteless monstrosity. The treasure chests and the bars of bullion were carried down to the wharf and loaded on board the waiting ships. I distributed these so that every ship carried at least one chest or a stack of bullion bars. In this way, the risk that the entire treasure could be lost at a single stroke of misfortune was greatly reduced.

There was much of the funerary treasure that we could not take with us, all the furniture and the statuary, the ceremonial armour and the boxes of *ushabti* statues, and of course the ungainly framework of the hearse from which I had stripped the gold. Rather than have it fall into the hands of the Hyksos, we piled all of this in the temple courtyard, and I personally hurled a burning torch on top of the mountain of treasure, and watched it burn to ashes.

All this was done in dreadful haste, and before the last ship was loaded the lookouts on the roof of the palace shouted the warning that the dust-clouds of the Hyksos chariots were in sight. Within the hour, our exhausted and battle-weary troops who, under command of Tanus and Kratas, had been fighting the long grim rear-guard action, began to pull back into the necropolis, and to embark on the waiting galleys.

I met Tanus as he came up on to the causeway at the head of a squad of the guards. So far, by dint of courage and sacrifice, he and his men had managed to win a few extra days for us to complete the evacuation. They could do no more, and the enemy was driving them in.

When I waved and called his name, Tanus saw me and shouted over the heads of the crowd, 'Queen Lostris and the prince? Have they gone aboard the *Breath of Horus?*'

'I forced my way through the throng to his side. 'My mistress will not leave until all her people are on board the ships. She ordered me to take you to her as soon as you arrived. She is waiting for you in her quarters in the palace.'

He looked at me aghast. 'The enemy are pressing us hard. Queen Lostris and the prince are more precious than all this rabble. Why did you not force her?'

I laughed. 'She is not an easy lady to force. You should know that as well as I do. She will leave none of her people to the Hyksos.'

'Seth blast that woman's pride! She will get all of us killed.' But his harsh words were belied by the expression of pride and admiration on his dusty, sweat-streaked face, and he grinned at me. 'Well, if she will not come on her own, we shall have to go and fetch her.'

We pushed our way through the long lines of passengers, laden with bundles of their possessions and carrying their infants, that were streaming down to the dock to go aboard the ships. As we hurried along the causeway, Tanus pointed over the battlements at the ominous clouds of dust bearing down upon us from both directions.

'They are moving faster than I had believed possible. They have not even halted to water their horses. Unless we speed up the embarkation, they will catch us with half our people still ashore,' he said grimly, and pointed down on to the wharf below us.

The wharf was wide enough to allow only two vessels to come alongside at one time. The masses of refugees clogged the causeway and congested the entrance gates to the dock. Their weeping and lamentation added to the confusion, and at that moment someone at the rear of the column screamed, 'The Hyksos are here! Run! Save yourselves! The Hyksos are here!'

The panic spread through the crowd and it surged forward mindlessly. Women were crushed against the stone gates, and children were trampled under foot. All order and control were breaking down, decent and dignified citizens and disciplined soldiers were being reduced to a desperate mob struggling for survival.

I had to use the sharpened stave I carried to force a way through them, as Tanus and I fought our way back towards the palace. At last we broke out of the crowd and ran to the palace gates.

The halls and corridors were empty and deserted except for a few looters who were picking through the empty rooms. They ran when they saw Tanus. He was a dreadful sight, gaunt and dusty and battle-worn, with a ruddy stubble of beard covering his jaw. Ahead of me, he burst into the private quarters of the queen, and we found her chamber unguarded and the door standing wide. We rushed through it.

My mistress sat alone on the terrace under the spreading vine, with Prince Memnon on her lap. She was pointing out to him the fleet of ships on the Nile below the terrace, and the two of them were enthusing over the spectacle.

'Look at the pretty ships.'

Queen Lostris stood up smiling when she saw us, and Memnon slid off her lap and ran to Tanus.

Tanus swung him up on to his shoulder, and then embraced my mistress with his free hand.

'Where are your slaves? Where are Aton and Lord Merseket?' Tanus demanded.

'I sent them to the ships.'

'Taita says that you refused to go yourself. He is very angry with you, and rightly so.'

'Forgive me, dear Taita.' Her smile could light my life, or break my heart.

'Rather beg the forgiveness of King Salitis,' I suggested stiffly. 'He will be here soon enough.' I seized her arm. 'Now that this rude soldier of yours has at last arrived, can we please go to the ships?'

We hurried from the terrace and back through the palace corridors. We were entirely alone, even the looters and the thieves had disappeared like rats into their holes. The only one of us who was completely unconcerned was Prince Memnon. For him it was another jolly game. Sitting astride Tanus' shoulders, he dug in his heels and shouted, 'Hi up!' as he had learned from me when we were riding Patience.

We raced across the palace gardens to the stone staircase that led up on to the causeway. That was the shortest way to the temple dock. As we hurried along the causeway, I realized that circumstances had changed drastically in the time that had passed since we had left to fetch my mistress and the prince from the palace. Ahead of us the causeway was deserted, the last of the refugees had gone on board the ships in the dock. Beyond the stone battlements I could see their masts moving slowly down the canal towards the open river.

With a hollow feeling in the pit of my stomach, I realized that we were the last persons left ashore, and that we still had half a mile to cover before we reached the empty dock. All of us stopped together, and watched the last galleys sail away.

'I told the captain to wait,' I groaned, 'but with the Hyksos so close, their only concern is with their own safety.'

'What can we do now?' my mistress breathed, and even Memnon's happy cries dried up.

'If we can reach the river-bank, surely Remrem or Kratas will see us and send in a skiff to pick us up?' I suggested, and Tanus agreed immediately.

'This way! Follow me!' he cried. 'Taita, see to your mistress.'

I took her arm to help her along, but she was as strong and agile as a shepherd boy and ran easily at my side. Then suddenly I heard the horses, and the squeal of chariot wheels. The sounds were unmistakable and terrifyingly near at hand.

Our own horses had left three days ago, and must be well on their way to Elephantine by this time. Our own chariots were dismantled and loaded in the holds of the departing fleet. The chariots I heard now were still out of sight below the wall of the causeway, but we knew to whom they belonged.

'The Hyksos!' I said softly, and we stopped in a tight little group. 'It must be one of their advance scouting parties.'

'It sounds like only two or three of their chariots,' Tanus agreed, 'but that is enough. We are cut off.'

'It seems that we have left it a little late,' said my mistress with a calmness that I knew was feigned, and she looked at Tanus and myself with complete trust. 'What do you suggest now?'

Her effrontery flabbergasted me. Her obstinancy was entirely responsible for our predicament. If she had followed my urging we would all of us have been on the *Breath of Horus* and making our way up-river to Elephantine by this time.

Tanus held up his hand for silence, and we stood and listened to the sounds of the enemy chariots driving along the pathway at the foot of the wall. The closer they came, the more certain it became that this was only a small advance party.

Suddenly the sounds of turning wheels stopped, and we heard the horses blowing and stamping, then men's voices speaking a harsh and guttural tongue. They were just below us, and Tanus made another urgent signal for silence. Prince Memnon was not accustomed to restraint, nor to keeping the peace against his inclinations. He also had heard and recognized the sounds.

'Horses!' he shouted in his usual high and ringing tones. 'I want to see the horses.'

There was an instant outcry. Hyksos voices shouted orders, and weapons rattled in their scabbards. Then heavy footfalls pounded upon the stone staircase as a party of the enemy came dashing up on to the causeway.

Their tall helmets appeared above the stone balustrade just ahead of us, and then the rest of them came into view. There were five of them in a body and they rushed up at us with drawn swords, big men with fish-scale shirts of mail and brightly coloured ribbons in their beards. But one of them was taller than the rest. I did not recognize him at first, for he had grown a beard and decorated it with ribbons in the Hyksos fashion, and the visor of his helmet hid half his face. Then he shouted in that voice that I would never forget, 'So it's you, young Harrab! I killed the old dog, and now I will kill his puppy!'

I should have known that Lord Intef would be the very first of them to come sniffing like a hungry hyena after Pharaoh's treasure. He must have raced ahead of the main Hyksos division to be the first into the funerary temple. Despite his boast, he did not rush to meet Tanus, but waved the band of Hyksos charioteers forward to do the job for him.

Tanus swept Prince Memnon from his shoulders and tossed him to me as though he were a doll.

'Run!' he ordered. 'I will buy you a little time here.' He rushed the Hyksos while they were still bunched on the staircase and had no room to wield their swords. He killed the first one cleanly, with that thrust through the throat which he always performed so skilfully.

'Don't stand there gawking,' he shouted over his shoulder. 'Run!'

I was not gawking, but with the child clutched to my chest, I knew how futile was his command. Burdened as I was, I would never reach the river-bank.

I stepped to the parapet of the causeway and glanced over. There were two Hyksos chariots parked directly below me, with the horses blowing and stamping in the traces. Only one man had been left to hold them, while his companions rushed up the staircase. He stood at the heads of the two teams and his whole attention was fixed on his charges. He had not seen me on the causeway above his head.

Still clutching Memnon, I threw my legs over the parapet and pushed myself outwards. The prince shrieked with alarm as we dropped. From the top of the causeway to where the Hyksos charioteer stood was four times the height of a tall man. I might easily have broken a leg in the fall, except that I landed neatly on the unsuspecting Hyksos' head. The impact broke his neck; clearly I heard the vertebrae snap, and he crumpled under us, breaking our fall.

I scrambled to my feet, with Memnon howling in outrage at this rough treatment, but there was more of it to follow. I dropped him into the cockpit of the nearest chariot and looked up at my mistress. She was peeping over the parapet high above me.

'Jump!' I shouted. 'I will catch you!' She never even hesitated, but flung herself over the edge so promptly that I was not yet braced to receive her. She came hurtling down on top of me, with her short skirts blowing up and exposing those long sleek thighs. She hit me squarely and knocked the wind out of my lungs. We went down together in a heap.

I scrambled up wheezing for breath, and dragged her to her feet. I shoved her roughly over the footplate of the chariot and shouted at her, 'See to Memnon!' She grabbed him just as he tried to escape from the cockpit of the chariot. He was still howling with anger and fright. I had to scramble over the top of them to reach the reins and take control of the horses.

'Hang on tight!' The pair of horses responded instantly to my hands, and I wheeled the whole rig smartly under the wall. One wheel bounced over the body of the man that I had killed with my fall.

'Tanus!' I screamed. 'This way!'

High above us he jumped up on to the parapet, and balanced there easily, exchanging parry and thrust with the group of charioteers who bayed around him, like hounds around a treed leopard.

'Jump, Tanus, jump!' I yelled, and he stepped out over the edge of the stone wall and let himself drop. With his cloak billowing around his head and shoulders, he landed astride the back of the off-side horse. His sword jerked out of his hand and clattered on the hard earth, and Tanus threw both arms around the animal's neck.

'Hi up!' I called to the pair, and whipped the end of the reins around their hindquarters. They surged forward into a full gallop. I steered them across the pathway and into the open fields that led down to the river-bank. I could see the sails of our fleet out there in midstream, and I could even recognize the pennant of the *Breath of Horus* flying amongst the forest of masts. We had half a mile to go to reach the bank, and I glanced over my shoulder.

Lord Intef and his men had rushed down the staircase. Even as I watched, they were climbing up into the other chariot. I cursed myself that I had not disabled it. It would have taken only a moment to cut the traces and chase away the horses, but I had been in a panic to get my mistress and the prince away.

Now Lord Intef was coming after us. His chariot had not covered a hundred paces before I realized that it was faster than the one I was driving. Tanus' weight on the back of the off-side horse was hampering its gallop; he was a heavy man and he still clung to its neck with both arms. He seemed frozen with terror. I think that this was the first time that I had ever seen him truly afraid. I have seen him stand firm and shoot down a charging lion with his bow, but the horse terrified him.

I tried to ignore the following chariot, and I looked ahead and concentrated all my newly acquired skill on piloting us over the open cultivated fields and through the maze of irrigation canals and ditches to the bank of the Nile. The Hyksos chariot was heavy and unwieldy, compared to my Taita vehicle. The solid wooden wheels with their glinting and turning knives around the rims bit deeply into the clay loam of the ploughed lands, and all that bronze armour and ornamentation on the dashboard and side-frames weighed us down. The horses must have been driven hard before I took control of them. They were lathered with sweat and white froth dripped from their muzzles.

We had not covered half the distance to the river-bank when I heard the shouts of the Hyksos charioteer closing with us, and the pounding of hooves. I glanced back to see them not three lengths behind. The driver was lashing the horses with a whip of knotted leather tails and yelling at them in that coarse and ugly language. Beside him, Lord Intef was leaning out eagerly over the dashboard. His ribboned beard was streaming back on either side of his jaw, and his handsome features were lit by the rapture of the hunter.

He shouted at me, and his voice carried over the sounds of the two labouring teams of horses. 'Taita, my old darling, do you still love me? I want you to prove it once more before you die.' And he laughed. 'You are going to kneel in front of me and die with your mouth full.' My skin prickled with insects' feet of horror at the image his words conjured up.

There was an irrigation ditch ahead of us, and I swerved to run alongside it, for the sides were deep and sheer. The Hyksos chariot followed us round, gaining on us with every stride.

'And you, my lovely daughter, I will give you to the Hyksos soldiers to play with. They will teach you a few tricks that Harrab forgot to show you. I don't need you, now that I have your brat.' Queen Lostris clutched the prince closer to her chest and her face was pale and set.

I understood Lord Intef's design immediately. A child of the royal blood of Egypt, even as a satrap of the Hyksos, would command the loyalty of all our people. Prince Memnon was the puppet through which

King Salitis and Lord Intef intended to rule the two kingdoms. It was an ancient and effective device of the conqueror. I pushed my horses to their utmost, but they were tiring and slowing, and Lord Intef closed with us so swiftly that he no longer needed to shout to make himself heard.

'Lord Harrab, this is a pleasure long delayed. What shall we do with you, I wonder? First, you and I will watch the soldiers entertain my daughter—' I tried to stop my ears to his filth, but his voice was insidious.

I was still gazing ahead, concentrating on the rough and dangerous ground, but from the corner of my eye I saw the heads of the Hyksos pair draw level with our vehicle. Their manes flowed back, and their eyes were wild as they tore up beside us at full gallop.

I looked back at them. The burly Hyksos archer on the footplate behind Intef nocked an arrow to his short recurved bow. The range was so short that even from the bouncing and leaping platform, he could not miss hitting one of us.

Tanus was out of the fight. He had dropped his sword. He was still clinging to the neck of the horse on the side furthest from the overtaking chariot. I had only my little dagger, and Queen Lostris was down on her knees trying to shield the prince with her own body.

It was only then that I realized the mistake that the Hyksos driver had made. He had pushed his team of horses into the gap between us and the deep irrigation ditch. He had left himself no room to manoeuvre.

The archer lifted his bow and drew the fletchings of the arrow to his lips. He aimed at me. I was looking into his eyes over the barbed flint of the arrow-head. His brows were black and dense and bushy, his eyes as dark and implacable as those of a lizard. The Hyksos horses were running level with the hub of my near-side wheel, and I gathered my reins and swerved towards them. The flashing bronze knives that stood out of my wheel-rims buzzed softly as they spun towards the legs of the horses.

The Hyksos driver shouted with consternation as he realized his error. His horses were trapped between the ditch and those cruel knives. The blades were less than a hand-span from the knees of the big bay stallion running nearest to me.

At that same instant, the Hyksos archer loosed his arrow, but my sudden swerve had beaten him also. The arrow seemed to fly quite slowly towards my head, but this was an illusion produced by my terror. In reality it flashed like a beam of sunlight over my shoulder, the flint edge touched my ear, and a drop of blood dripped from the grazed skin on to my chest.

The other driver had tried to counter my swerve by turning away from me, but now his far wheel was running along the lip of the irrigation ditch. It was crumbling away beneath the bronze-bound rim, and the chariot lurched and teetered on the edge.

I gathered my horses and swung them again, turning into the other chariot. My wheel-blades hacked into the legs of the nearest horse, and the poor beast squealed with agony. I saw pieces of skin and hair fly into the air above the sideboard of my chariot, and I steeled myself to the whinnying cry of the horse, and turned hard into him again. This time blood and bone chips flew in a mush from the broken legs, and the horse went down, kicking and squealing, pulling his team-mate down with him. The Hyksos chariot went over the edge of the ditch. I saw the two passengers in the cockpit thrown clear, but the driver was carried over and crushed beneath the capsized truck and the heavy, spinning wheels.

Our own chariot was now tearing along dangerously close to the edge of the ditch, but I managed to gather the horses and bring them back in hand.

'Whoa!' I slowed them, and turned to look back. A cloud of dust hung over the ditch where the Hyksos chariot had disappeared. I brought my team down to a trot. The river-bank was two hundred paces ahead, and nothing stood in our way to safety.

I turned for one last look behind me. The Hyksos archer, who had fired his arrow at me, lay in a crumpled and broken heap where he had been thrown. Lord Intef lay a little further from the edge of the ditch. I truly believe I might have left him there if he had not stirred, but at that moment he sat up and then pushed himself unsteadily to his feet.

Suddenly all my hatred of him came back to me with such force and clarity that my mind seethed with it. It was as though a vein had burst behind my eyes, for my vision darkened, and was glazed over with the reddish sheen of blood. A savage, incoherent cry burst from my throat, and I wheeled the horses in a tight circle until we were headed back towards the causeway.

Lord Intef stood directly in my path. He had lost his helmet and his weapons in the fall, and he seemed half-dazed, for he swayed upon his feet. I whipped the horses up into a gallop once more, and the heavy wheels rumbled forward. I aimed the chariot directly at him. His beard was dishevelled and the ribbons in it sullied with dust. His eyes also were dull and bemused, but as I drove the horses down on him, suddenly they cleared and his head came up.

'No!' he shouted, and began to back away, throwing out his hands towards me as if to fend off the massive carriage and the running horses. I aimed directly for him, but at the last moment, his dark gods defended him one last time. As I was right upon him, he threw himself to one side. I had seen him staggering and I had supposed that he was weak and helpless. Instead, he was as quick and nimble as a jackal pursued by the hounds. The chariot was heavy and unwieldy, and I could not turn it swiftly enough to follow his side-step and dodge.

I missed him and went on by. I wrestled with the reins, but the horses carried me on a hundred paces before I could get them under control and swing the heavy vehicle round again. By the time we came around, Intef was running for the shelter of the ditch. If he reached it, he would be safe – I realized that. I swore bitterly as I drove the team after him.

It was then that his gods finally abandoned him. He had almost reached the ditch, but he was looking back over his shoulder at me, and he was not watching his footing. He ran into a patch of clay clods, hard as rocks, and his ankle turned under him. He fell heavily but rolled back on to his feet like an acrobat. He tried to run again, but the pain in his broken ankle brought him up. He hobbled a pace or two and then tried to hop forward towards the ditch on one leg.

'You are mine at last!' I screamed at him, and he spun around to face me, balanced on one leg as I drove the chariot down on him. His face was pale, but those leopard eyes blazed up at me with all the bitterness and hatred of his cruel and twisted soul.

'He is my father!' my mistress cried at my side, holding the prince's face to her bosom so that he would not see it. 'Leave him, Taita. He is of my blood.'

I had never disobeyed her in my life, this was the first time. I made no move to check the horses, but gazed into Lord Intef's eyes, for once without fear.

At the very end, he almost cheated me again. He flung himself sideways, and such were his agility and his strength that he twisted himself clear of the truck and the wheels of the chariot, but he could not quite avoid the wheel-knives. One of the spinning blades hooked in the fish-scale links of his coat of mail. The point of the knife tore through the armour and hooked in the flesh of his belly. The knife was spinning and his entrails snagged and wrapped around it, so that his guts were drawn out of him, as though he was one of those big blue perch from the river being disembowelled by a fishwife on the market block.

He was towed along behind us by the slippery ropes of his own entrails, but he fell slowly behind as more coils and tangles of his gut were torn from his open stomach cavity. He clutched at them with both hands, as they were stripped out of him, but they slid through his fingers like some grotesque umbilical cord that bound him to the turning wheel of the chariot.

His screams were a sound that I wish never to hear again as long as I live. The echoes of them still sometimes haunt my nightmares, so that in the end he inflicted his last cruelty upon me. I have never been able to forget him, as I would so dearly have wished.

When at last the gruesome rope by which he was being dragged across the black earth snapped, he was left lying in the centre of the field. At last those cries of his were stilled, and he lay without movement.

I pulled up the horses and Tanus slid down off the back of his mount and came back to the chariot. He lifted my mistress and the prince down and held them close to his chest. My mistress was weeping.

'Oh, it was so terrible! Whatever he did to us, he was still my father.'

'It's all right now,' Tanus hugged her. 'It's all over now.'

Prince Memnon was peering back over his mother's shoulder at the sprawling figure of his grandfather with all the fascination that children have with the macabre. Suddenly he piped up in that ringing treble, 'He was a nasty man.'

'Yes,' I agreed softly, 'he was a very nasty man.'

'Is the nasty man dead now?'

'Yes, Mem, he is dead. Now we can all sleep better at nights.'

I had to drive the horses hard along the river-bank to catch up with our departing flotilla, but at last I drew level with Kratas' galley, and he recognized us in the unfamiliar vehicle. Even across that wide stretch of water, his astonishment was apparent. Later he told me that he had believed we were safely aboard one of the leading ships of the flotilla.

I turned the horses loose before I left the chariot. Then we waded out into the water to reach the small boat which Kratas sent in to pick us up.

THE HYKSOS would not let us go that easily. Day after day, their chariots pursued our flotilla down both banks of the Nile as we fled southwards.

Whenever we looked back over the stern of the *Breath of Horus*, we saw the dust of the enemy columns following us. Very often the dust was mingled with the darker clouds of smoke that rose from the towns and villages on the river-banks which the Hyksos burned as they sacked them. As we passed each of the Egyptian towns, a flock of small craft sailed out to join our fleet, so that our armada increased in numbers with each day that passed.

There were times, when the wind was unfavourable, that the columns of chariots overhauled us. Then we saw their cohorts gleaming on the banks on either side of us, and heard their harsh but futile jeers and challenges ring out across the water. However, eternal Mother Nile gave us her protection, as she had over the centuries, and they could not reach us out on the stream. Then the wind would veer back into the north and we drew ahead of them once more, and the dust-clouds fell back on to the northern horizon.

'Their horses cannot keep up this chase much longer,' I told Tanus on the morning of the twelfth day.

'Don't be too smug about it. Salitis has the lure of the treasure of Pharaoh Mamose and the legitimate heir to the double crown,' Tanus replied simply. 'Gold and power have a marvellous way of stiffening a man's resolve. We have not seen the last of the barbarian yet.'

The next morning the wind had changed again, and the chariots slowly gained upon us once more, and overtook the leading ships of our flotilla just as we approached the Gates of Hapi, the first of the granite walls that constricted the river below Elephantine. Between them the Nile narrowed to less than four hundred paces across from bank to bank, and the black granite cliffs rose almost sheer on each side. The flow of the current was full against us as it swirled through the Gates of Hapi, so that our speed bled off and Tanus ordered fresh men to the rowing-benches.

'I think you are right, Taita. This is where they will be waiting,' he told me grimly, and then almost immediately afterwards he pointed ahead. 'There they are.'

Leading the fleet, the *Breath of Horus* was just entering the gates, so we had to throw our heads back to look up the cliff-faces. The figures of the Hyksos archers high up on the rocky ledges were foreshortened by the angle, so that they appeared as grotesque dwarfs.

'From that height they could shoot their arrows clear across from bank to bank,' Tanus muttered. 'We will be in easy range for most of this day. It will be hard on all of us, but more especially on the women and the children.'

It was even worse than Tanus expected. The first arrow, fired at our galley from the cliffs above us, left a trail of smoke against the blue vault of the sky as it arced down and struck the water only a cubit ahead of our bows.

'Fire-arrows,' Tanus nodded. 'You were right once again, Taita. The barbarian does learn quickly.'

'It's easy enough to teach an ape new tricks.' I hated the Hyksos as much as any man in the fleet.

'Now let us see if your bellows can pump water into a ship as well as they pump it out,' Tanus said.

I had anticipated this attack with fire and so, for the last four days, I had been working on those galleys that Tanus had fitted with the water-pumps which I had designed for him. Now, as each of our vessels came up, Tanus ordered the captain to lower his sails, and we pumped water over the decks and soaked the rigging. Leather buckets were filled and placed ready upon the decks, and then one of the galleys escorted the ship into the granite-lined gut of the river and the rain of Hyksos fire-arrows.

It took two full days to get the flotilla through, for the cliffs blanketed the wind. It was hot and still in the gap, and each ship had to be rowed all the way against the current. The arrows fell upon us in pretty, sparking parabolas, rapping into the masts and the decks. Each of them started its own blaze that had to be quenched by the bucket chains or by the leather hoses of the pumps on the escort galley. There was no way for us to retaliate against this attack, for the archers were high up on the cliff-faces. They were well out of range of our own less powerful bows. When Remrem led a shore party to dislodge them from their perches, they were able to fire down on his men and drive them back into the boats with heavy losses.

Those vessels that won through were all scarred with black scorched patches. Many others were less fortunate. The flames aboard them had beaten the buckets and the pumps and engulfed them. They had to be cut free and left to drift down on the current, causing pandemonium amongst the rest of the fleet coming up into the gap. In most cases we managed to take the crew and passengers off before the flames were out of hand, but with some we were too late. The screams of the women and the children in the heart of the flames were enough to stop the blood in my heart. I am left for ever with an image from that dreadful day of a young woman leaping from the deck of a burning barge with her long hair wreathed in flames, like a wedding garland.

We lost over fifty ships in the Gates of Hapi. There were mourning banners flying on every ship as we sailed on towards Elephantine, but at least the Hyksos seemed to have exhausted themselves and their horses in this long chase southwards. The dust-clouds no longer besmirched our northern horizon, and we had a respite in which to mourn our dead and repair our vessels.

However, none of us believed that they had given up entirely. In the end, the lure of Pharaoh's treasure must prove too much to resist.

CONFINED AS we were to the deck of the galley, Prince Memnon and I spent much time together sitting under the awning on the poop-deck. There he listened avidly to my stories, or watched me design and whittle the first model of a new bow for our army, based on the Hyksos recurved type. He had by now learned the old trick of asking questions to keep my attention focused upon him.

'What are you doing now, Tata?'

'I am making a new bow.'

'Yes, but why?'

'All right, I will tell you. Our own single-curve bows, apart from lacking the same power and carry, are too long to be used from the chariot.' He listened gravely. Even when he was an infant I had tried never to indulge in baby-talk with him, and I always addressed him as an equal. If sometimes he did not understand, at least he was happy with the sound of my voice.

'I am now totally convinced that our future lies with the horse and chariot, I am sure that Your Royal Highness agrees with me.' I looked up at him. 'You love horses too, don't you, Mem?'

He understood that well enough. 'I love horses, especially Patience and Blade,' he nodded vehemently.

I had already filled three scrolls with my musings and diagrams of how I conceived these military assets could be used to best advantage. I wished that I was able to discuss these in detail with Tanus, but the Great Lion of Egypt's interest in matters equine was grudging and superficial.

'Build the cursed things if you must, but don't keep chattering about them,' Tanus told me.

The prince was a much more receptive audience, and while I worked, we conducted these long discussions, which were only much later to bear their full harvest. As a companion, Memnon's first choice was always Tanus, but I was not far behind in his affections, and we spent long, happy hours in each other's company.

From the very first he was an exceptionally precocious and intelligent child, and under my influence he developed his gifts more swiftly than any other I had ever instructed. Even my mistress at the same age had not been as quick to learn.

I had made Memnon a toy bow of the design I was studying, and he mastered it almost immediately and could soon shoot one of his tiny arrows the full length of the galley's deck, much to the agitation of the slave girls and nursemaids who were usually his targets. None of them dared bend over when the prince was armed with his bow, he seldom missed an inviting pair of feminine buttocks at under twenty paces.

After his bow, his favourite toy was the miniature chariot and horse that I had carved for him. I had even made the tiny figure of a charioteer to stand in the cockpit, and reins for him to drive the pair. The prince promptly named the mannikin Mem, and the horses were christened Patience and Blade. He crawled tirelessly up and down the deck, pushing the chariot in front of him, making appropriate horsey noises and uttering cries of 'Hi up!' and 'Whoa!'

For such a small boy he was always aware of his surroundings. Those sparkling dark eyes missed very little of what was happening around him. It was no surprise to me when he was the first of any of the crew of the *Breath of Horus* to spot the strange figure far ahead of us on the right bank of the river.

'Horses!' he shrieked, and then moments later, 'Look, look! It is Hui!'

I rushed up to where he stood in the bows, and my heart soared as I realized that he was right. It was Hui astride Blade coming down the river-bank to meet us at a full gallop.

'Hui has got the horses through to Elephantine. I forgive him all his other sins and stupidities. Hui has saved my horses.'

'I am very proud of Hui,' said the prince gravely, imitating my words and intonation so exactly that my mistress and all those around us burst out laughing.

WE WERE given a respite once we reached Elephantine. There had been no sign of the pursuing chariots for so many days that a new optimism spread through the fleet and the city. Men started speaking of abandoning the flight to the south, and of remaining here below the cataracts to build up a new army with which to oppose the invader.

I never allowed my mistress to be seduced by this spirit of confidence which was rooted in such shallow soil. I convinced her that my vision of the Mazes had shown us the true path and that our destiny still lay to the south. In the meantime, I continued my preparations for the voyage unabated. I think that by this time, it was the adventure itself that had cast its spell over me, even more than the necessity of running from the Hyksos.

I wanted to see what lay beyond the cataracts, and in the nights after a full day's work in the docks, I sat up into the late watches in the palace library, reading the accounts of men who had taken that first step into the unknown before us.

They wrote that the river had no end, that it ran on to the very ends of the earth. They wrote that after the first cataract, there was another more formidable, one that no man or ship could ever surmount. They said that to voyage from the first cataract to the next was a full year of travel, and still the river ran on.

I wanted to see it. More than anything in my life I wanted to see where this great river, that was our life, began.

When at last I fell asleep in the lamplight over the scrolls, I saw again in my dream the vision of the welcoming goddess seated on a mountain-top, with the twin spouts of water gushing from her great vagina.

Although I had slept but little, I awoke with the dawn, refreshed and excited, and I rushed back to the docks to continue the preparations for the journey.

I was fortunate in that most of the ropes for our shipping were woven and braided in the sail-yards here in Elephantine. Thus I had the pick of the finest linen cables at my disposal. Some of these were as thick as my finger, and others as thick as my thigh. With them I filled every available space in the holds of the ships not already crammed with stores. I knew just how desperately we would need these, when we came to the cataracts.

It was not surprising that here in Elephantine those of our company with faint hearts and weak resolve made themselves known. The rigours of the flight from Thebes had convinced many of these that the compassion and mercy of the Hyksos were preferable to a continuation of the voyage into the burning southern deserts where even more savage men and beasts awaited them.

When Tanus heard that there were so many thousands of these citizens anxious to desert from the fleet, he roared, 'Damned traitors and renegades! I know what to do with them.' And he expressed his intention of turning his legions upon them, and driving them back on board the ships.

At first he had my mistress's support in this. Her motives were very different from his. She was concerned only with the welfare of her subjects, and her vow that she would leave none of them to the Hyksos terror.

I had to spend half the night arguing with both of them before I could convince them that we were better off without reluctant passengers. In the end, Queen Lostris issued a decree that any person who wished to remain in Elephantine might do so, but she added a neat little touch of her own to the proclamation. This was read aloud in every street of the city, and upon the docks where our ships lay.

> I, Queen Lostris, regent of this very Egypt, mother of Prince Memnon, the heir to the double crown of the two kingdoms, now deliver to the people of this land my solemn promise.
>
> I make oath before the gods and call upon them to witness it. I swear to you that on the majority of the prince, I shall return with him to this city of Elephantine, here to elevate him to the throne of Egypt and place the double crown upon his brow that he may cast out the oppressor and rule over you with justice and in mercy all the days of his life.
>
> It is I, Queen Lostris, regent of this very Egypt, who speaks thus.

This act and declaration increased one hundredfold the love and the loyalty that the common people felt towards my mistress and the prince. I doubt that in all our history there had ever been a ruler so cherished as was she.

When the lists were drawn up of those who would come with us beyond the cataracts, I was not surprised to see that it comprised most of those whose loyalty and skills we most valued. Those who wished to stay in Elephantine were the ones we were happiest to lose, including most of the priesthood.

However, time would prove that those who remained behind us in Elephantine were of great value to us also. During the long years of the exodus they kept alive the flame in the hearts of the people, the memory of Prince Memnon and the promise of Queen Lostris to return to them.

Gradually, through all the long, bitter years of the Hyksos tyranny, the legend of the return of the prince spread through the two kingdoms. In the end, all the people of Egypt, from the first cataract to the seven mouths of the Nile in the great Delta, believed that he would come back, and they prayed for that day.

HUI HAD my horses waiting for me on the fields of the west bank, below the orange dunes hard by the river. The prince and I visited them every day, and although he was growing heavier, Memnon rode upon my shoulder to have a better view over the herd.

By now Memnon knew all his favourites by name, and Patience and Blade came to eat corn-cakes from his hand when he called them. The first time he rode upon her back without my hand to steady him, Patience was as gentle with him as she was with her own foal, and the prince shouted out loud with the thrill of cantering alone around the field.

Hui had learned a great deal about the management of the herds on the march, and using this knowledge, we planned in detail for their welfare on the next stage of the journey. I also explained to Hui the role that I wished the horses to play in the passage of the cataracts, and set him and the charioteers and grooms to work plaiting and splicing harness.

At the very first opportunity, Tanus and I went up-river to scout the cataract. The water was so low that all the islands were exposed. The channels between them were so shallow that in places it was possible for a man to wade through without the water covering his head.

The cataracts extended for many miles, a vast confusion of shining, water-worn granite boulders and serpentine streams that wriggled and twisted their way between them. Even I was daunted and discouraged by the task that lay ahead of us, while Tanus was his usual brutally straightforward self.

'You won't be able to push a skiff through here without ripping the belly out of it. What will you do with a heavily laden galley? Carry it through on the back of one of your cursed horses?' he laughed, but without the least trace of humour.

We started back to Elephantine, but before I reached the city, I had made up my mind that the only way forward was to abandon the ships and go on overland. The hardships that this course would bring down upon us were difficult to imagine. However, I reckoned that we might be able to rebuild the flotilla on the river-banks above the cataracts.

When we returned to the palace on Elephantine Island, Tanus and I went directly to the audience chamber to report to Queen Lostris. She listened to everything that we told her, and then shook her head.

'I do not believe that the goddess has deserted us so soon,' and she led us and all her court to the temple of Hapi on the south tip of the island.

She made a generous sacrifice to the goddess, and we prayed all that night and asked for the guidance of Hapi. I do not believe that the favour of the gods can be bought by cutting the throats of a few goats and placing bunches of grapes upon the stone altar, nevertheless, I prayed with all the fervour of the high priest, although by dawn my buttocks ached hideously from the long vigil on the stone benches.

As soon as the rays of the rising sun struck through the doors of the sanctuary and illuminated the altar, my mistress sent me down the shaft of the Nilometer. I had not reached the bottom step before I found myself ankle-deep in water.

Hapi had listened to our prayers. Although it was weeks early, the Nile had begun to rise.

THE VERY day after the waters began to rise, one of our fast scouting galleys that Tanus had left to watch the movements of the Hyksos cohorts came speeding up-river on the wings of the north wind. The Hyksos were on the march again. They would be in Elephantine within the week.

Lord Tanus left immediately with his main force to prepare for the defence of the cataracts, leaving Lord Merkeset and myself to see to the embarkation of our people. I was able to prise Lord Merkeset off the belly of his young wife just long enough for him to sign the orders which I had prepared for him so meticulously. This time we were able to avoid the chaos and panic that had overtaken us at Thebes, and the fleet prepared to sail for the tail of the cataracts in good order.

Fifty thousand Egyptians lined both banks of the river, weeping and singing psalms to Hapi and waving palm-fronds in farewell as we sailed away. Queen Lostris stood in the bows of the *Breath of Horus* with the little prince at her side, and both of them waved to the crowds on the bank as they passed slowly up-river. At twenty-one years of age, my mistress was at the zenith of her beauty. Those who gazed upon her were struck with an almost religious awe. That beauty was echoed in the face of the child at her side, who held the crook and the flail of Egypt in his small, determined hands.

'We will return,' my mistress called to them, and the prince echoed her, 'We will return. Wait for us. We will return.'

The legend that would sustain our blighted and oppressed land through its darkest times was born that day on the banks of the mother river.

WHEN WE reached the tail of the cataract the following noon, the rock-studded gorge had been transformed into a smooth green chute of rushing waters. In places it tumbled and growled in white water and froth, but it had not yet unleashed its full and terrible power.

This was the moment in the life-cycle of the river most favourable to our enterprise. The waters were high enough to allow our ships through without grounding in the shallows, but the flood was not yet so wild and headstrong as to hurl them back and dash them to driftwood on the granite steps of the cataract.

Tanus himself managed the ships, while Hui and I, under the nominal command of Lord Merkeset, managed the shore party. I placed the jovial old man, with a large jar of the very best wine on his one hand and his pretty little sixteen-year-old wife on the other, under a thatched shelter on the high ground above the gorge. I ignored the garbled and contradictory orders that the noble lord sent down to me from time to time over the ensuing days, and we got on with the business of the transit of the first cataract.

The heaviest linen lines were laid out upon the bank, and our horses were harnessed in teams of ten. We found out quickly enough that we were able to bring forward ten teams at a time – one hundred horses – and couple them to the main ropes. Any greater numbers were unmanageable.

In addition to the horses, we had almost two thousand men upon the secondary ropes and the guide-lines. Horses and men were changed every hour so that the teams were always fresh. At every dangerous turn and twist of the river, we stationed other parties upon the bank, and on the exposed granite islands. These were all armed with long poles to fend the hulls off the rocks as they were dragged through.

Our men had been born on the river-banks and understood their boats and the moods of the Nile better than they did their own wives'. Tanus and I arranged a system of horn signals between the ships and the shore party that functioned more smoothly even than I had hoped.

On board the vessels, the sailors were also armed with poles to punt themselves forward and to fend off the bows. They sang the ancient river shanties as they worked, and the *Breath of Horus* was the first to make the attempt. The sound of song and the cries of the horse-handlers mingled with the muted thunder of the Nile waters as we hauled her forward and she thrust her bows into the first chute of smoothly racing waters.

The green waters piled up against her bows, but their thrust was unable to overcome our determination and the strength of two thousand men and one hundred straining horses. We dragged the *Breath of Horus* up the first rapid, and we cheered when she glided into the deep green pool at the head.

But there were six miles still to go. We changed the men and horses and dragged her bows into the next tumbling, swirling stretch of broken water in which the rocks stood like the heads of gigantic hippopotami ready to rip out her frail timbers with fangs of granite. There were six miles of these hellish rapids to negotiate, with death and disaster swirling around every rock. But the ropes held, and the men and the horses plodded on and upwards in relays.

My mistress walked along the bank beside the teams of sweating men. She looked as fresh and cool as a flower, even in the baking sunlight, and her laughter and banter gave them fresh purpose. She sang the working songs with them, and I joined with her in the chorus. We made up fresh words as we went along. The men laughed at the saucy couplets and hauled on the ropes with renewed strength.

Prince Memnon rode on the back of Blade, in the leading team of horses. Hui had tied a rope around the horse's chest behind the front legs to give him a hand-hold, because Memnon's legs were still too short to afford him a firm grip, and stuck out at an undignified angle on each side of Blade's broad back. The prince waved back proudly at his father on the poop-deck of the galley.

When at last we broke out into the deep, unruffled flow of the main river above the rapids, the working chant of the boatmen turned to a hymn of praise to Hapi, who had seen us through.

Once my mistress had gone back on board the galley, she called for the master mason. She ordered him to cut an obelisk from the granite massif that hemmed in the gorge. While we laboured to bring the rest of the fleet through the gorge, the masons worked with fire and chisel to lift a long, slender column of mottled stone from the mother lode. When they had freed it from the matrix, they chiselled the words that my mistress dictated to them, using the pharaonic hieroglyphics in which her name and that of the prince were enclosed in the royal cartouche.

AS WE proceeded with the transit of the cataract, we became more expert with each pace we gained against the river.

It had taken us a full day to bring the *Breath of Horus* up the rapids. Within the following week we were making the transit in half that time, and we had five or six vessels in the gorge simultaneously. It was almost a royal procession with one galley coming up behind the other, stem to stern. Ten thousand men and nearly a thousand horses were in the traces at any one time.

There were over a hundred vessels moored along the bank in the quiet, deep green reach of the Nile above the rapids, when the Hyksos fell upon us once more.

King Salitis had been delayed by his sack and plunder of the city of Elephantine, and he had not realized immediately that we had continued on up-river with the great bulk of Pharaoh's treasure in the holds of our galleys. Everything that he knew about the river, all that his spies and Lord Intef had been able to tell him, had convinced him that the cataracts were a barrier that could not be navigated. He had wasted all that time in the city of Elephantine before setting after us again.

He had ransacked the city and the palace on the island; he had paid informers and tortured captives in an attempt to learn what had become of the treasure and the prince. The citizens of Elephantine had served their prince well. They had held out against the Hyksos in order to give our flotilla a chance to complete the transit.

Of course, it could not last indefinitely, and at last some poor soul broke under the torture of the tyrant. King Salitis harnessed up his horses yet again and came storming after us into the gorge of the cataract.

However, Tanus was well prepared to meet him. Under his command, Kratas and Remrem and Astes had made their dispositions with care. Every single man who could be spared from the work of hauling the ships through the gorge was sent back to help defend it.

The terrain was our greatest ally. The gorge was steep and rocky. The path along the bank was narrow and twisted with the broken ground crowding down upon it. At every turn of the river there rose high bluffs and cave-riddled cliffs, each of them a natural fortress for us to exploit.

In the confines of the gorge the chariots were unable to manoeuvre. They were unable to leave the river and make a detour around the gorge through the open desert. There was neither water nor fodder for their horses out there in the sandy wastes, and the going was soft and treacherous. Their heavy chariots would have bogged down and been lost in the trackless desert, before they could reach the river again. There was no alternative for them, they were forced to come at us in single file along the narrow river-bank.

On the other hand, Kratas had been given ample grace in which to improve the natural defences of the ground by building stone walls in the most readily defensible places. He positioned his archers in the cliffs above these obstacles, and set up man-made rock-slides on the high ground overlooking the pathway.

As the Hyksos vanguard came up the gorge, they were met with a downpour of arrows from stone-walled redoubts on the high ground above them. Then, when they dismounted from their chariots and went forward to clear the stone barriers that had been placed across the track, Kratas yelled the order and the wedges were knocked from under the rock-slides balanced on the lip of the precipice.

The landslides came tumbling and rolling down upon the Hyksos, sweeping men and horses and chariots off the bank into the surging green waters of the Nile. Standing on the top of the cliff with Kratas, I watched their heads go bobbing and spinning through the cascades, and heard their faint and desperate cries echoing from the cliffs, before the weight of their armour pulled them below the surface and the river overwhelmed them.

King Salitis was tenacious. He sent still more of his legions forward to clear the pathway, and others to climb up the cliffs and dislodge our troops from the heights. The Hyksos' losses in men and horses were frightful, while we were almost unscathed. When they laboured up the cliffs in their heavy bronze armour, we rained our arrows down upon them. Then, before they could reach our positions, Kratas ordered our men to fall back to the next prepared strongpoint.

There could be only one outcome to this one-sided encounter. Before he had fought his way halfway up the gorge, King Salitis was forced to abandon the pursuit.

Tanus and my mistress were with us on the cliff-tops when the Hyksos began their retreat back down the gorge. They left the path strewn with the wreckage of their chariots and cluttered with abandoned equipment and the detritus of their defeat.

'Sound the trumpets!' Tanus gave the order, and the gorge echoed to the mocking fanfare that he sent after the retreating Hyksos legions. The last chariot in that sorry cavalcade was the gilded and embossed vehicle of the king himself. Even from our perch on top of the precipice, we could recognize the tall and savage figure of Salitis, with his high bronze helmet and his black beard flowing back over his shoulders. He raised his bow, that he held in his right hand, and shook it at us. His face was contorted with frustration and rage.

We watched him out of sight. Then Tanus sent our scouts after them to follow them back to Elephantine, in case this was a ruse, a false withdrawal. In my heart I knew that Salitis would not come after us again. Hapi had fulfilled her promise, and offered us her protection once more.

Then we turned, and followed the pathway made by the wild goats along the precipice, back to where the flotilla was moored.

THE MASONS had finished work on the obelisk. It was a shaft of solid granite three times the height of a man. I had marked out the proportions and the shape of it upon the mother rock before the masons had made their first cut. Because of this, the lines of the monument were so elegant and pleasing that it appeared to be much taller, once it was set on the summit of the bluff above the last wild stretch of the cataract, overlooking the scene of our triumph.

All our people gathered below it, as Queen Lostris dedicated the stone to the goddess of the river. She read aloud the inscription that the masons had engraved upon the polished stone.

> I, Queen Lostris, Regent of Egypt and widow of Pharaoh Mamose, the eighth of that name, mother of the Crown Prince Memnon, who shall rule the two kingdoms after me, have ordained the raising of this monument.
>
> This is the mark and covenant of my vow to the people of this very Egypt, that I shall return to them from the wilderness whence I have been driven by the barbarian.
>
> This stone was placed here in the first year of my rule, the nine-hundredth year after the building of the great pyramid of Pharaoh Cheops.
>
> Let this stone stand immovable as the pyramid until I make good my promise to return.

Then, in sight of all the people, she placed the Gold of Valour upon the shoulders of Tanus and Kratas and Remrem and Astes, all those heroes who had made possible the transit of the cataract.

Then, last of all, she called me to her, and as I knelt at her feet, she whispered so I alone might hear, 'How could I forget you, my dear and faithful Taita? We could never have come this far without your help,' she touched my cheek lightly, 'and I know how dearly you love these pretty baubles.' And she placed around my neck the heavy Gold of Praise. I weighed it later at thirty deben, five deben heavier than the chain that Pharaoh had bestowed upon me.

On the way back down the side of the gorge, I walked beside my mistress to hold the sun-shade of ostrich feathers over her head, and she smiled at me more than once. Each smile was more precious to me than the heavy chain upon my shoulders.

The following morning we went back on board the *Breath of Horus* and turned our bows once more towards the south. The long voyage had begun.

WE FOUND that the river had changed its mien and character. It was no longer the broad and serene presence that had comforted and sustained us all our lives. This was a sterner, wilder being. There was little gentleness and compassion in its spirit. It was narrower and deeper. The land on each side of it was steeper and more rugged, and the gorges and nullahs were crudely gouged from the harsh earth. The brooding and darkling cliffs frowned down upon us with furrowed brows.

In some places the bottom lands along the banks narrowed down so that the horses and cattle and sheep had to pass in single file along the crude track that the wild goats had trodden between the cliffs and the water. In other places the track disappeared completely, as the bluffs and the cliffs pushed boldly into the flood of the Nile. Then there was no way forward for our herds. Hui was forced to drive them into the river and swim them across the green expanse of water to the far bank, where the cliffs had retreated and left the way open for them to pass.

As the weeks wore on, we saw little sign of any human presence. Once, our scouts found the worm-eaten hull of a crude dugout canoe washed up on a sand-bank, and upon the bottom land an abandoned cluster of huts. The sagging roofs were thatched with reeds and the sides were open. There were the remains of fish-smoking racks and the ashes of the fires, but that was all. Not a shard of pottery or a bead to hint at who these people might be.

We were anxious to make our first contact with the tribes of Cush, for we needed slaves. Our entire civilization was based on the keeping of slaves, and we had been able to bring very few of them with us from Egypt. Tanus sent his scouts far ahead of the fleet, so that we might have good warning of the first human habitations in ample time to organize our slave-catchers. I found no irony in the fact that I, a slave myself, spent so much of my time and thought in planning the taking of other slaves.

All wealth can be counted in four commodities, land and gold and slaves and ivory. We believed that the land that lay ahead of us was rich in all of these. If we were to grow strong enough to return and drive the Hyksos from our very Egypt, then we must discover this wealth in the unexplored land to which we were sailing.

Queen Lostris sent out her gold-finders into the hills along the river as we passed. They climbed up through the gorges and the dry nullahs, scratching and digging in every likely spot, chipping fragments off the exposed reefs of quartz and schist, crushing these to powder, and washing away the dross in a shallow clay dish, hoping always to see the gleaming precious tail remaining in the bottom of the dish.

The royal huntsmen went out with them to search for game with which to feed our multitudes. They searched also for the first sign of those great grey beasts who carry the precious teeth of ivory in their monstrous heads. I made vigorous enquiry through the fleet for any man who had ever seen one of these elephant alive, or even dead. Though their teeth were a commonplace throughout the civilized world, there was not a single man who could help me in my enquiries. I felt a strange and unaccountable excitement at the thought of our first encounter with these fabulous beasts.

There was a host of other creatures inhabiting this wild land, some of them familiar to us and many that were strange and new.

Wherever reeds grew upon the river-bank, we found herds of hippopotami lying like rounded granite boulders in the shallows. After long and erudite theological debate, it was still uncertain whether these beasts above the cataract belonged to the goddess, as did those below, or whether they were royal game belonging to the crown. The priests of Hapi were strongly of one persuasion, and the rest of us, with an appetite for the rich fat and tender flesh of these animals, were of the opposite opinion.

It was entirely by coincidence that at this point the goddess Hapi chose to appear to me in one of my celebrated dreams. I saw her rise from the green waters, smiling beneficently, and place in my mistress's hand a tiny hippopotamus no bigger than a wild partridge. As soon as I awoke, I lost no time in relaying the substance of this weird and thrilling dream to the regent. By now my dreams and divination were accepted by my mistress, and therefore by the rest of our company, as the manifest will and law of the gods.

That evening we all feasted on luscious river-cow steaks grilled on the open coals on the sand-bank against which the ships had moored. My reputation and popularity, which were already high throughout the fleet, were much enhanced by this dream. The priests of Hapi alone were not carried along by the general warmth of feeling towards me.

The river teemed with fish. Below the cataract, our people had fished the river for a thousand years and longer. These waters were untouched by man or his nets. We drew from the river shining blue perch heavier than the fattest man in our company, and there were huge catfish, with barbellate whiskers as long as my arm, that were too strong and weighty to be captured in the nets. With a flick of their great tails they ripped the linen threads as though they were the fragile webs of spiders. Our men hunted them in the shallows with spears, as though they were river-cows. One of these giants could feed fifty men with rich yellow flesh that dripped fat into the cooking-fires.

In the cliffs above the river hung the nests of eagles and vultures. From below they appeared like masses of driftwood, and the droppings of the huge birds painted the rocks beneath them with streaks of shining white. The birds floated above us on wide pinions, circling and swaying on the heated air that rose from the black rocks of the gorge.

From the heights, flocks of wild goats watched us pass with regal and disdainful mien. Tanus went out to hunt them on their airy crags, but it was many weeks before he succeeded in bringing back one of these trophies. They had the eyesight of vultures and the agility of the blue-headed rock lizards that could run effortlessly up a vertical wall of granite.

One of these old rams stood as tall as a man's shoulder. His beard flowed from his chin and throat to sweep the rock on which he posed. His horns curled upon themselves from mighty crenellated bases. When Tanus finally brought him down, it was with an arrow shot across a gorge a hundred paces deep, from peak to pinnacle of these rugged hills. The goat dropped into the gulf and twisted over and over in the air before it hit the rocks below.

Because of my passionate interest in all wild things, after he had skinned out and butchered the carcass, Tanus carried the head and the horns home for me. It took all his vast strength to bring down such a burden from those murderous crags. I cleaned and bleached the skull and set it up on the bows of our galley as a figurehead, as we sailed on into the unknown.

THE MONTHS passed, and below our keels the river began to dwindle away as the inundation abated. As we passed the sheer headlands, we could see the height of the river measured upon the cliff where all the previous inundations had left their watermarks.

At night Memnon and I sat up on deck as late as his mother would allow us, and together we studied the stars that illuminated the firmament of the sky with a milky radiance. I taught him the name and the nature of each of these fiery points of light and how they affected the destiny of every man born under them. By watching the heavenly bodies, I was able to determine that the river was no longer taking us directly into the south, but that we were veering towards the west. These observations stirred up another heated controversy amongst the scholars and the wise men of our company.

'The river is taking us directly to the western fields of paradise,' suggested the priests of Osiris and Ammon-Ra. 'It is a ruse of Seth. He wishes to confuse and confound us,' argued the priests of Hapi, who up until now had exerted undue influence over our councils. Queen Lostris was a child of their goddess, and it had been generally accepted by most of us that Hapi was the patron of our expedition. The priests were angry to see their position weakened by this wayward perambulation of the river. 'Soon the river will turn south once more,' they promised. It always appalls me to watch how unscrupulous men manipulate the wishes of the gods to coincide with their own.

Before the matter could be resolved, we came to the second cataract.

This was as far as any civilized man had ever ventured, and not one of them had reached further. When we scouted and surveyed the cataract, the reason for this was abundantly evident. These rapids were more extensive and formidable than those we had already negotiated.

Over a vast area, the stream of the Nile was split by several massive islands and hundreds of smaller ones. It was low-water now, and at most places the bed of the river was exposed. A maze of rock-strewn canals and branches extended for miles ahead of us. We were awed by the grandeur and menace of it.

'How do we know that there is not another cataract, and then another, guarding the river?' those who were easily discouraged asked each other. 'We will expend our strength and in the end find ourselves trapped between the rapids without the strength to advance or retreat. We should turn back now, before it is too late,' they agreed amongst themselves.

'We will go on,' decreed my mistress. 'Those who wish to turn back now, are free to do so. However, there will be no vessels to carry them nor horses to draw them. They will return on their own, and I am certain the Hyksos will bid them a hearty welcome.'

There were none who accepted her magnanimous offer. Instead, they went ashore on the fertile islands that choked the course of the river.

The spray from the rapids during the flood, and the water filtering up through the soil during low ebb, had transformed these islands into verdant forests, in stark contrast to the dry and terrible deserts on either bank. Springing from seeds brought down by the waters from the ends of the earth, tall trees, of a kind that none of us had ever seen before, grew on the silt that Mother Nile had piled up on the granite foundation of the islands.

We could not attempt a transit of these rapids until the Nile brought down her next inundation and gave us sufficient depth of water for our galleys. That was still many months away.

Our farmers went ashore and cleared land to plant the seeds that we had brought with us. Within days the seed had sprouted, and in the hot sunlight the plants seemed to grow taller under our eyes. Within a few short months the dhurra corn was ready to be harvested, and we were gorging on the sweet fruits and vegetables that we had missed so much since leaving Egypt. The muttering amongst our people died away.

In fact these islands were so attractive, and the soil so fertile, that some of our people began to talk about settling here permanently. A delegation from the priests of Ammon-Ra went to the queen and asked for her permission to erect a temple to the god on one of the islands. My mistress replied, 'We are travellers here. In the end we will return to Egypt. That is my vow and promise to all my people. We will build no temples or other permanent habitation. Until we return to Egypt we will live as the Bedouin, in tents and huts.'

I NOW had at my disposal the timber from those trees we had felled upon the islands. I was able to experiment with these and to explore their various properties.

There was an acacia whose wood was resilient and strong. It made the finest spokes for my chariot wheels of any material which I had so far tested. I put my carpenters and weavers to work on reassembling the chariots that we had brought with us, and building new ones from the woods and bamboos that grew on the islands.

The flat bottom lands were several miles wide on the left bank below the cataract. Soon our squadrons of chariots were training and exercising upon these smooth and open plains once more. The spokes of the wheels still broke under hard driving, but not as frequently as they once had. I was able to entice Tanus back on to the footplate; however, he would not ride with any driver but myself.

At the same time, I was able to complete the first successful recurved bow upon which I had been working since we had left Elephantine. It was made from the same composite materials as was Lanata, wood and ivory and horn. However, the shape was different. When it was unstrung, the upper and lower limbs were curved out and away from the archer. It was only when the weapon was strung that they were forced back into the familiar bow shape, but the tension in the stock and the string was multiplied out of all proportion to the much shorter length of the bow.

At my gentle insistence, Tanus finally agreed to shoot the bow at a series of targets that I had erected upon the east bank. After he had shot twenty arrows he said little, but I could see that he was astonished by the range and accuracy of it. I knew my Tanus so well. He was a conservative and a reactionary to the marrow of his bones. Lanata was his first love, both the woman and the bow. I knew it would be a wrench for him to acknowledge a new love, so I did not pester him for an opinion, but let him come to it in his own time.

It was then that our scouts came in to report a migration of oryx from out of the desert. We had seen several small herds of these magnificent animals since we had passed the first cataract. Usually they were grazing upon the river-bank, but they fled back into the desert as our ships sailed towards them. What our scouts reported now was a massive movement of these animals such as took place only very occasionally. I had witnessed it just once before. With the freak occurrence of a thunderstorm in the desert fastnesses once in twenty years or so, the flush of green grass that sprang from the wet earth would attract the scattered herds of oryx from hundreds of miles around.

As they moved towards the fresh grazing grounds, the herds amalgamated into one massive movement of animals across the desert. This was happening now, and it offered us the chance of a change of diet and the opportunity to run our chariots in earnest.

For the first time, Tanus showed a real interest in my chariots, now that there was game to pursue with them. As he took his place on the footplate of my vehicle, I noticed that it was the new recurved bow that he hung on the rack, and not his faithful old Lanata. I said not a word, but shook up the horses and headed them towards the gap in the hills that offered us a route out of the narrow valley of the Nile and gave access to the open desert.

We were fifty chariots in the squadron, followed by a dozen heavy carts with solid wheels that carried sufficient fodder and water for five days. We trotted in column of route, two vehicles abreast, and with three lengths between the files. This had already become our standard travelling formation.

To keep down the weight, we were stripped to loin-cloths, and all our men were in superb physical condition from long months of work on the rowing-benches of the galleys. Their muscled torsos were all freshly oiled and gleamed in the sunlight, like the bodies of young gods. Each chariot carried its brightly coloured recognition pennant on a long, whippy bamboo rod. We made a brave show as we came up the goat track through the hills. When I looked back down the column, even I, who never was a soldier, was affected by the spectacle.

I did not clearly recognize the truth then, but the Hyksos and the exodus had forced a new military spirit upon the nation. We had been a race of scholars and traders and priests, but now, with the determination of Queen Lostris to expel the tyrant, and led by Lord Tanus, we were fast becoming a warlike people.

As we led the column over the crest of the hills, and the open desert lay ahead of us, a small figure stepped out from behind the last pile of rocks where it had been lying in ambush.

'Whoa!' I reined down the horses. 'What are you doing out here so far from the ships?'

I had not seen the prince since the previous evening, and had believed that he was safe with his nursemaids. To come across him here on the edge of the desert was a shock, and my tone was outraged. At that time he was not quite six years of age, but he had his toy bow over his shoulder and a determined expression on his face that mirrored that of his father, when Tanus was in one of his most intractable moods.

'I am coming on the hunt with you,' said Memnon.

'No, you are not,' I contradicted him. 'I am sending you back to your mother this very instant. She will know how to deal with small boys who sneak out of the camp without telling their tutors where they are going.'

'I am the crown prince of Egypt,' declared Memnon, but his lip trembled despite this weighty declaration. 'No man durst forbid me. It is my right and my sacred duty to lead my people in time of need.'

We had now moved on to dangerous ground. The prince knew his rights and his responsibilities. It was I who had taught them to him. However, in all truth, I had not expected him to exercise them so soon. He had made it an affair of royal protocol, and it was difficult, even impossible, to argue with him. Desperately I sought for an escape.

'Why did you not ask me before?' I was merely bidding for time.

'Because you would have gone to my mother,' he said with simple honesty, 'and she would have supported you, as she always does.'

'I can still go to the queen,' I threatened, but he looked back into the valley where the ships were small as toys, and he grinned at me. We both knew that I could not order the entire squadron to drive all that way back.

'Please let me come with you, Tata,' he changed his tune. The little devil was attacking me on all fronts. I found it impossible to resist him when he exerted all his charm. Then I was struck with inspiration. 'Lord Harrab is the commander of this expedition. You must ask him.'

The relationship between these two was a strange one. Only three of us – the two parents and myself – were aware of Memnon's true paternity. The prince himself thought of Tanus as his tutor and the commander of his armies. Although he had come to love Tanus, he still held him in considerable awe. Tanus was not the type of man that a small boy, even a prince, would trifle with.

The two of them looked at each other now. I could see Memnon was pondering his best plan of attack, while I could feel Tanus trembling with the effort of holding back his laughter.

'Lord Harrab,' Memnon had decided on the formal approach, 'I wish to come with you. I think it will be a very useful lesson for me. After all, one day I will have to lead the army.' I had taught him logic and dialectic. He was a student to be proud of.

'Prince Memnon, are you giving me an order?' Tanus managed to cover his amusement with a horrific scowl, and I saw tears begin to well up in the prince's eyes.

He shook his head miserably. 'No, my lord.' He was a small boy once more. 'But I would very much like to come hunting with you, please.'

'The queen will have me strangled,' said Tanus, 'but hop up here in front of me, you little ruffian.'

The prince loved Tanus to call him a ruffian. It was a term that he usually reserved for the men of his old Blues regiment, and it made Memnon feel that he was one of them. He let out a yelp of glee and almost tripped over his own feet in his haste to obey. Tanus reached down and caught his arm. He swung him up and placed him securely between us on the footplate.

'Hi up!' Memnon shouted to Patience and Blade, and we drove out into the open desert, but not before I had sent a messenger back to the fleet with a message for the queen to tell her that the prince was safe. No lioness could be as fierce as my mistress in the care of its cub.

When we struck the migration road, it was a broad swathe of churned sand many hundreds of yards wide. The hooves of the oryx are broad and splayed to cover the soft desert sands. They leave a distinctive track, the shape of a Hyksos spear-head. Many thousands of the huge antelope had passed this way.

'When?' Tanus asked, and I dismounted to examine the trail. I took

Memnon down with me, for I never missed an opportunity to instruct him. I showed him how the night breeze had eroded the spoor, and how small insects and lizards had superimposed their own tracks over those of the herd.

'They passed here yesterday evening at sunset,' I gave my opinion, and had it endorsed by the prince. 'But they are travelling slowly. With luck we can catch them before noon.'

We waited for the wagons to come up. We watered the horses, and then went on, following the broad trodden road through the dunes.

Soon we found the carcasses of the weaker animals that had succumbed. They were the very young and the oldest, and now the crows and the vultures squawked and squabbled over their remains, while the little red jackals slunk around the fringes, hoping for a mouthful.

We followed the broad road until at last we saw the thin filtering of dust upon the southern horizon, and we quickened our pace. When we topped a line of rugged hills whose crests danced in the heat-mirage, we saw the herds spread out below us. We had reached the area where the thunderstorm had broken weeks before. As far ahead as we could see, the desert had been transformed into a garden of flowers.

The last rains might have fallen here a hundred years ago. It seemed impossible, but the seeds of that harvest had lain sleeping all that time. They had been burned and desiccated by sun and desert wind, while they waited for the rains to come once again. For any who doubted the existence of the gods, this miracle was proof. For any man who doubted that life was eternal, this held out the promise of immortality. If the flowers could survive thus, then surely the soul of man, which is infinitely more wonderful and valuable, must also live for ever.

The landscape below us was painted with shades of soft greens, the contours and the outlines of the hills were picked out with sweeps of darker green. This formed a background to the wonderful rainbow of colour that lit the earth. The flowers grew in banks and drifts. The blooms of each variety seemed to seek the company of their own kind, as do the herds of antelope and the flocks of birds. The orange-coloured daisies grew in pools and lakes together, those with white petals frosted entire hillsides. There were fields of blue gladiolus, scarlet lilies and yellow ericas.

Even the wiry brush plants in the gorges and nullahs, that had seemed seared and dried as mummies of men dead a thousand years, were now decked in fresh robes of green, with wreaths of yellow blooms crowning their ancient blasted heads. Lovely as it now was, I knew that it was ephemeral. Another month and the desert would triumph again. The flowers would wither on the stem, and the grass would turn to dust and blow away on the furnace blasts of the winds. Nothing would remain of this splendour except the seeds, tiny as grains of sand, waiting out the years with a monumental patience.

'Such beauty should be shared with the one you love,' Tanus breathed in awe. 'Would that the queen were with me now!'

That Tanus had been so moved by it proved the glory of the spectacle. He was a soldier and a hunter, but for once he gave no thought to the quarry, but gazed upon the spectacle with a religious awe.

It was a shout from Kratas in one of the following chariots that roused us from this reverie of beauty. 'By Seth's stinking breath, there must be ten thousand of them down there.'

The oryx were spread out to the green silhouette of the farther hills. Some of the old bulls were solitary, keeping all others away, but the rest of them were in herds of ten or a hundred, and some of the herds were beyond count. They were merely huge tawny stains, like cloud shadow upon the plains. It seemed to me that every oryx in all of Africa was gathered here.

We watered the horses again before the hunt began. This gave me a chance to go forward and to gaze down upon this great concourse of living things. Of course, I took Memnon with me, but when I tried to lead him by the hand he disentangled his fingers from my grip. 'Don't hold my hand in front of the men, Tata,' he told me solemnly. 'They will think I am still a baby.'

As we stood on the sky-line, the nearest animals raised their heads and regarded us with mild curiosity. It occurred to me that they had probably never before seen a human being, and that they detected no danger in our presence.

The oryx is a magnificent creature, standing as tall as a horse, with the same full, flowing, dark tail that sweeps the ground. Its face is painted with intricate whorls and slashes of black upon a pale, sand-coloured mask. A stiff, dark mane runs down the neck, enhancing the horse-like appearance, but its horns are like those of no other animal created by the gods. They are slim and straight and tipped like the dagger on my belt. Almost as long as the animal that bears them is tall, they are formidable weapons. Whereas all other antelope are meek and inoffensive, preferring flight to aggression, the oryx will defend itself even against the attack of the lion.

I told Memnon of their courage and their powers of endurance, and explained how they could live their entire lives without drinking water from pool or river. 'They take their water from the dew, and from the desert roots and tubers which they dig out of the earth with their hooves.'

He listened avidly, for he had inherited the love of the chase in his father's blood, and I had taught him to revere all wild things.

'The true huntsman understands and respects the birds and the animals that he hunts,' I told him, and he nodded seriously.

'I want to be a true huntsman and a soldier, just like Lord Tanus.'

'A man is not born with such gifts. He must learn them, in the same way that you must learn to be a great and just ruler.'

I felt a pang of regret when Tanus called to me that the horses were watered, and I looked back to see the charioteers mounting up. I would have preferred to spend the rest of that day with my prince watching the royal show upon the plains below me. I went back reluctantly to take up the reins and to drive our chariot back to the head of the column.

On the footplates of the other chariots, the archers had their bows strung, and the fever of the hunt gripped every man. They were like hounds on a short leash with the scent in their nostrils.

'Ho, Lord Tanus!' Kratas shouted across to us. 'A wager on the outcome?'

Before Tanus could reply, I murmured, 'Take one for me. The old braggart has never shot from the back of a flying chariot.'

'Clean kills only,' Tanus called back to him. 'Any animal with another man's arrow in it, not to count.' Every archer marked the shaft of his arrow with his own motif, so that he might claim it later. Tanus' mark was the Wadjet, the wounded Eye of Horus. 'One gold deben for each oryx with your arrow in it.'

'Make it two,' I suggested. 'One for me.' I am not a gambling man, but this was not a gamble. Tanus had his new recurved bow, and I was the best charioteer in the whole of our army.

We were still novices, but I had studied the Hyksos' use of the chariot. Every evolution that their squadrons had performed on that terrible day on the plain of Abnub was graven on my memory. To me this was not merely a hunt for meat and sport, but practice and training for the much greater game of war. We had to learn to run our formations to the very best advantage and to control them in the full flight and confusion of battle, while circumstances changed with every movement of the enemy, and every chance and hazard of war.

As we trotted down on to the plain, I gave the first signal, and the column split into three files. Smoothly we opened up like the petals of a lily. The flankers curled out like the horns of a bull to surround the quarry, while my column in the centre deployed into line abreast, with three chariot lengths between our wheel-hubs. We were the chest of the bull. The horns would hold the enemy while we came up and crushed him in our savage embrace.

Ahead of us, the scattered herds of gazelle threw up their heads and gazed at us with the first stirring of alarm. They began to drift away, gathering up their fellows as they passed, small herds combining into larger, the way that a single boulder rolling down the slope will bring down the landslide. Soon the entire plain was alive with moving oryx. They cantered with a peculiar rocking motion, and dust rose in a pale mist and hung over their swaying backs. Their long, dark tails swished from side to side.

I held my own squadron down to a walk. I did not want to tire the horses too soon with a long, stern chase. I was watching the denser, taller dust-clouds thrown up by the two flanking columns circling swiftly out on each side of the herd.

At last they came together far ahead, and the ring was closed. The herds of oryx slowed down as they found their escape-route blocked. They began to mill in confusion as those in the lead turned back and ran into the ranks that followed.

Obedient to my orders, once the flanking columns had completed the encircling movement, they also slowed to an easy walk, and turned in towards the centre of the circle. We had the huge herd of oryx in our fist, and slowly we closed our grip upon them. Most of the bewildered animals came to a halt, uncertain in which direction to run. Every way they gazed, they saw the lines of chariots bearing down upon them.

Closer we came, at a steady walk, and our horses were still fresh and eager to run. They had sensed the excitement, and threw their heads, fighting with the traces, snorting and rolling their eyes until the whites showed. The oryx herd began to move again, but in no definite direction. They milled upon themselves, making uncertain dashes in one direction before coming up short and then swinging around and rushing back again.

I was pleased with the control and discipline of our squadrons. They held their formations rigidly, without bunching up and leaving gaps in the ranks. The signals that I gave were repeated down the line and acted upon instantly. We were at last becoming an army. Soon we would be able to meet any foe on favourable terms, even the Hyksos veterans who had spent their entire lives on the footplate of a chariot.

I reached behind me and took Prince Memnon by the arm. I drew him forward and placed him against the dashboard. I wedged him there with my own body, and he gripped the front panel. Now Tanus had both hands free to shoot his bow, and the prince was safe.

'Let me take the reins, Tata. I will drive,' Memnon pleaded. I had let him drive before, so he meant it seriously, though he was barely tall enough to see over the dashboard. I dared not laugh at him, for he took himself very seriously.

'Next time, Mem. This time just watch and learn.'

At last we were less than a hundred paces from the nearest oryx, the pressure was too great for them to tolerate. Led by one scarred old cow, a hundred of them charged straight at our line in a mass. At my signal we shortened our line until we were running hub to hub, a solid wall of horses and men, and the trumpeters sounded the charge. I lashed my team into a full gallop and we raced headlong to meet them.

Tanus was firing past my right shoulder. I could watch each of his arrows fly out across the closing gap. This was the first time he had shot from a running chariot, and his first three arrows flew wide of the mark, as the chariot careered into the herd of racing oryx. But he was a master archer, and he adjusted his aim swiftly. His next arrow took the old cow, who was still leading the charge, full in the chest. It must have split her heart, for she went down, nose into the sand, and rolled over her own head. The animals following her swerved out on either side of her, offering Tanus broadside targets. It was fascinating to watch his next two arrows curl away and fall behind the racing oryx.

The temptation is always to shoot directly at a running target, and not at the place in the empty air ahead of it, where it will be when the arrow reaches it. This calculation of forward aim is further complicated by the movement of the chariot in relation to the target. I was trying to give him the easiest shot by turning the chariot with the run of the game. All the same, I was not surprised when two more of Tanus' arrows missed behind the target.

Then, like the master of the bow that he is, he adjusted his aim, and the following arrow plunged feathers-deep into the chest of the next oryx. He killed three more with three arrows, while all around us the hunt disintegrated into the wild confusion of battle, and dust obscured all but the closest glimpses of running chariots and racing animals.

I was driving close behind a pair of oryx, overhauling them slowly, when the flying hooves of one of them threw up a chip of sharp flint the size of the last joint of my thumb. Before he could duck, it struck Memnon on the forehead, and when he looked up at me I saw the blood trickling from the shallow cut above his eye.

'You are hurt, Mem,' I cried, and started to rein down the horses.

'It is nothing,' he told me, and used the corner of his shawl to mop the blood. 'Don't stop, Tata! Keep after them. Kratas will beat us, if you don't.'

So I drove on into the dust, and beside me Tanus' bow sang its awful song, and the prince yipped and yelped with excitement like a puppy the first time that it chases a rabbit.

Some of the oryx broke free of our lines and escaped into the open desert, while others were turned back into the trap. Men shouted with excitement and triumph, horses whinnied, and the oryx snorted and bellowed as the arrows slapped into them and brought them crashing down in a tangle of flying hooves and scimitar horns. All around us was the thunder of hooves and wheels, and we were immersed in the yellow fog of dust.

There is a limit to how long even the finest and most willing team of horses can be driven at full gallop. When finally I reined Patience and Blade down to a walk, the dust had caked like mud in the sweat that lathered their flanks, and they hung their heads with exhaustion.

Slowly, the dust-clouds that had obscured the field drifted aside and dissipated. The field was a terrible sight.

Our squadron was scattered over the entire plain. I counted five chariots whose wheels had shattered during the chase, and the up-ended vehicles looked like the broken toys of a petulant giant. The injured men lay on the sandy earth beside their shattered chariots, with their comrades kneeling over them as they tended their wounds.

Even those chariots that had survived undamaged were halted. The horses were blown and exhausted. Their flanks heaved as they strained for breath, and the white froth dripped from their muzzles. Each one of them was soaked with sweat, as though it had swum across the river.

The game was scattered upon the field in the same disorder and lack of purpose or design. Many of the great beasts were dead, and their carcasses lay stretched out on their sides. Many others were crippled and maimed. Some stood with their heads hanging. Others limped away through the dunes with slow and halting gait. Each arrow-shaft left a dark stain of wet blood upon the pale, roan-coloured hide.

This was the pitiful end to every hunt, when the heat and excitement have cooled and the wounded game has to be gathered up and put out of its misery.

Near us I saw one old bull oryx sitting on his paralysed haunches with his front legs stiff in front of him. The arrow that had crippled him stood out so high from his back that I knew that the point had severed his spine. I took the second bow from the rack on the side-panel of our chariot, and I jumped down from the footplate to the ground. As I walked towards the crippled bull, he swung his head to watch me. Then he made one last courageous effort, and dragged his crippled back legs as he came at me. He slashed those long black horns at me, but his eyes swam with the tears of mortal agony. I was forced to drive two arrows deep into the cavity of his chest before he gave one last groan and rolled over on to his side, kicked once convulsively, and was still.

When I climbed back into the chariot, I glanced at the prince's face. His eyes were wet with tears and his blood-smeared face was crumpled into an expression of pity for the oryx. He turned his face away from me, so that I could not see his tears, but I was proud of them. He who lacks compassion for the game he pursues is no true huntsman.

I took his curly head in my hands and turned his face back to me. Gently, I cleaned the wound on his forehead and bandaged it with a strip of linen.

We camped that night upon the plain of flowers, and their sweet perfume scented the darkness, and overlaid the smell of fresh-spilled blood.

There was no moon, but the stars filled the entire sky. The hills were bathed in their silver luminosity. We sat late at the camp-fires and feasted on the livers and hearts of oryx roasted on the coals. To begin with, the prince sat between Tanus and me at the fireside, but the officers and men vied for his attention. He had stolen all their hearts, and at their invitation he moved easily from one group to the next. They mended their language and banter to fit his ears, and the prince was at ease in their company.

They made a great fuss of his bandaged head. 'Now you are a real soldier,' they told him, 'just like one of us.' And they showed him their own scars.

'You did the right thing by allowing him to come with us,' I told Tanus, as we both watched him proudly. 'This is the best training any young cadet can ever have.'

'The men love him already,' Tanus agreed. 'There are two things that a general needs. One is luck and the other is the devotion of his troops.'

'Memnon must be allowed to go out with every expedition, just as long as it is not too dangerous,' I decided, and Tanus chuckled.

'I leave you to convince his mother of that. There are some things that are beyond my powers of persuasion.'

On the other side of the camp-fire, Kratas was teaching Memnon the expurgated version of the lyrics of the regimental marching songs. The prince had a sweet, clear voice, and the men clapped the time, and came in on the chorus. They protested loudly and rudely when at last I tried to send Memnon to the bed I had prepared for him under the body of the chariot, and even Tanus supported them.

'Let the boy stay with us a little longer,' he ordered, and it was well after midnight when at last I was able to roll the prince in my sheepskin rug.

'Tata, will I ever be able to shoot the way that Lord Tanus does?' he asked sleepily.

'You will be one of the great generals of our very Egypt, and one day I will carve an account of your victories on obelisks of stone, so that all the world will know of them.'

He thought about that for a while and then sighed. 'When will you make me a real bow, not just a baby's toy?'

'As soon as you can draw it,' I promised.

'Thank you, Tata. I should like that.' And he went to sleep as suddenly as I would blow out the flame of a lamp.

WE RETURNED in triumph to the fleet, the wagons loaded with the salted and sun-dried meat of the oryx herd. I had expected my mistress to tax me severely for having abducted the prince. I had prepared my defence and was determined to place the blame squarely on the broader shoulders of Lord Harrab.

However, her censure was milder than I had anticipated. She told Memnon that he was a wicked child for having caused her worry, and then hugged him until he was in danger of suffocation. When she turned to me, I launched into a long explanation of Tanus' role in the affair, and the valuable training and experience that the prince had received, but she seemed to have dismissed the entire episode.

'When did you and I last go fishing together?' she asked. 'Fetch your fishing-spears, Taita. We will take one of the skiffs. Just the two of us on the river, the way we used to be in the old days.'

I knew that we would do little fishing. She wanted me alone on the water where we could not be overheard. Whatever was troubling her was of serious importance.

I paddled downstream on the shrunken and slow green waters until the bend of the river and the high rocky bluff hid us from the fleet. All my attempts at conversation had failed, so I put aside my paddle and took up my lute. I strummed and sang the tunes she loved best, and waited for her to speak.

At last she looked up at me, and her eyes were filled with a strange mixture of joy and worry.

'Taita, I think I am going to have another baby.'

I can think of no reason why this statement should have surprised me so. After all, every night since we had left Elephantine, she and the commander of her army had been locked in secret conclave, while I kept guard at the door of her cabin. Nevertheless, I was so alarmed that my hand froze on the lute strings and the song died in my throat. It was some moments before I could regain my voice.

'My lady, did you use the infusion of herbs that I prepared for you?' I asked diffidently.

'At times I did, but at others I forgot.' She smiled shyly. 'Lord Tanus can be a very impatient man. Besides which, it is so unromantic to fiddle with pots and jars, when there are better and more urgent things waiting to be done.'

'Things like making babies who have no royal father to claim them.'

'It is rather serious, isn't it, Taita?'

I struck a chord on the lute while I framed a reply. 'Rather serious? Oh, I think that is the wrong word. If you give birth to a bastard, or if you take a husband, then you will be obliged to relinquish the regency. That is the custom and the law. Lord Merkeset would be the next in line as regent, but there will be covert warfare amongst all the nobility for the position. Without your protection as regent, the prince would be in great danger. We would be torn by internecine strife—' I broke off, and shuddered at the prospect of it.

'Tanus could become regent in my stead, and then I could marry him,' she suggested brightly.

'Don't think I have not thought of that before,' I told her sombrely. 'It would be the solution to all our difficulties. But then there is Tanus.'

'If I ask him, he will do it gladly, I am sure of that,' she smiled with relief, 'and I will be his wife. We need no longer play these shams and subterfuges to be alone together.'

'I wish it were that easy. But Tanus will never agree. He cannot—'

'What is this silliness?' The first sparks of anger lit her eyes, and I hurried on.

'That night at Thebes, the night that Pharaoh sent men to arrest Tanus on charges of sedition, we tried to force Tanus to declare for the crown. Kratas and all his officers swore their support, and that of all the army. They wanted to march on the palace and place Tanus on the throne.'

'Why did Tanus not agree to them? He would have been a fine king, and it would have saved all of us so much heartache.'

'Tanus spurned their offer. He declared that he was not a traitor, and that he would never mount the throne of Egypt.'

'That was long ago. Things have all changed,' she cried with exasperation.

'No, they have not changed. Tanus swore an oath that day, and he called on the god Horus to witness it. He swore that he would never take the crown.'

'But it no longer counts. He can go back on that oath.'

'Would you go back on an oath that you had sworn in the sight of the god Horus?' I demanded, and she looked away and hung her head.

'Would you?' I insisted, and she shook her head reluctantly.

'No,' she whispered, 'I could not.'

'The same code of honour binds Tanus. You cannot call upon him to do what you dare not do yourself,' I explained gently. 'Of course, we can put it to him, but you and I both know what his reply must surely be.'

'There must be something that you can do?' She looked at me with that blind trust that angered me. Whenever she had run herself into the deepest danger, she simply turned to me and said, 'There must be something that you can do?'

'There is something, but you will not agree to it, any more than Tanus will agree to wear the crown.'

'If you care anything for me, you will not even suggest it.' She understood me immediately, and recoiled from me as though I had struck her. 'I would rather die myself than kill this miracle of love that Tanus has placed in my womb. The child is him and me and our love. I could never murder all of that.'

'Then, Your Majesty, there is nothing more that I can suggest to you.'

She smiled at me with such sublime trust and confidence that it took my breath away. 'I know you will think of something, my darling Taita. You always do.'

And so I had a dream.

I RELATED my dream before a full session of the council of state called by the regent of this very Egypt.

Queen Lostris and Prince Memnon were seated upon the throne high on the poop-deck of the *Breath of Horus*. The galley was moored to the west bank of the Nile. The members of the council were seated upon the beach below her.

Lord Merkeset and the nobility represented the secular arm of the state. The high priests of Ammon-Ra and Osiris and Hapi represented the sacred arm. Lord Harrab and fifty of his senior officers stood for the military.

I stood upon the open deck below the throne and faced this distinguished gathering. I had taken even greater pains than usual with my appearance. My make-up was subtle and cunning. My hair was dressed with fragrant oils, and coiled in the fashion that I had made popular. I wore the two chains of the Gold of Praise around my neck, and my chest and arms were shaped and hardened by chariot-driving. I must have presented an extraordinary figure of beauty to them, for many of them gaped at me, and I saw the lust in the eyes of those whose inclinations ran in that direction.

'Your Majesties,' I made the low salutation to the pair upon the throne, and Prince Memnon grinned at me cheekily. His head was still bandaged, although it was no longer necessary. He was so proud of his war wound that I had let him keep it on. I frowned at him, and he adjusted his expression to be more in keeping with the occasion.

'Your Majesties, last night I dreamed a strange and wonderful dream which I feel it is my duty to relate. I beg your leave to speak.'

Queen Lostris replied graciously, 'Every person in this company is aware of the sacred gift that you have. The prince and I know that you are able to see into the future, and to divine the will and the wishes of the gods through dreams and visions. I command you now to speak of these mysteries.'

I bowed again and turned to face the council.

'Last night I slept at the door to the royal cabin, as is my duty. Queen Lostris lay alone upon her couch, and the prince slept in his alcove beyond her bed.'

Even Lord Merkeset leaned forward and held his cupped hand behind his good ear, the other being stone-deaf. They all loved a good story and a fruity prophecy.

'In the third watch of the night I awoke, and there was a strange light glowing throughout the ship. I felt a cold wind blowing upon my cheek although every door and porthole was closed.'

My audience stirred with interest. I had struck the right ghostly tone.

'Then I heard footsteps echoing through the hull, slow and majestic footsteps, such as never were made by mortal man.' I paused dramatically. 'These weird and eerie sounds came from the hold of the galley.' I paused again for them to absorb this.

'Yes, my lords, from the hold where the gold coffin of Pharaoh Mamose, the eighth of that name, lies awaiting burial.'

Some of my audience shuddered with awe, while others made the sign against evil.

'These footsteps drew closer to where I lay at the queen's door. The heavenly glow of light grew stronger, and while I trembled, a figure appeared before me. It was the shape of a man, but it was not human, for it glowed like the full moon and its face was a divine reincarnation of the king as I had known him, yet altered and filled with all the terrible divinity of his godhead.'

They were rapt and silent. Not a man stirred. I searched their faces for any sign of incredulity, but I found none.

Then suddenly a child's voice broke the silence, as the prince cried out high and clear, '*Bak-Her!* It was my father. *Bak-Her!* It was Pharaoh!'

They took up the cry, '*Bak-Her!* It was Pharaoh. May he live for ever!'

I waited for the silence, and when it returned I let it draw out to the point where they were almost overwhelmed by the suspense.

'Pharaoh came towards me, and I could not move. He passed me and entered the cabin of Her Gracious Majesty, Queen Lostris. Though I could neither move nor utter a sound, I saw all that came to pass. While the queen still slept, the divine pharaoh mounted upon her in all his splendour, and he took his husbandly pleasure with her. Their bodies were joined as man and woman.'

There was still no sign of disbelief on any face. I waited for the full effect of my words and then I went on, 'Pharaoh rose from the bosom of the sleeping queen, and he looked upon me and he spoke thus.'

I am able to mimic the sound of other men's voices so faithfully that others believe they hear the one I am imitating. I spoke now in the voice of Pharaoh Mamose.

'I have endowed the queen with my godhead. She has become one with me and the gods. I have impregnated her with my divine seed. She who has known no man but me, will bear a child of my royal blood. This will be a sign to all men that she enjoys my protection, and that I will watch over her still.'

I bowed once more to the royal pair upon the throne. 'Then the king passed back through the ship, and entered once more his golden coffin where he now rests. That was all my vision.'

'May Pharaoh live for ever!' shouted Lord Tanus, as I had coached him, and the cry was taken up.

'Hail, Queen Lostris! May she live for ever! Hail, the divine child she bears! May all her children live for ever!'

That night when I prepared to retire, my mistress called me to her, and she whispered, 'Your vision was so vivid and you told it so well that I shall not be able to sleep lest Pharaoh come again. Guard the door well.'

'I dare say there may be one bold and importunate enough to disturb your royal slumber, but I doubt that it will be Pharaoh Mamose. If some rascal does come to take advantage of your kind and loving nature, what should I do?'

'Sleep soundly, dear Taita, and stop your ears.' Her cheeks glowed pink in the lamplight as she blushed.

Once again my premonition of future events was proved accurate. That night there came a secret visitor to my mistress's cabin, and it was not the ghost of Pharaoh. I did what Queen Lostris had ordered. I stopped my ears.

THE NILE flooded once again, reminding us that another year had passed. We had reaped the corn that we had planted upon the islands, and we gathered in our herds. We broke down the chariots and packed them on the open decks of the galleys. We rolled up the tents and stowed them in the holds. Finally, when all was ready for our departure, we laid out the ropes upon the bank and put every able-bodied man and horse into the traces.

It took us almost a month of heart-breaking labour to make the transit of this fearsome cataract. We lost sixteen men drowned, and five galleys broken and chewed to splinters by the fangs of black rock. But at last we were through, and we set sail upon the smooth flow of the river above the rapids.

As the weeks turned to months, the Nile described a slow and majestic bend beneath our keels. Since leaving Elephantine, I had charted the course of the river. I had used the sun and the stars to give me direction, but I had come upon a great difficulty in measuring the distance that we travelled. At first I had ordered one of the slaves to walk along the bank and count every pace he took, but I knew that this method was so inaccurate that it would set all my calculations to nought.

The solution came to me one morning while we were out on chariot manoeuvres. I watched my right-hand wheel turning, and realized that each revolution of the rim made an exact measure of the ground that it had covered. Thereafter a chariot followed the bank of the river. One wheel had a flag on the rim, and a reliable man sat on the footplate and made a mark on a scroll for each time the flag came around.

Each evening I calculated the direction and distance we had travelled during the day, and marked it up on my chart. Slowly, the design and shape of the river made itself clear to me. I saw that we had made a vast loop out into the west, but that now the river had turned back into the south, as the priests of Hapi had predicted.

I showed my findings to Tanus and the queen. Many nights we sat late in the royal cabin, discussing the course of the river and how it would affect our plans to return to Egypt. It seemed that every mile along the river that we travelled, far from dimming my mistress's determination, served but to enhance the force of the vow she had made to return.

'We will build no temple nor palace of stone in the wilderness,' she ordered. 'We will set up no monument or obelisk. Our sojourn here is transitory. We will build no cities, but will live in our ships, or under tents and huts made of grass and reeds. We are a caravan on a journey that in the end will take us back to the city of my birth, beautiful Thebes of a hundred gates.'

In private she counselled me, 'Keep your charts well, Taita. I trust you to find the easy way home for us.'

So our river caravan journeyed onwards, and the desert on either hand changed its face with every mile, and yet in the end was unchanged.

We who sailed upon the river had become a close-knit community, almost an itinerant city without walls or permanent structure. Life burgeoned and faded. Our numbers increased, for most of those who had come with us from Elephantine were in the full bloom of life, and the women were fruitful. Young couples married upon the river-bank, and broke the jar of Nile water between them. Children were born, and we watched them grow.

Some of our old people died, and there were accidents and dangers that took toll of the younger ones. We embalmed them and dug tombs for them in the wild hills and left them to their slumber, and went onwards.

We observed the festivals and prayed to our gods. We feasted and fasted in the correct season, and danced and sang and studied the sciences. I held lessons for the older children upon the deck of the galley, and Memnon was the prize of all my students.

Before the year had run out, and while the course of the river still ran southwards, we came upon the third cataract that bestrode the course of the Nile. Once again we went ashore and cleared the land and planted our crops, while we waited for the Nile to rise and help us through.

IT WAS here at the third great cataract that another joy came to fill my life to overflowing.

In a linen tent upon the bank of the river, I attended my mistress in her labour, and brought forth into this world the Princess Tehuti, the acknowledged daughter of the long-dead Pharaoh Mamose.

In my eyes Tehuti was beautiful as only a miracle might be. Whenever I had the opportunity, I sat beside her cot and examined her tiny feet and hands with wonder and awe. When she was hungry and waited for her mother's nipple, I would sometimes place my little finger in her mouth for the pleasure of feeling her chewing on it with her bald gums.

The river rose at last and allowed us to make the transit of the third cataract. We sailed onwards, and almost imperceptibly the river turned back into the east, describing a vast loop beneath our keels.

Before the year was out it was necessary for me to dream another of my famous dreams, for my mistress had once more suffered a virgin pregnancy that could only be explained by supernatural means. The ghost of the dead pharaoh had been on the prowl again.

My mistress was huge with child when we reached the fourth great cataract of the river. This chute of tumbling waters and rocks like the teeth of crocodiles was even more formidable than those that had come before, and there was much despondency in our company. When they thought that no one could overhear them they complained to each other, 'We are beset by these infernal rock barriers. The gods have placed them across the river to prevent us going onwards.'

I read their lips as they huddled together on the bank of the river. None of them realized that I was able to understand what they said without hearing their words.

'We will be trapped behind these terrible rapids, and we will never be able to return down-river. We should turn back now, before it is too late.'

Even at the councils of state, I saw the words on the lips of some of the great lords of Egypt who sat at the back of the gathering and spoke to each other in muted tones. 'If we go on, we shall all die in this desert, and our souls will wander eternally through it without rest.'

There was an element amongst the young nobility that was both arrogant and headstrong. They were fostering discontent, and hatching insurrection. I knew that we had to act swiftly and with resolution, when I saw the Lord Aqer say to one of his henchmen, 'We are in the hands of this woman, this little harlot of a dead king, when what we really need is a strong man to lead us. There must be some way we can rid ourselves of her.'

Firstly, with the help of my old friend Aton, I ferreted out the names of all the malcontents and potential traitors. It did not surprise me that at the head of this list was this same Lord Aqer, the eldest son of Lord Merkeset, on whose lips I had read those traitorous sentiments. Aqer was an angry young man with inflated ideas of his own worth and importance. I suspected that he had the gall to see a vision of himself seated upon the throne of the two kingdoms with the double crown upon his head.

When I explained to Tanus and my mistress what I thought must be done, they called a full and solemn state council on the river-bank.

Queen Lostris opened the conclave. 'I know very well how you pine for your own land, and how you weary of this long voyage. I share with you every dream of Thebes.'

I saw Aqer exchange meaningful glances with his cronies, and had my suspicions strengthened.

'However, citizens of Egypt, nothing is as bad as it seems. Hapi has watched over our expedition, as he promised. We are much closer to Thebes than any one of you can imagine. When we return to our beloved city, we will not have to retrace our same weary footsteps. We will not have to face once again the dangers and the hardships of those hellish cataracts that block the course of the river.'

There was a stirring through her audience, and whispers of doubt and disbelief. Aqer laughed, not loud enough to cross the borders of respect and propriety, nevertheless my mistress singled him out. 'I see, Lord Aqer, that you question my word?'

'By no means, Your Majesty. I curse such a disloyal thought.' Aqer made a hasty retreat. He was not yet strong enough, nor sure enough of his support, to force a confrontation. I had caught him out before he was prepared.

'My slave, Taita, has plotted the course of the river that we have covered in these last years,' Queen Lostris went on. 'You have all seen the chariot with the flagged wheel that has measured the ground, and Taita has studied the heavenly bodies to find the direction of our journey. I order him now to arise before the council and reveal to us his calculations.'

Prince Memnon had helped me to trace copies of my chart on to twenty new scrolls. At nine years of age, the prince was already a fine pen-man. I passed these out to all the senior nobles, so that they might follow my lecture more clearly. I drew their attention to the almost circular course that we had followed since we had left Elephantine.

Their astonishment was evident. Only the priests had some prior knowledge of what had occurred, they also studied the stars and had some expertise in navigation. But even they were taken aback by the extent of the river's loop. This was not surprising, since the copies of the map that I showed them were not entirely accurate. I had taken certain liberties with the facts for the benefit of Aqer and his faction, and made the distance across the bight seem shorter than my calculations suggested was the case.

'My lords, as you can see by these charts, since we left the second cataract we have travelled very nearly a thousand miles, but we stand now not much more than a few hundred miles from the point of our departure.'

Kratas rose to his feet to ask a question that I had placed in his mouth before the meeting began. 'Does this mean that it should be possible to take this short cut across the desert and reach the second cataract in the same time as it takes to travel from Thebes to the Red Sea and return? I have made that journey several times.'

I turned to him. 'I was your companion on that same journey. Ten days in each direction it took us, and we did not have horses then. The crossing of this narrow strip of desert would be no more onerous. It means that from here one could be back in the city of Elephantine within a few short months, and it would be necessary to transit only the first cataract at Assoun.'

There was a buzz of comment and amazement. The maps were passed from hand to hand and scrutinized avidly. The entire mood of the assembly changed, as I watched. There was a pathetic eagerness amongst all of them to accept my theory. This unexpected proximity to home and the land they knew cheered all of them.

Only Aqer and his friends were out of countenance. He had been deprived of the top dice in the game he was playing. As I had hoped he would do, he rose angrily to his feet now to put the next question to me.

'How accurate are this slave's scribblings?' His tone was offensive and his expression haughty. 'It is a simple matter to make a few pen-strokes on a scroll, but when those are turned into miles of sand and rock, it is another matter entirely. How will this slave prove that these wild theories of his are fact?'

'My lord Aqer has come to the very heart of the matter,' my mistress intervened pleasantly, 'and, in so doing, has proven his astute grasp of the problem that faces us. I intend to send an expedition of good men to cross the neck of the desert and to open up our return route to the north, the road home to beautiful Thebes.'

I saw Aqer's expression change suddenly as he caught the slant of the queen's speech and realized the trap that had been set for him. He sat down again hurriedly, and tried to appear remote and disinterested. However, my mistress continued remorselessly, 'I was undecided as to who was best suited to lead this expedition, but now Lord Aqer has, by his perception and understanding, proposed himself for this vital task. Is that not the case, my lord?' she asked sweetly, and then went on smoothly before he could refuse.

'We are grateful to you, Lord Aqer. You are to have whatever men and equipment you require. I command that you make your departure before the next full moon. The moon will make it easier for you to travel during the night, and so avoid the heat of the day. I will send with you men who are able to navigate by the stars. You could win through to the second cataract and be back here before the end of the month, and, if you succeed, I will place the Gold of Praise upon your shoulders.'

Lord Aqer stared at her with open mouth, and he was still sitting rigid with shock on his stool after all his companions had dispersed. I fully expected him to find some excuse to back out of the task that we had tricked him into, but in the end he surprised me by coming to me to ask for my advice and help in arranging the scouting party. It seemed that I might have misjudged him, and that now he had been given some worthwhile mission, there was a chance that he would change from a trouble-maker to a useful member of the company.

I selected some of our best men and horses for him and gave him five of our most sturdy carts, which could carry water-skins that, if used sparingly, would last them for thirty days. By the time the full moon came around, Aqer was quite cheerful and optimistic, and I felt guilty about having minimized the distance and the hazards of the journey.

When the expedition set out, I went a short way into the desert with them to point them on the right road, and then I stood alone and watched them merge into the silvery moonlit wastes, aimed at that set of stars we call the Lute which marks the northern horizon.

I thought of Aqer every day over the weeks that followed while we lay below the fourth cataract, and I hoped that the map I had given him was not as inaccurate as I feared it was. At least the immediate threat of a rebellion had disappeared with him into the north.

While we waited, we planted our crops on the cleared islands and the river-banks. However, the lie of the land was steeper than at the other sites lower down the river. It was more difficult to raise the water to irrigate our crops, and I could see that the quantity and the quality of the harvest must suffer in consequence.

Naturally, we had set up the traditional shadoofs on their long, counter-balanced arms to lift the water from the river. These were worked by a slave who swung the clay pot at the end of the arm into the water and then lifted and spilled it into the irrigation ditch on the bank. It was a slow and back-breaking task. When the bank was high, as it was here, it was also an extremely wasteful method of collecting water.

Each evening Memnon and I drove our chariot along the river-bank, and I was troubled by the paucity of the harvest that we watched growing there. We had many thousands of mouths to feed, and cornmeal was still the staple of our diet. I foresaw a time of famine, unless we were able to bring more water to the fields.

I do not know what made me think of the wheel for this purpose, except that the science of the wheel had by this time become an obsession and a passion in my life. I was still plagued by the problem of the bursting of the wheels of our chariots. My dreams were filled with turning and spinning and shattering wheels, wheels with bronze knives on the rim or with flags to measure the distance run. Large wheels and small, the images haunted me and troubled my sleep.

I had heard from one of the priests of Hapi that some varieties of timber can be made harder and more resilient by soaking them in water for a long period, so I was driven to experiment with this idea. As we were lowering one of the chariot wheels into the river for this purpose, the current playing on the rim began to turn the wheel on its hub. I watched this idly, but as the wheel sank lower in the water, the movement ceased, and I thought no more about it.

Some days later, one of the small boats crossing between the islands capsized, and the two men in it were swept into the rapids and drowned.

Memnon and I watched this tragedy from the bank, and we were both distressed by it. I took the opportunity to warn the prince once more of the danger and the power of the river.

'It is so strong that it will even turn the wheel of a chariot.'

'I don't believe you, Tata. You are saying that to frighten me. You know how I love to swim in the river.'

So I arranged an exhibition for him, and we were both duly impressed by the wheel turning, seemingly of its own accord, when it was dipped into the running water.

'It would go faster, Tata, if it had paddles fixed around the rim,' Memnon gave his opinion at last, and I stared at him in wonder. He was a little over ten years old at the time, and yet he saw all things with a fresh and enquiring eye.

By the time the full moon came around again, we had built a wheel driven by the river which lifted the water in a series of small baked-clay jars and spilled it into a canal lined with clay tiles at the top of the high Nile bank. Even with her big belly, my mistress came ashore to watch this wondrous contraption. She was delighted by it.

'You are so clever with the things you do with water, Taita,' she told me. 'Do you remember the water-stool you built for me at Elephantine?'

'I could make another for you now, if only you would allow us to live in a decent home like civilized people.'

Tanus was similarly impressed with the water-wheel, though of course he would not show it. Instead, he grinned at me.

'Very clever, but when will it burst like one of your famous chariot wheels?' he demanded, and Kratas and those other military oafs thought that was hugely funny. Thereafter, whenever a chariot wheel broke, they said that it had 'gone Tata', the pet name that the prince called me.

Despite this levity, the fields of dhurra soon grew dense and green in the loamy soil on the high banks, and the ears of golden corn drooped heavily in the bright Nile sunlight. This was not the only harvest that we gathered in at the fourth cataract. Queen Lostris gave birth to another little royal princess. If anything, the infant was more exquisite than her elder sister.

It was passing strange that Princess Bekatha was born with a cap of golden-red curls. Her divine and ghostly father, Pharaoh Mamose, had been of swarthy cast, and her mother's hair was dark as the wing of the black eagle. No one could think of any reason for this aberrant coloration, but all agreed how pretty it was.

Princess Bekatha was two months old when the Nile began to rise once more, and we made our preparation for the transit of the fourth cataract. By now we were experienced in what had become an annual labour, and we had learned every trick and artifice to beat the rapacious river.

WE HAD not yet begun the transit, when there was tremendous excitement in the encampment. I heard the shouting and the cheering from the far bank of the river where Prince Memnon and I were inspecting the horses and making certain that all was ready for the ascent of the cataract.

We hurried back to the boats and crossed to the east bank, to find the camp in an uproar. We pushed our way through the crowds who were all waving palm-fronds and singing the songs of welcome and honour. At the centre of all this we found a small caravan of battered wagons and skeletal horses, and a band of lean, travel-hardened veterans, burned black by the sun and tempered by the desert.

'Seth damn you and that map of yours, Taita,' Lord Aqer shouted at me from the leading wagon. 'I don't know which of you lies worst. It was almost twice as far as you promised us.'

'Did you truly reach the north side of the river loop?' I shouted back at him, hopping with excitement and trying to fight my way through the crowd.

'There and back!' he laughed, mightily pleased with his accomplishment. 'We camped at the second cataract and dined on fresh fish from the Nile. The road back to Thebes is open.'

My mistress ordered a feast to welcome back the travellers, and Lord Aqer was the man of the day. At the height of the celebration, Queen Lostris placed the Gold of Praise around his neck, and promoted him to the rank of Best of Ten Thousand. My gorge rose to see the fellow preen and strut. As if that was not enough, she gave him command of the fourth division of chariots, and issued him a warrant that would entitle him to one hundred feddan of prime land on the river-bank when we returned to Thebes.

I thought all this a little excessive, especially the gift of so much land which must come out of my mistress's own estate. After all, Aqer had been on the brink of mutiny, and though his achievement had been laudable, it was I who had proposed and planned the expedition. In the circumstances, it seemed to me that another gold chain for the poor slave Taita might not have been out of place.

Nevertheless, I had to applaud my mistress's cunning and statesmanship. She had transformed Lord Aqer, who had been potentially one of her most dangerous enemies, into an ardent and loyal adherent who would prove his value to her many times in the years ahead. She had a way with all men, and was gaining in statecraft each day.

The taming of Lord Aqer and the discovery of the route across the bight had secured our rear, and we could go on above the fourth cataract with high spirits and brave heart.

WE HAD not travelled more than a month before we realized how our fortunes had changed and how the goddess had made good her promise.

It was clearer each day that we had come through the worst. The desert was behind us at last, and the broad, smooth flow of the river turned into the south once more and carried us into a land such as none of us had seen before.

It was here that for the first time many of our company witnessed the miracle of rain. Although of course I had seen it in the Lower Kingdom, they had never seen water fall from the sky. The rain beat down into our upturned and astonished faces, while the thunder rolled across the heavens and the lightning blinded us with its white fire.

These copious and regular rains engendered a new and exciting landscape, the like of which we could only wonder at. On either bank of the Nile, as far as we could see from the deck of the leading galley, stretched a broad savannah grassland. This magnificent plain, rich with grazing for our horses, set no boundaries to the range of our chariots. We could drive out at will, with no dunes or rocky hills to block our progress.

This was not the only blessing that the goddess had bestowed. There were trees. In the narrow valley that was our home, there might once have been forests, no man could tell. But they had fallen centuries before to the appetite and axes of man. Wood was to us Egyptians a rare and treasured commodity. Each stick of it had to be carried in by ship or on the back of beasts of burden, from far and foreign lands.

Now, wherever we looked, we saw great trees. They grew, not in the same dense forests that we had found on the islands in the cataracts, but in lofty groves with broad grassy spaces between the majestic trunks. There was timber enough upon these plains to rebuild all the fleets of all the nations on all the seas of the worlds. More than that, there was enough to rebuild the cities of all the civilized world, and to roof and furnish every room in them. After that there would still be enough left over to burn as fuel over the centuries to come. We who all our lives had cooked our food on bricks made from the dung of our animals, stared around us in wonder.

This was not the only treasure that we found for our taking in this legendary land of Cush that we had reached at last.

I saw them first in the distance and thought that they were monuments of grey granite. They stood upon the yellow grass plains and in the shade beneath the spreading branches of the acacia groves. Then, as we watched in perplexity, these great rocks began to move.

'Elephants!' I had never seen one before, but they could be nothing else. The cry was taken up by those on the deck around me.

'Elephants! Ivory!' These were riches that Pharaoh Mamose, with all his funerary treasure, could not have dreamed of. Wherever we looked, the vast herds stood.

'There are thousands of them.' Tanus gazed around him, the passion of the huntsman beginning to dawn in his eyes. 'Just look at them, Taita. There is no end to their numbers.'

The plains were thronged with living creatures, not only the herds of elephant. There were antelopes and gazelle, some of which we knew, and others that we had never seen or heard of before. We would come to know all of them well in the future, and find names for their abundant and diverse species.

Oryx mingled with herds of purple waterbuck whose horns curved like the bow that I had built for Tanus. There were spotted giraffe with necks that reached to the top branches of the acacia trees. The horns that grew from the snouts of the rhinoceros were as tall as a man and as sharp as his spear. The buffalo wallowed in the mud at the river's edge. They were huge bovine beasts, black as Seth's beard, and every bit as ugly. We would soon learn the malevolence behind that melancholy stare with which they regarded our passing, and the menace of those drooping black horns.

'Unload the chariots from the holds,' Tanus roared with impatience. 'Put the horses into the traces. The hunt is on!'

If I had known the danger that we were riding into, I would never have allowed Prince Memnon to mount the footplate behind me as we drove out on our first elephant hunt. To us who knew no better, they appeared such docile brutes, slow and clumsy and stupid. Surely they would be easy game.

Tanus was bristling with impatience to go out against this new quarry, and he would not wait for all four divisions of our chariots to be reassembled. As soon as the first division of fifty vehicles was ready, he gave the order to mount up. We shouted challenges to the other drivers, and made our wagers on the outcome of the hunt as the long columns of chariots rolled out through the groves along the river-bank.

'Let me drive, Tata,' the prince demanded. 'You know I drive as well as you do.' Although he was a natural horseman with gentle hands and an instinctive way with his team, and he practised the art almost every day, the prince's boast was unfounded. He certainly was not as good a charioteer as I was, no man in the army could make that claim, certainly not a scamp of eleven years.

'Watch me and learn,' I told him sternly, and when Memnon turned to Tanus, he supported me for once.

'Taita is right. This is something none of us has done before. Keep your mouth closed and your eyes open, boy.'

Ahead of us a small herd of these strange grey beasts were feasting on the seed-pods that had fallen from the top branches of the trees. I studied them with avid curiosity as we approached at a trot. Their ears were enormous, and they fanned them out and turned to face us. They lifted their trunks high, and I guessed that they were taking up our scent. Had they ever smelled a man or a horse before, I wondered.

There were small calves with them, and the mothers gathered them into the centre of the herd and stood guard over them. I was touched to see this maternal concern, and I had the first inkling then that these animals were not as slow and stupid as they appeared to be. 'These are all females,' I called over my shoulder to Tanus on the footplate. 'They have young at heel, and their ivory is small and of little value.'

'You are right.' Tanus pointed over my shoulder. 'But look beyond them. Those two must surely be bulls. See how tall they stand and how massive is their girth. Look how their tusks shine in the sun.'

I gave the signal to the chariots that followed us, and we veered away from the breeding herd of cows and calves. We ran on, still in column, through the acacia grove towards those two great bulls. As we drove forward, we were forced to swerve around the branches that had been torn from the trees, and to dodge the trunks of giant acacia that had been uprooted. As yet we knew nothing of the unbelievable strength of these creatures, and I called back to Tanus, 'There must have been a great storm through this forest to wreak such destruction.' It did not even occur to me then that the elephant herds were responsible; they seemed so mild and defenceless.

The two old bulls we had selected had sensed our approach and turned to face us. It was only then that I realized the true size of them. When they spread their ears they seemed to block out the sky, like a dark grey thunder-cloud.

'Just look at that ivory!' Tanus shouted. He was unperturbed, and concerned only with the trophy of the chase, but the horses were nervous and skittish. They had picked up the scent of this strange quarry, and they threw their heads up and crabbed in the traces. It was hard to control them and keep them running straight.

'That one on the right is the biggest,' squeaked Memnon. 'We should take him first.' The pup was every bit as keen as his sire.

'You heard the royal command,' Tanus laughed. 'We will take the one on the right. Let Kratas have the other, it's good enough for him.'

So I raised my fist and gave the hand-command that split the column into two files. Kratas wheeled away on our left with twenty-five chariots following him in line astern, while we ran on straight at the huge grey beast that confronted us with the yellow shafts of ivory, thick as the columns of the temple of Horus, standing out from his vast grey head.

'Go hard at him!' Tanus shouted. 'Take him before he turns to run.'

'Hi up!' I called to Patience and Blade, and they opened up into a gallop. We both expected the huge animal to run from us as soon as he realized that we menaced him. No other game we had ever hunted had stood to receive our first charge. Even the lion runs from the hunter until he is wounded or cornered. How could these obese animals behave differently?

'His head is so big, it will make a fine target,' Tanus exulted, as he nocked an arrow. 'I will kill him with a single shaft, before he can escape. Run in close under that long, ridiculous nose of his.'

Behind us the rest of our column was strung out in single file. Our plan was to come in and split on each side of the bull, firing our arrows into him as we passed, then wheeling around and coming back in classic chariot tactics.

We were right on the bull now, but still he stood his ground. Perhaps these animals were every bit as dull-witted as they looked. This would be an easy kill, and I sensed Tanus' disappointment at the prospect of such poor sport.

'Come on you old fool!' he shouted contemptuously. 'Don't just stand there. Defend yourself!'

It was as though the bull heard and understood the challenge. He threw up his trunk and loosed a blast of sound that stunned and deafened us. The horses shied wildly, so that I was thrown against the dashboard with a force that bruised my ribs. For a moment I lost control of the team, and we swerved away.

Then the bull squealed again, and he ran.

'By Horus, look at him come!' Tanus roared with astonishment, for the beast was not running from us, but directly at us, in a furious charge. He was swifter than any horse, and nimble as an angry leopard set upon by the hounds. He kicked up bursts of dust with each long flying stride, and was on us before I could get the horses under control again.

I looked up at him, for he towered directly over us, reaching out with his trunk to pluck us from the cockpit of the chariot, and I could not believe the size of him, nor the fury in those eyes. They were not the eyes of an animal, but those of an intelligent and alert human being. This was no porcine sloth, but a courageous and terrible adversary that we had challenged in our arrogance and ignorance.

Tanus got off a single arrow. It struck the bull in the centre of his forehead, and I expected to see him collapse as the bronze point pierced the brain. We did not know then that the brain of the elephant is not situated where you would expect it to be, but is far back in the mountainous skull and protected by a mass of spongy bone that no arrow can penetrate.

The bull did not even check or swerve. He merely reached up with his trunk and gripped the shaft of the arrow with the tip, as a man might do with his hand. He pulled the shaft from his own flesh and threw it aside and came on after us, reaching out towards us with the blood-smeared trunk.

Hui in the second chariot of our line saved us, for we were defenceless against the old bull's fury. Hui came in from the side, lashing his horses and yelling like a demon. His archer from the footplate behind him fired an arrow into the bull's cheek a hand's-span below the eye, and that pulled his attention from us.

The elephant wheeled to chase after Hui, but he was at full gallop and raced clean away. The next chariot in line was not so fortunate. The driver lacked Hui's skill, and his turn away was inept. The bull lifted his trunk high and then swung it down like an executioner's axe.

He struck the near-side horse across the back, just behind the withers, and broke its spine so cleanly that I heard the vertebrae shatter like a brittle potsherd. The maimed horse went down and dragged its teammate down with it. The chariot rolled over and the men were hurled from it. The elephant placed one forefoot on the body of the fallen charioteer and, with its trunk, plucked off his head and tossed it aloft like a child's ball. It spun in the air spraying a bright feather of pink blood from the severed neck.

Then the next chariot in line tore in, distracting the bull from his victim.

I pulled up my horses at the edge of the grove, and we stared back aghast at the carnage of our shattered squadron. There were broken chariots scattered across the field, for Kratas out on the left had fared no better than we had.

The two great bull elephants bristled with arrow-shafts, and the blood streamed down their bodies, leaving wet streaks on their dusty grey hide. However, the wounds had not weakened them, but seemed only to have aggravated their fury. They rampaged through the grove, smashing up the capsized chariots, stamping the carcasses of the horses under those massive padded feet, throwing the bodies of screaming men high in the air and trampling them as they fell back to earth.

Kratas raced up alongside us, and shouted across at us, 'By the itching crabs in Seth's crotch, this is hot work! We have lost eight chariots in the first charge.'

'Better sport than you expected, Captain Kratas,' Prince Memnon yelled back at him. He would have done better to keep his opinion to himself, for up until that moment we had forgotten about the boy in the confusion. Now, however, both Tanus and I rounded on him together.

'As for you, my lad, you have had enough sport for one day,' I told him firmly.

'It's back to the fleet with you, and that right swiftly,' agreed Tanus, and at that moment an empty chariot cantered by. I do not know what had happened to the crew, they had probably been thrown from the cockpit or been plucked out of it bodily by one of the infuriated beasts.

'Catch those horses!' Tanus ordered, and when the empty chariot was brought back to us, he told the prince, 'Out you get. Take that chariot back to the beach and wait there for our return.'

'My Lord Tanus,' Prince Memnon drew himself to his full height, reaching as high as his father's shoulder, 'I protest—'

'None of your royal airs with me, young man. Go back and protest to your mother, if you must.' He lifted the prince with one hand and dropped him into the vacant cockpit of the other vehicle.

'Lord Tanus, it is my right—' Memnon made one last despairing attempt to remain in the hunt.

'And it is my right to wrap the scabbard of my sword around your royal backside, if you are still here when I look around again,' said Tanus, and turned his back on him. Both of us put the boy out of our minds.

'Gathering ivory is not quite as easy as picking up mushrooms,' I remarked. 'We will have to think up a better plan than this.'

'You cannot kill these creatures by shooting them in the head,' Tanus growled. 'We will go in again and try an arrow through the ribs. If they have no brain in their skull, then surely they have lungs and a heart.'

I gathered up the reins, and lifted the heads of the team, but I could feel that Patience and Blade were as nervous as I was at the prospect of returning to the field. None of us had enjoyed our first taste of elephant hunting.

'I'll go at him head-on,' I told Tanus, 'and then turn out to give you a broadside shot into his ribs.'

I put the horses into a trot, and then gradually pushed up their speed as we entered the acacia grove. Dead ahead of us our bull rampaged over the ground that was littered with the wreckage of overturned chariots and the bodies of dead men and broken horses. He saw us coming and let out another of those terrible squeals that chilled my blood, and the horses flicked their ears and shied again. I gathered them up with the reins and drove them on.

The bull charged to meet us, like a landslide of rock down a steep hillside. He was a terrible sight in his rage and his agony, but I held my team steady, not yet pushing them to the top of their speed. Then, as we came together, I lashed them up and yelled them into a full, mad gallop. At the same moment I swung out hard left, opening the bull's flank.

At a range of less than twenty paces, Tanus fired three arrows in quick succession into his chest. All of them went in behind the shoulder, finding the gaps between the ribs, and burying themselves full-length in the seared grey skin.

The bull squealed again, but this time in mortal agony. Though he reached out for us, we raced clear of the stretch of his trunk. I looked back and saw him standing in our dust, but when he bellowed again, the blood spurted from the end of his trunk, like steam from a kettle.

'The lungs,' I shouted. 'Good work, Tanus. You have hit him through the lungs.'

'We have found the trick of it now,' Tanus exulted. 'Take us back. I will give him another one through the heart.'

I wheeled about and the horses were still strong and willing.

'Come on, my beauties,' I called to them. 'One more time. Hi up!'

Though he was mortally struck, the old bull was still far from death. I would learn just how tenacious of life these magnificent beasts were, but now he charged to meet us once again with a courage and splendour that filled me with reverence. Even in the heat of the hunt and terror for my own safety, I felt shame at the torture we were inflicting on him.

Perhaps it was because of this that I let the horses go in very close. Out of respect for him, I wanted to match his courage with my own. When it was almost too late, I swung my horses out of the charge, meaning to pass him just out of reach of that wicked trunk.

Just then the off-side wheel of the chariot burst under us. There was that giddy moment as I somersaulted through the air like an acrobat, but this was not the first time I had been thrown, and I had learned to fall like a cat. I rode the shock and let myself roll twice. The earth was soft and the grass as thick as a mattress. I came up on my feet unhurt and with my wits still all about me. I saw at a glance that Tanus had not come through as well as I had. He was sprawled flat out and unmoving.

The horses were up, but anchored by the dead weight of the broken chariot. The bull elephant attacked them. Blade was nearest to him and he broke my darling mare's back with a single blow of the trunk. Blade went down on her knees screaming, and Patience was still linked to her. The bull thrust one thick tusk through Blade's chest and jerked his head up, lifting the kicking and struggling animal high in the air.

I should have run then, while the bull was so distracted, but Patience was still unhurt. I could not leave her. The elephant was turned half-away from me, his own ears, spread like a ship's sail, blanketed me from his view, and he did not see me run in. I snatched Tanus' sword from the scabbard on the rack of the capsized chariot, and darted to Patience's side.

Although the great bull was dragging her along by the leather harness that attached her to Blade, and although the blood from the other horse splashed over her neck and shoulders, she was still unhurt. Of course, she was wild with terror, squealing and kicking out with both back legs, so that she almost cracked my skull as I darted up behind her. I ducked as her hooves flew past my head and grazed my cheek.

I hacked at the rawhide tackle that pinned her to the drive-shaft of the chariot. The sword was sharp enough to shave the hair from my head, and the leather split under that bright edge. Three hard strokes, and Patience was free to run. I snatched at her mane to pull myself up on to her back, but she was so terror-struck that she bounded away before I could find a grip. Her shoulder crashed into me and sent me spinning away. I was thrown heavily to the ground, under the side of the wrecked chariot.

I struggled up to see Patience dashing off through the grove; she ran with a free and light stride, so I knew she was unhurt. I looked for Tanus next. He lay ten paces away from the chariot, face down against the earth, and I thought he was dead, but at that moment he raised his head and looked around at me with a bewildered and groggy expression. I knew that any sudden movement might draw the bull elephant's attention to him, and I willed him to lie still. I dared not utter a sound, for the enraged animal was still standing over me.

I looked up at the bull. Poor Blade was impaled upon his tusk, and the rawhide traces were entangled with his trunk. The bull started to move off, dragging the battered chariot with him. He was attempting to dislodge the weight of Blade's dangling carcass from his tusk. The point of the tusk had ripped open the horse's belly, and the stink of the stomach contents mingled with the reek of blood and the elephant's peculiar rank and gamey odour. Stronger than all that, the stench of the sweat of my own fear filled my nostrils.

I made sure that the bull's head was still turned away from me, before I pushed myself up and ran doubled-over to where Tanus lay. 'Up! Get up!' I croaked in a hoarse whisper, and I tried to lift him to his feet, but he was a heavy man and still only half-conscious. Desperately I looked back at the bull. He was moving away from us, still dragging the whole tangle of broken equipment and the dead horse with him.

I draped Tanus' arm around my neck and put my shoulder into his armpit. With all my strength I managed to lever him to his feet, and he hung against me unsteadily. I swayed under his weight. 'Brace up!' I whispered urgently. 'The bull will spot us at any moment.'

I tried to drag Tanus along with me, but he took only one pace before he gave a groan and fell back against me. 'My leg,' he grunted. 'Can't move. Knee gone. Twisted the cursed thing.'

The full realization of our predicament struck me then, as it had not before. My old sin of cowardice overwhelmed me once more, and the strength went out of my own legs.

'Get out of it, you old fool,' Tanus grated in my ear. 'Leave me. Run for it!'

The elephant lifted his head and shook it in the same way that a dog shakes the water from its ears after it has swum back to the shore. Those vast leathery ears slapped and rattled against his own shoulders, and Blade's crushed carcass slid off the tusk and was hurled aside as if it were no heavier than a dead rabbit. The strength of the elephant bull was past all belief. If he could toss the weight of horse and chariot so easily, what might he do with my own frail body?

'Run, for the love of Horus, run, you fool!' Tanus urged me, and tried to push me away, but some strange obstinacy prevented me from leaving him, and I hung on to his shoulder. Afraid as I was, I could not leave him.

The bull had heard the sound of Tanus' voice and he swung around with those ears flaring wide open like the mainsail of a fighting galley. He stared full at us, and we were less than fifty paces from him.

I did not know then, as I would learn later, that the eyesight of the elephant is so poor that he is almost blind. He relies almost entirely on his hearing and his sense of smell. Only movement attracts him, and if we had stood still he would not have seen us.

'He has seen us,' I gasped, and I dragged Tanus with me, forcing him to hop on his good leg beside me. The bull saw the movement and he squealed. I shall never forget that sound. It deafened and stunned me, sending us both reeling so that we staggered together and almost fell.

Then the bull charged straight at us.

He came with long, driving strides, and his ears flapped about his head. Arrows bristled from the great weathered forehead, and blood streamed down his face like tears. Each time he squealed, the lung blood spurted in a cloud from his trunk. As tall as a cliff, and as black as death, he came at us in full charge. I could see every seam and crease in the folded skin around his eyes. The lashes of his eyes were thick as those of a beautiful girl, but such a glare of rage shone through them that my heart turned to a stone in my chest, and weighed down my legs so I could not move.

The passage of time seemed to slow down, and I was overcome with a sense of dreamlike unreality. I stood and watched death bear down upon us with a slow and stately deliberation, and could make no move to avoid it.

'Tata!' A child's voice rang in my head, and I knew that it was a delusion of my terror. 'Tata, I am coming!'

In total disbelief I swung my head away from the vision of death before me. Across the open ground of the grove a chariot was tearing towards us at full gallop. The horses were stretched out and their heads were going like the hammers on a coppersmith's anvil. Their ears were laid back, and their nostrils flared wide open, pink and wet. I could see no driver at the reins.

'Get ready, Tata!' Only then did I see the neat little head, barely showing above the dashboard. The reins were gripped in two small fists, the knuckles white with tension.

'Mem,' I cried, 'go back! Turn back!'

The wind blew his hair out in a cloud behind his head, and the sunlight struck ruby sparks from the thick dark curls. He came on without a pause or check.

'I'll thrash the little ruffian for disobeying me,' growled Tanus, as he teetered on one leg. We had both of us forgotten our own danger.

'Whoa!' Memnon cried, and brought the team down from a full gallop. He wheeled the carriage into such a sharp turn that the inside wheel stopped dead and swivelled on its rim. He had cut in front of the two of us, shielding us for an instant from the charging bull, and as the chariot spun about there was a moment when it was standing still. It was beautifully done.

I heaved my shoulder up under Tanus' armpit and threw him sprawling on the footplate. The very next instant I hurled myself headlong on top of him. As I landed, Memnon gave the horses their heads, and we bounded forward so sharply that I was almost jerked backwards off the platform, but I grabbed at the side-panel and steadied myself.

'Go, Mem,' I screamed, 'for all you're worth!'

'Hi-up!' Memnon screamed. 'Yah hah!' The chariot careered away with the frightened horses driven to full flight by the enraged squeals of the charging bull close behind.

All three of us stared back over the tail-board. The head of the bull hung over us, seeming to fill all my vision. The trunk reached out for us, so close that each time the bull squealed, the bloody cloud sprayed over us and speckled our upturned faces, so that we looked like the victims of some horrible plague.

We could not draw clear of his rush, and he was unable to overtake us. Matched in speed, we went racing through the glade with the great bloody head hanging over us as we cowered on the floorboards of the bouncing chariot. It needed only one small mistake from our driver to send us into a hole or rip our wheels off against a stump of a fallen tree, and the bull would have been upon us in an instant. But the prince handled the traces like a veteran, picking his route through the grove with a cool hand and practised eye. He sent the chariot careening through the turns on one wheel, within an ace of capsizing, holding off the bull's mad charge. He never faltered once, and then suddenly it was all over.

One of the arrows buried in the bull's chest had worked itself in deeper and sliced open the heart. The elephant opened his mouth wide, and a flood of bright blood shot up his throat and he died in his tracks. His legs went out from under him and he came down with a crash that jarred the earth under us, and lay upon his side with one long curved tusk thrust up in the air as if in a last defiant and regal gesture.

Memnon pulled in the horses, and Tanus and I stumbled down out of the carriage and stood together staring back at that mountainous carcass. Tanus clung to the side of the chariot to favour his damaged leg, and slowly turned back to look at the boy who did not know he was his father.

'By Horus, I have known some brave men in my time, but none of them better than you, lad,' he said simply, and then he lifted Memnon in his arms and hugged him to his chest.

I did not see much more of it, for those everlasting and tedious tears of mine blotted out my vision. Even though I knew myself for a sentimental fool, I could not staunch them. I had waited too long to see this happen, to watch the father embrace his son.

I only managed to regain control of my errant emotions when I heard the faint sound of distant cheers. What none of us had realized was that the chase had taken place in full view of the fleet. The *Breath of Horus* lay close in against the bank of the Nile, and I could see the slim figure of the queen upon the high poop. Even at this distance her face looked pale and her expression set.

THE GOLD of Valour is the warrior's prize, higher in honour and in esteem than the Gold of Praise. It is only ever worn by heroes.

We gathered on the deck of the galley, those closest to the queen and the commanders of all the divisions of her army. Stacked against the mast, the tusks of the elephants were on display like the spoils of war, and the officers wore all their regimental finery. The standard-bearers stood to attention behind the throne, and the trumpeters blew a fanfare as the prince knelt before the queen.

'My beloved subjects!' the queen spoke out clearly. 'Noble officers of my council, generals and officers of my army, I commend to you the crown prince, Memnon, who has found favour in my sight and in the sight of you all.' She smiled down on the eleven-year-old boy who was being treated like a victorious general.

'For his courageous conduct in the field, I command that he be received into the regiment of the Blue Crocodile Guards, with the rank of subaltern of the second class, and I bestow upon him the Gold of Valour, that he may wear it with pride and distinction.'

The chain had been especially forged by the royal goldsmiths to fit the neck of a boy of Memnon's age, but with my own hands I had sculpted the tiny golden elephant that was suspended from the chain. It was perfect in every detail, a miniature masterpiece with garnet chips for eyes and real ivory tusks. It looked well as it hung against the smooth, unblemished skin of the prince's chest.

I felt my tears coming on again as the men cheered my beautiful prince, but I fought them back with an effort. I was not the only one who was wallowing in sentiment like a wart-hog in a mud bath; even Kratas and Remrem and Astes, for all their hardbitten and cavalier attitudes which they usually cultivated so assiduously, were grinning like idiots, and I swear I saw more than one pair of wet eyes in their ranks. In the same way as his parents, the boy had a way with the affections and loyalties of men. Every officer of the Blues came forward at the end to salute the prince and embrace him gravely as a comrade-in-arms.

That evening, as we drove together along the bank of the Nile in the sunset, Memnon suddenly reined in the horses and turned to me. 'I have been called to my regiment. I am a soldier at last, so you must make me my own bow now, Tata.'

'I will make you the finest bow that any archer has ever drawn,' I promised.

He considered me gravely for a while, and then he sighed, 'Thank you, Tata. I think this is the happiest day of all my life.' The way he said it made eleven years seem like hoary old age.

The next day after the fleet had moored for the night, I went to look for the prince and found him alone upon the bank in a spot that was hidden from casual observation. He had not seen me, so I could observe him for a while.

He was stark naked. Despite my warnings about currents and crocodiles, it was obvious that he had been swimming in the river, for his hair was sopping wet upon his shoulders. However, I was puzzled by his behaviour, for he had selected two large round stones from the beach and was holding one of these in each hand, raising and lowering them in some strange ritual.

'Tata, you are spying on me,' he said suddenly, without turning his head. 'Do you want something from me?'

'I want to know what you are doing with those stones. Are you worshipping some strange new Cushite god?'

'I am making my arms strong so that I can draw my new bow. I want it to have a full draw-weight. You are not to fob me off with another toy, Tata, do you hear?'

THERE WAS one more cataract across the river, the fifth and what would later prove to be the penultimate that we would encounter upon our voyage. However, this was not the same barrier to our progress that the other four had been. With the change in the surrounding terrain, we were no longer restricted to the course of the river.

While we waited for the Nile to rise again, we planted our crops as usual, but we were able to send out our chariots to range far and wide across the savannah. My mistress despatched expeditions southwards to pursue the elephant herds and bring back the ivory.

Those vast herds of the magnificent grey beasts that had greeted us so trustingly when first we had sailed into Cush, were now flown and scattered. We had hunted them ruthlessly wherever we found them, but these sage creatures learned their lesson well and right swiftly.

When we arrived at the fifth cataract, we found the herds grazing in the groves on either bank. The elephant were in their thousands, and Tanus ordered the chariots into action immediately. We had refined our tactics of hunting them and we had learned how to avoid the losses that those first two bulls had inflicted upon us. At the fifth cataract, on the very first day, we killed one hundred and seven elephant, for the loss of only three chariots.

The following day there was not a single elephant in sight from the decks of the ships. Although the chariots pursued the herds, following the roads they had left through the forest as they fled, it was five days before they caught up with them again.

Very often now the hunting expeditions returned to our encampment below the cataract after being out for many weeks on end without having found a single elephant or gathered a single tusk. What had seemed to us at first to be an endless supply of ivory had proved an illusion. As the prince had remarked on that very first day, elephant-hunting was not as simple as it first seemed.

However, those chariots ranging southwards did not return entirely empty-handed. They had found something even more valuable to us than ivory. They had found men.

I had not left the encampment for several months for I had been involved in the eternal experimentation with my chariot wheels. It was at this period that I at last found the solutions to the problem which had plagued me from the very beginning, and which had been such a source of amusement and ridicule to Tanus and his military cronies – the occasional failure of some of my designs.

In the end, it was not a single answer, but a combination of factors, beginning with the material from which the spokes of the wheels were made. I now had an almost unlimited selection of various types of wood to work with, and the horn of oryx and rhinoceros which we hunted close to our settlement, and which, unlike the elephant herds, did not move away after being harassed.

I found that soaking the red heartwood of the giraffe acacia rendered it so hard that it would turn the edge of the sharpest bronze axe-head. I compounded this wood with layers of horn and bound it all up together with bronze wire, very much in the same fashion as I had done with the bowstock of Lanata. The result was that at last I had a wheel that could be driven to the utmost over any type of terrain without collapsing. When Hui and I had completed the first ten chariots with these new wheels, I challenged Kratas and Remrem, who were the most notoriously heavy-handed and destructive drivers in all the army, to try to smash them up. The wager that we agreed on was ten deben of gold a side.

This was a game much to the liking of those two overgrown children, and they entered into the spirit of it with boyish gusto. For weeks thereafter, their raucous cries and the sound of pounding hooves rang through the groves on the banks of the Nile. By the time their limit was up, Hui came to me complaining bitterly that they had worn out twenty teams of horses. However, it was some consolation to him that we had won the wager. Our new wheels had stood the most stringent test.

'If you had given us a few days more,' Kratas groused as he handed over his gold with a marked lack of sporting grace, 'I know I would have managed another Tata.' And he treated us to a pantomime which he thought amusing and which was supposed to suggest a shattering wheel and a somersaulting driver.

'You are a gifted clown, brave Kratas, but I have your gold.' I jingled it under his nose. 'All you have is a tired old jest that has gone sour on you.'

It was then that the scouting expedition, led by Lord Aqer, that had gone out to find elephant, came back with the news that instead they had found human habitation further to the south.

We had expected to come across the tribes as soon as we passed the first cataract. For centuries the land of Cush had produced slaves. These had been captured by their own people, probably in tribal warfare, and carried down with other commodities of trade – ivory and ostrich feathers and rhinoceros horn and gold dust – to the outposts of our empire. Queen Lostris' saucy black handmaidens were natives of this land and had come to her from the slave-markets in Elephantine.

I still cannot explain why we had not found people before this. Perhaps they had been driven back by wars and slave raids, in the same way as we had scattered the elephant herds. They may have been wiped out by famine or plague, it was impossible to say. Up until now we had found scant evidence of human presence.

However, now that we had finally caught up with them, the excitement was an epidemic in our company. We needed slaves more even than we needed ivory or gold. Our whole civilization and way of life was based upon the system of slave ownership, a system that was condoned by the gods and sanctified by ancient usage. We had been able to bring very few of our own slaves with us from Egypt, and now it was imperative for our survival and growth as a nation that we capture more to replace those we had been forced to abandon.

Tanus ordered a full-scale expeditionary force to be sent out immediately. He would lead it himself, for we were uncertain what we would find up-river. Apart from those taken as prisoners of war, we Egyptians had always purchased our slaves from foreign traders, and this was the first time in centuries, as far as I knew, that we were forced to resort to catching our own. It was sport as new to us as elephant-hunting, but at least this time we did not expect our quarry to be either docile or dull-witted.

Tanus would still not ride with any other driver than me, and even Kratas' and Remrem's unsuccessful efforts to destroy them had not yet convinced him of the virtue of my new chariots. We led the column, but the second chariot in line was driven by the youngest subaltern of the Blues, the crown prince, Memnon.

I had chosen the two very best charioteers to act as crew for Memnon. His own weight was so light that the chariot could carry an extra man, and the prince's strength had not developed sufficiently for him to be able to lift his end of the chariot when it was necessary to dismount and carry it over the obstacles that could not be driven over. He needed that extra man to help him.

The first villages we came across were on the river-bank, three days' travel above the cataract. They were groups of miserable grass shelters too rudimentary to be called huts. Tanus sent scouts forward to reconnoitre, and then in the dawn we surrounded them with a single swift rush.

The people that stumbled out of these crude shelters were too dazed and shocked to offer any resistance, or even attempt to run from us. They clung together and chattered and gaped at the ring of chariots and shields that we had thrown around them.

'A fine catch!' Tanus was delighted as we looked them over. The men were tall and lean, with long, slim limbs. They towered over most of the men in our ranks; even Tanus seemed short in comparison as we walked amongst them, sorting them into groups as a farmer might apportion his herds.

'There are some really good specimens,' he enthused. 'Look at that beauty.' He had picked out a young man of exceptional physique. 'He would fetch ten rings of gold on the slave-market at Elephantine on any day.'

Their women were strong and healthy. Their backs were straight and their teeth were white and even. Every mature female carried an infant on her hip and led another by the hand.

Yet they were the most primitive peoples I had ever encountered. Neither men nor women wore a shred of clothing, and they left their pudenda shamelessly bared, though the younger girls wore a single string of beads made from the shells of ostrich eggs around their waist. I could see at once that the mature women had all been circumcised in the most brutal fashion. Later I learned that either a flint knife or a sliver of bamboo was used for this operation. Their vaginas were scarred and deformed into open pits, and then infibulated with slivers of bone or ivory. The younger girls had not yet suffered this mutilation, and I determined that this custom would be outlawed in the future. I was certain that I could rely on the support of my mistress in this.

Their skins were so dark that their naked bodies appeared purple in the early sunlight, the colour of an over-ripe black grape. Some of them had smeared themselves with a paste of ashes and white clay, on which they had daubed crude patterns with their fingertips. They had dressed their hair with a mixture of ox-blood and clay into a tall, shiny helmet which exaggerated their already impressive height.

One thing that struck me immediately was that there were no old people among them. I learned later that it was their custom to break the legs of the elderly with their war clubs and leave them on the bank of the river as a sacrifice to the crocodiles. They believed that the crocodiles were reincarnations of their dead ancestors, and that by feeding them, the victim became a part of this process.

They had forged no metal artefacts. Their weapons were wooden clubs and sharpened sticks. The potter's art had eluded them and their vessels were the gourds of wild plants. They planted no crops, but lived on the fish they caught in basket-traps, and on the herds of stunted long-horned cattle which were their most prized possessions. They bled them from a vein in the neck and mixed the blood with milk warm from the udder, and drank the curdled mess with the utmost relish.

When I studied them over the months that followed, I found that they could neither read nor write. Their only musical instrument was a drum hollowed from a tree-trunk, and their songs were the grunting and braying of wild animals. Their dances were flagrant parodies of the sexual act in which ranks of naked men and women approached each other, stamping and grinding their hips until they met. When this happened, the imitation was transformed into reality, and the most licentious debaucheries were enacted.

When Prince Memnon questioned me as to what right we had to capture these people and take possession of them like cattle, I told him, 'They are savages, and we are civilized people. As a father has a duty to his son, it is our duty to lift them from their brutish state, and to show them the true gods. Their part of the bargain is that they repay us with their labour.' Memnon was a bright lad, and after I had explained it to him he never again questioned the logic or the morality of it.

At my suggestion, my mistress had allowed two of her black handmaidens to accompany the expedition. My personal relationship with these little hussies had not been entirely untroubled, but now they rendered invaluable service. Both these girls had childhood memories of the time before their capture, and they retained a rudimentary knowledge of the language of these tribes of Cush. This was just sufficient for us to begin the process of taming our captives. As a musician, I have an ear tuned to the sounds of the human voice; added to this, I have also a natural linguistic ability. Within a very few weeks I was able to speak the language of the Shilluk, which was what these people were called.

Their language was as primitive as their customs and their way of life. Their entire vocabulary did not exceed five hundred words, which I recorded on my scrolls and taught to the slave-masters and to the army instructors whom Tanus appointed over the fresh-caught slaves. For among these people Tanus had found his infantry regiments to complement the chariot divisions.

This first raid gave us no real warning of the true warlike nature of the Shilluk. It had all gone too easily, and we were unprepared for what followed when we swept down on the next straggle of villages. By this time the Shilluk had been alerted, and they were ready to meet us.

They had driven away their cattle herds and hidden their women and children. Naked and armed only with wooden clubs, they came in their hordes against our chariots and recurved bows and swords, with a courage and tenacity that surpassed belief.

'By the putrid wax in Seth's ear-hole,' Kratas swore with delight after we had driven back another charge, 'every one of these black devils is a soldier born.'

'Trained and armed with bronze, these Shilluk will stand out against any other foot-soldiers in the world,' Tanus agreed. 'Leave the bows on the racks. I want as many of them as we can catch alive.'

In the end, Tanus ran them to exhaustion with the chariots, and only when they fell to their knees with even their extraordinary stamina and reckless courage totally expended, could the slave-masters put the ropes on them.

Tanus selected the best of them for his infantry regiments, and he learned their language as readily as I did. The Shilluk soon looked upon him as a god to replace their crocodiles, and Tanus came to love them almost as much as I loved my horses. In the end it was no longer necessary to catch the Shilluk like animals. These marvellously tall and willowy spearmen came out of their hiding-places in the reeds and bushy gulleys of their own accord, to seek Tanus out and to beg to be allowed to join his regiments.

Tanus armed them with long bronze-tipped spears and shields made from elephant hide, and he uniformed them in kilts of wild-cat tails and head-dresses of ostrich feathers. His sergeants drilled them in all the classic evolutions of war, and we learned swiftly to integrate these tactics with those of the chariots.

Not all the Shilluk were selected for the army. The others proved to be indefatigable oarsmen on the rowing-benches of the galleys, and dedicated herdsmen and grooms, for they were born to tend their herds.

We very soon learned that their hereditary enemies were the tribes that lived further to the south, the Dinka and the Mandari. These other tribes were even more primitive, and lacked the fighting instincts of our Shilluk. Nothing pleased Tanus' new Shilluk regiments better than to be sent south with their Egyptian officers and supported by the chariots against their ancient foes. They rounded up the Dinka and Mandari in their thousands. We used them for the heavy unskilled work. None of them came in willingly, as some of our Shilluk had done.

ONCE WE had brought the fleet up through the fifth cataract, the entire land of Cush lay open to us. With our Shilluk now to guide us, the fleet sailed on up-river, while our chariot divisions ranged widely along each bank, and returned with more ivory and fresh levies of slaves.

Soon we reached a wide river-course that joined the main flow of the Nile from the east. The flow of this river was restricted to a sullen trickle down its shrunken pools. However, the Shilluk assured us that in its season this river, which we named the Atbara, would become a raging torrent, and its waters would augment the annual flood of the Nile. Queen Lostris despatched an expedition of gold-seekers, with Shilluk guides, to follow the Atbara as far as they were able. The fleet sailed on southwards, hunting and slave-raiding along the way.

I worried to see it, and tried to prevent it, but so often these days Prince Memnon's chariot was at the head of one of these flying columns. Naturally, he was supported by good men, I could at least see to that, but there was constant hazard and danger out there in the African bush, and he was still only a boy.

I felt he should spend more time with me and his scrolls studying on the deck of the *Breath of Horus*, rather than disporting himself with the likes of Kratas and Remrem. Those two hooligans had as little concern for the prince's safety as they had for their own. They egged him on with wagers and challenges and extravagant praise for his more daring feats. He was soon as much of a dare-devil as any of them, and when he returned from these forays, he took great pleasure in horrifying me with accounts of his escapades.

When I protested to Tanus, he merely laughed. 'If he is to wear the double crown one day, he must learn to spurn danger and lead men.' My mistress agreed with Tanus in the training of Memnon. I had to content myself with making the most of what time I still had to be alone with my prince.

At least I had my two little princesses. They were a wonderful consolation. Tehuti and Bakatha grew more enchanting each day, and I was their slave in more than name alone. Because of our peculiar circumstances I was closer to them than their true father could be. The first word that Bakatha ever said was 'Tata', and Tehuti refused to sleep unless I first told her a story. She pined when I was obliged to leave the fleet on other business. I think that this was the most happy period of my life. I felt that I was at the centre of my family, and solid in the affections of all of them.

The fortunes of our nation were almost as bright as my own. Soon one of our gold-seekers returned from the expedition up the Atbara river. He knelt before Queen Lostris and laid a small leather bag at her feet. Then, at her bidding, he opened the neck of the bag and poured from it a stream of gleaming pebbles. Some of these were as small as grains of sand, and others as large as the end of my thumb. All of them shone with that peculiar radiance that cannot be mistaken.

The goldsmiths were summoned and they worked with their furnaces and clay crucibles, and finally declared these nuggets to be veritable gold of an extraordinary purity. Tanus and I rode back up the Atbara to the site where this gold had been discovered. I helped to plan the methods that were used to mine the gravel-beds in the water-course of the river in which the gold had been trapped.

We used thousands of Mandari and Dinka slaves to scoop out basketloads of gravel and carry these up to the sluices that the masons had carved out of the granite slopes in the hills above the river.

To take back to my mistress I sketched pictures of the long lines of naked black slaves, their wet skins gleaming in the sunlight, toiling up the hillside, each with a heavy basket balanced on his head. When we left the miners hard at work and went back to rejoin the fleet, we carried with us five hundred deben of newly smelted gold rings.

WE ENCOUNTERED yet another cataract on our voyage southwards. This was the sixth and final set of rapids, but this transit proved swifter and easier than any of the others. Our chariots and wagons were able to detour around the rapids, and so at last we reached the mystical confluence of two mighty rivers that between them became the Nile we knew and loved so well.

'This is the place that Taita saw in his vision of the Mazes of Ammon-Ra. Here Hapi lets her waters flow and mingle. This is the sacred site of the goddess,' Queen Lostris declared. 'We have completed our voyage. It is at this place that the goddess will strengthen us for the return to Egypt. I name it Qebui, the Place of the North Wind, for it is that wind which blew us here.'

'It is a propitious place. Already the goddess has shown her favour by providing us with slaves and gold,' the great lords of the state council agreed. 'We should voyage no further.'

'It remains only to find a site for the tomb of my husband, Pharaoh Mamose,' Queen Lostris decreed. 'Once the tomb is built and Pharaoh sealed in it, then my vow will have been fulfilled and it will be time to return in triumph to our very Egypt. Only once that has been done can we go up against the Hyksos tyrant and drive him from our mother-land.'

I think that I was one of the very few of all our company who was not happy and relieved by this decision. The others were consumed by homesickness and weary of the long years of travel. I, on the other hand, had been stricken by a malady even more pernicious, that of wanderlust. I wanted to see what lay beyond the next bend of the river and over the crest of the next hill. I wanted to go on and on, to the very end of the world. Therefore I was delighted when my mistress chose me as the one to seek out the site of the royal tomb, and ordered Prince Memnon to escort me on this expedition with his squadron of chariots. Not only would I be able to indulge this new appetite of mine for travel, but I would once more have the undiluted pleasure of the prince's company.

At fourteen years of age, Prince Memnon was placed in command of the expedition. This was not exceptional. There have been pharaohs in our history who commanded great armies in battle when they were no older. The prince took his responsibilities on this his first independent command most seriously. The chariots were made ready, and Memnon inspected each horse and vehicle personally. We had two spare teams of horses for each chariot, so that these could be changed and rested regularly.

Then the two of us deliberated at great length and in even greater detail as to which direction we should follow in our search for the ideal site for the king's tomb. This should be in some rugged and uninhabited area not readily accessible to grave-robbers. There must be a cliff into which the tomb with all the subsidiary passages could be cut.

There was no area that we had come upon since we had entered the land of Cush that satisfied these requirements. We reviewed what we knew of the land behind us and tried to divine what lay ahead. Where we stood now at Qebui, the meeting-point of the two rivers, was the loveliest place we had visited on all the long voyage.

It seemed that all the birds of the air had gathered here, from tiny jewelled kingfishers to stately blue cranes, from whistling flocks of duck that darkened the sun in their multitudes to plovers and lapwings that scurried along the water's edge, pausing only to ask the plaintive question, 'Pee-wit? Pee-wit?' In the silvery acacia groves and out on the open savannah, the herds of antelope grazed in their countless millions. It was almost as though this seat of the goddess was sacred to all degrees of life. The waters below the juncture of the rivers roiled with shoals of fish, while in the sky above the white-headed fish eagles turned slow circles against the startling blue of the African sky and uttered their weird, yelping chant.

Each of these twin rivers expressed a different character and mood, just as two infants sprung from the same womb can vary in every detail of body and mind. The right-hand branch was slow and yellow, greater in volume than the other, but not so assertive. The eastern branch was a murky grey–blue, an angry, overbearing flood that shoved its twin aside when they met, refusing to mingle its waters, crowding the other against the bank and retaining its own turbid character for many miles downstream before sullenly allowing itself to be absorbed by the gentler yellow stream.

'Which river must we follow, Tata?' Memnon demanded, and I sent for the Shilluk guides.

'The yellow river comes out of a vast and pestilent swamp that has no end. No man can enter there. It is a place of crocodiles and hippopotamus and stinging insects. It is a place of fever where a man might lose his way and wander for ever,' the Shilluk told us.

'What of the other river?' we asked.

'The dark river comes out of the sky, down cliffs of stone that rise up into the clouds. No man can climb the dreadful gorges.'

'We will follow the dark left-hand fork,' the prince decided. 'In those rocky places we will find a resting-place for my father.'

So we journeyed into the east until we saw the mountains rise on the horizon. They formed a blue rampart so tall and formidable as to surpass anything that we had ever seen or believed possible. Beside these great mountains, the hills we had known in the Nile valley were like the scratching of little birds in the sand-banks of the river. Each day as we journeyed towards them they climbed higher into the heavens and dwarfed all the world below.

'No man can go up there,' Memnon marvelled. 'That must be the abode of the gods.'

We watched the lightning play upon the mountains, flickering and flaring inside the tumbling banks of cloud that blanketed the peaks from our view. We listened to the thunder growling like a hunting lion amongst the gorges and the sheer valleys, and we were awestruck.

We ventured no further than the foothills of this terrible range, and then the cliffs and gorges barred our way and turned our chariots back. In these foothills we found a hidden valley with vertical sides of stone. For twenty days the prince and I explored this wild place, until at last we stood before a black cliff-face and Memnon spoke quietly. 'This is where my father's earthly body will rest for all eternity.' He stared up at the sheer stone with a dreamy and mystical expression. 'It is as though I can hear his voice speaking in my head. He will be happy here.'

So I surveyed this place and marked out the cliff, driving bronze pegs into the cracks in the rock, setting out the direction and the angle of the entrance passage for the masons who would come to begin this work. When this was done, we extricated ourselves from the maze of valleys and snarling gorges, and returned down the Nile to the meeting-place of the rivers, where our fleet lay.

WE WERE camped on the great plains only a few days' travel from Qebui when I was awakened in the night by the eerie grunting cries and the sound of a moving mass of animals that seemed to come from the darkness all around us.

Memnon ordered the trumpeter to blow the call to arms, and we stood to, within the circle of chariots. We threw wood on the watch-fires and stared out into the night. In the flicker of the flames we saw a dark flood, like the spate of the Nile, streaming past us. The eerie honking cries and the snorting sounds were almost deafening, and the press of animals in this throng was so heavy that they bumped into the outer ring of chariots, and some of the vehicles were thrown over on their sides. It was not possible to rest in this uproar, and we stood to arms all the rest of that night. The flood of living creatures never abated in all that time.

When dawn lit the scene, we were presented with the most extraordinary spectacle. In every direction as far as the eye could see, the plains were covered with a carpet of moving animals. They were all travelling in the same direction, trudging onwards with a strange fatalistic determination, heads hanging, shrouded in the dust of their own passage, uttering those weird, mournful cries. Every so often, some section of this endless herd took fright, for no reason, and tossed up their heels. They cavorted and snorted and chased each other in aimless circles, like whirlpools in the surface of a smoothly flowing river. Then they would settle back into the same plodding gait and follow the swarms ahead of them into the hazy distance.

We stood and stared in amazement. Every animal in this vast concourse was of the same species, and each individual was identical in every respect to the next. They were all of a dark purplish hue, with a shaggy-maned dewlap and horns shaped like the crescent moon. Their heads were misshapen, with ugly bulbous noses, while their bodies sloped back from high shoulders to spindly hindquarters.

When at last we harnessed the chariots and resumed our own journey, we passed through this living sea of animals like a fleet of galleys. They opened to allow us passage, streaming by on either hand so close that we could reach out and touch them. They were completely unafraid, and stared at us with dull, incurious eyes.

When it was time for the midday meal, Memnon strung his bow and killed five of these antelope with as many arrows. We skinned and butchered the carcasses as their fellows streamed by us at arm's-length. Despite the animals' strange appearance, their flesh, when grilled on the coals of an open fire, was as good to eat as any wild game I had tasted.

'This is another gift from the gods,' Memnon declared. 'As soon as we rejoin the main army, we will send out an expedition to follow these herds. We will be able to smoke enough meat to feed all our armies and our slaves from now until these beasts come again next year.'

From our Shilluk guides we learned that this incredible migration was an annual occurrence as the herds moved from one grazing-ground to another, several hundred miles apart. The Shilluk called these beasts gnu, in imitation of their strange honking cry. 'This will be a never-ending supply, one that is replenished each year,' I informed the prince.

None of us was then able to foresee the catastrophic events which would flow from this visitation of the ungainly gnu. I might have been warned by the manner in which they threw up their heads and snorted without reason, or by the discharge of mucus from the nostrils of some of these beasts, that I noticed as they streamed past us. However, I gave little thought to this behaviour, and judged them to be mild and harmless creatures who could bring us nothing but great benefit.

As soon as we reached the twin rivers, we reported the migration of gnu to Queen Lostris, and she agreed with Prince Memnon's suggestion. Assisted by Kratas and Remrem, she put him in command of a column of two hundred chariots, supported by wagons and several thousand Shilluk. She ordered him to slaughter as many gnu as could be cut up and smoked for army rations.

I did not accompany the expedition, for the role of butcher's assistant was not to my fancy. However, we could soon see the smoke from the fires, on which the meat was curing, darkening the horizon, and before many more days had passed, the wagons started to return, each one loaded high with blackened slabs of cured meat.

Exactly twenty days from our first encounter with the gnu herds, I was sitting under a shady tree on the bank of the Nile, playing bao with my old and dear friend Aton. As a small indulgence to myself and out of deference to Aton, I had opened one of the precious jars of three-palm quality wine that remained from the stock which I had brought from Egypt. Aton and I played and haggled as old friends do, and sipped the wine with deep appreciation.

We had no means of knowing that catastrophe was rushing down upon us to overwhelm us all. On the contrary, I had every reason to be pleased with myself. The previous day I had completed the drawings and plans for the building of Pharaoh's tomb, in which I had incorporated several features to deter and frustrate the depredations of any grave-robber. Queen Lostris had approved these plans and appointed one of the master masons as the overseer. She told me that I might requisition all the slaves and equipment that I needed. My mistress was determined that she would not stint in making good her vow to her dead husband. She would build him the finest tomb that my genius could design.

I had just won the third successive board of bao from Aton and was pouring another jar of the truly excellent wine, when I heard the beat of hooves and looked up to see a horseman coming at full gallop from the direction of the chariot lines. When he was still at a distance I recognized Hui. Very few others rode astride, and certainly not at such a headlong pace. As he raced towards where we sat, I saw the expression on his face, and it alarmed me so that I stood up abruptly enough to spill the wine and upset the bao board.

'Taita!' he screamed at me from a hundred yards. 'The horses! Sweet Isis have mercy on us! The horses!'

He reined down his mount, and I swung up behind him and seized him around the waist. 'Don't waste time talking,' I shouted in his ear. 'Ride, fellow, ride!'

I went to Patience first. Half the herd was down, but she was my first love. The mare lay upon her side with her chest heaving. She was old now, with grey hairs frosting her muzzle. I had not used her in the traces since the day that Blade had been killed by the elephant bull. Although she no longer pulled a chariot, she was the finest brood mare in all our herds. Her foals all inherited her great heart and vivid intelligence. She had just weaned a beautiful little colt who stood near her now, watching her anxiously.

I knelt beside her. 'What is it, my brave darling?' I asked softly, and she recognized my voice, and opened her eyes.

The lids were gummed with mucus. I was appalled by her condition. Her neck and throat were swollen to almost twice their normal girth. A vile-smelling stream of yellow pus streamed from her mouth and nostrils. The fever was burning her up, so that I could feel the heat radiate from her, as though from a camp-fire.

She tried to rise when I stroked her neck, but she was too weak. She fell back, and her breath gurgled and wheezed in her throat. The thick, creamy pus bubbled out of her nostrils, and I could hear that she was drowning in it. Her throat was closing, so that she had to battle for each breath.

She was watching me with an almost human expression of trust and appeal. I was overcome with a sense of helplessness. This affliction was beyond my previous experience. I slipped the snowy-white linen shawl from my shoulder and used it to mop the streaming pus from her nostrils. It was a pathetically inadequate attempt, for as fast as I wiped it away, fresh trickles of the stinking stuff poured from her.

'Taita!' Hui called to me. 'Every one of our animals has been stricken by this pestilence.' Grateful for the distraction, I left Patience and went through the rest of the herd. Half of them were down already, and those still upright were mostly staggering or beginning to drool the thick yellow pus from their mouths.

'What must we do?' Hui and all the charioteers appealed to me. I was burdened with their trust. They expected me alone to avert this terrible disaster, and I knew that it was beyond my powers. I knew of no remedy, and could not think of even the most drastic and unlikely treatment.

I stumbled back to where Patience lay, and wiped away the latest flood of stinking discharge from her muzzle. I could see that she was sinking away swiftly. Each breath she drew now was a terrible struggle. My grief weakened me, and I knew that in my helplessness I would soon melt into tears and be of no further use to any of them, neither horses nor men.

Somebody knelt beside me, and I looked up to see that it was one of the Shilluk grooms, a willing and likely fellow whom I had befriended and who now looked upon me as his master. 'It is the sickness of the gnu,' he told me in his simple language. 'Many will die.'

I stared at him, as what he said began to make sense in my muddled mind. I remembered the snorting, drooling herds of slate-coloured animals darkening the plains with their numbers, and how we had thought it a gift of the benevolent gods.

'This sickness kills our cattle when the gnu come. Those that live through it are safe. They are never sick again.'

'What can we do to save them, Habani?' I demanded, but he shook his head.

'There is nothing to be done.'

I was holding Patience's head in my arms when she died. The breath choked away in her throat and she shuddered and her legs stiffened and then relaxed. I let out a low moan of grief and was on the very edge of the abyss of despair, when I looked up and through my tears saw that Patience's colt was down, with the yellow slime bubbling up from his throat.

In that moment my despair was replaced with a burning anger. 'No!' I shouted. 'I will not let you die also.'

I ran to the foal's side and shouted to Habani to bring leather buckets of hot water. With a linen cloth I bathed the colt's throat in an attempt to reduce the swelling, but it had no effect. The pus still poured from his nostrils, and the hot skin of his neck stretched out as the flesh ballooned like a bladder filling with air.

'He is dying.' Habani shook his head. 'Many will die.'

'I will not let it happen,' I swore grimly, and sent Hui to the galley to fetch my medicine chest.

By the time he returned, it was almost too late. The colt was in extremis. His breath was choking out of him and I could feel his strength draining away under my frantic hands. I felt for the ridged rings of his windpipe at the juncture of his throat and his chest. With one shallow cut through the skin I exposed the white sinewy pipe, and then I pressed the point of my scalpel into it and pierced the tough sheath. Immediately air hissed through the aperture and I saw the colt's chest swell as his lungs inflated. He began to breathe again to a steady and even rhythm, but I saw almost immediately that the puncture-wound in his throat was closing again with blood and mucus.

In frantic haste I hacked a length of bamboo from the framework of the nearest chariot, and I cut a hollow tube from the end of it and pushed this into the wound. The bamboo tube held the wound open and the colt relaxed his struggles as the air sucked and blew unimpeded through it.

'Hui!' I yelled for him. 'I will show you how to save them.'

Before night fell, I had trained a hundred or more of the charioteers and grooms to perform this crude but effective surgery, and we worked on through the night by the wavering, uncertain light of the oil lamps.

There were over thirteen thousand horses in the royal herds by this time. We could not save them all, although we tried. We worked on, with the blood from the severed throats caking black up to our elbows. When exhaustion overcame us, we fell on a bale of hay and slept for an hour and then staggered up and went back to work.

Some of the horses were not as badly affected by this pestilence, which I had named the Yellow Strangler. They seemed to have an in-born resistance to its ravages. The discharge from their nostrils was no more copious than I had seen in the gnu herds, and many of these remained on their feet and threw off the disease within days.

Many others died before we were able to open the windpipe, and even some of those, on which we had successfully operated, died later from mortification and complication of the wound which we had inflicted. Of course, many of our horses were out on expeditions into the plains and beyond my help. Prince Memnon lost two out of every three of his steeds and had to abandon his chariots and return to the Qebui rivers on foot.

In the end we lost over half our horses, seven thousand dead, and those that survived were so weakened and cast down that it was many months before they were strong and fit enough to pull a chariot. Patience's colt survived and replaced his old dam in my affections. He took the right-hand trace in my chariot, and was so strong and reliable that I called him Rock.

'How has this pestilence affected our hopes of a swift return to Egypt?' my mistress asked me.

'It has set us back many years,' I told her, and saw the pain in her eyes. 'We lost most of our best-trained old horses, those like Patience. We will have to breed up the royal herds all over again, and train young horses to take their places in the traces of the chariots.'

I waited for the annual migration of the gnu the following year with dread, but when it came and their multitudes once more darkened the plains, Habani was proved correct. Only a few of our horses developed the symptoms of the Yellow Strangler, and these in a mild form that set them back for only a few weeks before they were strong enough to work again.

What struck me as strange was that the foals born in the period after the first infection of the Yellow Strangler, those who had never been exposed to the actual disease, were as immune as their dams who had contracted a full dose. It was as though the immunity had been transferred to them in the milk that they sucked from their mother's udder. I was certain that we would never again have to experience the full force of the plague.

MY MAJOR duty now, laid upon me by my mistress, was the construction of Pharaoh's tomb in the mountains. I was obliged to spend much of my time in that wild and forbidding place, and I became fascinated by those mountains and all their moods.

Like a beautiful woman, the mountains were unpredictable, sometimes remote and hidden in dense moving veils of clouds that were shot through with lightning and riven with thunder. At other times they were lovely and seductive, beckoning to me, challenging me to discover all their secrets and experience all their dangerous delights.

Although I had eight thousand slaves to prosecute the task, and the unstinted assistance of all our finest craftsmen and artists, the work on the tomb went slowly. I knew it would take many years to complete the elaborate mausoleum which my mistress insisted we must build, and to decorate it in a fashion fit for the Lord of the Two Kingdoms. In truth there was no point in hurrying the work, for it would take as long to rebuild the royal horse herds and train the Shilluk infantry regiments until they were a match for the Hyksos squadrons against which they would one day be matched.

When I was not up in the mountains working at the tomb, I spent my time at Qebui, where there were myriad different tasks and pleasures awaiting me. These ranged from the education of my two little princesses to devising new military tactics with Lord Tanus and the prince.

By this time it was clear that, whereas Memnon would one day command all the chariot divisions, Tanus had never outgrown his first distrust of the horse. He was a sailor and an infantryman to the bone, and as he grew older, he was ever more conservative and traditional in his use of his new Shilluk regiments.

The prince was growing into a dashing and innovative charioteer.

Each day he came to me with a dozen new ideas, some of them far-fetched, but others quite brilliant. We tried them all, even the ones that I knew were impossible. He was sixteen years old when Queen Lostris promoted him to the rank of Best of Ten Thousand.

Now that Tanus rode with me so seldom, I slowly took over the role of Memnon's principal driver. We developed a rapport which became almost instinctive, and which extended to our favourite team of horses, Rock and Chain. When we were on the march, Memnon still liked to drive, and I stood on the footplate behind him. However, as soon as we engaged in action, he would toss me the reins and seize his bow or his javelins from the rack. I would take the chariot into the fray and steer it through the evolutions we had dreamed up together.

As Memnon matured and his strength increased, we began to win some of the prizes at the games and the military tattoos that were a feature of our lives at Qebui. First, we triumphed in the flat races where our team of Rock and Chain could display its paces to the full; then we began to win the shooting and javelin contests. Soon we were known as the chariot that had to be beaten before anyone could claim the champion's ribbon from Queen Lostris.

I remember the cheers as our chariot flew through the final gate of the course, myself at the traces and Memnon on the footplate hurling a javelin right and left into the two straw-filled dummies as we passed, then the mad dash down the straight, with the prince howling like a demon and the long wind-blown plait of his hair standing out behind his head, like the tail of a charging lion.

Soon there were other encounters in which the prince began to distinguish himself, and those without any assistance from me. Whenever he strode past the young girls, with the Gold of Valour gleaming on his chest and the champion's ribbon knotted into his plait, they giggled and blushed and slanted their eyes in his direction. Once I entered his tent in haste with some important news for him, only to come up short as I found my prince well mounted and oblivious to all but the tender young body and the pretty face beneath him. I withdrew silently, a little saddened that the age of his innocence was past.

Of all these pleasures, none for me could compare with those precious hours that I was still able to spend with my mistress. In this her thirty-third year she was in the very high summer of her beauty. Her allure was enhanced by her sophistication and her poise. She had become a queen indeed, and a woman without peer.

All her people loved her, but none of them as much as I did. Not even Tanus was able to surpass me in my devotion to her. It was my pride that she still needed me so much, and relied upon me and my judgement and my advice so trustingly. Notwithstanding the other blessings that I had to adorn my existence, she would ever be the one great love of my life.

I SHOULD have been contented and replete, but there is a restlessness in my nature that was exacerbated by this new wanderlust that had come to plague me. Whenever I paused from my labours at Pharaoh's tomb, and looked up at them, the mountains beckoned me. I began to make short excursions into their lonely gorges, often alone but sometimes with Hui or some other companion.

Hui was with me when I first saw the herds of wild ibex high above us in the lofty crags of the mountain. They were of a species we had never seen before. They stood twice as tall as the wild goats that we knew from the Nile valley, and some of the old billy-goats carried such a mass of curling horn that they seemed as monstrous as some fabulous beast.

It was Hui who carried reports of these huge ibex back to the twin rivers where the fleet lay at Qebui, and within the month, Lord Tanus arrived at the valley of the king's tomb, with his bow over his shoulder and Prince Memnon at his side. The prince was fast becoming as ardent a huntsman as his father, and was every bit as eager for the chase. As for myself, I welcomed the chance to explore those fascinating highlands in such company.

We had meant to venture only as far as the first line of peaks, but when we climbed to their crest, we were presented with a vista that was breathtaking. We saw other mountains against the sky that were shaped like flat-topped anvils, and were the tawny colour of lions. They dwarfed the peaks on which we stood and lured us onwards.

The Nile climbed in concert with us up through precipitous valleys and dark gorges that churned its waters to gleaming white. We could not always follow its course, but in places were forced to climb above it and follow giddy goat-tracks across the face of a frowning mountain.

Then, when we had been lured deep into its maw, the mountain loosed its full fury upon us.

We were one hundred men in our company, with ten pack-horses to carry our provisions. We were camped in the depths of one of these fathomless gorges, with the fresh trophies of Tanus' and Memnon's latest hunt laid out upon the rocky floor for our appraisal and admiration. These were two goat's heads, the largest we had seen in all our travels, so heavy in horn that it took two slaves to lift one of them. Suddenly it began to rain.

In our Egyptian valley it may rain once in twenty years. None of us had ever imagined anything even remotely like the rain that fell upon us now.

First, dense black clouds roofed over the narrow strip of sky that showed between the cliffs that walled us in, so that we were plunged from sunny noon into deep twilight. A cold wind raced down the valley and chilled our bodies and our spirits. We huddled together in dismay.

Then lightning lanced from the sombre belly of the clouds and shattered the rocks around us, filling the air with the smell of sulphur and sparks struck from flint. Thunder burst upon us, magnified as it rolled from cliff to cliff, and the earth jumped and trembled beneath our feet.

Then the rain fell. It did not come down upon us in the form of drops. It was as though we stood under one of the cataracts of the Nile when the river was in full flood. There was no longer air to breathe, water filled our mouths and our nostrils so that we felt that we were drowning. The rain was so thick that we could see only the blurred outline of the man who stood an arm's-length away. It battered us so that we were thrown down and cringed beneath the nearest rock for shelter. Still it assaulted all the senses and stung our exposed skin like a swarm of angry hornets.

It was cold. I had never known such cold, and we were covered only with our thin linen shawls. The cold sucked the force out of my limbs, and we shivered until our teeth clattered together in our mouths, and we could not still them even though we bit down with all the strength of our jaws.

Then, above the sound of the falling rain, I heard a new sound. It was the sound of water which had become a ravening monster. Down the narrow valley where we lay swept a wall of grey water. It stretched from cliff to cliff, and carried everything before it.

I was caught up in it and tumbled end over end. I felt life being beaten out of me as I was thrown against the rocks, and icy water filled my throat. Darkness overwhelmed me, and I thought that I was dead.

I have a vague recollection of hands dragging me from the flood, and then I was wafted away to some dark and distant shore. The voice of my prince called me back. Before I could open my eyes I smelled wood-smoke, and felt the warmth of the flames on one side of my body.

'Tata, wake up! Speak to me.' The voice was insistent, and I opened my eyes. Memnon's face floated before me, and he smiled at me. Then he called over his shoulder, 'He is awake, Lord Tanus.'

I found that we were in a rock cave and that outside, the night had fallen. Tanus came across from the smoky fire of damp wood and squatted beside the prince.

'How are you, old friend? I don't think you have broken any bones.'

I struggled into a sitting position, and gingerly tested every part of my body before I replied, 'My head is cracked through, and every limb aches. Apart from that, I am cold and hungry.'

'You will live then,' Tanus chuckled, 'though a while ago I doubted any of us would. We have to get out of these cursed mountains before something worse happens. It was madness ever to venture into a place where the rivers come out of the sky.'

'What about the others?' I asked.

Tanus shook his head. 'They are all drowned. You were the only one that we were able to drag from the flood.'

'What about the horses?'

'Gone,' he grunted. 'All gone.'

'Food?'

'Nothing,' Tanus replied. 'Even my bow is lost in the river. I have only the sword at my side and the clothes on my body.'

AT DAWN we left our rock shelter and started back down that treacherous valley. At the foot of the gorge we found the bodies of some of our men and the horses strewn upon the rocks where they had been stranded when the flood receded.

We scavenged amongst the rocks and scree, and we managed to recover some of our stores and equipment. To my great joy I found my medicine chest still intact, though flooded with water. I laid out the contents on a rock, and while they dried, I fashioned a sling from a leather harness to carry the chest upon my back.

In the meantime, Memnon had cut strips of meat from the carcass of one of the horses and grilled them over another fire of driftwood. When we had eaten our fill, we saved the rest of the meat, and set out on the return.

The journey slowly descended into nightmare as we scaled steep rocky slopes and dropped into the gorges beyond. There seemed to be no end to this terrible wilderness, and our bruised feet in open sandals protested each step. At night we shivered miserably around a smoky little fire of driftwood.

By the second day we all knew that we had lost the way, and that we were wandering aimlessly. I was certain that we were doomed to die in these terrible mountains. Then we heard the river and, as we topped the next saddle between peaks, we found the infant Nile winding through the depths of the gorge below us. That was not all. On the banks of the river we saw a collection of coloured tents, and amongst them moved the shapes of men.

'Civilized men,' I said immediately, 'for those tents must be of woven cloth.'

'And those are horses,' Memnon agreed eagerly, pointing out the animals tethered on the lines beyond the encampment.

'There!' Tanus pointed. 'That was the flash of sunlight off a sword-blade or a spear-head. They are metal-workers.'

'We must find out who these people are.' I was fascinated by what tribe could live in such an inhospitable land.

'We will get our throats cut,' Tanus growled. 'What makes you believe these mountaineers are not as savage as the land in which they live?' Only later would we come to know these people as Ethiopians.

'Those are magnificent horses,' Memnon whispered. 'Our own are not so tall, or so sturdy. We must go down and study them.' The prince was a horseman above all else.

'Lord Tanus is right.' His warning had aroused my usual prudent nature, and I was ready to counsel caution. 'These might be dangerous savages, with but the trappings of civilized men.'

We sat upon the shoulder of the mountain and debated for a while longer, but in the end curiosity got the better of all three of us and we crept down through one of the ravines to spy upon these strangers.

As we drew closer, we saw that they were tall, well-built people, probably more robust in stature than we Egyptians are. Their hair was thick and dark and curled profusely. The men were bearded, and we are clean-shaven. They wore full-length robes, probably woven of wool, and brightly coloured. We go bare-chested and our kilts are usually pure white in colour. They wore soft leather boots, as opposed to our sandals, and a bright cloth wound around their heads.

The women we saw working amongst the tents were unveiled and cheerful. They sang and called to each other in a language I had never heard before, but their voices were melodious as they drew water, or squatted over the cooking-fires, or ground corn on the millstones.

One group of men was playing a board-game that, from where I hid, looked very much like bao. They were wagering and arguing over the play of the stones. At one stage, two of them leapt to their feet and drew curved daggers from their belts. They confronted each other snarling and hissing, like a pair of angry tom-cats.

At that stage a third man, who had been sitting alone, rose to his feet and stretched, like a lazy leopard. He sauntered across and, with his sword, knocked up the daggers. Immediately the two protagonists subsided and slunk away.

The peace-maker was clearly the chief of the party. He was a tall man, with the wiry frame of a mountain goat. He was goat-like in other ways. His beard was as long and thick as that of an ibex ram, and his features were coarse and goaty; he had a heavy, hooked nose and a wide mouth with a cruel slant to it. I thought that he probably stank like one of the old rams that Tanus had shot from the cliff-face.

Suddenly I felt Tanus grip my arm, and he whispered in my ear, 'Look at that!'

This chieftain wore the richest apparel of any of them. His robe was striped in scarlet and blue and his earrings were stones that glowed like the full moon. But I could not see what had excited Tanus.

'His sword,' Tanus hissed. 'Look at his sword.'

I studied it for the first time. It was longer than one of our weapons and the pommel was obviously of pure gold filigree-work, of a delicacy that I had never seen before. The hand-guard was studded with precious stones. It was a masterpiece that clearly had occupied some master craftsman his lifetime.

This was not what had captured Tanus' attention, however. It was the blade. As long as the chief's own arm, it was made of a metal that was neither yellow bronze nor red copper. In colour it was a strange silvery glittering blue, like the living scales of a Nile perch taken fresh from the river. It was inlaid with gold, as if to highlight its unique value.

'What is it?' Tanus breathed. 'What metal is that?'

'I do not know.'

The chief resumed his seat in front of his tent, but now he laid the sword across his lap, and, with a phallus-shaped piece of volcanic rock, began lovingly to stroke the edge of the blade. The metal emitted a ringing thrill of sound to each touch of the stone. No bronze ever resounded like that. It was the purr of a resting lion.

'I want it,' Tanus whispered. 'I will never rest until I have that sword.'

I gave him a startled glance, for I had never heard such a tone in his voice. I saw that he meant what he said. He was a man struck with a sudden overpowering passion.

'We cannot remain here longer,' I told him softly. 'We will be discovered.' I took his arm, but he resisted. He was staring at the weapon.

'Let us go to look at their horses,' I insisted, and at last he allowed me to draw him away. I led Memnon by the other hand. At a safe distance we circled the camp, and crept back towards the horse-lines.

When I saw the horses close up, I was struck with a passion as fierce as Tanus had conceived for the blue sword. These were a different breed from our Hyksos horses. They were taller and more elegantly proportioned. Their heads were noble and their nostrils wider. I knew those nostrils were the mark of stamina and good wind. Their eyes were situated further forward in the skull and were more prominent than those of our animals. They were great soft eyes, shining with intelligence.

'They are beautiful,' whispered Memnon at my side. 'Look at the way they hold their heads and arch their necks.'

Tanus longed for the sword, we coveted the horses with a passion that equalled his.

'Just one stallion like that to put to our mares,' I pleaded to any god who was listening. 'I would exchange my hope of eternal life for a single one.'

One of the foreign grooms glanced in our direction, then said something to the fellow beside him and began to walk in our direction. This time I had no need to insist, and all three of us ducked down behind the boulder that sheltered us and crawled away. We found a secure hiding-place further down-river, amongst a tumbled heap of boulders, and immediately launched into one of those discussions in which all spoke together and none listened.

'I will go in and offer him a thousand deben of gold,' Tanus swore, 'I must have that sword.'

'He would kill you first. Did you not see him stroke it as though it was his first-born son?'

'Those horses!' marvelled Memnon. 'I never dreamed of such beauty. Horus must have beasts like that to draw his chariot.'

'Did you see those two fly at each other?' I cautioned. 'They are savage men, and bloodthirsty. They would rip out your guts before you opened your mouth to utter a word. Besides, what do you have to offer in return? They will see we are destitute beggars.'

'We could steal three of their stallions tonight and ride them down on to the plain,' Memnon suggested, and though the idea had appeal, I told him sternly, 'You are the crown prince of Egypt, not a common thief.'

He grinned at me. 'For one of those horses, I would cut throats like the worst footpad in Thebes.'

As we debated thus, we were suddenly aware of the sound of voices approaching along the river-bank from the direction of the foreign camp. We looked about for better concealment and hid away.

The voices drew closer. A party of women came into view and they stopped below us at the water's edge. There were three older women, and a girl. The women wore robes of a drab hue, and cloths of black around their hair. I thought that they were servants or nursemaids. It did not occur to me then that they were gaolers, for they treated the girl with unusual deference.

The girl was tall and slim, so that when she walked, she moved like a papyrus stem in the Nile breeze. She wore a short robe of rich wool, striped in yellow and sky blue, which left her knees bared. Though she wore short boots of soft stitched leather, I could see that her legs were lithe and smooth.

The women stopped below our hiding-place, and one of the older women began to disrobe the girl. The other two filled the clay jars that they had carried down on their heads with water from the Nile. The river was still swollen with flood-water. No one could safely enter that icy torrent. It was clear that they intended bathing the girl from the jars.

One of the women lifted the girl's robe over her head and she stood naked at the water's edge. I heard Memnon gasp. I looked at him and saw that he had forgotten entirely about stealing horses.

While two of the women poured the water from the jars over the girl, the third woman wiped her down with a folded cloth. The girl held her hands above her head and circled slowly to allow them to wet every part of her body. She laughed and squealed at the cold, and I saw tiny goose-bumps rise around her nipples, which were the rich ruby of polished garnets, mounted like jewels on the peak of each smooth, round breast.

Her hair was a dark bush of tight curls, her skin was the colour of the heart-wood of the acacia, when it has been buffed and oiled to a high patina. It was a rich, ruddy brown, that glowed in the high sunlight of the mountains.

Her features were delicate, her nose narrow and chiselled. Her lips were soft and full, but without any thickness. Her eyes were large and dark, slanted above high cheek-bones. Her lashes were so thick that they tangled together. She was beautiful. I have only known one other woman who was more so.

Suddenly she said something to the women with her. They stood aside, and she left them and climbed on those long naked legs towards us. But before she reached our hiding-place, she stepped behind a boulder that shielded her from her companions, but left her full in our view. She glanced around quickly, but did not see us. The cold water must have affected her, for she squatted quickly and her own water tinkled on the rock beneath her.

Memnon groaned softly. It was instinctive, not intentional, a sound of longing so intense as to have become agony. The girl sprang to her feet and stared directly at him. Memnon was standing a little to one side of Tanus and me. While we were concealed, he was full in her view.

The two of them stared at each other. The girl was trembling, her dark eyes enormous. I expected her to run or scream. Instead, she looked back over her shoulder in a conspiratorial gesture, as if to make certain that the women had not followed her. Then she turned back to Memnon and, in a soft sweet voice, asked a question, at the same time holding out her hand to him in a gesture of appeal.

'I do not understand,' Memnon whispered, and spread his own hands in a gesture of incomprehension.

The girl stepped up to him and repeated the question impatiently, and when Memnon shook his head, she seized his hand and shook it. In her agitation, her voice rose as she demanded something of him.

'Masara!' One of her attendants had heard her. 'Masara!' It was obviously the girl's name, for she made a gesture of silence and caution to Memnon and turned to go back.

However, the three women had all started up the slope after Masara. They were chattering with alarm and agitation, and they came round the side of the boulder in a pack and stopped when they saw Memnon.

For a moment nobody moved, and then all three women screamed in unison. The naked girl seemed poised to run to Memnon's side, but as she started forward, two of the women seized her; all four of them were screaming now, as the girl struggled to be free.

'Time to go home,' Tanus jerked my arm, and I was after him in a bound.

From the direction of the camp came the shouts of many men aroused by the screams of the women. When I paused to look back, I saw them coming over the ridge in a body. I saw also that Memnon had not followed us, but had leaped forward to the girl's assistance.

They were all big women and held the girl hard, redoubling their screams. Although Masara was trying desperately to pull free, Memnon could not get her away from them.

'Tanus!' I yelled. 'Memnon is in trouble.'

We turned back and between us grabbed him and hauled him away. He came reluctantly. 'I will come back for you,' he shouted to the girl, looking back over his shoulder as we ran with him between us. 'Be brave. I will come back for you.'

When somebody tells me nowadays that there is no such thing as love at first sight, I smile quietly to myself and think of the day that Memnon first saw Masara.

We had lost time in the struggle to get Memnon away, and our pursuers were already pressing us hard as we took to one of the goat-tracks and ran for the crest of the slope. An arrow flitted past Memnon's shoulder and clattered against the rocks beside the path. It spurred us to greater speed.

We were in single file along the narrow path. Memnon led us and Tanus followed him. I was last in the file, and, burdened by the heavy medicine chest on my back, I began to fall further behind. Another arrow passed over our heads, and then the third struck the pack on my back with a force that made me stagger. But the chest stopped the arrow that would otherwise have transfixed my body.

'Come on, Taita,' Tanus shouted back at me. 'Throw off that cursed box of yours, or they will have you.'

He and Memnon were fifty paces ahead of me and drawing away, but

I could not discard my precious chest. At that moment the next arrow struck, and this time I was not so fortunate. It hit me in the leg, in the fleshy part of the thigh, and I went tumbling across the path and fell hard.

I rolled into a sitting position and looked with horror at the reed shaft of the arrow that protruded from my leg. Then I looked back at our pursuers. The bearded chieftain in the striped robe led them, and he had outdistanced his own men by a hundred paces. He was coming up the track in a series of great elastic bounds, covering the ground as swiftly as one of the ibex rams that he resembled in so many other ways.

'Taita!' Tanus called back at me. 'Are you all right?' He had paused on the brow of the slope, and was looking back anxiously. Memnon had crossed over and was out of sight.

'I am arrowed!' I yelled back. 'Go on and leave me. I cannot follow.'

Without a moment's hesitation, Tanus turned back, and came leaping down towards where I lay. The Ethiopian chieftain saw him coming and bellowed a challenge. He drew the glittering blue sword and brandished it as he came on up the hillside.

Tanus reached the spot where I sat, and tried to lift me to my feet. 'It's no use. I am hard hit. Save yourself,' I told him, but the Ethiopian was almost upon us. Tanus dropped my arm, and drew his own sword.

The two of them came together, going for each other in a murderous rush. I was not in any doubt as to the outcome of this duel, for Tanus was the strongest and most skilled swordsman in all Egypt. When he killed the Ethiopian, we would all be doomed, for we could expect no mercy from his henchmen.

The Ethiopian swung first with a full-blooded overhand cut at Tanus' head. It was an imprudent stroke to aim at a swordsman of his opponent's calibre. I knew that Tanus' response would be a parry in the line of the head and a natural riposte, with all the momentum of his shoulder behind it, that would drive the point through the chieftain's beard and into his throat. It was one of Tanus' favourite strokes.

The two blades met, but there was no ringing clash. The blue blade hacked clean through Tanus' yellow bronze, as though it were a wand of green willow. Tanus was left with the hilt in his hand and a finger's-length remaining from that once long and deadly bronze blade.

Tanus was stunned by the ease with which the Ethiopian had disarmed him, and he was slow to defend himself from the next stroke that followed like a thunderbolt. He leaped backwards just in time, but the blue point opened a long, shallow cut across the bulging muscles of his naked chest, and the blood came swiftly.

'Run, Tanus!' I screamed. 'Or he will kill us both.'

The Ethiopian went for him again, but I was lying in the middle of the narrow path. He was forced to leap over me to get at Tanus. I seized him around the knees with both arms, and brought him down on top of me in a snarling, thrashing heap.

The Ethiopian was trying to drive the point of the blue sword into my belly, as I lay under him, and I twisted so violently aside that both of us rolled off the path and began to slide away down the steep slope of loose scree. As we rolled more swiftly, gathering momentum, I had one last glimpse of Tanus peering down over the edge of the path, and I screamed in a despairing wail, 'Run! Take care of Memnon!'

The shale and loose scree were as treacherous as swamp quicksands, and gave no anchor or purchase. The Ethiopian and I were flung apart, but both of us were carried to the edge of the torrent. I was battered and hammered to the edge of consciousness, and lay there groaning until rough hands dragged me to my feet, and blows and harsh curses rained upon my head.

The chieftain stopped them from killing me and throwing my body into the river. He was covered with dust, as I was, and his robe was torn and filthy from the fall, but the blue sword was still gripped in his right fist and he snarled at his men. They began to drag me away towards the encampment, but I looked around me desperately and saw my medicine chest amongst the rocks. The leather harness had snapped, and it had come off my back.

'Bring that,' I ordered my captors with as much force and dignity as I could muster, and pointed to the chest. They laughed at my insolence, but the chieftain sent one of his men to retrieve it.

Two men were obliged to support me, for the shaft in my thigh was beginning to cause me crippling pain. Every pace back to the camp was agony, and when they reached it, they threw me roughly to the ground in the open space in the centre of the ring of tents.

Then they argued long and fiercely. It was obvious that they were puzzling over my origins and my motives, and trying to decide what they should do with me. Every once in a while, one of them would stand over me and kick me in the ribs, while he shouted questions at me. I lay as quietly as I could, so as not to provoke further violence.

There was a distraction when the party that had pursued Tanus and Memnon returned empty-handed. There was more shouting and arm-waving as bitter recriminations and insults were exchanged. I was cheered by the thought that the two of them had got clean away.

After a while my captors remembered me, and they came back to vent their frustration on me with more kicks and blows. In the end their chieftain called them off, and ordered them not to torment me further. After that, most of them lost interest in me and wandered away. I was left lying on the bare ground, covered with dirt and bruises, with the arrow still lodged in my flesh.

The Ethiopian chieftain resumed his seat in front of the largest tent, which was clearly his own, and while he stropped the edge of his sword, he regarded me with a steady but inscrutable expression. Occasionally he exchanged a few low words with one of his men, but it seemed that my immediate danger was past.

I judged my moment carefully, and then addressed him directly. I pointed to my medicine chest, which had been thrown against one of the tents, and I made my voice mild and placatory. 'I need my chest. I must tend this wound.'

Although the chieftain did not understand the words, he understood my gestures. He ordered one of his men to bring the chest across to him. He made them set it down in front of him and opened the lid. He unpacked the chest methodically, examining each separate item. Anything that particularly caught his attention he held up, and asked a question to which I tried to give an answer with signs.

He seemed satisfied that, apart from my scalpels, the chest contained no dangerous weapon. I am not sure if he realized at this stage that these were medical items. However, with signs I showed him what I needed to do, pointing to my leg and making a pantomime of pulling the arrow. He stood over me with the sword in his hand, and made it clear that he would lop off my head at the first sign of treachery, but he allowed me to use my instruments.

The arrow had entered at an angle and position which made it awkward for me to reach. In addition to this, the pain that I inflicted upon myself, as I used the Taita spoons to trap and mask the barbs that were buried deep in my flesh, brought me more than once to the point of fainting away.

I was panting and drenched in sheets of sweat when at last I was ready to draw the arrow-head. By this time I had an audience of half the men in camp. They had returned to crowd around me and watch my surgery with garrulous interest.

I took a firm hold on the handles of the spoons, placed a wooden wedge between my teeth and bit down on it hard, and drew the clamped arrow-head out of the wound. There were shouts of wonder and amazement from my audience. Obviously none of them had ever seen a barb drawn with such ease and with so little damage to the victim. They were impressed even further when they watched the skill and dexterity with which I laid on the linen bandages.

In any nation and in any culture, even the most primitive, the healer and the physician have a special place of honour and esteem. I had demonstrated my credentials in the most convincing manner, and my status in the Ethiopian camp was drastically altered.

At the orders of the chief, I was carried to one of the tents and laid on a straw mattress. My medicine chest was placed at the head of my bed, and one of the women brought me a meal of corn-bread and chicken stew and thick sour milk.

In the morning, when the tents were struck, I was placed in a pole-litter behind one of the horses in the long caravan, and pulled along the rough and precipitous tracks. To my dismay, I saw from the angle of the sun that we were headed back into the fastness of the mountains, and I feared that I was lost to my own people, probably for all time. The fact that I was a physician had probably saved my life, but it had also placed such value on me that I would never be turned free. I knew that I was now a slave in more than name alone.

DESPITE THE jolting of the litter, my leg began to heal cleanly. This further impressed my captors, and soon they were bringing to me any member of the band who was sick or injured. I cured a ringworm and lanced a whitlow under a thumbnail. I sewed together a man who had won too much gambling with his quick-tempered friends. These Ethiopians had a penchant for settling arguments with the dagger. When one of the horses threw its rider down a gulley, I set his broken arm. It knitted straight, and my reputation was enhanced. The Ethiopian chieftain looked at me with a new respect, and I was offered the food-bowl after he had made his selection of the choice cuts, before any of the other men were allowed to eat.

When my leg had healed sufficiently for me to walk again, I was given the run of the camp. However, I was not allowed out of sight. An armed man followed me and stood over me, even when I was on the most private and intimate business amongst the rocks.

I was kept away from Masara and only saw her from afar at the start of each day's journey, and again when we camped for the night. During the long day's ride through the mountains we were separated; I rode near the head of the caravan, while she was brought along at the rear. She was always accompanied by her female gaolers, and usually surrounded by armed guards.

Whenever we did catch sight of each other, Masara cast the most desperate and appealing looks at me, as though I would be able to help her in some way. It was obvious that she was a prisoner of rank and of importance. She was such a lovely young woman that I often found myself thinking of her during the day, and trying to fathom the reason for her captivity. I decided she was either an unwilling bride, being taken to meet her future husband, or that she was a pawn in some political intrigue.

Without a knowledge of the language I could not hope to understand what was taking place, or to learn anything about these Ethiopians. I set out to learn the Geez tongue.

I have the ear of a musician, and I played my tricks upon them. I listened attentively to all the chatter around me, and picked up the cadence and the rhythm of their speech. Very early on, I was able to deduce that the chieftain's name was Arkoun. One morning before the caravan set out, Arkoun was giving orders for the day's march to his assembled band. I waited until he had delivered a long and heated harangue, and then I repeated it in precisely the same tone and cadence.

They listened to me in stunned silence, and then burst into uproar. They roared with laughter and beat each other on the back, tears of mirth streamed down their cheeks, for they had a direct and uncomplicated sense of humour. I had not the least idea what I had said, but it was obvious that I had got it exactly right.

They shouted excerpts from my speech at each other, and wagged their heads, mimicking Arkoun's pompous manner. It took a long time for order to be restored, but at last Arkoun strutted up to me and shouted an accusatory question at me. I did not understand a word of it, but I shouted the same question back at him, word for exact word.

This time there was pandemonium. The joke of it was too rich to be borne. Grown men clung to each other for support, they screamed and wiped their streaming eyes. One of them fell into the fire and singed his beard.

Even though the joke was on him, Arkoun laughed along with them and patted me on the back. From then onwards, every man and woman in the camp was my teacher. I had only to point at any object and the Geez word for it was shouted at me. When I began to string those words into sentences, they corrected me eagerly, and were inordinately proud of my progress.

It took me some time to fathom the grammar. The verbs were declined in a manner which had no relationship to Egyptian, and the gender and plurals of the nouns were strange. However, within ten days I was speaking intelligible Geez, and had even built up a good selection of choice curses and invective.

While I learned the language and treated their ailments, I studied their mores and manners. I learned that they were inveterate gamblers, and that the board-game that they played endlessly was a passion. They called it dom, but it was a simplified and rudimentary form of bao. The number of cups in the board and the quantity of stones brought into play varied from bao. However, all the objects and the principles were similar.

Arkoun himself was the dom champion of the band, but as I studied his play, I saw that he had no inkling of the classic rule of seven stones. Nor did he understand the protocol of the four bulls. Without a thorough knowledge of these, no bao player could aspire to even the lowly third grade of masters. I debated with myself the risk that I would run in humiliating such a vain and overbearing tyrant as Arkoun, but in the end I decided that it was the only way to gain ascendancy over him.

The next time he sat in front of his tent and set up the board, smirking and twirling his moustaches as he waited for a challenger to step forward, I elbowed aside the first aspirant and settled myself cross-legged opposite Arkoun.

'I have no silver to wager,' I told him in my still rudimentary Geez. 'I play for love of the stones.'

He nodded gravely. As an addict of the board, he understood that sentiment. The news that I was taking the board against Arkoun ran through the camp, and they all came laughing and jostling to watch.

When I allowed Arkoun to lay three stones in the east castle they nudged each other and chuckled with disappointment that the game would be so swiftly lost. One more stone in the east, and the board was his. They did not understand the significance of the four bulls that I had banked in the south. When I loosed my bulls, they strode invincibly across the board, splitting his unsupported stones and isolating the east castle. He was powerless to prevent it. Four moves and the board was mine. I had not even been called upon to demonstrate the rule of seven stones.

For some moments they all sat in shocked silence. I do not think that Arkoun realized the extent of his defeat for a while. Then, when it sank in upon him, he stood up and drew the terrible blue sword. I thought that I had miscalculated, and that he was about to lop my head, or at least an arm.

He lifted the sword high and then swung it down with a shout of fury. With a dozen strokes he hacked the board to kindling and scattered the stones about the camp. Then he strode out into the rocks, tearing his beard and shouting my death threats to the towering cliffs, that hurled them onwards down the valleys in a series of diminishing echoes.

It was three days before Arkoun set up the board again, and gestured to me to take my seat opposite him. The poor fellow had no inkling of what lay in store for him.

EACH DAY my command of the Geez language increased, and I was at last able to glean some understanding of my captor and the reason for this long journey through the canyons and gorges.

I had underrated Arkoun. He was not a chieftain but a king. His full name was Arkoun Gannouchi Maryam, Negusa Naghast, King of Kings and ruler of the Ethiopic state of Aksum. It was only later that I learned that in this land any mountain brigand with a hundred horses and fifty wives was likely to set himself up as a king, and that at any one time there might be as many as twenty Kings of Kings on the rampage for land and loot.

Arkoun's nearest neighbour was one Prester Beni-Jon, also claiming to be King of Kings and ruler of the Ethiopic state of Aksum. There appeared to be a certain amount of ill-feeling and rivalry between these two monarchs. They had already fought a number of inconclusive battles.

Masara was the favourite daughter of Prester Beni-Jon. She had been kidnapped by one of the other robber chieftains, one of those who had not yet crowned himself, nor taken the obligatory title of King of Kings. In a straightforward trading arrangement, Masara had been sold to Arkoun for a horse-load of silver bars. Arkoun intended using her to gain political ground from her doting father. It seemed that hostage-taking and ransom were very much a part of Ethiopian statesmanship.

Not trusting any of his own men with such a valuable commodity, Arkoun had gone himself to take possession of Princess Masara. Our caravan was carrying her back to Arkoun's stronghold. I gathered this and other information from the gossipy women slaves who brought me my meals, or in casual conversation over the dom board. By the time we reached Amba Kamara, the mountain fortress of King Arkoun Gannouchi Maryam, I was an expert on the complicated and shifting politics of the various Ethiopic states of Aksum, and the numerous claimants to the throne of the empire.

I was aware of an increasing excitement running through our caravan as we approached our journey's end, and at last we climbed the narrow winding pathway, no more than just another goat-track, to the summit of yet another amba. These ambas were the massifs that made up the mountain ranges of central Ethiopia. Each of them was a flat-topped mountain with sheer sides that plunged like a wall into the valley that divided it from the next mountain.

It was easy to see, when I stood at the top of the precipice, how the land was fragmented into so many tiny kingdoms and principalities. Each amba was a natural and impregnable fortress. The man on top of it was invincible, and might call himself a king without fear of being challenged.

Arkoun rode up beside me and pointed to the mountains on the southern sky-line. 'That is the hiding-place of that horse-thief and scoundrel, Prester Beni-Jon. He is a man of unsurpassed treachery.' He hawked in his throat and spat over the edge of the cliff in the direction of his rival.

I had come to know Arkoun as a man of not inconsiderable cruelty and treachery himself. If he conceded Prester Beni-Jon as his master in these fields, Masara's father must be a formidable man indeed.

We crossed the tableland of the Amba Kamara, passing through a few villages of stone-walled hovels, and fields of sorghum and dhurra corn. The peasants in the fields were all tall, bushy-haired ruffians, armed with swords and round copper shields. They appeared as fierce and warlike as any of the men in our caravan.

At the far end of the amba, the path led us to the most extraordinary natural stronghold that I had ever seen. From the main table of the mountain a buttress had eroded until it stood alone, a sheer pinnacle of rock with precipitous sides, separated from the table by an awe-inspiring abyss.

This gulf was bridged by a narrow causeway, a natural arch of stone, that joined it to the tableland. It was so narrow that two horses could not pass each other on the pathway, so narrow that once a horse started out across the bridge, it could not turn round and return, until it had reached the other side.

The drop under the causeway was a thousand feet, straight into the river gorge below. It was so unnerving to the horses that the riders were forced to dismount, blindfold them, and lead them over. When I was halfway across, I found myself trembling with vertigo, and I dared not peer over the edge of the pathway into the void. It required all my self-control to keep walking, and not to throw myself flat and cling to the rocks beneath my feet.

Perched on top of this pinnacle of rock was an ungainly, lopsided castle of stone blocks and reed thatch. The open windows were covered with curtains of rawhide, and the raw sewage and odious refuse running from the fortress stained and littered the cliff beneath it.

Festooning the walls and battlements like pennants and decorations celebrating some macabre festival, were the corpses of men and women. Some had hung there so long that their bones had been picked white by the flocks of crows that circled above the abyss or roosted squawking upon the roofs. Other victims were still alive, and I watched their feeble last movements with horror as they hung by their heels. However, most of them were already dead and in various stages of decomposition. The smell of rotting human carcasses was so thick that even the wind that whined eternally around the cliffs could not disperse it.

King Arkoun called the crows his chickens. Sometimes he fed them on the walls, and at other times he threw their food from the causeway into the gorge. The dwindling wail of another unfortunate victim falling away into the depths was a feature of our life on the pinnacle of Adbar Seged, the House of the Wind Song.

These executions and the daily floggings and chopping-off of hands or feet, or the pulling-out of tongues with red-hot tongs were King Arkoun's principal diversions when he was not playing dom, or planning a raid on one of the other neighbouring king of kings. Very often Arkoun wielded the axe or the tongs in person, and his roars of laughter were as loud as the screams of his victims.

As soon as our caravan had crossed the causeway and pulled into the central courtyard of Adbar Seged, Masara was whisked away by her female gaolers into the labyrinth of stone passageways, and I was led to my new quarters which abutted those of Arkoun.

I was allotted a single stone cell. It was dark and draughty. The open fireplace blackened the walls with soot and gave out little heat. Though I wore the woollen robes of the land, I was never warm in Adbar Seged. How I longed for the sunlight on the Nile and the bright oasis of my very Egypt! I sat on those wind-swept battlements and pined for my family, for Memnon and Tanus, for my little princesses, but most of all for my mistress. Sometimes I woke in the night with the tears chilling my face, and I had to cover my head with my sheepskin blanket, so that Arkoun would not hear my sobs through the thick stone wall.

Often I pleaded with him to release me.

'But why do you want to leave me, Taita?'

'I want to go back to my family.'

'I am your family now,' he laughed. 'I am your father.'

I made a wager with him. If I won a hundred successive boards of dom from him, he agreed that he would let me go and give me an escort back down the Nile to the great plains. When I won the hundredth game, he chuckled and shook his head at my naïvety.

'Did I say a hundred? I think not. Surely it was a thousand?' He turned to his henchmen. 'Was the bargain a thousand?'

'A thousand!' they chanted. 'It was a thousand!'

They all thought it a grand joke. When in a pique I refused to play another board with Arkoun, he hung me naked from the walls of the citadel by my heels until I squealed for him to set up the board.

When Arkoun saw me naked, he laughed and prodded me. 'You may have a way with the dom board, but it seems you have lost your own stones, Egyptian.' This was the first time since my capture that my physical mutilation had been revealed. Once again, men called me 'eunuch', much to my shame and mortification.

However, in the end the consequences were beneficial. If I had been a man entire, they would never have let me go to Masara.

THEY CAME for me in the night and led me shivering through the passages to Masara's cell. The room was lit by a dim oil lamp and smelled of vomit. The girl was curled on a straw mattress in the centre of the floor, with her vomit puddled on the stone floor beside her. She was in terrible pain, groaning and weeping and holding her stomach.

I set to work immediately, and examined her carefully. I was afraid that I would find her stomach as hard as a stone, the symptom of the swelling and bursting of the gut that would drench her insides with the contents of her intestines. There was no remedy for this condition. Not even I, with all my skills, could save her, if this was her affliction.

To my great relief I found her stomach warm and soft. There was no fever in her blood. I continued my examination, and though she groaned and screamed with agony when I touched her, I could not find any cause for her condition. I was puzzled and I sat back to think about it. Then I realized that although her face was contorted with agony, she was watching me with a candid gaze.

'This is worse than I feared.' I turned to her two female attendants and spoke in Geez. 'If I am to save her, I must have my chest. Fetch it immediately.'

They scrambled for the door, and I lowered my head to hers and whispered, 'You are a clever girl and a good actress. Did you tickle your throat with a feather?'

She smiled up at me and whispered back, 'I could think of no other way to meet you. When the women told me that you had learned to speak Geez, I knew that we could help each other.'

'I hope that is possible.'

'I have been so lonely. Even to speak to a friend will be a joy to me.' Her trust was so spontaneous that I was touched. 'Perhaps between us we will find a way to escape from this dreadful place.'

At that moment we heard the women returning, their voices echoing along the outside passage. Masara seized my hand.

'You are my friend, aren't you? You will come to me again?'

'I am and I will.'

'Quickly, tell me before you must go. What was his name?'

'Who?'

'The one who was with you on that first day beside the river. The one who looks like a young god.'

'His name is Memnon.'

'Memnon!' She repeated it with a peculiar reverence. 'It is a beautiful name. It suits him.'

The women burst into the room, and Masara clutched her healthy little belly and groaned as though she were at the point of death. While I clucked and shook my head with worry for the benefit of her women, I mixed a tonic of herbs that would do her some good, and told them that I would return in the morning.

In the morning Masara's condition had improved, and I was able to spend a little longer with her. Only one of the women was present, and she soon became bored and wandered away to the far side of the room. Masara and I exchanged a few quiet words.

'Memnon said something to me. I could not understand. What was it he said?'

'He said, "I will come back for you. Be brave. I will come back for you."'

'He could not mean that. He does not know me. He had met me only fleetingly.' She shook her head, and tears filled her eyes. 'Do you think he meant it, Taita?' There was a haunting plea in her tone that moved me, and I could not allow her to suffer more than she had already.

'He is crown prince of Egypt, and a man of honour. Memnon would not have said it unless he meant every word.'

That was all we could say then, but I came back the next day. The very first thing she asked of me was, 'Tell me again what Memnon said to me,' and I had to repeat his promise.

I told Arkoun that Masara was improving in health, but that she must be allowed out each day to walk on the battlements. 'Otherwise I cannot answer for her health.'

He thought about that for a day. However, Masara was a valuable asset for which he had paid a horse-load of silver bars, and at last he gave his permission.

Our daily exercise periods slowly extended, as the guards became accustomed to seeing us together. In the end Masara and I were able to spend most mornings in each other's company, strolling around the walls of Adbar Seged and talking endlessly.

Masara wanted to know everything that I had to tell about Memnon, and I racked my memory for anecdotes about him to entertain her. She had favourite stories which I was obliged to repeat until she knew them by heart, and she corrected me when I erred in the retelling. She particularly enjoyed the account of how he had rescued Tanus and me from the wounded bull elephant, and how he had received the Gold of Valour for his deed.

'Tell me about his mother the queen,' she demanded, and then, 'Tell me about Egypt. Tell me about your gods. Tell me about when Memnon was a baby.' Always her questions returned to him, and I was glad to appease her demands, for I longed for my family. Speaking about them made them seem closer to me.

One morning she came to me distraught. 'Last night I had a dreadful dream. I dreamed that Memnon came back to me, but I could not understand what he said to me. You must teach me to speak Egyptian, Taita. We will start today, this very minute!'

She was desperate to learn and she was a clever little thing. It went very quickly. Soon we were talking only Egyptian between ourselves, and it was useful to be able to speak privately in front of her guards.

When we were not talking about Memnon, we were discussing our plans to escape. Of course, I had been thinking of this ever since our arrival at Adbar Seged, but it helped to have her thoughts on the same subject to compare with my own.

'Even if you escape from this fortress, you will never pass through the mountains without help,' she warned me. 'The paths are like a skein of twisted wool. You will never unravel them. Every clan is at war with the next. They trust no strangers, and they will cut your throat as a spy.'

'What must we do, then?' I asked.

'If you are able to get away, you must go to my father. He will protect you and guide you back to your own people. You will tell Memnon where I am, and he will come to save me.' She said this with such shining confidence that I could not meet her eyes.

I realized then that Masara had built up an image of Memnon in her mind that was not based on reality. She was in love with a god, not a stripling as young and untried as she was herself. I was responsible for this, with my clever stories about the prince. I could not wound her now and shatter her hope by telling her how forlorn all these imaginings truly were.

'If I go to Prester Beni-Jon, your father, he will think I am one of Arkoun's spies. He will have my head.' I tried to extricate myself from the responsibilities she had laid upon me.

'I will tell you what to say to him. Things that only he and I know. That will prove to him that you come from me.'

She had blocked me there, so I tried a different escape. 'How would I find my way to your father's fortress? You have told me that the path is a tangled skein.'

'I will explain the way to you. Because you are so clever you will remember everything I tell you.'

By this time, naturally, I loved her almost as much as I loved my own little princesses. I would take any risk to shield her from hurt. She reminded me so strongly of my mistress at the same age that I could deny her nothing.

'Very well. Tell it to me.' And so we began to plan our escape. It was a game for me, which I played mostly to keep her hopes alive and her spirits buoyant. I had no serious expectation of finding a way off this pinnacle of rock.

We discussed ways of making a rope to lower ourselves down the cliff, although every time I looked over the causeway from the terrace outside her cell, I shuddered at that gaping void of space. She began to collect scraps of wool and cloth which she hid under her mattress. From these she planned to plait a rope. I could not tell her that a rope long enough and strong enough to support our weight and take us down to the floor of the valley would fill her cell to the ceiling.

For two long years we languished on the height of Adbar Seged, and we never were able to devise a plan of escape, but Masara never lost faith. Every day she asked me, 'What did Memnon say to me? Tell me again what he promised.'

'He said, "I will come back for you. Be brave."'

'Yes. I am brave, am I not, Taita?'

'You are the bravest girl I know.'

'Tell me what you will say to my father when you meet him.'

I repeated her instructions, and then she would reveal to me her latest plan of escape.

'I will catch the little sparrows that I feed on the terrace. You will write a letter to my father to tell him where I am. We will tie it to the sparrow's leg, and it will fly to him.'

'It is more likely to fly to Arkoun, who will have us both thrashed, and we will not be allowed to see each other again.'

In the end I escaped from Adbar Seged by riding out on a fine horse. Arkoun was going out on another raid against King Prester Beni-Jon. I was commanded to accompany him, in the capacity of personal physician and dom player.

As I walked my blindfolded horse across the causeway, I looked back and saw Masara standing on her terrace looking down at me. She was a lovely, lonely figure. She called to me in Egyptian. I could just make out her words above the sough of the wind.

'Tell him I am waiting for him. Tell him I have been brave.' And then softly, so I was not certain that I had heard the words right, 'Tell him I love him.'

The wind turned the tears upon my cheeks as cold as ice, as I rode away across Amba Kamara.

THE NIGHT before the battle, Arkoun kept me sitting late in his tent. While he gave his last orders to his commanders, he stropped the edge of the blue sword. Once in a while he would shave a few hairs off his wrist with the steely, glittering blade to test the edge, and nod with satisfaction.

At last he rubbed down the blade with clarified mutton fat. This strange, silver-blue metal had to be kept well greased, otherwise a red powder would form upon it, almost as though it was bleeding.

The blue sword had come to exert the same fascination on me as it had on Tanus. Occasionally, when he was in a specially benevolent mood, Arkoun would allow me to handle it. The weight of the metal was surprising, and the sharpness of the edge was incredible. I imagined what havoc it could wreak in the hands of a swordsman like Tanus. I knew that if we ever met again, Tanus would want every detail of it, and so I questioned Arkoun, who never tired of boasting about it.

He told me that the sword had been forged in the heart of a volcano by one of the pagan gods of Ethiopia. Arkoun's great-grandfather had won it from the god in a game of dom that had lasted for twenty days and twenty nights. I found all this quite plausible, except the part of the legend about winning the weapon in a dom game. If Arkoun's great-grandfather had played dom at the same standard as Arkoun, then it must have been a very stupid god who lost the sword to him.

Arkoun asked my opinion of his battle plan for the next day. He had learned that I was a student of military tactics. I told him his plan was brilliant. These Ethiopians had as much grasp of military tactics as they had of the play of the dom stones. Of course, the terrain would not allow full use of the horses, and they had no chariots. Nevertheless, their battles were fought in a haphazard and desultory manner.

Arkoun's grand strategy for the morrow would be to split his forces into four raiding parties. They would hide among the rocks and rush out, seize a few hostages, slit a few throats, and then run for it.

'You are one of the great generals of history,' I told Arkoun, 'I would like to write a scroll to extol your genius.' He liked the idea, and promised to provide me with whatever materials I required for the project, as soon as we returned to Adbar Seged.

It seemed that King Prester Beni-Jon was a commander of equal panache and vision. We met his forces the following day in a wide valley with steep sides. The battlefield had been mutually agreed upon some months in advance, and Prester Beni-Jon had taken up his position at the head of the valley before we arrived. He came forward to shout insults and challenges at Arkoun from a safe distance.

Prester Beni-Jon was a stick of a man, thin as a staff, with a long white beard and silver locks down to his waist. I could not make out his features over that distance, but the women had told me that as a young man he had been the most handsome swain in Ethiopia and that he had two hundred wives. Some women had killed themselves for love of him. It seemed clear to me that his talents might be more gainfully employed in the harem than on the battlefield.

Once Prester Beni-Jon had had his say, Arkoun went forward and replied at length. His insults were flowery and poetic, they rolled off the cliffs and echoed down the gorge. I committed some of his pithier remarks to memory, for they were worth recording.

When Arkoun subsided at last, I expected that battle would be joined, but I was mistaken. There were several other warriors on both sides who wished to speak. I fell asleep against a rock in the warm sun, smiling to myself as I imagined what sport Tanus and a company of his Blues would enjoy against these Ethiopian champions of rhetoric.

It was afternoon when I woke and started up at the clash of arms. Arkoun had loosed his first assault. One of his detachments raced forward against Prester Beni-Jon's positions, beating their swords against their copper shields. Within a remarkably short space of time they returned with great alacrity to their starting-point, without having inflicted or suffered casualties.

Further insults were exchanged, and then it was Prester Beni-Jon's turn to attack. He charged and retired with equal verve and similar results. So the day passed, insult for insult, charge for charge. At nightfall both armies retired. We camped at the foot of the valley and Arkoun sent for me.

'What a battle!' he greeted me triumphantly, as I entered his tent. 'It will be many months before Prester Beni-Jon will dare take the field again.'

'There will be no battle on the morrow?' I asked.

'Tomorrow we will return to Adbar Seged,' he told me, 'and you will write a full account of my victory in your scrolls. I expect that after this salutary defeat Prester Beni-Jon will soon sue for peace.'

Seven of our men had been wounded in this ferocious encounter, all by arrows fired at extreme range. I drew the barbs and dressed and bandaged the wounds. The following day I saw the wounded loaded on to the litters and walked beside them, as we started back.

One of the men had received a stomach wound and was in much pain. I knew he would be dead from gangrene within the week, but I did my best to ease his suffering and to cushion the bouncing of the litter over the rougher sections of the track.

Late that afternoon we came to a ford in the river, one that we had crossed on our way to give battle to Prester Beni-Jon. I had recognized this ford from the description that Masara had given me of the countryside and the route to her father's stronghold. The river was one of the numerous tributaries of the Nile that descended from the mountains. There had been rain over the preceding days, and the level of the ford was high.

I began the crossing, wading beside the litter of my patient with the stomach wound. He was already delirious. Halfway across the ford I realized that we had under-estimated the height and strength of the water. The flood caught the side of the litter and swung it sideways. It twisted the horse around, dragging the poor animal into deeper water where its hooves lost purchase on the gravel bottom.

I was hanging on to the harness, and the next moment the horse and I were both swimming. We were washed away downstream in the icy green flood. The wounded man was tumbled out of the litter, and when I tried to reach him, I lost my hold on the horse's harness. We were swept apart.

The wounded man's head disappeared below the surface, but by this time I was swimming for my own life. I rolled on to my back and pointed my feet downstream. This way I was able to fend off the rocks with my feet, as the current hurled me against them. For a short while some of Arkoun's men ran along the bank beside me, but soon the river swept me through a bend and they could not find a way around the base of the cliff. The horse and I were alone in the river.

Below the bend, the speed of the current slackened, and I was able to swim back to the horse and throw one arm over its neck. For the moment I was safe. For the first time I thought of escape, and realized that the gods had made an opportunity for me. I muttered a prayer of thanks, and used a handful of the horse's mane to steer it on down the middle of the river.

We had come downstream several miles and it was dark before I steered my horse into the bank. We clambered ashore on a sand-bar. I judged that I was safe from pursuit and recapture until morning. None of Arkoun's men would venture down the gorge in darkness. However, I was so chilled that my whole body shivered in uncontrollable spasms.

I led the horse to a sheltered place out of the wind, and then pressed my body to his flank. His wet hide steamed in the moonlight. Gradually the warmth of the animal permeated me, and my shivering subsided. Once I was half-warmed, I was able to gather up driftwood from the sand-bank. Using the Shilluk method, I managed with much difficulty to start a fire. I spread my robes out to dry, and crouched over the fire for the rest of that night.

As soon as it was light enough to see the path, I dressed myself and mounted the horse. I headed away from the river, for I knew that Arkoun's men would concentrate their search along the banks.

Two days later, following the directions that Masara had given me, I reached one of the fortified hilltop villages in the domain of Prester Beni-Jon. The headman of the village expressed the intention of cutting my throat immediately and taking my horse. I made full use of all my persuasive gifts, and eventually he agreed to keep the horse but lead me to the fortress of Prester Beni-Jon.

THE GUIDES who were escorting me to King Prester Beni-Jon spoke of him in warm and affectionate terms. The villages that we passed along the way were cleaner and more prosperous than those of Arkoun. The herds of kine were fatter, the crops well cultivated and the people better fed. The horses I saw were magnificent. Their beauty brought tears to my eyes.

When at last we came in sight of the castle high on another amba, it was in a better state of repair than that of Arkoun, and no grisly trophies decorated the walls.

From close at hand, King Prester Beni-Jon was indeed an extemely handsome man. His silver hair and beard endowed him with a singular air of dignity. His complexion was fair and his eyes dark and intelligent. At first he was highly sceptical of my story, but gradually his manner changed towards me, as I recited the intimate knowledge with which Masara had armed me.

He was deeply affected by the messages of love and duty that I brought to him from his daughter, and he questioned me eagerly as to her health and welfare. Then his servants led me to quarters that, by Ethiopian standards, were sumptuous, and I was provided with fresh woollen robes to replace my rags.

After I had eaten and rested, the servants led me back to the dank and smoky cell that was Prester Beni-Jon's audience chamber.

'Your Majesty, Masara has been a prisoner of Arkoun these past two years,' I pointed out to him immediately. 'She is a young and tender girl. She pines away in his stinking dungeons.' I embroidered the facts a trifle, to bring home to him the urgency of her plight.

'I have tried to assemble the ransom that Arkoun demands for my daughter,' Prester Beni-Jon excused himself. 'But I would have to melt down every plate and bowl in Aksum to put together such a hoard of silver as would satisfy his greed. In addition, he demands great tracts of my land and scores of my principal villages. To relinquish these to him would weaken my realm and condemn tens of thousands of my subjects to his tyranny.'

'I could lead your army to his stronghold of Adbar Seged. You could lay siege to the castle and force him to hand over Masara to you.'

Prester Beni-Jon looked startled by this proposal. I do not think such a course of action had occurred to him. It was not the Ethiopian way of waging war.

'I know Adbar Seged very well, but it is impregnable,' he answered me primly. 'Arkoun has a mighty army at his back. We have fought many fierce battles against him. My men are lions, but we have never been able to defeat him.' I had seen the lions of Prester Beni-Jon in battle, and I saw that his estimate of the situation was correct. The army he commanded could never hope to storm Adbar Seged and free Masara by force of arms.

The following day I returned with another proposal. 'Great Emperor of Aksum, King of Kings, as you well know, I am of the Egyptian nation. Queen Lostris, the regent of Egypt, lies with her armies at the confluence of the two rivers, where the Nile meets its twin.'

He nodded. 'This I know. These Egyptians have entered my territory without my leave. They are digging mines in my valleys. Soon I will fall upon them and annihilate them.'

It was my turn to be startled. Prester Beni-Jon was aware of the work on Pharaoh's tomb, and our people there were in danger of attack. Accordingly, I modified the suggestion that I was about to put to him.

'My people are skilled in the art of siege and war,' I explained. 'I have influence with Queen Lostris. If you send me safely back to her side, I will prevail on her to extend you her friendship. Her troops will storm the fortress of Adbar Seged and free your daughter.'

Although Prester Beni-Jon tried to disguise the fact, I saw that my suggestion appealed to him. 'What would your queen require in return for her friendship?' he asked carefully.

We haggled for five days, but in the end the bargain was struck. 'You will allow Queen Lostris to continue the mining work in your valley, and you will declare those valleys a prohibited area. Your own people will be forbidden to enter there on pain of death,' I told him. This was for my mistress. It would secure the tomb of Pharaoh from desecration.

'I agree,' said Prester Beni-Jon.

'You will deliver to Queen Lostris two thousand horses that I will choose from your herds.' This was for me.

'One thousand,' said the king.

'Two thousand.' I was firm.

'I agree,' said Prester Beni-Jon.

'Once she is free, the Princess Masara shall be allowed to marry any man she chooses. You will not forbid it.' That was for Memnon and the girl.

'It is against our custom,' he sighed. 'But I agree.'

'When we capture them, Arkoun and the stronghold of Adbar Seged will be handed over to you.' He looked more cheerful and nodded vigorously.

'Finally, we Egyptians shall be allowed to keep all the spoils of war that we capture from Arkoun, including the legendary blue sword.' That was for Tanus.

'I agree,' said Prester Beni-Jon, and I could see that he thought that he had made a bargain.

He gave me an escort of fifty men, and I set out the following day on the return to Qebui, riding a fine stallion that was the king's parting gift to me.

WE WERE still five days' ride from Qebui, when I saw the swift dust-cloud ahead of us, racing towards us across the plain. Then I saw the chariots dancing through the heat-mirage. As they approached, the columns deployed into attack formation at the gallop. It was beautiful to watch. The dressing was perfect, and the spacing between each vehicle so exact that they looked like a string of beads. I wondered who commanded them.

I shaded my eyes as they drew closer, and my heart leaped as I recognized the horses of the leading chariot. They were Rock and Chain, my own darlings. However, I did not immediately recognize the charioteer behind them. It was almost three years since last I had laid eyes on Memnon. The difference in age between seventeen and twenty is the difference between the boy and the man.

I had taken to riding with saddle-cloth and stirrups, in the Ethiopian manner, and so now I stood high in the stirrups and waved. I saw the chariot swerve, as Memnon recognized me and whipped up the team to full charge.

'Mem!' I howled. 'Mem!' and his answering shout came back to me on the wind.

'Tata! By the sweet milk of Isis, it's you!'

He pulled up the horses, sprang from the footplate and dragged me from my horse. First he hugged me, then he held me at arm's-length and we studied each other avidly.

'You are pale and thin, Tata. The bones are sticking out of you. Are those grey hairs I see here?' He tugged at my temples.

He was taller than I was now, lean in the waist and broad in the shoulder. His skin was tanned and oiled to the colour of burnished amber, and cords of muscle stood out in his throat when he laughed. He wore wrist-guards of gold and the Gold of Valour on his bared chest. Although it seemed impossible, he was more handsome than when I had last seen him. He reminded me of a leopard, supple and sleek.

He lifted me bodily and set me on the footplate of the chariot. 'Take up the traces,' he ordered. 'I want to see if you have lost any of your old skill.'

'Which way?' I asked.

'West, to Qebui, of course,' he ordered. 'My mother will be angry if I do not bring you directly to her.'

That night we sat at a camp-fire together, away from the other officers, so that we could talk in private. We sat in silence for a while, looking up at the silver blaze of stars, and then Memnon said, 'When I thought I had lost you, it was as though I had lost a part of myself. You are woven into my very first memory of life.'

I, who deal in words, could find no words to answer him. We were silent again, and then at last he laid a hand on my shoulder.

'Did you ever see the girl again?' he asked, and though his tone was casual, his grip upon my shoulder was not.

'Which girl?' I asked, to tease him.

'The girl at the river, on the day we were parted.'

'Was there a girl?' I frowned, as I tried to remember. 'What did she look like?'

'Her face was a dark lily, and her skin was the colour of wild honey. They called her Masara, and the memory of her still troubles my sleep.'

'Her name is Masara Beni-Jon,' I told him, 'and I have spent two years imprisoned with her in the fortress of Adbar Seged. There I learned to love her, for her nature is even sweeter than her face.'

He seized me with both hands now and shook me without mercy. 'Tell me about her, Tata! Tell me everything. Leave nothing out.'

So we sat the rest of that night beside the fire and we talked about the girl. I told him how she had learned to speak Egyptian for his sake. I told him how his promise to her had sustained her through the dark, lonely days, and in the end I told him the message that she had sent to him, the message she had called out to me from the battlements of Adbar Seged as I rode away and left her.

'Tell him I was brave. Tell him I love him.'

He was silent for a long while, staring into the flames, and then he said softly, 'How can she love me? She does not know me.'

'Do you know her any better than she knows you?' I asked, and he shook his head.

'Do you love her?'

'Yes,' he answered simply.

'Then she loves you in the same way.'

'I made her a promise. Will you help me make good my promise to her, Tata?'

I HAVE never in my life known such joy as was mine on my return to Qebui when I went aboard the *Breath of Horus*.

Memnon had sent a messenger ahead to warn them of my return, and they were all waiting for me.

'By the stinking crust between Seth's toes!' Kratas shouted. 'I thought we had got rid of you at last, you old rogue.' And he crushed me to his chest until I thought my ribs were all staved in.

Tanus seized my shoulders and stared into my eyes for a moment before he grinned, 'But for you, that hairy Ethiop would have had me. He got the better bargain when he took you instead. Thank you, old friend.' I saw how Tanus had aged. Like me, there was grey in his hair now, and his face was weather-beaten, beginning to erode like a granite cliff.

My little princesses were no longer little, but they were still adorable. They were shy towards me, for their memory of me had faded. They stared at me with big eyes as I made my obeisance. The colour of Bekatha's hair had darkened to copper. I looked forward to rekindling her affection.

Tehuti recognized me at last. 'Tata!' she said. 'Did you bring me a present?'

'Yes, Your Highness,' I replied, 'I have brought you my heart.'

My mistress smiled at me as I walked towards her along the deck. She wore the light *nemes* crown and the golden head of the cobra on her brow. When she smiled, I saw that she had lost her first tooth, and the gap marred her smile. She had thickened around the waist, and the heavy affairs of state had furrowed her brow and etched crow's feet at the corners of her eyes. To me, however, she was still the most lovely woman in the world.

She stood up from the throne as I knelt before her. This was the highest mark of her favour. She laid her hand on my bowed head, and it was a caress.

'You have been away from us too long, Taita,' she said, so softly that only I could hear her. 'Tonight you will sleep at the foot of my bed once more.'

That night, when she had drunk the bowl of herb broth that I had prepared for her, and I had covered her with a fur blanket, she murmured softly as she closed her eyes, 'Can I trust you not to kiss me when I am asleep?'

'No, Your Majesty,' I replied, and stooped over her. She smiled as my lips touched hers.

'Never leave us again for so long, Taita,' she said.

MEMNON AND I had planned our tactics meticulously, and we executed them with the same precision as one of our chariot manoeuvres.

Tanus was easy to convince. His defeat by Arkoun still rankled. In his presence Memnon and I discussed the ease with which the blue sword had sheered his bronze blade, and how Arkoun would certainly have killed him, if I had not intervened. Tanus bristled with humiliation.

Then Memnon questioned me on the magical origins and properties of the legendary weapon. Tanus forgot his pique and joined in with avid questions of his own.

'This Prester Beni-Jon has declared the blue sword a prize of war. Whoever can seize it, may hold it,' I told them.

'If we went against Arkoun, we would not be able to use chariots in those valleys,' Memnon mused. 'It would have to be the infantry. How do you think your Shilluk would fare against the Ethiops, Lord Tanus?' Memnon still addressed Tanus formally. Obviously he had not learned in my absence that Tanus was his real father.

By the time we had finished with him, Tanus was as hot for the venture as either of us. He was totally in league with us as we started our campaign on Queen Lostris.

From the very beginning my mistress had understood, as Tanus never had, just how vital the horses and chariots would be, if ever we were to fulfil the dream of the return to our very Egypt. I displayed the stallion that Prester Beni-Jon had given me, and pointed out to my mistress his finer points of breed.

'Look at his nostrils, Majesty. See the depth of his chest, and the balance of muscle to bone. The Hyksos have nothing to match these Ethiopian horses.'

Then I reminded her of her promise to the dead pharaoh, and told her, 'Prester Beni-Jon will cede the valley of the tomb to you. His warriors will guard it against the grave-robbers. He will place a taboo upon the valley, and these Ethiops are superstitious people. They will respect the prohibition even long after we have returned to Thebes.'

I warned Memnon not to mention to Queen Lostris his amorous interest in an expedition against Arkoun. It would do our cause no good.

Every mother is also a lover; she seldom takes any pleasure in seeing her son led away by another younger woman.

No woman, not even a queen, could resist the combined charm and cunning of the three of us, Tanus and Memnon and myself. Queen Lostris gave her consent to our expeditionary force marching on Adbar Seged.

WE LEFT the wagons and the chariots at the valley of Pharaoh's tomb, and struck out into the mountains. Prester Beni-Jon had sent a company of guides to meet us. They were a hundred of his best and most reliable men.

Tanus had selected a full division of his wild and bloodthirsty Shilluk, and promised them all the cattle they could capture. Each of these black pagans carried a cloak of thick jackal fur rolled upon his back, for we remembered the cold wind of the mountain passes.

For support we had three companies of Egyptian archers, led by Lord Kratas. That old ruffian had joined the company of nobles during my sojourn in Adbar Seged. He was spoiling for a real fight. He and every one of his men were armed with the new compound recurved bows that could outdrive the Ethiopian long-bows by two hundred paces.

Memnon had selected a small band of the finest swordsmen and rough fighters that we had. Remrem was one of these, of course, as were Lord Aqer and Astes. I was part of this special detachment, not for my warlike skills, but simply because I was the only one who had ever entered the fortress of Adbar Seged.

Hui wanted to come with us and offered me every bribe at his disposal. In the end I gave in to him, mainly because I needed an expert to help me select the horses that Prester Beni-Jon had promised me.

I impressed on both Tanus and the prince how vital it was to move swiftly, not only for reasons of surprise, but also because the rains must soon break upon the mountains. During my days in Adbar Seged I had studied the patterns of the weather and the seasons. If the rains caught us in the valleys, they would prove a more dangerous enemy than any Ethiop army.

We made the approach march to Amba Kamara in less than a month. Our column wound through the passes like a long, deadly cobra. The bronze spear-heads of the Shilluk glittered in the high sunlight like the scales of the serpent. We met no person to oppose us. The villages we passed through were deserted. The inhabitants had fled and taken their herds and their women with them. Although each day the clouds gathered black and sullen on the mountain peaks, and at night the thunder muttered at us, the rains held off and the fords of the rivers were low.

Twenty-five days after setting out, we stood in the valley below the massif of Amba Kamara, and looked up the winding track to the heights looming over us.

On my previous journeys up and down the mountain I had studied the defences that Arkoun had erected along the pathway. These comprised rockfalls and stone-walled redoubts. I pointed these out to Tanus, and we could make out the bushy, unhelmeted heads of the defenders showing above the walls of the strongpoints.

'The weakness of a rockfall is that you can only let it come down once, and my Shilluk are quick enough on their feet to dodge a charging buffalo,' Tanus said thoughtfully.

He sent them up the path in small parties, and when the defenders knocked out the wedges from under the rockfall and sent it rolling down on the track, those long-legged black spearmen ran out to the side with the agility of mountain goats. Once the slide of boulders had rumbled past them, they turned straight up the almost sheer mountainside. Bounding from rock to rock, and howling in such a horrible fashion that they started the hair on the nape of my neck, they drove the defenders up the mountain and over the crest.

They were held up only by Arkoun's archers hidden behind the walls of the stone redoubts. When this happened, Kratas led his archers up the mountain. With their superior bow-range, the Egyptians were able to stand back and shoot massed volleys, almost straight into the sky.

It was fascinating to watch a swarm of arrows climb into the air like a flock of black birds and then drop down on to the redoubt so steeply that the stone wall afforded the men behind it no protection. We heard their screams and then saw them break and scurry away up the slope. Immediately the Shilluk were after them, baying like a pack of hunting dogs. Even from the bottom of the valley I could hear their battle cry, '*Kajan*! *Kajan*! Kill! Kill!'

Though my legs were hard and my wind strong with so much marching, I had difficulty keeping up with Memnon and the rest of our small group. The years were beginning to take their toll.

We were all wearing long woollen Ethiopic robes, and we carried the traditional round shields of our enemies. However, we had not yet placed the horse-hair wigs on our heads. It would have been extremely unwise to resemble the Ethiopian too closely while the Shilluk were in their present mood.

When at last I came out on the flat tableland of the amba, I saw at a glance that Tanus was rallying and regrouping his infantry. The one fault of the Shilluk as fighting men is that once they have wet their spears with blood, they go berserk, and it is almost impossible to control them. Tanus was roaring like a bull elephant and laying about him with his golden whip of rank. Once more in hand, the Shilluk formed ranks and moved forward against the first village where the Ethiopians were waiting behind the stone walls. As the wave of tall black figures, topped by a foam of white ostrich-feather head-dresses, washed towards them, they loosed a shower of arrows from their long bows. But the Shilluk had their tall shields up.

As the Shilluk charge burst upon them, some of the Ethiopians rushed forward, brandishing their swords. They were not lacking in courage, but this type of warfare was new to them. They had never been forced to meet a charge that was carried through to the death.

I stayed long enough to see them heavily engaged, and then I called to Memnon and his band, 'The wigs!' Each of them pulled one of the wigs of black horse-hair over his scalp. I had made these with my own hands, and styled them on the Ethiopian model of beauty, full and floccose. Clad in the long striped robes and with the wigs on our heads, we could pass as a mob of Arkoun's clansmen.

'This way! Follow me!' I cried, and let out an ululating Ethiopic war cry. They yodelled and howled behind me, as we skirted the village where the fight was still raging, and ran in a disorderly bunch through the cornfields.

We had to reach the fortress and be at Masara's side to protect her when Arkoun finally realized that he had lost the day. I knew that he would not hestitate to kill her as soon as she was no longer of value to him. I thought that he would probably take the blue sword to her or throw her from the causeway into the gorge. Those were his favourite means of despatching his victims.

As we made our way across the amba, we found the entire tableland in turmoil. Bands of bushy-headed warriors milled about in confusion. Women dragged their children by the arm, their possessions piled on their heads, wailing with terror as they ran about like frightened chickens who smell the fox. Herds of goats bleated, and cattle lowed and churned the dust. The herd-boys had fled. Nobody paid us the least attention as we trotted through the fields and kept clear of the villages.

We followed the general movement towards Adbar Seged at the far end of the table, and as we neared the causeway the crowds thickened and congealed until we were obliged to force our way through them. There were guards at the head of the causeway. They were turning the fugitives back with drawn swords and clubs. Women were screaming and pleading for shelter in the fortress, holding up their babies for mercy's sake. Some of them were knocked down in the press and were trampled under the feet of those coming on from behind.

'Form the tortoise.' Memnon gave the order quietly, and our small band closed up and locked the edges of our Ethiopian shields. We cut through the crowd like a shark through a shoal of sardines. Some of the weaker ones at the front were pushed forward and forced over the edge of the precipice. Their screams added to the panic. When we reached the head of the causeway, the guards there tried to stop us, but they were themselves so crowded by the mob that they could not swing their weapons, and were in danger of being overwhelmed and thrown over the cliff.

'We are under King Arkoun's direct orders. Stand aside!' I shouted at them in Geez.

'The password?' the captain of the guard yelled at me, as he struggled to stay on his feet. The crowd surged back and forward in panic. 'You must give the password.' He poked his sword at me, but Memnon struck the blade aside.

During my imprisonment I had heard the password repeated a thousand times, for my cell had been above the main gate. It might have been changed since then, and I was ready to have the captain killed, as I yelled the old password at him: 'The mountain is high!'

'Go across!' He stood aside, and we struggled out of the throng, kicking and shoving back those who tried to follow us. We ran out on to the bridge. So urgent was the need to reach Masara that I barely noticed the drop on either hand, and without a qualm I led them across the gaping void.

'Where is King Arkoun?' I shouted at the guards who blocked the gateway. When they hesitated, I told them, 'The mountain is high! I have urgent despatches for the king. Stand aside! Let us pass!' We barged through the open gate before they could decide to oppose us, and, with twelve good men at my back, I raced for the outer staircase that led to the upper terrace.

There were two armed men at the door to Masara's chamber, and I rejoiced to see them. I had worried that the girl might have been moved to another part of the fort, but the presence of the guards assured me that she had not.

'Who are you?' one of them shouted, and drew his sword. 'By what authority—' He did not finish the challenge. I stepped aside and allowed Memnon and Remrem to brush past me. They flew at the guards and cut them down before they could defend themselves.

The door to Masara's chamber was barred from within, and when we hurled our combined weight against it, there came a chorus of feminine screams and wails from the other side. At the third attempt the door gave way and I was propelled through the opening into the room beyond.

It was in deep gloom, and I could barely make out the huddle of women in the far corner.

'Masara!' I called her name, as I plucked the wig from my head, and let my own hair fall around my shoulders. She recognized me by it.

'Taita!' She bit the wrist of the woman who tried to hold her, and ran to me. She flung both arms around my neck, and then she looked over my shoulder and her grip slackened, her dark eyes opened wide and the colour flooded her cheeks.

Memnon had pulled off his wig. Without it, he was strikingly and unmistakably a prince. I stepped aside and left Masara standing alone. The two of them stared at each other. Neither of them moved or spoke for what seemed like an eternity, but was a moment only. Then Masara said softly and shyly in Egyptian, 'You came. You kept your promise. I knew that you would.'

I think that this was the only time that I ever saw Memnon at a loss. He could only nod his head, and then I witnessed an amazing phenomenon. Blood flooded up his neck and suffused his face, so that even in the gloom of the chamber it glowed. The Crown Prince of Egypt, son of Pharaoh, commander of the first division of chariots, Best of Ten Thousand, holder of the Gold of Valour, stood there blushing and as tongue-tied as a peasant clod.

Behind me one of the women squawked like a startled hen, and before I could put out a hand to hold her, she had ducked under my arm and darted down the inner staircase. Her screams reverberated up the stairwell. 'Guards! The enemy has broken into the east wing. Come quickly!' and almost immediately there was a rush of booted feet on the staircase.

On the instant, Memnon was transformed from the blushing young lover to a hard-faced guardsman. 'Take care of her, Tata. Let no harm come to her,' he told me grimly, and stepped past me to the head of the stairs.

He killed the first man coming up with that classic thrust to the throat that Tanus had taught him. Then he placed his foot in the centre of his chest. As he jerked his blade free, he kicked the dead man backwards down the stair-well. The falling corpse tumbled into the other men coming up from below, and swept the stairs clean.

Memnon looked at me. 'Do you think we can reach the gate before they close it?'

'We must,' I answered. 'Our best route is back down the outer staircase.'

'Remrem, lead us. Tata and the princess in the centre. I will bring up the rear-guard,' he said crisply, and stabbed the next man coming up the stairs in the eye.

The Ethiopian dropped his weapon and clutched his face with both hands. Memnon stabbed him again through the chest and pushed him backwards down the stairs, clearing them a second time. 'Follow Remrem,' he shouted at me. 'Don't stand there. After him as fast as you can.'

I grabbed Masara's arm, but there was no need to pull her along. She came with me readily, so quick and agile that she was leading me.

The sunlight struck us as we ran out on to the terrace. After the dark room it dazzled me. I blinked to clear my vision, and then I looked across the causeway to the edge of the tableland on the far side of the gulf. Tanus' Shilluks were there. I saw their feathers dancing and their shields held high.

'*Kajan*! Kill! Kill!' they sang, and their spear-heads were dulled with fresh blood. The panic-stricken peasants scattered before them, and they reached the head of the causeway.

There were two or three hundred of Arkoun's soldiers there. They had the abyss at their backs, and necessity made heroes of every one of them. Now they had truly become lions. Although a score of them were driven back over the edge, and plunged to their death in the valley far below, the survivors hurled back the first charge of the Shilluk.

I saw Tanus then, exactly where I expected him to be, holding the centre. His helmet shone like a beacon in the dark sea of Shilluk warriors. I saw him throw back his head and begin to sing.

The savage Shilluk words carried over the gulf to where I stood on the terrace of the fortress. The men around him took up the chorus, and they surged forward, still singing. This time nothing could stand before them. They stabbed and hacked their way through the defenders, and Tanus was the first man on to the causeway. He ran lightly for such a big man, and he was still singing. His Shilluk followed him on to the stone arch, but it was so narrow that they were forced into single file.

Tanus was halfway across, when the song died on his lips, and he stopped.

From the gateway of Adbar Seged, below where I stood, another man stepped out on to the causeway to confront Tanus. I was looking down and so could not see his face, but there was no mistaking the weapon in his right hand. The blue sword caught the sunlight and flashed like a sheet of summer lightning.

'Arkoun!' Tanus bellowed. 'I have been looking for you.'

Arkoun could not understand the words, but the sense of them was unmistakable. He laughed into the wind, and his beard blew out like smoke around his goaty face.

'I know you!' He swung the silver-blue blade around his head, and it hissed and whined in the air. 'This time I will kill you.' He started forward, out along the narrow arch of stone, running with long, lithe strides straight at Tanus.

Tanus altered his grip on the handle of his bronze shield, and tucked his head in behind it. He now knew the power in that glittering blade, and I saw that he did not intend meeting it with his own softer bronze. Arkoun had also learned discretion from their last brief encounter. From the way he carried the blue sword, I guessed that he would not attempt another rash overhand stroke.

As they came together, Arkoun gathered himself. I saw his shoulders brace and his weight swing forward. He used the impetus of his charge to send the straight thrust at Tanus' head. Tanus lifted the shield and caught the blue blade in the centre of the heavy bronze target. It would have snapped a sword of inferior metal, but the blue sword sheared through it as if it were goat-skin. Half its silver length was buried in the yellow bronze.

Then I realized Tanus' intention. He twisted the shield at an angle so that the blade was trapped. Arkoun struggled to withdraw his weapon, he wrestled and heaved, throwing his full weight backwards, but Tanus had the blue sword in a vice of bronze.

Arkoun gathered all his strength and pulled back again. This time Tanus did not resist him. He leaped forward in the direction that Arkoun was heaving, and this unexpected move threw Arkoun off-balance.

Arkoun staggered away, tripped and teetered on the brink of the chasm. In order to keep his balance, he was forced to relinquish his grip on the hilt of the blue sword, and to leave it still embedded in the shield.

He windmilled his arms as he swayed out over the drop. Then Tanus shifted his ground, put his shoulder behind the shield and barged forward. The shield crashed into Arkoun's chest, and the pommel of the blue sword caught him in the pit of his belly with all Tanus' weight and strength behind it.

Arkoun was thrown backwards, out into empty space. He turned a slow somersault in the air and then went straight down, with his robe ballooning around him, and his beard streaming like a chariot pennant in the wind of his fall.

From where I stood, I watched him make the same last journey on which he had sent so many other unfortunate souls. From the causeway until he struck the rocks a thousand feet below, he screamed all the way down, on a high, receding note that was cut off abruptly at the end.

Tanus stood alone in the middle of the causeway. He still held the shield on high with the sword buried in the metal.

Slowly the tumult and the fighting died away. The Ethiopians had seen their king vanquished and cast down. The heart went out of them.

They threw down their weapons and grovelled for mercy. The Egyptian officers were able to save some of them from the blood-crazed Shilluk, and these were dragged away to where the slave-masters waited to bind them.

I had no eyes for any of this, for I was watching Tanus out there on the bridge. He began to walk towards the gateway of the fortress, and the men cheered him and raised their weapons in salute.

'There is plenty of fight in the old bull yet,' Memnon laughed in admiration, but I did not laugh with him. I felt the chill premonition of some awful tragedy, like the air stirred by the beat of vultures' wings as they settle to their gruesome feast.

'Tanus,' I whispered. He walked with a slow and hampered gait. He lowered the shield as he came down the bridge of stone, and only then did I see the stain spreading on his breastplate.

I thrust Masara into Memnon's arms and ran down the outer staircase. The Ethiopian guards at the gate tried to surrender their weapons to me, but I pushed my way past them and ran out on to the causeway.

Tanus saw me running towards him and he smiled at me, but the smile was lop-sided. He stopped walking and slowly his legs buckled beneath him, and he sat down heavily in the middle of the bridge. I dropped on my knees beside him, and saw the rent in the crocodile-skin of his breastplate. Blood oozed from it, and I knew that the blue sword had bitten deeper than I had believed possible. Arkoun had driven the point through the bronze shield, on through the tough leather breastplate, and into Tanus' chest.

Carefully I untied the straps that held his armour, and lifted away the breastplate. Tanus and I both looked down at the wound. It was a penetrating slit the exact width of the blade, like a tiny mouth with wet red lips. Every breath that Tanus drew frothed through that horrid opening in a rash of pink bubbles. It was a lung wound, but I could not bring myself to say it. No man can survive a sword-cut through one of his lungs.

'You are wounded.' It was an asinine remark, and I could not look at his face as I said it.

'No, old friend, I am not wounded,' he replied softly. 'I am killed.'

TANUS' SHILLUK made a litter with their spears, and covered it with a rug of sheepskin. They lifted him and carried him, gently and slowly, into the fortress of Adbar Seged.

We laid him on the bed of King Arkoun, and then I sent them all away. When they were gone, I placed the blue sword upon the bed beside him. He smiled and laid his hand on the gold and jewelled hilt. 'I have paid a high price for this treasure,' he murmured. 'I would have liked to wield it just once upon the battlefield.'

I could offer him no hope or comfort. He was an old soldier, and he had seen too many lung wounds. I could not hope to deceive him as to the final outcome. I bound up the wound with a pad of wool and a linen bandage. While I worked, I recited the incantation to quell the bleeding, 'Retreat from me, creature of Seth—'

But he was sinking away from me. Each breath he drew was an effort, and I could hear the blood stirring in his lungs like a hidden creature in the deep swamps.

I mixed a draught of the sleeping-flower, but he would not drink it. 'I will live every minute of my life,' he told me. 'Even the very last one.'

'What else is there that I can do for you?'

'You have done so much already,' he said. 'But there is no end to the demands that we all make upon you.'

I shook my head, 'There is no end to what I would give.'

'These last things then I ask of you. Firstly, you will never tell Memnon that I am his sire. He must always believe that the blood of the pharaohs runs in his veins. He will need every strength to meet the destiny that awaits him.'

'He would be as proud to share your blood as that of any king.'

'Swear to me you will not tell him.'

'I swear it,' I replied, and he lay a while gathering his strength.

'There is one other boon.'

'I grant it before you name it,' I said.

'Take care of my woman who was never my wife. Shield and succour her as you have done all these years past.'

'You know I will.'

'Yes, I know you will, for you have always loved her as much as I have. Take care of Lostris and of our children. I give them all into your hands.'

He closed his eyes, and I thought that the end was close, but his strength surpassed that of other men. After a while he opened them again.

'I wish to see the prince,' he said.

'He waits for you on the terrace,' I answered, and went to the curtained doorway.

Memnon stood at the far end of the terrace. Masara was with him, and the two of them stood close together but not touching. Their expressions were grave and their voices muted. They both looked up as I called.

Memnon came immediately, leaving the girl standing alone. He went directly to Tanus' bed and stood looking down at him. Tanus smiled up at him, but the smile was unsteady. I knew what effort it had cost him.

'Your Highness, I have taught you all I know of war, but I cannot teach you about life. Each man must learn that for himself. There is nothing else I have to tell you before I start out on this new journey, except to thank you for the gift of knowing and serving you.'

'You were ever more than a tutor to me,' Memnon answered softly. 'You were the father I never knew.'

Tanus closed his eyes, and his expression twisted.

Memnon stooped and took his arm in a firm grip, 'Pain is just another enemy to be met and overcome. You taught me that, Lord Tanus.' The prince thought it was the wound that had affected him, but I knew that it was the pain of the word 'father'.

Tanus opened his eyes. 'Thank you, Your Highness. It is good to have you to help me through this last agony.'

'Call me friend, rather than highness.' Memnon sank on one knee beside the bed, and he did not release the grip on Tanus' arm.

'I have a gift for you, friend.' The congealing blood in Tanus' lungs blurred his voice. He groped for the handle of the blue sword that still lay on the mattress beside him, but he did not have the strength to lift it.

He took Memnon's hand from his arm and placed it upon the jewelled hilt. 'This is yours now,' he whispered.

'I will think of you whenever I draw it from its scabbard. I will call your name whenever I wield it on the battlefield.' Memnon took up the weapon.

'You do me great honour.'

Memnon stood up, and with the sword in his right hand took the classic opening stance in the centre of the room. He touched the blade to his lips, saluting the man lying on the bed.

'This is the way you taught me to do it.'

Then he began the exercise of arms, in which Tanus had drilled him when he was still a child. He performed the twelve parries, and then the cuts and the lunges with an unhurried perfection. The silver blade circled and swooped like a glittering eagle. It fluted and whined through the air, and lit the gloom of the chamber with darting beams of light.

Memnon ended it with the straight thrust, aimed at the throat of an imaginary enemy. Then he placed the point between his feet and rested both hands upon the pommel.

'You have learned well,' Tanus nodded. 'There is nothing more that I can teach you. It is not too soon for me to go.'

'I will wait with you,' Memnon said.

'No.' Tanus made a weary gesture. 'Your destiny waits for you beyond the walls of this dreary room. You must go forward to meet it without looking back. Taita will stay with me. Take the girl with you. Go to Queen Lostris and prepare her for the news of my death.'

'Go in peace, Lord Tanus.' Memnon would not degrade that solemn moment with futile argument. He crossed to the bed and kissed his father on the lips. Then he turned and, without a backward glance, he strode from the room with the blue sword in his hand.

'Go on to glory, my son,' Tanus whispered, and turned to face the stone wall. I sat at the foot of his bed and looked at the dirty stone floor. I did not want to watch a man like Tanus weep.

I WOKE in the night to the sound of drums, those crude wooden drums of the Shilluk, beating out there in the darkness. The doleful sound of the Shilluk's voices chanting their savage dirge made me shudder with dread.

The lamp had burned low, and was guttering beside the bed. It threw grotesque shadows on the ceiling, like the beating and fluttering of the wings of vultures. I crossed slowly and reluctantly to where Tanus lay. I knew that the Shilluk were not mistaken — they have a way of sensing these things.

Tanus lay as I had last seen him, with his face to the wall, but when I touched his shoulder I felt the chill in his flesh. That indomitable spirit had gone on.

I sat beside him for the remainder of that night and I lamented and mourned for him, as his Shilluk were doing.

In the dawn I sent for the embalmers.

I would not let those crude butchers eviscerate my friend. I made the incision in his left flank. It was not a long, ugly slash, such as the undertakers are wont to perform, but the work of a surgeon.

Through it I drew his viscera. When I held Tanus' great heart in my

485

hands, I trembled. It was as though I could still feel all his strength and power beat in this casket of flesh. I replaced it with reverence and love in the cage of his ribs, and I closed the gash in his side and the wound in his chest, that the blue sword had made, with all the skill at my command.

I took up the bronze spoon, and pressed it up his nostril until I felt it touch the thin wall of bone at the end of the passage. This flimsy partition I pierced with one hard thrust, and scooped out the soft matter from the cavity of his skull. Only then was I content to deliver him over to the embalmers.

Even though there was no more for me to do, I waited with Tanus through the forty long days of the mummification in the cold and gloomy castle of Adbar Seged. Looking back upon it now, I realize that this was weakness. I could not bear the burden of my mistress's grief when first she heard the news of Tanus' death. I had allowed Memnon to assume the duty that was rightfully mine. I hid with the dead, when I should have been with the living who needed me more. I have ever been a coward.

There was no coffin to hold Tanus' mummified body. I would make him one when at last we reached the fleet at Qebui. I had the Ethiopian women weave a long basket for him. The mesh of the weave was so fine that it resembled linen. It would hold water like a pot of fired clay.

WE CARRIED him down from the mountains. His Shilluk easily bore the weight of his desiccated body. They fought each other for the honour. Sometimes they sang their wild songs of mourning as we wound our way through the gorges and over the windswept passes. At other times they sang the fighting songs that Tanus had taught them.

I walked beside his bier all that weary way. The rains broke on the peaks and drenched us. They flooded the fords so that we had to swim ropes across. In my tent at night, Tanus' reed coffin stood beside my own cot. I spoke aloud to him in the darkness, as if he could hear and answer me, just as we had done in the old days.

At last we descended through the last pass, and the great plains lay before us. As we approached Qebui, my mistress came to meet our sad caravan. She rode on the footplate of the chariot behind Prince Memnon.

As they came towards us through the grassland, I ordered the Shilluk bearers to lay Tanus' reed coffin under the spreading branches of a giant giraffe acacia. My mistress dismounted from the chariot and went to the coffin. She placed one hand upon it, and bowed her head in silence.

I was shocked to see what ravages sorrow had wrought upon her. There were streaks of grey in her hair, and her eyes were dulled. The sparkle and the zest had gone out of them. I realized that the days of her youth and her great beauty were gone for ever. She was a lonely and tragic figure. Her bereavement was so evident, that no person who looked upon her now could doubt that she was a widow.

I went to her side to warn her. 'Mistress, you must not make your grief clear for all to see. They must never know that he was more than just your friend and the general of your armies. For the sake of his memory and the honour that he held so dear, hold back your tears.'

'I have no tears left,' she answered me quietly. 'My grief is all cried out. Only you and I will ever know the truth.'

We placed Tanus' humble reed coffin in the hold of the *Breath of Horus*, beside the magnificent gold coffin of Pharoah. I stayed at the side of my mistress, as I had promised Tanus I would, until the worst agonies of her mourning had subsided into the dull eternal pain that would never leave her again. Then, at her orders, I returned to the valley of the tomb to supervise the completion of Pharaoh's sepulchre.

Obedient to my mistress, I also selected a site further down the valley for the tomb of Tanus. Though I did my very best with the material and craftsmen available to me, Tanus' resting-place would be the hut of a peasant compared to the funerary palace of Pharaoh Mamose.

An army of craftsmen had laboured all these years to complete the magnificent murals that decorated the passages and the subterranean chambers of the king's tomb. The store-rooms of the tomb were crammed with all the treasure that we had carried with us from Thebes.

Tanus' tomb had been built in haste. He had accumulated no treasure in his lifetime of service to the state and the crown. I painted scenes upon the walls that depicted the events of his earthly existence, his hunting of mighty beasts and his battles with the red pretender and the Hyksos, and the last assault on the fortress of Adbar Seged. However, I dared not show his nobler accomplishments, his love for my mistress and his steadfast friendship to me. The love of a queen is treason, the friendship of a slave is degrading.

When at last it was completed, I stood alone in Tanus' modest tomb, where he would spend all eternity, and I was suddenly consumed by anger that this was all I could do for him. In my eyes he was more a man than any pharaoh who had ever worn the double crown. That crown could have been his, it should have been his, but he had spurned it. To me he was more a king than ever Pharaoh had been.

It was then that the thought first dawned upon me. It was so outrageous that I thrust it from me. Even to contemplate it seriously was a terrible treason, and offence in the eyes of men and the gods.

However, over the weeks that followed, the thought kept creeping back into my mind. I owed Tanus so much, and Pharaoh so little. Even if I was damned to perdition, it would be a fair price to pay. Tanus had given me more than that over my lifetime.

I could not accomplish it alone. I needed help, but who was there to turn to? I could not enlist either Queen Lostris or the prince. My mistress was bound by the oath she had sworn to Pharaoh, and Memnon did not know which of the two men was his natural father. I could not tell him without breaking my oath to Tanus.

In the end there was one person only who had loved Tanus almost as much as I had, who feared neither god nor man, and who had the brute physical strength I lacked.

'By Seth's unwiped backside!' Lord Kratas roared with laughter when I revealed my plan to him. 'No one else but you could have dreamed up such a scheme. You are the biggest rogue alive, Taita, but I love you for giving me this last chance to honour Tanus.'

The two of us planned it carefully. I even went to the lengths of sending the guards at the entrance to the hold of the *Breath of Horus* a jug of wine heavily laced with the powder of the sleeping-flower.

When Kratas and I at last entered the hold of the ship where the two coffins lay, my resolve wavered. I sensed that the *Ka* of Pharaoh Mamose watched me from the shadows and that his baleful spirit would follow me all the days of my life, seeking vengeance for this sacrilege.

Big, bluff Kratas had no such qualms, and he set to work with such a will that several times during the course of the night, I had to caution him against the noise he was making as we opened the golden lids to the royal coffin and lifted out the mummy of the king.

Tanus was a bigger man than Pharaoh, but fortunately the coffin-makers had left us some space, and Tanus' body had shrunk during the embalming. Even so, we were obliged to unwind several layers of his wrappings before he fitted snugly into the great golden cask.

I mumbled an apology to Pharaoh Mamose as we lifted him into the humble wooden coffin, painted on the outside with a likeness of the Great Lion of Egypt. There was room to spare, and before we sealed the lid we packed this with the linen bandages that we had unwrapped from Tanus.

AFTER THE rains had passed and the cool season of the year returned, my mistress ordered the funeral procession to leave Qebui and set out for the valley of the tomb.

The first division of chariots, headed by Prince Memnon, led us. Behind followed fifty carts loaded with the funerary treasure of Pharaoh Mamose. The royal widow, Queen Lostris, rode on the wagon that carried the golden coffin. I rejoiced to see her take this last journey in the company of the one man she had loved, even though she thought it was another. I saw her glance back more than once towards the end of the long caravan that crept dolefully across the plains, five miles from its head to its tail.

The wagon at the rear of the column that carried the lighter wooden coffin was followed by a regiment of Shilluk. Their magnificent voices carried clearly to us at the head of the column as they sang the last farewell. I knew that Tanus would hear them and know for whom the song was sung.

WHEN WE at last reached the valley of the tomb, the golden coffin was placed beneath a tabernacle outside the entrance to the royal mausoleum. The linen roof of the tent was illuminated with texts and illustrations from the *Book of the Dead*.

There were to be two separate funerals. The first was the lesser, that of the Great Lion of Egypt. The second would be the grander and more elaborate royal funeral.

So it was that three days after our arrival at the valley, the wooden coffin was placed in the tomb that I had prepared for Tanus, and the tomb was consecrated by the priests of Horus, who was Tanus' patron, and then sealed.

During this ritual, my mistress was able to restrain her grief and to show nothing more than the decent sorrow of a queen towards a faithful servant, although I knew that inside her something was dying that would never be reborn.

All that night the valley resounded to the chant of the Shilluk regiment as they mourned for the man who had now become one of their gods. To this day they still shout his name in battle.

Ten days after the first funeral, the golden coffin was placed on its wooden sledge and dragged into the vast royal tomb. It required the efforts of three hundred slaves to manoeuvre the coffin through the passageways. I had designed the tomb so precisely that there was only the breadth of a hand between the sides and the lid of the coffin and the stone walls and roof.

To thwart all future grave-robbers and any others who would desecrate the royal tomb, I had built a labyrinth of tunnels beneath the mountain. From the entrance in the cliff-face, a wide passage led directly to an impressive burial vault that was decorated with marvellous murals. In the centre of this room stood an empty granite sarcophagus, with the lid removed and cast dramatically aside. The first grave-robber to enter here would believe that he was too late and that some other had plundered the tomb before him.

In fact, there was another tunnel leading off at right-angles from the entrance passage. The mouth of this was disguised as a store-room for the funerary treasure. The coffin had to be turned and eased into this secondary passage. From there it entered a maze of false passages and dummy burial vaults, each more serpentine and devious than the last.

In all there were four burial chambers, but three of these would remain forever empty. There were three hidden doors and two vertical shafts. The coffin had to be lifted up one of these, and lowered down the other.

It took fifteen days for the coffin to be inched through this maze, and installed at last in its final resting-place. The roof and walls of this tomb were painted with all the skill and genius with which the gods have gifted me. There was not a space the size of my thumbnail that was not blazing with colour and movement.

Five store-rooms led off from the chamber. Into these were packed that treasure which Pharaoh Mamose had accumulated over his lifetime, and which had come close to beggaring our very Egypt. I had argued with my mistress that, instead of being buried in the earth, this treasure should be used to pay for the army and the struggle that lay ahead of us in our efforts to expel the Hyksos tyrant and to liberate our people and our land.

'The treasure belongs to Pharaoh,' she had replied. 'We have built up another treasure of gold and slaves and ivory here in Cush. That will suffice. Let the divine Mamose have what is his – I have given him my oath on it.'

Thus on the fifteenth day, the golden coffin was placed within the stone sarcophagus that had been hewn out of the native rock. With a system of ropes and levers, the heavy lid was lifted over it and lowered into place.

The royal family and the priests and the nobles entered the tomb to perform the last rites.

My mistress and the prince stood at the head of the sarcophagus, and the priests droned on with their incantations and their readings from the *Book of the Dead*. The sooty smoke from the lamps and the breathing of the throng of people in the confined space soured the air, so it was soon difficult to breathe.

In the dim yellow light I saw my mistress turn pale and the perspiration bead on her forehead. I worked my way through the tightly packed ranks, and I reached her side just as she swayed and collapsed. I was able to catch her before she struck her head on the granite edge of the sarcophagus.

We carried her out of the tomb on a litter. In the fresh mountain air she recovered swiftly, but still I confined her to her bed in her tent for the rest of that day.

That night as I prepared her tonic of herbs, she lay quietly and thoughtfully, and after she had drunk the infusion she whispered to me, 'I had the most extraordinary sensation. As I stood in Pharaoh's tomb, I felt suddenly that Tanus was very close to me. I felt his hand touch my face and his voice murmur in my ear. That was when I fainted away.'

'He will always be close to you,' I told her.

'I believe that,' she said simply.

I can see now, though I could not see it then, that her decline began on the day that we laid Tanus in his grave. She had lost the joy of living and the will to go on.

I WENT back into the royal tomb the next day with the masons and the corps of slave labourers to seal the doorways and the shafts, and to arm the devices that would guard the burial chamber.

As we retreated through the maze of pasageways, we blocked the secret doorways with cunningly laid stone and plaster, and painted murals over them. We sealed the mouths of the vertical shafts so that they appeared to be smooth floor and roof.

I set rockfalls that would be triggered by a footstep on a loose paving slab, and I packed the vertical shafts with balks of timber. As these decayed over the centuries and the fungus devoured them, they would emit noxious vapours that would suffocate any intruder who succeeded in finding his way through the secret doorways.

But before we did all this, I went to the actual burial chamber to take leave of Tanus. I carried with me a long bundle wrapped in a linen sheet. When I stood for the last time beside the royal sarcophagus, I sent all the workmen away. I would be the very last to leave the tomb, and after me the entrance would be sealed.

When I was alone I opened the bundle I carried. From it I took the long bow, Lanata. Tanus had named it after my mistress and I had made it for him. It was a last gift from the two of us. I placed it upon the sealed stone lid of his coffin.

There was one other item in my bundle. It was the wooden *ushabti* figure that I had carved. I placed it at the foot of the sarcophagus. While

I carved it, I had set up three copper mirrors so that I could study my own features from every angle and reproduce them faithfully. The doll was a miniature Taita.

Upon the base I had inscribed the words: 'My name is Taita. I am a physician and a poet. I am an architect and a philosopher. I am your friend. I will answer for you.'

As I left the tomb, I paused at the entrance and looked back for the last time.

'Farewell, old friend,' I said. 'I am richer for having known you. Wait for us on the other side.'

IT TOOK me many months to complete the work on the royal tomb. As we retreated through the labyrinth, I personally inspected every sealed doorway and every secret device that we left behind us.

I was alone, for my mistress and the prince had gone up into the mountains to the fortress of Prester Beni-Jon. They had gone with all the court to prepare for the wedding of Memnon and Masara. Hui had accompanied them to select the horses from the Ethiopian herds that were part of our payment for the storming of Adbar Seged, and the recovery of Masara.

When at last my work in the tomb was completed and my workmen had sealed the outer entrance in the cliff-face, I also set off into the mountains, over those cold and windy passes. I was anxious not to miss the wedding feast, but I had left it late. The completion of the tomb had taken longer than I had planned. I travelled as hard as the horses could stand.

I reached Prester Beni-Jon's palace five days before the wedding, and I went directly to that part of the fortress where my mistress and her suite were lodged.

'I have not smiled since last I saw you, Taita,' she greeted me. 'Sing for me. Tell me your stories. Make me laugh.'

It was not an easy task she set me, for the melancholy had entered deeply into her soul, and the truth was that I was not myself cheerful or light-hearted. I sensed that more than sorrow alone was affecting her. Soon we abandoned our attempts at merriment, and fell to discussing affairs of state.

It might have been a love match, and a meeting of twin souls blessed by the gods as far as the two lovers were concerned, but for the rest of us, the joining of Memnon and Masara was a royal wedding and a contract between nations. There were agreements and treaties to negotiate, dowries to be decided, trade agreements to draw up between the King of Kings and ruler of Aksum, and the regent of Egypt and the wearer of the double crown of the two kingdoms.

As I had predicted, my mistress had been at first less than enchanted by the prospect of her only son marrying a woman of a different race.

'In all things they are different, Taita. The gods they worship, the language they speak, the colour of their skins – oh! I wish he had chosen a girl of our own people.'

'He will,' I reassured her. 'He will marry fifty, perhaps a hundred Egyptians. He will also marry Libyans and Hurrians and Hyksos. All the races and nations he conquers in the years to come will provide him with wives, Cushites and Hittites and Assyrians—'

'Stop your teasing, Taita.' She stamped her foot with something of her old fire. 'You know full well what I mean. Those others will all be marriages of state. This, his first, is a marriage of two hearts.'

What she said was true. The promise of love that Memnon and Masara had exchanged in those fleeting moments beside the river was now blossoming.

I was especially privileged to be close to them in these heady days. They both acknowledged and were grateful for my part in bringing them together. I was for both of them a friend of long standing, somebody that they trusted without question.

I did not share my mistress's misgivings. Though they were different in every way that she had listed, their hearts were turned from the same mould. They both possessed a sense of dedication, a fierceness of the spirit, a touch of the ruthlessness and the cruelty that a ruler must have. They were a matched pair, he the tiercel and she the falcon. I knew that she would not distract him from his destiny, but rather that she would encourage and incite him to greater endeavour. I was content with my efforts as a matchmaker.

One bright mountain day, watched by twenty thousand men and women of Ethiopia and of Egypt who crowded the slopes of the hills around them, Memnon and Masara stood together on the river-bank and broke the jar of water that the high priest of Osiris had scooped from the infant Nile.

The bride and the groom led our caravan down from the mountains, laden with the dowry of a princess and the treaties and the protocols of kinship sealed between our two nations.

Hui and his grooms drove a herd of five thousand horses behind us. Some of these were in payment for our mercenary services, and the rest made up Masara's dowry. However, before we reached the junction of the two rivers at Qebui, we saw the dark stain on the plains ahead as though a cloud had cast its shadow over the savannah – but the sun shone out of a cloudless sky.

The gnu herds had returned on their annual migration.

Within weeks of this contact with the gnu, the Yellow Strangler disease fell upon our herd of Ethiopian horses, and it swept through them like a flash-flood in one of the valleys of the high mountains.

Naturally, Hui and I had been expecting the plague to strike when the gnu returned, and we had made our preparations. We had trained every groom and charioteer to perform the tracheotomy, and to treat the wound with hot pitch to prevent mortification until the animal had a chance to recover from the Strangler.

For many weeks none of us enjoyed much sleep, but in the end, fewer than two thousand of our new horses died of the disease, and before the next flooding of the Nile, those that survived were strong enough to begin training in the chariot traces.

WHEN THE floods came, the priests sacrificed on the banks of the river, each to his own god, and they consulted the auguries for the year ahead. Some consulted the entrails of the sacrificial sheep, others watched the flight of the wild birds, still others stared into vessels filled with water from the Nile. They divined in their separate ways.

Queen Lostris sacrificed to Hapi. Although I attended the service with her and joined in the liturgy and the responses of the congregation, my heart was elsewhere. I am a Horus man, and so are Lord Kratas and Prince Memnon. We made a sacrifice of gold and ivory to our god and prayed for guidance.

It is not usual for the gods to agree with each other, any more than it is for men to do so. However, this year was different from any other that I had known. With the exception of the gods Anubis and Thoth and the goddess Nut, the heavenly host spoke with one voice. Those three, Anubis and Thoth and Nut, are all lesser deities. Their counsel could be safely discounted. All the great gods, Ammon-Ra and Osiris and Horus and Hapi and Isis and two hundred others, both great and small, gave the same counsel: 'The time has come for the return to the holy black earth of *Kemit*.'

Lord Kratas, who is a pagan at heart and a cynic by nature, suggested that the entire priesthood had conspired to place these words in the mouths of their patron gods. Although I expressed shocked indignation at this blasphemy, I was secretly inclined to agree with Kratas' opinion.

The priests are soft and luxurious men, and for almost two decades we had lived the hard lives of wanderers and warriors in the wild land of Cush. I think they hungered for fair Thebes even more than did my mistress. Perhaps it was not gods, but men who had given this advice to return northwards.

Queen Lostris summoned the high council of state, and when she made the proclamation that endorsed the dictates of the gods, the nobles and the priests stood and cheered her to a man. I cheered as loud and as long as any of them, and that night my dreams were filled with visions of Thebes, and images of those far-off days when Tanus and Lostris and I had been young and happy.

SINCE THE death of Tanus, there had been no supreme commander of our armies, and the war council met in secret conclave. Of course, I was excluded from this assembly, but my mistress repeated to me every word that was spoken.

After long argument and debate, the command was offered to Kratas. He stood before them, grizzled and scarred like an old lion, and he laughed that great laugh of his and he said, 'I am a soldier. I follow. I do not lead. Give me the command of the Shilluk, and I will follow one man to the borders of death and beyond.' He drew his sword then and pointed with it at the prince. 'That is the man I will follow. Hail, Memnon! May he live for ever.'

'May he live for ever!' they shouted, and my mistress smiled. She and I had arranged exactly this outcome.

At the age of twenty-two years Prince Memnon was elevated to the rank of Great Lion of Egypt and commander of all her armies. Immediately he began to plan the Return.

Though my rank was only that of Master of the Royal Horse, I was on Prince Memnon's staff. Often he appealed to me to solve the logistical problems that we encountered. During the day I drove his chariot with the blue pennant fluttering over our heads as he reviewed the regiments, and led them in exercises of war.

Many nights the three of us, the prince and Kratas and I, sat up late over a jar of wine as we discussed the Return. On those nights Princess Masara waited upon us, filling the cups with her own graceful brown hand. Then she sat on a sheep-skin cushion at Memnon's feet and listened to every word. When our eyes met, she smiled at me.

Our main concern was to avoid the hazardous and onerous transit of all the cataracts on the way down-river. These could only be navigated in flood season, and would thus limit the periods in which we could travel.

I proposed that we build another fleet of barges below the fifth cataract;

with these we could transport our army down to the departure-point for the desert crossing of the great bight. When we regained the river above the first cataract, we would rebuild another squadron of fast fighting galleys and barges to carry us down to Elephantine.

I was sure that if we timed it correctly, and if we could shoot the rapids and surprise the Hyksos fleet anchored in the roads of Elephantine, we would be able to deal the enemy a painful blow and capture the galleys we needed to augment our force of fighting ships. Once we had secured a foothold, we would then be able to bring down our infantry and our chariots through the gorge of the first cataract, and engage the Hyksos on the flood-plains of Egypt.

We began the first stage of the Return the following flood season. At Qebui, which had been our capital seat for so many years, we left only a garrison force. Qebui would become merely a trading outpost of the empire. The riches of Cush and Ethiopia would flow northwards to Thebes through this entrepôt.

When the main fleet sailed back into the north, Hui and I, with five hundred grooms and a squadron of chariots, remained behind to await the return of the gnu migration. They came as suddenly as they always did, a vast black stain spreading over the golden savannah grasslands. We went out to meet them in the chariots.

It was a simple matter to capture these ungainly brutes. We ran them down with the chariots, and dropped a noose of rope over their ugly heads as we ran alongside them. The gnu lacked the speed and the spirit of our horses. They fought the ropes only briefly and then resigned themselves to capture. Within ten days, we had penned over six thousand of them in the stockades on the bank of the Nile which we had built for this purpose.

It was here in the stockades that their lack of stamina and strength was most apparent. Without cause or reason, they died in their hundreds. We treated them kindly and gently. We fed them and watered them as we would our horses. It was as though their wild wandering spirits would not be fettered, and they pined away.

In the end we lost over half of those that we had captured, and many more died on the long voyage to the north.

TWO FULL years after Queen Lostris had commanded the Return, our people assembled on the east bank of the Nile above the fourth cataract. Before us lay the desert road across the great bight of the river.

For the whole of the previous year the caravans of wagons had set out from here. Each of them had been laden with clay jars filled to the brim with Nile water, and sealed with wooden plugs and hot pitch. Every ten miles along the dusty road we had set up watering stations. At each of these, thirty thousand water jars had been buried to prevent them cracking and bursting in the rays of that furious sun.

We were nearly fifty thousand souls and as many animals, including my dwindling herd of captured gnu. The water-carts set out from the river each evening. Their task was unending.

We waited on the river-bank for the rise of the new moon to light our way across the wilderness. Although we had planned our departure for this the coolest season of the year, still the heat and the sun would be deadly to both man and beast. We would travel only at night.

Two days before we were due to begin the crossing, my mistress said, 'Taita, when did you and I last spend a day together fishing on the river? Make ready your fish-spears and a skiff.'

I knew that she had something of deep import that she wished to discuss with me. We drifted down on those green waters until I could moor the skiff to a willow tree on the far bank, where we were out of earshot of the inquisitive.

First we spoke of the imminent departure along the desert road, and the prospects of the return to Thebes.

'When will I see her shining walls again, Taita?' my mistress sighed, and I could only tell her that I did not know.

'If the gods are kind, we might be in Elephantine by this time next season when the Nile flood carries our ships down the first cataract. After that, our fortunes will ebb and flow like the river, with the hazards and fortunes of war.'

However, this was not what she had brought me out on to the river to discuss, and now her eyes swam with tears as she asked, 'How long has Tanus been gone from us, Taita?'

My voice choked as I answered, 'He set out on his journey to the fields of paradise over three years ago, mistress.'

'So it is longer than that by many months that I last lay in his arms,' she mused, and I nodded. I was uncertain in which direction her questions were leading us.

'I have dreamed of him almost every night since then, Taita. Is it possible that he might have returned to leave his seed in my womb while I still slept?'

'All things in heaven are possible,' I replied carefully. 'We told the people that was how Tehuti and Bekatha were conceived. However, in all truth and seriousness, I have never heard of it happening before.'

We were both silent for a while, and she trailed her hand in the water and then lifted it to watch the drops fall from her fingertips. Then she spoke again without looking at me. 'I think I am to have another child,' she whispered, 'My red moon has waned and withered away.'

'Mistress,' I answered her quietly, and with tact, 'you are approaching that time of your life when the rivers of your womb will begin to dry up.' Our Egyptian women are like desert flowers that bloom early but fade as swiftly.

She shook her head. 'No, Taita. It is not that. I feel the infant growing within me.'

I stared at her silently. Once again I felt the wings of tragedy brush lightly past me, stirring the air and raising the hair upon my forearms.

'You do not have to ask me if I have known another man.' This time she looked directly into my eyes as she spoke. 'You know that I have not.'

'This I know full well. Yet I cannot believe that you have been impregnated by a ghost, no matter how beloved and welcome that ghost might be. Perhaps your desire for another child has fathered your imagination.'

'Feel my womb, Taita,' she commanded. 'This is a living thing within me. Each day it grows.'

'I will do so tonight, in the privacy of your cabin. Not here upon the river where prying eyes might discover us.'

MY MISTRESS lay naked upon the linen sheets, and I studied first her face and then her body. When I looked upon her with the eyes of a man, she was still lovely to me, but as a physician I could see clearly how the years and the hardships of this life in the wilderness had wrought their cruel change. Her hair was more silver than sable now, and bereavement and the cares of the regency had chiselled their grim message on her brow. She was growing old.

Her body was the vessel which had given life to three other lives. But her breasts were empty now, there was none of the milk of a new pregnancy swelling them. She was thin. I should have noticed that before. It was an unnatural thinness, almost an emaciation. Yet her belly protruded like a pale ivory ball out of proportion to those slim arms and legs.

I laid my hands lightly upon her belly, upon the silvery streaks where the skin had once stretched to accommodate a joyful burden. I felt the thing within her and I knew at once that this was not life beneath my fingers. This was death.

I could not find words. I turned away from her and went out on to the deck and I looked up at the night stars. They were cold and very far away. Like the gods, they did not care. There was no profit in appealing to them, gods or stars.

I knew this thing that was growing within my mistress. I had felt it in the bodies of other women. When they died, I had opened the dead womb and seen the thing that had killed them. It was horrible and deformed, bearing no resemblance to anything human or even animal. It was a shapeless ball of red and angry flesh. It was a thing of Seth.

It was a long time before I could gather the courage to return to the cabin.

My mistress had covered herself with a robe. She sat in the centre of the bed and looked at me with those huge, dark green eyes that had never aged. She looked like the little girl I once had known.

'Mistress, why did you not tell me about the pain?' I asked gently.

'How do you know about the pain?' she whispered back. 'I tried to hide it from you.'

OUR CARAVAN set out into the desert, travelling by moonlight across the silver sands. Sometimes my mistress walked at my side, and the two princesses frolicked along with us, laughing and excited by the adventure. At other times, when the pain was bad, my mistress rode in the wagon that I had equipped for her comfort. Then I sat beside her and held her hand until the powder of the sleeping-flower worked its magic and gave her surcease.

Every night we travelled just as far as the next watering-station along the road that was now well beaten by the thousands of vehicles that had preceded us. During the long days we lay beneath the awning of the wagon and drowsed in the sweltering heat.

We had been thirty days and nights upon the road when in the dawn we saw a remarkable sight. A disembodied sail upon the desert, moving gently southwards over the sands. It was not until we had journeyed on for many more miles that we saw how we had been deceived. The hull of the galley had been hidden from us by the bank of the Nile, and below the dunes the river ran on eternally. We had crossed the loop.

Prince Memnon and all his staff were there to greet us. Already the squadron of new galleys had almost completed fitting out. It was the sail of one of these that we had first descried as we approached the river again. Every plank and mast had been cut and sawn on the great plains of Cush, and transported across the loop of the river. All the chariots were assembled. Hui had herded all the horses across the desert, and the wagons had carried their fodder with them. Even my gnu were waiting in their stockades upon the river-bank.

Although the wagon caravans carrying the women and the children still followed, the main body of our nation had been brought across. It had been an undertaking that almost defied belief, a labour of godlike proportions. Only men like Kratas and Remrem and Memnon could have accomplished it in so short a time.

Now only the first cataract still stood between us and the sacred earth of our very Egypt.

We went on northwards again. My mistress sailed in the new barge that had been built for her and the princesses. There was a large and airy cabin for her, and I had equipped it with every luxury that was available to us. The hangings were of embroidered Ethiopian wool, and the furniture was of dark acacia wood inlaid with ivory and the gold of Cush. I decorated the bulkheads with paintings of flowers and birds and other pretty things.

As always, I slept at the foot of my mistress's bed. Three nights after we sailed, I woke in the night. She was weeping silently. Although she had stifled her sobs with a pillow, the shaking of her shoulders had awakened me. I went to her immediately.

'The pain has come again?' I asked.

'I did not mean to wake you, but it is like a sword in my belly.'

I mixed her a draught of the sleeping-flower, stronger than I had ever given to her before. The pain was beginning to triumph over the flower.

She drank it and lay quietly for a while. Then she said, 'Can you not cut this thing out of my body, Taita?'

'No, mistress. I cannot.'

'Then hold me, Taita. Hold me the way you used to do when I was a little girl.'

I went into her bed, and I took her in my arms. I cradled her, and she was as thin and light as a child. I rocked her tenderly, and after a while she slept.

THE FLEET reached the head of the first cataract above Elephantine, and we moored against the bank in the quiet flow of the river before the Nile felt the urging of the cascades and plunged into the gorge.

We waited for the rest of the army to be ferried down to us, all the horses and the chariots and Lord Kratas' pagan Shilluk regiments. We waited also for the Nile to rise and open the cataract for us to pass down into Egypt.

While we waited, we sent spies down through the gorge. They were dressed as peasants and priests and merchants with goods to trade. I went down with Kratas into the gorge to map and mark the passage. Now, at low water, every hazard was exposed. We painted channel-markers on the rocks above the high-water line, so that even when the flood covered them, we would still know where those obstacles lurked.

We were many weeks at this labour, and when we returned to where the fleet was moored, the army was assembled there. We sent out scouting parties to find a route for the chariots and the horses through the rock desert down into Egypt. We could not risk such a precious cargo to the wild waters of the cataract.

Our spies began to return from Elephantine. They came in secretly and singly, usually in the night. They brought us the very first news of our mother-land that we had heard in all the years of exile.

King Salitis still reigned, but he was old now, and his beard had turned silver-white. His two sons were the mighty men of the Hyksos legions. Prince Beon commanded the infantry and Prince Apachan commanded the chariots.

The might of the Hyksos exceeded all our estimates. Our spies reported that Apachan disposed of twelve thousand chariots. We had brought down only four thousand from Cush. Beon had forty thousand archers and infantry. Even with Kratas' Shilluk, we could muster only fifteen thousand. We were heavily outnumbered.

There was cheering news also. The great bulk of the Hyksos force was held in the Delta, and Salitis had made his capital at the city of Memphis. It would take months for him to move his forces south to Elephantine and Thebes. He would not be able to bring his chariots up-river until the floods abated and the land dried. There was only a single squadron of chariots guarding the city of Elephantine, one hundred chariots to oppose our entry. They were of the old solid-wheel type. It seemed that the Hyksos had not yet perfected the spoked wheel.

Prince Memnon laid out his battle plan for us. We would pass through the cataract on the flood, and seize Elephantine. Then, while Salitis moved southwards to oppose us, we would march on Thebes, raising the populace in insurrection as we went.

We could expect Salitis to give battle with his full army on the floodplains before Thebes, once the Nile waters had subsided. By then we could hope that the disparity in the numbers of the two armies would be redressed in part by the Egyptian troops that would rally to our standard.

We learned from our spies that the Hyksos did not suspect the presence of our army of liberation so close to their border, and that we could expect to gain the element of surprise with our first assault. We learned also that Salitis had adopted our Egyptian way of life. These days he lived in our palaces and worshipped our gods. Even his old Sutekh had changed his name to Seth, and was, very appropriately, still his principal god.

Although all his senior officers were Hyksos, many of Salitis' captains and sergeants had been recruited from amongst the Egyptians, and half the common soldiers were of our own nation. Most of these would have been infants or not yet born at the time of our exodus. We wondered where their loyalties would lie, when Prince Memnon led our army down into Egypt.

All was in readiness now. The scouts had marked a road through the desert of the west bank, and the water wagons had laid down stores of fodder and water jars along the length of it, enough to see our chariots through to the fertile plains of our very Egypt. Our galleys were rigged and manned for battle. When the Nile flooded, we would sail, but in the meantime there was one last ritual to complete.

We climbed the bluff above the river to where the obelisk that my mistress had raised over two decades before, still stood, a tall and elegant finger of stone pointing into the cloudless blue of the African sky.

My mistress was too weak to climb the rugged pathway to the summit. Ten slaves carried her up in a sedan-chair, and set her down below the tall monument. She walked painfully slowly to the foot of the pillar on the arm of Prince Memnon, and gazed up at the inscription carved in the granite. Our whole nation watched her, all those souls who had found their way back to this point from which we had set out so long ago.

My mistress read the inscription aloud. Her voice was soft, but still so musical that it carried clearly to where I stood behind the great lords and the generals.

'I, Queen Lostris, Regent of Egypt and widow of Pharaoh Mamose, the eighth of that name, mother of the Crown Prince Memnon, who shall rule the two kingdoms after me, have ordained the raising of this monument . . .'

When she had finished the reading, she turned to face her people and spread her arms.

'I have done that which was required of me,' she said, and her voice regained some of its old power. 'I have led you back to the border of your land. My task is completed and I relinquish the regency.' She paused, and for a moment her eyes met mine over the heads of the nobles. I nodded slightly to encourage her, and she went on.

'Citizens of Egypt, it is fitting that you have a true Pharaoh to lead you the last steps of the way home. I give to you the divine Pharaoh Tamose, who once was the Crown Prince Memnon. May he live for ever!'

'May he live for ever!' the nation roared in one voice. 'May he live for ever!'

Pharaoh Tamose stepped forward to face his people. 'May he live for ever!' they shouted the third time, and our new pharaoh drew the blue sword from its jewelled scabbard and saluted them with it.

In the silence that followed, his voice rang and echoed from the gaunt red crags of the hills.

'I take up this sacred trust. I swear on my hope of eternal life to serve my people and my land all my days. I shall not flinch from this duty, and I call upon all the gods to witness my oath.'

THE FLOOD came. The waters rose up the rocks that guarded the entrance to the gorge, and the colour changed from green to grey. The cataract began to growl like a beast in its lair and the spray-cloud rose into the sky and stood as high as the hills that flanked the Nile.

I went aboard the leading galley with Lord Kratas and Pharaoh. We dropped our mooring and shoved off into the stream. The rowers on the benches were stripped to their breech-clouts, their faces turned up to watch Kratas as he stood high in the stern, gripping the steering-oar in his bear-like fists.

In the bows two teams of sailors under the king stood ready with heavy oars to fend off. I stood beside Kratas, with the map of the rapids spread on the deck in front of me, ready to call the twists and turns of the channel to him as we came to them. I did not really need the map, for I had memorized every line drawn upon it. In addition to which, I had stationed reliable men on the sides of the gorge and on the islands in the main stream ahead of us. They would use signal flags to show us the way through.

As the current quickened beneath our keel, I cast one last glance backwards and saw the rest of the squadron fall into line astern behind us, ready to follow us down the cataract. Then I looked forward again, and felt the fist of fear tighten on my bowels so that I was forced to squeeze my buttocks together. Ahead of us the gorge smoked like the mouth of a furnace.

Our speed built up with deceptive stealth. The rowers touched the surface lightly with the blades of the oars, just enough to keep our bows pointed downstream. We floated so lightly and so smoothly that we seemed to be drifting. It was only when I looked at the banks, and saw them streaming past us, that I realized how fast we were running. The rock portals of the gorge flew to meet us. None the less, it was only when I noticed the grin on Kratas' craggy face that I realized the true danger of what we were attempting. Kratas only grinned like that when he saw death crook a bony finger at him.

'Come on, you rogues!' he shouted at his crew. 'This day I'll make your mothers proud of you, or I'll find work for the embalmers.'

The river was split by three islands, and the channel narrowed.

'Bear to port, and steer for the blue cross,' I tried to sound casual, but at that moment I felt the deck tip beneath my feet, and I clutched at the rail.

We flew down a chute of grey water, and our bows swung giddily. I thought that we were already out of control, and waited for the crunch of rock and for the deck to burst open beneath my feet. Then I saw the bows steady, and the blue cross painted on the wall of rock was dead ahead.

'Hard to starboard as we come up to the flag!' my voice squeaked, but I picked out the man on the centre island flagging us into the turn, and Kratas put the steering-oar over and yelled at the benches, 'All back right, pull together left!' The deck canted sharply as we spun into the turn.

The wall of rock flashed past us, and we were going at the speed of a galloping horse. One more turn and the first rapids lay ahead. Black rock stood across our path, and the waters piled upon it. The water took on the shape of the rocks beneath it. It bulged and stood in tall static waves. It opened into smooth green gulleys. It curled upon itself and exploded into veils of white through which the rock snarled at us with black fangs. My stomach clenched as we leaped over the edge and dropped down the slope. At the bottom we wallowed and spun, like a stalk of dry grass in a whirlwind.

'Pull left!' Kratas bellowed. 'Pull till your balls bounce!' We steadied and aimed for the next gap in the rock, and the white water dashed over the deck and into my eyes. It hissed alongside, running in tandem with us, and the waves stood taller than our poop-deck.

'By Seth's tattered and festering foreskin, I've not had so much sport since I tupped my first ewe!' Kratas laughed, and the rock sprang at us like a charging bull elephant.

We touched once, and the rock rasped along our belly. The deck shuddered beneath our feet, and I was too afraid to scream. Then Memnon's team poled us free and we raced on down.

Behind us I heard the shattering crash as one of the other galleys struck hard. I dared not look round as I judged our next turn, but soon there were wreckage and the heads of drowning men bobbing and swirling in the torrent on both sides of us. They screamed to us as they were borne away and dashed upon the spurs of rock, but we could offer them no succour. Death pressed hard upon our heels and we ran on with the stench of it in our nostrils.

In that hour I lived a hundred lives, and died in every one of them. But at last we were hurled from the bottom of the cataract into the main body of the river. Of the twenty-three galleys that had entered the gorge, eighteen followed us out. The others had been smashed to flotsam, and the corpses of their drowned crew washed down beside us in the grey Nile flood.

There was not time for us to celebrate our deliverance. Dead ahead lay the Island of Elephantine, and on both banks of the river stood the well-remembered walls and buildings of the city.

'Archers, string your bows!' King Tamose called from the bows. 'Hoist the blue pennant! Drummer, increase the beat to attack speed!'

Our tiny squadron flew into the mass of shipping that clogged the roads of Elephantine. Most of it was made up of trade barges and transports. We passed these by, and went for the Hyksos galleys. The Hyksos had manned their fighting ships with Egyptian sailors, for nobody knew the river better. Only their officers were Hyksos. Most of them were ashore, carousing in the pleasure-palaces of the docks.

Our spies had told us which was the flag of the southern admiral, a swallowtail of scarlet and gold so long that the end of it dipped in the water. We steered for the ship that flew her, and Memnon boarded her over the side with twenty men at his back.

'Freedom from the Hyksos tyrant!' they roared. 'Stand up for this very Egypt!'

The crew gaped at them. They had been taken completely by surprise, and most of them were unarmed. Their weapons were locked away below decks, for the Hyksos officers trusted them not at all.

The other galleys of our squadron had each picked out one of the enemy fighting-ships and boarded it as swiftly. On all of them the reaction of the crew was the same. After the first surprise they shouted the question, 'Who are you?'

And the reply was, 'Egyptian! The army of the true Pharaoh Tamose. Join with us, countrymen! Cast out the tyrant!'

They turned on their Hyksos officers and cut them down before we could reach them. Then they embraced our men, roaring out a welcome.

'For Egypt!' they cheered. 'For Tamose! For Egypt and Tamose!'

The cheering jumped from ship to ship. Men danced upon the rails and swarmed up the masts to tear down the Hyksos banners. They broke open the arms stores and passed out bows and swords.

Then they poured ashore. They dragged the Hyksos from the taverns and hacked them to bloody shreds, so that the gutters discharged a scarlet flood into the harbour waters. They ran through the streets to the barracks of the garrison, and fell upon the guard.

'For Egypt and Tamose!' they chanted.

Some of the Hyksos officers rallied their men, and held out for a while in pockets surrounded by the rabble. Then Kratas and Memnon came ashore with their veterans, and within two hours the city was ours.

Most of the Hyksos chariots were abandoned in their lines, but half a squadron was escaping through the east gate and galloping away over the causeway that crossed the inundated fields to the dry ground beyond.

I had left the ship and hurried through the back alleys, that I knew so well, to the north tower on the city walls. From there I knew I would have the best view over the city and the surrounding countryside. Bitterly, I watched the escaping detachment of chariots. Every one that got away now would have to be fought later, and I wanted those horses. I was about to turn away and watch what was happening in the city below me, when I saw a little finger of dust rising from the foot of the harsh southern hills.

I shaded my eyes and stared at it. I felt the quickening of excitement. The dust was coming towards us swiftly, I could make out the dark shapes beneath it.

'By Horus, it's Remrem!' I whispered with delight. The old warrior had brought the first division of chariots through the bad ground of the hills quicker than I would have believed possible. It was only two days since we had parted.

I watched with professional pride as the first division opened from columns of four into line abreast. Hui and I had trained them well. It was perfectly done, and Remrem had the Hyksos in enfilade. Half their vehicles were still on the causeway. It seemed to me that the enemy commander was not even aware of the massed squadrons bearing down upon his exposed flank. I think he must still have been looking back over his shoulder. At the very last moment he tried to swing into line abreast to meet Remrem's charge, but it was far too late. He would have done better to have turned tail and run for it.

Remrem's chariots poured over him in a wave, and he was washed away like debris in the stream of the Nile. I watched until I was certain that Remrem had captured most of the Hyksos horses, and only then did I sigh with relief and turn to look down into the city.

The populace had gone wild with the joy of liberation. They were dancing through the streets, waving any piece of blue cloth that came to hand. Blue was the colour of Pharaoh Tamose. The women tied blue ribbons in their hair, and the men wound blue sashes around their waists and tied on blue arm-bands.

There was still some isolated fighting, but gradually the surviving Hyksos were cut down or dragged from the buildings they were trying to defend. One of the barracks with several hundred men still inside it was put to the torch. I heard the screams of the men as they burned, and soon the aroma of scorched flesh drifted up to me. It smelled like roasting pork.

Of course there was looting, and some of our upstanding citizens broke into the taverns and the wine shops and carried the jars out into the street. When one of the jars broke, they went down on all fours and guzzled the wine out of the gutter like hogs.

I saw three men chase a girl down the alley below where I stood. When they caught her they threw her down and ripped her skirt away. Two of them pinned her limbs and held her spread-eagled while the third man mounted her. I did not watch the rest of it.

As soon as Memnon and Kratas had stamped out the last pockets of Hyksos resistance, they set about restoring order to the city. Squads of disciplined troops trotted through the streets, using the shafts of their war spears as clubs to beat sense into the drunken and delirious mob.

Memnon ordered a handful of those taken in the act of rape and looting to be strangled on the spot, and their corpses were hung by the heels from the city gates. By nightfall the city was quiet, and decent men and women could once more safely walk her streets.

Memnon set up his headquarters in Pharaoh Mamose's palace, which had once been our home on Elephantine Island. The moment I stepped ashore I hurried to our old quarters in the harem.

They were still luxuriously appointed and had escaped the looters. Whoever had occupied them had treated my murals with the respect they warranted. The water-garden was a profusion of lovely plants, and the ponds were filled with fish and lotus. The Egyptian gardener told me that the Hyksos garrison commander who had lived here had admired our Egyptian ways, and had tried to ape them. I was thankful for that.

Within days I had restored the rooms and garden to a state in which they were once more fit to receive my mistress. Then I went to Memnon to ask permission to bring the queen home.

Pharaoh was distracted by the burden of taking firm hold of his kingdom. There were ten thousand matters that demanded his attention, but he put them aside for the moment and embraced me.

'It all goes well, Tata.'

'A happy return, Your Majesty,' I replied, 'but there is still so much to do.'

'It is my royal command that when you and I are alone like this, you continue to call me Mem.' He smiled at me, 'But you are right, there is much to do, and little time left to us before Salitis and all his host marches up from the Delta to oppose us. We have won the first little skirmish. The great battles lie ahead of us.'

'There is one duty that will give me great pleasure, Mem. I have prepared quarters for the queen mother. May I go up-river and bring her home to Elephantine? She has waited too long already to set foot on Egyptian soil.'

'Leave at once, Tata,' he commanded, 'and bring Queen Masara down with you.'

The river was too high and the desert road too rough. One hundred slaves carried the litters of the two queens along the banks of the Nile, through the gorge and down into our green valley.

It was not pure coincidence that the first building we came to as we crossed the border was a small temple. I had planned our route to bring us here.

'What shrine is this, Taita?' my mistress drew aside the curtain of her litter to ask.

'It is the temple of the god Akh-Horus, mistress. Do you wish to pray here?'

'Thank you,' she whispered. She knew what I had done. I helped her down from the litter, and she leaned heavily upon me as we entered the cool gloom of the stone building.

We prayed together, and I felt certain that Tanus was listening to the voices of the two people in all the world who had loved him most. Before we went on, my mistress ordered me to hand over all the gold that we had with us to the priests, and promised to send more for the upkeep and the beautification of the temple.

By the time we reached the Palace of Elephantine, she was exhausted. Each day the thing in her womb grew larger as it fed upon her wasting body. I laid her on a couch under the barrazza in the water-garden, and she closed her eyes and rested for a while. Then she opened them again and smiled at me softly. 'We were happy here once, but will I ever see Thebes again before I die?' I could not answer her. It was idle to make promises to her that were not mine to keep.

'If I die before that, will you promise to take me back and build me a tomb in the hills from where I can look across and see my beautiful city?'

'That I promise you with all my heart,' I replied.

IN THE days that followed, Aton and I resuscitated our old spider's web of spies and informers across the Upper Kingdom. Many of those who had once worked for us were long dead, but there were also many who were not. With the bait of gold and patriotism, they recruited other younger spies in every village and city.

Soon we had spies in the palace of the Hyksos satrap in Thebes, and others as far north as the Delta of the Lower Kingdom. Through them we learned which Hyksos regiments were billeted in each town, and which of them were on the march. We learned their strength, and the names and foibles of their commanders. We had an exact count of the numbers of their ships and their chariots, and as the flood-waters of the Nile receded, we were able to follow the southward movement of this huge mass of men and fighting machines, as King Salitis marched on Thebes.

I smuggled secret messages in the name of Pharaoh Tamose to those Egyptians in the regiments of the enemy, urging them to revolt. They started to trickle in through our lines, bringing more valuable intelligence with them. Soon the trickle of deserters from the Hyksos armies became a flood. Two full regiments of archers came marching in under arms, with the blue banner waving over them, and chanting, 'Egypt and Tamose!'

The crews of a hundred fighting galleys mutinied and slew their Hyksos officers. When they came sailing up-river to join us, they drove before them a fleet of barges that they had captured in the port of Thebes. These were laden with grain and oil and salt and flax and timber, all the sinews of war.

By this time, all our own forces were down through the cataract and deployed around the city, except only the small herd of tame gnu. These I had left until the very last. From my lookout in the north tower, I could see the horse-lines extending for miles along both banks, and the smoke from the cooking-fires of the regimental encampments turned the air blue.

Each day we were growing stronger, and the whole of Egypt was in a ferment of excitement and anticipation. The heady aroma of freedom perfumed each breath we drew. *Kemit* was a nation in the process of rebirth. They sang the patriotic anthems in the streets and the taverns, and the harlots and the wine merchants grew fat.

Aton and I, poring over our maps and secret despatches, saw a different picture emerging. We saw the Hyksos giant shaking itself awake, and stretching out a mailed fist towards us. From Memphis and every city and town in the Delta, King Salitis' regiments were on the march. Every road was crowded with his chariots, and the river ran with his shipping. All of this was moving south upon Thebes.

I waited until I knew that Lord Apachan, the commander of the Hyksos chariots, had reached Thebes and was encamped outside the city walls with all his vehicles and all his horses. Then I went before the war council of Pharaoh Tamose.

'Your Majesty, I have come to report that the enemy now have one hundred and twenty thousand horses and twelve thousand chariots massed at Thebes. Within two months, the Nile will have subsided to the level that will enable Apachan to begin his final advance.'

Even Kratas looked grave. 'We have known worse odds—' he began, but the king cut him short.

'I can tell by his face that the Master of the Royal Horse has more to tell us. Am I right, Taita?'

'Pharaoh is always right,' I agreed. 'I beg your permission to bring down my gnu from above the cataract.'

Kratas laughed. 'By Seth's bald head, Taita, do you intend riding out against the Hyksos on one of those clownish brutes of yours?' I laughed with him politely. His sense of humour has the same subtlety as that of the savage Shilluk he commands.

The next morning Hui and I set off up-river to bring down the gnu. By this time there were only three hundred of these sorry creatures left alive out of the original six thousand, but they were quite tame and could be fed from the hand. We herded them down at a gentle pace, so as not to weaken them further.

The horses that Remrem had captured in that first brief battle with the escaping Hyksos chariots had on my orders been kept separated from our own horses that we had brought down with us from Cush. Hui and I moved the gnu into the same pasture with them, and after the first uneasiness between the two species, they were all feeding peaceably together. That night we penned gnu and Hyksos horses in the same stockade. I left Hui to watch over them and returned to the palace on Elephantine Island.

I will admit now to a great deal of uncertainty and worry over the days that followed. I had invested so much faith in the success of this ruse, which, after all, depended on a natural event that I did not fully understand. If it failed, we would be faced with the full fury of an enemy that outnumbered us by at least four to one.

I had worked late with Aton and had fallen asleep over my scrolls in the palace library, when I was shaken awake by uncouth hands, and Hui was shouting in my ear. 'Come on, you lazy old rascal! Wake up! I have something for you.'

He had horses waiting at the landing. We hurried to them as soon as the ferry put us ashore, and mounted up. We galloped all the way along the river-bank in the moonlight, and rode into the horse-lines with our mounts in a lather. The grooms had lamps lit and were working in the stockade by their feeble yellow light.

Seven of the Hyksos horses were down already with the thick yellow pus pouring from their mouths and nostrils. The grooms were cutting into their windpipes and placing the hollow reeds to save them from choking and suffocating.

'It worked!' Hui shouted, and seized me in a coarse embrace and danced me in a circle. 'The Yellow Strangler! It worked! It worked!'

'I thought of it, didn't I?' I told him with all the dignity that his antics allowed me. 'Of course it worked.'

The barges had been moored against the bank these weeks past, ready for this day. We loaded the horses immediately, all of those who could still stand upright. The gnu we left in the stockade. Their presence would be too difficult to explain where we were going.

With one of the captured Hyksos galleys towing each of the barges, we rowed out into the current and turned northwards. With fifty oars a side and the wind and current behind us, we made good speed as we hurried down to Thebes to deliver our gift to Lord Apachan.

AS SOON as we passed Kom-Ombo we lowered the blue flag, and hoisted captured Hyksos banners. Most of the crew of the galleys that were towing the barges had been born under Hyksos rule, some of them were of mixed parentage and spoke the foreign language with colloquial fluency.

Two nights north of Kom-Ombo, we were hailed by a Hyksos galley. They laid alongside and sent a boarding party over to inspect our cargo.

'Horses for the chariots of Lord Apachan,' our captain told them. His father was Hyksos but his mother was an Egyptian noblewoman. His deportment was natural and his credentials convincing. After a cursory inspection they passed us through. We were stopped and boarded twice more before we reached Thebes, but each time our captain was able to deceive the Hyksos officers who came aboard.

My chief concern by this time was the state of the horses. Despite our best efforts, they were beginning to die, and half of those still alive were in a pitiful condition. We threw the carcasses overboard, and ran on northwards at our best speed.

My original plan had been to sell the horses to the Hyksos quartermasters in the port of Thebes, but no man who knew horseflesh would look at this pitiful herd. Hui and I decided upon another course.

We timed the last leg of our voyage to arrive at Thebes as the sun was setting. My heart ached as I recognized all the familiar landmarks. The walls of the citadel glowed pinkly in the last rays of the sun. Those three elegant towers that I had built for Lord Intef still pointed to the sky, they were aptly named the Fingers of Horus.

The Palace of Memnon on the west bank, which I had left uncompleted, had been rebuilt by the Hyksos. Even I had to admit that the Asiatic influence was pleasing. In this light the spires and watch-towers were endowed with a mysterious and exotic quality. I wished that my mistress was there to share this moment of homecoming with me. We had both longed for it over half her lifetime.

In the fading light we were still able to make out the vast concourse of men and horses and chariots and wagons that lay outside the city walls. Although I had received accurate reports, it had not been possible to visualize such multitudes. My spirits quailed as I looked upon them, and remembered the gallant little army I had left at Elephantine.

We would need every favour of the gods, and more than a little good fortune to triumph against such a host. As the last light faded into night, the fires of the Hyksos bloomed and twinkled upon the plain, like a field of stars. There was no end to them – they stretched away to the limit of the eye.

As we sailed closer, we smelled them. There is a peculiar odour that a standing army exudes. It is a blend of many smells, of dung-fires and of cooking food, the sweet smell of new-cut hay and the ammoniacal smell of the horses, and the stench of human sewage in open pits, of leather and pitch and horse-sweat and woodshavings and sour beer. Most of all it is the smell of men, tens of thousands of men, living close to each other in tents and huts and hovels.

We sailed on, and the sounds floated across the star-lit waters to our silent ship; the snort and the whinny of horses, the sound of the coppersmiths' hammers on the anvil beating out spear-heads and blades, the challenges of the sentries, and the voices of men singing and arguing and laughing.

I stood beside the captain on the deck of the leading galley and guided him in towards the east bank. I remembered the wharf of the timber merchants outside the city walls. If it still stood, it would be the best point at which to disembark our herd.

I picked out the entrance to the dock, and we pushed in under oars. The wharf was exactly as I remembered it. As we came alongside, the harbour-master came fussing on board, demanding our papers and our licence to trade.

I fawned upon him, bowing and grinning obsequiously. 'Excellency, there has been a terrible accident. My licences were blown from my hand by the wind, a trick of Seth, no doubt.'

He blew himself up like an angry bullfrog, and then subsided again as I pressed a heavy gold ring into his fat paw. He tested the metal between his teeth, and went away smiling.

I sent one of the grooms ashore to douse the torches that illuminated the wharf. I did not want curious eyes to see the condition of the horses that we brought ashore. Some of our animals were too weak to rise, others staggered and wheezed, they drooled the stinking mucus from mouth and nostrils. We were forced to place head-halters on them and coax them out of the barge on to the wharf. In the end there were only a hundred horses strong enough to walk.

We led them down the wagon-track to the high ground where our spies had told us the main horse-lines were laid out. Our spies had also provided us with the password of the Hyksos first division of chariots, and the linguists among us replied to the challenges of the sentries.

We walked our horses the entire length of the enemy encampment. As we went, we began to turn our stricken animals loose, leaving a few of them to wander through the lines of every one of the Hyksos' twenty chariot divisions. We moved so casually and naturally that no alarm was raised, we even chatted and joked with the enemy grooms and horse-handlers we met along the way.

As the first streaks of dawn showed in the eastern sky, we trudged back to the timber wharf on which we had disembarked. Only one of the galleys had waited to take us off, the rest of the flotilla had cast off and turned back southwards as soon as they had discharged their cargo of diseased horses.

We went aboard the remaining ship, and although Hui and the other grooms threw themselves exhausted upon the deck, I stood at the stern-rail and watched the walls of my beautiful Thebes, washed by the pure early light, sink from view behind us.

Ten days later, we sailed into the port of Elephantine, and after I had reported to Pharaoh Tamose, I hurried to the water-garden in the harem. My mistress lay in the shade of the barrazza. She was pale and so thin that I could not keep my hands from trembling as I stretched out to her in obeisance. She wept when she saw me.

'I missed you, Taita. There is so little time left for us to be together.'

THE NILE began to shrink back into her bed. The fields emerged from under the inundation, glistening black under a thick new coat of rich mud. The roads began to dry out, opening the way northwards. Soon it would be time for the plough, and the time for war.

Aton and I waited anxiously, perusing every report from our spies in the north. It came at last, the intelligence for which we had waited and prayed. The news was carried by a fast felucca, flying to us on the wings of the north wind. It docked in the third watch of the night, but the messenger found Aton and me still working by lamplight in his cell.

I hurried with the dirty scrap of papyrus to the royal apartments. The guards had orders to let me pass at any hour, but Queen Masara met me at the curtained doorway to the king's bedchamber.

'I will not let you wake him now, Taita. The king is exhausted. This is his first night's uninterrupted sleep in a month.'

'Your Majesty, I must see him. I am under his direct orders—'

While we still argued, a deep young voice called to me from beyond the curtain, 'Is that you, Tata?' The curtain was thrown aside and the king stood before us in all his naked splendour. He was a man as few others I have ever known, lean and hard as the blade of the blue sword, majestic in all his manly parts, so that I was all the more conscious of my own disability when I looked upon him.

'What is it, Tata?'

'Despatches from the north. From the camp of the Hyksos. A terrible pestilence is sweeping through the lines of the Hyksos. Half their horses are stricken, and thousands of others fall prey to the disease with each new day.'

'You are a magician, Tata. How could we have ever mocked you and your gnu!' He gripped my shoulders and stared into my eyes. 'Are you ready to ride to glory with me?'

'I am ready, Pharaoh.'

'Then put Rock and Chain into the traces, and fly the blue pennant over my chariot. We are going home to Thebes.'

SO WE stood at last before the city of a hundred gates with four divisions of chariots and thirty thousand foot. King Salitis' host lay before us, but beyond his multitudes the Fingers of Horus beckoned to us, and the walls of Thebes shone with a pearly radiance in the dawn light.

The Hyksos army deployed ponderously in front of us, like the uncoiling of some gigantic python, column after column, rank upon rank. Their spear-heads glittered and the golden helmets of the officers blazed in the early sunlight.

'Where is Apachan and his chariots?' the king demanded, and I stared at the Finger of Horus that stood nearest the river. I had to strain my eyesight to make out the tiny coloured scraps that waved from the top of the tower.

'Apachan has five divisions in the centre, and he holds six more in reserve. They are hidden beyond the city wall.'

I read the flag signals of the spy I had posted in the tallest of the three towers. I knew that from there he had a falcon's view across the battlefield.

'That is only eleven divisions, Tata,' the king fumed. 'We know he has twenty. Where are the others?'

'The Yellow Strangler,' I answered him. 'He has fielded every horse that can still stand.'

'By Horus, I hope you are right. I hope that Apachan is not planning a pretty little surprise for us.' He touched my shoulder. 'The dice are in the cup, Tata. It is too late to change them now. We must play this coup with what the gods have given us. Drive out in review.'

I took up the reins and wheeled the chariot out in front of our army. The king was showing himself to his troops. His presence would give them heart, and stiffen their spines. I took the horses down the long ranks at a tight hand-trot. Rock and Chain were brushed until their coats shone like polished copper in the sunlight. The carriage of the royal chariot was dressed in a thin skin of gold-leaf. This was the only concession I had made, in my quest for lightness.

The gold was beaten thinner than a papyrus sheet, and it added less than a hundred deben to the overall weight of our vehicle, yet it made a dazzling display. Friend or enemy who looked upon it could not doubt that this was Pharaoh's chariot, and take heart or be struck by awe in the thick of battle. On its long, whippy bamboo rod the blue pennant nodded and streamed in the breeze high above our heads, and the men cheered us as we drove down their ranks.

On the day we had left Qebui to begin the Return, I had made a vow not to cut my hair until I had made sacrifice in the temple of Horus in the centre of Thebes. Now my hair reached to my waist, and to hide the streaks of grey in it, I had dyed it with henna imported from those lands beyond the Indus river. It was a ruddy gold mane that set off my beauty to perfection. I wore a simple starched kilt of the whitest linen, and the Gold of Praise upon my naked chest. I did not wish in any way to detract from the glory of my young pharaoh, so I wore no make-up and no other ornament.

We passed in front of the massed regiments of the Shilluk spearmen in the centre. Those magnificent bloodthirsty pagans were the rock that anchored our line. They cheered us as we rode by, '*Kajan!* Tanus! *Kajan!* Tamose!' Their ostrich feathers seethed white as the foam of the river in the cataracts as they raised their spears in salute. I saw Lord Kratas there in the midst of them, and he shouted at me. His words were lost in the roar of ten thousand voices, but I read his lips: 'You and I will get puking drunk tonight in Thebes, you old hooligan.'

The Shilluk were stacked in depth, file upon file and regiment upon regiment. Kratas had exercised them ceaselessly in the tactics that I had helped him evolve to deal with chariots. Apart from their long spears, each of them carried a bundle of javelins, and a sling of wood and leather to launch these with added power. They had set the sharpened wooden staves into the earth to form a palisade in front of their line. The Hyksos chariots had to break through that spiny barrier to reach them.

The Egyptian archers were drawn up behind them, ready to move forward through their ranks or retreat again, as the vagaries of the battle called for each differing tactic. They raised their recurved bows on high and cheered Pharaoh. 'Tamose! Egypt and Tamose!'

Pharaoh wore the blue war crown, with the golden circlet of the *uraeus* around his brow, the heads of the vulture and the cobra of the two kingdoms entwined, their jewelled eyes glittering. He returned their salute with the bare blade of the blue sword held high.

We wheeled around our own left flank, and before we started back, Memnon stopped me with a hand on my shoulder. For a short while we looked back over the field. The Hyksos were moving forward already. Their front line was twice the length of our own.

'From your own treatise, Tata,' he quoted, '"A circumspect defence until the enemy is committed, and then the rapid and audacious attack."'

'You have remembered the lesson well, sire.'

'It is certain we will be outflanked, and Apachan will probably throw in his first five chariot divisions at the start.'

'I agree with you, Mem.'

'But we know what we have to do, don't we, Tata?' He tapped my shoulder and we started back to where our own chariots were holding in the rear.

Remrem headed the first division, Astes had the second, and Lord Aqer the third. Newly promoted to the rank of Best of Ten Thousand, Captain Hui commanded the fourth division. Two regiments of Shilluk guarded our baggage and the spare horses.

'Look at that old hunting dog,' Memnon nodded at Remrem. 'He is chafing to be away. By Horus, I'll teach him a little patience before this day is done.'

We heard the horns sounding in the centre.

'It begins now.' Memnon pointed to the front, and we saw the Hyksos chariots looming through the dust-clouds. 'Yes, Apachan has turned loose his chariots.'

He looked back at our divisions, and Remrem raised his sword high. 'The first is ready, Majesty,' he called eagerly, but Memnon ignored him and signalled to Lord Aqer. The third division came forward in column of fours behind us, and Pharaoh led them out.

The Hyksos chariots lumbered forward, heavy and majestic, aimed at the centre of our line. Memnon cut across in front of them, interposing our thin column between their hordes and the infantry. Then, at his signal, we wheeled into line abreast and we flew straight at them. It seemed suicidal, as futile as charging one of our frail wooden galleys at the rocks of the cataract.

As we came together, our archers fired head-on into the Hyksos, aiming for the horses. Gaps opened in their line as the animals were brought down by our arrows, then at the last possible moment our own line dissolved like wind-driven smoke. Our drivers used their superior speed and manoeuvrability. Instead of coming into collision with the Hyksos line and being crushed beneath the juggernaut, we swerved into the gaps and raced through them. Not all our chariots escaped, and some were broken and overturned, but Lord Aqer led four out of every five of them through.

We emerged in the rear of the Hyksos charge and spun around in a full-locked turn, re-forming the line at the gallop and again using our speed to overhaul the Hyksos, coming into them from the rear, firing our arrows into them at shortening range.

The Hyksos chariots were designed to give protection to the crew from the front, and their archers were stationed on the footplate to fire their arrows forward. Confusion spread down their line as they tried to meet our attack from the rear. Hard-pressed, some of the drivers attempted to turn back to confront us, and they collided with the chariots alongside. Those fearsome wheel-scythes cut into the legs of the neighbouring horses, and brought them down in a screaming, whinnying tangle.

The confusion spread among them just as the first volley of arrows from the Egyptian archers rose up over the massed ranks of Shilluk and dropped among the Hyksos. Immediately this happened, Memnon gave the order, and we wheeled away and let them run down on that palisade of sharpened staves. Half their horses were maimed or killed by those fierce points. Those who broke through were met by the Shilluk and a cloud of javelins. Struck by stake and arrow and javelin, their horses panicked, kicking and rearing in the traces.

Those chariots that were still under control hurled themselves into the Shilluk phalanx. They met no resistance. The black ranks opened before them, allowing the horses to run through, but then they closed up behind them.

Every one of those tall, willowy black devils was an athlete and an acrobat. They leaped up on to the footplate of the racing chariots from behind, and they stabbed and hacked at the crew with dagger and spear. They swallowed that first charge of chariots the same way a jellyfish engulfs a swift silver sardine in its myriad arms and amorphous body.

The Hyksos spearmen were moving forward to follow up and exploit the chariot charge, but now they were exposed. Loose horses and the surviving chariots tore back into their massed ranks, and forced them to open up and let them through. For the moment they were stranded in disorder in the middle of the field, and Memnon skilfully seized the opportunity.

Lord Aqer's horses were blown, and Memnon led them back into reserve. He and I changed teams. It was but a moment's work for the grooms to loosen the tack that coupled Rock and Chain, and to lead in a fresh team from the horses being held in reserve. We had six thousand fresh horses ready in the rear. I wondered how many Hyksos horses had escaped the Strangler, how many fresh teams they were holding.

As we wheeled back into line, Remrem called to us desperately, 'Your Majesty! The first! Let my first division go!'

Pharaoh ignored him and signalled to Astes. The second moved forward behind us and formed up at the trot.

The Hyksos infantry was still tangled in the middle of the field. They had extended to overlap our shorter line, but had lost their dressing. The line was crumpled and twisted. With a general's eye, Memnon picked out the weakest point, a salient in their left flank.

'The second division will advance. Trot-march! Forward! Pods of eight, charge!'

We tore into the salient in the line, eight chariots abreast. Pod after pod, we crashed into them and ripped them open. Their left flank buckled, while their right still pressed forward. We had them canted across the field, their centre was shearing, and Memnon re-formed the third division at the gallop, and set them up to tear open the enemy centre.

At the moment before we were committed to the charge, I glanced across at the city. Dust had almost obscured the range, but I glimpsed the two white flags on the summit of the Finger of Horus. It was the warning signal from my lookout posted there, and I swivelled round and looked back at the eastern fort of the city.

'Sire!' I cried, and pointed back. The king followed my arm, and saw the first squadron of Hyksos chariots trot out from concealment behind the curve of the wall. The others followed, like a column of black warrior ants on the march.

'Apachan is throwing in his reserves to save his infantry,' Memnon shouted, above the din of battle. 'A moment more, and he would have had us in enfilade. Well done, Tata.'

We had to let the infantry escape, as we wheeled into line to face Apachan's chariots. We charged at each other across a field littered with smashed and overturned chariots, loose arrows and javelins, dead and wounded horses and dying men. As we came together, I stood taller on the footplate and peered ahead. There was something unusual about the run of the enemy chariots, and then it dawned upon me.

'Sire,' I cried, 'look at the horses! They are running sick animals.' The chests of the leading teams were painted with a glistening coat of yellow mucus that streamed from their gaping mouths. Even as I watched, one of the horses coming towards us staggered and fell headlong, bringing its team-mate down with it.

'Sweet Isis, you are right. Their horses are finished before they have begun,' Memnon answered. He saw instantly what he had to do. It was the measure of his superb control that he was able to deflect a charge of his chariots once it was fully launched. At this very last moment he declined the head-on engagement.

We opened like a flower before their charge, peeling away on either side of them, turning and running back for our own lines, drawing them on, straining their sick and gasping horses to their utmost.

We ran before them in a tight, compact formation. Their own line began to waver and fall apart as the weaker horses broke down. Some of them fell as though struck in the head by an arrow. Others merely slowed and stopped, standing with their heads hanging, mucus pouring from their mouths in shiny golden ropes.

Lord Aqer's own horses were almost blown by now. They had driven two furious charges without a rest. Still pursued by the remnants of Apachan's division, Memnon led them back to where Hui's fourth division was drawn up alongside Remrem and his first.

'Pharaoh! The first is ready. Let me go! In the name of all the gods, let me go!' Remrem howled with frustration.

Memnon hardly glanced in his direction. I turned my chariot in alongside that of Hui. A team of grooms slipped our sweat-soaked horses from the traces and led in a fresh pair. While Lord Aqer's exhausted division streamed back past us, we faced the oncoming Hyksos.

'Are you ready, Captain Hui?' Memnon called to him, and Hui raised his bow in salute.

'For Egypt and Tamose!' he shouted.

'Then forward march. Charge!' Memnon laughed, and our horses jumped against the traces and we shot forward.

There were six full divisions of Apachan's chariots scattered across the field in front of us. Half of them were broken down, with the horses fallen or drooping in the traces, suffocated and dying from the Yellow Strangler. Most of the others were reduced to a walk, the horses staggering and wheezing. However, the remaining chariots came on in good order.

We went out to meet them face to face. In the centre of their charge rode a tall chariot, its coachwork clad in shining bronze. On the footplate stood a man so tall that he towered above his driver. He wore the high golden helmet of Hyksos royalty, and his dark beard was plaited with coloured ribbons that fluttered in the wind like pretty butterflies hovering over a flowering shrub.

'Apachan!' Memnon challenged him. 'You are a dead man.'

Apachan heard him, and he picked out our golden chariot. He swerved to meet us, and Memnon tapped my shoulder.

'Lay me alongside the bearded hog. It's time for the sword, at last.'

Apachan loosed two arrows at us as we closed. Memnon caught one on his shield. I ducked under the other, but I never lost my concentration. I was watching those terrible spinning scythes on the hubs of Apachan's wheels. They could hack my horses' legs out from under them.

Behind me I heard the gravelly rasp as Memnon drew the blue sword from its scabbard on the side panel, and from the corner of my eye I caught the steely flash of the blade as he went on guard.

I swung my horses' heads over, feinting to the right to confuse the Hyksos driver, but the instant we started to turn away, I changed direction again. I avoided his scythes and passed him close, then I turned in sharply behind him. With my free hand I snatched up the grappling-hook and tossed it over the side-panel of the other chariot. Now we were locked together, but I had achieved the advantage, for we lay across his stern.

Apachan swivelled around, and aimed a sword-cut at me, but I fell to my knees under it, and Memnon gathered up the blow on his shield, then swung the blue sword. A shard of bronze curled from the edge of Apachan's weapon, sliced away by the steel, and he shouted in angry disbelief, and flung up his copper shield at the next blow.

Apachan was a superb swordsman, but no match for my king and the blue sword. Memnon mangled his shield to strips, and then swung hard at his bronze blade, as Apachan tried to defend his head. The blue blade sheared the bronze cleanly, and Apachan was left with only the hilt in his fist.

He opened his mouth wide and bellowed at us. The teeth in the back of his jaw were black and rotten, and his spittle blew into my face in a cloud. Memnon used that classic straight thrust to end it. He drove the point of the blue blade through Apachan's open mouth, deeply into the back of his throat. His angry bellow was drowned out by the torrent of bright blood that burst through his hairy lips.

I cut the rope of the grappling-hook, and let the Hyksos chariot run free. The horses were out of control and they slewed away and ran down the line of locked and battling chariots. Apachan clutched at the dashboard, holding himself erect even though he was dying, and the blood spurted from his mouth and cascaded down his breastplate.

It was a sight that struck dismay into the hearts of his charioteers. They tried to disengage their sick and staggering horses, but we ran hub-to-hub with them and hurled our javelins into them. We followed them all the way back, until we came within range of their archers, and flocks of arrows fell around us and forced us to break off.

'It is not over yet,' I warned Memnon, as we walked our tired horses back. 'You have broken Apachan's chariots, but you still have to deal with Beon's infantry.'

'Take me to Kratas,' Pharaoh ordered.

I stopped our chariot in front of the massed regiments of Shilluk, and Memnon called across to Kratas, 'What heart, my Lord?'

'I fear, sire, that my fellows will fall asleep if you cannot find a little work for us to do.'

'Then let us hear a tune from them as you take them forward to seek employment.'

The Shilluk began their advance. They moved with a curious shuffling gait, and every third pace they stamped in unison with a force that made the ground jump beneath their horny bare feet. They sang in those deep, melodious African voices, a sound like a swarm of angry black bees, and they drummed their spears upon their rawhide shields.

The Hyksos were disciplined and brave, they could not have conquered half the world if they had not been so. We had smashed up their chariots, but they stood to meet Kratas' advance behind a wall of bronze shields.

The two armies came together like fighting temple bulls. The black and the white bulls locked horns and fought it out breast-to-breast and spear-to-spear.

While the two armies of foot-soldiers mauled each other, Pharaoh held back his chariots, using them with skill and daring only when there was an opening or a weakness in the enemy positions. When a pocket of the Hyksos infantry was isolated on the left, he sent in Aqer's division, and annihilated them with two swift charges. When Lord Beon tried to send reinforcements forward to assist his beleaguered front, Pharaoh despatched Astes with five hundred chariots to frustrate him.

The Hyksos rallied every one of their remaining chariots, and every one of their horses that could still stand, and threw them against our right. Memnon sent Hui and Astes out to meet them, and to break up their attack. He left Remrem cursing and pleading and stamping up and down beside his chariot, and ignored his pleas.

Pharaoh and I circled the fighting in the golden chariot, watching each shift and change in the conflict. He pushed in his reserves in exactly those places where they were most needed, and with the timing and anticipation that can never be taught or learned. It was as though the pulse and the tempo of the battle beat in his heart, and he sensed it in his blood.

Always I looked for Kratas in the thick of it. Many times I lost him, and I dreaded that he was down, but then his helmet showed again with the ostrich-feather plume cut away, and the bronze splattered with his own blood and the blood of other men.

It was there in the centre where Kratas fought that the Hyksos ranks began to give. It was like the first trickle through the earth wall of a dam, their line bulged and stretched to the breaking-point. Their rear ranks began to fall in upon themselves under the relentless pressure.

'By the love of Horus and the compassion of all the gods, Tata, this is the moment of our victory.' Memnon saw it even before I did.

We galloped across to where Remrem still waited, and Pharaoh hailed him, 'Are you ready, my Lord Remrem?'

'I have been ready since dawn, sire, but I am no lord.'

'Would you argue with your king, sir? You are a lord now. The enemy centre is breaking. Take your chariots and chase them back to Memphis!'

'May you live for ever, Pharaoh!' Lord Remrem roared, and he sprang to the footplate. He led out the first. Their horses were fresh and strong, and their fighting spirit was chafed raw and angry with long restraint.

They crashed into the Hyksos right flank. They cut through them with barely a check, and swung round and went into the enemy centre from the rear. It was the perfect moment when the battle teetered, and the Hyksos centre broke. Within the time it takes to draw and hold a long breath, they were in rout.

They streamed back towards the city gates, but even Kratas' Shilluk were too far-gone to follow them. They stood knee-deep in the piles of dead and dying men, they rested on their spears and let the Hyksos go. This was when the genius of Memnon was made apparent. He had kept the first in hand for this moment. They took up the chase, and I saw Remrem's sword rise and fall to a terrible rhythm as he drove them on.

The first of the fleeing enemy reached the city gates, but they found them slammed closed in their faces. My spies and agents had done their work well. The populace of Thebes was in revolt, and the city was ours. They barred the gates to the broken Hyksos legions.

Remrem pursued the Hyksos until night fell and his horses were exhausted. He drove them back thirty miles, and every yard of the north road was littered with their discarded weapons and the bodies of the slain.

I DROVE Pharaoh's golden chariot up to the main gate of the city, and he stood tall on the footplate and shouted to the sentinels on the parapet above us. 'Open the gates! Let me pass through!'

'Who is it that demands entry to Thebes?' they called down.

'I am Tamose, ruler of the two kingdoms.'

'Hail Pharaoh! May you live for ever!'

The gates swung open, and Memnon touched my shoulder. 'Drive through, Tata.'

I turned to face him. 'Forgive me, Majesty. I have taken oath that I will not enter the city, except at the side of my mistress, Queen Lostris. I must pass the reins to you.'

'Dismount,' he ordered me gently. 'Go! Fetch your mistress and make good your oath.'

He took the reins from my hand, and I climbed down into the dusty roadway. I watched him drive the golden chariot through the gateway, and the sound of cheering was like the thunder of waters in the cataracts at high flood. The people of Thebes greeted their king.

I stood at the roadside as our depleted and battered army followed Pharaoh into the city. I realized what a bitter price we had paid for our victory. We would not be fit to pursue the Hyksos until we had rebuilt our army. By this time King Salitis would be strong again, and his horses recovered from the Yellow Strangler. We had won the first battle, but I knew that many more lay ahead of us before the tyrant could be cast out of this very Egypt.

I looked for Kratas as the Shilluk regiments marched past, but he was not there.

Hui had a chariot and fresh horses for me. 'I will ride with you, Taita,' he offered, but I shook my head.

'I will travel faster alone,' I told him. 'Go into the city and enjoy your triumph. A thousand pretty maids are waiting to welcome you home.'

Before I took the south road, I drove first to the battlefield. The jackals and the hyena were already at the feast that we had set for them, their growls and howls blended with the groans of the dying. The dead were piled like the flotsam on the river-bank when the flood-waters recede.

I drove the chariot through to where I had last seen Kratas, but this was the most gruesome corner of that awful field. The corpses were piled high as my chariot wheels. I saw his helmet lying in the dust that blood had turned to thick mud. I dismounted and took it up. The crest was gone and the helm was all dented and battered in by heavy blows.

I threw the helmet aside and began to search for Kratas' body. I saw his leg protruding like the branch of a giant acacia from beneath a pile of bodies. They were Shilluk and Hyksos lying together in the truce of death. I dragged them aside and found Kratas on his back. He was drenched in clotted black blood, his hair was matted with it and his face was a black, crusted mask.

I knelt beside him, and I whispered softly, 'Must they all die? Every one I truly love, must they all die?' I leaned forward and kissed his bloody lips.

He sat up and stared at me. Then he grinned that wide boyish grin of his. 'By the plug of dried snot in Seth's left nostril, that was a real fight,' he greeted me.

'Kratas!' I stared at him with delight. 'You will truly live for ever.'

'Never doubt it for a moment, my lad. But right now I need a noggin.'

I ran to the chariot and fetched the wine flask. He held it at arm's-length and let the red wine squirt down his throat without swallowing. When the flask was empty he threw it aside and belched.

'That will do well enough for a start,' he winked at me. 'Now point me towards the nearest tavern, you old reprobate.'

FASTER THAN any ship could sail against the current, I carried the news to Elephantine. I was one man in the chariot, and the horses ran lightly. I changed the teams at every relay station along the south road, and galloped on without a check. The grooms handed me a flask or a crust of corn-bread and cheese as they changed the horses, and I never slept or even rested.

During the night, the stars and the moon revealed the path to me, and Horus guided my weary hands upon the traces, for though I ached in every limb and I reeled on the footplate with fatigue, I met with no mishap.

At each relay station and in each village along the way, I shouted the joyous news. 'A victory! A mighty victory! Pharaoh has triumphed at Thebes. The Hyksos is cast down.'

'Praise to all the gods!' they cheered me. 'Egypt and Tamose.'

I galloped on, and they still speak of my ride to this day along the south road. They tell of the gaunt rider with wild bloodshot eyes, his robe thick with dust and the stains of dried blood, his long hair blowing in the wind, the harbinger of victory, bringing the news to Elephantine of the battle that set Egypt on the road to freedom.

I drove from Thebes to Elephantine in two days and two nights, and when I reached the palace, I barely had the strength left to stagger into the water-garden where my mistress lay, and throw myself down beside her couch.

'Mistress,' I croaked through cracked lips and a throat that was parched with dust, 'Pharaoh has won a mighty victory. I have come to take you home.'

WE SAILED down-river to Thebes. The princesses were with me to keep their mother company and to cheer her. They sat with her on the open deck and sang to her. They rhymed and riddled and laughed, but there were tones of sadness in their laughter and deep concern in their eyes as they watched over my mistress.

Queen Lostris was as frail as a wounded bird. There was no weight to her bones and her flesh was as translucent as mother-of-pearl. I could lift and carry her as easily as I had done when she was ten years of age. The powder of the sleeping-flower was no longer able to still the pain that gnawed into her belly like some terrible clawed crab.

I carried her to the bows of the galley when at last the walls of Thebes opened to our view around the last bend in the river. With an arm around her thin shoulders I supported her, as we delighted together in all those long-remembered scenes, and lived again a thousand joyous memories of our youth.

But the effort tired her. When we docked below the Palace of Memnon, half the populace of Thebes was waiting to welcome her. Pharaoh Tamose stood at the head of this vast throng.

When the litter-bearers carried her ashore, they cheered her. Although most of them had never laid eyes upon her, the legend of the compassionate queen had persisted during her long exile. Mothers lifted up their infants for her blessing, and they reached out to touch her hand as it trailed from the edge of the litter.

'Pray to Hapi for us,' they pleaded. 'Pray for us, Mother of Egypt.'

Pharaoh Tamose walked beside her litter like the son of a commoner, and Tehuti and Bekatha followed close behind. Both the princesses smiled brightly, though the tears jewelled their eyelids.

Aton had prepared quarters for the queen. At the door I sent them all away, even the king. I laid her on the couch beneath the vine arbour on the terrace. From there she could look across the river to the shining walls of her beloved Thebes.

When darkness fell, I carried her to her bedchamber. As she lay upon the linen sheets, she looked up at me. 'Taita,' she murmured, 'one last time, will you work the Mazes of Ammon-Ra for me?'

'Mistress, I can refuse you nothing.' I bowed my head and went to fetch my medicine chest.

I sat beside her bed, cross-legged upon the stone slabs, and she watched me prepare the herbs. I crushed them in the alabaster pestle and mortar, and heated the water in the copper kettle.

I raised the steaming cup and saluted her with it.

'Thank you,' she whispered, and I drained the cup. I closed my eyes and waited for the familiar but dreaded slide over the edge of reality, into the world of dreams and visions.

When I returned, the lamps were guttering and smoking in their brackets, and the palace was silent. There was no sound from the river or from the sleeping city on the far bank, only the sweet trill of a nightingale in the gardens, and the light breath of my mistress as she lay upon her silken pillow.

I thought she was sleeping. But the moment I lifted my trembling hand to wipe the cold and nauseous sweat from my face, she opened her eyes. 'Poor Taita, was it so bad?'

It had been worse than ever before. My head ached and my vision swam. I knew that I would never work the Mazes again. This was the last time, and I had done it for her alone.

'I saw the vulture and the cobra stand on either side of the river, divided by the waters. I saw the waters rise and fall one hundred seasons. I saw one hundred sheaths of corn, and one hundred birds fly over the river. Below them, I saw the dust of battle and the flash of swords. I saw the smoke of burning cities mingle with the dust.

'At last I saw the cobra and the vulture come together in congress. I saw them mating and entwined on a sheet of pure blue silk. There were blue banners on the city walls and banners of blue flew on the temple pylons.

'I saw the blue pennants on the chariots that drove out across the world. I saw monuments so tall and mighty that they would stand for ten thousand years. I saw the peoples of fifty different nations bow down before them.'

I sighed and pressed my fingers into my temples to still the throbbing in my skull, and then I said, 'That was all my vision.'

Neither of us spoke or moved for a long while thereafter, then my mistress said quietly, 'One hundred seasons must pass before the two kingdoms are united, one hundred years of war and striving before the Hyksos are at last driven from the sacred soil of this very Egypt. It will be hard and bitter for my people to bear.'

'But they will be united under the blue banner, and the kings of your line will conquer the world. All the nations of the world will pay homage to them,' I interpreted the rest of my vision for her.

'With this I am content.' She sighed and fell asleep.

I did not sleep, for I knew that she still needed me near her.

She woke again in that hour before dawn which is the darkest of the night. She cried out, 'The pain! Sweet Isis, the pain!'

I mixed the Red Shepenn for her. After a while she said, 'The pain has passed, but I am cold. Hold me, Taita, warm me with your body.'

I took her in my arms and held her while she slept.

She awoke once more as the first timid rays of dawn crept in through the doorway from the terrace.

'I have loved only two men in my life,' she murmured, 'and you were one of those. Perhaps in the next life, the gods will treat our love more kindly.'

There was no reply I could give. She closed her eyes for the last time. She stole away quietly and left me. Her last breath was no louder than the one before, but I felt the chill in her lips when I kissed them.

'Goodbye, my mistress,' I whispered. 'Farewell, my heart.'

I HAVE written these scrolls during the seventy days and nights of the royal embalming. They are my last tribute to my mistress.

Before the undertakers took her away from me, I made the incision in her left flank, as I had done for Tanus. I opened her womb and took from it that terrible incubus that had killed her. It was a thing of flesh and blood, but it was not human. When I cast it into the fire, I cursed it, and I cursed the foul god Seth who had placed it in her.

I have prepared ten alabaster jars to hold these scrolls. I will leave them with her. I am painting all the murals of her tomb with my own hand. They are the finest I have ever created. Each stroke of my brush is an expression of my love.

I wish that I could rest with her in this tomb, for I am sick and weary with grief. But I still have my two princesses and my king to care for.

They need me.

AUTHOR'S NOTE

On 5 January 1988, Doctor Duraid ibn al Simma of the Egyptian Department of Antiquities opened and entered a tomb on the west bank of the Nile in the Valley of the Nobles. The reason why this tomb had not been previously excavated was that in the ninth century AD an Islamic mosque had been built over the site. It was only after long and delicate negotiations with the religious authorities that the excavation was permitted.

Immediately upon entering the passage that led to the burial chamber, Dr Al Simma was greeted by a marvellous display of murals which covered all the walls and the ceilings. They were the most elaborate and vivacious that he had ever encountered in a lifetime spent studying the monuments.

He told me that he knew at once that he had made a significant find, for from amongst the hieroglyphics on the walls stood out the royal cartouche of an Egyptian queen who had not been previously recorded.

His excitement and anticipation increased as he approached the burial chamber, only to be dashed as he saw that the seals upon the doorway had been damaged, and the entrance had been forced. In ancient times, the tomb had been robbed and stripped of its sarcophagus and all its treasures.

Nevertheless, Dr Al Simma was able to date the tomb with reasonable accuracy to that dark night of strife and disaster that overwhelmed Egypt in about 1780 BC. For the next century the Two Kingdoms were in a state of flux. We have little record of the events of this period, but from the chaos eventually rose a line of princes and pharaohs that finally expelled the Hyksos invader, and lifted Egypt into its period of greatest glory. It gives me pleasure to think that the blood of Lostris and Tanus and Memnon ran strongly in their veins.

It was almost a year after the tomb was first opened, while Dr Al Simma's assistants were copying and photographing the decorations of the walls, that a section of the plaster fell away to reveal a hidden niche in which stood ten sealed alabaster vases.

When Dr Al Simma asked me to assist in the transcription of the scrolls contained in the vases, I was both honoured and filled with trepidation. I was not, of course, qualified to work on the original scrolls, which were written in the hieratic script. This work was done at Cairo Museum by a team of international Egyptologists.

Dr Al Simma asked me to rewrite this original transcription in a style that would make it more accessible to the modern reader. With this end in view I have included some anachronisms in the text. For instance I have, in places, used such comparatively modern measures of distance and weight as miles and ounces. I have also indulged myself with words such as 'djinn' and 'houri' and 'hooligan' which Taita never employed, but which, I feel certain, he would have used if they had formed part of his vocabulary.

Very soon after beginning work on the texts all my reservations began to evaporate as I became totally involved in the times and character of the ancient author. Despite all his bombast and vainglory, I developed an affinity and affection for the slave Taita that reached back over the millennium.

I am left with a realization of how little the emotions and aspirations of man have changed in all that time, and a lingering excitement that to this day somewhere in the Abyssinian mountains near the source of the Blue Nile the mummy of Tanus still lies in the unviolated tomb of Pharaoh Mamose.

W.S.

WILBUR SMITH

WARLOCK

MACMILLAN

For my new love

MOKHINISO

*Spirits of Genghis Khan and Omar Khayyam
reincarnated in a moon as lucent as
a perfect pearl*

Like an uncoiling serpent, a line of fighting chariots wound swiftly down the gut of the valley. From where he clung to the dashboard of the leading chariot the boy looked up at the cliffs that hemmed them in. The sheer rock was pierced by the openings to the tombs of the old people that honeycombed the cliff. The dark pits stared down at him like the implacable eyes of a legion of *djinn*. Prince Nefer Memnon shuddered and looked away, furtively making the sign to avert evil with his left hand.

Over his shoulder he glanced back down the column and saw that from the following chariot Taita was watching him through the swirling clouds of dust. The dust had coated the old man and his vehicle with a pale film, and a single shaft of sunlight that penetrated to the depths of this deep valley glittered on the mica particles so that he seemed to glow like the incarnation of one of the gods. Nefer ducked his head guiltily, ashamed that the old man had witnessed his fleeting superstitious dread. No royal prince of the House of Tamose should show such weakness, not now when he stood at the gateway to manhood. But, then, Taita knew him as no other did, for he had been Nefer's tutor since infancy, closer to him than his own parents or siblings. Taita's expression never changed but even at that distance his ancient eyes seemed to bore into the core of Nefer's being. Seeing all, understanding all.

Nefer turned back and drew himself up to his full height beside his father, who flipped the reins and urged the horses on with a crack of the long whip. Ahead of them the valley opened abruptly into the great amphitheatre that contained the stark and tumbled ruins of the city of Gallala. Nefer thrilled to his first sight of this famous battlefield. As a young man Taita himself had fought on this site when the demigod Tanus, Lord Harrab, had destroyed the dark forces that were threatening this very Egypt. That had been over sixty years ago but Taita had related to him every detail of the fight, and so vivid was his storytelling that Nefer felt as if he had been there on that fateful day.

Nefer's father, the god and Pharaoh Tamose, wheeled the chariot up to the tumbled stones of the ruined gateway, and reined in the horses. Behind them a hundred chariots in succession neatly executed the same manoeuvre, and the charioteers swarmed down from the footplates to begin watering the horses. When Pharaoh opened his mouth to speak the coated dust crumbled from his cheeks and dribbled down his chest.

'My lord!' Pharaoh hailed the Great Lion of Egypt, Lord Naja, his army commander and beloved companion. 'We must be away again before the sun touches the hilltops. I wish to make a night run through the dunes to El Gabar.'

The blue war crown on Tamose's head gleamed with mica dust, and his eyes were bloodshot with tiny lumps of tear-wet mud in the corners as he glanced down at Nefer. 'This is where I will leave you to go on with Taita.'

Although he knew that it was futile to protest, Nefer opened his mouth to do so. The squadron was going in against the enemy. Pharaoh Tamose's battle plan was to circle south through the Great Dunes and weave a way between the bitter natron lakes to take the enemy in his rear and rip an opening in his centre through which the Egyptian legions, massed and waiting on the Nile bank before Abnub, could pour. Tamose would combine the two forces and before the enemy could rally, drive on past Tell el-Daba and seize the enemy citadel of Avaris.

It was a bold and brilliant plan which, if it succeeded, would bring to a close, at one stroke, the war with the Hyksos that had already raged through two lifetimes. Nefer had been taught that battle and glory were the reasons for his existence on this earth. But, even at the advanced age of fourteen years, they had so far eluded him. He longed with all his soul to ride to victory and immortality at his father's side.

Before his protest could pass his lips, Pharaoh forestalled him. 'What is the first duty of a warrior?' he demanded of the boy.

Nefer dropped his eyes. 'It is obedience, Majesty,' he replied softly, reluctantly.

'Never forget it.' Pharaoh nodded and turned away.

Nefer felt himself spurned and discarded. His eyes smarted and his upper lip quivered, but Taita's gaze stiffened him. He blinked to clear his vision of tears, and took a pull from the waterskin that hung on the side rail of the chariot before turning to the old Magus with a jaunty toss of his thick dust-caked curls. 'Show me the monument, Tata,' he commanded.

The ill-assorted pair made their way through the concourse of chariots, men and horses that choked the narrow street of the ruined city. Stripped naked in the heat, twenty troopers had climbed down the deep shafts to the ancient wells, and formed a bucket chain to bring the sparse, bitter water to the surface. Once those wells had been bountiful enough to support a rich and populous city that sat full upon the trade route between the Nile and the Red Sea. Then, centuries ago, an earthquake had shattered the water-bearing stratum and blocked the subterranean flow. The city of Gallala had died of thirst. Now there was scarcely sufficient water to slake the thirst of two hundred horses and top up the waterskins before the wells were dry.

Taita led Nefer through the narrow lanes, past temples and palaces now inhabited only by the lizard and the scorpion, until they reached the deserted central square. In its centre stood the monument to Lord Tanus and his triumph over the armies of bandits who had almost choked the life out of the richest and most powerful nation on earth. The monument was a bizarre pyramid of human skulls, cemented together and protected by a shrine made of red rock slabs. A thousand and more skulls grinned down upon the boy as he read aloud the inscription on the stone portico: 'Our severed heads bear witness to the battle at this place in which we died beneath the sword of Tanus Lord Harrab. May all the generations that follow learn from that mighty lord's deeds the glory of the gods and the power of righteous men. Thus decreed in the fourteenth year of the reign of the God Pharaoh Mamose.'

Squatting in the monument's shadow Taita watched the Prince as he walked around the monument, pausing every few paces with hands on hips to study it from every angle. Although Taita's expression was remote his eyes were fond. His love for the lad had its origins in two other lives. The first of these was Lostris, Queen of Egypt. Taita was a eunuch, but he had been gelded after puberty and had once loved a woman. Because of his physical mutilation Taita's love was pure, and he had lavished it all on Queen Lostris, Nefer's grandmother. It was a love so encompassing that even now, twenty years after her death, it stood at the centre of his existence.

The other person from whom his love for Nefer sprang was Tanus, Lord Harrab, to whom this monument had been erected. He had been dearer than a brother to Taita. They were both gone now, Lostris and Tanus, but their blood mingled strongly in this child's veins. From their illicit union so long ago had sprung the child who had grown up to become the Pharaoh Tamose, who now led the squadron of chariot that had brought them here; the father of Prince Nefer.

'Tata, show me where it was that you captured the leader of the robber barons.' Nefer's voice cracked with excitement and the onset of puberty. 'Was it here?' He ran to the broken-down wall at the south side of the square. 'Tell me the story again.'

'No, it was here. This side,' Taita told him, stood up and strode on those long, stork-thin legs to the eastern wall. He looked up to the crumbling summit. 'The ruffian's name was Shufti, and he was one-eyed and ugly as the god Seth. He was trying to escape from the battle by climbing over the wall up there.' Taita stooped and picked up half of a baked-mud brick from the rubble and suddenly hurled it upwards. It sailed over the top of the high wall. 'I cracked his skull and brought him down with a single throw.'

Even though Nefer knew, at first hand, the old man's strength, and that his powers of endurance were legend, he was astonished by that throw. He is old as the mountains, older than my grandmother, for he nursed her as he has done me, Nefer marvelled. Men say he has witnessed two hundred inundations of the Nile and that he built the pyramids with his own hands. Then aloud he asked, 'Did you hack off his head, Tata, and place it on that pile there?' He pointed at the grisly monument.

'You know the story well enough, for I have told it to you a hundred times.' Taita feigned modest reluctance to extol his own deeds.

'Tell me again!' Nefer ordered.

Taita sat down on a stone block while Nefer settled at his feet in happy anticipation and listened avidly, until the rams' horns of the squadron sounded the recall with a blast that shattered into diminishing echoes along the black cliffs. 'Pharaoh summons us,' Taita said, and stood up to lead the way back through the gate.

There was a great bustle and scurry outside the walls, as the squadron made ready to go on into the dune lands. The waterskins were bulging again and the troopers were checking and tightening the harness of their teams before mounting up.

Pharaoh Tamose looked over the heads of his staff as the pair came through the gateway, and summoned Taita to his side with an inclination of his head. Together they walked out of earshot of the squadron officers. Lord Naja made as if to join them. Taita whispered a word to Pharaoh, then Tamose turned and sent Naja back with a curt word. The injured lord, flushed with mortification, shot a look at Taita that was fierce and sharp as a war arrow.

'You have offended Naja. Some day I might not be at hand to protect you,' Pharaoh warned.

'We dare trust no man,' Taita demurred. 'Not until we crush the head of the serpent of treachery that tightens its coils around the pillars of your palace. Until you return from this campaign in the north only the two of us must know where I am taking the Prince.'

'But Naja!' Pharaoh laughed dismissively. Naja was like a brother. They had run the Red Road together.

'Even Naja.' Taita said no more. His suspicions were at last hardening

4

into certainty, but he had not yet gathered all the evidence he would need to convince Pharaoh.

'Does the Prince know why you are going into the fastness of the desert?' Pharaoh asked.

'He knows only that we are going to further his instruction in the mysteries, and to capture his godbird.'

'Good, Taita.' Pharaoh nodded. 'You were ever secretive but true. There is nothing more to say, for we have said it all. Now go, and may Horus spread his wings over you and Nefer.'

'Look to your own back, Majesty, for in these days enemies are standing behind you as well as to your front.'

Pharaoh grasped the Magus' upper arm and squeezed hard. Under his fingers the arm was thin but hard as a dried acacia branch. Then he went back to where Nefer waited beside the wheel of the royal chariot, with the injured air of a puppy ordered back to its kennel.

'Divine Majesty, there are younger men than me in the squadron.' The Prince made one last despairing effort to persuade his father that he should ride with the chariots. Pharaoh knew that the boy was right, of course. Meren, the grandson of the illustrious General Kratas, was his junior by three days and today was riding with his father as lance-bearer in one of the rear chariots. 'When will you allow me to ride into battle with you, Father?'

'Perhaps when you have run the Red Road. Then not even I will gainsay you.'

It was a hollow promise, and they both knew it. Running the Red Road was the onerous test of horsemanship and weapons that few warriors attempted. It was an ordeal that drained, exhausted and often killed even a strong man in his prime and trained to near perfection. Nefer was a long way from that day.

Then Pharaoh's forbidding expression softened and he gripped his son's arm in the only show of affection he would allow himself before his troops. 'Now it is my command that you go with Taita into the desert to capture your godbird, and thus to prove your royal blood and your right one day to wear the double crown.'

Nefer and the old man stood together beside the shattered walls of Gallala and watched the column fly past. Pharaoh led it, the reins wrapped around his wrists, leaning back against the pull of the horses, his chest bare, linen skirts whipping around his muscular legs, the blue war crown on his head rendering him tall and godlike.

Next came Lord Naja, almost as tall, almost as handsome. His mien was haughty and proud, the great recurved bow slung over his shoulder. Naja was one of the mightiest warriors of this very Egypt and his name had been given to him as a title of honour: Naja was the sacred cobra in the royal *uraeus* crown. Pharaoh Tamose had bestowed it upon him on the day that, together, they had won through the ordeal of the Red Road.

Naja did not deign to glance in Nefer's direction. Pharaoh's chariot had plunged into the mouth of the dark gorge before the last vehicle in the column went racing past where Nefer stood. Meren, his friend and companion of many illicit boyhood adventures, laughed in his face and made an obscene gesture, then raised his voice mockingly above the whine and rattle of the wheels. 'I will bring you the head of Apepi as a toy,' he promised, and Nefer hated him as he sped away. Apepi was the King of the Hyksos, and Nefer needed no toys: he was a man now, even if his father refused to recognize it.

The two were silent for long after Meren's chariot had disappeared, and the dust had settled. Then Taita turned without a word and went to where their horses were tethered. He tightened the surcingle around his mount's chest, hiked up his kilts and swung up with the limber movement of a much younger man. Once astride the animal's bare back he seemed to become one with it. Nefer remembered that legend related he had been the very first Egyptian to master the equestrian arts. He still bore the title Master of Ten Thousand Chariots, bestowed upon him with the Gold of Praise by two pharaohs in their separate reigns.

Certain it was that he was one of the few men who dared to ride astride. Most Egyptians abhorred this practice, considering it somehow obscene and undignified, not to mention risky. Nefer had no such qualms and as he vaulted up on to the back of his favourite colt, Stargazer, his black mood started to evaporate. By the time they had reached the crest of the hills above the ruined city he was almost his usual ebullient self. He cast one last longing glance at the feather of distant dust left on the northern horizon by the squadron then firmly turned his back upon it. 'Where are we going, Tata?' he demanded. 'You promised to tell me once we were on the road.'

Taita was always reticent and secretive, but seldom to the degree that he had been over the matter of their ultimate destination on this journey. 'We are going to Gebel Nagara,' Taita told him.

Nefer had never heard the name before, but he repeated it softly. It had a romantic, evocative ring. Excitement and anticipation made the back of his neck prickle, and he looked ahead into the great desert. An infinity of jagged and bitter hills stretched away to a horizon blue with heat-haze and distance. The colours of the raw rocks astounded the eye: they were the sullen blue of stormclouds, yellow as a weaver bird's plumage, or red as wounded flesh, and bright as crystal. The heat made them dance and quiver.

Taita looked down on this terrible place with a sense of nostalgia and homecoming. It was into this wilderness that he had retired after the death of his beloved Queen Lostris, at first creeping away like a wounded animal. Then, as the years passed and some of the pain with them, he had found himself drawn once more to the mysteries and the way of the great god Horus. He had gone into the wilderness as a physician and a surgeon, as a master of the known sciences. Alone in the fastness of the desert he had discovered the key to gates and doorways of the mind and the spirit beyond which few men ever journey. He had gone in a man but had emerged as a familiar of the great god Horus and an adept of strange and arcane mysteries that few men even imagined.

Taita had only returned to the world of men when his Queen Lostris had visited him in a dream as he slept in his hermit's cave at Gebel Nagara. Once more she had been a fifteen-year-old maiden, fresh and nubile, a desert rose in its first bloom with the dew upon its petals. Even as he slept his heart had swollen with love and threatened to burst his chest asunder.

'Darling Taita,' Lostris had whispered, as she touched his cheek and stirred him awake, 'you were one of the only two men I have ever loved. Tanus is with me now, but before you can come to me also there is one more charge that I lay upon you. You never once failed me. I know that you will not fail me now, will you, Taita?'

'I am yours to command, mistress.' His voice echoed strangely in his ears.

'In Thebes, my city of a hundred gates, this night is born a child. He is the son of my own son. They will name this child Nefer, which means pure and perfect in body and spirit. My longing is that he carry my blood and the blood of Tanus to the throne of Upper Egypt. But great and diverse perils already gather around the babe. He cannot succeed without your help. Only you can protect and guide him. These years you have spent alone in the wilderness, the skills and knowledge you have acquired here were to that purpose alone. Go to Nefer. Go now swiftly and stay with him until your task is completed. Then come to me, darling Taita. I will be waiting for you and your poor mutilated manhood shall be restored to you. You will be whole and entire when next you stand by my side, your hand in my hand. Do not fail me, Taita.'

'Never!' Taita had cried in the dream. 'In your life I never failed you. I will not fail you now in death.'

'I know you will not.' Lostris smiled a sweet, haunting smile, and her image faded into the desert night. He woke, with his face wet with tears, and gathered up his few possessions. He paused at the cave entrance only to check his direction by the stars. Instinctively, he looked for the bright particular star of the goddess. On the seventieth day after the Queen's death, on the night that the long ritual of her embalmment had been completed, that star had appeared suddenly in the heavens, a great red star that glowed where none had been before. Taita picked it out and made obeisance to it. Then he strode away into the western desert, back towards the Nile and the city of Thebes, beautiful Thebes of a hundred gates.

That had been over fourteen years ago, and now he hungered for the silent places, for only here could his powers grow back to their full strength, so that he could carry through the charge that Lostris had laid upon him. Only here could he pass some of that strength on to the Prince. For he knew that the dark powers of which she had warned him were gathering around them.

'Come!' he said to the boy. 'Let us go down and take your godbird.'

On the third night after leaving Gallala, when the constellation of the Wild Asses made its zenith in the northern night sky, Pharaoh halted the squadron to water the horses and to eat a hasty meal of sun-dried meat, dates and cold *dhurra* millet cakes. Then he ordered the mount-up. There was no sounding of the ram's horn trumpet now for they were into the territory where often the patrolling Hyksosian chariots ranged.

The column started forward again at the trot. As they went on the landscape changed dramatically. They were out of the bad lands at last, back into the foothills above the river valley. Below them they could make out the strip of dense vegetation, distant and dark in the moonlight, that marked the course of great Mother Nile. They had completed the wide circuit around Abnub and were in the rear of the main Hyksosian army on the river. Although they were a tiny force to go in against such an enemy as Apepi, they were the best charioteers in the armies of Tamose, which made them the finest in the world. Moreover, they held the element of surprise.

When Pharaoh had first proposed this strategy and told them he would lead the expedition in person, his war council had opposed him with all the vehemence they could muster against the word of a god. Even old Kratas, once the most reckless and savage warrior in all the armies of Egypt, had torn at his thick white beard and bellowed, 'By Seth's ragged and festering foreskin, I did not change your shit-smeared swaddling sheet so that I could send you straight into the loving arms of Apepi.' He was perhaps the one man who might dare to speak to a god-king in this fashion. 'Send another to do such menial work. Lead the breakthrough column yourself if it amuses you, but do not disappear into the desert to be devoured by ghouls and *djinn*. You are Egypt. If Apepi takes you he takes us all.'

Of all the council only Naja had supported him, but Naja was always loyal and true. Now they had won through the desert, and were into the enemy rear. In tomorrow's dawn they would make the one desperate charge that would split Apepi's army, and allow five more of Pharaoh's squadrons, a thousand chariots, to come boiling through to join him. Already he had the melliferous taste of victory on his tongue. Before the next full moon he would dine in the halls of Apepi's palace in Avaris.

It was almost two centuries since the Upper and Lower Kingdoms of Egypt had been split apart. Since then either an Egyptian usurper or a foreigner invader had ruled in the northern kingdom. It was Tamose's destiny to drive out the Hyksos and unite the two lands once more. Only then could he wear the double crown with justification and the approval of all the ancient gods.

The night air blew in his face, cool enough to numb his cheeks, and his lance-bearer crouched low behind the dashboard to shield himself. The only sound was the crunch of the chariot wheels over the coarse gravel, the lances rattling softly in their scabbards, and the occasional low warning cry of 'Beware! Hole!' passed on down the column.

Suddenly the wide wadi of Gebel Wadun opened ahead of him and Pharaoh Tamose reined down the team. The wadi was the smooth roadway that would lead them down on to the flat alluvial plain of the river. Pharaoh tossed the reins to his lance-bearer and vaulted down to earth. He stretched his stiff, aching limbs and, without turning, heard the sound of Naja's chariot come up behind him. A low command and the wheels crunched into silence, then Naja's light, firm footsteps came to his side. 'From here the danger of discovery will be stronger,' Naja said, 'Look down there.' He pointed with a long, muscular arm over Pharaoh's shoulder. Where the wadi debouched on to the plain below them a single light showed, the soft yellow glow of an oil lamp. 'That is the village of El Wadun. That is where our spies will be waiting to lead us through the Hyksosian pickets. I will go ahead to the rendezvous to make safe the way. Do you wait here, Majesty, and I will return directly.'

'I will go with you.'

'I beg you. There may be treachery, Mem.' He used the King's childhood name. 'You are Egypt. You are too precious to risk.'

Pharaoh turned to look into the beloved face, lean and handsome. Naja's teeth gleamed white in the starlight as he smiled, and Pharaoh touched his shoulder lightly but with trust and affection. 'Go swiftly, and return as swiftly,' he acceded.

Naja touched his own heart, and ran back to his chariot. He saluted again as he wheeled past where the King stood, and Tamose smiled as he returned the salute then watched him go down the side of the wadi. When he reached the flat hard sand of the dry riverbed, Naja whipped up the horses, and they sped down towards the village of El Wadun. The chariot left black-shaded wheel-tracks behind it on the silvery sands, before it disappeared beyond the first bend of the wadi. When it had gone Pharaoh walked back down the waiting column, speaking quietly to the troopers, calling many by name, laughing softly with them, encouraging and cheering them. Small wonder they loved him, and followed him so gladly wherever he led them.

Lord Naja drove warily, hugging the south bank of the dry riverbed. Every now and then he glanced upwards at the crest of the hills, until at last he recognized the tower of wind-blasted rock that leaned slightly askew against the skyline, and grunted with satisfaction. A little further on he reached the point where a faint footpath left the wadi bottom and wound up the steep slope to the foot of the ancient watchtower.

With a curt word to his lance-bearer he jumped down from the footplate, and adjusted the cavalry bow over his shoulder. Then he unslung the clay fire-pot from the rail of the chariot, and started up the pathway. It was so well disguised that if he had not memorized every turn and twist he would have lost his way a dozen times before he reached the top.

At last he stepped out on to the upper rampart of the tower. It had been built many centuries ago and was in ruinous condition. He did not approach the edge for there was a precipitous drop into the valley below. Instead he found the bundle of dry faggots hidden in the niche of the wall where he had left it and dragged it into the open. Quickly he built up a tiny pyramid of the kindling, then blew on the charcoal nuggets in the fire-pot, and when they glowed he crumbled a handful of dried grass on to them. They burst into flame and he lit the small signal beacon. He made no attempt to hide himself but stood out where a watcher below would see him illuminated on the height of the tower. The flames died away as the kindling was consumed. Naja sat down to wait in the darkness.

A short while later he heard a pebble rattle on the stony path below the walls and he whistled sharply. His signal was returned, and he stood up. He loosened the bronze blade of his sickle sword in its scabbard and nocked an arrow in the bow, standing ready for an instant draw. Moments later a harsh voice called to him in the Hyksosian language. He replied fluently and naturally in the same tongue, and the footsteps of at least two men sounded on the stone ramp.

Not even Pharaoh knew that Naja's mother had been Hyksosian. In the decades of their occupation the invaders had adopted many of the Egyptian ways. With a dearth of their own women to choose from, many of the Hyksos had taken Egyptian wives, and over the generations the blood-lines had become blurred.

A tall man stepped out on to the rampart. He wore a skull-hugging basinet of bronze, and multicoloured ribbons were tied in his full beard. The Hyksos dearly loved bright colours.

He opened his arms. 'The blessing of Seueth on you, cousin,' he growled, as Naja stepped into his embrace.

'And may he smile on you also, Cousin Trok, but we have little time,' Naja warned him, and indicated the first light fingers of the dawn stroking the eastern heavens with a lover's touch.

'You are right, coz.' The Hyksosian general broke the embrace, and turned to take a linen-wrapped bundle from his lieutenant, who stood close behind him. He handed it to Naja, who unwrapped it as he kicked life back into the beacon fire. In the light of the flames he inspected the arrow quiver it contained. It was carved from a light tough wood and covered with finely tooled and stitched leather. The workmanship was superb. This was the accoutrement of a high-ranking officer. Naja twisted free the stopper and drew one of the arrows from the container.

He examined it briefly, spinning the shaft between his fingers to check its balance and symmetry

The Hyksosian arrows were unmistakable. The fletching feathers were dyed with the bright colours of the archer's regiment and the shaft was branded with his personal signet. Even if the initial strike was not fatal, the flint arrowhead was barbed and bound to the shaft in such a way that if a surgeon attempted to draw the arrow from a victim's flesh, the head would detach from the shaft and remain deep in the wound channel, there to putrefy and cause a lingering, painful death. Flint was much harder than bronze, and would not bend nor flatten if it struck bone.

Naja slipped the arrow back into the quiver and replaced the stopper. He had not taken the chance of bringing such distinctive missiles with him in his chariot. If discovered in his kit by his groom or lance-bearer, its presence would be remembered, and difficult to explain away.

'There is much that we still should discuss.' Naja squatted down and gestured for Trok to do the same. They talked quietly until at last Naja rose. 'Enough! Now we both know what must be done. The time for action has at last arrived.'

'Let the gods smile upon our enterprise.' Trok and Naja embraced again, and then, without another word, Naja left him, ran lightly down the rampart of the tower and took the narrow path down the hill.

Before he reached the bottom he found a place to cache the quiver. It was a niche where the rock had been split open by the roots of a thorn tree. Over the quiver he placed a rock the size and roughly the shape of a horse's head. The twisted upper branches of the tree formed a distinctive cross against the night sky. He would recognize the place again without difficulty.

Then he went on down the path to where his chariot stood in the wadi bottom.

Pharaoh Tamose saw the chariot returning, and knew by the impetuous manner in which Naja drove that something untoward was afoot. Quietly he ordered the squadron to mount up and stand with drawn weapons, ready to meet any eventuality.

Naja's chariot rattled up the pathway from the wadi bottom. The moment it drew level with where Pharaoh waited he sprang down.

'What's amiss?' Tamose demanded.

'A blessing from the gods,' Naja told him, unable to stop his voice shaking with excitement. 'They have delivered Apepi defenceless into our power.'

'How is that possible?'

'My spies have led me to where the enemy king is encamped but a short distance from where we now stand. His tents are set up just beyond the first line of hills, yonder.' He pointed back with his drawn sword.

'Can you be certain it is Apepi?' Tamose could barely control his own excitement.

'I saw him clearly in the light of his campfire. Every detail of his features. His great beaked nose and beard shot with silver shining in the firelight. There is no mistaking such stature. He towers above all those around him, and wears the vulture crown on his head.'

'What is his strength?' Pharaoh demanded.

'With his usual arrogance he has a bodyguard of less than fifty. I have counted them, and half of them are asleep, their lances stacked. He suspects nothing and his watchfires burn bright. A swift charge out of the darkness and we will have him in our grasp.'

'Take me to where Apepi lies,' Pharaoh commanded, and leaped to the footplate.

Naja led them, and the soft silvery sands of the wadi muffled the sounds of the wheels, so that in a ghostly silence the squadron swept around the last bend and Naja raised his clenched fist high to order the halt. Pharaoh drew up alongside him and leaned across.

'Where lies Apepi's camp?'

'Beyond the ridge. I left my spies overlooking it.' Naja pointed up the pathway towards the watchtower on the crest. 'On the far side is a hidden oasis. A sweet-water well and date palms. His tents are set among the trees.'

'We will take a small patrol with us to scout the camp. Only then can we plan our attack.'

Naja had anticipated the order, and with a few terse orders selected a scouting party of five troopers. Each one was bound to him by blood oath. They were his men, hand and heart.

'Muffle your scabbards,' Naja ordered. 'Make not a sound.' Then, with his recurved bow in his left hand, he stepped on to the pathway. Pharaoh came close behind him. They went upwards swiftly, until Naja saw the crossed branches of the thorn tree silhouetted against the dawn sky. He stopped abruptly, and held up his right hand for silence. He listened.

'What is it?' Pharaoh whispered close behind him.

'I thought I heard voices on the crest,' Naja answered, 'speaking the Hyksosian tongue. Wait here, Majesty, while I clear the path ahead.' Pharaoh and the five troopers sank down and squatted beside the path, while Naja went on stealthily. He stepped around a large boulder and his dim figure disappeared from view. The minutes passed slowly and Pharaoh began to fret. The dawn was coming on swiftly. The Hyksosian king would soon be breaking his camp, and moving on, out of their grasp. As a soft whistle came down to him he sprang to his feet eagerly. It was a skilful imitation of a nightingale's dawn call.

Pharaoh hefted his fabled blue sword. 'The way is clear,' he murmured, 'Come, follow me.'

They went on upwards, and Pharaoh reached the tall rock that blocked the pathway. He stepped round it then stopped abruptly. Lord Naja faced him at a distance of twenty paces. They were alone, hidden by the rock from the men who followed. Naja's bow was at full draw and the arrow was aimed at Pharaoh's naked chest. Even before he could move, the full realization of what confronted him blazed in Pharaoh's mind. This was the foul and loathsome thing that Taita, with his clairvoyant powers, had smelt in the air.

The light was strong enough for him to make out every detail of the enemy he had loved as a friend. The bowstring was pulled hard against Naja's lips, twisting them into a dreadful smile, and his eyes were honey gold and fierce as those of the hunting leopard as he glared at Pharaoh. The fletching of the arrow was crimson and yellow and green, and in the Hyksosian fashion the arrowhead was made from razor-sharp flint, designed to tear through the bronze of an enemy's helmet and cuirass.

'May you live for ever!' Silently Naja mouthed the words as though they were a curse, and he loosed the arrow. It flew from the bowstring with a twang and a hum. It seemed to come quite slowly, like some poisonous flying insect. The feathers spun the shaft, and it made one full revolution as it covered the twenty paces. Though Pharaoh's eyesight was sharpened and his other senses were heightened by the mortal danger in which he found himself, he could move only with the slowness of nightmare, too slowly to avoid the missile. The arrow took him high in the centre of his chest, where his royal heart pounded in its cage of ribs. It struck with the sound of a boulder dropped from a height into a bed of thick Nile mud, and half the length of the shaft was driven through his chest. He was spun round by the force of the impact, and thrown against the red rock of the boulder. For a moment he clung to the rough surface with his hooked fingers. The flint arrowhead had pierced him through and through. The blood-clotted barb stood out of the knotted muscles that ran down the right side of his spine.

The blue sword dropped from his fist, and a low cry burst from his open mouth, the sound muffled by a gout of his own bright lung blood. He began to slide down to his knees, his legs buckling under him, his fingernails leaving shallow scratches on the red rock.

Naja sprang forward with a wild cry, 'Ambush! Beware!' and he slipped one arm around Pharaoh's chest below the protruding arrow.

Supporting the dying king he bellowed again, 'On me, the guards!' and two stout troopers appeared almost instantly from around the rock wall, responding to his rallying cry. They saw at a glance how Pharaoh was struck and the bright bunch of feathers on the base of the arrow.

'Hyksos!' one yelled, as they snatched Pharaoh from Naja's grasp and dragged him back behind the shelter of the rock.

'Carry Pharaoh back to his chariot while I hold off the enemy,' Naja ordered, and whirled around, pulling another arrow from his quiver and loosing it up the path towards the deserted summit, bellowing a challenge, then answering himself with a muffled counter-challenge in the Hyksosian language.

He snatched up the blue sword from where Tamose had dropped it, bounded back down the path and caught up with the small party of charioteers who were carrying the king away, down to where the chariots were waiting in the wadi.

'It was a trap,' Naja told them urgently. 'The hilltop is alive with the enemy. We must get Pharaoh away to safety.' But he could see by the way the king's head rolled weakly on his shoulders that he was past any help, and Naja's chest swelled with triumph. The blue war crown toppled from Pharaoh's brow and bumped down the path. Naja gathered it up as he ran past, fighting down the temptation to place it on his own head.

'Patience. The time is not yet ripe for that,' he chided himself silently, 'but already Egypt is mine, and all her crowns and pomp and power. I am become this very Egypt. I am become part of the godhead.'

He held the heavy crown protectively under his arm, and aloud he cried, 'Hurry, the enemy is on the path hard behind us. Hurry! The king must not fall into their hands.'

The troops below had heard the wild cries in the dawn, and the regimental surgeon was waiting for them beside the wheel of Pharaoh's chariot. He had been trained by Taita, and though lacking the old man's special magic he was a skilled doctor and might be capable of staunching even such a terrible wound as had pierced Pharaoh's chest. But Lord Naja would not risk having his victim returned to him from the underworld. He ordered the surgeon away brusquely. 'The enemy is hard upon us. There is no time for your quackery now. We must get him back to the safety of our own lines before we are overrun.'

Tenderly he lifted the king from the arms of the men who carried him and laid him on the footplate of his own chariot. He snapped off the shaft of the arrow that protruded from the king's chest and held it aloft so that all his men could see it clearly. 'This bloody instrument has struck down our Pharaoh. Our god and our king. May Seth damn the Hyksosian pig-swine who fired it, and may he burn in eternal flame for a thousand years.' His men growled in warlike agreement. Carefully Naja wrapped the arrow in a linen cloth, and placed it in the bin on the side wall of the chariot. He would deliver it to the council in Thebes to substantiate his report on Pharaoh's death.

'A good man here to hold Pharaoh,' Naja ordered, 'Treat him gently.'

While the king's own lance-bearer came forward, Naja unbuckled the sword-belt from around Pharaoh's waist, sheathed the blue sword and carefully stowed it in his own weapons bin.

The lance-bearer jumped on to the footplate and cradled Tamose's head. Fresh bright blood bubbled from the corners of his mouth as the chariot wheeled in a circle then sped back up the dry wadi with the rest of the squadron driving hard to keep up with it. Even though he was supported by the strong arms of his lance-bearer Pharaoh's limp body was jolted cruelly.

Facing forward so that none could see his expression, Naja laughed softly. The sound was covered by the grinding wheels and the crash of the chassis over the small boulders he made no attempt to avoid. They left the wadi and raced on towards the dunes and the natron lakes.

It was mid-morning and the blinding white sun was halfway up the sky before Naja allowed the column to halt and the surgeon to come forward again to examine the king. It did not need his special skills to tell that Pharaoh's spirit had long before left his body and started on its journey to the underworld.

'Pharaoh is dead,' the surgeon said quietly, as he stood up with the royal blood coating his hands to the wrists. A terrible cry of mourning started at the head of the column and ran down its entire length. Naja let them play out their grief then sent for his troop captains.

'The state is without a head,' he told them. 'Egypt is in dire peril. Ten of the fastest chariots must take Pharaoh's body back to Thebes with all haste. I shall lead them for it may be that the council will wish me to take up the duties of regent to Prince Nefer.'

He had planted the first seeds and saw by their awed expressions that they had taken root almost immediately. He went on, with a grim, businesslike air that suited the tragic circumstances which had overtaken them, 'The surgeon must wrap the royal corpse before I take it home to the funeral temple. But in the meantime we must find Prince Nefer. He must be informed of his father's death and of his own succession. This is the single most urgent matter of state, and of my regency.' He had assumed that title smoothly, and no man questioned him or even looked askance. He unrolled a papyrus scroll, a map of the territory from Thebes down to Memphis, and spread it on the dashboard of his chariot. He pored over it. 'You must split up into your troops and scour the countryside for the prince. I believe that Pharaoh sent him into the desert with the eunuch to undertake the rituals of manhood, so we will concentrate our search here, from Gallala where we last saw him towards the south and east.' With the eye for ground of a commander of armies Naja picked out the search area, and ordered a net of chariots to be spread out across the land to bring in the prince.

The squadron returned to Gallala with Lord Naja in the van. Next in line came the vehicle carrying the partially embalmed body of Pharaoh. On the shore of the natron lake Waifra, the surgeon, had laid out the royal corpse and made the traditional incision in his left side. Through this he had removed the viscera and internal organs. The contents of the stomach and intestines had been washed in the viscous salt water of the lake. Then all the organs were packed with the white crystals of evaporated natron from the lake edge and stored in pottery wine jars. The king's body cavity was packed with natron salts, then wrapped in linen bindings soaked with the harsh salt. When they reached Thebes he would be taken to his own funerary temple and handed over to the priests and embalmers for the ritual seventy days of preparation for burial. Naja grudged every minute spent upon the road, for he was in desperate haste to return to Thebes before the news of the King's death preceded him. Yet at the gates of the ruined city he took more precious time to instruct the troop captains who were to undertake the search for the prince.

'Sweep all the roads to the east. The eunuch is a wily old bird and will have covered his tracks, but smell him out,' he ordered them. 'There are villages at the oases of Satam and Lakara. Question the people. You may use the whip and the hot iron to make certain they hide nothing. Search all the secret places of the wilderness. Find the prince and the eunuch. Fail me not, at your peril.'

When at last the captains had refilled their waterskins and were ready to take their divisions out into the desert, he held them with a final order, and they knew from his voice and his ferocious yellow eyes that this was the most fateful order of all, and that to disobey would mean death. 'When you find Prince Nefer, bring him to me. Give him into no other hand but mine.'

There were Nubian scouts with the divisions, black slaves from the wild southlands highly skilled in the art of tracking down men and beasts. They trotted ahead of the chariots as they fanned out into the wilderness, and Lord Naja spent another few precious minutes watching them go. His jubilation was tempered with unease. He knew that the ancient eunuch, Taita, was an adept; that he possessed strange and wonderful powers. If there is one single man who can stop me now, it is he. I wish that I could run them down myself, the eunuch and the brat, rather than send underlings to pit themselves against the Warlock's wiles. But my destiny calls to me from Thebes and I dare not linger.

He ran back to his chariot and seized the reins. 'Onwards!' He gave the command to advance with a clenched fist. 'Onwards to Thebes!'

They drove the horses hard, so that when they raced down the escarpment of the eastern hills on to the wide alluvial plain of the river, the lather had dried white on their heaving flanks and their eyes were red and wild.

Naja had withdrawn a full legion of the Phat Guards from the army encamped before Abnub. He had explained to Pharaoh that these were the strategic reserves to throw into the gap and prevent a Hyksosian break-out should the offensive fail. However, the Phat Guard was his own special regiment. The commanders were oath-bound to him. Following his secret orders they had pulled back from Abnub, and were waiting for him now at the oasis of Boss, only two leagues from Thebes.

The guards' pickets saw the dust of the approaching chariots and stood to arms. The colonel, Asmor, and his officers were turned out in full armour to meet Lord Naja. The legion, under arms, was drawn up behind them.

'Lord Asmor!' Naja hailed him from the chariot. 'I have dreadful news to take to the council at Thebes. Pharaoh is killed by a Hyksosian arrow.'

'Lord Naja, I stand ready to carry out your orders.'

'Egypt is a child without a father.' Naja halted his chariot in front of the ranks of plumed and glittering warriors. Now he raised his voice so it carried clearly to the rear ranks. 'Prince Nefer is a child still, and not yet ready to rule. Egypt stands in desperate need of a regent to lead her, lest the Hyksos take advantage of our disarray.' He paused and stared significantly at Colonel Asmor. Asmor lifted his chin slightly in acknowledgement of the trust that Naja had placed in him.

He had been promised rewards greater than any he had ever dreamed of.

Naja raised his voice to a bellow: 'If Pharaoh falls in battle, the army has the right by acclamation to appoint a regent in the field.' He fell silent and stood with one fist clenched on his breast and the lance in his other hand.

Asmor took a pace forward and turned to face the ranks of heavily armed guards. With a theatrical gesture he removed his helmet. His face was dark and hard. A pale scar from a sword slash twisted his nose to one side, and his shaven pate was covered by a plaited horsehair wig. He pointed his drawn sword to the sky, and he shouted, in a voice that had been trained to carry over the din of battle, 'Lord Naja! Hail to the Regent of Egypt! Hail to Lord Naja!'

There was a long moment of stunned silence before the legion erupted in a roar, like a pride of hunting lions, 'Hail to Lord Naja, Regent of Egypt.'

The cheering and the uproar lasted until Lord Naja raised his fist again, and in the silence that followed he spoke clearly: 'You do me great honour! I accept the charge you place upon me.'

'*Bak-her!*' they shouted, and beat upon their shields with sword and lance until the echoes broke like distant thunder on the hills of the escarpment.

In the uproar Naja summoned Asmor to him. 'Place pickets on all the roads. No man leaves this place until I do. No word of this must reach Thebes ahead of me.'

The journey from Gallala had taken three days of hard riding. The horses were worn out, and even Naja was exhausted. Yet he allowed himself only an hour to rest, bathe away the dust of the journey and change his apparel. Then, with his jaw shaven, his hair oiled and combed, he mounted the ceremonial chariot that Asmor had ready and waiting at the entrance to the tent. The gold leaf that decorated the dashboard shone in the sunlight.

Naja wore a white linen skirt, with a pectoral plate of gold and semi-precious stones covering his bare muscled chest. On his hip he carried the fabulous blue sword in its golden scabbard that he had taken from Pharaoh's dead body. The blade was beaten from some marvellous metal, heavier, harder and sharper than any bronze. There was none other like it in all Egypt. It had once belonged to Tanus, Lord Harrab, and had come to Pharaoh by his bequest.

The most significant of all his accoutrements, however, was the least eye-catching. On his right arm, held in place by a plain band of gold above the elbow, was the blue hawk seal. Like the sword Naja had taken it from Tamose's royal corpse. As Regent of Egypt, Naja was now entitled to wear this potent badge of imperial power.

His bodyguard formed up around him, and the full legion fell in behind him. With five thousand men at his back the new Regent of Egypt began his march on Thebes.

Asmor rode as his lance-bearer. He was young for the command of a full legion, but he had proved himself in battle against the Hyksos, and he was Naja's close companion. He, too, had Hyksosian blood in his veins. Once, Asmor had thought the command of a legion was the summit of his ambition, but now he had scaled the foothills and suddenly before him rose the glorious alps of exalted office, of power unfettered, and – dare he even think it? – elevation to the highest ranks of the nobility. There was nothing he would not do, no act so reckless or base that he would not undertake it willingly to hasten his patron Lord Naja's ascension to the throne of Egypt.

'What stands before us now, my old comrade?' It seemed that Naja had read his thought, for the question was so appropriate.

'The Yellow Flowers have cleared all but one of the princes of the House of Tamose from your path,' Asmor answered, and pointed with his lance across the grey silt-laden waters of the Nile to the far hills in the west. 'They lie there in their tombs in the Valley of the Nobles.'

Three years previously the plague of the Yellow Flowers had swept through the two kingdoms. The disease was named for the dreadful yellow lesions that covered the faces and bodies of the stricken before they succumbed to the pox's burning fevers. It was no respecter of persons, choosing its victims from every station and level of society, sparing neither Egyptian nor Hyksos, man nor woman nor child, neither peasant nor prince, it had mown them down like fields of *dhurra* millet before the sickle.

Eight princesses and six princes of the House of Tamose had died. Of all Pharaoh's children, only two girls and Prince Nefer Memnon had survived. It was as though the gods had set out deliberately to clear the path to the throne of Egypt for Lord Naja.

There were those who vowed that Nefer and his sisters would have died also, had not the ancient Magus Taita wrought his magic to save them. The three children still bore the tiny scars on their left upper arms where he had cut them and placed in their blood his magical charm against the Yellow Flowers.

Naja frowned. Even in this moment of his triumph he could still give thought to the strange powers possessed by the Magus. No man could deny that he had found the secret of life. He had already lived so long that no one knew his age; some said a hundred years and others two hundred. Yet he still walked and ran and drove a chariot like a man in his prime. No man could better him in debate, none could surpass him in learning. Surely the gods loved him, and had bestowed upon him the secret of life eternal.

Once he was Pharaoh, that would be the only thing that Naja lacked. Could he wring the secret out of Taita the Warlock? First, he must be captured and brought in along with Prince Nefer, but he must not be harmed. He was far too valuable. The chariots Naja had sent to scour the eastern deserts would bring him back a throne in the form of Prince Nefer, and life eternal in the human guise of the eunuch, Taita.

Asmor interrupted his thoughts: 'We of the loyal Phat Guard are the only troops south of Abnub. The rest of the army is deployed against the Hyksos in the north. Thebes is defended by a handful of boys, cripples and old men. Nothing stands in your way, Regent.'

Any fears that the legion under arms would be denied entrance to the city proved baseless. The main gates were thrown open as soon as the sentries recognized the blue standard, and the citizens ran out to meet them. They carried palm fronds and garlands of water-lilies, for a rumour had swept through the city that Lord Naja brought tidings of a mighty victory over Apepi of the Hyksos.

But the welcoming cries and laughter soon gave way to wild ululations of mourning when they saw the swaddled royal corpse on the floorboards of the second chariot and heard the cries of the leading charioteers: 'Pharaoh is dead! He has been slain by the Hyksos. May he live for ever.'

The wailing crowds followed the chariot that carried the royal corpse to the funerary temple, clogging the streets, and in the confusion no one seemed to notice that divisions of Asmor's men had taken over from the guards at the main gates, and had swiftly set up pickets at every corner and in every square.

The chariot bearing Tamose's corpse had drawn the crowds along with it. The rest of the usually swarming city was almost deserted, and Naja galloped his chariot team swiftly through the narrow crooked streets to the river palace. He knew that every member of the council would hurry to the assembly chamber as soon as they heard the dreadful news. They left the chariots at the entrance to the gardens, and Asmor and fifty men of the bodyguard formed up around Naja. They marched in close order through the inner courtyard, past the ponds of the water garden filled with hyacinth and fish from the river, which shone like jewels below the surface of the limpid pools.

The arrival of such a band of armed men took the council unawares. The doors to the chamber were unguarded, and only four members were already assembled. Naja paused in the doorway and looked them over swiftly. Menset and Talla were old and past their once formidable powers; Cinka had always been weak and vacillating. There was only one man of force in the chamber with whom he had to reckon.

Kratas was older than any of them, but in the way that a volcano is old. His robes were in disarray – clearly he had come directly from his pallet, but not from sleep. They said that he was still able to keep his two young wives and all of his five concubines in play, which Naja did not doubt, for the tales of his feats with arms and amours were legion. The fresh, damp stains on his white linen kilt and the sweet natural perfume of female concupiscence that enveloped him were apparent even from where Naja stood. The scars on his arms and bare chest were testimony to a hundred battles fought and won over the years. The old man no longer deigned to wear the numerous chains of the Gold of Valour and the Gold of Praise to which he was entitled – in any case, such a mass of the precious metal would have weighed down an ox.

'Noble lords!' Naja greeted the members of the council. 'I come to bring you dire tidings.' He strode down into the chamber and Menset and Talla shrank away, staring at him like two rabbits watching the sinuous approach of the cobra. 'Pharaoh is dead. He was cut down by a Hyksosian arrow while storming the enemy stronghold above El Wadun.'

The council members gawked at him in silence, all except Kratas. He was the first to recover from the shock of that news. His sorrow was matched only by his anger. He rose ponderously to his feet, and glowered at Naja and his bodyguard, like an old bull buffalo surprised in his wallow by a pride of half-grown lion cubs. 'By what excess of treasonable impudence do you wear the hawk seal upon your arm? Naja, son of Timlat out of the belly of a Hyksosian slut, you are not fit to grovel in the dirt under the feet of the man from whom you looted that talisman. That sword at your waist has been wielded by hands more noble by far than your soft paws.' The dome of Kratas' bald head turned purple and his craggy features quivered with outrage.

For a moment Naja was taken aback. How did the old monster know that his mother had been of Hyksosian blood? That was a close secret. He was forcefully reminded that this was the only man, besides Taita, who might have the strength and the power to wrest the double crown from his grasp.

Despite himself he took a step backwards. 'I am the Regent of the royal Prince Nefer. I wear the blue hawk seal by right,' he answered.

'No!' Kratas thundered. 'You do not have the right. Only great and noble men have the right to wear the hawk seal. Pharaoh Tamose had the right, Tanus, Lord Harrab had the right, and a line of mighty kings before them. You, you slinking cur, have no such right.'

'I was acclaimed by my legions in the field. I am the Regent of Prince Nefer.'

Kratas strode towards him across the chamber floor, 'You are no soldier. You were thrashed at Lastra and Siva by your Hyksos jackal kin. You are no statesman, no philosopher. You have gained some small distinction only by Pharaoh's lapse in judgement. I warned him against you a hundred times.'

'Back, you old fool!' Naja warned him. 'I stand in the place of Pharaoh. If you handle me, you give offence to the crown and dignity of Egypt.'

'I am going to strip the seal and that sword off you.' Kratas did not check his step. 'And afterwards I might give myself the pleasure of whipping your buttocks.'

At Naja's right hand Asmor whispered, 'The penalty for lèse-majesté is death.'

Instantly Naja realized his opportunity. He lifted his chin and looked into the old man's still bright eyes. 'You are an ancient bag of wind and dung,' he challenged. 'Your day has passed, Kratas, you doddering old idiot. You dare not lay a finger on the Regent of Egypt.'

As he had intended, the insult was too great for Kratas to bear. He let out a bellow and rushed the last few paces. He was surprisingly quick for a man of his age and bulk, and he seized Naja, lifted him off his feet and tried to rip the hawk seal from his arm.

'You are not fit—'

Without looking round, Naja spoke to Asmor, who stood only a pace behind his shoulder with his drawn sickle sword in his right hand.

'Strike!' said Naja softly. 'And strike deep!'

Asmor stepped to the side, opening Kratas' flank above the waistband of the kilt for the thrust low in the back, into the kidneys. In his trained hand the blow was true and powerful. The bronze blade slipped in silently, easily as a needle into a sheet of silk, right in to the hilt, then Asmor twisted it in the flesh to enlarge the wound channel.

Kratas' whole body stiffened and his eyes opened wide. He loosed his grip and let Naja drop back to his feet. Asmor pulled out the blade. It came away reluctantly against the suck of clinging flesh. The bright bronze was smeared with dark blood, and a sluggish trickle ran down to soak into Kratas' white linen kilt. Asmor stabbed again, this time higher, angling the blade upwards under the lowest rib. Kratas frowned and shook his great leonine head, as though annoyed at some childish nonsense. He turned away and began to walk towards the door of the chamber. Asmor ran after him and stabbed him again in the back. Kratas kept walking.

'My lord, help me kill the dog,' Asmor panted, and Naja drew the blue sword and ran to join him. The blade bit deeper than any bronze as Naja hacked and stabbed. Kratas reeled out through the doors of the chamber into the courtyard, blood spurting and pulsing from a dozen wounds. Behind him the other members of the council shouted, 'Murder! Spare the noble Kratas.'

Asmor shouted just as loudly, 'Traitor! He has laid hands on the Regent of Egypt!' And he thrust again, aiming for the heart, but Kratas staggered against the surrounding wall of the fish pond, and tried to steady himself. However, his hands were red and slick with his own blood and found no grip on the polished marble. He collapsed over the low coping and, with a heavy splash, disappeared under the surface.

The two swordsmen paused, hanging over the wall to catch their breath as the waters were stained pink by the old man's blood. Suddenly his bald head thrust out of the pool and Kratas drew a noisy breath.

'In the name of all the gods, will not the old bastard die?' Asmor's voice was filled with astonishment and frustration.

Naja vaulted over the wall into the pond and stood waist-deep over the huge, floundering body. He placed one foot on Kratas' throat and forced his head beneath the surface. Kratas struggled and heaved beneath him, and the waters were stained with blood and churned river mud. Naja trod down with all his weight and kept him under. ''Tis like riding a hippopotamus.' He laughed breathlessly, and immediately Asmor and the soldiers joined in with him, crowding the edge of the pool. They roared with laughter and jeered, 'Have your last drink, Kratas, you old sot.'

'You will go to Seth bathed and sweet smelling as a babe. Even the god will not recognize you.'

The old man's struggles grew weaker, until a vast exhalation of breath bubbled to the surface and at last he was still. Naja waded to the side of the pool and stepped out. Kratas' body rose slowly to the surface and floated there face down.

'Fish him out!' Naja ordered. 'Do not have him embalmed, but hack him into pieces and bury him with the other bandits, rapists and traitors in the Valley of the Jackal. Do not mark his grave.' Kratas was thus denied the chance to reach Paradise. He would be doomed eternally to wander in darkness.

Dripping wet to the waist Naja strode back into the council chamber. By this time all the other members of the council had arrived. They had been witness to Kratas' fate and huddled, pale and shaken, on their benches. They stared at Naja aghast as he stood before them with the reeking blue blade in his hand. 'My noble lords, death has always been the penalty for treason. Is there any man among you who would question the justice of this execution?' He looked at each in turn and they dropped their eyes: the Phat Guards stood shoulder to shoulder around the wall of the chamber and, with Kratas gone, there was no man to give them direction.

'My lord Menset,' Naja singled out the president of the council, 'do you endorse my action in executing the traitor Kratas?'

For a long moment it seemed that Menset might defy him, but then he sighed and looked at his hands in his lap. 'The punishment was just,' he whispered. 'The council endorses the actions of the Lord Naja.'

'Does the council also ratify the appointment of Lord Naja as the Regent of Egypt?' Naja asked softly but his voice carried clearly in the fraught and silent chamber.

Menset raised his eyes and looked around at his fellow members, but not one would catch his eye. 'The President and all the councillors of this assembly acknowledge the new Regent of Egypt.' At last Menset looked directly at Naja, but such a dark, scornful expression blighted his usually jovial features that before the full of this moon he would be found dead in his bed. For the time being Naja merely nodded.

'I accept the duty and heavy responsibility you have placed upon me.' He sheathed his sword and mounted the dais to the throne. 'As my first official pronouncement in my capacity of Regent in Council I wish to describe to you the gallant death of the divine Pharaoh Tamose.' He paused significantly, then for the next hour he related in detail his version of the fatal campaign and the attack on the heights of El Wadun. 'Thus died one of Egypt's most gallant kings. His last words to me as I carried him down the hill were, "Care for my only remaining son. Guard my son Nefer until he is man enough to wear the double crown. Take my two small daughters under your wings, and see that no harm befalls them."'

Lord Naja made little attempt to hide his terrible grief and it took him some moments to bring his emotions under control. Then he went on firmly, 'I will not fail the god who was my friend and my pharaoh. Already I have sent my chariots into the wilderness to search for Prince

Nefer and bring him back to Thebes. As soon as he arrives we will set him on the throne, and place the scourge and the sceptre in his hands.'

There was the first murmur of approval among the councillors, and Naja continued, 'Now send for the princesses. Have them brought to the chamber immediately.'

When they came hesitantly through the main doors, Heseret the elder was leading her little sister, Merykara, by the hand. Merykara had been playing pitch and toss with her friends. She was flushed from her exertions and her slim body was dewed with sweat. She was still several years from womanhood so her legs were long and coltish and her bare chest was as flat as a boy's. She wore her long black hair in a side-lock that hung over her left shoulder, and her linen breech clout was so diminutive that it left the lower half of her little round buttocks exposed. She smiled shyly around this formidable gathering of famous men, and clung harder to her elder sister's hand.

Heseret had seen her first red moon and was dressed in the linen skirts and wig of a marriageable woman. Even the old men looked at her avidly for she had inherited in full measure her grandmother Queen Lostris' celebrated beauty. Her skin was milky. Her limbs were smooth and shapely, and her naked breasts were like celestial moons. Her expression was serene but the corners of her mouth lifted in a secret, mischievous smile, and there were intriguing lights in her huge dark green eyes.

'Come forward, my pretty darlings,' Naja called to them, and only then they recognized the man who was the close and beloved friend of their father. They smiled and came towards him trustingly. He rose from the throne, went down to meet them and placed his hands on their shoulders. His voice and his expression were tragic. 'You must be brave now, and remember that you are princesses of the royal house, because I have bitter news for you. Pharaoh your father is dead.' For a minute they did not seem to understand, then Heseret let out the high keening wail of mourning, followed immediately by Merykara.

Gently Naja put his arms around them, and led them to sit at the foot of the throne, where they sank to their knees and clung to each other, weeping inconsolably.

'The distress of the royal princesses is plain for all the world to see,' Naja told the assembly. 'The trust and the duty that Pharaoh placed upon me is equally plain. As I have taken Prince Nefer Memnon into my care, so now I take the two princesses, Heseret and Merykara, under my protection.'

'Now he has all the royal brood in his hands. But no matter where he is in the wilderness, and how hale and strong the Prince Nefer may seem,' Talla whispered to his neighbour, 'methinks he is already sickening unto death. The new Regent of Egypt has made abundantly clear his style of government.'

Nefer sat in the shadow of the cliff that towered above Gebel Nagara. He had not moved since the sun had first shown its upper rim above the mountains across the valley. At first the effort of remaining still had burned along his nerve endings and made his skin itch as though poisonous insects were crawling upon it. But he knew that Taita was watching him so he had forced his wayward body slowly to his will and risen above its petty dictates. Now at last he sat in a state of exalted awareness, his every sense tuned to the wilderness about him.

He could smell the water that rose from its secret spring in the cleft in the cliff. It came up a slow drop at a time and dripped into the basin in the rock that was not much larger than the cup of his two hands, then overflowed and dribbled down into the next basin, green-lined with slippery algae. From there it ran down to disappear for ever into the ruddy sands of the valley bottom. Yet much life was supported by this trickle of water: butterfly and beetle, serpent and lizard, the graceful little gazelle that danced like whiffs of saffron dust on the heat-quivering plains, the speckled pigeons with their ruffs of wine-coloured feathers that nested on high ledges all drank here. It was because of these precious pools that Taita had brought him to this place to wait for his godbird.

They had begun to make the net on the day of their arrival at Gebel Nagara. Taita had bought the silk from a merchant in Thebes. The hank of thread had cost the price of a fine stallion, for it had been brought from a land far to the east of the Indus river on a journey that had taken years to complete. Taita had shown Nefer how to weave the net out of the fine threads. The mesh was stronger than thick strands of linen or thongs of leather but almost invisible to the eye.

When the net was ready Taita had insisted that the boy catch the decoys himself. 'It is your godbird. You must take it yourself,' he had explained. 'That way your claim will be more secure in the sight of the great god Horus.'

So, in the baking daylight out on the valley floor, Nefer and Taita had studied the route up the cliff. When darkness fell Taita had sat beside the small fire at the base of the cliff and softly chanted his incantations, at intervals throwing a handful of herbs on to the fire.

When the crescent moon rose to illuminate the darkness of midnight Nefer had started the precarious climb to the ledge where the pigeons roosted. He had seized two of the big, fluttering birds while they were still disorientated and confused by the darkness and the spell that Taita had cast over them. He brought them down in the leather saddlebag slung on his back.

Under Taita's instruction Nefer had plucked the feathers from one wing of each bird, so that they were no longer able to fly. Then they had selected a spot close to the base of the cliff and the spring, but exposed enough to make the birds clearly visible from the sky above. They tethered the pigeons by the leg with a thread of horsetail hair and a wooden peg driven into the hard earth. Then they had spread the gossamer net above them, and supported it on stalks of dried elephant grass, which would snap and collapse under the stoop of the godbird.

'Stretch the net gently,' Taita had shown him, 'not too tight, nor again too slack. It must catch in the bird's beak and his talons and tangle him so that he cannot struggle and damage himself before we can free him.'

When all was set up to Taita's satisfaction, they began the long wait. Soon the pigeons had become accustomed to their captivity, and pecked greedily at the handfuls of *dhurra* millet that Nefer scattered for them. Then they sunned and dusted themselves contentedly under the silken net. One day succeeded the next hot, sun-riven day, and still they waited.

In the cool of the evening they brought in the pigeons, furled the net, and then they hunted for food. Taita climbed to the top of the cliff where he sat cross-legged on the edge, overlooking the long valley. Nefer waited in ambush below, never in the same place so that the game were always surprised when they came to drink at the spring. From his vantage-point Taita wove his spell of enticement, which seldom failed to seduce the dainty gazelle within fair shot of where Nefer lay with his arrow nocked and bow held at draw. Every evening they grilled gazelle steaks over the fire at the entrance to the cave.

The cave had been Taita's retreat during all the years after the death of Queen Lostris when he had lived here as a hermit. It was his place of power. Although Nefer was a novice, and had no deep understanding of the old man's mystical skills, he could not doubt them, for every day they were demonstrated to him.

They had been at Gebel Nagara for many days before Nefer began to understand that they had not come here to find the godbird alone: this interlude was an extension of the training and instruction Taita had lavished upon him from as far back as Nefer's young memory stretched.

Even the long hours of waiting beside the decoys was a lesson in itself. Taita was teaching him control over his body and being, teaching him to open doors within his mind, teaching him to look inward, to listen to the silence and hear whispers to which others were deaf.

Once he had been conditioned to the silence, Nefer was more amenable to the deeper wisdom and learning that Taita had to impart. They sat together in the desert night, under the swirling patterns of the stars that were eternal but ephemeral as the winds and the currents of the oceans, and Taita described to him wonders that seemed to have no explanation but could only be perceived by an opening and extension of the mind. He sensed that he stood merely on the shadowy periphery of this mystical knowledge, but he felt growing inside him a great hunger for more.

One morning when Nefer left the cave in the grey light before dawn, he saw a huddle of dark, silent figures sitting out in the desert beyond the spring of Gebel Nagara. He went to tell Taita, and the old man nodded. 'They have been waiting all night.' He spread a woollen cloak over his shoulders and went out to them.

When they recognized Taita's gaunt figure in the half-light they burst into wails of supplication. They were people of the desert tribes and they had brought children to him, children stricken by the Yellow Flowers, hot with fever and covered with the terrible sores of the disease.

Taita ministered to them, while they remained camped beyond the spring. None of the children died, and after ten days the tribe brought gifts of millet, salt and tanned hides, which they left at the entrance to the cave. Then they were gone into the wilderness. After that there came others, suffering from disease and wounds inflicted by men and beasts. Taita went out to all of them, and turned none away. Nefer worked beside him and learned much from what he saw and heard.

No matter if there were the sick and ailing Bedouin to care for, or food to be gathered, or instruction or learning to be imparted, each morning they set out the decoys under the silken net and waited beside them.

Perhaps they had fallen under the calming influence of Taita, for the once-wild pigeons became docile and quiescent as chickens. They allowed themselves to be handled without any sign of fear, and uttered soft throaty coos as their legs were secured to the pegs. Then they settled and fluffed up their feathers.

On the twentieth morning of their stay, Nefer took up his position over the decoys. As always, even without looking directly at Taita, Nefer was deeply aware of his presence. The old man's eyes were closed and he, like the pigeons, seemed to be dozing in the sunlight. His skin was criss-crossed with innumerable fine wrinkles and dappled with age spots. It seemed so delicate that it might tear as easily as the finest papyrus parchment. His face was hairless, no trace of beard or eyebrows; only fine lashes, colourless as glass, surrounded his eyes. Nefer had heard his father say that neutering had left Taita's face beardless and little marked by the passage of time, but he was certain that there were more esoteric reasons for his longevity and the persistence of his strength and life-force. In vivid contrast to his other features, Taita's hair was dense and strong as that of a healthy young woman, but bright burnished silver in colour. Taita was proud of it and kept it washed and groomed in a thick plait down his back. Despite his learning and age, the old Magus was not inured to vanity.

This little touch of humanity heightened Nefer's love for him to the point where it stabbed his chest with a strength that was almost painful. He wished that there was some way in which he could express it, but he knew that Taita already understood, for Taita knew everything.

He reached out surreptitiously to touch the old man's arm as he slept, but suddenly Taita's eyes opened, focused and aware. Nefer knew that he had not been asleep at all, but that all his powers had been concentrated on bringing in the godbird to the decoys. He knew that, in some way, his wandering thoughts and his movement had affected the outcome of the old man's efforts, for he sensed Taita's disapproval as clearly as if it had been spoken.

Chastened, he composed himself, and brought his mind and body under control again in the manner that Taita had taught him. It was like passing through a secret doorway into the place of power. The time passed swiftly, without being counted or grudged. The sun climbed to its zenith and seemed to hang there for a long while. Suddenly Nefer was blessed with a marvellous sense of prescience. It was almost as if he, too, hung above the world and saw everything happening below him. He saw Taita and himself sitting beside the well of Gebel Nagara, and the desert stretching away around them. He saw the river that contained the desert like a mighty barrier and marked out the boundaries of this very Egypt. He saw the cities and the kingdoms, the lands divided under the double crown, great armies in array, the machinations of evil men, and the striving and sacrifice of the just and good. In that moment he was aware of his destiny with an intensity that almost overwhelmed and crushed his courage.

In that same moment he knew that his godbird would come on this day, for he was ready to receive it at last.

'The bird is here!'

The words were so clear that, for an instant, Nefer thought Taita had spoken, but then he realized his lips had not moved. Taita had placed the thought in Nefer's mind in the mysterious manner that Nefer could neither fathom nor explain. He did not doubt that it was so, but in the next instant it was confirmed by the wild fluttering of the decoy pigeons who had sensed the menace in the air above them.

Nefer made no move to show that he had heard and understood. He did not turn his head or lift his eyes to the sky. He dared not look upwards lest he alarm the bird, or incur the wrath of Taita. But he was aware with every fibre of his being.

The royal falcon was such a rare creature that few men had ever seen it in the wild. For the previous thousand years the huntsmen of every pharaoh had sought out the birds, had trapped and netted them, and to fill the royal mews had even lifted their young from the nest before they were fledged. Possession of the birds was proof that Pharaoh had the divine approval of the god Horus to reign in this very Egypt.

The falcon was the *alter ego* of the god: statues and depictions of him showed him with the falcon head. Pharaoh was a god himself so might capture, own and hunt the bird, but any other man did so on pain of death.

Now the bird was here. His very own bird. Taita seemed to have conjured it out of heaven itself. Nefer felt his heart held in a suffocating grip of excitement and the breath in his lungs seized up so that he thought his chest might burst. But still he dared not turn his head to the sky.

Then he heard the falcon. Its cry was a faint lament, almost lost in the immensity of sky and desert, but it thrilled Nefer to the core, as though the god had spoken directly to him. Seconds later the falcon called again, directly overhead, its voice shriller and more savage.

Now the pigeons were wild with terror, leaping against the thongs that secured them to the pegs, beating their wings with such violence that they shed feathers, and the downdraught of air raised a pale cloud of dust around them.

High overhead Nefer heard the falcon begin its stoop on the decoys, with the wind singing over its wings in a rising note. He knew that at last it was safe to raise his head, for all the falcon's attention would be focused on its prey.

He looked up and saw the bird drop against the aching blue of the desert sky. It was a thing of divine beauty. Its wings were folded back, like half-sheathed blades, and its head was thrust forward. The strength and power of the creature made Nefer gasp aloud. He had seen other falcons of this breed in his father's mews, but never before like this in all its wild grace and majesty. Miraculously the falcon seemed to swell in size, and its colours grew more intense as it fell towards where he sat.

The curved beak was a lovely deep yellow with a tip sharp and black as obsidian. The eyes were fiercest gold with tear-like markings in the inner corners, the throat was creamy and dappled like ermine, the wings were russet and black, and the whole creature was so exquisite in every detail that he never doubted it was an incarnation of the god. He wanted to possess it with a longing he had never imagined possible.

He braced himself for the moment of impact when the falcon would strike the silken net and ensnare itself in the voluminous folds. Beside him he felt Taita do the same. They would rush forward together.

Then something happened that he could not believe was possible. The falcon was fully committed to its stoop, the velocity of its dive was such that nothing could have stopped it but the impact of the strike into the pigeons' soft-feathered bodies. But, against all probability, the falcon flared out. Its wings changed their profile and for an instant the wind-force threatened to rip away the pinions at their juncture with its body. The air shrieked over the spread feathers and the falcon had changed direction, was hurtling aloft once more, using its own momentum to arc up into the sky until in seconds it was only a black speck against the blue. Its cry sounded once more in the air, plaintive and remote, and then it was gone.

'He refused!' Nefer whispered. 'Why, Taita, why?'

'The ways of the gods are not for us to fathom.' Although he had been still for all those hours, Taita stood up with the lithe movement of a trained athlete.

'Will he not return?' Nefer asked. 'He was my bird. I felt it in my heart. He was my bird. He must return.'

'He is part of the godhead,' Taita said softly. 'He is not part of the natural order of things.'

'But why did he refuse? There must be some reason,' Nefer insisted.

Taita did not reply immediately, but went to release the pigeons. After all this time their wing feathers had grown again, but as he freed their legs from the horsehair fetters they made no attempt to escape. One fluttered up and perched on his shoulder. Gently Taita took it in both hands and threw it aloft. Only then did it fly up the cliff face to its roost on the high ledge.

He watched it go then turned and walked back to the entrance of the cave. Nefer followed him slowly, his heart and legs leaden with disappointment. In the gloom of the cave Taita seated himself on the stone ledge below the back wall, and leaned forward to build up the smoky fire of thorn branches and horse dung until it burst into flames. Heavily, filled with foreboding, Nefer took up his accustomed place opposite him.

They were both silent for a long while, Nefer containing himself, although his disappointment at the loss of the falcon was a torment as intense as if he had thrust his hand into flames. He knew that Taita would only speak again when he was ready. At last Taita sighed, and said softly, almost sadly, 'I must work the Mazes of Ammon Ra.'

Nefer was startled. He had not expected that. In all their time together Nefer had only seen him work the Mazes twice before. He knew that the self-induced trance of divination was a little death that drained and exhausted the old man. He would only undertake the dreaded journey into the supernatural when no other course was open to him.

Nefer kept silent, and watched in awe as Taita went through the ritual of preparing the Mazes. First he crushed the herbs with a pestle in a mortar of carved alabaster, and measured them into a clay pot. Then he poured boiling water from the copper kettle over them. The steam that rose in a cloud was so pungent it made Nefer's eyes water.

While the mixture cooled, Taita brought the tanned leather bag that contained the Mazes from its hiding-place at the back of the cave. Sitting over the fire, he poured the ivory discs into one hand and rubbed them gently between his fingers as he began to chant the incantation to Ammon Ra.

The Mazes comprised ten ivory discs, which Taita had carved. Ten was the mystical number of the greatest potency. Each carving depicted one of the ten symbols of power, and was a miniature work of art. As he sang he fondled the discs so that they clicked between his fingers. Between each verse of the invocation, he blew on the discs to endow them with his life force. When they had taken on the warmth of his own body he passed them to Nefer.

'Hold them and breathe upon them,' he urged, and while Nefer obeyed these instructions, Taita began to sway in rhythm to the magical verses he was reciting. Slowly his eyes seemed to glaze over as he retreated into the secret places in his mind. He was already in the trance when Nefer stacked the Mazes in two piles in front of him.

Then with one finger Nefer tested the temperature of the infusion in the clay pot as Taita had taught him. When it was cool enough not to scald the mouth, he knelt before the old man and with both hands offered it to him.

Taita drank it to the last drop, and in the firelight his face turned white as building chalk from the quarry at Aswan. For a while longer he kept up the chant, but slowly his voice dropped to a whisper, then descended into silence. The only sound was his hoarse breathing as he succumbed to the drug and the trance. He subsided on to the floor of the cave, and lay curled like a sleeping cat beside the fire.

Nefer covered him with his woollen shawl, and stayed beside him until he started to twitch and groan, and the sweat streamed down his face. His eyes opened and rolled back in their sockets until only the whites glared blindly into the dark shadows of the cave.

Nefer knew there was nothing he could do for the old man now. He had journeyed far into the shadowy places where Nefer could not reach him, and he could no longer bear the terrible distress and suffering that the Mazes inflicted upon the Magus. Quietly he stood up, fetched his bow and quiver from the back of the cave and stooped to see out through the entrance. Across the hills the sun was low and yellow in the dust haze. He climbed the western dunes, and when he reached the top and looked out across the valleys he felt so strongly his disappointment at the lost bird, his concern for Taita in his agony of divination, and his sense of foreboding at what Taita would discover in his trance, that he was seized by the urge to run, to escape as though from some dreadful predator. He bounded away down the face of the dune, the sand cascading and hissing beneath his feet. He felt tears of terror brim in his eyes and stream down his cheeks in the wind, and he ran until the sweat poured down his flanks, his chest heaved and the sun was on the horizon. Then at last he turned back towards Gebel Nagara and covered the last mile in darkness.

Taita was still curled under the shawl beside the fire, but he was sleeping more easily now. Nefer lay down beside him, and after a while he, too, fell into a sleep that was restless with dreams and haunted by nightmares.

When he awoke dawn was glimmering at the entrance to the cave. Taita was sitting at the fire, grilling gazelle cutlets on the coals. He still looked pale and sick, but he skewered one on the point of his bronze dagger and offered it to Nefer. The boy was suddenly ravenous, and he sat up and gnawed on the bone. When he had devoured the third portion of sweet tender meat he spoke for the first time. 'What did you see, Tata?' he asked. 'Why did the godbird refuse?'

'It was obscured,' Taita told him, and Nefer knew that the omen had been unpropitious, that Taita was protecting him from it.

They ate in silence for a while, but now Nefer hardly tasted the food and at last he said softly, 'You have freed the decoys. How can we set the net tomorrow?'

'The godbird will not come to Gebel Nagara again,' said Taita simply.

'Then am I never to be Pharaoh in my father's place?' Nefer asked.

There was deep anguish in his voice, so Taita softened his answer. 'We will have to take your bird from the nest.'

'We do not know where to find the godbird.' Nefer had stopped eating. He stared at Taita with pitiful appeal.

The old man inclined his head in affirmation. 'I know where the nest is. It was revealed in the Mazes. But you must eat to keep up your strength. We will leave before first light tomorrow. It is a long journey to the site.'

'Will there be fledglings in the nest?'

'Yes,' said Taita. 'The falcons have bred. The young are almost ready for flight. We will find your bird there.' Silently he told himself, Or the god will reveal other mysteries to us.

In the darkness before dawn they loaded the waterskins and the saddlebags on to the horses then swung up bareback behind them. Taita led the way, skirting the cliff face and taking the easy route up the hills. By the time the sun was above the horizon they had left Gebel Nagara far below them. When Nefer looked ahead he started with surprise: there ahead of them was the faint outline of the mountain, blue against the blue of the horizon, still so far off that it seemed insubstantial and ethereal, a thing of mist and air rather than of earth and rock. The sensation that he had seen it before overcame Nefer, and for a while he was at a loss to explain it to himself. Then it came rushing back and he said, 'That mountain.' He pointed it out. 'That is where we are going, is it not, Tata?' He spoke with such assurance that Taita looked back at him.

'How do you know?'

'I dreamed it last night,' Nefer replied.

Taita turned away so that the boy would not see his expression. At last the eyes of his mind are opening like a desert bloom in the dawn. He is learning to peer through the dark curtain that hides the future from us. He felt a deep sense of achievement. Praise the hundred names of Horus, it has not been in vain.

'That is where we are going, I know it is,' Nefer repeated, with utmost certainty.

'Yes,' Taita agreed at last. 'We are going to Bir Umm Masara.'

Before the hottest part of the day, Taita led them to where a clump of ragged acacia thorn trees grew in a deep ravine, their roots drawing up water from some deep source far below the surface. When they had unloaded the horses and watered them, Nefer cast around the grove and within minutes had discovered sign of others who had passed this way. Excitedly, he called Taita over and showed him the wheel-marks left by a small division of chariots, ten vehicles by his reckoning, the ashes of the cooking fire, and the flattened earth where men had lain down to sleep with the horses tethered to the acacia trunks nearby.

'Hyksos?' he hazarded anxiously, for the dung of the horses in their lines was very fresh, not more than a few days old – it was dry on the outside, but still damp when he broke open a lump.

'Ours.' Taita had recognized the tracks of the chariots. After all, he had made the first designs of these spoked wheels many decades before. He stooped suddenly and picked up a tiny bronze rosette ornament that had fallen from a dashboard and was half buried in the loose earth. 'One of our light cavalry divisions, probably from the Phat regiment. Part of Lord Naja's command.'

'What are they doing out here, so far from the lines?' Nefer asked, puzzled, but Taita shrugged and turned away to cover his unease.

The old man cut short their period of rest and they went on while the sun was still high. Slowly the outline of Bir Umm Masara hardened and seemed to fill half of the sky ahead of them. Gradually they could make out the etching and scarification of gorge, bluff and cliff. As they reached the crest of the first line of foothills, Taita checked his horse and looked back. Distant movement caught his attention, and he held up his hand to shade his eyes. He could see a tiny feather of pale dust many leagues out in the desert below. He watched it for a while and saw that it was moving eastwards, towards the Red Sea. It might have been thrown up by a herd of moving oryx, or by a column of fighting chariots. He did not remark on it to Nefer, who was so intent on the hunt for the royal falcon that he could not tear his eyes from the silhouette of the mountain ahead. Taita thumped his heels into the flanks of his horse and moved up beside the boy.

That night, when they camped halfway up the slope of Bir Umm Masara, Taita said quietly, 'We will make no fire this night.'

'But it's so cold,' Nefer protested.

'And we are so exposed here that a fire could be seen for ten leagues across the desert.'

'Are there enemies out there?' Nefer's expression changed, and he gazed down over the darkening landscape with trepidation. 'Bandits? Raiding Bedouin?'

'There are always enemies,' Taita told him. 'Better cold than dead.'

After midnight when the icy wind woke Nefer, and his colt, Stargazer, stamped and whinnied, he rolled out of his sheepskin blanket and went to calm him. He found Taita already awake, sitting a little apart.

'Look!' he ordered, and pointed down on to the lowland. There was a distant glimmer and flicker of light. 'A campfire,' Taita said.

'They might be one of our own divisions. Those who made the tracks we saw yesterday.'

'They might indeed,' agreed Taita, 'But then again, they might be somebody else.'

After a long, thoughtful pause Nefer said, 'I have slept enough. It's too cold, anyway. We should mount again and move on. We don't want the dawn to catch us here on the bare shoulder of the mountain.'

They loaded the horses and in the moonlight found a rough path made by wild goats that led them round the eastern shoulder of Bir Umm Masara, so that when the light began to strengthen they were already out of sight of any watchers in the distant encampment.

The chariot of Ammon Ra, the sun god, burst furiously out of the east, and the mountain was suffused with golden light. The gorges were dark with shadow, made more sombre by the contrast, and far below the wilderness was vast and grand.

Nefer threw back his head, shouted with joy, 'Look! Oh, look!' and pointed up past the rock peak. Taita followed his gaze and saw the two dark specks, turning in a wide circle against the heavens. The sunlight caught one, so that it glowed for a second like a shooting star.

'Royal falcons.' Taita smiled. 'A mating pair.'

They unloaded the horses and found a vantage-point from which they were able to watch the circling birds. Even at this distance they were regal and beautiful beyond Nefer's ability to express it. Then suddenly one of the birds, the smaller male, the tiercel, broke the pattern of flight, and angled up against the wind, his leisurely wingbeats taking on a sudden ferocity.

'He has discovered,' Nefer shouted, with the excitement and joy of the true falconer. 'Watch him now.'

When it began the stoop was so swift that to have taken the eye off it for even a moment would have meant missing the kill. The tiercel dropped down the sky like a thrown javelin. A single pigeon was coasting unsuspectingly near the base of the cliff. Nefer recognized the moment when the plump bird became suddenly aware of the danger, and tried to avoid the falcon. It turned so violently towards the safety of the rock face that it rolled over on to its back in full and frantic flight. For an instant its belly was exposed. The tiercel tore into it with both sets of talons, and the big bird seemed to dissolve in a burst of puce and blue smoke. The feathers drifted away in a long cloud on the morning wind and the falcon bound on, locking its talons deep into its prey's belly, and plunged with it into the gorge. The killer and its victim hit the rocky scree slope only a short distance from where Nefer stood. The heavy thud of their fall echoed off the cliff and resounded down the gorge.

By this time Nefer was dancing with excitement, and even Taita, who had always been a lover of the hunting hawks, gave voice to his pleasure.

'Bak-her!' he cried, as the falcon completed the ritual of the kill with the mantling: it spread its magnificently patterned wings over the dead pigeon, covering it and proclaiming the kill as its own.

The female falcon came down to join him in a series of graceful spirals and landed on the rock beside her mate. He folded away his wings to let her share the kill, and between them they dismembered and devoured the carcass of the pigeon, ripping into it with their razor-sharp beaks, and pausing between each stroke to lift their heads and glare at Nefer, with those ferocious yellow eyes, while they gulped down the bloody fragments of flesh and bone and feathers. They were fully aware of the presence of the men and horses, but tolerated them as long as they kept their distance.

Then, when all that was left of the pigeon were a blood spot on the rock and a few drifting feathers, and the usually sleek bellies of the falcons were crammed with food, the pair launched into flight again. Wings flogging now to carry them, they rose up the sheer cliff face.

'Follow them!' Taita hitched up his kilt and scampered over the treacherous footing of the scree slope. 'Don't lose them.'

Nefer was faster and more agile, and he kept the rising birds in sight as he raced along the shoulder of the mountain beneath them. Below the peak the mountain was split into twin needles, mighty pinnacles of dark stone, terrifying even from below. They watched the falcons rise up this mighty natural monument, until Nefer realized where they were headed. Where the rock overhung, halfway up the eastern tower, there was a V-shaped cleft in the stone face. Stuffed into it was a platform of dried branches and twigs.

'The nest!' Nefer shrieked. 'There is the nest!'

They stood together, heads thrown back, watching the falcons alight, one after the other, on the edge of the nest, and begin to heave and strain to regurgitate the pigeon flesh from their crops. Another faint sound came to Nefer on the wind that soughed along the cliff-face: a chorus of importunate cries from the young birds demanding to be fed. From this angle he and Taita could not glimpse the falcon chicks, and Nefer was hopping with frustration. 'If we climb the western peak, there,' he pointed, 'we should be able to look down into the nest.'

'Help me with the horses first,' Taita ordered, and they hobbled them, and left them to graze on sparse clumps of mountain grass nurtured by the dews carried by the breeze from the distant Red Sea.

The climb up the western peak took the rest of the morning, but even though Taita had unerringly picked out the easiest route around the far side of the peak, in places the drop beneath them made Nefer draw in his breath sharply, and look away. They came out at last on to a narrow ledge just below the summit. They crouched there for a while to compose themselves, and to stare out at the grandeur of land and distant sea. It seemed that the whole of creation was spread beneath them, and the wind moaned around them, tugging at the folds of Nefer's kilt and ruffling his curls.

'Where is the nest?' he asked. Even in this lofty and precarious place, high above the world, his mind was fixed on one thing only.

'Come!' Taita rose and shuffled sideways along the ledge with the toes of his sandals overhanging the drop. They made their way round the angle and slowly the eastern peak came into view. They looked across to the vertical rock face only a hundred cubits away, but separated from them by such an abyss that Nefer swayed with vertigo.

On this side of the gulf they were slightly higher than the nest, and could look down upon it. The female falcon was perched on the edge, obscuring its contents. She turned her head and stared implacably at them as they rounded the shoulder of the peak. She raised the feathers along her back, as an angry lion lifts its mane in threat. Then she let out a wild cry and launched herself out over the drop, to hang almost motionless on the wind, watching them intently. She was so close that every feather in her wings was clearly revealed.

Her movement had exposed the interior of the cleft that contained the nest. A pair of young birds was crouched in the cup of twigs and branches lined with feathers and the wool of wild goats. They were fully fledged already, and almost as large as their mother. As Nefer stared across at them in awe, one raised itself and spread its wings wide, then beat them fiercely.

'He is beautiful.' Nefer groaned with longing. 'The most beautiful thing I have ever seen.'

'He practises for the moment of flight,' Taita warned him softly. 'See how strong he has grown. Within days he will be gone.'

'I will climb for them this very day,' Nefer vowed, and made as if to go back along the ledge, but Taita stopped him with a hand on his shoulder.

'It is not something to enter into lightly. We must spend a little precious time in planning it carefully. Come, sit beside me.'

As Nefer leaned against his shoulder Taita pointed out the features of the rock opposite them. 'Below the nest the rock is smooth as glass. For fifty cubits sheer there is no handhold, no ledge on which to place a foot.'

Nefer tore his eyes from the young bird and peered down. His stomach churned, but he forced himself to ignore it. It was as Taita had said: not even one of the rock hyrax, those furry, sure-footed rabbit-like creatures that made these lofty places their home, could have found a footing on that pitch of vertical rock. 'How can I get to the nest, Tata? I want those chicks – I want them so.'

'Look above the nest.' Taita pointed across. 'See how the cleft continues upwards, to the very top of the cliff.'

Nefer nodded – he could not speak as he stared at the perilous road Taita was showing him.

'We will find a way to reach the summit above the nest. We will take up the harness ropes with us. From the top I will lower you down the crack. If you wedge your bare feet and bunched fists sideways into the opening they will hold you, and I will steady you with the rope.'

Still Nefer could not speak. He felt nauseated by what Taita had suggested. Surely no living person could make that climb and survive. Taita understood what he was feeling and did not insist on a reply.

'I think . . .' Hesitantly Nefer started to refuse, then fell silent and stared at the pair of young birds in the nest. He knew that this was his destiny. One of them was his godbird, and this was the only way to achieve the crown of his fathers. To turn away now was to deny everything for which the gods had chosen him. He must go.

Taita sensed the moment when the boy beside him accepted the task and thus became a man. He rejoiced deep in his heart, for this also was his destiny.

'I will make the attempt,' Nefer said simply, and rose to his feet. 'Let us go down and prepare ourselves.'

The next morning they left their rudimentary camp and started upwards while it was still dark. Somehow Taita was able to place his feet on a path that even Nefer's young eyes could not discern. Each of them carried a heavy coil of rope, plaited from linen and horsehair and used to tether the horses. They had also brought one of the small waterskins: Taita had warned that it would be hot on the pinnacle once the sun reached its height.

By the time they had worked their way round to the far side of the eastern pinnacle the light had strengthened and they could see the face above them. Taita spent an hour surveying the route up it. At last he was satisfied. 'In the name of great Horus, the all-powerful, let us begin,' he said, and made the sign of the god's wounded eye. Then he led Nefer back to the point he had chosen from which to begin the ascent.

'I will lead the way,' he told the boy, as he knotted one end of the rope around his waist. 'Pay out the rope as I go. Watch what I do, and when I call you, tie it to yourself and follow me. If you slip I will hold you.'

At first Nefer climbed cautiously, following the route that Taita had taken, his expression set and his knuckles white with tension as he fastened on each hold. Taita murmured encouragement from above, and the boy's confidence grew with each move upwards. He reached Taita's side and grinned at him. 'That was easy.'

'It will grow harder,' Taita assured him drily, and led up the next pitch of rock. This time Nefer was scampering behind him like a monkey, chattering with excitement and enjoyment. They stood below a chimney in the rock face that tapered near the top into a narrow crack.

'This is like the climb you will have to make down to the nest when we reach the top. Watch how I wedge my hands and feet into the crack.' Taita stepped up into the chimney and went up slowly but without pause. When the chimney narrowed he kept on steadily, like a man climbing a ladder. His kilts flapped about his skinny old legs, and Nefer could see up under the linen to the grotesque scar where his manhood had been cut away. Nefer had seen it before, and grown so accustomed to it that the terrible mutilation no longer appalled him.

Taita called to him from above, and this time Nefer danced up the rock, falling naturally into the rhythm of the ascent.

Why should it not be so? Taita tried to keep his pride within reasonable bounds. In his veins runs the blood of warriors and great athletes. Then he smiled and his eyes sparkled as though he were young again. And he has had me to teach him – of course he excels.

The sun was only halfway up the sky when at last they stood together on the summit of the eastern peak. 'We will rest awhile here.' Taita took the waterskin from his shoulder and sank down.

'I am not tired, Tata.'

'Nevertheless, we will rest.' Taita passed him the skin and watched as he gulped down a dozen mouthfuls. 'The descent to the nest will be more difficult,' he said, when Nefer stopped for breath. 'There will be nobody to show you the way, and there is one place where you cannot see your feet when the rock leans away from you.'

'I will be all right, Tata.'

'If the gods allow,' Taita agreed, and turned away his head as if to admire the glory of mountain, sea and desert spread below them but in fact so that the boy would not see his lips move as he prayed. 'Spread your wings over him, mighty Horus, for this is the one you have chosen. Cherish him, my mistress Lostris, who has become a goddess, for this is the fruit of your womb and the blood of your blood. Turn your hand from him, foul Seth, and touch him not, for you cannot prevail against those who protect this child.' He sighed as he reconsidered the wisdom of challenging the god of darkness and chaos, then softened his admonition with a small bribe: 'Pass him by, good Seth, and I will sacrifice an ox to you in your temple at Abydos when next I pass that way.'

He stood up. 'It is time to make the attempt.'

He led the way across the summit and stood on the far lip, looking down at the campsite and the grazing horses, which were rendered tiny as new-born mice by the drop. The female falcon was in flight, circling out over the gorge. He thought there was something unusual in her behaviour, particularly when she uttered a strange, forlorn cry, such as he had never before heard from a royal falcon. There was no sign of her mate, though he searched the heavens for him.

Then he lowered his eyes and looked across the abyss at the main peak of the mountain and the ledge on which they had stood the previous day. This enabled him to orientate himself, for the bulge of the rock face under him hid the nest from sight. He moved slowly along the lip until he found the beginning of the crack, which he recognized as the one that ran down and opened into the cleft in which the falcons had built their nest.

He picked up a loose pebble and dropped it over the edge. It clattered as it dropped down the wall and out of sight. He hoped that it might alarm the tiercel off the nest and so confirm its exact position, but there was still no sign of it. Only the female bird continued her aimless circles and uttered her strange, lonely cries.

Taita called Nefer to him and tied the end of the rope around his waist. He checked the knot carefully and then, an inch at a time, drew the full length of the rope through his fingers, checking for any frayed or weakened spot. 'You have the saddlebag to carry the fledgling.' He checked the knot with which Nefer had secured it over his shoulder so that it would not hamper his movements on the climb.

'Stop fussing so, Tata. My father says that sometimes you are like an old woman.'

'Your father should show more respect. I wiped his arse when he was a mewling infant, just as I wiped yours.' Taita sniffed, and again checked the knot at the boy's waist, delaying the fateful moment. But Nefer walked to the edge and stood straight-backed above the drop without any sign of hesitation.

'Are you ready?' He looked over his shoulder, and smiled with a flash of white teeth and a sparkle of his dark green eyes. Those eyes reminded Taita so vividly of Queen Lostris. With a pang he thought Nefer even more comely than his father had been at the same age.

'We cannot dally here all day.' Nefer uttered one of his father's favourite expressions in lordly tones, aping the royal manner faithfully.

Taita sat down and wriggled into a position in which he could anchor his heels in the crack and lean back to brace himself against the rope over his shoulder. He nodded at Nefer, and saw the cocky grin leave the boy's face as he edged down over the drop. He paid out the rope as Nefer worked his way down.

Nefer reached the bulge in the wall and, hanging on grimly with both hands, let his legs down to grope for a foothold beneath the overhang. He found the crack with his toes and thrust his bare foot into it, twisting his ankle to lock the hold, then slithered down. He glanced up one last time at Taita, tried to smile, but made a sickly grimace, then swung round the overhang. Before he could find another hold he felt his foot slip in the crack and he started to swivel on the rope. If he lost his footing he would pivot and swing out helplessly over the drop. He doubted that the old man above would have the strength to haul him back.

He snatched desperately at the crack, and his fingers hooked on, steadying him. He lunged with his other hand and grabbed the next hold. He was round the bulge, but his heart was hammering and his breath hissed in his throat.

'Are you all right?' Taita's voice came down to him.

'All right!' he gasped. He looked down between his knees and saw the crack in the rock widen into the top of the cleft above the nest. His arms were tiring and beginning to shake. He stretched his right leg down, and found another foothold.

Taita was right: it was more difficult to descend than to climb upwards. When he moved his right hand down he saw that already his knuckle was raw and he left a small bloody smear on the rock. Inching down, he reached the point where the crack opened into the main cleft. Again he was forced to reach round the lip and find a hidden hold.

Yesterday, when he and Taita had discussed it, sitting together on the other side of the gulf, this transition point had looked so easy, but now both his feet were swinging out freely over the lip of the cleft, and the abyss seemed to suck at him like some monstrous mouth. He moaned and hung on with both hands, freezing to the rock face. He was afraid now, the last vestige of courage blown away on the gusts of hot wind that tugged at him, threatening to tear him from the cliff. He looked down and tears mingled with the sweat on his cheeks. The drop beckoned, pulled at him with claws of terror, sickening him to the guts.

'Move!' Taita's voice drifted down to him, faint but filled with urgency. 'You must keep moving.'

With a huge effort Nefer rallied himself for another effort. His bare toes groped under him and he found a ledge that seemed wide enough to give him purchase. He lowered himself on aching, juddering arms. Abruptly his foot slipped from the ledge, and his arms were too tired to support his weight any longer. He fell and screamed as he went.

He dropped only the span of his two arms, and then the rope bit cruelly into his flesh, binding up under his ribs and choking the breath out of him. He came up short and dangled out into space, held only by the rope and the old man above him.

'Nefer, can you hear me?' Taita's voice was rough with the strain of holding him. The boy whimpered like a puppy. 'You must catch a hold. You cannot hang there.' Taita's voice calmed him. He blinked the tears out of his eyes, and saw the rock only an arm's length from his face.

'Latch on!' Taita goaded him, and Nefer saw that he was hanging opposite the cleft. The opening was deep enough to accommodate him, the sloping ledge wide enough for him to stand on, if only he could reach it. He stretched out a shaking hand and touched the wall with his fingertips. He started to swing himself back towards it.

It seemed an eternity of struggle and heartbreaking effort, but at last he swung into the opening and managed to place both bare feet on the ledge, and to crouch doubled over in the opening. He wedged himself there, panting and gasping for air.

Above him Taita felt his weight go off the rope, and called down encouragement. '*Bak-her*, Nefer, *Bak-her*! Where are you?'

'I am in the cleft, above the nest.'

'What can you see?' Taita wanted to keep the boy's mind fixed on other things, so that he would not dwell on the void beneath his feet.

Nefer wiped the sweat from his eyes with the back of his hand and peered down. 'I can see the edge of the nest.'

'How far?'

'Close.'

'Can you reach it?'

'I will try.' Nefer braced his bowed back against the roof of the narrow cleft, and shuffled slowly down the sloping floor. Below him he could just make out the dried twigs that protruded from the nest site. As he went down further, his view into the nest opened slowly an inch at a time.

The next time he called out his voice was stronger and excited. 'I can see the tiercel. He is still on the nest.'

'What is he doing?' Taita shouted back.

'He is crouched down. It seems as though he is sleeping.' Nefer's voice was puzzled. 'I can only see his back.'

The male bird was motionless, lying on the high side of the untidy nest. But how could he be sleeping and unaware during the commotion above him, Nefer wondered. His own fear was forgotten now in the excitement of having the falcon so close and the nest almost within touching distance.

He moved faster, more confidently, as the floor of the cleft levelled out under his feet, and there was more headroom for him to stand erect.

'I can see his head.' The tiercel was stretched out with his wings spread as though he was mantling a kill. He is beautiful, Nefer thought, and I am almost close enough to touch him, yet he still shows no fear.

Suddenly he realized he could seize the sleeping bird. He braced himself for the effort, wedging his shoulder into the cleft, his bare feet in a secure stance under him. Slowly he leaned out towards the tiercel, then stopped with his hand poised above it.

There were tiny droplets of blood on the russet back feathers. Bright as polished rubies, they twinkled in the sunlight, and with a sudden, swooping sensation in the pit of his stomach, Nefer realized that the tiercel was dead. He was overcome with a dreadful sense of loss, as though something of great value to him had been taken away for ever. It seemed more than just the death of the falcon. The royal bird represented something more: it was the symbol of a god and a king. As he stared at it, the carcass of the tiercel seemed to be transformed into the dead body of Pharaoh himself. A sob choked Nefer and he jerked away his hand.

He had moved only just in time, for then he heard a dry, rasping sound and an explosive hiss of air. Something huge and glittering black whipped out at where his hand had been the moment before, and slammed into the mattress of dried twigs with such force that the whole nest shook.

Nefer recoiled as far as the cramped space in the cleft would allow, and stared at the grotesque creature that now swayed and wove before his face. His vision seemed sharpened and magnified, time moved with the slow horror of nightmare. He saw the dead fledglings huddled in the cup of the nest beyond the carcass of the tiercel, the thick, glittering coils of a gigantic black cobra twisted around them. The snake's head was raised, its hood, marked with a bold pattern of black and white, was spread.

The slippery black tongue flickered out between the thin, grinning lips. Its eyes were fathomless black, each with a star of reflected light in the centre as they held Nefer in a mesmeric stare.

Nefer tried to scream a warning to Taita, but no sound came from his throat. He could not tear away his gaze from the cobra's dreadful stare. It's head swayed gently, but the massive coils that filled the falcon's nest to overflowing pulsed and clenched. Every polished scale was burnished like a jewel as they rasped against the twigs of the nest. Each coil was as thick as Nefer's arm, and slowly they revolved upon themselves.

The head swayed back, the mouth gaped, and Nefer could see the pale lining of the throat. The almost transparent fangs came erect in the folds of soft membrane: there was a tiny bead of colourless venom on the tip of each bony needle.

Then the wicked head flashed forward, as the cobra struck at Nefer's face.

Nefer screamed and hurled himself sideways, lost his balance and tumbled backwards from the cleft.

Even though Taita was braced to take any sudden weight on the rope, he was almost jerked from his stance on top of the cliff as Nefer's weight hit the line. A coil of the horsehair rope slid through his fingers, scorching the flesh, but he held hard. He could hear the boy screaming incoherently below him, and feel him swinging at the end of the rope.

Nefer pendulumed out from the cleft then swung straight back towards the falcon's nest. The cobra had recovered swiftly from its abortive strike, and was once more poised and erect. It fixed its gaze on the boy and swivelled its head to face him. At the same time a harsh hiss erupted from its throat.

Nefer screamed again and kicked out wildly at the snake as he flew straight towards it. Taita heard the terror in that scream and lay back on the rope, hauling until he felt his old muscles crack under the strain.

The cobra struck instinctively at Nefer's eyes as he came within range, but at that instant Taita's heave on the rope end jerked Nefer off-line. The snake's gaping jaws passed a finger's width from his ear and then, like the lash of a chariot whip, the heavy body flogged across his shoulder. Nefer screamed again, knowing he was fatally bitten.

As he swung out once more over the open drop he glanced down at the spot on his shoulder into which the serpent had sunk its fangs, and saw the pale yellow venom splashed across the thick leather fold of the saddlebag. With a wild lift of relief he tore the bag free and as he started to swing back towards where the cobra still stood menacingly, he held the bag like a shield in front of him.

The instant he was within range the cobra struck again, but Nefer caught the blow on the thick leather folds of the bag. The beast's fangs snagged in the leather and held fast. As Nefer swung back the snake was dragged with him. It was hauled cleanly out of the nest, a writhing, seething ball of coils and polished scales. It thrashed against Nefer's legs, the heavy tail lashing him, hissing fearsomely, clouds of venom spraying from its gaping jaws and dribbling down the leather bag. So great was its weight that Nefer's whole body was shaken violently.

Almost without thought, Nefer hurled the leather bag away from him, the cobra's fangs still hooked into the leather. The bag and the snake dropped away together, the sinuous body still curling, coiling and whipping furiously. The penetrating hisses grew fainter as it plunged away down the cliff. It seemed to fall for ever until at last it struck the rocks far below. The impact did not kill or stun it, and it whipped about as it rolled down the scree slope, bouncing over the rocks like a huge black ball until Nefer lost sight of it among the grey boulders.

Through the mists of terror that clouded his mind, Taita's voice reached him. It was hoarse with effort and concern. 'Speak to me. Can you hear me?'

'I am here, Tata.' Nefer's voice was weak and shaky.

'I will pull you up.'

Slowly, one heave at a time, Nefer was drawn upwards. Even in his distress Nefer marvelled at the old man's strength. When the rock came within reach, he was able to take some of his weight off the rope and it went quicker. At last he clawed his way round the overhang, and saw, with vast relief, Taita looking down at him from the summit, the ancient features, like those of a sphinx, riven into deep lines by his exertions on the rope.

With one last heave Nefer tumbled over the top and fell into the old man's arms. He lay there gasping and sobbing, unable to speak coherently. Taita hugged him. He too was shaking with emotion and exhaustion. Slowly they calmed and regained their breath. Taita held the waterskin to Nefer's lips and he gulped, choked and gulped again. Then he looked into Taita's face so abjectly that the old man hugged him closer.

'It was horrible.' Nefer's words were barely intelligible. 'It was in the nest. It had killed the falcons, all of them. Oh, Tata, it was terrible.'

'What was it, Nefer?' Taita asked gently.

'It killed my godbird, and the tiercel.'

'Gently, lad. Drink some more.' He offered the waterskin.

Nefer choked again and was seized with a paroxysm of coughing. The moment he could speak again he wheezed, 'It tried to kill me also. It was huge, and so black.'

'What was it, boy? Tell me clearly.'

'A cobra, a huge black cobra. In the nest, waiting for me. It had bitten the chicks and the falcon to death, and it went for me as soon as it saw me. I never imagined a cobra could grow so large.'

'Are you stricken?' Taita demanded, with dread, and hauled Nefer to his feet to examine him.

'No, Tata. I used the bag as a shield. It never touched me,' Nefer protested, but Taita stripped off his kilt and made him stand naked while he went over his body looking for puncture wounds. One of his knuckles and both his knees were grazed but otherwise the strong young body was marked only by the pharaonic cartouche on the smooth skin of his inner thigh. Taita had tattooed the design himself, and it was a miniature masterpiece that would for ever endorse Nefer's claim to the double crown.

'Thanks be to the great god who protected you,' Taita murmured. 'With this cobra apparition, Horus has sent you a portent of terrible events and dangers.' His face was grave, and touched with the marks of grief and mourning. 'That was no natural serpent.'

'Yes, Tata. I saw it close. It was enormous, but it was a real snake.'

'Then how did it reach the nest site? Cobras cannot fly, and there is no other way to scale the cliff.'

Nefer stared at him aghast, 'It killed my godbird,' he whispered aloud.

'And it killed the royal tiercel, Pharaoh's other self.' Taita agreed grimly, sorrow still in his eyes. 'There are mysteries here revealed. I saw their shadows in my vision, but they are confirmed by what has happened to you this day. This is a thing beyond the natural order.'

'Explain it to me, Tata,' Nefer insisted.

Taita handed him his kilt. 'First we must get down off this mountain, and fly from the great dangers that beset us before I can consider the omens.'

He paused and looked to the sky, as if in deep thought. Then he lowered his eyes and looked into Nefer's face. 'Put on your clothes,' was all he said.

As soon as Nefer was ready, Taita led him back to the far side of the summit and they began the descent. It went swiftly, for they had opened the route, and the urgency in every move Taita made was infectious. The horses were where they had left them, but before they mounted Nefer said, 'The place where the cobra struck the rocks is but a short way from here.' He pointed to the head of the scree slope below the cliff on which the falcons' nest was still visible. 'Let us search for the carcass. Perhaps if we find its remains you could work some charm to destroy its powers.'

'It would be precious time wasted. There will be no carcass.' Taita swung up on to the mare's back. 'Mount, Nefer. The cobra has returned to the shadow places from which it sprang.'

Nefer shivered with superstitious awe, then scrambled up on to the back of his colt.

Neither of them spoke again until they were off the upper slopes and into the broken eastern foothills. Nefer knew well that when Taita was in this mood it was wasted effort to speak to him, but he urged his horse alongside and pointed out respectfully, 'Tata, this is not the way to Gebel Nagara.'

'We are not going back there.'

'Why not?'

'The Bedouin know that we were at the spring. They will tell those who search for us,' Taita explained.

Nefer was puzzled. 'Who searches for us?'

Taita turned his head and looked at the boy with such pity that he was silenced. 'I will explain when we are off this cursed mountain and in a safe place.'

Taita avoided the crests of the hills, where they might be silhouetted on the skyline, and wove a path through the gorges and valleys. Always he headed east, away from Egypt and the Nile, towards the sea.

The sun was setting before he reined in his mare again, and spoke: 'The main caravan road lies just beyond the next line of hills. We must cross it, but enemies may be watching for us there.'

They left the horses tethered in a hidden wadi, with a few handfuls of crushed *dhurra* millet in their leather nosebags to keep them contented, then climbed cautiously to the crest of the hills and found a vantage-point behind a bank of purple shale from which they could look down on to the caravan road below.

'We will lie here until dark,' Taita explained. 'Then we will cross.'

'I don't understand what you are doing, Tata. Why are we travelling east? Why don't we return to Thebes, and the protection of Pharaoh, my father?'

Taita sighed softly and closed his eyes. How do I tell him? I cannot hide it much longer. Yet he is a child still, and I should shield him.

It was almost as if Nefer had read his thoughts, for he laid his hand on Taita's arm and said quietly, 'Today, on the mountain, I proved that I am a man. Treat me as one.'

Taita nodded. 'Indeed, you proved it.' Before he went on he swept another look along the well-beaten road below them, and immediately ducked his head, 'Someone coming!' he warned.

Nefer flattened himself behind the shale bank and they watched the column of dust coming swiftly down the caravan road from the west. By this time the valley was in deep shadow and the sky was filled with all the glorious shades of the sunset.

'They are moving fast. Those are not merchants, they are fighting chariots,' Nefer said. 'Yes, I can see them now.' His bright young eyes had picked out the shape of the leading chariot, with the teamed horses trotting ahead of the charioteer on his high carriage. 'They are not Hyksos,' he went on, as the shapes hardened and drew closer, 'they are ours. A troop of ten chariots. Yes! See the pennant on the leading vehicle.' The fluttering pennant on the long, limber bamboo rod rode high above the rolling dustcloud. 'A cohort of the Phat Guards! We are safe, Tata!'

Nefer sprang to his feet and waved both hands over his head, 'Here!' he yelled. 'Here, the Blues. Here I am. I am Prince Nefer!'

Taita reached up a bony hand and hauled him down violently. 'Get down, you little fool. Those are the minions of the cobra.'

He shot another quick glance over the bank, and saw that the leading charioteer must have spotted Nefer on the skyline, for he had whipped his team into a canter and was tearing up the road towards them.

'Come!' he told Nefer. 'Hurry! They must not catch us.'

He dragged the boy off the ridge and started down the slope. After his initial reluctance, Nefer was spurred on by Taita's haste. He began to run in earnest, jumping from rock to rock, but he could not catch the old man. Taita's long skinny legs flew and the silver mane of his hair streamed out behind him. He reached the horses first, and was on the mare's bare back in a single leap.

'I don't understand why we are running from our own people,' Nefer panted. 'What is happening, Tata?'

'Mount! No time now to talk. We must get clear.'

As they galloped out of the mouth of the wadi and into the open, Nefer shot a longing look back over his shoulder. The leading chariot came soaring over the top of the ridge, and the driver let out a shout, but the distance and the rumble of the wheels muffled his voice.

Earlier, Taita had led them through an area of broken volcanic rock through which no chariot would find a way. Now they rode for it, the horses running shoulder to shoulder, and stride for stride.

'If we can get among the rocks, we can lose them during the night. There is only a whisper of daylight left.' Taita looked up at the last glow of the sun that had already sunk behind the western hills.

'A single horseman can always hold off a chariot,' Nefer declared, with a confidence he did not truly feel. But when he looked back over his shoulder he saw it was true. They were pulling away from the troop of bouncing, jolting vehicles.

Before Nefer and Taita reached the broken ground the chariots had dropped so far behind that they were almost obscured by their own dustcloud and by the gathering blue dusk. As soon as they reached the fringe of rocks they were forced to bring the horses down to a cautious trot, but the footing was so dangerous and the light so bad that they were quickly reduced to a walk. In the last glimmer of the light Taita looked back and saw the dark shape of the leading chariot of the squadron halt at the edge of the bad ground. He recognized the voice of the driver who shouted after them, even though his words were faint.

'Prince Nefer, why do you flee? You need not fear us. We are the Phat Guards, come to escort you home to Thebes.'

Nefer made as if to turn his horse's head. 'That is Hilto. I know his voice so well. He is a good man. He is calling my name.'

Hilto was a famous warrior, who wore the Gold of Valour, but Taita ordered Nefer onwards sternly.

'Don't be deceived. Trust nobody.'

Obediently Nefer rode on into the wilderness of broken rock. The faint shouts behind them dwindled and were snuffed out by the eternal silence of the desert. Before they had gone much further the darkness forced them to dismount and walk through the difficult places where the twisting path narrowed, and sharp pillars of black stone might maim a careless horse or shatter the wheels of any vehicle that tried to follow them through. At last they had to stop to water and rest the horses. They sat close together and, with his dagger, Taita sliced a loaf of *dhurra* bread, and they munched it as they talked softly.

'Tell me of your vision, Tata. What did you truly see when you worked the Mazes of Ammon Ra?'

'I told you. They were obscured.'

'I know that is not true.' Nefer shook his head. 'You said that to protect me.' He shivered from the chill of the night, and from the sense of dread that had been his constant companion ever since that visitation of evil at the falcons' nest. 'You saw something of terrible portent, I know you did. That is why we are fleeing now. You must tell me all your vision. I must understand what is happening to us.'

'Yes, you are right.' Taita agreed at last. 'It is time for you to know.' He put out one thin arm and drew Nefer close under his shawl – the boy was surprised by the warmth of the old man's skinny frame. Taita seemed to be collecting his thoughts, and then at last he spoke.

'In my vision I saw a great tree growing on the banks of Mother Nile. It was a mighty tree and its blooms were blue as hyacinth and over it hung the double crown of the Upper and Lower Kingdoms. In its shade were all the multitudes of this very Egypt, men and women, children and greybeards, merchants and farmers and scribes, priests and warriors. The tree gave them all protection, and they prospered mightily and were content.'

'That was a good vision.' Eagerly Nefer translated it, the way Taita had taught him: 'The tree must have been Pharaoh, my father. The colour of the House of Tamose is blue, and my father wears the double crown.'

'That is the meaning as I read it.'

'Then what did you see, Tata?'

'I saw a serpent in the muddy waters of the river, swimming towards where the tree stood. It was a mighty serpent.'

'A cobra?' Nefer guessed, and his voice was small and fearful.

'Yes,' Taita affirmed, 'it was a great cobra. And it crawled from the waters of the Nile and climbed into the tree, twisting itself around the trunk and the branches until it seemed part of the tree, supporting it and giving it strength.'

'That I do not understand,' Nefer whispered.

'Then the cobra reared up above the uppermost branches of the tree, struck down and buried its fangs in the trunk.'

'Sweet Horus.' Nefer shuddered. 'Was it the same snake that tried to bite me, do you think?' He did not wait for an answer, but went on quickly, 'What did you see then, Tata?'

'I saw the tree wither, fall and shatter. I saw the cobra still reared triumphantly on high, but now it wore on its evil brow the double crown. The dead tree began to throw out green shoots but as they appeared the serpent struck at them, and they, too, were poisoned and died.'

Nefer was silent. Although the meaning seemed evident, he was unable to voice his interpretation of the vision.

'Were all the green shoots of the tree destroyed?' he asked eventually.

'There was one that grew in secret, beneath the surface of the earth, until it was strong. Then it burst out like a mighty vine and locked itself in conflict with the cobra. Although the cobra attacked it with all its strength and venom, still it survived and had a life of its own.'

'What was the end of the conflict, Tata? Which of them triumphed? Which one wore the double crown at the end?'

'I did not see the end of the conflict, because it was obscured in the smoke and dust of war.'

Nefer was silent for so long that Taita thought he had fallen asleep, but then the boy began to shake and he realized he was weeping. At last Nefer spoke, with a dreadful finality and certainty. 'Pharaoh is dead. My father is dead. That was the message of your vision. The poisoned tree was Pharaoh. That was the same message at the falcons' nest. The dead tiercel was Pharaoh. My father is dead, killed by the cobra.'

Taita could not answer him. All he could do was tighten his grip around Nefer's shoulders, and try to impart strength and comfort to him.

'And I am the green shoot of the tree,' Nefer went on. 'You saw this. You know that the cobra is waiting to destroy me as he did my father. That is why you would not let the soldiers take me back to Thebes. You know that the cobra waits for me there.'

'You are right, Nefer. We cannot return to Thebes until you are strong enough to defend yourself. We must fly from this very Egypt. There are lands and mighty kings to the east. It is my purpose to go to them and seek an ally to help us destroy the cobra.'

'But who is the cobra? Did you not see his face in the vision?'

'We know that he stands close to your father's throne. For in the vision he was entwined with the tree and gave it support.' He paused, and then, as if making a decision, went on, 'Naja is the name of the cobra.'

Nefer stared at him. 'Naja!' he whispered. 'Naja! Now I understand why we cannot return to Thebes.' He paused for a while, then said, 'Wandering in the eastern lands we will become two outcasts, beggars.'

'The vision showed that you will grow strong. We must put our trust in the Mazes of Ammon Ra.'

Despite his grief for his father, Nefer slept at last, but Taita roused him in the darkness before dawn. They mounted again and rode eastwards until the bad ground fell away behind them and Nefer thought he smelt the salt of the sea on the dawn wind.

'At the port of Seged we will find a ship to take us across to the land of the Hurrians.' Taita seemed to read what was in his mind. 'King Sargon of Babylon and Assyria, those mighty kingdoms between the Tigris and the Euphrates, is your father's satrap. He is bound in treaty to your father against the Hyksos, and all our mutual enemies. I think that Sargon will hold to that treaty, for he is an honourable man. We must trust that he will take us in and foster your claim to the throne of united Egypt.'

Ahead of them the sun came up in a furnace glow, and when they topped the next rise they saw the sea below them blazing like a freshly forged bronze war shield. Taita judged the distance. 'We will reach the coast before the sun sets this evening.' Then, with narrowed eyes, he turned to look back over his mount's rump. He stiffened as he made out not one but four separate plumes of yellow dust rising on the plain behind them. 'Hilto, again,' he exclaimed. 'I should have known better than to think that old rogue had given up the chase so readily.' He jumped up and stood erect on his horse's back for a better field of view, an old cavalryman's trick. 'He must have detoured around the rocky ground in the night. Now he has thrown out a ring of chariots in an extended line to sweep for our tracks. He did not need a necromancer to tell him we must be heading east for the coast.'

Swiftly he looked in every direction for cover. Although the open stony plain over which they were travelling seemed devoid of any feature, he picked out an insignificant fold of ground that might offer concealment if they could reach it in time.

'Dismount!' he ordered Nefer. 'We must keep as low as possible and raise no dust for them to spot us.' Silently he rebuked himself for not having taken more care to cover their tracks during the night. Now as they turned aside and led the horses towards the concealing fold of ground, he took care to avoid the patches of soft earth and keep to a natural rock pavement, which would leave no tracks. When they reached the hidden ground they found it was too shallow to cover a standing horse.

Nefer looked back anxiously. The nearest column of moving dust was less than half a league behind them, and coming on fast. The others were spread out in a wide semicircle.

'There is no place to hide here, and it's too late to run now. Already they have us surrounded.' Taita slipped down from the back of his mare, spoke to her softly and stooped to caress her front legs. The mare stamped and snorted, but when he insisted, she lowered herself reluctantly and lay flat on her side still snorting in mild protest. Taita took off his kilt and used it to blindfold her, so that she would not attempt to stand up again.

Then he came quickly to Nefer's colt and performed the same trick. When both horses were down he told Nefer sharply, 'Lie at Stargazer's head and hold him down if he tries to stand.'

Nefer laughed for the first time since he had learned of his father's death. Taita's way with animals never failed to enchant him. 'How did you make them do that, Tata?'

'If you speak to them so that they understand, they will do whatever you tell them. Now, lie beside him and keep him quiet.'

They lay behind the horses and watched the encircling columns of dust sweep across the plain around them. 'They won't be able to pick out our tracks on the stony ground, will they, Tata?' Nefer asked hopefully.

Taita grunted. He was watching the approach of the nearest chariot. In the dancing mirage it seemed insubstantial, wavering and distorted as an image seen through water. It was moving quite slowly, weaving from side to side as it cast for spoor. Suddenly it moved forward with more determination and purpose, and Taita could see that the charioteer had picked up their tracks and was following them.

The chariot came on until they could make out the men on the footplate more clearly. They were leaning out over the dashboard, examining the earth as they passed over it. Suddenly Taita muttered unhappily, 'By Seth's stinking breath, they have a Nubian scout with them.'

The tall black man was made even taller by the headdress of heron's feathers he wore. Five hundred cubits from where they lay concealed, the Nubian jumped down from the moving vehicle and ran ahead of the horses.

'They are at the spot where we turned aside,' Taita whispered. 'Horus conceal our spoor from that black savage.' It was said that Nubian scouts could follow the track left by a swallow flying through the air.

The Nubian brought the chariot to a halt with a peremptory hand signal. He had lost the tracks where they turned on to the stony ground. Bent almost double, he circled out over the bare earth. At that distance he looked like a secretary bird hunting for serpents and rodents.

'Can you not weave a spell of concealment for us, Tata?' Nefer whispered uneasily. Taita had worked the spell for them often when they were hunting gazelle out on the open plains, and most times had enticed the dainty little animals within easy bow-shot without them becoming aware of the hunters. Taita did not reply, but when Nefer glanced across to where he lay he saw that the old man already had his most potent charm in his hand, a golden five-pointed star of exquisite workmanship, the Periapt of Lostris. Nefer knew that sealed within it was a lock of hair Taita had snipped from the head of Queen Lostris as she lay on the embalmer's table before her deification. Taita touched it to his lips as he silently recited the canticle for Concealment from the Eyes of an Enemy.

Out on the plain the Nubian straightened with a fresh air of purpose, and gazed straight in their direction.

'He has found the twist in our tracks,' Nefer said, and they watched the chariot pull in behind him as the Nubian started towards them over the rocky ground.

Taita said softly, 'I know that devil well. His name is Bay and he is a shaman of the Usbak tribe.'

Nefer watched in trepidation as the chariot and its outrider came on steadily. The charioteer was standing high on the footplate. Surely he could look down on them from there. But he made no sign of having spotted them.

Closer still they came and Nefer recognized Hilto as the charioteer, even down to the white battle scar on his right cheek. For a moment it seemed he stared straight at Nefer with those hawk-sharp eyes, then his gaze slid away.

'Do not move.' Taita's voice was soft as the light breeze over the bright plain.

Now Bay, the Nubian, was so close that Nefer could see every charm in the necklace that dangled on his broad bare chest. Bay stopped abruptly and his scarified features creased into a frown, as he turned his head, slowly questing all around, like a hunting dog with the scent of game in his nostrils.

'Still!' Taita whispered. 'He senses us.'

Bay came on a few slow paces then stopped again and held up his hand. The chariot pulled up behind him. The horses were restless and fidgeting. Hilto touched the dashboard with the shaft of the lance in his hand. The small rasping sound was magnified in the silence.

Now Bay was staring directly into Nefer's face. Nefer tried to hold that dark implacable stare without blinking, but his eyes watered with the strain. Bay reached up and clasped one of the charms on his necklace. Nefer realized it was the floating bone from the chest of a man-eating lion. Taita had one in his armoury of talismans and magical charms.

Bay began to chant softly in his deep melodious African bass. Then he stamped one bare foot on the hard earth, and spat in Nefer's direction.

'He is piercing my curtain,' Taita said flatly. Suddenly Bay grinned and pointed directly at them with the lion charm in his fist. Behind him Hilto shouted with astonishment, and gaped at where Taita and Nefer were suddenly revealed, lying on the open ground only a hundred cubits away.

'Prince Nefer! We have searched for you these thirty days past. Thank great Horus and Osiris, we have found you at last.'

Nefer sighed and scrambled to his feet, and Hilto drove up, leaped out of the chariot and went down on one knee before him. He lifted the bronze skull helmet from his head, and cried, in a voice pitched to giving commands on the battlefield, 'Pharaoh Tamose is dead! Hail, Pharaoh Nefer Seti. May you live for ever.'

Seti was the Prince's divine name, one of the five names of power that had been given him at birth, long before his accession to the throne was assured. No one had been allowed to use the divine name until this moment when he was first hailed as Pharaoh.

'Pharaoh! Mighty bull! We have come to bear you to the Holy City that you may be risen in Thebes in your own divine image as Horus of Gold.'

'What if I should choose not to go with you, Colonel Hilto?' Nefer asked.

Hilto looked distressed. 'With all love and loyalty, Pharaoh, it is the strictest order of the Regent of Egypt that you be brought to Thebes. I must obey that order, even at the risk of your displeasure.'

Nefer glanced sideways at Taita, and spoke from the side of his mouth: 'What must I do?'

'We must go with them.'

They began the return to Thebes with an escort of fifty fighting chariots led by Hilto. Under strict orders the column rode first to the oasis of Boss. Fast horsemen had been sent ahead to Thebes and Lord Naja, the Regent of Egypt, had come out from the city to the oasis to meet the young Pharaoh Nefer Seti.

On the fifth day the squadron of chariots, dusty and battered from months in the wilderness, trotted into the oasis. As they entered the shade of the canopy of the palm groves a full regiment of the Phat Guards formed up in parade order to welcome them. The troopers had sheathed their weapons and instead carried palm fronds, which they waved as they chanted the anthem to their monarch.

> 'Seti, mighty bull.
> Beloved of truth.
> He of the two ladies, Nekhbet and Wadjet.
> Fiery serpent, great of strength.
> Horus of Gold, who makes hearts live.
> He of the sedge and the bee.
> Seti, son of Ra, god of the sun, living for ever and eternity.'

Nefer stood between Hilto and Taita on the footplate of the leading chariot. His clothing was ragged and dusty, and his thick locks were matted with dust. The sun had burnt his face and arms to the colour of ripe almonds. Hilto drove the chariot down the long alley formed by the soldiers, and Nefer smiled shyly at those men in the ranks whom he recognized and they cheered him spontaneously. They had loved his father, and now they loved him.

In the centre of the oasis an assembly of multicoloured tents had been set up beside the well. In front of the royal tent Lord Naja, surrounded by a concourse of courtiers, nobles and priests, waited to receive the king. He was mighty in the power and grace of regency, glistening and beautiful in gold and precious stones, redolent of sweet unguents and fragrant lotions.

On his either hand stood Heseret and Merykara, the princesses of the royal House of Tamose. Their faces were pearly white with makeup, eyes huge and dark with kohl. Even the nipples of their bare breasts had been rouged red as ripe cherries. The horsehair wigs were too large for their pretty heads, and their skirts were so heavy with pearls and gold thread that they stood as stiffly as carved dolls.

As Hilto brought the chariot to a halt in front of him, Lord Naja stepped forward and lifted down the dirty boy. Nefer had not had an opportunity to bathe since leaving Gebel Nagara, and he smelt like a billy-goat.

'As your regent I salute you, Pharaoh. I am your foot servant and your loyal companion. May you live a thousand years,' he intoned, so that all those in the closest ranks could hear every word. Lord Naja led Nefer by the hand to the dais of council, carved from precious black woods from the interior of the African continent and inlaid with ivory and mother-of-pearl. He placed him upon it, then went down on his knees and kissed Nefer's grazed and grubby feet without any sign of repugnance. The toenails were torn and caked with black dirt.

He stood up and lifted Nefer to his feet, stripped away the torn kilt so the pharaonic tattoo on his thigh was revealed. He turned the boy slowly so that everyone in the audience could see it clearly.

'Hail, Pharaoh Seti, god and son of the gods. Behold thy sign. Look upon this mark, all the nations of the earth, and tremble at the power of the king. Bow down before the might of Pharaoh.'

A great shout went up from the soldiers and the courtiers packed around the dais. 'Hail, Pharaoh! In his might and majesty may he live for ever.'

Naja led the princesses forward, and they knelt before their brother to take their oaths of allegiance. Their voices were inaudible until Merykara, the younger, could contain herself no longer and sprang up on to the dais in a flurry of jewelled skirts. She rushed to her brother.

'Nefer,' she squealed, 'I have missed you so very much. I thought you were dead.' Nefer returned her embrace awkwardly, until she pulled away and whispered, 'You smell terribly,' and giggled.

Lord Naja signalled for one of the royal nursemaids to take the child away, and then, one by one, the mighty lords of Egypt, headed by the members of the council, came forward to take the loyal oath. There was one uncomfortable moment when Pharaoh surveyed the gathering and asked, in a clear, penetrating voice, 'Where is my good uncle Kratas? He of all my people should have been here to greet me.'

Talla mumbled a placatory explanation. 'Lord Kratas is unable to attend. It shall be explained later to Your Majesty.' Talla, old and feeble, was now president of the council of state. He had become Naja's creature.

The ceremony ended when Lord Naja clapped his hands. 'Pharaoh has come on a long journey. He must rest before leading the procession into the city.'

He took Nefer's hand in a proprietary manner and led him into the royal tent whose spacious galleries and saloons could have accommodated a full regiment of the guards. There the master of the wardrobe, the perfumers and hairdressers, the keeper of the royal jewels, the valets, manicurists, masseurs and the maids of the bath were waiting to receive him.

Taita had determined to stay at the boy's side where he could protect him. He tried unobtrusively to include himself among this entourage, but his lanky frame and head of silver hair marked him out, while his fame and reputation were such that he could never have passed inconspicuously anywhere in the land. Almost immediately a serjeant-at-arms confronted him. 'Greetings, Lord Taita. May the gods always smile upon you.' Although Pharaoh Tamose had elevated him to the nobility on the day that he had sealed the deed of his manumission, Taita still felt awkward at being addressed by his title.

'The Regent of Egypt has sent for you.' He looked down at the Magus' filthy clothing and dusty old sandals. 'It would be as well not to attend him in your present state of dress. Lord Naja detests uncouth odours and unwashed apparel.'

Lord Naja's tent was larger and more luxuriously appointed than Pharaoh's. He sat on a throne of carved ebony and ivory decorated in gold and the even rarer and more precious silver with representations of all the principal gods of Egypt. The sandy floor was covered with woollen rugs from Hurria, woven in wonderful colours, including the bright green that signified the verdant fields that covered both banks of the Nile. Since his elevation to the stature of regent, Naja had adopted that green as the colour of his house.

He believed that pleasing aromas encouraged the gods to draw nigh, and incense burned in the silver pots suspended on chains from the ridge-pole of the tent. There were open glass vases filled with perfume on the low table in front of the throne. The Regent had discarded his wig, and a slave held a cone of perfumed beeswax on his shaven pate. As the wax melted it ran down his cheeks and neck, cooling and soothing him.

The interior of the tent smelt like a garden. Even the ranks of courtiers, ambassadors and supplicants who sat facing the throne had been induced to bathe and perfume their bodies before entering the presence of the Regent. Likewise, Taita had followed the advice of the serjeant-at-arms. His hair was washed and combed into a silver cascade over his shoulders, and his linen was freshly laundered and bleached to purest white. At the entrance to the tent, he knelt to make obeisance to the throne. There was a hum of comment and speculation as he rose to his feet. The foreign ambassadors stared at him curiously, and he heard his name whispered. Even the warriors and priests nodded and leaned close together as they told each other, 'It is the Magus.'

'The holy Taita, adept of the Mazes.'

'Taita, the Wounded Eye of Horus.'

Lord Naja looked up from the papyrus he was scanning and smiled down the length of the tent. He was truly a handsome man, with sculpted features and sensitive lips. His nose was straight and narrow, and his eyes were the colour of golden agate, lively and intelligent. His naked chest was devoid of fat, and his arms were lean and covered with hard muscle.

Swiftly Taita surveyed the ranks of men who now sat closest to the throne. In the short time since the death of Pharaoh Tamose there had been a redistribution of power and favour among the courtiers and nobles. Many familiar faces were missing, and many others had emerged from obscurity into the sunshine of the Regent's goodwill. Not least of these was Asmor of the Phat Guards.

'Come forward, Lord Taita.' Naja's voice was pleasant and low. Taita moved towards the throne, and the ranks of courtiers opened to let him pass. The Regent smiled down at him. 'Know you that you stand high in our favour. You have discharged the duty that Pharaoh Tamose placed upon you with distinction. You have given the Prince Nefer Memnon invaluable instruction and training.' Taita was astonished by the warmth of this greeting, but he did not let it show. 'Now that the prince has become Pharaoh Seti, he will stand in even greater need of your guiding hand.'

'May he live for ever.' Taita responded, and the gathering echoed his words.

'May he live for ever.'

Lord Naja gestured. 'Take your seat here, in the shadow of my throne. Even I will have much need of your experience and wisdom when it comes to ordering the affairs of Pharaoh.'

'The royal Regent does me more honour than I deserve.' Taita turned a gentle face to Lord Naja. It was prudent never to let your hidden enemy recognize your animosity. He took the seat that was offered him, but declined the silken cushion, and sat on the woollen rug. His back was straight, and his shoulders square.

The business of the Regency proceeded. They were dividing up the estate of General Kratas: as a declared traitor everything Kratas owned was forfeited to the Crown. 'From the traitor Kratas, unto the temple of Hapi and the priests of the mysteries,' Naja read from the papyrus, 'all his lands and the buildings on the east bank of the river between Dendera and Abnub.'

As Taita listened he mourned his oldest friend, but he let no shadow of grief show on his face. During the long journey back from the desert, Hilto had related the manner of Kratas' death, then gone on to tell him, 'All men, even the noble and the good, walk softly in the presence of the new Regent of Egypt. Menset is dead, he who was president of the council of state. He died in his sleep, but there are those who say he had a little help to start him on the journey. Cinka is dead, executed for treason, though he had no longer the wits to cheat on his ancient wife. His estates are confiscated by the Regency. Fifty more have gone in company with the good Kratas to the underworld. And the council members are all Naja's dogs.'

Kratas had been Taita's last link with the golden days when Tanus, Lostris and he had been young. Taita had loved him well.

'From the traitor Kratas, unto the Regent of Egypt, all the store of millet held in his name in the granaries of Athribis,' Lord Naja read from the papyrus.

That was fifty bargeloads, Taita calculated, for Kratas had been a shrewd investor in the millet exchanges. Lord Naja had paid himself generously for the onerous work of assassination.

'These stores to be used for the common good.' The expropriation was qualified, and Taita wondered expressionlessly who would determine the public good.

The priests and the scribes were busily recording the division on their clay tablets. These would be stored in the archives of the temple. While Taita watched and listened, he kept his anger and his sorrow locked away in his heart.

'We will move on now to another important royal matter,' Lord Naja said, when Kratas' heirs had been deprived of all their inheritance, and he was richer by three lakhs of gold. 'I come to the consideration of the well-being and status of the princesses royal, Heseret and Merykara. I have consulted earnestly with the members of the council of state. All are agreed that, for their own good, I should take both the Princess Heseret and the Princess Merykara in marriage. As my wives, they will come under my full protection. The goddess Isis is the patron of both the royal maidens. I have ordered the priestesses of the goddess to consult the auguries, and they have determined that these marriages are pleasing to the goddess. Therefore, the ceremony will take place in the temple of Isis at Luxor on the day of the next full moon after the burial of Pharaoh Tamose, and the coronation of his heir, Prince Nefer Seti.'

Taita remained unmoving, his face blank, but all around him there was a rustle and murmur at this pronouncement. The political considerations of such a double marriage were monumental. All of those present knew that Lord Naja was intent on making himself a member through marriage of the royal House of Tamose, and thus the next in line of succession.

Taita felt chilled to his bones, as though he had just heard the death sentence of Pharaoh Nefer Seti cried aloud from the White Tower in the centre of Thebes. There remained only twelve more days of the required seventy for the Royal embalming of the dead pharaoh. Immediately after the interment of Tamose in his tomb in the Valley of the Kings on the west bank of the Nile, the coronation of his successor and the weddings of his surviving daughters would take place.

Then the cobra will strike again. Taita felt the certainty of it. He was roused from his preoccupation with the dangers that surrounded the prince by a general stir in the gathering around him, and he realized that, without him hearing it, the Regent had just declared the levee closed, and was rising and retiring through the tent flap behind the throne. He rose with the others to leave the tent.

Colonel Asmor stepped forward to stop him, with a smile and a courteous bow. 'Lord Naja, the Regent of Egypt, asks you not to leave. He invites you to a private audience.'

Asmor was now colonel of the Regent's bodyguard, with the rank of Best of Ten Thousand. In a short time he had become a man of power and influence. There was no point in or possibility of refusing the summons, and Taita nodded. 'I am the servant of Pharaoh and of his regent. May they both live a thousand years.'

Asmor led him to the back of the tent, and held open the curtaining for him to pass through. Taita found himself out in the open palm groves, and Asmor led him through the trees to where a smaller, single-roomed tent was pitched on its own. A dozen guards were posted in a ring around this pavilion, for this was a place of secret council which no person was permitted to approach without the Regent's summons. At a command from Asmor, the guards stood aside and the colonel ushered Taita into the shaded interior.

Naja looked up from the bronze bowl in which he was washing his hands. 'You are welcome, Magus.' He smiled warmly, and waved to the pile of cushions in the centre of the rug-covered floor. While Taita seated himself, Naja nodded to Asmor, who went to take up a guard position at the tent opening, his sickle sword drawn. There were only the three of them in the tent, and their conversation would not be overheard.

Naja had discarded his jewellery, and insignia of office. He was affable and friendly as he came to take a seat on one of the cushions facing Taita. He indicated the tray of sweetmeats and sherbet in golden bowls that stood between them. 'Please refresh yourself.'

Taita's instinct was to decline, but he knew that to refuse the Regent's hospitality would advertise his own hostility, and alert Naja to his deadly opposition.

As yet, Lord Naja had no reason to know that Taita was aware of his intentions towards the new Pharaoh, or of Naja's crimes and his further ambitions. He inclined his head in thanks and selected the golden bowl furthest from his hand. He waited for Naja to pick up the other bowl of sherbet. The Regent took it, raised it, drank and swallowed without hesitation.

Taita lifted the bowl to his lips, and sipped the cordial. He held it on his tongue. There were those who boasted of possessing poisons that were tasteless and undetectable, but Taita had studied all the corrosive elements, and even the tart fruit could not mask their flavours from him. The drink was uncontaminated, and he swallowed it with pleasure.

'Thank you for your trust,' said Naja gravely, and Taita knew that he referred to more than his acceptance of the refreshment.

'I am the servant of the King, and therefore of his regent.'

'You are a person of inestimable value to the Crown,' Naja countered, 'You have faithfully served three pharaohs and all of them have relied on your advice without question.'

'You overestimate my worth, my lord Regent. I am an old man and feeble.'

Naja smiled. 'Old? Yes, you are old. I have heard it said that you are more than two hundred years old.' Taita inclined his head, neither confirming nor denying it. 'But feeble, no! You are old and as monumental as a mountain. All men know that your wisdom is boundless. Even the secrets of eternal life are yours.'

The flattery was blatant and unashamed, and Taita searched behind it for the hidden reason and meaning. Naja was silent, watching him expectantly. What was he waiting to hear? Taita looked into his eyes, and tuned his mind to catch the other man's thoughts. They were as fleeting and evanescent as the darting shapes of cave bats against the darkling sky at sunset.

He captured one thought entire, and suddenly understood what Naja wanted from him. The knowledge gave him power, and the way ahead opened before him like the gates of a captured city.

'For a thousand years, every king and every learned man has searched for the secret of eternal life,' he said softly.

'Perhaps one man alone has found it.' Naja leaned forward eagerly, with his elbows on his knees.

'My lord, your questions are too profound for an old man like me. Two hundred years is not life eternal.' Taita spread his hands deprecatingly, but dropped his eyes, allowing Naja to read what he wanted to hear in the half-hearted denial. The double crown of Egypt, and eternal life, he thought, and smiled inwardly, keeping his expression solemn. This regent's wants are few and simple.

Naja straightened. 'We will speak of these deep matters another time.' There was a triumphant light in his yellow eyes. 'But now there is something else I would ask of you. It would be a way for you to prove that my good opinion of you is fully justified. You would find my gratitude without bounds.'

He twists and turns like an eel, Taita thought, and I once believed him to be a dull clod of a soldier. He has been able to hide the light of his lantern from all of us. Aloud he said simply, 'If it is within my power, I would deny Pharaoh's regent nothing.'

'You are an adept of the Mazes of Ammon Ra.' Naja said, with a finality that brooked no denial.

Once more Taita glimpsed the shadowy depths of this man's ambition. Not only the crown and eternal life! He wishes also to have the future revealed to him, Taita marvelled, but nodded humbly and replied, 'My lord Naja, all my life I have studied the mysteries, and perhaps I have learned a little.'

'All your very long life.' Naja placed his own emphasis on the phrase. 'And you have learned a very great deal.'

Taita bowed his head and remained silent. Why did I ever dream that he would have me killed? he asked himself. He will protect me with his own life, for that is what he believes I hold in my hands – the key to his immortality.

'Taita, beloved of kings and gods, I wish you to work the Mazes of Ammon Ra for me.'

'My lord, I have never worked the Mazes for anyone who was not a queen or a pharaoh, or one who was not destined to sit upon the throne of this very Egypt.'

'It may well be that one such person asks you now,' said Lord Naja, with deep significance in his tone.

Great Horus has delivered him to me. I have him in my hands, Taita thought, and said, 'I bow to the wishes of Pharaoh's regent.'

'Will you work the Mazes for me this very day? I am most anxious to know the wishes of the gods.' Naja's handsome features were alive with excitement and avarice.

'No man should enter the Mazes lightly,' Taita demurred. 'There are great dangers, not only for me but also for the patron who requests the divination. It will take time to prepare for the journey into the future.'

'How long?' Naja's disappointment was evident.

Taita clasped his forehead in a pantomime of deep thought. Let him sniff the bait for a while, he thought. It will make him more eager to swallow the hook. At last he looked up. 'On the first day of the festival of the Bull of Apis.'

The next morning, when he emerged from the great tent, Pharaoh Seti was transformed from the dusty and odorous little rapscallion who had entered the oasis of Boss the previous day.

With a regal fury and fire that had dismayed his entourage, he had resisted the attempts of the barbers to shave his head. Instead, his dark curls had been shampooed and combed until they shone in the early sunlight with russet lights. On top of them he wore the *uraeus*, the circlet of gold depicting Nekhbet, the vulture goddess, and Naja, the cobra. Their images were entwined on his forehead, with eyes of red- and blue-coloured glass. On his chin was the false beard of kingship. His makeup was skilfully created so that his beauty was enhanced, and the packed crowds who waited before the tent sighed with admiration and awe as they sank to the ground in adoration. His false fingernails were of beaten gold, and there were gold sandals on his feet. On his chest was one of the most precious of the Crown Jewels of Egypt: the pectoral medallion of Tamose, a jewelled portrait of the god Horus the Falcon. He walked with a stately tread for one so young, carrying the flail and the sceptre crossed over his heart. He stared solemnly ahead until, from the corner of his eye, he glimpsed Taita in the front rank of the crowd: he rolled his eyes at the old man then made an impish moue of resignation.

In a cloud of perfume, Lord Naja walked a pace behind him, splendid with jewels and awesome with authority. On his hip hung the blue sword, and on his right arm he wore the hawk seal.

Next came the princesses, with the golden feathers of the goddess Isis on their heads, and golden rings on their fingers and toes. They were no longer in the stiff, encrusted robes of yesterday: from throat to ankles they were encased in long dresses, but the linen was so fine and transparent that the sunlight struck through it, as though through the river mist at dawn. Merykara's limbs were slim, and her chest boyish. The outline of Heseret's body was moulded into voluptuous curves, her breasts were rosy-tipped through the diaphanous folds, and at the base of her belly, in the fork of her thighs, nestled the shadowy triangle of womanhood.

Pharaoh mounted the processional carriage and took his seat on the elevated throne. Lord Naja stood at his right hand, and the princesses sat at his feet.

The companies of priests from every one of the fifty temples of Thebes fell in ahead, strumming the lyre, beating drum and shaking sistrum, sounding the horns, chanting and wailing praises and supplications to the gods.

Then Asmor's bodyguard took up their positions in the procession, and after them came Hilto's squadron of chariots, all freshly burnished and decked with pennants and flowers. The horses were curried until their hides glowed like precious metal, and ribbons were plaited into their manes. The bullocks in the traces of the royal carriage were all of unblemished white, their massive humps decorated with bouquets of lilies and water-hyacinth. Their widespread horns and even their hoofs were covered with gold leaf.

The drivers were stark naked Nubian slaves. Every hair had been plucked from their heads and bodies which greatly emphasized the size of their genitals. They had been anointed from head to foot with rich oils so that they glistened in the sunlight, black as the eye of Seth, in magnificent contrast to the snowy hides of their bullocks. They goaded the team forward, and the bullocks plodded through the dust. A thousand warriors of the Phat Guards fell in behind them and burst with one voice into the anthem of praise. The populace of Thebes had opened the main gates of the city in welcome and were lining the tops of the walls. From a mile outside it they had covered the dusty surface of the road with palm fronds, straw and flowers.

The walls, towers and buildings of Thebes were all built of sun-baked mud bricks – stone blocks were reserved for the construction of tombs and temples. It hardly rained in the Nile valley so these constructions never deteriorated; they had all been freshly whitewashed and hung with banners in the sky blue of the House of Tamose. The procession passed through the gates, with the crowds dancing, singing and weeping with joy, filling the narrow streets so that the pace of the royal carriage was that of a giant tortoise. At every temple along the way the royal carriage came to a ponderous halt, and Pharaoh dismounted in solemn dignity to sacrifice to the god who dwelt within.

It was late afternoon before they reached the docks at the riverside where the royal barge waited to ferry Pharaoh's party across to the palace of Memnon on the west bank. Once they had gone on board, two hundred rowers in massed banks plied their paddles. To the beat of the drum they rose and fell in unison, wet and shining like the wings of a gigantic egret.

Surrounded by a fleet of galleys, feluccas and other small craft they made the crossing in the late sunlight. Even when they reached the west bank the King's duties for his first day were not completed. Another royal carriage bore him through the crowds to the funerary temple of his father, Pharaoh Tamose.

It was dark before they rode up the causeway, lit on both sides by bonfires, and the populace had indulged themselves all that day on beer and wine provided by the royal treasury. The uproar was deafening as Pharaoh dismounted at Tamose's temple, and climbed the stairway between ranks of granite statues of his father and of his patron god Horus in all his hundred divine guises – Horus as the child Harpocrates, with side-lock and a finger in his mouth, suckling at the breast of Isis, or squatting on a lotus blossom, or falcon-headed, or as the winged sun disc. It seemed that king and god had become one.

Lord Naja and the priests led the boy Pharaoh through the tall wooden gates into the Hall of Sorrow, that holy place where Tamose's mummy lay on its embalming slab of black diorite. In a separate shrine in the side wall, guarded by a black statue of Anubis, the god of cemeteries, stood the pearly alabaster canopic jars that held the king's heart, lungs and viscera.

In a second shrine against the opposite wall the gold-covered sarcophagus stood ready to receive the royal corpse. The lid of the coffin bore a portrait of Pharaoh in gold so lifelike that Nefer's heart twisted, impaled with grief, and tears started in his eyes. He blinked them away, and followed the priests to where his father's body lay in the centre of the hall.

Lord Naja took up his position opposite him on the far side of the diorite slab, facing Nefer, and the high priest stood at the head of the dead king. When all was in readiness for the ceremony of Opening the Mouth of the dead king, two priests drew aside the linen sheet that covered the corpse, and Nefer recoiled involuntarily as he looked down on his father.

For all the weeks after his death, while Nefer and Taita had been in the desert, the embalmers had been at work on the King's body. First they had probed a long-handled silver spoon up his nostril and, without marking his head, scooped out the soft custard of the brains. They removed the eyeballs, which would putrefy swiftly, and filled the eye sockets and the cavity of the skull with natron salts and aromatic herbs. Then they had lowered the corpse into a bath of highly concentrated salts, with the head exposed, and let it soak for thirty days, daily changing the harsh alkali fluids. The fats were leached out of the corpse and the skin peeled away. Only the hair and skin of the head were unaffected.

When at last the corpse was removed from the natron bath it was laid on the diorite slab and wiped down with oils and herbal tinctures. The empty stomach cavity was stuffed with linen pads soaked in resins and waxes. The arrow wound in the chest was sewn closed, and amulets of gold and precious stones placed over it. The barbed and broken shaft that had killed the king had been removed from Pharaoh's body by the embalmers. After it had been examined by the council of state, the missile had been sealed in a golden casket and would go into his tomb with him, a powerful charm against any further evil that might befall him on his journey through the netherworld.

Then, during the remaining forty days of the embalming, the corpse was allowed to dry thoroughly with the hot desert wind through the open doorways streaming over it.

Once it was as desiccated as firewood, it could be bound up. The linen bandages were laid on it in an intricate design, as incantations to the gods were chanted by choirs of priests. Under them were placed more precious talismans and amulets, and each layer was painted with resins that dried to a metallic hardness and sheen. Only the head was left uncovered, and then for the week before Opening the Mouth, four of the most skilful makeup artists of the guild of embalmers, using wax and cosmetics, had restored the King's features to lifelike beauty.

They replaced the missing eyes with perfect replicas of rock-crystal and obsidian. The whites were translucent, the iris and pupils an exact match of the king's natural colour. The glass orbs seemed endowed with life and intelligence, so that now Nefer gazed into them with awe, expecting to see the lids blink and his father's pupils widen in recognition. The lips were shaped and rouged so that at any moment they might smile, and his painted skin looked silken and warm, as though bright blood still ran beneath it. His hair had been washed and set in the familiar dark ringlets that Nefer remembered so well.

Lord Naja, the high priest and the choir began to chant the incantation against dying for the second time, but Nefer could not tear his gaze away from his father's face.

> *'He is the reflection and not the mirror,*
> *He is the music and not the lyre,*
> *He is the stone and not the chisel,*
> *He will live for ever.'*

The high priest came to Nefer's side and placed the golden spoon in his hand. Nefer had been coached in the ritual, but his hand trembled as he placed the spoon on his father's lips and recited, 'I open thy lips that thou might have the power of speech once more.' He touched his father's nose with the spoon. 'I open thy nostrils that thou might breathe once more.' He touched each of the magnificent eyes. 'I open thine eyes that thou might behold the glory of this world once more, and the glory of the world to come.'

When at last it was done, the royal party waited as the embalmers wrapped the head and painted it with aromatic resins. Then they laid the golden mask over the blind face, and once more it glowed with splendid life. Contrary to custom and usage, there was only one death mask and one golden sarcophagus for Pharaoh Tamose. His father had gone before him to his tomb covered by seven masks and seven sarcophagi, one within the other, each larger and more ornate than the next.

For the rest of that night Nefer stayed beside the golden sarcophagus, praying and burning incense, entreating the gods to take his father among them and seat him in the midst of the pantheon. In the dawn he went out with the priests on to the terrace of the temple where his father's head falconer waited. He carried a royal falcon on his gloved fist.

'Nefertem!' Nefer whispered the bird's name. 'Lotus Flower.' He took the magnificent bird from the falconer and held it high upon his own fist, so that the populace gathered below the terrace might see it clearly. Around its right leg the falcon wore a tiny goldtag on a golden chain. On it was engraved his father's royal cartouche. 'This is the godbird of Pharaoh Tamose Mamose. It is the spirit of my father.' He paused to regain his composure, for he was near to tears. Then he went on, 'I set my father's godbird free.' He slipped the leather rufterhood from the falcon's head. Fierce eyes blinked at the light of the dawn and the bird ruffled its feathers. Nefer unknotted the jesses from its leg, and the bird spread its wings. 'Fly, divine spirit!' Nefer cried. 'Fly high for me and my father!'

He threw the bird up, it caught the dawn wind and soared on high. Twice it circled overhead, and then, with a wild and haunting cry, it sped away across the Nile.

'The godbird flies to the west!' the high priest called out. Every member of the congregation upon the steps of the temple knew that that was a most unpropitious omen.

Nefer was so physically and emotionally exhausted that as he watched the bird fly away he swayed on his feet. Taita steadied him before he fell and led him away.

Back in Nefer's bedchamber in the palace of Memnon, Taita mixed a draught at his bedside and knelt beside him to offer it. Nefer took one long swallow then lowered the cup and asked, 'Why does my father have only one small coffin when you tell me my grandfather was entombed in seven heavy golden sarcophagi and that it took twenty strong oxen to draw his funeral wagon?'

'Your grandfather was given the richest funeral in all the history of our land, and he took a great store of grave goods to the underworld with him, Nefer,' Taita agreed. 'But those seven coffins consumed thirty lakhs of pure gold, and almost beggared the nation.'

Nefer looked thoughtfully into the cup, then drained the last few drops of the draught. 'My father deserved such a rich funeral, for he was a mighty man.'

'Your grandfather thought much of his afterlife.' Taita explained patiently. 'Your father thought much of his people and the welfare of this very Egypt.'

Nefer thought about this for a while, then sighed, settled down on the sheepskin mattress and closed his eyes. He opened them again. 'I am proud of my father,' he said simply.

Taita laid his hand upon his forehead in blessing and whispered, 'And I know that one day your father will have reason to be proud of you.'

It did not need the ill omen of the flight of the falcon Nefertem to warn Taita that they had reached the most dire and fateful period in all the long history of this very Egypt. When he left Nefer's bedchamber and started out into the desert, it was as though the stars stood frozen in their courses and all the ancient gods had drawn back and deserted them, abandoning them in this their most dangerous hour.

'Great Horus, we need your guidance now. You hold this *Ta-meri*, this precious land, in the cup of your hands. Do not let it slip through your fingers and shatter like crystal. Do not turn your back upon us now that we are in our agony. Help me, mighty falcon. Instruct me. Make your wishes clear to me, so that I may follow your will.'

Praying as he went, he climbed the hills at the periphery of the great desert. The clicking of his long staff against the rocks alarmed a yellow jackal and sent it scampering away up the moonlit slope. When he was certain that he was not observed he turned parallel to the river, and quickened his stride. 'Horus, well you know that we are balanced on the sword edge of war and defeat. Pharaoh Tamose has been struck down and there is no warrior to lead us. Apepi and his Hyksos in the north are grown so mighty as to have become almost invincible. They gather against us, and we cannot stand against them. The double crown of the two kingdoms is rotten with the worm of treachery, and cannot survive against the new tyranny. Open my eyes, mighty god, and show me the way, that we might triumph against the invading Hyksosian hordes from the north and against the destroying poison in our blood.'

For the rest of that day Taita journeyed through the stony hills and the silent places, praying and searching to discover the way forward. In the late evening he turned back towards the river, and came at last to his ultimate destination. He could have chosen to come here by the direct means of a felucca, but too many eyes would have remarked his passing, and he had needed that time alone in the desert.

In the deep darkness when most men slept he approached the temple of Bes on the riverbank. A guttering torch burned in its niche above the gate. It lit the carved figure of the god Bes, which guarded the entrance. Bes was the deformed dwarf god of drunkenness and joviality. His tongue lolled out between his leering lips. In the wavering light of the torch he gave Taita an inebriated grin as he passed.

One of the temple acolytes was waiting to receive the Magus. He led him to a stone cell in the depths of the temple where a jug of goat's milk stood on the table beside a platter of *dhurra* bread and honey in the comb. They knew that one of the Magus' weaknesses was honey from the pollen of the mimosa blossom.

'There are three men already waiting your arrival, my lord,' the young priest told him.

'Bring Bastet to me first,' Taita instructed.

Bastet was the chief scribe of the Nomarch of Memphis. He was one of Taita's most valued sources of information. Not a rich man, he was burdened with two pretty but expensive wives and a brood of brats. Taita had saved his children when the Yellow Flowers devastated the land. Although of little consequence in the scheme of things, he sat close to the seat of power, using his ears and phenomenal memory to good effect. He had much to tell Taita of what had transpired in the nome since the accession of the new Regent, and received his payment with genuine gratitude. 'Your blessing would have been sufficient payment, mighty Magus.'

'Babes don't grow fat on blessings.' Taita dismissed him.

Next came Obos, the high priest of the great Horus temple at Thebes. He owed his appointment to Taita, who had interceded for him with Pharaoh Tamose. Most of the nobles came to the temple of Horus to worship and make sacrifice, and they all confided in the high priest. The third man to report to Taita was Nolro, the secretary of the army of the north. He also was a eunuch, and there was a bond between those who had suffered such mutilation.

From the days of his youth, when Taita had first found himself directing affairs of state from the shadows behind the throne, he had been aware of the absolute necessity of having impeccable intelligence on which to base decisions. All the rest of that night and most of the following day he listened to these men and questioned them narrowly, so that when he was ready to return to the palace of Memnon he was informed of all the important events that had transpired, and the significant undercurrents and political whirlpools that had developed while he had been away in the wilderness of Gebel Nagara.

In the evening he started back towards the palace, taking the direct route along the bank of the river. The peasants returning from their labours in the fields recognized him, made the sign for good luck and long life, and called to him, 'Pray to Horus for us, Magus,' for they all knew he was a Horus man. Many pressed small gifts upon him, and a ploughman called to him to share his dinner of millet cakes and crisply roasted locusts and goat's milk warm from the udder.

As night fell Taita thanked the friendly ploughman, bade him farewell, and left him sitting beside his fire. He hurried on through the night, anxious not to miss the ceremony of the royal rising. It was dawn before he reached the palace, and he had barely time to bathe and change his raiment before he hurried to the royal bedchamber. At the door his way was barred by the two guards, who crossed their spears across the entrance.

Taita was astonished. This had never happened before. He was the royal tutor, appointed thirteen years ago by Pharaoh Tamose. He glared at the sergeant of the guard. The man dropped his eyes but remained steadfast in his denial of entry. 'I mean no offence, mighty Magus. It is on the specific orders of the commander of the bodyguard, Colonel Asmor, and the palace chamberlain. No person not approved by the Regent is allowed in the royal presence.'

The sergeant was adamant, so Taita left him and strode down the terrace to where Naja was at breakfast with a small circle of his particular favourites and toadies. 'My lord Naja, you are fully aware that I was appointed by Pharaoh's own father as his tutor and mentor. I was given the right of access at any time of day and night.'

'That was many years ago, good Magus.' Naja replied smoothly, as he accepted a peeled grape from the slave who stood behind his stool and popped it into his mouth. 'It was right for that time, but Pharaoh Seti is a child no more. He no longer needs a nursemaid.' The insult was casual, but that did not make it less cutting. 'I am his regent. In future he looks to me for advice and guidance.'

'I acknowledge your right and duty to the King, but to keep me from Nefer's side is unnecessary and cruel,' Taita protested, but Naja waved a lordly hand to silence him.

'The safety of the King is paramount,' he said, and stood up from the breakfast board, to indicate that the meal and the interview were over. His bodyguard closed in around him so that Taita was forced to fall back.

He watched Naja's entourage set off down the cloister towards the council chamber. He did not follow immediately but turned aside and sat down on the coping of one of the fish pools to ponder this development.

Naja had isolated Nefer. He was a prisoner in his own palace. When the time came he would be alone, surrounded by his enemies. Taita searched for some means to protect him. Once again he considered the idea of flight from Egypt, to spirit Nefer away across the desert to the protection of a foreign power until he had grown old and strong enough to return to claim his birthright. However, he could be certain that Naja had not only barred the door to the royal quarters but that every escape route from Thebes and Egypt would have already been closed.

There seemed no easy solution, and after an hour of deep thought, Taita rose to his feet. The guards at the door to the council chamber stood aside for him, and Taita went down the aisle and took his accustomed seat on the front bench.

Nefer was seated on the dais beside his regent. He wore the lighter *hedjet* crown of Upper Egypt, and he looked pale and peaky. Taita felt a flare of concern that he might already be the victim of slow poison, but he could detect no deadly aura surrounding the boy. He concentrated on sending a current of strength and courage to him, but Nefer gave him a cold, accusing stare to punish him for missing the royal rising ceremony.

Taita turned his attention to the council business. They were considering the latest reports from the northern front, where King Apepi had recaptured Abnub after a siege that had lasted the previous three years. That unfortunate city had changed hands eight times since the first Hyksosian invasion in the reign of Pharaoh Mamose, Tamose's father.

If Pharaoh Tamose had not been struck down by the Hyksosian arrow, his bold strategy might have averted this tragic reversal of arms. Instead of now being forced to prepare for the next Hyksosian strike towards Thebes, the armies of Egypt might have been surging towards the enemy capital of Avaris.

Taita found that the council was bitterly divided in every consideration of the crisis. They were seeking to place the blame for this most recent defeat, when it was plain for any fool to see that Pharaoh's untimely death had been the main cause. He had left his army without a head and a heart. Apepi had taken immediate advantage of his death.

Listening to them argue Taita felt more strongly than ever that this war was a running abscess in the body of this very Egypt. Exasperated, he rose quietly and left the council chamber. There was nothing further he could accomplish here, for they were still wrangling over who should be given command of the northern armies to replace the dead Pharaoh Tamose. 'Now that he has gone, there is not one of our commanders who can match Apepi, not Asmor or Teron or Naja himself,' Taita muttered, as he stalked away. 'The land and our armies are bled white by sixty years of warfare. We must have time to build up our strength again, and for a great military leader to emerge from our ranks.' He thought of Nefer, but it would be years before the lad could take over the role that Taita knew, from his study of the Mazes of Ammon Ra, destiny had devised for him.

I have to win him that time and keep him safe until he is ready.

Next he went to the women's quarters of the palace. Because he was a eunuch he could pass through the gates, which were barred to other men. It was three days since the princesses had learned that they were soon to become brides, and Taita knew he should have visited them before. They would be confused and distressed, and sorely in need of his comfort and advice.

Merykara was the first to see him when he entered the courtyard. She sprang up from where a priestess of Isis had been instructing her with writing tablet and brush, and flew to him on those long legs, her sidelock bouncing on her shoulder. She flung her arms around his waist and hugged him with all her strength. 'Oh, Taita, where have you been? I have searched for you these last days.'

When she looked up at him, Taita saw that she had been weeping for her eyes were red-rimmed and heavily underscored with dark bruises. Now she started again, her shoulders shaking with her sobs. Taita picked her up and held her in his arms until she had quieted a little. 'What is it, my little monkey? What has made you so unhappy?'

'Lord Naja is going to take me to a secret place and do terrible things to me. He is going to put something huge and sharp inside me that will hurt me and make me bleed.'

'Who told you that?' Taita controlled his anger with difficulty.

'Magara and Saak.' Merykara sobbed. 'Oh, Taita, can't you stop him doing these things to me? Please, oh, please.'

Taita should have known that the two Nubian slave girls had been responsible for her terror. Usually their tales were of African hobgoblins and ghouls, but now they had something else with which to torment their charge. Grimly Taita swore retribution on both little hussies, and set about calming the princess's fears. It needed all his tact and gentleness, for Merykara was terrified.

He led her to an arbour in a quiet corner of the garden, sat down and she scrambled up on to his lap and pressed her cheek to his chest.

Of course, her fears were unfounded. Even after marriage, it was beyond nature, law and custom that Naja would take her to the marriage bed before Merykara had seen her first red moon, and that event was still years away. He succeeded at last in calming her then took her down to the royal stables to admire and fondle the colt that had been born that morning.

When she was smiling and chattering again, Taita led her back to the *zenana*, and performed a few minor miracles for her amusement. He transformed a jug of Nile water into delicious sherbet by dipping his finger into it, and they drank this together. Then he threw a pebble into the air, which turned into a live canary and flew to the top branches of a fig tree. There it hopped and trilled while the child danced and squealed with glee beneath it.

He left her, went to find the two slave girls, Magara and Saak, and gave them such a verbal lambasting that soon they were clinging together and wailing dolefully. He knew that Magara was always the ringleader in any such unpleasantness, so he produced a live scorpion from her ear and held it inches in front of her face, which reduced her to such paroxysms of terror that she urinated in little squirts down her legs.

Satisfied, he went to look for Heseret. As he had anticipated, she was down on the bank of the river with her lyre. She looked up at him with a sad little smile but went on strumming. He sat down beside her, on the grassy verge under the trailing branches of the willow. The tune she was playing had been her grandmother's favourite. Taita had taught it to her, and now she began to sing the words.

> 'My heart flutters up like a wounded quail
> when I see my beloved's face.
> and my cheeks bloom like the dawn sky
> to the sunshine of his smile.'

Her voice was sweet and true, and Taita felt his own tears brimming. It was as though he were listening to Lostris once again. He joined in with the chorus. His voice still clear and steady, without the quavering of age. Out on the river the rowers on a passing galley rested on their oars while they listened with rapt expressions as the current carried the vessel past where the pair sat together.

When the song ended Heseret laid aside the lyre, and turned to him. 'Darling Taita, I am so glad you have come.'

'I am sorry to have kept you waiting, moon of all my nights.' She smiled faintly at the pet name, for she had always had a romantic side to her nature. 'What service do you wish of me?'

'You must go to Lord Naja, and present him with my sincere apologies, but I cannot marry him.'

She was so much like her grandmother had been at the same age. Lostris, too, had saddled him with an impossible task, with the same assurance and confidence in his ability to accomplish it. Heseret now turned those enormous green eyes on him. 'You see, I have already promised Meren that I will be his wife.' Meren was the grandson of Kratas, and the boon companion of Prince Nefer.

Taita had noticed him looking at Heseret with calf's eyes, but had never suspected that she returned his feelings. Fleetingly he wondered how far they had gone towards the consummation of their passions, but put aside the thought. 'Heseret, I have explained to you many times that you are not like other girls. You are a princess royal. Your marriage cannot be undertaken in the light fancy of youth. It is something of dire political consequence.'

'You don't understand, Taita,' Heseret said softly, but with the sweet obstinacy he dreaded. 'I love Meren, I have loved him since I was a little girl. I want to marry him, not Lord Naja.'

'I cannot overrule the decree of the Regent of Egypt,' he tried to explain, but she shook her head and smiled at him.

'You are so wise, Taita. You will think of something. You always do,' she told him, and he felt as though his heart would break.

'Lord Taita, I refuse to discuss your access to Pharaoh or my impending marriage to the royal princesses. In both these matters my mind is set.' To emphasize that he had closed the subject, Naja returned his full attention to the scroll spread on the writing table in front of him. Enough time passed for a flock of wild geese to rise from the swampland on the east bank, cross the wide grey Nile waters on heavy wingbeats and pass over the palace gardens where they sat. At last Taita brought his eyes down from the sky, and rose to leave. As he bowed to the Regent and began to back away, Naja looked up at him. 'I have not given you leave to go.'

'My lord, I thought you had no further need of me.'

'On the contrary, I have the most urgent need.' He glared at Taita and gestured for him to sit again. 'You are testing my good temper and favour. I know that you were wont to work the Mazes for Pharaoh Tamose whenever he called upon you to do so. Why do you procrastinate with me? As the Regent of this land, I will brook no further delay. I ask this not for my own profit, but for the very survival of our nation in this war with the north. I need the guidance of the pantheon of the gods. You are the only one who can provide that for me.'

Naja stood up so suddenly that the table in front of him overturned, spilling scrolls of papyrus, brushes and ink on to the terracotta tiles. He paid it no attention, but his voice rose to a shout: 'I command you, with all the authority of the hawk seal . . .' he touched the amulet on his right arm '. . . I command you to work the Mazes of Ammon Ra on my behalf.'

Taita bowed his head in theatrical resignation. For weeks past he had been prepared for this ultimatum, and had delayed only to extend to the limit that period of grace during which Nefer would be relatively safe from the ambitions of the Regent. He was still convinced that Lord Naja would make no fatal move towards Nefer until he had been given the sanction of the Mazes.

'The full of the moon is the most propitious period for the Mazes,' Taita told him. 'I have already made the preparations.'

Naja sank back on his stool. 'You will you do it here, in my quarters,' he said.

'Nay, Lord Regent, that would not be ideal.' Taita knew that if he were to gain ascendancy over Naja, he must keep him off-balance. 'The closer we can be to the influence of the gods, the more accurate will be the predictions. I have arranged with the priests at the temple of Osiris at Busiris. That is where I will work the Mazes at midnight in the full of the moon. I will conduct the mystery in the inner sanctum of the temple. The backbone of the god, the *djed*-pillar, dismembered by his brother, Seth, is held there. This holy relic will magnify the force of our deliberations.' Taita's voice was heavy with arcane meaning. 'Only you and I will be present in the sanctuary. No other mortal must overhear what the gods have to tell you. One of Asmor's regiments will guard the approaches to the sanctuary.'

Naja was an Osiris man, and his expression was solemn. Taita had known that he would be impressed by the time and place he had chosen.

'As you say, so let it be,' Naja agreed.

The journey to Busiris in the royal barge took two days, with Asmor's regiment following in four naval galleys. They landed on the yellow beach under the walls of the temple, and the priests were waiting to welcome the Regent with psalms and offerings of gum arabic and myrrh. The Regent's delight in sweet-smelling substances was already known throughout the land.

They were shown to the quarters that had been prepared for them. While Naja bathed, perfumed and refreshed himself with fruit and sherbet, Taita visited the sanctuary in company with the high priest and made sacrifice to the great god Osiris. Afterwards, at Taita's subtle suggestion, the high priest withdrew and left him alone to make his preparations for the evening. Lord Naja had never been present at the working of the Mazes – there were few living persons who had. Taita would put on an impressive show for him, but he had no intention of subjecting himself to the exhausting and harrowing ordeal of the authentic ritual.

After sunset the high priest entertained the Regent at a banquet. In his honour he served the famous wine from the vineyards that surrounded the temple. It had been at Busiris that the great god Osiris had first introduced the grape to Egypt. When the luscious vintage had mellowed the Regent and the rest of the company, the priests presented a series of theatrical acts representing the life-history of the great god. In each of these Osiris was depicted with different skin colorations, white as the wrappings of a mummy, black for the realm of the dead, red for the god of retribution. Always he held the crook and the flail, the insignia of the ruler, and his feet were held together like those of a corpse. In the final act his face was painted green to symbolize his vegetable aspect. As with the *dhurra* millet, which signified life and sustenance, Osiris was buried in the earth, which signified death. In the darkness of the netherworld he germinated like the millet seed, then emerged into the glorious cycle of life eternal.

While the tableaux were enacted, the high priest recited the god's names of power: 'Eye of the Night', 'The Eternally Good Being', 'Son of Geb' and 'Wennefer, Perfect in Majesty.'

Then, surrounded by the smoke of the incense pots, to the beat of gong and drum, the priests chanted the epic poem of the struggle between good and evil. The legend related how Seth, envious of his virtuous brother, locked Osiris in a chest and threw him into the Nile to drown. When his dead body washed up on the riverbank, Seth hacked it to pieces and hid the various parts. Here at Busiris he hid the *djed*-pillar, the backbone. Isis, their sister, searched for and found all the parts of the corpse and reassembled them. Then she copulated with Osiris. While they were locked in union her wings fanned the breath of life back into him.

Long before midnight the Regent of Egypt had consumed a flagon of the rich and heady wine, and was in a nervous, susceptible condition, his religious superstitions titillated by the priests. As the silver beam of the full moon entered through the precisely aligned aperture in the roof of the temple and moved softly across the flags of the nave towards the closed door of the sanctuary, the high priest gave a signal and all the other priests rose and moved out in procession leaving Lord Naja and Taita alone.

When the chanting of the departing priests had dwindled with distance into a heavy silence, Taita took the Regent by the hand and led him down the moonlit nave to the doors of the sanctuary. As they approached the great bronze-covered doors swung open of their own accord. Lord Naja started and his hand trembled in Taita's. He might have drawn back, but the Magus led him forward.

The sanctuary was lit by four braziers, one in each corner of the small chamber. There was a low stool in the centre of the tiled floor. Taita led Naja to it and gestured for him to be seated. As he did so, the doors swung closed behind them, and Naja looked round at them fearfully. He would have started up again, but Taita placed a hand on his shoulder to restrain him. 'No matter what you see and what you hear, do not move. Do not speak. As you value your life, do nothing. Say nothing.'

Taita left him sitting and, with stately tread, approached the statue of the god. He raised his hands, and suddenly he was holding a golden chalice by its stem. He lifted it on high and called on Osiris to bless the contents, then brought it back to Naja and urged him to drink. The honey-viscous liquid tasted of crushed almonds, rose petals and mushrooms. Taita clapped his hands and the chalice was gone.

He held out his empty hands and made a mystical pass back and forth before Naja's face, and in the blink of an eye the Mazes of Ammon Ra filled his cupped hands. These ivory counters Naja recognized from the fanciful accounts he had heard of the ritual. Taita invited him to cover them with his own hands, while he recited an invocation to Ammon Ra and the host of the pantheon. 'Greatness in light and fire, furious in divine majesty, approach and hearken to our pleas.'

Naja squirmed on his stool as the Mazes grew hot to the touch, and it was with relief that he passed them back to Taita. He was sweating heavily as he watched the old man carry them across the sanctuary and place them at the feet of the gigantic statue of Osiris. The Magus knelt there, bowed over them. For a while there was no sound within the chamber except the hiss of the flames, no movement except the shadows, cast by the lambent light of the braziers, dancing on the stone walls.

Then, abruptly, a terrible disembodied shriek rang through the sanctuary. It sounded as though once again the god's vitals were being ripped from his body by his evil brother. Naja moaned softly and covered his head with his shawl.

Again there was silence until suddenly the flames of the braziers flared as high as the roof, and turned from yellow to fierce shades of green and violet, crimson and blue. Great clouds of smoke boiled from them and filled the chamber. Naja choked and coughed. He felt as though he were suffocating, and his senses reeled. He could hear his own breath reverberating in his head.

Taita turned slowly to face him, and Naja shuddered in horror, for the Magus was transformed. His face glowed with green light, like the face of the resurrected god. Green foam frothed from his gaping mouth and poured down his chest, and his eyes were blind orbs that flashed silver rays in the light of the braziers. Without moving his feet he glided towards where Naja sat, and from his gaping frothing mouth issued the voices of a wild horde of demons and *djinns*, a terrible chorus of screams and moans, hisses and grunting, retching and insane laughter.

Lord Naja tried to rise, but the sounds and the smoke seemed to fill his skull, and blackness overwhelmed him. His legs gave way beneath him and he slumped forward off the stool on to the tiles in a dead faint.

W hen the Regent of Egypt regained consciousness the sun was high, sparkling on the waters of the river. He found himself lying on the silken mattress on the poop deck of the royal barge under the yellow awning.

He looked around him blearily, and saw the sails of the escort galleys white as egret wings against the lush green of the riverbanks. The sunlight was dazzling, and he closed his eyes again. He had a consuming thirst, his throat felt as though he had swallowed a handful of sharp gravel chips, and there was a pounding in his skull as though all the demons of his vision were trapped within it. He moaned, shuddered and vomited copiously into the bucket that a slave held for him.

Taita came to his side, raised his head and gave him a cool draught of some miraculous brew that soon eased the pounding in his head, and loosened the gases trapped in his swollen belly, allowing them to erupt from his nether orifice in spluttering gusts of foul-smelling wind. When he had recovered enough to speak again, he whispered, 'Tell it all to me, Taita. I remember nothing. What did the Mazes reveal?'

Before he would reply Taita sent all the crew and slaves out of earshot. Then he knelt beside the mattress. Naja laid a trembling hand on his arm and whispered pitifully, 'I remember nothing after...' He hesitated as the terrors of the previous night came back to him, and shuddered.

'We have almost reached Sebennytos, Majesty,' Taita told him. 'We will be back at Thebes before nightfall.'

'What happened, Taita?' He shook Taita's arm. 'What did the Mazes reveal?'

'Great wonders, Majesty.' Taita's voice trembled with emotion.

'Wonders?' Naja's interest quickened, and he struggled to sit up. 'Why do you call do you call me "Majesty"? I am not Pharaoh.'

'It is part of what was revealed.'

'Tell it to me! Tell it all to me!'

'Do you not remember how the roof of the temple opened like the petals of the lotus, and the great causeway descended to us from the night sky?'

Naja shook his head, and then nodded uncertainly. 'Yes, I think so. The causeway was a ladder of gold?'

'You do remember,' Taita commended him.

'We ascended the golden ladder.' Naja looked at him for confirmation.

'We were borne upwards on the backs of the two winged lions.' Taita nodded.

'Yes, I remember the lions, but after that it is all shadowy and vague.'

'These mysteries numb the mind and dim eyes unaccustomed to them. Even I, an adept of the seventh and final degree, was amazed by what we endured,' Taita explained kindly. 'But do not despair, for the gods have commanded me to explain them to you.'

'Speak, good Magus, and spare no detail.'

'On the backs of the flying lions we crossed high above the dark ocean and over the peaks of the white mountains, with all the kingdoms of earth and heaven spread below us.'

Naja nodded avidly. 'Go on!'

'We came at last to the citadel in which the gods dwell. The foundations reached to the depths of the netherworld, and the pillars supported the sky and all the stars. Ammon Ra rode above us in fiery splendour, and all the other gods of the pantheon were seated on thrones of silver and gold, of fire, crystal and sapphire.'

Naja blinked at him, focusing with difficulty. 'Yes. Now that you tell me, I remember it. The thrones of sapphire and diamonds.' The desperate need to believe was like a fire within him. 'Then the god spoke?' he hazarded. 'He spoke to me, did he not?'

'Yes, In a voice loud as the fall of a mountain the great god Osiris spoke thus: "Beloved Naja, you have always been faithful in your devotion to me. In this you shall be rewarded."'

'What was his meaning? Did he make it clear, Taita?'

Taita nodded solemnly. 'Yes, Majesty.'

'You use that title again. Tell me why.'

'As you command, Majesty. I shall tell you every word. Great Osiris rose up in all his terrible glory, and lifted you off the back of the winged lion and placed you beside him on the throne of fire and gold. He touched your mouth and your heart, and he greeted you with the title Brother Divine.'

'He called me Brother Divine? What did he mean by that?'

Taita suppressed a twinge of irritation. Naja had always been a clever man, sharp and perceptive. He did not usually need to have every detail spelt out so laboriously. The effects of the essence of the magical mushroom, which Taita had administered to him the night before, and the drugged smoke of the braziers had not yet worn off. It might be days before he was thinking clearly again. I shall have to ply a heavy paintbrush, he decided, and went on, 'I too was puzzled by his words. The meaning was not clear to me, but then the great god spoke again: "I welcome you to the pantheon of heaven, Brother Divine."'

Naja's face cleared, and his expression became proud and triumphant. 'Was he not deifying me, Taita? Surely there can be no meaning other than that.'

'If there had been any doubt it was immediately dispelled, for Osiris took up the double crown of Upper and Lower Egypt, placed it upon your head and spoke again. "Hail, Brother Divine! Hail, Pharaoh who shall be."' Naja was silent now, but he stared at Taita with glittering eyes. After a long silence Taita went on, 'With the crown upon your brow, your holiness was manifest. I knelt before you and worshipped you with the other gods.'

Naja made no effort to hide his emotions. He was in transport. He was as vulnerable as if he had been in orgasm. Taita seized the moment. 'Then Osiris spoke again, "In these wondrous things, your guide shall be the Magus Taita, for he is an adept of all the mysteries, and the master of the Mazes. Follow his instruction faithfully, and all the rewards I have promised will be yours."'

He watched Naja's reaction. Had he made it too pointed, he wondered, but the Regent seemed to accept the stricture without resistance.

'What else, Taita? What more did the great god have to say to me?'

'Nothing more to you, my lord, but now he spoke directly to me. His words struck through to the depths of my soul, for he laid a heavy charge upon me. These are his exact words, each one branded in fire upon my heart. "Taita, master of the Mazes, from henceforth you have no other love, loyalty or duty. You are the servant of my royal and divine brother, Naja. Your only concern is to help him fulfil his destiny. You will not cease until you see the double crown of Upper and Lower Egypt placed upon his head."'

'"No other loyalty or love,"' Naja repeated softly. He seemed now to have thrown off most of the ill-effects of his ordeal. His strength was flooding back, and the familiar light of cunning grew stronger in his yellow eyes. 'And did you then accept the charge that great Osiris placed upon you, Magus? Say fair and true, are you my man now, or would you deny the word of the great father?'

'How could I deny the great god?' Taita asked simply. He lowered his head and pressed his forehead to the planking of the deck. With both hands he took Naja's bare right foot and placed it on his own head. 'I accept the charge that the gods have placed upon me. I am your man, divine Majesty. Heart and head and soul, I belong to you.'

'What of your other duties? What of the oath of allegiance you swore to Pharaoh Nefer Seti at his birth, and even more recently at his coronation?'

'Majesty, the great god Osiris has absolved me from anything that came before. No oath counts for me other than the one I now make to you.'

Naja raised him up and stared into his eyes, searching for any trace of deceit or guile. Taita looked back at him serenely. He could sense the Regent's doubts, hopes and suspicions swarming together like a basket of live rats waiting to be fed to the falcons in the royal mews. The wish is father to the deed, Taita thought. He will allow himself to believe, because he longs for it to be so.

He watched the doubts clear in those yellow eyes and Naja embraced him. 'I believe you. When I wear the double crown you will have rewards beyond your expectation or imagination.'

Over the days that followed Naja kept Taita close to his side, and the old man used this new position of trust to change some of the Regent's undeclared intentions. At Naja's urging, Taita made another examination of the auguries. He slaughtered a sheep and examined its entrails, he released a falcon from the royal mews and watched its flight pattern. From these he was able to determine that the god would sanction no marriage of Naja to the princesses until at least the beginning of the next inundation of the Nile waters or the flooding would certainly fail. This would be a disaster that even Naja could not risk. The life of this very Egypt depended upon the inundations of the great river. With this prophecy Taita had delayed the danger to Nefer, and the agony of the two princesses.

Naja protested and argued, but since that terrible night at Busiris he had found it almost impossible to resist Taita's predictions. In this he was made more amenable by the ominous news from the northern war front. On Naja's orders, and against Taita's counsel, the Egyptians had launched a desperate counter-attack to try to retake Abnub. They had failed, losing three hundred chariots and almost a regiment of foot in the dreadful fighting around the city. Now Apepi seemed poised to deliver a crushing stroke through the demoralized and weakened Egyptian regiments, and come storming on to Thebes. It was not the time for a wedding, which even Naja conceded, and Nefer's safety was ensured for a while longer.

Already a constant stream of refugees fled from Thebes by road and river towards the south. The volume of trade caravans from the east fell alarmingly, as the merchants waited to see the outcome of the imminent Hyksosian offensive. All commodities were in short supply and prices shot up.

'The only way in which you can stave off an annihilating defeat at the hands of Apepi is to negotiate a truce,' Taita advised the Regent.

He was about to qualify this by adding that the truce would in no circumstances be a surrender, that they would merely use the respite to strengthen their military position, but Naja did not allow him the chance to elaborate. 'This I believe also, Magus,' he agreed eagerly. 'Oft-times I tried to convince my beloved companion, Pharaoh Tamose, of the wisdom of this course. He would never listen to me.'

'We need time,' Taita explained, but Naja waved a hand to silence him.

'Of course you are right.' Naja was excited by this unexpected support.

He had tried without success to convince the individual members of the council to agree to a peace with the Hyksos, but none, not even Cinka, had supported him. Even the loyal Asmor had risked his wrath by vowing to fall on his own sword rather than surrender to Apepi. It had been a sobering revelation to find honour flowering in such unlikely ground, and to learn that even as regent there were limits to what he could force through the council.

Peace with the Hyksos was the cornerstone of Naja's vision, a vision of the two kingdoms reunited and a single pharaoh ruling both. Only a pharaoh who was part Egyptian and part Hyksosian could hope to achieve that, and he knew, without any doubt, that this was what the gods had promised him through the Mazes.

He went on earnestly, 'I should have known that you, Taita, were the one person who would not let yourself be blinded by prejudice. All the others cry, "No surrender," and "Death rather than dishonour".' He shook his head. 'You and I can see that what we could not achieve by force of arms, we can bring about perhaps in a more gentle fashion. After sixty years in the Nile valley, the Hyksos are becoming more Egyptian than Asian. They have been seduced by our gods, our philosophy and our women. Their savage blood has been softened and sweetened by ours. Their wild ways have been tempered by our noble manners.'

The Regent's response to his tentative suggestion was so overpowering that Taita was taken aback. There was much more here than he had suspected. To gain time to think it out, and garner some inkling of Naja's true intentions, he murmured, 'Those are words of wisdom. How could we hope to bring about this truce, Lord Regent?'

Naja was eager to explain. 'I know there are many among the Hyksos who agree with these sentiments. It would take little for them to join us. Then we can bring peace and unity to the two kingdoms.'

The veils began to part. Taita was reminded suddenly of a suspicion he had once heard expressed but had rejected at the time.

'Who are these Hyksos sympathizers?' he asked. 'Are they highly placed? Close to Apepi?'

'Noblemen, indeed. One sits on Apepi's war council.' Naja seemed about to enlarge on this, but he stopped himself with an obvious effort.

It was enough for Taita. That faint rumour of Hyksosian connections in Naja's background must have had substance, and if it was true the rest fell neatly into place. Once again, he was amazed at the width and breadth of Naja's ambitions.

'Would it be possible to meet these noblemen and speak to them?' Taita asked carefully.

'Yes,' Naja confirmed. 'We could reach them within days.'

For Taita the implications of that simple statement were enormous. The Regent of Egypt had covert allies in the ranks of the traditional enemy. What else about him was hidden? Where else had his avaricious fingers reached? A chill ran down Taita's spine, and the silver hairs on the back of his neck came erect.

This is the loving friend who was at Pharaoh's side when he was struck down. Here is the only witness to the manner of Pharaoh's death. This creature of boundless ambition and cruel purpose admits to being an intimate and confidant of Hyksosian noblemen, and it was a Hyksosian arrow that killed Pharaoh. How deep does the plot run?

He let nothing of this show on his face, but nodded thoughtfully, and Naja went on quickly, 'I am certain that we can reach agreement with the Hyksos, and I envisage a co-regency between Apepi and myself with a joint council of state. Then your influence would be needed to persuade our own councillors to ratify it. Perhaps you could consult the Mazes again, and make the wishes of the gods known.'

Naja was suggesting that he make a fraudulent divination. Did he suspect that that was what had happened at Busiris? Taita did not think so, but he must quash the idea at once. His expression became stern. 'In any matter to do with the Mazes, to take the word or name of the god Ammon Ra in vain or to misrepresent his oracle would be to court terrible retribution.'

Quickly Naja retracted. 'I suggested no such impiety, but through the Mazes the gods have already given sanction to me.'

Taita grunted. 'First we must determine if this treaty is feasible. Apepi might believe his military position is unassailable and refuse to meet us. Despite any approaches from us for peace, he might decide to prosecute this war to the bitter end.'

'I do not think that will happen. I will give you the names of our allies on the other side. You must go to them secretly, Taita. You are well known and respected even among the Hyksos, and I will give you a talisman that will prove you come from me. You are the best emissary for our cause. They will listen to you.'

Taita sat a while longer in thought. He tried to see if he could wring any further advantage to Nefer and the princesses from the situation, but at this stage he could find none. Whatever happened, Nefer would still be in mortal danger.

There was only one certain course open to Taita if he were to ensure Nefer's survival and that was to get him out of Egypt while Naja was still in power. Was there an opportunity to do that now? Naja was offering him a safe conduct to the frontier. Could he use that to take

Nefer with him? Within seconds he realized he could not. His contacts with the boy Pharaoh were still severely circumscribed by Naja. He was never allowed to be alone with him. He was not even allowed to sit close to him at sessions of the council, or to exchange even the most innocent messages with him. The only time in the last few weeks that he had been allowed close to him was when Nefer had developed an agonizing septic throat. Then Taita had been allowed into the royal bedchamber to tend him, but both Naja and Asmor had been present, watching everything that transpired, listening to every word that was spoken. Because of his affliction Nefer had not been able to speak above a whisper, but his eyes never left Taita's face and he clung to his hand when the time came for them to part. That had been almost ten days ago.

Taita learned that Naja had chosen tutors to replace him, and Asmor had provided instructors from the Blue Guards to continue Nefer's exercises in horsemanship and chariot handling, swordsmanship and archery. None of his old friends were allowed to visit him. Even his crony Meren had been ordered out of Pharaoh's quarters.

If he made an attempt to get Nefer away and failed, not only would he have sacrificed Naja's confidence, he would have placed Nefer in terrible peril. No, he could use this sortie across the lines into the Hyksosian territory only to make more careful and secure arrangements for the young Pharaoh's safety.

'It is my duty, a duty placed upon me by the gods, to help you in every way. I will undertake this mission,' Taita said. 'What is the safest way for me to pass through the Hyksosian lines? You say I am well known among them, and that I will be recognized.'

Naja had foreseen this query. 'You must use the old chariot road through the dunes and down the wadi at Gebel Wadun. My friends on the other side keep the road under surveillance.'

Taita nodded. 'That is the road along which Pharaoh Tamose met his death. I have never travelled beyond Gallala. I will need a guide to show me the rest of the way.'

'I will send my own lance-bearer and a squadron of the Blues to take you through,' Naja promised. 'But the road is long and hard. You must leave at once. Every day, every hour might make the difference.'

Taita had driven the chariot all the way from the ruined city of Gallala with only four halts. They had made the run in half a day less than it had taken Naja and Tamose to cover the same route, and at less cost to the condition of the animals.

The troopers in the nine vehicles that followed him were in awe of the Magus' reputation. They knew him as the father of the corps of cavalry, for he had been the first Egyptian ever to build a chariot and harness a team to it. His celebrated ride from Thebes to Elephantine to carry the news of the victory of Pharaoh Tamose over the Hyksos was the stuff of legend. Now, as they followed his chariot through the dunes, they learned that the legend was well founded. The old man's stamina was amazing, and his concentration never wavered. His gentle but firm hands on the reins never tired, as hour after hour he coaxed the horses into giving their best. He had impressed every man in the squadron, not least the one riding beside him in the cockpit.

Gil was Naja's lance-bearer. He had a rugged, sun-darkened face and was lightly built, which was desirable for a charioteer, but he possessed also a wiry strength and cheerful disposition. He had to have been one of the best to be selected to ride in the commander's chariot.

With the moon waxing and the weather at its hottest they had driven through the cool of the night. Now, in the dawn, they halted to rest. When he had watered the horses, Gil came to where Taita sat on a boulder overlooking the wadi of Gebel Wadun and handed him a ceramic water jug. Taita took a long swig from the spout and swallowed the bitter water they had carried with them from Gallala with no sign of repugnance. It was the first drink he had taken since their last stop at midnight.

The old devil-rouser is tough as a Bedouin raider, Gil thought, with admiration, and squatted at a respectful distance to await any order that Taita might issue.

'Where is the place at which Pharaoh was struck down?' Taita asked at last.

Gil shaded his eyes against the glare of the rising sun and pointed down the wadi towards where the dry riverbed debouched on to the plains. 'Down there, my lord. Near that distant line of hills.'

The first time Taita had questioned Gil had been before the council when the lance-bearer had given evidence on the circumstances of Pharaoh's death. The council had called every person who might have any knowledge of it to testify at the inquiry. Taita remembered that

Gil's evidence had been coherent and credible. He had not been overawed by the pomp of the council and its illustrious members, but had spoken out like the honest, simple soldier he was. When it was shown to him, he had recognized the Hyksosian arrow as the one that had struck down Pharaoh Tamose. The shaft had been snapped in two. Lord Naja had broken it off to ease the pain of the wound.

That had been the first occasion of their meeting. They had spoken briefly one or twice since leaving Thebes, but until now there had not been the opportunity for any long conversation.

'Are any other men here who were with you on that day?' Taita asked now.

'Only Samos, but he was waiting with the chariots in the wadi when we were attacked,' Gil replied.

'I want you to point out the exact place to me, and I want you to take me over the battleground,' Taita told him.

Gil shrugged. 'It was no battle, just a skirmish. There will be precious little to see. 'Tis a barren place. However, it shall be as the mighty Magus commands.'

The troop mounted and descended the steep side of the wadi in single file. There had been no rain here in a hundred years and even the desert wind had not wiped away the tracks of Pharaoh's chariots, which were still deeply scored and plain to read. When they reached the floor of the wadi Taita continued to follow them, his own wheels riding in the deep grooves that they had left.

They were alert for a Hyksos ambush and watched both banks of the wadi, but although the raw rock danced in the heat mirage, there was no sign of an enemy.

'There is the watchtower.' Gil pointed ahead, and Taita saw its gnarled silhouette leaning drunkenly again the unblemished pale blue of the sky.

They swept around another bend in the riverbed, and even from two hundred paces Taita could make out the area of confused wheel-tracks where the chariots of Pharaoh's squadron had halted and circled, and where many men had dismounted and remounted in the soft sand of the wadi bottom. Taita signalled his small force to slow down and they moved forward at a walk.

'This is where Pharaoh dismounted and we went forward with Lord Naja to scout the camp of Apepi.' Gil pointed over the side of the dashboard.

Taita halted the chariot and signalled the others to do the same. 'Wait for me here,' he ordered the sergeant of the following vehicle, then turned to Gil. 'Come with me. Show me the battleground.'

Gil led the way up the rude pathway. At first he went slowly, in deference to the old man, but soon realized that Taita was matching him step for step and speeded up. The gradient increased and the surface became more uneven as they went on. Even Gil was breathing hard when at last they reached the tumble of large boulders halfway up the hill that almost blocked the pathway.

'This is as far as I went,' Gil explained.

'So where did Pharaoh fall?' Taita looked around him at the steep but open hillside, 'Where were the Hyksosian troops hidden? From where was the fatal arrow fired?'

'I cannot tell you, lord.' Gil shook his head. 'I and the rest of the men were ordered to wait here, while Lord Naja went forward beyond that outcrop of boulders.'

'Where was Pharaoh? Did he go forward with Naja?'

'No. Not at first. The King waited with us. Lord Naja heard something up ahead, went to scout and disappeared from our view.'

'I do not understand. At what point were you attacked?'

'We waited here. I could see that Pharaoh was becoming impatient. After a while Lord Naja whistled from beyond the rocks. Pharaoh sprang up. "Come on, lads!" he told us, and went up the path.'

'Were you close behind him?'

'No, I was near the rear of the file.'

'Did you see what happened next?'

'Pharaoh disappeared behind the boulders. Then there was shouting and the sound of fighting. I heard Hyksos voices and arrows and spears striking the rocks. I ran forward but the path was crowded with our men who were trying to get round the boulders here to reach the fight.'

Gil ran forward to show him how the path narrowed and wove around the tallest boulder. 'This was as far as I got to. Then Lord Naja was shouting that Pharaoh had been struck down. The men ahead of me were milling around, and suddenly they dragged the King down to where I was standing. I think he was dead even then.'

'How close were the Hyksos? How many were they? Were they cavalry or infantry? Did you recognize their regiments?' Taita demanded. All the Hyksos wore distinctive regalia, which the Egyptian troops had come to know well.

'They were very close,' Gil told him, 'and there were a lot of them. At least a squadron.'

'What regiment?' Taita insisted. 'Did you pick out their plumes?'

For the first time Gil looked uncertain and a little shamefaced. 'My lord, I did not actually set eyes on the enemy. You see, they were behind the rocks up there.'

'Then how do you know their strength and numbers?' Taita frowned at him.

'Lord Naja was shouting—' Gil broke off and dropped his eyes.

'Did any of the others, apart from Naja, see the enemy?'

'I do not know, honourable Magus. You see, Lord Naja ordered us back down the pathway to the chariots. We could see that the King was mortally wounded, probably already dead. We had all lost heart.'

'You must have discussed it later with your companions. Did any of them tell you he had engaged an enemy? That he had hit one of the Hyksos with arrow or lance?'

Gil shook his head doubtfully. 'I don't remember. No, I don't think so.'

'Apart from the King, were any others wounded?'

'None.'

'Why did you not tell this to the council? Why did you not tell them that you had not seen an enemy?' Taita was angry now.

'Lord Naja told us to answer the questions simply and not to waste the council's time with idle boasting and long tales of our part in the fighting.' Gil hunched his shoulders with embarrassment. 'I suppose that none of us wanted to admit that we ran without a fight.'

'Do not feel ashamed, Gil. You carried out your orders,' Taita told him, in a kinder tone. 'Now, climb up on the rocks there, and keep your eyes open. We are still deep in Hyksosian territory. I shall not be long.'

Taita went forward slowly and stepped round the boulder that blocked the path. He paused and surveyed the ground ahead. From this angle he could just make out the top of the ruined watchtower. The path went up towards it in a series of dog-legs. Then it disappeared over the crest of a slope, which was fairly open, with little cover for a Hyksosian ambush, just a few clumps of rock and scattered sun-blasted thorn trees. Then he remembered that it had happened at night. But something disturbed him. Taita felt a vague sense of evil, as though he was being watched by a powerful malignant force.

This feeling grew so strong that he stood motionless in the sunlight and closed his eyes. He opened his mind and his soul, becoming a dry sponge to soak up any influence from the air around him. Almost at once the feeling grew stronger still: there were terrible things here, but the focus of evil emanated from somewhere not far ahead of him. He opened his eyes and walked slowly towards it. There was nothing to be seen, other than heat-blasted rock and thorn, but now he could even smell evil in the hot air, a faint but rank odour like the breath of a carrion-eating wild beast.

He stopped and sniffed, like a hunting dog, and immediately the air smelt dusty and dry, but clean. This proved to him that the elusive stench was something outside natural law. He was catching the faint echo of an evil that had been perpetrated in this place, but when he tried to pinpoint it, it disappeared. He took a pace forward then another, and once more the nauseating stench wafted around him. Another pace, and now the smell was accompanied by a feeling of great sorrow, as though he had lost something of inestimable value, something that could never be replaced.

He had to force himself to take the next step up the rocky pathway, and at that instant something struck him with a force that drove the air from his lungs. He cried out in agony and dropped to his knees, clutching his chest, unable to breathe. It was extreme pain, the pain of death, and he struggled with it as though with a serpent that had wound its coils about him. He managed to throw himself back down the path, and immediately the pain fell away.

Gil had heard him cry out and came bounding up the path. He seized Taita, and helped him to his feet. 'What is it? What ails you, my lord?'

Taita thrust him away. 'Go! Leave me! You are in danger here. This is a thing not of men but of gods and demons. Go! Wait for me at the bottom of the hill.'

Gil hesitated, but then he saw the look in those glittering eyes and recoiled as if from a ghost.

'Go!' Taita said, in a voice Gil wanted never to hear again, and he fled.

For a long time after he had gone Taita struggled to bring his body and mind back under his own control, to enable him to counter the forces arrayed against him. He reached into the pouch on his belt and brought out the Periapt of Lostris. He held it in his right hand and stepped forward again.

As he came to the exact spot on the pathway the pain struck once more with even more savage intensity, like a flint-tipped arrow through the chest, and he could barely prevent himself screaming as he reeled backwards and the pain fell away as it had before.

Panting, he stared down at the stony ground. At first it seemed unmarked and no different from any other point on the rugged pathway he had traversed. Then, a small ethereal shadow appeared on the earth. As he watched, it changed, became a shimmering dark scarlet pool. Slowly he sank to his knees. 'The heart blood of a king and a god,' he whispered. 'Here, on this very spot, died Pharaoh Tamose.'

He rallied himself and in a quiet yet firm voice spoke the invocation to Horus, so potent that only an adept of the seventh degree dared voice it. On the seventh repetition he heard the rustle of unseen wings, which stirred the desert air around him. 'The god is here,' he whispered, and he began to pray. He prayed for his Pharaoh and his friend, entreating Horus to relieve his suffering and lift his torture.

'Allow him to escape from this dread place,' he beseeched the god. 'It must have been murder for his soul to have been trapped here.'

As he prayed he made the signs for the exorcism of evil. Before his eyes the pool of blood began to shrink, as though it were soaking away into the dry earth. As the last drop disappeared Taita heard a soft, formless sound, like the cry of a sleepy child, and the terrible weight of loss and sorrow that had burdened him fell from his shoulders. As he stood up he felt a great sense of release. He stepped forward on to the spot where the pool of blood had been. Even when his sandalled feet were firmly planted upon it he felt no pain and his sense of well-being remained intact.

'Go in peace, my friend and my king, and may you live for all eternity,' he said aloud, and made the sign for long life and happiness.

He turned away, and would have started back down the hill to where the chariots waited but something stopped him in his tracks. He lifted his head and tested the air again. There was still a faint whiff of that evil smell, just an elusive trace of it. Warily he turned back up the slope, passing the place where Pharaoh had died, and went on. With each pace the stench of evil grew stronger, until it caught in his throat and made his gorge rise. Once again, he realized that this was something from beyond the natural order. He went on, until after twenty measured paces the odour began to fade. He stopped and retraced his steps. Immediately the stench grew stronger. He quested back and forth until it was at its zenith. Then he stepped off the path and found it stronger still, almost suffocating.

He was standing under the twisted branches of a thorn tree that grew next to the path. He looked up and saw that the branches were strangely shaped, as though they had been fashioned by a human hand into a distinctive cross that stood out against the blue of the sky. He looked down and a rock the size and shape of a horse's head caught his attention. It had recently been dislodged then replaced in its original position. Taita lifted it out of the depression in which it sat, and saw that it had covered a niche between the roots of the thorn tree. He laid it aside and peered into the niche. There was something in it and he reached in gingerly – it was the kind of shelter that might hide a snake or scorpion.

He brought out a magnificently carved and tooled object. He stared at it for a moment before he realized that it was an arrow quiver. There was no doubting its origin, for the design was in the Hyksosian heraldic style, and the image tooled into the leather cover was Seueth, the crocodile god of war revered by Hyksosian warriors.

Taita twisted off the stopper cover and found that the quiver contained five war arrows, fletched in green and red. He drew out one of the shafts and his heart beat fiercely as he recognized it. There could be no mistake. He had minutely examined the broken, blood-caked one that Naja had brought before the council. This was identical to the arrow that had killed Pharaoh.

He held it to the light and peered closely at the signet etched into the painted shaft. It was a stylized head of a leopard, holding the hieratic letter T in its jaws. This was the device he had seen on the fatal arrow. This was its identical twin. Taita turned it over and over in his hands, as though trying to draw from it the last grain of information. He held it to his nose and sniffed it. There was just the smell of wood, paint and feathers. The foul odour that had guided him to the cache had disappeared.

Why should the assassin of Pharaoh hide his quiver? After the fight the Hyksos had been left in possession of the field. They would have had all the time they needed to recover their weapons. This is a beautiful and valuable object. No warrior would abandon it, unless he were forced to, Taita thought.

For another hour he searched the hillside, but found no other item of interest, nor did he detect again the supernatural odour of putrefaction and evil. When he went down to where the chariots waited in the sand of the wadi he carried the quiver concealed under his apron.

They waited hidden in the wadi until after nightfall. Then, the wheel-hubs freshly greased with mutton fat to stop them squealing, the horses' hoofs covered with leather boots, and all the loose weapons and tack carefully muffled, they went on deep into Hyksosian territory, with Gil guiding them.

The lance-bearer knew the area well, and although Taita made no comment, he wondered how often the man had travelled this way with his master, and what other rendezvous they had kept with the enemy.

By now they were down on the alluvial plain of the Nile. Twice they had to turn off the road and wait while parties of armed men, anonymous in the darkness, rode past their hiding-place. After midnight they came to an abandoned temple of some forgotten god that had been hollowed out of the side of a low clay hill. The cave was large enough to shelter the entire squadron, vehicle, horses and men. It was immediately apparent that it had been used before for this purpose: lamps and an oil amphora were hidden behind the ruined altar, and bales of horse fodder were stacked in the sanctum.

As soon as they had removed the horses' harness and fed them, the troopers ate their own meal then settled down on mattresses of dried straw and were soon snoring. In the meantime Gil had changed from his cavalry uniform to the nondescript attire of a peasant. 'I cannot use a horse,' he explained to Taita. 'It would attract too much interest. On foot it will take me half a day to reach the camp at Bubasti. Do not expect me back before tomorrow evening.' He slipped out of the cave and disappeared into the night.

Honest Gil is not such a simple bluff soldier as he seems, Taita thought, as he settled down to wait for Lord Naja's allies to answer the message that Gil was taking to them.

As soon as it was light he posted a sentry at the top of the hill, where the air shaft from the subterranean temple emerged. Just before noon a low whistle down the shaft warned them of danger and Taita climbed up to join the sentry. From the east a caravan of heavily laden donkeys was heading directly for the temple entrance, and Taita guessed that it was these merchants who used the temple as a makeshift caravanserai. It was almost certainly they who had left the store of fodder in the sanctum. He scrambled down the hillside, keeping out of sight of the approaching caravan. In the middle of the roadway he arranged a pattern of white quartz stones while he recited three verses from the Assyrian Book of the Evil Mountain. Then he retired to await the arrival of the caravan.

The leading donkey was fifty cubits or so ahead of the rest of the column. It was clear that the animal knew of the temple and the delights it contained, for he needed no encouragement from his driver to come on at a trot. As he reached the pile of white quartz stones in the path the little animal shied so violently that the pack slid over and hung under his belly. He started to buck and gallop at the same time, heading out across the plain away from the temple, hoofs flying in every direction. His hoarse honking and braying affected the rest of the animals in the column, and soon they were rearing and throwing their heads against the lead reins, kicking out at their drivers and running in circles as though attacked by a swarm of bees.

It took the caravan drivers half of the rest of the afternoon to catch and reassemble the runaways, to pacify the terrified animals and to set off again on the road towards the temple. This time the portly and richly robed figure of the head driver marched in the van, dragging the reluctant donkey behind him on a long rein. He saw the stones in the middle of the road and stopped. The column crowded up behind him, and the other drivers came forward. They held an impromptu conference with raised voices and arms waving. Their voices carried to where Taita sat hidden among the olive trees on the hillside.

At last the head driver left the others and came on alone. At first his step was bold and assured, but soon it slowed and became timid until at last he stood ill-at-ease and, from a distance, studied the pattern of quartz stones. Then he spat towards the stones and jumped back, as if he expected them to return the insult. Finally he made the sign against the evil eye, turned and trotted back with alacrity to join his fellows, shouting and waving them back. The others needed little convincing. Soon the entire caravan was in full retreat along the road it had come. Taita went down the hill and scattered the stones, allowing the influences they contained to disperse, and opening the way for the other visitors he was expecting.

They came in the short summer dusk, twenty armed men riding hard, Gil leading them on a borrowed steed. They swept down past the scattered stones and up to the entrance of the temple, where they dismounted with a clatter of weapons. The leader was a tall man, wide across the shoulders with a heavy beetling brow and a fleshy hooked nose. His heavy black moustaches were trained to droop down on to his chest, and coloured ribbons were plaited into his beard.

'You are the warlock. Yes?' he said, in a thick accent.

Taita did not think it opportune to let them know he spoke Hyksos like one of them, so he replied modestly in Egyptian, neither claiming nor denying magical powers. 'My name is Taita, a servant of the great god Horus. I call his blessing down upon you. I see that you are a man of might, but I do not know your name.'

'My name is Trok, Paramount Chief of the Clan of the Leopard, and commander of the north in the army of King Apepi. You have a token for me, Warlock?'

Taita opened his right hand and showed him the broken shard of blue glazed porcelain, the upper half of a tiny votive statue of the god Seueth. Trok examined it briefly, then took another fragment of porcelain from the pouch on his sword-belt and fitted the two pieces together. The broken edges matched perfectly, and he grunted with satisfaction. 'Come with me, Warlock.'

Trok strode out into the gathering night with Taita beside him. They climbed the hill in silence, and squatted down facing each other in the starlight. Trok kept his scabbard between his knees and his hand on the hilt of his heavy sickle sword. From habit more than distrust, Taita thought, but nevertheless the war chief was a man to reckon with.

'You bring me news of the south,' Trok said, in a statement, not a question.

'My lord, you have heard of the death of Pharaoh Tamose?'

'We know of the death of the Theban pretender from prisoners captured when we took the city of Abnub.' Trok was careful not to acknowledge by word or inference the authority of the Egyptian Pharaoh. To the Hyksos, the only ruler in either of the two kingdoms was Apepi. 'We heard also that a child now pretends to the throne of Upper Egypt.'

'Pharaoh Nefer Seti is only fourteen years of age,' Taita confirmed, equally careful to insist on the title of Pharaoh when he spoke of him. 'He will not attain his majority for some years. Until then Lord Naja acts as his regent.'

Trok leaned forward with sudden intense interest. Taita smiled inwardly. The Hyksosian intelligence was poor indeed if they did not know at least that much about the affairs of the Upper Kingdom. Then he recalled the campaign that, just before the King's death, he and Pharaoh Tamose had waged against Hyksosian spies and informers in Thebes. They had winkled out and arrested over fifty. After interrogation by torture, they had executed every one. Taita felt a smug satisfaction at this confirmation that they had cut off the flow of information to the enemy.

'So, then, you come to us with the authority of the Regent of the south.' Taita detected a strange air of triumph about Trok, as he demanded, 'What message do you bring from Naja?'

'Lord Naja wants me to carry his proposal directly to Apepi,' Taita hedged. He did not want to give Trok any more information than was strictly necessary.

Trok took immediate umbrage at this. 'Naja is my cousin,' he said coldly. 'He would wish me to hear every word he has sent.' Taita had such control over his emotions that he showed no surprise, although it was a grave indiscretion on Trok's part. His suspicions as to the Regent's antecedents were confirmed, but his voice was measured as he answered, 'Yes, my lord, this much I know. However, what I have for Apepi is of such moment . . .'

'You underestimate me, Warlock. I have the complete confidence of your regent.' Trok's voice was rough with exasperation. 'I know full well that you have come to offer Apepi a truce, and to negotiate a lasting peace with him.'

'I can tell you nothing more, my lord.' This Trok might be a warrior, but he is no conspirator, Taita thought, but his voice and manner did not change as he said, 'I can give my message only to the Shepherd

Chieftain, Apepi.' This was how the Hyksosian ruler was referred to in Upper Egypt. 'Can you take me to him?'

'As you wish, Warlock. Keep your mouth shut, if you will, though there is no purpose in it.' Trok stood up angrily. 'King Apepi is at Bubasti. We will go there immediately.'

In stilted silence they returned to the subterranean temple, where Taita called Gil and the sergeant of the bodyguard to him. 'You have done your work well,' he told them, 'but now you must return to Thebes as secretly as you have come.'

'You will return with us?' Gil asked anxiously. Clearly he felt responsible for the old man.

'No.' Taita shook his head. 'I will remain here. When you report to the Regent tell him that I am on my way to meet Apepi.'

By the dim light of the oil lamps the horses were harnessed to the chariots, and within a short time they were ready to leave. Gil brought Taita's leather saddlebag from the chariot and handed it to him. Then he saluted respectfully. 'It has been a great honour to ride with you, my lord. When I was a child my father told me many tales of your adventures. He rode with your regiment at Asyut. He was captain of the left wing.'

'What was his name?' Taita asked.

'Lasro, my lord.'

'Yes.' Taita nodded. 'I remember him well. He lost his left eye in the battle.'

Gil gazed at him with awe and wonder. 'That was forty years ago, and still you remember.'

'Thirty-seven,' Taita corrected him. 'Go well, young Gil. I cast your horoscope last night. You will have a long life, and attain much distinction.'

The lance-bearer took up the reins and rode out into the night, speechless with pride and gratification.

By this time Lord Trok's troop was also mounted and ready to leave. They had given Taita the horse on which Gil had returned to the temple. Taita threw the saddlebags over its withers then swung up behind them. The Hyksos did not have the same scruples about riding astride as the Egyptians, and they clattered out of the cave entrance and turned west, in the opposite direction to that taken by the column of chariots.

Taita rode in the centre of the party of heavily armed Hyksos. Trok led them and he did not invite Taita to ride alongside him. He had been distant and aloof since Taita had refused to give Naja's message to him directly. Taita was content to be ignored, for he had much to think about. In particular the revelation of Naja's confused blood-lines opened a host of fascinating possibilities.

They rode on through the night, heading west towards the river and the main enemy base at Bubasti. Even though it was still night-time, they encountered more and more traffic on the road. There were long lines of wagons and carts, all heavily laden with military supplies, moving in the same direction as they were. Returning towards Avaris and Memphis were equal numbers of empty vehicles that had discharged their cargo.

As they came closer to the river, Taita saw the fires of the Hyksosian troops encamped around Bubasti. It was a field of flickering light that stretched many miles in both directions along the riverbank, a huge agglomeration of men and animals unseen in the darkness.

There was nothing on earth like the smell of an army encamped. It grew stronger as they approached until it was almost overpowering. It was a mixture of many odours, the smell of the cavalry lines, manure and the smoke of dung fires, of leather and mouldy grain. On top of this was the smell of unwashed men and their festering wounds, cooking food and fermenting beer, unburied rubbish, and filth, the ammoniacal reek of the latrine pits and the dung heaps, and the even more biting stench of unburied corpses.

Underlying this stifling blend of odours Taita picked out another sickly taint. He thought he recognized it, but it was only when one of the sufferers staggered drunkenly in front of his horse, forcing him to rein in sharply, that he saw the rose-coloured blotches on the pale face and he was certain. He knew now why Apepi had failed so far to follow up his victory at Abnub, why he had not yet sent his chariots tearing southwards towards Thebes where the Egyptian army was in disarray, and at his mercy. Taita pushed his horse up alongside Trok's mount, and asked him quietly, 'My lord, when did the plague first strike your troops?'

Trok reined in so roughly that his mount danced and circled under him, 'Who told you that, Warlock?' he demanded. 'Is this cursed disease one of your spells? Is it you who have laid this pestilence upon us?' He spurred away angrily without waiting for a denial. Taita followed at a discreet distance, but his eyes were busy taking in every detail of what was happening around him.

By this time the light was strengthening, and a weak, hazy sun barely showed through the heavy bank of mist and woodsmoke that blanketed the land and blotted out the dawn sky. It gave the scene a weird, unearthly aspect, like a vision of the underworld. Men and animals were transformed by it into dark and demoniacal figures, and under the hoofs of their horses the mud of the recent inundation was black and glutinous.

They passed the first of the burial carts, and the men around Taita used their cloaks to cover their mouths and noses against the stink and the evil humours that hung over the heap of naked, bloated corpses piled high in the back of the cart. Trok spurred his horse to overtake it quickly, but ahead there were many more similarly laden vehicles almost blocking the roadway.

Further on they passed one of the cremation fields, on which more carts were unloading their grisly burden. Firewood was a scarce commodity in this land, and the flames were not fierce enough to consume the heaps of corpses. They spluttered and flickered as the fats oozed out of the decaying flesh, and sent up clouds of oily black smoke that coated the mouths and throats of the living men who breathed it.

How many of the dead are victims of the plague? Taita wondered. And how many from the fighting with our army?

The plague was like some grim spectre that marched in step with any army. Apepi had been here at Bubasti for many years in camps that swarmed with rats, vultures and the carrion-eating marabou storks. His men were crowded together in their own filth, their bodies crawling with fleas and lice, eating rotten food and drinking the water from the irrigation canals into which the effluent from the graves and dung heaps drained. These were the conditions in which the plague flourished.

Closer to Bubasti the encampments became more numerous, tents, huts and hovels crowded right up to the walls and ditches that surrounded the garrison town. The more fortunate among the plague victims lay under tattered roofs of palm fronds, scant protection from the hot morning sunlight. Others lay out in the trampled mud of the fields, abandoned to thirst and the elements. The dead were mixed with the dying, those wounded in the fighting lying side by side with those ravaged by streaming dysentery.

Although his instincts were those of a healer, Taita would do nothing to succour them. They were condemned by their own multitudes, for what could one man do to help so many? What was more, they were the enemies of this very Egypt, and it was clear to him that the pestilence was a visitation from the gods. Should he heal a single Hyksos, it would mean that there was one more to march on Thebes and put his beloved city to flame and rapine.

They entered the fortress and found that conditions were not much better within its walls. Plague victims lay where they had been struck down by the disease, and the rats and pariah dogs gnawed at their corpses, and even at those still alive but too far gone to defend themselves.

Apepi's headquarters was the principal building in Bubasti, a massive sprawling mud-brick and thatch palace in the centre of the town. Grooms took their horses at the gates, but one carried Taita's saddle-bags. Lord Trok led Taita through courtyards and the dark shuttered halls where incense and sandalwood burned in bronze braziers to cloak the plague stench that wafted up from the town and the surrounding encampments, but whose guttering flames made the heated air scarcely bearable. Even here in the main headquarters the groans of plague victims rang eerily through the rooms, and huddled figures lay in dark corners.

Sentries stopped them outside a barred bronze door in the deepest recesses of the building, but as soon as they recognized Trok's hulking figure they stood aside and allowed them to pass through. This area was Apepi's private quarters. The walls were hung with magnificent carpets and the furniture was of precious wood, ivory and mother-of-pearl, much of it plundered from the palaces and temples of Egypt.

Trok ushered Taita into a small but luxuriously furnished ante-chamber, and left him there. Female slaves brought him a jug of sherbet and a platter of ripe dates and pomegranates. Taita sipped the drink but ate only a little of the fruit. He was always abstemious.

It was a long wait. A sunbeam through the single high window moved sedately along the opposite wall measuring the passage of time. Lying on one of the carpets, he used his saddlebags as a pillow, dozing, never sinking into deep sleep, and coming instantly awake at every noise. At intervals he heard the distant sound of women weeping, and the keening wail of mourning somewhere behind the massive walls.

At last there came the tramp of heavy footsteps down the passage outside, and the curtains over the doorway were thrown open. A burly figure stood in the doorway. He wore only a crimson linen kilt belted below his great belly with a gold chain. His chest was covered with grizzled wiry curls, coarse as the pelt of a bear. There were heavy sandals on his feet and greaves of hard polished leather covered his shins. But he carried no sword or other weapon. His arms and legs seemed massive as the pillars of a temple, and were covered with battle scars, some white and silky, long-ago healed; others, more recent, were purple and angry-looking. His beard and dense bush of hair were grizzled also, but lacking the usual ribbons or plaits. They had not been oiled or combed and were in careless disarray. His dark eyes were wild and distracted, and his thick lips under the great beaked nose were twisted as if with pain.

'You are Taita, the physician,' he said. His voice was powerful, but without accent for he had been born in Avaris and had adopted much of the Egyptian culture and way of life.

Taita knew him well: to him Apepi was the invader, the bloody barbarian, mortal enemy of his country and his Pharaoh. It took the exercise of all his self-control to keep his expression neutral and his voice calm as he replied, 'I am Taita.'

'I have heard of your skills,' said Apepi. 'I have need of them now. Come with me.'

Taita slung the saddlebags over his shoulder and followed him out into the cloister. Lord Trok was waiting there with an escort of armed men. They fell in around Taita as he followed the Hyksosian king deeper into the palace. Ahead the sound of weeping became louder, until Apepi threw aside the heavy curtains that covered another doorway, and took Taita's arm to push him through.

Dominating the crowded chamber was a large contingent of priests from the temple of Isis in Avaris. Taita's lip curled as he recognized them by their headdress of egret feathers. They were chanting and shaking sistrums over the brazier in one corner in which cauterizing tongs glowed red hot. Taita's professional feud with these quacks went back two generations.

Apart from the healers, twenty others were gathered around the sickbed in the centre of the floor, courtiers and army officers, scribes and other officials, all looking solemn and funereal. Most of the women were kneeling on the floor, wailing and keening. Only one was making any attempt to nurse the young boy who lay on the couch. She seemed not much older than her patient, probably thirteen or fourteen years of age, and she was sponging him down with heated, perfumed water from a copper bowl.

With a single glance Taita saw that she was a striking-looking girl, with a determined, intelligent face. Her concern for her patient was evident, her expression loving and her hands quick and competent.

Taita switched his attention to the boy. His naked body was also well formed, but wasted by disease. His skin was blotched with the characteristic stigmata of the plague, and dewed with perspiration. On his chest were the raw and inflamed wounds where he had been bled and cauterized by the priests of Isis. Taita saw that he was in the final stages of the disease. His thick dark hair was sodden with sweat, it hung over his eyes, which were sunk into plum-coloured cavities, open and bright with fever but unseeing.

'This is Khyan, my youngest son,' Apepi said, as he went to the bedside, and looked down at the child helplessly. 'The plague will take him, unless you can save him, Magus.'

Khyan groaned and rolled on to his side with his knees drawn up in agony to his lacerated chest. With an explosive spluttering sound a mixture of liquid faeces and bright blood spurted from between his shrunken buttocks on to the soiled bed linen. The girl who was nursing him at once cleaned his backside with the cloth, then wiped up the mess on the sheets without any sign of distaste. In the corner the healers renewed their chants, and the high priest took up a pair of hot tongs from the charcoal brazier and came towards the bed.

Taita stepped forward, barring the man's way with his long staff. 'Get out!' he said softly. 'You and your butchers have done enough damage here.'

'I must burn the fever out of his body,' the man protested.

'Out!' Taita repeated grimly, then to the others who crowded the chamber, 'Out, all of you.'

'I know you well, Taita. You are a blasphemer, and a familiar of demons and evil spirits.' The priest stood his ground, and brandished the glowing bronze instrument menacingly. 'I do not fear your magic. You have no authority here. The prince is in my charge.'

Taita stepped back and dropped his staff at the feet of the priest, who shrieked and sprang back as the rod of tambootie wood began to writhe, hiss and snake towards him over the tiles. Suddenly it reared up head-high, its forked tongue darting between thin grinning lips and its beady black eyes glittering.

Instantly there was a yelling stampede for the door. Courtiers and priests, soldiers and servants panicked, clawing and elbowing their way through the press to be the first out. In his haste to escape, the high priest knocked over the brazier, then screamed as he danced barefoot on the scattered coals.

Within seconds the chamber was deserted except for Apepi, who had not moved, and the girl at the sickbed. Taita stooped and picked up the writhing serpent by the tail. Instantly it was straight, rigid and wooden in his grasp. He pointed the restored staff at the girl at the bedside. 'Who are you?' he demanded.

'I am Mintaka. This is my brother.' She laid her hand protectively on the boy's sweat-damp curls, and lifted her chin with a defiant air. 'Do your worst, Magus, but I will not leave him.' Her lips trembled and her dark eyes were huge with terror. She was clearly overawed by his reputation and by the serpent staff that Taita was pointing at her. 'I am not afraid of you,' she told him, then moved around the bed until it was between them.

'Good,' said Taita briskly, 'Then you will be of more use to me. When did the boy last drink?'

It took a moment for her to gather herself. 'Not since this morning.'

'Can't those quacks see that he is dying of thirst as much as of the disease? He has sweated and voided most of the water from his body,' Taita grunted, and picked up the copper jug from beside the bed to sniff the contents.

'This is foul with priest poison and plague humours.' He hurled it against the wall. 'Go to the kitchens and find another jug. Make sure it is clean. Fill it from the well, not with river water. Hurry, girl.' She fled and Taita opened his bag.

Mintaka returned almost immediately with a brimming jug of clean water. Taita prepared a potion of herbs, and heated it on the brazier.

'Help me give it to him,' he ordered the girl when it had brewed. He showed her how to position her brother's head and to stroke his throat as he dribbled the water into his mouth. Soon Khyan was swallowing freely.

'What can I do to help you?' the king asked.

'My lord, there is nothing for you here. You are better at destroying than at healing.' Taita dismissed him without looking up from his patient. There was a long silence, then the tramp of Apepi's bronze-studded sandals as he left the chamber.

Mintaka soon lost her terror of the Magus, and as a helper she was quick and willing. She seemed able to anticipate Taita's wishes. She forced her brother to drink while Taita brewed up another cup of medicine from his bag on the brazier. Between them they were able to get this down his throat without losing a drop. She helped him smear a soothing ointment on the burns that covered his chest. Then between them they wrapped Khyan in linen sheets and soaked them with well water to cool his burning body.

When she came to sit beside him to rest for a moment Taita took her hand and turned it palm up. He examined the red lumps on the inside of her wrist, but Mintaka tried to pull her hand away. 'Those are not plague spots.' She flushed with embarrassment. 'They are only flea-bites. The palace is crawling with fleas.'

'Where the flea bites, the plague follows,' Taita told her. 'Take off your shift.'

She stood up without hesitation and let her it drop around her ankles. Her naked body, though slim and nubile, was also athletic and strong. Her breasts were in first bud, the perky nipples pricking out like ripening mulberries. A triangle of soft fluff nestled between her long shapely legs.

A flea hopped from her pale belly. Deftly Taita picked it out of the air and crunched it between his fingernails. The insect had left a chain of pink spots around her neatly puckered belly button.

'Turn round,' he ordered, and she obeyed. Another of the loathsome insects ran down her back towards the deep cleft between her hard round buttocks. Taita pinched it between his fingers and crushed its shiny black carapace. It popped in a spot of blood. 'You will be the next patient if we don't get rid of these little pets of yours,' he told her, and sent her to fetch a bowl of water from the kitchens. On the brazier he boiled up the dried purple flowers of the pyrethrum plant and washed her down from head to toe in the brew. He snapped four or five more fleas that tried to escape the pungent douche by leaping off her drenched skin.

Afterwards Mintaka sat beside him while her naked body dried, and chatted unselfconsciously as they picked over her clothes companionably, removing the last fleas and their eggs from the seams and pleats. They were fast becoming good friends.

Before nightfall Khyan's bowels voided once more, but sparingly, and there was no blood in the stool. Taita sniffed the faeces, and the stench of the plague humours was milder. He administered a stronger distillation of the herbs, and between them they forced Khyan to drink another jugful of well water. By next morning the fever had broken and Khyan was resting more comfortably. He urinated at last, which Taita declared to be beneficial, even though his water was dark yellow and acrid. An hour later he passed more water, lighter in colour and not so evil-smelling.

'Look, my lord,' Mintaka exclaimed, stroking her brother's cheek, 'the red blotches are fading, and his skin feels cooler.'

'You have the healing touch of a nymph of paradise,' Taita told her, 'but do not forget the water jug. It is empty.'

She raced away to the kitchens, and came back almost immediately with a brimming jug. While she gave it to him, she began to sing a Hyksosian lullaby, and Taita was delighted by the sweetness and clarity of her voice:

> 'Listen to the wind in the grass, little darling,
> Sleep, sleep, sleep.
> Hear the sound of the river, my little baby,
> Dream, dream, dream.'

Taita studied her face. In the Hyksosian way, it was a little too broad, and her cheekbones too prominent. Her mouth was large, her lips full, her nose strongly bridged. Not one of these features was perfect in itself, but each was finely balanced with and matched to all the others, and her neck was long and graceful. Her almond-shaped eyes were truly magnificent under arched black brows. Her expression was alert and bright. Hers was a different kind of beauty, he thought, but beauty none the less.

'Look!' She broke off the song and laughed. 'He is awake.'

Khyan's eyes were open and he was looking up at her.

'You have come back to us, you horrid little beast.' When she laughed her teeth were square and very white in the lamplight. 'We were so worried. You must not do that again, ever.' She hugged him to hide the tears of joy and relief that suddenly sparkled in her eyes.

Taita looked beyond the pair on the bed and saw the bulky figure of Apepi in the doorway. Taita did not know how long he had been there, but now he nodded at Taita without smiling, then turned and disappeared.

By that evening Khyan was able to sit up with a little help from his sister, and to drink from the soup bowl she held to his lips. Two days later his rash had disappeared.

Three or four times a day Apepi visited the chamber. Khyan was still too weak to rise, but as soon as his father appeared, he touched his heart and his lips in a gesture of respect.

On the fifth day he tottered from the couch and tried to prostrate himself before the King, but Apepi stopped him and lifted him back on to the pillows. Even though his feelings for the boy were clear, Apepi had little to say and left again almost immediately, but in the doorway he looked back at Taita and ordered him to follow with a curt inclination of his head.

They stood alone on the summit of the highest tower of the palace. They had climbed two hundred steps to reach this height, and from here they had a view upriver over the captured citadel of Abnub, which lay ten miles upstream. Thebes was less than a hundred miles beyond that.

Apepi had ordered the sentries to go down and leave them alone in this lofty place, so that they would not be spied upon or overheard. He stood staring out over the great grey river towards the south. He was in full war costume, hard leather greaves and breastplate, sword-belt studded with gold rosettes, and his beard was plaited with crimson ribbons to match his ceremonial apron. Incongruously he wore the golden *uraeus*, the vulture and cobra crown, over his dense silver-shot curls. It infuriated Taita that this invader and despoiler considered himself Pharaoh of all Egypt, and wore the sacred regalia, but his expression was serene. Instead he tuned his mind to catch Apepi's thoughts. They were a tangled web, so deep and devious that even Taita could not discern them clearly, but he could sense the force within that made Apepi such a dreadful adversary.

'At least something they say of you is true, Magus.' Apepi broke the long silence. 'You are a physician of great skill.' Taita remained silent.

'Can you work a charm to heal the plague in my army as you have in my son?' Apepi asked. 'I would pay you a lakh of gold. As much gold as ten strong horses can carry.'

Taita smiled bleakly. 'My lord, if I could work such a charm I could as well conjure a hundred lakhs out of the thin air without the effort of curing your ruffians.'

Apepi turned his head and returned his smile, but it lacked any humour or goodwill. 'How old are you, Warlock? Trok says you are over two hundred years old. Is that true?'

Taita gave no indication of having heard him, and Apepi went on, 'What is your price, Warlock? If not gold then what can I offer you?' The question was rhetorical and he did not wait for an answer, but stamped away to the northern parapet of the tower, and stood with his fists on his hips. He looked down over the encampments of his army, and the cremation fields beyond. The fires were still burning and the smoke drifted low across the green waters of the river and out into the desert beyond.

'You have won a victory, my lord,' Taita said softly, 'but you do well to contemplate the pyres of your dead. Pharaoh will have reinforced and regrouped his forces before the plague burns itself out and your men are ready to fight again.'

Apepi shook himself with annoyance, like a lion shaking off flies. 'Your persistence irks me, Warlock.'

'Nay, lord, it is not me but the truth and the logic that irk you.'

'Nefer Seti is a child. I have defeated him once, I will do it again.'

'What is more crucial to you, there is no plague in his army. Your spies will have told you that Pharaoh has five more legions at Aswan, and another two at Asyut. They are already on the river coming north with the current. They will be here before the new moon.'

Apepi growled softly, but made no response. Taita went on relentlessly, 'Sixty years of war have bled both kingdoms white. Would you pass on the legacy of Salitis, your own father, sixty years of bloodshed? Is that what your sons will inherit from you?'

Apepi rounded on him, scowling, 'Do not press me too hard, old man. Do not insult my father, the divine god Salitis.' After an interval long enough to express his disapproval, Apepi spoke again. 'How long will it take you to arrange a parley with this so-called Regent of the Upper Kingdom, this Naja?'

'If you give me safe conduct through your lines, and a fast galley to carry me, I can be in Thebes in three days. The return with the current will be even swifter.'

'I will send Trok with you to see you safely through. Tell Naja I will meet him at the temple of Hathor on the west bank at Perra beyond Abnub. Do you know it?'

'I know it well, my lord,' Taita said.

'We can talk there,' Apepi said. 'But tell him not to expect too many concessions from me. I am the victor, and he the vanquished. You can go now.'

Taita stood his ground.

'You may go, Warlock.' Apepi dismissed him a second time.

'Pharaoh Nefer Seti is almost of an age with your daughter, Mintaka,' Taita said stubbornly. 'You might wish to bring her with you to Perra.'

'To what purpose?' Apepi stared at him suspiciously.

'An alliance between your dynasty and that of the Tamosian pharaohs might seal a lasting peace in the two kingdoms.'

Apepi stroked the ribbons in his beard to hide his smile, 'By Seueth, you intrigue as cunningly as you mix a potion, Warlock. Now, get you gone before you irk me past forbearance.'

The temple of Hathor had been excavated out of the rocky hillside above the river in the reign of Pharaoh Sehertawy hundreds of years previously, but had been added to by every pharaoh since then. The priestesses were a rich, influential sisterhood who had contrived somehow to survive during the long civil wars between the kingdoms and even to prosper in difficult times.

Dressed in their yellow robes they were gathered in the courtyard of the temple, between the two massive statues of the goddess. One of these depicted Hathor as the piebald cow with golden horns, and the other was her human manifestation, the tall, beautiful lady wearing the crown of horns and the golden sun disc on her head.

The priestesses chanted and rattled the sistrum as the suite of Pharaoh Nefer Seti filed into the courtyard from the eastern wing, while King Apepi's courtiers entered through the western colonnade. The order of arrival at the conference had been a matter of such heated debate that the negotiations had almost broken down before they had begun. The first arrival would have the prestige of the incumbent in the position of power, while the second arrival would appear as the supplicant begging for peace. Neither side had been willing to forgo the advantage.

It was Taita who had suggested the expedient of a simultaneous arrival. He had also tactfully settled the equally vexing question of the regalia to be worn by the two protagonists. Both would eschew the double crown. Apepi would wear the red *deshret* crown of Lower Egypt, while Nefer Seti would confine himself to the white *hedjet* crown of Upper Egypt.

The entourages of both rulers packed the spacious courtyard, their ranks facing each other unsmiling and grim. Only a few paces separated them physically, but the bitterness and hatred of sixty years' strife formed a mighty barrier between them.

The hostile silence was shattered by a rolling fanfare of rams' horns, and the thunder of bronze gongs. This was the signal for the royal parties to emerge from the opposite wings of the temple.

Lord Naja and Pharaoh Nefer Seti paced out solemnly and took their places on the high-backed thrones, while the two princesses, Heseret and Merykara, followed them meekly and took their seats at the foot of Naja's throne, for they were his betrothed. Both girls were so heavily made-up that their faces were as expressionless as that of the statue of Hathor in whose shadow they sat.

At the same time the Hyksosian royal family emerged from the opposing wing of the temple. Apepi led them, an impressive, warlike figure in full battle armour. He glared across the courtyard at the boy pharaoh. Eight of his sons followed him; only Khyan, the youngest, had not recovered sufficiently from the plague to make the journey upriver. Like their father they were armed and armoured, and strutted and posed with the same bravado.

A formidable coterie of bloodthirsty ruffians, Taita thought, as he surveyed them from where he stood close to Nefer's throne.

Apepi had brought only one of his many daughters with him. Like a desert rose in a thicket of spiny cactus, the contrast to her brothers made Mintaka's beauty shine out. She picked out Taita's tall lank figure and silver hair in the crowd opposite and her face lit in a smile so radiant that it seemed for a moment that the sun had burst through the awnings stretched over the courtyard. None of the Egyptians had ever laid eyes on her before, and there was a subdued rustle and murmur through their ranks. They had been unprepared for her. The myth was that all Hyksosian women were as heavily built as their menfolk and twice as ugly.

Pharaoh Nefer Seti leaned forward slightly and despite the solemnity of the occasion tugged at his earlobe under the bottle-shaped white crown. It was a habit Taita had tried to break, and Nefer only did it when he was intensely interested in something, or when he was distracted. Taita had not seen Nefer for over two months – Naja had kept them separated since his return from Apepi's headquarters at Bubasti – yet he was so familiar with the boy, so attuned to his mind, that he could still read his thoughts with ease. He sensed that Nefer was in a ferment of elation and excitement, as intense as if he had just spotted a gazelle moving within arrow range, or was about to mount an unbroken colt, or had launched a hawk at a heron and was watching it begin its stoop.

Taita had never known him react like this to the presence of a member of the opposite sex. Nefer had always looked upon all females, including his sisters, with a regal disdain. However, it was less than a year since he had been launched on to the troubled waters of puberty, and most of that time he had been sequestered with Taita in the wilderness of Gebel Nagara where there had been nothing to rivet his attention in the way that Mintaka was now doing.

Taita felt smug at what he had achieved with so little effort. It would have complicated all his plans and enhanced the danger in which they found themselves if Nefer had taken a violent dislike to the Hyksosian girl. If the two married, Nefer would be the son-in-law of Apepi and come under his protection. Even Naja must pause before giving offence to someone so powerful and dangerous. Mintaka might unwittingly save Nefer from the Regent's machinations and ambitions. That at least was Taita's intention in fostering the union.

During the short time they had nursed and cared for her brother Taita and Mintaka had formed a firm friendship. Now Taita nodded almost imperceptibly and returned her smile. Then Mintaka's gaze moved past him. She looked with interest at the noble Egyptian women opposite her. She had heard much about them, but these were the first she had seen. Swiftly she singled out Heseret. With sure feminine instinct she recognized someone as attractive as herself, and a possible future rival. Heseret reacted to her in exactly the same way, and they exchanged a brief but haughty and mutually hostile glance. Then Mintaka raised her eyes to the impressive figure of Lord Naja and stared at him with fascination.

He was such a splendid sight, so different from her own father and brothers. He shone with gold and precious stones, and his linen was dazzling in its purity. She could smell his perfume across the distance that separated them, like a field of wild flowers. His face was a mask of makeup, his skin almost luminous and his eyes outlined and enhanced with kohl. Yet she thought that his was the fatal beauty of a snake or a poisonous insect. She shivered and turned her eyes to the figure on the throne beside the Regent.

Pharaoh Nefer Seti was staring at her with such intensity that she caught her breath. His eyes were so green – that was the first thing that struck her and she wanted to look away but found she could not. Instead she started to blush.

Pharaoh Nefer Seti looked so dignified and divine under the white crown and with the false goatee beard on his chin that she felt flustered. Then, suddenly, Pharaoh gave her a warm and conspiratorial smile. Instantly his face was boyish and appealing, and unaccountably her breath came faster and she blushed deeper. With an effort she tore away her eyes, and studied the cow statue of the goddess Hathor with great attention.

It took her some time to bring herself under control, and by that time Lord Naja, the Regent of Upper Egypt, was speaking. In measured tones he greeted Apepi, diplomatically referring to him as King of the Hyksos but avoiding any reference to his claims to Egyptian territory. Mintaka watched his lips intently, but she was aware of Nefer's eyes on her, and determined not to look at him.

Lord Naja's voice was sonorous and boring, and at last she could hold out no longer. She sneaked a quick sideways glance at Nefer, intending to look away again immediately, but his eyes were still fastened on her. They glinted with silent laughter and fascinated her. Hers was not a timid nature, but this time her smile was shy and hesitant, and she felt her colour rise again. She dropped her eyes and looked at her hands in her lap, twisting her fingers together until she realized that she was fidgeting and stopped herself. She kept her hands still, but now she was irritated with Nefer for having ruffled her calm. He is only a precious Egyptian fop. Any one of my brothers is more of a man and twice as handsome. He is only trying to make me look a fool by staring at me in that boorish way. I will not look at him again. I will ignore him completely, she decided, and her resolve lasted until Lord Naja stopped speaking, and her father rose to answer him.

She shot Nefer another quick look from under her thick dark lashes. He was gazing at her father, but the moment her glance touched his face his eyes swivelled to her. She tried to make her expression severe and forbidding, but as soon as he smiled her lips twitched in sympathy. He really is as handsome as some of my brothers, she conceded, then took another quick peek. Or perhaps as any of them. She looked back at her lap and thought about it. Then she took another peep just to make certain. Perhaps even more handsome than any of them, even Ruga. Immediately she felt that she had betrayed her eldest brother and qualified her opinion: But in a different kind of way, of course.

She glanced sideways at Ruga: with his beribboned beard and dark brow, he was all warrior. Ruga is a fine-looking man, she thought loyally.

In the ranks opposite, Taita did not seem to be watching her but he missed not a single nuance of the surreptitious exchanges between Nefer and Mintaka. He saw more than that. Lord Trok, Naja's cousin, was standing close behind Apepi's throne, almost within arm's reach of Mintaka. His arms were folded over his chest, and he wore embossed wristlets of solid gold. Over one shoulder was slung a heavy recurved bow, over the other an arrow quiver covered with gold leaf. Around his neck were the gold chains of valour and praise. The Hyksos had adopted Egyptian military honours and decorations as well as their beliefs and customs. Trok was watching the Hyksosian princess with an unfathomable expression.

There was another brief exchange of glances between Mintaka and Nefer, which Trok followed with his dark, brooding gaze. Taita could sense his anger and jealousy. It was as though the hot and oppressive cloud of the *khamsin*, the terrible Saharan sandstorm, was building up on the desert horizon. I had not foreseen this. Is Trok's interest in Mintaka romantic or political? he wondered. Does he lust for her, or see her merely as a staircase to power? In either case it is dangerous, and something else we must take into account.

The speeches of greeting were coming to an end and nothing of significance had been said: negotiation of the truce would begin in secret session the next day. Both sides were rising from their thrones and exchanging bows and salutations, and the gongs began to beat and the ram's horns to sound again as they withdrew.

Taita took one last look at the Hyksosian ranks. Apepi and his sons disappeared through a gateway guarded by tall granite pillars, topped with the twin cow heads of the goddess. With a final backward look Mintaka followed her father and brothers. Lord Trok followed her closely, and also shot a last glance at Pharaoh Nefer Seti over his shoulder. Then he, too, strode out between the pillars. As he did so the arrows in his quiver rattled softly, and their coloured fletchings caught Taita's eye. Unlike the workaday leather war quiver with its stopper to prevent the arrows spilling out, this ceremonial one was covered in gold leaf, and the barrel end was open so that the fletched tips of the arrows protruded above his shoulder. The feathers were red and green, and something evil stirred in Taita's memory. Trok marched away through the gateway, leaving Taita gazing after him.

Taita returned to the stone cell in the temple annex that had been allocated to him for the duration of the peace conference. He drank a little sherbet, for it had been hot in the courtyard, then went to the window in the thick stone wall. A flock of bright-coloured weavers and tits hopped and twittered on the sill, and on the flagged terrace below. While he fed them with crushed *dhurra* millet, and they sat on his shoulders or pecked from his cupped hands, Taita thought about the events of the morning and began to piece together all the disparate perceptions he had garnered during the opening ceremony.

His amusement and pleasure at what had transpired between Mintaka and Nefer were forgotten as he went on to think of Trok. He considered the man's relationship to the Hyksosian princess, and the complications that might ensue when he tried to force through his plans for the young couple.

His train of thought was interrupted as he noticed a stealthy shadow creeping along the edge of the terrace outside the window. It was one of the temple cats, gaunt, scarred and flayed in patches with mange. It was stalking the birds that hopped on the flags outside the window, picking up the spilled grains of *dhurra* millet.

Taita's pale eyes slitted as he concentrated on the cat. The old tom stopped and peered around suspiciously. Suddenly its back arched and every hair on its body stood erect as it stared at an empty spot on the stone flags in front of it. It uttered a spitting shriek, spun round and raced away down the terrace until it came to a palm tree. It flew up the tall trunk until it reached the crowning top fronds where it clung pathetically. Taita threw another handful of grain to the birds and picked up his thoughts.

Even during their long ride together, Trok had kept his war quiver firmly stoppered and it had not occurred to Taita to compare one of the arrows it contained to those he had found at the site of Pharaoh's murder. How many other Hyksosian officers had red and green fletchings he could only guess, but it was probably a great number, though each would have his unique signet. There was only one way to connect Trok to the death of Pharaoh Tamose, and through him to implicate his cousin Naja. That was to study one of his arrows. How to do this without arousing his suspicions, he wondered.

Once again he was distracted from his thoughts. There were voices in the passage outside the door of his cell. One was young and clear, and he recognized it at once. The others were gruff, pleading and protesting.

'Lord Asmor has given specific orders—'

'Am I not Pharaoh? Are you not bound to obey me? I wish to visit the Magus, and you dare not prevent me. Stand aside, both of you.' Nefer's voice was strong and commanding. The uncertain timbre of puberty was gone, and he spoke with the tones of a man.

The young falcon is spreading his wings and showing his talons, Taita thought, and turned from the window, dusting the millet powder from his hands, to greet his king.

Nefer jerked aside the curtain that covered the doorway, and stepped through. Two armed bodyguards followed him helplessly, crowding into the doorway behind him. Nefer ignored them and faced Taita with his hands on his hips.

'Taita, I am much displeased with you.' Nefer said.

'I am distraught.' Taita made a deep obeisance. 'In what way have I given you offence?'

'You have been avoiding me. Whenever I send for you they tell me that you are gone on a secret mission to the Hyksos, or that you have returned to the desert, or some other such moonlit tale.' Nefer scowled to mask his delight at being with the old man again. 'Then suddenly you pop up from nowhere, as though you had never left, but still you ignore me. You did not even look in my direction during the ceremony. Where have you been?'

'Majesty, there are long ears about.' Taita glanced at the hovering guards.

Immediately Nefer turned upon them wrathfully. 'I have ordered you more than once to be gone. If you do not go this instant I will have you both strangled.'

They withdrew unhappily, but not too far. Taita could still hear their murmurs and the clink of their weapons as they waited in the passage beyond the curtain. He jerked his head at the window and whispered, 'I have a skiff at the jetty. Would Your Majesty like to go fishing?' Without waiting for his reply, Taita hitched up the skirts of his *chiton* and hopped on to the window-sill. He glanced over his shoulder. Nefer had forgotten his anger and was grinning delightedly as he ran across the cell to join him. Taita jumped down on to the terrace outside and Nefer followed him nimbly. Like truants from the classroom, they sneaked across the terrace and down through the date palms to the river.

There were guards at the jetty, but they had received no orders to restrain their young Pharaoh. They saluted and stood aside respectfully as the pair scrambled into the small fishing skiff. Each took up a paddle and shoved off. Taita steered into one of the narrow passages in the banks of waving papyrus, and within minutes they were alone on the swamp waters, hidden from the banks in the maze of secret waterways.

'Where have you been, Taita?' Nefer dropped the regal air. 'I have missed you so.'

'I will tell you everything,' Taita assured you, 'but first you should tell me all that has happened to you.'

They found a quiet mooring in a tiny papyrus-enclosed lagoon, and Nefer related everything that had happened to him since they had last been able to talk in private. He had been held on Naja's orders in a gilded prison, without being able to see any of his old friends, not even Meren or his own sisters. His only distractions had been his studies of the scrolls from the palace library, his chariot drills and arms practice under the coaching of the old warrior, Hilto.

'Naja will not even let me go out hawking or fishing without Asmor to wet-nurse me,' he complained bitterly.

He had not known that Taita was to be at the welcoming ceremony in the temple courtyard until he had seen him there. He had believed him to be at Gebel Nagara. At his first opportunity, when Naja and Asmor were locked in the truce conclave with Apepi, Trok and the other Hyksosian warlords, he had browbeaten his guards and blustered his way out of the quarters to which he had been confined to come to Taita.

'Life is so dull without you, Taita. I think I might die of boredom. Naja must let us be together again. You should cast a spell on him.'

'It is something we can consider,' Taita avoided the suggestion adroitly, 'but now we have little time. Naja will send the whole army out to search for us once he finds that we are missing from the temple. I must tell you my own news.' Rapidly, in simple outline, he told Nefer what had happened to him since their last meeting. He explained the relationship between Naja and Trok, and described how he had visited the scene of Pharaoh Tamose's death and the discovery he had made there.

Nefer listened without interruption, but when Taita spoke of the death of his father his eyes filled with tears. He looked away, coughed and wiped his eyes on the back of his hand.

'Now you can appreciate the danger you are in,' Taita told him. 'I am certain that Naja had much to do with Pharaoh's murder, and the closer we come to the proof of it, the greater that danger becomes.'

'One day I will avenge my father.' Nefer vowed, and his voice was cold and hard.

'And I will help you do it,' Taita promised, 'but now we must protect you from Naja's malice.'

'How do you plan to do that, Taita? Can we escape from Egypt as we planned before?'

'No.' Taita shook his head. 'Naturally I have considered that course, but Naja has us too securely imprisoned here. If we tried to run for the frontier again we would have a thousand chariots hot behind us.'

'What can we do, then? You are in danger also.'

'No. I have convinced Naja that he cannot succeed without my help.' He described the false divination ceremony at the temple of Osiris, and how Naja believed that Taita could share with him the secret of eternal life.

Nefer grinned at the Magus' cunning. 'So what do you plan?'

'We must wait until the right time either to escape or rid the world of Naja's evil presence. In the meantime I will protect you as best I can.'

'How will you do that?'

'Naja sent me to Apepi to arrange this peace conference.'

'Yes, I know that you went to Avaris. They told me that when I demanded to see you.'

'Not to Avaris, but to Apepi's battle headquarters at Bubasti. Once Apepi had agreed to the meeting with Naja, I was able to convince him that they should seal the treaty by a marriage between you and Apepi's daughter. Once you are under the protection of the Hyksosian king, Naja's knife will be blunted. He could not risk plunging the land back into civil war by voiding the treaty.'

'Apepi is going to give me his daughter as a wife?' Nefer stared at him in wonder. 'The one in the red dress whom I saw at the ceremony this morning?'

'Yes.' Taita agreed. 'Mintaka is her name.'

'I know her name,' Nefer assured him vehemently. 'She is named after the tiny star in the belt of the Hunter constellation.'

'Yes, that's her.' Taita nodded. 'Mintaka, the ugly one with the big nose and funny mouth.'

'She is not ugly!' Nefer flared at him, springing to his feet so that he almost overturned the skiff and dumped them in the mud of the lagoon. 'She is the most beautiful . . .' When he saw the expression on Taita's face, he subsided. 'I mean, she is quite pleasing to look at.' He grinned ruefully. 'You always catch me out. But you must admit to me that she's beautiful, Taita.'

'If you like big noses, and funny mouths.'

Nefer picked up a dead fish from the bilges and threw it at his head. Taita ducked. 'When can I speak to her?' he asked, trying to sound as though it was a request of no real importance to him. 'She does speak Egyptian, doesn't she?'

'She speaks it as well as you do,' Taita assured him.

'Then when can I meet her? You can arrange it for me.'

Taita had anticipated this request. 'You could invite the princess and her suite to a hunt here in the swamps, and perhaps a picnic afterwards.'

'I will send Asmor to invite her this very afternoon,' Nefer decided, but Taita shook his head.

'He would go to the Regent first, and Naja would immediately see the danger. He would never allow it, and once he was alerted he would do everything in his power to prevent you coming together.'

'What shall we do, then?' Nefer looked agitated.

'I will go to her myself,' Taita promised, and at that moment there were faint shouts from different directions in the papyrus swamps around them, and the splash of paddles. 'Asmor has found out that you are missing, and has sent his hounds to bring you in,' Taita said. 'It proves how difficult it will be to elude him. Now, listen carefully for we have little time before we will be separated again.'

They spoke quickly, making arrangements to exchange messages in any emergency and to put other plans into place, but all the time the shouting and splashing was growing louder, drawing nearer. Within minutes a light fighting galley packed with armed men burst through the screen of papyrus, thrust onward by twenty oars. A shout went up from the command deck: 'There is Pharaoh! Steer for the skiff!'

The Hyksos had set up a practice field on the alluvial plain abutting the papyrus swamp of the river. When Taita came down from the temple, two battalions of Apepi's guards were exercising at arms under a cloudless sky from which the morning sun blazed down. Two hundred fully armed men were running relay races through the swamp, toiling waist deep through the mud, while squadrons of chariots performed complicated evolutions out on the plain, from columns of four forming a single line ahead, then fanning out into line abreast. Dust swirled out behind the racing wheels, the lance tips shot beams of sunlight and the brightly coloured pennants danced in the wind.

Taita stopped by the butts to watch for a while as the line of fifty archers shot at a hundred cubits, each man loosing five rapid arrows. Then they raced forward to the straw man-shaped targets, retrieved their arrows and shot again at the next line of targets two hundred cubits further on. The flail of the instructor fell heavily on the back of any man who was slow to cross the open ground or who missed the mark when he shot. The bronze studs on the leather thongs left spots of bright blood where they bit through the linen tunics.

Taita walked on unchallenged. As he passed, the matched pairs of lancers who were practising the standard thrusts and blocks with warlike shouts, broke off their bouts and fell silent. They followed him with a respectful gaze. His was a fearsome reputation. Only after he had passed did they engage each other again.

At the far end of the field, on the short green grass beside the swamp, a single chariot was speeding through a course of markers and targets. It was one of the scout chariots, with spoked wheels and bodywork of woven bamboo, very fast, and light enough for two men to lift and carry over an obstacle.

It was drawn by a pair of magnificent bay mares from the personal string of King Apepi. Their hoofs threw up lumps of turf as they spun round the markers at the end of the course and came back at full gallop with the light chariot bouncing and swerving behind them.

Lord Trok was driving, leaning forward with the reins wrapped around his wrists. His beard fluttered in the wind, his moustaches and the coloured ribbons were blown back over his shoulders as he urged the horses on with wild shouts. Taita had to acknowledge his skill: even at such speed he had the pair under perfect control, running a tight line between the markers, giving the archer on the footplate beside him the best chance at the targets as they sped past.

Taita leaned on his staff as he watched the chariot come on at full gallop. There was no mistaking the slim straight figure and royal bearing. Mintaka was dressed in a pleated crimson skirt that left her knees bare. The cross-straps of her sandals were wound high around her shapely calves. She wore a leather guard on her left wrist, and a hard leather cuirass moulded to the shape of her small round breasts. The leather would protect her tender nipples from the whip of the bowstring as she loosed her arrows at the targets as they sped by.

Mintaka recognized Taita, called a greeting and waved her bow over her head. Her dark hair was covered by a fine-woven net and it bounced on her shoulders at each jolt of the chariot. She wore no makeup but the wind and exertion had rouged her cheeks and put a sparkle in her eyes. Taita could not imagine Heseret riding as lance-bearer in a war chariot, but Hyksosian attitudes towards women were different.

'Hathor smile upon you, Magus!' She laughed as Trok brought the chariot to a broadsiding halt in front of him. He knew that Mintaka had adopted the gentle goddess as her patron, rather than one of the monstrous Hyksosian deities.

'May Horus love you for ever, Princess Mintaka.' Taita returned her blessing. It was a mark of his affection that he accorded her the royal title when he would not acknowledge her father as king.

She jumped down in the dust cloud and ran to embrace him, reaching up to throw her arms around his neck so that the hard edge of her cuirass dug into his ribs. She felt him wince and stepped back. 'I have just shot five heads straight,' she boasted.

'Your warlike skills are exceeded only by your beauty.' He smiled.

'You do not believe me,' she challenged. 'You think that just because I am a girl I cannot draw a bow.' She did not wait for his disclaimer but ran back to the chariot and leaped up on to the footplate. 'Drive on, Lord Trok,' she commanded. 'Another circuit. At your best speed.'

Trok shook out the reins and turned the chariot so sharply that the inside wheel stood still. Then, as he lined up, he shouted, 'Ha! Ha!' and they sped away down the course.

Each target was set on top of a short pole, at the level of the eye of the archer. They were in the shape of human heads, each carved from a block of wood. There was no mistaking their nationality. Each dummy head was a caricature of an Egyptian warrior, complete with helmet and regimental insignia, and the painted features were as grotesque as ogres.

Little doubt of the artist's opinion of us, Taita thought wryly.

Mintaka plucked an arrow from the bin on the dashboard, nocked and drew. She held her aim, the bright yellow fletchings touching her pursed lips as though in a kiss. Trok brought the chariot in towards the first target, trying to give her a fair shot, but the ground was rough. Even though she flexed from the knees to ride the bumps, she swayed with the motion of the carriage.

As the target flashed by Mintaka loosed, and Taita found he was holding his breath for her. He need not have worried for she handled the light bow with perfect aplomb. The arrow slapped into the left eye of the dummy and quivered there, the yellow fletching bright in the sunlight.

'*Bak-her!*' He applauded, and she laughed with delight as the chariot raced on. Twice more she shot. One arrow lodged deep in the forehead, the next in the mouth of the target. It was excellent shooting even for a veteran charioteer, let alone a slip of a girl.

Trok spun the chariot around the far marker and they came back again. The horses' ears were laid back, their manes flying. Mintaka shot again, scoring another hit right on the tip of the dummy's oversized nose.

'By Horus!' Taita said, with surprise. 'She shoots like a *djinn*!'

The last target came up fast and Mintaka was balancing gracefully, cheeks flushed and white teeth gleaming as she bit her lip in concentration. She shot and the arrow flew high and right missing the head by the breadth of a hand.

'Trok, you clumsy oaf! You drove straight into that hole just as I was loosing!' she yelled at him.

She jumped down from the chariot while it was still moving and blazed up at Trok, 'You did that on purpose to make a fool of me in the sight of the Magus!'

'Your Highness, I am mortified by my own incompetence.' The mighty Trok was as awkward as a small boy in the face of her anger. Taita saw that his feelings for her were every bit as ardent as he had suspected.

'You are not forgiven. I shall not allow you the privilege of driving me again. Not ever.'

Taita had not seen her show such spirit before, and this, together with her recent exhibition of marksmanship, sent his good opinion of her to an even higher level. This is a fitting wife for any man, even a pharaoh of the Tamosian dynasty, he decided, but he was careful not to show any sign of levity, lest Mintaka switch her wrath to him. He need not have worried, though, for as soon as she turned to face him her smile bloomed again.

'Four out of five is good enough for a warrior of the Red Road, Your Highness,' Taita assured her, 'and it was indeed a treacherous hole that you hit.'

'You must be thirsty, Taita. I know I am.' She took his hand artlessly and led him to where her maids had spread a woven woollen rug at the edge of the river, and laid out platters of sweetmeats and jugs of sherbet.

'There is so much I have to ask you, Taita,' she told him, as she settled on the sheepskin rug beside him. 'I have not seen you since you left Bubasti.'

'How is your brother, Khyan?' He forestalled her question.

'He is his usual self,' she laughed, 'if not even naughtier than before. My father has ordered that he join us here as soon as he has fully recovered. He wants all his family around him when the truce is signed.'

They chatted of trivialities for a while longer, but Mintaka was distracted. He waited for her to broach the subject uppermost in her mind. She surprised him by turning suddenly to Trok, who was standing nearby with a hang-dog air.

'You may leave us now, my lord,' she said to him coolly.

'Will you ride with me again tomorrow morning, Princess?' Trok was close to pleading.

'Tomorrow I shall probably be otherwise occupied.'

'Then the day after?' Even his moustache seemed to droop pitifully.

'Fetch me my bow and my quiver before you go,' she ordered, ignoring his question. He brought them to her like a lackey, and placed them close to her hand.

'Farewell, my lord.' She turned back to Taita. Trok hovered for a few minutes longer, then stumped off to his chariot.

As he drove off Taita murmured, 'How long has Trok been in love with you?'

She looked startled then laughed delightedly. 'Trok in love with me? Why, that's ridiculous! Trok is as ancient as the Pyramids at Giza – he must be almost thirty years old! And he has three wives and Hathor only knows how many concubines!'

Taita drew one of her arrows from the magnificently decorated quiver and inspected it casually. The fletchings were blue and yellow, and he touched the tiny carved signet on the shaft.

'The three stars of the Hunter's belt,' he remarked, 'with Mintaka the brightest.'

'Blue and yellow are my favourite colours.' She nodded. 'My arrows are all made for me by Grippa. He is the most famous fletcher in Avaris. Each of the arrows he makes is perfectly straight and balanced to fly true. His decorations and signets are works of art. Look how he has carved and painted my star.' Taita turned the arrow between his fingers and admired it at length, before returning it to the quiver.

'What is Trok's arrow signet?' he asked casually.

She made a gesture of annoyance. 'I do not know. For all I care it is probably a wild hog, or an ox. I have had enough of Trok for this day and many days to come.' She poured sherbet into Taita's bowl. 'I know how you like honey.' Ostentatiously she changed the subject, and Taita waited for her to choose the next.

'Now, I have certain delicate things to discuss with you,' she admitted shyly. She picked a wild flower from the grass on which they sat and began to twist it into the beginning of a garland, still not looking at him, but her cheeks, which had lost the flush of exertion, turned rosy once more.

'Pharaoh Nefer Seti is fourteen years and five months old, almost a year older than you. He was born under the sign of the Ibex, which makes a fine match for your Cat.'

Taita had anticipated her, and she looked up at him in astonishment. 'How did you know what I was going to ask you?' Then she clapped her hands. 'Of course you knew. You are the Magus.'

'Speaking of Pharaoh, I have come to deliver a message from His Majesty,' Taita told her.

Immediately all her attention was fixed on him. 'A message? Does he even know I exist?'

'He is very much aware of that fact.' Taita sipped his sherbet. 'This needs a little more honey.' He poured some into the bowl, and stirred.

'Do not tease me, Warlock,' she snapped at him. 'Give me my message at once.'

'Pharaoh invites you and your suite to a duck hunt in the swamps tomorrow at dawn, and afterwards to a picnic breakfast on the Isle of the Little Dove.'

The dawn sky was the glowing shade of a sword-blade fresh from the coals of the forge. The top of the papyrus formed a stark black frieze below it. In this time before the sunrise there was no breath of air to set them nodding, or any sound to break the stillness.

The two hunting skiffs were moored at opposite ends of a small lagoon, hard against the wall of reeds that surrounded the open water. Less than fifty cubits separated them. The royal huntsmen had bent the tall papyrus stems over to form a screening roof over the hunters.

The surface of the lagoon was still and unruffled, reflecting the sky like a polished bronze mirror. It was just light enough for Nefer to make out the graceful form of Mintaka in the other boat. She had her bow across her lap, and she sat as motionless as a statuette of the goddess Hathor. Any other girl he could think of, particularly his own sisters Heseret and Merykara, would have been hopping around like a canary on a perch and twittering twice as loudly.

In his mind he ran lingeringly over their brief meeting this morning. It had been dark, not the faintest glow of dawn to dim the glory of the star panoply that hung over the world, each star so plump and bright that it seemed he could reach up and pluck them like ripe figs from the tree. Mintaka had come down the pathway from the temple, her way lit for her by torch-bearers, and her maids following close behind her. She wore a woollen hood over her head to ward off the river chill, and no matter how hard he stared her face remained in darkness.

'May Pharaoh live a thousand years.'

These were the first words he had ever heard her speak. Her voice was sweeter than the music of any lute. It was as though ghostly fingers were stroking the back of his neck. It took him some moments to find his own voice. 'May Hathor love you through all eternity.' He had consulted Taita on the form of greeting he should employ, and he had rehearsed it until he had it off pat. He thought he saw the flash of her teeth as she smiled under the hood, and he was encouraged to add something else that Taita had not suggested. It came to him in a flash of inspiration. He pointed up at the star-bright sky. 'Look! There is your own star.' She raised her head to look up at the constellation of the Hunter. The starlight fell on her face, so that he saw it for the first time since she had come down the pathway. He caught his breath sharply. Her expression was solemn, but he thought that he had never seen anything more enchanting. 'The gods placed it there especially for you.' The compliment tripped off his tongue.

Immediately her face lit up, and she was even more beautiful. 'Pharaoh is as gallant as he is gracious.' She made a small, slightly mocking obeisance. Then she stepped into the waiting skiff. She did not look back as the royal huntsmen rowed her out into the swamp.

Now he repeated her words to himself as though they were a prayer: 'Pharaoh is as gallant as he is gracious.'

Out in the swamp a heron boomed. As though this was a signal, the air was filled suddenly with the sound of wings. Nefer had almost forgotten the reason they were out on the water, which was a measure of his distraction for he loved the hunt with a singular passion. He tore his eyes off the dainty figure in the boat across the water, and reached for his throwing sticks.

He had decided to use the sticks rather than the bow, because he was certain that she did not have the brawn or skill to handle the heavier weapons. This would give him a distinct advantage. When skilfully thrown the spinning stick cut a wider swathe than the arrow. Its bludgeoning weight was more likely to knock down a bird than the blunt-tipped arrow, which might be deflected by the dense plumage of the waterfowl. Nefer was determined to impress Mintaka with his hunting skills.

The first flight of ducks came sweeping in low out of the dawn. They were glossy black and white, and each had a distinctive knob on top of its beak. The lead bird shied away, leading the others out of range. At that moment the traitor ducks began to call seductively. They were captured and tamed birds that the huntsmen had placed out on the open waters of the lagoon, held there by a line around the leg that was anchored to a stone on the muddy bottom.

The wild ducks turned back in a wide circle then started to drop and line up to settle on the open water alongside the traitors. They set their wings and streamed in, losing height swiftly, passing directly over Nefer's skiff. Pharaoh judged his moment neatly, and rose to his feet with the stick cocked and ready to throw. He waited for the lead bird to flare out and then let fly, sending the stick cartwheeling up. The duck saw the missile coming and dropped a wing to avoid it. For an instant it seemed it might have succeeded, but then there was a thud, a burst of feathers and the duck dropped into an uncontrolled dive, trailing a broken wing. It hit the water with a heavy splash but almost instantly recovered and dived under the surface.

'Quickly! Go after him!' Nefer shouted. Four naked slave boys were hanging in the water alongside, only their heads showing. They clutched at the side of the skiff with numb fingers. Already their teeth were chattering with cold.

Two swam to retrieve the fallen bird, but Nefer knew that it would be in vain. With no injury other than a broken wing the duck could outdive and outswim the retrievers indefinitely.

Lost bird, he thought bitterly, and before he could throw the second stick the flight of duck had angled across the lagoon, directly towards Mintaka's boat. They were still keeping low, unlike teal who would have rocketed almost straight up. However, they were going very fast, their blade-shaped wings whistling through the air.

Nefer had almost discounted the hunter in the other boat. At that height and speed the targets were too difficult for all but the most expert archer. In quick succession two arrows rose to meet the struggle of ducks. The sound of the double impact carried clearly across the lagoon. Then two birds were falling with that peculiar inert look, wings loose and head flopping, killed cleanly, stone dead in the air at the same time. They plopped on to the water and floated there, motionless. The swimmers picked them up easily and swam back to Mintaka's skiff, carrying the carcasses gripped in their teeth.

'Two lucky arrows,' Nefer voiced his opinion.

In the bows of the skiff, Taita added, without a smile, 'Two unlucky ducks.'

Now the sky was filled with birds, which rose in dark clouds as the first rays of the sun struck the waters. So dense were the flocks that from a distance it looked as though the reed beds were smouldering and spewing up clouds of dark smoke.

Nefer had ordered twenty light galleys and as many smaller boats to patrol all the open waters within three miles of the temple of Hathor, and to chase up any waterbirds that settled. The winged multitudes never thinned. Not only a dozen varieties of duck and geese, but ibis and herons, egrets, spoonbills and openbills were in flight. At every level, from high overhead to low down over the waving tops of the papyrus, they wheeled in dark cohorts or raced low in V-formations with rapid wingbeats. They squawked and honked and quacked and bleated and wailed.

At intervals through the avian cacophony sounded a peal of sweet laughter and squeals of girlish glee as Mintaka's slave girls urged her to greater efforts.

Her light bow was well suited to the task. It was quick to align and draw without taxing her strength unduly. She was not firing the traditional blunt-tipped arrows but using instead sharp metal heads that had been especially forged for her by Grippa, the famous armourer. The needle-points drove through the dense layer of plumage and went straight to the bone. She had realized, without a word being exchanged, that Nefer intended to make a contest of the hunt, and she was proving that her competitive instincts were every bit as fierce as his.

Nefer had been badly rattled both by his first failure and by Mintaka's unexpected skill with the bow. Instead of concentrating on his own task, he was distracted by what was happening in the other skiff. Every time he glanced in that direction it seemed to him that dead birds were falling from the sky. This flustered him further. His sense of judgement deserted him, and he began to hurl the sticks too soon or too late. To try to compensate he strained and started to jerk his arm into the stroke instead of using his whole body to launch the club. His right arm tired quickly, so instinctively he shortened the arc of his throwing arm and bent his elbow, almost spraining his wrist as a result.

Usually he could count on hitting with six out of ten throws, now he was missing more than half. His frustration increased. Many of these birds he brought down were only stunned or crippled, and eluded his slave boys by diving under the surface and swimming into the thick papyrus beds, staying submerged beneath the mat of roots and stems. The number of dead birds piled on the floorboards of the skiff grew pitifully slowly. In contrast the happy cries from the other skiff continued almost without a break.

In desperation Nefer discarded his curved sticks and snatched up the heavy war bow, but it was too late. His right arm was almost exhausted by his efforts with the sticks. His draw was laboured and he shot behind the faster birds and in front of the slower ones. Taita watched him flounder ever deeper into the trap he had set for himself. A little humiliation will do him no real harm, he told himself.

With a few words of advice he could have corrected Nefer's mistakes: almost fifty years ago Taita had written the standard texts, not only on chariot handling and tactics but also on archery. For once his sympathy was not wholeheartedly with the boy, and he smiled secretly as he watched Nefer miss again and Mintaka take down two birds from the same flight as they passed over her head.

However, he felt pity for his king when one of Mintaka's slaves swam across the lagoon, and hung on to the side of Nefer's skiff. 'Her Royal Highness Princess Mintaka hopes that mighty Pharaoh might enjoy jasmine-scented days and starry nights filled with the song of the nightingale. However, her boat begins to sink under the weight of her bag, and she is hungry for her breakfast, which she says was promised her these hours past.'

An untimely sally! Taita thought, as Nefer scowled furiously at this impertinence.

'You can give thanks to whatever god of apes and cur-dogs you worship, slave, that I am a man of compassion. Otherwise I would myself hack off your ugly head and send it back to your mistress to answer that jest.'

It was time for Taita to intervene smoothly: 'Pharaoh apologizes for his thoughtlessness, but he was enjoying the sport so much that he forgot the passage of time. Please tell your mistress that we shall all go in to breakfast immediately.'

Nefer glowered at him but put up his bow and made no effort to revoke Taita's decision. The two small boats paddled back towards the island in close formation, so that the piles of duck on the floorboards of each could be readily compared. Not a word was said by the crew of either skiff, but everyone was conscious of the results of the morning's hunt.

'Your Majesty,' Mintaka called across to Nefer, 'I must thank you for a truly diverting morning. I cannot remember when last I enjoyed myself so much.' Her voice was lilting and her smile angelic.

'You are too kind and forgiving.' Unsmilingly Nefer made a regal gesture of dismissal. 'I thought it was rather poor sport.'

He turned half away from her and stared broodingly out at the horizon of reeds and water. Mintaka showed not the least distress at the pointed snub, but turned to her slave girls. 'Come, let us give Pharaoh a few verses of "The Monkey and the Donkey".' One of her maids handed her the lute, and she strummed the opening bar then launched into the first verse of the silly children's song. The maids joined in with the chorus, which involved raucous animal imitations and uncontrolled hilarity.

Nefer's lips twitched with amusement but he had taken up a position of frosty dignity from which he could not retreat. Taita could see that he longed to join in the fun, but once again he had trapped himself.

First love is such unmitigated joy, Taita thought, with sympathetic irony, and to the delight of all the girls in the other boat he improvised a new version of what the monkey said to the donkey, which was much funnier than any that had preceded it. They squealed anew and clapped their hands with delight. Nefer felt himself further excluded and sulked ostentatiously.

They came in to the landing on the island still singing. The bank was cut away steeply, and the mud below it black and glutinous. The boatmen jumped over the side into the knee-deep ooze and held the first skiff steady while the slaves handed the princess and her maids across the gap onto the firm dry ground at the top of the bank.

As soon as they were safely ashore the royal skiff came in and the slaves made ready to hand Nefer across to join Mintaka on the high bank. He waved them aside imperiously. He had suffered enough humiliation for one morning, and he was not about to lower his dignity further by clinging to a pair of half-naked wet slaves for support. He balanced easily on the transom and the entire company watched respectfully for he was a splendid sight. Mintaka tried not to let her emotions show, but she thought he was the most beautiful creature she had ever seen, slim and sleek with his boyish body just starting to take on the hard contours of manhood. Even his haughty, sullen expression enthralled her.

He is of the stuff from which heroes and great pharaohs are moulded, she thought, in a surfeit of romantic ardour. I wish I had not angered him so. It was unkind, and before this day is ended I shall make him laugh again, as Hathor is my witness.

Nefer launched himself across the gap between skiff and landed like a young leopard springing from the branch of an acacia tree. He landed gracefully on the high bank almost within arm's length of where she stood. He paused there conscious of every eye upon him.

Then the bank collapsed beneath him. A chunk of the friable dry clay on which he was standing broke off under his feet. For an aching moment he windmilled his arms, trying to keep his balance, then toppled backwards into the swamp.

Everyone stared down at him in horror, appalled by the spectacle of Royal Egypt sitting waist deep in sticky black Nile mud with a startled expression on his face.

For long moments nobody moved or spoke. Then Mintaka laughed. She had not meant to do so, but it was too much for her self-control and once it began she could not stop herself. It was a delightful, infectious laugh, that none of her maids could resist. They burst into merry squeals and giggles that set the huntsmen and boatmen off. Even Taita joined in, cackling unrestrainedly.

For a moment Nefer looked as though he might burst into tears, but then his anger, kept so long on a tight rein, exploded. He snatched up a handful of thick black mud and hurled it up at the laughing princess.

His humiliation gave strength to his arm and improved his aim while Mintaka was so helpless with mirth that she could neither duck nor dodge and it hit her full in the face. Her laughter died and she stared at Nefer with huge eyes in a running black mask.

It was Nefer's turn to laugh. Still sitting in the swamp he threw back his head and gave vent to all his frustration and humiliation with a howl of mocking laughter. When Pharaoh laughs all the world laughs with him. The slaves, boatmen and huntsmen redoubled their shouts of merriment.

Mintaka recovered swiftly from her shock, and then, without any warning, launched herself over the bank into the attack. She dropped on top of Nefer with all her weight. He was taken so completely by surprise that he could not even draw a full breath before he was driven clean under with her sitting on his head.

He floundered about beneath the surface, trying to get purchase on the muddy bottom but her weight kept him pinned. She had both arms locked around his neck. He tried to throw her off, but she was nimble and slippery as an eel with the coating of mud. With a huge effort he lifted her just long enough to allow him to stick his head out and catch a quick breath, then she plunged him under again. He managed to get on top of her but it took a mighty effort to hold her. She wriggled and kicked with surprising strength. Her tunic had rucked up round her waist and her legs were bare and smooth. She hooked her one leg through his and hung on. Now they were face to face, and he could feel her body warmth through the slippery mud.

Their filthy faces were only inches apart, her hair was streaming down into her eyes, and he was startled to realize that she was grinning at him through the slimy coating. He grinned back, and then they were both laughing. But neither would concede defeat, and they kept up the struggle.

His chest was bare, and her shift so wet and flimsy that it might not have existed. Her bare legs were still hooked around his. He reached down with one hand to prise himself free of their tenacious grip. Unintentionally his right hand came upon a hard round buttock that was wriggling around with great energy.

Nefer became aware of a strange and pleasurable sensation that seemed to suffuse his entire body, and the urgency went out of his efforts to subdue her. He was content to hold her and let her struggle against him while he enjoyed this new and extraordinary feeling.

Abruptly she stopped laughing as she in her turn made a momentous discovery. Between their lower bodies had grown up a protuberance that, only moments before, had not existed. It was so rubbery and large that she could not previously have overlooked it. She pushed her hips out to test its nature, but every time she did that it grew harder and larger. This was something beyond her experience, and in a spirit of discovery she repeated the movement.

She hardly noticed that he had stopped his violent efforts to dislodge her, and that his left arm was wrapped around her upper body. His right hand was cupped around her posterior and when next she pushed out her hips to examine the lump, he imitated her movement thrusting out to meet her and his cupped hand drew her closer still. The lump prodded against her as though it were some small animal with a life of its own.

She had never anticipated the sensation that overcame her. Suddenly that mysterious creature took on an importance far beyond anything she had dreamed of up to that time. Her entire being was filled with a dreamy, pleasurable warmth. Without conscious intent she reached down with one hand to catch hold of it, to capture it as though it were a kitten or a puppy.

Then, with a shock like a blow to her stomach, she remembered the wild tales her slave girls had told her about that thing, and what men did with it. On more than one occasion they had described it to her in startling detail. Up to that time she had discounted these descriptions as pure invention, for they bore no resemblance to the small dangling appendages that her younger brothers carried in that area of their anatomy.

She particularly remembered what Saak, the Numidian slave girl, had told her: 'You won't waste any more prayers on Hathor once you have seen the one-eyed god when he is angry.'

Mintaka threw herself backwards out of Nefer's embrace and sat in the mud staring at him in consternation. Nefer struggled into a sitting position and returned her stare with a bemused air. Both were panting as though they had run a gruelling race.

The guffaws and shrieks of laughter from the high bank slowly petered out as the spectators became aware that something untoward had taken place, and the silence became uncomfortable. Taita covered it up smoothly: 'Your Majesty, if you extend your swim much longer you will offer a fine breakfast to any passing crocodile.'

Nefer jumped up and sloshed across to where Mintaka sat. He lifted her to her feet as gently as if she were made of the most delicate Hurrian glass.

Dripping slime and Nile water, with her hair dangling in a muddy tangle over her face and shoulders, her maids led the princess away to find a clean pool well screened by reeds. When she reappeared some time later she was washed clean of the last traces of slime and ooze.

The maids had brought with them a change of apparel, so Mintaka was resplendent in a clean dry apron embroidered with silk and seed pearls and there were golden bracelets on her arms and a necklace of turquoise and coloured glass at her throat. Her hair, though damp, was combed and plaited neatly.

Nefer hurried to meet her and led her to her a giant kigelia tree under whose spreading branches a breakfast feast was laid out in the shade. At first the young couple were restrained and shy, still overawed by the momentous awakening that they had shared, but soon their natural high spirits reasserted themselves, and they joined in the banter and the chatter, although their eyes kept meeting and almost every word they uttered was aimed at the other.

Mintaka loved to riddle and she challenged him to an exchange. She made it more difficult for Nefer by couching her clues in the Hyksosian language.

'I have one eye and a sharp nose. I run my victim through and through, but I draw no blood. What am I?'

'That's easy!' Nefer laughed triumphantly. 'You are a sewing needle.' And Mintaka threw up her hands in surrender.

'Forfeit!' cried the slave girls. 'Pharaoh is right. Forfeit!'

'A song!' Nefer demanded. 'But not the monkey. We have had enough of him for one day.'

'I shall give you "The Song of the Nile",' she agreed, and when she finished Nefer demanded another. 'Only if you help me, Majesty.'

His voice was a robust tenor but whenever he slipped off-key she covered his mistake and made him sound much better than he was.

Of course Nefer had brought his bao board and stones. Taita had taught him to love it, and he had become expert. When he tired of the singing he inveigled Mintaka into a game.

'You will have to be patient with me. I am a novice,' she warned him, as he set out the board. Bao was an Egyptian game, and this time he expected confidently to outmatch her.

'Don't feel bad about it,' Nefer encouraged her. 'I will coach you.'

Taita smiled because he and Mintaka had wiled away a few hours at bao in the palace of Bubasti when they were nursing her little brother. Within eighteen moves her red stones dominated the west castle and were menacing his centre.

'Have I done the right thing?' she asked sweetly.

Nefer was saved by a hail from the riverbank and looked up to see a galley flying the Regent's pennant coming swiftly down the channel. 'What a pity. Just when the game was getting interesting.' He began to pack up the board with alacrity.

'Can't we hide from them?' Mintaka asked, but Nefer shook his head.

'They have seen us already.' He had been expecting this visitation all morning. Sooner or later the Regent must hear about this illicit outing and send Asmor to bring in his errant charge.

The galley nosed into the bank below where they sat and Asmor sprang ashore. He strode up to the picnic party. 'The Regent is much displeased by your absence. He bids you return at once to the temple, where matters of state await your attention.'

'And I, Lord Asmor, am much displeased by your ill manners.' Nefer tried to retrieve some of his hurt dignity. 'I am not a groom or a house servant to be addressed in that manner, and neither have you shown respect for the Princess Mintaka.' But there was no escaping that he was being treated like a child.

Still, he tried to put a good face on it and invited Mintaka to sail back with him in the skiff while her maids followed in the second vessel. Taita kept tactfully to the bows as this was their first opportunity to hold a private conversation. Not quite certain what to expect of her Nefer was startled when, rather than bothering with polite niceties, she launched immediately into a discussion of the chances of success or failure of the peace conference between their opposing sides. She soon impressed him with her political acumen and her strong views. 'If only we women were allowed to run this world, there would never have been a stupid war in the first place,' she summed up, but he could not let that go unchallenged. They argued animatedly all the way back to the temple. The journey was far too short for Nefer's liking, and as they came into the landing he took her hand. 'I should like to see you again.'

'I should like that well enough,' she replied, without withdrawing her hand.

'Soon,' he insisted.

'Soon enough.' She smiled and gently took back her hand. He felt strangely bereft as he watched her walk away towards the temple.

'My lord, you were present at the divination of the Mazes of Ammon Ra. You know of the dire charge placed upon me by the gods. You know that I can never flout their express wishes and that therefore I am committed to your interest. I had good reason to assist the boy in what was only, after all, a harmless escapade.'

Naja was not so easily placated. He was still furious that Nefer had given Asmor the slip and managed to spend the morning out in the swamps with the Hyksosian princess.

'How can I believe that when you aided Nefer? Nay! You instigated this piece of folly.'

'My lord Regent, you must realize how crucial to our enterprise it is that I retain the young Pharaoh's complete trust. If I appear to flout your orders and authority, then this will make the boy believe that I am still his man. It will make the difficult task laid upon me by the Mazes easier to accomplish.'

Diplomatically Taita turned aside each of the Regent's accusations, until he was no longer ranting but merely grumbling bitterly. 'It must not happen again, Magus. Of course I trust your loyalty. You would be a fool indeed to fly against the express strictures of the gods. However, in future whenever Nefer leaves his quarters he must be accompanied by Asmor and a full escort of his men. I cannot take the chance that he will disappear.'

'My lord, how goes the negotiation with the Shepherd Chieftain? Is there aught that I can do to help you ensure a successful outcome in this matter?' Adroitly Taita set the hounds on a different scent, and Naja followed them.

'Apepi is indisposed. This morning he had a coughing fit so intense he brought up blood and had to leave the conference chamber. Even though he cannot attend himself, he will not let any other speak on his behalf, not even Lord Trok who usually has his confidence. Only the gods know how long it will be before the great bear returns to the conference. We may be forced to waste days or even weeks.'

'What is Apepi's ailment?' Taita asked.

'I do not know—' Naja broke off as an idea occurred to him. 'Why did I not think of it before? With your skills, you will be able to cure whatever ails him. Go to him at once, Magus, and do your utmost.'

As he approached the king's apartments, Taita could hear Apepi from across the courtyard. He sounded like a black-maned lion caught in trap, and the roars grew louder as Taita entered the chamber. As he stepped over the threshold he was almost knocked over by three priests of Osiris fleeing the royal presence in terror, and a heavy bronze bowl crashed into the doorsill. It had been thrown across the room by the Hyksosian king, who sat naked on a muddle of furs and tangled bedsheets in the middle of the chamber.

'Where have you been, Warlock?' he roared, as soon as he saw Taita. 'I sent Trok to find you before dawn. Why do you come only in the middle of the afternoon to save me from those infernal priests with their stinking poisons and hot tongs?'

'I have not seen Trok,' Taita explained, 'but I came as soon as Lord Naja told me you were indisposed.'

'Indisposed? I am not indisposed, Warlock. I am at the point of death.'

'Let us see what can be done to save you.'

Apepi rolled over on to his hairy belly and Taita saw the grotesque purple swelling on his back. It was the size of both the king's bunched fists. When he touched it lightly with a fingertip Apepi bellowed again and broke out in a running sweat. 'Gently, Taita. You are as bad as all the priests in Egypt together.'

'How did this come about?' Taita stepped back. 'What were your symptoms?'

'It started with a bitter pain in my chest.' Apepi touched it. 'Then I started coughing, and the pain became sharper. I felt something move in here, and then the pain seemed to move to my back, and there was this lump.' He reached over his shoulder with one hand to touch the swelling, and groaned again.

Before going further, Taita administered a draught of the Red Shepenn, the sleeping flower. It was a draught that would have knocked a baby elephant off its feet, but though Apepi's eyes crossed and his voice was slurred he was still lucid. Taita palpated the swelling again, and the king groaned but made no other protest.

'There is some foreign object lodged deep in your flesh, my lord,' he stated at last.

'This comes as no great surprise to me, Warlock. Evil men, most of them Egyptians, have been sticking foreign objects into my flesh since I last sucked on my wet-nurse's paps.'

'I would have thought it was an arrowhead or a blade, but there is no entry wound,' Taita mused.

'Use your eyes, fellow. I am covered with them.' The king's hairy carcass was indeed laced and blotched with old battle scars.

'I am going to cut for it,' Taita warned him.

Apepi snarled, 'Do it, Warlock, and stop yapping about it.'

While Taita selected a bronze scalpel from his chest, Apepi picked up his thick leather belt from the floor and doubled a length of it. He bit down on it, and composed himself to the knife.

'Come here!' Taita called to the guards at the door. 'Come and hold the king.'

'Get out, you idiots!' Apepi countermanded the order. 'I need no man to hold me still.'

Taita stood over him, calculated the angle and depth of the cut, then made one swift, deep incision. Apepi let out a muffled bellow from between clamped teeth, but did not move. Taita stood back as a fountain of dark blood and thick yellow pus erupted from the wound. A gut-wrenching stench filled the chamber. Taita laid aside the scalpel and ran his forefinger deep into the opening. Blood bubbled up around it but he felt something hard and sharp in the bottom of the incision. He picked up the ivory forceps that he had placed ready to hand, and probed the opening until he felt the tip strike something solid.

Apepi had stopped yelling, and he lay without movement, except the involuntary shuddering of his back muscles. He breathed with loud porcine snuffles through his nose. At the third attempt Taita gripped the object with the jaws of the forceps, and tugged at it until he felt it give and start to rise towards the surface. It came out – the last inch with a rush of pus and detritus – and Taita held it up so that the light from the window fell upon it.

'An arrowhead,' he announced, 'and it's been in there for a long time. I am amazed it did not mortify years ago.'

Apepi spat out the belt and sat up, chuckling shakily. 'By the hairy testicles of Seueth, I recognize that pretty little bauble. One of your ruffians shot that into me at Abnub ten years ago. At the time, my surgeons said it lay so close to my heart that they could not reach it, so they left it in and I have been gestating it ever since.'

He took the triangle of shaped flint from Taita's bloody fingers and beamed at it with proprietary pride. 'I feel like a mother with her first-born. I will have it made into a charm to wear around my neck on a gold chain. You can weave a spell over it. That should ward off any other missiles. What do you think, Warlock?'

'I am sure it will prove highly efficacious, my lord.' Taita filled his mouth with hot wine and honey from the bowl he had prepared and used a hollow brass tube to syringe out the pus and blood, squirting it deep into the wound.

'What a waste of good wine,' Apepi said, lifted the bowl with both hands and drained the remainder of the contents to the dregs. He hurled it against the far wall and belched. 'Now, as a reward for your services, I have an amusing tale for you, Warlock, that harks back to our last conversation on the tower top at Bubasti.'

'I am listening with fixed attention to your lordship's every word.' Taita bent over him and began to bandage the open wound with linen strips, murmuring the incantation for the binding up of wounds as he did so:

> 'I bind thee up, thing of Seth.
> I stop thy red mouth, thing of great evil.'

Apepi interrupted harshly, 'Trok has offered a lakh of gold as a bride price for Mintaka.'

Taita's hands stopped moving. He stood with the bandage wound half around Apepi's barrel chest. 'What did you answer him, Majesty?'

He was so distressed that the royal title slipped out before he could check himself. This was a dangerous and unforeseen development. 'I told him the bride-price was five lakhs.' Apepi grinned. 'The dog is so hot for my little bitch that his prong is standing up between his eyes and blinding him, but despite the booty he has stolen from me over the years, even he can never find five lakhs.' He belched again. 'Do not worry, Warlock, Mintaka is too valuable to waste on someone like Trok, when I can use her to chain your little pharaoh into my realm.'

He stood up and lifted one thickly muscled arm, trying to peer under it at his bandaged back, like an old rooster with its head under its wing. 'You have made me into a mummy before my time,' he laughed, 'but it's a neat job. Go and tell your regent that I am ready to risk another whiff of his perfume, and I will meet him in the conference chamber again in an hour's time.'

Naja was mollified by Taita's success, and the message from Apepi. Any inkling he might have had of Taita's disloyalty was expunged. 'I have that old rogue Apepi at the brink,' Naja gloated. 'He is about to make even more concessions than he realizes, which is why I was so angry when he broke off the conference and went to his couch.' He was so delighted with himself that he could not remain seated. He jumped up and paced the stone floor. 'How is he, Magus? Did you give him any potion that might cloud his mind?'

'I sent a dose down his gullet that would have stunned a bull buffalo,' Taita assured him. Naja crossed to his cosmetics chest and sprinkled perfume from a green glass vial into the cup of his hand and stroked it down the back of his neck. 'Well, I shall take full advantage.' He started towards the door, then looked back over his shoulder. 'Come with me,' he ordered. 'I might have use of your powers before I am done with Apepi.'

Binding Apepi to the treaty was not the easy task that Naja had suggested it would be. He showed no ill effect from either his wound or from the medication, and he was still ranting, shouting and banging his clenched fist on the table long after the watchman on the temple walls had called the midnight hour. No compromise Naja offered seemed enough for him, and at last even Taita was exhausted by his intransigence. Naja adjourned the conference and, to the crowing of the roosters in the courtyard, staggered off to bed.

The next day, when they met again at noon, Apepi was no more amenable to reason, and if anything the negotiations were even more stormy. Taita used his best influences to calm him, but Apepi allowed himself to be wooed only very slowly. So it was only on the fifth day that the scribes could begin to write down the terms of the treaty on the clay tablets in both the hieratic script and in hieroglyphics, translated into Hyksosian and Egyptian. They laboured late into the night.

Up to this time Naja had excluded Pharaoh Nefer Seti from the conclave. He had kept him occupied with trivial tasks, lessons with his tutors, and practice at arms, meetings with ambassadors and delegations of merchants and priests, all of whom sought concessions or donations. In the end Nefer had rebelled so Naja sent him out hawking and hunting with Apepi's younger sons. These outings were not the most amiable of events, and the first day had ended in a loud dispute over the bag, which had almost led to an exchange of blows.

On the second day, at Taita's suggestion, Princess Mintaka joined the hawking party to act as peace-maker between the two factions. Even her older brothers held her in considerable awe, and deferred to her when at any other time they might have drawn their weapons and rushed to wreak havoc on the Egyptian party. In like manner, when Mintaka was riding beside him in his hunting chariot, Nefer's warlike instincts were lulled. He took little notice of the threatening, boastful behaviour of her loutish siblings and enjoyed her wit and erudition, to say nothing of her close physical presence. In the confined cockpit of the chariot they were often thrown together as they bounced over the rough ground in pursuit of the fleeing gazelle herds. Then Mintaka would grab and hold him, even when the immediate danger was past.

When Nefer returned to the temple after the first outing, he sent for Taita, ostensibly to describe the day's sport to him but he was vague and distracted. Even when Taita questioned him on the performance of his favourite falcon, Nefer showed no great enthusiasm. Until he suddenly remarked dreamily, 'Does it not amaze you, Taita, just how soft and warm girls are?'

By the morning of the sixth day the scribes had completed their work and the fifty tablets of the treaty were ready to be ratified. Now Naja sent for Pharaoh to take part in the proceedings. Likewise, all Apepi's offspring, including Mintaka, were to be present at the ceremony.

Once again the courtyard of the temple was filled with a glittering congregation of royalty and nobility as, in stentorian tones, the Herald Royal began to read out the text of the treaty. Immediately Nefer was absorbed by what it contained. He and Mintaka had discussed it in detail during the days they had spent together, and exchanged significant glances whenever they thought they had detected a flaw or an oversight in the terms. However, these were few, and Nefer was certain that he detected Taita's shadowy influence in many areas of the long document.

At last it was time to affix the seals. To a series of blasts on the rams' horns Nefer pressed his cartouche on to the damp clay and Apepi did the same. It annoyed Nefer to see that the Hyksosian king had usurped the pharaonic prerogative by adopting the sacred cartouche.

While Naja watched, with an enigmatic expression behind his heavy makeup, the new co-rulers of the two kingdoms embraced. Apepi folded Nefer's slim form in his bearlike embrace and the congregation exploded in loud shouts of *'Bak-her! Bak-her!'* Men rattled their weapons against their shields, or hammered the butts of their spears and lances on the stone flags.

Nefer found himself almost overcome by Apepi's powerful bodily odours. One of the Egyptian mores that the Hyksos had not adopted was their concept of personal hygiene. Nefer consoled himself with the thought that if he found the odour repugnant, then Naja was in for a shock when the king bestowed his affection upon him. Gently he eased himself out of the arms of his co-pharaoh, but Apepi beamed down on him in avuncular fashion and placed one hairy paw on his shoulder. Then he turned to face the crowded courtyard. 'Citizens of this mighty land, which is once again united, I pledge you my duty and my patriotic love. In token of these, I offer the hand of my daughter, Princess Mintaka, in marriage to the Pharaoh Nefer Seti who is my co-ruler of this very Egypt. Pharaoh Nefer Seti, who shares with me the double crown of the Upper and Lower Kingdoms, and who shall be my son and whose sons shall be my grandsons!'

There was a long moment of utter stillness in the courtyard as the assembly came to terms with this startling announcement. Then they burst out in even more enthusiastic cries of approval while the drumming of weapons and the stamp of armoured sandals became deafening.

Pharaoh Nefer Seti had an expression on his face that in any lesser mortal would have been described as an idiotic grin. He was gazing across the courtyard at Mintaka. She was frozen, with one hand covering her mouth, as though to stop herself shrieking or squealing, and her eyes were wide open with astonishment as she gazed at her father. Slowly a dark blush suffused her face and shyly she turned her eyes to meet Nefer's. The two gazed at each other as if no other person was in the crowded courtyard.

Taita watched from the foot of Pharaoh's throne. He realized that

Apepi's timing of the announcement had been masterly. Now there was no possible way in which anybody – Naja, Trok or any other – could stand in the way of the marriage.

Taita stood close to Naja's throne. Under his makeup the Regent was plainly in a state of deep consternation, especially aware of his own predicament. If Nefer married the princess he was beyond Naja's reach. He saw the double crown slipping from his grasp. Naja must have sensed Taita's eyes upon him, for he glanced in his direction. For a moment only Taita looked into his soul, and it was as though he had looked into a dry well filled with the live cobras for which the Regent was named. Then Naja veiled his fierce yellow eyes, smiled coolly and nodded in agreement and approval, but Taita knew that he was thinking furiously. However, those thoughts were so swift and complex that even he could not follow them.

Taita turned his head and sought out the burly figure of Lord Trok in the Hyksosian ranks opposite. Unlike the Regent, Trok was making no attempt to disguise his feelings. He was in a black rage. His beard seemed to bristle and his face was swollen with dark blood. He opened his mouth as if to shout an insult or a protest, then closed it, and placed one hand on the hilt of his sword. His knuckles glazed white with the pressure of his grip, and briefly Taita thought that he was about to draw his blade and rush across the courtyard to Nefer's slim figure. With a huge effort he regained control of himself, smoothed down his beard then turned abruptly and pushed his way out of the courtyard. The commotion was such that almost no one noticed him go. Only Apepi watched him with a cynical smile.

As Trok disappeared between the tall granite Hathor pillars, Apepi dropped his hand from Nefer's shoulder and crossed to Naja's throne. He lifted the Regent easily off his cushions and embraced him with even more vigour than he had Pharaoh. His lips were pressed to Naja's ear when he whispered softly, 'No more Egyptian tricks now, my sweet-smelling flower, or I shall ram them as far up your arse as my arm can reach.'

He dropped Naja back on his cushions, then took the throne that had been placed alongside for him. Naja blanched and held a linen pad soaked in perfume to his nose while he gathered his wits. Wave after wave of applause swept over the courtyard. As it died away Apepi slammed his huge paws on the arms of his throne to encourage them to fresh efforts, and the cheering began all over again. He was enjoying himself hugely and he kept them at it until they were almost exhausted.

With the *deshret* crown of lower Egypt on his head, his was the dominant figure. Beside him Nefer, even under the authority of the tall *hedjet* crown, was a mere stripling. At last, after a final burst of applause, Naja rose to his feet and held up both arms. A grateful silence at last descended.

'Let the holy virgin come forward!' Led out in procession by her acolytes from behind the carved screen of the chancel, the high priestess of the temple advanced to the double throne. Before her, two priestesses carried the *pshent* crowns of the double kingdom. While the temple choir sang praises to the goddess the venerable old woman removed the single crowns from the heads of the co-rulers and replaced them with the double crowns, signifying the reunification of Egypt. Then she pronounced her quavering blessing on the two pharaohs and the new land, and retired into the depths of the temple. There was a short pause of indecision, for this was the first time in the long history of Egypt that a ceremony of reunification had been held and there were no established protocols to follow.

Adroitly Naja seized his opportunity. Once again he rose and stepped in front of Apepi. 'On this auspicious and joyous day, we rejoice not only in the joining of the two kingdoms, but also in the betrothal of Pharaoh Nefer Seti and the beautiful Princess Mintaka. Therefore, be it known throughout the two kingdoms that the marriage will take place in this temple on the day that Pharaoh Nefer Seti celebrates his majority, or fulfils one of the conditions to ratify his claim to the crown and rules in his own right without a regent to protect and advise him.'

Apepi frowned and Nefer made a small gesture of dismay, but it was too late. It had been announced in full session and, as regent, Naja spoke with the authority of both crowned heads. Unless Nefer captured his own godbird, or succeeded in running the Red Road, thereby ratifying his claim to the throne, Naja had effectively prevented the marriage taking place for a number of years.

That was a masterly stroke, Taita thought bitterly, but he admired the political acumen behind it. Naja had averted disaster for himself by his quick thinking and timely intervention. Now, while his opposition was off-balance, he went even further. 'On an equally happy note, I invite Pharaoh Apepi and Pharaoh Nefer Seti to celebrate my own marriage to the princesses Heseret and Merykara. This joyous ceremony will take place ten days from now, on the first day of the festival of Isis Ascending at the temple of Isis in the city of Thebes.'

So, in ten days' time Lord Naja will be a member of the Tamosian royal family, and will stand next in succession to Pharaoh Nefer Seti, Taita thought grimly. Now we know, past all doubt, who was the cobra in the nest of the royal falcon on the cliffs of Bir Umm Masara.

By the terms of the treaty of Hathor, Apepi's seat would remain at Avaris and Nefer Seti's at Thebes. Each would govern his former kingdom, but in the name of the biumvirate. Twice every year, at the beginning and the end of the inundation of the Nile, the two kings would hold a combined royal assize at Memphis where all matters concerning the two kingdoms would be dealt with, new laws enacted and legal appeals considered.

However, before the two pharaohs parted, each to take up his seat in his respective capital, Apepi and his train would sail upriver in company with Nefer Seti's fleet to Thebes. There they would attend Lord Naja's double wedding.

The simultaneous embarkation of both trains from the wharf below the temple was a chaotic affair that took up most of the morning. Taita mingled with the throng of boatmen and dockers, slaves and important passengers. Even he was amazed by the mountains of luggage and equipment piled upon the beach, waiting to be loaded on the lighters, feluccas and galleys. Rather than drive the long, rough road back downriver, the regiments of both Thebes and Avaris had broken down their chariots and were loading them and the horses on to the lighters. This contributed greatly to the confusion on the riverbank.

For once Taita was not the centre of attraction: there was work to keep everyone fully occupied. Occasionally a man would look up from what he was doing, recognize him and ask for his blessing, or a woman would bring him a sick child to tend. However, he was able to work his way gradually along the beach, casually looking out for the chariots and equipment of Lord Trok's regiment. He recognized them by their green and red pennants, and as he approached he made out the unmistakable figure of Trok among his men. Taita edged closer and saw him standing over a pile of equipment and weapons, haranguing his lance-bearer: 'You brainless baboon, how have you packed my kit? That is my favourite bow lying there unprotected. Some oaf is sure to drive the horses over it.' His mood of the previous day had not improved, and he stamped away down the wharf, lashing out with his chariot whip at any unfortunate who stood in his way. Taita watched him pause to talk to another of his sergeants, then take the path up to the temple.

As soon as he had disappeared Taita approached the lance-bearer. The trooper was stripped to breech-clout and sandals, and as he stooped over one of the chests of Trok's equipment and staggered with it to the waiting lighter, Taita saw the distinctive circular rash of the ring-worm on his naked back. The lance-bearer handed up the chest to a boatman on the deck of the galley then came back. For the first time he noticed Taita standing nearby and touched his own breast with a clenched fist, saluting respectfully. 'Come here, soldier.' Taita called him across. 'How long have you had the itch on your back?'

Instinctively the fellow twisted up one arm between his shoulder-blades, and scratched himself so vigorously that he drew blood. 'Cursed thing has been bothering me ever since we captured Abnub. I think it's a gift from one of those dirty Egyptian whores—' He broke off guiltily. Taita knew that he was speaking about a woman he had raped during the capture of the city. 'Forgive me, Warlock, we are allies and fellow countrymen now.'

'That is why I will attend to your affliction, soldier. Go up to the temple, ask at the kitchens for a jar of lard and bring it to me. I will mix an ointment for you.' Taita sat down on the pile of Trok's luggage and equipment, and the lance-bearer hurried away down the beach. Among the luggage were three war bows – Trok had been unfair in his accusations for each of the bows was unstrung and carefully wrapped in its leather cover.

Taita's seat was a stack of wooden chests. This was not by chance for he had seen that the top chest bore the seal of Grippa, the Avaris fletcher who made arrows for all the high-ranking Hyksosian officers. Taita remembered that he had discussed Grippa's work with Mintaka. He slipped the little dagger from the sheath under his *chiton*, cut the cord that secured the lid, and lifted it. A layer of dry straw protected the arrows, and under it they were packed alternately, flint head to gaudy red and green feathers. Taita picked one out and turned it in his fingers.

The carved signet leaped out at him, the stylized head of the leopard with the hieratic letter T held in its snarling jaws. The arrow was identical to the ones he had found in the quiver at the scene of Pharaoh's murder. It was the last thread in the fabric of treason and treachery. Naja and Trok were linked inextricably in the bloody plot, whose whole shape as yet he could only guess at.

Taita slipped the incriminating arrow under the folds of his *chiton* and closed the lid of the chest. Deftly he retied the cord, and waited for the lance-bearer to return.

The old soldier was volubly grateful for Taita's ministrations, then went on to plead for a further favour: 'A friend of mine has the Egyptian pox, Magus. What should he do about it?' It always amused Taita how the Hyksos called it the Egyptian pox, and the Egyptians returned the compliment. It seemed that no man ever contracted it himself but always had a friend suffering from the disease.

The wedding ceremony and feast to celebrate the marriage of Lord Naja to the two Tamosian princesses was the most lavish ever recorded. Taita recalled that it far exceeded in splendour any of those of either Pharaoh Tamose or his father Pharaoh Mamose, both divine sons of Ra, may they live for ever.

To the common citizens of Thebes, Lord Naja gave five hundred head of prime oxen, two lighters of millet from the state granaries, and five thousand large clay pots of the best beer. The feasting continued for a week but even the hungry mouths of Thebes could not devour such quantities of food in so short a time. The remains of the millet and the meat, which they smoked to preserve it, fed the city for months thereafter. However, the beer was another matter: they drank it in the first week.

The wedding was celebrated in the temple of Isis before both pharaohs, six hundred priests and four thousand invited guests. As they entered the temple each guest was presented with a commemorative carved jewel, ivory, amethyst, coral or some other precious gemstone, with the guest's own name engraved upon it between the names of the Regent and his brides.

The two brides came to meet their groom on one of the state carriages drawn by the sacred white hump-backed oxen, driven by naked Nubian coachmen. The road was strewn with palm fronds and flowers, and a chariot drove ahead of the wedding coach throwing rings of silver and copper to the deliriously happy crowds that lined the way. Their enthusiasm was due in no small measure to Lord Naja's largesse of beer.

The girls were clad in cloud-white linen of gossamer quality, and little Merykara was almost weighed down by the gold and jewels that covered her small body. Her tears had cut runnels through the kohl and antimony makeup. Heseret squeezed her hand tightly to try to console her.

When they reached the temple they were met by the two pharaohs as they disembarked from the great state coach. Nefer whispered to Merykara, as he led her into the nave of the temple, 'Don't cry, little kitten. Nobody is going to hurt you. You will be back in the nursery before your bedtime.'

To register his protest at the marriage of his sisters, Nefer had tried to avoid the duty of leading his little sister into the sanctuary, but Taita had reasoned with him. 'We cannot prevent it happening, although you know how we have tried. Naja is determined. It would be cruel of you not to be there to comfort her in this the most dread episode of her short life.' Reluctantly Nefer had acquiesced.

Close behind them Apepi led Heseret. She was as lovely as a nymph of paradise in her snowy robes and glittering jewellery. Months ago she had come to terms with the fate the gods had apportioned her and her initial dismay and horror had slowly given way to curiosity and a sneaking anticipation. Lord Naja was a magnificent-looking man, and her nurses, handmaidens and playmates had discussed him in avid detail, endlessly pointing out his more obvious virtues and, with breathless giggles, speculating in salacious detail on his hidden attributes.

Perhaps as a consequence of these discussions Heseret had recently been experiencing intriguing dreams. In one she had run naked through a lush garden on the bank of the river pursued by the Regent. When she looked back at him over her shoulder she saw that he also was naked, but that he was human only as far as his waist. From there down he was a horse, exactly like Nefer's favourite stallion, Stargazer. When he was with the mares, she had often seen Stargazer in the same amazing condition as the Regent now exhibited, and she had always found herself strangely moved by the sight. However, just as the Regent caught up with her and reached out a bejewelled hand to seize her the dream ended abruptly and she found herself sitting bolt upright on her mattress. Without realizing what she was doing she reached down and touched herself. Her fingers came away wet and slippery. She was so disturbed that she could not sleep again and pick up the dream where it had broken off, although she tried hard to do so. She wanted to know the outcome of this enthralling experience. The next morning she felt restless and irritable, and took out her bad temper on all those around her. From that time onwards her girlish interest in Meren began to fade. She saw him seldom, these days, anyway: since the death of his grandfather at Lord Naja's hands his fortune had been forfeit, and the family had fallen into disgrace. She came to realize that he was an impecunious boy, a common soldier without favour or prospects. Lord Naja's social rank almost matched hers, and his fortune far exceeded her own.

Now she kept a demure and chaste demeanour as Apepi led her down the long hypostyle gallery of the temple to the sanctuary. Lord Naja was waiting there for the bridal party, and although he was surrounded by courtiers and officers in fine costumes and magnificent uniforms, Heseret had eyes for him alone.

He wore a plumed headdress of ostrich feathers to emulate the god Osiris and stood tall above even Asmor and Lord Trok, who flanked him. As Heseret approached him she became aware of his perfume. It was a blend of essences of blooms from a land beyond the Indus and also contained the precious ambergris, found only rarely on the seashore, a bounty from the gods of the ocean depths. The aroma stirred her, and she took the hand that Naja offered her without hesitation, and looked up into those fascinating yellow eyes.

When Naja offered his other hand to Merykara she burst into loud sobs, and it was all Nefer could do to comfort her. She sobbed softly at intervals during the long ceremony that followed.

When at last Lord Naja broke the jars of Nile water to mark the culmination of the ceremony, the crowds gasped with amazement: the waters of the great river, on whose bank the temple stood, turned a brilliant blue. Around the first bend Naja had caused a line of barges to be anchored from bank to bank, and at a signal relayed from the temple roof they had released jars of dye into the waters. The effect was breathtaking, for blue was the colour of the Tamosian dynasty. Naja was declaring to the world his new pharaonic connections.

Watching from the roof of the western enclosure, Taita saw the river change colour and shuddered with a sense of foreboding. It seemed that for a moment the sun darkened in the tall Egyptian sky while the blue waters took on the colour of blood. But when he looked up there was no cloud, no passing flock of birds to dull its rays, and when he looked down the waters were once more cerulean blue.

Now Naja is of the blood royal, and Nefer is stripped of even that protection. I am the only shield he has, and I am one man and old. Will my powers be enough to turn away the cobra from the fledgling falcon? Give me your strength, divine Horus. You have been my buckler and my lance down all the years. Do not forsake me now, mighty god.

Lord Naja and his two new wives rode back in splendour down the sacred avenue guarded by the ranks of granite lions to the palace gates. There they dismounted and went in procession through the gardens to the banquet hall. Most of the guests had arrived ahead of them, and had been sampling the wine from the vineyards of the temple of Osiris. The commotion as the wedding party entered was deafening. Naja led a new young wife on each hand. The trio processed with dignity through the throng and briefly inspected the heaps of gifts stacked in the centre of the banquet hall, which were fitting to such a momentous occasion. Apepi had sent a chariot covered in gold leaf. It was so brilliant that even in the dimly lit hall it was difficult to look at it directly. From Babylon King Sargon had sent a hundred slaves, each bearing a sandalwood chest filled with jewellery, precious stones or golden vessels. They knelt before the Regent and offered their burdens. Naja touched each as a sign of acceptance. Pharaoh Nefer Seti, at the suggestion of Lord Naja, had deeded to his new brother-in-law five expansive estates on the riverbank. The scribes had calculated that all these treasures were worth upward of three lakhs of pure gold. The Regent had become almost as rich as his pharaoh.

When the connubial trio took their seats at the head of the wedding board, the palace cooks laid a feast before them and their guests that consisted of forty different dishes served by a thousand slaves. There were trunks of elephants, tongues of the buffalo and fillets of Nubian mountain goat, the flesh of wild boar and warthog, gazelle and Nubian ibex, of monitor lizard and python, of crocodile and hippopotamus, oxen and sheep. Every type of Nile fish was served, from barbelled catfish, whose flesh ran with rich yellow fat, to white-fleshed perch and bream. From the northern sea there was tuna, shark, grouper, crayfish and crab, sent up by fast river galley from the delta. The birds of the air, including mute swans, three types of goose, numerous varieties of duck, and lark, bustard, partridge and quail, were roasted, baked or grilled, marinated in wine or wild honey, or stuffed with herbs and spices from the Orient. The aromatic smoke from the fires and the smell of cooking was savoured by the crowds of beggars and commoners at the palace gates, and by those who lined the far bank of the river, or filled the feluccas in mid-stream all vying for a closer view of the festivities.

To entertain the guests there were musicians and jugglers, acrobats and animal trainers. Maddened by the uproar, one of the huge brown bears broke its chain and escaped. A party of Hyksosian nobles, led by Lord Trok, pursued it through the gardens with drunken shouts and slew the cringing animal on the riverbank.

King Apepi was titillated by the suppleness and athleticism of two of the Assyrian female acrobats: so he picked up one under each arm and carried them, kicking and squealing, from the dance floor into the private quarters of the palace. When he returned he confided to Taita, 'One of them, the pretty one with long curls, was a boy. I was so surprised when I discovered what he had between his legs that I almost let him escape.' He roared with laughter. 'Luckily I did not, for he was by far the most succulent of the two.'

By nightfall most of the guests were drunk or so stuffed with food that few could stand when Lord Naja and his brides retired. As soon as they were in the private apartments Naja called for the nursemaids to take Merykara to her own quarters. 'Treat her gently,' he warned them. 'The poor child is asleep on her feet.'

Then he took Heseret by the hand and led her to his own sumptuous apartments, which overlooked the river. The Nile's dark waters were spangled with the reflection of the golden stars.

As soon as they entered the chamber, Heseret's handmaidens took her behind the screen of bamboo to remove her wedding dress and jewellery.

Covering the marriage bed was a sheepskin that had been bleached shining white. Lord Naja inspected it carefully, and when he was assured of its perfection he went out on to the terrace and inhaled deeply the cool river air. A slave brought him a bowl of spiced wine, and he sipped appreciatively. It was the first he had allowed himself all evening. Naja knew that one of the most vital secrets of survival was to keep his wits clear in the presence of his enemies. He had watched all the other guests drink themselves into a pitiful state. Even Trok, in whom he placed so much trust and confidence, had succumbed to his animal nature – Naja had last seen him puking copiously into a bowl held for him by a pretty Libyan slave girl. When he had finished Trok had wiped his mouth on the girl's skirts then lifted them over her head, pushed her down on the grassy sward and mounted her from behind. Naja's fastidious nature had been offended by this display.

He returned to the chamber as two slaves staggered in, bearing between them a cauldron of hot water, in which floated lotus petals. Naja set aside the wine bowl and went to bathe. One of the slaves dried and braided his hair, while the other brought him a clean white robe. He dismissed them and returned to the marriage bed. He lay upon it, stretched out his long, elegant limbs and rested his braided head on the gold-inlaided ivory headrest.

From the far end of the chamber came the rustle of clothing and feminine whispers. Once he recognized Heseret's giggle and the sound aroused him. He propped himself up on one elbow and looked across at the bamboo screen. The gaps in it were just large enough to afford him tantalizing glimpses of pale smooth skin.

Power and political aspiration were the main reasons for this marriage, but they were not the only ones. Although he was a warrior by trade and an adventurer by disposition, Naja had a voluptuous and sensual nature. For years he had watched Heseret surreptitiously, and his interest had increased at each stage in her journey towards womanhood; from infancy through gawky girlhood, and then that tantalizing period when her breast buds had bloomed and the puppy fat had melted away, to leave her body delicate and graceful. The smell of her had changed too: whenever she was close he had detected the faint sweet musk of womanhood, which enthralled him.

Once when out hawking Naja had come across Heseret and two of her friends collecting lotus blooms to plait into garlands. She had looked up at him as he stood above her on the riverbank, and her wet skirts had clung to her legs so the skin shone through the fine linen. She had brushed the hair off her cheeks with an innocent gesture that was nevertheless intensely erotic. Even though her expression had remained serious and chaste, the slanted eyes had hinted at a sly, lascivious streak in her that had fascinated him. This revelation had lasted only a moment before she had called to her friends and splashed to the bank then raced away across the grassy field towards the palace. He had watched her long wet legs glinting, the round buttocks oscillating and changing shape beneath the linen skirt, and suddenly his breath had come short and fast.

At the memory his loins stirred and quickened. He longed for her to come out from behind the screen, but perversely he wanted to delay the moment so that he could savour the anticipation to the full. It happened at last. Two of the handmaidens led her out, then slipped away quietly leaving her standing alone in the middle of the floor.

Her nightrobe fell from her throat to her ankles. It was of a rare and precious silk from the eastern lands, creamy in colour and so fine that it seemed to float around her like river mist, stirring with every breath she took. There was an oil lamp on a tripod in the corner behind her, and the soft yellow light shone through the silk, highlighting the curves of her hips and shoulders so they shone softly as polished ivory. Her bare feet and her hands were dyed with henna. Her face had been washed clean of makeup so the young blood beneath the flawless skin delicately rouged her cheeks, and her lips trembled as though she were on the point of tears. She hung her head in an appealingly girlish manner and looked up at him from under lowered lashes. Her eyes were green, and his blood thrilled again as he detected that same wicked glint in them that had originally intrigued him.

'Turn round,' he said gently, but his throat was as dry as if he had sucked the juice from a green persimmon. She obeyed him, but with a dream-slow movement, rolling her hips, her belly gleaming softly through the silk. Her buttocks undulated, round and lustrous as ostrich eggs, and the shining tresses of her hair swayed.

'You are beautiful.' His voice caught. Now a hint of a smile lifted the corners of her lips, and she wet them with the tip of a tongue that was as pink as that of a kitten. 'I am glad that my lord regent finds me so.'

He rose from the bed and went to her. He took her hand, which was warm and soft in his. He led her to the bed, and she followed him without hesitation. She knelt upon the white sheepskin and hung her head so that her hair veiled her face. He stood over her and leaned forward until his lips touched it. She exuded the elusive fragrance of a healthy young woman in the first flush of physical arousal. He stroked her hair and she looked up at him through the dark curtain. Then he parted the tresses and cupped her chin with one hand. Slowly, teasing himself, he lifted her face.

'You have eyes like Ikona,' she whispered. Ikona was his tame leopard: the beast had always frightened and fascinated her. She felt those same emotions now for he was as sleek and feline as the great cat, his eyes yellow and implacable. With a woman's instinct she sensed the cruelty and ruthlessness in them, which evoked in her emotions that she had never before experienced. 'You also are beautiful,' she whispered, and it was true. In this moment she realized that he was the most beautiful creature she had ever known.

He kissed her and his mouth startled her. It tasted of some ripe fruit she had never eaten before, and quite naturally she opened her own mouth to savour it. His tongue was as flickeringly quick as a snake's, but it did not revolt her. She closed her eyes and touched it with her own. Then he placed one of his hands behind her head and pressed his mouth harder against hers. She was so lost in his kiss that when his hand closed over her breast she was unprepared. Her eyes flew open and she gasped. She tried to pull away but he held her, and now he caressed her with a gentle but skilful touch that stilled her fears. He teased out her nipple, and the sensation flowed through her body, rippling down her arms to her fingertips. She felt a sharp disappointment when he took away his hand. He lifted her to her feet so she stood on the sheepskin above him with her breasts at the level of his face.

With a single movement he swept off her silken robe and let it fall to the floor. Then, as he sucked her engorged nipple deep into his mouth, she cried aloud. At the same time one of his hands came up between her thighs and cupped the soft nest of dark fluff.

She had not the slightest inclination to resist what he was doing to her. Instead she surrendered herself to it. From what her slave girls had told her she had been terrified that he might hurt her, but his hands, though swift and strong, were gentle. He seemed to know her body better than she did herself, and he played upon it with such skill that she found herself drawn deeper and deeper, faster and faster beneath the surface, sinking away and drowning in this sea of new sensations.

She surfaced only once more when suddenly she opened her eyes and found that his own robe was gone, and that he stood over her naked. She remembered the dream in which he had had the same thing down there as Stargazer, the stallion. She looked down in trepidation, but it was nothing like the dream: it was smooth and rosy, yet hard as bone, perfect and clean in form as a temple column. Her fears evaporated and once again she surrendered herself to his hands and his mouth. There was only one sharp moment of stinging pain, but that was much later, and it was fleeting, replaced almost as swiftly by an unaccustomed but wonderful feeling of fullness. Then later still she heard him cry out above her. The sound triggered something in her own body, turning almost unbearable pleasure into its own kind of pain, and she held him with all the strength of her encircling arms and legs and cried out with him.

Twice more during that too-short enchanted night he forced her to cry out in that same frenzy of pleasure, and when the dawn suffused the chamber with its rose and silver light she lay still in his arms. She felt as though the life force had been drawn out of her, as though her bones had turned soft and malleable as river clay, and there was a soft ache deep in her belly that she savoured.

He slipped out of her arms and she just had the strength left to protest, 'Don't go. Oh! Please don't go, my lord. My beautiful lord.'

'Not for long,' he whispered and gently drew out the sheepskin from under her. She saw the stains upon the snowy fleece, the blood bright as the petals of a rose. She had experienced only that brief pain at the piercing of her womanhood.

He carried the fleece to the terrace and she watched him through the doorway as he hung it over the parapet wall. From far below there came the faint sound of cheering as the citizens waiting below saw this proof of her virginity displayed. She cared nothing for the approbation of the peasant hordes, but watched the naked back of her new husband and felt her chest and her aching womb swell with love for him. As he came back to her she held out both arms to him.

'You are magnificent,' she whispered, and fell asleep in his arms. Much later she came gradually awake and found that her whole being was filled with a lightness and a feeling of joy that she had never known before. At first she was not certain of the source of her well-being. Then she felt his hard muscular warmth stir in her arms.

When she opened her eyes he was watching her with his strange yellow ones, and he smiled gently. 'What a splendid queen you would make,' he said softly. This he meant sincerely. During the night he had discovered in her qualities that he had not before suspected. He sensed that he had found in her someone whose desires and instincts were in perfect harmony with his own.

'And what a splendid pharaoh you would make for this very Egypt.' She smiled back at him and stretched voluptuously. Then she laughed softly, reached up and touched his cheek, 'But that could never happen.' She stopped smiling abruptly and asked softly, seriously, 'Could it?'

'There is only one thing that stands in our way,' he answered. He did not have to say anything more, for he saw a sly acquisitive expression bloom in her eyes. She was entirely in step with him.

'You are the dagger, and I shall be the scabbard. No matter what you ask of me, I shall never fail you, my beautiful lord.'

He laid one finger on her lips, which were inflamed and swollen with his kisses. 'I see clearly that there is little need of words between us, for our hearts beat in unison.'

King Apepi's entourage remained in Thebes for almost a month after the wedding. They were the guests of Pharaoh Nefer Seti and of his regent, and were entertained in royal fashion. Taita encouraged this delay. He felt certain that Naja would take no action against Nefer while Apepi and his daughter were in Thebes.

The royal visitors spent their days hunting or hawking, visiting the numerous temples on both banks of the river dedicated to all the gods of Egypt, or in tournaments between the regiments of the northern and southern kingdom. There were chariot races, archery contests, and foot races. There were even swimming races, in which the chosen champions swam the full width of the Nile for a prize of a golden statue of Horus.

Out in the desert they hunted gazelle and oryx from speeding chariots, or hawked for the great bustards with the swift Sakers. No royal falcons remained in the palace mews, for they had been released into the wild during the funeral rites of Nefer's father. Along the riverbank the guests hawked for herons and duck, and speared the huge whiskered catfish in the shallows. They hunted the river horse, the mighty hippopotamus, from the fleet war galleys, with Nefer at the tiller of his own galley named the *Eye of Horus*. Princess Mintaka stood beside him and shrieked with excitement as the great beasts broke the surface, their backs studded with spears, and the waters turned pink with their blood.

During these days Mintaka was often at Nefer's side. She rode in his chariot when they hunted and handed him the lance when they drove up alongside a galloping oryx. She carried her own falcon on her arm as they quartered the reed beds for heron. At the hunting picnics in the desert, she sat beside him and prepared little treats for him. She selected the sweetest grapes for him and peeled them with her long, tapered fingers and then popped them into his mouth.

Every evening there were banquets in the palace and there also she sat at his left side, the traditional place for a woman so that she never blocked her man's sword arm. She made him laugh with her wry wit and she was a marvellous mimic: she imitated Heseret to perfection, simpering and rolling her eyes, and speaking of 'my husband, the Regent of Egypt' in the portentous tones as Heseret now employed.

Though they tried, they could never be completely alone. Naja and Apepi saw to that. When Nefer appealed to Taita for assistance, not even he could manoeuvre a secret meeting for them. It never occurred to Nefer that Taita did not exert himself to do so, or that he was as set on keeping them innocent as the others were. Long ago Taita had engineered a tryst for Tanus and his beloved Lostris, and the consequences still echoed like thunder down the years. When Nefer and Mintaka played bao there was always an audience of slave girls, while courtiers and the ubiquitous Lord Asmor hovered nearby. Nefer had learned his lesson well, and no longer underrated Mintaka's skill on the board. He played against her as if he were matched against Taita. He came to learn her strengths, and to recognize her few weaknesses: she was always overprotective of her home castle, and if he pressed her hard in that quadrant she might sometimes offer an opening in her flanks. Twice he exploited this and broke up her defence, but the third time he discovered too late that she had anticipated his tactic and had laid a trap. When he had exposed his west castle she rammed a phalanx through the gap, and laughed so deliciously when he was forced to capitulate that he almost, but not quite, forgave her. Their bouts became ever more keenly contested and in the end were of epic proportions, so that even Taita spent hours watching them and occasionally nodding in approval or smiling his thin, ancient smile.

Their love was so apparent that it cast a glow upon all those around them, and wherever they went together there were smiles and laughter. As Nefer's chariot sped through the streets of Thebes with Mintaka on the footplate as his lance-bearer, her dark hair flowing in the wind like a banner, the goodwives ran out of their houses and the men paused from their labours to shout greetings and good wishes. Even Naja smiled benignly upon them, and none would have believed that he fiercely resented the attention of the populace having been diverted from his own nuptials and brides.

Lord Trok was the only sombre presence at the hunting parties, the picnics in the countryside and the banquets in the palace.

Their time together sped by too fast.

'There are always so many people around us,' Nefer whispered over the bao board. 'I long to be alone with you even for just a few minutes. There are only three more days before you have to return to Avaris with your father. It might be months, even years, before we meet again, and there is so much I want to tell you, but not with all these eyes and ears pointed at us like nocked arrows.'

She nodded, then reached across and moved a stone that in his preoccupation he had overlooked. He glanced down and almost discounted it, until he realized that his west castle was now under a forked attack. Three moves later she had broken his front. He kept up the losing battle for a while longer, but his forces were in disarray and the outcome was inevitable. 'You caught me when I was distracted by other things,' he groused. 'So much like a woman.'

'Your Majesty, I make no claims to being anything else than a woman.' She used his title with an irony that bit like the jewelled dagger she wore on her belt. Then she leaned close and whispered, 'If I were alone with you, would you promise to respect my chastity?'

'I swear by the wounded eye of the great god Horus that I will never, as long as I live, cause you shame,' he told her earnestly.

She smiled at him. 'My brothers will not be overpleased to hear that. They would welcome an excuse to slit your throat.' She slanted those magnificent dark eyes at him. 'Or, failing your throat, some other part of you might satisfy them.'

Their chance came the next day. One of the royal huntsmen came in from the hills above the village of Dabba to report that a lion had come out of the eastern wilderness and raided the cattle pens during the night. It had jumped the stockade and killed eight of the terrified beasts. In the dawn a horde of villagers, brandishing burning torches, blowing horns, beating drums and screaming wildly, had driven it off.

'When did this happen?' asked Naja.

'Three nights ago, Your Grace.' The man was prostrate before the throne. 'I came upriver as soon as I could, but the current runs strongly and the winds were flukey.'

'What has happened to the beast?' King Apepi interrupted eagerly.

'It has gone back into the hills, but I have sent two of my best Nubian trackers to follow it.'

'Did any man see it? What size is it? Lion or lioness?'

'The villagers say that it is a large male, with a full mane, thick and black.'

Up until the last sixty years lions had been almost unheard-of in the lands along the river. They were royal game, and had been hunted ruthlessly by successive pharaohs, not only because of the damage they inflicted on the livestock of the peasant farmers but also because they were the most sought-after trophy of the royal hunt.

During the long, bitter struggle of the Hyksos wars the pharaohs of both kingdoms had been preoccupied and the lions had been hunted seldom. In addition the human corpses left on the battlefields had provided an easy source of food for the lion prides. In the last few decades they had flourished, their numbers had increased many-fold and so had their boldness.

'I will have the chariots loaded on to the boats at once,' Apepi decided. 'With the state of the river we can be at Dabba early tomorrow morning.' He grinned and punched his fist into the horny palm of his sword hand. 'By Seueth, I would like a chance at this old black-mane. Since I have had to give up killing Egyptians, I am starved for real sport.'

Naja frowned at the sally. 'Majesty, you are expected to sail back to Avaris the day after tomorrow morning.'

'You are right, Regent. However, most of our baggage is already loaded and the fleet lies ready to depart. Moreover, Dabba lies on my way homewards. I can afford a day or two to join in the hunt.'

Naja hesitated. He was not so addicted to the hunt that he wished to neglect the numerous affairs of state that awaited his attention. He had looked forward to the departure of Apepi, whose boisterous, uncouth presence in Thebes had long since palled. Also he had other plans afoot, which could only be furthered once Apepi had left Thebes. Yet he could not allow the Hyksosian Pharaoh to hunt alone in the Upper Kingdom. Not only would it be churlish to do so, but it would be impolitic to let Apepi behave in the southern kingdom as though he had sole right to it.

'Your Majesty,' Nefer intervened, before Naja could compose a suitable refusal, 'we will join in the hunt with the greatest of pleasure.' He saw an opportunity for magnificent sport, for he had never had the chance to run down a lion in his chariot and test his own courage by standing down the charge. But, a hundred times more important, the hunt might also delay Mintaka's dreaded departure. This happy circumstance might even provide the opportunity that had so far eluded them of spending a short time alone. Before Naja could prevent him Nefer had turned to the huntsman, who still lay with his forehead pressed to the tiled floor. 'Well done, my good fellow. The chamberlain will give you a gold ring for your trouble. Return to Dabba at once in the fastest felucca in our fleet. Make ready for our arrival. We will go after this beast in full array.'

Nefer's only cause for regret was that Taita would not be with him during his first lion hunt to offer counsel and advice. The old man had disappeared into the wilderness on another of his periodic and mysterious forays, and no one knew when he would return.

In the early morning of the next day the hunting party disembarked on the bank of the river below the village of Dabba. Then all the horses and twenty chariots were off-loaded from the small convoy of lighters and galleys. While this was being done, the lance-bearers sharpened the spear blades, restrung the hunting bows and checked the arrows for balance and straightness. While the horses were watered, fed and groomed, the hunters ate a hearty breakfast that the villagers had provided.

The mood was ebullient, and Apepi sent for the tracker who had returned from the hills to report. 'It is a very big lion. The biggest I have ever seen east of the river,' the man told them, increasing their excitement.

'You actually saw him?' Nefer demanded. 'Or did you only read his sign?'

'I saw him clearly but only at a distance. He stands as tall as a horse and he walks with the dignified tread of a monarch. His mane waves like a sheaf of *dhurra* millet stalks in the wind.'

'By Seth, the fellow is a poet,' Naja sneered. 'Stick to the facts and eschew the fine words, knave.'

The huntsman touched his heart with his fist to show his contrition, and went on with his report in a subdued tone. 'He lay up yesterday in a wooded wadi two leagues from here, but he left at the fall of night to prowl. It is four days since he last fed and he is hungry and hunting again. During the night he tried to drag down an oryx, but it kicked him off and ran free.'

'Where do you hope to find him today?' Nefer asked, in a kinder voice than Naja had used. 'If he hunted he will be thirsty as well as hungry. Where will he drink?'

The huntsman looked at him with respect, not only for his royal eminence but also for the knowledge of the wild he displayed. 'After his attempt to bring down the oryx, he went into stony ground where we could no longer read his tracks.' Apepi made a gesture of annoyance, and the huntsman hurried on, 'But I expect him to have drunk this morning at a small oasis. A hidden place little known to any except the Bedouin.'

'How long to reach this place?' Nefer asked, and the man swept his arm through part of an arc, indicating the sun's progress over the passage of three hours.

'Then we have little time to waste.' Nefer smiled at him, and turned away to shout at the troop captain of the chariots, 'How much longer, soldier?'

'All is ready, Majesty.'

'Sound the mount up,' Nefer ordered, and the ram's horns blared as the hunters scattered to the waiting chariots. Mintaka walked at Nefer's side. In these informal circumstances all royal dignity was forgotten, and they were simply boy and girl on an exciting outing. Lord Trok spoiled the illusion: just as he leaped into his own chariot and gathered up the reins, he called across to King Apepi, 'Your Majesty, it is not wise to let the Princess ride with an untried boy. This is not a gazelle we are hunting now.'

Nefer froze and stared at Trok with outrage. Mintaka laid a small hand on his bare arm. 'Do not provoke him. He is a formidable fighter with a terrible temper, and if you challenge him even your rank will not protect you.'

Nefer shrugged off her arm furiously. 'My honour will not allow me to ignore such an insult.'

'Please, my heart, for my sake, let it pass.' It was the first time she had used such an endearment. She did it deliberately, knowing the effect it must have on him: she was already learning to manage his volatile moods and tempers with a loving woman's instinct far beyond her years and experience. In the instant Nefer forgot Trok and the slur to his honour.

'What did you call me?' he asked huskily.

'You are not deaf, my darling.' He blinked at this second endearment. 'You heard quite clearly.' And she smiled into his face.

Apepi bawled into the silence, 'Do not worry, Trok. I am sending my daughter to take care of Pharaoh. He will be quite safe.' He gave a snort of laughter and shook the reins. As his team jumped forward he shouted again, 'We have wasted half the morning here. Huntsmen, take up the chase!'

Nefer steered his chariot behind Apepi, cutting steeply past the noses of Lord Trok's team. As he went by he gave Trok a cold glare, and told him, 'You are impudent. Rest assured that this is not the end of it. We will speak further on this matter, Lord Trok.'

'I fear he is now your enemy, Nefer,' Mintaka murmured. 'Trok has an evil reputation and an even more evil temper.'

Led by the royal huntsman, who rode bareback astride a scrubby but tough little pony, the hunting column climbed into the bare, stony hills. They went at the trot, saving the horses, letting them blow after every steep gradient. Within the hour they found one of the Nubian trackers waiting for them on a hilltop, and he ran down to report to the huntsman. They spoke to each other earnestly, then the huntsman trotted back to report to the royal party. 'The Nubians have cast the hills but without finding the spoor again. They are sure that he will drink at the waterhole, but not wanting to disturb him they have waited for us to catch up.'

'Lead us to the water,' Apepi ordered, and they went on.

Before midday they came down into a shallow valley. They were not far from the river, but this seemed like the deep desert, waterless and forbidding. The huntsman trotted alongside Apepi's chariot and said, 'The waterhole is at the head of this valley. The beast will probably be lying up nearby.'

Naturally Apepi, the old warrior, took command, and Nefer did not dispute his right to do so. 'We will split into three squadrons, and surround the oasis. If the chase breaks cover we will have him surrounded. My lord Regent, do you take the left wing. Pharaoh Nefer Seti, take the centre. I will cover the right flank.' He brandished his heavy war bow over his head. 'Whoever draws first blood will win the trophy.'

They were all expert charioteers and the new formation evolved swiftly and without check. They threw out a wide net to encircle the waterhole. Nefer had his bow over his shoulder and the reins unwrapped from his wrists, ready to drop them in an instant to leave both hands free to draw. Mintaka pressed close to his side. She held the long lance ready to hand to him. They had perfected this change of weapons over the past weeks, and he knew he could rely upon her to slap the grip of the lance into his palm at the very moment he needed it.

They approached the oasis at a walk, closing in steadily. The horses sensed the tension in their drivers, and perhaps they had picked up the lion scent. They flung up their heads, and rolled their eyes and blew through their nostrils, stepping high and nervously.

The line of vehicles closed slowly around the patch of low scrub and rank grass that concealed the waterhole. When the encirclement was complete, Apepi raised his hand above his head to signal the halt. The royal huntsman dismounted and went forward on foot, leading his pony. He approached the sparse brown cover cautiously.

'If the lion was here, surely we would have seen such a large animal by now.' Mintaka's voice shook, and Nefer loved her all the more for this little show of fear.

'A lion can flatten himself until he becomes part of the earth, and you could walk close enough to touch him without ever suspecting his presence,' he told her.

The huntsman went forward a few paces at a time, stopping to listen and search every bush and clump of rank grass in his path. An the edge of the scrub he stooped and picked up a handful of small stones, and began to lob them systematically at each possible hiding place.

'What is he doing?' Mintaka whispered.

'The lion will growl before it charges. He is trying to provoke it and make it reveal itself.'

The silence was broken only by the plop of the pebbles, the snorting of the horses and the restless stamping of their hoofs. Every one of the hunters had nocked an arrow and was poised to draw at an instant. Suddenly there was a squawk and clatter in the grass. Every bow went up at once and the lance-bearers hefted their weapons. They all relaxed and looked sheepish as a chocolate brown hammerhead stork launched itself into the air and flapped away down the valley in the direction of the river.

The huntsman took a minute to recover his nerve, then began to work his way, a pace at a time, deeper into the cover until he reached the seep. The brackish water came up a sluggish drop at a time, and filled a shallow basin in the rocky ground, hardly enough to quench the thirst of a great predator. The huntsman went down on one knee to search the rim of the basin for sign, then shook his head and stood up. More quickly he worked back through the scrub, and at last mounted the pony and trotted back to Apepi's chariot. The other hunters drove across to hear his report, but the huntsman was crestfallen. 'Majesty, I was mistaken in my judgement,' he told Apepi. 'The lion has not come this way.'

'What now, fellow?' Apepi was making no effort to hide his disappointment and irritation.

'This was the most promising place to look, but there are others. From where we last saw him, he could have crossed the valley, or he may be lying up close to here and waiting for darkness before drinking. There is cover further down.' He pointed back to the stony slopes.

'Where else?' Apepi demanded.

'There is another waterhole in the next valley, but there are Bedouin encamped there. They might have scared off the beast. There is another small water seep below those hills to the west.' He pointed out a low line of purple peaks on the horizon. 'The lion could be at any of those places, or at none,' the man admitted. 'Also he might have doubled back and be on the edge of the plain where there is an abundance of water. Perhaps he has been drawn by the smell of cattle and goats as well as by thirst.'

'You have not the least idea where he is hiding, have you?' Lord Naja demanded. 'We should call off the hunt and get back to the boats.'

'No!' Nefer cut in. 'We have barely begun. How can we give up so soon?'

'The boy is right,' Apepi agreed. 'We must go on, but there is much ground to cover.' He paused for a moment, then reached a decision. 'We will have to split up and search each area separately.' He looked across at Naja. 'My lord Regent, you take your squadron to the Bedouin encampment. If they have seen the chase they will direct you. I will ride to the seep below the hills.' He turned to Trok. 'Take three chariots down the valley. One of the trackers will go with you to search for sign.' To Asmor he said, 'Take three chariots and cast back along the edge of the plain to Dabba, in case he has returned to where he last killed.' Then he looked at Nefer. 'Pharaoh, you cast in the opposite direction, north towards Achmim.'

Nefer realized that he was being given the least promising ground to cover, but he had no complaint. This new plan meant that for the first time he and Mintaka would be away from the direct surveillance of his guardians. Naja, Asmor and Trok were being sent in different directions. He waited for someone to point this out, but they were all so wrapped up in the hunt that no one seemed to realize the significance of this move. Except Naja.

He looked hard at Nefer. Perhaps he was weighing the advisability of countermanding Apepi's orders, but in the end he must have realized that this would be unwise and concluded that Nefer was guarded by the desert as effectively as he would have been by Asmor: there was no place for him to run to, and if he took Mintaka with him on some wild adventure he would have the entire armies of both kingdoms upon him like swarms of wild bees.

Naja looked away from him as Apepi went on to nominate an assembly point, and to give his final orders. At last the ram's horns sounded the mount-up and the advance, and the five columns drove out of the valley. On the level ground they split into their separate squadrons and headed out in diverging directions.

As the last of the other squadrons disappeared among the stark hills, Mintaka leaned even closer to Nefer and murmured, 'At last Hathor has shown mercy to us.'

'I believe it is Horus who has granted us his favour,' Nefer grinned down at her, 'but I will accept this benevolence from whomsoever it comes.'

There were two other chariots in Nefer's squadron, commanded by Colonel Hilto, the old soldier who had discovered him and Taita when they had tried to escape from Egypt. He had served under Nefer's father and was loyal unto death: Nefer knew he could trust him without reservation.

Nefer led them fast, wanting to make the most of the remaining daylight, and within an hour's ride the vast vista of the river plain opened beneath them. He reined in to admire it for a few minutes. The river was an emerald mounted in the luscious green of fields and plantations that enclosed it.

'How beautiful it is, Nefer.' Mintaka spoke almost dreamily. 'Even when we are married, we must always remember that this land owns us, and that we do not own it.'

Sometimes he forgot that she had been born in Avaris and had as strong claim to the land as he had. He felt his heart swell with pride that she loved it as he did, and felt the same patriotic duty.

'I will never forget it, not with you at my side.' She lifted her face to him and her lips were parted slightly. He could smell her sweet breath, and the temptation to reach down for those lips with his own mouth was almost irresistible. Then he felt the gaze of Hilto and the other men on them, and from the corner of his eye saw one smile knowingly. He drew back and looked at Hilto coolly. He had been rehearsing his next order since they had left the rest of the hunting party. 'Colonel, if the lion is here it will probably be lying up somewhere on the slope of the hills down below us.' He indicated the area with a sweep of his arm. 'I want to extend in line abreast. The left flank must be on the edge of the plain and our right up here on the crest of the hills. We will sweep northwards.' He made a wide gesture, but Hilto looked dubious and scratched the scar on his cheek.

'That is a broad front, Your Majesty. It's almost half a league to the valley bottom. At times we will be out of sight of each other.'

Nefer could see that it went against all his military instincts to spread his front too thin, and he went on swiftly to mollify him. 'If we do become separated we will reassemble on the third ridge ahead of us, under that small hillock over there. It will give us a good landmark.' He pointed out a distinctive rock pile four miles ahead. 'If any of us is late to the rendezvous the others must wait until the sun is at that angle before coming back to look for the missing vehicle.'

He had given himself a few hours before they would begin to search for him and Mintaka. Still Hilto hesitated. 'I beg Your Majesty's indulgence, but the Lord Naja charged me most strictly—'

Nefer cut in with a sharp tone and cold expression: 'Do you presume to argue with your pharaoh?'

'Never, Majesty!' Hilto was shocked at the accusation.

'Then do your duty, fellow.'

Hilto saluted with deep respect and hurried back to his own chariot shouting urgent orders to his men as he ran. As the squadron wheeled out down the slope, Mintaka nudged Nefer and smiled. 'Do your duty, fellow!' She mimicked his haughty tone then laughed. 'Please never look at me like that or use that tone to me, Your Majesty. I am sure I would die of fright.'

'We have only a little time,' he replied. 'We must make the most of it, and find a place where we can be alone.'

He swung the chariot back over the skyline so that they could no longer be seen from the river valley or by the chariots lower down the slope, and as they trotted forward they were both craning eagerly ahead.

'Look, over there.' Mintaka pointed to the right. A small grove of thorn trees was almost hidden by a fold in the ground, only the dull green tops showing. Nefer turned towards it, and they found a narrow ravine that had been cut, over millennia, into the hillside by wind and weather, and rare thunderstorms. There must have been subterranean water for the thorn trees were robust. Their thick foliage offered shade and privacy in this hot midday. Nefer drove down the bank and into the shade. As soon as he stopped Mintaka hopped down from the footplate.

'Loosen the harness, and give the horses a rest,' she suggested.

Nefer hesitated, then shook his head. It was against his training: in a detached and unsupported position such as this, he must have the vehicle ready for any sudden alarm or excursion. He jumped down and went to fill the bucket from the waterskin to water the horses. Mintaka came to help him. They worked side by side in silence.

Now that the moment they had both longed for had arrived, they were shy and tongue-tied. Suddenly they turned to each other simultaneously, and spoke in unison.

Nefer said, 'I wanted to tell you—'

Mintaka said, 'I think that we should—'

They stopped and laughed shyly, standing close together in the shade. Mintaka blushed and looked down at her feet, and Nefer stroked the head of his stallion.

'What were you going to say?'

'It was nothing. Nothing important.' She shook her head and he saw that she was blushing. He so loved to watch the colour bloom in her cheeks. She was still not looking at him, and her voice was so soft as to be barely audible as she asked in her turn, 'What were you going to say?'

'When I think that you will be gone in just a few more days' time, I feel as though my right arm has been cut off, and I want to die.'

'Oh, Nefer.' She looked up at him and her eyes were huge and liquid with the turmoil and rapture of first love. 'I love you. I do truly love you.'

In the same instant they both lunged for each other, and their teeth came together with a click. His lower lip was caught between them and a drop of blood oozed from the nick, so their kiss was salt flavoured. Their embrace was unpractised and unrehearsed, clumsy and frenzied. It evoked wild and uncontrolled feelings in both of them. They clung together, moaning with the strength of these new sensations. Even though her body was flattened against his, he tried to pull her closer still, while she clung harder as though to weld their separate flesh into one entity, like potter's clay. She reached up and twisted her fingers into his thick dusty curls and said, 'Oh! Oh!' but her voice was blurred.

'I don't want to lose you.' He broke the kiss. 'I never want to lose you.'

'I don't want to leave you ever – ever!' she gasped, and they kissed again, if possible even more furiously than before. From here onwards they were in unexplored realms of mind and body. They rode together on a chariot that was out of their control drawn by the runaway horses of love and desire.

Still clinging together they sank down on the soft white sand of the wadi bottom, and clawed at each others bodies as though they were enemies. Their eyes were wild and unseeing, their breathing ragged and broken. The linen of her skirt tore like papyrus parchment in his hands, and he reached through the opening. She moaned as though in mortal agony but her thighs fell apart and she went limp and pliable. Neither had any inkling of where this was leading. All Nefer wanted was to feel his bare skin against her smoothness. It was a deep need on which his very life seemed to depend. He ripped away his own apron and they pressed their bodies together, both absorbed in the ecstatic sensation of her warm young flesh against his hardness. Then without any conscious thought he began to move against her, rocking rhythmically, and she rode his movements as thought she were flying in a chariot over rough ground.

Then abruptly she felt something hard pressing imperiously at the very portals of her womanhood, and she experienced the almost undeniable urge to meet thrust with thrust, to help him break through, to welcome him into her soft, secret places.

Then reality rushed back upon her. She kicked out wildly, arching her back and struggling with renewed strength like a gazelle in the jaws of a hunting cheetah. She tore her mouth from his and screamed, 'No, Nefer! You promised! By Horus' wounded eye, you promised!'

He sprang away from her, recoiling as though from a slash with a chariot whip. He stared at her with wide and terrified eyes. His voice was hoarse and panting, as though he had run far and fast. 'Mintaka, my love, my darling. I don't know what happened to me. It was a madness. I did not intend it.' He made a despairing gesture. 'I would rather die than break my oath, and bring dishonour upon you.'

Her breathing was so laboured that she could not answer him at once. She averted her eyes from his naked body, and he went on piteously, 'Please don't hate me. I did not know what was happening.'

'I don't hate you, Nefer. I could never hate you.' His distress was too much to bear, she wanted to throw herself back into his arms and to comfort him. But she knew how dangerous that would be. She used the wheel of the chariot to pull herself to her feet. 'I am as much at fault as you are. I should never have let that happen.' Her legs trembled under her, and she tried to push her hair back off her face with both hands.

He stood up guiltily, took one step towards her but when she recoiled he stopped at once. 'I have torn your skirt,' he said. 'I did not mean to.'

She looked down, and saw how blatantly she was exposed – she was almost as naked as he was. Hastily she pulled the ripped ends together and stepped further from him. 'You must dress yourself,' she whispered, and despite herself she looked down at him. He was so lovely, and she felt desire rise again. She forced herself to look away. He stooped quickly, gathered up the discarded *chiton* and fastened it around his waist.

They stood in guilty, awkward silence. Desperately Mintaka searched for words to distract them both from this terrible moment. Her own body came to her aid. She became aware of a real and pressing fullness in her bladder. 'I must go!'

'No,' he pleaded. 'I did not mean it. Forgive me. It won't happen again. Stay with me. Don't leave me.'

She smiled shakily, 'No. You don't understand. I will be gone for a short while only.' She made an unmistakable gesture with the hands holding her torn skirt together. 'I won't be long.'

His relief was almost pathetic. 'Oh, I understand. I will make the chariot ready.' He turned to the horses, and she left him and picked her way deeper into the grove of thorn trees.

The lion watched her come through the trees towards where he lay. He flattened his ears against his skull, and pressed his body closer to the stony earth.

He was an old beast, past his prime. There were grey hairs in the dark, shaggy bush of his mane. His back had once had a bluish sheen, but now it was lightly frosted with age. His teeth were worn and stained, and one of the long fangs was broken off close to the gum. Although he could still pull down a full-grown bullock and kill it with a single blow of one of his huge paws, his claws were worn and blunted so that it was difficult for him to cling to more agile prey. The previous night he had missed an oryx, and his hunger was a dull, insistent pain in his gut.

He watched the human creature with yellow eyes, and his upper lip lifted in a silent snarl. As a cub his dam had taught him to feed on the dead flesh that they scavenged from the battlefields. He did not have the natural repugnance that most other carnivorous animals feel for the taste of human flesh. Over the years he had killed and feasted upon this meat whenever the opportunity presented itself. He saw this creature come towards him through the low scrub as natural prey.

Mintaka stopped fifty paces short of where he lay, and looked around her. The instinct of the lion during the stalk was to avoid the direct gaze of its prey. He kept his head low to the ground and hooded his eyes to slits. This was not the moment for the attack, and his tail was held stiff and low.

Mintaka stepped behind the trunk of one of the trees, crouched down and voided her bladder. The lion's snout creased into deep wrinkles as he picked up the sharp scent of her urine. It quickened his interest. Mintaka stood again and let her torn skirt drop back around her thighs. She turned away from the lion, and started back towards where Nefer waited.

The lion slashed its tail back and forth, the prelude to the charge. He lifted his head, and the black tufted tail whipped against his flanks.

Mintaka heard the rhythmic swish and thud of the tail, stopped and looked back, puzzled. She looked straight into the yellow gaze of the beast. She screamed, a high-pitched sound that struck Nefer to the heart. He whirled round and in an instant took in the situation: the girl and the crouching beast facing her.

'Don't run!' he shouted. He knew that if she ran it would trigger the feline reflex of the lion to chase. 'I am coming!'

He snatched his bow and quiver from the rack on the dashboard, and raced towards her, nocking an arrow as he ran.

'Don't run!' he repeated desperately, but at that moment the lion growled. It was a terrible sound that seemed to vibrate in Mintaka's bones and make the ground tremble under her feet. She could not control the terror that overwhelmed her. She whirled and ran back blindly towards Nefer, sobbing with each stride.

Instantly the lion's mane rose like a dark aura around his head and he launched himself into his charge, coming straight after her, a dark, tawny streak through the trees. He overtook her as though she were still rooted to the earth.

Nefer stopped dead and dropped the quiver to free both hands, and he threw up the bow. He drew the fletching to his lips and set his aim on the massive heaving chest. Even though the range was short, it was a difficult shot. The beast was coming at an angle, so the deflection was critical, and Mintaka was in the direct line of his fire. On top of that, he knew that a wounding would not save Mintaka. He must drive an arrowhead through the beast's vital organs to pin it down, and give her the chance to get clear. Yet there was no time for precise calculation, the lion was almost on top of her.

It came grunting at each bound, clods and pebbles spurting up under the drive of its great paws. The yellow eyes were terrible. Nefer swung just a touch ahead, allowing a hand's breadth for the drop of the arrow in flight and he yelled, with all the urgency he could muster, 'Down, Mintaka! Clear my shot!'

They had developed a close accord over the weeks in which they had hunted together, and she had learned to trust him implicitly. Even in her transport of terror he could still reach her. She did not hesitate but from full run she threw herself flat upon the stony earth almost under the jaws of the onrushing lion.

In the same instant that she went down, Nefer let fly. The arrow sprang from his bowstring. To Nefer's fear-crazed eyes it seemed to move across the gap that separated them with the leisurely flight of some overburdened bird of prey. It passed over where Mintaka lay, already beginning to drop, seeming tiny, slow and ineffectual against such a massive animal.

Then it struck soundlessly and Nefer half expected the flimsy shaft to snap, be thrown aside contemptuously by the grunting, bounding animal.

Just as the lion's mouth gaped wide, showing the full array of ragged stained fangs, the flint arrowhead disappeared into the thick coating of dark hair that covered its chest. There was no sound of the impact but the slim straight shaft of the arrow slid in after it, until only a hand's span of shaft and the bright feathers of the fletching protruded.

Nefer thought that he had struck the heart. The lion leaped high in a monumental convulsion and its grunting changed to a barrage of continuous roars that shook a cloud of dried leaves from the thorn branches over its head. Then the beast spun in a circle snapping at its own chest, chewing the projecting end of the shaft of the arrow to splinters. Mintaka lay almost under his flying, slashing paws.

'Get away from him!' Nefer screamed. 'Run!'

He stooped and grabbed a second arrow from the quiver at his feet, and ran forward, nocking the arrow as he closed in. Mintaka sprang up. She had recovered enough of her wits not to impede his aim by racing to him for protection, and dodged behind the trunk of the nearest thorn tree.

The movement was enough to draw the wounded lion's attention back to her. Now in pain and fury, rather than in hunger, it lashed out at her. The hooked yellow claws tore a slab of wet bark from the tree trunk behind which Mintaka crouched.

'Come! Here I am! Come to me!' Nefer yelled wildly, trying to pull the lion off her. It swung its huge, mane-shaggy head towards him, and Nefer drew and shot the next shaft with one desperate movement. His arms were shaking and his aim was hurried and wild. The arrowhead took the beast too far back, lancing deep into its belly, and it coughed at its sting. It left Mintaka and hurled itself towards Nefer.

Though it was mortally wounded and already slowing, there was no chance for Nefer to evade this fresh charge. He had shot his last arrow and the quiver lay on the hard ground well out of his reach. He reached down and drew his dagger from the sheath on his belt.

It was a flimsy weapon against this furious beast. The thin bronze blade was not long enough to stab through to the heart, but he had heard the royal huntsman tell tales of miraculous escapes from just such a deadly predicament. As the lion launched itself into the death spring, Nefer fell backwards, not even attempting to resist the beast's weight and impetus. He lay between its forepaws, and the lion opened its jaws to full stretch and thrust its head down to crush Nefer's skull with those terrible fangs. Its breath was so foul, with the stench of rotten meat and open graves, that Nefer felt hot vomit rise in his throat. He steeled himself for the moment and thrust his right hand, with the dagger, deep into the open jaws. The lion bit down instinctively.

Nefer had the dagger held firmly in his fist, with the blade aligned upright, and as the lion's jaws closed the bronze point was driven up through the roof of its mouth. Nefer snatched away his hand before the fangs could crush the bones of his wrist, but the lion's jaws were fixed open by the dagger held between them, and it could not bite down.

It was ripping at him with both its forepaws, the claws fully extended. He wriggled and writhed beneath the heavy body, evading some of the claw strokes, but his apron was ripped from him, and he felt the bony hooks tearing into his flesh. He knew he could not hold out much longer. Involuntarily he screamed at the lion above him, 'Leave me, you filthy creature! Get off me!'

The lion was still roaring and the blood from its skewered palate blew out in a crimson cloud, mingled with its stinking breath and hot saliva, into Nefer's face.

His shouts galvanized Mintaka, and when she peered out from behind the bole of the thorn tree Nefer was a blood-soaked spectacle beneath the lion's bulk. He was being mauled to death, and her own fear was forgotten.

Nefer's bow was trapped under his body, and without it the quiver full of arrows was useless to her. She sprang out from behind the tree and raced towards the chariot. The screams and roars behind her goaded her on and she ran until her heart seemed on the point of bursting.

Ahead of her the horses were terrified by the scent of the beast and its roaring. They reared and threw their heads, kicking out at the traces. They would have bolted long ago had not Nefer secured the locking brake on one wheel so they could only turn in a tight, right-handed circle. Mintaka ran in under their flying hoofs, and jumped up on to the footplate. She seized the loose reins and called to the team, 'Ho there, Stargazer! Hold hard, Hammer!'

On many of their previous outings, Nefer had let her drive, so the horses knew her voice and recognized her touch on the traces. Swiftly she brought them under control, but it seemed to her an eternity for she could hear Nefer's screams and the lion's deafening bellows. The moment she had the pair in hand she leaned over the side and knocked off the brake. She brought the horses round in a hard left-hand turn then drove them forward straight at the lion and its victim.

Hammer balked, but Stargazer held true. She snatched up the whip that Nefer had never used on them, and laid a stroke across Hammer's glossy haunches that raised a welt as thick as her thumb.

'Ha!' she yelled. 'Pull, curse you, Hammer!'

Startled, Hammer leaped forward, and they pounded down on the lion. All its attention was on the shrieking, writhing victim between its front paws, and it did not look up at the chariot bearing down on it.

Mintaka dropped the whip, and instead snatched the long lance from its rack. She had carried it for Nefer during hours of hunting, and now it felt light and familiar in her right hand. Guiding the racing team with the reins in her left hand, she leaned far out over the side panel and raised the lance high. As they ran past the crouching lion, its head was lowered and the back of its neck was fully exposed. The exact juncture of spine and skull in the back of its neck was covered by the dense black bush of its mane, but she guessed at the spot and thrust down with all the strength of her fear and her love for Nefer.

Her lance hand had the impetus of the flying chariot behind it. To her amazement the blade slid in readily, full length through the taut hide, and deep into the back of the animal's neck. She felt the slight tick in her hand as the point found the joint between the vertebrae of the spine and went on to sever the spinal column.

As the chariot raced past, the haft of the lance was plucked from her grip. But the lion collapsed in a loose, inert heap on top of Nefer. It did not twitch again, killed on the instant.

It took her fifty cubits to bring the crazed horses to a halt, wheel them round and force them back to where Nefer lay beneath the huge carcass. She had the presence of mind to throw on the wheel brake before she jumped down from the footplate.

It was obvious how badly Nefer was hurt. From the sheets of blood that covered him she thought he might even be dead. She fell to her knees beside him. 'Nefer, speak to me. Can you hear me?'

To her immense relief he rolled his head towards her and his eyes were open and focused. 'You came back,' he breathed. '*Bak-her*, Mintaka, *bak-her!*'

'I will get this off you.'

She could see that the enormous weight of the dead beast was crushing the wind from his lungs. She jumped up and tugged at its head.

'The tail,' Nefer whispered painfully through a running mask of blood. 'Roll him over by the tail.'

She was quick to obey him, and seized the long tufted tail then heaved with all her strength. Slowly the hindquarters began to swing, the whole carcass flopped over and he was free.

Mintaka knelt beside him and helped him into a sitting position, but he swayed drunkenly and reached out to her for support.

'Hathor help me,' she pleaded. 'You are desperately wounded. There is so much blood.'

'Not all of it is mine,' he blurted, but from his right thigh rose a feathery crimson fountain where the claws had ripped open a blood vessel. Taita had instructed him long and earnestly in the treatment of war wounds, and he thrust his thumb down into the torn flesh and pressed until the jet of blood shrivelled.

'Get the waterskin,' he said, and Mintaka ran to the chariot and brought it back to him. She held it for him while he drank thirstily, and then, tenderly, she washed the blood and filth from his face, relieved to find it unmarked. However, when she inspected his other injuries she had difficulty in hiding her shock at how grievous they were.

'My bedroll is in the chariot.' His voice was weaker. When she brought it to him he asked her to undo the bundle, where she found his housewife roll. She selected a needle and silk thread. He showed her how to tie off the spurting blood vessel. It was work that came easily to her, and she did not hesitate or flinch from it. Her hands were bloody to the wrists as, with nimble fingers, she pulled a thread around the open artery then closed the deeper rents in his flesh. Still under his instruction she used strips torn from his tattered *chiton* to bind up the wounds. It was rough, rudimentary surgery, but sufficient to stem the worst of the bleeding.

'That is all we can do now. I must help you into the chariot and get you to where a surgeon can do the rest. Oh, if only Taita were here.'

She ran to Stargazer's head and led the pair back to where he lay. Nefer was up on one elbow staring longingly at the carcass of the lion that lay beside him.

'My first lion,' he whispered ruefully. 'Unless we skin it, the trophy will spoil. The hair will slip and slough off.'

In the heat of emotion and her terrible concern for him, she lost her temper. 'That is the most stupid piece of man's nonsense I have ever heard uttered. Would you risk your very life for a stinking bit of fur?' Angrily she came to help him to his feet. It took the extreme efforts of both off them to raise him up. He leaned on her with all his weight as he hobbled to the chariot and collapsed weakly on to the footplate.

Mintaka used the sheepskin from the bedroll to make him as comfortable as she could, then climbed up and stood over him with the reins in her hands.

'Which way?' she asked.

'The rest of the squadron will be far up the valley by now, and they will be driving too fast for us to catch them. Also they are heading in the wrong direction,' he told her. 'The other hunters are scattered across the desert, We could search for them all day without finding them.'

'We must return to where the fleet is lying at Dabba. There is a surgeon with the ships.' She had reached the only feasible conclusion, and he nodded. She urged the horses into a walk, and they left the grove and climbed to the high ground heading south once again.

'It's three hours or more to reach Dabba,' she said.

'Not if we cut across the loop of the river,' he answered. 'We can shorten the return by at least four leagues.'

Mintaka hesitated and looked eastwards into the bleak desert, which he wanted her to attempt. 'I might lose the way,' she murmured fearfully.

'I will guide you,' he answered, confident in the instruction that Taita had given him in desert travel. 'It's our best chance.'

She swung the team to the left, marking a blue shale hillock in the direction Nefer had pointed out to her.

When they were strong and well they both delighted in the motion of a chariot running hard over broken ground, and they rode the pitch and roll with young legs. But now, even though she kept the horses down to a walk or a trot, the collision with every stone or hump, the drop into every hole, was transmitted through the rigid chassis into Nefer's torn body. He winced and sweated, but tried to hide his pain and discomfort from her. Yet as the hours wore on, his wounds stiffened, and the pain became unbearable. He groaned aloud at a particularly nasty impact, and slumped into unconsciousness.

Immediately Mintaka reined the pair to a halt, and tried to revive him. She soaked a pad of linen with water and squeezed a few drops between his lips. Then she sponged his pale, sweating face. But when she tried to rebandage his wounds she found that the gash in his thigh was bleeding again. She worked to staunch it, but succeeded only in reducing it to a slow leak. 'You are going to be all right, my darling,' she told him, with a confidence she did not feel. She embraced him gently, kissed the top of his dusty blood-caked head, and took up the reins again.

An hour later she gave the last of the water to Nefer and the horses, not drinking herself. Then she stood as high as she could on the dashboard of the chariot and looked about her at the gravel and shale hills that danced and wavered in the heat mirage. She knew she was lost. Have I drifted too far eastwards? she wondered, glancing up at the sun and trying to calculate its angle. At her feet Nefer stirred and moaned, and she looked down with a brave face and smiled. 'Not much further now, my heart. We should see the river over the next crest.'

She rearranged the sheepskin from the bedroll under his head, then stood up, gathered the reins and braced herself. Suddenly she realized how exhausted she was: every muscle in her body ached and her eyes were sore and red from the sun's glare and the dust. She forced herself and the team onwards.

Soon the horses were showing signs of distress. They had stopped sweating and the salt rime dried white across their backs. She tried to urge them into a trot but they could not respond, so she climbed down, took the stallion's head and led them on. Now she was staggering herself, but at last she found the tracks of a chariot in a sandy valley bottom, and her spirits lifted.

'They are heading west,' she whispered, through lips that were beginning to swell and crack. 'They will lead us back to the river.' She kept moving along the wheel ruts for some time, until she stopped in confusion as she found her own footprints in front of her. It took her some time to realize that she must have walked in a circle and was following her own tracks.

At last despair overtook her. She sank down to her knees, helpless and lost, and whispered to Nefer as he lay, still unconscious, 'I am sorry, my darling. I have failed you.' She stroked the matted hair from his face. Then she looked up at the low hilltop to the east, and blinked. She shook her head to clear her vision, glanced away to rest her burning eyes, then looked back. She felt her spirits surge upwards once again, but still she could not be sure that what she was seeing was illusion or reality.

On the crest of the hills above them, a gaunt figure stood on the skyline, leaning on his long staff. His silver hair shone like a cloud, and the hot light breeze off the desert flapped his skirts against his heron-thin legs. He was staring down at them.

'Oh, Hathor and all the goddesses, it can't be so,' she whispered.

Beside her, Nefer opened his eyes. 'Taita is near,' he murmured. 'I feel him close.'

'Yes. Taita is here.' Her voice was faint, and she held her own throat in shock. 'But how did he know where to find us?'

'He knows. Taita knows,' Nefer replied, closed his eyes and slumped back into unconsciousness.

The old man was striding down the rugged slope towards them now, and Mintaka pulled herself to her feet and tottered to meet him. Swiftly her fatigue fell away and she waved and screamed greetings at him, almost delirious with joy.

Taita drove down the escarpment towards the river and the village of Dabba. The horses responded to his touch, moving to an easy motion that cosseted the wounded boy on the footplate. Taita seemed to have known with some deep instinct just what medicines and dressings Nefer would need, and he had carried these with him. After he had re-dressed the wounds he had led the horses to a hidden water seep nearby, where the bitter water had revived them. He had taken Mintaka up on the footplate and turned the horses' heads unerringly in the direction of Dabba and the river.

Beside him, Mintaka had pleaded with him, almost tearfully, to explain to her how he had known that they needed him, and where to find them. Taita had smiled gently, and called to the horses, 'Gently now, Hammer! Steady, Stargazer!'

On the floorboards Nefer was deep in the drugged sleep of the Red Shepenn, but his wounds were staunched, cleaned and bound with linen bandages.

A red and angry sunset was fading over the Nile like a dying bush-fire. The boats of the fleet were still anchored in the stream, like children's toys in the fading light.

Apepi and Naja rode out to meet them from the village of Dabba. Lord Naja was highly agitated, and Apepi bellowed at his daughter as soon as they were in range of his bull voice, 'Where have you been, you stupid child? Half the army is out looking for you.'

Lord Naja's agitation abated as soon as he came close enough to see Nefer bandaged and unconscious in the bottom of the chariot cockpit. He became almost sanguine when Taita explained to him the extent of Pharaoh's injury.

Barely conscious, Nefer was carried down to the riverbank on a litter and lifted gently aboard one of the galleys by a party of boatmen. 'I want Pharaoh taken up to Thebes with all possible speed,' Taita told Naja, 'even if it means a night journey. There is a very real danger that the wounds will putrefy. This happens with injuries received from one of the great cats. It is almost as though their fangs and claws are steeped in some virulent poison.'

'You can order the galley to sail at once,' Naja said, in front of the company, but then took Taita's arm and led him a short way along the riverbank to where they could not be overheard. 'Bear in mind, Magus, the charge laid on you by the gods. Clearly I discern their divine intervention in these extraordinary circumstances. If Pharaoh were to die from his wounds no person in either kingdom would take it as unnatural.' He said no more but gazed into Taita's face with those piercing yellow eyes.

'The will of the gods will prevail against all else,' Taita agreed quietly, but enigmatically.

Naja read in his reply what he wanted to hear. 'We are in accord, Taita. I place my trust in you. Go in peace. I will follow you back to Thebes after Apepi has been taken care of.' The phrasing of this last remark struck Taita as unusual, but he was too distracted to ponder it. Naja smiled mysteriously and went on, 'Who knows? We may have momentous news for each other when we meet again.'

When Taita hurried back on board the galley, and went to the small deck cabin in which Nefer lay, he found Mintaka kneeling beside the litter in tears.

'What is it, my darling?' he asked her gently. 'You have been as brave as a lioness. You have fought like a warrior of the guards. How can you dissolve into despair now?'

'My father is taking me back to Avaris in the morning, but I should be with Nefer. I am his betrothed. He needs me. We need each other.' She looked up at him piteously, and he could see that she was both physically and emotionally exhausted.

She seized his hand. 'Oh, Magus! Will you not go to my father and ask him to let me go back to Thebes to help you to take care of Nefer? My father will listen to you.'

But Apepi snorted with laughter when Taita attempted to persuade him. 'Place my lamb in Naja's pen?' He shook his head with amusement. 'I trust Naja as I would a scorpion. Who knows what tricks he would try if I gave him that coin to bargain with? As for that young puppy, Nefer, he would be up her skirts as quick as a hawk on a bustard, if he hasn't travelled that road already.' He laughed again. 'I don't want to debase the currency of her virginity. No, Warlock, Mintaka comes back under my wing to Avaris until her wedding day. And none of your magic spells will change my mind on that.'

Sadly Mintaka went to take her leave of Nefer. He was on the edge of consciousness, weak from the blood he had lost and the drug. But when she kissed him he opened his eyes. She spoke quietly, pledging her love, and he watched her eyes as she spoke. Before she rose to leave him, she took the golden locket that hung at her throat. 'This contains a lock of my hair. It is my soul, and I give it to you.' She placed it in his hand and he folded his fingers tightly around it.

So Mintaka stood alone on the bank of the Nile as the swift galley bearing Nefer and Taita breasted the current. With twenty oarsmen a side and a white curl under her prow she headed upstream towards Thebes. Mintaka did not wave at Taita's tall silhouette on the stern, but watched him forlornly.

The next morning there was a final meeting between Apepi and the Regent, Lord Naja, on board the Hyksosian royal barge. All Apepi's nine sons were present and Mintaka was seated beside her father. Apepi had kept her on a tight rein since the previous evening when the ship bearing Pharaoh Nefer Seti had left. From long experience, he knew his headstrong daughter well enough to trust neither her judgement nor her sense of filial duty and obedience when she had set her heart on a course of action.

The farewell ceremony took place on the deck of Apepi's galley, with protestations of mutual trust and devotion to the peace.

'May it last a thousand years!' Naja intoned, as he bestowed upon Apepi the Gold of Eternity, an honour he had created for this auspicious occasion.

'A thousand times a thousand,' Apepi replied, with equal gravity, as the chain of the order, encrusted with precious and semi-precious gems, was placed around his shoulders. The Regent and the king embraced with the affection of brothers, then Naja was rowed across to his own galley. As the two fleets diverged, one to return to Thebes the other to run down with the current hundreds of leagues to Memphis and Avaris, the crews cheered each other out of sight. Garlands and wreaths of palm fronds and blossoms tossed from one vessel towards the other bestrewed the surface of the wide river.

The urgency of King Apepi's voyage did not dictate that his fleet should sail on in the darkness of this moonless night, so that evening they anchored at Balasfura, opposite the temple of Hapi, the half hippopotamus hermaphroditic god of the Nile. The king and his family went ashore and made sacrifice of a pure white ox at the altar in the sanctuary. The high priest disembowelled the bellowing beast, and while it still lived he drew and inspected the entrails to read the auspice for the king. He was appalled to find that the animal's guts were infested with stinking white worms, which spilled on to the temple floor in a seething mass. He tried to hide this hideous phenomenon from the king by spreading his cloak and beginning to make up some mendacious nonsense, but Apepi shouldered him aside and stared at the horrible sight. Even he was visibly shaken, and for once he was subdued as they left the temple and went down to the riverbank where Trok and the officers under his command had arranged a banquet and entertainment for him.

Even the sacred black cockerels of the temple refused to peck at the contaminated entrails of the sacrifice. The priests threw the grisly mess on the temple fire, but rather than consume the entrails the fire, which had burned since antiquity, was extinguished by them. The signs could not have been more inauspicious, but the high priest ordered the entrails to be buried and the fire to be relit. 'I have never seen such an unhappy omen,' he told his acolytes. 'Such a sign from the god Hapi can only presage some terrible event, such as war or the death of Pharaoh. We must pray through all this night for the recovery of Pharaoh Nefer Seti from his wounds.'

On the riverbank Lord Trok had set up pavilions hung with vivid red, yellow and green curtains to receive the royal family. Whole oxen were grilling over the pits of glowing ash, and amphorae of the choicest wines were cooling in the river waters. Slaves staggered up the bank under the weight of them as one after the other they were drained by the company and Apepi bellowed for fresh jars to be brought.

The king's sombre mood lightened with each bowl he lowered, and soon he encouraged his sons to join him in singing the ribald marching songs of his army. Some were so scurrilous that Mintaka pleaded exhaustion and a sick headache, and she and her slave girls rose to retire to the royal barge anchored offshore. She tried to take her youngest brother, Khyan, with her, but Apepi intervened. The good wine had helped him to throw off the misgivings brought upon him by the divination in the temple. 'Leave the boy where he is, you little vixen. He should be taught to appreciate good music.' He hugged the boy to him in an excess of affection, and held the wine bowl to his lips. 'Take a sup. It will make you sing all the sweeter, my princeling.'

Khyan adored his father, and such public comradeship reduced him to a transport of pride and hero-worship. At last his father was treating him like a man and a warrior. Even though he gagged upon it, he managed to drain the bowl and the company, led by Lord Trok, cheered him as though he had killed his first enemy in battle.

Mintaka hesitated. She felt an almost maternal sense of protection for her little brother, but she realized that her father was beyond reason. With all dignity she led her maids down to the riverbank and, to the ironic and inebriated cheers of the company, they went aboard the barge.

Mintaka lay on her mattress and listened to the sounds of revelry. She tried to compose herself to sleep, but Nefer was in the forefront of her mind. The sense of loss that she had held at bay all day, and her concern for Nefer's injuries, flooded back, and though she tried to prevent them, tears welled up. She smothered her sobs in her pillows.

At last she sank into a black, dreamless sleep, from which she woke with difficulty. She had sipped only a little of the wine, but she felt drugged and her head ached. She wondered what had roused her. Then she heard raucous voices through the side of the hull, and the barge rocked under her as a weight of men clambered aboard. There was drunken laughter and voices, and heavy footfalls from the deck over her head. From their comments it seemed that her father and her brothers were being carried on board. It was not unusual for the men in her family to drink themselves into this condition, but she was worried about little Khyan.

She dragged herself from her bed and began to dress, but she felt strangely listless and confused. She staggered as she climbed up on deck.

The first person she met was Lord Trok. He was directing the men who were carrying her father. It took six of them to handle his huge inert bulk. Her elder brothers were in no better case. She felt angry and ashamed of them.

Then she saw Khyan being carried by a boatman, and she ran to him. Now they have done it to Khyan also, she thought bitterly. They will not rest until they have turned him into a drunkard too.

She directed the boatman to carry Khyan down to the mattress in her father's cabin where she undressed him and forced a distillation of herbs between his lips to revive him. The potion was a cure-all that Taita had mixed for her, and it seemed to be efficacious. At last Khyan murmured and opened his eyes, then fell back immediately into a deep but natural sleep. 'I hope he learns from this,' she told herself. There was nothing more she could do other than leave him to sleep it off. Besides, she still felt lethargic and her headache was unbearable. She went back to her own cabin and, without bothering to undress, she dropped on to the mattress, and almost immediately succumbed to sleep again.

The next time she woke she believed that she was in nightmare for she could hear screams and she was choking on clouds of thick smoke that scalded the back of her throat. Before she was fully conscious she found herself bundled out of her bed, swaddled in a blanket of furs and carried on deck. She struggled, but she was as helpless as an infant in a powerful grip.

On deck the moonless night was lit by leaping flames. They were roaring out of the open forward hatch of the royal barge, climbing the masts and rigging in a hellish orange torrent. She had never seen a wooden hull burn before and the speed and ferocity of the flames appalled her.

She could not stare at it for long, for she found herself carried swiftly across the deck and down the side into a waiting felucca. Her senses returned to her in a rush, and she began again to struggle and scream. 'My father! My brothers! Khyan! Where are they?'

The felucca pushed off into the stream and now she fought with all her strength to free herself, but the arms that pinioned her were remorseless. She managed to twist her head and see the face of the man who held her.

'Trok!' She was angered by his presumption, at the way he was handling her, and ignoring her cries. 'Let me go! I command you!'

He did not respond. He held her easily but he was watching the burning galley with a calm, detached expression.

'Go back!' shrieked at him. 'My family! Go back and fetch them!'

His only response was to snap an order to the oarsmen. 'Hold the stroke!' They shipped their paddles and the felucca rocked on the current. The crew watched the burning hulk with fascination. There were agonizing screams from those trapped below the decks.

Abruptly part of the after-deck collapsed in a tower of flame and sparks. The mooring cables burned through and the galley swung round slowly on the current and drifted downstream.

'Please!' Mintaka changed her tone. 'Please, Lord Trok, my family! You cannot let them burn.'

Now the screams from inside the hull died away and were replaced by the low thunder of the flames. Tears poured down Mintaka's cheeks and dripped from her chin, but still she was helpless in his grasp.

Suddenly the main hatch on the burning deck was thrown open, and the crew of the felucca gasped with horror as a figure emerged. Lord Trok's arms tightened around Mintaka until it seemed that he would crush in her ribs. 'It cannot be!' he grated.

Seen through the smoke and flames it seemed like an apparition from the shades of the underworld. Naked and covered with hair, great belly bulging, Apepi staggered towards the side of the barge. He carried the body of his youngest son in his arms, and his mouth was wide open, gasping for air in the holocaust of flame.

'The monster is hard to kill.' Trok's anger was tinged with fear. Even in her own distress Mintaka read the meaning of his words.

'You, Trok!' she whispered. 'You have done this to them.' Trok ignored the accusation.

The hair on Apepi's body singed and in a puff of heat was gone, for a moment leaving him naked and blackened. Then his skin began to blister and fall away in tatters. His bush of beard and the hair upon his head burst into flame like a pitch-soaked torch. He was no longer moving forward, but he stood with legs astraddle and lifted Khyan high above his head. The boy was as scorched as he was, and the raw flesh showed red and wet where his skin had been burned away. Perhaps Apepi was attempting to throw him over the ship's side into the river to escape the flames, but his strength failed him at last and he stood like a colossus with his head in flames, unable to summon the last reserves to hurl his son to safety in the cool Nile waters.

Mintaka could not move and she was silenced by the horror of the spectacle. To her it seemed to last an eternity, until suddenly the deck under Apepi's feet burst open. He and his son dropped through, and in a tall fountain of flame, sparks and smoke were gone into the guts of the hull.

'It's over.' Trok's voice was dispassionate and detached. He released Mintaka so suddenly that she fell into the bilges of the felucca. He looked at his horrified crew. 'Row to my galley,' he ordered.

'You did this to my family,' Mintaka repeated, as she lay at his feet. 'You will pay for it. I swear it to you. I will make you pay.'

But she felt numbed and bruised as though she had been beaten with the knotted leather lashes of a flail. Her father was gone, that monumental figure in her life whom she had hated a little and loved a great deal. Her family was gone, all of her brothers, even little Khyan, who had been more a son than a sibling to her. She had watched him burn and she knew that the horror of it would stay with her all her days.

The felucca drew alongside Lord Trok's galley and she made no protest as he picked her up as though she were a doll and carried her on board, then down to the main cabin. He laid her on the mattress with uncharacteristic gentleness. 'Your slave girls are safe. I will send them to you,' he said, and went out. She heard the locking bar placed across the door then the sound of him climbing the companion ladder, and crossing the deck above her head.

'Am I a prisoner, then?' she whispered, but that seemed of little importance in the light of what she had just witnessed. She hid her face in pillows that smelt of Trok's stale sweat, and wept until her tears were exhausted. Then she slept.

The burning hull of Apepi's royal barge drifted up on to the riverbank opposite the temple of Hapi. In the dawn the smoke rose high into the still air. It was tainted by the stench of burned flesh. When Mintaka awoke the smell had penetrated into the cabin and sickened her. The smoke seemed to act like a beacon, for the sun had hardly risen above the eastern hills before the fleet of Lord Naja came sweeping around the bend of the river.

The slave girls brought the news to Mintaka. 'Lord Naja has come in full array,' they told her excitedly. 'Yesterday he left us to return to Thebes. Is it not strange that he could reach here so soon when he should be twenty leagues upriver?'

'Surpassing strange,' Mintaka agreed grimly. 'I must dress and be ready for whatever new atrocity awaits me now.'

Her baggage had all gone up in flames in the royal barge, but her maids borrowed clothing from the other noble ladies in the fleet. They washed and curled her hair, then dressed her in a simple linen shift, gold girdle and sandals.

Before noon an armed escort came aboard the galley, and she followed them on deck. Her eyes went first to the blackened timbers of the royal barge that lay on the far bank, burned down to the waterline. No effort was being made to recover any bodies from the wreck. It was her family's funeral pyre. The Hyksosian tradition called for cremation, not embalmment and elaborate funeral procedures and ceremonials.

Mintaka knew that her father would have approved of the manner of his own going, and this gave her some small comfort. Then she thought of Khyan and averted her eyes. It was with an effort that she held back further tears as she went down into the waiting felucca and was taken to the bank below the temple of Hapi.

Lord Naja was waiting with all his company assembled to meet her. She remained aloof and pale when he embraced her. 'This is a bitter time for all of us, Princess,' he said. 'Your father, King Apepi, was a mighty warrior and statesman. In view of the recent treaty between the two kingdoms, and the combining of this very Egypt into one sacred and historical whole, he leaves a dangerous gap. For the good of all, this must be filled immediately.'

He took her hand and led her to the pavilion, which had last evening been the scene of feasting and festivity, but where now were assembled in solemn conclave most of the nobility and officialdom of both the kingdoms.

She saw Trok in the forefront of this throng. He was a striking figure in full regimentals. He wore his sword on a gold-studded belt and carried his war bow over his shoulder. Behind him in packed ranks were all his officers, grim, cold-eyed and menacing despite the gay ribbons plaited in their beards. They stared at her, unsmilingy, and she was bitterly aware that she was the last of the Apepi line, abandoned and unprotected.

She wondered to whom she could appeal, and whose loyalty she still commanded. She searched for friendly familiar faces in the multitude. They were all there, her father's councillors and advisers, his generals and comrades of the battlefield. Then she saw their eyes slide away from her face. None smiled at her or returned her scrutiny. She had never felt so alone in her life.

Naja led her to a cushioned stool at one side of the pavilion. When she sat down Naja and his staff formed a screen around her, hiding her from view. She was certain that this had been deliberately arranged.

Lord Naja opened the conclave with a lamentation for the tragic death of King Apepi and his sons. Then he launched into a eulogy of the dead pharaoh. He recounted his numerous military triumphs and his feats of statesmanship, culminating with his participation in the treaty of Hathor, which had brought peace to the two kingdoms torn by decades of internecine warfare and strife.

'Without King Apepi, or a strong pharaoh to guide the affairs of the Lower Kingdom and to rule in conjunction with Pharaoh Nefer Seti and his regent in Thebes, the treaty of Hathor is in jeopardy. A return to the horrors and warfare of the last sixty years prior to the treaty is unthinkable.'

Lord Trok beat his sword scabbard against his bronze buckler, and shouted, *'Bak-her! Bak-her!'* Immediately the applause was taken up by all the military commanders behind him, and spread slowly through the entire assembly until it was a deafening thunder.

Naja let it continue for a while, then held up both arms. When silence fell he continued, 'In the tragic circumstances of his death, King Apepi leaves no male heir to the Crown.' Smoothly he passed over any mention of Mintaka. 'As a matter of urgency I have consulted the senior councillors and nome governors of both kingdoms. Their choice for the new Pharaoh has been unanimous. With one voice they have asked Lord Trok of Memphis to pick up the reins of power, to take the double crown upon himself and steer the nation forward in the noble tradition set by King Apepi.'

The silence that followed this announcement was profound and drawn-out. Men looked at each other in blank astonishment, and only then became aware that while they had been absorbed in Lord Naja's address two regiments of the northern army commanded by, and loyal to Trok, had come silently out of the palm groves and surrounded the assembly. Their swords were sheathed, but every gloved hand was on the hilt. It would take a moment only to draw the bronze blades. An air of dismay and consternation fell upon them all. Mintaka seized the moment. She sprang off the stool where she had been hidden and cried, 'My lords and loyal citizens of this very Egypt...'

She got no further. Four of the tallest Hyksosian warriors crowded around her, hiding her. They rattled their drawn swords against their shields and shouted in unison, 'Long live, Pharaoh Trok Uruk.' The shout was taken up by the rest of the army. In the joyous uproar that followed strong hands took Mintaka and spirited her away through the cheering press. She struggled ineffectually, her movements smothered and her voice unheard in the storm of cheering. On the riverbank she twisted in the arms of her captors and glanced back. Over the heads of the crowd she glimpsed Lord Naja raising the double crown over the head of the new Pharaoh.

Then she was hustled down the bank to the waiting felucca, and back to her locked and guarded cabin on board Lord Trok's galley.

Mintaka sat with her slave girls in the crowded little cabin and waited to learn what was to be her fate when the new Pharaoh returned on board. Her girls were terrified and as confused as she was. However, she tried to comfort them. When they had calmed a little she started them playing their favourite games. These soon palled so she called for a lute. Her own had been lost on her father's barge, but they borrowed one from a guard.

Mintaka held a competition, making each girl dance in turn in the confined space of the little cabin. They were laughing and clapping when they heard the new Pharaoh returning on board. The girls fell silent but she urged them to continue, and soon they were as rowdy as before.

Mintaka did not join in the merriment. Previously she had carefully explored her surroundings. Attached to her main cabin was a much smaller one, little more than a cupboard, which served as a latrine. It contained a large pottery toilet bowl with a lid and, beside it, a pitcher of water for washing. The bulkhead dividing it from the next cabin was thin and flimsy. The boat-builders had been concerned to save weight.

Mintaka had been on board this galley in happier times, when she and her father had been guests of Lord Trok. She knew that the main cabin lay on the other side of this bulkhead.

Mintaka slipped into the latrine. Even above the noise her girls were making, she heard men's voices from beyond the partition. She recognized Naja's clear, commanding tones, and Trok's gruff replies. Carefully she laid her ear against the planking of the bulkhead and immediately the voices were clearer, the words intelligible.

Naja was dismissing the guards who had accompanied them on board. She heard them stump away, and there was a long silence. So long that she thought Naja might be alone in the saloon. She heard the gurgle of wine being poured into a drinking bowl, and Naja's voice, heavy with sarcasm. 'Your Majesty, have you not over-refreshed yourself already?'

Then Trok's unmistakable laugh, and Mintaka could hear from the impediment to his speech that he was indeed already in his cups as he replied to Naja's jibe, 'Come, cousin, be not so severe. Take a bowl with me. Let us drink to the successful outcome of all our endeavours. Drink to the crown on my head, and the one that will soon bless yours.'

Naja's tone mellowed a little. 'A year ago, when we first began to plan, it all seemed so impossible, so remote. Then we were disparaged and overlooked, as far from the throne as the moon is from the sun, and yet here we are, two pharaohs holding between us the whole of Egypt.'

'And two pharaohs gone on ahead of us,' Trok joined in, 'Tamose with your arrow through his heart and Apepi, the great hog, fried in his own lard along with all his piglets.' He shouted with triumphant laughter.

'Pray, not so loud. You are indiscreet, even if we are alone,' Naja rebuked him gently. 'It would be best if we never repeated those things. Let our little secrets go with Tamose to his tomb in the Valley of the Kings, and with Apepi to the bottom of the river.'

'Come!' Trok insisted. 'Drink with me to all that we have achieved.'

'To what we have achieved,' Naja agreed. 'And to all that is to follow.'

'Today Egypt, and tomorrow the treasures and riches of Assyria, Babylon and the rest of the world! Nothing can stand in our way.'

Mintaka heard Trok gulp noisily. Then there was a crash against the bulkhead at the level of her ear. It startled her and she jumped back, then realized that Trok had hurled the empty wine bowl against the panel smashing it to shards. He belched loudly, and went on, 'Yet there is one detail that remains. Tamose's puppy has your crown upon his head still.'

As she listened Mintaka was in a whirlpool of emotion that tugged her one way then the other, and spun her until her senses reeled. She had listened in horror as, dispassionately, they discussed the murders of her father, her brothers and Pharaoh Tamose, but she was ill-prepared for what they had to say about Nefer.

'Not for much longer,' Naja said. 'That will be taken care of as soon as I return to Thebes. It is all arranged.'

Mintaka clamped her hands across her mouth to prevent herself crying out. They were going to murder Nefer as coldly as they had all the others. Her heart seemed to shrivel within her, and she felt helpless. She was a prisoner and without friends. She tried to think of some way in which she could send a warning to Nefer, for only in that moment did she know the full extent of her love for him: she would do anything in her power to save him.

''Tis a pity the lion did not do your work for you,' said Trok, 'instead of only scratching him a little.'

'The beast set the stage nicely. Nefer needs just a little push, and I will give him a funeral even more splendid than I gave his father.'

'You were always a generous man.' Trok chuckled drunkenly.

'While we speak of Tamose's brat, let us also speak of what remains of Apepi's brood,' Naja suggested silkily. 'The little princess was meant to burn with the rest of them, was that not what we agreed?'

'I decided to change that.' Trok's tone had become sulky. She heard him fill another wine bowl.

'It is dangerous to leave any seed of Apepi unreaped,' Naja warned him. 'Mintaka might easily become a figurehead in the years ahead, a rallying point for rebellion and insurrection. Get rid of her, cousin, and that soon.'

'Why did you not do the same with Tamose's girls? Why do they still live?' Trok challenged him defensively.

'I married them,' Naja pointed out, 'and Heseret dotes on me already. She would do anything I ask of her. We share the same ambitions. She is as hot to see her brother Nefer buried as I am. She lusts for the crown almost as much as for my royal sceptre.'

'Once she has felt my honey bee in her little pink lotus flower, Mintaka will be the same,' Trok declared.

Mintaka's flesh crawled. Once again she was thrown into the maelstrom. She was so appalled at the picture that Trok's boast conjured up that she almost missed Naja's next remark.

'So she has you by the testicles, cousin,' Naja said, but his tone was unamused. 'She is too bold and unruly for my taste, but I wish you joy of her. Be careful of her, Trok, there is a wildness in her. She may take more managing than you think.'

'I will marry her immediately and breed her as swiftly,' Trok assured him. 'With a bundle in her belly she will be more tractable. But for these many years past she has lighted a fire in my loins that cannot be extinguished except by her sweet young juices.'

'You should use your head more, cousin, and your prong less.' Naja's voice was resigned. 'Let us hope that we do not live to regret this passion of yours.' Mintaka heard the deck creak under his feet as Naja stood up, 'So, then, may the gods love and protect you, cousin.' Naja took his leave. 'We both have grave matters to attend. We must part on the morrow, but let us meet as already planned in Memphis at the end of the inundation of the Nile.'

During the rest of the voyage downriver from Balasfura, Mintaka was confined to Trok's galley. While they were under way she had the freedom of the deck, but at anchor or at moorings she was locked in her cabin, and there was a guard at the door.

That happened often, for at every temple along the way Trok went ashore to sacrifice and give thanks to the resident god or goddess for his elevation to the throne of Egypt. Though no others knew it as yet, Trok was also giving notice to those gods that he would soon be joining them in the pantheon as their equal.

Apart from these restrictions, Trok's attempts to ingratiate himself with Mintaka made up in perseverance for what they lacked in subtlety. Each day he presented her with at least one marvellous gift. Once it was a pair of white stallions, which she gave to the captain of the galley. The next day it was a gilt and jewelled chariot that had been captured from the king of Libya by her father. She gave it to the colonel of the palace guard, who had been a stalwart of Apepi. Another time it was a roll of gorgeous silk from the Orient, and on another a silver casket of gemstones, which she distributed among her slave girls. When they were decked in their finery Mintaka paraded them in front of Trok. 'These tawdry pieces look well enough on slaves,' she remarked dismissively, 'but not on any lady of quality.'

The new Pharaoh was undeterred and as soon as they sailed past Asyut into the Lower Kingdom he pointed out a lush and fertile estate that extended for almost a league along the east bank. 'That is yours now, Your Highness, my gift to you. Here is the deed of ownership.' Trok handed it to her with a flourish and a smirk.

She sent for the scribes that same day and had them draw up a charter of manumission, freeing all the slaves who were owned by the estate, and a second deed transferring the entire estate to the priestesses of the temple of Hathor in Memphis.

When Mintaka tried to throw off her sorrow and mourning by relaxing with her girls on the after-deck, dancing and singing, playing bao and setting riddles, Trok tried to join in the sport. He made two of the girls dance the Flight of the Three Swallows with him, then turned to Mintaka. 'Set me a riddle, Princess,' he pleaded.

'What smells like a buffalo bull, looks like a buffalo bull, and when it cavorts with the gazelles does so with all the grace of a buffalo bull?' she asked sweetly. The girls giggled while Trok scowled and flushed. 'Forgive me, Your Highness, that is too obscure for me,' he replied, and stalked away to join his officers.

The next day he had forgiven, but not forgotten, the insult. When they anchored at the village of Samalut, he ordered a troupe of itinerant entertainers, acrobats and musicians to come aboard the galley to entertain Mintaka. One of the magicians was a handsome fellow, with an amusing patter. However, his repertoire of tricks was stale and his execution lacking in finesse. Yet as soon as Mintaka learned that the troupe was taking advantage of the peace that had come with the treaty of Hathor and was on its way upriver to Thebes, where they hoped to play before the court of the southern Pharaoh, Mintaka became enthralled with their performances, particularly that of the magician whose name was Laso. After the performance she invited them to join her for refreshments of sherbet and honeyed dates. She gestured at the magician to sit on the cushions at her feet. He soon overcame his awe of her and regaled her with a few stories at which she laughed merrily.

Under the cover of the chatter and giggling of her girls she asked Laso to deliver a message to the famous Magus, Taita, when he reached Thebes. Almost overcome with her condescension Laso agreed readily. First she impressed upon him the secrecy and the delicacy of the task, then slipped into his hand a small roll of parchment, which he hid under his *chiton*.

She felt a great lift of relief as she watched the troubadours go ashore. She had been desperately seeking some means to convey a warning to Taita and Nefer. The parchment contained protestations of her love for Nefer as well as a warning of Naja's murderous intentions, and that his sister Heseret could no longer be trusted as she had joined their enemies. She went on to tell of the true circumstances surrounding the death of her father and brothers. Finally she told of how Trok planned to take her to wife, despite her betrothal to Nefer, and asked Nefer to intervene with all his authority to prevent this happening.

She estimated that it might take the troupe ten days or more to reach

Thebes and prostrated herself on the deck to pray to Hathor that her warning would not arrive too late. That night she slept better than she had since the terrible events at Balasfura. In the morning she was almost gay, and her girls remarked on how beautiful she looked.

Trok insisted that she joined him for breakfast on the foredeck. His cooks had provided a lavish banquet. There were twenty other guests and Trok seated himself next to Mintaka. She determined that she would not allow even this imposition to dampen her spirits. Pointedly she ignored Trok and directed all her charm and wit to the officers of his army who made up most of the rest of the company.

At the end of the meal Trok clapped his hands for attention, and was rewarded with an obsequious silence. 'I have a gift for the Princess Mintaka.'

'Oh, no!' Mintaka shrugged. 'And what shall I do with this one?'

'I believe Your Highness will find it more to her taste than my other poor offerings.' Trok was looking so pleased with himself that she began to feel uneasy.

'Your generosity is misplaced, my lord.' She would not address him by any of his numerous new royal titles. 'Thousands of your subjects, victims of war and plague, are starving and stand in greater need than I.'

'This is something special, which will have value to you alone,' he assured her.

She threw up her hands in resignation. 'I am only one of your loyal subjects.' She made no effort to hide her sarcasm. 'If you insist, far be it from me to deny you anything.'

Trok clapped his hands again and two of his guardsmen came down the deck from the bows, carrying between them a large bag of untanned leather. The smell it gave off was strong and unpleasant. Some of the girls exclaimed with disgust, but Mintaka remained expressionless as the two soldiers stopped in front of her.

Trok nodded at them and they loosened the drawstring at the mouth of the bag, then tipped out the contents on to the deck. The girls shrieked with horror, and even some of the men started and exclaimed with disgust.

The severed human head rolled across the planking to Mintaka's feet, and lay there, staring up at her with a wide and startled gaze. The long dark locks were stiff with dried black blood.

'Laso!' Mintaka whispered the name of the inept magician whom she had entrusted with her message to Thebes.

'Ah! You recall his name.' Trok smiled. 'His tricks must have impressed you as much as they did me.'

In the summer heat the head had begun to decompose, and the smell was strong. The flies came swiftly and crawled on the open eyeballs. Mintaka's gorge rose, and she swallowed hard. She saw that a scrap of papyrus parchment protruded from between Laso's purple lips.

'Alas, it seems that his last trick was his most amusing.' Trok leaned over and retrieved the blood-smeared parchment. He held it so that Mintaka could be certain it was her own cartouche that sealed the message, then dropped the papyrus into the charcoal brazier on which the lamb kebabs were roasting. It burned quickly and the ashes curled into grey powder.

Trok gestured for the head to be removed. One of the soldiers picked it up by the hair, dropped it back into the bag and took it away. The company sat for a long minute in shocked silence, except that one of the girls was sobbing softly.

'Your Royal Highness, your divine father of illustrious memory must have had some premonition of the fate that awaited him,' Trok addressed her gravely. Mintaka was too disturbed to reply. 'Before his tragic death he spoke to me. He placed you under my protection. I gave him my oath, and I accepted this as a sacred charge. You need never appeal to any other for protection. I, Pharaoh Trok Uruk, am your oath man.' He placed his right hand upon her bowed head, and in the other hand he raised another scroll of parchment.

'This is my royal proclamation setting aside the betrothal of Princess Mintaka of the House of Apepi to Pharaoh Nefer Seti of the House of Tamose. Furthermore, it contains a proclamation of the marriage of the Princess Mintaka to Pharaoh Trok Uruk. The proclamation has been ratified by the cartouche of Lord Naja, accepting and confirming it in the name of Pharaoh Nefer Seti.' He handed the scroll to his chamberlain with a terse instruction. 'Have one hundred copies made of this proclamation and cause them to be publicly displayed in every city in every nome of this very Egypt.'

Then, with both hands, he lifted Mintaka to her feet. 'You will not be alone for much longer. You and I will be husband and wife before the rise of the Moon of Osiris.'

Three days later Pharaoh Trok Uruk arrived at Avaris, his military capital in the Lower Kingdom, and immediately plunged with indefatigable energy into securing to his own hand all the affairs of state, and the trappings of power.

The populace was delirious with joy at the news of the treaty of Hathor, and at the promise of peace and prosperity in the years ahead. However, there was some puzzlement and dismay when one of the first acts of the new Pharaoh was to put in hand another massive enforced draft of men for the army. It soon became clear that he was intent on doubling the size of his infantry regiments and building two thousand more fighting chariots.

The question was asked, but not to Trok's face, where he expected to find a new enemy now that Egypt was once more united and at peace. The loss of working men from the millet fields and pastures to the army resulted in a shortage of food and a sharp increase in the prices in the markets. The expenditure on new chariots, weapons and military equipment necessitated an increase in taxation. There were mutters now that Apepi, despite his warmongering, taxation and contempt of the gods, had not been as bad a ruler as they had believed him to be.

Within weeks Trok ordered work to commence on the extensive enlargements and refurbishment to the palace in Avaris into which he intended to move with his bride, Princess Mintaka. The architects estimated that these works would cost over two lakhs of gold. The muttering grew louder.

Well aware of the rising discontent, Trok met it with the proclamation of his own divinity and elevation to the pantheon. Work was to begin within the week on the construction of his temple on a choice site alongside the magnificent temple of Seueth in Avaris. Trok was determined that his temple would exceed that of his brother god in splendour. The architects estimated that the completion of the temple would require at the very least five thousand labourers, five years and another two lakhs of gold.

The revolt started in the delta where a regiment of foot, who had been unpaid for over a year, murdered their officers and marched on Avaris, calling on the population to rise and join them against the tyrant. Trok met them with three hundred chariots near Manashi and cut them to pieces with his first charge.

He emasculated and impaled five hundred mutineers on stakes. Like a macabre forest, they decorated both sides of the road for half a league beyond the village of Manashi. The ringleaders of the revolt were roped to the back of chariots and dragged to Avaris to state their grievances. Unfortunately none of the prisoners survived the journey: by the time they arrived they were barely recognizable as human – their skin and much of their flesh had been ripped away as they were dragged over the rough ground. Ragged pieces of flesh and splinters of bone were scattered over twenty leagues of the roadway, to the delight of the pi-dogs, jackals and carrion crows.

A few hundred mutineers escaped the massacre and disappeared into the desert. Trok did not bother to pursue them beyond the eastern borders, for this petty matter had already occupied too much of his attention and delayed his wedding by months. He hurried back to Avaris, using up three pairs of horses in his furious impatience.

While Trok was away, Mintaka had tried twice more to send a message to Taita in Thebes. The first of her messengers had been one of the eunuchs of the harem, a fat, kindly black man she had known all her life. There was a special bond between the eunuchs in both kingdoms that transcended race or country. Even during the years when the two kingdoms were split asunder, Soth, for that was the eunuch's name, had honoured this special tie to Taita, and had been his friend and confidant.

However, Trok's spies were ubiquitous and unsleeping. Soth never reached Assyut but was brought back in a leather bag barely alive. He died when his head was plunged into a cauldron of boiling water. His skull, with the flesh boiled away, the bone bleached and polished, the eye-sockets filled with orbs of lapis lazuli, was presented to Mintaka as a special gift from Pharaoh Trok.

After that Mintaka could not bring herself to recruit another messenger, and thus condemn him or her to a gruesome death. Nevertheless, one of her Libyan slave girls, Thana, who knew the depth of her mistress's love volunteered to carry her message. She was the not the prettiest of the girls, for she had a cast in one eye and a large nose, but she was loyal, loving and true. At her suggestion Mintaka sold her to a merchant who was travelling to Thebes the following day. He took Thana with him, but three days later she was back in Avaris, bound by wrists and ankles to the side frame of a chariot of the border guards.

Trok dealt with Thana on his return from Manashi: he condemned her to death by love and she was given to the regiment that had led the charge at Manashi. Over four hundred men took their pleasure with her until, at sunset on the third day, she bled to death.

For three days Mintaka wept for her without cease.

The wedding of Pharaoh Trok Uruk and Princess Mintaka Apepi was played out in the ancient Hyksosian tradition that had its origins a thousand years earlier, and a thousand leagues to the east, on the vast treeless steppe beyond the mountains of Assyria from which their ancestors had ridden to the conquest of Egypt.

At dawn on the day of the wedding, a party of two hundred of the relatives and members of the tribe of Princess Mintaka burst into the royal apartments where she had been kept captive ever since her return to Avaris. There was no resistance from the guards who had been expecting this incursion. The members of her faction carried Mintaka away, and rode towards the east in a tight formation with the princess in their midst, shouting defiance and brandishing clubs and staves. Edged weapons of any sort were banned from the festivities.

When the bridal party had been given a head-start the bridegroom led a party of his own tribe, the leopards, in pursuit. The fugitives had shown no urgency to escape, and as soon as the pursuers came into view they turned back and gleefully launched themselves into the fray. Even though swords and daggers were not allowed, two men suffered fractured limbs, and there were a few cracked skulls. Not even the bridegroom escaped without cuts and bruises. In the end Trok claimed his prize. He snatched up Mintaka with an arm around her waist and lifted her into his chariot.

Mintaka's resistance was not in the least play-acting, and with her fingernails she inflicted a deep scratch down the right side of Trok's face, which narrowly missed his eye, and the dripping blood spoiled the colourful splendour of his costume.

'She will give you many warlike sons!' his supporters shouted in admiration for the ferocity of the Mintaka's resistance.

Grinning delightedly at the belligerent spirit of his bride Trok drove her triumphantly back to his temple where the newly appointed priests of his order waited to perform the final rituals.

The temple was as yet only open foundation trenches and tall heaps of stone building blocks, but this did not detract from the pleasure of the wedding guests or the enthusiasm of the bridegroom as they stood under the canopy of woven reeds while the high priest bound Mintaka to him with a halter rope.

At the culmination of the ceremony, Trok cut the throat of his favourite war horse, a beautiful chestnut stallion, as a sign that he placed a higher value on his bride than on this other precious possession.

As the animal fell kicking and spurting blood from the open carotid artery the company shouted their acclamation and lifted the couple into the flower-bedecked chariot.

Trok drove back to the palace with one arm still firmly around his bride, taking no chances on a second escape. The army lined the way, swarming around the vehicle, and showered gifts of amulets and good-luck charms into the cockpit. Others held up bowls of wine to Trok as he drove past, and he gulped them, spilling much of it down his tunic where it mingled with the blood from his torn cheek.

By the time they reached the palace Trok was soaked with blood and red wine, sweating and dusty from the ride and the fight to claim his bride, reckless with wine and wild-eyed with lust.

He carried Mintaka through the crowd into their new apartments, and the guards at the door turned back the wedding guests with drawn swords. However, they did not disperse but surrounded the palace, chanting encouragement to the bridegroom and ribald advice to the bride.

In the bedchamber Trok threw Mintaka on to the white sheepskin that covered the mattress and used both hands to struggle with his sword-belt, trying to loosen the clasp and cursing it lustily when it would not yield. Mintaka hit the bed and bounced off it like a rabbit startled from her burrow by a ferret.

She raced to the terrace door and tried to wrest it open. The locking bars on the outside had been put in place by Trok's orders. Desperately she tried to tear open the panel with her fingernails, but the doors were solid and thick and did not even tremble to her onslaught.

Behind her Trok had at last rid himself of the sword-belt and the scabbard clattered on the mosaic tiles. He came lumbering unsteadily after her. 'Fight as much as you wish, prettyling,' he slurred. 'It sets my prong on fire when you kick and scream.'

He placed one arm around her waist, and reached around with the other hand to seize one of her breasts. 'By Seueth, what ripe, juicy fruit is this?' He squeezed hard with fingers calloused by the hilt of sword and by the reins of his chariot. The pain shot through her chest, and she screamed and twisted in his arms, raking for his eyes again. He caught her wrist. 'You'll not play that little trick twice.' He swung her off her feet and carried her back to the bed.

'Baboon!' she cried. 'You smelly hairy ape. You foul animal.'

'You sing a sweet love song, little one. My heart and my prong swell when I hear how much you desire me.'

He threw her down again and this time pinned her with one huge muscular arm across her chest. His face was inches from hers. His beard prickled her cheeks, and his breath smelt of sour wine. She twisted her face away. He laughed and hooked one finger in the neck of her shift and ripped the silk to below her waist.

He prised out her breasts and one after the other squeezed them hard enough to leave red fingermarks on the tender flesh. He pinched her nipples and pulled them out until they darkened in colour, then ran his right hand over her belly. Playfully he prodded one thick finger into her belly button, then tried to force his hand between her thighs. She locked her legs, one over the other, to deny him.

Suddenly he reared up, straddled her, sitting across her lower body with all his weight so that she could not struggle, and ripped off his tunic. Under it he was naked. His body was trained by war, hunting and rough games, and although her vision was distorted by pain, tears and terror, she had an impression of wide shoulders and bulging muscle, limbs thick and thewy as the branches of a cedar of Lebanon.

Still pinning her under him, he twisted round until his belly pressed against hers, and the coarse hair that covered his chest rasped against her breasts. With mounting terror she felt his massive penis prodding against her.

She fought not only for her dignity and modesty, but as if for her very life. She tried to bite his face but her small sharp teeth were smothered in his beard. She clawed at his back and the skin peeled away to jam under her nails, but he did not seem to feel it.

He was trying to force a knee between her thighs, but she kept them locked together, hooking one of her legs over the other. Every muscle in her lower body was frozen in a rigor of fear and revulsion, hard and as impenetrable as a granite statue of the goddess.

Both of them were sweating, he more heavily. It poured from his body, greasing their skin so that his huge member slithered over her belly and pounded at the junction of her thighs.

Suddenly he heaved his upper body free, and swung a heavy blow, flat-handed, across her face. It jarred her clenched jaws, crushing her lips and nose. She felt blood flood into her mouth and darkness fill her head.

'Open up, bitch!' he panted above her. 'Open that hot little slit and let me in.' He was thrusting hard with his hips, and she felt the loathsome thing slithering over her. Even in the pain and darkness of the blow she managed to deny him entry, but she knew she could not last out much longer. He was too heavy and powerful.

'Hathor, help me!' She closed her eyes and prayed. 'Sweet goddess, do not let it happen!'

She heard him groan above her, and her eyes flew open. His face was swollen and dark with congested blood. She felt him arch his back, and he moaned as though in pain. His eyes were wide, sightless and shot with blood. His mouth opened in a terrible rictus.

Mintaka did not understand what was happening. For a moment she thought that the goddess must have heard her plea and struck him through the heart with a divine dart. Then she felt hot liquid spray over her stomach, so hot it seemed to scald her skin. She tried to twist away to avoid it, but he was too heavy and strong. At last the loathsome stream shrivelled and dried up. Suddenly he groaned again and collapsed on top of her. He lay quiescent, and she dared not move lest it incite him to further efforts. They lay for a long time, until in the quiet chamber they both became aware of the lewd cries of the crowd waiting outside the palace walls. Trok roused himself and looked down at her. 'You have shamed me, you little slut. You have made me spill my seed in vain.'

Before she knew what he was about, he grabbed her by the back of her neck and forced her face into the white sheepskin.

'Never fear, I shall use the blood from your nose if I can't have it from your honeypot.'

He rolled her aside and inspected the crimson stain from her bleeding face on the pure white wool with grim satisfaction. Then he jumped to his feet, strode, stark naked, to the shutters and kicked them open with a crash of shattering timber. He disappeared out into the bright daylight.

With a fold of the bed linen Mintaka wiped away the loathsome slime that was clotting on her ivory smooth belly. There were angry red marks on her breasts and on her limbs. Her fear turned to fury.

His sword-belt lay where he had dropped it. Quietly she slipped from the bed and drew the burnished bronze blade from its scabbard. She crept to the door that led on to the terrace and flattened herself against the jamb.

Outside, Trok was acknowledging the applause of the crowd and flapping the stained sheepskin for all to see. 'She loved it!' he answered some shouted comment. 'When I finished with her, she was wide and wet as the delta swamps, as hot as the Sahara.'

Mintaka tightened her grip on the haft of the heavy sword and gathered herself.

'Farewell, my friends,' Trok shouted. 'I am going back for another bite at that sweet fig.'

She heard his bare feet swish on the tiles as he returned and then his shadow fell across the entrance. She drew back the sword with both hands, and held the point at belly height.

As he stepped into the chamber she braced herself and then with all her strength thrust at him, aiming halfway between the pit of his navel and the dense black bush from which dangled the heavy excrescence of his genitals.

Once, long ago, while hunting with her father, she had watched him aim at a monster male leopard that was unaware of their presence. The cat had been alerted by the twang and hum of her father's bowstring, and instantly leaped aside before the arrow reached its mark. Trok possessed the same feral instinct for danger and survival.

Her thrust was still in the air, when he twisted away from the sharp bronze point. It flew the width of a finger past his hairy stomach, without cutting skin or drawing a drop of blood. Then he clamped both her wrists in one of his huge paws. He squeezed until she felt the bones in her wrist crushing and she had to let the weapon drop and clatter on the floor.

He was laughing as he dragged her across the room, but it was an ugly sound. He threw her back on to the rumpled and sweat-sour bed. 'You are my wife now,' he said, as he stood over her. 'You belong to me, like a brood mare or a bitch-dog. You must learn to obey and respect me.'

She lay face down, pressing her face into the soiled linen, refusing to look at him. He picked up the sword scabbard from where it lay beside the bed. 'This lesson in obedience is for your own good. A little pain now will save us both a great deal of unhappiness and suffering later.'

He weighed the scabbard in his right hand. It was of polished leather, bound with gold and electrum bands, studded with metal rosettes. He swung it down across the back of her naked legs. It slapped across the white flesh and left a welt with the raised pattern of rosettes in brighter scarlet. She was so taken by surprise that despite herself she shrieked aloud.

He laughed at her pain, and lifted the scabbard again. She tried to roll away from him but the next blow caught her across her raised right arm, and the next across her shoulder. She stopped herself crying out again, and tried to hide her distress by forcing a wicked smile and spitting at him like a lynx. This infuriated him, and he struck with more venom.

He knocked her off the bed and followed her as she crawled across the floor. He beat her across the back, and when she rolled herself into a ball he lashed her across her back, shoulders and buttocks. He spoke to her while he kept the blows falling to a steady rhythm, punctuating his words with the exhalation of effort as he struck. 'You will never lift a hand to me again, hah! Next time I come to you, hah! You will behave as a loving wife, hah! Or I will have four of my men hold you down, hah! While I mount you, hah! Then when I have finished, hah! I will beat you again, hah! Like this, hah!'

She clenched her jaws as the blows rained down upon her until at last she could no longer fight back, but mercifully he stepped away, breathing heavily.

He pulled on his stained and dust-streaked tunic, belted the scabbard around his waist and thrust his sword into the scabbard that was smeared with her blood, and stalked to the door of the chamber. There he paused and looked back at her. 'Remember one thing, wife, either I break my mares,' he said, 'or, by Seueth, they die under me.' He turned and was gone.

Mintaka lifted her head slowly and stared after him. She could not speak. Instead she filled her mouth with spittle and spat it after him. It splattered on the tiles streaked with blood from her swollen mouth.

***

It was long after the waning of the Moon of Isis before the scabs fell off Mintaka's injuries and the bruises faded to greenish-yellow stains on her smooth, creamy skin. Either by design or luck, Trok had not knocked out any of her teeth, broken any bones or left her face scarred.

Since their calamitous wedding day he had left her alone. Most of that time he was campaigning in the south. Even when he returned for brief periods to Avaris he avoided her. Perhaps he was repelled by her unsightly injuries, or perhaps he was shamed by his inability to consummate their marriage. Mintaka did not ponder the reason too deeply, but she rejoiced in being free for a while of his brutish attentions.

There had been further serious rebellion in the south of the kingdom. Trok had responded savagely. He had fallen on the insurgents and had slaughtered those who opposed him, seized their property and sold their families into slavery. Lord Naja had sent two regiments to assist in these operations against the rebels, supporting his cousin and pharaoh, and at the same time sharing in the spoils.

Mintaka knew that Trok had returned triumphantly to Avaris three days ago, but she had still not seen him. She thanked the goddess for that, but it was premature. The summons came from him on the fourth day. Mintaka was to attend an extraordinary session of the state council. So urgent was the matter that she was allowed only an hour to prepare herself. His message warned her that should she choose to ignore his summons he would send his bodyguards to drag her to the conclave. She had no option, and her girls dressed her.

This was the first occasion on which Mintaka had appeared in public since her wedding. With her makeup carefully applied she was as lovely as ever as she took her seat on the queen's throne, below of that of Pharaoh, in the lavishly redecorated assembly hall of the palace. She tried to make her expression remote, and to keep aloof from the proceedings, but her reserve slipped as she recognized the royal herald who came in and prostrated himself before the twin thrones. She leaned forward attentively.

Trok acknowledged the herald then called upon him to rise and state his news to the council. When he rose to his feet Mintaka saw that he was in the grip of deep emotion. He had to clear his throat several times before he could utter a word, and then at last he spoke, in a voice so shaken that at first Mintaka did not understand what he was saying. She heard the words but could not bring herself to accept them.

'Your Sacred Majesty Pharaoh Trok Uruk, Queen Mintaka Apepi Uruk, distinguished members of the state council, citizens of Avaris, brothers and fellow countrymen of this reunited Egypt, I bring tragic tidings from the south. I would rather die outnumbered a hundred to one in battle than have to tell you this.' He paused and coughed again. Then his voice rose stronger and clearer.

'I have made the voyage by fast galley downriver from Thebes. Travelling day and night, stopping only to change rowers, I have taken twelve days to reach Avaris.'

He paused again and spread his arms in a gesture of despair. 'Last month, on the eve of the festival of Hapi, the young Pharaoh Nefer Seti whom we all loved, and in whom we placed so much trust and hope, died of the grievous wounds that he received at Dabba while hunting a cattle-raiding lion.' There was concerted sigh of despair. One of the councillors covered his eyes and began to weep silently.

The herald spoke into the silence: 'The Regent of the Upper Kingdom, Lord Naja, who is of the royal family of Tamose by marriage, and who is next in the line of succession, has been raised to the throne in the place of the departed Pharaoh. He purifies the land in his name of Kiafan, he endures unto eternity in his name of Naja, the fear of him through all the world is great in his name of Pharaoh Naja Kiafan.'

The cries of mourning for the dead Pharaoh, and the clamour of acclamation for his successor filled the hall.

In the uproar, Mintaka stared at the herald. Under the makeup she had turned chalky pale and her eyes needed no kohl to make them huge and tragic. The world seemed to turn dark around her, and she swayed on her stool. Although she had heard Nefer's death being planned and plotted, she had convinced herself that it would not happen. She had made herself believe that, even without her warnings, Nefer, with Taita to help him, would somehow avoid the malignant web spun by Naja and Trok.

Trok was watching her with a sly, gloating smile, and she knew he was revelling in her pain. She did not care any longer. Nefer was gone and with him her will and her reason to resist and to go on living herself. She stood up from the throne and, like a sleep-walker left the hall. She expected her husband to order her back, but he did not. In the general consternation and lamentation few of the other guests noticed her leave. Those who did were aware of her terrible sorrow. They recalled that she had once been betrothed to the dead Pharaoh, and they forgave her this breach of decorum and protocol.

Mintaka stayed in her own chamber for three days and nights without eating. She drank only a little wine mixed with water. She ordered everyone to leave her, even her girls. She would see nobody, not even the physicians Trok sent to her.

On the fourth day she asked for the chief priestess of the temple of Hathor. They were alone together for the entire morning, and when the old woman left the palace she had covered her shaven head with her white shawl as a sign of mourning.

The next morning the priestess returned with two of her acolytes, who carried a large basket of woven palm fronds. They placed the basket in front of Mintaka, then covered their heads and withdrew.

The priestess knelt beside Mintaka and asked her quietly, 'Are you certain that you wish to take the way of the goddess, my daughter?'

'There is nothing further for me to live for,' Mintaka said simply.

The priestess had tried for hours the previous day to dissuade her, but now she made one last attempt. 'You are young still . . .'

Mintaka held up one slim hand. 'Mother, I may not have lived many years, but in that short time I have experienced more pain than most encounter in all their long lives.'

The priestess bowed her head and said, 'Let us pray to the goddess.' Mintaka closed her eyes as she went on, 'Blessed lady, mighty cow of the sky, mistress of music and love, all-seeing, all-powerful, hear the prayers of your daughters who love you.'

Something in the basket in front of them moved and there was a faint susurration like the river breeze in the papyrus beds. Mintaka felt the coldness in her stomach, and knew that it was the first chill of death. She listened to the prayer, but her thoughts were with Nefer. She recalled vividly so much that they had shared together, and in her mind a picture of him appeared as though he still lived. She saw again his smile and the way he held his head so perfectly balanced on his strong, straight neck. She wondered what point he had reached on his dread journey through the netherworld, and she prayed for his safety. She prayed for him to reach the green hills of paradise, and that she should soon be reunited with him there. I shall follow you soon, my heart, she promised him.

'Your beloved daughter, Mintaka, the wife of the divine Pharaoh Trok Uruk, begs from you the favour you have promised to those who have suffered too much in this world. Allow her to meet your dark messenger, and through him to find peace in your bosom, mighty Hathor.'

The priestess ended her prayer and waited. The next step must be taken by Mintaka alone. Mintaka opened her eyes, and studied the basket as though seeing it for the first time. Slowly she reached out with both hands and lifted the lid. The interior of the basket was dark, but there was movement within, a heavy, languid coiling and uncoiling, a glinting of black upon black like oil spilled on water in a deep well.

Mintaka leaned forward to peer within, and slowly a scaled head rose to meet her. As it emerged into the light the hood distended until it was wide as a woman's fan, patterned in black and ivory. The eyes were as shiny as glass beads. The thin lips were curved in a sardonic grin, and the feathery black tongue flickered out between them, tasting the air, and the scent of the girl who sat in front of it.

They stared at each other, the girl and the cobra, for a hundred slow beats of her heart. Once the serpent swayed back as though to strike, then came gently upright once more like some fatal flower on a long stem.

'Why will it not do its work?' Mintaka asked, with her lips close enough to those of the cobra to exchange a kiss. She reached out her hand and the serpent turned his head to watch her fingers come towards him. Mintaka showed no fear. Gently she stroked the back of the cobra's widely distended hood. Instead of attacking the cobra turned half away from her, almost like a cat offering its head to be caressed.

'Make it do what has to be done,' Mintaka begged the priestess, but the old woman shook her head in puzzlement.

'This I have never seen before,' she whispered. 'You must strike the messenger with your hand. That will surely make him deliver the gift of the goddess.'

Mintaka drew back her hand, with open palm and fingers spread. She aimed at the ophidian head of the serpent and was on the point of striking, when she started with surprise and lowered her hand. Puzzled, she glanced around the darkened chamber, into the shadowed corners, then looked directly at the priestess.

'Did you speak again?' she asked.

'I said nothing.'

Mintaka raised her hand again, but this time the voice was closer and clearer. She recognized it with a rush of superstitious fear, and felt the hairs rise upon the back of her neck.

'Taita?' she whispered, looking around. She expected him to be standing at her shoulder, but the chamber was still empty except for the two of them kneeling in front of the basket. 'Yes!' Mintaka said, as though replying to a question or an instruction. She listened to the silence and twice nodded, then softly, 'Oh, yes!'

The priestess heard nothing, but she knew and understood that there had been some mystical intervention in their proceedings. She was unsurprised when the cobra sank back slowly into the depths of the basket. She replaced the lid, and stood up.

'Forgive me, Mother,' Mintaka said softly, 'I will not take the way of the goddess. There is still much for me to do in this world.'

The priestess picked up the basket, and said to the girl, 'May the goddess bless you and grant you eternal life hereafter.' She backed away to the door of the chamber, and left Mintaka sitting in the gloom. She seemed to be listening still to a voice that the old woman could not hear.

Taita brought Nefer back to Thebes from Dabba in the deep sleep of the Red Shepenn. As soon as the galley carrying them moored at the stone jetty below the palace, Taita had him carried ashore on a litter, curtained from the gaze of the common people. It would have been unwise for Pharaoh's critical condition to become widely known in the city. There had been previous occasions when the death of a king had plunged the city and the entire state into wild despair, and caused devastating speculation in the millet exchange, riots, looting and a breakdown of all the mores and conventions of society.

Once Nefer was safely ensconced in his royal quarters at the palace, Taita was able to work on him in safety and seclusion. His first concern was to examine again the terrible lacerations down the front of the boy's legs and lower abdomen and assess if there had been any morbid changes.

His greatest fear was that the entrails had been punctured and that their contents had leaked into the stomach cavity. If this had happened then his skills would be to little avail. He unwrapped the bandages, probed the openings gently, sniffed the effluent for the stink of faeces, and was greatly relieved to find no taint of that contamination. He syringed the deepest wounds with a mixture of vinegar and Oriental spices. Then he stitched them closed with cat-gut and bandaged them with all his skill, touching them with the golden Periapt of Lostris, commending her grandson to the goddess with each wrap of the linen strip.

Over the days that followed Taita gradually reduced the dosage of the Red Shepenn and was rewarded when Nefer recovered consciousness, and smiled at him. 'Taita, I knew you were with me.' Then he looked around him, still drowsy with the drug. 'Where is Mintaka?'

When Taita explained her absence, Nefer's disappointment was almost palpable, and he was too weak to conceal it. Taita tried to console him by telling him that the parting was only temporary, and that he would soon be well enough to make the voyage northwards to visit Avaris. 'We will find a fine excuse for Naja to allow you to make the journey,' Taita assured him.

For a while Nefer's recovery was encouraging. The following day he was sitting up, and ate a hearty meal of *dhurra* bread and chick-pea soup. The next day he took a few steps on the crutches Taita had carved for him, and asked for meat with his meal. In order not to heat his blood, Taita forbade red meat, but allowed him fish and poultry.

The next day Merykara came to visit her brother, and spent most of the day with him. Her merry laughter and her childlike prattle cheered him. Nefer asked after Heseret, and wanted to know why she had not come also. Merykara answered evasively and invited him to play another game of bao. This time he deliberately opened his centre castle to let her win.

The next day the terrible news of the tragedy at Balasfura reached Thebes. The first reports were that Apepi and his entire family, including Mintaka, had perished in the flames. Nefer was stricken down again, this time by grief. Taita had to mix him another potion of the Red Shepenn, but within hours the wounds in his leg had turned. Over the next few days his condition worsened, and soon he was at the very frontiers of death. Taita sat with him and watched him tossing and raving in delirium while the livid scarlet lines of morbidity ran like rivers of fire up his limbs and his belly.

Then news came from the Lower Kingdom that Mintaka had survived the tragedy that had engulfed the rest of her family. When Taita whispered these wonderful tidings in his ear Nefer seemed to understand and respond. The next day he was weak but lucid, and he tried to convince Taita that he was strong enough to make the long journey to be with Mintaka in her bereavement. Gently Taita dissuaded him, but promised that as soon as Nefer was strong enough he would use all his influence to convince Lord Naja to allow him to go. With this goal to strive towards, Nefer rallied strongly once again. Taita could see him subduing the fevers and evil humours in his blood by sheer strength of will.

Lord Naja returned from the north, and within hours Heseret came to visit Nefer for the first time since his mauling by the lion. She brought him gifts of sweetmeats, a pot of wild honey in the comb, and a magnificent bao board made of coloured agate, with stones of carved ivory and black coral. She was sweet, infinitely gentle and concerned with his suffering, excusing herself for having neglected him.

'My dear husband, the Regent of the Upper Kingdom, the illustrious Lord Naja, has been away all these weeks,' she explained, 'and I have pined so much for his return that I was not fit company for anyone as ill as you have been. I was afraid that my unhappiness might affect you badly, my poor darling Nefer.' She stayed an hour, sang to him, and related some of the doings of the court, much of it scandalous. At last she excused herself: 'My husband, the Regent of the Upper Kingdom, does not like me to leave his side for long. We are so much in love, Nefer. He is a wonderful man, so kind and dedicated to you and Egypt. You must learn to trust him completely, as I do.' She rose to her feet and then, as though as an afterthought, she remarked lightly, 'You must have been relieved to hear that Pharaoh Trok Uruk and my dear husband, the Regent of Upper Egypt, have agreed for reasons of state to cancel your betrothal to that little Hyksosian barbarian, Mintaka. I was so sorry for you when I heard that such a disgraceful marriage was thrust upon you. My husband, the Regent of Upper Egypt, was against it from the very beginning, as I was.'

After she had gone Nefer sank back weakly on the pillow and closed his eyes. When Taita came to him a little later he was puzzled by the way in which he had relapsed. He removed the bandages and found that the infection in his injuries had flared up again, and that the malodorous pus streaming from the deepest wound was thick and yellow. He stayed with him through that night, exerting all his skill and his powers to ward off the shadows of evil that surrounded the young Pharaoh.

At dawn Nefer was in a coma. Taita was truly alarmed by his condition. It could not be explained entirely by the boy's grief. Suddenly he was startled and angered by a commotion at the door. He was about to call for silence when he heard Lord Naja's commanding voice ordering the guards to stand aside. The Regent strode into the chamber and, without greeting Taita, stooped over Nefer's still form and peered into his pale, drawn face. After a long moment he straightened up and signed to Taita to follow him on to the terrace.

When Taita came out behind him he was gazing across the river. On the far bank a squadron of chariots was practising their evolutions, changing formations at full gallop. Strangely, there had been much warlike preparation since the treaty of Hathor. 'You wished to speak to me, my lord?' Taita asked.

Naja turned to him. His expression was grim. 'You have disappointed me, old man,' he said, and Taita bowed his head but made no reply. 'I had hoped that my way forward, my destiny as predicted by the gods, would be cleared by now of impediment.' He stared hard at Taita. 'Yet it seems that, far from allowing this come to pass, you have done all in your power to prevent it.'

'This has been pretence. I have made a show of caring for my patient, while in reality I have been fostering your interests. As you can see for yourself, Pharaoh hangs over the great abyss.' Taita made a gesture towards the sick chamber where Nefer lay. 'Surely you can sense the shades drawing in more closely around him. My lord, we have almost obtained our object. Within days the way ahead will be cleared for you.'

Naja was not convinced. 'I am reaching the limit of my patience,' he warned, and strode from the terrace. He passed through the chamber without another glance at the still form upon the bed.

During that day Nefer's condition fluctuated between deep coma and bouts of restless sweating and delirious ravings. When it became clear that the leg was giving him intense agony, Taita removed the linen bandages and found the whole of his thigh grotesquely swollen. The stitches holding the wound closed were strained and cutting deeply into the hot, purple flesh. Taita knew that he dared not move the boy while his life hung on such a slender thread. The plans that he had laid so carefully over the past weeks could not go forward unless he took drastic action. To interfere further with the wound in this condition was to risk a fatal poisoning of the blood, but there was no other course open to him. He laid out his instruments and bathed the entire leg in a solution of vinegar. Then he forced another heavy dose of the Red Shepenn between Nefer's lips, and while he waited for the drug to take effect he prayed to Horus and to the goddess Lostris for their protection. Then he took up the scalpel and cut one of the stitches that held the lips of the wound together.

He was taken aback by the way in which the flesh burst open and at the gagging flood of yellow corruption that poured out. He used a gold spoon to scrape it clean, and when he felt the metal strike some hard obstruction in the depths of the wound, he probed with ivory forceps and gripped the object in the jaws. At last he prised it free. He took it to the light from the doorway and found that it was a ragged splinter of the lion's claw, half as long as his little finger, which must have broken off as the beast was savaging Nefer.

He placed a gold tube in the wound to allow it to drain, then rebandaged it. By evening Nefer's recovery was miraculous. In the morning he was weak but the fever in his blood had abated. Taita gave him a tonic to fortify him, and placed the Periapt of Lostris on his leg. While he sat beside him in the noonday, gathering his resolve, there was a soft scratching at the shutters. When he opened them a crack, Merykara slipped into the chamber. She was distraught and had been weeping. She flung herself against Taita and hugged his legs.

'They have forbidden me to come here,' she whispered and she did not have to explain who 'they' were, 'but I know the guards on the terrace and they let me pass.'

'Gently, my child.' Taita stroked her hair. 'Do not distress yourself so.'

'Taita, they are going to kill him.'

'Who are they?'

'The two of them.' Merykara started sobbing again and her explanation was barely coherent. 'They thought I was asleep or that I would not understand what they were discussing. They never said his name, but I knew they were talking about Nefer.'

'What did they say?'

'They will send for you. When you leave Nefer alone, they say that it won't take long.' She broke off and gulped, 'It's so horrible, Taita! Our own sister, and that awful man – that monster.'

'When?' Taita shook her gently to brace her.

'Soon. Very soon.' Her voice steadied.

'Did they say how, Princess?'

'Noom, the surgeon from Babylon. Naja says that he will push a thin needle up through Nefer's nostril and into his brain. There will be no bleeding or any other sign.' Taita knew Noom well: they had debated against each at the library of Thebes, arguing the correct treatment for fractured limbs. Noom had come away smarting from the lash of Taita's eloquence and knowledge. He was deeply jealous of Taita's reputation and his powers. He was a rival and a bitter enemy.

'The gods will reward you, Merykara, for daring to come and warn us. But you must go now, before they find out that you have been here. If they suspect you, they will treat you as they plan to do Nefer.'

When she had gone Taita sat for a while collecting his thoughts, reviewing his plans. He could not do it alone, and he would have to rely on others, but he had chosen the best and most reliable. They were ready to act, and they had been waiting for his word. He could delay no longer.

At his bidding the slaves brought kettles of hot water and Taita washed Nefer carefully from head to foot and rebandaged his wounds, placing a dressing of lambswool over the gaping opening in his thigh that was still draining.

When he had finished, he warned the guards not to let anybody pass, and barred all the entrances to the chamber. He prayed for a while and then threw incense on the brazier and in the blue and aromatic smoke made an ancient, potent incantation to Anubis, the god of death and cemeteries.

Only then did he prepare the elixir of Anubis in a new and unused oil lamp. He warmed the mixture on the brazier until it was the temperature of blood, and took it to the bed where Nefer was sleeping quietly. Gently he turned his head to one side and placed the spout of the lamp in his ear. He poured the elixir into the eardrum, a heavy viscid drop at a time. Carefully he wiped away the excess, taking care that it should not touch his own skin. Then he plugged Nefer's ear with a small ball of wool and pushed it deeply into the passage until it could not be detected by any but a detailed examination.

He emptied what remained of the elixir on to the coals of the brazier, and it flared in a puff of acrid steam. Then he filled the lamp with oils and lit the wick. He placed it with the other lamps in the corner of the chamber.

He went back to the bed and squatted beside it. He watched Nefer's chest rise and fall to his breathing. Each breath was slower and the intervals between them longer. At last they ceased altogether. He placed two fingers on Nefer's throat beneath his ear, and felt the slow deliberate pulsing of the life force within him. Gradually that also faded away until it was only a flutter like the wing of tiny insect that took all his skill and experience to detect. With the fingers of his left hand he counted the beating of the life force in his own neck, and compared the two.

At last his own beat was three hundred to a single barely detectable flutter in Nefer's neck. Gently he closed the boy's eyes, placed an amulet on the lids in the traditional preparation of the corpse. Next he bound a strip of linen over them, and another strip under his jaw to keep his mouth from gaping open. He worked quickly for there was danger in every minute that Nefer remained under the influence of the elixir. At last he went to the door and removed the locking bar.

'Send word to the Regent of the Upper Kingdom. He should come immediately to hear terrible tidings of Pharaoh.'

Lord Naja arrived with surprising alacrity. Princess Heseret was with him, and they were followed by a crowd of their intimates, which included Lord Asmor, the Assyrian doctor Noom, and most of the members of the council.

Naja ordered the others to wait in the corridor outside the royal apartments, while he and Heseret came into the chamber. Taita rose from beside the bed to greet them.

Heseret was weeping ostentatiously and covering her eyes with an embroidered linen shawl. Naja glanced at the bandaged body laid out stiffly on the couch, then glanced at Taita with a question in his eyes. In reply Taita nodded slightly. Naja masked the gleam of triumph in his eyes, then knelt beside the bed. He laid one hand on Nefer's chest and felt the warmth slowly ebbing to be replaced by a spreading coolness. Naja prayed aloud to Horus, who was the patron god of the dead pharaoh. When he rose to his feet again he took Taita's upper arm in a firm grip.

'Console yourself, Magus, you did all that we could require of you. You will not lack reward.' He clapped his hands, and when the guard hurried through the door he ordered, 'Summon the members of the council to assemble.'

They filed into the room in solemn procession and formed up around the bed three deep.

'Let the good doctor Noom come forward,' Naja ordered. 'Let him confirm the Magus' pronouncement of Pharaoh's death.'

The ranks opened for the Assyrian to reach the couch. His long locks had been curled with hot tongs and dangled to his shoulders. His beard had also been curled in the fashion of Babylon. His robe swept the floor and was decorated with embroidered symbols of strange gods and magical patterns. He knelt beside the deathbed and began an examination of the corpse. He sniffed at Nefer's lips with a huge hooked nose from whose nostrils protruded clumps of black hair. Then he placed his ear against Nefer's chest and listened, during a hundred beats of Taita's anxious heart. He had placed much store in the Assyrian's ineptitude.

Then Noom took a long silver pin from the hem of his robe and opened Nefer's limp hand. He pricked the point deeply up under the fingernail and watched for a muscular reaction or for a drop of blood to form.

At last he stood up slowly, and Taita thought that there was evidence of deep disappointment in his curled lip and lugubrious expression as he shook his head. Taita reflected that he had certainly been offered untold rewards to use the silver pin to other effect. 'Pharaoh is dead,' he announced, and those around the bed made the sign against the evil eye and the wrath of the gods.

Lord Naja threw back his head and gave the first cry of lamentation, and Heseret, standing behind him, took up the wailing cry in her lovely soaring voice.

Taita hid his impatience while he waited for the mourners to file past the couch, and one by one to leave the chamber. When only Naja and Heseret, Noom and the viziers of the nomes of the Upper Kingdom remained, Taita stepped forward again. 'Lord Naja, I beg your indulgence. You are aware that I have been Pharaoh Nefer Seti's tutor and servant since his birth. I owe him respect and duty, even now in death. I beg you to grant me a boon. Will you allow me to be the one to convey his corpse to the Hall of Sorrow, and there to make the incision to remove his heart and viscera? I would take that as the greatest honour you could bestow on me.'

Lord Naja thought for a while, then nodded. 'You have earned that honour. I charge you with the duty of conveying Pharaoh's sacred body to the funeral temple, and of beginning the process of embalming by making the incision.'

※

The old warrior, Hilto, came swiftly to Taita's summons. He had been waiting in the guardroom at the palace gates. With him he brought the Nubian shaman, Bay, and four of his most trusted men. One of these was Meren, the friend and companion of Nefer's childhood. He was now a handsome ensign of the guards, tall of stature and clear of eye. Taita had asked for him particularly to take part in these duties.

Between them they carried the long woven basket that the embalmers used to transport their cadavers to the funerary temple. The empty basket appeared heavier than one might have expected.

Taita let them into the death chamber and whispered to Hilto, 'Swiftly now! Every second is precious.'

He had already wrapped Nefer in a long white winding sheet, with a loose fold of linen covering his face. The pall-bearers laid the basket beside the couch and lifted Nefer reverently into it. Taita packed bolsters around the body to cushion it during the move, then closed the lid, and nodded. 'To the temple,' he said. 'All is in readiness.'

Taita trusted his bag to Meren, and they moved quickly through the passages and courtyards of the palace. The sounds of mourning and lamentation followed them. The guards lowered the points of their weapons and knelt as the dead Pharaoh passed. The women covered their faces, and wailed. All the lamps had been extinguished, and the fires in the kitchens had been drawn so that no smoke rose from the chimneys.

In the entrance courtyard a squadron of Hilto's chariots was drawn up with the horses in the traces. The bearers laid the long basket on the footplate of the leading chariot and secured it with leather straps. Meren placed Taita's leather instrument bag in the cockpit, and Taita mounted and took the reins. The ram's horns of the regiment sounded a dirge, and the column moved out through the gates at a walk.

The news of Pharaoh's death had spread through the city like the plague. The citizens crowded around the gates, wailing and ululating as the column passed. Crowds lined the route along the river. Women, howling their grief, ran forward and threw the sacred lotus blossoms on to the basket.

Taita pushed the horses into a trot, then into a canter. He was desperate to get the basket into the sanctuary of the funerary temple. The temple of Nefer's father had not yet been demolished even though Pharaoh Tamose had been taken months ago to his tomb in the bleak hills to the west. No temple had yet been built for Nefer: he was so young that the expectation of his life stretched far ahead of him. His death now was untimely and left them no alternative but to use the building prepared for his father.

The tall, rose-coloured granite walls and portico of the temple were set upon a low prominence overlooking the green river. The priests, hastily assembled, were waiting to greet the column. Their heads were freshly shaven and anointed with oil. The drums and sistrum beat a slow tempo as Taita drove up the wide causeway and halted the chariot at the foot of the staircase that mounted to the Hall of Sorrow.

Hilto and his warriors lifted the basket and climbed the staircase with it balanced on their shoulders. The priests fell in behind them, singing mournfully. Before the open wooden doors of the Hall of Sorrow the pall-bearers paused, and Taita looked back at the priests,

'By the grace and authority of the Regent of Egypt, I, Taita, have been charged with lifting Pharaoh's viscera.' He fixed the high priest with a mesmeric gaze. 'All others will wait without while I perform this sacred charge.'

There was a hum of consternation among the brotherhood of Anubis. This was a solecism, against tradition and their own authority. But Taita held the priest's eye sternly, then slowly lifted his right hand holding the Periapt of Lostris. The priest knew, by fearful repute, the power of that relic. 'As the Regent of Egypt has decreed,' he capitulated. 'We will pray without while the Magus performs his duty.'

Taita led Hilto and the bearers through the doorway and they solemnly laid the basket on the floor beside the black diorite slab in the centre of the Hall of Sorrow. Taita glanced at Hilto, and the grizzled old commander marched to the doors with great dignity and shut them in the faces of the assembled priests. Then he hurried back to Taita's side. Between them they opened the basket and lifted out Nefer's wrapped body. They laid it on the black slab.

Taita turned back the fold of cloth that covered Nefer's face. He looked pale and lovely as an ivory carving of the young god Horus. Gently Taita turned his head to one side, and nodded at Bay who placed the leather instrument bag close to his right hand and opened it. Taita selected the ivory forceps, slipped the points into Nefer's ear and drew out the woollen plug. He filled his own mouth with dark ruby-coloured liquid from a glass jar, and through a gold tube carefully sluiced the dregs of the elixir of Anubis from Nefer's eardrums. When he looked deep into the ear passages he was relieved to see that there was no inflammation. Next he introduced a soothing ointment into the ear orifices and replugged them. Bay had the antidote to the elixir ready in another phial. When he opened the stopper it released a sharp odour of camphor and sulphur. Hilto helped them to lift Nefer into a sitting position and Taita administered the entire contents of the phial.

Meren and the others had been watching this with blank incomprehension. Suddenly Nefer coughed harshly and, with superstitious dread, they sprang back from the slab and made the sign against evil. Taita massaged Nefer's bare back and he coughed again, vomiting a little yellow bile. While Taita kept working steadily at reviving him, Hilto ordered his men to their knees and made them swear a dreadful oath of secrecy as to all that they were witnessing. Shaken and pale they swore their lives into jeopardy.

Taita placed his ear to Nefer's back, listened for a while then nodded. He massaged him again, and listened once more. He signed to Bay, who took a twist of dried herbs from the bag and lit the end at one of the temple lamps. He held it under Nefer's nose. The boy sneezed and tried to turn his head away. Satisfied at last Taita rewrapped him in the linen sheet, and made another sign to Bay and Hilto.

The three turned back to the basket. The others gaped as Taita lifted out the false bottom and revealed another corpse laid in the compartment beneath. This body also was wrapped in a white linen winding-sheet.

'Come!' Hilto ordered. 'Lift it out!'

Under Taita's sharp eye and Hilto's stern instruction they exchanged the two bodies. They laid Nefer in the hidden compartment in the bottom of the basket, but did not yet replace the false bottom. Bay squatted beside the basket to watch Nefer and to check his condition. The others laid the strange corpse on the diorite slab.

Taita swept away the winding sheet and revealed the body of a youth of about the same age and bodily shape of Nefer. He had the same thick dark hair. It had been Hilto's responsibility to procure this corpse. In the present climate in the land this had not been difficult. The plague was still flourishing in the poorer outlying areas of the nome. In addition, there were the nightly gleanings from the streets and alleys of the city, the victims of brawling, outright murder, or footpads.

Hilto had considered all these sources. However, in the end he had found, in circumstances so perfect to the quest that they could not have been coincidental, the ideal substitute for the young Pharaoh. The city bailiffs had arrested this lad in the very act of slitting the purse of one of the most influential millet merchants in Thebes, and the magistrates had not hesitated to sentence him to death by strangulation. The condemned lad was so like in body and general complexion to Nefer as to be able to pass as his brother. In addition he was well set-up and healthy, not like the starvelings and plague victims. Hilto had spoken to the commander of the city guards who had been charged with carrying out the execution, and during this friendly exchange three heavy gold rings had found their way into that worthy's purse. It was agreed that the strangulation be delayed until Hilto gave him the word, and that it would be carried out with as little apparent damage to the victim as the executioner's skill could encompass. The prisoner had been given justice that very morning and his body was not yet cold.

The canopic jars were arranged in the small shrine at the end of the hall. Taita ordered Meren to fetch them and open the stoppers ready for filling. While he was doing this, Taita rolled the corpse over and made a sweeping incision down his left side. There was little time for surgical finesse. He thrust his hand into the opening and drew forth the viscera then, using both hands, he worked the scalpel deep into the interior of the corpse. First he cut through the diaphragm to gain access to the chest cavity, then reached deeper, past the lungs, liver and spleen, until he could sever the windpipe above its juncture with the lungs. Finally he rolled the corpse over, ordered Meren to hold the buttocks apart and with sure strokes freed the sphincter muscles of the anus. Now all the contents of the interior of the chest and abdomen were unanchored.

He brought them out on to the diorite slab in a single mass. Meren blanched, swayed on his feet and clapped his hand over his mouth.

'Not on the floor, in the sink,' Taita ordered brusquely. Meren had fought against Apepi's regiments in the north. He had killed a man and been unaffected by the carnage of the battlefield, but now he fled to the stone basin in the corner and puked noisily into it.

Bloodied to the elbows, Taita began to separate the liver, lungs, stomach and entrails into piles. As soon as this was done he took the entrails and stomach to the sink, wherein already reposed Meren's contribution. He flushed out the contents of the dismembered stomach and entrails and packed them into their jars. He filled every jar with the pickling natron salts, and sealed the stoppers. Then he washed his hands and arms in the bronze basins filled with water expressly for that purpose.

He glanced enquiringly at Bay, and the Nubian nodded his bald, scarified head, reassuring Taita as to Nefer's condition. Working with controlled haste Taita stitched the abdominal incision closed. Then he bandaged the head until its features were hidden. When that was done, he and Hilto carried the corpse to the large natron bath and lowered it into the harsh alkali mixture, until only the bandaged head was not immersed. It would remain in the bath, with the head covered, for the next sixty days. At the end of that time the priests would remove the bandage, and discover the substitution. By that time, however, Taita and Nefer would be far away.

It took only a little longer to sluice down the slab with leather buckets of water, and to pack Taita's instruments, before they were ready to leave. Taita knelt beside the basket in which Nefer lay, and laid a hand on his naked chest to feel the warmth of his skin and to check his breathing. It was slow and even. He drew down one eyelid and watched the pupil react to the light. Satisfied, he stood up and gestured for Hilto and Bay to cover the hidden compartment. When this was done and they began to replace the basket lid, Taita stopped them. 'Leave it open,' he ordered. 'Let the priests see that it is empty.'

The bearers lifted the basket by its handles and Taita led them to the doors. As they approached Hilto threw them open, and the assembly of priests craned forward. They gave the empty basket only a cursory glance as it was carried out, then rushed into the Hall of Sorrow with almost indecent haste to take over the duties that had been usurped from them.

Ignored by the crowds that had gathered outside the temple, Taita's men loaded the basket on to the leading chariot and drove in column back to the city.

When they entered the main gates they found the narrow streets almost deserted. The populace had either flocked to the funerary temple to pray for the young pharaoh, or they had hurried to the palace to await the announcement of his successor, although there was little doubt in anyone's mind as to who would be the next pharaoh of the upper kingdom.

Hilto drove the chariot to the guards' barracks near the east gate, and the basket was carried through the back entrance of his private quarters. Here, everything was in readiness to receive Nefer. They lifted him out of the bottom compartment and Taita, with Bay assisting him, went to work to revive Nefer fully. Within hours he was well enough to eat a little millet bread and drink a bowl of warm mare's milk and honey.

At last Taita judged it safe to leave him for a while in Bay's charge, and drove through the narrow empty streets. Ahead of him he heard the sudden din of wild cheering. When he reached the environs of the palace he found himself enveloped in a dense crowd of citizens celebrating the ascension of the new pharaoh. 'Eternal life to His Sacred Majesty Pharaoh Naja Kiafan!' they howled, with loyal fervour, and passed the wine jugs from hand to hand.

So thick were the crowds that Taita was forced to leave the chariot with Meren to go the rest of the way on foot. At the palace gate the guards recognized him, and used the butts of their spears to clear the way for him to pass. Once he was in the grounds he hurried to the great hall, and there he found another press of obsequious humanity. All the military officers, courtiers and state dignitaries were waiting to swear loyalty and fealty to the new pharaoh, but Taita's reputation and his unnerving gaze ensured that the crowd made way for him to pass to the front ranks.

Pharaoh Naja Kiafan and his queen were in the private cabinet beyond the doors at the end of hall, but Taita had to wait only a short while before he was granted access to the royal presence.

To his astonishment he found that Naja was already wearing the double crown, and holding the flail and the crook crossed over his chest. Beside him Queen Heseret seemed to have blossomed like the desert rose under the caress of rain. She was as lovely as Taita had ever known her, pale and serene under her makeup, her eyes made enormous by skilfully applied kohl.

When Taita entered Naja dismissed those around him and soon the three were alone. This, in itself, was a sign of high favour. Then Naja laid aside the flail and the crook and came to embrace Taita. 'Magus, I should never have doubted you,' he said, his voice even more sonorous and commanding than before. 'You have earned my gratitude.' He took from his right hand a magnificent ring of gold and ruby, and placed it on Taita's right index finger. 'This is but a small token of my favour.' Taita wondered that he had placed such a powerful talisman in his hands: only a lock of Naja's hair or the clippings of his nails would have been more potent.

Heseret came forward and kissed him. 'Dearest Taita, you have always been faithful to my family. You shall have gold, land and influence beyond anything you have ever coveted.'

After all these years she knew so little of him. 'Your generosity is exceeded only by your beauty,' he said, and she simpered. Then he turned back to Naja. 'I have done what the gods required of me, Your Grace. But it has cost me dear. It is not a light or easy matter to go against my sense of duty and the dictates of my own heart. You know that I loved Nefer. Now I owe you that same duty and love. But for a space I must mourn Nefer, and make my peace with his shade.'

'It would be strange indeed if you did not feel for the dead Pharaoh,' Naja agreed. 'What do you wish of me, Magus? You have only to speak the words.'

'Your Grace, I ask your dispensation to go out into the desert to be alone for a time.'

'How long?' Naja asked, and Taita could see he was alarmed by the thought of losing the key to eternal life, which he truly believed Taita held in his hands.

'Not too long, Majesty,' Taita assured him.

Naja thought about it for a while. He was never a man for hasty decisions. At last he sighed and went to the low table upon which stood stylus and papyrus. Swiftly he wrote out a safe pass and sealed it with his royal cartouche. It was clear that the seal had been carved long ago in anticipation of his succession. While Naja waited for the ink to dry he said, 'You may absent yourself until the next inundation of the Nile begins, but then you must return to me. This safe-conduct will allow you to travel at large and to avail yourself of whatever food and equipment you may need from my royal storehouses anywhere in my domains.'

Taita prostrated himself in gratitude, but Naja lifted him to his feet in another extraordinary act of condescension. 'Go, Magus! But return to us on the appointed day to receive the rewards you so richly deserve.'

Clutching the roll of papyrus Taita backed towards the door, making the signs of blessing and benediction.

They left Thebes in the early hours of the next morning while most of the city still slept and even the guards at the east gate were yawning and heavy-eyed.

Nefer was laid in the back of the wagon drawn by a team of four horses. These draught animals had been chosen carefully by Hilto. They were strong and healthy, but not exceptional in any way that might excite envy or comment. The wagon was loaded with essential supplies and the equipment they might need once they had left the river valley. Hilto was dressed as a wealthy farmer, Meren as his son and Bay as their slave.

Nefer was laid on a straw mattress in the bed of the wagon, under a screen of tanned leather. He was now fully conscious and able to understand all that Taita had to tell him. Despite the royal safe-conduct the sergeant of the guard was officious. He did not recognize Taita under his hood, so he climbed into the back of the wagon to inspect the contents. When he pulled back the screen and Nefer peered out at him with his gaunt, pale features spotted with the unmistakable scarlet stigmata of the plague that Taita had applied, the sergeant of the guard swore with horror and leaped down from the wagon signing so vehemently against evil that he dropped his lamp, which shattered at his feet.

'Get you gone!' he shouted frantically at Hilto on the reins. 'Take that filthy poxy wretch out of the city.'

Twice more during the days that it took them to cross the littoral plain of the river and to reach the hills that marked the frontiers of the cultivated lands and the desert they were stopped by military patrols. Each time the royal scroll and the plague victim were enough to send them on their way again with only the briefest delay.

It was clear from the attitude of the patrols that in Thebes the substitution of corpses had not been discovered, and that no alarm had been raised. All the same Taita was relieved when they climbed the hills into the desert and followed the old trade route eastwards towards the Red Sea.

Now Nefer was able to climb down from his bed in the wagon, and for short periods limp along beside it. At first it was clear that, despite his denials, the leg was painful, but soon he was walking more easily and for longer periods.

They rested for three days at the ancient ruined city of Gallala. They refilled the waterskins at the meagre and bitter well and let the horses recover from the rigours of the hard, stony road. Bay and Taita tended their hocks and hoofs. When they were fit to resume the journey, they turned aside from the known way: travelling in the cool of the night, they took the path known only to Taita that led to Gebel Nagara. Bay and Hilto swept their back-trail and covered all signs of their passage.

They arrived at the cave in the middle of a night lit by bright stars. There was not enough water in the tiny seep to supply so many men and horses, so once the wagon was unloaded Hilto and Bay started back, leaving only Meren to serve Taita and Nefer. Hilto had resigned from his regiment on the pretext of ill-health, so he was free, with Bay, to return with every full moon to bring supplies, medicine and news from Thebes.

The first month at Gebel Nagara passed swiftly. In the clean, dry desert air Nefer's wounds closed without further reverses, and soon he was limping out into the desert to hunt with Meren. They startled the desert hares and bowled them over with their throwing sticks, or Taita sat on the crags of the hills above the spring and worked his charm of concealment to entice the herds of gazelle within arrow shot.

At the end of that month Hilto returned from Thebes with Bay. They brought the news that Taita's subterfuge had not yet been discovered and Pharaoh Naja Kiafan, along with all the populace, still believed that Nefer's corpse was pickling in the natron bath in the Hall of Sorrow.

They also brought news of insurrections in the Lower Kingdom, and the terrible reprisals by Pharaoh Trok at Manashi. Unrest had also flared in the Upper Kingdom where Naja, like Trok, had increased taxation and ordered an enlistment of men into the army. 'The people are angry that there should be such an enlargement of the armed forces when there is peace throughout the land,' Hilto reported. 'I think that the armed insurrection will soon spread to the Upper Kingdom, where Naja will deal with it as kindly as Trok has in the north. Those who cheered the ascension of these two pharaohs will soon have reason to regret it.'

'What other news have you from the Lower Kingdom?' Nefer asked eagerly. Hilto launched into a long recitation of trade news and millet prices, of the visit of the Assyrian special envoy to the court of Pharaoh Trok. Nefer listened impatiently, and when Hilto had finished he asked, 'What news is there of Princess Mintaka?'

Hilto looked puzzled. 'None that I know of. I should think she is in Avaris, but I cannot be certain.'

On the incoming leg of his journey Hilto had crossed the spoor of a large herd of oryx, and asked Taita's permission to follow them up and hunt them. Dried venison would eke out their supplies, so Taita agreed readily. But he decreed that Nefer was not yet strong enough to join the hunting party. Strangely, this did not seem to make Nefer unhappy: instead, he suggested that Taita go out with the hunting party to use his powers to find the game, and to conceal the hunters when they closed in.

As soon as he was alone in the cave, Nefer unpacked the small cedarwood chest of fresh papyrus scrolls and writing material that Hilto had brought him, and began to compose a letter to Mintaka. He knew with all certainty that by now the reports of his death would have been received in Avaris. He remembered his own terrible suffering when he had heard the false reports of Mintaka's death with her family at Balasfura, and he wanted to spare her the same kind of agony. He wanted also to explain that it was Naja and Trok who had annulled their betrothal, but that as far as he, Nefer, was concerned he still loved her beyond his own hope of eternal life, and would never rest until she was his wife.

All this had to be couched in language that, should the scroll fall into the wrong hands, would be meaningless to any person other than Mintaka.

He saluted her in his opening as 'The First Star'. She would remember how, when they had discussed the derivation of her name, she had told him, 'I am called after the third star in the belt of the celestial Hunter.'

He had replied, 'No, not the third. The very first in all the firmament.'

He drew the symbols of the hieratic with great care – he had always excelled at penmanship. He signed himself as the 'Fool from Dabba', sure that she would recognize the reference to his solecism when they had been alone in the desert.

That evening when the hunters had returned and they were feasting on fresh oryx steaks, Nefer waited his opportunity to speak to Hilto in private. This came when Taita left the circle around the camp fire to stalk out into the desert night for a while. Hilto had brought several large jars of beer among the load of supplies from Thebes, and Taita had enjoyed a bowl or two, but one of the few signs he showed of his age was the rate at which the brew passed through him.

As soon as he was out of earshot, Nefer leaned closer to Hilto and whispered, 'I have a special duty for you to perform for me.'

'I shall be greatly honoured, Your Majesty.'

Nefer passed him the tiny roll of papyrus. 'Guard this with your very life,' he ordered, and when Hilto had hidden it in his shawl Nefer gave him the orders for its delivery to the princess in Avaris. He ended with a further caution: 'Tell nobody of this. Not even the Magus. On your sacred oath!'

The following evening Hilto and Bay left Gebel Nagara at the setting of the sun, when the air had started to cool. They made their loyal obeisance to Nefer, asked Taita for his blessing and a charm of protection, then struck out into the starlit wilderness. The horses toiled up the first slope of the dune hills and into the jumble of moon silver rocks that crackled as they cooled in the night.

Walking ahead of the horses, Bay suddenly recoiled, gave a startled exclamation in his savage tongue and reached for the lion-bone charm on his necklace. He pointed it at the strange shape that had emerged from the shadows of the rocks.

Hilto was even more agitated, 'Stand aside, evil shade,' he shouted, cracked his whip, and made the sign against evil then gabbled an incantation to turn aside all ghosts and hobgoblins.

'Peace, Hilto!' The apparition spoke at last. The moon was so bright that it threw a long shadow along the shale-hard earth and made the head of the creature glow like molten silver in the crucible. 'It is I, Taita the Magus.'

'It cannot be you!' Hilto shouted. 'I left Taita at Gebel Nagara at sunset. I know you. You are some dreadful shade from the netherworld, pretending to be the Magus.'

Taita strode forward and seized Hilto's whip hand. 'Feel the warmth of my flesh,' he said, then lifted Hilto's hand to his face. 'Feel my face, and listen to my voice.'

However, it was only when Bay had touched Taita's breast with the lion bone, smelt his breath for the stench of the tomb and declared him to be who he claimed he was that the old warrior was reluctantly convinced. 'But how did you reach this place ahead of us?' he demanded plaintively.

'These are the ways of the adept,' Bay told him mysteriously. 'It is best never to ask that question.'

'Hilto, you have something on your person that places all of us in mortal danger.' Taita cut through the trivialities. 'It exudes the smell of death and confusion.'

'I cannot think what that might be,' Hilto said uneasily.

'It is something that was entrusted to you by the very Egypt,' Taita insisted, 'and you know it well enough.'

'By the very Egypt.' Hilto scratched his beard, and shook his head.

Taita held out his hand, and Hilto sighed and capitulated without further resistance. He reached into the leather purse on his belt and brought out the roll of parchment. Taita took it from him. 'Say nothing of this,' Taita warned him, 'not to anybody, not to Pharaoh himself. Do you hear me, Hilto?'

'I hear you, Magus.'

Taita held the papyrus in his right hand and stared hard at it. After a few seconds a tiny glowing spot appeared on the scroll, a wisp of smoke curled up into the night air, then abruptly it burst into flame.

Taita let it burn out between his fingers without flinching at the heat, then crumbled the ashes to dust.

''Tis magic,' Hilto gasped.

'A simple feat,' Bay muttered, 'one that even an apprentice could perform.'

Taita raised his right hand in benediction. 'May the gods keep you safe during your journey,' he said, and watched the wagon roll away and merge with the gloom.

When Taita stood once again beside the small hearth fire in the cave of Gebel Nagara, warming his old bones from the desert chill, he studied Nefer's sleeping form covered by a sheepskin, against the back wall.

He felt no anger at the boy's pathetic attempt to outwit him. Age had not withered his humanity, or dimmed his memories of the torments of passion, and he empathized with Nefer's wish to allay Mintaka's fears and her suffering. Added to which was the deep affection, verging on love, that he had conceived for Mintaka.

He would never confront Nefer with what might have been the consequences of this deed of compassion. He would allow him the opiate of believing that Mintaka would soon know that he still lived.

He squatted down beside Nefer and, without touching him, gently worked his way into the boy's inner being. From long exercise of this power over his patient, he achieved it readily. Nefer stirred, groaned and gabbled something that made no sense. Even in deep sleep Taita's power, cast like a web over him, had touched him and brought him almost awake.

His body has journeyed well along the road to full recovery. Taita delved deeper. His spirit is strong, and he has lost nothing by the ordeal through which he has passed. It will not be long now before we can move on to our next endeavour.

He went back to the fire, and placed a few more acacia sticks upon it. Then he settled back, not to sleep, for at his age he needed only a few hours each night, but to open his mind to the currents generated by events, some distant and others much closer. He let them eddy around him as though he were a rock in the stream of existence.

The next moon passed more swiftly than the last, as Nefer grew stronger and more restless. Each day his limp became less noticeable until at last it disappeared. Soon he was racing Meren from the valley floor to the crest of the hills. These contests became a regular part of their lives at the oasis. At first Meren won easily, but soon that changed.

At dawn on the twentieth day after the departure of Hilto, they started at the mouth of the cave and flew across the stony valley bottom shoulder to shoulder, but when they started the climb up the dune face Nefer edged ahead. Halfway up he unleashed a sudden, powerful rush and left Meren struggling after him. On the crest of the hill he turned back and laughed down at Meren, placing his hands on his hips in a triumphant gesture. In the dawn wind his long dense tresses floated on his shoulders. The early sun was rising behind him and the golden rays cast a nimbus of light around his head.

Taita had watched it all from below, and was about to turn back into the cave when an eerie sound in the desert silence stopped him. He lifted his face to the sky to see a dark speck describing a high circle against the blue, and felt the divine presence of the god close at hand. The cry sounded again, small and faint, but it pierced to the heart: the unforgettable cry of a royal falcon.

On the crest of the dune Nefer heard it also, and turned his head to search for the source. He picked out the tiny shape and lifted both hands towards it. As though the gesture was a command the falcon dropped into a stoop, seeming to swell in size. The wind across its cocked wings sighed as it dived straight at Nefer. If it struck at that speed it would rip flesh and break bone, but Nefer did not flinch as it came straight for his upturned face.

At the last possible second the falcon flared out of the stoop, and hovered above the boy's head. Nefer reached up and could almost touch the sleek, beautiful plumage of its breast. For a moment Taita thought that the bird might allow itself to be captured, but then it changed its wingbeats and rose on high. Once again it uttered that forlorn and lovely cry, then sped away towards the sun and seemed to disappear into the flaming orb.

On his last visit to Gebel Nagara Hilto had brought with him a full-weight war bow. Under Taita's instruction Nefer practised with it every day, building up the muscles in his back and shoulders until he had the strength to throw up the weapon, draw to full stretch and hold his aim without his arms beginning to tire and shake. Then, at Taita's word of command, he would send an arrow arcing high to drop on to the target two hundred cubits distant.

Nefer cut himself a heavy acacia-wood staff from a hidden grove in the foothills and shaped, scraped and polished it until it had perfect balance and length in his hands. In the cool of the dawn, he and Taita fought in the traditional fashion. At first Nefer held back in deference to Taita's age, but the Magus bloodied his shins and raised a lump on his scalp. Furious and humiliated, Nefer attacked in earnest, but the old man was quick and nimble. He hopped just out of reach of Nefer's slashing staff, then darted in to impart a painful rap on an unprotected elbow or knee.

Taita had lost little of his skill with the blade. Hilto had brought them a rack of heavy sickle swords, and when Taita decided that they had had sufficient practice with the fighting staffs, he brought out the swords and led Nefer and Meren through the entire repertoire of cuts, thrusts and parries. He made them repeat every manoeuvre fifty times, then start again. By the time he called a halt for supper both Nefer and Meren were flushed and running with sweat as though they had plunged into a pool of the Nile. Taita's skin, though, was dry and cool. When Meren remarked ruefully on this, he chuckled. 'I sweated my last drop of juice before you were ever born.'

On other evenings Nefer and Meren stripped naked, oiled their bodies and wrestled, while Taita umpired their bouts and called advice and instruction. Although Meren was taller by a hand and heavier in the shoulders and limbs, Nefer had natural balance and Taita had taught him how to use his opponent's weight against him. They matched each other throw for throw.

In the evenings and late into the night Taita and Nefer sat by the fire and debated every subject from medicine and politics to war and religion. Often Taita would outline a theory, then require Nefer to discover any flaws in his postulates and arguments. He placed hidden traps and illogicalities in these lessons, and more often now, and with greater alacrity, Nefer would uncover and question them. Then there was always the bao board to puzzle over in the attempt to unravel the laws and infinite possibilities inherent in the movements and patterns of the stones.

'If you could understand all there is to know of the bao stones, you would know all there is to know of life itself,' Taita told him. 'The subtleties and nuances of the game tune and sharpen the mind to the greater mysteries.'

The month passed so swiftly that it was with a small shock of surprise that Nefer, while running hard through the desert in pursuit of a mortally wounded gazelle, suddenly descried on the horizon, distorted by the mirage, a tiny cloud of yellow dust, and beneath it the distant shape of the wagon returning from the river valley. On the instant, he forgot the gazelle he was chasing and raced to meet Hilto. Even though Hilto was accustomed to feats of physical prowess from his men, he was impressed with the speed at which Nefer covered the ground through the shimmering heat.

'Hilto!' Nefer yelled, still at a distance, and without any sign of laboured breathing. 'May the gods love you and grant you eternal life! What news? What news?'

Hilto pretended to misunderstand the significance of the question, and as Nefer walked at his side he began a long-winded recital of political and social events in the kingdoms. 'There has been another rebellion in the north. This time Trok found it harder to put down. He lost four hundred men in three days of hard fighting, and half the rebels escaped his wrath.'

'Hilto, you know that is not what I wanted to hear from you.'

Hilto indicated Bay with a jerk of his head. 'Perhaps this is not the time to touch on certain matters,' he suggested tactfully. 'Your Majesty, should we not speak later and in private?'

Nefer was forced to contain his impatience.

As they sat that evening around the campfire in the cave, it was agony for Nefer to have to listen to Hilto making another long, detailed report to Taita, the most important part of which was that the substitution of bodies had been discovered when the priests of Anubis had unwrapped the head of the corpse in the Hall of Sorrow. Pharaoh Naja Kiafan had done his best to suppress the news and to prevent it becoming public knowledge for the foundations of his throne would be undermined if the populace suspected that Nefer was still alive. However, it was impossible to keep such an extraordinary event secret when many people, priests and courtiers were privy to it. Hilto reported that rumours were rife in the streets and market-places of the city of Thebes and the outlying towns and villages.

Partly as a result of these rumours, the unrest in both kingdoms had become more widespread and concerted. The rebels were calling themselves the Blue Faction. Blue was the colour of the Tamosian dynasty; Naja had selected green as his own royal colour, and Trok's was red.

Added to this, trouble was brewing in the east. The Egyptian pharaohs had sent the Hurrian ambassador back to his master, King Sargon of Babylon, that mighty kingdom between the Tigris and Euphrates, demanding that Sargon's annual tribute be increased to twenty lakhs of gold. It was a crippling amount to which Sargon could never agree.

'So, this accounts for the build-up of the armies in both kingdoms,' Taita said, as Hilto paused in his report. 'It is clear at last that the two pharaohs are greedy for the riches of Mesopotamia. They are intent on conquest. After Babylon, they will turn on Libya and Chaldea. They will not rest until the entire world comes under their sway.'

Hilto looked amazed. 'I had not considered that, but you must be right.'

'They are as cunning as two old baboons raiding the farmers' fields along the riverbank. They know that war is a uniting factor. If they march on Mesopotamia the populace will rally behind them in a patriotic frenzy. The army loves the prospect of booty and glory. The merchants love the prospect of increased trade and profit. It is a marvellous way to take the minds of the people off their grievances.'

'Yes.' Hilto nodded. 'I see it now.'

'Of course, this is to our advantage,' Taita mused. 'I have been seeking a haven for us. If he is at war with Trok and Naja, then Sargon will welcome us to his side.'

'We are leaving Egypt?' Hilto interjected.

Taita explained, 'Now that Naja and Trok know that Nefer still lives, they will come after us. The road to the east is the only one open to us. It will not be for long, just until we have built up our strength and support throughout the two kingdoms and have made ourselves powerful allies. Then we will return to reclaim Pharaoh Nefer's birthright.'

They all stared at him silently as they recovered from the shock of this prospect. They had not thought so far ahead, and it had never occurred to them that they would be forced to leave their native land.

It was Nefer who broke the silence. 'We can't do that,' he said. 'I cannot leave Egypt.'

Taita glanced at the others, and jerked his head in dismissal. Obediently Hilto, Bay and Meren stood up and filed out of the cave.

Taita had been anticipating this situation. He knew it would take all his cunning to resolve it, for Nefer wore his set expression and had made his declaration in a stubborn tone that Taita recognized. He knew it was going to be difficult to move Nefer from this position. The boy was staring into the fire, and Taita realized he must force him to break his silence. When he did so, Taita's position would be strengthened.

'You should have discussed this plan with me,' Nefer said at last. 'I am no longer a child, Taita. I am man and Pharaoh.'

'I told you my intentions,' Taita said quietly.

They sat in silence again, staring into the flames of the fire, and Taita could sense the cracks appearing in Nefer's resolve.

At last Nefer spoke again. 'You see, there is Mintaka.'

Still Taita said nothing. Intuitively he understood that they were approaching a crisis in their relationship. It had had to come at some time, so he made no effort to avoid it.

'I sent Mintaka a message,' Nefer said. 'I told her I loved her, and I gave her an oath on my life and eternal spirit that I would not desert her.'

Now Taita broke his silence. 'Are you certain that Mintaka received this foolhardy oath of yours that placed you, her and all around you in mortal danger?'

'Yes, of course. Hilto—' Nefer stopped and his expression changed as he stared at Taita across the flames of the campfire. Suddenly he sprang up and strode to the cave entrance. He moved not like a boy but like a man, an angry man. In these last few short months he had changed completely. Taita experienced a deep satisfaction. The way ahead would be hard, and Nefer would need all this new-found strength and determination.

'Hilto!' Nefer called into the darkness. 'Come to me.' Perhaps Hilto heard the new authority in his tone because he came swiftly and dropped to one knee before Nefer.

'Majesty?' he asked.

'Did you deliver the message I entrusted to you?' Nefer demanded.

Hilto glanced at Taita beside the fire.

'Don't look to him,' Nefer snapped. 'I am asking you the question. Answer me.'

'I did not deliver the message,' Hilto answered. 'Do you wish to know the reason why I did not?'

'I know the reason well enough,' Nefer said ominously. 'But hear this. If ever you wilfully disobey me at any time in the future you will pay the full penalty.'

'I understand,' Hilto said stolidly.

'If there is ever again a choice between Pharaoh and an interfering old man, you will choose Pharaoh. Is that clear to you?'

'It is clear as the midday sun.' Hilto hung his head penitently, but smiled into his beard.

'You have been evading my questions, Hilto. Now, what news do you have of the princess?'

Hilto stopped smiling, and opened and closed his mouth, trying to find the courage to tell him the dire news.

'Speak!' Nefer ordered. 'Have you so soon forgotten your duty?'

'Gracious Majesty, the news will not please you. Six weeks ago the Princess Mintaka was married in Avaris to Pharaoh Trok Uruk.'

Nefer stood as still as if he had been turned into a granite statue. For a long time the only sound in the cave was the crackle of the acacia logs in the fire. Then, without another word, Nefer walked past Hilto, out into the desert night.

When he returned the dawn was a faint red promise in the eastern sky. Hilto and Meren were wrapped in their sheepskins at the back of the cave, but Taita sat in exactly the same position as Nefer had left him. For a moment he thought that the old man was asleep also. Then Taita raised his head and looked at him with eyes that were bright and alert in the firelight.

'I was wrong, and you were right. I need you now, more than ever, old friend,' said Nefer. 'You will not desert me?'

'You need not ask,' Taita said softly.

'I cannot leave her with Trok,' Nefer said.

'No.'

Nefer came back to his seat opposite Taita, who took a slow, deep breath. The storm had passed. They were still together.

Nefer picked up a charred stump of firewood and pushed it deeper into the flames. Then he looked up at Taita again. 'You have tried to teach me to overlook at a distance,' he said. 'I have never acquired the gift. Not until this last night. Out there in the darkness and the great silence, I tried again to overlook Mintaka. This time I saw something, Taita, but only dimly and I did not understand it.'

'Your love for her has made you sensitive to her aura,' Taita explained. 'What did you see?'

'I saw only shadows, but I felt devastating sorrow and grief. I sensed despair so insupportable that it made me wish for death myself. I knew that these were Mintaka's emotions and not my own.'

Taita stared expressionlessly into the fire, and Nefer went on, 'You must overlook her for me. There is something terribly wrong. Only you can help her now, Taita.'

'Do you have anything of Mintaka's?' he asked. 'Any gift or token that she gave you?'

Nefer's hand went to the necklace at his throat. He touched the tiny golden locket that hung in the centre of the chain. 'It is my most precious possession.'

Taita held out his hand across the fire. 'Give it to me.' Nefer hesitated, then opened the clasp and held the amulet in his closed fist.

'Other than my own, hers were the last fingers to touch it. It contains a lock of her hair.'

'Then it is highly potent. It contains her essence. Give it to me, if you wish me to help her.' Nefer passed it to him.

'Wait here,' Taita said, and stood up. Although he had squatted cross-legged through all the hours of darkness, there was no stiffness in his movements, which were those of a young, virile man. He went out into the dawn and climbed to the crest of the dunes, then gathered the skirts of his *chiton* around his skinny shanks and squatted in the sand, facing the dawn.

He pressed Mintaka's amulet to his forehead and closed his eyes. He began to rock slightly from side to side. The sun cleared the horizon and struck fully into his face.

The amulet in his right hand seemed to take on some strange life of its own. Taita felt it pulse softly in rhythm to his own heartbeats. He opened his mind and let the currents of existence enter freely, swirling around him like a great river. His own spirit broke free of his body and he soared aloft. As though he was borne on the wings of some gigantic bird, he saw fleeting, confused images of lands and cities, forests, plains and deserts far below him. He saw armies on the march, the squadrons throwing up thunderclouds of yellow dust in which spearheads glinted. He saw ships on high seas battered by wave and wind. He saw cities burning as they were sacked, and he heard strange voices in his head, and knew they were from the past and the future. He saw the faces of those long dead, and those not yet born.

He moved on, his spirit ranging wide, always with the amulet his lodestone. In his mind he called for her, Mintaka! and felt the amulet grow warm then burning hot in his hand.

Slowly the images cleared away, and he heard her sweet voice reply, 'I am here. Who is it that calls?'

'Mintaka, it is, Taita,' he replied, but he was aware that something evil had intervened and broken the stream between them. Mintaka had gone and instead there was a fateful presence. He focused all his powers upon it, trying to disperse the dark clouds. They seemed to coalesce, and took the shape of a rearing cobra, the same baleful influence that he and Nefer had encountered in the nest of the royal falcon on the cliffs of Bir Umm Masara.

In his mind he wrestled with the cobra, extending his powers to drive it back, but rather than succumbing, the image of the serpent became clearer and more menacing. Suddenly he knew that this was not a psychic manifestation, but a direct and mortal threat exerted against Mintaka. He redoubled his efforts to break through the curtains of evil and to reach her, but so much pain and grief was interposed between them that it was an impenetrable barrier.

Then, suddenly, he saw a hand, slim and graceful, reach out towards the sinister scaly head. He knew it was Mintaka's hand, for the blue lapis lazuli ring on the index finger was engraved with her cartouche. He held the venomous serpent in check with all his life force, and prevented it striking at Mintaka's hand as she stroked the back of its extended hood. The cobra turned half away from her, almost like a cat offering its head to be caressed.

'Make it do what has to be done.' Taita heard Mintaka's voice, and another voice he recognized replied, 'This I have never seen before. You must strike the messenger with your hand. That will surely make him deliver the gift of the goddess.' It was the voice of the high priestess of the temple of Hathor in Avaris, and Taita understood. Mintaka, overwhelmed with grief, was about to take the way of the goddess.

'Mintaka!' He exerted himself to reach her, and was rewarded at last.

'Taita?' she whispered, and because Mintaka was at last aware of him, Taita's view expanded so that he could see it all clearly.

Mintaka was in a stone-walled bedchamber. She was kneeling in front of a basket. The holy priestess was at her side, and in front of her reared the deadly snake.

'You must not take this road,' Taita ordered her. 'It is not for you. The gods have prepared a different destiny for you. Do you hear me?'

'Yes!' Mintaka turned her head towards him, as though she could see his face.

'Nefer is alive. Nefer lives. Do you hear me?'

'Yes! Oh, yes.'

'Be strong, Mintaka. We will come for you. Nefer and I will come for you.'

So fierce was his concentration that he dug his fingernails deeply into the palms of his hands until the blood welled, but he could hold her no longer. She began to slip away from him, her image blurred and faded, but before she was gone he saw her smile, a beautiful thing, full of love and renewed hope.

'Be strong!' he urged her. 'Be strong, Mintaka!' The echo of his voice came back to him as though from a great distance.

Nefer was waiting for him at the foot of the dunes. When Taita was only halfway down the boy realized that something momentous had taken place. 'You saw her!' he shouted, and it was not a question. 'What has happened to her?' and he ran forward to meet Taita.

'She needs us,' Taita said, and laid a hand on Nefer's shoulder. He could never tell him of the extremes of sorrow and despair in which he had found Mintaka, nor of the fate she had prepared for herself. Nefer could never bear that. It might easily drive him to some wild endeavour that would destroy both the lovers. 'You were right,' Taita went on. 'All my plans to leave this land and find sanctuary in the east must be set aside. We have to go to Mintaka. I have promised her that.'

'Yes!' Nefer agreed. 'When can we leave for Avaris?'

Taita replied, 'There is great urgency. We will leave at once.'

It took them fifteen days of hard travel to reach the tiny garrison and remount station of Thane a day's travel south of Avaris. They had changed horses four times on the road – Taita used the royal requisition order that Naja had given him to replace the worn-out animals and to replenish their supplies at the military garrisons and camps they had passed along the way.

Since leaving Gebel Nagara they had discussed their plans endlessly, knowing that they were pitted against the might of Pharaoh Trok Uruk. The officers they spoke to at the garrisons estimated that Trok now had twenty-seven fully trained and equipped regiments at his disposal, and almost three thousand chariots. To oppose this multitude they had a wagon showing the effects of long, hard service with a back wheel that showed a marked propensity to fall off at the most inappropriate times and bodywork held together with twine and leather strips. There were only the four of them: Nefer and Meren, Hilto and Bay. But the fifth was Taita.

'The Magus is worth twenty seven regiments at least,' Hilto pointed out, 'so we are evenly matched against Trok.'

Hilto knew the captain in charge of the encampment at Thane, a scarred and grizzled old warrior named Socco. Long ago they had run the Red Road together. They had fought, roistered and whored together. After they had reminisced for an hour and shared a pot of sour beer,

Hilto handed him the requisition scroll. Socco held it upside down at arm's length and looked wise.

'See the cartouche of Pharaoh.' Hilto touched the seal.

'If I know you at all, Hilto, and by Horus I do, you probably drew that pretty picture yourself.' Socco handed the scroll back to Hilto. 'What do you need, you old rogue?'

They selected fresh horses from the herd of several hundred in the remount herd, then Taita went over the ranks of parked chariots in the garrison pool that had just been sent out from the makers in Avaris. He selected three vehicles, and they harnessed the fresh horses.

When they left Thane, Taita was driving the old wagon. Meren, Hilto and Nefer each drove a chariot, while Bay brought up the rear herding twenty spare horses. They did not head directly for Avaris but made a detour to the east of the city.

On the edge of the desert there was a small oasis used by the Bedouin and by merchant caravans heading out to and returning from the Orient.

While the others unloaded the fodder they had carried from Thane in the wagon, hobbled the horses and greased the wheel hubs of the new chariots, Taita went to barter with the Assyrian master of the caravan that was encamped nearby. He bought an armful of dirty, tattered clothing, and twenty woollen rugs woven in the land along the Further Sea. They were of inferior workmanship and material, but he was forced to pay an extortionate price for them. 'That Assyrian ape is a cut-throat and a robber,' he muttered, as they loaded the carpets on to the wagon.

'Why do we need them?' Nefer wanted to know, but Taita pretended not to hear the question.

That night Taita dyed his mane of silver hair with an extract of mimosa bark, which altered his appearance dramatically. In the darkness of early morning they left Bay in charge of the herd of horses and the chariots, climbed into the dilapidated wagon and, sitting high on the pile of dusty carpets, headed west towards Avaris. They were dressed in the rags and cast-offs that Taita had procured. Taita wore a long robe and sash, and the lower half of his face was veiled in the fashion of a citizen of Ur of the Chaldeas. With his dyed dark hair he was unrecognizable as the Magus.

It was evening when they reached the royal city of the north. There was a permanent encampment of several thousand souls outside the walls, mostly beggars, itinerant players, foreign traders and other riff-raff. They set up camp among them, and early the next morning they left Meren to watch the wagon and went to join the throng waiting outside the city for the gates to open at sunrise.

Once they were past the city guard, Hilto went to tour the taverns and brothels in the narrow streets of the old quarter where he hoped to find some of his cronies and former comrades-in-arms and gather the latest news from them. Taita took Nefer with him and they made their way through the crowded streets of the awakening city to the palace gates. Here they joined the beggars, tradesmen and supplicants. Taita made no effort to gain entry to the palace, rather they spent the morning listening to the chatter of those around them, and gossiping with the other idlers.

At last Taita struck up a conversation with a merchant from Babylon, dressed in similar style to himself, who introduced himself as Nintura. Taita spoke the Akkadian language like a native of Mesopotamia, which was why he had chosen this particular disguise. The two shared a pot of coffee brewed with rare and expensive beans imported from Ethiopia, and Taita exerted all his wiles to charm Nintura, who had been loitering outside the palace for the last ten days, waiting for his turn to display his wares to Trok's new bride. He had already paid the exorbitant *baksheesh* demanded by the palace vizier to be allowed to enter the presence of the young consort, but many others were ahead of him.

'They say that Trok has been cruelly treated by his young wife. She will not allow him into her bed.' Nintura chuckled. 'He is wild for her, like a stag in rut, but she keeps her legs crossed and the door to her chamber locked. Trok is trying to win her favours with expensive gifts. They say he will refuse her nothing. Also she buys everything that is offered to her and then, to spite him, she immediately resells it for a fraction of what he was forced to pay and distributes the proceeds to the poor of the city.' He slapped his knee and roared with laughter. 'They say she buys the same things over and over, and Trok keeps paying.'

'Where is Trok?' Taita asked.

'He is campaigning in the south,' Nintura replied. 'He is stamping out the flames of rebellion, but no sooner does he turn his back than they flare up again behind him.'

'Whom should I approach to enter the presence of this Queen Mintaka?'

'The palace vizier. Soleth, is his name, the fat, gelded freak.' Nintura had not realized Taita's own physical status.

Taita knew Soleth only by reputation and that he was one of the secret brotherhood of eunuchs. 'Where can I find him?' Taita asked.

'It will cost you a gold ring just to enter his presence,' Nintura warned him.

Soleth was sitting beside the lotus pond in his own walled garden. He did not rise when one of the harem-keepers brought Taita to him.

The Hyksos had so forsaken their ancient customs, and taken to Egyptian ways, that they no longer kept their wives sequestered in the *zenana*. The eunuchs still exercised much of their former power over the royal women, but when suitably chaperoned their charges were allowed much freedom. They could walk abroad, sail on their pleasure barges on the river, have merchants visit them to display their wares or dine, sing, dance and play games with their friends.

Taita made a dignified salutation as he introduced himself to Soleth under an assumed name. He followed that with the recognition sign of the brotherhood, crooking both his little fingers and touching them together. Soleth blinked with surprise and ran his eyes down Taita's lean frame: he did not have the shape or the look of a eunuch. Nevertheless he waved to Taita to seat himself on the cushions opposite him. Taita accepted the bowl of sherbet a slave offered, and they talked for a while of seemingly trivial matters, but swiftly they established Taita's credentials and common acquaintances within the brotherhood. Without seeming to do so, Soleth was studying Taita's features thoughtfully, looking beyond the veil and the dyed hair. Slowly recognition bloomed in his eyes and at last he asked softly, 'In your travels you might have met the famous Magus, known through both kingdoms, and beyond, as Taita?'

'I know Taita well,' Taita agreed.

'Perhaps as well as you know yourself?' Soleth asked.

'At least as well as I know myself,' Taita affirmed, and Soleth's chubby face creased in a smile.

'Say no more. What service can I perform for you? You need only ask.'

That evening Nefer, Meren and Hilto were on the carpet load when Taita drove the creaking wagon, its incorrigible back wheel wobbling lopsidedly, up to one of the side gates of the palace where a gang of ragged urchins skulked in the mean, narrow lane. Taita gave one a copper ring to guard the wagon, then banged on the gate with the butt of his staff. It swung open at once, but they were confronted by a file of levelled spears. The entrance to the *zenana* was heavily guarded: Trok was taking good care of his little hind.

Soleth was not there to greet him – obviously, he was keeping his nose clean – but he had sent one of his underlings, an old black slave, to usher Taita past the guards and to act as a guide. Although Taita was armed with the papyrus scroll that Soleth had given him, the captain of the guard insisted on searching them before he would allow them to pass. He ordered Hilto to unroll the carpets and prodded every fold with his spear point. At last he was satisfied, and waved them through.

The ancient slave hobbled ahead of them, guiding them through a labyrinth of narrow passages. As they progressed the surroundings became grander, until they stopped before an elaborately carved sandalwood door guarded by two huge eunuchs. There was a whispered exchange between them and the old slave, then the sentries stood aside and Taita led the others through into a large airy room redolent of flowers, perfume and the tantalizing aroma of young womanhood. Beyond there was a wide terrace, from which floated the sounds of a lute and feminine voices.

The old slave went out on to the terrace. 'Your Majesty,' he quavered, 'there is a merchant with fine silk carpets from Samarkand to wait upon Your Grace.'

'I have seen enough rubbish for one day,' a woman's voice replied, and Nefer thrilled to those familiar well-beloved tones so that his breathing came short. 'Send them away.'

The guide looked back at Taita and pulled a face, spreading his hands helplessly. Nefer dropped the rolled carpet off his shoulder on to the stone floor tiles with a weighty thump, and strode to the entrance on to the terrace where he paused. He was dressed in tatters and a grubby cloth was wrapped around his head, covering the lower half of his face. Only his eyes were visible.

Mintaka was sitting on the parapet wall with two of her slave girls at her feet. She did not look in his direction but started singing again. It was the monkey and donkey song, and Nefer felt every word twist his heart as he studied the sweet curve of the cheek turned half away from him and the tresses of thick dark hair that hung down her back.

Abruptly she broke off and looked at him with annoyance. 'Don't stand there gawking at me, you insolent oaf,' she snapped. 'Take your wares and go.'

'Forgive me, Majesty.' He spread his arms in supplication, 'I am but a poor fool from Dabba.'

Mintaka screamed and dropped her lute, then covered her mouth with both hands. Patches of bright crimson rouged her cheeks and she stared into his green eyes. The black slave drew his dagger and tottered forward feebly to attack Nefer, but Mintaka recovered herself at once. 'No, leave him.' She raised her right hand to reinforce the command. 'Leave us. I will speak with the stupid fellow.' The slave looked dubious and hesitated, the naked dagger still aimed uncertainly at Nefer's belly.

'Do as I tell you,' Mintaka snarled, like a leopardess. 'Go, fool. Go!'

Confused, the old fellow sheathed his blade and backed away. Mintaka was still staring at Nefer, her eyes huge and dark. Her girls could not fathom what ailed her. They knew only that something strange was afoot. The curtains over the entrance fell back into place as the slave withdrew. Nefer whipped off the cloth that covered his head and his curls fell to his shoulders.

Mintaka screamed again. 'Oh, by the grace of Hathor, it is you. It is really you! I thought you would never come.' She flew to him and he ran to meet her, enfolding her in his embrace. They clung to each other, both talking at the same time, incoherently trying to tell each other of their love and how much they had missed each other. The slave girls recovered from their astonishment and danced around them, clapping their hands and weeping with joy and excitement until Taita silenced them with a few well-directed prods of his staff.

'Stop that mindless squealing. You will have all the sentries here in a minute.' Once he had them under control, he turned back to Hilto and Meren. At his direction they spread the largest carpet out on the tiles.

'Mintaka, listen to me! There will be time for that later.'

She turned her face to him, but kept her hands locked around Nefer's neck. 'It was you who called to me, wasn't it, Taita? I heard your voice so clearly. If you hadn't stopped me I would have—'

'I thought you more sensible than to stand here chattering when so much is at stake,' Taita cut across her. 'We are going to hide you in the carpet to get you out of the palace. Hurry now.'

'Do I have time to fetch my—'

'No,' Taita said. 'You have time for nothing other than to obey me.'

She kissed Nefer once more, a lingering embrace, then ran into the chamber and threw herself full length on the carpet. She looked up at her girls, who stood amazed in the doorway. 'Do whatever Taita tells you.'

'You cannot leave us, mistress,' her favourite, Tinia, wailed. 'Without you we are nothing.'

'It will not be for long,' Mintaka said. 'I promise I will send for you, Tinia, but until then be brave, and do not fail me.'

Nefer helped Hilto and Meren roll Mintaka in the patterned red carpet, and placed one end of a long hollow reed between her lips. The other end, protruding a few inches from the heavy folds, would enable her to breathe.

In the meantime Taita instructed the weeping slave girls: 'Tinia, you are to go into the bedchamber and bar the door. Cover yourself with bed linen, as though you were your mistress. The rest of you will stay here in the vestibule. You must not open the door to any demands. Tell anyone who asks that your mistress is laid low by her moon sickness and can see no one. Do you understand that?' Tinia nodded, broken-hearted, not trusting herself to speak. 'Delay them as long as you are able, but when you are discovered and can no longer dissemble, tell them what they want to know. Do not try to hold out under torture. Your death or crippling will serve little purpose, except to prey upon the conscience of your mistress.'

'Can I not go with the Queen?' Tinia blurted. 'I cannot live without her.'

'You heard your mistress's promise. Once she is safe she will send for you. Now, bar the door behind us when we leave.'

The old slave was waiting in the passage when they carried out the rolled carpet on their shoulders.

'I am sorry. I did my best for you, as Soleth ordered me. Queen Mintaka was once a kind and happy girl,' he told them, 'but no longer. Since her marriage she has become sad and angry.' He beckoned them to follow and led them back through the warren of the *zenana* until at last they reached the small side gate, where the sergeant of the guards confronted them once more.

'Unroll those carpets!' he ordered brusquely.

Taita stepped closer to him and stared into his eyes. The sergeant's hostile expression faded. He looked mildly confused. 'I can see that you are feeling contented and happy,' Taita said softly, and a slow grin spread over the man's ugly, wrinkled features. 'Very happy,' Taita said, and laid his hand gently on the man's shoulder.

'Very happy,' the sergeant repeated.

'You have already searched the carpets. Surely you do not want to waste your valuable time. Do you?'

'I don't want to waste my time,' the sergeant declared, as though it was his own idea.

'You want us to pass.'

'Pass!' said the sergeant. 'I want you to pass.' And he stood aside. One of his men raised the locking bar and let them out into the lane. The last glimpse they had of the sergeant as the door closed showed them that he was grinning benignly after them.

The wagon stood where they had left it with the urchins guarding it. Gently they loaded the carpet into the wagon bed and Nefer called quietly into the mouth of the roll, 'Mintaka, my heart, are you all right?'

'It is hot and stuffy, but that is a small price to pay to know that you are near.' Her voice was muffled and he reached down the tube formed by the roll and touched the top of her head.

'You are as brave as a lioness.' he said, and scrambled up behind Taita on the wagon box as he urged the horses forward.

Taita whipped up the horses. 'The city gates will soon be closed for the night. When Mintaka's escape is discovered the first thing they will do is seal off the city, search every building and vehicle, and question every stranger within the walls.'

They galloped down the wide avenue leading to the eastern gate. As they approached they saw that the way was blocked with other wagons and chariots lined up in front of the gate. There had been a religious festival and procession earlier in the day, and these were worshippers and revellers returning to the outlying villages around Avaris. Their forward progress was tantalizingly slow.

The sun had already sunk behind the walls and the light was fading, but there were still two vehicles ahead of them when the captain of the guard came out of the gate house and yelled at his men, 'That is enough! The sun has set. Close the gates!'

There were yells of protest from all the travellers still trying to pass out.

'I have a sick child. I must take her home.'

'I have paid my toll, let me pass. My load of fish will spoil.'

One of the smaller wagons drove forward deliberately and blocked the efforts of the guards to force the gates shut. A small riot broke out, with shouting guards swinging clubs, outraged citizens screaming back at them and frightened horses rearing and whinnying. Suddenly there was a further commotion from without the walls. Louder voices drowned the protests of travellers and guards alike.

'Make way for Pharaoh! Clear the road for Pharaoh Trok Uruk!'

The boom of a war-drum enforced the order. The guards ceased their efforts to shut the gates and instead fell over each other in their haste to throw them wide open again to reveal on the roadway outside a squadron of fighting chariots. Over the leading vehicle waved the red leopard pennant. Standing tall on the footplate, his bronze helmet gleaming and his beribboned beard thrown over one shoulder, stood Pharaoh Trok Uruk, whip and reins in his gauntleted hands.

As soon as the gates were wide open he drove his four-horse team straight into the mass of people and wagons in the roadway, lashing out indiscriminately with his whip at any who stood in his way. His men ran ahead of him, overturning any vehicle that blocked the road, and dragging it aside, spilling loads of wet slippery fish and vegetables into the gutters.

'Make way for Pharaoh!' they roared, above the screams of those caught up in the confusion. The troopers reached Taita's vehicle and began to tip it over to clear the path for Trok. Taita stood up and lashed at them with the whip, but his blows fell on their helmets and their bronze epaulettes. They laughed at him and heaved together. The wagon went over. The rolled carpet slid across the wagon bed and might have been crushed under the capsizing vehicle.

'Help me!' shouted Nefer, and jumped back to hold the carpet roll and cushion its fall. Hilto caught one end and Bay the other. As the wagon crashed on its side with a crackle of breaking timber they dragged Mintaka, still cocooned in the roll, to safety against the wall of the nearest building.

Pharaoh Trok forced his chariot through the wreckage and spilled loads, cracking his whip over the heads of his team, roaring commands at his warhorses.

'Strike! Strike!' The horses were battle-trained, and at his urging they reared and struck out at anyone in their way with their bronze-shod hoofs. Nefer saw one old woman scurry straight under the flying hoofs. One caught her full in the face. Her head split open, and her teeth flew from her mouth like a burst of white hailstones. They rattled on the cobbles and she sprawled in front of Trok's chariot.

The bronze wheel rims bumped over her body as he drove on, passing so close to where Nefer crouched protectively over Mintaka's carpet roll that for an instant they looked into each other's eyes. Trok did not recognize him in his rags with the headcloth wound around his head, but with casual cruelty he snapped the whip over Nefer's shoulder. The metal tips of the lash cut through the cloth and raised a line of bright blood spots. 'Out of my way, peasant!' Trok snarled, and Nefer gathered himself to leap on to the footplate and drag Trok out of the chariot by his beard. This was the beast who had defiled Mintaka, and Nefer's rage was a red veil over his vision.

Taita grabbed his arm to restrain him. 'Let it pass. Get the carpet out of the gates, you fool. We will be trapped here.' Nefer strained to be free of his grip, and Taita shook him. 'Do you want to lose her again so soon?'

Nefer regained control of his temper. He stooped to seize the end of the roll and the others helped him. They ran with it to the gates, but the squadron of chariots was through and once more the guards were swinging the heavy wooden doors to. Taita ran ahead and scattered the guards with his staff. When one of the sentries raised a club over his head, Taita turned on him and stared into his face with those mesmeric eyes. The man recoiled as though confronted by a man-eater.

Carrying the rolled carpet between them they squeezed through the narrow gap between the closing gates, then ran into the encampment below the city walls. Although angry shouts followed them, they disappeared from the guards' view into the gathering darkness among the leather tents and shacks. Behind the walls of a goat pen they lowered their burden to the ground and unrolled it. Dishevelled and hot, Mintaka sat up and smiled to see Nefer kneeling in front of her. They reached for each other and embraced as the others looked on.

Taita brought them back to reality. 'Trok has returned unexpectedly,' he told Mintaka, 'It will not be long before he discovers that you are missing.' He pulled Mintaka to her feet. 'We have lost the wagon. Ahead of us we have a long journey on foot. Unless we set out now it will be after daylight tomorrow before we reach the oasis where we left the chariots.'

Mintaka sobered immediately. 'I am ready,' she said.

Taita glanced down at her flimsy gold sandals decorated with turquoise studs, and strode away among the huts. He returned in a few minutes with a slatternly old woman following close behind him. He was carrying a pair of hard-worn but sturdy peasant's sandals. 'I have exchanged these for yours,' he said.

Mintaka did not demur but slipped off the lovely sandals and handed them to the old woman, who scuttled away before anyone could take them back from her. Then Mintaka stood up. 'I am ready,' she said. 'Which way, Magus?'

Nefer took her hand and they fell in behind Taita as he strode out into the desert.

Trok drove through the palace gates and reined in his dusty, lathered horses in the front courtyard before his own magnificent quarters. Two colonels of his cavalry, both members of the leopard clan and his particular cronies, stumped after him into the banquet hall with weapons and bucklers clattering. The house slaves had laid out a feast to welcome Pharaoh home. Trok drained a bowl of sweet red wine, and seized the boiled haunch of a wild boar.

'There is something I need more than food or drink.' He winked at his companions, who guffawed and nudged each other. Trok was aware that his marital reverses were common gossip in the army, and that the manner in which his new wife treated him was weakening his reputation. Despite his victories over the rebels in the south, and the harsh retribution he had imposed upon them, his prestige as a man was suffering. He was determined to change that this very night.

'There is more food than even you two oxen can eat, and enough wine in which to drown a hippopotamus.' Trok waved at the groaning board. 'Do your worst, but don't expect me to join you before morning. I have a field to plough, and an incorrigible filly to break to my will.'

He strode from the hall gnawing at the bone in his hand, and gulping down mouthfuls of the fat pork as he went. Two slaves with burning torches ran ahead of him to light his way down the gloomy passages to the *zenana*. In front of the doors to Mintaka's quarters the eunuch sentries had heard him coming. They flourished their weapons and crossed them over their fat chests in salute.

'Open up!' Trok ordered. He tossed aside the pork bone and wiped his greasy hands on the skirts of his tunic.

'Your Majesty,' one of the sentries saluted again nervously, 'the doors are barred.'

'By whose orders?' Trok demanded furiously.

'By orders of Her Majesty Queen Mintaka.'

'By Seueth, I'll have none of that! The arrogant hussy knows I am here,' Trok stormed, drew his sword and pounded on the door with the bronze pommel. There was no reply, so he tried again. The sound of the blows echoed down the silent passages, but still there was no sign of life beyond the doors. He backed away then charged the door with his shoulder. It shook but did not yield. He snatched the pike from the hands of the nearest sentry and hacked at the panel.

Splinters of timber flew under the blade and with a few more blows he had chopped a hole wide enough for him to reach through and dislodge the locking bar on the far side. He kicked open the door and marched into the room beyond. The slave girls were against the far wall in a terrified huddle. 'Where is your mistress?'

They gabbled and cackled incoherently, but could not prevent their collective eyes from turning towards the door of the bedchamber. Trok went to it, and there was an immediate outcry from the girls.

'She is sick.'

'She cannot see you.'

'Her moon has come.'

Trok laughed. 'She has used that excuse too often.' He hammered on the door. 'If there is blood, then there had better be a river of it – more than I spilled on the field of Manashi. By Seueth, I will wade through it to reach the happy portals.'

He kicked at the bedchamber door. 'Open up, you little witch! Your husband has come to show you his duty and respect.'

At his next kick the door flew open, torn off its leather hinges, and

Trok swaggered through. The couch was carved from African ebony, and inlaid with silver and mother-of-pearl. The feminine form upon it was hidden under a pile of linen bedclothes but one small foot protruded. Trok let his sword-belt drop to the floor and called, 'Have you missed me, my little lily? Have you been pining for my loving arms?'

He grabbed the bare foot and hauled the girl out from under the bedclothes. 'Come my, sweet ewe lamb. I have another gift for you, so long and hard, that you will not be able to sell it or give it away—' He broke off and gawked at the terrified, snivelling girl. 'Tinia, you dirty little harlot, what are you doing in your mistress's bed?' He did not wait for her reply, but threw her on to the floor, and rampaged through the room, ripping down the curtains and wall hangings. 'Where are you?' He kicked in the doors to her closet. 'Come out! This childishness will serve you little.'

It took him only a minute to make certain that Mintaka was not hiding. Then he rushed back to Tinia and seized her by the hair. He dragged her across the floor. 'Where is she?' He kicked her in the belly. She screamed and tried to roll away from his metal-shod foot. 'I will beat it out of you, I will flay every inch of skin from your miserable body.'

'She is not here!' Tinia screamed. 'She has gone!'

'Where?' Trok kicked her again. His war sandals were studded with bronze nails. They cut her tender flesh like knives. 'Where?'

'I know not,' she howled. 'Men came and took her away.'

'What men?' He kicked her again, and she rolled into a ball, sobbing and shivering.

'I don't know.' Despite Taita's instruction, she would not betray her beloved mistress. 'Strange men. I had never seen them before. They covered her with a carpet and carried her away.' Trok gave her a last brutal kick, then strode to the door. He shouted at the eunuch sentries, 'Find Soleth. Bring the fat slug here immediately.'

Soleth came cringing and wringing his smooth, plump hands. 'Divine Pharaoh! Greatest of the gods! Might of this very Egypt!' He threw himself at Trok's feet.

Trok kicked him with a full swing of his armoured sandal. 'Who were these men you allowed to enter the *zenana*?'

'On your orders, gracious Pharaoh, I allowed any vendor of fine merchandise to display it before the Queen.'

'Who was the carpet-seller? The last one to enter these quarters.'

'Carpet-seller?' Soleth seemed to ponder the question.

Trok kicked him again. 'Yes, Soleth, carpets! What was his name?'

'I remember now. The carpet-merchant from Ur. I forget his name.'

'I will help your memory.' Trok called the eunuch sentries to him. 'Hold him over the bed.'

They dragged Soleth to the rumpled couch and pinned him face down. Trok picked up his discarded sword-belt and drew the weapon. 'Lift his robes.' One of them hoisted Soleth's skirts and exposed his chubby buttocks. 'I know that half the palace guard have passed this way,' Trok touched his anus with the point of the sword, 'but none of them were as hard or as sharp as this one will be. Now, tell me, who was the carpet merchant?'

'I swear on bread and Nile water that I never saw him before.'

'For you that is a great pity,' Trok said, and ran the point of the sword the length of a forefinger up Soleth's rectum. Soleth shrieked on a high, quavering note of agony.

'That was only the tip,' Trok warned him. 'If you are enjoying it so much, I can give you another cubit of bronze right up to your gullet.'

'It was Taita,' Soleth screamed, with the blood spraying out of him. 'Taita took her away.'

'Taita!' Trok exclaimed with astonishment and jerked the blade free. 'Taita, the Magus.' There was superstitious dread in his tone. Then he was silent for a long pause. At last he ordered the eunuchs who still held Soleth. 'Release him.'

Soleth sat up moaning. At the movement the gas from his bowels rushed out through the slack opening in a long, bubbling fart.

'Where has he taken her?' Trok ignored the sound and the sickening faecal odour that filled the chamber.

'He did not tell me.' Painfully Soleth bundled the linen bed-sheet and thrust it in between his legs to staunch the bleeding. Trok lifted the point of the sword and touched one of his naked pendulous breasts.

Soleth whimpered and farted again. 'He did not tell me, but we spoke of the land between the two rivers, the Tigris and the Euphrates. Maybe that is where he intends taking the Queen.'

Trok thought about it only briefly. It was logical. By now Taita would know of the strained relationships between Egypt and the eastern kingdoms. He would know that he might find sanctuary and protection there, if he could run that far.

But what was his reason for abducting Mintaka? Surely it could not be for ransom. Taita was famous for his scorn of gold and riches. It could not be for some salacious desire. As an ancient eunuch, Taita was not capable of physical lust. Was it the friendship that had grown up between the old man and the girl? Had she appealed to him to help her escape from Avaris and the marriage that was so insufferable to her?

Certainly, she must have gone with him willingly and probably gladly. The manner in which her slave girls had tried to cover her escape proved that, and clearly she had made no outcry, for if she had the sentries would have heard it.

He put aside those considerations for the moment. The main concern now was to get the pursuit in hand and to recapture her and the Warlock before they reached the shores of the Red Sea and crossed into the territories loyal to Sargon of Babylon. He smiled down at Soleth. 'I hope that your paramours will find the alterations I have made to your joy passage to their liking. I will deal with you further when I return. There are hungry hyenas and vultures to be fed.'

The two colonels were still in the banquet chamber, hogging the food and wine, although they had not been at it long enough to drink themselves stupid.

'How many chariots can we have manned and running eastward before midnight?' Trok demanded. They looked startled, but they were warriors and responded swiftly to his angry mood.

Colonel Tolma spat out the mouthful of wine he was about to swallow and leaped to his feet, only slightly unsteadily. 'I can have fifty on the road within two hours,' he blurted.

'I want that to be a hundred,' Trok demanded.

'I will have a hundred under command before midnight.' Colonel Zander sprang up, eager not to be outdone. 'And another hundred running east before dawn.'

Taita led them through the night under a moon only days from full. The tip of his staff clicked on the stony path, and his shadow flitted ahead of him like a monstrous black bat. The others had to stretch their legs to keep him in sight.

After midnight Mintaka began to fail. She was limping heavily and falling back steadily. Nefer shortened his stride to stay with her. He had not expected this from her: usually she was as strong as any boy he knew, and could outrun most of them. He murmured encouragement to her, not loud enough to reach the ears of Taita. He did not want the Magus to realize Mintaka's weakness, and to shame her in the sight of the others.

'It is not far now,' he told her, and took her hand to lead her faster. 'Bay will have the horses ready for us. We will ride the rest of the way to Babylon in royal style.' She laughed but it was a strained, painful sound. It was only then that he realized something was wrong with her.

'What is it that ails you?' he demanded.

'Nothing,' she said, 'I have been locked up in the palace too long. My legs have gone soft.'

He would not accept it. He took her arm and forced her to sit on a rock beside the path, lifted one of her small feet and unlaced the strap of the sandal. He pulled it off and gasped, 'Sweet Horus, how did you manage a single step on this?' The rough ill-fitting sandal had galled her grievously. The blood was black and shining in the moonlight. He lifted the other foot and gently eased off its sandal. Slabs of skin and flesh peeled away with it.

'I am sorry,' she whispered, 'but don't worry, I can go on barefoot.'

Furiously he hurled the bloodied footwear out among the rocks. 'You should have warned me of this earlier.' He stood up, lifted her to her feet, turned his back to her and braced himself to receive her weight. 'Put your arms around my neck and jump up'. Then he set off after the others who, by this time, were merely a dark moving shadow on the moonlit desert far ahead.

Her mouth was close to his ear, and she whispered to him as he toiled on, trying to distract him, and to encourage him. She told him how she had missed him, and how when she had heard of his reputed death she had not wanted to live without him. 'I wanted to die, so that I could be with you again.' Then she told him about the priestess of Hathor and how she had brought the serpent to her. Nefer was so appalled that he lowered her to the earth and scolded her angrily.

'That was stupid.' In his agitation he shook her roughly. 'Don't ever think like that again, whatever happens in the future.'

'You cannot know how much I love you, my darling. You cannot imagine the devastation I felt when I thought you were gone.'

'We must make a pact. We must live for each other from this day onwards. We must never think of death again until it comes to us uninvited. Swear it to me!'

'I swear it to you. From now onwards I will live only for you,' she said, and kissed him to seal their bargain. He lifted her on to his shoulders again and they went on.

Her weight seemed to increase with every pace he took. Where the road was soft and sandy he lowered her and she leaned upon him, hobbling along beside him on her raw and bleeding feet. When the ground became rough and stony he lifted her again and trudged onwards. She told him of how Taita had overlooked her and saved her from her resolve to die. 'It was the most extraordinary feeling,' she said, 'As though he stood at my side and spoke to me in a strong clear voice.

He told me that you were still alive. How far away were you when he overlooked me?'

'We were at Gebel Nagara in the south, fifteen days' travel from Avaris.'

'He could reach so far?' she asked incredulously. 'Is there no end to his powers?'

Once more they stopped to rest in the darkness and she leaned against his shoulder and whispered to him, 'There is something I want to tell you, about my wedding night with Trok . . .'

'No!' he said vehemently. 'I don't want to hear. Do you think I have not tortured myself each day with the thought of it?'

'You must listen to me, my heart. I was never wife to him. Though he tried to force me, I was able to resist him. My love for you gave me the strength to deny him.'

'I have heard that he displayed the red-stained sheepskin on the palace walls.' The words were painful to him and he turned away his face.

'Yes, it was my blood,' she said, and he tried to pull away from her embrace but she held him. 'It was not my virgin blood. It was the blood from my nose and mouth where he had beaten me to force me to submit. I swear to you on the love I have for the goddess, and on my hope to bear your sons, that I am virgin still and will be until you accept my maidenhead from me as a proof of my love.'

He took her in his arms and kissed her and wept with relief and joy, and she wept with him.

After a time he stood up again and he lifted her on to his back. It was as though her vow had given him new strength and they went on more strongly.

It was after midnight before the others realized that something had befallen them, and came back to search for them. Taita bound up Mintaka's feet and after that Hilto and Meren took their turns at carrying her. They went on faster, but the stars were fading and the dawn light growing stronger when they finally reached the oasis where Bay waited for them with the horses.

All of them were exhausted by that time, but Taita would not allow them to rest. They watered the horses for the last time and refilled the waterskins until they were tight and shiny, with drops of moisture oozing from them.

While they were doing this Taita half filled a bucket with water from the well, and, using some foaming unguent, washed the dye from his hair until once more it shone silver.

'Why does he wash his hair at a time like this?' Meren wondered.

'Perhaps it restores some of his force that he lost when he dyed it,' Mintaka suggested, and no one questioned this.

When they were ready to leave Taita forced them to drink again from the well, to fill their bellies with all the water they could swallow without vomiting. While they were doing so Taita spoke quietly to Bay. 'Can you feel it?'

Bay scowled and nodded. 'It is in the air and I can feel it reverberating through the soles of my feet. They are coming.'

Despite the urgency of the moment and the menace of an enemy close at hand, Taita took one last opportunity to treat Mintaka's feet. He smeared the raw and bruised places with salve and re-bandaged them. Then at last he ordered them to mount.

Taita took Meren in the leading chariot as his lance-bearer. Nefer followed with Mintaka clinging to the dashboard to take the weight off her feet. Hilto and Bay brought up the rearguard in the last chariot.

The Assyrian merchant who had sold them the carpets was supervising his servants and slaves as they loaded up his wagons and draught animals. He turned to watch them as they passed, and he called a farewell to Taita. But his interest quickened as he saw the girl in the second chariot. Not even her dusty clothing and dishevelled hair could hide her striking looks. He was still staring after them as they topped the last rise and disappeared into the wilderness, heading east along the caravan road that would lead eventually to the shores of the Red Sea.

***

While Trok was waiting impatiently for his squadrons to assemble before the city gates he ordered Colonel Tolma to send his men to search the encampment of beggars and foreigners outside the walls of Avaris. 'Turn out every hovel. Make certain that Queen Mintaka is not hiding in any of them. Search for Taita the Warlock. Bring me any tall, thin old man you find. I will question him myself.'

There were screams and cries among the huts, the sounds of doors being broken down and flimsy walls smashed in as Tolma's men carried out his orders. Within a short time two of the troopers returned, dragging a filthy old Bedouin harridan to where Trok stood beside his chariot. The woman was screaming hysterical abuse at her captors as she kicked and struggled in their grip.

'What is it, soldier?' Trok demanded, as they threw the woman down at his feet. The trooper held up a pair of delicate golden sandals, decorated with turquoise studs that glittered in the torchlight.

'Your Majesty, we found these in her hut.'

Trok's face darkened with fury as he recognized them and he kicked the woman in the belly. 'Where did you steal them, you foul old she-baboon?'

'I never stole nothing, divine Pharaoh,' she whined. 'He gave them to me.'

'Who was he? Answer me straight or I will push your head up your cunt until you drown in your own stinking juices.'

'The old man, he gave them to me.'

'Describe him to me.'

'Tall, he was, and skinny.'

'How old?'

'Old as the rocks of the desert. He gave them to me.'

'Was there a girl with him?'

'Three other men and a pretty little harlot dressed in fine stuff with paint on her face and ribbons in her hair.'

Trok jerked her to her feet and shouted into her startled face, 'Where did they go. Which way?'

With a shaking finger the woman pointed along the road that led into the hills and the desert beyond.

'When?' Trok demanded.

'That much of the moon's journey,' she said, indicating an arc of the sky that corresponded to four or five hours of the lunar orbit.

'How many horses did they have?' Trok snarled. 'Chariots? Wagons? How were they travelling?'

'No horses,' she answered. 'They went on foot, but in great haste.'

Trok pushed her away. He grinned at Tolma who stood beside him. 'They will not get far on foot. We will have them just as soon as you can get your idle ruffians out of their sleeping rugs and mounted.'

◈

The sun was hot and halfway up the sky when Trok topped the hills above the oasis at the threshold of the wilderness. Two hundred chariots followed him in a column of fours. Five miles further back, their dustcloud clearly visible in the bright sunlight, came Zander with another two hundred. Each vehicle carried two heavily armed troopers, and was loaded with waterskins and sheaths of spare javelins and arrows.

Below them they saw the Assyrian trader coming up the slope from the well at the head of his caravan. Trok rode forward to meet him, and hailed him from a distance. 'Well met, stranger. Whence come you, and what is your business?'

The trader looked up at this warlike host in trepidation, not certain what to expect. Trok's friendly greeting meant little. On the long road from Mesopotamia he had met robbers, bandits and warlords.

Trok reined in his chariot in front of him. 'I am His Divine Majesty Pharaoh Trok Uruk. Welcome to the Lower Kingdom. Fear not. You are under my protection.'

The trader fell to his knees and made his obeisance. For once Trok was impatient of the honours being paid to him, and he cut the man short. 'Stand and speak up, my brave fellow. If you are honest with me and tell me what I need to know, I shall give you a licence to trade throughout my kingdom free of any tax, and send ten chariots to escort you to the gates of Avaris.'

The merchant scrambled to his feet, and began to express his deep gratitude, although he knew from long experience that such royal condescension was usually costly. Trok cut him short. 'I am in pursuit of a band of criminal fugitives. Have you seen them?'

'I have met a number of travellers along the way,' the Assyrian replied cautiously. 'Would Your Divine Majesty deign to describe these villains to me, and I will do my best to place you upon their tracks?'

'Probably five or six in number. They will be heading towards the east. One young woman with them, and the rest of them men. Their leader is an ancient rogue. Tall and thin. He may have dyed his hair black or brown.'

Trok got no further with his description, before the Assyrian broke in excitedly. 'Your Majesty, I know them well. Some days ago the old man with dyed hair purchased carpets and old clothing from me. At that time the woman was not with him. He left horses and three chariots at the oasis down yonder, in the charge of an ugly black ruffian. With the others in an old wagon loaded with the carpets I had sold him, he took this high road we are standing on towards Avaris.'

Trok grinned triumphantly. 'That is the one I want. Have you seen him since? Did he return to pick up the chariots?'

'He and the other three came back early this morning, on foot from the direction of Avaris. With them was the young woman you asked after. She seemed to be injured in some way, for they carried her.'

'Where have they gone, fellow? Which way?' Trok demanded eagerly, but the Assyrian would not be hurried.

'The woman was young. Though she was injured and could only walk with difficulty, she wore fine cloth. She was clearly of high rank and beautiful, with long dark hair.'

'Enough of that. I know the woman well enough without your description. After they left the oasis, which way did they go?'

'They harnessed the horses to the three chariots and left immediately.'

'Which way, man? Which direction did they take?'

'East along the caravan road.' He pointed out the winding track that climbed the low hills into the dune country. 'But the old man's hair was no longer dyed. When last I saw him, it shone like a cloud in the summer sky.'

'When did they leave?'

'An hour after sunrise, Majesty.'

'What was the condition of their horses?'

'Well watered and rested. They had been lying up at the oasis for three days and they had brought a load of fodder with them when they arrived. When they left this morning their waterskins were filled at the well and they seemed to be provisioned for the long journey to the sea.'

'Then they are only hours ahead of us.' Trok exulted. 'Well done, fellow. You have earned my gratitude. My scribes will issue you with the licence to trade, and Colonel Tolma will assign you an escort to Avaris. You will be further rewarded when I return to the city with the fugitives in bonds. You shall have a fine seat in the front row of spectators at their execution. Until then I wish you a good journey and much profit in my kingdom.'

He turned from him and began issuing orders to Colonel Tolma who followed him closely in the second chariot of the column. 'Give this fellow a trade licence and an escort to Avaris. Top up the waterskins at the well, and let the horses drink their fill. But swiftly, Tolma. Be ready to leave again before noon. In the meantime send your wizards and the regimental priests to me.'

The troopers took the horses down to the well in batches of twenty at a time to drink. The men who were not busy with this work stretched out in the shade thrown by their own vehicles to rest and eat a frugal meal of millet bread and dried meat, the staple diet of the cavalry.

Trok found a patch of shade under a gnarled tamarind near the well. The wizards and holy men came in response to his summons and squatted in a circle around him. There were four of them, two shaven priests of Seueth in their black robes, a Nubian shaman hung with necklaces and bracelets of charms and bones, and a sorcerer from the east known as Ishtar the Mede. Ishtar had one wall eye and his face was tattooed with purple and red whorls and circles.

'The man we are pursuing is an adept of the occult arts,' Trok warned them. 'He will exert all his powers to frustrate us. It is said that he can weave a spell of concealment, and that he can conjure up images that might dismay our legions. You will have to work your own spells to turn aside his powers.'

'Who is this charlatan?' asked Ishtar the Mede. 'You can be certain that he will not prevail against our combined force.'

'His name is Taita,' Trok replied, and only Ishtar showed no dismay at the identity of their adversary.

'I know Taita only by reputation,' he said, 'but I have long looked for an opportunity to match him.'

'Weave your magic,' Trok ordered them.

The priests of Seueth went aside a short distance and laid out their accoutrements and mystical trappings on the sand. They began to chant softly and shake their rattles over them.

The Nubian searched among the rocks around the well, until he found a venomous horned adder under one of them. He lopped off its head and dribbled the blood over his own head. With it running down his cheeks and dripping off the tip of his nose, he hopped in circles like a great black toad. As he completed each turn he spat copiously towards the east where Taita lay.

Ishtar built a small fire near the well and squatted over it, rocking on his heels and muttering incantations to Marduk, the most powerful of all the two thousand and ten gods of Mesopotamia.

Once he had given his orders to Tolma, Trok went across to watch him at work. 'What magic are you making here?' he asked at last, as Ishtar opened a vein in his wrist and let a few drops of his own blood drip and sizzle in the flames of the fire.

'This is the hex of fire and blood. I am placing obstacles and hardships in Taita's path.' Ishtar did not look up. 'I am confusing and confounding the minds of his followers.'

Trok grunted sceptically, but secretly he was impressed. He had seen Ishtar work before. He walked a short way along the road and glared at the line of eastern hills. He was hot for the pursuit and grudged this stay. On the other hand he was enough of a general to realize the absolute necessity of resting and watering the horse after the long night ride.

He knew well the nature of the ground ahead. As a young captain of chariots he had patrolled there on many occasions. He had crossed the shale beds that cut hoofs and hocks like flint knives, and had endured the terrible heat and thirst of the dunes.

He walked back to where he had left his chariot, but he had to pause and turn his back as a sudden dust devil came swirling across the yellow plain, spinning upon itself and rising several hundred cubits into the sultry air. The vortex encompassed him. The air was as hot as the breath from a bronze furnace, and he had to cover his nose and eyes with his headcloth and breathe through the material to strain out the flying sand. It swept past and spun away across the hot earth with the grace of a harem dancer, leaving him coughing and wiping his eyes.

It was a little before noon and they had just finished the watering when the second column under Colonel Zander caught up with them and came down the slope to the well. They were as much in need of water as the first column and now there was danger of congestion at the oasis. Already the water was depleted and muddied. They would be forced to fall back on the precious waterskins to eke out the supply.

Trok held a brief conference with Zander and Tolma, explaining his plan of action, and the formation he wanted to employ to prevent Taita from twisting and turning out of the net they were spreading for him. 'Warn the regimental commanders to be on the alert for any magical snares that Taita puts out to confuse us,' he ended. 'Ishtar the Mede has worked a potent spell. I have much faith in him. He has never failed me before. If we are fully aware of the wiles of the Warlock we will succeed. After all, how can he prevail against such an array?' With a sweep of his arm he indicated the huge gathering of chariots and horses and élite troops, 'No! By the breath of Seueth, this time tomorrow I will be dragging Taita and Mintaka behind my chariot on the way back to Avaris.'

He ordered the leading column to mount. Four chariots abreast and in a column half a league long they headed out into the wilderness. On the soft sandy earth ahead the wheel tracks of their quarry were clearly etched.

Taita signalled the two vehicles that followed him to halt. They stopped in the purple shade thrown across the sands by a tall slip-faced dune shaped like the elegant curve of a gigantic seashell.

The horses were already showing signs of distress. They hung their heads and their chests heaved as they breathed. The sweat had dried in salt white rime on their dust-dulled hides.

Carefully they measured out a water ration from the waterskins into the leather buckets and the horses drank eagerly. Taita treated Mintaka's feet and was relieved to find no evidence that the injuries were mortifying. When he had retied the bandages he led Bay out of earshot of the others.

'We are being overlooked,' he said flatly. 'There is a baleful influence slowly enveloping us.'

'I have felt it also,' Bay agreed, 'and I have begun to resist it. But it is powerful.'

'We can best frustrate it if we combine our powers against it.'

'We must be careful of the others. They are more vulnerable.'

'I will warn them to be on their guard.'

Taita walked back to where the others were just finishing the watering. 'Be ready to go on,' he told Nefer. 'Bay and I are going to scout the ground ahead. We will return in a short while.'

The two adepts went forward on foot and disappeared around the curved sand wall of the slip-face. Out of sight of the chariots they halted. 'Do you know who Trok has with him who can work such a potent spell?'

'He has priests and sorcerers with all his regiments, but the most powerful of them is Ishtar the Mede.'

'I know of him.' Taita nodded. 'He works in fire and blood. We must try to turn his influence back on him.'

Bay started a small fire of dried horse dung, and when it was burning steadily they pricked the end of their thumbs and squeezed out a few red drops into the flames. With the whiff of burnt blood in the air they faced the enemy, for they could feel that the influence was in the western segment, from the direction that they had come. They exerted their combined powers and after a while they felt it begin to diminish, and disperse like the smoke of the dying fire.

When they had completed the ritual, and were smothering the fire with sand, Bay said softly, 'It is still there.'

'Yes,' Taita said. 'We have weakened it, but it is still dangerous, especially to those who have not learned how to resist it.'

'The youngest will be more susceptible,' Bay suggested. 'The two boys, Pharaoh and Meren, and the girl.'

They went back to where the chariots waited. Before they mounted again Taita spoke to the others. He knew that they would be frightened if he mentioned the true reason for his concern, so he said, 'We are entering the most inhospitable and dangerous area of the dune-lands. I know you are all tired and thirsty, drained by the rigours of the journey, but it could be fatal for any of you to become careless. Watch the horses and the ground ahead. Do not allow yourselves to be distracted by any strange sound or by an unusual sight, a bird or an animal.' He paused and looked directly at Nefer. 'That applies to you particularly, Your Majesty. Be on your guard at all times.'

Nefer nodded and for once did not argue. The rest of them also looked grave, realizing that Taita had some reason of his own to give them this warning.

As they went forward again, following the valleys between the high dunes the heat seemed to increase with every turn of the chariot wheels. The loose sand walls that rose on either hand took on a motley of vivid colours, lemon yellow and gold, plum, purple and heron blue, fox-red and tawny lion-brown. In places the dunes were streaked with frosty talc, or etched with patterns of black sand like the soot of an oil lamp.

Overhead the sky turned brazen and ferocious. The quality of light changed: it became yellow and ethereal. Distances were rendered confusing and distorted. Nefer slitted his eyes against the shimmering glare of the brassy sky. It seemed close enough to touch with the end of his whip. At the same time the shape of Taita's vehicle only fifty cubits ahead seemed to recede to a blurred and distant horizon.

The heat scorched any exposed skin on face or body. Nefer felt a formless dread take hold of him. There was no reason for it, but he could not shake it off.

When Mintaka shuddered against him and gripped his whip arm he knew that she had sensed it too. Great evil hung in the air. He wanted to call out to Taita, to ask him for guidance and reassurance, but his throat was closed by dust and heat. No sound issued from it.

Suddenly at his side he felt Mintaka stiffen and her fingers dug painfully into the biceps of his whip arm. He looked down at her face and saw that she was terrified. With her free hand she pointed frantically to the crest of the dune that seemed to hang suspended above them.

Something colossal and dark detached itself from the heights and began to tumble down towards them. He had never seen anything like it. It had the same weighty amorphous shape as a monstrous waterskin, but was so large that it covered the entire side of the dune, large enough to engulf and squash not only the three chariots below it but an entire regiment. As it rolled down the almost sheer slope it gathered speed, undulating, wobbling and bouncing silently, coming down on them so swiftly that it blotted out the yellow desert sky. In the heat it exuded a sudden cold that squeezed their breath from their lungs as if they had plunged into an icy pool in a high mountain stream.

The horses had seen it also: they plunged wildly and swung off the sandy track and bolted across the valley bottom, trying to outrun the terrifying apparition. There was a field of ragged black lava rocks directly ahead of them and they were racing straight into it. Nefer realized the danger and tried to turn their heads but they were out of control. As he wrestled with the reins Mintaka was screaming beside him.

Certain that they were about to be overwhelmed by the dark monstrosity, Nefer glanced over his shoulder. He expected it to be looming over them, for he could feel the cold emanation on the back of his neck, but there was nothing. The side of the dune was bare, smooth and silent. The yellow sky above was empty and bright. The other two chariots were halted under the slope, the horses calm and under control. Taita and the others were staring at them, astonished.

'Whoa!' Nefer yelled at the runaway team, and threw his full weight on the reins, but the horses never checked. At full gallop they flew into the field of lava rock with the chariot bounding and swerving behind them. 'Whoa!' he screamed again. 'Stop, curse you, stop!'

The horses were mad with terror, far beyond restraint. They arched their necks to fight the reins, striding out at full stretch, grunting with every stride.

'Hold hard, Mintaka!' Nefer shouted, and threw one arm around her shoulders to protect her. 'We are going to strike!'

The black rocks were worn and carved by windblown sand into strange shapes. Some were the size of a man's head and others as big as the chariot under them. Nefer managed to steer the crazed horses clear of the first, but they ran on into a gap between two of the largest rocks. It was too narrow for them to pass through: the off-wheel struck with a rending crash, and disintegrated. Shattered spokes and sections of the rim were hurled into the air. The carriage dropped on to its axle, dragging down the off horse, which was thrown into the next rock. Nefer heard its front legs snap like kindling, even as he and Mintaka were hurled clear of it.

They hit the soft sand, narrowly avoiding being thrown into the rock that had maimed the horse. When they came to a standstill, Nefer was still holding Mintaka in his arms. He had cushioned her fall, and now he demanded breathlessly, 'Are you all right? Are you hurt?'

'No,' she answered at once, 'Are you?'

Nefer came to his knees, and stared in horror at the wreckage of the chariot and the crippled horses.

'Sweet Horus!' he cried. 'We are finished.' The chariot was smashed beyond any hope of repair. One horse was down for ever, both front legs shattered. The other was standing, still in its traces and harnessed to the single shaft of the chariot, but one leg was swinging loosely from its dislocated shoulder.

Unsteadily he came to his feet, and pulled Mintaka up after him. They clung to each other as Taita drove his chariot to the edge of the lava field, tossed the reins to Meren and jumped down from the footplate. He came to them with long strides. 'What happened? What caused the horses to bolt?'

'Did you not see it?' Nefer asked, still shaken and bewildered.

'What was it?' Taita insisted.

'A thing. Dark and huge as a mountain. It rolled down the dune on top of us.' Nefer groped for words to describe what they had seen.

'It was big as the temple of Hathor.' Mintaka supported him. 'It was terrifying. You must have seen it also.'

'No,' Taita replied. 'It was an aberration of your mind and vision. Something placed there by our enemies.'

'Witchcraft?' Nefer was bemused. 'But the horses saw it also.'

Taita turned away from them and called to Hilto as he drove up, 'Destroy those poor beasts.' He pointed to the maimed horses. 'Help him, Nefer.' Taita wanted to distract him from the disaster and its consequences.

With a heavy heart Nefer held the head of the downed horse. He stroked its forehead and covered its eyes with his headcloth so that it would not see death coming.

Hilto was an old trooper and had done this sad work on many far-flung battlefields. He placed the point of the dagger behind the animal's ear and with a single thrust drove it into the brain. The horse stiffened, shivered and then relaxed. They went to the second animal. It dropped instantly to Hilto's thrust and lay without moving again.

Taita and Bay stood together, watching this harrowing act of mercy, and Bay said softly, 'The Mede is stronger than I thought him to be. He has singled out the most vulnerable among us and directed his powers at them.'

'He has Trok's other sorcerers to reinforce his influence. From now onwards we will have to watch over Hilto and Meren also,' Taita agreed. 'Until I can gather my own force to oppose Ishtar we are in great danger.'

He left Bay's side. It would trouble the others if they saw the two of them conferring secretly together. It was of the utmost importance to keep up their spirits.

'Bring the waterskins,' Taita ordered. One had burst in the crash and the other two were only half full, but they strapped them on to the remaining chariots.

'From here onwards, Meren will ride with Hilto and Bay. I will take Their Majesties with me.'

With the waterskins and the weight of the extra passengers the chariots were now overloaded. The horses were straining as they went forward into the glaring heat, with the lurid sun almost obscured by the strange yellow overcast.

Taita held the golden Periapt of Lostris in his right hand, and chanted softly to himself, warding off the evil that was thickening everywhere around them. In the following chariot Bay was singing also, a monotonous repetitive refrain.

They came to a section of the road where the wind had wiped away the tracks of other caravans and travellers. There were no signs to follow except for the small cairns of stones that had been placed at intervals. Eventually even these petered out, and they went on into the trackless sands. They relied now on Taita's experience, his knowledge of the desert, and his deep instincts.

At last they came out into flat ground between two ranges of high dunes. The sand here was smooth and level, but Taita stopped at the edge of it and considered it carefully. He climbed down from the footplate and beckoned to Bay. The black man came to his side and together they examined the innocuous surface.

'I like it not at all,' Taita said. 'We must look for a detour around this plain. There is something here.'

Bay walked a short way out on to the firm level sand and sniffed the hot air. He spat twice and studied the pattern of his own spittle. Then he came back to Taita. 'I can find nothing troublesome here. If we look for a way round it may cost us hours, even days. The pursuit is not far behind. We must decide which is the greatest risk.'

'There is something,' Taita repeated. 'Like you, I also feel an impulse to cross here. That feeling is too strong and illogical. The idea has been placed in our minds by the Mede.'

'Mighty Magus,' Bay shook his head, 'In this case I do not agree with you. We must take the risk and cross this valley. Otherwise Trok will catch up with us before nightfall.'

Taita took him by the shoulders and stared into his black eyes. He saw that they were slightly unfocused, as though he had been smoking the bhang weed. 'The Mede has penetrated your armour,' he said, and placed the Periapt on Bay's forehead. Bay blinked and opened his eyes wide. Taita could see him struggling to throw off the influence. He exerted his own will to help him.

At last Bay shivered and his gaze cleared. 'You are right,' he whispered. 'Ishtar had overlooked me. There is great danger in this place.'

They looked down the length of the narrow valley. It was a river of yellow sand with no beginning and no end in sight. The far bank was close, no more than three hundred cubits across at the narrowest places, but it might have been two hundred leagues, and Trok's regiments were close behind them.

'South or north?' Bay asked. 'I cannot see the way round.'

Taita closed his eyes and exerted all his powers. Suddenly there was a sound in the terrible silence. A faint high cry. They all looked up and saw the tiny shape of a royal falcon turning high in the furious yellow sky. It circled twice then sped south along the valley, and disappeared into the haze.

'South,' Taita said. 'We will follow the falcon.'

They had been so intent on these deliberations, that neither of them had noticed that Hilto had eased his own chariot up closer to where they stood. He and Meren were leaning over the dashboard and listening to this exchange. Hilto was frowning with impatience. Suddenly he exclaimed, 'Enough of this! The way is clear ahead. We cannot afford any delay. Will you dare to follow if Hilto leads the way?'

He whipped up his team, and the startled horses jumped forward. Meren was taken so completely by surprise that he was almost thrown backwards over the footplate but he grabbed a handhold and managed to stay on the racing vehicle.

Taita shouted at Hilto, 'Come back! You are bewitched. You do not know what you are doing.'

Bay jumped up to catch the harness of the off-side horse, but he was too late: the chariot sped past him and out on to the flat ground. It gathered speed and Hilto's laughter floated back to them. 'The way is open. 'Tis smooth and fast.'

Nefer snatched up the reins of the stationary vehicle, and shouted, 'I will stop him or turn him.'

'No!' Taita turned back to him, desperately raising his hand in a command to stop, 'Don't go out there. There is danger. Stop, Nefer!'

But Nefer ignored his cries. With Mintaka beside him he lashed up the team and the wheels sang over the smooth hard sand. He was catching up with Hilto rapidly.

'Oh, sweet Horus!' Taita groaned. 'Watch the wheels.'

A fine feather of silver sand began to rise from behind the spinning wheels of Hilto's chariot. Then, as they watched in horror, the feather became a thick plume of yellow slush, then slabs of loose mud. The horses slowed as they sank to their hocks in the soft footing and lumps of mud were thrown up so high from their driving hoofs that they flew over Hilto's head. He made no attempt to stop or turn back but drove them on deeper into the quagmire.

'The sinking sands!' Taita cried bitterly. 'This is the work of the Mede. He has hidden the true road from us and led us into this trap.'

Abruptly Hilto's team broke through the crust into the treacherous swamp beneath. As its wheels dropped in over the rims, the chariot came to such a sudden halt that both Hilto and Meren were catapulted over the dashboard. They rolled across the innocent-seeming surface, but when they came to a stop and tried to stand up their bodies were coated with sticky yellow mud, and immediately they sank in to their knees.

The horses were completed mired. Only their heads and front quarters were free, but as they whinnied and plunged they sank deeper and deeper still.

Nefer was bemused and reacted too slowly to the disaster taking place before his eyes. By the time he attempted to turn back it was too late. Within ten cubits his wheels were in over the hubs and both horses were bogged down to the shoulders. He jumped down to help them, to try to unharness them and lead them back, but immediately he was trapped in the slimy mud, sinking in to the knees and then to the waist.

'Don't try to stand,' Mintaka warned him frantically. 'It will swallow you under. Throw yourself flat and swim.'

She threw herself headlong from the sinking vehicle, and lay flat on the quaking mud. 'Like this, Nefer. Do as I do.'

He recovered his wits and stretched out flat on the surface. In an awkward swimming motion, like a child learning to doggy-paddle, he reached the chariot before it disappeared completely. With his dagger he cut the leather straps that held the floorboards in place and, in desperate haste, ripped them up and threw them clear. They floated on the surface of the deadly quicksands, but the heavy-laden chariot slid inexorably below the surface and drew the horses down with it. Within minutes there was only a lighter patch on the dun-coloured plain to mark their grave.

Hilto's chariot had also been drawn under and his horses with it. He and Meren were floundering about, yelling with terror, managing only to keep their mud-daubed heads and shoulders clear.

Nefer shoved one of the floorboards to Mintaka. 'Use this!' he ordered her, and she crawled on to it.

He did the same with another board, which supported his weight. Towing two more boards with him by their leather straps he propelled himself across the swamp until he was close enough to throw them to Hilto and Meren. They dragged themselves out of the glutinous clutches of the mud. All four started to swim laboriously back towards where Taita and Bay watched in horror from firm ground.

Taita waved his arms and shouted urgently, 'You are already halfway across. Don't return here. Go on. Cross to the other side.'

Nefer saw the sense in this immediately. They turned for the far bank. It was slow, hard work, for the mud clung tenaciously to their arms and legs and to the bottom of the boards. Mintaka's lighter weight soon told and she drew ahead of the others. She was first to reach firm ground and to drag herself from the clutches of the sinking sands. At last Nefer, Hilto and Meren followed her. They were almost exhausted. They threw themselves down at the foot of the eastern dunes.

While they crossed, there had been time for Taita to consider their predicament. It seemed hopeless. They were split into two groups, with a gulf between them two hundred cubits wide. They had lost all of their horses and vehicles, their weapons and equipment, but the worst loss of all was the precious waterskins.

Now Bay touched his arm and whispered, 'Listen!'

It was a susurration in the air, far off, sometimes fading away, then growing louder again, a distant echo reverberating from the enclosing dunes. Though faint, it was unmistakable: the sound of a column of chariot cavalry on the march.

The three mud-soaked figures on the far side of the valley heard it also, and came to their feet. All of them stared back into the dunes and listened to Trok and his men coming on apace.

Suddenly Mintaka ran back to the edge of quagmire where they had abandoned the boards that had carried them across. Nefer stared after her, trying to fathom out what she intended. She gathered up the boards and waded out knee-deep, dragging the boards after her by their leather straps.

Nefer realized suddenly what she was doing, but he was too late to stop her. She threw herself flat on one of the boards and began to skim out over the yellow mud. She was out of his reach when at last he was forced to stop waist-deep.

'Come back,' he shouted after her. 'I will go.'

'I am lighter and faster than you,' she called back, and though he went on pleading with her she ignored him and used all her breath and strength on skimming forward.

The sound of chariots grew louder, and spurred Mintaka on to greater effort. Watching her Nefer was torn with fear for her safety and anger for her intransigence, but even stronger was his pride in her courage. 'She has the heart of a warrior and a queen,' he whispered, as she drew closer to the far bank.

Now they could hear the voices of the pursuers and the rattle of wheels and the clank of weapons, magnified by the sounding board of the dunes.

Taita tucked his staff under his belt to leave his hands free, then he and Bay waded out to meet Mintaka. Each took a spare board from her and launched themselves out on the treacherous surface. All three started to swim back to the east bank.

From out of the dunes behind them debouched the head of the column of pursuing chariots. The unmistakable figure of Trok was in the leading vehicle, and his bull voice roared out triumphantly and echoed from the dune walls.

'Forward! Charge!'

The leading phalanx of chariots broke into full gallop and came tearing towards the edge of the sinking sands. The three fugitives sculled themselves frantically on to the yellow morass. Behind them the yells of the charioteers grew louder.

Trok's bulk forced his wheels to sink deeper into the loose sand than those of the other vehicles, and though his horses strained under the whip, he fell back behind the first rank of the charge.

The other three chariots of the leading file ran headlong into the sinking sands, and were sucked in as swiftly as the other vehicles had been engulfed. Thus, Trok was alerted to the danger. He managed to bring his own team under control and swerve away from the morass.

He seized his short recurved bow from the rack and leaped down. Behind him the other chariots broke the charge and drew up in a mass.

'Bows!' shouted Trok. 'Massed volleys. Don't let them get away. Shoot them down.'

The archers ran forward and formed into ranks four deep at the edge of the swamp, full quivers on their backs and bows strung taut.

Mintaka had once more pulled ahead of her companions. She had passed the halfway mark, and though they were sculling frantically Taita and Bay were lagging ever further behind her.

Trok strode down the ranks, giving his orders. 'Archers, nock your arrows!' A hundred and fifty men fitted arrow to bow string.

'Archers, draw and aim!' They lifted their weapons and drew to the lip, aiming into the lowering yellow sky.

'Loose!' Trok yelled, and they fired a massed volley. The arrows rose in a dark cloud. They reached the zenith of their trajectory and fell towards the three small figures out in the swamp.

Taita heard them coming and looked back into the sky. The deadly cloud dropped towards them, whistling softly as the wings of a flight of wild geese.

'Into the mud!' Taita called urgently, and all three slipped off the boards and were immersed in the thick mud until only their heads protruded. The arrows fell thick as hail around them. One pegged deeply into the board on which Mintaka had lain only seconds before.

'Onward!' Taita ordered, and they hauled themselves back on to the boards and sculled forward again, gaining only a few yards before the air was once more filled with the hum of falling arrows, and they threw themselves back into the protection of the yellow mud.

Three times more they were forced to dive off the boards, but each time the range was longer for the archers and the volleys less accurate. Mintaka pulled away even faster than before and was soon out of range.

Trok's bellows of rage and frustration followed them as he urged his men to shoot. The arrows plopped into the mud around them, but the fall of the volleys was less concentrated.

Taita turned his head to look across at Bay. His huge scarified head was shining with mud and sweat. His bloodshot eyes bulged from their sockets, and his mouth was wide open, his filed teeth sharp as those of a shark.

'Courage, Bay!' Taita called to him. 'We are almost across.' As he said it, he realized that the words were a direct challenge to the gods.

On the bank behind them Trok saw them slipping slowly from his grasp. His troopers were using the shorter and less powerful bows designed to be shot from a running chariot. Two hundred cubits was the limit of their effective range. Trok turned and glared back at his lance-bearer, who was managing the horses of his team.

'Bring my war bow,' he shouted. Trok was the only man in the regiment who carried the long bow in his chariot: he had decided that for the rest of his troops the war bow's awkward length did not compensate for the added strength and range.

However, Trok's massive strength and the reach of his long arms set him above the strictures placed on lesser men. He used the short recurved bow in most situations. However, he had designed a special rack on the side of his chariot to accommodate the extra length of the more powerful but unwieldy weapon.

His lance-bearer ran to him and placed the great bow in his hands. He brought also the quiver holding the special arrows, emblazoned with the head of the leopard, that fitted the long weapon.

Trok shouldered his way into the front row of archers, and they made way for him. He nocked a long arrow and measured the range with half-closed eyes.

The heads of the two swimmers were tiny blobs on the yellow expanse. The men around him were still shooting rapidly, but their arrows fell short, dropping ineffectually into the mud. Mentally he calculated the angle of release and took his stance with his left foot leading. He sucked in a deep breath and drew with straight left arm, until the string touched the tip of his hooked nose. The bow challenged even his strength. The muscles in his bare arms stood proud, and his features contorted with the effort. He held it for a heartbeat, adjusting his aim fractionally. Then he released, and the great bow-stock flexed and pulsed in his hands like a living creature.

The long arrow blurred as it climbed, high above the clouds of lesser missiles, outstripping them effortlessly. It reached its noon and dropped like a stooping falcon.

In the mud Taita heard the sharper shriller sound of its flight and looked up. He saw it coming straight at him, and there was no time for him to fall off his primitive craft or even to duck to avoid it.

Involuntarily he closed his eyes. The arrow passed so close over his head that he felt his hair stirred by the wind of its passage. Then he heard the solid thump of the strike.

He opened his eyes and rolled his head towards the sound. The long arrow had taken Bay in the middle of his naked back. It had transfixed his body, and the flint head had buried itself in the board on which he lay, pinning him to the wood like a shiny black beetle.

Bay's face was only an arm's length from his own. Taita looked into the deep black eyes, and saw the agony of death flare in them. Bay opened his mouth to cry out or to speak, but the copious rush of bright blood through his lips drowned any sound. Painfully he reached up to the necklace around his neck, and pulled it loose. He reached out to Taita offering him, as his last gift, the priceless relic that was twisted around his clawed fingers.

Taita gently untangled it from the rigid fingers and dropped the string around his own neck. He felt the essence of the dying shaman flowing from it into his own body, reinforcing his powers.

Bay's head dropped forward, but the arrow prevented him rolling off the board. Taita recognized the leopard inlay on the shaft of the arrow, and knew who had fired it. He reached across, placed two fingers on Bay's throat and felt the moment of his passing. Bay was gone, and no effort on his part could save him. He left him and swam onwards to where Nefer and Mintaka stood on the far bank calling encouragement to him. Four more of the long arrows dropped close to him, but none touched him and he drew slowly out of their reach.

Nefer met him and helped him to his feet in the thick mud. Taita used his staff to help himself out on to firm ground. He sagged down, gasping for breath. After only a minute he sat up again, and stared across the sinking sands to where Trok stood on the far bank, arms akimbo, every line of his body and head betraying his rage and frustration. Then Trok cupped his hands around his mouth and shouted,

'Think not that you have escaped me, Warlock. I want you and I want my bitch back. I will have you both. I will run you down. I will never lose the scent.'

Mintaka walked forward as far as she could go. She knew exactly where he was most vulnerable, and how to humiliate him most painfully in front of his men. 'Dear husband, your threats are as flaccid and empty as your loins.' Her high sweet voice carried clearly and two hundred Hyksos warriors heard every word. There was a shocked silence, and then a great roar of mocking laughter went up from their ranks. Even his own men hated Trok enough to take pleasure in his humiliation.

Trok brandished his bow above his head and stamped with helpless rage. At last he turned, snarling, on his men and they fell silent, abashed by their own temerity.

In the silence Trok shouted, 'Ishtar! Ishtar the Mede, come forward!'

Ishtar stood at the edge of the sinking sands and faced the little party on the far bank. His face was covered by the patterns of tattoos. His eyes were surrounded by purple whorls; his one wall eye shone like a silver disc. A double row of red dots ran down his long nose. There were fern-like tracings across his chin and cheeks. His hair was set into long hard spikes with red shellac. Deliberately he loosened his robe and let it fall to the sand.

He stood stark naked, and his back and shoulders were covered with leopard rosettes. A huge star of red was tattooed on his belly and his pubic hair was shaven, which emphasized his enormous dangling penis. Tiny bells of gold and silver were hooked through his pierced foreskin. He stared at Taita, and the Magus stepped forward to confront him. The gap between them seemed to shrink as they stared at each other.

Slowly Ishtar's member swelled and the bells tinkled as it stiffened into a massive erection. He thrust his hips forward, pointing the angry red head at Taita's. It was a direct challenge, emphasizing Taita's eunuch status, and exerting Ishtar's masculinity over him.

Taita lifted his staff and pointed at the Mede's groin. Neither moved for a long while, projecting all their strength against each other like thrown javelins.

Suddenly Ishtar groaned and ejaculated, spurting all his seed into the sand. His penis shrivelled, becoming small, wrinkled and insignificant. Ishtar sank to his knees and hurriedly pulled on his robe to cover his humiliation. He had lost the first direct confrontation with the Warlock.

He turned his back on Taita and shuffled back to where the two priests of Seueth and the Nubian shaman squatted. He joined their circle, and they linked hands and began to chant.

'What are they doing?' Nefer asked nervously.

'I think that they are trying to divine the way around the sinking sands,' Mintaka whispered.

'Taita will stop them,' Nefer said, with a confidence he did not feel.

Suddenly Ishtar sprang to his feet, with renewed vitality. He let out a cry like a raven's hoarse croak, and pointed south down the sand valley.

'He has chosen the route the falcon revealed to us,' Taita said quietly. 'We are not yet safe.'

Trok's regiments mounted. With Ishtar riding beside Trok in the leading chariot they trotted away southwards following the winding river of fatal mud. As they passed, the troopers shouted threats and defiance at the forlorn group on the opposite bank.

After the dust settled they saw that Trok had left a small force, five chariots, ten men, camped under the dunes on the far bank to keep them under observation. soon the last chariot in the pursuit column was gone into the yellow heat haze, and was hidden by the bend in the valley walls.

'Before nightfall Trok will have found the way across to our side,' Taita predicted.

'What can we do?' Nefer asked.

Taita turned to him. 'You are Pharaoh. You are the Lord of Ten Thousand Chariots. Give us your orders, Majesty.'

Nefer stared at him, speechless at this taunt. Surely Taita was jeering at him. Then he stared into those ancient pale eyes and saw that there was no mockery in them. His anger rose in his throat with the bitter taste of bile.

He was about to protest, to point out that they had lost everything, all their vehicles and water, and that there was a burning desert ahead of them and a relentlessly pursuing army behind them but Mintaka touched his arm, which steadied him. He stared into Taita's eyes and the inspiration came to him.

He told them his plan, and before he was finished Hilto was grinning and nodding, and Meren laughed and rubbed his hands together. Mintaka stood closer to him, proud and straight.

When he had given his orders, Taita nodded. 'That is the battle plan of a true pharaoh,' he said. His voice was flat and without emotion, but in his eyes was a spark of approval. He knew at last that the task Lostris had set for him would soon be finished. Nefer was almost ready to take charge of his own destiny.

They had covered no more than a few leagues when Ishtar pointed forward. Trok halted the column and strained his eyes in the strange yellow light and the shimmering heat-haze. Ahead the valley of the sinking sands narrowed sharply.

'What is that?' Trok demanded. It seemed that some sinuous sea monster was swimming across the gap. The crest of its dorsal fin stuck up from the yellow mud, black and sharp-edged.

'It is our bridge,' Ishtar told him, 'a ridge of shale running from one bank to the other. This is our crossing.'

Trok sent two of his best men ahead on foot to scout the shale bridge. They ran lightly across and reached the far side with dry sandals. They shouted and waved to Trok and he whipped up his horses and followed them across. In single file the rest of the column crossed behind him.

As soon as they were all safely on the far bank, Trok turned towards the north following the valley back to where they had last seen Taita's fugitive party.

But they had covered less than half the distance before the overcast cloud turned to a yellow fog, a brooding miasma that brought on the night prematurely. Within minutes the last of the light had been snuffed out, and the utter darkness forced the column to halt.

'The horses are tired.' Trok tried to put a brave face on the decision to halt for the night when his commanders gathered around him in the darkness for their orders. 'Water them and let them and the men rest. We will go on at first light. Even the Warlock will not have gone far on foot and without water. We shall have them before noon tomorrow.'

Taita unwrapped Mintaka's feet and nodded with satisfaction. Then he dampened them in the strong alkali moisture of the sinking sands, and rebandaged them. Over her protests Nefer made her don his own sandals. They were too large for her by far, but the bandages made them fit closer.

They had nothing to carry, no water or food, no weapons or baggage, nothing except the floorboards from the sunken chariots. With the Hyksos troopers on the far bank watching them curiously, Nefer led them up the face of the high dune, heading east. Panting, they reached the crest. Already their thirst was a raging torment.

Nefer took one last look across the sinking sands. Trok's troopers on the far bank had removed their horses' harness, laagered their chariots and were lighting their watchfires. Nefer gave them an ironic salute, and followed the rest of the party down the far side of the dune. As soon as they were hidden from the watchers they rested awhile. 'Every effort will cost us dear,' Nefer warned them. 'We will have no water for many hours more.'

As they lay panting in the heat they listened anxiously for the sound of the men and chariots. Mintaka gave voice to their fears: 'Pray to all the gods that Trok does not find his crossing and come back to us before dark.'

When they had recovered Nefer led them, under cover of the intervening sand dune, parallel to the valley of the sinking sands. They went only a short distance, but in the heat the effort taxed them severely. Once again they settled down to rest in the enervating yellow fog. They did not have long to wait before the darkness descended on them.

Night brought little relief from the heat. They climbed back to the top of the dune and below them saw the watchfires of the men on the opposite side of the valley. The flames gave just sufficient light for them to make out the layout of the Hyksos camp.

The enemy chariots were drawn up in a hollow square with the horses' heads hitched to the wheels. Two sentries sat beside the fires, and the rest of the men were lying on their sleeping mats within the shelter of the laager.

'They have seen us set out towards the east. We must hope that they believe we are still heading in that direction, and that they are off their guard,' Nefer said, and led them slipping and sliding down the face of the dune. They reached the bottom a few hundred cubits down the valley from the camp. This was just far enough to hide their movements and muffle any sounds they might make.

Using the glow of the campfires for orientation, linking arms so that no one would lose the way in the dark, they groped their way to the edge of the sinking sands.

They launched the wooden boards and sculled across the quagmire. They had become practised at this form of travel and within a short time they reached the far side.

Keeping close together they crept towards the camp, and crouched down just beyond the circle of firelight. Except for the two sentries the enemy camp seemed asleep. The horses were quiet and the only sound was the soft crackle of the flames. Suddenly one of the sentries stood up and walked across to where his comrade sat. The two talked softly. Nefer fretted at the delay, and was about to ask Taita for help when the old man anticipated him. He pointed his staff at the two dark figures. Within minutes their voices sounded drowsy, and at last the one sentry stood up, stretched and yawned. He sauntered back to his own fire, and settled down with his sword across his lap.

Taita kept the staff pointed at him, and slowly the man's head sank forward, his chin resting on his chest. From the other fire came a soft snore. Both men were fast asleep.

Nefer touched Hilto and Meren. Each knew his job. They crept forward again leaving Taita and Mintaka at the edge of the firelight.

Nefer came up behind the nearest sentry. The sword had slipped from his lap and lay beside him in the sand. Nefer picked it up and in the same movement slammed the bronze pommel into the man's temple. Without a sound the sentry toppled over and lay stretched full-length beside his fire.

With the sword in his fist Nefer glanced across at the other fire. Hilto and Meren had dealt with the sentry, who lay curled up like a sleeping dog. Hilto had his sword. The three ran forward and reached the nearest chariot. The javelins were still in the side-bins.

Nefer grabbed one. It felt heavy and comforting in his grip. Meren, too, had armed himself. Suddenly one of the horses whinnied softly and stamped its hoof. Nefer froze. For a moment he thought that they had remained undetected. Then a sleepy voice called from within the square of chariots.

'Noosa, is that you? Are you awake?'

A trooper staggered into the firelight, still more than half asleep, naked except for his loincloth. He held a sword in his right hand.

He stopped and gawked at Nefer. 'Who are you?' His voice rose in alarm.

Meren hurled the javelin. It struck in the centre of the man's chest. He threw up his hand and slumped to the sand. Meren jumped forward and picked up his fallen sword. Howling like maddened *djinns* the three of them leaped over the shafts and rushed into the square of vehicles. Their shrieks had thrown the awakening men into wild confusion. Some had not even drawn their weapons and the captured swords rose and fell to a murderous rhythm. The blades dulled with blood.

Only one of the enemy rallied and turned upon them. He was a big brute of a man, and he beat them back, roaring like a wounded lion. He aimed a full cut at Nefer's head, and although Nefer caught it with a high parry, the blow numbed his arm to the shoulder. The bronze blade snapped off at the guard.

Nefer was disarmed and his adversary swung up his sword and aimed at his head to finish it. Taita stepped out of the darkness behind him, and rapped him over the skull with his staff. The man collapsed, and Nefer snatched the sword from his nerveless fingers before it struck the ground.

The fight was over. Five of the survivors knelt with their hands on their heads, while Hilto and Meren stood over them. Mintaka and Taita built up the fires, and by the light of the flames they made out that three of the troopers were dead, and two others gravely wounded.

While Taita treated their injuries, the others used spare tackle from the chariots to pinion the hand and feet of the prisoners. Only then could they drink their fill from the waterskins, help themselves from the bread bag and cut slices of dried meat from the provisions they found.

By the time they had eaten and drunk the light of the new day was strengthening. It was another threatening scarlet dawn, and the heat was already suffocating. Nefer selected three chariots, and the best of the horses to draw them. They stripped the chosen vehicles of any unnecessary equipment, such as the troopers' personal baggage and spare weapons beyond their own requirements. Nefer turned the unwanted horses loose and sent them galloping into the wilderness by waving a blanket in their faces.

Every minute the ruddy light of that eerie dawn grew stronger, and they mounted in haste. When they were ready to leave Nefer went to the group of bound prisoners.

'You are Egyptians, as we are. It pains me deeply that we have killed and wounded some of your companions. This was neither our choice nor our pleasure. The usurper Trok forced this upon us.'

He squatted down next to the big man who had nearly killed him. 'You are a brave fellow. I wish that some day we could fight side by side against the common enemy.'

The skirt of Nefer's apron had drawn up as he sat, and the prisoner's eyes went down to the smooth muscles of his right thigh. His mouth fell open. 'Pharaoh Nefer Seti is dead. Why do you bear the royal cartouche?' he asked.

Nefer touched the tattoo that Taita had inscribed there so long ago. 'I bear it by right,' he said. 'I am Pharaoh Nefer Seti.'

'No! No!' The prisoner was agitated and afraid, as he had probably never been on a battlefield.

Mintaka jumped down from the chariot and came to them. She spoke to the man in a friendly tone. 'Do you know who I am?'

'You are Her Majesty Queen Mintaka. Your father was my god and commander. I loved him well. Therefore I love and respect you.'

Mintaka slipped her dagger from its sheath and cut away his bonds, 'Yes,' she said. 'I am Mintaka, and this is Pharaoh Nefer Seti who is my betrothed. One day we shall return to Egypt to claim our birthright, and to rule in peace and justice.'

Nefer and Mintaka stood up and she went on, 'Give this message to your comrades-in-arms. Tell the people that we are alive and that we shall return to this very Egypt.'

The man crept forward on his knees and kissed her feet, then he crawled to Nefer and picked up one of his feet. He placed it upon his own head.

'I am your man,' he said. 'I shall carry your message to the people. Return to us soon, divine Pharaoh.'

The other prisoners joined him with protestations of loyal love. 'Hail, Pharaoh! May you live and rule a thousand years!'

Nefer and Mintaka mounted their captured chariot, and the freed prisoners shouted, '*Bak-her! Bak-her!*'

The three vehicles pulled out of the wrecked camp. Taita rode alone in the van, because he was best able to resist the wiles of Ishtar the Mede, and to discover the true road that had been hidden from them. Nefer and Mintaka followed closely, and Hilto and Meren brought up the rearguard. They headed back the way they had come.

They had gone only a short way, the valley of the sinking sands and the camp still in sight, when Taita stopped and looked back. The other two vehicles halted behind him. 'What is it?' Nefer asked, and Taita held up his hand. In the silence they heard the distant sound of Trok's division coming on along the far bank. Then suddenly, through the lowering red dawn, they saw the head of his column appear from out of the far dunes.

In the leading chariot Trok reined in sharply and shouted at Ishtar, 'By the blood and seed of Seueth, the Warlock has outwitted you again. Did you not foresee that they would cross back and seize the chariots of our picket?'

'Did you also not foresee it?' Ishtar snarled at him. 'You are the great general.'

Trok threw back his whip arm to lash him across his tattooed face for such insolence, but when he looked into the Mede's dark eyes he thought better of it and lowered the whip. 'What now, Ishtar? Will you let them get clear away?'

'There is only one road back for them and Zander is coming down it with two hundred chariots. You still have them between the grindstones.' Ishtar pointed out darkly. Trok's face lit in a savage smile. In his fury he had almost forgotten Zander.

'The sun has hardly risen. You have all this long day to recross the shale bridge and follow them up,' Ishtar went on. 'I have their scent in my nostrils. I will cast my web to ensnare them and, like a faithful hound, I will lead you to the kill.'

Trok lashed his horses forward and rode out on to the firm sand at the edge of the swamp, directly opposite the three chariots on the other bank. He managed to summon up a laugh and a wide smile that were almost convincing.

'I am enjoying this more than you are, my friends. Revenge is a meal best eaten cold! By Seueth, I will enjoy the taste of it.'

'You must catch your rabbit before you can cook it,' Mintaka called back.

'I will. Be sure that I still have some surprises to amuse you.'

His smile faded as the three chariots started forward into the dunes, Mintaka waving back at him gaily. Although he knew that it was her intention to anger him, it galled him so much that his guts felt hot and sour with rage.

'Back!' he shouted at his men. 'Back across the bridge.'

As they went on Taita looked to the sky more frequently, and his expression was sober and thoughtful as the brimstone clouds sank closer to the earth.

'I have never see a sky like this,' Hilto said, when they stopped to water the horses in the middle of the forenoon. 'The gods are angry.'

It was strange how readily they found the true road. The fork where they had made the wrong turning was plain to see from far off. It seemed that they could not possibly have missed the tall cairn of stones that marked it, and the main road to the Red Sea, travelled by so many trading caravans, was more deeply trodden and apparent than the rudimentary track they had followed into the valley of the Sinking Sands.

'Ishtar blinded us,' Nefer murmured, as they rode towards the crossroads, 'but this time we will not be so easily duped.' Then he looked up uneasily at the sky and made the sign against evil. 'If the gods are kind.'

It was Hilto, with his warrior's eyes, who picked out the dustcloud ahead of them. The low, clouded sky had obscured it until now when it was close. Hilto galloped alongside Taita's chariot and shouted to him, 'Magus! Those are chariots ahead of us, and many of them.'

They reined in and stared ahead. The dustcloud was moving even as they studied it.

'How far ahead?' Taita asked

'Half a league or less.'

'Do you think that Trok has a second division coming up behind him?'

'You know better than I do, Magus, that that is the common tactic of the Hyksos. Do you not recall the Battle of Dammen? How Apepi caught us there between his two divisions?'

'Can we reach the crossroads before they cut us off?' Taita asked, and Hilto narrowed his eyes.

'Maybe so. But it will be a close race for it.'

Taita turned and looked back. 'Trok will be on the road behind us already. We dare not turn back into his arms.'

'It would be certain disaster to leave the road and enter the sands. We would leave a clear sign for them to follow. The horses would fail before the end of the day.'

'No wonder Trok laughed at us,' said Mintaka bitterly.

'We are once again between the hammer and the anvil,' Meren agreed.

'We must run for it,' Nefer decided. 'We must try to reach the crossroads and get on to the main road ahead of them. It is our only escape.'

'At our best speed, then, even if we use up the horses in the effort,' Hilto agreed.

They surged forward three abreast. The chariots bumped and swerved as their wheels caught the ruts in the track, but the horses were going well. The dustcloud ahead became more menacing as they ran towards it. The cairns of stones seemed never to grow closer. They were still more than five hundred cubits from the turning when the first chariots of the approaching division hove into sight, half obscured by dust and the awful yellow light.

They stopped as though uncertain of the identity of the three racing vehicles they saw coming towards them, then suddenly started forward again, coming straight at the fugitives.

Taita tried to force a last turn of speed out of the horses, but felt the weariness overtaking them. They held on until the last possible moment, but the enemy was charging head-on at them, and it gradually became certain that they could not reach the crossroads before them. At last Taita held up his clenched fist in the command to halt. 'Enough!' he cried. 'We can never win this race.'

They halted across the track, the horses lathered and heaving for breath. The charioteers were pale under the dust that coated their features and despair bloomed in their eyes.

'Which way, Pharaoh?' Hilto shouted. They were already beginning to turn to Nefer for leadership.

'There is only one way open. Back the way we have come.' And then, so low that only Mintaka could hear him, 'Into Trok's arms. But at least it gives me a last chance to settle the score with him.'

Taita nodded agreement, and was the first to swing his chariot into a tight full turn. He led them back towards the sinking sands. The others wheeled around and followed in his dust. At first the dust covered their view of the pursuit, but then a puff of hot wind blew it aside momentarily and they saw that they had already lost ground.

They tore onwards, but Nefer felt his horses start to fail. Their gait was heavy and laboured, their legs flopping and their hoofs starting to throw out sideways. Nefer knew that it was nearly over. He placed one arm around Mintaka's waist. 'I loved you from the first moment I saw you. I shall love you through eternity.'

'If you truly love me, then you will never let me fall into Trok's hands again. At the end, it will be the way for you to prove your love.'

Nefer turned to look down at her, puzzled. 'I do not understand,' he said, and she touched the captured sword that hung at his side.

'No!' He almost screamed the word, and hugged her to him with all his strength.

'You must do it for me, my heart. You cannot give me back to Trok. I do not have the courage to do it myself so you must be strong for me.'

'I cannot,' he cried.

'It will be quick and painless. The other way . . .'

He was in such distress that he almost ran full tilt into the back of Taita's chariot as it came to an abrupt swerving halt across the track ahead of them. Taita pointed ahead.

Trok was there. Even at distance they could make out his bear-like form at the head of his moving column, coming straight towards them. They looked back and the other enemy was closing in as fast.

'One last fight!' Hilto loosened his blade in its scabbard. 'The first the worst. The second the same. The last the best of all the game.' It was one of the adages of the Red Road, and he quoted it with genuine anticipation.

Taita looked up at the bile-coloured sky as another sultry gust rippled his hair, like wind through a field of silver grass.

Mintaka tugged Nefer's arm. 'Promise me!' she whispered, and his eyes filled with tears.

'I promise you,' he said, and the words scalded his mouth and throat. 'And afterwards I shall kill Trok with my own hands. When I have done that I will follow close behind you on the dark journey.'

Taita did not raise his voice but it carried to all of them: 'This way. Mark well my wheel tracks and follow them faithfully.'

To their astonishment Taita turned his horses off into the sand heading at a right-angle from the track, north into the unmarked shifting dunes. Nefer expected him to sink to the hubs immediately, but somehow he must have found a hard crust under the soft surface. He went on at a steady trot and they followed him closely, although they knew that this was a last, doomed attempt.

Looking back Nefer could still make out both clouds of dust from the two enemy divisions converging on them from the east and the west. There was not the least chance that, when they reached it, they would not find the place where the three chariots had left the track. Unless, of course, Taita could weave a spell of concealment to outwit Ishtar, but that was a despairing chance. Ishtar had proved that he was not susceptible to such trivial witchcraft and Trok with his own eyes must have seen them turn aside from the track.

Yet when he looked ahead he saw that Taita had the golden Periapt of Lostris in his right hand and around his wrist he had wrapped the necklace that had been the gift of Bay. He was not looking back at the pursuit, but his face was raised to the menacing sky and his expression was rapt.

Their plight seemed hopeless, but Nefer felt an illogical and perverse glow of hope. He realized that, in some mysterious fashion, the gift of Bay had enhanced the old man's already formidable powers. 'Look at Taita,' he whispered to Mintaka. 'Perhaps it is not yet the end. Perhaps there will be one more move of the bao stones left to us before the game is decided.'

Trok galloped down the track until he reached the spot where he had seen the three chariots turn aside and head into the dunes. Their tracks were so deeply etched into the sand that they might have been made by a single pair of wheels. At that moment Zander rode up from the opposite direction at the head of the second column.

'Well done! You have turned the quarry. We have them now,' Trok shouted at him.

'It has been a good chase,' Zander roared back. 'What formation do you want me to keep?'

'Take the rearguard once again. In column of fours. Follow me.' As he turned off to follow the fugitives, his two divisions of chariots fell in behind him. He looked ahead. Taita and his tiny party had already disappeared into a funnel of high sandhills, whose tops were purple and blue. The depths between them were sombre and shaded under the lowering sky. He had not gone two hundred cubits when the outside chariots of the column were bogged down in the soft sand. He knew then why Taita had maintained such a tight formation. Only in the centre line was the earth hard enough to support a chariot.

'In single line ahead!' He altered his formation. 'Stay in my tracks.'

The two combined divisions stretched out over half a league as they followed Trok into the uncharted wilderness, and the troopers looked up with mounting trepidation at the towering sand walls and the ugly sky above. Trok could not press his horses at the same killing pace and they came down to a walk, but he could judge by the tracks Taita had left that he, too, was moving more slowly.

They kept on for almost another league until abruptly the land ahead changed character. From the soft sand waves rose a dark island of rock. It was like some small craft lost in the ocean of the dunes. Its sides were honeycombed and eaten away by the abrasive sand-laden winds of millennia, but the peak was as sharp as the fang of some fabulous monster.

On the peak, tiny with distance, stood an unmistakable figure, sparse and tall with a wild bush of silver hair that glinted like a helmet in the strange and awful light.

''Tis the Warlock,' Trok gloated to Ishtar. 'They have taken refuge in the rocks. I hope they try to fight us there.' Then to his trumpeter, 'Sound the battle call.'

When Nefer and Mintaka saw the rockpile looming ahead they were both astonished.

'Did Taita know it was here?' Mintaka asked.

'How could he have known?' Nefer replied.

'You told me once that he knows everything.' And Nefer was silenced. He looked back to cover his uncertainty, and saw the dust of the pursuit close behind, rising to mingle with the yellow glare of the sunless sky.

'It matters not at all. How can it avail us?' he asked. 'We might be able to defend those rocks for a very little while, but there are hundreds of Trok's men. This is almost the end.' He touched the waterskin that hung from the rail beside him. It was almost empty, not even enough left to keep the horses alive for another day.

'We must trust Taita.' Mintaka said, and he laughed bitterly.

'It seems the gods have deserted us. Who else is there to trust but Taita?'

They went forward, with the horses down to a hampered walk. Behind them they heard the faint sounds of the pursuit: the cries of the captains urging their troopers to keep the line, the jingle of loose equipment and the groan and whine of dry wheel hubs.

At last they came up under the hill of black and ochre-coloured rock. It was a hundred feet high and the accumulated heat radiated from it like a bonfire. Not a single plant had found a foothold on it, but the wind had carved fissures and cracks in its cliffs.

'Drive the chariots close in against the cliff,' Taita ordered, and they obeyed. 'Now free the horses and bring them this way.' Taita set the example by leading his own team around the angle of the rockface. Here there was a deep fissure with sheer sides cutting into the rock pile.

'This way.' He led them as far as they could go along the sandy floor of the deep, vertical crack. 'Now make the horses lie down.'

All cavalry horses were trained to perform this trick. At the urging of their handlers they lowered themselves to their knees and then, grunting and blowing, they went flat on their sides on the floor of the fissure.

'Like this!' Taita told them. He had brought a bedding roll from the chariot. With strips torn from it he blindfolded the horses to keep them quiet and submissive. Then he drove a javelin deep into the loose earth and used it as an anchor to tie down the horses' swathed heads and prevent them from rising again. The others followed his example.

'Now bring what remains of the water. 'Tis a pity there is not enough to give the horses a last drink, but we will need every drop for ourselves.'

Almost as if he knew of its existence, Taita led them to a shallow overhang in the cliff. The head room under the overhang was so low that anyone trying to enter would have to go down on hands and knees.

'Use the loose scree from the cliff to wall this in.'

'A *zareba* wall?' Nefer looked puzzled. 'We cannot defend this place. Once we are in the cave we could not even stand, let alone swing a sword.'

'There is no time to argue.' Taita glared at him. 'Do as I tell you.'

Nefer's nerves were raw with fear for Mintaka, and he was wearied by the hardships they had lived through these last days. He glared back at Taita. The others watched with interest: the young bull challenging the older one. The seconds drew out until abruptly Nefer realized his own foolishness. Only one person could save them now and he capitulated. He stooped and picked up a large rock from the scree pile and staggered with it to the shallow cave. He placed it in position and ran back for another. The others joined in the work. Even Mintaka carried her share of the rough lumps of schist. The skin of her hands was raw and torn before they had closed in a narrow space behind the wall.

'What do we do now?' Nefer asked stiffly, still smarting from his encounter with the Magus.

'Drink,' said Taita,

Nefer poured from the skin into a leather bucket and handed it to Mintaka. She took a few sips then offered it to Taita.

He shook his head. 'Drink, and drink deep.'

When they had all drunk as much as their stomachs would hold, Nefer turned on Taita again. 'What now?'

'Wait here.' Taita ordered and picked up his long staff, he began to climb the jagged side of the hillock.

'What about this *zareba*?' Nefer shouted after him, 'What purpose is it to serve?'

Taita paused on a narrow ledge thirty feet above them and looked down. 'Your Majesty will know when the time comes.' Taita began to climb again.

'A hiding-place? A tomb, perhaps?' Nefer called sarcastically after him, but Taita did not answer or look back.

He climbed without rest or pause until he reached the peak of the hillock. He stood there gazing back in the direction from which Trok would come.

The little party in the gully at the foot of the hillock watched him, some puzzled, some with hope and one angrily.

Nefer roused himself. 'Fetch the javelins and the rest of the weapons from the chariots. We must be ready to defend ourselves.' He ran to where they had left the chariots. He came back with an armful of javelins, and Meren and Hilto following behind him similarly laden.

'What is Taita doing?' he asked Mintaka. She pointed up at the crest.

'He has not moved.'

They stacked the weapons then settled down at the entrance to the rough shelter. All their eyes went up to Taita again.

He was outlined against that dreadful sulphur sky. Nobody spoke, nobody moved, until they heard that dreaded sound again. They turned their heads to listen to the faint rattle and squeal of chariot wheels, hundreds of them, the voices of men, sometimes muffled by the dunes, at others clear and menacing.

Slowly Taita raised both arms and pointed them to the sky. All their eyes followed the movement. In his right hand he held his staff, in the left the Periapt of Lostris, and at his throat he wore the gift of Bay.

'What is he doing now?' Hilto asked, in an awed tone. Nobody answered him.

Taita stood as still as if he had been chiselled out of the living rock. His head was thrown back, his hair fluffed out silver on his shoulders.

His robes were belted up, so that his thin shanks were exposed. He looked like an old bird at roost.

The heavens swirled with low, heavy cloud. The light was transient, fading as the hidden sun was covered more heavily, flaring as the clouds thinned and fumed.

Still Taita did not move, his staff aimed at the pregnant belly of the heavens. The sound of the approaching column became clearer still, and suddenly there was a distant blare of a ram's horn trumpet.

'That is the battle call. Trok has seen Taita,' Mintaka said quietly.

Trok shouted at his trumpeter, 'Sound the advance!' but the warlike sound seemed to be swallowed up by the empty desert and the low, angry heavens.

'Wait!' said Ishtar the Mede. He was watching Taita's tiny figure on the peak of the rock hill. 'Wait!'

'What is it?' Trok demanded.

'As yet I cannot fathom it,' Ishtar said, without taking his gaze off the Warlock, 'but it is pervasive and powerful.'

The column remained halted, every man in it staring at the figure on the peak with awe. A terrible silence fell on the desert. There was no sound at all. Even the horses were still – there was no rattle or jingle of equipment.

Only the sky moved. It formed a whirlpool over the head of the Magus, a great turning wheel of smouldering cloud. Then slowly the centre of the whirlpool opened like the single eye of an awakening monster. From the heavenly eye a shaft of dazzling sunlight burst forth.

'The eye of Horus!' Ishtar breathed. 'He has called up the god.' He made a sign of protection, and at his side Trok was silent and rigid with superstitious dread.

The brilliant shaft of light struck the peak, and lit the figure of the Warlock like a bolt of blinding lightning. Around his head it spun a nimbus of silver radiance.

He made a slow circular pass with his long staff, and the Hyksosian charioteers cringed like curs under the whip. The clouds opened wider, and the sky was clear. The sunlight danced on the dunes and was reflected like a sheet of polished bronze into their eyes, dazzling and blinding them. They lifted their shields or their hands to protect their eyes from the strange radiance, but they made no sound.

On the peak Taita described another deliberate circle with his staff, and there was a sound at last: soft as a lover's sigh, it seemed to issue from the very heavens. Men's heads turned questioningly as they sought the source.

Once again Taita gestured and the sigh became a soughing, a gentle whistling. It came from the east, and slowly all their heads turned towards it.

Out of that strange, cloudless brilliance, they saw it coming. It was a solid dun wall that reached from the earth to the highest heavens.

'Khamsin!' Trok whispered the dread word.

The wall of airborne sand marched towards them with a terrible deliberation. It undulated and pulsed like a living creature, and its voice changed. No longer a whisper, it became a rising howl, the voice of a demon.

'Khamsin!' The word was yelled from chariot to chariot. They were no longer warriors hot for war, but small terrified creatures in the face of this destroyer of men, cities and civilizations, this eater of worlds.

The column of chariots lost its formation and broke up into fragments as the drivers wheeled their teams and tried to run from it.

As soon as they left the narrow path of harder ground the sand sucked down their wheels. Men leaped from the cockpits and abandoned their vehicles, leaving the horses in the traces. Instinctively the horses sensed the menace and reared and screamed, trying to escape by kicking themselves free of the traces.

The *khamsin* bore down upon them inexorably. Its voice changed from a howl to a bellow. Men ran before it in mindless panic. They slipped and fell in the loose sand, dragged themselves up and ran on. They looked back and saw the great storm come on apace roaring like a crazed monster, rolling and roiling upon itself, twisting curtains of sand, brazen where the sunlight struck them, dun and sombre where their own mountainous heights shaded them.

Taita stood with his arms and staff outstretched and watched the army below him engulfed. He saw Trok and Ishtar still frozen like a pair of statues in the sunlight, and then, as the front of the storm reached them, they were gone with magical swiftness, they and all their men, chariots and horses, gone in the rolling billows of the *khamsin*.

Taita lowered his arms, turned his back on the monster and, without haste, started down the hillock. His long legs spanned the difficult places and he leaned upon his staff as he stepped from ledge to ledge.

Nefer and Mintaka were standing hand in hand at the base of the cliff. They welcomed him with a bemused expression, and Mintaka's tone was subdued and incredulous as she asked, 'You called up the storm?'

'It has been brewing all these last days.' Taita said, his face neutral and his tone equivocal. 'You have all remarked the heat and the dolorous yellow mists.'

'No,' said Nefer. 'It was not in nature. It was you. You knew and understood all along. You called it up. And I doubted you.'

'Go into the shelter now,' said Taita. 'It is almost upon us.' His voice was lost in the shrieking cacophony of the *khamsin*. Mintaka led the way, crawling into the low narrow cave through the opening in the rude wall. The others followed her, crowding into the tiny space. Before he entered Hilto handed in the almost empty waterskins.

In the end, only Taita stood outside the shelter. Almost as though the storm was his creature, his face was intent as it loomed over him. It struck with a force that made the living rock around them seem to quiver and vibrate and Taita was gone, his tall figure obliterated. The first gust lasted only a few seconds, but when it passed Taita was still there, unmoved and serene. The storm gathered itself bellowing, like a berserk monster, and as it hurled down on them in all its terrible majesty Taita stooped through the opening and sat with his back to the inner wall.

'Close it up,' he said, and Meren and Hilto blocked the entrance with the rocks they had placed at hand.

'Cover your heads,' said Taita, and wound his headcloth over his face. 'Keep your eyes closed, or you will lose your sight. Breathe carefully through your mouth or you will drown in sand.'

The storm was so overwhelming that its first front picked up Trok's chariot and rolled it over with the horses screaming as the lashing shaft broke their backs.

Trok was thrown free. He fought his way to his feet, but the storm struck him down again. He managed to pull himself up, using all his brute strength, but he had lost all sense of direction. When he tried to open his eyes he was blinded by sand. He did not know in which direction he was facing, or where he should try to escape. The storm was swirling upon itself so that it seemed to be coming from every direction at once. He dared not open his eyes again. The *khamsin* ripped at his face, and its harsh rush abraded the skin from his cheeks and lips until he covered them with his headcloth.

In the turmoil of sand and wind Trok screamed, 'Save me! Save me, Ishtar, and I will reward you beyond your greediest dreams.'

It seemed impossible that anyone could have heard his cry in the deafening uproar. Then he felt Ishtar seize his hand and squeeze it hard to caution Trok to hold fast.

They stumbled on, at times sinking to the knees in the sand, which ran like water. Trok tripped over an obstacle and lost contact with Ishtar. When he groped for him in panic he touched the object that had tripped him, and realized that it was one of the abandoned chariots lying on its side.

He screamed for Ishtar, staggering in a circle and Ishtar's hand grabbed his beard and led him on. He was scorched by sand, blinded by sand, drowning in sand.

He fell to his knees and Ishtar hauled him up again, ripping out a handful of his beard. He tried to speak but when he opened his mouth the sand rushed in and he choked. He knew he was dying, that no man could survive this terrible thing that had them in its grip.

It seemed endless, their tormented journey to nowhere. Then, abruptly, he felt the force of the wind diminish. For a minute he thought that the storm had already passed them by, but the roar had not abated – to the contrary, it seemed still to be rising. They staggered onwards, reeling and bumping into each other like two drunkards trying to lead each other home from the tavern. Still the wind force dropped. In a vague and confused way Trok thought that somehow Ishtar had worked a spell to shield them, but then a sudden gust almost lifted him off his feet and broke the grip that Ishtar had on his beard. He crashed into a wall of rock with such force that he felt his collar-bone break.

He dropped to his knees and clung to the rock, like a child to its mother's breast. How Ishtar had brought them to it he neither knew nor cared. All that mattered was that the cliff above them was breaking the full force of the storm. He felt Ishtar kneel at his side and pull up his tunic until it covered his head. Then Ishtar pushed him down flat in the shelter of the cliff and lay down beside him.

In the tiny cave Nefer crawled close to Mintaka and took her in his arms. He tried to speak to her, to comfort and encourage her but both their heads were swathed with cloth, and the wind drowned out all sound. She laid her head on his shoulder and they clung to each other. They were entombed in the roaring darkness, dumb and blinded and half suffocated. Each hot breath they drew had to be strained through cloth and taken only a sip at a time to prevent a rush of talcum fine sand passing between their lips.

After a while the roar of the wind deafened them and dulled all their other senses. It went on and on, without ceasing or relenting. They had no way to judge the passage of time, except the tiniest awareness of light and darkness through their closed eyelids. To mark the arrival of the day there was a faint rosy aura; when night fell it faded into utter darkness. Nefer had never known such complete and endless dark. If it had not been for Mintaka's body pressed close to his, he thought that he would have gone mad.

Every once in a long while she stirred against him and answered the pressure of his arms with her own. He might have slept, but there were no dreams, just the roaring of the *khamsin* and the darkness.

After another long while he tried to move his legs, but he could not. In a blind panic he thought he had lost control of his body. That he was weak and dying. He tried again with all his strength, and managed to move his foot and toes. Then he knew that he was entrapped by the sand that was filtering into their shelter through the chinks in the *zareba* wall. It had already piled up as high as his waist. They were slowly being buried alive. The thought of that insidious death filled him with terror. With his bare hands he scraped away enough sand to be able to move his legs then did the same for Mintaka.

He felt the others working at the same task in the crowded cave, trying to fight back the sand, but it trickled in like water. It was deposited on them from the dense clouds of swirling dust.

And the storm raged on.

For two days and three nights the wind never relented. During this time Nefer managed to keep back the sand just enough to move his head and his arms, but his lower body was encased solidly. He could not begin to dig himself out, for there was no where to which he could move the sand.

He reached up one hand and touched the stone roof inches above his head. He ran his fingers across it, and realized it was slightly domed. Their heads were in this small space, but the sand had sealed off the cave entrance so that no more sand could penetrate. But he could still hear the storm bellow endlessly.

He waited. At times he felt Mintaka sobbing quietly beside him and tried to comfort her with a gentle pressure of his arms. The air trapped with them in the tiny head space became fetid and stale. He thought that soon it would no longer keep them alive, but some fresh air must have been filtering through the sand, for although each breath was a struggle they were still alive.

They drank most of the water that remained in the waterskins, leaving only a tiny amount in the bottom. Then the thirst came. Even though they were unable to move their bodies to use up moisture, the hot dry sand and air sucked it out of them. Nefer felt his tongue slowly cleave to the roof of his mouth. Then it began to swell so his breathing, already difficult, became almost impossible because of the huge spongy thing that filled his mouth.

With the fear and the thirst he lost track of time, and it seemed that years had passed. Nefer aroused himself from the stupor that was slowly overtaking him. He realized that something had changed. He tried to fathom what it was, but his mind was numb and unresponsive. Mintaka was very still beside him. He squeezed her fearfully. In reply he felt a tiny shudder of movement. She was still alive. Both of them were alive, but entombed, able only to move some small part of their bodies.

He felt himself drifting back into that dark stupor, into haunted dreams of water, of cool green expanses of the great river, of cascades and bright rivulets of water. He forced himself up from the darkness, and listened. He heard nothing. That was what had roused him. There was no sound. The roaring clamour of the *khamsin* had given way to a profound silence. The silence of a sealed tomb, he thought, and the horror returned full force.

He began to struggle again, to try to work his way out of the sand. He managed at last to free his right arm, reached out and found Mintaka's covered head. He stroked it and in the silence heard her whimper. He tried to speak, to reassure her, but his swollen tongue would let no word pass. Instead he reached out beyond her to see if he could touch Hilto, who had been sitting on the far side of her. Either Hilto was gone or was beyond the reach of his arm, for he touched nothing.

He rested a while then roused himself once more, and made an effort to clear the sand from around the entrance to the cave. But there was little space to store what he scraped away. A handful at a time he scooped it away and pushed it into a nook in their tiny cell. Soon he was working at the furthest reach of his right arm, scraping away a few grains at a time. It was a despairing attempt but he knew that he had to keep trying or give up hope.

Abruptly he felt the sand cascade out from under his fingers, and even through the folds of his headcloth fresh air that had not been breathed seeped into the cave. And he was aware of the faintest glimmer of light beyond his closed eyelids. Painfully he began to pull away the cloth from his face. The light grew stronger and the air was sweet in his dry mouth and aching lungs. When his face was free of the cloth he half opened one eye, and was almost dazzled by the light. When his vision had adjusted he saw that he had opened a hole to the outside that was no larger than the circle of his thumb and forefinger, but from beyond there was quiet. The storm had passed.

Excited and with new hope he tugged at the cloth that covered Mintaka's head and heard her breathe the fresh air. Again he tried to speak, but again his voice failed him. He tried to move, to escape from the deadly grip of the heavy sand, but his body was still encased to the armpits.

With all his remaining strength, he struggled silently to free himself, but the effort soon exhausted him and his throat burned and ached with thirst. He thought how cruel it would be to die here with the promise of air and light mocking him through that tiny cleft.

He closed his eyes again wearily, giving up. Then he was aware of another change in the light, and he opened his eye again. With a sense of disbelief he saw a hand reaching through the opening towards him. An ancient hand, with desiccated skin covered with the dark blotches of age.

'Nefer!' He heard a voice so strange, so hoarse and altered, that for a moment he doubted it was the Magus. 'Nefer, can you hear me?'

Nefer tried to reply but still could not speak. He reached out and touched Taita's fingers. Immediately the old man's fingers closed over his with surprising strength.

'Hold hard. We will dig you out.'

He heard other voices then, rough and faint with thirst and effort, and hands scraped away the sand that entrapped him until at last they could lay hold of him and pull him free of the soft, deadly grasp of the sand.

Nefer slithered out through the narrow cleft as though the rocky hillock was giving birth to him. Then Hilto and Meren reached in again and dragged Mintaka out of the soft dark womb into the brilliant sunlight.

They lifted the pair to their feet and held them from falling again, for their legs had no strength. Nefer shrugged off Meren's hands, lurched across to Mintaka and embraced her silently. She was shivering as though in the crisis of malaria. After a while he held her at arm's length and studied her face with horror and pity. Her hair was white with sand, which clung thickly in her eyebrows. Her eyes had receded into deep purple cavities, and her lips were swollen black, so that when she tried to speak they cracked open and a drop of blood, bright as a ruby, trickled down her chin.

'Water,' Nefer managed to articulate at last. 'She must have water.'

He dropped to his knees and began frantically to dig into the sand that still blocked the cave. Meren and Hilto were working beside him and they uncovered the waterskin. They pulled it out, and found that most of the water that had remained had evaporated or been squeezed from it. There remained only sufficient for a few mouthfuls each, but even that amount was enough to keep them alive a little longer. Nefer felt strength return to his dehydrated body, and for the first time looked about him.

It was the middle of the morning. He did not know what morning or for how many days they had been buried. There was still a haze of fine sand like gold-dust in the still air.

He shaded his eyes, looked out over the desert and did not recognize it. The landscape had changed completely: the high dunes had marched away to be replaced by others, of different shape and alignment. There were valleys where there had been mountains, and vales where hills had stood. Even the colours had changed: the sullen purples and bruised blues had been replaced by reds and golden yellows.

He shook his head in wonder, and looked at Taita. The Magus was leaning on his staff, watching Nefer with those pale, ancient but ageless eyes.

'Trok?' Nefer managed to say. 'Where?'

'Buried,' Taita replied, and now Nefer could see that he also was dried out like a stick of firewood, and suffering the same agonies as they were.

'Water?' Nefer whispered, touching his swollen and bleeding mouth.

'Come,' said Taita.

Nefer took Mintaka's hand and slowly they followed the Magus out into the brazen sands. Now at last thirst and exposure had taken their toll on Taita and he moved slowly and stiffly. The others staggered along behind him.

Taita seemed to be wandering aimlessly through the new valleys of fine sand that ran beneath their feet. He held out his staff in front of him, making a sweeping motion with it. Once or twice he lowered himself to his knees and touched the earth with his forehead.

'What is he doing?' Mintaka whispered. The water they had drank had not been enough to sustain her and she was weakening again. 'Is he praying?'

Nefer only shook his head: he would not squander his own meagre reserves by speaking unnecessarily. Taita moved on slowly, and by the way he was sweeping with his staff Nefer was reminded of a water-diviner at work.

Once again Taita knelt and placed his face close to the earth. This time Nefer watched him with more attention, and saw that he was not praying but sniffing the air close to the surface of the sand. Then he knew what Taita was doing. 'He is searching for the buried chariots of Trok's division,' he whispered to Mintaka. 'His staff is his divining rod, and he is sniffing for the scent of putrescence below the sand.'

Taita stood up painfully and nodded at Hilto. 'Dig here,' he ordered.

They all crowded forward and began to scrape away the loose sand with cupped hands. They had not far to go. An arm's span deep they struck something hard, and redoubled their efforts. Quickly they exposed the wheel rim of a chariot that was lying on its side. Another few minutes of frantic digging and they pulled out a waterskin. They stared at it in despair for it had burst open, perhaps when the chariot had capsized. It was dry, and though they squeezed it frantically it yielded not a single drop of the precious fluid.

'There must be another.' Nefer spoke through dry swollen lips. 'Dig deeper.'

They clawed at the sand in a last despairing burst of strength, and as the excavation deepened the stench of the dead horses in the traces grew stronger and more nauseating. They had been lying in the heat all these days.

Suddenly Nefer reached deeper into the hole and felt something soft and yielding. He pressed it and they all heard the gurgle and slosh of water. He swept away more of the loose sand and between them they lifted out a bulging waterskin. They were mumbling and whimpering with thirst, as Taita opened the stopper and poured it into the leather bucket that had lain beside the waterskin in the bottom of the excavation.

The water was the temperature of blood, but when Taita held the bucket to Mintaka's lips she closed her eyes and drank in a quiet ecstasy.

'Not too much at first,' Taita warned her, took the bucket from her and passed it to Nefer. They drank in turn, then Mintaka drank again, and the bucket made another circuit.

In the meantime Taita left them to continue his search. In a short time he called them to dig again. This time they were lucky: not only was the chariot under less sand, but there were three waterskins, and none was damaged.

'The horses now,' Taita told them, and they looked at each other guiltily. In their desperate preoccupation they had forgotten them. Carrying the waterskins they trudged back through the sand to the base of the cliff.

The narrow gully in which they had pegged down the horses must have been well aligned to avoid the full force of the *khamsin*. When they began to dig, using the wooden spade they had found among the equipment of the buried chariot, they found the first horse almost at once. However, the stink warned them what to expect. The beast was dead and its stomach ballooned with gas. They left it and dug for the next animal.

This time they were more fortunate. It was a mare, the most willing and robust of the horses they had captured at the sinking sands. She was alive, but barely so. They cut the retaining halter that had held her down, but she was too weak to come to her feet unaided. The men lifted her between them. She stood weak and shivering, reeling and threatening to fall again, but she drank greedily from the bucket Mintaka held for her and seemed at once to improve.

In the meantime the men were digging for the other horses. They found two more dead of thirst or suffocation, but another two still alive. They also responded immediately they were given water.

They left Mintaka to care for the three pathetic beasts and went back to the chariots they had uncovered to find fodder. They brought back bags of grain and another waterskin.

'You are doing good work with them,' Nefer told Mintaka, as he stroked the mare's neck, 'but I fear they are too far gone ever to pull another chariot.'

She rounded on him fiercely: 'I will bring all of them through, I swear to the goddess. There must be hundreds more fodder bags and waterskins out there under the sand. We may have to stay here many more days, but when we leave, these gallant creatures will take us out.'

Nefer laughed at her through his cracked, scabbed lips. 'I am in deep awe of your passionate nature.'

'Then provoke me no further,' she warned him, 'or you will see more proof of it.' It was the first time she had smiled since the passing of the *khamsin*. 'Now go back to help the others. We cannot have too great a supply of water.'

He left her, and went down into the sands where Taita was divining further afield. Not all the Hyksos chariots were so lightly covered with sand as the ones they had first found. Many were hidden for ever beneath the high new dunes.

They moved further and further away from the rocky hillock as the search went on. Beneath the sands they found many corpses, swollen bellies stinking.

Soon they were out of earshot of where Mintaka was tending the horses like a syce.

The cessation of all sound roused Trok, and he groaned as he tried to move. The sand was a stifling weight upon him. It seemed to crush in his ribs and force the breath from his lungs. Nevertheless, he knew that the spot Ishtar had chosen for them to ride out the storm was, either by chance or design, a good one. In any other place they might have been buried for ever. Here he had been able to keep close to the surface of the earth. In the past days as the layers of blown sand had built up over him and the weight had become unbearable he had managed to wriggle free, leaving only enough covering him to protect him from the full abrasive force of the *khamsin*.

Now he struggled up towards the light and air like a diver coming up from the depths of a deep pool. As he swam up laboriously through the sand his damaged shoulder was a burning agony. He struggled on until his head, still swathed in folds of cloth, broke free. He unwrapped it and blinked about him in the dazzling light. The wind had passed but the air was luminous with fine particles of suspended dust. He rested like that for a while until the pain in his shoulder abated a little. Then he pushed aside the layer of sand that still covered his lower body and tried to call out, 'Ishtar! Where are you?' but his voice was a formless croak. He turned his head slowly and saw the Mede, sitting near him, his back to the rocky cliff face. He looked like an exhumed corpse that had been dead for days. Then Ishtar opened his one good eye.

'Water?' Trok's voice was only just intelligible, but the Mede shook his head.

'So we have survived the storm just to die in the same grave,' Trok tried to say, but no sound came out from his ravaged throat and mouth.

He lay for a while longer, and felt any instinct to survive being extinguished under the slow seep of exhaustion and resignation. It would be so much easier just to close his eyes and drift off to sleep, never to wake again. That thought spurred him and he forced open his crusted eyelids, felt the grit under the lids scraping at his eyeballs.

'Water,' he said. 'Find water.'

Using the cliff side as a support he lurched to his feet and stood there swaying, hugging his useless arm to his chest.

Ishtar watched him, his one blind eye like that of a reptile or a corpse. Trok started forward drunkenly, bumping into the cliff at every few paces he took, making his way along the base of the rock until he could look out over the desert. The dunes were pristine and unblemished, as voluptuously curved as the body of a lovely young girl.

There was no trace of men or vehicles. His fighting divisions, the finest in all Egypt, had vanished without trace. He tried to lick his lips, but there was no spittle in his chalky mouth. He felt his legs give way under him and knew that if went down he would never rise again. Using the wall of stone as a support he tottered on, not knowing where he was going and with no thought in his head but to go on.

Then he heard human voices, and knew he was hallucinating. There was silence again. He went a few steps further, stopped and listened. The voices came again. This time they were closer and clearer. He felt unexpected strength flow back into his body, but when he tried to call out no sound came from his parched throat. There was silence once more. The voices had ceased.

He started forward again, then stopped suddenly. A woman's voice, no mistaking it. A sweet, clear voice.

Mintaka. The name formed silently on his swollen lips. Then another voice. This time a man's. He could not make out the words or recognize the speaker, but if he was with Mintaka he must be one of the fugitives Trok had been pursuing. The enemy.

Trok looked down at himself. His sword-belt was gone, and his weapons with it. He was unarmed, dressed only in his tunic, which had so much sand in the weave that it chafed his skin like a hair-shirt. He looked around him for a weapon, a stick or a stone, but there was nothing. The scree had been covered by sand.

He stood undecided, and the voices came again. Mintaka and the man were in a gully among the rocks. While he still hesitated he heard the sand crunching like salt crystals under someone's feet. That person was coming down the gully towards where Trok stood.

Trok shrank back against the stone wall and a man emerged from the mouth of the gully, twenty paces from where Trok hid. The stranger set off with a determined stride into the dunes. He was strongly familiar, but recognition eluded Trok until the man turned and called back towards the gully, 'Do not tax yourself unduly, Mintaka. You have come through a trying ordeal.' Then he walked on.

Trok gaped after him. He is dead, he thought. It cannot be him. The message from Naja was clear... He considered the possibility that a *djinn* or some evil spirit was impersonating the young Pharaoh Nefer Seti as he watched the young man go out into the desert. Then, through eyes bleary with sand, he saw him join three others, among them the unmistakable figure of the Warlock, who, Trok realized, must be responsible, in some strange and miraculous way, for the resurrection of Nefer Seti. But now he had neither the time nor the inclination to ponder this further. There was only one thought in his mind and that was water.

As stealthily as he could he crept forward into the gully where he had heard Mintaka's voice and peered round the corner of the cliff. He did not recognize her at first: she was as bedraggled as a peasant. Her hair and her tattered tunic were stiff with sand, and her eyes were sunken and bloodshot. She was kneeling at the head of one of a small herd of horses, holding a water bucket for it to drink.

Water was the only thing Trok could think about. He could smell it and his whole body craved it. He staggered towards Mintaka. Her back was turned to him and the soft sand covered the sound of his approach. She was not aware of him until he seized her arm. She turned, saw him, and screamed. He snatched the bucket from her hands and knocked her down. As his arm was useless he knelt on the small of her back to pin her down, while he drank from the bucket.

He swallowed huge gulps, gurgled and belched, then drank some more. Mintaka was wriggling under him and screaming, 'Nefer! Taita! Help me.'

He belched again, pushed her face into the sand to silence her, and swallowed the last drops from the bucket. He looked around him, still crouching over her like a lion on its kill. He saw the waterskin against the wall of the gully and the javelins and swords stacked beside it.

He stood up quickly and started towards them. Instantly Mintaka tried to jump to her feet, but he kicked her down again. 'None of that, you bitch,' he croaked, and seized a handful of her thick sand-drenched hair. He dragged her after him through the sand until he could reach the waterskin. Then he had to drop her. He placed one huge sandalled foot on her back again, reached for the waterskin and held it between his knees while he unfastened the wooden stopper. He lifted the nozzle to his lips and let the warm, brackish liquid flow down his throat.

Although she was face down in the sand Mintaka realized that Trok was engrossed in his craving for water. She must act before he had satisfied it and turned his full attention on her. She knew that he had suffered more humiliation than he could bear and that he would kill her now rather than let her escape him again.

Desperately she reached out to the bundle of weapons stacked against the rock. Her fingers closed around the shaft of a javelin. Trok was still drinking with his head thrown back, but he felt her movement and lowered the waterskin just as Mintaka twisted to stab up at his belly and groin with the short but deadly weapon. However, the blow was aimed from her prone position under him and lacked force.

Trok saw the bright bronze point flash and, with a startled exclamation, jumped back to avoid it. 'You treacherous little slut!' He dropped the waterskin and lunged for her, but the moment his weight was off her Mintaka jumped up. She tried to slip past him and run out of the gully into the open desert, but he cut her off and reached for her with his long arm. He caught the hem of her tunic, but she leaped aside. The linen tore in his fingers and she twisted away from him, but he still had her trapped in the gully.

He lumbered after her but she ran to the cliff wall and started to scale it, lithe and quick as a cat. Before he could catch her she was out of his reach. She went up swiftly and he could not hope to follow her. He picked up the javelin she had dropped and hurled it up at her, but he was using his left hand and there was little power in the throw.

Mintaka ducked as the javelin flew over her head and struck the rock in front of her face. She climbed faster, driven by fear. Trok staggered to where the other weapons were stacked, and grabbed another javelin. He threw again. It missed her by a hand's width.

Trok grunted with fury and frustration and snatched a third javelin, but at that moment Mintaka reached a ledge in the cliff and crawled over it out of his sight. She lay there pressing herself to the rock. She heard him raving and swearing at her. Even in her distress she was sickened by the filthy words he sent after her.

Then another javelin flashed over where she lay and clattered against the rock face above her. It dropped back on to the ledge and she grabbed it before it could fall back to the gully floor. She peered over the edge of the ledge, ready to duck back.

Trok was staring up at her uncertainly, his injured arm dangling at his side. When her head appeared his face contorted with rage and the pain of his injury, and he started forward as if to climb up to her.

She showed him the point of the javelin. 'Yes, come up,' she hissed at him, 'and let me stick this in your great hog belly!'

He stopped. He would have to climb and defend himself with only one arm. He saw that her threat was real. While he hesitated, Mintaka began to scream again. 'Nefer! Taita! Hilto! Help me!'

Her voice echoed off the cliff and rang down the gully. He looked about him nervously, as if expecting to see a rush of armed enemies coming at him. Suddenly he reached a decision. He picked up the waterskin and slung it over his shoulder. 'Do not think you can evade me for ever. One day I will sample all the delights of your body and afterwards I will give you as a plaything to my troopers,' he shouted up at her. Then he tried to mount the mare, but she was still too weak to support his bulk and collapsed under him.

Trok hauled himself to his feet and lumbered away down the gully.

Mintaka feared that his withdrawal might be a trick. She dared not descend from her perch on the cliff. She screamed wildly, 'Nefer! Help me.'

She was still screaming when Nefer came racing back to her down the rocky gully, a sword in his hand, Hilto and Meren close behind him.

'What is it?' Nefer demanded, as she slid down the cliff into his arms.

'Trok!' She sobbed with relief to feel him hold her safely. 'Trok is alive. He was here.'

She blurted out an account of what had happened, but before she had ended Nefer was giving orders to the others to arm themselves and prepare to go after Trok.

Taita had come back to join them. He stayed with Mintaka while the three men followed Trok's footprints in the sand as cautiously as if they were tracking a wounded lion. They moved along the base of the cliff until they reached the fissure where Trok had weathered the fury of the *khamsin*. Nefer examined the disturbed sand and interpreted the signs. 'Two of them,' he said. 'They were buried by the storm, as we were. They dug themselves out. One waited here.' He picked up a thread of wool that had adhered to the rock, and held it to the light. 'Black.' It was a colour seldom worn by Egyptians. 'Almost certainly the Mede.'

Hilto nodded agreement. 'Ishtar would have the witchcraft to survive the storm. 'Tis certain he saved Trok, just as Taita saved us.'

'Here.' Nefer stood up and pointed out the sign. 'Carrying the waterskin, Trok returned to find the Mede, and they went this way.'

They followed the footprints a short way out into the desert. 'They have gone west. Back towards Avaris and the Nile. Will they ever reach it?'

'Not if I catch up with him.' Nefer said grimly, and hefted the javelin he was carrying.

'Majesty.' Hilto was respectful but firm. 'They have the waterskin and a long start. They will be well away from here by now. You dare not follow without water.'

Nefer hesitated. Though he saw the sense in what Hilto said it galled him sorely to let Trok escape. From what Mintaka had told him, Trok was injured and would not be too dangerous an opponent, even though Nefer himself was still weak.

In the end he turned aside and ran to the top of the nearest dune.

Shading his eyes he looked westward, along the string of footsteps on the pristine, windswept sands until in the distance, half a league or more away, he made out two tiny figures moving steadily towards the west. He watched them fiercely until they disappeared in the wavering heat mirage.

'There will be another time,' Nefer whispered. 'I will come for you. I swear it on the hundred sacred names of Horus.'

They found and uncovered another sixteen of the buried chariots. With such an abundant supply of water and food, horses and men recovered swiftly. In addition, they had uncovered many more corpses of Trok's troopers. From these they were able to dress themselves. Nefer altered a pair of sandals to fit Mintaka, whose injured feet were almost completely healed.

By the tenth day they were ready to move. The four remaining horses were not strong enough to drag the chariots back through the loose sand, so Nefer decided to use them as pack horses, and load them with as much water as they could carry.

At nightfall, leading the horses, they started out across the dunes. Although the mare could not carry Mintaka's weight as well as its load, Nefer rigged a leather strap around its shoulders and insisted that Mintaka hang on this to help herself through the soft footing.

The *khamsin* had altered the landscape so greatly that Taita had to navigate by the stars. They kept going steadily through the whole of that night, and the one that followed. Before dawn on the second day they reached the old caravan road. It had been obliterated in places by the *khamsin*, but before they had gone much further the light strengthened and they saw the cairn of stones that marked the crossroads ahead.

They discovered that, since the storm had ended, someone had been on the road before them. Two pairs of footprints led westwards along the road, heading back towards the Nile valley and Avaris. One pair was large, the other smaller. Taita and Nefer examined them carefully.

'This one is Trok. Nobody else has feet like that, the size of a Nile barge. Mintaka was correct. He is injured, on his right side. He favours it as he walks.' Taita read the sign. 'As yet I cannot be certain about the other. Let us see if he leaves some clue as to his identity.' They followed the tracks as far as the marked cairn.

'Ah! There!' Close by the cairn someone had recently arranged an intricate pattern of stones in the sand. 'No doubt now. It is Ishtar the Mede.' Angrily Taita scattered the stones. 'This is an invocation to his foul Marduk the Devourer.' He hurled one of the smaller stones down the road that Trok and Ishtar had taken. 'If Ishtar had an infant with him, he would likely have sacrificed it. Marduk thirsts for human blood.'

Here, at the marker cairn, Nefer had a difficult decision to make. 'If we are to make the long journey to the east, we will need supplies and gold. We should not arrive at the court of the Assyrian as indigent outcasts.'

Taita nodded. 'There are many powerful men in Egypt who would lend us full support if only they could be certain that their pharaoh was still alive.'

'Hilto and Meren must go back to Thebes,' Nefer said. 'I would go myself but all the world will be searching for Mintaka and me.' He removed one of his royal finger rings and handed it to Hilto. 'This will be your token of recognition. Show it to our friends. You must return bringing us men and gold, chariots and horses. When we go to King Sargon we must arrive in some state to show him the support we still command in Egypt.'

'I will do as you command, Majesty.'

'Almost as vital to us will be intelligence. You must gather news. We must must be informed of every action of the false pharaohs.'

'I will leave at nightfall, Pharaoh.' Hilto agreed.

They spent that long hot day lying under the shade of an awning they had salvaged from one of the buried chariots, discussing their plans. When the sun sank towards the horizon and began to lose its heat they parted company, Hilto and Meren to head back west towards Thebes, and Taita, Nefer and Mintaka to go eastwards.

'We will wait for you at the ruins of Gallala,' were Nefer's last words to Hilto. Then they watched him and Meren take the high road and disappear into the gathering dusk.

Taita, Mintaka and Nefer took the caravan road towards Gallala. Twelve days later, with only a few drops remaining in the waterskins, they reached the deserted ruins.

The weeks became months, and still they waited at Gallala.

Taita spent days at a time in the hills that surrounded the city. Nefer and Mintaka caught occasional glimpses of him from a distance as he prowled the valleys and harsh gullies. Often they saw him tapping and prodding the rocks with his staff. At other times he sat by the almost dried-up wells outside the city walls, staring down the deep shafts.

When Nefer questioned him obliquely, he was distant and evasive. 'An army needs water,' was all he would volunteer.

'There is hardly enough water for us,' Nefer pointed out, 'let alone an army.' Taita nodded, stood up and walked away into the hills with his staff tapping against the rocks.

Mintaka set up quarters for them among the ruins, and Nefer roofed them over with the tattered tent. As a royal Hyksosian princess, Mintaka had never been called upon to cook a meal or sweep out a chamber, so her first efforts were disastrous. As he chewed a charred mouthful Taita remarked, 'If we want to destroy Trok's army the most effective way would be to send you to them as a cook.'

'If you are so skilled, then perhaps you might honour us with your great culinary skills.'

'It is either that or starve,' Taita agreed, and took her place at the hearth.

Nefer resumed his old role of hunter, and after his first day out in the desert returned with a plump young gazelle and four marvellously patterned giant bustard eggs that were only slightly addled. Mintaka sniffed her share of the omelette Taita made and pushed it away. 'Is this the same man who complained of my cooking?' She looked across the fire at Nefer. 'You are as guilty as he is. Next time I will go with you to make sure that what you bring back is edible.'

They lay side by side in one of the shallow wadis that cut through the hills and watched a herd of gazelle feeding towards them.

'They are dainty as fairies,' Mintaka whispered. 'So beautiful.'

'I will shoot if you have qualms,' Nefer told her.

'No.' She shook her head. 'I did not say I would not do it.' Her tone was determined, and by now he knew her well enough not to query her decision.

The ram moved ahead of his herd. His back was a delicate cinnamon shade and his underbelly was the silvery white of one of the thunderheads that rose above the horizon. His horns were lyre-shaped and polished between his pricked, trumpet-shaped ears. He turned his head on the long curved neck and gazed back at his small herd. One of the lambs began to stot, bouncing on stiff legs with its nose almost touching its bunched hoofs. This was the alarm behaviour.

'The little creature is just practising and showing off.' Nefer smiled.

The ram lost interest in this juvenile display, and came on towards where they lay in ambush. He picked his way over the stony ground with studied grace, stopping every few paces to look about warily for danger.

'He has not seen us, but he soon will,' Nefer whispered. 'We do not have Taita to gull him.'

'He is out of range,' she whispered back.

'Fifty paces, no more. Shoot or he will be gone in an instant.'

Mintaka waited until the ram once more turned away his head. Then she rose slowly to her knees and drew the bow. It was one of the short recurved weapons they had salvaged from a buried chariot. She released the arrow and it rose in a gently arc against the pale desert sky.

With those huge dark eyes, the gazelle had instantly picked out her small movement of rising. His head switched round and he stared at her, on the point of flight. At the twanging release of the bowstring he leaped forward while the arrow was still in the air. He skimmed away, tiny puffs of dust rising where his hoofs touched the earth. The arrow rattled against the stones, where moments before, he had been standing. Mintaka jumped to her feet and laughed to watch him go, showing no sign of chagrin at having missed the shot.

'Watch him run, like a swallow in flight.'

Taita had taught Nefer that the true hunter loves and honours his quarry. He admired Mintaka the more for her compassion towards the creatures she hunted. She turned to him, still laughing. 'I am sorry, my heart. You will go hungry to bed this night.'

'Not with Taita at the cooking fire. He will pluck a feast from the very air.'

They raced each other to retrieve her spent arrow. She had a headstart, and reached it ahead of him. She stooped to pick it up, and the back of her short tattered skirt flew up. Her thighs were smooth and brown and her buttocks perfect rounds, the skin pale and unblemished where the sun had never touched it, lustrous as precious Oriental silk.

She straightened and turned in a flash to catch the expression in his eyes. Though she was virgin and unversed in sensuality, her feminine instincts were full blown. She could see what passion her innocent gesture had roused in him, and the knowledge stirred her too. Seeing how he desired her made her want him with an intensity that was painful. She felt her loins melt with love for him, overflowing sweet and viscous like a honeycomb left in the heat of the midday sun.

Timidly she swayed towards him, but Nefer felt hot shame at the carnal desire that had almost overwhelmed him again. He remembered his promise to her. 'I would rather die than break my oath, and bring dishonour upon you,' he had told her, and at the memory he forced himself to turn away. He found that his hands were shaking and his voice was gruff as he said, with his eyes averted, 'I know where there is another herd, but we must hurry if we are to find them before dark.' He set off without looking back at her, and she felt bereft. She had wanted more than anything on this earth to feel his arms around her and his hard young body pressed to hers.

She gathered herself quickly and followed him, trying to push away the strange feelings that had so nearly engulfed her, but they would not so easily be set aside. She caught up with him, and trotted a few paces behind him.

She studied his back. She watched how his thick dark curls bounced on his shoulders. She wondered at how wide his shoulders had grown since she had first met him. Then she looked further down, and felt her cheeks burn as she watched his buttocks moving under the thin stuff of his short apron. She enjoyed a delicious sense of shame at her own lascivious feelings.

Too soon they reached the rim of the long wadi that cleaved the mountains. He turned his head to look back at her and almost caught her studying his body. She raised her eyes to his just in time.

'There are hundreds of old tombs in the bottom of the cliff here. I first saw them when my father brought me this way, just before he was—' He broke off, saddened by the memory of the last day he had spent with Tamose.

'Whose tombs are they?' she asked, to distract him from something so painful.

'Taita says they are a thousand years old, from the time of Cheops and Chephren who built the great Pyramids at Giza.'

'Then they must be almost as old as the Magus himself.' She smiled and he laughed.

'Have you ever explored them?' she asked.

He shook his head, 'Since we first arrived here, I have thought of doing so often, but there has never been an opportunity.'

'Let us do it now,' she said.

He hesitated. 'We should have ropes and lamps.' But she was already scrambling down the cliff, and he was forced to follow her.

At its base, they soon found that most of the tombs were out of their reach, set high in the sheer cliff face with a deadly drop below them.

After a while Nefer picked out an opening he thought they might be able to reach. They climbed a section where the cliff face had collapsed, and reached a narrow ledge. They worked their way along it cautiously, Nefer leading. He reached the dark opening and stooped to peer into it. 'Of course, it will be guarded by the spirits of the dead.' He tried to make it sound like a joke, but she sensed his unease and was affected by it.

'Of course!' she joked back, but behind her back made the sign against evil.

'It's very dark in there,' Nefer said thoughtfully. 'We should return tomorrow with an oil lamp.'

Mintaka looked over his shoulder. A short passageway led at a slight upward angle into the solid rock. Even after the passing of centuries, engravings were still clearly visible on the walls.

'Look.' Mintaka touched one. 'This is a picture of a giraffe, and this is a man.'

'Yes,' Nefer grinned, 'and a very friendly man, at that. There is no mistaking it.'

She pretended to bridle, but could not hide her smile. The ancient artist had endowed the figure with a huge erect member.

'Here.' She moved deeper into the passage. 'These are writings. I wonder what they mean.'

'Nobody will ever know,' Nefer said, and stepped past her, 'The key to that ancient script has long been lost. We should go back.'

The floor was covered with a layer of soft windblown sand. After a short distance the recesses of the shaft were obscured by sinister darkness.

'We can explore just a short way further,' Mintaka said stubbornly.

'I don't think that's a good idea.'

'Here.' She pushed past him. 'Let me go first.'

'Wait!' He tried to restrain her, but she laughed and pulled away. He placed one hand on the hilt of his dagger and followed her, shamed by her example and his own reluctance.

The gloom thickened with each step forward until even Mintaka stopped and peered uneasily ahead. He stooped to pick up a chip of flint from the sandy floor and threw it over her shoulder into the dark reaches of the shaft. It rattled on the stone walls. 'Nothing,' she said in the silence that followed, but before she could take another step forward something moved in the darkness ahead. They heard a rustling sound that was magnified in the narrow space. They froze in their tracks, and stared into the darkness. There was a high-pitched shriek, echoed immediately by a chorus, the rustle became a rushing roar, and out of the darkness straight into their faces hurled a squeaking, fluttering cloud of darting shapes, whose wings lashed their startled faces.

Mintaka screamed, whirled around, ran straight into Nefer and threw both her arms around his neck. He seized her and held her hard, drawing her down on to the sandy floor.

'Bats,' he told her. 'Only bats.'

'I know!' she said breathlessly.

'They can't hurt you.'

'I know.' Her voice was calmer, but she made no effort to unwind her arms from around his neck. He pressed his face into her thick, springy hair. It smelt rich and perfumed as new-mown grass.

She made a soft, murmuring sound of pleasure, buried her face against his throat, and moved softly against him.

'Mintaka,' he tried gently to push her away, 'I gave you my promise that this would not happen again.'

'I release you from that promise.' Her voice was so soft as to be barely audible. She lifted her face to his. Her breath was warm and sweet-smelling. Her lips were tender and full, and quivered as though she were on the point of tears. 'I want to be your wife more than I have ever wanted anything in my life.'

He reached down and took her mouth with his own. It was wet and so hot that it seemed to scald his. He lost himself in it. She felt that she belonged nowhere else but in his embrace. Still kissing her he explored the angles and curves and plains of her back with his fingertips. He traced the outline of her spine, like a string of pearls running down between the firm ridges of muscle.

He placed a hand on her hip, and felt the curve of her waist like the shape of a precious ceramic vase. He reached behind her and enclosed one buttock in each hand, astonished by their symmetry and elastic firmness.

She thrust her hips forward to meet his, and he pulled her even harder to him. He felt his loins swell and stiffen, and tried to arch his back to hide it from her. She made a small sound of remonstrance, forbidding him to avoid her. She moved against him, glorying in this proof of his arousal, of how much he wanted her.

She had a fleeting memory of Trok thrusting his monstrous blue-veined thing at her, but that horrid episode had no relevance to what was happening here. Without effort the memory was expunged from her mind.

She felt Nefer's fingers running slowly down the cleft between her buttocks, and she concentrated on the sensation, marvelling that she could feel it echoed in the swelling tips of her breasts and in her secret depths.

'Touch me.' She spoke into his mouth. 'Yes! Touch me. Hold me. Stroke me. Love me.'

The sensations blended so that they seemed to envelop her every fibre, every part of her mind and body. He broke the kiss at last, and she felt his lips nuzzling her bare shoulder. She knew instinctively what he needed, and opened the front of her tunic and took out one of her breasts. It felt heavy in her hand, the tip aching and swollen. She entwined the fingers of her other hand in the thick curling hair at the back of his head, and placed her nipple in his mouth. When he sucked it, like a hungry infant, she felt something spasm and contract deep in her belly, and realized with wonder that it was her own womb.

Gently she changed him from one breast to the other, and the sensation did not fade, but instead grew fiercer.

In a daze of pleasure she became aware of his fingers lifting the front of her skirts and fumbling with her loincloth. She moved her legs apart to allow him to reach her more easily, and then, with her free hand, she helped him untie the knot at her hip. The cloth fell away and the air of the tomb was cool on her naked bottom and belly.

She felt him stroke the crisp pelt of curls that covered her pudenda, then he found the swollen lips that bulged from her cleft and parted them gently with trembling fingers. She cried out as if in pain and, without conscious volition, pulled aside the skirts of his apron and reached in to find him. She was startled by its girth and encircled it with thumb and forefinger. It leaped like a living thing in her grasp, and she wanted to look at it. Without releasing her grip, she pushed him back so that she could see down between them.

'You are so beautiful,' she breathed, 'so smooth, so strong.'

Then she kissed him again, and holding her mouth to his she fell backwards dragging him down upon her belly, spreading her thighs to welcome him, sensing his lack of experience. It made her feel maternal and possessive. In her own ignorance, she was guiding him, feeling him sliding and slipping in her overflowing desire, probing at the entrance to her very self. She altered the angle of her hips and he flew deeply into her, his belly flat against hers, filling her until she felt he might cleave her apart, crying out triumphantly in the bittersweet pain of it.

He was riding her like a runaway horse, and she paced him, meeting the thrusting drive of his hips with her own, mounting with him higher and faster, until she knew that she had reached the limit. Then, unbelievably, they went on far past that limit. Breaking free of earth and its bonds, then at the ends of the heavens, feeling it burst out of him, and flood her with liquid heat, swelling up within her so that she matched and met him, their separate beings welding together, so that they became a single entity. Their voices a single jubilant cry.

Long afterwards, when they had returned together from those distant heights, they lay in each other's arms, their sweat and their breath mingling and cooling, still linked by his flesh deep within hers.

'I don't want this ever to end,' she whispered at last. 'I want to stay like this with you for ever.'

A long while later he sat up languidly and looked towards the opening of the shaft. 'It is becoming dark already,' he said, in a wondering tone. 'The day has passed so swiftly.'

She came up on her knees, smoothed down her skirts, and he touched the fresh stains upon the hem. 'Your maiden's blood,' he whispered in awe.

'My gift to you,' she answered. 'The proof of my love for you alone.'

He reached up and tore from the hem of her skirt an encarmined shred the size of her little fingernail.

'What are you doing?' she asked.

'I will keep this for ever as a memory of this wonderful day.' He opened the locket he wore at his throat and placed the fragment of cloth with the lock of her dark hair that it already contained.

'Do you really love me, Nefer?' she asked, as she watched him close the locket.

'With every drop of blood that flows through my veins. More than life eternal.'

When they came into the room in the ancient building that they had restored and made habitable, Taita was at the hearth stirring the contents of the pot upon the coals. He looked up at Mintaka as she stood in the open doorway with the last light of the day behind her. Her skirt was still damp where she had washed it in the scanty waters of the well and it clung to her thighs. 'I am sorry we are so late back, Taita,' she said shyly. 'We followed the gazelle out into the desert.'

She had never apologized for their late return before, and Taita looked up at the two of them. Nefer was hovering over her with a soft, dazed expression. The emanation of their love was so strong that it seemed to form a shimmering aura around them and Taita could almost smell it in the air, like the fragrance of a wild flower.

So what was inevitable has happened at last, he mused. The only wonder is that it took so long. He grunted, noncommittal. 'It is evident that you did not catch up with them. Did they run too fast or were you distracted?' They stood awkwardly, covered with confusion and guilt, knowing that to him they were transparent.

Taita turned back to the cooking pot. 'At least there is one provider among us. I have been able to snare a brace of wild pigeon. We need not go hungry to bed.'

The days that followed passed for the two of them in a golden haze of delight. They thought they were being subtle and discreet in Taita's presence, trying to keep their eyes off each other, and touching only when they thought he was not looking.

Mintaka had made a boudoir for herself in a bare cell that led off the main living room of their quarters. Each night Nefer waited until Taita was snoring softly before he rose surreptitiously and crept to her sleeping mat in this little room. Each morning she would rouse him long before dawn and send him back to his own mat in the main room, when they thought Taita was still sleeping.

On the third morning Taita announced inscrutably, 'It seems that these rooms are inhabited by rats or other strange creatures for I am kept from sleep by their scurrying and whispering.' They both looked stricken, and he went on, 'I have found more tranquil accommodation.'

He moved his own sleeping mat and possessions to a small ruin across the square, and to these he retired each evening after they had eaten dinner together.

During the days the lovers wandered out into the desert, to pass their time in talking, making love, and forming a thousand plans for the future, deciding when and how they might marry, how many sons and how many daughters she would bear him and finding names for each.

They were so lost in each other that they forgot the world that lay beyond the lonely desert spaces, until one morning when they left the ruined city before dawn, carrying a coil of rope and two oil lamps, determined to explore the ancient tombs more thoroughly. By a circuitous route they reached the top of the cliff, where they sat down to catch their breath and watch the magnificent spectacle of the dawn breaking over the blue, secret hills.

'Look!' cried Mintaka suddenly, starting out of his arms and pointing back towards the west along the old trade route that led down into Egypt. Nefer jumped up, and they gazed down the valley at the strange caravan coming towards them. There were five ramshackle vehicles leading, followed by a straggling column of humanity.

'There must be a hundred men, at least,' Mintaka exclaimed. 'Who can they be?'

'I don't know,' Nefer admitted grimly, 'but I want you to run back and warn Taita of their approach while I go and spy on them.'

She did not argue, but set off immediately for Gallala, racing down the back slope of the hills, leaping from rock to rock with the agility of a wild ibex. Nefer cached the rope and the lamps, then restrung his bow and checked the arrows in his quiver, before creeping along the crest of the hills, keeping off the skyline and out of sight until he reached a point from where he could look down on the slow-moving caravan.

It was a sorry spectacle. As it came closer, Nefer saw that the first two vehicle were knocked-about fighting chariots drawn by thin, overworked horses. They were designed to carry two men, but each contained four or five. Behind them came an assortment of wagons and carts in no better case than the leading chariots. Nefer saw that they were laden with sick or wounded men, huddled miserably together or lying on makeshift litters. Behind the wagons straggled a long file of walking men, some hobbling along on crutches or leaning on staffs. Others carried litters on which lay other sick or wounded figures.

'In the name of Horus, they look like fugitives from a battlefield,' Nefer muttered, as he strained his eyes to make out the features of the men in the leading chariot.

Suddenly he stood up from behind the rock that had hidden him, and shouted with excitement. 'Meren!' He had at last recognized the tall figure who held the reins of the first chariot. Meren pulled up the horses and shaded his eyes to stare into the eye of the rising sun. Then he, too, shouted and waved as he saw Nefer on the skyline. Nefer ran down the slope, slipping and sliding in the loose scree, and he and Meren embraced, laughing and both speaking at once.

'Where have you been?'

'Where are Mintaka and Taita?'

Then Hilto was hurrying to Nefer, and making loyal salutations. Behind him crowded the host of exhausted and wounded men. Their faces were drawn and gaunt, and blood and pus had soaked through their dirty bandages and dried to a crust. Even the men in the wagons and on the litters, who were too far gone to stand, lifted themselves to stare in awe at Nefer.

With a quick appraisal Nefer could see that these were warriors, but warriors beaten in battle, their bodies and spirits broken.

After Hilto had greeted Nefer he turned back to them, and shouted, 'It is even as I promised you! Here before you stands your true Pharaoh, Nefer Seti. Pharaoh is not dead! Pharaoh lives!'

They were silent and apathetic, sick and demoralized. They stared at Nefer uncertainly.

'Your Majesty,' Hilto whispered to him, 'please stand on this rock so that they may have a clear view of you.'

Nefer sprang up on to it and surveyed them with interest. They stared back at him in silence. Most had never laid eyes on their king before. Even the few who had seen him in formal palace processions had done so from a distance. Then he had been a doll-like figure, covered from throat to foot in splendid robes and jewels, his face a white mask of makeup, sitting stiffly on the royal carriage drawn by the white bullocks. They could not reconcile that remote, unnatural figure with this strapping young man, virile and hard-looking, his face tanned by the sun and his expression alive and alert. He was not the child-pharaoh they had known by reputation alone.

While they still stared without comprehension, or exchanged dubious glances, another figure seemed to materialize out of the air. Like a *djinn* he appeared beside Nefer on the rock. This one they knew well, both by repute and by sight.

''Tis Taita the Warlock,' they breathed with awe.

'I know what you have suffered,' Taita told them, in a voice that carried clearly to every ear, even to the sick and wounded on the wagons. 'I know what price you have paid to resist the tyranny of the assassins and usurpers. I know that you have come here to find if your true king still lives.'

They murmured in agreement. and suddenly Nefer knew now who they were. These were some of the survivors from the rebellion against Naja and Trok. Where Hilto had found them was a mystery, but these shattered remnants had once been fighting troopers, élite charioteers and warriors.

'This is where it begins,' Taita said softly at his side. 'Hilto has brought you the seeds of your future legions. Speak to them.'

Nefer surveyed them for a moment longer, standing proud and tall before them. He picked out a man in the ranks, who was older than the others, with the first snows in his hair. His eyes were sharp and his expression intelligent. Despite his rags and half-starved body he had the air of authority and command. 'Who are you, soldier? What is your rank and your regiment?'

The man lifted his head and squared his gaunt shoulders, 'I am Shabako. Best of Ten Thousand. Adept of the Red Road. Commander of the centre of the Mut regiment.'

A lion of a man! Nefer thought, but said only, 'I greet you, Shabako.' He lifted the skirt of his *chiton* and exposed the tattooed cartouche upon his thigh, 'I am Nefer Seti, the true Pharaoh of Upper and Lower Egypt.'

A sigh and a hum went through the scarecrow ranks when they recognized the royal cartouche. As one man they threw themselves to earth in obeisance.

'*Bak-her*, Divine One, beloved of the gods!'

'We are your loyal subjects, Pharaoh. Intercede for us with the gods.'

Mintaka had come with Taita and now stood below him. Nefer

reached down and took her hand. He lifted her on to the rock beside him. 'I give you the Princess Royal, Mintaka of the House of Apepi. Mintaka, who will be my queen and your sovereign lady.'

They greeted her with another shout of acclamation.

'Hilto and Shabako will command you,' Nefer decreed, 'For the time being Gallala will be our base, until we return victoriously to Thebes and Avaris.'

They rose to their feet, even the gravely wounded attempting to climb from their litters, and they cheered him. Their voices were thin and almost lost in the great silences of the desert, but the sound filled Nefer with pride and renewed his determination and resolve. He climbed up into the leading chariot, took the reins from Meren and led his little raggle-taggle army down into his ruined capital city.

When they had set up their barracks among the ruins, Nefer sent for Shabako and Hilto and the other officers among them. Late into that first night, and for many nights that followed, he sat with them and listened to their accounts of the rebellion, the fighting, and their ultimate defeat by the combined forces of the two pharaohs. They told him of the terrible retribution that Trok and Naja had visited on those rebels who had fallen into their clutches.

At Nefer's orders they detailed the order of battle of the new Egyptian army, the names of the commanders, the numbers and names of their regiments and the total of men, chariots and horses that Naja and Trok had at their disposal. There were three army scribes among the fugitives and Nefer set them to work, writing down all these details and the lists of the enemy garrisons and fortifications on clay tablets.

In the meantime Taita, with Mintaka assisting him, set up an infirmary where all the wounded and the sick were housed. Hilto had brought a dozen or so women with him, wives of some of the fugitives, or merely camp-followers. Taita brought them in to act as nurses and cooks. Taita worked during all the daylight hours, setting broken bones, drawing barbed arrowheads from the flesh with his golden spoons, stitching sword-cuts and in one case even trepanning a cracked, depressed skull that had received a blow from a hardwood war club.

When the light faded and he could no longer work with the sick, he joined Nefer and his commanders as they pored over the maps drawn on tanned lambskins, planning and scheming by the light of the oil lamps. Although Nefer was nominally their supreme commander, in reality he was a student of the art of war and these experienced old soldiers were his instructors, the lessons he learned from them invaluable.

It was after midnight usually before Nefer could adjourn these grave councils, and sneak away to join Mintaka on the sheepskin mat where she patiently waited for him. Then they made love and whispered together. Although they were both exhausted by their labours, the dawn was often creeping over the silent desert before they fell asleep in each other's arms.

In total there were less than a hundred and fifty souls and fifty horses in Gallala, but within the first few days it became evident that the bitter wells of the city could not support even these meagre numbers. Each day they emptied them and each night it took longer for them to refill. Even the quality of the water began to deteriorate: it became more bitter and brackish every day, until it was only barely potable unless mixed with mare's milk.

They were forced to ration the water. The horses were distressed and the mares lost their milk. Still the trickle of underground water shrivelled.

At last Nefer called an emergency council of his commanders. At the end of an hour of solemn talk, Hilto summed up gloomily, 'Unless Horus works a miracle for us, the wells will dry completely, and we will be forced to abandon the city. Where then will we flee?'

They looked at Nefer, who turned expectantly to Taita. 'When the water dries up, where do we go, Magus?' he asked.

Taita opened his eyes. He had sat in silence through the long debate and they had thought he was dozing. 'Tomorrow, at first light, I want every man who can walk and wield a spade assembled before the gates of the city.'

'To what end?' Nefer asked, but Taita smiled enigmatically.

In the cool of the dawn fifty-six men were waiting before the ancient gates when Taita stepped through. He was wearing all his regalia, the Periapt and the gift of Bay, and his other necklaces, bracelets and amulets. He had washed his hair until it shone, and Mintaka had braided it for him. He carried his staff with the carved serpent's head. Nefer was beside him, a solemn expression covering his mystification. Taita looked over the assembled men. As he had ordered, they all carried digging tools – wooden spades and shovels, metal-tipped digging staves. He nodded with satisfaction then descended the steps and set off up the valley.

At a word from Nefer the men shouldered their tools and followed the old man, falling naturally into a military marching formation. However, they had not far to go, for Taita stopped at the foot of the hills and stared up at the heights.

Nefer recalled that this was the area where Taita had spent so much time over the last few months. Often he and Mintaka had seen him sitting here, drowsing in the sun with hooded eyes like a blue-headed lizard, or prodding and tapping among the rocks with his staff.

For the first time Nefer studied the rock formation of this section of the hills and realized that they were different. The rock was friable and veins of grey limestone had intruded into the schist. A profound fault ran diagonally through the face on the bare, burned hills, edged with strata of different colours. Then he noticed something else. Recently someone had placed marks on some of the stones, esoteric hieroglyphs painted with a white paste, probably made from crushed limestone mixed with well water. There were also cairns of stones placed in a pattern on the earth.

'Nefer, the men must be divided into the five teams,' Taita told him, and Nefer gave the orders. When they were ready, Taita ordered the first forward. 'Start driving an adit into the hillside here.' He pointed out the hieroglyphs that marked the opening to the horizontal shaft where he wanted them to begin digging.

The men looked at each other, puzzled and uncertain, but when Taita glared at them wordlessly, Shabako took over quite naturally. 'You heard the Magus. Get on with it, now, and handsomely!'

It was hard work, even though the underlying rock was shattered along the line Taita had chosen. They had to prise out each lump, then dig out the loose earth that lay behind it. Clouds of dust rose around them, and soon their bodies were powdered with it. Even though their hands were toughened by use of club and sword, their palms blistered, tore and bled. They wrapped them with linen strips and worked on without complaint. The heat came up swiftly with the rising sun, and Shabako pulled the first team out of the excavation and sent in the next.

They rested for an hour at noon when the heat was at its height. Taita went into the shallow cave and inspected the rock face intently. He emerged into the sunlight without comment, and Shabako ordered the work to continue. It went on until it was too dark to see what they were doing, then Shabako released them and sent them down the hill to their frugal dinner. The supplies of *dhurra* millet were dwindling almost as swiftly as the well waters.

Taking advantage of the coolness, they started again before dawn. By nightfall they had driven the adit only twenty cubits into the hillside.

There they struck a solid stratum of blue, crystalline rock. The bronze-tipped staves made no mark upon it, and the men began to mutter.

'Are we warriors or miners?' mumbled one old veteran, as he inspected his bruised and blistered palms.

'What are we supposed to be digging? Our own tombs?' asked another, as he bound up the deep cut in his shin inflicted by a carelessly wielded stave.

'How can we dig through solid rock?' Yet another wiped the running sweat and mingled dust from his bloodshot eyes.

Taita sent them down the valley to where a thick grove of dead acacia trees stood as a silent monument to the water that had long ago dried. They cut cords of the dried branches and carried the bundles back to the diggings. Under Taita's instructions they stacked the firewood on the adamantine rock, and lit it. They let the fire burn through the night, stoking it at intervals, and the next morning, when the rock glowed with the heat, they quenched it with skins filled from the failing wells. In clouds of hissing steam, the rock crackled, burst and exploded.

One man was hit by a sharp flying fragment, and lost his right eye. Taita removed its remains, and stitched the lids closed.

'The gods gave us two eyes for just such a mishap,' he assured his patient. 'You will see just as well with one as you did with two.'

They let the shattered rock cool then prised out great blackened chunks of it. Behind these the rock was still solid and impenetrable. They stacked fresh cords of firewood upon it and repeated the arduous, dangerous process, with the same result. They had gained a few cubits for the expenditure of days of heartbreaking labour.

Even Nefer was discouraged, and told Mintaka so when they lay together in the darkness that night.

'There are many things that we do not understand, my heart,' she cradled his head and whispered.

'We don't even know why he is making us dig this hole, and when I ask him he gives me that infuriating look of his, like an ancient tortoise. The men have almost had enough of it, and so have I.'

She giggled. 'Ancient tortoise! You had better make sure he doesn't hear that. He might turn you into a toad, and I should not like that at all.'

Early the following morning, the teams of weary, disgruntled men traipsed up the valley and assembled around the mouth of the tunnel to await the arrival of the Magus.

With his usual sense of the dramatic, Taita came up the slope with the first rays of the rising sun behind him, suffusing his silver bush of hair with light. He carried a roll of linen cloth over one shoulder. Nefer and the other officers stood to welcome him, but he ignored their salutations and gave instructions to Shabako to hang the linen over the mouth of the shaft like a curtain. When it was in place he entered the screened shaft alone, and a silence fell over the men gathered outside.

It seemed like a long wait but was in reality less than an hour, for the sun had risen only a hand's breadth above the horizon, when the linen curtain was jerked aside and Taita stood in the entrance of the cave. Either by chance or the Magus' design, the sunlight shone directly into the shaft. The blank face of the adit was brilliantly lit, and the ranks of men crowded forward expectantly. They saw that now a representation of the wounded eye of the great god Horus was painted on the blue rock.

Taita's expression was rapt as he began to chant the invocation to the Horus of Gold. The waiting congregation fell to their knees and came in with the chorus:

> '*Horus of Gold, mighty bull!*
> *Invincible in strength!*
> *Master of his foes!*
> *Holy in his rising!*
> *Wounded eye of the universe!*
> *Attend our endeavours.*'

After the last verse Taita turned and, with every eye fixed avidly upon him, strode back down the adit until he stood before the blue-grey wall of newly exposed rock at the end. Tiny crystals of feldspar were embedded in it and sparkled as the sun played on them.

'*Kydash!*' Taita cried, and struck the wall with his staff. The men at the entrance shrank back, for this was one of the words of power.

'*Mensaar!*'

They gasped with awe, and he struck again.

'*Ncube!*' He struck for the third and last time, then stepped back.

Nothing happened, and Nefer felt a sinking disappointment and anticlimax. Taita stood unmoving, and slowly the sun climbed higher and the shadow spread across the rock wall.

Abruptly Nefer felt a tingle of excitement, and the men around him stirred and whispered. In the centre of the rock face, under the painted eye, a dark damp spot appeared. It spread gradually, and a single drop of moisture oozed out, sparkling like a tiny gem in the sunlight. Then it trickled slowly down the wall and balled in the dust of the floor.

Taita turned and walked out of the shaft. Behind him there was a sharp sound, like the breaking of a dry branch, and a fine crack split the rock from top to bottom. Water dripped to the floor, drop after drop, the tempo accelerating into a rapid patter. Another sound, like a shard of pottery snapping in flames, and a chunk of rock fell out of the wall. A sluggish trickle of yellow mud oozed out of the opening it left. Then, with a roar, the entire rock face collapsed, there was a rush of mud and a gushing fountain of crystal-bright water. Knee-deep, it swept the length of the shaft, burst from the mouth and spilled down the hillside, bounding and rippling over the rocks.

There were shouts of amazement, praise and disbelief from the dusty ranks. Suddenly Meren ran forward and plunged headlong into the rushing torrent. He came up spluttering with his wet hair slicked down over his face. He scooped up a double handful and gulped it down. 'Sweet!' he shouted. 'It tastes sweet as honey.'

Men threw off their clothing and rushed naked into the stream, splashing sheets of spray, throwing handfuls of mud, ducking each other and shouting with laughter. Nefer could not long resist the temptation before he shed all dignity and jumped in on top of Meren and wrestled him beneath the surface.

Taita stood on the bank of the stream and looked down on the mayhem with a benign expression. Then he turned to Mintaka. 'Put the thought out of your mind,' he said.

'What thought?' She feigned innocence.

'It would be an outrage to have a princess of Egypt cavorting with a rabble of rough, naked soldiers.' He took her hand and led her away down the hill, but she looked back wistfully at the revels.

'How did you do it, Taita?' she asked. 'How did you make the fountain appear? What kind of magic was it?'

'The magic of common sense and observation. The water has been there for centuries, just waiting for us to dig down to it.'

'But what about the prayers and the words of power? Were those of no effect?'

'Sometimes men need encouragement.' He smiled and touched the side of his nose. 'A little magic is a sovereign tonic for flagging spirits.'

For months thereafter every man was employed in the digging of a channel to lead the sweet flood of water down the hillside and into the old wells. These now became storage cisterns for the settlement. When they brimmed over, Taita surveyed the old fields at the lower end of the valley that were now a stony desolation. However, the outlines of ancient irrigation ditches were still visible. Their levels had been set out by the old inhabitants, and it took small effort to clean out the contour lines and divert the overflowing waters into them.

The desert earth was fertile; the goodness had not been leached out of it by heavy rainfall. The continuous sunshine, and abundant water had a miraculous effect. They planted the millet seed smuggled in from Egypt. All Egyptians were farmers and gardeners by nature and tradition, and they lavished their skills upon the land and the crops. Within months they had reaped their first harvest of *dhurra*. Then they planted grass fields for grazing, which flourished and provided far beyond their present needs. The women joined in the cutting, drying and stacking of fodder, and within the year they had sufficient to sustain an army of cavalry, though yet they lacked the horses.

Almost every day fugitives drifted into the city, having braved the desert crossing to escape the tyranny of the false pharaohs. They came singly or in small parties, weary and almost dying of thirst and starvation. The guards posted along the hills intercepted them, and sent them in to Hilto. He made them swear the oath of fealty to Pharaoh Nefer Seti, then issued them with rations and, depending on their suitability, sent them to the training regiments or put them to work in the fields or on restoring the dilapidated buildings of the old city. These waifs and foundlings were not the only recruits, however. A cohort of deserters from the armies of the false pharaohs marched in smartly with their javelins, shouting the praises of Nefer Seti as soon as they were in sight of the walls. Then a squadron of twenty chariots, driven by crack troopers of the Ankh regiment with a colonel named Timus at their head, came in under arms and joyously swore themselves in as the liegemen of Pharaoh Nefer Seti. Timus brought the momentous news that Naja and Trok were prepared at last to march on their combined offensive against King Sargon of Babylon and Assyria.

Over the last few months the two pharaohs had mustered their expeditionary force of three thousand chariots at Avaris, and now they had almost finished their preparations to cross the land bridge that linked Egypt with the eastern lands to the north of the Great Bitter

Lake and Lake Timsah. First they had sent a column to drive in the Babylonian pickets along the border then, once the road was cleared, they had shipped in tens of thousands of water jars in carts and wagons and placed them at strategically located storage stations across the dry lands. The country beyond was fertile and well watered.

They planned to cross the land bridge in the full of the moon, using its light and the cool nights to sweep past Ismailiya and up over the Khatmia Pass and on to Beersheba, gathering up the forces of their vassal satraps as they went.

Nefer and Taita had been preparing the defences of Gallala against an imminent attack by the false pharaohs. They knew that their presence in the ancient city must by now be common knowledge throughout the two kingdoms. They had confidently expected Naja and Trok to move against them first, before starting on the Mesopotamian adventure. Therefore they were amazed to have this reprieve.

'They have not taken seriously the threat that our presence so close to their borders poses,' Nefer exulted. 'If they had attacked us now while we are still so weak, we would have had no choice but to fly.'

'Perhaps they took that possibility into their calculations,' Taita agreed. 'Perhaps they are intent on conquering Mesopotamia and cutting off any support that we might have attracted in the Orient. Then they would have us surrounded. I think they have miscalculated, for they leave us to grow stronger for at least another year.'

'Can we be certain that this is not a diversion?' Nefer asked thoughtfully. 'Is the eastern expedition a pretence? Perhaps their true offensive will be directed against us after they have lulled us into a sense of false security.'

'There is always that possibility. Trok is a bull, but Naja especially is cunning and devious. It is the type of bluff he might try.'

'We must keep the expeditionary army under observation,' Nefer decided. 'I will take a scouting party north to watch the road through Ismailiya, and make certain that they pass that way.'

'I will go with you,' Taita agreed.

'No, Magus,' Nefer demurred. 'You will best be employed here, to keep our defences alert, and ensure that if Naja leads three thousand chariots down upon us, the populace is poised for instant flight. Also, there is another service I require of you . . .' He hesitated. 'That is to care for Mintaka. I believe she might be discontented here with the other women, and may attempt something unwise.'

Taita smiled. 'Precipitous action on the part of the princess is always a distinct possibility. However, I know well enough where my first duty lies. I will go with you.' Though Nefer argued long and strenuously,

Taita was adamant, and in the end Nefer was secretly relieved to know that the old man would be at his side, as always.

Even with the latest arrival of troops to their cause, they could muster only thirty-two battle-ready chariots, and less than a hundred horses fit enough to draw them.

They left half of the chariots under the command of Shabako to defend Gallala. Taking Hilto and Meren with them, they set out with sixteen fighting vehicles to drive around the eastern shore of the Great Bitter Lake and intercept the main route north of Ismailiya. The new moon was only days past full, the nights dark but pleasantly cool, so they made good progress, and completed the journey through the uncharted wilderness before the moon was into its second quarter.

At dawn on the fifteenth day after leaving Gallala they lay hidden on the hills to the east of Ismailiya, from where they could overlook the town. The main highway ran below their lookout post and the army of the two pharaohs would have to pass this way. Ismailiya was the Egyptian border fortress, and the natural starting point for the campaign.

'It seems that our intelligence is good enough,' Nefer called down to Taita. He had climbed one of the tall cedar trees on the front slope of the hill, and from there he had a fine uninterrupted view over many leagues of terrain. 'The town is swarming with activity. There are horse lines and a city of tents outside the walls of the fort.' He shaded his eyes. 'There are clouds of dust coming up the road from the delta. It looks like all the wagons and chariots of Egypt are on the march.'

He continued to call down his sightings to the Magus through the rest of that morning, until the heat had built up to the point where all activity around the city and upon the roads fell off into the somnolent noonday. Then he climbed down and went to find shade, like the rest of the squadron, to wait out the hot hours.

In the late afternoon as the air cooled, they roused themselves to feed and water the horses. Then Nefer climbed once more to his vantage-point.

It was at once apparent that they had arrived just in time. The road to the east was an artery pulsing with the life force of a mighty army. Squadron after squadron, fifty chariots strong, wound out through the gates of Ismailiya, each followed by wagons carrying their baggage and fodder, and streamed down the road towards their hiding-place. The vanguard passed so close to where Nefer sat in the high branches of the cedar tree that he could make out individuals among them.

The army flowed by like an endless river, glinting with the reflections of bronze weapons, and the dust rose in a dense cloud over it all until it threaten to obscure the sun.

Four cohorts made up the vanguard, and then came a gap. Obviously this was to let the dust settle a little and to alleviate the discomfort of the royal party that followed.

Next came two chariots riding abreast. Both vehicles were so massive, and covered with gold leaf, that each needed six horses to draw it. Nefer's hatred rose with the taste of gall into the back of his throat as he recognized the drivers.

Trok had the reins of the nearest chariot. There was no mistaking his broad shoulders nor the dark, beribboned bush of his beard. He wore a gold helmet shaped like a beehive, decorated with a crest of foaming white ostrich plumes. On his shoulder clanged the double shield, each leaf as thick as his thumb, so weighty that it was said that he alone of all his army could wield it, just like the great war bow in the rack at his right hand.

In the other great chariot rode Pharaoh Naja Kiafan. Like his namesake the cobra, he cut a slimmer, more graceful figure. He wore a pectoral of gold and precious stones that sparkled in the red sunlight that filtered through the dustclouds. On his head he wore the blue war crown of Egypt, and at his side, sheathed in silver and electrum, studded with turquoise and lapis lazuli, was the legendary blue sword, that he had plundered from the body of Nefer's father.

Strangely, though he lacked the physical stature of Trok, Naja was the more threatening of the two.

The golden chariots passed and were hidden by their own dustclouds, but Nefer remained stretched out on the main branch of the cedar tree as the warlike phalanxes rolled by below him.

The sun had slipped below the horizon, but there was still just enough light to make out the next section of the endless procession. Nefer straightened up with renewed interest and attention.

Swaying and rolling over the surface of the highway, which was already rutted by the passage of the hundreds of chariots and wagons that had preceded them, came two litters drawn by teams of bullocks. They were so capacious, the silk curtains decorated with golden stars and rosettes, that Nefer knew the passengers within must be women of the royal harem. Nefer could not imagine Trok taking his wives or concubines on campaign with him – he had heard that Trok relied for his pleasure on the prisoners he took from the captured enemy towns and that he enjoyed boys or girls with equal gusto. So if they did not belong to Trok, they must be Naja's women. Nefer wondered if Naja had tired of Heseret and taken other wives.

Then the curtain of the second litter jerked open, a girl jumped down into the dusty roadway and skipped along beside the bullocks. Though she had changed markedly since he had last seen her, he could not doubt that this lovely creature was Merykara, his younger sister. She no longer wore the side-lock of childhood, her hair was bobbed upon her shoulders and cut in a thick straight fringe at the level of her eyebrows. The loss of her side-lock was the token that she had seen her first red moon. Nefer felt a pang that his funny little monkey was a child no more. Then it occurred to him that there was no longer any impediment to Naja taking Merykara to the connubial bed. He had heard that Naja was a voluptuous satyr and the idea of him ravishing his little sister revolted Nefer so much that he could taste it in the back of his throat, like rotten fish.

He felt an overwhelming desire to speak to Merykara, to learn if she was happy, if there was aught he could do to make her lot easier. Then it ocurred to him to rescue her and take her back to Gallala. He knew that such thoughts were dangerous, and that his comrades would try to dissuade him from such suicidal fantasy.

Following close behind the litters he saw the carts carrying the war chests of the false pharaohs. Here was a motive that the others would understand. They were unornamented carts painted a dull, sombre blue, but sturdily built and with the trucks reinforced to withstand the great weight of their cargo. The metal-shod wheels cut deeply into the road surface. The doors at the rear of the truck bed were chained and locked, and armed men marched beside them. These were the standard conveyances of the treasures without which no army marched. Nefer knew that they contained gold bullion cast into bars and fingers, rings and beads. These would be used to pay the troops, and to buy the allegiance of minor kings and satraps, to subvert the allies of Babylon and Assyria, and to bribe spies and informers in the ranks of the enemy.

Nefer slid down the trunk of the cedar to the ground. Taita was dozing quietly there, but he opened his eyes before Nefer could touch his arm. 'The war chests of the false pharaohs,' Nefer whispered in his ear. 'Enough to pay an army or buy a throne.'

For many nights that followed Nefer and the Magus stalked the column from the moonlit shadows, moving parallel to the carts that carried the treasure, observing the routine and behaviour of the guards. From the first they realized that it would be impossible to seize the carts and carry away that mass of bullion without the entire army coming down upon them.

'At the speed those oxen are capable of maintaining, Naja's chariots would catch us before we had gone a league with them,' Nefer observed ruefully.

'We will need to be a little more subtle than that,' Taita agreed. 'The only time when we might be able to tamper with the chests would be when they go into laager during the day.'

'What about the guards?'

'Ah!' said Taita. 'The guards will present some small problem.'

Each day when the sun rose high and the heat became oppressive the entire army went into laager. The litters bearing the royal wives, and treasure carts were usually placed in a separate encampment a short distance from the main army. At first there was a great bustle as the animals were loosed from their harness, fed and watered, the sentries posted and the tents of the wives erected. Then the fires were lit and the midday meal was cooked and eaten, washed down with beer. After that Heseret, Merykara and their maids retired to their tents. The men who were not on sentry duty lay down under makeshift shelters to rest after the long night's journey. Gradually a languid silence fell over the huge muster of men and animals, and the camp slept.

Nefer and Taita left the rest of their party lying in a patch of dense thornbush up in the valley and crept to the camp. They were able to get within a few hundred paces of the sentries and lie there unobserved for an hour, whispering together, trying to find some manner of reaching the war chests without being discovered by the sentries.

'Is there no way we can distract them?' Nefer asked.

'For that we will need help from inside the camp,' Taita said.

'Merykara?' Nefer looked at him sharply.

'Merykara,' Taita agreed.

'How can we get a message to her?' Nefer looked puzzled, but Taita smiled, touched the Periapt of Lostris that hung on his necklace and closed his eyes. After a while Nefer thought he had fallen asleep. The old man knew exactly how to infuriate him.

His age is catching up with him at last, he thought irritably, and was about to shake him awake, when he heard voices from the camp, and looked up.

Merykara had come out of her tent. She had obviously been sleeping for her face was flushed and marked by the pillow. She stretched and yawned. She wore only a blue linen skirt, whose pleats hung below her knees. Her upper body was bare. Despite himself Nefer was astonished at the way her breasts had bloomed: they were pear-shaped and the nipples stood proud and rosy. Merykara was arguing with the guard at the entrance to her tent and her voice rose imperiously so that Nefer could hear every word. 'I cannot sleep, and I am going out to walk awhile.' The sentry was trying to restrain her, but she shook her head until her hair danced on her shoulders. 'No, I will not let you escort me. I want to be alone.' The sentry insisted and she flared at him, 'Stand aside, you insolent creature, or I will report your behaviour to my husband.' Reluctantly the sentry acceded to her orders and grounded his spear. He called after her anxiously, 'Please, Your Majesty, be not too long nor venture too far. It will be more than my miserable life is worth should Pharaoh find out about this.'

Merykara ignored him, ducked through the horses' lines, and came out through the gate of the thornbush fence that surrounded the camp. She looked back only once to make certain that she was not observed by any of the sentries. Then as though to an assignation, she came directly to where Nefer and Taita lay among the desert scrub.

Nefer saw that her green eyes were rapt and that there was an intent expression on her lovely face, as though she were listening to music that she alone could hear.

When she was close enough to touch, Nefer said softly, 'Merykara, don't be afraid. It's Nefer.'

She started like an awakening sleep-walker and stared down at him. Then her face lit with an expression of untrammelled joy and she sprang forward to embrace him.

'Wait!' Nefer ordered. 'Don't betray us to the guards.'

He was proud of her, for she obeyed him and stopped instantly. She had always been an intelligent child. She glanced around quickly and her voice trembled when she said softly, 'I was sound asleep, but suddenly I woke and knew that I had to come out into the desert. It was almost as though a voice in my head was calling to me.' She looked at Taita. 'Was it your voice, Magus?' Then her eyes went back to Nefer.

'Darling brother, you will never know how I have missed you. First I thought you were dead, and I mourned in your funeral procession with ashes on my head. Look here are the scars where I cut my arms to bleed for you.'

'I am alive, Merykara. Believe me, this is no shade you are looking at.'

'I know, Nefer. All the world knows now how you took Mintaka away from Avaris into the desert, and I knew in my heart that you would come for me also, one day.' She smiled through happy tears. 'I knew you would come.'

'Yes,' Nefer said, 'we will take you away with us. But first there is something you must do to help us.'

'Anything for you and Taita,' she agreed readily.

Speaking swiftly and urgently, Taita told her what she had to do and then he made her repeat it. She did so faultlessly. 'You are a clever girl, my little one.' Taita said. 'That is exactly what we want you to do.' He handed her a small packet. 'Here is the powder. Remember, just enough to cover your fingernail in each jar.'

'First you call me clever, and then you treat me as though I were stupid,' she snapped.

'Forgive me, Your Majesty.' Taita made a gesture of penitence.

'Don't call me that either. I hate being married to that slimy serpent, and now I know what he is going to do to me, I hate it even more.'

'You are not easy to please, Merykara. Now, go back to the camp before the guards come looking for you.'

She stooped quickly and kissed Nefer on the lips. 'Until tomorrow then, my beloved brother.'

***

The following noon the mighty army of Egypt camped below the high plateau where the sandy desert and the dry lands ended. They had almost completed the crossing and tomorrow they would go up through the pass into the cooler lands where the oases were only a day's journey apart, where forests and fields and vineyards grew and mountain streams flowed all year round.

When the escort of the royal wives began to set up camp for the day, they found that the young Queen Merykara was fractious and overbearing, not at all her usual sweet and gracious self. She wanted her own tent set further apart from that of her sister, Queen Heseret, and when this was done she insisted that they move the carts that carried the army war chests down into a narrow wadi two hundred paces from the main encampment. In vain the commander of the guard pointed out that the bed of the wadi was soft and sandy and the wheels of the heavy vehicles would sink in deeply.

'I don't care if they disappear into the sand completely,' she told him. 'I am sick of looking at those ugly carts and listening to the mooing of the bullocks. Get them out of my sight.'

The commander thought of appealing to Pharaoh Naja Kiafan to ratify this unreasonable order from his youngest wife. Then he contemplated the fact that the column was spread out over almost four leagues of desert. It would take an hour of hard riding to reach Pharaoh at it's head, and the return ride would be just as arduous. The day was even hotter than those that had preceded it and, besides, he had a tryst with one of Merykara's slave girls, an enchanting little black Nubian who knew more tricks than a performing monkey. He moved the carts into the wadi bottom and, as a sop to his conscience, doubled the guard upon them.

Having got her own way, Merykara became once again the endearing girl they all loved so well.

'I am so sorry I was hard on you, Moram. It must be this awful heat that affects us all,' she told the commander of the guard sweetly in front of his men. 'I am going to have Misha bring you five jars of the finest beer from my private stores to make it up to you. But be certain that you share it equally with all your men for I have given them extra work and trouble too.'

Misha, the statuesque Nubian maid with an imperious carriage and a legendary pair of buttocks, brought the beer jars to Moram's tent, and the men lined up to receive their share, calling down the gods' blessings on Queen Merykara and toasting her health as they swigged down the first draught of the frothing liquor.

Despite his promise to Merykara, the beer was of such surpassing excellence that Moram drank more than his share. As soon as they were alone in his tent he pounced on Misha who, squealing and resisting playfully, finally allowed him to lift her clothing and unveil her prodigious buttocks. They sprang out from under her short linen skirts, shining black as new mined anthracite, great quivering rounds, dark full moons that overflowed his clutching hands.

In a transport of lust he mounted her, but after less than a dozen mighty thrusts, he keeled over slowly, fast asleep before he reached the floor. Misha stared at him in astonishment. Nothing like this had ever happened to her in all her short but busy lifetime. Moram let out a snore that reverberated like distant thunder, and she sprang to her feet, pulled on her skirt, delivered one furious kick to his sleeping form and stormed out of the tent back to her mistress. The guard at the entrance to the royal tent was also sleeping like a dead man.

'All men are pigs,' Misha said, in her savage native tongue, and kicked him with all the strength of her long and shapely right leg.

Nefer led a small party of his men down the dry riverbed. They kept close under the bank, and the soft sand muffled their footsteps.

The four treasure carts were drawn up side by side, and their wheels were chained together so that they could not be driven off in haste by bandits or robbers.

Eight armed men were posted around them as sentries, and every one was laid out on the soft sand like a corpse awaiting the embalmers. Taita went to each in turn, felt for the pulse in the throat then drew back a lid to examine the eye of the unconscious man. Finally he nodded to Nefer, and went to the rear door of the first cart.

He took a long bronze probe from his pouch and worked intently on the massive bronze lock. It fell open and the hasp snapped back. Taita swung open the heavy metal door to reveal the four small cases that were tied down to ringbolts in the wagon bed. The lids of the treasure chests were sealed with a clay tablet that carried the cartouche of Pharaoh Naja Kiafan.

Taita used his dagger blade to lift the seals, and dropped them into his pouch so that they would not be evidence of tampering when next the cart doors were opened. He used the point of the dagger to unscrew the fastenings that held down the lid, then lifted it. The chest was filled with small leather pouches. Taita weighed one in his hand, and smiled. He opened the mouth of the pouch to see the unmistakable glint of the precious metal within.

While he had been busy, Nefer and Meren had dug a shallow hole in the soft sand under the wagon truck. Taita passed down the leather pouch to Nefer, who laid it in the bottom of the hole. In all Taita selected fifty of the heaviest leather bags from the first chest. Then he screwed back the lid. Using a lump of fresh damp clay that he had brought with him he resealed the lid. With the engraved ruby ring that Naja had given him as a gift when he had left Thebes, he imprinted the clay seal with the royal cartouche. Then he went on to the next chest in the row of four.

'We are not taking enough,' Meren grumbled. 'We are leaving more than half of it for Naja and Trok.'

'Greed would be our undoing,' Taita grunted, as he prised up the lid of the last case. 'This way they will not know that any of the bullion is missing until the paymaster opens the cases again and counts it, which may not be for several more months.'

From each case in the four carts they lifted fifty leather bags and buried them in the loose sand of the wadi bed. Though they worked as swiftly as care would allow, the sun was low in the western sky when they resealed the final chest and locked the rear doors of the last cart. One of the sleeping guards stirred and mumbled, and tried to sit up. Taita went to him and laid a gentle hand on his brow. The man sighed and lay back. Taita pulled open his mouth and sprinkled a pinch of white powder under his tongue, and he lay quiet.

'We must hurry now. They are beginning to revive.'

They spread sand over the rows of bags in the bottom of the hole beneath the last wagon, and then roughed and dotted the surface with footprints so that the smooth sand would not be conspicuous.

'How much do you estimate we took?' Nefer asked.

'Impossible to tell until we weigh it,' Taita said, 'but I would guess we have at least three lakhs.'

'Enough to recruit and equip an army,' Nefer muttered, as he worked.

They made one last quick but thorough inspection of the carts and the area around them, to make sure that they had overlooked nothing. Then leaving the guards still in heavy drugged sleep, they slipped away down the wadi.

They climbed into the foothills below the plateau, back to where they had left Hilto with the chariots. From this vantage-point they kept watch on where they had buried the plundered gold. They observed no evidence of any outcry or unusual activity in the wadi. Perhaps the guards felt too guilty when they woke to make any report on their dereliction of duty.

Just before dark they saw the straining teams of bullocks heave the four carts out of the sandy riverbed, and trudge away behind the royal litters as the host of the false pharaohs resumed the night march.

For five more days and nights the great army of Egypt streamed past this spot. There were successive squadrons of chariots, regiments of slingers, archers and spearmen. These were followed by marching columns of slaves who would be used for the heavy labour of building fortifications and sapping the walls of besieged cities. Then came the craftsmen, the chariot builders and carpenters, the armourers and arrow makers, and after them the camp-followers, the wives, sweethearts and whores with their slaves, servants and infants. They were followed by the merchants with wagonloads of goods and luxuries of every possible description to sell to the troops when they were rich with loot and plunder.

Yet out of all this multitude the watchers on the hills saw nobody enter the dried wadi where the gold was buried, and though each day companies and regiments camped nearby no one approached the wadi to use it as a latrine or a camping site.

When the last vehicle in that mighty host had trundled past and climbed up through the rocky Khatmia Pass, and the last straggler had limped by, Nefer and Taita were certain that the short-weight of bullion in the treasure carts had not been discovered by the army paymasters, and they were almost certain that the cache in the riverbed had not been stumbled upon by chance.

When at last the eastern highway was deserted they came down from the hills during the night and left the chariots on the high bank of the wadi with the horses still in the traces, ready for instant flight. Nefer and Meren went down into the sandy bed, and in the moonlight the tracks left by the treasure carts and the oxen were still plain to see. After only a few thrusts with the wooden spade Meren whistled with glee and turned up the first pouch of gold. As they lifted each bag from the hole they counted them, making certain that they overlooked not a single one. Then they carried them up the wadi bank, staggering under their weight, and stacked them beside the waiting chariots. Eight hundred leather bags filled with fine gold made an impressive pile.

'Too much! We will not be able to carry away all of it,' Nefer said doubtfully.

'It is one of the natural laws of this wicked world.' Taita shook his head. 'Of gold there can never be too much.'

The light fighting chariots had not been designed as transport carts, but they loaded them until the axles sagged and the coachwork groaned. Still they had not taken half of it on board. Nursing the horses, leading them by the reins, they took the overloaded chariots up into the hills then came back for the next load. It required two more trips to carry it all away.

They divided the treasure into five equal parts and buried four in separate caches, well dispersed, taking great care to conceal them and leave no sign. Thus, if one hoard was discovered they would not lose all. The fifth part they loaded on to thirteen of the chariots and Nefer sent them back to Gallala under the command of Hilto. Once he reached the city Hilto would return with a convoy of heavy wagons to fetch in the remainder.

Nefer kept back the remaining three chariots. They would be driven by himself, Taita and Meren. The two squadrons parted company, Hilto taking his laden vehicles south again, and Nefer leading his smaller group eastwards, shadowing the army of the two pharaohs.

Nefer travelled by day, knowing that the army they were following would be resting in camp, and with a daylight view ahead they were unlikely to run into any surprises.

They went up through the pass on to the plateau where they found ample water, although much of it had been fouled by the thousands of animals and men who had been there ahead of them. The horses were well rested, and they travelled fast in the lightly laden chariots. They passed hundreds of abandoned campsites, marked by dead fires and sagging lean-to shelters, litter and scattered filth. There were also hastily dug graves, for an army on the march suffers constant attrition. Some had already been dug open by the hyena and the jackal, the corpses dragged out and partially consumed.

'We will need her,' Nefer said, as he dismounted and stood over the body of a young woman, probably one of the army whores. There was no way of telling how she had died for the vultures had almost completed what the hyena had begun. Her eyes and lips were missing and her skull grinned at them through blood blackened teeth.

'In all love of the gods,' Meren cried, 'have you lost your senses? That thing stinks to the skies.'

'Help me wrap her.' Nefer ignored his protest. He had found a length of discarded linen, so torn and dirty that even the Bedouin who scavenged behind the army had found no use for it. Between them they lifted the remains of the dead woman on to it and wrapped her neatly. Then, to his loudly expressed disgust, they tied the bundle to the back of Meren's chariot.

Though they had been travelling under the dust pall since dawn, it was mid-morning before they caught up with the rearguard of the army. The entire expeditionary force had already gone into laager for the day, and the smoke from the cooking fires marked the position of hundreds of separate encampments along the road ahead.

Nefer led them off the road, and they circled out to avoid the baggage train, keeping out of sight of the road. Scouting the terrain ahead, they went forward cautiously. Eventually they caught up with the convoy of treasure carts and the tall litters of the royal wives halted in a grove of olive trees. It was well past noon when Nefer crept up close to them, and climbed a tamarind tree from which he could spy over the thornbush *zareba* that surrounded the camp.

Queen Merykara's pavilion was set up at some distance from that of Heseret, but the two sisters were sitting under a linen awning, protected from the sun and picking at the lavish meal their serving maids had brought from the cooking fires.

Nefer was not close enough to overhear their conversation. Heseret sat facing him, chattering and laughing gaily. She was even more beautiful than Nefer remembered her. Even in these informal circumstances she was wearing carefully applied makeup, which was intended to make her resemble the statue of Hathor in Memphis. She was decked out in a suite of magnificent jewels, and her thick dark hair had been freshly oiled and crimped. Misha, the tall black slave girl with the legendary posterior, leaned over her shoulder to refill her golden bowl. A splash of the red wine spilled down the front of Heseret's dress. She sprang to her feet and thrashed Misha over the head with a heavy fan of silver and ostrich feathers. The girl fell to her knees and covered it with both hands but the blood sprang up between her fingers. Merykara tried to restrain her elder sister, but Heseret rained blows on Misha's head until the shaft of the fan snapped in two, then hurled the broken end at Merykara and flounced away, yelling threats and abuse over her shoulder.

Merykara lifted the slave girl to her feet and led her away to her own pavilion. Nefer waited patiently, hidden in the top branches of the tamarind tree. Some time later, Misha left the tent with her head bandaged. Still weeping she disappeared among the trees. Nefer did not move, until Merykara appeared in the opening of her pavilion.

When they had last spoken, Nefer had warned her to keep alert and to wait for him to come to her. Now she looked around her carefully, spoke to the guard at the door of the tent, and began to wander, without any apparent purpose, around the periphery of the camp. Clearly she had taken Nefer's instructions seriously and was searching the surrounding countryside for a glimpse of her rescuers. She was the only person stirring: most of the others were sheltering from the sun and the heat, and even the sentries showed no interest in her.

Nefer took a small polished silver mirror from his pouch, picked up the sun's reflection and shot a ray of light into Merykara's face. She stopped instantly, shaded her eyes, and peered in his direction. He flashed thrice more, the agreed signal and, even from that distance, saw her smile become as radiant as the reflected sunbeam that danced over her lovely face.

Merykara lay in the swaying, jolting litter, on cushions and a mattress stuffed with swansdown. Misha was curled at her feet like a sleeping puppy, but Merykara was awake and alert. The curtains of the litter were drawn back to let in the cool night air and she could hear the sounds of the army on the march: the clatter of hoofs, the creak and rattle of the wagons, the lowing of the draught oxen, the cries of the wagoners and the tramp of the guards alongside the litter.

Suddenly there was a commotion ahead, the swish and crack of whips, the crash of wheels over rocks, the sound of running water and the splashing of animals and vehicles. Then Merykara heard her sister's querulous voice: 'Ho there! What is happening?'

'Your Majesty, we are fording a small stream. I must beg you to dismount, lest the litter capsize. The safety of your divine person is all our concern.'

She heard Heseret complain bitterly about the inconvenience, and Merykara took advantage of the diversion to whisper her final instructions to Misha. Then they climbed down from the litter. Slaves waited with lanterns to lead them down to the riverbank, where Heseret was already waiting.

'They woke me when I was sleeping,' she told Merykara. 'I shall report that oaf of a caravan master to my husband, the Pharaoh of Upper Egypt.'

'I am sure that it will be beneficial to your health to have the skin flogged from his back,' Merykara agreed, with sweet irony. Heseret tossed her head and turned away.

At that moment a nightingale called upstream from where they stood, and Merykara thrilled to the sound. As children Nefer had tried to teach her how to imitate that low, warbling note, but she had never mastered it. Three times the bird called, but only she took notice of it. The others were engrossed in getting the ungainly litters and the heavy treasure carts across the treacherous riverbed. The thousands of vehicles ahead of them had cut up the entrance to the ford, and churned the bottom to a morass. It was after midnight before the crossing was accomplished and the last treasure cart was dragged through with loud exhortations to the oxen to 'Heave away!' and the flourish and cracking of whips up the far bank.

Then the caravan master brought up sedan chairs for the royal wives. They were helped into the seats and carried over by teams of slaves.

When they reached the far bank there was further consternation and confusion for one of the treasure carts had lost a wheel and was blocking the road ahead. Now, in addition to this mishap, the slaves who had carried Heseret across in the sedan chair had allowed the water to flow over her feet and ruin her sandals. Heseret insisted that they were punished on the spot, and the slash of the overseers' whips and the howls of the miscreants added to the uproar.

Over it all Merykara heard the nightingale call again, this time close at hand and on the same side of the stream. 'Do not fail me,' she said to Misha.

'My life is yours, mistress,' the girl replied, and Merykara kissed her.

'You have proved that often, and I shall never forget it.' She turned from Misha and walked calmly into the darkness.

Only Heseret paid her the least notice. 'Where are you going, Merykara?'

'To drown the bad fairies.' Merykara used their childhood euphemism. Heseret shrugged, climbed back into her own litter and drew the curtains.

As soon as she was hidden from the road, Merykara stopped and gave her own inept version of the bird call. Almost at once a firm hand closed on her upper arm and her brother whispered in her ear, 'Pray desist, little one, you will terrify every nightingale from here to Beersheba.'

She spun round, threw her arms about his neck, and hugged him with all her strength, too overcome to speak. Gently he loosened her grip then took her hand and led her along the dark riverbank. He went swiftly and he seemed to have the night eyes of a leopard for he never stumbled or hesitated. He did not speak except to whisper a warning when there was a hole or an obstacle in the path. She followed him blindly. After what seemed half the night, he stopped to allow her to rest.

'Does Misha know what to do?' he asked.

'She will keep the curtains of the litter closed and tell anyone who asks that I am sleeping and will not be disturbed. No one will know that I am gone.'

'Until they halt tomorrow,' he qualified. 'We have only that much time to get away. Are you ready to go on? We must cross back over the river here.'

He picked her up easily and carried her across, and she was amazed at how strong he had grown. She was a doll in his arms. He set her down again on the opposite bank, and they went on.

After a while she tugged on his hand. 'What is that awful smell?' She gagged.

'It's you,' he told her. 'Or, at least, one who shall take your place.'

Before he finished speaking two dark figures stepped out into the starlight on the path ahead of them, and Merykara gave a small gasp of fright.

''Tis only Taita and Meren,' Nefer reassured her. They led her into a coppice in which they were screened by the dense growth of leafy branches, and Meren opened the shutter of the lantern he carried. Merykara gasped again as, by the feeble yellow light, she saw the gruesome object stretched on the ground. It was a corpse, but so dreadfully mutilated that it was difficult to tell that it was human and female.

'Quickly, now!' Nefer told her. 'Give me all your jewellery and your clothing.'

Merykara stripped herself naked, and handed everything to Nefer. Taita handed her a small bundle of spare clothing, tunic, skirt and sandals, to replace her own.

Nefer knelt beside the corpse and placed the strings of necklaces around the dead girl's neck, and the rings and bracelets on her skeletal fingers and wrists. He could not work Merykara's skirt and loincloth up over the rigid legs, so he ripped them to tatters and rubbed them in the dirt, then he stabbed his own thumb with the point of his dagger and dribbled fresh blood on the fine cloth. From near at hand there came the shrieking, whooping chorus of a pack of hungry hyena.

Merykara shuddered. 'They have smelt the body.'

'They will leave only enough evidence to convince Naja that you were devoured by wild animals.' He stood up. 'Now we must go.'

The chariots were waiting a little further upstream. Nefer had not wanted to leave their tracks too close to the body of the dead girl. As he pulled his sister up on to the footplate beside him, he looked into the east. 'The morning star,' he said quietly. 'It will be light in an hour. We must make the most of the darkness that remains.'

When the dawn bloomed, like a bouquet of roses and mimosa blossom, across the sky behind them they were already halfway down the escarpment of the plateau, and the desert was spread out below them.

It was such a grand sight that involuntarily they reined in the horses and stared out across the ocean of golden sands in awe. All except Meren. With the air of a pilgrim who has travelled across half the world to reach the shrine of the goddess he worshipped, he stared at Merykara as she stood beside her brother in the leading chariot. Through the long night ride she had been hidden from him by the darkness, but now the early sun played upon her, and he stared. He had known her for most of his life as the saucy, impish little sister of his best friend, but this was the first time in two years that he had laid eyes upon her. Time had wrought a miracle of change. Now, every movement she made, each gesture and turn of her head, was perfect grace. Every angle and plane of her face, every curve and line of her slim body was exquisite. Her skin was cream and mother-of-pearl, her eyes greener and brighter than any emerald, her voice and laughter the most enchanting music he had ever heard.

Taita caught his expression and smiled inwardly. Even in the most dire situations, life struggles to renew itself, he thought, but aloud he said, 'Majesty, we must not linger here. The horses are in need of water.'

At the foot of the hills they left the highway and struck out in a southerly direction towards the Great Bitter Lake. They kept going until they reached the first cache of water jars they had left for their return journey, and found that Hilto had been there before them. From his tracks they could tell that his chariots, heavily laden with gold bullion, were moving only slowly, and that he was not far ahead.

They found with relief that he had not used up all the water but had left four jars untouched, enough to keep their horses going until they reached the next oasis at Zinalla.

Although Merykara had been sparkling and animated when she chatted and jested with Nefer and Taita, by some chance she had not acknowledged Meren or even glanced in his direction, except when she knew it was safe to do so. Although once not long ago he had treated her with lordly disdain, Meren was now too overcome to approach her directly. For she was a queen, albeit to a false pharaoh, and in his eyes at least a goddess.

For the hundredth time since they had halted he placed himself artlessly in her direct line of vision as she rested in the scant shade of a flowering acacia tree. This time she lifted her eyes and inclined her head. He made a loyal obeisance. 'Greetings, Your Majesty. I am delighted to see you safe. I was infernally worried for your safety.'

She gave him a single long look, searching and calculating, to take in his increased height and the confident, powerful set of his shoulders. She saw how long and thick his hair had grown, and not for the first time that day she was aware of a strange congestion in her breathing. 'Meren Cambyses,' she said sternly, 'the last time I had any truck with you, you broke my favourite kite. Can I ever trust you again?'

'With your very life,' he said fervently.

When the horses were fed and rested and it was time to move on, Merykara told her brother casually, 'Your horses have borne my extra weight all night. I think I should relieve them now.'

'How will you do that?' He looked puzzled.

'I will ride in another chariot,' she said, and went to where Meren waited for her.

The following day they reached the oasis of Zinalla and found Hilto's squadron there before them. Now Nefer redistributed the weight of men and bullion equally between the fifteen chariots and they went on towards Gallala at a much better pace.

Mintaka was on the roof of the temple of Hathor, which she and some of the women and old men were making habitable for the goddess so that they might resume their worship in her presence. The building might have been a thousand years old, there was no way of telling, but many of the murals were in a marvellous state of preservation and needed only a little touching up. The roof was another matter. However, the elements were kindly and so consistent that the great holes mattered little. It was only necessary to remove the rotten rafters, which placed the worshippers below in mortal jeopardy. Mintaka was supervising this work. She was dressed like the other women in simple, well-worn clothing, and like them she was burnt brown by the sun. This life was so different from that closeted existence in the *zenana* of Avaris, and she revelled in her new freedom, the friendship and company of her common companions.

She straightened and stretched her aching back, balancing easily on the high wall. Then she shaded her eyes and looked out over the green fields of young *dhurra*, and the patterns of irrigation ditches filled with sparkling water from Taita's fountain. Herds of cattle and a flock of fat-tailed sheep were grazing in the lush paddocks, but very few horses. Like every other person in Gallala, she felt the lack of them keenly.

Then, as she had every hour over the past long and lonely days since Nefer had left the city, she raised her eyes and looked down the length of the valley, between the bare, forbidding hills that stood in such bleak contrast to the green fields clustered around the city. This was the direction from which Nefer would come. She searched the blue distance without real hope for she had been disappointed too often recently.

Suddenly she narrowed her eyes against the glare, and her heartbeat quickened. Something was there, tiny against the soaring immensity of the sky, insubstantial and ethereal as a feather blowing in the wind. A dust-devil, perhaps, one of the whirlwinds born of the heated desert airs.

She looked away and wiped the sweat from her thick dark brows, resting her eyes. When she looked again the dustcloud was closer, and she allowed herself to hope. At that moment a ram's horn sounded a single long blast. The lookouts on the crest of the hills had seen it also. Around her the others stopped work and peered down the valley. From the streets below came the excited shouts of the children, grooms ran to the stables, the charioteers to where their vehicles lay beyond the market-place. All was happy bustle.

Mintaka could restrain herself no longer. She went down the scaffolding that covered the outer wall of the temple with the alacrity of a vervet caught stealing fruit in an orchard. Shabako was driving his chariot across the forum, past the battle memorial of Tanus, heading for the gates.

'Shabako!' She ran to intercept him. He swerved to meet her, and as he pulled up the team she leaped on to the footplate behind him. They raced out through the gates and down the rutted track. Ahead, the dustcloud was coming on apace.

'Is it them, Shabako? Tell me it is.'

'I do believe it is, Majesty,' he shouted, above the rush of the wind.

'Then why do you drive so slowly?'

Over the rise ahead came a single vehicle, and she clung to the dashboard, trying to make out the charioteer, but he was still too far away.

'Look, mistress! He flies the blue pennant.' Shabako pointed to the scrap of dyed cloth that fluttered on the long bamboo rod above the chariot.

''Tis Nefer! Oh, all praise to the goddess, it is him!'

She ripped off her headcloth and waved it, while Nefer lashed up his team and came on at the charge.

'Let me off!' She beat on Shabako's shoulder to enforce the order and he slowed the horses to a trot. She jumped from the moving vehicle and landed gracefully in balance. Then she ran to meet the advancing chariot with her arms open wide.

Coming up behind, Taita thought that in his eagerness Nefer might run her down, but at the last moment he swerved and, as the chariot lost speed, he leaned far out over the side of the cockpit and reached down for her. Trustingly she threw herself into the circle of his arm. If she had hesitated or flinched she might have been dashed beneath the galloping team or crushed under the metal-shod wheels but he caught her up, swung her high and she laughed in his arms.

Nefer called his council to assemble in the old city forum and made a full report to them. He described in detail the lifting of the bullion out of the treasure carts and they listened agog. Then he presented Merykara to them and related how she had been rescued from under the very noses of Trok and Naja. They shouted, 'Bak-her!' and stood to applaud him.

Then Nefer sent for the scribes, and they weighed the gold bullion in front of the members of the council. The final tally was well over half a lakh. 'My lords, this is only a fifth part of what we have won. Hilto will take a convoy of wagons back to retrieve the rest. He will leave tomorrow but he will need men to go with him.'

It seemed that every able-bodied man in Gallala was desperate to volunteer, but when Shabako and the most tried and experienced of his warriors were passed over, they protested bitterly. 'Will Pharaoh have us sit here in Gallala, dreaming at the hearth like old women?' Shabako asked.

Nefer smiled. 'I will have sterner work for you. But now the sun is well set, and a victory feast is prepared for us. We will meet again soon in war council, I give you my oath on it,' he assured them, and adjourned the assembly. They went away grumbling, but their mood revived after the first jars of freshly brewed beer had been disposed of.

Nefer had ordered the slaughter of two bullocks and a dozen fat sheep, and the women had spent every minute since his return preparing a celebratory feast. Every man and woman in the city was invited, and even the garrisons of hilltop forts and watchtowers were sent their share. Like the digging of the fountain, the winning of the gold was an achievement that had knit the community closer.

Taita had composed a heroic poem to honour the occasion and, like all his creative efforts, it was an instant, overwhelming success. They would not let him sit down when he had finished, but yelled and banged their bowls on the board until he had repeated all sixty verses. By then they had memorized the entire epic and the musicians had extemporized a musical score. The entire company joined with gusto in the third and final rendition.

Then Nefer called upon any citizen who felt an oratorical urge to stand up and speak out. Some of the speeches were incoherent but well received, others were hilarious or so poignant that most of the women and many men were reduced to tears. In this emotional atmosphere Merykara leaned across Mintaka to speak to her brother. The din around them was so great that she had to raise her voice to be heard. 'Royal and divine brother!' she teased him, for she had also sampled the contents of the beer pots. 'I have a boon to ask of you.'

'Little sister, who is little no more, ask what you wish and if it is in my power you shall have it.'

'It is very much in your power.' She broke off, looked down the table at Meren, caught his avid eye, lowered her gaze and blushed an appealing shade of pink. 'You know that as a child I was married without my consent and against my will. That marriage was never consummated. I want you to proclaim my divorce from Naja. I want you to set me free so that I can go to a husband of my own choice. This would be the most precious gift you could ever give me.'

'Is that possible?' Nefer sobered at once, and looked at Taita. 'Do I have it in my power to divorce a husband and wife in the sight of the gods?'

'You are Pharaoh,' Merykara cut in, before Taita could reply. 'Just as Trok divorced Mintaka, so you are able to divorce me from Naja.'

'Trok divorced Mintaka?' Nefer demanded, so sharply that all those within hearing fell silent.

'Did you not know?' Merykara asked. 'Forgive me for breaking it to you in such a tactless, thoughtless fashion. I thought that such momentous news would have reached even here.' Nefer took Mintaka's hand and shook his head, too overcome with emotion to speak. Merykara went on blithely. 'Oh, yes! On his own sacred holy-day, in his own new temple, Pharaoh Trok sacrificed a ram and proclaimed three times "I divorce her."' Merykara clapped her hands. 'And, poof! the dread deed was done.'

Nefer drew Mintaka a little closer to him, and looked at Taita. The old man knew the law better than any temple scribe in Egypt, and now, in answer to Nefer's silent enquiry, he nodded solemnly.

Merykara was rattling on. 'Of course, immediately after the divorce he sacrificed another ram and passed sentence of death upon Mintaka for adultery and sacrilege in dishonouring a god.'

Nefer turned his head and stared deeply into Mintaka's eyes. She stared back as they considered the implication of Merykara's revelations. Slowly a strange expression spread over Nefer's face, like that of a condemned man hearing of his reprieve. 'You are free, my one true love,' he said. 'And your freedom has set me free.'

Before dawn the following morning, while most of the city was still sleeping off the effects of the good strong beer, Nefer sought out Taita in his private quarters in one of the old buildings. Taita looked up from the papyrus scroll he was reading by the flickering yellow light of an oil lamp.

'Are you occupied with some important matter?' Nefer asked, with strange diffidence.

'You can see that I am,' said Taita, but resignedly he began to roll the scroll on to its wooden spine. For a while Nefer wandered aimlessly around the room, pausing to examine some articles that the old man had collected since they had been here in Gallala: preserved skins of colourful birds, skeletons of small mammals and reptiles, oddly shaped pieces of dried wood or plants, and other amorphous substances in bowls or bottles or bags that were piled on the benches or in odd recesses. Taita waited patiently for him to come to the reason for this visit, though he knew well enough what it must be.

Nefer picked up a fossil of some antediluvian crustacean and held it to the lamplight. 'Mintaka is no longer married to Trok,' he said, without looking up.

'Stone deaf as I may be in both ears, even I was able to make that out.'

Nefer replaced the fossil and took up a copper statuette of Isis with the infant Horus sitting on her lap and nursing at her breast that Taita had dug up from beneath the city walls. It was coated with a rich layer of green verdigris.

'What are the restrictions placed on the marriage of a king under the statutes of Chephren?' he enquired casually.

Taita picked his nose thoughtfully and examined what he had retrieved on the end of his forefinger. 'Like any other bride his wife should be free to marry, either a virgin or a widow,' he said.

'Or divorced by her husband.'

'Or divorced by her husband, or by the decree of the reigning Pharaoh.' Taita nodded. 'And before he is deified or married the king should be ordained in his sovereignty.'

'To be ordained, Pharaoh must have reached his majority, which I have not, or taken his godbird, which I have attempted but failed, or he must have become an adept of the Red Road.' Nefer paused then went on, 'Which I have not. Yet.' He emphasized the last word and Taita blinked, but did not reply.

Nefer set down the idol and looked at Taita with determination. 'I intend to run the Red Road.'

Taita studied him in silence. 'You are not yet at your full growth and strength.'

'I am grown enough and strong enough.'

'Who will ride with you?'

'Meren,' said Taita firmly.

'There are others stronger and more experienced who might be of greater help to you. There will be many who would dearly love to gather the hair braid of a pharaoh of the Tamosian line.'

'I have promised Meren,' said Nefer firmly.

Two puppies, tripping over their own paws in their enthusiasm and ignorance, Taita thought, but instead he said, 'There are no unbroken horses in Gallala – at least none that would answer the purpose.'

'I know where to find them. Naja and Trok have left all the remaining herds of Egypt unguarded.' Taita did not bother to point out the fallacy of that assertion. The false pharaohs had left more veteran troops to guard Egypt than ever they had taken with them on the adventure to Mesopotamia, but he knew that Nefer was not inclined to listen to any argument that ran contrary to his fixed intention.

'If you fail in the attempt you will lose much more than your hair. You will lose so much prestige that your claim to the throne might fail also.'

'I shall not fail,' Nefer said quietly. Taita had anticipated that exact reply.

'When do you intend to attempt the Red Road?' he asked.

'First I must have my horses.'

As soon as they had dug the fountain and it had become feasible to use Gallala as a permanent base Nefer, advised by Taita, had instituted a cleansing system for the city. The human waste, the manure from the cattle pens and horse lines were gathered up by the dung carts and spread on the fields as fertilizer, while the rest was carried out to dumps at the end of the valley, which soon became the home of a permanent population of crows and kites, vultures and the offal-eating marabou storks, with their obscenely naked heads. The baboons came down from the hills, and hundreds of jackals and pariah dogs picked over the heaps of rubbish.

At Nefer's orders traps were set each evening on the dumps, and the following morning the captured animals were taken away in cages.

In the meantime Shabako and his most trusted men were sent as scouts and spies back to the towns and villages of the Nile valley. They drank in the taverns and questioned the travellers they met on the road. They scouted each fort and garrison, and counted the troops they saw entering, leaving and drilling. When they returned weeks later the intelligence they brought back was detailed and accurate.

They reported that the false pharaohs had left at least half of their infantry, spearmen, slingers and archers, to counter any threat to their rear. All the border forts were fully manned and guarded, and the garrisons seemed alert and vigilant.

'What of the remount divisions?' Nefer asked, when Shabako had come to the end of his long report.

'Trok has taken most of his chariots with him to Mesopotamia. He has left less than two regiments in reserve in Egypt. However, all the army workshops are hard at work building more chariots.'

'Horses?' Nefer demanded.

'They have commandeered every animal in both kingdoms that they could lay their thieving hands on. They have even sent army dealers to Libya to buy what they could find. It seems that the remount depots at Thane and Manashi are at full strength. However, most of these animals appear young and untrained. The battle-hardened animals have been taken with the main army to the east.'

'Thane,' Nefer decided. 'It's much closer to the edge of the desert than Manashi.' He recalled that Thane was where Taita had used his requisition order from Naja to obtain fresh horses and chariots from Socco, Hilto's old comrade-in-arms, while they were on their way to rescue Mintaka from Avaris. He cast his mind back and tried to memorize the layout of the garrison and the surrounding terrain, but it had all been a long time ago.

'Tell me all you can about Thane. Is Socco still in command there?'

'We drank beer in the local brothel with a sergeant of the garrison. He told me that Socco has done such a good job there that Trok has promoted him to the rank of Best of Ten Thousand.'

Ten days later Nefer and Taita sat in the thick green grass and pretended to watch over the herd of goats that grazed around them. Although the land around the garrison of Thane was well irrigated and rich in grazing, it was also flat, treeless and featureless. There were no hills from which they could overlook the camp. The nearest high ground was along the edge of the desert, a league to the east.

The two of them were dressed in the ragged dusty black robes of the Bedouin. In this guise they were able to blend into the landscape as readily as a pair of hares or crows. At intervals they stood and herded the goats a little closer to the garrison, then squatted down again in the characteristic attitude of the Bedouin herdsman.

Not far from where they sat the herds of remounts were also grazing, tended by armed and uniformed herders. 'I would think there are upward of two thousand animals here,' Nefer guessed.

'Perhaps not as many as that.' Taita shook his head. 'Closer to fifteen hundred, but still more than we can handle.'

They watched and waited through the long, lazy afternoon. In the stockades alongside the cavalry lines the handlers were at work breaking the young animals to the chariot harness. Their shouted commands and the crack of the stock whips carried faintly to where Nefer and Taita sat. In the late afternoon the herds of horses were driven in from the fields and stockades to the long horse lines beyond the fort. From a distance they watched them tethered and bedded down for the night.

As the sun was setting Nefer and Taita rounded up their goats and drove them slowly back towards the desert. In the dusk a small detachment of four chariots came bowling down the road from Avaris. At the reins of the leading vehicle stood a burly officer wearing the silver pectoral plate of the Best of Ten Thousand. As he came closer they both recognized him.

'The curse of Seth on it,' Nefer murmured. ''Tis Socco, Hilto's old comrade-in-arms. Will he recognize us?'

They bowed their heads, slumped their shoulders in a submissive attitude, and shuffled along after the goats. Socco swerved off the road and drove directly at them. 'You stinking scum!' he shouted. 'How often must I warn you to keep your filthy, disease-ridden beasts off my grass and away from my horses?' He leaned out and struck Nefer across the shoulders. The whiplash hummed and cracked against his flesh, and red rage blinded Nefer. Before he could drag Socco out of the chariot, though, Taita made a restraining gesture that riveted him where he stood. It seemed to affect Socco too, for his tone moderated a little as he coiled his whip and said, 'If I catch you people here again, I'll lop off your balls and stick them up your bung-hole.' He steered the chariot back on to the road and trotted off towards the fort.

Six nights later in the dark of the new moon, they returned to Thane in force, every man from Gallala who could ride astride, forty horsemen with black-dyed robes and soot-daubed faces. Each rider carried a large bag slung behind him over his horse's haunches. The contents of the bags squirmed and writhed, emitting muffled yips and whimpers: for each contained two or three live jackals. Their legs were tied, and strips of flax twine were bound around their muzzles to gag them.

The horses' hoofs were muffled with leather boots so they made no sound as Nefer led them in single file in a wide circuit round to the westerly side of the fort, keeping well clear of the cavalry lines so that they did not alarm the sentries.

Every man knew what was expected of him for they had practised this manoeuvre many times, and they kept silently in their formation, a half-moon of dark horsemen between Thane and the river. They were spaced at intervals just close enough together that a quiet command could be passed down the line. Nefer was in the centre, Meren on the left wing and Shabako on the right.

When Nefer was satisfied that they were in position he gave the warbling call of a nightingale, three times repeated, and saw the red line of glowing spots in the darkness as his men opened the lids of the clay firepots they all carried and blew the tinder into flame. He did the same, and then he opened the mouth of one of the bags on his horse's rump and reached in. He brought out a fat vixen by the scruff of the neck. She writhed in his grip.

There was a harsh, tarry smell, strong enough to mask the natural odour of the animals. The fur and brush had been soaked in a black viscous liquid. Taita had gathered this sticky substance from a natural seep that he knew of in the wilderness. It oozed from the earth and Taita said that it came up from great depth. It was highly inflammable, but he had mixed it with another substance, a yellow crystalline powder, that made it even more so. Every one of the captured jackals had been treated with this mixture.

With his dagger Nefer cut the twine that secured the vixen's four paws together. When she sensed freedom, she kicked and thrashed in his grip. He touched the firepot to her furry brush, which burst into spluttering, smoking flame. She redoubled her efforts to escape, but before he released her he slipped the point of the dagger between her lips and cut the loop of twine that muzzled her. She opened her jaws wide and let loose a screech, unearthly and terrifying. Nefer dropped her to the ground and the little creature shot away, spreading a stream of fire and sparks behind her, howling and shrieking in a fashion that set even his nerves on edge and made the hair rise down the back of his neck.

He pulled another jackal out of the bag. All down the line balls of flame flared in the darkness and steamed out across the open fields and those terrible agonized howls made the night hideous. A few of the tormented creatures broke back towards the river valley but the rest headed instinctively for their home in the desert, with the garrison of Thane directly in their path. In a pack they bore down on the cavalry lines.

As Nefer released the last screaming jackal, he drew his sword and kicked his mount into a gallop. He raced after the burning animals, and on either hand his troopers rode with him. They were all yelling like demons, adding their voices to the uproar.

Some of the jackals dragged their flaming tails through the dry horse fodder and bedding, which burst into flame also. The scene was lit by an eerie flickering light that made the dark riders seem monstrous.

Ahead Nefer saw the nearest sentries hurl aside their weapons and flee, screaming as loudly as the burning animals.

'Djinns!' they howled.

'Save us! The dark legions of Seth are upon us!'

'The hordes of hell! Run! Run!'

The tethered horses were rearing and plunging. When a stake was pulled up from the earth, or one of the long lines snapped under the strain, twenty horses were freed at once and wheeled away before the line of yelling, shrieking riders that swept into the camp.

Nefer leaned from his horse's back and sabred one of the running guards, striking deeply between his shoulder-blades and letting the slack body slide off the blade. Then he swerved to where a bunch of terrified horses struggled against a line that resisted their combined efforts to break free. With a single slash he cut the rope and whooped to send them to join the panic-stricken horde, then rounded up another bunch of milling disorientated animals and pushed them out of the lines into the open fields. Shabako and his men rode with him, shouting and whipping the horses along, a racing tide of men and animals compressed into a single entity and lit only by the flames of the burning garrison behind them. The last of the jackals had burnt to death and their black, smouldering carcasses were left in the grass as the riders thundered towards the hills.

Shabako appeared out of the night and rode at Nefer's side. 'By the sweat and seed of Seth!' he shouted. 'That was fun!' Then he turned and looked back. 'No sign yet of any pursuit, more is the pity. A good hack and slash now would be the perfect ending to an entertaining evening.'

'I promise you much entertainment later,' Nefer laughed, 'but now, we must head off the herd, before they run their guts out.'

They pushed their mounts hard, moving through the galloping mass until they rode in the first rank, then cut across them flagging them down from the gallop into a trot and then a walk, turning them in the direction of the open desert and Gallala.

Dawn found the long herd of loose horses spread out down a gaunt, rocky defile, moving at an easy but steady pace with Nefer and Shabako pointing them while Meren and his drovers brought up the stragglers from behind.

Nefer squinted into the first rays of the sun, and called to Shabako, 'Keep them headed up and moving. I am going back to see if Socco and his men are after us yet.'

As he rode back, Nefer singled out Meren and three others, all skilled with javelin and sword. He signalled to them and they galloped up to join him. 'If they are after us, we should try to change their minds for them.'

Nefer led them along their back trail, and at a point where the rock defile narrowed they left the three troopers to hold their horses, and he and Meren climbed the steep rock-strewn slope.

By the time they reached the top the sun was clear of the horizon, but had not yet dissipated the cool of the night and the dust and heat-haze had not built up. The land glowed with that peculiar lambency of the desert dawn. Each distant detail of rock and dune, cliff and gnarled tree, was etched with breath-stopping beauty.

'There!' said Nefer. Meren's eyes were sharp, but his were more so.

'Ten riders.' Meren tried to hide his chagrin at not finding them first.

'Eleven,' Nefer corrected him, and he did not argue.

Instead he grinned delightedly. 'Fair odds to our five.'

'We will take them there.' Nefer pointed down into the gorge. 'There, where it narrows. We don't want them to carry back their news to Avaris. There must be no survivors.'

'That suits me above all things.' Meren laughed.

They waited among the boulders, standing by the heads of their horses, hands over their nostrils to prevent them whickering or snorting and springing the trap prematurely. In the middle of the gap, Nefer had placed a leather bag, that had earlier contained captured jackals. It was now stuffed with their cloaks, which were no longer needed in the rising morning warmth.

Their heads went up as, from lower down the gorge, they heard the click of hoof against stone and the rattle of a dislodged pebble. Nefer looked across the open ground to where Meren and one of the other men were hidden on the far side of the defile. He held up his left hand with fingers spread. The signal for silence and vigilance. His father had taught him that hand signals were always preferable to spoken commands, especially in the heat of battle when they might be lost and drowned in the tumult, or in situations when stealth was paramount.

Now he picked out other small sounds, loud in the great silence of the sands: the creak of tackle and the rattle of arrows in quivers. Nefer glanced around the boulder that hid him and two of his troopers. A scrubby growth of bottlebrush broke up the silhouette of his head.

A rider appeared in the mouth of the gorge, and halted his horse as he saw the leather bag lying in the path. He looked around carefully and the rest of his troop crowded up behind him. Even under the crocodile-skin helmet Nefer recognized Socco, and his back itched where the whip had raised a bloody welt.

Time to return a favour, he thought grimly. Socco took his time, an old soldier, wary and suspicious. Then he walked his horse forward and the others followed him. They halted in a tight group, all leaning out and staring down at the bag. Socco grunted an order, 'Steady now! Watch my back,' and swung down from his horse. He stooped over the bag, and Nefer gave the command, a chopping motion with his raised left hand.

The throwing thongs were wrapped around every one of their right wrists and the range was point-blank. They threw as one man, and because Hilto and Shabako had trained them to perfection no two picked the same target. Five javelins buzzed like enraged bees, and struck where no armour could deflect them, three in the throat and two in the back of the neck. Five men toppled from horseback, and fell under the hoofs of their startled steeds.

Nefer and his men burst from ambush at the gallop, swords drawn and screaming their war-cry, 'Horus and Seti!'

The survivors of that first murderous flight of javelins turned instinctively to meet them but did not have time to clear their swords from the scabbards before they crashed into them, their horses trained to charge in chest to chest. Two more of Socco's horses were taken off-balance and dashed off their feet, throwing their riders. Nefer picked the nearest man, who was still mounted, and killed him with a thrust to the throat. Now Socco cleared his sword and thrust up at Nefer's belly. Nefer turned the blow and his horse reared and lashed at Socco with both hoofs, one of which struck him a solid blow. He was thrown sprawling into the sand. Before Nefer could finish him another of the enemy rode at him, sword lifted high. Nefer rode in under the stroke and engaged him, cut and parry, as they milled and shouted, struggling at close quarters.

Socco's men had only just rallied from the first shock when Meren chose his moment perfectly and led the trooper with him in a furious charge into the mêlée. He sent a thrust to the heart and yelled in triumph. Then immediately he reversed his blade and killed again, a cut across the neck. His victim slid down on to the earth with his head half severed from the trembling jerking trunk.

Socco had lost his helmet and his sword and crawled desperately on his knees to try to retrieve the weapon. He was the only one of all his men still able to resist. Nefer leaned out from his horse's back and aimed at the opening where his breastplate of crocodile-skin armour was fastened between his shoulder-blades, but at the last moment could not bring himself to drive home. He changed his blow smoothly, rolling his wrist to present the flat of the sickle-shaped blade and cracked Socco across the back of his grizzled pate. The man dropped face down in the sand.

Nefer glanced round to make certain that Meren had everything in hand. Then slid off his horse to the ground just as Socco groaned, shook his head and tried to sit up. Nefer slammed his heel into his adversary's chest and thrust him back, then placed the point of his sword at his throat. 'Yield, Socco, or I will send the news of your passing to your mother and all the one hundred stinking goatherds who had a hand in fathering you.'

Socco's dazed expression cleared and became a defiant glare. 'Let me reach my sword, puppy, and I will teach you how to lift your leg when you piss.' He was about to add more to the insult, when suddenly the bellicose light in his eyes faded. He stammered wordlessly. He was gawking at the cartouche on Nefer's thigh.

'Majesty,' he gasped. 'Forgive me! Strike! Take my worthless life as forfeit for those gross and stupid words of mine. I heard the rumours that you still lived, but I had wept at your funeral and could not believe in such a miracle.'

Nefer smiled with relief. He had not wanted to kill him – he was an attractive old rogue, and Hilto said that he was one of the finest horse-handlers in all the armies of Egypt. Hilto should know. 'Will you swear the loyal oath to me as Pharaoh?' he demanded sternly.

'Gladly, for all the earth fears you in your name of Nefer Seti, beloved of all the gods, and light of this very Egypt. My heart beats only for you and my soul will sing my duty to you until the hour of my death.'

'Then, Socco, I promote you to Master of a Thousand Chariots, and Taita had best guard his title of Poet Laureate, for you turn a pretty phrase.'

'Let me kiss your foot, Pharaoh,' Socco pleaded.

'Give me your hand, rather,' Nefer said, seized his horny fist and pulled him to his feet. ''Tis a pity about your men.' Nefer glanced at the corpses. 'If they had shared your loyal sentiments, they need not have died.'

'They died at the hand of a god,' Socco pointed out. 'There is no greater honour. Besides, Taita the Warlock may be able to save the few who are still groaning and twitching.'

Three days later, when they rode into Gallala, they were droving nigh on four hundred horses, and Socco rode proudly at the right hand of his new pharaoh with his helmet sitting high on the bandages that were wound around his injured head.

Socco was not only quartermaster general of the armies of the false pharaohs with the rank of Best of Ten Thousand, but he was also an adept of the Red Road. He was able to give Nefer the exact tally of all the enemy fighting chariots and transport wagons, and where they were deployed. From memory he drew up a list of the numbers of horses and bullocks in depots of the delta, and the latest inventory of weapons stored in the armouries.

'Trok and Naja have taken almost the last serviceable fighting chariot with them on the expedition to the east. There are less than fifty left in Egypt, in either the Upper or Lower Kingdom. The military workshops at Avaris, Thebes and Aswan are working day and night, but every chariot they turn out is sent immediately along the road to Beersheba and Mesopotamia.'

'Horses we now have, thanks to Pharaoh's bold stroke at Thane, even though most are young and unbroken, but we cannot fight a campaign without chariots,' said Hilto gloomily. 'We cannot seize what does not exist, and all the gold now in the royal treasury cannot buy a single squadron.'

While they had been away from Gallala on the great horse raid, Hilto had brought in the remaining gold from the caches along the eastern highway. There was over three lakhs of the precious metal in the ancient cisterns under the city of Gallala. He went on, 'Soon Trok must hear of our successes. He will realize that we have become a real threat. As soon as he has captured Babylon, he will divert part of his army to attack us here. If he sent only a hundred chariots, we could not stand against them in our present state.'

When all the others had had their say, Nefer stood to address the council. He did not speak long. 'Socco, you train the horses for me,' he said. 'Taita and I will find the chariots.'

'That, Majesty, will take a minor miracle,' said Socco gloomily.

'Be not so parsimonious, Master of a Thousand Chariots.' Nefer smiled at him. 'How can we make good your title with only a minor miracle? Let us put our faith in a major one.'

Taita stood on the black rock outcrop. Around him the sand dunes stretched away to the limit of the eye. From the base of the rock a hundred men watched him, puzzled but intrigued. The fame of the Magus was as boundless as the desert in which they found themselves. All of them were warriors who had come to Gallala of their own accord, forsaking the false pharaohs to offer their allegiance to Nefer Seti. That allegiance was wearing a little thin, for here they found themselves without weapons or chariots, and daily there were fresh rumours that either Trok or Naja or both were on the march to seek vengeance for their desertion.

Pharaoh Nefer Seti stood beside the Warlock on the pinnacle of rock. They were in deep discussion. Occasionally one or the other would gesticulate or point out towards the west, where there was nothing to see but sand, sand and more sand.

They waited patiently through the heat of the day. Not one expressed disenchantment or disbelief for they were all in awe of Taita. As the shadows in the hollows of the dunes deepened to purple, that ill-assorted pair, young monarch and ancient Magus, came down from the pinnacle and walked out into the dunes. Without any apparent purpose the Warlock wandered back and forth along one of the dune faces. He stopped at intervals and made strange, esoteric gestures with his long staff, then went on again with Pharaoh and his officers following him.

At last in the gathering dusk the Magus planted his staff in the soft sand and spoke quietly to Pharaoh Nefer Seti. Now, suddenly, they were all galvanized by the shouted orders of the officers.

Twenty men ran forward carrying the digging tools with which they had been issued. Under the direction of Hilto and Meren, and under the daunting eyes of their king and the Magus, they began to dig. When the hole was shoulder deep the loose sand ran back into it almost as fast as they shovelled it out, and they were forced to redouble their efforts to make any gains. The heads of the diggers sank slowly below the level of the surrounding earth, until abruptly there came an excited shout from the bottom of the excavation. Nefer strode forward and stood on the lip.

'There is something here, divine Majesty.' A man was kneeling in the bottom of the hole, and he looked up with sweat mixed with the grit that coated his face and body.

'Let me see.' Nefer jumped down and pushed the man out of the way.

A patch of hide was exposed, still covered with hair but hard as cedarwood.

Nefer looked up at Taita. 'It is the body of a horse!' he called.

'What colour?' Taita asked. 'Is it black?'

'How did you know that?' Nefer was not really surprised.

'Does the halter carry the golden cartouche of Pharaoh Trok Uruk?' Taita answered his question with another.

'Dig it open!' Nefer ordered the sweating men around him. 'But gently now. Do no damage.'

They worked with great care, using their bare hands to sweep away the sand. Gradually they exposed the complete head of a black horse that wore on its forehead the cartouche of Trok, embossed on a gold disc, just as Taita had foreseen.

Then they went on to uncover the rest of the carcass. The animal had been wonderfully preserved by the hot dry sand. The embalmers in Thebes would have difficulty in matching what the desert had achieved. Beside it lay its harness mate, another stallion. Nefer recalled how he had last seen these magnificent animals as they drew Trok's chariot forward under the louring dustclouds of the *khamsin*.

By this time night had fallen and the workmen lit the oil lamps and placed them on the lip of the excavation. They went on with the work through the night. The dead horses were unbuckled from the traces and lifted out. Their desiccated carcasses were so light that four men could carry them with ease.

Then they recovered the harness. It was in a perfect state of preservation, and Nefer set his grooms to work immediately, oiling the leather and polishing the gold and bronze parts.

Now they worked back to the chariot itself and a gasp went up from the diggers as the dashboard was cleared of the engulfing sand: it was covered with gold leaf, and gleamed in the lamplight, shooting out darts of light that pricked their eyes. The javelins and lances were still in their bins on either side of the cockpit, ready to the hand of the charioteer. Each weapon was a work of art in itself, the lance handles laminated for strength and the metal heads sharp as the scalpels of a surgeon. The arrows had been made by Grippa of Avaris, the shafts straight and true, the fletchings dyed crimson, yellow and green, the royal cartouche carved into the shaft.

Trok's great war bow was still in its rack, and only the bowstring needed to be replaced. Nefer flexed the shaft in his hands and wondered if he had the strength to wield it in battle.

When the entire chariot had been uncovered they passed ropes under the chassis and lifted it out of the excavation. The gold leaf had been beaten so thin that it added no more than two taels to the total weight of the vehicle, and to compensate for this the chassis had been carved from dark hard woods, hewn in the sinister rain-forests far to the south of Egypt's borders. These timbers were more resilient than the finest bronze, but light and tough. They could be fined down to save weight without sacrificing strength.

Now it was morning, and the sun was climbing above the horizon. Nefer and Taita circled the chariot as it gleamed in the light. It was so sleek and graceful that it seemed already in motion. Its single shaft seemed to pine like a lover for the touch of two proud horses. Nefer stroked the gold work. It was smooth as a lovely woman's skin and warm beneath his hand.

'It seems to be a living creature,' he breathed. 'Surely there was never a more magnificent weapon of war ever conceived.'

'Fifty years ago I built a chariot for Lord Tanus.' Taita sniffed and shook his head. 'You should have seen that one. But it rests with him in his tomb in far-off Ethiopia.'

Nefer hid a smile – the old man would never admit second best. 'Then I shall have to be content with this inferior work cart,' he said seriously. 'I need only the blue sword that Naja stole from my father to complete my armoury.'

Over the weeks and months that followed Taita pinpointed the other buried vehicles and their accoutrements. Teams of workmen dug them out and sent them to the chariot-makers who had set up a workshop in the lee of the rock pinnacle, roofed over with palm thatch. Here, fifty of them and nearly a hundred armourers laboured through the daylight hours, never letting up even in the furious heat of noon. The armourers polished and sharpened swords, javelins and lances. They rebound the shafts and reset the heads. Over slow fires they straightened the arrows that had warped. The chariot-makers stripped each vehicle as it came out from under the sand, checked each component, painted and lacquered the chassis and the panels, and balanced and lubricated the wheels to run true and sweetly. Then they reassembled them and sent them on to Gallala, loaded with the restored weapons, to equip the army that Hilto, Shabako and Socco were training.

Many of the vehicles were so deeply buried under the burning yellow dunes that they were lost for ever, or until the next great storm uncovered them, but in the end they salvaged a hundred and five. Enough to equip five squadrons.

When Nefer drove through the gates of Gallala in the royal chariot, Meren was on the footplate by his side.

Mintaka and Merykara stood together on the roof pediment of the temple of Hathor, and strewed oleander petals upon them as they passed below.

'He is so handsome.' Merykara's voice was husky with awe. 'So tall and handsome.'

'So tall and handsome and strong,' Mintaka agreed. 'He will be the greatest pharaoh in the history of this very Egypt.'

'I did not mean Nefer,' said Merykara.

By this time a thriving smuggling route existed between the city and Egypt, and other caravans came in regularly from the port of Safaga on the eastern sea. Since the capture of the treasure of Trok and Naja, Gallala had become a city rich with gold. Like hyenas the merchants sniffed the aroma of the yellow metal from afar and brought in their wares from the ends of the world. Nowadays there was no luxury or necessity that could not be obtained in the city's souks, so Mintaka was able to procure a wagonload of the finest red wine from the vineyards of the temple of Osiris at Busiris for the welcome banquet she had arranged for the evening that the charioteers returned.

At her orders, the butchers spitted and roasted ten whole oxen, and chickens and geese by the hundred. Fast relays of the new chariots brought up fresh fish, and baskets of lobsters in seaweed from the coast. Most of the long-whiskered crustaceans were still alive when they were dropped squeaking into the boiling pots. Hunters scoured the surrounding desert and came in with gazelle, oryx, and the flesh and eggs of the ostrich.

The banquet was a joyous celebration of their achievements and small victories over the false pharaohs. The wine had flowed to great effect when Nefer rose to welcome the guests and announce the recovery of the five squadrons of chariots from under the sands. 'With the horses that we freed from the tyranny of Trok . . .' there were hoots and guffaws at this '. . . and the weapons and chariots we now have, we are well able to defend ourselves against Trok and Naja. As you are aware, every day that passes sees fresh recruits to the blue banner. Soon it will not be merely a case of defending ourselves, but of taking back what was stolen from us and avenging the terrible deeds that those two monsters have perpetrated. They have the blood of true and noble kings upon their hands. They are the murderers of King Apepi, who was the father of the noble lady at my side, and they slew my own father, Pharaoh Tamose.'

The guests were silent and puzzled now, looking at each other for guidance. Then Hilto rose to his feet. Nefer had primed him, and placed the question on his lips. 'Divine Majesty, forgive my ignorance for I am just a simple man, but I do not understand. All the world knows that King Apepi died in an accident when his barge caught fire while anchored at Balasfura. Now you lay the guilt for his death on the pretenders. How can that be?'

'There is one among us who was a witness to the true events of that tragic night.' Nefer reached down and drew Mintaka to her feet. The company cheered her, for they had all come to love her for her beauty and her gracious spirit. When Nefer held up his hand they fell silent and listened to her with all their attention as she related the story of the murder of her father and brothers. She used simple words and spoke to them as friends and comrades, yet she was able to share with them her own horror and grief. When she had finished they were growling like a cage of hungry lions at feeding time.

Now Shabako rose and asked his prepared question: 'But, divine Pharaoh, you spoke also of the death of your own father, King Tamose of blessed memory. How was he murdered – and by whom?'

'For the answer to this question I must call upon the Magus, Lord Taita, from whom no secret, however devious and grisly, can be hidden.'

Taita faced them and spoke in a whisper that riveted their attention. His every word carried to the ears of even those on the outskirts of the gathering, and the softness of those words contrasted so effectively with the gruesome circumstances they described that men shuddered and women wept.

At the end Taita held up the broken arrow with its crimson, green and yellow feathers. 'This is the instrument of Pharaoh Tamose's death. The arrow that bears the signet of Trok, but which was loosed by Naja, the man whom Pharaoh loved and trusted as a brother.'

They howled their outrage and their craving for justice to the starlit skies above Gallala. Taita hurled the arrow on to the nearest fire over which one of the oxen was roasting. It would not have borne closer inspection, for it was not the arrow that had killed Pharaoh but one of those he had taken from the buried chariot. He sat down and closed his eyes, as if composing himself to sleep.

Nefer let the guests give full vent to their feelings and when they began to quieten a little he signalled for more wine flagons to be carried out.

There was one last proclamation he had to make, and he waited until the mood had mellowed further before he stood up again. All fell silent and watched him in anticipation heightened by the good wine from

Busiris. The night had already held so many marvels and they wondered what was yet to come.

'Before a king leads his armies against the enemies of this sacred land of our forefathers, he should be a king indeed, a true and veritable king. I purpose to lead you against the usurpers, but I am not yet ordained as Pharaoh. I can achieve this confirmation if I wait until the year of my majority, but that is still far off, and I do not choose to wait that long. Nor will my enemies allow me that grace.' He paused and they watched him, fascinated – so young yet so tall and straight, as his father had been before him. Now he raised his right hand in the gesture of oath-taking.

'In the sight of my people and my gods, I will run the Red Road to prove to you that I am your king.'

Some sighed and shook their heads, others started to their feet and cried out, 'No! Pharaoh, we will not see you killed,' while others called, '*Bak-her!* If he fails then he fails as a brave man.'

That night Mintaka wept as she asked him, 'Why did you not tell me first?'

'Because you would have tried to stop me.'

'But why must you do it?'

'Because my gods and my duty require it.'

'Even if it kills you.'

'Even if it kills me.'

She stared long into his green eyes and saw how steadfast was his resolve. Then she kissed him and said, 'I am proud that I am to be wife to such a man as you.'

The astrologers among the priests of Horus, assisted by the Magus, consulted the calendars and set the date for the trial of the Red Road to be held on the day of the new moon of the god. Therefore, as Taita had remarked, Nefer had little time to prepare for the ordeal. He withdrew from all his other duties, leaving even the conduct of affairs of state to Taita and the council while he gave all his attention to the first task required of him. Before a novice could present himself for trial he must break and train his own team of horses to carry him on the Red Road.

Nefer had to pick out a team of horses from the herd they had captured at Thane, then train them to the shaft of the chariot. He would have liked to ask Socco to help him with the selection of his team: not only was he a famous horseman but he knew each of the captured animals. However, Socco was one of only five Red Road warriors in Gallala and was one of those who would examine Nefer. He could not assist him in his preparations for the ordeal.

There was another to whom Nefer could appeal: Taita's knowledge, understanding and experience of horsemanship and chariot tactics exceeded even Socco's. Yet Taita was not a Red Road warrior. His physical imperfections precluded him from the brotherhood, and added to that he had religious scruples. He would never forswear Horus and the other gods of the pantheon to pledge himself to the mysterious Red God of war, a god whose name was known only to his adepts.

The two spent the first day on the hillside above the green fields where the unbroken horses grazed. They sat together and watched the animals below them, discussing those that caught the eye. Nefer pointed out a handsome white colt, but Taita shook his head. 'A grey looks good in the traces, but I have always been wary of them. I have found they lack stamina and heart. Let us look for either black or bay, matched in colour.'

Nefer picked out a filly with a white blaze on her forehead, but again Taita shook his head. 'The Bedouin say that a white mark is the touch of a devil or a *djinn*. I want not a trace of white on the animals we choose.'

'Do you believe what they say?'

Taita shrugged. 'A blaze or a sock mars their symmetry. You and your team should have the look of a pharaoh when you ride out.'

Taita and Nefer stayed on the hillside until nightfall, and went out again the next morning, as soon as it was light enough to see the path, with Meren and three grooms. They began to sort the horses, driving any imperfect animal into the adjacent field. By noon they had whittled down the herd to twenty-three animals, all clean-limbed and strong, no scars, no blemish, no obvious impediment in their gait. There was not a single white hair on any of them.

They let them settle down, and when the horses were grazing quietly they sat in the grass and watched them.

'I like that black colt,' Nefer said.

'He is lame. Almost certainly he has a cracked left front hoof.'

'He does not limp,' Nefer protested.

'Watch his left ear. He flicks it at every pace. Tell Meren to drive him out.'

A little later Nefer marked a black filly. 'She has a fine head and a bright eye.'

'She is too highly strung. The eye is more nervous than intelligent. She will wilt in the din of battle. Meren can let her go.'

'What of the black colt with the long tail and mane?'

'The tail disguises the fact that he is half a thumb's length short in the back.'

By late afternoon there were only six horses left in the field. In a pact of silence, they had avoided speaking of one particular colt. He was too obviously the choice they must make. He was a marvellous beast, not too tall or heavy, well proportioned, with strong legs and back. His neck was long and his head noble. They watched him a while longer.

At last Magus spoke, 'I can find no vice in him. There is a spark in his eyes that comes from the fire in his heart.'

'I will call him Krus,' Nefer decided. 'It is the Bedouin name for fire.'

'Yes, the name is important. I never knew a good horse with an ugly name. It as if the gods are listening. Let Krus be your right-hander, but now you need a left hander.'

'Another colt—' Nefer started, but Taita stopped him.

'No, we need a filly on the left. A feminine influence to keep Krus in check, and steady him in the heat of the fight. A great heart to pull with him when the road is hard.'

'You have chosen already, have you not?' Nefer asked.

'And so have you.' Taita nodded. 'We both know who she must be.'

Their eyes went back to the filly grazing placidly beside the main irrigation channel, a little separated from Krus and the rest of the herd. Almost as though she knew they were speaking about her, she raised her head and stared back at them, with large shining eyes behind thick lashes.

'She is beautiful,' Nefer murmured. 'I would love to take her without having to put a rope on her.' Taita was silent, and after another minute Nefer said impulsively, 'I am going to try.' He stood up and called to Meren. 'Take the others out of the field. Leave only the bay filly.'

When Nefer and the filly had the field to themselves, he left the fence, and moved casually in her direction, not going straight at her but strolling obliquely across her front. As soon as she showed the first sign of agitation he squatted down in the green grass and waited. She began feeding again but all the while she was watching him from the corner of her eye. Nefer began to sing the monkey song softly, and she raised her head and looked at him again. He took out a *dhurra* cake from the pouch on his belt, and without standing up offered it to her. She flared her nostrils and snuffled loudly.

'Come, my darling.'

She took an uncertain step towards him, then stopped and threw up her head.

'Sweetheart,' he crooned, 'my lovely darling.'

A step at a time she came in, then extended her neck to full stretch and sniffed noisily at the cake. Terrified by her own audacity she jerked back and galloped away, making a wide circuit of the field.

'She moves like the wind,' Meren called.

'Dov.' Nefer used the Bedouin word for the north wind, the soft cool wind of the winter season. 'Dov, that is her name.'

Having shown him her feminine capriciousness, Dov circled back flirtatiously and came to him from the other side. This time she accepted his offering readily and drooled saliva as she crunched it up. She ran her velvet muzzle over his open palm searching for crumbs, and when she found none she reached for his pouch and bumped it so demandingly that she knocked Nefer over backwards. He scrambled up and fished out another cake.

While she ate it he touched her neck with the other hand. As though flies were crawling over her, she made her dark mahogany-coloured hide dance, but did not pull away. There was a tick in her ear-hole, and Nefer plucked it off then crushed it between his fingernails and offered the bloody fragment for her to smell. She shuddered with disgust and rolled her eyes at the offensive odour, but allowed him to examine and fondle the other ear. When he left the field she followed him like a dog to the fence. Then she hung her head over the rail, and whickered after him.

'I am consumed with jealousy.' Mintaka had watched the encounter from the temple roof. 'Already she loves you almost as much as I do.'

The next morning Nefer came down to the field alone. Taita and Meren were watching from the roof of the temple. This was something between Nefer and Dov. No others should interfere.

Nefer whistled as he came down to the fence and Dov threw up her head and galloped across the field to meet him. As soon as she reached him she pushed her muzzle into his pouch.

'You are a typical woman,' Nefer scolded her. 'You are interested only in the gifts I bring you.'

While she ate the cake he fondled and caressed her, until he could slip one arm around her neck. Then he walked her along the fence and back again, and she leaned her shoulder against him. He fed her one more cake and as she savoured it he moved back along her left flank, stroking her and telling her how beautiful she was. Then in one smooth movement he swung up and straddled her back. She started under him and he braced himself for her first wild plunge, but she stood trembling with her legs slightly splayed. Then she turned her head and stared at him in such comical astonishment that he could not help laughing. 'It's all right, my sweetling. This is what you were born to.'

She stamped her forefoot and snorted.

'Come now,' he said. 'Are you not going to try to throw me off? Let us get this question settled at once.' She reached back and sniffed his toe, as if she could not bring herself to believe the extraordinary solecism he had committed against her dignity. She shuddered and stamped her hoof again, but she stood firm.

'Come then!' he said. 'Let's try a canter.' He touched her flanks with his heels and she jumped with surprise, then walked forward. They went down the fence sedately, and he touched her again. She broke into a trot, then a gentle canter. Meren was whooping and shouting from the temple roof, and the men and women working in the fields straightened up and watched with interest.

'Now let's see you really move.' Nefer slapped her lightly on the neck and urged her forward with a thrust of his hips. She stretched out and floated away, her dainty hoofs seeming barely to touch the earth, like the gentle wind for which she had been named. She ran so that the wind stung his eyes and the tears streamed over his temples and wet the dense tresses of his hair.

Round and round the paddock they sped, while on the roof of the temple Mintaka clapped her hands and cried out with amazement.

Beside her, Taita smiled distantly. 'A royal pair,' he said. 'They will be hard to catch on the Red Road.'

※

The entire city had heard of the instant love affair between Pharaoh and his filly. Now the word spread rapidly through Gallala that Nefer was going to put the rope on Krus. Horsemen all, they knew that the colt would be a different proposition from the filly. They were in a ferment of excitement at the prospect of Nefer's first attempt to break him in. Nobody went out into the fields that morning and all work in the vehicle shops and on the buildings was suspended. Even the training regiments were given a day's holiday to watch the attempt. Thus, there was fierce competition for the best positions on the city walls and rooftops that overlooked the field below the fountain of Horus.

Nefer and Meren went out through the gates to ironical cheers and ribald advice shouted down from the walls by the wags among the crowd. Krus was in the centre of the herd. He stood out among the other animals, taller by a hand and his head was distinguished. All the horses had sensed the mood of the watchers, and were skittish and nervous as the two men paused at the gate and hung the coils of flax ropes over the fence.

'I will try him first with a cake,' Nefer said, and Meren laughed.

'Look in his eye. I think he would eat you before the cake.'

'Nevertheless, I will try. Wait here.'

Nefer went through the gate, and moved in slowly as he had with Dov. Krus disliked this attention. He arched that long neck and rolled his eyes. Nefer stopped and let him settle down to graze again. He took a *dhurra* cake from his pouch and held it out, but when he moved forward Krus tossed his head, kicked his heels to the sky and galloped furiously away down the fence line. Nefer chuckled ruefully. 'So much for my gifts. He will not make it easy.'

'Look at him run,' Meren called. 'Sweet Horus, if Dov is the north wind then this one is the *khamsin*.'

Krus was running with the other horses now, leading them. Nefer and Meren went into the field together and between them worked the herd gently down to the corner of the fence of heavy poles. There they milled around nervously in the dust as the men came up. Then they broke the wrong way, galloping back to the top end of the field before Nefer could cut them off. Twice more Krus led them out of the trap, but then Nefer sent Meren to cut him off on the far side of the field and Krus made his first mistake. He came thundering back towards Nefer.

Nefer shook out the loop on the end of the long flax rope he carried coiled over his shoulder, and waited for the colt to come through the narrow gap between him and the wooden slats of the fence. Nefer judged his moment and put the loop into flight, a spinning circle over his head, then as Krus galloped through with his neck stretched out, Nefer shot out the loop, which dropped neatly over his head and slipped back to the front of his shoulder. The coils of rope were whipped off Nefer's shoulder, one after the other, as Krus bore away. Nefer braced himself with legs spread wide, leaning back with the end of the rope wrapped half a dozen times around his wrist.

The rope came up hard with the running colt at the other end, and Nefer was yanked off his feet, and hauled face down on to his belly. The colt felt the grab of the rope and the weight, panicked and bolted. Nefer was dragged after him like a sledge, bouncing and rolling at the rope's end.

The crowds on the rooftops and the walls exploded into hysterical mirth and cheers. Mintaka stuffed her fingers into her mouth to stop herself screaming and Merykara covered her eyes and turned away. 'I cannot watch!' she cried.

The colt reached the fence at the end of the field and swung parallel to it. For a moment there was slack in the rope and Nefer used it to roll on to his feet. His belly and legs were grazed and covered with green grass stains, but the rope was tight around his wrist. It came up hard again and he was jerked forward brutally, but he kept on his feet. Using the impetus he went after Krus with long strides, dragged along on the rope's end.

After one circuit of the field Krus slowed to the heavy drag, and Nefer consolidated his gain by digging in the heels of his bronze-cleated sandals. Then as they slowed he swung himself out on the rope's end, catching the colt by surprise. The animal stumbled at the changed direction of the pull, and as soon as he steadied Nefer swung himself the other way. Twice more Nefer was pulled down, but each time he fought his way to his feet again and put pressure on the colt.

In the meantime Meren had opened the gate and driven the rest of the herd into the adjacent field, then he closed it so that man and horse had the empty field in which to fight it out.

Nefer dug in for a foothold and swung the colt's head towards the fence, forcing him to back up on the rope or crash into the heavy poles. He gathered up the slack in the rope then raced forward. Before Krus could recover he had taken three turns of rope around the heavy corner post of the fence and pinned him. Krus reared and plunged, shaking his head and rolling his eyes until the whites showed.

'I have you now,' Nefer gasped, and worked himself hand over hand down the rope towards him. Krus rose on his hind legs and struck out at the rope, whinnying shrilly. 'Gently, gently. Will you kill us both?'

Krus reared again and lifted Nefer off his feet. He came down foursquare and they confronted each other, the colt trembling wildly and sweating down his back and shoulders. Nefer was in no better case, the front of his body covered with scratches and grass burns, from which blood and pale lymph oozed. He, too, was running with sweat, and his face was contorted with the effort of holding down the colt.

They both rested for a space, then Nefer started creeping hand over hand down the rope towards Krus again. He reached the horse's head and flung one arm around his neck. Krus reared again and lifted Nefer high, but he kept his grip. Again and again Krus tried to break away, but Nefer hung on.

At last the colt stood trembling, and before he could recover Nefer had thrown a loop of the rope around his back leg and pulled it tight.

When Krus tried to bolt again his nose was almost touching his right flank and he could only turn in a tight circle. Nefer secured the knots in the rope, so that they would not slip and strangle Krus, then staggered back.

He was so exhausted that he could barely keep his feet. Krus tried to run, but managed only to follow his nose in another tight circle. Round and round he went in a right-hand turn, slower and slower, until at last he stood confused and helpless, nose pointing at his rump.

Nefer left him and dragged his battered body to the gate.

The next morning the rooftops and walls were crowded once more with men and women, as Nefer made his way out of the gates and down to the field. He was trying not to limp. Despite the salves and unguents that Taita had mixed and that Mintaka had applied, his injuries had stiffened overnight. Krus was still standing in the same attitude in which Nefer had left him the previous evening, nose to tail.

Nefer began to sing softly as he came through the gate into the field. Krus did not move but laid his ears flat on his neck and bared his teeth in a vicious grin.

Nefer moved around him slowly, singing and whispering to him, and Krus fidgeted and tried to move away, but he was locked in that monotonous circle. Nefer seized the head rope and gently adjusted his knots so that they could be released and dropped with a single movement.

Then he moved quietly down Krus' left flank where he was hidden from the colt. He stroked his back and kept talking as he gathered himself. Then, in one easy movement, he swung up and straddled Krus' back. The colt's entire body convulsed then froze with terror and outrage. He tried to run but his head was held down. He made another uneasy circle. He tried to buck but the rope jerked up hard around his neck. He stood again, but with his ears laid back.

Nefer jerked the tag end of the slip-knot, first the one that secured his back leg and then the loop around his neck. The rope dropped away, and Krus lifted his head and arched his neck. For another moment nothing happened. Then he realized that he was free. Like a gull launching into flight, Krus seemed to rise straight up into the air on four stiff legs with his nose touching his front hoofs. He came down and jumped again spinning on his tail, switching from side to side. Nefer stuck to his back like a growth. Krus started to buck, kicking viciously at the sky with both back legs together. In a series of these wild running lunges he crossed from one side of the field to the other.

Then he rose high on his back legs and flung himself over, crashing down on his own spine with a thud that carried clearly to the watchers on the walls, attempting to crush his rider between himself and the earth.

Mintaka screamed, expecting to hear the crackle of breaking bone, but Nefer had jumped clear, landing like a cat, and crouched beside the colt as Krus lay on his back and thrashed his legs in the air.

'Only a clever and warlike horse will try like that to kill a man,' Taita remarked, without emotion.

Frustrated, Krus raised himself on his front legs, but before he could scramble back on to all four feet Nefer had vaulted firmly on to his back. The colt stood under him, trembling and shaking his head, then burst into a furious gallop. He tore across the field stretched in full stride, and aimed straight at the fence. Nefer lay stretched out on his neck and shouted at him, 'Yes! As fast as you like!'

Krus went at the high fence without a check, and Nefer shifted his weight to help him over. They rose together on a great wave of power, and sailed clear over the top bar, landing cleanly in balance.

Nefer laughed with exhilaration, and urged him forward with a thrust of his hips. 'Come on! Let's see your best speed.'

Krus went up the lower slopes of the bleak bare hills like a wild oryx, and disappeared over the skyline, headed out into the desert. The cheering and hubbub on the city walls died away, and a profound silence fell.

'We must send someone after them,' Mintaka cried in the silence. 'Nefer may be thrown. He could be lying out there in the wilderness with his back broken.'

Taita shook his head. 'It is between the two of them now. Nobody should intervene.'

They waited on the walls and rooftops while the sun made its noon then began to sink towards the horizon, but nobody left their position – they would not chance missing the climax of this trial of strength and nerve between man and beast.

'They have killed each other,' Mintaka fretted. 'That horse is a monster. If it has hurt Nefer I will have it destroyed,' she vowed furiously.

Another hour passed, slowly as dripping honey, and then a stir ran along the top of the wall. Men jumped to their feet and stared up at the crest of the hills, and a murmur rose slowly to an excited chorus of shouts and laughter.

On the skyline appeared a sorry pair. The colt's head was hanging, and his coat was dark with sweat, limed with the salt the had dried upon him. His utter exhaustion was evident in every halting pace he took. On his back Nefer drooped wearily, and as Krus picked his way down the slope they could see how Pharaoh's body had been bruised and battered.

Krus reached the foot of the hills. He was too far gone to jump the fence again, but he came submissively down the dusty road towards the city gates.

Mintaka shouted, 'Bak-her! Well done, Your Majesty!' and immediately the cry was taken up and flung from man to man until it echoed from the hills above the fountain of Osiris.

'Bak-her! Bak-her!'

Nefer straightened on the colt's back and raised one fist high in a triumphant salute. The cheering redoubled.

Below the walls he showed his mastery by putting Krus through a series of turns, first one way then the other. Then he stopped him with a hand on his withers and made him back up. His commands were almost imperceptible, light pressure of his knees or a toe pressed behind Krus' elbow, or subtle shifts of his weight, but the horse responded submissively.

'I feared he had broken the colt's spirit,' Taita told Mintaka, 'but Krus is one of those rare creatures who needs firm treatment rather than kindness. Nefer had to establish his mastery and, Horus is my witness, I have never seen it done so swiftly and completely.'

Nefer rode in through the city gates and waved up at Mintaka, then went down the long avenue to the cavalry lines. He tethered Krus and held the leather bucket for him to drink. Once the colt had slaked his thirst he washed off the dust and dried sweat with hot water, then took him out of the stable to roll in the sand lot. He filled his nosebag with crushed *dhurra* sweetened with honey, and while Krus ate greedily, Nefer rubbed him down, telling him how brave he was, how they would run the Red Road together, and Krus switched his ears back and forth as he listened to him.

As the sun went down Nefer spread the straw bedding thickly on the stable floor. Krus sniffed at it, nibbled a mouthful then lowered himself wearily and stretched out upon his side. Nefer lay down in the straw beside him and pillowed his head on Krus' neck. They fell asleep together, and Mintaka lay alone that night.

The next day Nefer introduced Krus to Dov. The horses circled each other warily, sniffed each other's mouths and circled again. When Krus thrust his nose under Dov's tail she feigned outrage and lashed out at him with both back legs, then raced away flirtatiously with Krus prancing after her. Nefer let them graze together for the rest of the day, and the following morning showed them the chariot. This was not the magnificent royal vehicle, but an older, well-used one. He let them smell the shaft, which had been rubbed and polished smooth by contact with the flanks of many other horses. When they both lost interest in such a mundane object, Meren led Krus away while Nefer took Dov through the next step.

Stroking and caressing her, he placed the harness carefully over her shoulders and fastened the straps. She fidgeted unhappily but allowed him to place these unaccustomed restraints on her. He went up on her back and took her on two circuits of the field. When he brought her back, Meren had the shaft ready. It was not attached to the chariot, although it had the ring bolt at one end. Nefer hitched the harness to it, and Dov rolled her eyes nervously as she felt the weight hanging down her side. She turned her head to examine the shaft, and once she had satisfied her curiosity he took her head and led her forward.

She snorted and crabbed as the shaft followed her, but Nefer gentled and reassured her. After they had circled the field a few times she was no longer skittering sideways. Now came the crucial step. Nefer had borrowed Hilto's placid old mare and placed her in the right-hand traces. She stood there stolidly. He hitched Dov into the left-hand position. The calm nature of the old mare reassured Dov and she stood quietly. Nefer put their nosebags on them and fed them a ration of crushed *dhurra*. When she was relaxed and content, he padded Dov's back legs with strips of linen bandage so that she did not damage herself if she started kicking when she felt the full weight of the chariot behind her.

He need not have worried. He took her head and led her forward and she moved easily beside the old mare. Nefer touched her shoulder and she leaned into the harness and took her share of the weight like a veteran. Nefer broke into a run and Dov trotted at his side. Then he jumped up into the cockpit and gathered up the reins. He put the pair through a series of turns, each one tighter than the last, and though Dov had never felt the reins before she mimicked her right-hand partner faithfully. By the end of that first day she recognized the commands and responded to them instantly, rather than waiting for the old mare to show her the way. For another five days he ran the two mares together and Dov learned fast.

Now it was time to take Krus through the same routine. It was three days before he stopped bolting as soon as he felt the drag of the shaft. Nefer almost gave up on him, but Taita made him persevere. 'Give him your patience now and he will reward you a thousand times over,' he counselled. 'He has intelligence and heart. You will never find another to replace him.'

Eventually Krus resigned himself to the pole that slithered after him and aped his every move so alarmingly. Nefer was at last able to place him in the traces beside Dov. She turned her head and nuzzled his neck, like a mother with a fractious child. Krus calmed down and ate his *dhurra*. When Nefer led them forward he tried to turn sideways and balk but Nefer slapped him sternly across the haunch. He straightened up and fell in line with Dov, but he was shirking. Another slap and he put his shoulder into the traces and took his fair share. The sensation must have pleased him for soon he was hauling with a will. The only difficulty was to make him stop.

Meren threw open the gate of the paddock and jumped up on to the footplate as the chariot rolled past. They took the trade road and swept up the hills in a cloud of their own red dust.

It was the route they took at dawn every day over the months that followed. Each evening when they returned to Gallala the horses were quicker and ran truer, shoulder to shoulder like a single beast with two heads and eight legs. The two young warriors on the footplate were harder and tougher, burned dark by the desert sun.

Mintaka learned how it must feel to be a widow.

There were only five warriors of the Red Road in the fortress city of Gallala: Hilto, Shabako, Socco, Timus and Toran. Many others had tried but had lost their hair braids in the attempt.

Hilto and Shabako were adepts of the third and highest degree of the order, worshippers of the nameless god, the Bull of Heaven, the Sumerian god of war. Only his adepts knew his true name; from all others he was concealed behind the covert name of the Red God. He had no temple or shrine dedicated to him. He came when two or more of his adepts invoked his name upon any field where men had died in battle. Such a place was Gallala, for here Lord Tanus had vanquished the enemies of Egypt and piled their severed heads in the plaza of the city.

Secret catacombs honeycombed the limestone beneath the central square, making it a most suitable temple for the worship of the nameless one.

After midnight, while the rest of the city slept above, Hilto led a prime white bullock down the narrow tunnel that was the entrance to the catacombs, and he sacrificed it upon the stone altar they had built in the dark recesses of the main cistern. In the wavering torchlight the blood spurted and puddled on the paved floor. Then the five warriors of the order dipped their swords in the blood and prayed for the blessing of the secret god on their deliberations and implored him to help them choose wisely. Then they considered the ordeal to be set for Pharaoh Nefer Seti and his companion.

'There must be no concession made to Pharaoh. He must be tested as relentlessly as any other novice,' said Hilto.

'To do otherwise would be to give offence to the mighty and warlike one.' Even in this distinguished company he hesitated to use the god's true name. 'It would degrade the honour of those warriors who have ridden the Red Road before Nefer Seti,' Shabako agreed.

Their conclave lasted most of that night and, wrapped in their woollen cloaks, the two novices waited outside the entrance to the tunnel that led down to the catacombs. They spoke little for they were intensely aware that their very lives would be decided by the five warriors in the dark cave beneath where they sat. The light of the dawning day had not yet washed out the pinprick of the morning star from the eastern horizon when Shabako came to summon them before the conclave.

They followed him along the stone-lined tunnel. The torch he carried shone into the niches in which lay the painted mummy cases of men and women dead five hundred years and more. The air was dry and cool. It smelt of earth and mushrooms, decay and antiquity. Their footsteps echoed eerily, and there were faint whispers in the air, perhaps the voices of the dead or the rustle of bats' wings.

Then they smelt fresh blood, which splashed under their feet as they passed the carcass of the sacrificial bullock. There were torches in the brackets upon the walls of the echoing cavern where the warriors waited for them.

'Who approaches the mysteries?' called the voice of Hilto, but his face was hidden in the folds of his cloak.

'I am Nefer Seti.'

'And I am Meren Cambyses.'

'Do you wish to attempt the Red Road?'

'We do.'

'Are you both natural men, entire in body and mind?'

'We are.'

'Have you killed your first man in fair combat?'

'We have.'

'Is there a warrior who sponsors you, Nefer Seti?'

'I am the sponsor.' Shabako spoke up for him.

'Is there a warrior who sponsors you, Meren Cambyses?'

'I am the sponsor,' replied Socco.

When the catechism had been completed, Nefer and Meren were inducted into the first grade of the order. 'In the blood of the Bull, and the fire of his might, you are accepted by the god as his novices. You are not yet entitled to sit in conclave with the anointed warriors of the second and third grades, nor to worship the Red God, nor even to learn his hidden name. You have only the right to attempt the road that the god lays out for you. Knowing that it might mean death, do you accept this challenge?'

'We do.'

'Then know that there are five stages along the road and the first of these is . . .'

Each of the anointed warriors spoke in turn, explaining the ordeal Nefer and Meren faced and setting out the rules to which they must adhere. The five stages were designated as the javelin, the wrestler, the bow, the chariot and the sword. The two novices felt their spirits quail.

In the end Hilto spoke again. 'You have heard what the god has ordained. Are you determined to embark upon this endeavour?'

'We are.' Their voices were unnaturally loud, the tone cracked with false bravado, for now they knew the full extent of what lay ahead of them.

'Then from this point onwards there is no turning back,' said Hilto.

'The chariot is the main discipline,' Taita told them. 'Remember that it is a race. There will be ten chariots pursuing you. Speed is all. You must learn to get the very best out of your team.'

They worked relentlessly. By the time the new moon of Osiris was a sliver of bronze on the horizon, Dov and Krus had learned all that Nefer and Meren could teach them. They ran like one horse, leading with the same stride, aware of the balance and stability of the chariot behind them, using their weight and strength to hold true in the tightest turns, bringing it down from full gallop to dead stop in its own length, responding to the most subtle commands instantly.

Mintaka brought Merykara out into the desert, driving her own chariot, to watch them in training. At noon when they halted to water and rest the pair, Mintaka called out spontaneously, 'Perfection! Surely there is nothing more you can teach them. Nothing more for them to learn.'

Nefer gulped from the water jug then wiped his mouth on the back of his hand and looked up at the crest of the black rock hills.

'There is one who would not agree with you.'

The girls shaded their eyes and followed the direction of his gaze. They saw the figure perched up there, sitting so still that he might have been part of the rock.

'Taita. How long has he been watching?'

'Sometimes it seems that he has been watching for ever.'

'Is there something more he can show you?' Mintaka demanded. 'If there is, then why has he not already done so?'

'He is waiting for me to ask him,' Nefer said.

'Go to him at once,' Mintaka ordered. 'If you don't I will.'

Nefer climbed the hill and sat down beside Taita. They were silent for a while, and then Nefer said, 'I need you again, Old Father.'

Taita did not respond at once, except to blink like an owl caught out of his nest by the rising sun. He would never have a son, and no man had ever called him father before.

'You can help me. What must I still do?'

After a long pause Taita spoke softly. 'Krus senses when you are going to loose the javelin or shoot the arrow. He steps high at the moment, chopping with his right fore. Dov feels it and flinches.'

Nefer thought about it. 'Yes! I have felt the break in their stride at the moment of release.'

'It can throw your aim by a thumb's breadth.'

'What can I do?'

'You must teach them the fifth gait.'

'There are only four. Walk, trot, canter and gallop.'

'There is another. I call it the glide, but it must be taught. Most horses will never learn.'

'Help me teach them.'

They took the horses out of the harness, and Nefer went up on Dov's back. He took her for a short canter then brought her back to where Taita stood. The old man made her lift her right front hoof and tied a leather thong around her fetlock. Attached to the thong was a perfectly round, water-worn pebble wrapped in leather. Dov put her head down and sniffed it curiously. 'Take her round again,' said Taita.

Nefer prodded his toes behind her shoulder and she started forward. The pebble dangled on her leading foot, and instinctively she tried to rid herself of the nuisance, flipping her leading hoof with each pace. It changed her whole motion. Her back no longer came up to slap into his buttocks, there was no longer that rocking movement, that lunge. 'She flows like a river under me!' Nefer shouted with delight. 'Like the Nile herself!'

Within two days he was able to take off the bobber, and she would change from the canter or gallop into the glide at his command. The word of command was 'Nile'.

When they first brought it to him, Krus behaved as though the bobber was a venomous cobra. He reared and pawed the air. When he saw it coming in Nefer's hands, he rolled his eyes and quivered all over.

For three days he and Nefer pitted their wills against each other, and then suddenly, on the fourth day, he flicked out his right hoof and glided away. The next day he was gliding on command as readily as Dov.

On the tenth day Taita watched from his hilltop as they came galloping down on the line of targets, Nefer with the javelin thong wrapped around his wrist. Krus was watching the painted wooden circles on their tripods, his ears pricked forward nervously, but before he could break and chop Nefer called, 'Nile!'

Dov and Krus changed gait simultaneously, the chariot steadied and glided forward like a fighting galley under sail. Nefer's first javelin slapped into the red central ring of the target.

Taita observed Nefer nock, draw and hold his aim. He was watching the yellow flag on its staff behind the row of targets that were set up two hundred paces in front of them. The flag stirred and flapped, filled for a moment then sagged limply as the hot breeze died away. Nefer loosed and the arrow rose on its lazy parabola of flight. It reached its zenith and as it started to drop the breeze puffed again on Taita's cheek.

The arrow felt the breeze also and veered perceptibly in flight. It dropped towards the target, and struck three hands' breadth to the leeward side of the red bullseye.

'Seth vomit on this treacherous wind!' Nefer swore.

'The light arrow feels it more,' Taita said, and walked back to the little cart that carried the spare bows and the quivers. He came back with a long bundle wrapped in a leather sheath.

'No!' Nefer said, as he unwrapped Trok's great war bow. 'It outdoes me!'

'When did you last attempt to draw it?' Taita asked.

'On the day we unearthed it,' Nefer replied. 'You should know. You were there.'

'That was six months ago.' Taita said, and glanced significantly at Nefer's bare chest and arms. The muscles had grown hard as carved cedarwood. He handed the bow to him.

Reluctantly Nefer took it and turned it in his hands. He saw that the stock had been rebound recently with fine electrum wire and lacquered. The bowstring was new – the sinews of a lion's forelegs, cured and twisted until they were hard and unyielding as bronze.

The refusal rose to his lips again but did not pass them for Taita was watching him. He lifted the bow and, without an arrow in place, raised it and tried to draw. It came back half a cubit, then his arms locked and although the muscles flattened and hardened across his chest it would move no further. Carefully Nefer released the pressure and the bow stock returned to rest.

'Let me have it back.' Taita reached out to take the weapon from him. 'You have neither the strength nor the determination.'

Nefer jerked it away from him, and his lips went thin and white, his eyes blazed.

'You don't know everything, old man, even though you think you do.'

He reached into the cart and snatched one of the long heavy arrows from the quiver that carried the cartouche of Trok embossed in the polished leather. Like the bow it had been salvaged from the buried chariot. He strode back to the firing-line and took his stance. He nocked the arrow. His chest swelled as he sucked in a full breath. His jaw clenched and he began the draw. It came back slowly at first and reached the median line. He grunted and his breath hissed out through his throat, the muscles in his arms stood proud and hard and he came back to the full draw, kissing the bowstring like a lover. In the same movement he loosed, and the heavy arrow leaped away, singing against the blue, made its noon and dropped, flying high over the line of targets, going on and on, twice the distance. Then the flint head struck a bright spur of sparks from a distant rock and the shaft snapped with the terrible power of the strike.

Nefer stared after the arrow in astonishment, and Taita murmured, 'Perhaps you are right.'

359

Nefer dropped the bow and embraced him. 'You know enough, Old Father,' he said. 'Enough for all of us.'

Taita took Nefer and Meren into the desert, three days' travel through the harsh and beautiful land. He led them to the hidden valley where the black liquid oozed to the surface through a deep cleft in the rock. This was the same thick, tarry substance that they had used to set alight the jackals' fur on the night raid at Thane.

They filled the clay pots they had brought with them and returned to the workshop at Gallala. Taita refined the black liquid, boiling it down over a slow fire until it felt slippery as fine silk between the fingers. 'It will lubricate the wheel hubs smoother and longer than clarified pigs lard, or any other concoction. It will give you an advantage of fifty paces in a thousand. Perhaps the difference between success or failure, or even life and death.'

Nefer was inclined to run the royal chariot on the Red Road, but Taita asked, 'Do you really want to ride in a golden sarcophagus?'

'The goldwork weighs only two taels. You weighed it yourself.'

'It might just as well be two hundred when you go out there.'

Taita went over every one of the one hundred and five chariots they had exhumed from the sands, selected ten and stripped them down. He weighed the chassis and tested the strength of the joints in the carriagework. He spun the wheels on their hubs, judging by eye the slightest wobble in their rotation. At last he made his final choice.

He modified the hub assembly on the chosen vehicle so that the wheels were held by a single bronze pin that could be removed with a mallet blow. When he reassembled the chariot he discarded the dashboard and side panels, ridding it of every last tael of superfluous weight. Without the support of the struts and panels the riders would have to rely on their own sense of balance and a single loop of rope spliced to the footplate to steady themselves over the roughest ground. Finally he lubricated the wheel hubs with the black grease from the desert well.

Under Taita's supervision, they went over the harness an inch at a time, and Mintaka, Merykara and their maids sat up late into the night stitching and double stitching the joins and seams.

Then they chose the weapons they would carry, rolling the javelins and the arrows to detect any imperfection, suspending them on the special balance board Taita had designed, adding a bead of lead at haft or head until they were perfect. They sharpened the points so they would bite and hold in the targets. They resoled their sandals and filed the bronze cleats into spikes. They shaped new leather guards to protect their forearms from the whip of the bowstring and the javelin thong. They selected three swords each, for the bronze blades often snapped in the heat of combat. They sharpened the edges then burnished them with powdered pumice stone until they could shave the hair from their own forearms.

They cured and twisted spare bowstrings, to be carried as belts tied around their waists. Other than leather helmets and jerkins, they would wear no armour on the road, to lighten the load that Dov and Krus must draw. They worked behind the locked doors of the workshop, so that no others would learn of their preparations.

But above all else they trained and practised, built up their strength and stamina, and the trust of the horses.

For Dov and Krus the fire would be the worst of the ordeal. They built their own fires out in the desert, stacking faggots of wood and bundles of dry straw. They let the horses see the flames and smell the smoke, then blindfolded them. Though at first Krus balked and whinnied with terror, in the end he would run blind, trusting the man upon his back, so close to the crackling flames that they singed his mane.

Mintaka and Merykara spent long hours during the waiting days in the newly renovated temple of Hathor, sacrificing for their men and praying for the protection and intervention of the goddess on their behalf.

Thirty-five days before the full of the moon of Horus a strange caravan arrived in Gallala. It had come up from the coast, from the port of Safaga. It was led by a one-eyed and one-armed giant of a man named Aartla. The five warriors of the Red Road went out to meet him when he was still three leagues outside the city walls. They carried him back to Gallala in honour, for he was a brother warrior of the third degree who had run the Red Road almost thirty years before. Twenty years ago an arrow had pierced his eye during the Libyan campaign of Pharaoh Tamose, and five years later a Nubian axeman had sheared his arm with a single stroke below the elbow.

Aartla was a wealthy man now. He owned a travelling company of entertainers, men and women of special talents and skills. One of his troupe was reputed to be the strongest woman in the world. She could lift two horses into the air, one with each hand, and she could bite the end off a bronze rod and then bend the metal stump with the grip of her vagina. Another of his women was famed as the most beautiful in the world, though few had set eyes on her face. She came from a land so far to the north that at certain seasons of the year the rivers turned to white stone and ceased to flow. Aartla charged ten taels of silver for the privilege of seeing her face unveiled. They said she had golden hair that hung to the ground, and eyes of different colours, one golden and the other blue. The price that Aartla charged for viewing the rest of her charms was in proportion, and only a rich man might sample all her delights.

In addition Aartla possessed a black slave girl who ate fire, covered herself from head to foot with a cloak of live scorpions, and draped a great python around her neck. At the climax of her performance she enticed the serpent to crawl into the secret opening of her body until all its length had disappeared into her womb.

These wonders were intended merely to whet the appetite of the audience for the main attractions of Aartla's circus, which were his champions: a company of fighting men, wrestlers and swordsmen who stood to meet all contenders in combat. Aartla offered a purse of a hundred taels of pure gold to any man who could defeat one of his champions. The side wagers made on these contests were legendary and were the source of Aartla's immense wealth. Though nowadays he never fought, he was still a warrior at heart and a devotee of the Red God.

When word reached him that a pharaoh of the Tamosian dynasty was determined to run the Red Road, he brought his champions across half the world to oppose him. He loved the game so well that he made no charge for this service.

His brother warriors had prepared one of the ancient palaces of the city to house Aartla and his troupe. On the night after his arrival they held for him a great welcome banquet, to which only Nefer and Meren were not invited. 'We could not have accepted,' Nefer explained to Mintaka. 'We are not brothers of the order. Besides, to sit down with the men who will oppose us would be flying in the face of convention and tradition.'

The day after the welcoming banquet the champions resumed their never-ending practice and training, under the sharp eye of Aartla. They worked in the courtyard of the ancient palace, and all strangers were excluded. Aartla was too shrewd to let other gamblers assess the form and style of his champions without paying good gold for the privilege.

However, Taita was no stranger. When Aartla had lost his arm Taita had trimmed and sewn up the stump, and saved him from the gas gangrene that had infected the wound and threatened Aartla's life. Aartla welcomed him to the practice courtyard and sat him on a pile of cushions on the side of his good eye. The most beautiful woman in the world served him honey-flavoured sherbet in a golden bowl, and smiled at him with those haunting mismatched eyes from behind her veil.

First, Aartla gave Taita the latest news of the Egyptian campaign in Mesopotamia, whence he had come. It seemed that King Sargon, with his armies broken and scattered, had retreated behind the walls of Babylon, his capital city. The final outcome could not be in doubt. The armies of the false pharaohs would soon be free to return to Egypt and deal with the other threat posed to their monarchy by the little army of Gallala. When he said this his look was significant, a timely warning to an old friend.

While they sat on the cushions and discussed many other things, politics, power and war, medicine, magic and the gods, Taita seemed engrossed in their discussion, hardly glancing at the athletes who struggled and sweated in the sunlight. But his pale ancient eyes missed not a single throw or swordstroke.

The champions lived by their murderous skills. They were devotees of the Red God, and their endeavours were a form of worship. When Taita returned to his cell that evening, where Nefer and Meren waited for him, he was grave. 'I have watched your adversaries at practice, and I warn you that there is still much work for us to do,' he said, 'and only days left to us.'

'Tell us, Old Father,' Nefer said.

'First there is Polios, the wrestler...' Taita began, and he outlined the character and strength of each champion, his style of combat and his particular strengths. Then he discussed any weakness he had discerned in them, and how that might best be exploited.

The five warriors of the order, assisted by Aartla, began to lay out the course to be run. They spent day after day in the wilderness, surveying a wide circular track that began in the central forum of Gallala, went up into the hills and the broken lands, then three leagues later came back down the long valley past the fountain of Taita, and through the city gates to finish back in the forum. Once they had laid out the course, they sent parties of workman to build the obstacles along the way.

Ten days before the contest, Hilto and Shabako read out the proclamation to the populace of the city. They described the course in detail, and the rules governing the trial. Then they named the champions who would oppose the novices.

'In the ordeal of wrestling, Pharaoh Nefer Seti will be matched against Polios of Ur.' The crowd sighed for Polios was a famous fighter. His nickname was the Backbreaker. Recently he had killed a man in Damascus, his seventeenth victim in the ring.

'Meren Cambyses will be matched against Sigassa of Nubia.' They knew him almost as well. He was called the Crocodile, for some strange disease had made his skin as hard, lumpy and black as that of one of the great reptiles.

'In the ordeal by sword, Pharaoh Nefer Seti will meet Khama of Taurine.'

'Meren Cambyses will meet Drossa of Indus.'

That night Mintaka and Merykara sacrificed a white lamb to the goddess, and wept as they pleaded for her protection over the men they loved.

For seven days before the running of the Red Road the five warriors held trials to select the chasers. There were no shortage of contenders for the honour. Any man who plucked the hair braid of a king could expect immortality. Hilto promised that there would be a carved stele five cubits high raised in the temple of his preferred god or goddess to commemorate his feat. He would receive a thousand taels of gold, sufficient to purchase a fine estate when at last they returned to the motherland. In addition he would take as trophies all the weapons and accoutrements of the novice he succeeded in running down.

The five warriors made the final selection by a process of elimination, and proclaimed it from the stone platform in the centre of the forum. 'They have chosen the ten best and most experienced men available, and given them their pick of chariots and horses. There will be great danger both behind and in front,' Taita warned the pair, as he went over the list again. 'Consider this one, Daimios. He is a captain of chariots. He knows how to get the best out of a pair of horses.'

'It will all depend on the start,' Nefer said.

'And that will be decided by the Red God alone.'

For a seven-night before the trial Mintaka denied Nefer her couch. 'My love will weaken your resolve, and drain your strength. But I will miss you a hundred times more than you will me,' she told him as together they braided Krus' long mane.

The day before the full moon of Horus, Taita ordered them all to rest. Dov and Krus grazed quietly together in the field below the fountain. Merykara made up a basket of figs and oranges and *dhurra* cakes, and she and Meren sat beside the fountainhead watching the horses on the green grass below them. When they had eaten the simple meal, Merykara knelt behind him and plaited his hair into a rope that hung halfway down his back. 'It is so thick and lustrous,' she murmured, and buried her face in it. 'It smells so good. Let no other take it from you, but bring your braid back to me.'

'How will you reward me if I do?' He turned his head to smile at her.

'I will give you such a reward as you have never dreamed of.' She blushed as she said it.

'I have dreamed of it,' he assured her fervently. 'I dream of it every night of my life.'

In the morning Taita came to wake Nefer. He found him asleep, with one arm thrown over his face. At Taita's touch he sat up, stretched and yawned. The thick braid of his hair, which Mintaka had plaited, hung down his back. As he looked at Taita his eyes focused and hardened, as he remembered what the day would bring forth.

While Nefer drank a bowl of sour milk and ate a handful of figs, Taita went to the window and looked out over the rooftops to the grove of young palm trees they had planted above the wells. He saw the topmost fronds sway and nod to the breeze. They had all prayed for a still day, but this breeze carried with it the threat of failure. Now Nefer would have to rely more than ever on the great war bow to counter it.

Taita said nothing to Nefer of his misgivings. Instead, he turned and cast his eyes down the avenue. The sun was not yet risen, but it seemed that half the populace of Gallala was streaming out of the city gates.

'They are anxious to secure vantage-points along the course, and to watch as much of the run as possible,' he told Nefer. 'No one except the participants and the judges are allowed to ride. All others must follow the chase on foot. Some argue that it might be possible to watch the javelin and the wrestling, then cut across the hills to look down on the swordplay from close at hand. Those who are less fleet of foot will climb to the summit of Eagle Mount and watch the crossing of the chasm below them then run back here to see the finish.'

Despite the great exodus from the city many hundreds of others had chosen to watch the start and crowded into the forum. Others had climbed high above the square and were perched on the walls and balconies. Even so early in the day the air was festive and the mood feverishly excited. Some of those on the walls had brought their breakfast and chewed bones and scraps showered on to those below. Others shouted their wagers to Aartla and his scribes. Aartla was offering even money that Nefer and Meren would cross the chasm, two to one against them passing the swordsmen and four to one against them finishing the course without being overtaken by the pursuit.

As the sun rose above the walls the ten chariots of the pursuers filed into the forum. The gongs beat, the drums rolled and the sistrum rattled, women squealed and threw flowers, and children danced around them, but the charioteers were grim and intent as they lined up along the starting barrier.

There was an interval now of tense expectation and then the sound of cheering from the cavalry lines, swelling and coming closer. Then, to an explosion of *'Bak-her!'*, the stripped-down chariot of the novices entered between the eroded columns at the entrance to the forum.

Dov and Krus had been groomed until their coats shone like burnished metal in the early sunlight. Their manes were plaited, coloured ribbons twisted into the strands, their tails were clubbed.

Nefer and Meren wore only light leather armour, and their bodies were oiled for the wrestling. They stepped down from the footplate of the chariot and went down on their knees, with their hands resting on the hilts of their swords. Taita came forward and stood over them. He recited a prayer to Horus and the Red God, asking for their blessing and protection. Finally, he took an amulet from around his own neck and placed it over Nefer's bowed head.

Nefer looked down at the object as it dangled on his chest and felt a tingle of shock, almost as though a strange current of power flowed from it. It was the golden Periapt of Lostris, the locket of his grandmother, which nobody but Taita had ever touched.

Then Hilto, wearing the red cape of the third degree of the order, mounted to the stone platform in the centre of the forum. He read aloud the rules. When he had finished he asked, in a stern voice, 'Do you understand and undertake to abide by the rules of the order of the Red Road?'

'In the name of the Red God!' Nefer affirmed.

'Who will cut the hair braids?' Hilto asked, and Mintaka and Merykara stepped up behind the kneeling warriors. Mintaka's eyes were heavily underscored with purple, for she had not slept the previous night. They were both pale and tense with anxiety. Nefer and Meren bowed their heads, and lovingly the women lifted the braids and sheared them away. They handed them to Hilto, who attached them to the tips of the tall pennant rods on each side of the footplate of their chariot. These were the trophies that the pursuers must attempt to snatch, and which Nefer and Meren must defend with their lives.

'Mount your chariot,' Hilto ordered, and Nefer and Meren climbed to the footplate. Nefer gathered up the reins. Dov and Krus arched their necks, stamped and backed up a single turn of the wheels.

'Bring on the birds!' Hilto ordered.

The handlers climbed into the circular sanded cockpit, each with a fighting cock under his arm. The wattles of both birds had been cut away so their heads were sleek, almost reptilian, with no dangling flesh or skin to give the enemy bird purchase. The sunlight gleamed on their plumage with the iridescence of oil spilled on water.

A tense, aching silence fell over the crowded forum. The handlers knelt, facing each other, in the centre of the sanded pit, and held their birds in front of them. The birds did not have artificial spurs strapped to their feet: the long metal spikes would make a kill too swift and certain, but their natural spurs had been sharpened and polished.

'Bait your birds!' Hilto called, and the handlers thrust them at each other, without allowing them to touch. The eyes of the two roosters gleamed with malice, their heads began to swell with rage and the naked skin of their heads and throats turned an angry crimson. They beat their wings, and tried to break from the handlers' grip to fly at each other.

With his drawn sword Hilto pointed across the forum at the ruined roof of the temple of Bes, the patron god of Gallala, where a blue flag flapped idly in the hot breeze. 'The novices will start when the birds are released. The flag will be lowered when one of the birds is killed, and only then will the chase begin. The Red God, in his infinite wisdom, will determine how long the birds will survive and how long the lead time will be. Now, hold yourselves in readiness.'

Every eye, even those of Nefer and Meren, turned to the challenging cock-birds. Hilto lifted his sword. The birds' hackles were raised, they were crimson with rage, fighting to be at each other.

'Now!' cried Hilto, and the handlers set them free. They flew across the sand in a flutter of bright wings, leaping high, thrusting with claws and spurs.

'Ha, Dov! Ha, Krus!' Nefer called and they sprang away, throwing gravel and dust from under their hoofs. A mighty shout went up from the crowd and the chariot raced once around the forum then out into the open avenue. Behind them the cheering faded as they tore through the gates and turned on to the track that led into the hills, its length marked every two hundred paces with white linen flags, which shook and flapped lazily in the early breeze that came in off the desert. 'Keep the flags to the right!' Meren reminded Nefer. If they missed a flag on the wrong side the judges would send them back to round it fairly.

While he drove, saving the horses, bringing them down to a trot as the slope rose steeply under them Nefer assessed that breeze by flag and dust, judging its strength and direction. It was coming harsh and hot from the west, strong enough to blow the dustcloud aside behind them. This was the worst possible wind. It would drain the horses, and confuse the range when they came to the trial of javelin and bow. He thrust the thought aside to concentrate first on the ascent of the hills.

The gradient tilted sharply upwards, and at a word of command from Nefer they sprang down from the footplate and ran beside the horses, to lighten the burden. Dov and Krus surged ahead so strongly that they had to take a grip on the harness to keep pace with them. As they reached the crest, Nefer halted them and let them rest for a measured three hundred beats of his own heart.

He looked back at the city walls below and heard the regular roar swelling and subsiding like the sound of distant surf on a coral reef, the characteristic sound of the cockfight as the crowd hailed each attack of the birds. But the flag still flew on the crumbling top of the temple of Bes to signal that the fight had not been decided. He turned away and looked down the length of the level plain that stretched ahead, and picked out the line of javelin butts, five of them spaced at intervals of two hundred paces. There was a low fence of thorn brush running parallel to them that would keep the chariot at a range of fifty paces.

Nefer jumped to the footplate, and called, 'Come away!' and the pair strode forward. He glanced back and the blue flag still flew on the tower of Bes.

As they raced in on the line of targets, Nefer wound the thong around his wrist and composed himself, seeing in his mind's eye the target, imagining the flight of the missile from his hand to the inner red circle, ignoring the yellow outer. He watched the wind moving the flags.

He saw Shabako standing on a low knoll near the centre of the line. He would show a red flag for an inner, and a yellow for a miss. They carried only five javelins, and they would be allowed only one yellow. If they failed on the first run they must turn back, retrieve the thrown javelins, and run again until they had scored the four reds.

Nefer handed the reins to Meren, who steered in close to the dividing fence to give Nefer the best shot. The first target came up fast, and Nefer braced himself on the bouncing swerving footplate.

'Nile!' He gave the command and instantly Dov and Krus changed their gait into that wonderful gliding motion. The chariot steadied under him and he rode the easy movement with his legs and he threw. There was never a doubt from the moment the javelin left his hand, its velocity accelerated by the whip of the thong – he had allowed for the wind. It flew fifty paces swinging across the wind into the heart of the red circle, and from the corner of his eye Nefer saw Shabako wave the red flag to acknowledge the strike. He snatched another javelin from the bin, and wound the thong. He felt a supreme almost godlike confidence: he knew that the next four darts would fly as true as the first. He watched the second target come up, and he threw again. It was another perfect throw. He did not even have to glance at the flag, and beside him Meren shouted, '*Bak-her*, brother!' and steered for the third.

They were running in close, and the thorn fence flew by the off-wheel in a blur. Nefer lined up and whipped his right arm into the throw, and at exactly that moment the wheel touched the fence and the chariot swerved violently and hung for a moment on the verge of capsizing. The horses pulled it straight with their combined weight, but the javelin was already in flight. With despair in his heart Nefer saw it fly wide, missing the target completely, and the yellow flag went up.

'It was me,' Meren gritted. 'I ran too fine.'

'Hold her true now,' Nefer snapped at him. 'We need two more reds.'

The fourth target came up but Nefer felt the altered motion under him. Krus was leading with the wrong foot, the collision with the fence had unbalanced him.

'Ho, Krus,' Meren called, and tried to steady him with the touch of reins. Then Dov leaned lightly against him and he felt her rhythm and picked up the step from her just as the fourth target came up.

Nefer threw and beside him Meren called, 'Red! A clean hit. You have done it.'

'Not yet,' Nefer told him, and snatched the last javelin from the bin. 'One more to go.'

They came down fast on the last target, and the men were tense as drawn bow stocks, every muscle rigid and every nerve stretched tautly. Krus sensed it, felt it in the reins from Meren's right hand, with his right eye he saw the target come up, knew precisely the instant at which

Nefer would throw and instinctively fell into his wicked old habit and broke step. The carriage lurched and swayed just as Nefer released. Even then it might have scored, were it not for the wind. A hot gust swept over them, strong enough to flog the heavy hair braids on the flag staffs. The javelin was already slightly off-line, but the wind aggravated the error. It drifted even further to the right and missed the red inner by the width of two fingers and quivered in the outer ring. Shabako held raised the black flag high above his head and waved it from side to side so that folds of cloth volleyed and flogged loudly, the signal of failure.

Their first run had been disqualified. They must retrieve the javelins and run the butts again.

Grimly silent, Nefer snatched the reins back from Meren and spun the chariot into a tight turn around the end of the thorn fence and they started back. He pushed the horses to the top of their speed – there was no thought of husbanding their strength now. For all Nefer knew, one of the fighting cocks was already slain and ten chariots had begun the chase.

They flew back along the line of targets, passing them so closely that Meren was able to pluck the javelins from the packed straw bodies without having to bring the chariot to a complete stop. The fourth javelin that had missed the target completely lay in the open, but even from a distance Nefer saw that the impact with the rocky ground had snapped the shaft in two. They were left with only four missiles to score four red flags. A single miss would mean that they would have to make their stand here, two against ten picked warriors: they would have to capitulate or fight to the death.

With only four javelins in the bin, they reached the start of the line and Nefer halted the chariot and jumped down to the ground. He ran to Krus' head and stroked his forehead. 'Run true now, my darling. Don't fail me again.'

From a great distance came the sound of a long, sustained cheering. This time it did not fade away.

'One of the birds is dead!' Meren called. 'The chase has begun.'

Nefer knew it was true. One of the cocks had succumbed and the chasers were released to follow them. They had lost their starting advantage. The pursuing chariots did not have to run the test of the javelins. They would race past the butts without a check. Even if this time they managed a clean pass of the butts with four red flags, ahead of Nefer and Meren waited the wrestlers.

Mintaka and Merykara stood side by side, looking down into the cockpit. Though stools had been placed for them they could not sit for their blood was afire with anxiety as they watched the closing stages of the bloody conflict below them.

The two fighting cocks had been carefully matched, veterans of many epic battles, both had proved their courage and stamina. They were long-legged but their thighs were compact and balled with muscle. They could drive their wicked black spurs deeply through flesh to an adversary's bone. With serpentine necks and massive hooked beaks they could reach out to rip away feathers and flesh, and when they had bled and weakened their opponent, they would seize the death-hold, pinning him while they stabbed into his vitals.

The older bird had feathers of gold and copper, bright as the sunrise. His tail was a proud cascade shot with sapphire lights. The other bird was black, but lustrous sparkling black, and his bare head was purple red.

They circled each other now. They had fought hard and long, loose feathers strewed the sand and drifted in the hot puffs of the west wind. Both birds were bleeding, fat heavy drops that sparkled on their plumage. Their strength was draining away, and they were slightly unsteady on their feet. However, their eyes were bright and fierce as they had been at the beginning of the conflict.

'Please, adored and worshipful Hathor, give them both strength to survive,' whispered Merykara, as she clung tightly to Mintaka's hand. 'Let them fight until the setting of the sun.' Even she knew how vain was her appeal. 'And keep Meren and Nefer from harm.'

Suddenly the black bird flew up head high, and then with a powerful wingbeat shot forward with both legs fully extended. The red bird rose to meet him, but he was almost exhausted and his riposte lacked fire. He was slow to lift his legs to counter the thrust. They collided in a burst of feathers, rolled together and when they separated the red cock was dragging a wing. It was very close to the end now.

Merykara sobbed aloud, 'Oh, Hathor, do not let him die!' She seized Mintaka's arm and sank her fingernails into the flesh, leaving bright red half-moons on the skin, but Mintaka hardly felt it. She was watching with horror as the red bird staggered weakly and the crowd howled savagely.

The black bird knew he had won, and his strength revived. He went high again, springing on those long, hard legs, his wings wide and brightly glittering. He dropped and hit the red cock before he could recover his balance and knocked him flat and fluttering. He pecked murderously for the eye, caught a fold of the wattled cheek and hung on.

The red bird regained his feet, but the black was locked into him. The red bird ran painfully, carrying his opponent's weight, and the girls screamed in the uproar: 'Let him go, black shade of Seth. Let him live!'

A full circuit of the cockpit the red carried him, but every stride was weaker, and at last he collapsed just below where they stood at the barrier.

'He is dead!' somebody yelled. 'The fight is over. Let the chasers go.'

'No! He lives yet,' screamed Mintaka fiercely.

The black bird released his grip on the other's head, and stood over him. With the last of his strength and courage the red bird forced himself to his feet and stood swaying, with both wings dragging in the sand and the blood pouring from the gash in his cheek.

The black bird seemed to be measuring the distance between them, then once more he leaped high and for a moment towered over his victim. Then he fell upon him and drove both spurs in to their full length, through heart and lungs. The red rooster crumpled under him and lay upon his back, his beak wide open in a silent death cry and his wings shivering convulsively.

The black rooster stood over the carcass, threw back his head and gave vent to a raucous crow of triumph that seemed to rip down Mintaka's spine, and made her shudder.

'The god has spoken! It is finished.' Hilto lifted the torn and bloody carcass by the neck, and the flag on the tower of Bes dropped. He turned to the charioteers, who crouched behind their teams of horses.

'You are free to take the Red Road!' he cried. 'Ride to death or glory!' The long whips cracked, the horses threw their heads, tossed their manes, and the ten fighting chariots swept together once around the forum, while the crowds scattered from under their wheels, women screamed and men cheered. Then they burst through the city gates and tore away into the hills, following the line of flags.

Nefer took a moment longer to pamper and reassure the horses; he stood with an arm around each of their necks and whispered to them. Then he ran back and jumped on to the footplate. He started them at a walk then brought them gently to a canter. Only when they were running in perfect unison, leading together, did he change their gait with the command, 'Nile!'

Smoothly they swept down on the targets for the second attempt and he passed the reins to Meren. He gave him no admonition, for he knew that Meren was still smarting from the their first blundered attempt.

While he wrapped the thong around his wrist Nefer watched Krus' ears for any sign that he would break stride again, but he held them pricked forward and ran true. He held the line perfectly as they came level with the first target, and the javelin smacked into the red inner. It seemed that almost immediately the second target came up and he threw smoothly with just that final application of power in the stroke and the point sank deeply into the inner ring. Beside him Meren was silent, steering the team with his very breath and soul.

The third javelin twinkled like a beam of sunlight as it flew across the range and Shabako waved the red flag for another hit.

The last javelin was in Nefer's hand, the thong clinched firmly around his wrist, and he crooned to the horses, making his tone firm but reassuring. 'One more. Just one more for me!'

Krus seemed to gather himself and tuck in his chin and he held the line sweetly and as Nefer threw he knew it was going to strike in the very centre of the red. He shouted to them while it was still in flight.

'Ha! Ha! Come away.' And they surged forward, breaking from the glide into full gallop so strongly that Nefer had to brace his legs and clutch at the grab rope to prevent himself being thrown over backwards.

Shabako waved the red flag over his head and his voice carried clearly, '*Bak-her*, Majesty! You are through and clear!'

But Nefer knew they could never make up the ground they had lost, and the chasers were already coming up swift and hard behind them.

The line of flags led them in a wide circle to the north along the edge of a deep chasm with sheer sides, and on up a series of natural terraces where the bare earth was a soft peachy colour that belied its harsh and barren nature.

The step of the third and final terrace was lined with over fifty of the more hardy spectators who had climbed up from Gallala. As Nefer's chariot raced up towards them they cheered them onwards, and opened their ranks to let them through. The summit of the terrace was flat and level. In the centre of this open space the wrestlers waited.

Each stood in his own circle of white painted stones. Nefer steered down towards them, with the crowds running after them cheering and laughing with excitement. Just short of the stone rings, Nefer brought the horses to a halt, and two grooms who were standing ready ran forward to take their heads.

'See they drink only one bucket each,' Nefer ordered, as he jumped down. This was the first point at which they were permitted to water the horses, but Nefer did not want their bellies blown up with liquid.

Swiftly Nefer and Meren stripped off their leather armour and the short *chitons* beneath until they stood stark naked in the sunlight. The crowd hummed with admiration when their hard young bodies, trained to athletic perfection, were revealed, and some of the women of low status and dubious morality ululated and cavorted lewdly with excitement.

Now every second that passed brought the pursuing chariots closer. Nefer did not even glance at the dancing women but he and Meren strode forward, each towards the ring where his allotted opponent waited. Nefer paused outside the ring of white stones and looked at Polios of Ur who stood in the centre.

He was not exceptionally big or tall, no larger or heavier then Nefer, for the judges had matched them carefully and fairly. However, there was no fat or superfluous flesh on Polios. It was obvious that he had been limbering up, for he shone with sweat and oil and his muscles were engorged and flushed with blood. Everything about him was hard. His shoulders were in perfect proportion to his waist, his belly flat, his limbs long and supple. He stood with his arms folded over his chest and watched Nefer with a hard flat stare.

Nefer took one long breath and heard again Taita's words in his ear, as clearly as if he had spoken again in his ear, 'The left knee. That is his only weakness.'

He dropped his eyes to the limb but Polios' left knee seemed as sturdy as the right. Hard and impregnable as the main stem of an olive tree.

Nefer touched the golden charm at his throat, and stepped into the ring of stones. The crowd howled and yelped and shouted. Polios placed his hands on his knees and hunched his shoulders, and watched him with the flat implacable stare of a serpent. Nefer knew that he must make the first advance, for Polios was in no hurry. His task was to delay Nefer here until the pursuing chariots could catch up with him. Nefer circled him once, and Polios turned slowly to keep facing him.

'Yes,' Nefer told himself, 'there it is. He drags his left toe.' But it was so tiny a flaw that he would never have picked it out without Taita's advice.

'An old injury,' Taita had told him. 'Here!' and he had pressed his thumb into Nefer's knee to mark the exact site of it. But then Taita had gone on, 'Even so, do not rate him lightly. He is a man-killer. This is his favourite throw, and it is well nigh irresistible.' Taita had demonstrated it.

Nefer circled back the other way and Polios turned with him. He saw it now, a faint unnatural hollow below the bulge of the kneecap. He could not afford another moment and he closed.

Each of them fell into the classical prelude, grabbing at each other with both hands, seeking the throwing grip, changing the holds, shifting weight, pushing and then giving, feeling the other man's balance. Then suddenly Polios leaped forward, coming in low, under Nefer's guard, and though Nefer had been expecting it he could not prevent one long arm whipping around his waist. Suddenly he was lifted high so only the tips of his toes touched the earth, and Polios spun with him in his arms, turning him backwards so that he could not keep his balance. Then suddenly Polios dropped on his right knee, and brought Nefer down with him. His other leg was braced solid, left thigh parallel to the ground like a carpenter's bench, Nefer came down across it and it caught him in the small of his back, at the level of his kidneys. It should have snapped his spine, but Nefer had practised the counter a hundred times with Meren. He arched his back to take the strain and at the same time slammed both his heels in the ground to break the force of it. Even so he felt his spine creak as his vertebrae were strained to the very limit.

Polios came down on him with the full weight of his upper torso, but Nefer reached under his back and clamped his right hand on Polios' knee. Taita had made him spend hours hardening his right thumb, squeezing a ball of leather until he could leave a deep indentation in the surface. Even then Taita had not been satisfied. He had made Nefer continue these exercises until he could crack a cowrie shell between thumb and forefinger. Then time and again Taita demonstrated the exact point under the kneecap where the injury lay, and the direction of pressure he must apply to sunder it. Nefer found it now, and drove his thumb into the hollow between the head of the tibia and the unattached kneecap.

Every muscle in Nefer's right arm stood out with the effort and his eyes seemed to bulge from their sockets. Then suddenly he felt something give under the point of his thumb, and he made one final effort. His thumb went in deeper, the weakened cartilage and sinew crackling and popping as they tore, the kneecap lifted in Nefer's grip, ripped from its seat.

Polios screamed, a sound of such extreme agony that it hushed the roar of the spectators that crowded the edge of the ring. Polios released his own hold and tried to push Nefer away from him, but Nefer rolled easily with the throw, never releasing his grip on the mangled kneecap, tearing it further open. Suddenly, rendered helpless as an infant, Polios sobbed and choked on the pain of it.

Nefer came up on top of him and forced his face into the earth. He twisted his left leg up behind him, and Polios could not resist. Nefer bent the shattered knee back until the heel touched Polios' buttocks, and put all his weight upon it. The terrible cry that Polios gave out sounded not human.

'Yield!' Nefer commanded, but Polios was dumb and paralysed with agony. The umpire ran forward to touch Nefer's shoulder and signal his victory.

Nefer sprang to his feet and left Polios writhing and blubbering in the dirt. The spectators parted silently in front of him, stunned by the swiftness and completeness of his victory.

Nefer heard someone in the crowd say, 'He will never walk on that leg again,' but he never looked back as he ran to the other ring and pushed out of his way the men that surrounded it.

Meren and Sigassa, the Crocodile, were locked chest to chest. They rolled across the ring, first one on top then the other. Nefer saw at a glance that Meren was injured. Sigassa's diseased skin was thick and horny, impervious to pain, and he used it now like a weapon, rubbing himself against him, tearing Meren's flesh so the blood oozed up from the shallow lacerations across his chest and arms. Taita had warned them of that, but it was impossible to avoid his loathsome embrace, and Meren was being overpowered. Nefer had arrived only just in time.

The rules of the Red Road were deliberately stacked against the novices. However, they allowed one novice to come to the aid of the other, but only after he had defeated his own opponent. This was one of the few concessions they were granted. Nefer took full advantage of it.

The moment he was into the ring Nefer stooped and picked up a white pebble the size and shape of a dove's egg. As he ran to Meren's aid, he placed the stone in the centre of his palm, wrapped his fingers and thumb around it and clasped it so firmly that his knuckles whitened with the pressure. He had turned his fist into a weapon as effective as a carpenter's mallet.

The crowd shouted a warning to the Crocodile, and he released Meren and came to his feet in one swift movement. Head down he charged at Nefer. Taita had warned them that his bald and knobbly skull was a deadly battering ram. Sigassa had already cracked two of Meren's ribs with his first charge, and now he strove to do the same to Nefer.

Nefer let him come on, judging his moment, placing his feet firmly and then he swung his clenched right fist into the side of Sigassa's jaw, at the precise point that Taita had shown him. The weight and speed of Sigassa's own rush met the full power of Nefer's shoulders behind the blow. The great scaly head snapped back and Sigassa's legs turned soft as porridge under him. But his momentum carried him on, he sprawled full length over the line of marker stones.

No one in the crowd had ever seen a bare fist used as a weapon. They gaped in amazement. Even Nefer was startled by the result, for Sigassa lay without twitching. Nefer recovered in a moment and yelled at the umpire, 'Sigassa has left the ring! He must forfeit!'

The umpire shouted his agreement, 'Nefer Seti is the victor. Sigassa forfeits the bout. You are through and clear, Nefer Seti!'

Nefer ran to Meren and hauled him to his feet. 'Are you hurt?'

'My ribs! The swine butted like a bull,' he gasped.

'We must go on.'

'Of course.' Meren straightened and squared his shoulders. His face was grey as ashes with the pain. 'It is nothing.' But he clutched the side of his chest as they ran back to the chariot. Hastily they pulled on their discarded *chitons* and strapped on the leather armour.

'That took too long. We are losing ground every second.' As they scrambled up on to the footplate of the chariot they both looked back down the terraced slope of the hills towards the javelin butts on the plain below.

'There they are,' Meren grunted, and they saw the dustcloud boiling up pale and ethereal in the sunlight. The pursuing vehicles were still only dark specks beneath the hovering dust, but seemed to grow in size even as they watched them.

There was nothing to say. The pursuers would not be tested by the wrestlers. They would ride straight past the rings of stones. Nefer and Meren knew how meagre was their lead, and how swiftly they could lose even that small advantage. It needed only one more wrong step or miscalculation on their part.

Nefer shook out the reins and called to the team. Dov and Krus had rested while they had been wrestling. Now they were refreshed, they leaned their full weight into the harness and sped away. Ahead, the line of flags marking the course began the wide turn back into the south, in the direction from which they had come.

'Halfway through!' Meren tried to sound gay, but his voice was tight with the pain of his cracked ribs, and each breath he drew was agony. They crossed the plateau and reached the far side where the terraces dropped in a series of giant steps to the rim of the chasm. They looked down towards the paddocks and pastures of the irrigated lands, startlingly green against the ochre and dun hues of the surrounding landscape, and the towers and rooftops of Gallala, so tumbled and earth-coloured that from this distance they seemed not man-made but natural features of the desert.

They looked ahead and the chasm gaped at them like the maw of a monster. Its sides were sheer and unscaleable, falling to shaded purple depths. There were small groups of people on the path that skirted the top of the cliffs. These were the spectators who had watched the trial of the javelins and who had taken the short-cut and were hurrying to watch the archery trial.

Nefer drove hard down the terrace, pushing the horses to their best speed, trying to win back even a few yards from the pursuit. This was where Krus made up in full measure for his mistakes at the javelin butts: his great strength bore them on and gave new heart to Dov at his side. They reached the lip of the chasm and raced along the edge, so close to it that the small pebbles thrown up by the wheels were flung out over the void. Though Krus was on the side closest to it he never broke his stride but leaned into the traces and ran with all his heart and will. Nefer felt his spirits soar on high.

'We can still beat them to the bridge,' He shouted in the wind. 'Come away, Krus! Come away, Dov.'

Nefer looked ahead and saw the tall, unmistakable figure of Taita standing on the lip of the precipice. He was staring across the chasm at the archery targets on the far side, and he did not look round as they pulled up behind him and jumped down from the chariot.

The previous evening Taita had predicted, 'With the west wind blowing, the archery and the crossing of the chasm will determine the final outcome. I will wait for you there.'

They took down the bows and arrow quivers from the racks, and left the horse in the care of the waiting grooms as they hurried to join Taita at the edge of the cliff.

'We lost time at the javelin butts,' Nefer told him grimly, as he strung the great war bow, one end anchored on the ground between his feet as he exerted all his strength and weight on the other end to flex the stock.

'Krus was too eager,' Taita said, 'and so were you. But there is no profit in looking back. Look ahead!' He pointed across the deep void to where the targets were suspended on a light bamboo scaffolding.

As at the javelin butts, there were five targets. They were inflated pigs' bladders, each suspended on the crosspiece of the scaffold by a length of flax twine. They were well separated so that an arrow intended for one would not strike another by chance. The twine that held them was two cubits long, so that they had freedom of movement. Light as air they danced on the west wind, bobbing and ducking unpredictably.

The great open void between them made it almost impossible to judge the range accurately, and the west wind swirled and eddied along the cliffs. The force and direction of the wind that they felt on this side of the chasm would be different from that on the far bank. However, it would affect the arrows almost as much as the targets.

'What is the range, Old Father?' Nefer asked, as he chose a long arrow from the quiver. Earlier that morning Taita had paced out one side of a right-angled triangle along this lip of the chasm. Then he had gauged the angle subtended by the targets on the far side with a weird arrangement of pegs and strings on a board. He had used these measurements, in a manner that was unfathomable to Nefer, to calculate the range across the chasm.

'One hundred and twenty-seven cubits,' Taita told him now. Nefer added this information to his own calculations of wind speed and direction, as he took his stance on the crumbling edge of the cliff. Meren stepped up beside him with the lighter cavalry bow in his hand.

'In the name of Horus and the goddess,' Nefer prayed, 'let us begin!' They shot at the same time.

Nefer's arrow dropped over the crosspiece of the scaffold, too long and high. Meren's arrow rose at a steeper angle aimed wide into the wind. As it slowed at the top of its trajectory the wind took hold of it, and it veered to the left, almost at the limit of its range it dropped towards the dangling bobbing line of pigs' bladders. It struck the middle target cleanly and they heard the pop as it burst, and disappeared like a stroke of magic.

A joyous shout went up from the watchers, and the umpire called the hit in a loud voice, but Meren muttered as he nocked another arrow, 'That was a fluke.'

'I'll take any more flukes that you have in your quiver,' Nefer told him, '*Bak-her*, brother, *Bak-her*.'

They drew and fired again, this time Meren's arrow fell short, rattling against the rocks of the cliff. Nefer missed the bladder on the right-hand end by half a cubit, and cursed Seth for the wind he had sent.

Unlike the javelins, the rules of the Red Road placed no limit on the number of arrows they were allowed. The only stipulation was that they must carry them all on the chariot from the start, so it was a trade-off between weight and numbers. They had each brought fifty missiles, but one of Nefer's long arrows weighed half again as much as one of Meren's.

They shot and missed, and shot again and missed again.

Taita had watched the wind and the flight of each arrow. He had gathered all his powers around him to feel the strength and impetus of the treacherous wind. He could almost see it, the flow and the strength of it, like the currents in a clear stream of water.

'Hold the same point of aim!' he ordered Nefer. 'But wait for my command.'

Nefer drew to full strength and though every muscle in his right arm quivered with the strain he held it.

Taita read the wind, became part of it, felt it in the depths of his being. 'Now!' he whispered, and the arrow leaped out high over the void and wavered on the capricious airs. Then like a towering falcon it seemed to gather itself and stoop to the target. The bladder popped as it struck, and the crowd howled.

'The next one!' Taita ordered, and Nefer drew, held his aim high and to the right of the second bladder.

'Now!' Taita whispered. The old man seemed to control the flight of the arrow by the force of his mind. At the very last instant before it struck the west wind tried spitefully to turn it aside, but it held the line and the bladder burst with a sharp crack.

'The next one. Draw!' whispered Taita. 'Hold!' and a heartbeat later, 'Now!' This time the arrow almost touched the bladder, but at the last moment the ball bounced aside.

Nefer shot again on Taita's command and he missed by a full arrow length, high and left. The strain of working the great bow was too much, his right arm ached and his muscles cramped and jumped involuntarily.

'Rest!' Taita ordered. 'Take the Periapt of Lostris in your right hand, and rest.'

Nefer laid aside the bow and stood with his head bowed in an attitude of prayer, with the golden amulet in his right hand. He felt the strength begin to flow back into his bow arm. Meren was still trying with the smaller bow, but the pain of his cracked ribs almost doubled him over and the sweat of agony ran down his pale face.

At that moment the crowd along the top of the cliff stirred and turned and looked back up the terrace. Someone shouted, 'They come!' and the cry was taken up, until the shouting was deafening.

Nefer lifted his head and saw the first chariot come whirling over the skyline. It was close enough for him to recognize Daimios at the reins, his golden hair streaming back on the wind. Behind him came the other chariots of the pursuers strung out in a line. Faintly he heard the drivers shouting to the horses and the rumble of the wheels over the rough ground.

'Do not look at them,' Taita ordered him. 'Do not think about them. Think only of the target.'

Nefer turned his back on the approaching line of vehicles and lifted the bow.

'Draw and hold!' Taita said. The wind spurted and dropped. 'Now!' The arrow sped unerringly across the chasm and the fourth bladder burst.

Nefer slid another arrow from the quiver, then he paused with the shaft in his hand and felt despair in his heart. A dust-devil came spinning down out of the desert on to the line of targets. The dun-coloured curtains of dust and sand and debris obscured the range, and the single remaining bladder disappeared in its depths.

High on the hill behind them the pursuing charioteers shouted with triumph, and Nefer heard Daimios' voice above the roar of the whirlwind, 'Now you must stand and fight me, Nefer Seti.'

'One more target before you are clear,' Socco, the umpire, shouted sternly. 'Stand your ground.'

'There is no target,' Nefer protested.

'The will of the Nameless God,' Socco told him. 'You must submit to it.'

'There!' shouted Taita. 'There is the manifest will of a greater and more powerful goddess.' He pointed across the deep ravine at the impenetrable cloud of yellow dust.

Like a cork floating up from the depths of a turbid lake, the bladder with its broken string trailing under it rose to the top of the dustcloud, and skittered in the heated air.

'Now, in the name of the goddess Lostris!' Taita urged Nefer. 'She is the only one who can help you now.'

'In the name of the goddess!' Nefer shouted, threw up the great bow and shot at the tiny balloon in the wild embrace of the storm. Up and up climbed the arrow, and it seemed that it must miss to the left, but abruptly the bladder ducked and dived to meet it. The razor-sharp flint arrowhead slashed it open, it burst and whipped away like a rag on the wind.

'You are through and clear!' Socco released them with a shout. Nefer dropped the bow and ran to the chariot. Meren ran after him, favouring his injured ribs, and the crowd urged them on as Dov and Krus jumped away together. Behind them the cries of the pursuit were frustrated and angry, but Nefer did not look back.

A thousand paces ahead the suspension bridge spanned the gorge from cliff to cliff, with the terrible drop below, but before they reached it they must run the fire.

Shabako was the umpire of the bridge crossing. On horseback, he had galloped across from his post at the javelin butts as soon as Nefer and Meren had cleared them. Now he had taken his next station at the bridge. This was the most crucial stage of the entire Red Road.

The novices had a choice here. They could decline to breach the wall of fire to reach the bridge. Instead they might take the long route and cross further down the valley where the cliffs fell gently away. However, this added almost two leagues to the course.

Shabako stood at the head of the bridge and watched Nefer's chariot leave the archery butt and, with the pursuit close behind, come racing towards him along the lip of the precipice.

Shabako's sympathies were with his pharaoh. However, his loyalty to the Red God was even more compelling. Though he longed with all his heart to see Nefer succeed, he dared not show him favour. That would go against his sacred oath, and place his immortal soul in peril.

He considered the fence. Along the length of it his men crouched with burning torches. The fence was twice the height of a man and made of bundles of dried grass that would burn like tinder on this hot, dry wind. The fence was built in a semi-circle with each end anchored on the edge of the cliff. It held the head of the bridge in its arms. There was no way round it. To reach the bridgehead the novices must break through it.

Reluctantly Shabako shouted the order to set the fire. The torchbearers ran down its length, dragging the flames along the bottom of the fence. They caught instantly, rising in a towering wall of awful crimson flame and dark smoke.

Nefer saw the wall of flame rise ahead of them, and though he had anticipated it, still his spirits quailed and he feared for the horses, for they had already endured so much. He watched Krus' ears and saw them switching back and forth with alarm as he smelt the smoke and watched the flames leap and tumble on the wind.

Not far behind them he heard Daimios' derisive jeers: 'Take the long road, Nefer Seti. The fire is too hot for your tender skin.'

Nefer ignored him and studied the wall of fire as they bore down on it. There was no weak place that he could see, but the nearest end had been lit first and the flames burned faster and more furiously. As he watched, a heavy bundle of the dried grass fell out of the wall and left a narrow gap through which he could make out the wavering heat-obscured outline of the bridgehead beyond.

He steered for the gap and told Meren beside him, 'Cover your head!' They wound headcloths over their heads and splashed water from the skin over themselves, drenching their head clothes and *chitons*.

'Have the blindfolds ready,' Nefer told Meren.

They were so close now that they felt the heat blazing out to meet them, and Krus broke step and began to balk at the barrier of leaping flame that confronted him.

'Mount up!' Nefer ordered, and still at the gallop they ran out along the shaft between the horses and swung up on to their backs, riding astride. Nefer stretched out along Krus' neck and spoke to him calmly. 'It's all right, my darling. You know the blindfold. You know I will not hurt you. Trust me, Krus! Trust me!' And he covered his eyes with the thick woollen cloth, and steered him with his knees at the narrow gap in the burning wall. The heat poured over them in a wave. Their wet clothing steamed and Nefer felt the skin on the back of his hands blistering. The tips of Krus' mane blackened and crisped. But both horses ran on strongly.

They struck the wall of blazing grass, and it exploded around them. Nefer felt his eyes frying in his head and he closed them tightly and urged Krus on. They burst out of the far side, trailing sparks and fire.

Nefer looked back under his arm and saw Daimios aiming his chariot at the gap they had broached in the burning wall. Daimios horses were not blindfolded, and they saw the flames and shied off the line and began to rear and plunge, fighting to avoid the horror they saw ahead of them.

'Daimios' horses have refused!' Nefer shouted across at Meren on Dov's back. 'We have a chance now.'

They charged up to the bridgehead, reined the horses down and halted them just short.

'Keep them blindfolded!' Nefer ordered. 'Don't let them see the drop.'

The catwalk of the bridge had been built deliberately too narrow for a chariot to drive across, and it would not carry the weight. They would have to break the vehicle down and carry it across piecemeal. While Meren unbuckled the harness and hobbled the horses, Nefer seized the mallet and knocked the bronze retaining pins out of the hubs. Then he pulled off the wheels. He picked up one of them and Meren took the other. They ran to the head of the bridge.

The bridge swung gently and undulated to the impulse of the wind. It was not wide enough for the two of them to cross shoulder to shoulder. Nefer did not hesitate but ran out on to the narrow way, and Meren followed close behind him. The bridge moved under their feet like the deck of a ship at sea, but they balanced the motion and fixed their eyes on the far bank, never looked down at the terrible void beneath them and the gut of the gorge lined with jagged rock.

They reached the far side, dropped the wheels and ran back. At the burning fence, the flames were still too high and fierce to let Daimios pass, though they saw him flogging his team and screaming abuse at them.

They discarded the waterskin, the last of the arrows and every other piece of redundant equipment, and picked up the chassis of the chariot between them. They carried it out on to the bridge, where the wind caught their hair braids on the ends of the long staffs and whipped them jubilantly. Each careful step they took seemed to take a lifetime, but at last they reached the far side, dropped the chassis and ran back. Nefer picked up the shaft and balanced its weight across his shoulders. Meren carried the harness and the swords and they crossed again. Now only the horses remained to bring over.

When they started back they saw that the flames were dying, but where the fence had collapsed it had formed a thick bed of ash that still glowed with oven-like heat. Rastafa, one of the pursuers, forced his horses into it with whip and threatening shouts, but within a few paces the hide was burned from their legs and the raw red flesh showed through. They turned back despite their driver, screaming and kicking at the pain.

Nefer led Meren back at a run with the bridge swaying under them. They reached the horses. Dov and Krus stood patiently, hobbled and blindfolded. They unbuckled the knee hobbles.

'Take Dov across first,' Nefer ordered. 'She is the steady one.'

While Nefer waited on the near side, with his arm around Krus' neck, Meren led Dov out on to the catwalk of the bridge. She felt it move under her, lifted her head and snorted with alarm. Meren talked softly to her. Gingerly she took another pace and stopped again.

'Don't rush her,' Nefer called. 'Let her set her own pace.' A step at a time Dov moved out on to the high bridge. When she reached the middle she froze, and stood with all four legs splayed and trembling. Meren stroked her forehead and whispered to her and she went on. She reached the far side, stepped off the catwalk, felt the solid earth under her hoofs, whinnied and shook her head with relief.

Still blocked by the burning barrier Daimios shouted, 'They have got one of their team across. We have to stop them now. Rastafa, give me your horses. They are crippled already. I will ride them through, even if it kills them.'

Nefer glanced back and saw Daimios ride into the glowing bed of ash. It reached as high as his mount's knees, and the maimed animal stumbled and almost fell but Daimios drove it on in a torrent of sparks and the stench of burning hair and flesh. The terribly injured creature carried him through then collapsed as soon as it reached open ground. Daimios jumped from its back, drew his sword and rushed towards Nefer.

Nefer drew his own sword, and called to Meren across the chasm, 'Come back and take Krus over. I will hold this bastard in play.' He stepped forward to meet Daimios as he charged in. He met his cut high in the natural line, and the blades jarred and scraped their full length. Daimios reversed and cut again at his head. Nefer caught the stroke, then riposted, forcing him to jump back.

Nefer had one moment to glance back and saw that Meren was already leading Krus out on to the swaying catwalk. Krus felt it move under his hoofs, tossed his head and tried to back away.

'Come away, Krus!' Nefer shouted at him sternly, and at the sound of his voice the colt steadied and stepped gingerly on to the planking.

Daimios came in again and Nefer had to concentrate everything on him. He aimed a rapid series of thrusts at Nefer's throat and chest and when Nefer blocked and parried he reversed and cut low at his ankles. Nefer jumped over the glittering circle of the blade and went for his exposed shoulder. He touched him and saw the blood spring brightly on the tanned and oiled muscles.

But Daimios seemed not to feel the shallow wound. He came on as strongly as before. They exchanged parry for thrust and block for cut, then Daimios stepped back and circled to the left, trying to move in behind him and cut him off from the bridgehead, but Nefer went at him again and forced him to give ground.

A moment's respite and Nefer saw that the flames had died down, the grass fence burned almost entirely away. The other chasers had left their chariots and were jumping over the bed of glowing ash and running to join the fight.

'Form a ring around him, and cut him down!' Daimios shouted to them as they ran up.

Nefer glanced back and saw that Meren had led Krus far out on the catwalk. The colt was trembling and sweating at the sensation of the moving deck under his hoofs, but he could not see the terrible aching void below him.

Just then the other chasers ran up, brandishing their blades and jeering at Nefer: 'Now, we will ram your hair braid up your right royal arse.'

Nefer retreated quickly on to the head of the bridge. Now they could come at him only one at a time, and the jeers died away. They paused in a group at the head of the catwalk.

'He has nicked me,' said Daimios. 'Do you go after him, Rastafa, while I bind it up.' With his teeth he tore a strip off the hem of his tunic, and tied it over the shallow flesh wound. While he was doing this Rastafa ran out on to the bridge. He was bearded and swarthy with a dark and angry gaze, a big man but quick as a ferret. He balanced easily on the moving deck and thrust at Nefer's throat, coming on so strongly that Nefer had to fall back again.

Krus heard the clash of blades and the shouting close behind him and he reared up in protest. The bridge jumped and wobbled under him, and for a terrible moment it seemed that the colt might lose his balance and go over the side, but by some miraculous chance he came down on all four legs, and stood quivering on the wildly swinging catwalk.

It was Rastafa who stumbled and teetered on the edge. He windmilled his arms as he fought to regain his balance. Nefer took one quick step towards him and stabbed him under his lifted arm. The bronze blade slipped in between the ribs and went in deeply. Rastafa looked at him with mild surprise, and said, 'It hurts. In the name of Seth, it hurts!'

Nefer jerked the blade out and Rastafa's heart-blood fountained after it. Spouting crimson, he toppled backwards, and went spinning into the abyss, arms and legs spread like the spokes of a wheel. His voice was a wild screech, fading in volume as he fell away, and the sound was cut off abruptly as his armour clattered on the rocks in the gut of the gorge.

His comrades hesitated at the bridgehead, appalled by the horror of that death plunge, suddenly reluctant to step out on to the narrow way.

Nefer seized that moment to turn back and stroke Krus' trembling haunches, 'Steady, Krus. I am here, my darling. Walk on!' Krus calmed to his voice, and then, as the wild gyrations of the bridge eased, he took a step forward and another.

'Walk on, Krus, walk on.'

They were almost halfway across when Meren shouted a warning: 'Behind you, brother!'

Nefer whirled around just in time to meet another opponent. Nefer knew him by reputation. He was a Libyan slave, and was fighting for his freedom. Fearlessly, he ran down the narrow deck, straight at Nefer. He used the full impetus of his charge and Nefer was only just able to turn aside that first stroke. They locked blades and came chest to chest, clamping each other in a murderous embrace with their free arms. They heaved and wrestled, shifting and shoving for the advantage.

Krus heard the struggle behind him and it spurred him on. He lunged forward again, covering another few paces towards the safety of the far bank.

Nefer was face to face with his man. His teeth were black and jagged and his breath stank like rotten fish. He tried to sink those filthy fangs into Nefer's face, snapping at him like a dog, but Nefer pulled back then butted with his forehead, slamming the peak of his leather helmet into the bridge of the man's nose. He felt the bone and gristle break, and the man released his grip and reeled back. He lost his footing and grabbed the side rope of the bridge to steady himself, hanging on desperately, his back arched out over the drop. Nefer chopped off his grasping fingers, and the rope slipped from the bloody severed stubs. He went over backwards, screaming and twisting in the air. He seemed to fall for a long time before he struck the rocks far below with a meaty thump.

There were three men on the catwalk behind him, led by Daimios. He had bound up his wound, and seemed unhurt. But he had seen what had happened to his two comrades and now he was more wary. Nefer engaged him, keeping him off a full blade's length, giving him ground only as Krus moved forward slowly and hesitantly towards the far bank.

Suddenly Meren shouted triumphantly, 'We are across, Nefer.' And he heard Krus' hoofs clatter on the rock bank. 'Krus has come over.'

Nefer could not look round for Daimios blade flashed and gleamed before his eyes, but he shouted, 'Cut down the bridge, Meren, cut away the mainstays, and let her fall.'

Daimios heard the command and jumped back with alarm. He glanced over his shoulder and saw how far he had come out on to the catwalk, how far it was back to the other bank.

Meren stood over the two thick ropes that carried the full weight of the catwalk. He hacked at one, and his first stroke cut halfway through, the strands parted with a sharp popping sound and began to unravel like mating serpents.

Pale horror washed over Daimios' sweaty face and he turned and fled, his comrades with him, back along the narrow way. Nefer whirled and ran towards where Meren stood over the ropes. He reached the end of the bridge and jumped to safety. Immediately he attacked the other mainstay, chopping at it with full overhead blows. One of the stays parted and the entire bridge shivered then tilted violently to one side. Daimios flung himself forward and dragged himself on to firm ground just as the second stay gave way, and the bridge sagged and fell into the abyss.

Daimios recovered and stood on the edge of the precipice, glaring at them across the void. Nefer sheathed his sword and gave him a taunting wave. 'You have a long ride ahead of you.'

Then he ran to help Meren reassemble the chariot. They had practised this a dozen times under Taita's watchful eye. While Meren lifted one side of the chassis Nefer eased the wheels on to the hubs and drove the bronze locking pins home with the mallet. Then they lifted the shaft and fastened it to the ringbolt in the footplate.

Nefer wasted a few seconds to look back across the gorge. He saw that Daimios and the surviving chasers were already mounting their chariots, and through the last wisps of smoke from the smouldering grass fence, he saw them speed away in a line ahead, following the track along the edge of the gorge that would lead them eventually to where the cliffs flattened out, so that they would be able to bring their vehicles and horses across, and renew the pursuit.

'We have won enough time.' Meren tried to sound confident, but the effort of bringing the nervous horses across the bridge had taxed him severely, and he pressed a hand to his injured side.

Nefer feared for him. 'Perhaps, but that will depend on the Red God,' he said and touched the Periapt of Lostris at his throat.

They buckled the horses into the harness and hitched them to the long shaft. Then they scrambled up on to the footplate and started them along the line of marker flags. They could push the horses to the utmost on this stretch, for at the end of it waited Khama of Taurine and Drossa of Indus. The horses might have a long rest indeed while their drivers went into the ring with the two most notorious swordsmen in Aartla's troupe.

Nefer forced the pace, and the marker flags sped by in quick, regular succession. They crested the final rise and saw ahead of them, at the far end of the long, narrow valley, the city of Gallala with her gates standing wide open to welcome them.

But at the head of the valley, between them and the city, gathered in a shallow basin of hills, was a large crowd of many hundreds of persons. It seemed that every last citizen had come out from the city to watch the trial by swords.

They rode down fast, and heard the din of the crowd rise like the sound of storm surf to greet them.

There was a lane through the crowds demarcated by wooden railings that led them to the two rings of white stones in the centre. As they jumped down and the grooms ran forward to hold the horses, Nefer embraced Meren.

'You are sore hurt, brother,' he whispered to him. 'There is no shame in that, for it was a wound received with honour, but it will hamper you. You must not try to confront Drossa, and trade him blow for blow. He is fast and strong, and he wears full armour. Run from him and keep running until I can come to your aid.'

They parted then, each to the ring allotted to them by the umpires and Nefer halted at the line of white-painted stones, and looked at the warrior in the centre.

Khama of Taurine wore full armour, helm, breastplate and greaves. If Nefer and Meren had wanted the same protection they would have had to carry it in the chariot from the start, but the weight of the two suits would have drained even Krus' strength.

From the edge of the ring of stones Nefer studied his man. Khama's helmet was a hideous mask with spread wings above the ears, and the nosepiece was an eagle's beak. The eyes that glittered behind the sockets were inhuman and implacable. His chest was protected by a bronze cuirass. His gauntlets were covered with golden fish scales. He carried a small circular shield on his left shoulder.

'Throat, wrist, armpit, ankles and eyes,' Taita had instructed Nefer. 'All else is covered.'

Nefer lifted the Periapt of Lostris over his head and wound the long golden chain around his left wrist. Then he held the tiny golden figure to his lips and kissed it. He stepped over the white stones and went forward to meet Khama of Taurine.

They circled once to the right, then back, and suddenly Khama burst upon him with a blazing series of thrusts and cuts that were so rapid as almost to cheat the eye. Carrying that weight of armour, Nefer had not expected him to be so fast. He had to exert all of his skill and strength to hold him off, and still he received a cut through his leather body armour that scored his ribs. He felt the hot blood trickle down his flank as they disengaged and circled again.

The crowd was shouting and roaring like a storm sea all around them, but in the sudden quiet as they disengaged he heard a cry of pain from the other ring and he recognized Meren's voice. Meren had taken a hit, and by the sound of it a grievous one. He needed Nefer's help, probably his life depended upon it. But Nefer's own life was in terrible jeopardy, for he had never faced an opponent such as this Khama before.

Even Taita had not been able to divine any weakness in him, but as they came together again in the whirl and clangour of metal on metal, Nefer noticed a tiny flaw. When Khama made a low underhand cut, he opened his right side for an instant and thrust his head forward, an awkward gesture out of keeping with his otherwise fluid and graceful style.

Nefer knew that he could not hold out much longer. Khama was simply too skilful and powerful for him.

'Everything on one throw of the dice.' He took the gamble, and offered his right hip unguarded and like a striking adder Khama went for it with the low cut, his front opened and his head thrust forward. Prepared for it, Nefer swayed his hip out of the shot and the blade slit the hem of his *chiton* without drawing blood.

The golden Periapt of Lostris twinkled as he spun it on the end of its chain then Nefer whipped it in like a slingshot, using the chain to speed the throw so it became a darting beam of light. It flashed into the eye socket of Khama's helmet and the sharp metal edge sliced deeply through his eyeball.

Khama reeled back with a mixture of eye jelly and blood pouring down his golden mask. He was blinded and disorientated with pain, trying to wrench off his helmet to reach his burst eyeball. As the rim of his helmet lifted and exposed his throat, Nefer drove his point in a thumb's width above the lump of his Adam's apple. The point angled up into the back of his brain, and Khama flung his arms wide and went down, dead before his armour clanged on the sun-baked earth.

Nefer placed his cleated sandal on his throat and had to wrench with all his strength to draw the point of his sword free from where it was trapped between the metal of the helmet and the bone of his skull.

Nefer left the corpse lying, and wrapping the chain of the amulet around his wrist again, ran from the ring. He tried to reach the other ring where he knew Meren was in mortal danger, but the crowds impeded him. He swung his sword to clear the way and the spectators fled screaming ahead of him. He broke through the press and saw that in the second ring Meren had lost his weapon and was bleeding profusely from a terrible gash in his right side, and a cut that had half severed his ear. It dangled down his cheek on a thread of flesh. Somehow he was managing to stay out of Drossa's reach, backing frantically away from him.

Drossa was laughing, bellowing like a bull with the joy of killing, the sound echoing eerily within the confines of his crested war-helmet. He was goading Meren into a position for the killing stroke, taking his time, enjoying it.

Drossa's back was turned to Nefer. Nefer sprang at him and aimed a thrust through the lacing of his cuirass. With the instincts of a wild animal, Drossa sensed the danger and spun to face him, Nefer's thrust struck the metal breastplate and glanced aside and Drossa aimed a full-blooded cut at his head. Nefer ducked and recoiled, and they circled each other.

Meren saw his chance and stooped to pick up the sword he had dropped, but Drossa leaped at him. Meren was so weak that he stumbled backwards and fell. Drossa kicked the fallen sword out of the ring and placed his foot between Meren's shoulders and pinned him down.

'Behold, mighty Pharaoh, feared by all the world, I have your bum-boy in my power.' He feigned the stroke of a headsman, but stopped his blade against the back of Meren's neck. 'Shall I give you his head? A gift fit for a king.'

Nefer felt red blind anger sweep over him, and he rushed at Drossa to drive him off Meren's prostrate form. He felt the sting of the blade across his thigh, which sobered him. He jumped back, and saw by Drossa's eyes in the helmet slits that he was toying with him, drawing the last drop of sadistic pleasure from the encounter. Drossa was an entertainer, and the crowd were loving his performance. They howled their approval.

Suddenly Meren reached up and grasped Drossa's ankle with both bloody hands, and tried to trip him. Drossa stumbled, swore and kicked his foot free, but for an instant he was off-balance and Nefer seized the opportunity and rushed in. He aimed for the throat, into the gap between the chinpiece of the helmet and the top of the breastplate. Drossa twisted away and the point of Nefer's sword rang on metal.

Nefer had missed his chance for a kill, but he had driven Drossa off his victim, and Meren scrambled to his feet and staggered behind Nefer, using him as a protective shield.

They circled again, and Nefer felt the first cold draught of despair lift the hairs on his forearms. He knew he could not expect a man like Drossa to give him another chance. In despair he tried again with the Periapt, swinging it on the length of gold chain and aiming for the eye slits in Drossa's helmet. Drossa dropped his chin and the golden charm glanced off the brow of his helm. If it had not been upon the chain Nefer would have lost it, but he recovered it and let the chain wind itself around his left wrist again.

'That is no weapon but a child's toy.' Drossa laughed scornfully.

They circled and feinted, Drossa moving easily, but Nefer was hampered by his need to guard Meren. He could not launch an attack, and leave Meren unprotected.

Drossa was working the two of them like a sheepdog with a flock of lambs, pushing them back against the line of white stones. He wanted to make a spectacular kill to please the crowd, and enhance his own reputation.

'The chasers!' someone in the crowd yelled, and every head swung and lifted to the crest of the rise at the head of the long valley.

Daimios' chariot raced over the skyline. Desperate to make up for his humiliation at the bridgehead, he was riding hard and outstripped the rest of his troop. He came tearing down towards them at the top of his speed.

'You belong to me, mighty Egypt!' Drossa mocked Nefer. 'I will not let an upstart like Daimios take your hair braid from me.'

He moved in menacingly, and Nefer could see the icy determination in the pale eyes that watched him through the helmet slits.

Nefer whispered to Meren, 'If I fall, save yourself. Step out of the ring.'

'No, Pharaoh, I will ride with you as your lance-bearer on the road to paradise,' Meren said softly, and his strength failed him. His legs gave way under him, and bleeding he sagged to earth. Drossa seized the moment, and came down upon Nefer like an avalanche. His sword clanged and rang on Nefer's desperate guard like a coppersmith's hammer on the anvil.

Each blow jarred and numbed Nefer's right arm to the shoulder, and he knew he could not last out much longer. Still he watched Drossa's eyes to read each blow, and saw them narrow and gleam as he gathered himself for the killing stroke.

It came from on high, like a thunderbolt from the sky and all Nefer could do was lift his own blade above his head to meet it. He knew he could not turn or stop it with one hand, it was too powerful. So he braced his sword hand, gripping the right wrist with his left hand, the hand that held the golden Periapt.

The two swords came together with force that bronze could not resist. Both blades snapped cleanly and spun away, glittering out of the circle of white stones.

At a stroke they were both disarmed, and for an instant they stared at each other in astonishment. Nefer recovered first and hurled the hilt of the sword at Drossa's head. Instinctively Drossa blinked and ducked. Nefer charged him and they came chest to chest.

Like a pair of temple dancers they whirled together, first one way then back again, trying to throw each other. Irresistibly Drossa worked his arms under Nefer's armpits and locked his armoured fists between his shoulder-blades. With wristlets of silver and gauntlets of gold he started to grind Nefer against his bronze cuirass. Nefer had no response as he was lifted off his feet. He had no weapon to defend himself, except the Periapt of Lostris.

With the last of his strength he managed to throw a loop of the gold chain over Drossa's helmet. He took a turn around each of his own wrists and pulled the chain downwards until suddenly it found the gap below the rim of the helmet and closed around Drossa's neck. Nefer strained and sawed the ends of the chain, and felt the golden links biting deeply in living flesh.

Drossa gasped, released his grip and reached up with both hands to try to break free. He seized Nefer's wrists and tried to pull them away from his throat, but this increased the cutting power of the links. Staring into the slits of the helmet, Nefer saw Drossa's eyes start from their sockets and swell with blood. He took another turn around his right wrist and sawed the chain back and forth. Drossa made a gargling sound and a vein popped in one of his eyes. It bulged crimson as a ripe berry from the socket, and still clutching Nefer's wrists Drossa sank to his knees. Nefer stood over him and rolled his wrists, tightening the chain until suddenly he felt it cut through something gristly and Drossa's breath burst explosively from his severed windpipe. Nefer took another wrap of the chain and pulled again, feeling it cut its way down to bone. Blood erupted in thick gouts from under the rim of the helmet, and Nefer gathered himself and exerted all his remaining strength. The chain found the joint between two vertebrae in Drossa's neck and cut through. Drossa's head sprang from his shoulders and, still clad in the heavy helmet, rolled across the ring.

As Nefer staggered backwards he heard the umpire shout, 'You are free and clear,' and he slipped the bloody golden chain back over his head. As he did so he looked over the heads of the maddened crowd, back up the slope of the hill. Daimios' chariot was already halfway down, and coming straight towards him at full gallop.

Nefer stooped over Meren. 'Can you stand?' he asked, but when Meren made the effort his legs collapsed under him and he sprawled on the trampled earth. Nefer pulled him up by one arm then swung the arm over the back of his neck. Taking the weight across his shoulders, he raised Meren to his feet, grabbed him behind the knees and lifted his inert body off the ground, his head dangling down his back and his legs down his front.

Meren was a heavy man, and Nefer was almost exhausted, near the limit of his strength. He staggered with him to the waiting chariot and dropped him in a heap on the floorboards. For a moment he leaned panting against the near wheel, and looked back.

Daimios had reached the level ground at the bottom of the slope, and was less than four hundred paces away, coming on swiftly, so close that Nefer could see the triumphant expression on his face. Daimios leaned forward and cracked the long black lash over the backs of his team and the horses seemed to spring forward, coming on even faster. The chariots of the other chasers were following him down the slope, six of them all told. If he had any thought of standing to fight them, Nefer put it out of his mind at once. In his present state he could not even take on Daimios in a straight fight. He had to run.

Nefer took two turns of the grab rope around Meren's body, worked them up under his armpits and clinched the knot, strapping him to the floorboards. Then he dragged himself up on to the footplate and stood straddling Meren's body.

'Turn them loose!' he called to the grooms, who held the horses' heads, and they released them and jumped out of the way.

'Come away, Dov! Come away, Krus!' he called to them, and snapped the reins along their gleaming backs. They sprang forward together and the crowds scattered ahead of them. He pointed their heads down the valley towards the open gates of the city, and let them run.

Between his feet Meren groaned involuntarily as the chariot jolted and lurched, and Nefer tried to steer to miss the patches of rough ground. Behind him he heard the crack of the lash, he glanced back and saw Daimios bearing down on them. He was flogging on his team and shouting at them angrily, but Dov and Krus were holding them off despite Daimios' cruel work with the whip. Nefer looked ahead and judged the distance they still had to run.

It was less than half a league to the gates of Gallala. Already he could make out the wreaths of palm fronds that adorned the walls and decorated the red stone columns of the entrance.

At that moment he paid the price for his inattention. His off-wheel hit an outcrop of rock at the edge of the track, and the vehicle bounced high and slewed wildly under him. It almost capsized, but as he fought for control Krus leaned into the traces and helped him to pull it straight.

Now when Nefer looked back he saw that the mistake had cost them dear, for Daimios had gained a hundred paces on them. He was within javelin range, and Nefer saw him reach for the missiles in the bin at his side and wind the thong on to his wrist.

Nefer had no reply to him. He and used all his darts at the first stage. He had dropped his bow at the chasm, and his last sword had snapped in the bout with Drossa. He did not even have his whip. His only defence was speed.

He called to his horses, 'Come, Dov! Come away, Krus!' And their ears flicked back as they heard him call their names and their hoofs drummed on the hard earth and the wheel hubs squealed, for even Taita's black oil was running dry.

Then there was the sound of other hoofs, blending with those of Nefer's team, and this time when he looked back Daimios was closer still, his horses whipped and galled until their flanks and backs were bloody. Daimios had a javelin poised and now he hurled it. Nefer watched the dart leave his hand, and fly in like a poisonous insect. He flinched instinctively, as it slammed into the floorboards beside his right foot. It stood out quivering.

'Come away, my darlings.' His voice took on a strident note, and the horses heard it. 'Give me all you've got!' Krus found a little more in his great heart, and swept Dov along with him. They began to pull away from Daimios' scourged and bleeding pair.

'Pull, you swine!' Daimios screamed. 'Pull, or I'll take the hide off your backs.' And as his long lash sang, they raced together as though an invisible rope linked the two vehicles.

Daimios seized another javelin and wrapped the thong. As he swung his arm back for the throw, Nefer judged his moment skilfully and flicked the reins. With the javelin in the air, Dov leaned into Krus' shoulder and they swerved slightly, just enough for the dart to fly past Nefer's shoulder. But the turn had cost ground, and Daimios snatched his last javelin from the bin and wrapped the thong around his wrist. He was close now, very close.

Nefer watched him with a feeling of desperation, gathering his team with a firm rein so they could anticipate his command. The moment Daimios swivelled his right shoulder forward in the throw, Nefer turned his team back the other way, jinking their run at full gallop. But the javelin did not leave Daimios' hand: he had feinted. He raised the javelin again into the ready position, levelled and ready to throw.

Nefer was forced to swing back or leave the track and tear into the rough ground and scattered boulders. He changed the angle and this time Daimios aimed not at Nefer but at Dov, whose flank had been exposed by the turn.

The dart took her high in the shoulder. It cut through hide and bunched muscle, but then struck the bone and did not penetrate to her vitals. It was not a mortal blow, but a crippling one, for the javelin head was barbed and it dangled down her flank, hampering each stride she took.

She tried, she tried with all her heart, but she could no longer keep pace with Krus, and the blood ran back along her flank and splattered on Nefer's legs. He could feel the chariot slowing under him, and though he called to Dov, the javelin slapped against her flank with each stride she took, and tangled in her forelegs.

Daimios sped forward and from the corner of his eye Nefer saw the heads of his racing horses draw level with his near wheel, and Daimios' voice hoarse with effort and triumph sounded almost in his ear.

'It is over, Nefer Seti. I have you now.'

Nefer turned his head and looked across at him. Daimios' lips were drawn back in a horrible rictus, like that of a corpse who had died of the lock-jaw. He had thrown his last javelin, and had discarded his whip, but he had drawn his sword.

How far to run to the gates? Nefer thought. Less than five hundred paces. So close, so very close! But still too far.

Instinctively he looked to the roof of the temple. It was lined with tiny human figures, and among them, just where he expected to see it, he picked out the scarlet of Mintaka's tunic, and saw that she was waving a green branch over her head, her long dark hair tossing like a pennant on the north wind.

A prize beyond all others, he thought, and his hand fell upon Daimios' javelin that was pegged into the floorboard beside his foot. The head was buried deeply into the woodwork, but he braced himself. Twisting and jerking, he pulled it free.

He did not have a throwing thong, but he held it like a spear, and looked across at his adversary. Daimios' eyes narrowed as he saw the weapon in Nefer's hand and he took the guard position with the sword. He drew up inexorably alongside Nefer and lunged. Nefer turned the blow with the stock of the javelin. The two vehicles swerved apart then came back together and struck so hard that Nefer was almost thrown over the side and had to clutch wildly at the reins to steady himself.

Daimios swung a cut at the long staff on which flew Nefer's hair braid, but did not sever the hard bamboo. Nefer recovered his balance and thrust at Daimios with the javelin, driving him off. Now the two vehicles were running wheel to wheel, and hub to hub.

Nefer and Daimios were leaning across, hacking and stabbing at each other. The bronze blade slashed across Nefer's chest, and though he threw himself back against the reins it cut through the leather of his breastplate and he felt the sting of the razor edge. But he thrust the point of the javelin at Daimios' face, and forced him to swerve away.

Dov was labouring hard, the barbs of the javelin still fixed in her skin, and the shaft banging her legs at each stride.

Nefer heard the sound of many voices, soft at first and almost drowned in the drumming of hoofs and the squeal and rumble of the wheels, but the sound was growing louder at each stride. He looked up and through the running sweat that stung his eyes saw the gates directly ahead. The city walls and the rooftops were lined with the crowds. Through the hubbub of their cheering, he thought he heard the sound of Mintaka's voice. 'For me, my heart, do this for me!' It may have been but a figment of his own exhaustion, but it steeled him, and he called to the horses and gathered them with the reins. But Dov was staggering and failing.

Daimios came in again, and this time when Nefer thrust at him, he swung a full blow not at the man but at the javelin. His blade sheared through the shaft inches from Nefer's fist, leaving him with a useless stump. Nefer hurled it at Daimios' head but he ducked under it, and struck at Nefer again, forcing him to dodge to the far side of the footplate to avoid the bright blade.

Daimios took instant advantage, and forced his way ahead of Nefer. As he came past he reached across and seized the rod on which Nefer's hair braid danced and whipped in the wind. He tried to snap it off, but although it bent almost double it resisted his efforts. Still holding the staff in one hand Daimios reached up with the other hand for the thick dark hank of hair. It flicked and danced at his fingertips, but he was trying to keep a grip on the hilt of his sword at the same time, and he could not quite get a hold of the trophy. He dropped his sword, and this time caught hold of the braid and tried to tear it free, but the bamboo was resilient and tough, and the braid securely tied.

Krus and Daimios' off-side horse were galloping shoulder to shoulder. Daimios was completely absorbed with trying to wrest his trophy from the bamboo staff. He knew that Nefer was disarmed and no real danger, and he ignored the stone gates that loomed up ahead of them.

'Lean in!' Nefer shouted at Krus, 'Give him your shoulder!' Nefer sawed the reins. This was what they had trained for, all those months in the desert. With Taita driving the other team, Nefer had taught Krus to love this contest of strength, and now he bore in with his great right shoulder, tucking it in just behind the other horse, lifting him off-balance. The locked chariots veered to the right, and the gateway was coming up fast. The portals were columns of hewn red stone, and though the grit-laden winds of the centuries had polished and shaped them they were still massive and forbidding.

'Ride him off!' Nefer shouted to Krus, and encouraged him with a strong hand on the reins. Krus forced the other horse another yard over until he was headed straight for the solid red stone wall.

At the very last instant Daimios became aware of what was happening and, with a wild cry of alarm, he let go of the bamboo rod and tried to recover control of his racing chariot, but Krus dominated the other horse and drove him headlong towards the stone gateway.

Daimios realized that he could not stop the flying chariot and avoid the collision. He tried to jump from the hurtling cockpit, but he was too late. Both his horses ran full tilt into the stone column. It killed them instantly. Nefer heard their last terrified screams as they went in, the crash of the impact, the crackle of their breaking bones and the shattering and rending of timbers. One wheel was torn clean off and for a moment bounced along beside Nefer's vehicle. Daimios was hurled like one of his own javelins straight into the wall. He struck head first and his skull burst as though it were an overripe melon. His strong white teeth were embedded in the surface of the red stone, souvenirs to be prised out later by urchins, threaded on chains of gold and sold in the market-place.

Nefer steered Krus and Dov into the gateway, and though the hub of their near wheel scraped the red stone they tore through into the central avenue of the city, which was lined on both sides by the joyous crowds. They had strewn the paving with palm fronds and flowers and even with shawls and headcloths and other pieces of their own apparel.

Nefer's first concern was for Dov. He halted the horses, jumped down and ran to the wounded filly. The barbs of the javelin were buried deeply in her shoulder. He trusted only Taita to remove them, but he snapped off the shaft, so that it no longer dangled down her side. Then he climbed back to the footplate and took the reins again.

The crowds swarmed into the avenue and ran along beside the chariot as it moved on at a walking pace. They reached up to touch Nefer, using their headcloths to wipe up the blood that dribbled down his legs from his wounds. The blood of a god, a pharaoh and a Red Road warrior would transform the cloth into a sacred relic. Hysterically they screamed their praises.

'Pray for us, mighty Egypt. Pharaoh indeed!'

'Lead us, great Pharaoh. Let us share your glory.'

'Hail, divine brother of the Red God!'

'May you live a thousand and a thousand years, Nefer Seti, true Pharaoh!'

At the entrance to the forum the crowd was so dense that the city guards had to run ahead of the chariot and club them out of the way before Nefer could drive through into the forum.

In the centre of the forum on the raised stone dais Hilto and Shabako stood to welcome their new brother warriors.

Nefer halted the battered, dusty and blood-splattered chariot below the platform, and the two men came down and helped him lift Meren. Between them they carried him into the temple of Hathor where Taita waited to care for him. They laid Meren on the trestle Taita had prepared, and the old Magus began work on him immediately, first at tending to the deep sword thrust in his side. Merykara's tears fell upon Meren's broken and bleeding body, and anointed his wounds.

The warriors of the Red Road led Nefer back into the forum. Then Nefer went down the steps, lifted the two hair braids from the chariot, and carried them to the brazier that burned on its tripod in the centre of the raised stone dais. He knelt before the brazier, and declared, 'No enemy has laid hands upon these trophies of our honour and valour.' He held them high for all the world to witness, and then he spoke clear and proud: 'I dedicate them to the Red God.'

He flung the hair braids on to the fire. They burned up brightly. Nefer rose to his feet and, weakened by his wounds, swayed as he stood before them. 'I have run the Red Road! Though I lack the years, I have confirmed my right to the double crown of Egypt. I declare myself Pharaoh. The one true Pharaoh. Let any other pretend to the crown at his peril.'

They cheered him then while the warriors of the Red Road knelt before him, kissed his right hand and foot, and swore their allegiance unto death and beyond.

Nefer raised his right arm for silence, but his legs gave way under him and he might have fallen had not Mintaka rushed forward and steadied him. With one arm around her shoulders he looked into her eyes, and whispered, 'What I have done was for this very Egypt and for you, my love.'

His voice was so husky and low that only she heard him. She reached up and kissed him full on the lips, and the populace recognized this gesture as an open declaration of betrothal. They shouted until the echoes startled flocks of rock-pigeons from the cliffs beyond the walls.

Floating on the waters of the two great rivers, the city lay before them like a lotus flower, ready for plucking. Its walls were of burned brick. They were twenty-seven cubits thick and taller than the tallest palm trees of this fertile and well-watered land.

'What is their span?' Trok asked Ishtar the Mede. 'How far is it to ride around this city?'

'Ten leagues, Majesty.' Ishtar told him. 'Half a day's ride.'

Trok stood taller on the footplate of his chariot and shaded his eyes. 'Is that the Blue Gate of legend?' he demanded. He knew that Ishtar had lived in this royal city of Babylon for fifteen years, and had learned much of his magic here in the temple of Marduk.

Even at this distance the gateway glimmered like an enormous gemstone. The threshold was so wide that ten chariots could enter driving abreast, and the carved cedarwood gates were higher than ten men standing on each other's shoulders.

'It is truly blue in colour,' Trok marvelled. 'I have heard that it is covered with lapis lazuli.'

'Not so, Majesty.' Ishtar's face twisted in a condescending grimace. 'They are ceramic tiles. Each tile depicts one of the two thousand and ten gods of Babylon.'

Trok cast a general's eye along the miles of wall on each side of the Blue Gate. There were watchtowers at every two hundred paces, and at regular intervals the massive walls were heavily buttressed. Ishtar knew what he was thinking.

'There is a road along the top of the wall, wide enough for two chariots to ride abreast. Within an hour Sargon can move five thousand men along it to any point that is threatened by a besieging army.'

Trok grunted, to show that he was unimpressed. 'Still and all, any wall can be undermined and sapped. We need only one breach.'

'There is an inner wall, divine Pharaoh,' Ishtar murmured in a silky tone. 'It is almost as impregnable as the first.'

'If we cannot go through, we will find a way round.' Trok shrugged, 'Are those the gardens of Sargon's palace?' He jutted out his beribboned beard to indicate the terraces that rose in mighty tiers into the sky. They were so skilfully raised upon each other, a soaring inverted pyramid, that they seemed to float like a mighty eagle with spread wings, free of the bounds of earth.

Ishtar pointed with one sinewy, blue-tattooed arm. 'There are six terraces built around a vast courtyard, each wider than the one before.

The *zenana* alone has five thousand rooms, one for each of Sargon's wives. His treasury is buried in a deep dungeon below the palace. It is packed with gold to the height of a man's head.'

'Have you seen these wonders with your own eyes?' Trok challenged him.

'Not the *zenana*,' Ishtar admitted, 'but I have entered the main vault of the treasury, and I tell you straight, King-who-is-a-god, that in all your army you do not have sufficient wagons to carry away such a treasure as lies before you.'

'And I tell you straight, Ishtar the Mede, that I can always build new wagons.' And Trok threw back his head and laughed with animal high spirits.

The march to Babylon had been one long triumph, an unbroken string of victories. They had met Ran, Sargon's eldest son, on the banks of the Bahr al Milh: between the chariots of Trok and Naja they had ground his army like *dhurra*, and swept the chaff into the lake until the waters ran red with blood, and the bloated corpses floated from one bank to the other.

They had sent Ran's severed head to his father, skewered on a spear. Maddened with grief, Sargon had charged into the trap they had prepared for him. While Naja retreated before him to lure him on, Trok had circled out to the south then come at him from the rear with a thousand chariots. When Sargon turned back to defend his baggage train, they had him in a glittering ring of bronze.

Sargon had managed to break out with fifty chariots but he had left two thousand chariots and eleven thousand men behind him. Trok emasculated the prisoners, an undertaking that took two days to accomplish. But he joined in the work in person, bloody to the elbows like a butcher, and with a ribald jest to each of his victims as he dangled their severed genitalia in front of their eyes. Afterwards he allowed his victims to bleed to death, their blood an offering to Seueth, the hungry god who loved such fare. Trok sent the severed trophies to Sargon, packed in salt, in a hundred cedarwood chests. A subtle warning as to what he might expect when Trok and Naja came to Babylon.

Babylon was built upon the narrow spit of land between the two rivers, the Euphrates to the west and the Tigris to the east. In his headlong retreat Sargon had not been able to destroy the bridges. In any case, it would have taken an army to tear down those massive piers of burned brick on which they were built. Sargon no longer had an army. He had left one depleted regiment of foot to defend the bridges, but they were demoralized and without chariots to support them. They had not lasted long against the two pharaohs.

Trok had bound the survivors hand and foot and dropped them from the central span of the bridge into the broad brown river, and the Egyptian troops had lined the parapet to delight in their antics as they drowned.

Now Babylon lay before them, little more than a year since they had marched from Avaris.

'You know the defences, Ishtar. You helped design some of them. How long before the city falls?' Trok demanded impatiently. 'How long will it take me to breach the walls?'

'The walls are impregnable, Majesty,' said Ishtar.

'We both know that is not true,' Trok told him. 'Given enough time, men and determination, there is no wall built that cannot be breached.'

'A year,' Ishtar murmured thoughtfully. 'Or two, maybe three.' But there was a sly look on his tattooed face, and his eyes were shifty.

Trok laughed and playfully seized a handful of Ishtar's lacquered spiky beard. He twisted it until his blue whorled face contorted with pain and his eyes watered. 'You want to play games with me, wizard. You know how I love a good game, don't you?'

'Mercy, mighty Egypt,' Ishtar whimpered. Trok pushed him away so hard that he almost fell from the footplate of the chariot and had to clutch at the side of the dashboard to steady himself.

'A year, you say? Two? Three? I have not that amount of time to sit here and look upon the beauties and wonders of Babylon. I am in a hurry, Ishtar the Mede, and you know what that means, don't you?'

'I know, god without peer. And I am but a man, fallible and poor.'

'Poor?' Trok shouted in his face. 'By Seueth, you slimy charlatan, you have milked me of a lakh of gold already, and what do I have to show for it?'

'You have a city and an empire. After Egypt itself, the richest in the world. I have laid it at your feet.' He knew Trok well by now, knew just how far he could go.

'I need the key to that city.' Trok watched his face, happy with what he saw there. He knew Ishtar almost as well as the magician knew him.

'It would have to be a key made of gold,' Ishtar mused. 'Perhaps three lakhs of gold?'

Trok let out a great burst of laughter and aimed a blow at his head with a mailed fist. It was not intended to do damage, and Ishtar ducked under it easily.

'With three lakhs I could buy another army.' Trok shook his head and the ribbons in his beard danced like a cloud of butterflies.

'Yonder, in the treasury of Sargon, lie a hundred lakhs. Three from a hundred is a small price to pay.'

'Give me the city, Ishtar. Give it to me within three full moons and you shall have two lakhs of gold from the treasure of Sargon,' he promised.

'If I give it to you before the next full moon?' Ishtar scrubbed his hands together like a carpet trader.

Trok's grin slid from his face at the prospect, and he said seriously, 'Then you shall have your three lakhs, and a convoy of wagons to carry them away.'

***

The army of the two pharaohs went into camp before the Blue Gate, and Trok sent an emissary to Sargon to demand the immediate surrender of the city – 'to save such a prodigy of architecture from the flames, and your person and family and populace from the sword', as Trok humorously phrased his demand. In reply Sargon, sanguine and defiant behind his walls, sent the messenger's decapitated head back to Trok. The preliminaries having been dealt with, Trok and Naja made a circuit of the walls to allow the Babylonians to view their full might and splendour.

They drove the golden chariots, Trok's drawn by six black stallions, Naja's by six white. Heseret rode beside Naja, glittering with jewels and wearing the golden *uraeus* on her high-piled curls. Behind the golden chariots marched fifty prisoners, Babylonian women captured from the outlying towns and villages between the two rivers. All were pregnant, some very near their time.

They were preceded by a vanguard of five hundred chariots and followed by a rearguard of another five hundred. The slow, stately circuit of the city took all that day, and at sunset they came back to the Blue Gate. Sargon and his war council were gathered on the parapets above the shining gateway.

Sargon was tall and thin, with a shock of silver hair. In his youth he had been a mighty warrior and had conquered the lands as far north as the Black Sea to add to his domains. He had suffered defeat only once in all his campaigns and that had been at the hands of Pharaoh Tamose, the father of Nefer Seti. Now another pair of Egyptians stood at his gates, and he did not delude himself into believing that these would be as merciful as the first.

To confirm him in this belief, Trok had the pregnant women stripped naked and marched forward one at a time. Then, while all the city watched their swollen bellies were slit open, the unborn infants ripped out and the tiny bodies piled on the threshold of the Blue Gate.

'Add these to your army, Sargon,' Trok bellowed up at him. 'You will need every man you can get.'

It had been a long and exciting day for Heseret, and she retired to her tent with all her slave girls, leaving her husband and Trok to pore over a map of the city by lamplight. It was a work of art, drawn on a finely tanned sheepskin, the walls, roads and canals drawn to scale, each of the main buildings depicted in coloured detail.

'How came this into your possession?' Naja demanded.

'Twelve years ago, by the command of King Sargon, I surveyed the city and drew this map with my own hands,' Ishtar replied. 'No other could have achieved such accuracy and beauty.'

'If he commissioned it, why did you not deliver it to Sargon?'

'I did.' Ishtar nodded. 'I delivered the inferior draft to him, while secretly I kept the fair copy you see before you. I knew that one day someone would pay me more handsomely than Sargon ever did.'

For another hour they studied the map, muttering a comment now and then, but for the most part silent and absorbed. As fighting generals with a professional eye for the salient features of a battlefield, they were able to admire the depth and strength of the walls, towers and redoubts that had been built up layer upon layer over the centuries.

At last Trok stood back from the table. 'There is no weakness that I can divine, magician. You were right the first time. It will take three years of hard work to break through those walls. You will have to do better than this to earn your three lakhs.'

'The water,' whispered Ishtar. 'Look to the water.'

'I have looked to the water.' Naja smiled at him, but it was a serpent's smile, cold and thin-lipped. 'There are canals supplying every quarter of the city, enough water to grow Sargon's six terraces of gardens that reach up into the sky, and to water and feed the city for a hundred years.'

'Pharaoh is all-seeing, all-wise.' Ishtar bowed to him, 'but where does the water come from?'

'From two mighty rivers. After the Nile itself, the mightiest rivers in the world. A supply of water that has not failed in this millennium.'

'But where does the water enter the city? How does it pass through, under or over those walls?' Ishtar insisted, and Naja and Trok exchanged a look of dawning comprehension.

Half a mile north of Babylon, outside the city walls, on the east bank of the Euphrates, at a point where the flood broadened and ran sluggishly, stood the temple of Ninurta, the lion-headed winged god of the Euphrates. It was built on stone piers that extended out into the river. The multiple images of the god were engraved on a frieze that ran around all four outer walls. In the Akkadian language, chiselled into the stone lintel over the entrance, was a warning to all who sought to invade the sanctuary, calling down the wrath of the god upon them.

Ishtar the Mede worked a charm on the threshold to nullify the curse, slitting the throats of two captives and splashing their blood on the portals. Once the way was cleared Trok, with twenty troopers at his back, strode through into the temple courtyard where all the purple-robed priests of Ninurta were gathered. They were chanting and gesticulating, waving their arms towards the intruder, splashing water from the Euphrates in his path, invoking Ninurta to build up an invisible wall of magical power to turn Trok back.

Trok strode through the wall without a check and killed the high priest with a single thrust through the old man's throat. Wailing at such sacrilege, the other priests prostrated themselves before him.

Trok sheathed his sword and nodded to the captain, who commanded the guard. 'Kill them all. Make certain no one escapes.'

The work was done swiftly, and when the courtyard was littered with purple-clad bodies Trok commanded, 'Do not throw them into the river. We do not want the city guards to see them float past and guess what we are about.'

Then he turned to watch Ishtar who, once all the priests had been disposed of, had entered the courtyard to work another charm to counteract the baleful influence of the god they had invoked. At the four corners he burned bundles of herbs, which emitted a thick, greasy smoke that was repugnant to Ninurta and, as Trok remarked jovially, to all gods and lesser mortals equally. Once Ishtar had completed the purification, he led the way into the holy places of the temple, and Trok and his troopers followed him, with blood-caked blades bared.

Their cleated sandals rang hollowly in the gloomy recesses of the high, cavernous hall, and even Trok felt a religious chill as they approached the image of the god on his plinth. The lion's head snarled silently and the wings of stone were spread wide. Ishtar declaimed another lengthy prayer to the god to placate him, then led Trok into the narrow space between the rear wall and the idol's back. Here he pointed out a heavily grilled gate built into the body of Ninurta. Trok seized the bars of the grille, and shook them with all his bear-like strength. They did not move.

'There is an easier way, all-wise Pharaoh,' Ishtar suggested sweetly. 'The key will be on the body of the high priest.'

'Fetch it!' Trok snapped at the captain of his guard, who ran. When he returned there was blood on his hands, but he carried a bunch of heavy keys, some of them as long as his forearm. Trok tried two in the lock on the grille, and the second turned the ancient mechanism. The gate swung open on creaking hinges.

Trok peered down a descending spiral staircase into darkness. The air coming up the deep shaft was cold and dank, and he heard the sound of running water far below.

'Bring torches!' he ordered, and the captain sent four of his troopers to take down the burning torches from their brackets. With a torch held above his head, Trok started down the narrow, unprotected stairwell. He went gingerly, for the treads of the stone steps were slimy and slippery. The sound of running water grew louder as he went down.

Ishtar followed him closely. 'This temple and the tunnels beneath it were built almost five hundred years ago,' he told Trok. Now there was the gleam of water below them, and the sound of the torrent running swiftly in the darkness. At last Trok reached the bottom and stepped down on to a stone pier. By the wavering torchlight he saw that they stood in a wide tunnel with a curved roof, an aqueduct of impressive dimensions. The roof and walls were lined with ceramic tiles, laid in geometric patterns. Both ends of the tunnel shaded off into deep darkness.

Ishtar picked a fragment of fungus from the wall and tossed it into the flow. It was whisked away down the duct and disappeared from sight. 'It is deeper than a man's head,' he said, and Trok looked speculatively at the captain of the guard, as though he considered testing that statement. The captain shrank back into the shadows trying to appear insignificant.

'This footpath on which we stand runs the full length of the aqueduct,' Ishtar explained. 'The priests who repair and maintain the tunnel use it to gain access.'

'Where does it start and where does it end?' Trok demanded.

'There is a sump in the bed of the river, under the piers of the temple, into which the water flows. The far end of the aqueduct emerges in the other temple of Ninurta within the walls of Babylon, near the Blue Gate,' Ishtar explained. 'Only the priests know of the existence of this tunnel. All others believe that the water is a benevolent gift from the god. After it gushes from the fountain in the temple precinct, the water is lifted by *shadoof*, water wheels, to the gardens of the palace, or sent by canals to every quarter of the city.'

'I do believe, Ishtar the Mede, that you are close to earning your three lakhs.' Trok laughed with delight. 'It remains only for you to lead us down this rabbit-hole, and into the city of wonders and treasure, especially the treasure.'

Trok reasoned that the priests at the main temple of Ninurta within the city walls must regularly correspond with those in the river temple. Almost certainly they used this aqueduct as a thoroughfare between the two communities. It would not take long for them to discover that something untoward had happened to their brethren in the river temple. He had to make his plans swiftly.

Trok chose two hundred of his best and most reliable men, all members of his own leopard tribe. He divided them into two groups. Once they had fought their way through the aqueduct into the city, the first group were to secure the Blue Gate and keep it open until Pharaoh Naja Kiafan could lead the main force through it. The second, much smaller group were to make their way into the palace, and seize Sargon's treasury before he was able to dispose of the gold. 'Although it would take a thousand wagons to carry it all away,' Ishtar assured him.

The chosen two hundred were dressed in the uniforms of Sargon's army, taken from the prisoners and the dead men left on the battlefield. They wore the long ankle-length tunics of striped material, belted at the waist, and the tall beehive-shaped helmets. Ishtar showed them how to curl their beards and hair into the characteristic ringlets of the Mesopo-tamians. They wore only a red sash to distinguish them from the foe. Rough copies of the city map were hastily drawn by the army scribes and issued to the captains of both divisions so that they knew the lay-out of streets and buildings. By evening every man knew exactly what was expected of him once he entered the city.

As soon as it was dark Naja quietly moved his assault force up into position outside the Blue Gate, ready to dash through into the city as soon as Trok's men threw it open.

In the courtyard of the river temple of Ninurta, Trok mustered his division. While it was still daylight, he and Ishtar led them in single file down the spiral staircase to the level of the aqueduct. There was no hurry, for they had many hours in which to make the long subterranean journey. Their cleated sandals had been muffled with leather socks, so their heavy footsteps did not echo along the gloomy tunnel. They marched in silence, every tenth man carrying a torch, giving just sufficient light for the men who followed to make out their footing on the slimy stones of the pier. At their left hand the never-ending flow of water rustled darkly by. Every thousand paces Ishtar stopped to placate the god Ninurta with gifts and incantations, and to clear the way ahead of the magical obstacles and barriers placed by the dead priests.

Nevertheless, the silent march seemed endless to Trok, and it came as a surprise when abruptly Ishtar stopped and pointed ahead. The faint glimmer of light was reflected off the shiny ceramic walls. Trok signalled the men following him to halt, then went forward with Ishtar. Over their own garments they wore headdresses and purple robes taken from the bodies of the slaughtered priests.

As they went towards the source of the light, they saw another grille gate across the tunnel, and the distorted shadows of men thrown on the walls by the light of a torch set in a bracket above the gate. As they drew closer they saw that on the other side of the grille two robed priests were seated on stools, with the bao board between them, absorbed in their game. They looked up when Ishtar called softly to them. The fat one stood up and wobbled to the gate.

'Are you from Sinna?' he called.

'Yes!' Ishtar assured him.

'You are late. We have been waiting since nightfall. You should have been here hours ago. The high priest will be displeased.'

'I am sorry,' Ishtar sounded contrite, 'but you know Sinna.'

The fat priest chuckled. 'Yes, I know Sinna. He taught me my responses thirty years ago.'

His key jangled in the lock of the gate, and then he swung it open. 'You must hurry,' he said. Trok trotted forward with the hood over his face, holding his sword in the fold of his robe. The priest stood back against the wall to let him pass. Trok stopped in front of him, and whispered, 'Ninurta will reward you, brother,' and killed him with a thrust up under his chin into his brain.

With a shout of alarm, his companion leaped to his feet, knocking over the bao board and scattering the stones across the pier. With two long strides Trok reached him and chopped his head half off. Without another sound, the priest fell backwards into the dark stream and, with his robes ballooning about him buoying him up, he was carried away down the tunnel.

Trok gave a soft whistle and, with the muted tramp of muffled feet his men moved up into the torchlight with drawn swords. Ishtar led them forward until they reached the foot of another steep stone stairway. They went up it quickly until they came to a heavy curtain blocking their way. Ishtar peeped around its edge and nodded. 'The temple is empty.'

Trok stepped through, and looked about him. This temple was even larger and more impressive than the river temple. The ceiling was so high that the light from fifty torches was eaten up by the shadows. Below them the image of the god crouched over the mouth of the shaft from which the full force of the aqueduct spurted like a gigantic fountain into a deep pond with a white marble coping. The corpse of the priest that Trok had almost decapitated was floating in the pool, from which the water spilled over into the canal that carried it to the city. Although the smell of incense was thick in the air, the great hall of the temple was deserted.

Trok signalled his men to come forward. As soon as they emerged from the tunnel they formed up behind their captains in silence. Trok gave the hand signal and they went forward at a trot. Ishtar led the smaller band through a side door of the hall into a corridor that connected with the palace of Sargon. Trok led his men out into the narrow lane behind the temple and, working only from his memory of the map, turned at the second lane into the wide avenue that he knew led to the Blue Gate. It was still dark and the stars blazed above the sleeping city.

They met a number of cloaked figures on the way, one or two staggering drunk, but the others scurried out of their way and let the dark column of armed warriors pass. A woman with a child in her arms called after them, 'May Marduk smile upon you, brave warriors, and keep us safe from Trok, the barbarian of Egypt.' Trok understood just enough Akkadian to catch her meaning, and smiled into his beard.

Disguised in their plundered robes, they reached the end of the avenue without being challenged further, but as the gateway loomed ahead a voice sang out at them from the door of the guardhouse.

'Stand ho! Give the watchword for tonight.' The centurion of the gate with five men at his back, stepped out into the torchlight. But they were ill-prepared, without helmets and body armour, their eyes puffy and their faces still crumpled with sleep.

'The honourable emissary of King Sargon to the pharaohs of Egypt,' Trok mumbled in execrable Akkadian, and gave the hand signal for his troops to charge. 'Open the gate and stand aside!' He ran straight at the centurion.

For a moment longer the man stood uncertainly. Then he saw the glint of swords and shouted urgently, 'Stand to arms. Turn out the guard.' But it was too late. Trok was on him, and dropped him in his tracks with a single blow. His men swarmed over the other guards before they could defend themselves, but the noise had alerted the sentinels on the parapets above the gate. They sounded the alarm with braying ram's horns, and hurled their javelins down into the attackers.

'Winkle them out of there!' Trok ordered, and half of his men rushed up the ramps on either side of the gateway to reach the parapet. They were at once locked in close and desperate fighting with the guards on the wall. Trok kept half of his men with him.

Ishtar had described the gate room that housed the complicated machinery, a system of heavy winches and pulleys, that operated the massive gates. Trok led his men to the entrance before the defenders within could close the doors, and after only a few minutes of furious fighting they had killed or wounded most of them. The survivors threw down their weapons, some fell to their knees and pleaded in vain for quarter. They were stabbed and clubbed as they knelt. The others fled out of the postern gate, and Trok led his men to the massive winches. With two men on each spoke of the capstans they began to open the gates.

But the ram's horns had aroused the city guards, who swarmed out of their barracks, some without armour and still half asleep, and rushed to defend the gateway.

Trok barred the heavy door to the winch room and placed men at the entrance to defend it. On the parapets above the gateway his men had killed the defenders or thrown them from the top of the wall, and now they fought on the ramps, holding off the attacking Babylonians.

The door to the winch room trembled and bulged as the Babylonians battered at it, trying desperately to break in, but the winches revolved slowly to the efforts of Trok's men, and the mighty gates rose from their seatings, the gap under them widening inexorably.

The avenue leading to the gates was by now crowded with Babylonian defenders, but they were hampered by their own numbers. Only four abreast could mount the ramps to the top of the walls, and Trok's men met them and hurled them back. Others were still trying to break into the room that housed the winches, but the doors were sturdy. When at last they smashed them down they found Trok and his men waiting for them on the threshold.

Outside the walls Naja's men had swarmed forward with crowbars and levers. They forced the heavy gates wider and wider, until at last a squadron of chariots could pass through. Then they stood aside, and Naja led a phalanx of fighting chariots in a brutal charge through the gateway, and swept the avenue from side to side. The army of Egypt poured through behind them. Trok took command of them and led them rampaging through the city towards the palace.

The sack of Babylon had begun.

The defence of the palace was stubborn, led by Sargon himself. However, by that evening Trok had opened a breach in the outer walls of the first terrace. He led a strong contingent through and the defence collapsed. When they burst into Sargon's bedchamber he was kneeling before the image of Marduk, the devouring god of Mesopotamia, with a bloody sword in his hands. Beside him lay the body of his favourite wife, a grey-haired woman who had been with him for thirty years. He had given her a merciful death, compared to what she might have expected from Trok's men. However, Sargon had not been able to steel himself to fall on his own sword. Trok knocked the weapon out of his grasp.

'We have much to discuss, Your Majesty,' he promised him. 'Was it not you who referred to me as the Black Beast of Seueth? I hope to convince you that you painted me the wrong colour.'

The women from the *zenana* were herded out of the palace, only five hundred of them, not the five thousand of which Ishtar had spoken. Trok selected twenty, the youngest and prettiest, for his personal entertainment, and the rest were given to his senior officers. After they had enjoyed them, they would be passed on to the common soldiery.

It took another two days to break into the treasury buried deep in the earth below the palace, for many ingenious constructions and devices guarded it. Without the expertise and first-hand knowledge of Ishtar the Mede, it might have taken even longer to penetrate to the main treasure chamber.

When the way was clear, Trok and Naja, Heseret following them, descended the stairway and entered the chamber. Ishtar had lit the interior with a hundred oil lamps, their rays cunningly reflected by burnished copper mirrors to show off the booty to full effect.

Even the two pharaohs and Heseret were stunned into silence by the splendour of the treasure. The silver had been cast into bars, the gold into conical ingots that fitted into each other to facilitate stacking. They were all stamped with the goldsmiths' marks and the royal cartouche of Sargon.

Heseret, for once speechless, had to shade her delicate eyes against the dazzle of the masses of precious metal. Naja walked forward slowly between the stacks, which were higher than his head, stopping every few paces to stroke the ingots. At last he regained his voice and whispered, 'They feel warm and smooth as the body of a virgin.'

Trok picked up a heavy bar in each hand and laughed with delight. 'How much?' he demanded of Ishtar.

'Alas, splendid and divine Majesty, we have not yet had the opportunity to count it. But we have consulted the scrolls of Sargon's scribes. They record the total weight of silver at fifty-five lakhs, the gold at thirty-three.' He spread his tattooed hands deprecatingly. 'But who would trust the count of a Babylonian?'

'Sargon is a greater robber than I gave him credit for.' Trok made it sound like a compliment.

'At least there is enough here to pay me the pittance you promised me?' Ishtar suggested smoothly.

'I think we should discuss that further.' Trok smiled at him genially. 'I am a kindly and generous man, Ishtar, as you know full well. However, over-generosity is a form of stupidity. Stupid I am not.'

Once he had finished gloating over the contents of the treasury, there was much else to see and marvel at within the city. Trok and Naja toured the palace, climbing to the top terrace with its fountains, gardens and groves. From this height they could look down on both the great rivers and the vista of fields, marshes and papyrus beds outside the city walls.

Next they visited all the temples, for these magnificent buildings were also stuffed with bullion, beautiful furniture, statuary, mosaics and other works of art. As they removed these Naja and Trok spoke to the incumbent god in conversational tones, as brother gods and equals. Trok explained that Babylon was no longer a capital city but merely a satrapy of Egypt. Therefore the god should remove his earthly seat to Avaris, where Trok undertook to provide him with suitable accommodation. The removal of the god's wealth should be considered in the nature of a loan which would later be repaid.

The greatest of these temples was that of Marduk the Devourer. Trok found this to be not only a mine of precious metal and jewellery but a place of endless fascination.

Ishtar was a disciple of Marduk, and as a young man had studied the mysteries in this same temple under the high priest. As he had not yet been paid his reward, he stuck as close to Trok as a tick to the belly of a lion. He instructed Trok in the worship of Marduk, and Trok remarked, 'Marduk has tastes very close to those of my own familiar, Seueth. They might well be brothers.'

'As always, Your Majesty is perspicacious. However, Marduk had a far greater appetite for human sacrifice than Seueth. And he is particular about how it is presented to him.'

He led Trok through the maze of passageways and corridors, through gardens, courtyards and echoing halls into the holy of holies deep in the heart of the temple, which was a small city in itself. They came at last to the furnace complex.

When they stood above the main sacrificial chamber, Trok gazed down into the gut of it in total fascination. He was amazed by the design and the construction. 'Describe it to me,' he ordered Ishtar.

'There are two furnaces, not a single one, one behind each of those walls.' Ishtar pointed down at the walls of shining copper. 'When the charcoal fires are lit they are fanned with great bellows, until the metal walls glow like the rising sun with the heat. The walls are movable. By means of pulleys the priests are able to roll them forward, or pull them apart . . .'

When Ishtar had finished his explanation, Trok thumped his mailed fist into the palm of his other hand. 'In the names of Seueth and Marduk, I have never heard the like. I must see it demonstrated. If it is as you describe, I will have the same contraption built in my own temple in Avaris. Order the priests to fire up their infernal furnaces. We will celebrate my victory with a sacrifice to Marduk.'

'It will take several days for the furnaces to reach the desired heat,' Ishtar warned him.

'I have several days,' Trok said. 'I have to supervise the consignment of the booty, and also I must see to the contentment and well-being of twenty of Sargon's young wives.' He rolled his eyes. 'A most arduous task. In any event, my ruffians are still busy sacking the city. It will be some time yet before I can bring them back to their senses.'

Three days later Trok held a victory banquet for his senior officers on the upper terrace of the great palace. The guests reclined among groves of orange trees growing in huge clay pots, all in full blossom so the air was filled with their sweet perfume. Around them the fountains tinkled and burbled. The banquet table was covered with silken carpets. The bowls and vessels were of silver and gold and set with precious stones – they had been taken from the temple offertories. The stools on which the guests sat were Sargon's wives, kneeling naked except for their golden chains. Later when the flagons of foaming beer and the sweet wine had taken effect, the living stools were used as pillows and mattresses.

In the midst of this revelry Ishtar crept to Trok's side, and whispered in his ear, 'Pharaoh god, who swallows the seas and eats the stars, the furnaces are ready.'

Trok staggered to his feet and clapped his hands. 'Gentle brethren!' he addressed his officers, and they roared with laughter at the jest. 'I have an entertainment to offer you. Follow me!' And he made unsteadily for the staircase with his men crowding after him.

They lined the parapet of the gallery, and looked down into the sacrificial chamber. Smoke shimmered from the twin chimneys above their heads, and they began to sweat in the heat reflected from the glowing metal walls.

'We are gathered here today to make sacrifice to the great god Marduk, who has given us his city as a prize of war,' Trok told them, imitating the sing-song, sanctimonious tones of a high priest. They cheered him delightedly.

'What better sacrifice can we offer than a king and his royal family?' They cheered again.

Trok waved to Ishtar, who darted down the stairway to the chamber below where a hundred slaves stood at the windlasses ready to activate the mechanism. At a signal from the high priest they began to chant a hymn to Marduk.

The priest stepped out on to his pulpit above the open chamber with its glowing walls. With the chanting slaves as a background, he lifted both arms and began to sing a prayer to the god in a reedy falsetto voice.

At his signal a small door opened in the fixed stone wall of the furnace chamber, and another priest led in a file of human beings. They were clad in simple white tunics, and wore no adornment other than the halters around their necks.

They were of both sexes, and all ages. Some were mere infants carried in their mothers' arms; some were toddlers; others were on the verge of adolescence. But the tallest was a lean white-haired man with the carriage of a king and a warrior.

'Hail, Sargon, mighty ruler of heaven and the sacred earth between the two great rivers,' Trok mocked him. 'I am about to do for you what you did not have the courage to do for yourself. I am sending you as a messenger into the loving arms of your god, Marduk the Devourer. Because I am a compassionate man and I do not want your wives, your little sons and daughters to mourn you, I am sending them with you to keep you company on the way.' He paused to let the laughter of his men subside. Then he went on, 'Give this message to Marduk, when you stand face to face with him. Tell him that Trok, his divine brother, greets him, and demands his good favour.'

Sargon gathered his sons around him and did not deign to look up at Trok or to reply to his words.

Trok looked across at the high priest. 'Now, priest, show us how this machine of yours works.'

The high priest began to sing again, but a different prayer, harsh and primitive. In the room behind him the slaves sang with him, and in unison took a step forward then brought their bare soles down on the stone slabs with a sound like a clap of thunder. One step at a time the windlass began to turn.

At first nothing appeared to change then Ishtar whispered, 'Observe the burning walls, mighty Trok, greatest of all hero kings. See how they begin to move towards each other, slowly. Oh, so slowly. Until they meet at last, and the sacrifices crisp and blacken like moths in the lamp flame.'

Trok leaned forward, his face bright with sweat and anticipation.

'Marduk is pleased,' Ishtar announced, looking up from the bowl. 'The sacrifice that you made to him in the furnace was most acceptable to him.'

Trok nodded. 'Tell my brother Marduk that I am pleased he is pleased.'

Trok knelt on a pile of leopardskins spread on the stone floor in the inner sanctum of the temple before the altar of Marduk the Devourer. The golden image of the god was of a comely youth, with a smiling countenance. The statue was three or four times life-sized. The only characteristics that distinguished the god from a mortal, other than his size, were tiny goatlike horns on each side of his curly head and cloven hoofs instead of feet.

'You told me that Marduk was a terrible god, crueller and fiercer than any other in the pantheon, more ferocious even than Seueth,' Trok had challenged Ishtar when first he had seen the image, 'yet this is a pretty boy.'

'Divine Pharaoh, be not deceived!' Ishtar had warned him. 'This is the face that Marduk shows the world of men. His true aspect is so hideous that any man who looks upon it is instantly rendered blind and slobbering twitching mad.'

Sobered by that thought Trok had knelt before the image and remained silent while the priests had brought in twin newborn infants, and offered them to the god. Ishtar had slit their throats so skilfully that they made hardly a cry as they bled into the golden divination bowl that he held beneath them.

When the small exsanguinated bodies were dropped into the marble chute that led to the furnace beneath the sanctum, Ishtar had placed the golden bowl before the altar and lit the incense braziers. Chanting and mumbling, he threw handfuls of herbs on the flames until the vault filled with wreaths of blue smoke and the air became fragrant and enervating. After a while Trok found it difficult to think clearly and his vision became distorted so that the shadows seemed to waver and dance, and he heard the sounds of distant, mocking laughter. He closed his eyes and pressed his fingers to the lids. When he opened them again he saw that the sweet smile on the face of the god had become a leer so obscene and frightening that his skin crawled as though poisonous insects were creeping upon it. He tried to look away but found he could not.

'The great god Marduk is pleased,' Ishtar repeated, reading the auguries reflected in the surface of the blood-filled bowl. 'He deigns to answer your questions.'

'Tell Marduk that I honour him as my peer. I shall send a thousand more sacrifices into his furnace.'

'Marduk hears you.' Ishtar picked up the bowl and peered into it. After a long silence he began to rock gently back and forth with the bowl in his lap. He looked up at last. 'Behold Marduk, the great god of Babylon! Speak to us, dreadful one, we entreat you!'

He opened his arms to the golden statue, and the god spoke in the voice of a child, lisping and mellifluous.

'I greet you, my brother Trok,' said this strange voice. 'You wish to know about the fledgling falcon that spreads its wings and sharpens its talons in the desert places.'

Trok was startled not only by the disembodied voice but also by the accuracy of this statement. Indeed, he had intended asking for counsel on his plans to attack and destroy Nefer Seti. He tried to reply, but his throat was closed and as dry as the wrappings of an ancient mummy.

The sweet, childlike voice went on, 'You have had good counsel from my loyal servant Ishtar the Mede. It was as well that you hearkened to him. If you had not done so, if you had marched on Gallala when you purposed to do so, you would have encountered a disaster even greater than the *khamsin* winds that destroyed and buried your legions.'

Trok recalled bitterly how Ishtar had dissuaded him from leading another army into the eastern desert to attack Nefer Seti and to capture Mintaka, his runaway woman. Long ago his spies had reported to him the exact whereabouts of the pair at Gallala. He had assembled another force of chariots and foot soldiers for the expedition. He knew that if he did not rid himself of this challenge to his throne, if he did not crush the boy pharaoh before he attained his full strength, then soon the rebellions and insurrections would spread through his entire realm. Once that happened he knew that the dynasty he was founding would end in destruction and extinction. As much as he longed to rid himself of the challenge and the threat of Nefer Seti, he longed much more to recapture the only woman who had ever humiliated and defied him. His hatred for her surpassed any other of his emotions.

Ishtar had prevented him marching. With predictions of dire consequences, with warnings of disaster and death, Ishtar had persuaded him to divert his forces into this joint expedition with Naja to the fabled city of Babylon. Although, thus far, the expedition had turned out to be a triumph, although the booty and the slaughter had been beyond counting, still Trok felt himself unfulfilled.

He spoke as much to himself as to the golden god when he growled, 'I must have Nefer Seti. The double crown will sit uneasily on my head until I kill him and throw his body on the flames so that he will never know resurrection. Already I have expunged his name and the name of his sire from every edifice and monument in Egypt, but I must destroy him and his memory for ever.'

In his anger and hatred he sprang to his feet, and shouted at Ishtar and his god, 'You have cheated me of my destiny once before with your ill omens and baleful warnings. Now I address you as your peer, your equal, and not as a worshipper. I demand that you deliver the person and the soul of Nefer Seti to me, in justice and retribution. I will not accept another refusal from you and your minion here.' In his fury and frustration Trok aimed a kick at Ishtar. The Mede saw it coming and rolled aside. Trok's bronze-cleated sandal caught the divining bowl and the blood of the babes splattered across the flags and down the front of the altar.

Even Trok was appalled by what he had done. He stood frozen before the image waiting for the reaction of the god.

'Sacrilege!' Ishtar wailed. 'Trok Uruk, now your enterprise is surely doomed.' Then he prostrated himself in the puddle of blood, so terror-stricken that he could not raise his eyes to the image.

A dreadful hush had fallen over the sanctum. The faint rumble of the flames of the sacrificial furnace under the stone floor on which they stood seemed to enhance it.

Then there was a sound, soft but unmistakable. It was the sound of breathing, like that of a sleeping child to begin with but then growing harsher and stronger. Now it was the breathing of a wild beast, then of some monster that echoed through the temple. At last it became the furious sound of an outraged god, roaring like all the storms of the heavens, thundering like the galeswept waves of the ocean. So terrible was it that even Ishtar the Mede whimpered like a child.

'The god will never allow you to succeed now. You dare not march against Taita and his protégé, not until the Warlock is dead,' Ishtar whispered.

Then a terrible voice spoke, so harsh and unearthly that it raked Trok's nerves and made him shudder. 'Hear me! Trok Uruk, you mortal man who claims to be part of the godhead!' The thunder echoed and rolled around the dark recess of the sanctum. 'You know that you are no god. Hear me, blasphemer! If you march against Gallala in defiance of me and my prophet, Ishtar the Mede, I shall destroy you and your army just as I buried your other army in the sands of the desert. This time you shall not escape my wrath.'

Even though he was befuddled by the poisonous smoke of the incense braziers, and fearful of the rage of Marduk that filled the temple, Trok was still cunning enough to sense some false note in Ishtar's protestations, something not convincing in the force of Marduk's fury.

He gathered his courage, which had been scattered by the supernatural manifestations of the god, and tried to identify exactly what had given him pause. He realized that the sound of the bestial breathing, and the thunderous voice issued from the belly of the golden statue. He stared at it hard and saw that the navel of the god was a dark slit. He took a step towards the statue and Ishtar raised his head in alarm and cried, 'Beware, Pharaoh! The god is angry. Do not approach him.'

Trok ignored him and took another step forward, staring at the god's belly button. He saw a faint gleam in the depths of the aperture, a shadowy movement. Often in battle he had sensed the exact moment when the fates had swung in his favour and he felt it now. He steeled himself and shouted, above the awful sound of the god's breathing, 'I defy you, Marduk the Devourer! Strike me down if you are able. Heap your temple fires upon me, if you can!'

Suspicion became certainty as that glimmer showed again in the slit in the god's belly, and the breathing faltered. Trok drew his sword and, with the flat of the blade, knocked Ishtar out of his way. Then he ran forward, darting behind the golden image. Quickly he examined the back, tapping the metal with the tip of his blade. It sounded hollow as a drum, and when he looked more closely he discovered a removable panel that fitted almost perfectly.

'A trap-door!' he growled. 'It seems that there is more in Marduk's belly than ever went in through his mouth.'

He ducked back and peered into the slit in the god's belly. A human eye looked back at him. The pupil widened with astonishment, and Trok gave a mighty shout: 'Come out of there, you slime of the great beast!' He placed his shoulder against the idol and heaved with all his strength. The statue wobbled on its stone base, and Trok heaved again. Slowly the image went down with a crash on to the stone flags. Ishtar screamed and leaped out of the way as it threatened to crush him.

The head of the god was bent at an angle by the fall, and in the silence after the shattering impact there was a scrabbling sound, like startled rats, from the interior of the fallen idol. The trap-door flew open and a small figure crawled out. Trok seized it by its thick head of curls. 'Mercy, great King Trok,' the girl pleaded, in that honey-sweet voice. 'It was not I who tried to deceive you. I was doing the bidding of others.' She was such a lovely child that, for a moment, Trok felt his rage subside. Then he snatched her up by the ankles and dangled her upside-down in one fist. She was weeping and writhing in his grip.

'Who ordered you to this?' Trok demanded.

'Ishtar the Mede,' she wept.

Trok swung her twice in a circle around his head, building up speed and momentum, then dashed the child against the temple column. Her screams were cut off instantly. Trok let her corpse drop in a crumpled heap on the altar.

He turned back to the golden idol and thrust his sword into the opening of the trapdoor, rummaging around in the belly of the God. There was another squeal and a grotesque creature shot out of the opening. At first Trok thought it was a huge bullfrog, and jumped back in alarm. Then he saw that it was a hunch-backed dwarf, even shorter and smaller than the girl he had just killed. The dwarf bellowed with a voice like a bull, the deafening roars out of keeping with his diminutive stature. He was the ugliest man Trok had ever laid eyes upon, with eyes out of kilter and of disparate sizes. Clumps of black hair bushed out of his ears and nostrils, and from the huge moles that hung from his face.

'Forgive me, that I tried to deceive you, mighty god and King of Egypt!' Trok slashed at him with the sword, but the creature ducked and dodged and leaped nimbly about the sanctum, roaring with terror in that outlandish voice. Trok found himself laughing at his antics. The dwarf shot behind the curtains at the back of the chamber and disappeared through a secret doorway.

Trok let him go and turned back to Ishtar, just in time to seize a handful of his stiff-lacquered hair as he tried to flee from the chamber. He flung him full length on the stone floor and kicked him in the ribs, belly and back. 'You have lied to me.' Trok was no longer laughing, and his face turned dark purple with rage. 'You have deliberately misled me. You have diverted me from my purpose.'

'Please, master,' Ishtar wailed, rolling across the floor to avoid the savage kicks, 'it was for your good alone.'

'Was it for my good that you allowed the spawn of Tamose to flourish in Gallala unchecked, and to spread rebellion and sedition throughout my realm?' Trok bellowed. 'Do you think I am mad, and so stupid that I should believe that?'

'It is true,' Ishtar blubbered, as Trok's toe caught him in the ribs and knocked him over on his back. 'How could we go against a Warlock who commands the storm to his will as though it were his pet dog?'

'You are afraid of Taita.' Trok stood back to regain his breath. 'The Warlock?' he demanded incredulously.

'He overlooks us. He can turn my own spells back upon me! I cannot prevail against him. I sought only to save you from him, great Pharaoh.'

'You sought only to save your own blue-tattooed skin,' Trok snarled, and rushed in again to slam kicks into Ishtar's doubled-up body.

'I beg of you, first of all the gods,' Ishtar covered his head with both arms, 'give me my reward and let me go. Taita has dissipated my powers. I cannot confront him again. I can be of no further use to you.'

Trok stood with one foot drawn back, frozen in the act of delivering another kick. 'Your reward?' he demanded in astonishment. 'Surely you do not believe that I will reward your disloyalty with three lakhs of gold.'

Ishtar came up on his knees and tried to kiss Trok's foot. 'I have given you Babylon, great master. You cannot deny me what was promised.'

Trok laughed angrily. 'I can deny you anything I please to. Even life itself. If you wish to live another day then you will lead me to Gallala, and take your chances in a trial of magical strength with the Warlock.'

It seemed that all Egypt had heard that Nefer Seti had run the Red Road and was ordained in his kingship. Each day visitors from all over the country arrived in Gallala. Some were the colonels and captains of the regiments that Trok and Naja had left to guard Egypt in their absence. Others were emissaries of the elders of the great cities along the Nile – Avaris and Memphis, Thebes and Aswan – and the high priests from the temples in those cities. Sickened and saddened by the tyrannies and excesses of Naja and Trok, and emboldened by their absence in Babylon so far to the east, all had come to swear allegiance to Nefer Seti.

'The populace of Egypt is ready to welcome you,' the emissaries told him.

'Our regiments will declare for you as soon as you step again on to the sacred soil, and they see your face, and know that the rumours of your survival are true,' the captains assured him.

Nefer and Taita questioned them keenly, demanding to know the muster of their regiments and their state of readiness. It soon became apparent that Trok and Naja had skimmed the cream of the regiments for their Mesopotamian adventure, and left only the reserve battalions, made up mostly of new recruits, the very young and untried, or the elderly nearing the end of their military lives, tired and unfit, already looking forward to the retirement and their little plot of land near the river where they could sit in the sun and play with their grandchildren.

'What of the chariots and horses?' Nefer asked the crucial question. The captains shook their grey heads and looked grave. 'Trok and Naja stripped the regiments bare. Almost every vehicle went with them on the western road. They left hardly enough to patrol the eastern borders to discourage the Bedouin raiders from the desert.'

'What about the workshops in Memphis, Avaris and Thebes?' Nefer wanted to know. 'Each of them can turn out at least fifty chariots in a month.'

'As soon as horses are trained to pull them, they are sent to the east to join the army of the twin pharaohs in Babylon.'

Taita assessed this information. 'The false pharaohs are fully aware of the threat we pose to their rear. They want to ensure that if the regiments they have left in Egypt rebel against them and declare for the true Pharaoh, Nefer Seti, they will lack cavalry and chariots to be an effective force.'

'You must return to your regiments,' Nefer ordered the officers. 'We are too many in Gallala already, and we are near the limits of our food and water. Do not allow any more vehicles or horses to leave Egypt. Keep your men in training, and equip the best of them with the new chariots as they become available. I will come to you soon, very soon, to lead you against the tyrants.' They left, praising his name, and with renewed assurances of their loyalty.

'You dare not fulfil your promise to them prematurely. You can only return to Egypt with a powerful force under your command, well trained and well equipped,' Taita advised Nefer. 'These captains who have come over to you are good, loyal men, and I know you can count on them. However, there will be many others who remain true to Trok and Naja, either in fear of the consequences when the false pharaohs return or because they believe in their divine right to rule. Also, there will be many who are undecided, but who will turn against you if they detect any weakness.'

'Then we have much to do.' Nefer accepted this advice. 'We must still break the last of the horses we took at Thane and complete the repairs to the chariots from the dunes. Then our men must finish their training so that they can stand up against Trok and Naja's veterans. When we have done these things, we will return to Egypt.'

So the little army of Gallala redoubled its efforts to build itself into a force to challenge the might of the false pharaohs. They were inspired by their young commander, for Nefer worked harder than any of them. He rode out with the first squadrons long before dawn, and with the other warriors of the Red Road at his side, and Taita to advise him, he gradually forged his divisions into a cohesive body. When he rode back into the city, weary and dusty, in the evening, he would go to the workshops where he cajoled and argued with the foremen armourers and chariot builders. Then, after he had eaten, he would sit up in the lamp-light with Taita, going over the battle plans and the dispositions of their forces. Usually it was after midnight when he stumbled to his bedchamber. Mintaka woke and rose from the bed without complaint to help him strip off his armour and sandals and to bathe his feet and massage aching muscles with sweet oils. Then she warmed a bowl of wine and honey to help him sleep. Often the bowl dropped from his hand before he had finished it, and his head flopped back on to the pillow. Then she would slip off her *chiton*, take his head on to her bosom and hold him until he woke to dawn's first promise.

Each day Meren sank a little lower from the wounds he had received on the Red Road. Taita had strapped his broken ribs and they had healed swiftly enough. He had sewn back the torn ear so neatly that now it was cocked only slightly awry, and Merykara thought that the half-moon scar down his cheek made him look older and more distinguished. However, the sword thrust under his arm worried even Taita: when he probed it he knew from its angle and depth that the weapon must have penetrated Meren's lung. Twice, when it seemed to have healed over, the wound broke open again and leaked foul-smelling pus and fluid. Sometimes Meren was lucid, able to sit up and eat without assistance. Then, when the morbid humours welled up again, he sank back into semi-consciousness and fever.

Merykara stayed at his bedside, changing his dressings and anointing the wound with the unguent Taita brewed for her. When Meren was stronger she sang to him and related all the news of the city and the army. She played bao with him, and made up rhymes and riddles to amuse him. When the wound turned again, she fed him and bathed him like a baby, stroking his sweat-soaked head until he calmed. At night she slept at the foot of his bed, coming awake immediately every time he stirred and muttered in delirium.

She came to know his body as intimately as if he had been her own child. She cleaned his teeth with the green twigs of the acacia tree, chewing the ends into a stiff brush with her own small white teeth. She dressed his hair, brushing it until it grew out long enough to plait again. She trimmed his nails, and came to know and love the shape of his fingers calloused by the hilt of sword and chariot reins. She scraped the wax from his ears, and the dried mucus from his nostrils without the slightest revulsion. She used her own ivory comb on the soft dark hair that grew in thick clumps under his arms, curled on his chest and nestled at the base of his belly.

Each morning she washed every part of him, every crease, plane and bulge of hard muscle, and mourned as his flesh melted off him in the fevers and his bones began to show through.

At first she averted her eyes from his manly parts as she washed them, but soon this seemed prudish to her. Then she cupped them in the hollow of her hand and studied them closely. They invoked in her feelings of tenderness and compassion. They were so soft and warm, the skin so smooth and flawless. Then her emotions changed when she gently drew back the skin in the way that Mintaka had shown her, and the pink tip popped out, silky as an oleander petal. It stiffened and swelled in her hand until she could barely encompass its girth with her thumb and forefinger. When this happened she felt a strange, breathless sensation, and a warmth in the most unlikely parts of her own anatomy.

One night she woke with the moonlight from the window lying like a silver bar across the stone floor of the chamber. For a moment she thought she was in her own bedchamber in the river palace of Thebes, but then she heard Meren's painful breathing, the incoherent cries inspired by his nightmare, and it all came back to her with a rush of dread. She jumped up naked from her mattress at the foot of his couch and ran to him.

When she lit the lamp, she saw that his eyes were wide open but unseeing, and that his face was ashen and contorted, there was a white scum on his lips and his body was shining with running sweat. He was throwing himself about so violently on the crumpled linen sheets that she was terrified he would injure himself further. She knew that this was the crisis Taita had warned her to expect.

'Taita!' she screamed. 'Please, we need you now.' Taita's cell was across the courtyard from theirs, and he always slept with his door open so that he could hear her call.

'Taita!' she shrieked again, as she threw herself across Meren's chest to restrain him. Then she remembered that the Magus had gone into the desert with Nefer and a squadron of chariots on some mysterious expedition, and it was unlikely that they would return for many days. She thought of calling Mintaka, but her chamber was at the other end of the ancient palace, and she dared not leave Meren.

She was on her own. She knew that Meren's life was in her hands, and at that thought she felt her panic subside. A cool determination took its place. She lay against him and held him tightly, whispering encouragement and reassurance. After a while he calmed so that she could leave him for a moment. She went to the chest against the window wall, found the vial that Taita had left for her, mixed the pungent contents with wine and warmed it on the brazier as he had instructed her.

When she held the goblet to Meren's lips he tried to refuse, but she forced him to drink. When the bowl was empty she heated water and washed the sweat from his face, the scum from his lips. She was about to wash his body when a sudden seizure racked him, and he began to shake and groan. Her terror returned in full force. She flung herself on him and clung to him with all her strength. 'Do not die, my darling,' she pleaded with him, and then in a stronger voice, 'I will not let you die. O Hathor, help me. I will drag him back from the underworld with my own hands.' She knew she was in a battle, and she fought with him, extending all her strength and adding it to his. When she felt him go limp in her arms and his sweat-drenched body start to cool, she cried out, 'No, Meren, come back! Come back to me. You cannot go without me.'

She placed her mouth over his and tried to breathe her own life into him. Suddenly he gave an explosive gasp, emptying his lungs, and she thought it was all over. She hugged him with both arms around his bony chest, and when she released the pressure he took another noisy breath, then another and another. The flutter of his heart become a strong, regular thumping that reverberated through her frame.

'You have come back,' she whispered. 'You have come back to me.'

He was still cold, and when he shivered, she held him with both her arms around his chest, and wrapped her legs around his hips, warming him with her own body. Slowly, his breathing became deep and regular, and she felt the warm blood flowing back into his veins. She lay with him and felt a deep sense of fulfilment, for she knew that she had saved him, and that from this night onwards he would belong to her alone.

In the dawn another miracle occurred. She felt his body awaken, and what she had once held soft and small in the palm of her hand now swelled against her once more, becoming enormous, hard as bone, pressing up between her spread thighs.

She looked into his face and saw that he was conscious, his eyes dark and sunken in the wasted sockets, but with an expression of such awe and tenderness in them that her heart swelled within her chest so that she felt she might suffocate with the strength of her own torrential emotions.

'Yes?' he asked.

'Yes,' she answered. 'It is what I want more than anything else in all the world.' She spread herself, and reached down to guide him, aching inside with her need for him, taking him in deeply to the core of her existence, rising with him as if on wings to a place she had never been before, then crying out as she felt him fill her with a hot flood, as though she had drawn out of him and into her own body all his fever and pain and suffering, sensing the deep peace in him as he slumped against her and slept.

She lay quietly beside him, careful not to disturb him, revelling in the sound of his breathing and the warmth of his thin, ravaged body, savouring the ache where he had been deep within her.

She felt him coming awake and kissed him gently on the lips to welcome him back. He opened his eyes and looked into hers, first with bewilderment and then with dawning joy as the events of the night came back to him.

'I want you to be my wife,' he said.

'I am your wife already,' she replied, 'and I will be your wife until the day I die.'

Nefer looked back along the column of chariots. They were at full gallop, four abreast. The platoon commanders were watching for his signal. He looked ahead and saw the line of enemy foot soldiers out in the plain, distorted by the heat mirage so that they seemed to be a wriggling serpent, swimming in a lake of shimmering water where there was no water. He steered for their centre. Under Taita's care, Dov had fully recovered from her wound and now she ran strongly, matching Krus' long stride.

As they raced in he saw the enemy formation change: like a giant hedgehog, the line rolled itself into a ball, a tight circle two ranks deep, facing outwards, the outer rank with their long lances levelled, and the second rank with their lances thrust through the gaps, so that they offered a glittering wall of bronze spearheads. Nefer raced straight at the centre of the double row of lances, and then, when they were only two hundred paces away, he gave the hand signal for the 'wings of Horus'.

The formation of chariots opened like a blossom in the sun, successive ranks wheeling alternately right and left, spreading the wings of Horus to envelop the hedgehog of crouching infantrymen. The chariots whirled around them like the rim of a wheel around the hub, and the arrows from the short recurved cavalry bows flew into them in a dark cloud.

Nefer gave the signal to break off the attack and withdraw. Smoothly the chariots re-formed into columns of four and wheeled away. Another signal, and they split down the centre and came racing back, their javelins poised and the throwing thongs wound around their wrists.

As he swept past the infantry circle, Nefer raised his right fist in a salute, and shouted, 'Well done! That was much better.'

The foot-soldiers raised their lances to acknowledge his praise and shouted, 'Nefer Seti and Horus!'

Nefer slowed the horses and turned them, trotting back to halt his squadron in front of the ranks of infantry. Taita stepped out of the defensive circle to greet him.

'Any injuries?' Nefer asked. Even though the tips of the practice arrows they had shot into the hedgehog were padded with leather, they could still knock out an eye or inflict other damage.

'A few bruises.' Taita shrugged.

'They have done well,' Nefer said, then shouted to the centurion commanding the infantry, 'Let your lads fall out. I want to speak to them. Afterwards they can eat and drink. Then we will practise the false retreat again.'

There was an outcrop of rock that formed a natural podium, and Nefer climbed to the top of it while all the men, infantry and charioteers, gathered below him.

Taita squatted at the base of the rock and watched and listened. Nefer reminded him strongly of Pharaoh Tamose, his father, at the same age. He had the easy manner, and spoke simply but effectively in the colloquial language that his men understood best. At times like these he became one of them, and the warmth and respect they felt for him was evident in the way they responded, grinning and crowding closer to catch every word, laughing at his jests, scowling with shame at his rebukes, and glowing at his compliments.

Nefer reviewed the morning's exercises, giving them the credit they deserved, but ruthlessly picking out every deficiency in their performance.

'I think you are almost ready to give Trok and Naja the surprise of their pretty lives,' he ended. 'Now, get something to eat. We have not finished for the day – in fact we have barely begun.' They laughed and began to disperse.

Nefer jumped down from the rock, and as he did so Taita sprang to his feet and said quietly but urgently, 'Stop, Nefer! Do not move!' Nefer froze where he stood.

The cobra must have had its nest in the rock pile, but the noise and the trampling of feet and hoofs had disturbed it. It came slithering out of the crack in the dark rock just as Nefer jumped down and landed almost on top of it. The serpent reared up behind him, almost as high as his waist. Its hood was flared open, and its feathery black tongue flickered between the thin grinning lips. Its eyes were beads of polished onyx, with sparks of light in the black centres, and they were fastened on Nefer's long bare legs within easy striking distance in front of it.

The nearest men had heard Taita's warning and they turned back. Now almost five hundred men were gathered around Nefer, but none dared move. They stared in horror at the mortal predicament of their pharaoh.

The cobra gaped wide, the preliminary to the attack, and the bony fangs came erect in the pale roof of its mouth. Drops of venom sparkled on the needle points.

Taita swung the Periapt of Lostris on its long chain like a pendulum, and it twinkled in the sunlight. He sent it swinging past the cobra's raised head. Distracted, the serpent swivelled its eyes away from Nefer to stare at the glittering charm. Taita had his staff in his other hand, and he edged closer. 'When I strike, jump clear,' he whispered, and Nefer nodded. Taita moved gradually out to one side and the cobra turned with him, fascinated by the golden charm.

'Now!' said Taita, and thrust at the cobra with his staff. At the same instant Nefer jumped clear, and the snake struck at the staff. Taita jerked away, so the cobra missed and for an instant it was stretched out along the bare earth. With a movement even faster than the strike, Taita pinned it behind the head with the curved end of the staff, and a shout of relief went up from the watchers.

The cobra writhed and coiled into a glittering scaly ball around the end of the staff. Taita reached down and worked his hand through the heaving coils until he could grip the snake behind its head. Then he lifted it up and showed it to the men, who gasped with fear and horror. They shrank back instinctively as it coiled around Taita's long, thin arm. They had expected him to kill it but, still carrying the writhing snake, Taita walked through their ranks, out into the open desert.

There he threw the serpent from him. As it struck the ground it uncoiled and slithered away across the rocky earth. Taita watched it, rapt.

Suddenly there was a shrill cry from the sky above. They had all been so intent on the capture of the cobra that no one had seen the falcon hovering high in the blue above them. Now it stooped towards the earth, dropping towards the cobra. At the last moment the snake became aware of the danger and reared up again, its hood spread wide. In full flight the falcon sank its talons into the flared hood, an inch behind the head, then rose on heavily flogging wings, carrying the cobra dangling and twisting below it.

Taita watched the bird as it bore away the snake. It dwindled in size in the distance and at last disappeared into the blue-grey heat-haze that shrouded the horizon. Taita stood a long time staring after it. When he turned and walked back to where Nefer stood his expression was grave, and he was silent for the rest of that day. In the evening he rode back to Gallala in the chariot beside Nefer, still silent.

'It was an omen,' Nefer said, and glanced at him. He saw by Taita's face that this was so. 'I have listened to the men,' Nefer went on quietly. 'They are disturbed. None of them has ever seen the like before. The cobra is not the natural prey of the royal falcon.'

'Yes,' said Taita. 'It was an omen, a warning and a promise from the god.'

'What does it mean?' Nefer studied his face.

'The cobra threatened you. That means great danger. The royal bird flew towards the east with the snake in its talons. It means great danger in the east. But in the end the falcon triumphed.'

They both looked towards the east. 'We will take out a scouting expedition tomorrow at the first light of dawn,' Nefer decided.

In the chill darkness before the dawn Nefer and Taita waited on the mountain-top. The rest of the scouting party were encamped on the back slope. All told they were twenty men. For the sake of stealth they had left the chariots in Gallala and they travelled on horseback. Wheels threw more dust than hoofs alone, and hoofs made accessible these high, precipitous places along the coast where wheels could not travel.

Hilto and Shabako had taken other scouting parties to cover the terrain to the south; between them they could sweep all the eastern approaches to Gallala.

Nefer had brought his party from the Gebel Ataqa down along the western shores of the Red Sea, looking in on every port and fishing village along the way. Apart from a few trading caravans and wandering bands of Bedouin they had found nothing, no sign of the danger foreshadowed by the omen. Now they were camped above the port of Safaga.

Taita and Nefer had woken in the darkness and left the camp to climb to the look-out peak. They sat close together in companionable silence. Nefer spoke at last.

'Could it have been a false omen?'

Taita grunted and spat. 'A falcon with a cobra in his talons? It is not in nature. It was an omen, without doubt, but false perhaps. Ishtar the Mede and others are capable of setting such snares. It is possible.'

'But you do not think it is?' Nefer insisted. 'You would not have driven us so hard if you believed it to be false.'

'The dawn comes on apace.' Taita avoided the question, and looked instead to the darkling eastern sky, where the morning star hung, like a lantern, low on the horizon. The sky softened like a ripening fruit, turning the colour of persimmon and ripe pomegranate. The mountains of the far shore were black and sharp and ragged as the fangs of an ancient crocodile against the lightening backdrop of the heavens.

Taita stood up suddenly and leaned on his staff. Nefer never failed to be amazed by the acuity of those pale old eyes. He knew Taita had seen something. Nefer stood up beside him.

'What is it, Old Father?'

Taita laid a hand on his arm. 'The omen was not false,' he said simply. 'The danger is here.'

The sea was turning the grey of a dove's belly, but as the light strengthened the surface was speckled with white.

'The wind has whipped the sea into white horses,' Nefer said.

'No.' Taita shook his head. 'Those are not breakers. They're sails. A fleet under sail.'

The sun pushed its upper rim above the tops of the far mountains, and sparkled on the tiny triangles of white. Like a vast flock of egrets returning to the roost, a fleet of dhows was heading into the port of Safaga.

'If this is the army of Trok and Naja, why would they come by sea?' Nefer asked quietly.

'It is the direct and shortest route from Mesopotamia. The boat crossing will save the horses and the men from the hard road through the desert. Without the warning of the snake and the falcon, we would not have expected danger from this direction,' Taita answered. 'It is a cunning move.' He nodded approval. 'It seems that they have commandeered every trading vessel and fishing boat in the entire Red Sea to make the crossing.'

They scrambled back down the mountain to the camp in the gorge below. The troopers were awake and alert. Nefer called in the sentries and gave them their orders. Two would ride back with all speed to Gallala, carrying his orders to Socco, whom he had left in command of the city. Most of the other men he split into pairs and sent south to find the scouting parties under Hilto and Shabako and bring them in. He kept five troopers with him.

Nefer and Taita watched the men he had despatched ride away, then they mounted and rode down through the hills towards Safaga, with the five men Nefer had selected following them. They reached the high ground above the port in the middle of the morning. Taita led them to an abandoned watchtower that overlooked the port and the approaches. They left the horses in the care of the troopers and climbed the rickety ladder to the top platform of the tower.

'The first boats are entering the bay.' Nefer pointed them out. They were deeply laden but with the wind on the quarter they came in swiftly with the bow waves curling white as salt in the sunlight and the big lateen sails bulging.

They rounded up just off the beach and dropped the heavy coral anchors. From the top of the tower Nefer and Taita had a fine view down on to the open decks, which were crowded with men and horses.

As soon as the dhows were anchored the men removed the wooden gunwales along the dhows' sides. Their faint cries carried up to the ruined watchtower as they urged the horses to leap out. They struck the water with tall splashes of spray. Then the men stripped down to loincloths and jumped in after them. They seized the horses' manes and swam alongside them to the beach. The animals came ashore shaking the water from their bodies in a fine mist that turned to rainbows in the sunlight.

Within an hour the beach was swarming with men and horses, and defensive pickets had been set up around the mud-daub buildings of the little port.

'If only we had a squadron of chariots,' Nefer lamented, 'this would be the time to strike. With only half their force ashore and their chariots broken down, we could cut them to pieces.' Taita made no reply to such wishful speculation.

By now the bay was filled with shipping. The boats carrying the chariots and the baggage had anchored close in, and as the tide ran out from under them they took the ground and listed over. Soon the water was only knee deep around their hulls. The men from the beach waded out to begin unloading. They carried the parts of the broken-down chariots ashore and reassembled them on the beach.

The sun was setting over the western mountains when the last dhow entered the bay. This was the largest of them all, and at the peak of her stubby mast she flew the snarling leopard head gonfalon and the gaudy colours of the House of Trok Uruk.

'There he is.' Nefer pointed to the unmistakable figure in the bows.

'And that is Ishtar beside Trok, the dog and its master.' Taita had a fierce gleam in his pale eyes that Nefer had seldom seen before. They watched the strange pair wade ashore.

There was a stone jetty running out across the beach. Trok mounted it. It gave him a vantage-point from which to watch the disembarkation of the rest of his army.

'Do you see Naja's standard on any of the other ships?' Nefer asked, and Taita shook his head.

'Trok alone leads the expedition. He must have left Naja to hold Babylon and Mesopotamia. He has come to take care of personal business.'

'How do you know that?' Nefer demanded.

'There is an aura around him. It is like a dark red cloud. I can sense it even from here,' Taita said softly. 'All that hatred is focused on one person alone. He would never let Naja or anyone else share in the lust for revenge that has brought him here.'

'I am the object of his hatred?' Nefer asked.

'No, not you.'

'Who, then?'

'Above all else he comes for Mintaka.'

When the sun set, Nefer and Taita left the five troopers to shadow Trok's advance and rode hard through the night, back towards Gallala.

The morning after his landing at Safaga, Trok captured two Bedouin leading a string of donkeys down the road to Safaga. Unsuspecting, they walked out of the desert straight into the arms of his pickets. Trok's reputation had penetrated even into these desert fastnesses, so as soon as they learned who was their captor the Bedouin were desperate to please. They gave Trok tantalizing accounts of the resurrection of the ancient city. They told him of the fountain of sweet water that now flowed from the cave in the hills, and of the pastures of lush grass that surrounded Gallala. They also gave him an estimate of the numbers of chariots that Nefer Seti commanded, and Trok realized that he outnumbered his enemies five to one. Most important of all, they gave him details of the route from Safaga to the ancient city. Up to now Trok had had only second-hand knowledge of the approach march to Gallala, and it seemed that he had been misinformed. He had been told that even travelling fast it was a journey of three or four days, and he had planned on carrying his own water and fodder wagons with him from the coast. This would have been a long and laborious process. This new intelligence changed everything. The Bedouin assured him he could reach Gallala in a day and a night of hard riding.

He weighed the risks and dangers, then decided on a dash through the desert to Gallala to take the city by surprise. It would mean, of course, that they would ride straight into battle with the horses exhausted by the long march and with their waterskins empty. However, with numbers and surprise on their side they could seize the fountainhead and the pastures that the Bedouin had described. Once they had those prizes victory was assured.

It took him two more days to disembark all his squadrons, and to assemble the chariots. On the second evening he was ready to begin the forced march on Gallala.

With the waterskins filled, the leading cohorts pulled out of Safaga as soon as the heat went out of the sinking sun. Each of the chariots had two spare teams behind it on lead reins. They would not stop during the night to rest the horses, but would change them as they tired. Any exhausted animals would be turned loose and left behind for the remount herds to bring up.

Trok led the vanguard, and set a killing pace, alternately walking up the inclines, then whipping the horses into a trot or a canter downhill and on level ground. Once the waterskins were empty there was no turning back. By mid-morning the following day the heat had become fierce, and they had used up most of the spare horses.

The Bedouin guides kept assuring Trok that Gallala was not far ahead, but each time they topped a rise the same daunting vista of rock and baked earth shimmered in the heat mirage ahead.

In the late afternoon the Bedouin guides deserted. With the grace of *djinns* they melted away into the heat mirage, and though Trok sent a brace of chariots after them they were never seen again.

'I warned you,' Ishtar the Mede told Trok smugly. 'You should have listened to my advice. Those godless creatures were probably in the pay of Taita the Warlock. Almost certainly he has masked the road, and led us astray. We do not know how far it is to this mythical Gallala, or for that matter if it really exists.' For this uninvited opinion, Trok lashed him across his tattooed face. This did nothing to alleviate the sense of doom and despondency that threatened to overwhelm Trok. He whipped up the horses once more and took them up the next long, stony incline that faced them. He wondered how many more lay ahead. They were almost at the end of their tether, and he doubted they could keep going through the night.

Somehow they kept struggling onwards, or at least most of his force did. Fifty or sixty chariots burned out their last teams of horses, and Trok left them scattered back along the road.

The sun came up on the second day, warm as a kiss after the chill of the night, but it was a treacherous kiss. Soon it stung and dazzled their bloodshot eyes. For the first time Trok faced the possibility of dying here on this dreadful road to nowhere.

'One more hill,' he called to his last team of horses, and tried to whip them into a trot, but they stumbled up the easy incline with their heads hanging, and the sweat long ago dried to white salt on their flanks. Just below the crest Trok looked back down the straggling column of his army. Even without counting them he saw that he had lost half of his chariots. Hundreds of dismounted troopers were staggering along behind the column, but even as he watched he saw two or three fall and lie beside the track like dead men. There were vultures in the sky following them, hundreds of dark specks turning in high circles against the blue. He saw some slant down to the feast he had prepared for them.

'There is only one way,' he told Ishtar, 'and that is forward.' He cracked the whip over the backs of his team, and they went on painfully.

They reached the top of the hill, and Trok gawked in astonishment.

The scene in the valley below him was like nothing he had ever imagined. The ruins of the ancient city rose before him. Their outline seemed ghostly but eternal. As he had been promised, the city was surrounded by fields of cool green, and a network of sparkling water canals. His horses smelt the water and strained against the reins with renewed strength.

Even in his desperate haste, Trok took time to assess the tactical situation. He saw at once that the city was helpless and undefended. The gates stood wide open and from them poured the panic-stricken rabble of the escaping populace. Carrying their children and pathetic bundles of possessions they streamed away up the narrow but steep-sided valley to the west of Gallala. A few foot-soldiers mingled with the refugees, but they were obviously in rout and out of hand. There was no sign of cavalry or of fighting chariots. They were a flock of sheep before the wolf pack, but the wolves were parched and weak with thirst.

'Seueth has delivered them into our hands,' Trok shouted with triumph. 'Before the sun sets this day you will have more women and gold than you can use!'

The cry was taken up by the men who followed him over the ridge, and they rode down as fast as their exhausted horses could move to the first irrigation ditch. They spread out along the length of it, the horses sucking up the blessed liquid until their bellies swelled as though in pregnancy. The men threw themselves full-length along the bank, plunging their faces under, or filling their helmets and pouring it over their heads and down their throats.

'You should have let me poison the irrigation canals,' Nefer said flatly, as they watched from the other side of the valley.

'You know better than that.' Taita shook his silver head. 'That would have been an offence that the gods would never forgive. In this bitter land only Seth or Seueth could contemplate such a foul deed.'

'On this day I could play Seth willingly enough.' Nefer smiled bleakly, but he said it merely to provoke the Magus. 'Your two rogues have done well.' He glanced at the two ragged Bedouin who knelt beside Taita. 'Pay them and let them go.'

'They place no value on gold,' Taita explained. 'When I lived at Gebel Nagara they brought their children to me, and I cured them of the Yellow Flowers.' He made a sign of blessing over the crouching men and said a few words to them in their dialect, thanking them for risking their lives to mislead Trok, and promising them his future protection. They kissed his feet then slipped away among the boulders.

Taita and Nefer gave their full attention to the unfolding battle in the valley below. Trok's men and horses had drunk until their bellies bulged and now they were mounting. Even though he had lost so many chariots on the approach march, Trok still outnumbered Nefer's forces at least three to one.

'We dare not meet him on open ground,' Nefer mused, and looked down upon the mass of refugees escaping up the valley below them. To begin with there had been very few women in the city – Nefer had deliberately kept their numbers down to eke out the reserves of food for his fighting men – and even they, including Mintaka and Merykara, together with all the children, the sick and wounded, had been evacuated from Gallala two days before. Meren had gone on one of the wagons carrying the contents of the treasury, the gold they had lifted from the false pharaohs. Nefer had sent them all to Gebel Nagara, where Trok would never find them, and the tiny spring of water would just support them until after the battle was decided.

Now Gallala was stripped of everything of value, every chariot, weapon and piece of armour. He gazed down on the refugees with satisfaction. Even from this close it was difficult to tell that they were not women and civilians, but disguised foot-soldiers. Many of these stalwarts were tripping and stumbling in their long skirts and shawls. The bundles they carried in their arms were not swaddled infants, but their bows and swords wrapped in shawls. Their long lances had been cached among the rocks higher up the valley were his main force was concealed.

All Trok's chariots had finished watering and they were coming on across the pastures in tight and ordered formations, wave after wave of fighting vehicles. The water had revived then miraculously, and before them lay the promise of plunder and rapine.

'Pray Horus that we can entice Trok to take up the pursuit and enter the valley,' Nefer whispered. 'If he does not take the bait and seizes the undefended city instead, then he denies us the water and grazing. We would be forced to come to battle on the open ground where he would have every advantage.'

Taita said nothing. He stood with the golden Periapt pressed to his lips and his eyes turned upwards in the attitude the Nefer had come to know so well.

The enemy were close enough now for Nefer to be able to pick out Trok's chariot among the moving mass of vehicles, as it wheeled into a position across the mouth of the valley crowded with the fleeing refugees. Trok was in the centre of the leading rank, ten of his chariots on each of his flanks, on a front wide enough to sweep the valley from side to side. Behind him the rest of his chariots were formed up. The dust settled around them and a terrible silence fell over them. The only sound was the faint babble and hubbub of the fleeing rabble in the gut of the narrow valley ahead of them.

'Come, Trok Uruk!' Nefer whispered. 'Order the charge! Ride into history!'

In the leading chariot in the front rank of the massed forces, Ishtar the Mede crouched beside Trok's massive armoured figure. He was so agitated that he reached up to tug at the ribbons of Trok's beard.

'The smell of the Warlock hangs in the air like the reek of a ten-day-old corpse.' His voice was shrill, and saliva frothed on his lips and flew in a cloud with the force of his emotion. 'He waits for you up there, like a man-eating beast. I can feel his presence. Look up, mighty Pharaoh!'

Trok was distracted enough to glance up at the sky. The vultures had dropped lower.

'Yes! Yes!' Ishtar pressed the small advantage. 'They are Taita's chickens. They wait for him to feed them with your flesh.'

Trok looked back up the valley at the prize that lay before him, but the shadows of the vultures flitted over the earth between them and he hesitated.

Hidden among the boulders on the steep side of the valley Nefer watched him. He was so close now that Nefer fancied that he could read his expression.

'Forward, Trok!' Nefer murmured. 'Sound the charge. Lead your army into the valley.' He could sense doubt in the manner that Trok fiddled with the reins in his hand, and turned his head to look down at the skinny figure of Ishtar beside him.

The Mede's blue-painted face was turned up to him earnestly, and he touched Trok and tugged at his armour with the force of his entreaties. 'It is a snare laid for you by the Warlock. If you never trust me again, you must trust me now. There is death in the air, and the stench of treachery. I can feel Taita's spells like bats' wings beating against my face.'

Trok scratched his beard, and glanced over his shoulder at the ranks of chariots parked wheel to wheel and his troopers leaning forward in cruel anticipation of his order.

'Turn aside, mighty Trok. Seize the city and the water fountain. Nefer Seti and the Warlock will perish out there in the desert, as we so nearly did. That way is certain. The other way is madness.'

On the hillside Nefer narrowed his eyes as he watched his disguised troopers scurrying away up the valley, and he knew that the moment was passing. 'What is holding Trok? Will he not commit to the charge?' Nefer cried aloud. 'If he does not charge now . . .'

'Look to the head of the valley.' Taita had not opened his eyes. Even in his agitation Nefer glanced up the valley, and stiffened with alarm. His fist tightened on the hilt of his sword until the knuckles turned white as bone.

'It is not possible!' he growled.

Near the top end of the valley, but fully visible from where Trok's chariots were drawn up, was a slab of rock. Square and ochre-coloured, it stood like a man-made monument beside the road. On top of this, above the stream of fleeing refugees, had appeared a single figure. It was a woman, young and slim, with long dark hair that hung to her waist. Her *chiton* was the crimson of the royal House of Apepi: it stood out brilliantly, a speck of colour in the bleakness of bare rock and sand.

'Mintaka!' Nefer breathed. 'I ordered her to go with Meren and Merykara to Gebel Nagara.'

'We know that she would never have disobeyed you.' Taita opened his eyes and smiled ironically. 'Therefore, it seems that she must have misheard you.'

'This is your doing,' Nefer said bitterly. 'You are using her as bait for Trok. You have placed her in mortal danger.'

'Perhaps I can control the *khamsin*,' Taita said, 'but not even I can control Mintaka Apepi. What she does, she does of her own free will.'

Below them Trok had turned to give the order for his chariots to wheel away, to let the rabble escape, and to seize the fountain and the city of Gallala as Ishtar was urging him. Before he could speak he felt Ishtar stiffen beside him, and heard him whisper, 'This is something that Taita has conjured.'

Trok jerked around and stared up the long rising valley. He saw the tiny figure in the crimson dress, standing high on the yellow rock platform. He recognized in an instant the object of all his hatred and rage. 'Mintaka Apepi,' he snarled, 'I have come for you, you adulterous little dog-bitch. I will make you plead for death.'

'It is an illusion, Pharaoh. Don't let the Warlock deceive you.'

'That is no illusion,' Trok said grimly. 'I will prove it to you when I bury my prong in her warm flesh, and prod her until she bleeds.'

'The Warlock has blinded you,' Ishtar howled. 'There is death all around us.'

He tried to leap down from the footplate and run, but Trok seized him by his lacquered locks and hauled him back. 'Nay, stay with me,

Ishtar the Mede. I will let you have a taste of her sweet crevice before I throw her to my bully-boys to finish off.' He raised his clenched fist high above his head and shouted, 'Forward! March!'

The chariots on either hand rolled forward together, and the ranks behind followed Trok into the valley, the sun sparkling on the javelin heads and the dust rose around them like smoke. The tail of the fleeing refugees was three hundred paces ahead when Trok gave his next order.

'Forward at the gallop! Charge!'

The horses leaped away, and in a rising thunder of hoofs and wheels they swept up the narrow valley.

'Trok has committed,' Nefer said softly. 'But at what cost? If he takes Mintaka...' He could not bring himself to go on, but he stared in anguish at her tall lithe figure standing serenely in the path of the storm.

'Now you have something to fight for,' Taita said gently.

Nefer felt all his love and deadly concern for Mintaka become battle rage, but it was a cold hard rage that sharpened every one of his senses and filled his being to the exclusion of all else.

As the phalanx of chariots swept by below where he stood on the side of the valley, he stepped out from behind the rock that had concealed him. The complete attention of Trok and his troopers was fixed on the helpless victims ahead of their racing chariots. They had no eyes for the tall figure that appeared suddenly high on their flank. But all Nefer's men could see him clearly. They were hidden among the boulders down both slopes of the valley. Nefer raised his sword above his head, and as the last chariot sped past he brought it down sharply.

The wagons were poised on the steep gradient, with their wheels chocked and lashed to hold them. They were screened from view with dried grass the exact colour of their surroundings, and they were so heavily laden with rocks that the axles sagged. At Nefer's signal his wagoners pulled out the wooden chocks and slashed away the lashings that held the wheels. From both sides of the valley the wagons rolled forward, gathering speed, bounding down on top of the massed chariots below.

When Ishtar screamed at his side, Trok tore his eyes from the Mintaka's figure at the far end of the valley, and he saw the huge vehicles tearing down upon his squadrons. 'Back!' he shouted. 'Break away!' But even his bull voice was lost in the uproar. The charge once launched could not be stopped, and there was no space to manoeuvre in the narrow floor of the valley.

The first wagons crashed into the head of the charge. There was the rending of wood, the screams of crushed men and horses, the thunder of wagons overturning and capsizing, shedding their loads of rock.

Suddenly the way ahead of Trok was blocked by one of the cumbersome carts, and his horses swerved into the chariot running beside him. In an instant the magnificent charge was transformed into a shambles of shattered and overturned vehicles, and crippled horses.

The wagons had sealed off the valley at both ends. Even the chariots that had not been smashed and capsized were now bottled up in a struggling mass. The whole purpose of the chariot, its strength and threat, was its ability to run and turn, to charge and pull back at speed. Now they were immobilized, held by walls of stone, and Nefer's archers were on the slopes above them. The first volleys decimated the unprotected charioteers. Within minutes the valley was transformed into a slaughterhouse.

Some of Trok's men jumped down from their trapped vehicles and charged up the sides of the valley on foot. But they were exhausted by the gruelling approach march, and burdened with their armour. The ground was steep and rugged and they moved only slowly. From the cover of the boulders and walls of hastily erected stone *zarebas*, Nefer's men met them with long lances and hails of javelins. Most were cut down before they had reached the first rank of defenders.

Trok looked around him wildly, seeking some way out of the trap, but one of his horses was dead, crushed by the spilled load of rocks from the wagon that blocked his way forward. Behind him the other vehicles were so crowded that there was no room for him to turn or back up. Arrows and javelins were singing around him, clattering against the sides of the chariot, clanging off his helmet and breastplate.

Before Trok could restrain him, Ishtar took advantage of the confusion to spring down from the footplate and scuttle away between the wrecked chariots and plunging, shrilling horses. Then Trok looked ahead again, and incredulously he saw Mintaka still standing unmoved on the top of the ochre rock pile just ahead of him. She was staring at him with a cold look of revulsion on her lovely face that turned his rage to madness.

He snatched up his war bow from the rack at his side and reached for an arrow from the quiver, but then he changed his mind, threw the weapon aside and shouted at her over the heads of his rearing and plunging horses. 'No! An arrow is too good for a bitch in heat. I am coming to get you with my bare hands, I want to feel you struggling as I squeeze the last breath out of you, you filthy little harlot.'

He drew his sword and sprang down to the ground. He ran forward under the hoofs of his rearing horse, and scrambled over the overturned body of the wagon. Two of Nefer's men jumped out from behind the rocks to oppose him but he hacked them down and ran over their twitching corpses. His eyes were fastened hungrily on the girl in the crimson dress standing tall and proud ahead of him, the flame to the moth.

Nefer saw Trok break out of the trap, and he ran down the slope, springing from rock to rock. 'Run, Mintaka! Get away from him,' he shouted urgently, but either she did not hear him or she would not listen.

Trok did hear him, and he stopped and looked up. 'Come on, then, my pretty boy, I have enough blade for both you and your whore.'

Without breaking his run, Nefer hurled the javelin in his hand, but Trok caught it neatly in the centre of the light targe he carried on his shoulder, and the weapon spun away, clattering on the rock, and landed at Mintaka's feet. She ignored it.

The throw had been enough to divert Trok for the moment, and Nefer sprang down on to the level ground in front of him. Trok went on guard as Nefer confronted him and then his face twisted into a ferocious grin. He crouched behind the bronze shield and waved the sword in his right hand. 'Come, puppy,' he said. 'Let us test your claim to the double crown.'

Nefer used the impetus of his run down the slope and came at him without a pause. Trok caught the first blow on the circle of bronze. Nefer jumped back just as Trok cut at him over the top of the targe. Nefer closed in again, trading thrust for cut.

Nefer's men had seen him charge down the hillside. They followed his example, left the cover of the rocks and came bounding down in waves. Within seconds the full length of the valley was choked from side to side with struggling, hacking, thrusting men.

Nefer feinted at Trok's hip, aiming at the joint of his armour. When Trok covered, he swung backhanded at his face. Trok was surprised by the change of direction and by the speed of the stroke. Though he jerked his head back the point of Nefer's blade split his cheek open and the blood gushed into his beard. The wound galvanized him, and Trok roared and rushed at Nefer. He swung blows from every angle with such rapidity that his sword seemed to form an impenetrable wall of shining bronze around him. Nefer was forced to fall back before the attack until he felt the stone slab on which Mintaka stood pressing into his back.

He could no longer retreat or manoeuvre, and he was forced to pit himself against all Trok's bull-like strength, and trade him blow for blow. In a contest of this nature, there were few men who could stand against Trok, who never seemed to flag, and he laughed as Nefer managed to turn some of his blows. 'Let us see how long you can stem the tide, boy. I can go on like this all day, can you?' he asked, without missing a stroke. Metal clanged and rang on metal, while Trok moved gradually to the right blocking the only way that Nefer might slip out of his clutches.

Trok's strength was like some malignant force of nature. Nefer felt that he was caught in a great storm wind, as helpless as if he were carried away on a rip-tide of the ocean. As much as the years of battle training had hardened him, they had not prepared him for this. He felt his right arm tiring and slowing as he tried to match Trok.

Trok nicked the side of his neck, and then seconds later sliced open his leather corselet and scored him along the ribs. Nefer knew that his only chance of surviving the storm was to trade his speed and agility against Trok's brute strength, but he was pinned against the rock. He had to break away.

He caught the next cut high on his blade and deflected it just sufficiently to make an opening through which he could escape, but as he leaped into it he exposed his left flank. Trok recovered and drove in a low thrust that laid open his thigh just above the tattooed cartouche. The blood ran down into his sandal and squelched at every pace he took.

The last of Nefer's strength was ebbing away, and Trok swept up his blade and locked it with his own, forcing his guard higher and higher. Nefer knew that if he attempted to break away he would expose his chest for the killing thrust. Yet the cut in his thigh had weakened and slowed him still further. The grin on Trok's face was triumphant. 'Courage, boy! It is nearly over. Then you can rest – for ever,' he gloated.

Nefer heard Mintaka shout something, but it made no sense, and he could not afford the distraction. Gradually Trok forced aside his blade and towered over him, so they came chest to chest, then suddenly he shifted his weight to the left, towards Nefer's wounded leg. Nefer tried to counter, but his leg gave way under him. Trok hooked his foot behind Nefer's heel and threw him over backwards.

The sword flew from Nefer's weakened grip, and as he sprawled on the sunbaked earth, Trok lifted his blade above his head with both hands for the killing stroke. He was poised like that when suddenly his expression changed to one of surprise and bewilderment. Without completing the blow he reached up behind his own neck with one hand. He brought the hand back and held it before his face. It was wet with his blood. He opened his mouth to say something, but a double stream of bright blood trickled from the corners of his mouth and he turned slowly away from Nefer. Trok stared up at Mintaka who stood on the pinnacle of the rock above him. With a detached feeling of disbelief, Nefer saw the shaft of the javelin sticking out of the back of Trok's neck.

As she saw Nefer go down, Mintaka had snatched up the javelin that lay at her feet, the weapon that Nefer had thrown at the start of the engagement. She hurled it at Trok's back. The point took Trok beneath the rim of his bronze helmet and went in deeply, just missing the spinal column, but opening the carotid artery.

Standing like a gargoyle with his mouth wide open, blood spewing out in a fountain, Trok dropped his sword and reached up. He seized Mintaka around the waist and dragged her screaming from her perch above him. He was trying to say something, but the sheets of blood pouring from his mouth drowned his voice.

Mintaka screamed as he crushed her to his chest, and Nefer scrambled to his feet. He picked up Trok's sword from where he had dropped it, and limped up behind him.

Mintaka's cries had given renewed strength to his sword arm. He sent his first thrust through the lacings of Trok's corselet, deeply into his back. Trok stiffened, and dropped Mintaka. She scrambled away, and Nefer pulled out the blade and stabbed again. Swaying on his feet, Trok turned slowly to face him. He took a step towards Nefer, reaching out for him with bloody mailed hands. Nefer stabbed him in the throat, and Trok dropped to his knees, clutching at the blade. Nefer pulled it away, slicing deeply into Trok's fingers and palms, severing the sinews and nerves.

Trok toppled forward on his face, and Nefer stabbed him through the lacing, between his shoulder-blades to his heart. He left the blade in him, and turned to Mintaka who crouched in the shelter of the rock. She flew to him, and clung to him with all her strength. Now that the danger was past, Mintaka lost all her icy control and she was sobbing, barely coherently, 'I thought he was going to kill you, my love.'

'He almost did, but for you,' Nefer gasped. 'I owe you a life.'

'It was terrible.' Mintaka's voice quavered. 'I thought he would never die.'

'He was a god.' Nefer tried to laugh but it came out wrongly. 'They take a little killing.'

He became aware that the sounds of battle from further down the valley had changed. With his arm still around her, he turned to look back. Trok's men had seen their pharaoh cut down, and the fight had gone out of them. They were throwing down their weapons, and wailing, 'Enough! Enough! We yield. All praise to Pharaoh Nefer Seti, the one true king.'

With the realization of victory, Nefer felt the last vestiges of strength flow out of his battered and bleeding body. He had just enough left to raise his voice, and shout, 'Give them quarter. They are our brother Egyptians. Give them quarter!'

As Nefer slumped down, Taita materialized at his side and helped Mintaka lower him to the ground. While the two of them dressed his wounds, and staunched the bleeding from the deep cut in his thigh, his officers came to report to Nefer.

Nefer discounted his own injuries as he demanded to know who had survived the battle and who had been wounded and killed. With joy, and thanks to Horus and the Red God, Nefer saw that his trusted captains, Hilto, Shabako and Socco, were among the men who crowded around him, exulting in the victory, proud of themselves and their men, filled with joy to see him alive.

They made a litter of lances and carried him back down the valley to Gallala, but it was a long journey for Trok's captured officers, and men crowded the roadside, kneeling unarmed and bare-headed to plead for his mercy, shouting repentance and remorse that they had ever taken up arms against the true Pharaoh.

Three times before they reached the gates of the city, Nefer signalled for his litter to be lowered and allowed the captured centurions and captains to come forward and kiss his feet. 'I spare you from the traitor's death you so richly deserve,' he told them sternly, 'but you are all reduced to the rank of sergeants of the Blue, and you must prove once more your duty and loyalty to the House of Tamose.'

They praised him for his mercy, but Nefer frowned and shook his head when they addressed him as a god. 'I am not one of the pantheon, as the blasphemers Trok and Naja claim they are.' But they would not be dissuaded, and renewed their praises and entreaties, and his own men led by his brother warriors of the Red Road, joined their voices to those of the defeated, begging him to declare his divinity.

To distract them Nefer issued his orders with a frowning mien. 'The corpse of Trok Uruk, the false claimant to the double crown of this very Egypt, shall be burned without ceremony, here upon the battlefield so, that his soul shall wander through all eternity seeking but never finding a home.'

They murmured with awe for this was the most dreadful punishment that could be devised.

'The other enemy dead are to be treated with all respect, and allowed embalmment and a decent burial. The name of Trok Uruk shall be erased from every monument and building in the land, and the temple that he erected to himself in Avaris shall in his stead be dedicated to the winged Horus in memory of the victory that he gave us this day before the city of Gallala.'

They shouted their approbation at this decree, and Nefer went on, 'All the possessions of Trok Uruk, all his treasure and estates, his slaves and buildings, his warehouses and goods of whatsoever nature shall be forfeited to the state. Send water wagons back along the road to Safaga, with grooms and surgeons to bring in all the horses, chariots and men that Trok Uruk left along the way during his arrogant march on our capital here in Gallala. If they repudiate the false pharaohs and swear allegiance to the House of Tamose the prisoners shall be pardoned and recruited into our armies.'

By the time Nefer had given his last order, and issued his last decree for that day, his voice was hoarse, he was pale and almost exhausted. As they carried him through the city gates he asked Mintaka quietly, 'Where is Taita? Has anybody seen the Magus?' But Taita had disappeared.

Taita watched from the hillside above the battlefield as the jaws of the trap closed on Trok's army and his chariots were smashed by the rock-filled wagons, the arrows and the javelins falling like flights of locusts upon the survivors, when a single bizarre figure caught his eye in the chaos.

Ishtar the Mede scampered between the rocks. Like a running hare he disappeared from sight only to reappear further up the slope, ducking and dodging. By some chance or magical charm he avoided the arrows and javelins of Nefer's troops and at last dived over the crest and disappeared from sight.

Taita let him go. There would be time for him later. He watched the climax of the battle, extending all his powers to act as a shield over Nefer during his single combat with Trok at the base of the rock. Even at this distance he managed to deflect many of Trok's blows that should have been fatal, and when Trok went for the final thrust into Nefer's thigh his blade might have found the great femoral artery if Taita had not used all his influence to turn the point aside.

Since that time long ago when Taita had saved Mintaka from harm during the encounter with the cobra of the goddess, she had become a subject who responded readily to his influence. She had the intelligence and imagination that opened her mind to him. It was impossible to influence a fool. He had summoned her back to Gallala to show herself to Trok at the head of the valley, and to lure him into the trap. Then, when she had stood frozen with horror on the rock above the fighting pair, Taita had bent her to his will once again and put into her mind the impulse to reach down for the javelin that lay at her feet. He had bolstered her right arm as she steadied her aim and threw. Then, as the life went out of Trok, he had rushed down the slope to minister to Nefer and to bind up the wound that had cut so perilously close to the pulsing artery in his thigh.

When his brother warriors of the Red Road lifted the young pharaoh on to the litter of spears, Taita with his duty done for the present drifted away into the throng. Nobody paid him any heed as he went.

He picked up the tracks that Ishtar had left as he escaped out of the narrow valley and followed them until they were impossible to discern on the earth on the top of the hills, which was baked hard as mosaic tiles by the sun.

Taita stopped and crouched down. From his pouch he took out a sliver of dried root and slipped it into his mouth. As he chewed on it, he opened his mind and reached out to detect the Mede's aura, the trace he had left as he passed. As the root sharpened his senses Taita saw the aura in the corner of his vision. It was a shadow, dirty grey and ephemeral, that vanished when he looked directly at it. Each person had his own aura. Nefer Seti, on account of his noble and divine inner being, threw a rosy essence that to Taita was readily detectable. Taita had followed that faint rosy emanation to find Nefer after he had been mauled by the lion and he and Mintaka were lost in the desert beyond Dabba.

Ishtar the Mede's aura was dark and tainted. Taita stood up and went on again after it, striding out on his long legs with his staff tapping on the stones. Every so often he saw physical confirmation that he was on the right track, by a smudged footprint in a softer patch of earth or by a recently dislodged pebble.

Ishtar had circled round to the south then come back towards Gallala. Taita was alarmed and lengthened his stride. If Ishtar was trying to get close to Nefer again to work some mischief, Taita must intercept him. However, the pursuit led him to one of the chariots Trok had abandoned on his march up from the coast. From the wreck Ishtar had salvaged something, and Taita closed his eyes and worked out what it was.

'A waterskin,' he murmured, and Taita saw where he had scraped away the earth to drag the skin out from under the side of the capsized chariot. Another dry and empty skin was still hanging there. Ishtar had left it, probably because he knew he could carry the weight of only one full skin. Taita picked up the empty skin and slung it over his shoulder. He left the chariot, with the dead horses in the traces already beginning to stink, and followed Ishtar onwards.

Carrying the waterskin with him, Ishtar had gone back towards Gallala. When he topped the ridge above the city he had crept down to the bank of the closest irrigation canal. The imprint of his knees was clear in the wet clay where he had knelt to drink and then to fill the skin he carried. Taita drank himself. After that he filled his own waterskin. Then he rose and followed the traces Ishtar had left as he started back eastwards along the road towards Safaga and the coast. Taita strode after him.

Night fell and Taita kept on. Sometimes the aura of the Mede faded away completely, but Taita followed the road. At other times it grew stronger, until Taita smelt it, a faint, musty, unpleasant odour. When it was this strong he could fathom the essence of the Mede. He could detect his vindictive and vengeful nature. He divined that Ishtar was frightened and demoralized by the turn that the fates had taken against him, but his powers were still formidable. He constituted a great and real danger, not only to Nefer and Mintaka but to Taita himself. If he were allowed to escape and regenerate his scattered powers, he might threaten the future of the House of Tamose and Apepi. Ishtar was one of the higher adepts, an evil one, which made him all the more dangerous. He could certainly overlook his selected victims, and conjure up all manner of profanities to bring down disaster on Nefer and Mintaka. He could sicken and sour their love for each other, bring down suffering, miscarriage and plague, pains and disease with no focus or reason, mental aberrations, madness and eventually death.

Even Taita was not immune to his baleful spirit. If he were allowed to escape, Ishtar might gradually erode Taita's powers and frustrate his work. Unless Taita acted now, while he had the opportunity, to destroy him utterly.

The gibbous moon rose over the stark hills and lit Taita's way. He was in that long swinging stride with which he could cover the ground as swiftly as a mounted man. He could sense that ahead of him Ishtar was unaware that he was being followed and his pace was much slower. Every hour that passed Taita felt his aura stronger and nearer. I will be up to him before sunrise, he thought, and at that moment he doubled over and vomited in a projectile stream on to the stony track. Overwhelmed with a sudden, terrible nausea, Taita almost collapsed but regained his balance, and staggered back, wiping the bitter taste of bile from his mouth.

'Careless!' he rebuked himself angrily. 'So close to the quarry I should have taken greater care. The Mede has detected me.'

He drank a little water from the skin, then went forward cautiously. He pointed his staff ahead and swung it slowly from side to side. Suddenly it grew heavy in his hand. He followed that direction and saw ahead of him, glinting in the moonlight, the circle of pale pebbles laid out on the side of the track.

'A gift from the Mede,' he said aloud.

Nausea seized him once more, but he choked it back, struck the earth with the staff and spoke one of the words of power.

'*Ncube!*' His nausea receded, and he could approach the circle closer.

It is not enough that I should break his spell, he thought grimly. I must turn it back upon the Mede.

He used the tip of his staff to move one of the pebbles out of the circle, disrupting its power. Now he could squat beside the pattern without experiencing any harm. Without touching any of the pebbles he leaned close and sniffed at them. The smell of the Mede was strong upon them and he smiled with cold satisfaction.

'He touched them with his bare hands,' Taita whispered. Ishtar had left traces of his sweat on them. Taita could use that faint effluent. Careful not to make the same mistake, he moved the pebbles with the tip of his staff, forming them into a different pattern, an arrowhead pointing in the direction that Ishtar had taken. He took a mouthful of water from the skin and spat it on the pebbles, which shone wetly in the moonlight. Then he pointed his staff like a javelin along the same line as the arrowhead of pebbles.

'*Kydash!*' he shouted, and felt pressure build up in his eardrums as though he had plunged deeply below the surface of the ocean. Before it became unbearable, it began slowly to abate, and he felt a sense of well-being and pleasure. It was done. He had turned it back upon the Mede.

A league ahead Ishtar the Mede was hurrying along the track. He was by now fully aware of the pursuit. He was confident that the barrier he had placed across the track would stop most men, but he knew it would not long deter the one he feared most.

Suddenly he staggered in mid-stride and clutched his ears with both hands. The pain was blinding, as though a red hot dagger had been thrust deep into each of his eardrums. He groaned and dropped to his knees. 'It is the Warlock.' He sobbed. The pain was so intense that he could not think clearly. 'He has turned it back on me.'

With shaking hands he reached into the pouch on his belt and brought out his most potent talisman, the dry embalmed hand of one of Pharaoh Tamose's infants who had died soon after birth during the plague of the Yellow Flowers. Ishtar had robbed the little prince's tomb to obtain it. The hand was dark and clawed like a monkey's paw.

He held it to his pounding head, and felt the pain start to abate. He came unsteadily to his feet, and broke into a shuffling dance, chanting and wailing. The pain in his ears cleared. He gave one final leap in the air and stood facing back along the way he had come. He could feel the presence of the Warlock close, like the threat of thunder on a close summer's day.

He thought of laying another snare, but knew that Taita would send it back to him. I must turn aside and conceal my path, he decided. He ran on along the road seeking the place where he could turn. He found where the track crossed an intrusion of grey schist, so hard that even the passing of Trok's legions had left no mark upon it.

With his left forefinger he traced out lightly the sacred symbol of Marduk on the rock, spat on it and uttered the three hidden names of the god that would summon him.

'Hide me from my enemies, mighty Marduk. Bring me safely back to your temple in Babylon, and I will make for you the sacrifice you love so well,' he promised. Best of all Marduk loved little girls sent into his furnace.

Ishtar stood on one leg and hopped backwards five and fifty paces, the esoteric number of Marduk known only to the adepts. Then he turned sharply off the road and set out at right angles to it, heading into the northern wilderness. He went swiftly, trying to open the distance between him and the man who pursued him.

Taita reached the point where the ridge of grey schist crossed the road, and stopped abruptly. The aura that had been so strong only moments before had disappeared like mist in the warmth of the rising sun. There was neither taste nor smell nor a glimpse of the Mede remaining. He went on down the road a short way, but found that the trail was dead and cold. Quickly he retraced his steps until he reached the point where he had lost it. Ishtar would not have wasted his time with a simple spell of concealment. He knows that the Ashes or the Water and Blood would hardly give me pause, he thought.

He looked up at the sky, and from the starry firmament picked out the single red star low on the horizon, the star of the goddess Lostris. He held up her Periapt and began to chant the Praise to the Goddess. He had barely completed the first stanza when he felt an angry, alien presence. Another god had been invoked on this spot, and knowing Ishtar he could guess well enough who that was. He started on the second stanza of praise and on the bare rock ahead of him appeared a glow, like that of the copper walls of the furnace in the temple of Marduk when the sacrificial fires were burning.

Marduk is affronted, and shows his anger, he thought, with satisfaction. He went to stand over the faintly glowing spot and intoned. 'You are far from your own land and your temple, Marduk of the furnace. Few worship you in this very Egypt. Your powers are dissipated. I invoke the name of the goddess Lostris, and you cannot stand against it.'

He lifted the skirt of his *chiton*. 'I quench your fires, Marduk,' he said, and squatting like a woman, he urinated on the rock. It sizzled and steamed like a bar of metal from the forge of the coppersmith drenched in the trough. 'In the name of the goddess Lostris, Marduk the Devourer, stand aside and let me pass.'

The rock cooled quickly, and as the steam dispersed he could make out once more the shadowy traces of the Mede beyond as they turned off the track towards the north. The veil that Ishtar had laid was pierced and torn. Taita stepped through it and set off again after him.

The horizon paled and the light increased to a golden radiance in the east. Taita knew that he was gaining steadily, and he strained his eyes ahead in the gathering light for the first glimpse of his quarry. Instead he came to an abrupt halt. At his feet gaped a terrible abyss, whose sheer sides dropped into darkness far below. No man could scale those depths, and there was no way around this obstacle.

Taita looked across at the far side. It was at the very least a thousand paces across, and the precipice was even more daunting when seen from this angle. There were vultures soaring over the bottomless gulf. One of the grotesque birds circled in to alight on its shaggy nest of sticks and twigs built on a ledge high in the opposite cliff face.

Taita shook his head with admiration. 'Wonderful, Ishtar!' he murmured. 'Even the vultures. That was a masterful touch. I could not have improved upon it, but such an effort called for a great expenditure of strength. It must have cost you dearly.'

Taita stepped out over the edge of the cliff, and instead of plunging down into airy space, there was firm ground under his feet. The vista of cliffs and gorges, even the circling vultures, wavered and broke up as a mirage does when you walk towards it.

The abyss was gone and in its place was a gentle plain of stony ground, with low hills still blue with shadows at the far end. In the middle of this plain, not five hundred paces away, stood Ishtar the Mede. He was facing Taita with both arms held above his head, trying desperately to preserve the illusion that he had created. When he saw that he had failed and that Taita was striding towards him like an avenging *djinn*, he dropped his arms with a hopeless, resigned gesture and turned towards the limestone hills at the far end of the stony plain. He broke into a shambling run, his black robes swirling around his legs.

Taita followed him with his long indefatigable strides, and when Ishtar looked back there was desperation on his blue-whorled face. For a moment he stared in terror at the tall silver-haired figure, then he turned and ran faster. For a while he pulled away, opening the gap, then his run faltered, and Taita gained upon him inexorably.

Ishtar dropped the waterskin from his shoulder, and ran with a lighter step, but he was only a few hundred paces ahead of Taita when he reached the low hills that were grey blue with limestone outcrops in the early light. He disappeared into one of the gullies.

When Taita reached the mouth of the gully he saw Ishtar's footprints strung along the sandy floor ahead of him, but they disappeared round the corner where the gully turned sharply to the right. Taita followed him, but as he reached the corner of pale limestone pillars, he heard the thunderous grunting and roaring of a wild beast. As he stepped round he saw that the gully narrowed ahead of him, and standing foursquare in the way, its tail lashing from side to side, was a huge male lion.

The lion's black mane was erect, a great bush that shook like grass in a high wind at each roar that erupted from the gaping jaws. Its eyes were golden and the pupils were implacable black slits. The rank, bestial scent of the animal was thick in the hot air, the stench of the rotting carcasses on which it had feasted with those long yellow fangs.

Taita looked down at the sandy earth on which the massive paws were planted with all the claws unsheathed. He could still see Ishtar's footprints in the sand, but the paws of the lion had left no mark.

Taita never broke his stride. He raised the Periapt on its chain, and walked straight at the slavering animal. Instead of rising in pitch the roaring became muted, the outline of its head turned transparent so that he could see the rock walls of the gully through it. Then, like river mist, the animal faded and was gone.

Taita walked through the space where it had stood and rounded the corner. Ahead of him the gully became narrower still and the sides were steeper. It ended abruptly against a wall of rock.

Ishtar stood with his back against the rock, staring at Taita with mad eyes. The whites were yellowed and bloodshot, the pupils black and dilated. The smell of his terror was more rank than the odour of the phantom lion had been. He raised his right hand and pointed a long bony finger at Taita. 'Back, Warlock!' he screamed. 'I warn you!'

Taita walked towards him and he screamed again, this time in a guttural language, and made the gesture of hurling some unseen missile at Taita's head. Quickly Taita held the Periapt of Lostris before his eyes, and felt something fly close past his head, with the sound of a flighting arrow.

Ishtar turned and bolted into a narrow opening in the rock wall behind him, that had been screened from Taita by his body. Taita paused before the entrance, and tapped the stony portals with his staff. The rock rang true, and he heard Ishtar's blundering footsteps echoing out of the dark entrance. Taita was almost certain that this was no illusion, but the real entrance to a cavern in the limestone cliff.

Taita stepped through after him, and found that he was in a low, rocky passage, dimly lit by the sunlight through the entrance behind him. The floor of the cave sloped away in front of him, and he went on, stepping more cautiously. Now he was certain that the passage was real in time and dimension, not something conjured up by the Mede to thwart him and turn him aside.

He could hear the echoes of Ishtar's footsteps, distorted and magnified in the tunnel ahead. Taita counted his paces as he went forward into darkness. After a hundred and twenty the light strengthened again, a strong emanation from some source deeper in the hillside.

Suddenly the tunnel took a sharp bend, and as he stepped round it Taita found himself in a large cavern with a high roof. In the centre of the roof was an aperture which must lead to the outside world and open air for a beam of bright sunlight fell from it to the floor of the cavern.

From the floor rose sharp-pointed stalagmites, the crystals glimmering like the fangs of a man-eating shark. From the high roof hung down matching stalactites, some shaped like spearheads and others like the shining wings of the gods.

Across the cavern Ishtar crouched against the far wall. There was no escape that way. When he saw Taita appear in the mouth of the tunnel he began to shriek and blubber. 'Mercy, mighty Magus! There is a bond between us. We are brothers. Spare me and I will show you such mysteries as even you have never dreamed of. I will place all my powers at your disposal. I will be your faithful dog. I will devote my life to your service.'

So abject were his entreaties and his promises that, despite himself, Taita felt his resolve waver. It was just the mere flicker of doubt in his mind, but Ishtar picked up the tiny chink in his armour, and exploited it instantly. He flung out one hand with the thumb and forefinger forming a circle, the sign of Marduk, and shouted something in that strange guttural tongue.

From behind him Taita felt an insupportable physical weight bear down upon his shoulder, and something like the invisible tentacles of a giant octopus envelop his body, trapping his arms to his sides, wrapping around his throat in a strangler's grip. He smelt scorching human flesh, the aura of the Devourer, suffocating him. He could not move.

On the far side of the cavern Ishtar danced and capered, his tattooed face contorted in a grotesque mask, his tongue sticking out between his blue lips and lapping at the air like that of a cat. He lifted his skirts and thrust his hips out at Taita. His penis was in full erection, the skin peeled back from the swollen purple head like an obscene fruit. 'Your frail goddess cannot protect you here deep in the earth, Taita. You can no longer prevail against Marduk the Devourer and Ishtar, his minion,' he shrieked. 'Our contest is over. I have defeated you and all your wiles, Warlock! Now you will die.'

Taita turned his eyes up towards the high dim roof of the cavern and fixed all his attention on one of the long gleaming stalactites that hung down from it like a great shimmering dagger. He gathered all his reserves, lifted the staff in his right hand and pointed it upwards. With the last breath in his lungs he shouted, *'Kydash!'* the word of power.

There was a crack like the ice shattering in the depths of a glacier, the stalactite broke from the roof and plunged downwards. Driven by its own immense weight, the point struck Ishtar on the top of his shoulder, close to its juncture with his neck. It transfixed him through chest and belly and tore out through his anus. The long stone spike pegged him down on the cavern floor like a gutted fish on the drying rack.

As Ishtar twitched and shuddered and kicked convulsively in his death throes, Taita felt the weight lifted from his shoulders and the pressure on his throat relax. Marduk had retreated and Taita could breathe again. The smell of burnt flesh was gone. The air was ancient and sterile once again, cool and tainted only with the faint odour of fungus.

He picked up his staff, turned and walked back along the tunnel into the open air and the sunlight. At the entrance he turned back and with his staff struck the limestone portals of the tunnel, once, twice, three times.

Deep in the earth there was a rumble of collapsing rock, and a gust of air and dust blew from the tunnel mouth as, deep in the earth, the roof of the cavern caved in.

'With the stone spike driven through your heart, not even your foul god can free you from your tomb. Lie in it through all eternity, Ishtar the Mede,' Taita said, and turned away. With his staff tapping on the stones, he struck out along the road back to Gallala.

The three messengers reached Babylon in the spring when the snows were still thick upon the distant mountain-tops in the north where the two great rivers rise.

Pharaoh Naja Kiafan gave them audience on the uppermost terrace garden of the palace of Babylon. Queen Heseret sat beside his throne. She wore the most magnificent jewels that the treasury of King Sargon had yielded. Her high-piled dark hair was covered by a silken net on which gemstones sparkled like all the stars of the firmament. Her arms were laden with bracelets and her fingers with rings so heavy with emeralds and rubies and sapphires that she could barely lift them. Around her throat was a stone the size of an unripe fig, as clear as water from a mountain spring and so adamantine that it could cut through glass or obsidian. This marvellous gem came from the land beyond the Indus river, and when the sun caught it, the shafts of light it threw out pained the eye.

The messengers were all high officers from the army that Pharaoh Trok had taken westward four months before. They came in great fear of their lives, for they bore evil tidings. They had ridden so far and so fast that they were thin and burned dark by the suns of the desert and the high mountains. They threw themselves at the foot of the throne on which Naja sat in glory and splendour to overshadow even that of his wife. 'All hail to you, Pharaoh Naja, mightiest of the gods of Egypt,' they greeted him. 'We are bearers of terrible tidings. Have mercy upon us. Though what we have to tell you will displease you, be merciful and turn away your wrath from us.'

'Speak!' Naja commanded sternly. 'I alone shall judge if you are to be spared.'

'The news we bring is of Pharaoh Trok Uruk, your brother god and the co-ruler of Egypt,' said the officer who was a Commander of the Vanguard, bore the rank of Best of Ten Thousand and wore the Gold of Valour upon his chest.

'Speak!' Naja ordered again, for the man had faltered.

'In the desert that surrounds the ancient city of Gallala there took place a mighty battle between the armies of Pharaoh Trok Uruk and those of the usurper Nefer Seti.' He fell silent again.

'Continue!' Naja rose to his feet, and pointed the royal flail at the man's face, a gesture that threatened torture and death.

The messenger went on hurriedly, 'By the means of cowardly deceit and wicked witchcraft the army of your brother and our Pharaoh Trok Uruk was lured to destruction. He is slain and his army decimated. Those of his men who survived have gone over to the enemy, and have rallied to the standard of the false pharaoh Nefer Seti, may Seth visit him with a terrible vengeance and eradicate his name and all his works. This same wicked usurper with all his force marches on Avaris and both kingdoms of this very Egypt!'

Naja sank back on his throne and stared at him in astonishment. At his side Heseret smiled. When she did so, the cruel lines at the corners of her mouth vanished and she was transformed, becoming once more ineffably beautiful. She touched Naja's arm with a bejewelled finger, and when he leaned towards her she whispered in his ear, 'Praise to the gods, and all hail to the one and only Pharaoh of the Upper and Lower Kingdoms, the mighty Naja Kiafan!'

Naja tried to remain stern and expressionless but a tiny smile played for an instant over his lean and handsome features. It took him a moment to suppress it then he rose again. His voice was sibilant and soft, but menacing as the sound of a sword blade being swiped across the face of the whetstone. 'You bring the news of the death of a pharaoh and a god. Woe upon you for you are now contaminated and steeped in misery and misfortune.' He made a gesture to his bodyguard who stood around the throne. 'Take them away and give them over to the priests of the god Marduk that they be sacrificed in the furnace to appease the wrath of the god.'

When they were bound and led away to the sacrifice, Naja stood again and announced, 'The god and Pharaoh Trok Uruk is dead. We commend his soul to the gods. I declare before you all that there is now only one ruler over both kingdoms, and over all the territories and all the conquered lands and possessions of Egypt. I declare further that ruler to be myself, Pharaoh Naja Kiafan.'

'*Bak-her!*' cried all the courtiers and captains, who stood around his throne, and they drew their swords and beat them on their shields. '*Bak-her!* Exalted be the king-god Naja Kiafan!'

'Send word to all my commanders and the generals of all my armies. We will meet in war council at the noon hour this same day.'

For eleven days that followed, from dawn to dusk, Pharaoh Naja sat at the head of his council in the throne room of the palace of Sargon. With sentries at the doors to bar interlopers or spies they drew up their plans and their order of battle. On the twelfth day Naja commanded the muster of his armies in Mesopotamia, and sent ambassadors to the subservient kings and satraps in all the conquered territories between Babylon and the borders of Egypt. He ordered them to prepare all their forces for war, and place themselves under his command for the campaign against Nefer Seti.

In the full of the following moon, when the army mustered before the Blue Gate of the city of Babylon they were forty thousand strong, all veteran and blooded troops, well equipped with horse and chariot, bow and sword.

Heseret stood with her husband, the one and only true Pharaoh of Egypt, on the ramparts of the city to review the array.

'What a glorious sight,' she told him. 'Surely there was never such a muster as this in all the annals of war.'

'As we march westwards, back towards the motherland, our numbers will be swollen by the Sumerians and the Hittites, the Hurrians and all the armies of the conquered lands through which we pass. We will return to Egypt with two thousand chariots. The puppy dare not stand against us.' He looked down at her. 'Do you feel no pity for your brother Nefer?'

'None!' She shook her head so her jewellery glinted and sparkled in the sunlight. 'You are my pharaoh and my husband. Whosoever rises against you is a traitor, and deserves death.'

'Death he shall have, and the treacherous Warlock will share his funeral pyre and burn beside him,' Naja promised grimly.

They smelt the river from afar, the perfume of the sweet cool waters on the desert air. The horses lifted their heads and whickered. The infantry quickened their step and gazed ahead, eager for the first glimpse of the waters that, at this season of the year, would be swollen and dark with rich silts, the flesh and blood of the motherland.

Nefer and Mintaka rode together in his chariot at the head of the long cavalcade that wound down the caravan road from Gallala. Meren and Merykara rode at his right hand in the second chariot of the column. Over the protests of Merykara, who thought him still too weak and sick, Meren had insisted on being in the van. 'I missed the battle at Gallala, but I vow I will never miss another. As long as there is breath in my body I will ride with my king and my dearest friend.' Though he was thin and pale as an egret he stood proud on the footplate, with the reins in his hands.

The leading chariots topped the escarpment, and below them stretched the green valley of the Nile, with the mighty river itself gleaming like a spill of molten copper from the furnace, glowing red in the early sunlight. Nefer turned and smiled at Meren in the chariot alongside. 'We are coming home!'

Mintaka began singing, softly at first then more strongly as Nefer added his voice to hers.

> 'Temple of the Gods,
> Seat of ten thousand heroes,
> Greenest in all the earth,
> Our dearest love. Our sweetest home.
> Our very Egypt!'

Then Meren and Merykara were singing with them, and the singing spread back down the column. Squadron after squadron picked up the joyous chorus as they wound down the escarpment.

Another army came to meet them, armed charioteers in the van, generals and captains leading their regiments, and legions of foot-soldiers following them. Behind them followed the elders, the priests and the governors of every nome, all dressed in their robes, chains and decorations of office, some in carriages and others in litters borne by slaves, and still others riding astride or on foot. After them came the dense masses of citizenry, laughing and dancing. Some of the women were carrying their infants and weeping for joy, as they picked out their husbands, lovers, brothers and sons in the ranks of the army of exile coming home.

The two cavalcades came together and mingled, and elders and generals prostrated themselves before Pharaoh's chariot. Nefer dismounted, raised up those he recognized and embraced the mightiest and most powerful of them, calling down the blessings of the gods on all his people.

When he mounted again they fell in behind him, and followed him to the banks of the Nile. There Nefer dismounted again and, fully dressed, plunged into the waters. While they lined the bank and cheered and sang, he bathed ritually and drank of the muddy brown waters.

Mounted once again and dressed in fresh linen robes, with the blue war crown on his head, Nefer led the vast concourse along the riverbank towards the city of Avaris. For a league outside the city the road was lined with the welcoming crowds. They had allayed the dust by sprinkling the road with Nile water, and had spread palm fronds and flowers in his way.

When they reached the city the gates stood wide open and the populace lined the walls. They had hung banners and bunches of sweet flowers and fruits from the ramparts. They sang anthems of loyalty, praise and welcome as Nefer, with Mintaka beside him, drove under the arch of the gateway.

Beautiful as a young god and goddess, they drove first to the magnificent temple on the riverbank that Trok Uruk had built to celebrate his own divinity. Nefer had sent instructions ahead of him, and the stonemasons had already been at work for weeks. They had chiselled away every portrait of the false pharaoh and expunged his name from the walls and tall hypostyle columns. They were still busy engraving the portraits and titles of the winged Horus, and of Pharaoh Nefer Seti, together with descriptions of his victory at the battle of Gallala.

Nefer drove there as his first duty to give thanks to the god and to sacrifice a pair of perfect black bulls before the stone altar. After the religious service he declared a week of holiday, festivity and feasting, with free millet bread, beef, wine and beer for every citizen, and games and theatre to amuse them.

'You are a sly one, my heart,' Mintaka told him admiringly. 'They loved you before, but now they will adore you.'

For how long? Nefer wondered. As soon as the news of our ascension to the throne reaches Naja, in far off Babylon, he will be on the march, if he is not already. The common people will love me until he knocks upon the gates.

***

Pharaoh Naja Kiafan anointed his trusted general Asmor as King of Babylon, a satrap of his own throne. He left him five hundred chariots, two thousand archers and infantry to hold and secure his conquests. Then, with the bulk of his army, he began the march on Egypt to recover his crown and throne from the man who had seized it.

Like a snowball rolling down a mountainside, the army of Pharaoh Naja Kiafan gathered weight and impetus as it advanced westwards over plain and mountain pass towards the frontier of Egypt. As he went, the vassal kings flocked to his standard, and by the time he stood on the heights of the Khatmia Pass his army had almost trebled in size.

Naja looked westwards, across the wide sand desert towards the city of Ismailiya at the head of the Great Bitter Lake, and to the borders of his homeland. He had known all along that at this point on the march he would be hampered by the size of his host, embarrassed by multitudes.

Ahead of him lay a great expanse of desert, with neither a single spring nor an oasis to sustain his army until he reached Ismailiya. Once again he was reduced to laying down water points along the route ahead. When he strained his eyes against the glare he could make out the lines of water carts, loaded with clay pots, strung out along the rutted road below the escarpment, like dark worms wriggling through the dun and ochre landscape. For months they had been at work building up water dumps in the desert, burying the filled pots in the sand, then leaving detachments of infantry to guard them while they returned for the next load.

It would take his army almost ten days and nights to make the crossing. During that time they would be strictly rationed, allowed just enough water to sustain the long night marches, and to eke out the burning days when they lay up to rest, enduring the heat in any scrap of shade afforded by linen tents or shelters made from thorn branches and grass.

'I will ride with you in the vanguard.' Heseret spoke at his elbow, breaking into his train of thought.

He glanced at her. 'We have discussed this before.' He frowned. After years of marriage her charms and beauty had begun to pall, overshadowed by her petulance, jealousy and demanding tempers. These days, Naja spent more and more time among his concubines, enduring her jealous tirades when he returned to her bed.

'You will come up with the other women in the baggage train, under the wing of Prenn, the centurion of the rearguard.'

Heseret pouted. Once, that had been appealing but now it was merely irritating. 'So that you can put Lassa with child, just as you have her sister,' she complained. She was referring to the two princesses given to Naja as hostages by the satrap of Sumeria as evidence of his loyalty to the crown of Egypt. The princesses were both young, slim and nubile, with large breasts. They painted their nipples and, in the shameless Sumerian fashion, walked abroad with them naked and uncovered.

'You become tiresome, wife.' Naja lifted his upper lip in a smile that was more a snarl. 'You know that it is political expediency. I needed a son from at least one of the wenches to place upon the throne when the old man dies.'

'Swear on the breath and heart of Seueth that you are not taking Lassa with you in the vanguard,' Heseret insisted.

'I swear it readily.' Naja smiled that deadly smile again. 'I am taking Sinnal of Hurria.' She was another hostage, younger even than the Sumerians, barely fourteen years of age but with bright copper-coloured hair and green eyes. Her buttocks were large and rounded. Heseret knew from experience that Naja would enter through the back gate to the citadel, as readily as through the front.

'I need a son from her as well,' Naja explained, reasonably, 'to place on the throne of Assyria.' He laughed then, a soft, mocking snigger. 'The duties of royalty are onerous indeed.'

She gave him a furious glare, and called for her litter with its screens and cushions of silk to take her back down the column, to where Prenn was bringing up the rearguard.

On Taita's advice, Nefer had established a screen of scouts along the shores of the Red Sea to report any invasion by dhows, yet Taita was certain that Naja's main invasion force must come through the Great Sand Desert. Naja and Trok had passed this way on their Mesopotamian adventure. Naja knew the route well, and his army was too large to bring across the Red Sea in boats as Trok had done with his much smaller force.

Thanks to a marvellous innovation by the Magus, Nefer and his staff knew the exact numbers and composition of Naja's muster. One of the centurions, high in the chain of Naja's command, who was an old associate of Taita and who owed him a debt of gratitude, had sent a message to Taita declaring his loyalty to the Pharaoh Nefer Seti and his intention of defecting and coming to join Nefer's army. Through another of his minions, a trader in fine carpets, who was leading a caravan to Beersheba, Taita had sent the centurion a reply, instructing him to remain at the head of his division. 'You are more valuable to us as a source of intelligence than as a warrior,' he had told him, and through the carpet trader had sent him two unusual gifts: a basket of live pigeons and a papyrus scroll on which was set out a secret code.

When the pigeons were released by the centurion, they returned immediately to the coop in Avaris in which they had been hatched, and they carried with them, tied to one leg with a silken thread, a coded message written on a tiny roll of the finest and lightest papyrus sheet. Through these messages, Nefer had in his possession the precise numbers and disposition of the troops Naja commanded. He knew the exact day on which Naja had marched from Babylon, and how many troops he had left there under Asmor. Nefer was able to follow his advance westward, through Damascus and Beersheba and all the other towns and garrisons along his line of march.

Very soon it became apparent that Taita had assessed the situation correctly, and that Naja would not attempt a surprise crossing of the

Red Sea. He was indeed intent on a frontal assault through the Great Sand Desert.

Nefer pulled in his pickets from along the Red Sea coast, and immediately moved his headquarters and most of his army forward to the frontier garrison of Ismailiya on the edge of the desert. Here there were bountiful sweet-water wells, and ample grazing for the horses.

While they waited in Ismailiya, reports continued to be carried in by the returning pigeons. Not only did Nefer know Naja's strength, he knew also who commanded each of his divisions.

Mintaka sat on his war council in the fort of Ismailiya. Her contributions were invaluable: she was Hyksos born, and she knew well those officers on Naja's staff who had once been on her own father's staff. As a child she had listened to her father's assessment of each of them, and she had a formidable memory, trained and sharpened over the bao board. She was able to advise Nefer on the strengths, weaknesses and personal peculiarities of each of these men. She went over the lists they had received.

'Now this one, Centurion Prenn who commands Naja's rearguard, is related to me, for he was one of my father's cousins. I know him well. He taught me to ride. I used to call him Uncle Tonka, which means "Bear" in my language.' She smiled at the memory. 'My father said of him that he was loyal as a hound, cautious and slow, but once he had sunk his teeth into the throat of an enemy he would hang on to the death.'

By this time Meren had almost fully recovered his health and strength. He begged Nefer for employment in some useful role, so Nefer sent him forward with a division of chariots to cover Naja's further advance, once he came down from the heights into the desert.

Meren's scouts watched Naja's water carts carrying their loads of clay jars forward and building up the dumps in the arid land through which Naja must pass to reach the frontier of Egypt. Meren asked to be allowed to attack and disperse the convoys of water carts, but Nefer sent orders to him not to interfere with them, merely to keep them under observation and to note carefully were they placed the water stores.

Then Nefer ordered the last reserves that he had been holding on the river to be brought up, and when these were encamped around Ismailiya he called a council of all their commanders. 'Even with Trok's vehicles that we captured at Gallala, Naja outnumbers us by almost three to one,' he told them. 'All his men are battle-hardened, and his horses trained and in fine condition. We cannot afford to let him cross the frontier and reach the river. We must meet him and fight him here in the desert.'

All that night they sat in council, and Nefer laid out his battle plan and issued his orders. They were to let Naja advance unopposed for the first five days. Then, once he was deeply committed, they would raid and destroy his water stores, both in front and to the rear of his advance. This would trap him in the midst of the sands.

'I know Naja well enough to stake the battle on his arrogance and his overbearing confidence in his own fighting skills. I am certain that even once we cut off his water supply he will not turn back, but will thrust onwards. His forces will reach Ismailiya after a forced dry march of many days through the desert. We will be able to meet them with our horses and troops well rested and watered on a battleground of our own choosing. This will make up some of the deficit in our opposing strengths.'

During the long council, Taita sat silently in the shadows behind Nefer's campaign stool. It seemed that he was dozing, but once in a while he opened his eyes then, blinking like a sleepy owl, closed them again and let his chin droop back on to his chest.

'Our greatest lack is in the number and condition of our chariots.' Nefer went on, 'but we can almost match Naja in archers, slingers and spearmen. I am certain that once he realizes his shortage of water, Naja will drive ahead of his foot-soldiers with all his chariots. Taita and I have devised a plan to lead his vehicles into a trap in which we can exploit the small advantage that we have.

'In front of the town and the wells we will throw up a series of low stone walls behind which our archers and infantry can conceal themselves. These works will be just high enough to block the advance of a chariot.' With a charcoal stick Nefer sketched out a design on the sheet of papyrus spread on the table-top in front of him. Hilto, Shabako, Socco and the rest of his staff craned forward to watch.

'The walls will be laid out in the design of a fish trap.' He drew the inverted funnel shapes, with the apex aimed back towards the fort of Ismailiya.

'How will you lead him into the funnel?' Shabako asked.

'With a charge of our own chariots and the mock retreat you have practised so often,' Nefer explained, 'our archers and slingers will remain concealed behind the walls until Naja follows us into the funnel. The deeper they penetrate, the more tightly his squadrons will be compressed between the walls. They will offer a fine target for our slingers and archers as they pass at close range.'

Even Shabako looked impressed. 'You intend to shut them up in a stockade like cattle, just as you did with Trok.'

They discussed the plan with enthusiasm, offering suggestions and refinements. In the end Nefer put Shabako in charge of building the walls. Taita had spent the last five days surveying and marking them out for him, so the work could begin as soon as it was light the next day.

'We have little time left to us,' Nefer warned them. 'We know that Naja's forces are already drawn up on the heights of the Khatmia. His water wagons have almost finished laying down the dumps. I expect he will begin his descent of the escarpment within days.'

The council broke up at last and the officers hurried away to take up the tasks that Nefer had allocated to them. At last only three remained in the tower room of the old fort at Ismailiya, Nefer, Taita and Mintaka.

Mintaka spoke up for the first time. 'We have discussed already Prenn, my uncle Tonka,' she said, and Nefer nodded, but gave her a quizzical look. 'If I could meet him, if I could speak to him face to face, I am sure I could convince him to turn against Naja and throw in his lot with us.'

'What do you mean?' Nefer's voice was harsh and his expression stern.

'Dressed as a boy, with a small detachment of good men and fast horses, I could circle around Naja's main army and get through to Uncle Tonka in the rear. There would be little risk.'

Nefer's face blanched with anger. 'Madness!' he said quietly. 'Stark raving madness of the kind you exhibited at Gallala when you showed yourself as bait to Trok. I will not hear another word of it. Can you imagine what Naja would do to you if you fell into his hands?'

'Can you imagine what Naja would do if, in the critical moment of the battle, Uncle Tonka and his legions fell upon him from his own rear?' she flashed back at Nefer.

'We will not speak of it again.' Nefer came to his feet and slammed his fists down on the table-top. 'You will stay with Merykara here in the fort during the rest of the campaign. If you do not give me your word to put such stupidity out of you mind, I will have the door to your chamber barred and guarded.'

'You cannot treat me as a chattel.' Her voice crackled with fury. 'I am not even your wife. I will take no orders from you.'

'I am your king, and I demand your solemn word not to place yourself in jeopardy with this wild scheme of yours.'

'It is not a wild scheme, and I will not give you my word.'

Taita looked on, expressionless. This was their first serious argument, and he knew it would be all the more bitter because of the depth of their feelings for each other. He waited with interest to see how it would be resolved.

'You deliberately disobeyed my orders at Gallala. I cannot trust you not to do the same now. You leave me no alternative.' Nefer told her grimly, and shouted to the sentry outside the door to send for Zugga, the head eunuch of the royal harem.

'I can't trust Merykara either.' He turned back to Mintaka. 'She is completely under your influence, and if you put your mind to it you will turn her to this lunatic enterprise of yours. I am sending both of you back to the *zenana* in the Avaris palace. You are to remain there in the care of Zugga. You can amuse each other by playing bao until the battle is fought and the war is won.' And Zugga led Mintaka away. At the door she looked back over her shoulder at Nefer, and Taita smiled as he read her expression. Nefer had taken on a more stubborn adversary than both the false pharaohs combined.

That evening Taita went to visit her in the new accommodation that Mintaka now shared with Merykara in what had once been the commander's suite of the fort. A pair of large, placid eunuchs were at the door and another outside the barred window.

Mintaka was still seething with anger, and Merykara was every bit as outraged by her brother's treatment of herself and her dear Mintaka, and especially this humiliating incarceration.

'At least you have learned from this that it does not pay to confront a king, even if he loves you,' Taita told them gently.

'I don't love him,' Mintaka replied, with tears of anger and frustration in her eyes. 'He treats me like a child, and I hate him.'

'I hate him even more,' Merykara declared, not to be outdone. 'If only Meren were here!'

'Has it occurred to you that what Nefer is doing to you is evidence of his love and concern for your safety?' Taita suggested. 'He knows how dire will be your fate if you fall into the hands of Naja Kiafan and Heseret.' They turned upon him so roundly that he held up both hands to deflect their wrath and withdrew tactfully, their denials and recriminations still ringing in his ears.

The next morning both Nefer and Taita watched from the ramparts of the fort as the little caravan left Ismailiya, escorted by the eunuchs and a contingent of chariots, and headed back towards Avaris. Mintaka and Merykara were closeted together behind the silk curtains of the litter in the centre of the column. They did not show themselves or take their farewells of Nefer and Taita.

'Personally, I would have preferred to stir up a beehive with a short stick,' Taita murmured. 'It may have made for a more restful climate to have shown a little more tact.'

'They must learn that I am pharaoh, and that my word is law even to them. Besides, at the moment I have other concerns than female tantrums,' Nefer said, 'They will get over it.' But he stayed on the wall and watched until the swaying litter and the caravan disappeared in the hazy distance.

Taita and Nefer rode out and inspected the stone walls that Shabako had hastily thrown up along the eastern approaches to the oasis of Ismailiya.

'Shabako's efforts will not rank among the great architectural achievements of the age,' Taita gave his opinion, 'but that is all to the good. From the direction in which Naja will come, they appear to be natural features and will excite no suspicion until he enters the funnel and finds his front progressively narrowed.'

'Your plan has the towering virtue of allowing us to choose our own battleground.' Nefer nodded. 'With the help of Horus, we will turn it into a slaughter-ground.' Then he laid his hand upon Taita's skinny arm. 'Once again I find myself deeply in your debt, Old Father. This is all your work.'

'No.' Taita shook his head. 'It was a gentle nudge I gave to you. The rest of it is yours. You have inherited the military instincts of your father, Pharaoh Tamose. You will achieve the greatness that might have been his, had he not died so cruelly at the hands of the enemy who faces us now.'

'It is time for me to avenge that death,' Nefer said. 'Let us ensure that we do not let the cobra slither away again.'

Over the days that followed Nefer exercised his forces, and rehearsed in detail the plans and tactics of his defence. The battalions of archers and slingers marched out each morning and took up their positions behind the rough, ungainly walls. They placed small cairns of stones in front of the walls to mark the range, so that they would be able to judge precisely the moment to spring the trap. They concealed bundles of spare arrows close at hand so that they would not run short of missiles during the battle. The slingers moulded their clay balls and baked them in the fire until they were rock hard. Then they laid up mounds of these deadly missiles behind the walls, close at hand.

During the exercises, Nefer and his commanders played the role of Naja's troops and rode in from the desert, viewing their dispositions with a critical eye, making certain that they were completely concealed by the breastworks.

Then, while they waited, Nefer rehearsed his tactics before the walls, charging, wheeling and retreating, covering the ground so that his men came to know every fold, plain and gully, even the location of the aardvark holes and other small obstacles across the field. He chose carefully the secure points behind the walls where he could water the horses during the battle, and where his reserves would be held until they were needed. 'I doubt that there was ever a commander able to learn the board on which the game will be played as intimately as I,' Nefer told Taita, and ordered his squadrons out again to go through the same evolutions.

In the evening he rode back into the fort at the head of his squadron. The dust had mingled with his sweat and caked his face and body. He was weary to the bone, but content in the knowledge that he had done all in his power to ready his legions for what lay ahead.

When he pulled up Krus and Dov, threw the rein to the grooms and jumped down on to the hard-baked parade-ground, his sense of well-being evaporated. Zugga, the head eunuch of the royal *zenana*, was waiting for him, wringing his fat hands, his eyes red with weeping and his reedy voice whining with fear. 'Great Pharaoh, forgive me. I did my best but she is wily as a vixen. She has outwitted me.'

'Who is this vixen?' Nefer demanded, although he knew who it must be.

'The Princess Mintaka.'

'What has happened to her?' Nefer voice was harsh with alarm.

'She has run away, and taken the Princess Merykara with her,' blubbered Zugga, in sure expectation of the strangling garotte.

Mintaka and Merykara spent much of the journey back to Avaris huddled together in the screened litter, whispering as they planned their escape. They soon discarded the notion of seizing one of the chariots from their escort and riding away in it. In the unlikely event that they were able to trick or overpower one of the charioteers, they knew that within an hour they would have the entire army of Egypt on their heels, led by a wrathful pharaoh. Gradually a better plan emerged from their deliberations.

Mintaka's first endeavour was to make herself agreeable to Zugga, their guardian and gaoler, and to impress him with her submissive resignation to his authority. By the time they reached the palace in Avaris four days later, she had him completely gulled, believing only the best of her gentle, innocent nature. There, in the most pretty and convincing manner, she appealed to Zugga to allow her and Merykara to visit the temple of Hathor to pray for the safety of Nefer and his victory in the looming battle. With some misgivings, Zugga acquiesced and the two women were able to spend almost an hour alone with the high priestess in the sanctuary of the temple. Zugga waited anxiously at the door, for no man, not even a eunuch, was allowed to enter the sanctum.

Great was Zugga's relief, and all his suspicions set at rest, when Mintaka and Merykara at last re-emerged, both as beautiful, demure and innocent as any of the temple virgins. A few days later when they asked to be allowed to pray again in the temple, and to make sacrifice to the goddess, Zugga was amenable to the request and waddled beside their litter chatting blithely through the curtain, and relating to the princesses the most juicy items of scandal in the life of the palace.

Once again the high priestess was waiting in the forecourt of the temple to greet Mintaka and Merykara and lead them into the sanctum. Without misgivings Zugga settled down to await the return of the lovely royal pair. The high priestess sent out two of her acolytes to serve him an overflowing platter of grilled chicken and fish, together with a large jar of excellent wine. Zugga ate it all and polished off the contents of the jug, then fell asleep in the shadow of the cow effigy of the goddess. When he woke the sun had set and he was alone. He saw that the litter bearers had gone. He heaved his vast bulk upright and experienced twinges in his belly that were not caused by dyspepsia but by a pressing sense of alarm. He shouted for attention and beat on the temple door with his staff. It was a long time before a priestess came to him with a message: 'The two princesses have pleaded for sanctuary within the temple. The holy mother has granted their plea, and taken them under her protection.'

Zugga was thrown into turmoil. The sanctuary of the temple was inviolate. He could not demand the return of his charges, not even under the authority of Pharaoh. The only course open to him was to return to Ismailiya and confess his failure, but that was risky. The young pharaoh had not yet revealed his true nature, and his rage might well be fatal.

The moment the temple doors closed behind them Mintaka and Merykara dropped their pretence of resigned innocence.

'Have you made the arrangements, Holy Mother?' Mintaka demanded eagerly.

'Have no fear, daughter. All is in readiness.' The priestess's brown eyes sparkled with amusement. Clearly she was enjoying this escapade, a break from the tranquil routine of temple life. 'I took the liberty of slipping a mild sleeping draught into the eunuch's wine.' She giggled. 'I hope you will not think I have overstepped myself, and that you will forgive me.'

Mintaka kissed her smooth pale cheek. 'I am sure Hathor will be as proud of you as I am.'

The priestess led them to a cell where all the items that Mintaka had requested were laid out for them. They dressed hastily in the rough peasant garments, and covered their heads with woollen shawls. Then, carrying the leather pouches slung across their shoulders, they followed the high priestess through the maze of corridors. The temple backed on to Nile, and they became aware of the gentle swish of the river current against the outer walls growing louder ahead of them. At last they stepped out through a low doorway into the sunshine, and on to the jetty where a large dhow was moored. 'The captain has been paid with the gold you gave me, and he knows where to go. All the other items you asked for are stowed in your cabin on board,' she said.

'You know what to tell Zugga,' Mintaka said, and the old woman giggled again.

'I am sure that Hathor will forgive me such an insignificant falsehood. It is in such a good cause.'

As the pair jumped down on to the deck of the dhow, the crew, who had been dozing in the shade, scrambled to their feet and rushed to set the lateen sail. Without waiting for orders, the captain steered out into the main flow of the current and turned the bows downstream, heading for the delta. For the rest of that day Mintaka and Merykara stayed in the tiny cabin, taking no chance that they might be recognized from the shore, or from a passing riverboat. In the late afternoon the dhow moored briefly against the east bank and two armed men came aboard, carrying heavy sacks. Immediately the dhow captain hoisted the sail again and they pressed on with all speed downriver. The two men came to the cabin and prostrated themselves before Mintaka.

'May all the gods love you, Majesty,' said the bigger of the two, a bearded Hyksos with large nose and strong features. 'We are your dogs. We came as soon as we received your summons.'

'Lok!' Mintaka smiled with pleasure to see his well-remembered face, and then turned to the other man. 'And surely this is your son, Lokka.' He seemed as big and doughty as his father. 'You are both well met and welcome. You, Lok, served my father well. Will you and your son do the same for me?' She spoke in the Hyksosian language.

'With our lives, mistress!' they told her.

'I will have hard employment for you once we go ashore, but until then rest and prepare your weapons.'

The dhow captain selected one of the many mouths of the delta where the current slowed and meandered through swamps and lagoons over which hovered clouds of waterfowl. Darkness fell before they reached the open sea, but the dhow captain steered his craft unerringly through the shallows and the hidden sandbars, until at last the miasma of the swamps was blown away on the clean salt airs of the Mediterranean. The two girls came up on deck.

'Just about now, Zugga will realize that we have flown.' Mintaka smiled at Merykara. 'I wonder what he will tell Nefer. That we are safely locked up in the temple under the wing of the high priestess? I hope so.'

With half a moon in the sky they sailed out of the confined waterways and felt the scend of the open sea lift the deck beneath their feet. As soon as he had made his offing and there was deep water under his hull, the captain turned eastwards and hugged the coast throughout the night.

In the dawn Mintaka and Merykara stood in the bows, huddled in their shawls for warmth. They stared south at the low bleak desert shore to their right.

'To think that Nefer is only a few leagues out there,' Mintaka whispered. 'I feel as though I could reach out my hand to touch him.'

'Meren is there too, only a little further to the east. What a surprise they would have to know that we are so close.'

'My heart yearns for Nefer. I pray every hour to Horus and Hathor to keep him safe.'

'You no longer hate him, then?' Merykara asked.

'I never did,' Mintaka denied hotly, then hesitated. 'Well, perhaps for a moment and only a very little.'

'I know just how you feel,' Merykara assured her. 'At times, they can be so stubborn and bull-headed and . . .' she sought for a word to describe it '. . . and so male.'

'Yes!' Mintaka agreed, 'That's it exactly. Like children. I suppose we must forgive them, for they cannot help themselves.'

During the rest of that day and the following night they sailed eastwards along the coast, through the Khalig el Tina and along the string of islands and sandbars that enclosed the vast lagoon of the Sabkhet el Bardawill. The next morning the dhow edged in towards the beach at El Arish, and as soon as the water was waist deep the two bodyguards, Lok and Lokka, carried the women ashore then waded back to the boat to fetch the baggage. The small party stood and watched the crew of the dhow row off, then set the sail and head back out to sea for the return to Egypt and the delta.

'Well, we have done it,' said Merykara uncertainly. Despite Mintaka's company, she was feeling vulnerable and alone. 'But what do we do now?' She sounded close to tears.

'I will send Lok to find transport for us,' said Mintaka, and then to give her comfort and a little more confidence she went on to explain to Merykara, 'Nefer might have stopped us going southwards through the desert to find my uncle Tonka, but we have outwitted him.' She smiled more gaily than her spirits dictated, for she was even more aware than Merykara of their invidious position. 'Just think how furious Nefer and Meren would be if they only knew!' They laughed together, and Mintaka went on, 'Here we are in the rear of Naja's advancing army, and the road between Beersheba and Ismailiya lies a very few leagues south of us. When Lok finds a cart or wagon for us we can lose ourselves in the baggage train of Naja's army, hide among the camp-followers until we can reach the headquarters of Uncle Tonka.'

It was not quite as easy to find transport as Mintaka had made it sound. The quartermasters of Naja's army had been ahead of them, and had seized wagons and horses, as well as food and provisions from the local populace. In the end they had to settle for a string of five decrepit donkeys, and they had to pay dearly for these, with two heavy gold rings and two of silver. The animals were barely able to support the weight of even the two women, let alone their bodyguards, so they walked most of the rugged path southwards, until on the third day after landing they topped a rise and saw in the valley below them the tail of the army of Pharaoh Naja. This great host filled the main east-to-west road in both directions as far as the eye could see, and the dust it raised sullied the sky like the smoke from a forest fire.

They went down to join it, and found themselves in the baggage train. They fell in with the long caravan of wagons and pack animals. Mintaka and Merykara kept their heads and faces covered, and in their dusty, bedraggled clothing excited little notice. Lok and Lokka chaperoned them closely, and discouraged the attentions of any other travellers. The rate of march was of the slowest, so even on the poor donkeys they were moving a little faster than the rest of the cavalcade and, like a scrap of flotsam in the mighty river, they drifted forward towards the head. As they went they passed every type and condition of humanity, beggars and bawds, merchants and water-carriers, barbers, coppersmiths and carpenters, troubadours and jugglers. There were captains splendid in the Gold of Valour, driving their chariots furiously through the throng, lashing out of their path the limping cripples on their crutches, and the army women with their bastards at the breast, feeding on the march, toddlers whining at their skirts.

Mintaka and Merykara kept up the best speed the wretched donkeys could manage, and they camped that first night under the stars, surrounded by the campfires, the hubbub and stench of this immense agglomeration of humanity.

In the dawn, as soon as it was light enough to see the road underfoot, they set off again. Before noon they had caught up with the rearguard of the main army: the marching companies of spearmen, and the ranks of archers with bows unstrung, the battalions of slingers singing their marching songs in the barbaric language of the western islands. Next they passed the long lines of the horses of the remount division, twenty to a string, being led behind the fodder wagons and the water carts. Mintaka marvelled at the numbers: it did not seem possible that there were so many animals in all Egypt.

The soldiers looked at the two women, and not even their shoddy dress or the voluminous shawls wound around their heads could hide their youth and grace from such discerning eyes. They called suggestive compliments and lewd invitations as they passed, but the discipline of their officers and the stern presence of Lok and Lokka kept them from any further advances.

That evening they kept on travelling after the main army had encamped and after sunset they came upon a large *zareba* of poles and thornbushes just off the road. This had been set up in an easily defended defile of low hills. The entrance was heavily guarded, and there was much activity around it, the marching and counter-marching of the sentries, the scurrying of servants and orderlies, and the coming and going of chariots driven by officers of the Red. Above the gate of the stockade flew the gonfalon that Mintaka recognized at once: on it was depicted the severed head of a wild boar with its tongue lolling from the corner of its tusked jaws.

'This is the man we are looking for,' Mintaka whispered to Merykara.

'But how do we get in to see him?' Merykara asked doubtfully, eyeing the sentries.

They made their own rudimentary camp a little further down the road, but within sight of the gates of the regimental headquarters of

General Prenn, centurion of the Red, and the commander of the rearguard of the pharaonic army.

From one of the leather saddlebags Mintaka brought out the precious oil lamp that had so far survived the journey, and by its light she wrote a short message on a scrap of papyrus parchment. It was addressed to 'Uncle Bear' and signed 'from your little cricket'.

The two women washed the dust from their faces, dressed each other's hair, and shook out their *chitons*. Then, hand in hand to give each other courage, they approached the gate of the stockade. The sergeant of the guard saw them coming and stepped out in front of them to head them off. 'Come now, you two juicy pieces of prong bait. You know better than to come flaunting your joy-clefts hereabouts. Get away with you.'

'You look like a kind and good man,' Mintaka told him primly. 'Would you allow any ruffian to talk to your own daughters in that coarse fashion?'

The sergeant checked, and gawked at her. She spoke the Hyksos language in the cultured tones and accent of the aristocracy. He lifted his lantern and shone the light upon them. Their dress was common, but their features made him draw breath sharply. These were clearly young women of high rank. In fact their faces were disturbingly familiar, even though he could not immediately place them.

'Forgive me, ladies,' he mumbled. 'Mistook you for—' He broke off, and Mintaka smiled graciously.

'Of course, you are forgiven. Will you deliver a message for us to Centurion Prenn?' She proffered the rolled parchment.

The sergeant hesitated a moment before he took it. 'I am sorry but I will have to ask you to wait here until I have an instruction from him.'

He came hurrying back within a very short time. 'My ladies! I am desolated to have kept you waiting. Please follow me.'

He led them to a pavilion of coloured linen in the centre of the stockade, and there was another short delay as he whispered to the junior officer in charge of the entrance. Then they were led through into the tent. The interior was sparsely furnished and the floor was covered by animal skins, oryx, zebra and leopard. On these a man was sitting cross-legged with maps and scrolls spread about him, and a wooden platter on his lap containing grilled ribs and a lump of *dhurra* bread. He looked up as the girls entered. His face was gaunt, his cheeks sunken, and even the ribbons in his beard could not disguise the fact that it was more grey than black. A leather patch covered one eye. He scowled at them.

'Uncle Tonka!' Mintaka stepped into the lamplight and threw back her head shawl. The man came to his feet slowly and stared at her.

Then suddenly he grinned, and his single eye gleamed. 'I did not think it possible!' He embraced her and lifted her off her feet. 'I heard that you had deserted us and gone over to the enemy.'

When he put her down again and she had partially recovered from this display of affection, she gasped, 'That's what I have come to speak to you about, Uncle Tonka.'

'Who is this with you?' He glanced at Merykara, then blinked his one good eye. 'By Seth's foul breath, I know you.'

'It's the Princess Merykara,' Mintaka told him.

'Naja's runaway wife. He will be pleased to have you back.' Prenn chuckled. 'Have the two of you eaten?' Then, without waiting for a reply, he shouted to his servants to bring more meat and bread and wine. The two girls covered their faces again while they were served, but once the servants had gone Mintaka sat close to Prenn, on the side of his good ear, and dropped her voice so that they could not be overheard by a listener outside the tent walls.

He heard her out silently, but his expression changed as she described to him in detail the events of that terrible night when her father and all her brothers had died in the burning galley on the river at Balasfura. Mintaka thought she saw a tear gleam in the corner of his eye as she went on, but she knew that such a show of weakness was not possible in a centurion of the Red. Prenn turned away his face and when he looked back at her the tear was gone and she knew she had been mistaken.

When at last she finished speaking Prenn said simply, 'I loved your father, almost as much as I love you, little cricket, but what you are proposing is treason.' He was silent a while longer and then he sighed. 'All this I will have to think on. But in the meantime, you can't return whence you came. It is much too risky. You must stay under my care, both of you, until this affair is resolved.'

When they protested, he overrode them brusquely. 'It is not a request. It is an order.' He thought a moment. 'I will have you disguised as a pair of my pretty boys. That will cause little comment, for all my men know that I enjoy a slice of rump almost as much as a cut of breast.'

'Can I at least send a message to Nefer Seti?' Mintaka pleaded.

'That also is too great a risk. Have patience. It will not be for long. Naja is poised on the heights of the Khatmia. Within days he will begin the march on Ismailiya. The battle will be decided before the full moon of Osiris begins to wane.' His voice dropped to a growl. 'And I will be forced to a decision.'

From a distance Meren watched the great host of Pharaoh Naja come down the escarpment from the Khatmia Pass into the arid lands, and he released a pair of the pigeons that Taita had given to him. Two birds, so that if one was taken by a falcon or another predator the other might still win through. Both birds had a single strand of red thread looped around a leg, the signal that the advance had begun.

Meren shadowed the stately progress of the enemy legions across the desert, and at night crept closer to the camps to watch them watering from the stored jars and to eavesdrop on any of the loud conversations around the campfires.

By the fifth night Naja's full army was committed to the crossing, and the leading elements had passed the halfway mark between Khatmia and Ismailiya. Meren was able to cut in behind the rearguard and examine the now deserted water stores they had left behind them. He discovered that they were almost entirely used up, or had been carried away. Naja was so confident of his victory that he had left no contingency reserves for a possible retreat. From the unused jars that he did find Meren replenished his own waterskins, which were almost exhausted, and he smashed the few jars that remained.

Now he rode back parallel to Naja's line of march, but well out to the south and beyond the range of vision of his scouts, and circled out in front of the heavily encumbered, slowly moving host. He came back to where he had left the bulk of his force concealed. They were fifty chariots manned by crack troops and drawn by some of the finest horses in all Nefer's army. He paused only to water, and to change the pennants his chariots flew from the blue to the red of Naja's army. He consoled himself that this was a legitimate ruse of war. Then, at the head of his squadron, he cut back in front of Naja's vanguard and drove furiously along his intended line of march.

The men who had been left to guard the water dumps saw the approaching chariots coming from where they expected their comrades to arrive. When they recognized the false colours flying above them they were lulled. Meren gave them no time for second thoughts, but raced in upon them, and cut down any who tried to resist. The survivors were given a choice: death or defection. Most came over to Nefer Seti. A single mallet blow was sufficient for each of the clay jars, and the precious fluid poured out into the sand. Meren's squadron mounted again and went on to the next dump.

When at last they came in sight of Ismailiya Nefer rode out to greet them, and embraced Meren when he heard that he had fulfilled the task he had been set: Naja was now waterless in the wilderness. 'You have just earned your first Gold of Valour,' he told Meren, 'and you are promoted to the rank of Best of Ten Thousand.' He was relieved to see that Meren seemed to have recovered from his wound, and was now lean, eager and burned dark by the desert sun. 'In the battle that lies ahead, I am giving you command of the right wing.'

'Pharaoh, if I have pleased you, I beg a boon.'

'Of course, old friend. If it is in my power, you shall have it.'

'My rightful place is at your side. We rode the Red Road together, let us see this battle out together. Let me ride with you once again as your lance-bearer. That is all the honour I seek.'

Nefer gripped his arm, and squeezed hard. 'You shall ride in my chariot one more time. And it is I who will be honoured.' He dropped his hand. 'But we have no more time to chatter. Naja will not be far behind you. As soon as he discovers what you have done to his water supplies, he will be forced to come on at all speed.'

Instinctively they both looked back into the wilderness whence the enemy must come, but the heat-haze was grey and turbid and there was little to be seen across that grisly plain. However, they had not long to wait.

Pharaoh Naja reined in his chariot and gazed out over the remains of his water dump. Although the scouts had warned him, he was still appalled by the extent of the destruction. Slowly he dismounted and strode out into the littered field. Shards of shattered pottery crunched under his sandals, and suddenly his usual icy control snapped. He kicked one of the broken jars in fury and frustration, then stood with his hands clenched into fists at his sides and glared towards the west. Slowly he regained control of himself and his breathing slowed. He turned and walked back to where his staff waited.

'Will you give the order to turn back?' asked one of his captains diffidently.

Naja turned on him coldly. 'The next coward who suggests such a thing I will have stripped naked and tied feet first behind my chariot. I will drag him back to Egypt.' They dropped their eyes and shuffled their feet in the sand.

Naja lifted the blue war crown from his head, and when his lance-bearer handed him a square of linen cloth, he wiped the sweat from his shaven head. With the crown tucked under his arm he gave new orders. 'Collect all the waterskins from the entire army. From now on the water supply is under my direct control. No man or animal drinks without my permission. There is no turning back, no retreat. All the fighting chariots will move to the front of the column, even those of Prenn from the rearguard. The other vehicles and the foot must take their chances, and follow as best they can. I will take the cavalry ahead and seize the wells at Ismailiya...'

Heseret thrust her head out of the opening of her tent, and called to the captain of her bodyguard, 'What is the trouble, fellow? This is a royal and sacred enclosure, so what are those rogues doing in my stockade?' She pointed at the men who were taking the waterskins from one of her personal baggage carts parked alongside her tent. 'What do they think they are up to? How dare they remove our water? I have not yet bathed. Tell them to replace those skins at once.'

''Tis Pharaoh, your divine husband's order, Majesty,' the captain explained, although he was also agitated and alarmed at the prospect of being stranded waterless in this terrible desert. 'They say all the water is needed for the forward squadrons of cavalry.'

'Such orders cannot apply to me, the divine Queen of Egypt!' Heseret screamed. 'Put those waterskins back.'

The soldiers hesitated, but the sergeant touched the peak of his leather helmet with his sword. 'Forgive me, Your Majesty. My orders are to take all the water.'

'You dare defy me?' Heseret shouted in his face.

'Please forgive and understand my predicament, Your Majesty, but I have my orders.' The man stood his ground.

'By the sweet name of Isis, I shall have you strangled and your body burned, if you defy me.'

'My orders—'

'A plague on you and your orders. I shall go at once to General Prenn. I shall have new orders for you when I return.' Then she turned to the officer of her bodyguard. 'Ready my chariot and an escort of ten men.'

Across the flat and open plain, General Prenn's headquarters camp was in clear view of Heseret's tent. It took only minutes for her chariot to carry her there, but the guard at the gate of the stockade barred her way. 'Your Divine Majesty, General Prenn is not here,' he told her.

'I do not believe that,' Heseret flared at him. 'That is his standard flying there.' She pointed at the boar's head gonfalon.

'Your Majesty, the general left an hour ago with all his cavalry. He had orders from Pharaoh to join the vanguard.'

'I have to see him. It is a matter of extreme urgency. I know he would not have left without informing me. Stand aside and I will see for myself if he is here.' She drove the chariot straight at him and he jumped hurriedly out of her way. Her escort clattered after her.

Heseret went straight to the yellow- and green-striped command tent and tossed the reins to a groom. In her agitation she did not stand on ceremony, but jumped down and ran to the entrance of the tent. It was unguarded, and she began to believe that she had been told the truth, that Prenn had indeed left. Nevertheless, she stooped through the doorway, and stopped dead in the threshold.

Two boys were sitting on the piles of animal skins in the centre of the floor. They were eating with their fingers from wooden platters, but they looked up at her startled.

'Who are you?' Heseret demanded, though she knew from Prenn's reputation who and what they were. 'Where is the general?'

Neither replied, but they continued to stare wordlessly at her. Suddenly Heseret's eyes narrowed and she took a step towards them. 'You!' she screamed. 'You treacherous, poisonous bitches!' She pointed a quivering finger at the girls. 'Guards!' Heseret shrieked at the top of her voice. 'Guards, here, at once!'

Mintaka came to her senses, seized Merykara's hand and pulled her to her feet. The two darted across the tent and out through the rear opening.

'Guards!' Heseret yelled again. 'This way!' Her bodyguard burst in through the doorway behind her.

'Follow them!' She raced after the fleeing pair, with her bodyguard hard after her. When they ran out into the open, Mintaka and Merykara were halfway to the stockade gate.

'Stop them!' Heseret shouted. 'Don't let them escape. They are spies and traitors.'

Her bodyguard charged after them, shouting to the guards at the gate, 'Stop them. Seize them. Don't let them escape.' And the sentries drew their swords and ran to block the gate.

Mintaka stopped as soon as she saw that they were cut off. She looked around her wildly, then still pulling Merykara by the hand ran to the thorn fence of the stockade and tried to scale it. But the bodyguard came up under them, seized their ankles and pulled them down from the wall. The thorns had ripped their arms and legs, and they were both bleeding, but they fought desperately, kicking, scratching and biting. The soldiers overwhelmed them at last and dragged them back to the command tent to face Heseret. She was smiling vindictively. 'Bind them securely. I am sure that my husband, the sole ruler of this very Egypt, will devise a suitable punishment for their crimes when he returns. I shall delight in their screams as they are forced to pay the ultimate penalty. Until that time they are to be caged like wild animals, and kept at the door of my tent where I can keep them under my eye.'

The bodyguard lifted Mintaka and Merykara, bound at wrists and ankles, into a chariot and carried them back to Heseret's encampment. One of the carts of Heseret's baggage train carried her stock of livestock in cages, chickens, pigs and young goats for her kitchen. The cage that had contained the sucking pigs was now empty – they had been slaughtered and eaten. The cage was made from lengths of bamboo lashed together with rawhide strips, and stank of the pig dung that coated the floor. The guards shoved the two girls through the narrow door. The interior was not high enough to allow them to stand upright. They were forced to sit with their backs to the bamboo wall, and their wrists were lashed behind them with rawhide strips to one of the struts. There was no protection from the sun.

'There will be guards standing over your cage day and night,' Heseret warned them. 'Should you try to escape I will have one of your feet cut off, to discourage further attempts.'

From the look on her face they knew that Heseret meant every word of the threat. Merykara began to weep, but Mintaka whispered to her, 'No, my darling. Be brave. Do not give her the satisfaction of watching you break down.'

From the watchtower above the fort at Ismailiya the sentry shouted the warning, 'Pharaoh! The pickets are coming in!'

Nefer sprang up from the table under the awning in the courtyard where he and Taita were eating the midday meal and going over the details of the defence yet again. He climbed swiftly up the ladder to the platform and shaded his eyes to look towards the east. Through the yellow glare he made out the chariots of his forward pickets coming in. As they drove down the bank of the wadi, the guards threw open the gates and allowed them to enter the fort.

'The enemy comes on apace!' the sergeant of the pickets shouted up to Nefer on the high platform.

'Well done, sergeant,' Nefer called back to him, and then to the trumpeter on the wall above the gate, 'Sound the call to arms!'

The ram's horn blared out across the plain, and the entire army that was encamped down the length of the broad wadi began to stir. The trumpet call was picked up and repeated, flung from legion to legion and from squadron to squadron. From the tents and sun-shelters men poured out, seized their arms and hurried to join their formations. Soon lines of marching men and columns of chariots were moving forward to their prepared positions.

Taita clambered up on to the high platform, and Nefer smiled at him. 'So, even deprived of his water, Naja has not turned back.'

'We never thought he would,' Taita said softly.

In the east the horizon started to darken, as though night had come on prematurely. On a wide front the dustcloud of the advancing enemy army boiled like a brewing thunderstorm.

'It still lacks many hours of noon.' Nefer looked up at the pitiless sun. 'There is time to decide this battle before the close of day.'

'Naja's horses have drunk little in three days, and they must have been driven hard to reach us so soon. He knows he must win and reach the wells this day, or for him there will not be another.'

'Will you ride out to meet him with me, Old Father?' Nefer asked, as he strapped on the sword-belt that his orderly handed to him.

'No!' Taita lifted his left hand. On the second finger he wore a gold ring, set with a huge pigeon's-blood ruby. When it caught the sunlight and sparkled, Nefer recognized it as the token Naja had taken from his own finger and given to Taita in Thebes all those years ago, when he believed that the Magus had murdered the young pharaoh for him. Nefer understood that it was a talisman almost as powerful as would have been a lock of Naja's hair, a pellet of his dried excrement or the clippings of his nails. 'I will overlook the battle from here. Perhaps in my own feeble way I might be of more help to you than if I wielded a javelin or drew a bow.'

Nefer smiled. 'Your weapons are sharper and fly more truly than any I have ever held in my hand. Horus love and protect you, Old Father.'

They watched as the battalions of archers and slingers marched out of the wadi to take up their positions behind the breastworks. The ranks moved with purpose and swiftly, for every man among them knew what was expected of him, and had rehearsed this manoeuvre many times. As the last of them disappeared into the ambuscade, the field seemed deserted.

The dustcloud of Naja's advance was less than a league off when at last Nefer embraced Taita, and climbed down the ladder. When he strode out through the gates of the fort a roar went up from the massed squadrons of chariots. As he went down their ranks he picked out his captains and centurions among them, and called to them, 'Courage, Hilto! One more time for me, Shabako! Tonight we will drink a victory cup together, Socco.'

Meren had Dov and Krus in hand as he leaped up on to the footplate. Nefer took the reins from him and Dov recognized his touch and nickered, looking back at him with her great luminous eyes, with their long dark lashes. Krus arched his neck, and pawed at the ground with one front hoof.

Nefer lifted his right fist high and gave the command: 'March! Forward!'

The ram's horn sounded the advance and he led the van out, rank upon rank. They moved in majestic progress, down between the low breastworks from behind which not a single archer showed himself, out on to the open plain.

Nefer gave another hand signal, and the formations opened. Wheel to wheel the front rank moved forward to meet the great dustcloud that rolled towards them. On the markers he had laid out weeks before, Nefer halted his leading squadron, and let the horses rest while he studied the enemy advance.

Now where the dun dustclouds made a tenuous contact with the grey desert he saw the line of dark spots, and myriad flashes of metal wavering in the heated air. On they came and in the mirage the outlines of the chariots in the front rank of Naja's advance wriggled and changed shape like tadpoles in the depths of a pond.

Then they hardened and took on firm shape, and he could make out the horses and the armoured men on the vehicles behind them.

Meren murmured, 'Sweet Horus be praised. It seems he has committed all his vehicles. He holds no depth of chariots in reserve.'

'They must be desperate for water. His only chance of survival is to break our ranks with a frontal charge and win through to the wells.'

Closer and closer rolled the enemy, and now they could make out the features of the warriors in the front rank, and from their colours and pennants they identified each regiment, and recognized the captains who commanded them.

Two hundred paces away the mighty host rolled to a halt. A vast silence settled over the brooding landscape, broken only by the fretting susurration of the wind. The dust settled like a falling curtain and every detail of both armies was starkly revealed.

From the enemy centre a single chariot pulled forward. Even though dust coated the coachwork the gold leaf gleamed through, and the royal pennant flew above the driver's head. Naja halted less than a hundred paces to the front, so that Nefer recognized the cold, handsome face under the blue war crown.

'Hail, Nefer Seti, puppy of the dog I slew with my own hand!' Naja called in that sonorous voice. Nefer stiffened to hear him confess so openly to regicide. 'Upon my head I wear the crown I took from Tamose as he was dying. In my hand,' he raised the mighty blue sword, 'I carry the brand I took from his craven fist. Will you claim it from me, puppy?'

Nefer felt his hands begin to shake upon the reins and anger rose in a red cloud that obscured his vision.

'Steady!' Meren whispered at his side. 'Do not let him provoke you.'

With a huge effort Nefer forced aside the curtains of rage. He managed to keep his face expressionless, but his voice rang like metal on stone. 'Make ready!' and he lifted his own sword high.

Naja laughed soundlessly, wheeled his own chariot and drove back to his place in the centre of the opposing line.

'March! Forward!' Naja raised the blue sword. His front ranks gathered momentum, rolling towards Nefer's line. 'At the gallop! Charge!' They surged forward in a solid mass.

Nefer stood his ground and let them come on. Naja's taunts rang in his ears still, and he felt a terrible temptation to abandon his well laid-out plan, and rush forward to meet Naja head to head and pierce his traitor heart. With a violent effort he put aside the temptation, and lifted his sword. He described three flashing arcs with the blade above his head. His legions responded instantly. Like a flock of birds swerving in full flight or a shoal of fish avoiding the attacking barracuda, they turned as though possessed of a single controlling mind, and raced away over the plain, back the way they had come.

Naja's front rank had braced itself for the impact, but they met no resistance and, like a man stumbling over a step that did not exist, they lost impetus. By the time they had recovered, Nefer had pulled away another hundred paces. Now his squadrons smoothly changed their formation and drew together from extended order into a column of fours.

Naja tore after him, but within three hundred paces his flanks came upon a low stone breastwork that slanted across their front. They could not stop now, so they veered left and right towards their own centre. Like the current of a wide river forced suddenly into the mouth of a narrow rocky gorge they were squeezed together. Wheel snagged wheel, and horse teams were forced to give way to each other. The charge wavered and slowed as chariots and horses jammed into a solid mass.

At that fatal moment, the ram's horns brayed across the field, and at the signal the heads and shoulders of the archers and slingers rose from behind the breastworks on either hand. The arrows were already nocked and now the archers drew and flexed their short recurved bows. They held their aim a moment, choosing their targets with care. The first volley was always the most telling.

The slingers whirled their weapons on high, double-handed to counter the weight of the hard-baked clay balls in the leather pouches at the end of the long straps. They buzzed through the air as they built up a dreadful momentum.

Naja's leading squadrons were deep in the funnel between the breastworks, when the trumpets sang out again and the archers loosed, in a single concerted volley. They had been ordered to aim for the horses, and to pick out the enemy captains. The arrows flew in almost silently, with just the soft whisper of the fletchings through the air, but the range was short, and the strike of the arrowheads into living flesh sounded like a handful of gravel thrown into a mud-bank. The first rank of Naja's charge was shot down, and as the horses fell the chariots piled up over their carcasses, swerving out of control into the stone walls on either hand, or capsizing and rolling.

Then the slingers loosed their missiles with uncanny accuracy. The solid balls of burnt clay were the size of a ripe pomegranate but heavy as ivory. They could crack the skull of man or horse, snap a leg or shatter ribs as though they were dry twigs. They thudded into the next rank of charging chariots, and the havoc they wrought was terrible.

The vehicles that followed were unable to stop the charge, and crashed into the wreckage of those in front. The coachwork crackled and tore with the sound of green branches in a raging bushfire. Some of the long drive-shafts shattered and deadly splinters speared the horses that pulled them. Wheels burst and were torn from their axles. Men were hurled from the cockpits and trampled under the frantic hoofs of the rearing, milling horses.

At the head of his squadron, Nefer gave the hand signal that the men following him were expecting, and a swarm of foot-soldiers leaped out of hiding and dragged away the thornbushes that concealed the openings that had been deliberately left in the stone walls on either hand. In quick succession Nefer's chariots swerved through them and out into the open ground beyond the walls. No longer constricted, they were free to manoeuvre across the plain. They doubled back, circling in behind Naja's trapped squadrons, and falling on their rear echelons.

Now both armies were locked together, like fighting bulls, horn to horn. Not all of Naja's vehicles had been lured into the trap between the walls. There had simply not been enough space for them all to enter at one time. These loose chariots now came rushing forward to engage Nefer, and a traditional chariot battle swiftly developed. Running chariots circled, charged and withdrew, then charged again. The squadrons broke up into smaller units, and across the plain single vehicles viciously engaged each other, wheel to wheel, and man to man.

Despite the frightful losses he had inflicted on the enemy in the opening phase, Nefer was still heavily outnumbered. As the advantage swung back and forth, Nefer was forced to call in more and more of the reserves he had been holding concealed in the wadi behind the fort. Now he signalled in the last of them. He was fully committed. He had brought up every last chariot. But they were not enough. Slowly his horses and his men were being ground down by the sheer numbers of his enemy.

In the dust and clamour and turmoil, Nefer desperately searched the plain for Naja's golden chariot and the royal red pennant. He knew that if he could force Naja to single combat and kill him, he could still carry the day. But there was no sign of him. Perhaps he had been cut down in the defile between the walls, perhaps he was lying wounded or dead somewhere in the confusion of the battle.

Close by Nefer saw Hilto's chariot hemmed in by two of the enemy, and the old warrior wounded and thrown to earth. Hilto's squadron saw him go down, and broke up in confusion. Nefer felt the cold hand of despair squeeze his heart. They were losing the battle.

He saw a line of Red chariots circle out then sweep around behind the backs of his archers and slingers along the breastworks, and cut them down with arrows and javelins. The foot-soldiers scattered and fled, a screaming rabble, and their despair was infectious. Grimly Nefer remembered that Taita called it the 'little bird effect – when one flies they all fly.'

Nefer knew that his army would soon be in rout, and he shouted encouragement to the charioteers close enough to hear him, and tried to rally them by running down another enemy chariot and slaying the crew with a dozen strokes of the sword. Then he wheeled away in pursuit of another Red chariot, but by now Dov and Krus were almost worn out, and the enemy pulled away from them.

Then beside him Meren shouted, 'Look, Pharaoh!' and he pointed to the east out into the desert. With the back of his hand Nefer wiped his own sweat and splashes of enemy blood from his face, and stared out into the glare.

He knew then beyond all doubt that it was over, and that they had lost the battle. A fresh mass of enemy chariots was tearing in towards them. Where they had suddenly come from Nefer could not fathom. He had thought that Naja had committed all his vehicles. That did not matter now, for the battle was lost.

'How many?' Nefer wondered, with black desolation filling his soul.

'Two hundred,' Meren guessed. 'Maybe more.' His voice was resigned. 'It is all over, Pharaoh. We will die fighting.'

'One last charge.' Nefer shouted to the chariots nearest to him, 'On me the Blues! Death with glory.'

They cheered him hoarsely and wheeled in on either side of him. Even Dov and Krus seemed imbued with new strength, and the thin line of Blue chariots tore in at the new foe, going to meet them head to head. As they closed they saw that the leading enemy chariot flew the pennant of a general, a centurion.

'By Horus, I know him,' Meren cried. 'It's Prenn, the old sodomite.'

So close were they now that Nefer also recognized the gaunt figure, with the black patch over one eye. He had seen him on the staff of King Apepi, in the temple at Perra when they had met to negotiate the treaty of Hathor. The same wondrous day that he had first laid eyes on Mintaka.

'His arrival is untimely,' Nefer said grimly, 'but perhaps we can save the next generation of young boys from his amorous attentions.'

He steered Dov and Krus straight at Prenn, trying to force him to swerve and offer a flank shot for his javelin throw. But as they came closer together, Meren shouted, startled, 'He flies the Blue!' Prenn's pennant was streaming back, directly away from them, which was why Nefer had not noticed it until this moment, but Meren was right: Prenn was flying the Blue of the House of Tamose, and all his chariots with him.

Now Prenn slowed and held his right arm across his chest in salute to Nefer, and he shouted in a great voice that carried above the rumble of the chariot wheels, 'Hail, Pharaoh! May you live ten thousand years, Nefer Seti.'

In amazement Nefer lowered the javelin he had been about to hurl, and checked his horses.

'What are your orders, Pharaoh?' Prenn shouted.

'What strange business is this, General Prenn? Why do you call on me for orders?' Nefer called back.

'The Princess Mintaka delivered to me your message, and I have come to place myself under your command and to help you avenge the murders of King Apepi and Pharaoh Tamose.'

'Mintaka?' Nefer was confused, for surely she was still closeted in the sanctuary of the temple in Avaris. But then his warrior instincts took over, and he thrust aside those thoughts. There would be time for such musing later. 'Well met, General Prenn. You arrive none too soon. Lay your chariot alongside mine and we will sweep this field from end to end.'

They charged side by side, and Nefer's broken and scattered legions saw the blue pennants coming and heard the war-cry, 'Horus and Nefer Seti!' and the blaring of the ram's horn trumpets, and they took new heart. The Red squadrons of Naja Kiafan were in hardly better case and could offer only scant resistance as Prenn's fresh troops charged into them. They fought on for a while, but the heart was torn out of them. Some scrambled out of their chariots to kneel in the dust, hands raised in surrender, begging for quarter and shouting the praises of Nefer Seti. Their behaviour was infectious and spread across the battlefield, as the Red charioteers threw down their swords and knelt.

Nefer quartered across the field, searching for Naja. In his heart he knew that the victory would not be complete until he had avenged his father's murder. He came back towards the stone breastworks where last he had seen Naja at the head of his charge. He rode through the debris and detritus of battle, the shattered and overturned vehicles, the wounded and dying men and horses, the scattered corpses. Although most of the enemy were killed or had surrendered, there were still small isolated groups fighting on. Nefer's men had no mercy on these and cut them down, even when they tried to surrender. Nefer intervened where he could to halt the slaughter, and to protect the prisoners, but his men were mad with battle rage, and scores more died before he could save them.

He reached the stone breastworks and reined in Krus and Dov. From his height on the footplate he could see over the low wall into the narrow defile where he had trapped the forward legions of Naja's army. The smashed chariots were piled upon each other like the wreckage of a fleet thrown upon the rocks by a mighty storm at sea. Some of the horses had struggled to their feet and stood still tethered by the harness to their shattered vehicles. He saw a lovely bay mare standing on three legs with her off-fore broken by a slinger's clay ball, and near her a black stallion with its entrails dangling to the ground from a rent in its belly. Around each chariot lay the dead and the wounded. Some were still moving and weeping, calling to the gods and to their mothers for water and succour. Others sat dazed and slack-jawed with the agony of their wounds. One was trying feebly to pull out the arrow that was lodged deep in his stomach. Nefer looked for Naja's body among the dead, but all was confusion and many were buried in the wreckage. Then he picked out a flash of gold leaf, and the royal standard of Naja Kiafan lying in the dust and the puddles of congealing blood.

'I must find him,' Nefer told Meren. 'I must know he is dead.' He jumped down from the chariot.

'I will help you search.' Meren went to the horses' heads and tethered them to the wall. Nefer vaulted over the breastworks and scrambled over the other wreckage until he reached the golden chariot. It lay on its side, but the cockpit was empty. One of the horses was still alive, but both its front legs were broken, and it lifted its head and looked up at Nefer piteously. He took one of the javelins from the bin on the chassis, and killed the animal with a thrust behind the ear. Suddenly Meren shouted and stooped to pick up something from among the debris. He lifted his trophy high, and Nefer saw that he had found Naja's blue war crown.

'The swine's body must be close,' Nefer called to him. 'He would not have discarded that. It means too much to him.'

'Search beneath his chariot,' Meren called back to him. 'He might be trapped under it. I will help you lift it.' He came towards Nefer, scrambling over the wreckage, and at that moment Nefer caught a flash of movement from the corner of his eye. At the same instant Meren shouted an urgent warning: 'Look out! Behind you!'

Nefer ducked and whirled about. Naja had risen from where he had been crouching behind the dashboard of the chariot. His shaven head was pale and shiny as an ostrich egg, and his eyes were wild. He still carried the blue sword of Tamose and he launched a double-handed blow at Nefer's head, but Meren's warning had saved him and Nefer ducked under the hissing blade. His own sword was still in the scabbard at his hip, but he carried the javelin with which he had delivered the *coup de grâce* to the maimed horse. Instinctively he thrust at Naja's throat, but Naja was quick as the cobra that was his namesake and twisted aside. This gave Nefer a moment to reach for his own sword, but Naja stepped back and looked about him. He saw Meren coming to Nefer's aid with bared sword, and he saw the empty chariot hitched to the wall with Dov and Krus in the traces. He drove Nefer back with another thrust of the blue blade, then whirled and sprinted away. Nefer hurled the javelin after him, but the thong was not wound on and the throw was wide. Naja reached the wall. As he jumped over it he cut the horses free with a slash of the blue sword and leaped up on to the footplate. He did not have hold of the reins, but he seized the whip from the bin and lashed Krus and Dov across the haunches. Startled, the pair leaped forward together and within half a dozen strides they were both at full gallop.

Behind them Nefer jumped to the top of the wall and saw Naja being carried away across the plain. He drew a long breath and whistled, the high piercing blast that Dov and Krus knew so well. He saw their heads go up, their ears prick and swivel towards him. Then Krus changed gait and swung into a tight turn, and Dov came smoothly round with him. The chariot was flung hard over in the turn and Naja had to clutch at the dashboard to prevent himself being hurled overboard. The pair of horses came pounding back towards where Nefer stood poised on the wall. Naja recovered his balance and held the blue sword at guard, ready to strike out at Nefer as soon as he came within reach. Nefer knew that his own bronze could never stand against that terrible blade. It would be certain death to throw himself on top of a swordsman of Naja's calibre armed with that weapon.

As the horses swept by below him, Nefer leaped lightly on to Krus' back and with his knees steered him out on to the open plain still at full gallop. He glanced back and saw Naja climbing out of the cockpit. He edged out along the drive-shaft to get at Nefer.

Nefer leaned down from Krus' back and with his own blade sliced the knot in the plaited leather rope that hitched the horses to the drive-shaft. The chariot was running free and veered off to one side. Naja's weight drove down the drive-shaft and the end of it dug into the soft earth. The racing vehicle was flicked end over end, and Naja was thrown clear. He struck the ground with his shoulder and even above the sound of hoofs and the shattering woodwork of the chariot, Nefer heard the bone break.

Nefer turned Krus back, and they charged at Naja. He had climbed painfully to his feet and stood swaying, and clutching his damaged right arm across his chest. In his fall he had lost his grip on the hilt of the blue sword. It had spun out of his hand, and ten paces away from where he stood the point had pegged into the earth. The blade still quivered from the impact, and the wondrous blue metal threw slivers of blue light, and the jewelled hilt whipped from side to side.

Naja staggered towards the weapon, but then he saw Krus bearing down on him, and an expression of utter terror turned his face the colour of cold ashes. He turned and started to run.

Nefer leaned from Krus' back, plucked the sword out of the sand, and turned Krus in pursuit of Naja. Naja heard the rising crescendo of hoofbeats behind him, and looked back. The mascara had run down his cheeks like black tears, and terror distorted his features. He knew then that he could not escape the terrible vengeance that was bearing down upon him. He fell to his knees and lifted both hands in supplication. With a slap across the withers and a sharp whistle Nefer brought Krus to a plunging halt before the kneeling figure, jumped down and stood over Naja.

'Mercy!' Naja sobbed. 'I yield to you the double crown and all the kingdom.' He crawled pitifully to Nefer's feet.

'I already have that. I lack only one thing. Vengeance!'

'Mercy, Nefer Seti, in the name of the gods and for the sake of your sister, the goddess Heseret, and the infant she carries in her womb.' Suddenly there was a dagger in his right hand, and he stabbed up viciously at Nefer's groin. Nefer was almost taken in, but he twisted away only just in time, and the point of the dagger snagged in the skirt of his *chiton*. Nefer struck the weapon out of his grasp with a flick of the blue blade.

'I admire your constancy. To the very end you are true to your base nature.' Nefer smiled down on him coldly. 'I grant you the same mercy that you showed my father, Pharaoh Tamose.' He drove the point of the blue sword into the centre of Naja's chest, and it came out between his shoulder-blades. An expression of agonized disbelief played over Naja's face.

'You have defiled this sacred blade. Now I will wash it in your blood,' said Nefer, jerked it free, then drove it in again deeply.

Naja toppled face first into the dust, and drew one more ragged breath, but the air from his lungs bubbled out of the wound between his shoulder-blades and he shuddered and died.

Nefer hitched the body by its heels to the traces that dangled from Krus' harness, then mounted and dragged it back across the field. The cheering followed him, wave upon wave, as he rode up to the gates of the fort. He cut the rope and left Naja's bloody corpse lying in the dust.

'Have the usurper cut into separate parts and send them to be displayed in every nome in this land. Let every citizen of this very Egypt look upon the fruits of regicide and treachery.'

Then he looked up to the figure who stood high upon the watchtower of the fort, and raised the blood-smeared blue blade to him in salute. Taita lifted his right hand in acknowledgement and there was a flash of dark crimson light from the gemstone upon his finger, Naja's ruby ring.

He was on the tower through the whole day. What part did the Magus play in the battle? Nefer asked himself. Would we have triumphed without his influence? There was no answer, and he put the thought aside. He mounted the ladder to the top of the tower and stood beside Taita. From there he spoke to his men. He thanked them for their duty and their bravery. He promised them their rewards, a share of the plunder to all, and the honours of rank and chains of gold and titles of valour to the captains and centurions.

By the time he had named them all the sun was sinking through a low bank of purple thunderclouds towards the horizon. He ended his speech with a call to prayer: 'I dedicate this victory to the golden Horus, the falcon of the gods,' he cried, and as he prayed there was a strange omen. A fleeting ray of the last sunlight broke through the cloud bank and lit the tower of the fort. It glinted on the blue war crown on Nefer's head and on the blue sword in his hand.

At that same moment there was a wild cry from above: every head lifted and every eye turned towards the sky. A great murmur and sigh went up from the multitude. A royal falcon hovered in the air above the head of Pharaoh, and as they stared in wonder it uttered that strange, haunting sound again, then circled three times, and at last shot away in a straight line on rapid, incisive wingbeats into the darkling eastern sky and was gone in the gloom.

'A blessing from the god,' the soldiers chanted. 'Hail, Pharaoh! Even the gods salute you.'

But as soon as they were alone Taita spoke softly, so no one else outside the room could hear his words. 'The falcon brought a warning and not a blessing.'

'What is the warning?' Nefer demanded quietly, but with deep concern.

'When the bird called, I heard Mintaka cry out,' Taita whispered.

'Mintaka!' Nefer had forgotten her in the exigencies of the battle. 'What did Prenn tell me about her?' He turned to the entrance of the tent and shouted to the guards. 'Prenn! Where is the centurion Prenn?'

Prenn came at once, and knelt before Pharaoh. 'You have earned our deepest gratitude,' Nefer told him. 'Without you we could not have prevailed. Your reward will surpass that of all my other captains.'

'Pharaoh is gracious,'

'At the start of the battle, you spoke of the Princess Mintaka. I thought that she was safe in the temple of Hathor in Avaris. Where did you last see her and when?'

'Pharaoh, you are mistaken. Princess Mintaka is not in the temple. She came to me to bring your message. I could not bring her into battle with me, so I left her two days ago in my camp in the desert, on the road between here and the Khatmia.'

A terrible foreboding seized Nefer. 'Who else did you leave in the same encampment?'

'Some of the other royal women, the Princess Merykara, who had accompanied Mintaka, and Her Majesty Queen Heseret—'

'Heseret!' Nefer sprang to his feet. 'Heseret! If Mintaka and Merykara are in her power, what will she do to them when she hears that I have slain her husband?' He strode to the door of the tent and shouted for Meren. 'Mintaka and Merykara are in terrible jeopardy,' he told him.

'How do you know this?' Meren looked distraught.

'From Prenn. And Taita has read a warning in the cry of the falcon. We must ride at once.'

Heseret awoke in the darkness and chill of that dread time before the dawn when all the world is at its darkest and the human spirit at its lowest ebb. At first she was uncertain of what had interrupted her sleep, but then she became aware of the faint sound of many voices, still far off but growing stronger. She sat up, letting the fur blankets drop to her waist, and tried to make sense of the distant hubbub. She was able to make out words now: 'defeated' and 'slain' and 'flee at once'.

She screamed for her maids and two stumbled in to her, half awake and naked, carrying small oil lamps.

'What is going on?' Heseret demanded, and the eyes of the women were wide and dark with incomprehension.

'We know not, mistress. We were asleep.'

'You stupid girls! Go and find out at once,' Heseret ordered angrily. 'And make certain the prisoners are still in their cage, that they have not escaped.' They fled.

Heseret leapt from her bed. She lit all the lamps, then bound up her hair, pulled on a *chiton* and threw a shawl over her shoulders. All the time the din outside her stockade was growing louder, and now she could hear shouting, and carriages trundling past on the road, but still she made no sense what was happening.

The two maids came scampering back into the tent. The eldest was breathless and almost incoherent: 'They say there has been a great battle at a place called Ismailiya, Majesty.'

Heseret felt a great surge of joy. Naja had triumphed: in her heart she was certain of it. 'What was the outcome of the battle?'

'We don't know, mistress. We did not ask.'

Heseret seized the girl nearest to her by the hair, and shook her so violently that clumps came away in her hands. 'Have you not a speck of brain in your thick skull?' She slapped her across the face, and left her lying on the floor of the tent. She grabbed a lamp and hurried to the door.

The guards were gone, and she felt the first pangs of fear. She ran to the cart and held up the lamp, peering into the pig cage. Part of her anxiety was allayed as she saw that the two bedraggled figures were still pinioned and tied to the struts at the back of the cage. They looked up at her with pale, dirt-streaked faces.

Heseret left them and ran to the gate of the stockade. In the starlight she made out a dark cavalcade streaming past. She saw the loom of carts and wagons being drawn by teams of oxen. Some were piled high with bales and boxes, others were crowded with women clutching their children. Hundreds of soldiers hurried past on foot and Heseret saw that most had thrown away their weapons.

'Where are you going?' she called to them. 'What is happening?' No one answered her, or even seemed aware of her presence. Heseret ran out into the road and seized the arm of one of the soldiers. 'I am Queen Heseret, wife of the Pharaoh of all Egypt.' She shook his arm, 'Hearken to me, knave!'

The soldier gave a strange barking laugh, and tried to shrug her off. But Heseret held on to his arm with desperate strength, until he struck her a heavy blow and left her lying in the dust of the roadway.

She dragged herself to her feet and picked out another soldier in the passing throng, who wore the collar of a sergeant. She ran to him, with blood dribbling from her nose. 'What news of the battle? Tell me. Oh, please tell me,' she begged. He peered into her face and there was just light enough for him to recognize her.

'The most dire news, Majesty.' His voice was gruff. 'There has been a terrible battle and the enemy has prevailed. Our army has been defeated, and all the chariots destroyed. The enemy comes on apace and will be upon us soon. You must flee at once.'

'What of Pharaoh? What has happened to my husband'

'They say that the battle is lost and that Pharaoh is slain.'

Heseret stared at him, unable to move or speak.

'Will you come away, Your Majesty?' The sergeant asked. 'Before it is too late. Before the victors arrive, and the plundering and the rapine begin. I will protect you.'

But Heseret shook her head. 'It cannot be true. Naja cannot be dead.' She turned away. She stood alone on the roadside as the sun came up and the routed army still poured past her. This confused and disordered rabble bore no resemblance to the proud host that had assembled before the Blue Gate of Babylon only months before.

There were a few officers among them, and Heseret called to one, 'Where is Pharaoh? What has happened?'

The officer did not recognize her with blood on her face and in her dishevelled garments covered with dust. He shouted back, 'Naja Kiafan was cut down in single combat by Nefer Seti himself, and his corpse hacked into pieces and sent to be displayed publicly in all the nomes of Egypt. The enemy forces are coming on swiftly and will likely be here before noon.'

Heseret let out a keening wail. These details were too vivid for her to doubt longer. She gathered up a double handful of dust and poured it over her head. Still wailing she clawed her face with her own fingernails until fresh blood started and dribbled down her cheeks on to her *chiton*.

Her handmaidens and the captain of her own bodyguard came out of the stockade to fetch her in, but she was maddened with grief and screamed incoherent obscenities at them. She turned her face to the heavens and shouted blasphemy at the gods, blaming them for not protecting her husband who was a far greater god than any other in the pantheon.

Her sobs and screams grew louder, her behaviour wilder and madder. She ripped her own breast with the tiny jewelled dagger she always carried, urinated down her legs, and rolled in the mud she had created. Then suddenly she sprang up and rushed into the stockade. She ran to the pig cage on the cart, and screeched at Merykara through the bars: 'Our husband is dead. Slain by our own monstrous brother.'

'Praise be to Hathor and all the gods,' Merykara cried.

'You blaspheme!' Heseret raved at her. 'Naja Kiafan was a god, and you were his wife.' She was goading herself into deeper madness. 'You should have been a dutiful wife but you deserted him. You brought shame and humiliation upon him.'

'Meren is my husband,' Merykara told her. 'I despise that creature whom you call husband. He murdered our father, and he richly deserves the punishment that Nefer has given him.'

'Meren is a common soldier, and Naja is and was a god.'

Although Merykara's lips were swollen with thirst and sunburn, she forced herself to smile. 'Meren is more a god than Naja ever was. And I love him. He will be here very soon, and you had best set Mintaka and me free before he arrives, or he and Nefer will make you pay dearly for it.'

'Gently, sweet friend,' Mintaka whispered. 'She is mad. Look at her eyes. Do not provoke her. She is capable of any evil now.'

Heseret was far past reason or restraint. 'You love a common soldier?' she demanded. 'You dare compare him to my husband, the Pharaoh of this very Egypt? Then you shall have your fill of soldiers!'

She turned to the captain of her guards. 'Drag the sow from her filthy cage.' The captain hesitated. Merykara's warning haunted him: Nefer and his captains would be here soon.

Heseret gained a semblance of control over her emotions and sanity. 'I order you, Captain, obey me or face the consequences.' Reluctantly he gave the order to his men and they cut the leather thongs that bound Merykara's wrists to the strut, then reached into the door and dragged her out by her feet.

Merykara's hands and feet were blue and swollen where the ropes had restricted the blood-flow, and she could barely support her weight. The exposed skin of her face and limbs had been burned livid by the sun, and her hair hung down over her face in a tangle of knotted curls.

Heseret looked about her quickly and her attention fixed on a loose wheel that had been removed from one of the other wagons for repair. It was propped against the wall of the stockade.

'Bring that wheel here!' she ordered, and two men rolled it to where she indicated. 'Tie the bitch to it. No, not that way. Spreadeagled! With her arms and legs wide open to welcome her soldier lovers.'

They obeyed her, and strapped Merykara's wrist and ankles to the rim of the wheel, like a star fish. Heseret stood in front of her and spat in her face. Merykara laughed at her through cracked lips, 'You are mad, sister. Grief has addled your mind. I pity you, but nothing can bring Naja back to you. When his foul crimes are weighed in the scales of justice the monster at the gates of paradise will devour his black heart and he will pass into oblivion.'

Heseret slashed her across both her cheeks with the point of the dagger, superficial shallow wounds that nevertheless bled copiously. The blood dripped down the front of Merykara's *chiton*. Heseret used the dagger to split the linen cloth. Then with both hands she ripped it open from neck to hem. Merykara was naked under it.

Her body, untouched by the sun, was white and tender. Her breasts were small and tipped with clear pink, her belly was flat and white, and the hair at the base was a silky nest.

Heseret stood back and looked at her guards. 'Which of you will be the first?'

They gaped at the slender naked body on the wheel.

Mintaka called from the cage, 'Be careful what you do! Nefer Seti will be here very soon, and this is his sister.'

Heseret rounded on her, 'Shut your poisonous mouth. You will be next. Ten thousand men are out there, and you will pleasure most of them before this day is through.' She turned back to the men. 'Come, look at this sweet flesh. Will you not have a little taste of it? I can see your prongs growing stiff under your robes.'

'This is madness,' the captain whispered, but he could not tear his eyes from her pale body. 'She is a princess of the royal House of Tamose.'

Heseret grabbed the long spear out of the hand of the nearest soldier and struck him across the back with the shaft. 'Come, corporal, have you no balls? Let us see you plunge deep into this honey-filled hole.'

The man backed away, rubbing the welt across his back. 'You are mad. What punishment would Nefer Seti heap upon my head?' He turned suddenly and bolted from the stockade to join the flood of fleeing refugees in the roadway. His companions hesitated only a moment longer, then one muttered, 'She is mad! I am not waiting for Nefer Seti to arrive and find his sister like this,' and rushed to the gate with his companions hard after him.

Heseret ran after them. 'Come back! I order you!' But they mingled with the crowds and were gone. Heseret ran to a tall Nubian archer who was hurrying past, grabbed his arm and tried to lead him into the stockade. 'Come with me. I know you black animals, you have prongs big as that of a bull elephant and you love to give them employment. I have something that will please you.'

The archer shoved her away violently. 'Leave me, whore! I have no time for your trade now.'

She stared after him as he strode away up the long, congested road, and yelled after him, 'Not me, beast. How dare you insult the Queen of Egypt?'

Weeping and raving she ran back into the stockade. Mintaka called to her from the cage, 'It is over now, Heseret. Calm yourself. Free Merykara, and we will protect you.' She made her voice low and soothing for she knew that Heseret had crossed the borders of sanity and lost herself in the wilderness of dementia.

'I am the Queen of Egypt, and my husband is an immortal god,' Heseret screamed. 'Look at me and fear my beauty and my majesty.' She was covered in blood and filth, and she brandished the spear wildly.

'Please, Heseret,' Merykara added her entreaty, 'Nefer and Meren will be here very soon. They will care for you and protect you.'

Heseret glared at her. 'I need no protection. Don't you understand what I am telling you? I am a goddess, and you are a soldier's whore.'

'Darling sister, you are deranged with grief. Set me free so that I can help you.'

A cunning expression passed over Heseret's face. 'You think I cannot find a male prong to do for you? Well, you are wrong. I have one of my own.' She lifted the long spear and reversed the shaft, so that the blunt end pointed at Merykara. 'Here is your soldier lover, come to claim you.' She advanced on Merykara menacingly.

'No, Heseret!' Mintaka called urgently. 'Leave her be.'

'You will be next, you treacherous bitch. I will deal with you after I have serviced this one.'

'Heseret, no!' Merykara pleaded with her and writhed against her bonds. But Heseret seemed not to hear her, as she placed the shaft of the spear between her spread thighs.

'Sister, you cannot do this. Don't you remember—' Merykara broke off and her eyes flew wide open with shock and pain.

'There!' said Heseret, she thrust the end of the shaft deeply into her. 'There!' she screamed. 'And there!' Deeper with each thrust, until it slid almost arm's length into her belly and came out smeared with Merykara's blood.

Now both girls were screaming at her, 'Stop! Oh, please stop!' But Heseret kept shoving the shaft into her sister.

'There! Does this satisfy your lust?'

Merykara was pouring blood, but Heseret leaned all her weight on the weapon and thrust it full-length into her. Merykara shrieked for the last time then sagged against her bonds. Her chin dropped forward on to her naked chest.

Heseret left the shaft buried in her slim pale body, and stepped back. She stared at what she had done with a bemused expression. 'It was your fault. Don't blame me. It was my duty. You behaved like a whore. I treated you like a whore.' She began to weep again and wring her hands. 'It doesn't matter. Nothing matters any more. Naja is dead. Our dearly beloved husband is dead . . .'

Dazed as a sleep-walker she went to her tent and into the luxuriously appointed but deserted interior. She pulled off the blood- and urine-soaked *chiton* and dropped in the centre of the floor, then she picked another robe at random from the pile in the corner, and pulled sandals on to her feet.

'I am going to find Naja,' she said, with sudden resolve. Quickly she gathered a few items and stuffed them into a leather satchel. Then with new determination she headed for the door.

As she stepped out into the early sunlight, Mintaka called to her from the cage. 'Please release me, Heseret. I must tend your little sister. She is badly wounded. In all charity, let me go to her.'

'You don't understand.' Heseret shook her head wildly. 'I have to go to my husband, the Pharaoh of all Egypt. He needs me. He has sent for me.'

She did not glance at Mintaka again but hurried out of the stockade, shaking her head and muttering incoherently to herself. She turned towards the west, in the opposite direction from the flood of terrified humanity, and started to run back towards Ismailiya and Egypt.

Mintaka heard her scream once more, 'Wait for me, Naja, my one true love. I am coming. Wait for me!' and then her ravings faded with distance.

Mintaka struggled against her bonds, twisting and tugging, bracing her bare feet against the struts of the cage to give herself better purchase. She felt the skin smearing from her wrists, and warm blood dripping down her hands and her fingers, but the leather thongs were tight and strong and she could neither stretch nor snap them. She felt her hands becoming numb from lack of blood. Whenever she rested from her struggle her eyes went to Merykara's limp body on the wheel. She called to her, 'I love you, my darling. Meren loves you. Don't die. For our sakes, please don't die.' But Merykara's eyes were wide open and her stare was fixed. Soon her eyeballs began to dry out and glaze over with a thin film of dust, and the flies swarmed busily over them and drank from the puddle of blood between her legs.

Once Mintaka heard a stealthy scuffle at the entrance to the tent and when she twisted her head she saw Heseret's two maids creeping out of the tent. They were each carrying a large bag crammed with valuables they had looted. Mintaka called to them, 'Please set me free. You shall have your freedom and a great reward.' But they glanced at her with startled, guilty expressions, scurried from the stockade and out into the road to join the retreating rabble of the defeated army passing eastwards.

Later there were voices at the gate and Mintaka was on the point of crying out. In time she recognized the coarse accents, and managed to check herself. Four men crept cautiously into the stockade. By their features, dress and talk, she knew they were ruffians of the lowest sort, probably members of those gangs of jackals and scavengers that followed every army for loot and pickings. She let her head sag, and feigned death.

The men stopped to examine Merykara's body. One laughed and made such an obscene remark that Mintaka squeezed her eyelids closed, and forced herself to hold her tongue with the greatest difficulty.

Then they came to her cage and peered in at her. She lay completely still and held her breath. She knew what a dreadful appearance she must have, and she tried to play dead.

'This one stinks like a sow,' one remarked. 'I would rather have it with Mistress Palm and her five daughters.' They all guffawed at the jest, then scattered to ransack the camp for loot. After they had crept away, carrying what they could, Mintaka watched the shadows lengthen across the beaten earth of the stockade floor, while outside the sounds of passing wagons and carts and people on foot slowly diminished. Just before sunset the last of them passed, and the silence of the desert and the dead settled over the camp.

During the night Mintaka dozed at times, overtaken by exhaustion and pervading despair. Whenever she started awake she saw Merykara's pale body stretched out in the silver moonlight and the terrible cycle of her grief began again.

The dawn came and the sun rose, but the only sound was the soughing of the desert wind through the branches of the scrawny thorn tree at the gate, and at times her own sobs. But these grew softer and weaker as another day passed without water.

Then she heard something else, a distant murmur that grew into a soft rumble, and she knew it was the sound of wheels coming on at speed – chariots, for she could hear the hoofbeats now and the sound of men's voices growing stronger, and stronger still, until she could recognize one. 'Nefer!' She tried to scream his name, but her voice was a draughty whisper. 'Nefer!'

Then she heard shouts of horror and dismay, and she twisted her head slowly and saw Nefer storm through the gateway, Meren and Taita close behind him.

Nefer saw her at once, and ran to the cage. He tore the gate off its hinges with his bare hand then pulled his dagger from its sheath to slash loose the leather thongs from her wrists. Gently he drew her out of the stinking cage and held her to his chest. He was weeping as he carried her into the tent.

'Merykara!' she whispered, through cracked and swollen lips.

'Taita will see to her, but I fear it is too late.' Mintaka looked back over his shoulder and saw that Taita and Meren between them had cut Merykara free from the wheel and drawn the blood-clotted weapon from her body. Now they were spreading a clean white linen sheet over her body, covering the terrible mutilations.

Mintaka shut her eyes. 'I am exhausted by sorrow and grief but, my darling, your face is the most beautiful and welcome sight I have ever beheld. Now I will rest awhile.' And she slumped into unconsciousness.

Mintaka came awake slowly as though she were rising up from the depths of that dark and terrible pit where demons live.

When she opened her eyes the demons that had haunted her dreams fled away, and she saw with immense relief the two most beloved faces in her world. Taita sat at one side of her couch and Nefer at the other.

'How long?' she asked. 'How long was I gone?'

'A day and a night,' Taita answered her. 'I gave you of the Red Shepenn flower.' She raised her hand to her face and found a thick coating of salve upon it. She rolled her head towards Nefer, and whispered, 'I am ugly.'

'No!' he replied, 'You are the most beautiful woman I have ever laid eyes upon, and I love you past the counting of it.'

'You are not angry with me for disobeying you.'

'You have given me a crown and a land.' He shook his head and one of his tears fell upon her face. 'Above that you have given me your love, which is more precious to me than all of that. How could I ever be angry with you?'

Taita rose softly and left the tent, and they stayed together all the rest of that day, speaking softly to each other.

In the evening Nefer sent for the others. When they had gathered around Mintaka's couch, Nefer looked at their faces gravely and saw that all of them were there: Taita and Meren, Prenn, Socco and Shabako moving stiffly from the pain of his wounds garnered on the battlefield of Ismailiya.

'You have come to see justice done,' he told them, then turned to the guards at the door.

'Bring in the woman named Heseret,' he ordered.

Mintaka started and tried to sit up, but he pushed her gently back upon the bolster.

'Where? How did you find her?'

'Our pickets found her wandering in the desert on the road back to Ismailiya,' Nefer explained. 'At first they did not recognize her or believe her claims to be a queen. They thought her a mad woman.'

Heseret came into the tent. Nefer had allowed her to bathe and provided her with fresh raiment, and Taita had treated the cuts and grazes on her face and body. Now she shrugged off the hands of her guards and looked around her with a regal lift of her chin. 'Prostrate yourselves before me,' she ordered the men who faced her. 'I am a queen.'

No one moved, and Nefer said, 'Bring her a stool.'

When she was seated upon it, he stared at her so coldly that Heseret covered her face and started to weep. 'You hate me,' she blubbered. 'Why do you hate me?'

'Mintaka shall tell you why,' he answered, and turned to the girl on the couch. 'Please describe to us the manner of the death of Princess Merykara.'

Mintaka spoke for almost an hour, and during all that time one in the tent moved or uttered a sound, except to gasp and exclaim in horror at the most dreadful parts of what they were hearing. At the end Nefer looked at Heseret. 'Do you deny any part of this testimony?'

Heseret returned his cold stare. 'She was a whore, and she brought shame on my husband, the Pharaoh of Egypt. She deserved death. I am pleased and proud that I was able to be the instrument of justice.'

'Even now I might have forgiven you,' Nefer said softly, 'if you had shown a grain of remorse.'

'I am a queen. I am above your petty laws.'

'You are a queen no longer,' Nefer replied, and she looked confused.

'I am your own sister. You would not harm me.'

'Merykara was your sister also. Did you spare her?'

'I know you well, Nefer Seti. You will not harm me.'

'You are right, Heseret. I will not harm you. But there is one who will not scruple.' He turned to his assembled captains. 'It is the ancient law of the rights of the one most injured. Stand forth, Meren Cambyses.'

Meren rose and stepped forward, 'Pharaoh, I am your man.'

'You were betrothed to the Princess Merykara. Yours is the greatest injury. I give into your keeping the body and the life of Heseret Tamose, who was a princess of the royal house of Egypt.'

Heseret began to scream as Meren placed a golden chain around her neck: 'I am a queen and a goddess, you dare not harm me.'

No one took notice of her cries, and Meren looked at Nefer. 'Your Majesty, do you place any restriction upon me? Do you urge or order me to show mercy and compassion?'

'I give her to you without reservation. Her life is yours.'

Meren loosened the sword in its sheath on his hip, and pulled Heseret to her feet with the chain. He dragged her blubbering and wailing from the tent. Nobody followed them.

They sat in silence, and through the linen walls listened to Heseret's wailing, entreaties and blandishments. Then there was a sudden silence and they steeled themselves. They heard a high, piercing shriek that ended as abruptly as it had started.

Mintaka covered her face with both hands and Nefer made the sign against evil with his right hand. The others coughed, and moved restlessly.

Then the curtains at the entrance parted and Meren stepped back into the tent. In his right hand he carried the naked sword and in the other a dreadful object. 'Your Majesty,' he said, 'justice has been done.' By its dense hair-tresses he held high the severed head of Heseret, the wife of Naja Kiafan, the false pharaoh.

It was five more days before Mintaka had recovered sufficiently to begin the long journey back to Avaris. Even then Taita and Nefer insisted that she be carried in a litter to ease the jolting and lurching over the rough road that lay ahead. They travelled slowly, and it was fifteen days later that they reached the escarpment and looked down from the arid wastes upon the wide green valley of the Nile.

Nefer helped Mintaka from the litter, and together they walked a short way from the road, so that they could be alone and savour to the full this joyous moment of homecoming. They had not been there long when Nefer stood up and shaded his eyes.

'What is it, my heart?' Mintaka asked.

'We have visitors,' he said, but when she exclaimed with annoyance at the intrusion he went on, 'These visitors are always welcome.'

She smiled then as she recognized the two mismatched figures approaching them. 'Taita. And Meren! But what strange attire is this?'

They were both dressed in simple robes and sandals, and slung on their backs they carried the leather satchels of holy men on a pilgrimage.

'We have come to say our farewells, and to take our leave of you,' Taita explained.

'You will not leave me now.' Nefer was dismayed. 'Will you not attend my coronation?'

'You were crowned upon the field of Ismailiya,' Taita told him gently.

'Our wedding!' Mintaka cried. 'You must stay for our wedding.'

'You were married long since,' Taita smiled, 'perhaps on the day of your birth, for the gods intended you for each other.'

'But you, my brother of the Red Road and my dearest friend,' Nefer turned to Meren, 'what about you?'

'There is nothing more for me here, now that Merykara is gone. I must go with Taita.'

Nefer knew that there was nothing further to say, that more words would degrade this moment. He did not even ask where they were going. Perhaps they did not know themselves.

He embraced them and kissed them, and he and Mintaka stood and watched them walk away, and their distant shapes slowly dwindle in size in the shimmering wastes of the desert wilderness, and they shared the same deep ache of regret and bereavement.

'They have not really gone,' Mintaka whispered, when at last they had disappeared from view.

'No,' Nefer agreed. 'They will always be with us.'

With the high priestess and fifty acolytes from the temple of Hathor preceding her, the Princess Mintaka Apepi came for her marriage to Pharaoh Nefer Seti.

They stood together on the terrace of the palace of Thebes that overlooked the broad brown flow of the Nile in flood, in the season most propitious to all living things in the land of this very Egypt.

Mintaka had long since recovered from her injuries and her ordeal. Her beauty was fully restored, and in this joyous moment seemed to be enhanced ten-fold.

It seemed that all of Egypt had come to bear witness to the nuptials. The crowds stretched back along both banks of the river as far as the eye could see. When the couple embraced and broke the jars of Nile water, the shout that went up to heaven must have startled the gods themselves. Then Nefer Seti led his new queen out by the hand and showed her beauty to the populace, who fell to their knees, and wept and cried aloud their loyalty and their love.

Suddenly a silence fell over this vast congregation and slowly every eye turned upwards to the tiny speck in the vaulted sky above the palace.

In the silence there was the wild lonely cry of a royal falcon and the bird began its stoop out of the high blue. In the end, just as it seemed it must come into violent collision, the falcon flared its wings wide and hovered over the tall figure of Pharaoh. Nefer lifted his right arm and held it out, and softly as a feather the magnificent bird alighted upon his fist.

A sound like the sea on a stormy day rose from ten thousand throats as they greeted the miracle. But Nefer's eyes fell on the thin loop of pure gold that was fastened about the bird's right foot above the great hooked talons. Engraved into the precious metal was a symbol that made Nefer's heart race as he recognized it.

'The royal cartouche!' he whispered. 'This was never a wild bird. This is Nefertem, my father's falcon. That is why it came to me so often in times of greatest danger, to warn and guide me. It was always my father's spirit.'

'And now Nefertem has come to affirm before all the world that you are king indeed.' Mintaka stood closer to him and gazed into his face with eyes that glowed with pride and love.

AUTHOR'S NOTE

I ask my readers to remember that *Warlock* is a work of fiction. Many of the places that I have written about do exist, but the others never did – or at least those like Avaris have long ago been lost and forgotten. Gallala is another case in point. Taita's spring dried up a thousand years ago and another earthquake destroyed the city and buried the ruins.

Likewise, most of my characters are fictitious – even Taita lives on only in my imagination.

Wilbur Smith

Come and visit the new

WILBUR SMITH

website:

www.wilbursmith.net

∗ *Complete book summaries*

∗ *Author biography*

∗ *Family trees*

∗ *Links to Wilbur Smith Forum*

∗ *Wilbur Smith Events page*

∗ *Contact Author page*

∗ *Wilbur Smith Audio page*

THE COURTNEYS

When the Lion Feeds
'Mr Smith is a natural story-teller. . . .'
(*The Scotsman*)

The Sound of Thunder
'a violent saga-type story set in Boer War Africa and
told with vigour and enthusiasm'
(*Evening Standard*)

A Sparrow Falls
'He packs humanity into a bag already overflowing with
adventure, excitement, and realism.'
(*Yorkshire Post*)

THE COURTNEYS OF AFRICA

The Burning Shore
'Courage, drama, love and revenge on land, sea and in the air towards the end of the first world war and blended in fine style. Mr Smith's research into events and places is spot-on, as usual.'
(*Bolton Evening News*)

Power of the Sword
'a stupendous story, written in the grand old manner, from the master of thoroughgoing adventure'
(David Hughes, *The Mail on Sunday*)

Rage
'The prose is as lean and muscular as ever, the pace would do credit to a Porsche, and the invention is as bright and explosive as a firework display.'
(*The Sunday Telegraph*)

A Time to Die
'. . . one is enthralled by this ability to conjure up the sights, smells and sense of the bush.'
(Ted Willis)

Golden Fox
'We are caught up in a broad historical sweep, nothing less than the destabilisation of one entire continent . . . hot and steamy territory where action is never further than the turn of a page.'
(*Independent*)

THE BALLANTYNE NOVELS

A Falcon Flies
'There is throughout *A Falcon Flies* a genuine sense of excitement and wonder.'
(*Sunday Telegraph*)

Men of Men
'a splendid read'
(*Financial Times*)

The Angels Weep
'... action, adventure and romance....'
(*Yorkshire Post*)

The Leopard Hunts in Darkness
'... big, bold and bloody....'
(*The Scotsman*)

ALSO BY WILBUR SMITH

The Dark of the Sun
'If the phrase "a man's book" has any meaning, it describes this powerful savage story.'
(*Books & Bookmen*)

Shout at the Devil
'a fast and thrilling adventure'
(*Northern Echo*)

Gold Mine
'. . . violent action and informed technical detail. . . .' Mr Smith is at his liveliest and best.'
(*Evening Standard*)

The Diamond Hunters
'a gem of a suspense/adventure novel'
(*Daily Mirror*)

The Sunbird
'A splendid panoramic piece of writing, with colourful characters woven into an enthralling plot.'
(*Oxford Times*)

Eagle in the Sky
'Wilbur Smith . . . rarely misses a trick . . . Terribly competent. . . .'
(*Sunday Times*)

The Eye of the Tiger
'supreme professionalism, vividness, and attention to detail'
(*Sunday Express*)

Wild Justice
'For cold-blooded terror it would be difficult to equal.'
(*Evening News*)

Cry Wolf
'Another cracker . . . Africa, arms dealing, armoured cars, strong men with stronger women all combine beautifully for a real entertainment.'
(*Daily Mirror*)

'rattling good adventure.'
(*Evening Standard*)

Hungry as the Sea
'His narrative surges forward with a bone in its teeth, as irresistibly as the *Warlock* running south "at the top of the green".'
(*The Times Literary Supplement*)

Elephant Song
'Sex, money, ambition, fear and blood . . . an emotional stampede.'
(*Daily Mail*)